CLAUS BOXED 4

(VOL. 4)

TONY BERTAUSKI

TOYWORLD

HOME OF THE CHRISTMAS THIEF

TOYWORLD

Hiro's parents rearrange the furniture every December.

They make space in the corner for something tall. They plug in string lights and leave them on the floor. Sometimes, they cut down a tree but don't know what to do with it. It's not just Hiro's parents. Everyone does it. Come January, they all straighten up their living rooms and everything goes back to normal. They do this every year.

No one knows why.

Something's missing and they all feel it, but they never wonder what it is. And every year that passes, the world becomes colder and grayer. Until Hiro has a dream.

It's a world of magic, where he can taste sounds and hear thoughts, see things that defy the laws of physics and biology. It's a place where trees are decorated and stockings are hung above the fireplace. Every day is celebrated with gifts.

It's the last place where joy exists.

Someone has stolen the Christmas spirit from the universe and hidden it in the dream. Hiro doesn't remember a jolly fat man or flying reindeer, or elves on the North Pole. No one in Hiro's world remembers Christmas at all.

Hiro and others like him need to free the Christmas spirit. This is their one and only chance. If they fail, his world and all others like it will stay cold and gray without Christmas... unless they discover the thief's true identity.

It's closer than they think.

1

I'm not the hero in this story. Far from it.

To tell this story properly, we need to start at the beginning.

It was a night like any other. I had folded the covers back and smoothed the wrinkles. I drank the remains of chamomile tea, still warm, with a lemon wedge resting on the bottom of the mug. In my silk pajamas, cool and smooth, I slid into bed. I lay in the dark, listening to the downstairs grandfather clock count the seconds.

The house was empty. As usual.

An annoying red glow filled my window from across the street, strings of lights on my neighbor's gutters. I stared at a small water stain on the ceiling that I had yet to repair, and counted all my life's failures. It wasn't something I enjoyed doing. Just something I'd always done. Part of the ritual.

Then I took three deep breaths, exhaling slowly with each one, and closed my eyes. The breathing technique was something my father taught me as a child. It was habit. Comfortable. I made the mistake, once, of telling him of a dream I had. *Dreams are wasted thoughts,* he said with a voice as hard as an icy driveway. *Foolish entertainment.*

He believed in two things: hard work and harder work. The only thing that was real was what could be seen and touched. Dreams were stupid. It wasn't like I could stop dreaming, nor did I want to. There was no television in the house, and computer time was strictly monitored. Dreams were my only escape as a child. I recorded them in a notebook and hid it between my mattress and box spring. I would get so nervous he'd find it that occasionally I would burn it. A few weeks later, I would start a new one.

This night, where the story begins, I had a dream like no other. I traveled to somewhere beyond the galaxy. I floated without a spaceship, breathing as if air existed in the vacuum of space. Coasting weightless and effortless, past planets and moons, stars and black holes. I saw things I never imagined. It was the loveliest of dreams.

I didn't remember waking up, but I'd opened my eyes to stare at the water stain on the ceiling. Only it wasn't there. The grandfather clock wasn't ticking. I wasn't in my bed.

I was slumped on a shelf, frozen in postdormital sleep paralysis, locked in my body, staring helplessly across a room. How I got there was a mystery. This didn't feel like a dream. What else could it be? I was a grown man, a rational man. This was a dream; it could be nothing else.

A small Christmas tree was in the corner, casting a red glow across the room. I was thinking of my neighbor's repugnant lights. The light, however, caught pairs of eyes in dim corners. There were dozens of them. I'd had this dream before, being stalked by predators. Never like this, though. I'd read a fair share of dream books and knew they represented my fears. As always, I couldn't outrun them. Powerless, I endured their judgment. They weren't blinking. Neither was I.

I wanted to escape, to run away. *Wake up!* I thought. Sometimes that worked.

A terrifying jolt racked my entire being. I tumbled forward like a puppet. I heard the wind, then the hollow clatter of plastic sticks on laminate flooring. It sounded like pieces of an unassembled model dumped out of a box. I still remembered that sound like it was yesterday. Horrifying.

I was bones. Red, red bones.

Fibulas and tibias, phalanges and ribs. Crimson and polished and expertly crafted. No wires or twine, no glue or ties. I sat up with a clatter. One of my arms fell from my shoulder. Pulled from the socket, it looked like a chew toy the dog had forgotten. There was no time to panic. The predators were circling.

Keys jingled on a key ring. Long tubes of light flickered on the ceiling. Giants entered the room. *Ah, of course. They've come to grind my bones.*

They wore puffy coats and stocking caps. Boots crusted with snow. A man and a woman and a child in between. I gave them quite a fright, scrambling into the corner like a feral cat. The man spilled coffee. Imagine seeing a trembling pile of bones. I expected them to swat me with a broom.

The father, I correctly assumed, turned to the mother and said with all the nonchalance of calling attendance in homeroom, "I thought they were blank."

The mother looked more confused than terrified. She went to the shelves, which, by the way, weren't filled with predators, and picked up a stuffed dog with floppy ears, squeezed the nose on a giant orange cat. "This never happened before," she said, looking at me. "Christmas is ten days away."

Never happened before? I couldn't parse the meaning. Like this had never happened before, or this had never happened *ten days before Christmas?*

The girl walked around a workbench covered in bags of white stuffing, sewing needles and thread. A backpack strapped to her shoulders. She was ten years old or twelve. I'm not good with kids.

Madeline Bells.

That was her name. I didn't know how I knew it. The name just popped into my head. She picked up my lost arm like it was a stick. I squeezed into the corner, my joints protesting. Right about then I was thinking this dream was different. Like no other dream I'd ever had. I was about to pop another limb off my body when the mother said to the girl, "Easy, hon. He's frightened."

This was weird. Even for a dream. They squatted in front of me like I was a puppy who had just piddled on the floor.

"Hello, Viktor," the mother said. "We just want to help."

I was jammed into a corner with nowhere to go and wondering who Viktor was. Then I noticed a tag on my arm. The one Madeline was holding.

Viktor the Red.

Viktor was my family name of sorts, from the old country. I would wake up soon and write all of this down, tease out the symbolism. The predators were my father; I was bones that lacked self-worth or identity or fill in the blank. It would all make sense, it always did. When I woke up.

The mother popped my arm back into the socket. Her touch was warm and gentle. Madeline looked at her mother and said, "Can I keep him?"

I never forgot that, for as long as I lived. It was the way she said it. It filled me with a warmth I'd never felt. It was so kind. I began to melt.

I woke in my bed. In my home, in my silk pajamas. My pillow damp with sweat. I leaped out of the covers and touched my chest and stomach, ran my hands down to my toes. I went to the bathroom and looked in the mirror. There I was, in my forty years of flesh. Wrinkles had never made me so happy.

I showered in cold water till my teeth chattered, then sat in the kitchen with a cup of tea till it was time for work. I was different that day. Madeline's words were butterflies. *Can I keep him?*

I once read the barrier between reality and dreaming was gossamer thin, and the two were irrevocably inseparable. One side tugs on the other. I couldn't explain why the dream felt so real. I only knew one thing.

I wanted to go back.

2

His name was Hiro. A bit on the nose for a story, right? Why not call him Prince or Excalibur? It's quite simple: that was his name. He wasn't named after a grandfather or famous uncle or anything like that. They liked the sound of it. It's on his birth certificate, look it up. It's all very legal.

Our Hiro, as some of us called him, was eight years old when it began. He had no idea who he was or what was about to happen. No one did. This is all a fairy tale, you might think. And you can believe that if you want. It won't make it any less true than believing the world is flat.

His adoring parents were watching their son carefully peel tape from a Christmas present when this story began. His stack of gifts was almost as high as he was, sitting on the floor. Being an only child had its perks. This year was the year for a chemistry set, designer pants and name brand shirts, and a monogrammed parka for camping, if he ever went camping. There was also a telescope with a digital display, a block and hammer cityscape for budding engineers, a marble chess set with hand-carved pieces, an advanced magic module to expand last year's set, and, perhaps his favorite, hardcover books signed by his favorite authors.

This was the most favorite time of year in the Tanaka household.

"Do you like it?" his mother said.

Hiro unfolded a monogrammed apron. He liked chopping vegetables, stirring soup and watching bread rise. He liked making cookies best of all, licking batter from the spoon. But the apron wasn't for cooking. There were sketchbooks wrapped inside it and a set of graphite pencils, colored markers, paintbrushes and watercolors.

He would be embarrassed if friends saw the apron with his name stitched on it. Ah, but that was the one and only benefit of being a loner. No one to make fun of you, no one to prank you or always coming over to visit or talking to you. Hiro rarely spoke, even when a teacher called on him. He always looked at his Devin Claire shoes and muttered just above a whisper.

Imagination can be your very best friend, his grandfather used to say. He was a loner, too.

"Look at this." His mother pulled out three journals. "One for you, one for me and one for your father."

She passed them out, each of them splashed with glitter, the words written calligraphy style and surrounded by finely detailed mazes. *Dream Journal,* it read. His mother didn't click a button for Christmas. She made it. *That's the true spirit,* she would say.

"Now we can write them down," she said.

This was perhaps Hiro's favorite gift that Christmas (which, by the way, would turn out to be the last Christmas). It was such a simple gift. At breakfast, they always told each other their dreams from the night before. His father would go first, then his mother. He enjoyed hearing their dreams as much as he did telling his own. *Dreams are gateways,* his mother would say.

She had no idea how right she was.

Does it make you sad, a boy telling his dreams to his parents this way? Shouldn't he be spending the night with friends, playing video games, talking about girls or boys or whatnot? Don't be. Our Hiro was very happy.

"Coffee," his father announced. He shoved off the couch, tousling Hiro's hair.

Hiro dug a pencil out of the apron, turning it in the sharpener, watching the wood curl in scalloped leaves. When his father returned, they took turns reciting their dreams from the night before. His father didn't write his dream down. Hiro wasn't sad he didn't use the dream journal his mother had spent so much time on, since his father had had a very long dream about an elevator falling twenty stories. It was a bad dream, but his mother insisted there was no such thing as bad dreams. Only challenging ones. All dreams had something to say.

Hiro wrote his dream as he told his parents. It was about Santa Claus and his reindeer. He heard the bells and the hooves on the roof, the sleigh scuffing the shingles. His mother asked questions, to help him remember, her lips thinning in a broad smile. Hiro still believed in Santa. That would end soon enough. And not for reasons you might be thinking.

They played chess that afternoon. His father beat him three games, but the last one was close. Hiro helped his mother make cookies, then read his books in front of the fireplace. The whole scene was ripped from a Christmas calendar, it was all so very perfect.

And when *it* happened—the very reason for this story—no one felt a thing.

They didn't hear a sound or feel a tremor, didn't see a flash of light or smell a change in the air. It was much too subtle to know that everything, in that very moment, changed around the world.

Hiro went to his room that night, his belly full of melted marshmallows and lemon drops. The Christmas lights drooped from the eave outside his window, casting a white glow across his pillows. He stopped in the doorway, his hand reaching for the light switch. A purple monkey waited for him on the edge of his bed.

Yes, a purple monkey. You think you've heard this story before? Not even close.

Hiro didn't move for a full minute. You wouldn't think a stuffed animal would be surprising. Hiro had never owned a stuffed animal. He had toys from when he was very little, but never a doll or a teddy bear. A troll doll, once, with green hair that stood like flames. But that was it. Never a stuffed animal big enough to hug.

Hiro wrapped the long, skinny arms around his neck, the fur tickling his cheek. He fell asleep with a smile. In the morning, for some reason, he forgot to ask his parents who had put the monkey in his room. That wasn't like him to forget. His manners were impeccable. He was on Santa's gold star list.

But Hiro wasn't the only one who forgot that Christmas.

3

Long, crooked fingers scratched the bedroom window, an ancient creature that woke during winter storms. It wanted inside to hide under the bed, to crouch in the closet. Hiro no longer believed in those things. He was older now. Occasionally, though, he checked under his bed. Childhood beliefs never go away. Not entirely.

He opened his eyes, stared at the eggshell ceiling, listened to the *scritch, scritch, scritch* on the frosted pane. It was still dark. The outline of a tree branch, dusted with snow, swayed outside.

Thoughts of bedtime monsters dissolved like a snowball against a brick wall. He did not like feeling frightened of his own mind, the way his thoughts seemed to live in his head. He wasn't a child anymore. At the same time, he loved the way imagination created worlds to explore. Sometimes, though, it seemed imagination was beyond his control. That was exciting. At the same time, it made him nervous.

Tucked beneath thick blankets, a dream lurked just beyond reach. He relished these moments, waking before the alarm yanked him into a hard and cold world. Last night's dream wasn't frightening or whimsical. He didn't go to school in his underwear or forget to study for an exam. It was a big dream. A black and empty dream.

His grandfather would say memory was like a misty day. Names and places, thoughts he would have just moments before, would disappear in the fog. He knew they were out there, just beyond his reach. But some days were clear skies, and memories were as easy as picking apples. Hiro's dream wasn't lost in a mist. It was just so far away. Like reaching across an infinite galaxy.

The alarm blared from his dresser. He threw the blankets off, plunging into the cold air. He dressed quickly in beige pants, a white shirt and a black sweater with the school insignia, then made his bed and fluffed his pillow. The smell of coffee greeted him downstairs. He stopped next to the front door, stood in front of a mirror to straighten his collar. His hair was black and shiny, falling over his forehead, just above his eyes. A timid shadow darkened his upper lip. He leaned closer, combing the trace of whiskers with his finger. A lone hair had sprung from his chin like a weed. It took three attempts to pluck it.

The streetlight shined through the bay window, filling the front room, pale and yellow. The furniture had been rearranged, the couch shoved aside and the chair against the wall, leaving the corner of the room empty. His parents did that every year, the first week of December, pushing stuff around, then sitting down to read their phones or watch a program. In January, it went back the way it was before. One year, his father put a coat rack in the corner. They hung their coats on it, put their shoes beneath it. Now it was like they were expecting the delivery of a large appliance that never came.

"Good morning," Hiro said.

"Morning to you." His father was at the kitchen table, wearing a white shirt and skinny black tie, a tight knot cinched against his throat. He worked from home now, remotely, but still dressed up. He sipped coffee as black as his tie.

His mother offered a blanched smile, her complexion pale in the harsh kitchen light. She'd stopped wearing lipstick shortly after the art program was dropped from the school curriculum and cut her hair, a severe crop just below her ears. She'd been reassigned to teach technical writing. Her attire was as colorless as her lips. A silver beaded necklace was across a white blouse beneath a gray jacket.

Breakfast and a glass of water waited on the table.

Hiro wondered what his father had done differently this morning. The eggs looked like a wet sponge. He poked at the yellow mound, strings of cheese stretching across the plate. He rearranged the eggs in the center.

"Did you dream last night?" Hiro said.

His father chuckled, distracted by something on his phone. His mother smiled thinly, chewing with lips curved slightly downward. Hiro pulled a chunk of egg from the blob, twanged the cheese string with his fork.

"Don't play with it, Hiro," she said.

"I had this dream. It was different. Have you dreamed like that before? Like you, I don't know, went somewhere?"

"Can't say I have," his father said.

"It was like... *space*. Lots of it. Like a galaxy." He poked the eggs. "There was a planet."

"Did you finish your science proposal?" his mother said.

His father pointed. A more relevant question for breakfast conversation. Because dreams were just leftover thoughts, a symptom of a chaotic mind struggling to make sense of the world. Hiro couldn't remember who said that.

He told his mother he'd finished it. He wasn't exactly lying. *Is anything ever really finished?* She used to say that in art class. When there was an art class. He rearranged the eggs like satellites orbiting a space station, the stringy cheese tethering them together.

"I'm leaving in ten minutes. I can't take you home after school. I have a conference." His mother rinsed her plate.

"I wonder where the journals are," Hiro said.

"They're in your room," his father said.

Hiro wasn't talking about schoolwork. He searched the cabinets above the stove, then the pantry while explaining the journals they once had, where they wrote their dreams down at breakfast instead of scrolling through newsfeeds. It seemed like forever since he'd seen them. His mother had made them a long time ago. He couldn't remember why.

"They're not in the pantry, Hiro."

"I'm looking for salt."

"Why?"

Hiro didn't want to say the eggs were bland. They were bland. He didn't ask his father if he'd done something different with breakfast. It tasted like soppy cardboard. Hiro found old packets of salt and pepper from a restaurant. His mother returned with a square brief-case, watching him dust his eggs. His parents glanced at each other.

"It's supposed to rain this afternoon," his mother said. "Can you pick him up?"

"I've got a meeting at two," his father said.

"He can wait for you. I'd rather he not catch a cold." She brushed lint from her jacket. "I'm leaving, Hiro."

He took another bite, then washed the rest down the sink, wiping his mouth and checking his sweater for food that might have spilled. He stopped in the front room. The yard was washed in a gloomy soup, the sun struggling to find its way through the aluminum sky. Mother's car breathed ashy clouds from the tailpipe, staining the modest snowbank along the driveway. His mother honked.

"She might leave without you." His father sipped his coffee.

Hiro looked at the empty corner. "Why do we move the furniture every year?"

He shrugged. "That time of year."

That was all he said. It was something they did because they always did it. And forgot why they did it in the first place.

JACOB HERRINGTON'S shirt hung out from the bottom of his sweater. The desk etched an arc on the waxed tiles when he turned it, making a terrible sound. Jacob scrolled through his photos. James Popper nodded at him and said, "Do it, do it."

Jacob thumbed his phone. They looked across the classroom. A few seconds later, Missy Cabernet saw what Jacob had posted on the Social. They were laughing. She wasn't.

Hiro felt trapped in his desk, the way it wrapped around him, the way the molded plastic didn't quite fit his bottom. He tried not to fidget. The hardware creaked. Jacob and James looked at him. Hiro stared at the blue lines on his notebook. If he didn't look up, he would become part of the desk. Just another object in the room. Nothing worth noticing.

The door swung open. Silence seeped in like fog, leaving only the hard clap of Mr. Corker's shoes: a punishing sound that haunted the hallways. It could be heard around corners and across the gym, sending shivers down freshman spines. *Heel-toe, heel-toe.*

He stopped at the podium, sharpshooter eyes snapping on each student. They locked on Jacob. Corker turned his head, looking down the row. Flicked his fingers. Jacob turned his chair to fall in line with the rest of the chairs, as straight as Corker's spine. Five rows of chairs in perfect order.

Corker went to the closet and brought out a box. Setting it on the desk, he called for a volunteer. Gabriel Mankowicz—third seat, second row—wasted no time. Corker pulled out folded papers, maps and drawings, notes and calculations he did in his spare time, and stacked them on the desk. He threw his black tie over his shoulder and climbed onto his desk with legs as long as fishing poles. The shoes were black mirrors. Shoes he buffed in the teacher's lounge, so perfect a student could see their distorted reflection in the toe. He unfurled skinny fingers like a spider, and Gabriel reached into the box to hand him what was inside. He hung three planetary models from the ceiling.

"Thank you, Ms. Mankowicz."

Gabriel returned to the second seat in the third row. Corker reached into his pocket, blew his nose into a white handkerchief like someone playing an instrument poorly. Then promptly folded the contents into a neat square and returned it to his back pocket. Aimee Steiner looked away.

"Proposals are due." He touched the screen on the wall. A list appeared. Two names were in large, red font. "Mr. Jenkins and Mr. Tippitt are remiss."

He nodded. Two boys slid out of their seats to stand at attention. Corker's reprimand began, reminding all of them of their responsibility. Or as he called it, their *pupil duty.* Hiro kept his eyes forward. He stared at the mobiles hanging from the ceiling, the planets gently swaying on thin lines, each making a slow and wobbly course around their prospective stars.

"Sit," Corker said. He paced back to the podium, hands locked behind his back, stamping the floor. *Heel-toe.* "Proposal feedback will be posted tonight. You will respond in agreement or support your disagreement by tomorrow. Your report will be due upon our return from winter break. Ten pages with proper footnotes and a minimum of five legitimate references." He held up his hand. *Five.* "Social boards are not legitimate. It must be peer-reviewed publications of preapproval."

He paced with locked arms, reviewing examples of acceptable topics that had been submitted, primarily interstellar discoveries from the last one hundred years. Anything on a planet, other than the one where they currently existed, or moon or asteroid, comet, black hole or other galactic thing they'd covered in class was acceptable.

Penelope Partridge raised her hand. "Can the report not follow the proposal?"

He paused. "Elaborate, Ms. Partridge."

"I mean, if we decide to write about something other than our proposal?"

"Precisely!" He stabbed a skinny finger at the ceiling tiles. His favorite expression looked like popping a child's balloon. "This is the scientific method. Science is based on learning from mistakes. Mistakes are part of the process." A smile creased his face like a knife through a block of cheese. "Diverge from your proposal but do so with great care."

He marched stiff legged. His voice rose and fell on the sharp edge of consonants, enunciating words with a watchmaker's precision, reviewing various proposals, their weaknesses and strengths: discoveries on other planets and moons, current interstellar travel and, for the ambitious, the warping of time and space. A palpable haze of boredom hung over their heads, eyes glazed with milky condensation.

Hiro was thinking about breakfast.

An epiphany began taking shape. Shapes and colors projected in his imagination. Hiro pretended to be taking notes but didn't write a single word. A circle filled the page with hatched lines to capture tones and shapes. It felt like a planet, but not a planet that resembled one from Corker's mobile. Squiggly lines emanated from its atmosphere, jutting out into space. Color pencils ached to capture the vivid blends he was seeing.

Once upon a time, this classroom had been where his mother taught art. Hiro had helped her hang decorations after school when he was younger. He remembered long strands of artificial greenery and shiny orbs. A small tree in the corner and a vague memory of happiness.

Hiro sketched the outlines of land masses. There was distant laughter, a sound outlawed from Corker's class, but Hiro was too immersed. He had to grab the details while they hovered in his imagination, before they disappeared into the fog. The squiggly lines should be glowing. Yes! That was what he'd dreamed. Glowing, squiggly lines. If he had a yellow pencil, he could outline them. Instead, he applied a soft layer of shade.

He didn't hear the clapping of hard soles. Only saw the polished shoes, in perfect alignment, next to his desk, triggering an adrenaline flood in Hiro's chest. He slammed the book closed.

Corker's fingers unfurled like a clammy creature. Hiro had no choice. Corker studied the drawing, lips pursed like a lemon squeezed under his tongue. The longer he looked, the sourer it became. He squinted at Hiro and grunted. Perplexed was not one of Corker's personality traits. But, for a moment, he was exactly that. He took long, deliberate steps. The shiny shoes sounded like axes on a marble slab.

"Come."

Hiro was a petrified version of himself, an immovable carving that resembled a sixteen-year-old boy fused to a plastic seat. Cold vapor filled his legs; his cheeks could cook an egg. The students were looking at him. Some smiling. This was the only time everyone paid attention: a championship bout between a heavy favorite and a hopeless underdog. *Ding, ding.*

Corker taped the drawing on the wall. Hiro gripped the desk like he'd been pushed from a plane. Corker nodded ever so slightly. Then let the silence bake Hiro like a Thanksgiving turkey. Sweat tracked his spine. The silence was a microwave beam. Hiro let go before he was fully cooked.

He shoved his hands in his pockets. His legs were cold steel. He bit his lip to keep it from quivering. It wasn't just the march up to the front that disemboweled him or the twenty-five pairs of eyes that brought earth-shattering panic. *Mother will hear about this.*

Corker offered the podium like an honor. And then, to make matters worse, he abandoned him up front, walking stiffly down the aisle and folding his lanky body into Hiro's empty desk.

There were snickers and whispers that, ordinarily, Corker would snuff out with a cold eye. But he let them go. Sweat popped up on Hiro's upper lip. He tasted something metallic on his lower lip. Corker nodded, and Hiro knew what that meant. It had happened before when Jenny Skarsgard was caught on her phone. Corker hadn't sat in the audience when she marched up front. Hiro looked at the faux wood grain of the podium.

"Um." Hiro reflexively swallowed a rock in his throat. "This is—"

"Hands from pockets, Mr. Tanaka," Corker said. "Address the class."

Hiro swallowed again, but the rock wouldn't go down. He quickly grabbed the podium to keep his hands from flying off. Their eyes, all their eyes, were mini microwaves. He could smell his hair burning. Perry Parsons had his phone where Corker wouldn't see it. Hiro closed his eyes briefly. If Corker made him let go of the podium, he would crumble like a wooden puppet.

"Um, this is... I was—" He started to point at the drawing and quickly latched back onto the podium. His mouth filled with cotton. "I was working out my proposal."

"Proposal?" Corker said.

"I wasn't sure, you know, what to write yet. I started drawing."

Corker nodded with dead eyes. Hiro stammered. He wasn't sure if words came out.

Paul Baker raised his hand. "What is it?"

"The drawing?" Hiro said.

"Yeah. The drawing."

"Planet."

"Which one?"

Hiro shook his head. He didn't know.

Margaret Bleeker said, "What are the lines coming off it?"

Hiro didn't know what those were, either. He couldn't admit it was a dream. Not in front of the class. Corker raised his hand like one of the students. He didn't lower it until Hiro nodded.

"Where are the words?"

"Words?"

"Yes, words. It is a written assignment, five pages, and sourced. *Woooords.*" The class chuckled, and Corker let them. "Where are the words?"

"It's just, I was... ideas... and..."

"The lines are wormholes," Hazel Melblank said. "*Worlds Apart.* It was a movie where space is an illusion and—"

"There are no such things as wormholes." Corker turned a darker shade. The first sign he was human with a heart that pumped blood instead of antifreeze. He turned his icy lasers back to Hiro. "Why did you draw it?"

"Because I wasn't sure—"

"That's not what I'm asking. Why did you draw *that*?" He jabbed a finger at the wall behind Hiro.

"I-I-I don't know."

"You don't know?"

Hiro shook his head. Admitting it was a dream could make this last even longer.

"So you made it up?" Corker's eyes narrowed into deadly slits.

Hiro nodded. Corker rapped his fingernails on the desk like chisels. His lie detector was spinning. Hiro wasn't budging.

"*Worlds Apart*," Hazel said. "He probably saw it and—"

"Enough."

Corker vacated the desk and stepped aside. They watched Hiro return to his former bubble of anonymity, sitting in the perfectly straight row of perfectly matched uniforms. Hiro concentrated on not collapsing, grateful he hadn't fainted. Or worse.

"This is not a movie or a comic book," Corker said. "In this class, we work with facts. Things we know. A little thing we call proof. The purpose of this assignment is reality, not fantasy. It is not what you *wish* for, it is not about what you *believe*. No flying saucers or little stuffed animals running the world. No wormholes." He looked at Hazel. "Do not trust your senses. Trust only facts. This is science."

Hazel raised her hand, and Hiro wished she hadn't. "If we can't trust our senses, then how can we read facts? We need our eyes to see, which is one of our senses, and—"

Hiro could feel the heat shift to her side of the room. "Enough entertainment for the day, Ms. Melblank. Let's continue our class in reality. Because this reality is all there is. Mr. Tanaka, you will meet me after school to discuss reality a bit further."

Corker stripped the drawing off the board, wadded it into a tight ball and tossed it.

"That is where that belongs." He pointed at the trash can. "Precisely!"

HIRO PUT HIS PEN DOWN, held an apple by the stem. It rotated one way and then the other. He should be working on his outline, using words for his report instead of drawing, but couldn't stop thinking of round things hovering in space.

He closed his eyes. The conversations at other tables, the occasional glances in his direction, went away. The dream was still in the fog. The colorful planet surrounded by a radiant atmosphere. Glowing lines like ethereal vines twisting in solar winds, reaching into the galaxy. It was so real.

A chair scraped the floor. Hazel dropped her sharp elbows on the table. She leaned in, her eyes big and round, an amused smile half twisted into her cheek.

"You going to eat that?" she said. "Kidding. No one eats them." She took the apple from him, cupped it like a snowball. One of the points of her collar was tucked inside her sweater. The other one curled up. She whispered, "You're a terrible teacher. No offense. I mean, you had the floor. You could've said anything. But you sort of didn't."

Hiro stared at his notes.

"He's a turd, Hiro. Yeah," she said, "a turd. The kind that attracts flies." *Is there another kind?* "He's supersmart, like genius smart, and should be building rockets or something instead of designing sadistic teenage mind games. Maybe his mother didn't tuck him in at night or his father made him eat beets or someone didn't love him back. Although I can't see Corker loving anything. Either way, who pays the price? We do. We pay."

Hiro covered his writing with both hands, for some reason. He was uncomfortable with the way she looked at him, like she could see his thoughts and anxiety. His eyes were glassy portals that revealed the quivery dance his brain did whenever someone looked at him this long. And his notes would somehow betray him even more, like clues to his not-so-secret fears.

She leaned back, still watching. He hoped she'd get bored if he didn't look up; she'd go back to regular life and leave him alone. His stomach was pulling alarms in his head. He closed his notebook and started packing.

"Where is this?"

She unfolded a wad of paper and smoothed it on the table. The wrinkles made the squiggly lines crooked and wayward. The planet he drew was smudged.

"Did you really make this up?" she said. "Or were you trying to draw something else?"

He pulled the drawing closer. It was better than he remembered. If he closed his eyes, it would look just like his dream. All it needed was color.

"I dreamed it."

The words came out like snowflakes on a whisper, drifting in the cafeteria noise. She caught them with wrinkles between her eyes.

"I don't remember the last time I dreamed. Except..." She looked up, like her thoughts were floating near the ceiling. "Do daydreams count?"

She recounted, unabashedly, how she'd daydreamed about wearing shorts to school, like, really short ones. And didn't shave her legs.

"So are they?" She dropped her finger on the squiggly lines. "Wormholes? Like I said, remember? *Worlds Apart,* shortcuts through space. You never saw that movie?"

He shook his head. He didn't know what the lines were. Although they felt like tunnels, which, if they were in outer space, would make them wormholes.

"You should include that in your paper," she said. "The drawing. Staple it to the back."

His spine shivered. He could feel his legs solidify. Just the thought of Corker seeing his drawing on the table raised a fleet of perspiration. He even had the thought of putting it back in the trash in case Corker went looking for it. Hiro already had one detention to stay after school. When his mother found out, there would be more.

"Corker and his facts," she said. "What kind of facts did we have before microscopes? Germs were invisible fairies until the microscope was invented. And there was the one guy, the famous one, I don't remember his name, I should, but he said the sun doesn't orbit around our planet when everyone else said it did. And what did that get him? They threw him in jail or something. I guarantee you Corker would've marched to his house with pitchforks and torches because facts, Hiro. Facts!" She chopped the air. "Nothing exists without facts!"

People were looking at them. He covered the drawing.

"Look, what I'm saying is we don't know everything. Am I right? Like how'd we get here? Why are we here? What's the point? Corker can't answer that. No one can."

She stabbed the drawing with her finger.

"You put that with your report, make it part of some historical research. You know, like write about what astronomical science was like before the telescope when people thought gods made it rain when they threw someone in a volcano. What's the worst that can happen? He'll give you a bad grade because you had a dream?"

"My mother."

He bit his lip hard enough to taste it. His thoughts dripped from his brain and escaped out of his mouth. He had to get away before he confessed to something he didn't do. He gathered his notebook, put his pen in his pocket.

"Your mom, right," Hazel said. "Didn't she teach art? She can handle it, Hiro. I'll bet she'll be proud if you use the drawing."

He shook his head rabidly. She didn't know his mother. She was different now. The chair nearly tipped over when he stood. He didn't need it slamming on the floor like a gavel to get everyone's attention.

"I'll text you." She held up her phone. "Or I can email you, class chat, whatever. I'm not charging you; this advice is free. But if you want to help me with *my* report, we'll call it even. Help me help you help me."

Hiro dropped his pen. His hands were shaking.

"Or not," she said.

He took a deep breath, moving slowly, deliberately. No sudden movements, nothing to see here. Just two people talking. Or one person talking. But it was nothing, just a boy and girl and an apple. He started to walk off, then remembered the drawing. She snapped a picture of it.

"You on Social?" she said, taking three more pictures before he got it. "Stay off for a while. Perry Pinhead posted your guest lecture."

The sweat down his back turned into morning frost. Perry had had his phone out when Hiro was at the podium. Hiro wasn't on Social. And he'd never have known it was posted if she hadn't told him.

"You can still be a teacher." She took a bite of the apple, then spit in her hand. Wiped her tongue and made a face, then said, "Just saying, everyone doesn't start strong."

4

Corker wasn't in his classroom.

Maybe he forgot Hiro was coming. He doubted Corker had ever forgotten anything. Hiro was early; he wanted to get this over with. He'd never had detention before, didn't know what would happen. Maybe Corker would have him scrub the floors or straighten desks with a ruler. There was a hope, a tiny hope, that if he did everything just right, his mother wouldn't hear about it.

When this was his mother's classroom, there had been lamps in the corners and candles on the teacher's desk. Music played from a small speaker. The desks were never in the same place; sometimes they were arranged in a circle or facing different directions. Sometimes students sat cross-legged on a rug.

Now it smelled like a hospital.

Hiro sat in his assigned seat. His legs shook, so he walked up and down the aisle. Corker's desk was orderly. No candle wax drippings, no coffee cup filled with candy. There was a calendar with a stack of envelopes, names without addresses. December 25 was circled on the calendar. Maybe he was going on a trip for winter break. It was hard to imagine Corker on a ski slope or lounging on a beach.

The planetary mobiles hung from the ceiling, slowly turning in the draft from the ventilation ducts. The box was on the floor. Hiro went to the podium. He didn't shake or bite his lip. It was easy standing up there without all the eyes on him. Hazel was right. He should have done something besides grip the podium like a toy soldier.

"That's right," he whispered, "I dreamed of a planet. It isn't against the law. Just because no one else does or, or, or if they do, can't remember them. I did nothing wrong."

He looked at the empty seats, imagining his classmates no longer snickering. Their expressions slowly changing. They were nodding along. Perry was still secretly filming him. They all had their phones out now, not even trying to hide it.

"I'll bet you dream, too," he whispered, pointing. "Wishing for something different. Thinking something is missing. Dreaming the world could be different. I'm not different than you. We're the same."

Someone would say, *I had a dream, too!* And then someone else would say it and someone else. Mitzy Bennigan would be the first one to stand on her desk, because that was something she would do. Corker would tell them to be quiet because he wanted to hear what else Hiro had to say.

"*That* came from my imagination." Hiro pointed at the empty wall where Corker had taped his drawing. "I don't know where it came from. It spoke to me. It can speak to you. All you have to do is listen."

They would start clapping now. Corker would stand up with the others, walloping those big spidery hands together and then climbing onto the desk, his head brushing the ceiling.

Hiro went to the wall and pretended to take the drawing off. The cheers would be so loud the principal would come down. And once he saw the drawing, he'd burst into tears. Hiro's mother would rush into the room and hug him. They would be posting about him on the Social, where his inspiration would spread around the world.

"This is my dream."

Hiro thrust his empty hand above his head. Metal objects crashed on the table. Wires circled around his arm. He'd knocked one of the mobiles off the hook Corker had set into the ceiling tile.

Without hesitation, he climbed onto the table. The wires were tangled but hadn't kinked. The hook had fallen off the ceiling. He had to search for it, straighten out the planets and climb back onto the desk. He wasn't sure where Corker had exactly put it. The wires rang in his shaky hands. There was no way to know, so he just hung it above the podium. He moved it two times, stepping back, examining it, trying to remember where it had been exactly.

There were footprints all over the table.

He looked around, found a towel in the cardboard box where Corker had stored the mobiles. It sat on top of a stack of notebooks. Big sheets of folded paper were wedged between them. Hiro saw bright colored lines, and despite the paralyzing anxiety, his curiosity made him look.

He unfolded a large map on the table. There were dozens of them in the box, drawings of interstellar constellations crisscrossed with red lines and blue lines, orange and green and yellow. A thick purple line had clusters of Corker's indecipherable writing; words under-lined with exclamation points. Calculations with symbols and numbers, things circled. Nothing he could understand.

It felt familiar.

Maybe it was because it had to do with space, and that was all Hiro could think about: space. The notebooks had dates and times, long rambling entries without paragraphs or punctuation and barely a word he could read, a scribbling mess of lines from someone whose mind worked too fast for his hand to keep up.

Click-clack.

The heel-toe warning was coming down the hall. Hiro rushed everything back into the box, started for his seat, then ran back to wipe his footprints off the desk. The footsteps grew closer. There wasn't time to get back to his seat. He stood against the whiteboard as the door began to open. He tossed the towel into the box.

Corker stopped. His nostrils flared. Eyes shifting around the room, landing on the mobile above the podium still swaying. He blinked heavily.

"Sit."

Hiro went to his assigned seat far away from the front of the classroom. Corker looked inside the cardboard box. Hiro held onto his desk to keep from running away. Corker put the box in the closet, then went to his desk, sat down and began writing. This went on for several minutes. The dry scritching of a pointed pencil, the stabbing punctuation and abrupt folding of paper. He tucked the letter in an envelope, licked the flap and added it to the pile.

Maybe this was detention, listening to a teacher handwrite letters. Corker put the pencil down, tidied the desktop and stood up. Hiro stiffened as he walked down the aisle. He took the desk in front of Hiro, turned it around and folded his lanky body into it. With his back straight, he stared with dead eyes.

Corker was more gray than pink. His cheeks drawn, cheekbones protruding. He barely looked real, like a hollow version of a bitter physics teacher in a wax museum. A ghost who didn't want to be there any more than the students it haunted. His lips slowly parted.

"Did you take the drawing from the trash?"

"My what?" Hiro smacked his dry lips. They stuck together. Corker blinked with impatience. "Oh. No. No, I didn't take it from the trash."

Corker waited with heavy eyelids. His fingers unfolded, hand extended. Palm expectant. Hiro swallowed. There was no point in drawing this out. He dug his drawing out of his backpack.

"I didn't take it."

"Then why do you have it?"

"I found it in the cafeteria."

"How did it get there?"

Hiro sat still. He didn't shrug or lie. Nor did he say anything that would get Hazel in trouble.

Corker smoothed the drawing on his desk. He appeared to study it, nodding and grunting to himself. Following lines with a fingernail in need of trimming. He pondered it like a detailed map.

"You dreamed this?"

A cold rush of blood froze the hair on his head. He knew. He knew Hiro had dreamed it.

"How many times?"

"How many?"

"Yes. How many times did you dream this?" He held the drawing up.

"Just last night."

"Why?"

"Why?"

"Why did you dream *this*?"

That didn't make any sense. Why does anyone dream? "I, uh, I don't know."

Corker grunted, not satisfied. It was better not to lie, not even a little. Corker had lie detectors as good as Hiro's mother.

"Nothing more you'd like to share?" He drummed the fingernails like daggers. "About the dream?"

"No, sir."

"Anything else besides this?" He shook the drawing.

"No. No, I just remember that, that's all. I swear."

This was weird. Nothing about not paying attention in class or lying about taking it. Corker seemed distracted, but, thankfully, there was nothing more. If Hiro had dreamed something awful and embarrassing, he would have to say it to be spared the X-ray vision that was peeling through his thoughts like a card catalog. Corker narrowed his eyes, grunted.

"You are best served to stay in this world, Mr. Tanaka. Not fantasy land."

He methodically folded the drawing twice, running his finger down the crease, and handed it to Hiro. He crawled out of the desk, turned it around and put it in line with the others. Hiro watched him pace up front to resume letter writing.

"You may leave," Corker said without looking up.

Hiro wasn't sure if he'd heard that correctly, so he didn't move. It wasn't until Corker waved his hand that he grabbed his backpack. He ached to get away from the antiseptic smell and the sound of the pencil. He stopped with his hand on the doorknob. He couldn't explain what happened next. From somewhere unknown, a thought slipped over his tongue before he could stop it.

"I'm changing my proposal."

Corker stopped what he was doing. "Pardon?"

"I want to do a historical review of discoveries. Like what we believed was true before microscopes. I mean, we didn't know single-celled organisms existed. People thought spirits were causing disease. And telescopes, too. Before that, the sun orbited around the planet, and anyone who said different got punished. I think, you know, it would be interesting to look at how facts evolve with technology. Maybe this is a dream." The drawing quivered in his hand. "But what if it's more than that?"

Corker put his pencil down. The temperature dropped a few degrees. Hiro wanted to say more, like shouldn't the scientific method be curious? Maybe Hazel was right and these were wormholes that were somehow communicating through dreams like radio waves. If all we had was our senses to observe reality, why did we ignore dreams? Because this dream felt as real as the paper in his hand.

"Dreams, Mr. Tanaka, are thoughts. And thoughts are nothing more than thoughts." He half-heartedly pointed at the ceiling. "Precisely that."

He pushed away from his desk. His heavy, calculated footsteps pounded Hiro's chest like a hammer. Corker's hand wrapped around the doorknob. He looked down on Hiro like a superhero tired of saving the world, desperate to escape.

"This is science, not fiction writing. Keep your feet on the ground till after winter break. Whoever is teaching this class when you get back may feel differently than I do."

"You're not coming back?"

He pulled the door open and gestured. Hiro stepped into the hall. The heel-toe footsteps faded behind him.

5

Fifty-one days without dreaming.

I knew the exact number because I started a journal. I read a book about lucid dreaming, and that was what it said to do. I had dreams during that time, but they were petty: going to work in my underwear, house flooding. Those kinds of dreams. Still, I kept a notebook on the nightstand and wrote them down as soon as I woke.

I'd lost hope. *It was just a dream,* I told myself. *A vivid, lucid dream. It wasn't real. I wasn't a toy.*

On the fifty-second night, I smelled popcorn. I hate popcorn. Gets stuck in my teeth, always messy. *Why would I make popcorn?* I thought. I started to panic, thinking I'd left the stove on. I was going to get out of bed, check the kitchen.

A furry orange cat startled me. He was the size of a middle school child, slouched in the corner with round eyes. I was on a dresser. A purple monkey on one side, a floppy-eared dog on the other. Both wide-eyed and slumped over, staring at posters of puppet bands. A mobile of a solar system hung from the ceiling. There were planets and moons I'd never seen, like something a third grader would make.

There she was, Madeline Bells, lying on her bed, tapping on a laptop. Humming to a song in her earphones, watching a video. Face lit with electric light. Her hair was longer than the last time I'd seen her, when she picked my arm off the floor, crouching down while I cowered in the corner.

The air was crisp, but not cold. Like inhaling effervescent evergreen. It was so different than the air at home. It was vibrant, scintillating. Alive. I wanted to cry. *Am I breathing?*

I was wrapped in a flannel blanket. I squirmed until it fell from my collarbones. Two arms. I had two arms. And the tag, the Viktor the Red tag, was gone. Madeline looked up. I held still like the toys next to me. It was instinctual, automatic. Like I'd done something wrong. She pulled the earphones out. We stared at each other, and then slowly she slid off the bed and crept out of her room.

Music bled from the covers. Not a song I knew.

She returned with her mother, carefully stepping into the doorway, peeking inside. I could feel their apprehension. Their emotions were palpable, like I was running my fingers over tissue paper, feeling grains of sand beneath. Like the air between us was gritty.

Her mom whispered. Madeline approached with a hopeful smile.

"I wrapped you up so you wouldn't get cold." She looked at her mom, back to me. "Can I pick you up?"

I didn't say yes or no, but I didn't fight it when she reached for me like I was a feral cat. Her hands were warm. The warmth seeped through me like bathwater and all the goodness of innocence. That weepy feeling filled me again.

"I'm so glad you're back." She hugged me like a puppy.

"Gentle," the mom said.

It didn't hurt. She could squeeze as hard as she wanted.

"Can you hear me?" she said. I was too emotional to nod. "Can you talk? No? It's okay." She turned to the mom. "Where's Dad?"

"In his office. Why don't you show him around, and I'll get him."

Madeline gave me the grand tour of the house. I wrapped my boney arms around her neck, and she giggled, pointing out the kitchen, her parents' bedroom, and the bathroom. Her dad's office was in the back of the house. A fireplace was blazing in the living room. Fuzzy, red stockings hung from the mantel. Three of them. A Christmas tree in the corner, presents stacked beneath it. A half-finished puzzle was on a coffee table, a book on a beige sofa.

"It's the strangest thing," the mom muttered. "I can't explain it. He's back."

"How long has it been?" the dad said.

"Almost a year."

A year? I thought. I would solve that conundrum later.

The parents watched Madeline explain the puzzle to me. They did one every Christmas. It was a tradition. The dad had streaks of gray in a tightly clipped beard. He wore a black tie and white shirt. Creases in his slacks. He stared with intense fascination. It was a weird mix of surprise and curiosity. There was a living toy in their house. That didn't seem to be the root of his surprise, like of course the toy was living. It was something else.

"This is my dad, Philip."

The dad reached out his hand. I just looked at it, then realized what he was doing. I wrapped boney fingers around two of his fingers. Warm, like Madeline.

"Pleased to meet you, Viktor," he said.

"And you've met my mom, Polly. She made you. You're not a box job. You're original."

That sounded special.

"Is he talking?" the dad said.

"Let's not push it," the mom said. "He needs to acclimate."

"Maybe we should go into town."

"Not yet. I want to keep an eye on him today, not overwhelm him. Hon, keep holding him; I want to scan his charm."

The mom left the room. The dad looked me over, complimented my bone structure, how sturdy I was. The mom returned with something like a cell phone. This was what babies must feel like, all the fuss and smiles. The dad stepped back, made way for the mom and her cell phone.

"Okay. Um, this won't hurt, Viktor. I'm just going to wave this in front of you."

I squeezed Madeline's neck. When someone with a foreign object says this isn't going to hurt, it's going to hurt. The mom heard my bones shaking and stepped back. She pulled a silver marble from her pocket. It was an oversized ball bearing.

"See that?" Madeline said. "You have one just like it." She touched my head. "Usually, it's in the chest, but since you're all bones, Mom put it up there. Can we show him?"

"I don't think that's a good idea."

"Isn't that what you do to help with stabilization?" the dad said. "Once he sees the core, he'll know who he is. Right?"

The mom was thinking, and I was getting more nervous. She started nodding because, evidently, toys had come to life, and she'd done this before. I felt Madeline's hand cradle the back of my head. Once again, the warmth filled me with pleasurable wonder. She shushed and rocked me. A smile grew inside me. Her fingers were at the base of my skull.

There was a click.

I couldn't move. I'd lost all feeling in my bones, but I could see what was happening, hear what they were saying. Madeline held a silver marble like the one her mom had pulled from her pocket.

"This is you," she whispered.

This dream was impeccably detailed. I wasn't the toy. I was a marble inside the toy. The red skeleton was a vehicle. A body. That was how this worked. I had no idea how it could possibly work, but there was some logic to it. Like a brain inside a body.

"I think he's got it," the mom said. "You can put it back."

There was another click as the marble slid back into my skull. A little trapdoor closed. I was back in her arms. I made the mistake of touching my forehead, heard the hard plastic of my fingers touch my skull. It wasn't till my finger slipped inside an empty eye socket that I sort of lost my cool—scrambling on Madeline's shoulder to run away from the queer sensation.

"It's all right, it's all right." Madeline held me tight. That helped. Immensely.

The mom waited till I was no longer shaking to hold up the cell phone instrument. She told me, again, it wasn't going to hurt. I clung to Madeline. I would have closed my eyes if I had eyes.

She waved it over my head, then studied the reading. "Good. He's stable. Let's watch him for a bit. Want to put him down?"

Madeline lowered me to the floor. I hadn't thought about standing on my own. It was a bit like walking on stilts. I was a child all over again, waving my arms, dragging boney feet over the hardwood floor, knocking puzzle pieces off the table. It was like ice skating for the first time.

"Wow," the dad said. "He's not good at walking."

"Yes," the mom said. "I built him as a blank prototype, not expecting him to wake up. It's like some consciousness crossover occurred."

"From another toy?"

"What else could it be?"

The dad scratched his beard. "It's just, he acts like a newborn."

"I'll check around to see if a nearby toy went blank. Maybe there was some synchronous thought transmission that cross-connected with another charm. It's happened before, one toy moves into another if the frequencies suddenly match."

"The odds on that are—"

"A billion to one. Yes. What else could it be?"

"What about, I don't know, *somebody* switched into the wrong toy?"

I felt the chill between them. I didn't know what that meant, exactly, or why I felt it. I'd followed what they were saying up to that point. If my consciousness was inside that marble—they called it a charm, I guess—then perhaps it could sync up with another marble, like a wireless toy leaping from one toy to another. But when the dad said *somebody,* that meant something else. Something chilling.

Somebody switched into the wrong toy.

"No. That's not possible. There's not a switch bank near my shop," the mom said. "Even if there were, a person couldn't accidentally occupy a random toy."

"I know," the dad said. "Still."

The mom shook her head. "I'll check around, see if any activity matches up. What time did he wake?"

They noted the time I woke up on the dresser. And the date and time they found me in the toy shop, which, apparently, had been a year ago. It hadn't been a year when I last dreamed of this place. They were clearly confused. Not as much as I was, and not as much as they should be.

That night I was put on the dresser with the purple monkey and floppy-eared dog. I didn't sleep. Just sat there, listening to Madeline sleep. In the morning, I was still there, wrapped in the flannel blanket.

THEY WORE puffy coats and stocking caps. I had a green cloak the mom had fashioned from a blanket. It had a hood and tied around my neck, dragged behind me like a cape. Madeline didn't want me getting cold. I looked like a fairy tale.

The outside of the house was simple. Thick shutters, brick chimney, a cracked sidewalk. A car puffed smoke in the driveway, not a model I'd ever seen before. It was boxy, very wide. Madeline explained what snow was. It went up to my pelvis when I stepped in it. It wasn't cold. Slightly chilly, maybe. It felt like sponge cake.

Madeline and I got in the back seat. We drove past small houses decorated with ornaments and lights. Neighbors waved as we passed them. In the distance, the hills rose around this valley village that was quiet and friendly. It was all quite normal. Until we got downtown.

That was where the toys were.

There were teddy bears and skinny dolls, furry animals and action figures. Walking and talking, sitting inside cafés, dancing across the road. A panda bear dressed as Santa, ringing a bell in front of an empty bucket. Farther down, a fabric doll was facedown on a storm sewer. People walked past them without acknowledgment, as if they were pigeons in search of crumbs.

Toys are people.

This explained everything. It wasn't impossible, the more I thought about it. Technology could program a metal ball with artificial intelligence and insert it into a body. How the neural connections were made to control it, I had no idea. The proof was walking down the sidewalk. Although *I* wasn't artificial intelligence. If I were, would I know it?

This is a dream, I reminded myself. *An incredibly long, detailed dream.* I decided, for once in my life, I would stop trying to solve the equation and just go for the ride.

"That's where you woke up," Madeline said.

A small shop was tucked between a shoe store and an electronics repair shop. Words were painted on the window. *Toy Stitchery.*

I recalled, as the store receded through the back window, jolting awake on the shelf, losing my arm. It seemed like so long ago. So frightening. And now, it almost seemed normal to see toy elephants staring at pastries through a shop window and holding trunks.

According to Madeline, toy stitching ran in the family. The skill passed down from generation to generation. It went all the way back to the Great Toy Migration. I wanted to know more about that, but, seeing as I didn't know how to talk, I had no way to ask.

"I'm going to build my own shop in the city," she said. "Maybe you can be my assistant."

Well, here I was, not more than a day old in this dream and I already had a job.

Toys of different stripes and colors were queued up along an old brick building. I couldn't tell what they were waiting for, but they were dirty and wet. Matted fur and marred plastic. A yellow toy truck was missing a wheel. The car stopped in front of us. Someone threw a pink piggy out the window. It tumbled like a pillow, four short legs pointing at the blue sky, at the end of the line.

"Pull over," the mom said. She was out of the car before the dad had come to a complete stop. "Hey, no! You don't toss her like that."

The car drove off. The mom went a few more steps, still shouting at the driver. She came back to the car. "I need to see why the shelter isn't open. Can you go down to the experience café, engage Viktor's senses? I don't want him seeing this. I'll meet you down there."

The mom picked the pink piggy up, brushed her off and helped her get in line. She spoke to the toys on her way past them, unlocking the front door to let them in. Madeline wasn't looking. Her nose crinkled, dark eyebrows pinched. I thought she was avoiding me. I tapped her arm.

"It happens every Christmas." She put her arms around me. "It won't happen to you."

For the next two days, we sat around the fireplace and told stories, went to town to see the mom's workshop, built a snowman in the front yard, visited experience cafés, where I learned the full array of toy senses. We were working on the puzzle when the house started beeping. The room was suddenly cold. An alarm clock was making noise.

Then I was staring at a water stain on the ceiling.

6

A plywood boardwalk was beneath naked bulbs swaying on black cords, sharp shadows dancing on boxes of the old and forgotten: a baby crib, a hermetically sealed wedding dress, a plastic dog carrier. Hiro's father, bundled in a winter coat, breath steaming in the white light, walked between the rafters. Hiro hated the cold. His skin always tired beneath layers of sweaters.

"It's down there." His father pointed. "I think."

They walked to the end of the plank. He pulled the string on the last bulb. It swung over his stocking cap like a great idea. Hiro shivered, hugging himself, as his father pulled out boxes and glanced inside. Coffee mugs and glassware, wooden spoons and moldy towels.

"I've been looking for this." His father held up a meditation bench. Looked around. "We're getting warmer. I can feel it." *No, we're not,* Hiro thought.

They found a bronze sculpture of a stout little figure. That was from when Mother used to sculpt. When she used to make stuff. Her studio, in the back of the house, had smelled earthy. She would stay back there all day, coming out with more clay on her hands than there was dirt in the backyard. She would be glowing. Now that room was an office.

"Help me with this," his father said.

Hiro helped slide a long box onto the plank. He rubbed a layer of dust off the label. "Why do we have an artificial tree?"

"Why do we have these?" He opened a box of smooth black rocks with a pouch of white feathers. "Your grandparents were always bringing stuff back from their travels. We just put them up here."

They dug deeper, carefully stepping on the joists to keep from going through the ceiling. There was a cylinder of ornate canes, a pottery wheel, and a unicycle missing a pedal.

"Here we go." His father held a box in the light. There were brushes and pallet knives and rags stiff with paint. He handed it to Hiro, who set it on the boardwalk. "Why do you all of a sudden want art supplies?"

He shrugged. "Something to do."

"It wouldn't have anything to do with Mr. Corker's class, would it?" He paused with a grim smile.

Hiro thought he'd gotten away with that. Missteps were usually dealt with at dinner or, at the very latest, breakfast. It had been two days since detention. His mother hadn't said a word to Hiro. But, apparently, had said plenty to his father.

"Your mother said he's a good teacher, Hiro."

Hiro grunted, then covered his mouth.

"All right, a challenging teacher. A bit unusual, maybe. But there's a lot you can learn from him."

"He made me get up in front of class."

He turned with a jar of marbles. "Are you injured?"

"What?"

"Did you bruise a kidney?"

"He embarrassed me in front of everybody."

His father handed him the jar and pulled off his mittens, breathing into his fists. He nodded, thinking. The temperature was dropping by the second. Hiro wanted to cup his hands around the light bulb for warmth.

"There was this Buddhist temple. All the students there were very diligent about their studies. Among them was a foul old man. He cursed if someone bumped into him. Spat on the sidewalk during walking meditation. Then one day, to the relief of everyone, he decided he'd had enough and left the temple.

"The students were all excited. They approached the teacher and said now that the old man was gone, they could get serious about their meditations. The teacher asked if they really wanted to practice. They all agreed. Of course they did. That was why they were there. So the teacher left the temple. He returned two days later with the old man."

Hiro waited for the end of the story. "That's it?" he finally said.

"The best teachers push buttons, Hiro. They graciously reveal your shortcomings that you cannot see. They are neither naughty nor nice. They do what's required of life."

Hiro nodded. Even though it didn't make sense. "Someone put the whole thing on Social. They recorded me."

"So? You went in front of class, and you did it. You faced it and owned it. That, my son, is courage."

"I didn't have a choice."

"Sure you did."

Is he joking? It was hard to tell with the shadows across his face. *Choice?* This would be a very different conversation if Hiro had refused to do what Corker told him to do.

"Remember this?" His father reached into the clutter. Boxes tumbled over. Red paint flaked from the rails. Lacquer peeled from the boards. He handed it to Hiro. The sled dropped on the boardwalk with a bang.

He remembered this when he was little. There was this long slope in the park. In winter, everyone would bring disks and toboggans and sleds. Hiro's parents and grandparents would stand at the top with the other parents. Hiro remembered the park was decorated with lights and shiny round things in the trees.

There was this one time a kid asked if Hiro wanted to wax the rails, make it go faster. Hiro wasn't ready for just how fast it would go.

The wind whistled in his ears. He tried to steer away from the hump the big kids would hit. He was launched into the air. The landing knocked the wind out of him, and he tumbled all the way to the bottom. The big kids were down there, laughing. Someone called him a banger.

Hiro pulled the sled back up the hill. His ribs ached. He couldn't catch his breath. When he reached the top, his parents said that was probably enough for one day.

"And what did you do?" his father said.

"I went again."

"Why?"

Hiro insisted it was because he knew if he didn't, he'd be too afraid to ever go again. He avoided the hump the second time, went all the way to the bottom and climbed back to the top. Then they went home.

"Do you know what everyone has in common with heroes?" His father leaned the sled against a rafter, put his hands on Hiro's shoulders. "They're scared, too."

"Tomo!" Mother called from downstairs.

"That's my cue," he said, rubbing his arms. "Turn off the lights when you come down."

His footsteps echoed down the boardwalk. Hiro watched him climb quickly out of sight. He considered following him downstairs, where it was warm, but after that talk about heroes, he felt like he should keep looking. Not like there were dragons in the attic.

He carefully climbed through the rafters, ducking to avoid the pitched roof where nails were sticking through. They'd found the brushes. The rest of the supplies were somewhere. He pulled open flaps and dug through boxes of books, found a stash of old music on silver discs and a CD player. He'd never heard of any of the artists. The cover art was things like snow and strings of lights, warm fires and evergreen trees.

He lugged a box to the boardwalk to take downstairs and went back for more. He decided to keep going till he reached the corner. One of the plastic bins had spilled a stack of books. He put them back in the bin. The pages sparkled in the white light. The glitter had worn off the covers. His mother's handwriting had faded.

The dream journals.

The pages crackled when he opened them. Hiro's journal was half full of words and pictures, the pages dogeared and torn, sketches in the margins where he'd try to show his parents what a dream looked like during breakfast. But there in the middle, where the writing had stopped, the dreams were shorter. The drawings scarce. He couldn't remember when he quit writing them down. Or why.

His mother's journal was mostly poems written in flowing handwriting; so stylish it was as enticing to look at as it was to read. Her lyrics were like candy. They grew shorter and trite. Ending with one final thought, a single line without punctuation. *And to all a good night.*

To Hiro's surprise, his father had recorded a dream. It was only one. As dreams go, it was strange in the familiar way dreams distort reality into something believable until waking. A dream of waking on a wintery morning, his head filled with sugar plums and candy canes, running downstairs in bare feet to open presents.

It sounded nice.

Boxes tipped over, and a bigger mess lay before him. He was getting careless and would freeze before he finished. He didn't want to be a hero. But when something scampered beneath the clutter, he jumped back, nearly stepping through the ceiling, and stood on the boardwalk, bumping his head on the light bulb. The light swayed into the corner. Perhaps he hadn't caused the avalanche after all. It was a rodent. Or something bigger. Like the things that lived under his bed when the lights went out.

He reached for the drawstring on the light, prepared to run all the way to the ladder. An object rolled out of a box and bounced off the insulation, dribbling onto the boardwalk. Hiro picked it up. It was round and smooth and shiny with a hook made from a paperclip. A picture was pasted to the side. *Hiro's First... something.*

The last word was missing. *My first what?*

He looked as far back into the shadows as he could see, then grabbed a golf club from a moldy bag. Squeezing the rubber grip, he advanced like a swordsman, jabbing and poking. As the minutes went by, nothing scampered, nothing moved. It was his imagination that made this mess, a mess he would clean up after he warmed up in front of the fire. The last box he poked spilled colorful tubes crimped at the bottoms. Markers and pencils followed. The art supplies were buried under a tangle of lights and silver bells. He scooped them into the box and turned to leave.

The hair stood up on the back of his neck.

It was that feeling of someone breathing behind him. Of something beneath the bed. His knuckles ached around the golf club. He backed out, careful of where he stepped, when he saw something staring at him. The light caught two unblinking eyes. Hiro held still. He nudged a paper bag aside and peeked around the rafters.

It was furry.

THE SILVER DISC whirred in the player. The label, written in black marker, spun past a transparent window. It was his mother's handwriting. The player was too old for wireless earbuds. Hiro plugged headphones, the kind with spongy foam over the speakers, into the jack.

He propped pillows against the headboard. It was old-people music. You couldn't dance to it, wouldn't blare it from a car. There was no bass to boom. There were strings and bells. He wouldn't describe it as good. But it made him feel good.

He finished his sketch. Now he added color. The details were sharp. He'd dreamed the dream for the second time, the exact same dream, which was weird. It was like seeing a world through the most powerful telescope. The deep blue oceans and craggy chunks of land. He used a white pencil to color the polar caps and a cerulean blue marker to capture the atmosphere.

The squiggly lines were harder to reproduce. Their colors, in the dream, were always shifting from sienna to burnt orange to scarlet, forest green to navy blue to bright pink. He tried combining the colors, but they ended up murky. The planet looked the same in both dreams, but something was different about the second one.

Someone grabbed his foot.

Hiro leaped from the bed, and he wasn't sure, but he might have screamed. He definitely threw the CD player against the wall. The headphones ripped from his ears. Pencils and markers scattered on the floor. He stood beside his bed, covering himself, even though he was wearing three sweatshirts and two pairs of sweatpants.

"Your dad let me up," Hazel said. "He was calling you. You didn't answer."

Hiro retrieved the player. The lid was cracked. He threw it on the bed and wound the headphone wires. His heart was spinning faster than the disc. For a second, when he felt her grab his foot, he thought something had come down from the attic.

"He's nice, your dad. We talked for, like, ten minutes." She lifted a cup, holding a saucer below it. "He made tea."

She took a sip, then tossed her bookbag on the bed. Pencils and markers bounced on the sketchbook.

"Nice. You're going to use this for the report? I knew you would." She compared the colored drawing to the sketch he'd done in class, squinting back and forth.

"What are you doing here?" he said.

She frowned. "You're not as nice as your dad."

"I just mean... why are you in my house... my room?"

"So you can help with my report. Your dad was impressed. You know, teenagers on winter break doing homework, that sort of thing. I think that's why he made tea. These are different." She held up the drawings. "You're missing lines in this one."

That was it. There were fewer squiggly lines in the second dream. It was hard to remember the first dream. Maybe he had it wrong.

"I dreamed it again. Last night."

"Same dream?"

He nodded. He couldn't explain it, but it wasn't so much seeing the colors he remembered but how they felt. The squiggly lines *felt* sienna, burnt orange and scarlet. *Are there really fewer lines?*

"You're good," she said. "I wish I could draw like that."

She unpacked a laptop from her backpack. The monitor lit up. She sat on the corner of the bed, humming as she doodled the touchpad.

"Do you really need help?" he said.

"Yessss," she said. "But that's not why I'm here."

The rings on her fingers danced against each other as she tapped the keyboard. By the looks of it, she'd painted her fingernails cherry red a month ago and chewed at them ever since. He stepped around the bed. She slid the laptop toward him.

It was the Social with photos and comments and emojis: little hearts and angry faces, thumbs up and thumbs down. A video was streaming, the heading below it in all caps: TEACHER OF THE YEAR.

Hiro felt like he'd eaten a bad mushroom. His stomach recoiled. The image of Corker's classroom reached out from the screen and buried a fist in his gut. It wasn't Corker behind the podium, but a chalky student, eyes wide in terror. He wanted to slam it shut.

"They're on your side," she said. "Mostly. The video went viral. There's, like, I don't know"—she peeked at the screen—"over a thousand comments calling out bullies for putting this up. It's totally backfiring on them. I don't know why they haven't taken it down, but good."

"Why are you showing me this?" he stammered. "I-I-I never would've known."

"Because of this." She scrolled through the comments.

Hiro couldn't take his eyes off the disaster: his trembling lip caught between his teeth, sweat glistening on the bridge of his nose. And the whole world saw it.

"Here, look. Read that. Just read it." When he didn't read it, she turned the laptop back around. "*Who is this? Please tell me who you are. I dreamed that picture!* You hear that? She dreamed that sketch you did. You're not on Social, no one has your number or email. She knows nothing about you, and she said she dreamed what you drew. I thought you'd want to know. I mean, what are the odds?"

"She's just, she's playing along."

"Maybe." Hazel shrugged. "I messaged her. She sent her email. So, you know, that's it. You want it?"

"Want what?"

"Her email. Maybe there's, like, a viral dream going around, and you two are connected. Maybe it's, like, your future wife. Wouldn't that be a story? Tell your grandkids you met through this video. Sort of sweet."

He shook his head. He didn't want the email. He just wanted that video to go away. There were two weeks before they went back to school. How long did a viral video last? He knew nothing about these things.

"Look, sorry. I didn't mean to upset you. I just thought if she was for real, you should know. Maybe I shouldn't have showed you. I shouldn't have. But then you wouldn't have believed me. Anyways, I'll let you get back to whatever you're doing. Can I?" She aimed her phone at the new drawing and snapped a pic. "You want the rest of this?"

She offered the tea. When he didn't answer, she put it on the dresser.

"Oh, hey. Where'd you get this?" She grabbed the purple monkey by the gangly arms, pressed the Velcro hands together and looped them around her neck. The monkey hung against her like a baby in need of a serious bath.

"Found him in the attic." He didn't add how much it scared him. The way the purple monkey had been sitting there like a puppy.

"She smells old."

"She?"

"Yeah, she." She made a face. *Duh.* "She likes you more than me."

"She does?"

"Maybe." She took another sip of tea. "I can make up stuff, too."

She plopped the dusty monkey back on the dresser and packed

her laptop, humming again as she strapped the backpack over her shoulders.

"Anyways, bye," she said.

"Wait." Hiro went to his desk, shuffled through notebooks, found a stack of folders with bent corners. She was tickling the monkey's stomach when he handed them to her. "These are just, like, old notes and references. I'm not writing on the topic anymore, so you can use them, you know, if you want."

"Sure?"

He nodded vigorously.

"All right then. I didn't lie to your dad, then." She pulled fingerless gloves over her hands, the chipped fingernails poking through stubby holes she had cut with scissors. "It's nice to hear you say more than three words."

"Yeah, well. Okay."

"That's it?" She tilted her head, waiting. "Shouldn't you say something like…"

"Oh. Um, thanks, Hazel."

"Haze. My mom calls me *Hazel*."

She threw up two fingers, shouted, "Toots!" and headed for the stairs. Hiro stood in the doorway, heard his father ask if she was leaving already. They talked for a couple of minutes. He'd been working from home too long. When the front door closed, Hiro went back to his room. He didn't know why he'd thanked her. Then saw a scrap of paper on the bed.

It was an email.

7

The wire mesh was drawn aside; the heat from the fire blasted out like a furnace. Hiro stabbed the logs with a black poker, stirring the embers. Sometimes he'd sit in front of the fireplace until he tasted perspiration on his lip.

He stared at the mantel. Framed photos of family vacations, his grandparents, the time he played soccer in third grade (*why is that still up there?*). There were candles, too, and a painted gourd and one of those ugly mugs his mother used to sculpt. Nothing had changed. But it felt like something was missing.

"Your turn," his father said. "Hiro?"

"Sorry."

Hiro rolled dice across the board, then moved his piece, collected a power card. His mother organized her decks with one hand, eating popcorn with the other. Hiro had lost track of how many magic points he needed to advance his pod. His father had assembled a brigade of trolls outside his territory.

"Pass," Hiro said.

His father frowned. It wasn't like Hiro to pass, but he cared little about winning tonight. His mind was crowded. He found himself at a party of strange thoughts, all of them new and uninvited. There wasn't space to strategize. His father rattled the dice, tossed them on the board.

"Did you know a girl came to visit Hiro today?" he said.

"A girl?" his mother said.

"A very nice girl." He tapped his piece on the corner of the board. "We talked for several minutes. She was charming. She liked my tea."

"She liked your tea? That is charming."

Hiro shuffled his defense deck, pretended to focus. His mother held the bowl of popcorn out. Hiro shook his head.

"Who was it?" she said.

"Nobody."

"Nobody?" she said. "Does Nobody have a last name?"

"Haze," his father said.

"Haze," Mother repeated.

"You know her?"

"Hmm-mm."

Hiro's father ignored her, smiled at Hiro. "You should invite her over," he said. "There's room on the board for another player."

"She doesn't know how to play." Hiro had no idea if that was true.

It was his mother's turn. She played a strong-3 card and stacked a carriage of gnomes in the battery. Hiro took his time, played a series of giant cards and squeezed a gate across the moat. The fire crackled, and his mother dug through the popcorn in silence. His father jotted down some notes before throwing the dice.

"She's helping Hiro with his research project," he said. "She must be smart."

"Helping him? That's interesting."

Hiro scuttled away from the fire. He was suddenly hot. His stomach was twisted and empty. Ants marched up and down his skin.

"Everything all right?" his father said.

"I'm fine. Whose turn is it?"

There was nothing he could say that wouldn't make this worse. The truth would be worse than a lie. Besides, he couldn't make sense of the truth enough to tell them. The dream, the email. All of it.

His father said, "Is it the viral video?"

"No."

He'd told his mother about the video, how Corker had made him get up in front of the class, how one of the students had recorded it and posted it. Hiro looked at his socks, could feel his parents looking at him while his father gave her details of the video that only a person who had watched it would know. So now his father was on the Social. Hiro couldn't get any smaller. He didn't say anything about the comments. *Please tell me who you are. I dreamed that picture!*

There was a long pause. Then his mother took her turn and went to the kitchen. Hiro rushed through his turn. The game wasn't going to end soon enough. His father rattled the dice, dropped them on the board.

"You know, there was this girl in college—"

"I don't like her," Hiro said.

"Well, I liked this girl at college." He glanced at the kitchen, then scooted to the edge of the couch. "She was tall with long black hair that shined like a majestic bird."

"A bird?"

"Yeah, a bird. She had a magnetic smile, these big brown eyes like, like chocolate." He always struggled for analogies. "Anyway, she was very popular. She was president of a sorority, organized student activities, went to parties. Always impeccably dressed in the latest fashion."

"And you married her. I get it."

He slapped Hiro's knee. "I went weeks without saying a word to her. I was trapped in the lab or my apartment, wearing the same clothes for days at a time. There wasn't time to brush my teeth—don't tell your mother. I only thought about school and barely looked up when I walked across campus. This girl was in my English lit class, sat in the front row. I would stare at her hair, the way it flowed over her shoulders."

"Her bird hair."

"I'd wait for her to turn her head to catch a glimpse of her face. I'd get lost in daydreams. When class was over, I'd stay at my desk, pretend to write notes until she left."

"You sound a little stalkerish."

"I couldn't move when I was around her. She was this planet, and I was in her orbit. I wanted to be an asteroid soaring through the universe, but when I saw her, I just went round and round her. Like my body would fill with sand and my legs froze. I don't think I could swallow."

He shuffled his cards.

"I was coming out of a café with coffee. It was starting to drizzle, and I was waiting for a ride when she came walking down the sidewalk. She was on her phone, a sparkly scarf around her neck, her hair pulled back from her face. I was back in orbit. The coffee was shaking in my hand. She was going to see me staring, but I couldn't look away. She stopped next to me, answered a text. Her smile wrapped around me."

"I don't need to hear—"

"I opened the car door and then stopped. She was still there. And then I did it. I put the coffee on top of the car and turned around. I stuck out my hand." He held out his hand. "Hello. I'm Tomo, I said. At first, she didn't know I was talking to her. She looked up from her phone and smiled. She shook my hand. It felt like ice cream melted inside me. We're in lit class together, I said. She had no idea who I was or how much I'd studied the back of her head, but she smelled so nice. Fireworks were going off.

"It's nice to meet you, she said. I shook her hand way too long, and she was giggling, and I think I was laughing. My hand was sweaty when I let go. All I could do was nod. Then I waved, and she waved back."

He squinted across the room, seeing it happen.

"I started to duck into the car. I remembered my coffee and grabbed the door. The roof was slick, and the cup slid. Just as I was coming out of the car, it fell. The lid popped off, and all that coffee went over my head and inside my collar. It soaked my shirt, burned my back. I think she said something, but I was just... I was mortified. And you know what I did?"

"You asked her to marry you."

"I got in the car and went to class. I was completely embarrassed. The tight chest, the rotten stomach, the heat in my cheeks. I noticed the thoughts I was having and just let the sensations be there."

Another meditation lesson. Hiro had heard more than he could count. They were usually obvious, like the old man in the temple. He hadn't seen this one coming.

"I took the risk. And the next time I did it, it was easier. Still hard." He raised a finger. "The next time, I introduced myself to this lovely woman at a study group. A beautiful woman who loves to eat popcorn when she plays board games."

"I don't like Haze."

He shrugged. "You know what your grandfather always says. Jump—"

"Jump in the pool," Hiro said. "I know. I'm not asking her out."

"Where'd you find these?"

His mother returned to the game with the dream journals. Hiro told her they had been in the attic when he was looking for art supplies. She played a few cards, then opened one of the faded books, sliding her fingers over the yellowed pages. She couldn't remember making them.

Hiro's father made a card play, then opened one of the journals. Hiro's newest sketches were dated over the last couple of days.

"What's this?" he said.

It was the dream he'd told them about at breakfast, he explained. He'd had the same one almost every night, floating in space, looking down on a strange planet with squiggly lines. He didn't bother telling them there were fewer squiggly lines each time he had the dream. It would be hard to describe why that felt important.

"Do you ever think we don't see something when it's in front of us?" Hiro said.

"Like what?" his father said.

"You know the science project? Mr. Corker only wants us to use facts. But facts change. Like before microscopes were invented, no one knew about microorganisms. But they were still there. There could be planets out there, things we don't know about. Maybe someone or something is trying to tell us about them through dreams."

"Sounds like someone doesn't want to do a science project," his father muttered.

"What if I wrote a report about single-celled organisms causing disease instead of evil spirits?"

"You'd fail," his father said.

"But I wouldn't be wrong."

"He won't accept drawings of imaginary planets, Hiro," his mother said sharply. "Work with what we know.

"And don't get an F." His father put the dice in front of him.

How could someone be punished for the truth? They were right, though, if he was honest. He could make up anything and say it hadn't been discovered. He pushed a dragon scout through the primordial tunnel to open a hole in the wall of ogres and grabbed a gold card from his father's stack.

"So don't take risks, that's what you're saying," Hiro said.

"Hiro," his mother said sternly.

"Something on your mind, Hiro?" his father asked.

He shook his head. Heroes were courageous. They took risks to discover the unknown. But his parents wanted him to follow the rules. Hiro wondered how many risks his father had taken since spilling coffee on his head. Did he still jump in the pool? Or did he wait to get pushed?

"Take calculated risks." His father dropped a magician's net on the board that snared Hiro's dragon scout and claimed half of Hiro's gold. "There are consequences."

8

Hiro inhaled through his nostrils. Each breath was slow and fluid while he focused on an imaginary point in his mind. His heart rate settled. The meditation bench from the attic was solid. He rarely meditated on his own. It was only when his parents made him do it during Sunday morning ceremony.

Now seemed like a good time.

When he was done, he paced around his bed to the other side and back, slowing down just enough to read the email on his laptop before making another lap. His heart was racing again. Finally, after ten laps, he stopped in front of the mirror. The purple monkey, propped against an alarm clock, watched him fuss with his collar.

He'd already changed sweaters twice. The shirt beneath it once. No matter what he did with his hair, it always fell back into place. His hair was reliably straight, even when he got out of bed. He rubbed his finger over his teeth, tested his breath.

"Hi. Hi there. Howdy." He cleared his throat and loosened his collar. "What am I doing? Or, nothing. Just, you know."

Meditation didn't help. He went back to pacing. If he walked fast enough, he could outpace the claustrophobic feelings. But anxiety trailed like a tether of tin cans. He kept moving, glancing at the email, went back to the mirror. He turned the monkey toward the window, then turned him back around. He needed to practice in front of someone. Even a stuffed monkey.

He cleared his throat, pulled back his shoulders, and smiled. He looked like an advertisement for life insurance. "Hello. It's nice to—"

His phone buzzed. Hiro stepped back like it was the rodent from the attic (which he still hadn't told his parents about). A number popped up. *Oh, God. She's calling me.* It was a local area code, so it couldn't be her. He touched the screen.

"Hello?" he said.

"Hey." It took a moment to recognize her voice. Haze said, "I was going to text, but didn't. You still drawing?"

"How did you get my—"

"Your dad gave it to me." Hiro thought for a second, recalled their cell numbers taped to the refrigerator. "I was going to come over," she said, "but I didn't want your parents getting the wrong idea. And your mom's a little intense. So, hey, here I am. I was just—"

"What do you want?" he said.

There was a long pause. "You need to work on manners."

"Sorry." Tension had slung the words out of him. There were more that wanted out, and he couldn't stop them. "She wants to video chat."

"Who?"

"The girl. The, uh..." He studied his laptop. "Pride204. You know, from the video. The email?"

"Awww, you emailed her. I'm proud of you, stepping up like that. That's why I called, mostly. Also, to tell you they took the post down. Your video is viral no more. There were, like, a thousand comments, and they were all sticking up for you, talking about how brave you were to get up like that."

Brave? He didn't *want* to get up in front of the class. Certainly didn't want the world to see it.

"Anyways, when you calling her?" she said.

"I'm not." He looked in the mirror, phone pressed against his ear. "What would I say?"

"Most people start with hello."

"That's not what I mean."

"Talk about the drawing, Hiro. It's not a date."

Words didn't come easy for him. When he looked at someone, a snowstorm blew into his brain. The words were in there; he just couldn't see them. Then he ended up staring at the other person, and that never went well.

"What if I freeze?" he said.

"That's what you're scared of? You don't have a terminal disease, Hiro. You live in a house with heat and food and a mom and a dad. You'll survive. You've already been embarrassed in front of the class. You went up there, everyone was looking at you, and you were just staring back at us, biting your lip and hanging onto the podium like it teetered over a volcano. And then someone put it on the Social and—"

"You're not helping." He returned to pacing.

"Do you know how to ride a bike?"

"No," he lied.

"You don't know how to ride a bike?"

"Yes, I know how to ride a bike."

"You didn't do it the first time, did you? Same thing. Just click her number, stand back and say, 'Hi, my name is Hiro.' Here, practice. Do it now."

"It's easy for you. Everyone likes you."

Genuine laughter erupted. She snorted and sighed. "That's why I'm calling you on a Friday night, because everyone likes me. Please. What people think of me is none of my business. You're scared, Hiro. You can feel scared and call her at the same time."

"You sound like my mother."

"Aww. Take that back."

She sounded like she meant it. Haze only knew his mother when she was in teacher mode. Although teacher mode had become her default mode.

"Why are you doing this?" he said.

"Doing what?"

"Calling me. Helping."

"I don't know." He imagined she was chewing her nails. "You and her dreamed the same thing. It's weird, but it's also, I don't know, important. Or maybe I just wish I dreamed, too."

"I wished you dreamed this, too." Then she would be making the call. It would be easy for her, and she would love it. *Why me?*

"I'm not calling her, Hiro. Push the button. Oh, and one more thing. I need more notes for the report. And maybe you can write a paragraph for me, you know, just to get it started. Help me get in the flow. You don't have to write much, like half a page or a page or two, you know, if you find yourself in the flow and—"

"You're using me, Haze."

"Aww. That's sweet. Tell me how the call goes."

THE LAPTOP WAS on the bed, the desk chair facing it. Hiro adjusted the screen so the camera would capture the bookshelf behind him. He moved a family photo so it would be over his right shoulder, then adjusted the books so the most important ones were in frame. They were smart books, ones he'd never read. He considered lighting a candle.

He'd selected a maroon sweater that fit nicely. Made his shoulders look sharp. He experimented with different postures: slouching forward looked too casual; legs crossed was too proper. He tried the chair backwards and rested his chin on the back.

He opened the bedroom door. The television could be heard from downstairs. His father would be on his laptop, and his mother would be curled beneath a comforter. Hiro moved his dresser to block the door. He didn't have a lock.

After a few trips around the bed, he plopped down. Waiting was making it worse. Wading into a cold pool was a bad way to get in. *Just jump.* He tapped the keyboard and closed his eyes, stopped himself from slamming the laptop shut, forced himself to sit there and open his eyes. The call was spinning. She wasn't going to pick up. *At least I tried.*

A face appeared.

Her complexion was dark, lips full. Her eyes brown and wide, staring back from another dimension. Hiro started to bite his lip.

"Hi," he said. "My name is—"

The screen was a blur. He saw palm trees and a deck, then a door. A stove briefly flashed by. "Where are you going, young lady?" someone said, their voice fading. Hiro watched stairs with beige carpeting swing past. Heard a door slam. The ruffle of blankets. Then he was looking at a ceiling fan slowly turn. There was the sound of shuffling papers; the phone tipped to reveal a messy desk.

A painting filled his screen. Her fingers clutched the page, switching it to a drawing, then a sketch, then another drawing. There were five or six of them.

"How many times have you dreamed this?" She shook the paper. Flakes of paint fell off. "Wait, don't tell me. Write down your answer. We need to be objective. Do it, write it down."

Hiro turned to his desk, then hid an index card on his lap. She counted down to zero, and they both showed their answer to the camera. They both had dreamed it five times.

"I'm on the phone!" She left the screen and turned on music. She returned, her face filling the entire screen. She whispered, "It's not a dream. I mean, it is, but it's more than that. It's a place. It's a place, Hiro. She told me about a book. Look."

She left again. Things tumbled out of sight. A purple cover was suddenly on his computer. *Lucid Dreaming.*

"I found it at the library. It's old, really old. But it explains what's happening. Dreams aren't just dreams, they're windows. Not windows. *Doorways.* Most nights we're just looking through them, seeing what's over there. But you can crawl through a window if you open it. I thought the dream was noise until I saw your drawing. Your drawing! She told me you'd been going there, too. That's when I knew, I just knew she was right."

Haze told her? "What's that music?" Hiro said.

Everything was spinning so fast, he barely heard the song in the background until the bells began to chime. And then he recognized the tune. The words. It was what he'd heard on the CD. The music he'd found in the attic.

"Christmas music." She smiled. "You forgot about it. We all did. That's why we're dreaming the dream." She shook her drawing. "This is what took Christmas away. I started searching the library. There's this corner with really old books, where I found this one. It had fallen behind some other books. It's about Santa Claus and reindeer and snowmen..."

She continued naming names and things he'd never heard of but seemed distantly familiar. Like a memory from a time in the cradle, ushered from the fog by the timeless music. Was he really remembering it, or just thinking he did?

"Do your parents move furniture around this time of year?" she asked.

Hiro fidgeted. He began to shake.

"My parents chop down a tree and leave it in the backyard, like they don't know what to do with it. She told me they—"

"Who told you?" Hiro said.

"Someone who—never mind. You'll think I'm crazy."

That was exactly what he would have thought. If she didn't have those drawings. Didn't say that about the tree. *We have a tree in our attic.*

"We need to stick to facts," she said. "Fact, we're having the same dream. Fact, we live in different parts of the world. Fact, our drawings look the same, almost exactly. And this one, the last one... let me see the last one you did."

He showed it.

"See! Look, there are fewer portals."

She traced the squiggly lines.

"It's how we get there," she whispered. "And they're disappearing. If we don't get there soon, they'll be gone. She said he's cutting them off, one by one. And when the last one is gone, we'll never see Christmas again."

"Christmas?" He shook his head. *Why would that be important?* "Who's telling you all this?"

"Chase!" someone shouted.

She looked away. "I'm coming!"

"Mom said we're going!" someone replied.

"I said I'm coming!" She carried her phone to the corner of the room. "Don't ask your parents about Christmas. It'll upset them. Like something they want to remember but can't. Just, for now, don't say anything. And meet me there tonight."

"Where?" What was he going to do, board a plane?

She thumped the purple book. "Wake up inside the dream. It's all here. When you go to bed tonight, keep looking at your hands. I don't know why it works, but that's what they say. Look at your hands and ask yourself if you're dreaming. When you have a tiny doubt that you're not awake, then you're in the dream." She got up and peeked out the bedroom door. "I'll meet you there."

"Wait!" Hiro said. "How do I... are you serious?"

This wasn't what he expected. He didn't have time to be nervous. *Stick to the facts. And the facts are there.*

"Hello?" he said. "What do you mean by—"

She fumbled the phone. It bounced on the floor. He was looking at her dresser. The drawer was half open. He waited for her to pick it up, he had so many questions, and then he saw something that made all the doubt go away. All those facts were trumped by what was sitting on top of *her* dresser. The long arms with purple fur.

A monkey looking at him.

9

Most nights I made the journey.

Sometimes Madeline was sleeping, curled up with the purple monkey (I wasn't the cuddly type. Couldn't argue that). Other times no one was home. This morning, I smelled bacon and went to the kitchen.

"Good morning," Madeline said.

Madeline was always excited to see me. Like I'd sailed overseas and was home on leave. Truth was even stranger. I had done the math. Time went faster here. On an average night of sleep, I would be here for two and a half days, a one-to-seven ratio. One day at home was seven days here. I hadn't figured out where *here* was.

I climbed onto an empty chair and bumped knuckles with the dad. I'd never been cool. Not even a little. They were eating breakfast. Just a normal day with a normal family. With a red skeleton.

"I wonder if Viktor dreams," Madeline said to the mom. "Do you dream, Viktor?"

I shook my head. I didn't like to think about that. The more time I spent here, the more it made me dizzy. *Am I a man dreaming about being a toy, or the other way around?*

The mom put a bowl on my placemat. It looked like porridge. I smelled it first, let the aroma of cinnamon and sugar fill my senses, then stirred it with my finger. If I had eyes, they would have rolled back into my skull. Flavors surged through my bones. The satisfaction utterly complete. Food wasn't nourishing, not that I was aware of. The experience, though, was blissful. The sweeter, the better. I once dipped my feet in a bowl of peppermint corn syrup and wept in ecstasy.

"Off you go," the dad said. "See you after school."

Madeline packed her bookbag and went to school. The mom kissed the dad, and off to her workshop she went. The dad finished breakfast, and off to his office he went. I stirred the cinnamon porridge for thirty minutes.

The thing you don't understand about being a toy is that nothing else matters but the present moment. When I was here, I was completely content. Even cleaning the kitchen was fabulous. I never grew bored. Think of the greatest thing you've ever done in your life, the sweetest moment you've ever experienced—your first kiss, the perfect job, winning the lottery. It's like that. All the time.

Pure joy.

I watched the neighbor mow his lawn, then edge the driveway. It was wholly captivating. Like watching an award-winning movie, but without a plot or acting. It was sometime before lunch when I noticed something new in the living room: two columns anchored next to the fireplace, one on each side. They were shiny metal tubes, my distorted reflection in each one, with wires and conduit drilled into the floor. It was an odd choice, didn't match the sofa.

Curiosity tickled my bones. It would turn into a tidal wave of obsession before long. Things like this, discrepancies I couldn't understand, eroded my attention for anything else. Maybe the pipes were part of an entertainment system, speakers or projectors of some sort. I watched my reflection grow wider as I neared one of them.

The dad was in his office. He rarely came out. I didn't know what he did in there. Occasionally, there was tinkering. This time I heard him talking. That was a first. I gave up on the lawn care. The dad's one-sided conversation was heating up. I could feel what he was saying, like sound waves in my skull. I couldn't quite understand them, though, until his voice grew louder.

"It'll work this time," he said, pausing. "Christmas. Yes, I know. I know. Yes, because... right, time syncs. The math is sound, you've seen it yourself."

I put my head against the door.

"You have a hard time believing this? Where did the toys come from?! It's not much of a leap. Just... yes, Christmas. That's all I ask. Okay? Okay. When do you think you'll get an answer?"

The conversation trailed off. Then it was quiet. Just the occasional clink of glass or metal, a door closing. He was back to whatever he did. I couldn't reach the doorknob. Instead, I knocked. The dad opened the door.

"Viktor, everything all right? You need something?"

The room beyond him was a gravity field I couldn't deny. I was pulled inside, recognizing things on bench tops: magnets and pulleys, heat lamps and pendulums. A spectrometer, a voltameter, a potentiometer. Electromagnets. This wasn't an office. *It's a lab.*

"Sorry, buddy."

The dad swept me off the floor. He dropped me on the couch, threw a blanket over my lap, because that's what Madeline did. The television turned on.

"I won't be long."

He went back to his lab. Here I thought he was writing software programs or selling insurance. I'd just watched a man bag grass clippings with total fascination. I'd already calculated the time dilation between home and this place. *Imagine what I could discover with a complete physics lab!*

I had been plopped on the couch like the family pet. The dad was more likely to see if I'd fetch a ball than allow me to calibrate a spectrometer. I listened at the door again, but it was mostly silence.

I returned to staring at unknown talk shows, one that featured puppets on oversized couches. The audience was a mix of humans and toys. I watched numbly, barely aware of the story they were reporting of a human-sized wooden puppet pounding a podium. He had a red heart painted on his chest and wore a comical top hat. It was a satire of a political rally. Only it wasn't satire.

It was this place.

MY FIRST WORDS came out in lumps. How I said them, no idea. No tongue, no vocal cords. No lips, lungs, or air to produce sound. Yet there they were, vibrating in my skull like a cheap radio.

Madeline looked up from her homework. I pointed at the lab. She muted the television, twisted on the couch. I wasn't sure I could do it again. I focused on the words until they crystallized, felt them release like pebbles in a slingshot.

"What. Is. There?"

"Viktor!" She scrambled over the couch. "You talked! You did it, you did it." She slid on her knees, hugged me till my joints popped. "Can you say my name? Wait, wait."

She ran back to the couch, came back with her phone.

"Look at me, just like that. Okay, there. Now, say my name. Go."

I hobbled away from the door, then concentrated, saw the word. "Mads. Lynn."

She squealed like I was a winning lottery ticket.

"Oh, merry, merry." Whooshing sounds flew off her phone. "I'm sending this to Mom and Dad first. I'm going to say those were your first words. Oh, merry." She thumbed her phone with a grin that could float a balloon. "Viktor's... first... words..."

I knocked on the lab door. Pointed.

"We can't go in there," she said.

"What. In. There?"

"Dad stuff," she said, distracted. "Sciency stuff."

I gave her a moment. A toy's first words, apparently, was a big deal. Three more posts, twenty replies, and a selfie with me later, she sat back and shook her head, basking in the glow of new parenthood. Or toyparenthood, I suppose.

"What. Does. He do?" I managed two words in a sentence that time.

"He's looking for someone."

I nodded. There was more. She checked her phone, looked around.

"Don't tell anyone," she said. *Hilarious.* "He's looking for Santa Claus. Do you know who that is?"

I shook my head. Of course I did. Like a good scientist, I wanted to hear who she thought he was.

"He's a jolly fat man with a long, white beard. Wears a red coat. He's got this sleigh, right? It's pulled by flying reindeer. I don't know how they fly, but they do. They fly him to every house on Christmas, land on the roof. Santa comes down the chimney, I don't know how, but he does. And he delivers toys to good girls and boys."

"Toys?" I was intrigued. I didn't know why. *I'm a toy.*

"Toys, things we want. Whatever. He puts them under the tree and fills the stockings by the fireplace. I don't know how it all works, but that's what happens on Christmas."

She leaned back on the floor, satisfied with her answer. I had too many questions that had nothing to do with how Santa squeezed through a chimney or how reindeer flew without wings. The simple physics of visiting every house in a single night was impossible, for starters. At the rate I was producing words, it would take all night to ask the questions I wanted to ask.

I pointed at the door again. *What does your dad do?*

"Oh." She seemed to understand. "Yeah, well. He has a theory. Technically, it's a hypothesis. He says that every year on Christmas, when the clock strikes midnight, time synchronizes between all galaxies. Wait, that's not it." Her nose scrunched in thought. "Between realities, whatever that means. And Santa uses a time-warping bubble to travel through space portals to get here. Like time inside it stops so he can go everywhere. Something like that."

I didn't see that coming. But I was a toy, so my suspension of disbelief was fully engaged.

"He's not crazy." She sounded less bubbly. "I don't care what anyone says. The toys arrived, like, a hundred years ago. On Christmas. No one thinks that's crazy. Dad thinks they came here because of Santa. That Santa has some verve, like Christmas spirit or something, that did it. And that's why toys are alive."

"Verve?"

"Yeah, verve. He thinks that sounds better than magic. He should just call it Christmas spirit."

She picked me up. We went to the couch and opened the laptop. She scrolled through her social media, answering all the replies. Posted the selfie of us, splashed it with little hearts. I tapped her arm. She looked at me with a smile that could melt snow.

"Looking?" I said.

It took her a moment. She'd already forgotten our conversation. I couldn't think of anything else now.

"Oh. He's going to take a picture of him when he comes through the chimney next Christmas."

She glanced at the fireplace. The metal tubes anchored next to it.

That was all I was going to get. The mom got home and plopped on the couch with us, listening to Madeline tell the story of my first words (second words, technically). The mom was almost as happy as Madeline. Then the dad came home. Not as happy, but still excited. I said their names, just to make a show. We would celebrate with a special dessert. I dipped my fingers in a smoothie of fizzy nectarines. Yes, it was delicious.

But things had changed.

I couldn't quite get back into the flow of just being present. A train of thoughts plowed through my head. The Santa myth was a lot to digest. The theory of time bubbles and space portals? Maybe. I was a toy, after all. The only thing stranger than dreams was real life. This might not be a dream. And if it wasn't a dream... *how did I get here?*

10

"So what's her name?" Haze said.

Hiro paced in the front room with the phone on speaker. He parted the curtains. The driveway was empty. Mrs. Parsons was walking her dog, saw him looking out the window and waved.

"Chase." He closed the curtains. "She wants to meet me."

"She lives here?"

"No. Meet me, like, in the dream."

There was a long pause. "Uh, what?"

"She's having the same dream and told me to meet her there, said she read a book on lucid dreaming. I'm supposed to look at my hands. I never should have called her."

It wasn't just that. It was everything. It was all so insane he might never sleep again.

"So did you?" she said.

"Did I what?"

"Meet her in the dream. If you did—"

"No. No, Haze. I didn't meet her in the dream."

"Because if you did, that would be wild."

He walked faster now, pacing through the family room, into the kitchen, back to the front room, looked out the window again, then started the loop again. He hadn't slept much that night. The monkey had been staring at him. He'd put it in the closet and stared at the ceiling for hours, getting out of bed and walking until his legs were tired. At some point, he'd dreamed the dream. The planet hovered in space.

"I'm not doing it anymore," he said. He was just going to follow the rules, play it safe. Read a book. "I don't know why I called you."

"Because you need to talk."

"I've got to go."

"You're going to make another drawing?"

"I threw them away. This is stupid. It got me in trouble, and then the whole thing in front of the class and everyone laughing at me. I want everything to go back to the way it was."

He just wanted to forget any of it happened. Go back to being a boring, happy idiot. *Why did I have to dream?*

"What was the name of the book?" she said.

"What book?"

"The one you told me about five minutes ago. The one she read."

"*Lucid Dreaming.*"

Haze muttered to herself. He heard typing. "The library has it," she said. "Sounds donkey. I'm going to get it."

"Why? Forget it. I'm not doing any of it. Thank you for helping and everything, I guess, but no."

"That was heartfelt."

"I just mean, you know, talking to me. That's all." No one ever did that. "I'll help you with the report. I'll just write it for you. I'm good at that. I'll fill it with so many facts it'll choke a whale. Corker will love it. If he's still teaching."

"You're funny." She laughed. Actually laughed. "Wait. What do you mean still teaching?"

He told her about the strange conversation at detention, how it sounded like he might not be coming back. "Don't get your hopes up."

"Where's he going?"

"Nowhere. You know how he is."

"But he was writing letters?"

"I don't know what he was doing."

"Yeah. Yeah." She was typing. Then said, "Bye."

Hiro looked at the phone. She'd hung up. He wasn't expecting it. He was never very good at stopping a conversation. He didn't have much practice at it. But, if he was honest, he felt just a little bit better talking to Haze. He was going to write her report. It was the least he could do.

HIRO WAS LICKING a spoon when a car door slammed.

The cookies weren't done. His parents weren't supposed to be home for another fifteen minutes. He wanted to surprise them. At least the house smelled like cookies. *That's the best part,* his mother used to say. He couldn't remember the last time she made cookies. He washed his hands and dried them on the apron, gave the batter one last stir before dropping a dollop on the cookie sheet.

The doorbell rang.

A red truck was parked on the street, the door panels crusted with gray snow, the windshield sealed under a layer of ice with only a thin line scraped away. He cracked open the front door, cold air seeping in. Haze's nose was shiny. She shook her head and pushed past him.

"I think my snot froze." She shucked her boots by the door. "It's so warm in here. What is it, like, eighty degrees? My dad keeps it at sixty-eight. Wear more clothes, he says. They're free." She unzipped her coat, looked around. "Are you standing guard?"

He was holding the spoon like a club. She stripped off her bookbag and followed the smell. He shoved her boots into the corner where the snow would melt. She was at the kitchen counter with her finger in a metal bowl, a glob of cookie dough hooked on the end of her finger. She found a spoon for the next scoop.

"Um, I know I ask this a lot," he said, "but what are you—"

"What are you doing here?" she blurted. "Beat you."

She dropped her backpack on the table, licking the spoon like a lollipop, and fished into one of the pockets. She dropped a book. The dull cover was in a crinkly plastic sleeve. *Lucid Dreaming: How to Wake Up.*

"I can't believe they even had it," she said. "It's super old. Only been checked out once, like, ever."

She opened the refrigerator, put a gallon of milk on the counter. "It's about waking up *while* you're dreaming. Said you can become conscious in a dream world, have a body, fly, do whatever. Guy who wrote it has a PhD, does research and everything. So it's real."

She found a glass and a plate, sat at the table with a glob of cookie dough.

"I mean, if it was just some blogger saying it, then you probably couldn't. You know, like people who say you can live off eating air. No, this guy has a whole team who—hey!"

Hiro grabbed the plate. "You can't eat that."

"It's cookie dough."

"It's uncooked." He dumped it in the garbage disposal. "Raw eggs aren't good for you."

"I'll take my chances." She licked the spoon. "So the hands thing you said, it's supposed to be some sort of anchor. Like, I guess if you look at your hands when you're dreaming, you'll realize you're in the dream without actually waking up. It's down to a science, which is weird, because I've never heard of this. You'd think people would be talking about it. Are you even listening?"

"I told you I don't want to talk about it anymore. I mean, thank you and everything for getting the book. It's nice and all." He grabbed the spoon from her. "Let me bake it first; you'll get sick. You can take some home with you."

"Aww. That's so sweet. You're telling me to leave."

"No, that's not it. My parents aren't home."

She covered her mouth. "And you have a girl in the house. I'll bet that's against the rules."

He doled out lumps of cookie dough on the cookie sheet. The oven was preheating. He just wanted to bake some cookies and not think about anything for a while. Haze was at the table, slurping milk and licking her fingers, the sound of pages turning. He couldn't wait for the oven to preheat, set the timer and put the cookies in. Then give her a paper plate and push her out the door. Everything would go back to normal. He could not talk to anyone in class, no one would notice him, and he would get good grades. *Normal.*

"Tell me a story," she said.

"What?"

"A story about a boy named Jack and a girl named Jill. Jack doesn't know Jill, but he calls her anyway, and they talk. Tell me a story about that."

"I'm not telling you a story." He washed his hands.

"Pretend it's a story. And keep busy with whatever you're doing."

"I'm washing my hands."

"All right, then wash your hands and make some tea. Probably won't be as good as your dad's."

She started looking through the cabinets, found the dish soap and filled the sink with bubbles. Then she started washing the dishes, humming as she did it. Drying them, looking for where they went without asking, wiping the counters. Ignoring him when he asked her to stop. Not answering his questions. He thought about going to his room. But that would be strange if his parents came home. Worse if she followed him up there.

"Her drawings were just like mine." He sat at the table, staring at the book. "Even the new ones. She wasn't faking it. There were fewer of those squiggly lines on them, just like mine."

"Portals."

"That's what she said."

Haze snorted. "Go on."

"Yeah, well, she asked if my parents move the furniture around this time of year, which they do."

"I just got the chills."

"And her parents cut down a tree and drag it into the backyard."

"Why?"

"It's called Christmas." He looked up. "And we all forgot about it.

Everyone in the world did. Someone told her that's why we're having the dream."

"Who told her?"

"She wouldn't say." I shrugged. "I thought it was you."

She grimaced like there was a bad smell. "Why would everyone forget?"

"Do you remember Christmas?"

"Never heard of it. Anyway—furniture, dead trees and Christmas. Keep going."

He took a deep breath. "Remember that music I was listening to, the CD player? She was playing the same song when I called. Sleigh bells and one-horse open sleighs. Christmas music."

She wasn't looking at him. She was staring across the room, putting it all together. He couldn't make up a story like this.

"The planet, the one we're both dreaming about, that's what made everyone forget. If we don't stop it, no one will ever remember Christmas again."

She shook her head. "You're not making this up?"

"No."

"No wonder you're like... *gah*."

That was exactly how his brain felt. *Gah.* "That's not all."

He checked on the cookies, opening the oven just a bit, dry heat on his face, cookie smell filling the room. It made him feel comfortable. Or maybe it was the talking. Or the look on Haze's face.

"Well?" She shook her head. "What is it?"

"You remember my purple monkey?" He leaned against the counter.

"Don't tell me—"

"Just like it."

"She did not."

Haze walked around the kitchen table. Twice. She started to talk and stopped, flopped into a chair and squinted. Turned to him. "Seriously?"

He nodded.

"Where'd she get it?"

"I don't know."

"Where'd you get it?"

"It was in the attic."

"I know, but how did it get there?"

He had thought about it a great deal but couldn't remember. His only memory was that it was waiting on his bed one day. No one ever said anything about it.

"This isn't a scam," she muttered. "Have you tried calling her again?"

"I just want to forget about it."

She nodded, tapping the table, finding a small glob of cookie dough and licking it off her finger. Then pointed. "You need to meet her."

"I don't know where she lives."

Haze slid the book across the table. "Meet her."

He laughed. It felt good, releasing tension that had turned his stomach into a concrete mold. "You can't be serious," he said.

"I don't know, am I? You just told me an impossible story. You don't look like you're lying. Are you lying?"

He shook his head for a number of reasons.

"Yeah, well, then you need to try. Meet her in that dream. What do you have to lose? You're going to sleep anyway."

"That doesn't even make sense. If I meet her in my dream, it won't be her. It'll just be... *thoughts!*"

"Who told her about Christmas?"

"She read it in a book, something about Santa something and reindeer." That twisty feeling was returning. "Look, Haze, maybe you're right. Someone at school is just—"

"No, you said someone told her that's why you're having the dream. Who told her?"

"That's what I mean. Someone at school, Perry or Richard, is helping her."

A cold elixir of fear stirred into the pot of anxiety. This was an elaborate hoax. This kind of thing happened all the time. It was a matter of how they knew he was listening to music, had a purple monkey in his room, the furniture moved around. *How could they know that?*

He stepped back. He pointed. "You're helping them."

"What?"

"You knew all this stuff before I called her. You made me call her."

She nodded. She was admitting it. The fear and anxiety lit fumes of anger. She held up her hands. He backed against the refrigerator, pointing at the front room, stammering. Gently, she grabbed his arms.

"I know you don't have friends. Neither do I. If I did, it wouldn't be Perry or Dick. I wouldn't, in a million years, do this to anyone. Especially you, Hiro. You're right, I saw the monkey; I guess I could've seen the furniture. But I didn't hear the music, Hiro. You broke the player when I came to your room."

His breath was choppy. It was her touch that kept him from running. Her kind eyes. She was right. The player had been broken.

"Besides," she said, "if I did this to you, who's going to write my report?"

The emotions suddenly bubbled with intoxicating hope. When she smiled, he smiled. And he wanted to hug her. It was the relief, that was it. Someone was there with him in all this. Someone believed him. Wanted to help him. Wanted him to write a report.

"Hello?" his father called. "Someone here?"

Haze let go of Hiro and started moving the dishes around. They were already clean. She grabbed the tea kettle and started filling it with water. Hiro was pasted to the refrigerator, his arms still warm where she'd held onto him. His mother's voice snapped him out of it. He started to panic, going to the oven, then swiped the book off the table and hid it beneath his apron.

"Oh." His mother stopped in the doorway.

"Hello, Mrs. Tanaka," Haze said.

"Well, hello, Ms. Melblank."

"Please, call me Haze."

Mother peeled her gloves off one finger at a time. "Making cookies, are we?"

"She just got here," Hiro said, "and I just started a batch, so she was—"

"I thought I recognized that truck," his father said. "Hello there, young lady. It's good to see you. Hiro, I'm glad you have company. I see you *spilled the coffee*." He winked. Haze and his mother looked at him. "Are you making tea?"

"We heard you pull into the driveway," Haze said. "We thought we'd start the water."

"Would you look at that, honey?" He loosened his tie. "She started the water. What are you kids up to?"

"School," Hiro said.

His father went to the cabinet for a box of tea. He set four mugs on the counter, rubbing his hands together. Mother hadn't moved.

"We're almost done with Mr. Corker's report," Hiro said. "Haze was helping with references and doing a proofread for me. I was making, you know, cookies."

"Is that what those are?" his mother said. "Can I see your reports?"

"I put them away." Hiro swallowed the lie like a golf ball. "It's still pretty rough and—"

"Have a seat." His father pulled out chairs. "Anything we can do to help you, just ask. You have an engineer and a schoolteacher at your disposal."

"Oh, yes," his mother said. "We'd love to help. Let's see what you've written so far."

This was getting out of control for no reason at all. There were plenty of things he didn't want to tell her, but this was a pointless lie. There was no way around this. He was going to get out of this before it became something, tell her everything about the drawing and the phone call. He reached under his apron for the lucid dreaming book.

"I have a question," Haze said. "Have you ever heard of Christmas?"

Hiro's parents did something he'd never seen them do. Nothing ever surprised them. They never looked shocked. They met every moment, no matter how pleasant or stressful, with meditative introspection.

They winced. Like the question poked them in the stomachs.

"We were researching." Haze poured hot water in the mugs. "We came across the word and didn't know what it was. Someone named Santa. What did he do, Hiro?"

"I... I don't remember."

He was watching his parents deflate. They were struggling with the question. Not like when his father grappled with a difficult calculation or when his mother faced a creative block. They were lost.

His mother left the kitchen. His father dropped teabags on the floor. He picked them up and shoved them on the counter, then followed her out. Hiro and Haze waited for them to return. The bathroom door closed, then the bedroom door.

"What just happened?" Haze said.

"You weren't supposed to ask them about Christmas."

11

Hiro plugged in the laptop. He walked around his bedroom while it booted up, leaning over the desk to check the progress. Chase had sent twelve emails within the last forty-eight hours. He took another lap, debating whether to read them or not. But he'd come this far.

Where were you?

Did you read the book?

I can't wait any longer for you.

Ride the purple tail.

I'll go away soon. It's the only way to save Christmas.

Slowly, gently, he closed the laptop and sat there, feeling the words march through his head. He was expecting that. He wanted to have a calm conversation with Chase. Her messages sounded like aliens were invading. He was already walking a thin line of confidence. He wanted to jump in the pool. Not be pushed.

Where were you? Well, he wasn't there, wherever she expected him to be. Which was impossible. He assumed she was asking if he'd read the lucid dreaming book, which how did she know he had it? *I can't wait any longer for you.* Fine. Why was she waiting? *Ride the purple tail.* No idea what that could mean.

I'll go away soon. That bothered him. It was slightly cryptic. It sounded more like she was running away, not lucid dreaming. That was the thing with dreams. If things got too scary, she just had to open her eyes. She wasn't really going anywhere. *It feels like she means it.*

He pulled out the meditation bench, took long slow breaths and settled into a centered focus. After several minutes, he dug through the trash. The drawings were crumpled in tight balls. He smoothed them on the bed, arranged them in the order he drew them. They were in decent shape. He found some tape and put them on the wall.

"This is crazy," he muttered.

He went downstairs. His parents were reading by the fireplace. His father's face was illuminated in the tablet's soft glow. His mother was reading a hardcover with one hand in a bowl of popcorn.

"I'm going to read upstairs," Hiro said. "Probably fall asleep. Just wanted to say goodnight."

"Don't stay up late," his father said. "We're getting up early, don't forget."

They were going to his grandparents' for brunch. They did that at this time of year: got dressed up for it. It was more of a way-too-early dinner than brunch. He'd never wondered why they did that every year. Now he questioned everything.

"Your father would like to apologize about the *coffee*," his mother said without looking up from her book.

"What for?" Hiro said.

"It was inappropriate," she said. "Tomo?"

He cleared his throat. "I'm sorry, Hiro, for embarrassing you in front of your friend." He shook his head while he said it. Hiro smiled.

"Are you shaking your head, Tomo?"

"No." He nodded.

"Tomo, we talked about this."

"I'm sorry, she seems like a nice girl. Friendly and I'll bet funny. Right, Hiro?"

"She's a friend."

"Of course she is," he said. "I'm just saying, it took guts to have her over here. And when we were gone."

His mother looked up with tired eyes. She was not entertained. His father should be apologizing to her. He said something else but couldn't crack the lines furrowed in her cheeks. They seemed back to normal: Mother's anxiety delicately frosting her emotions; Father attempting to fan her sense of humor back to life. The blank sadness that had briefly hovered over them earlier in the day was gone.

"She is nice," Hiro said. "And I'm sorry about what she asked."

"Asked what?" his father said.

Hiro knew why he said that. It was a test. They were either great actors or completely forgot Haze had asked about Christmas, which brought on a temporary bout of melancholy.

"Never mind," Hiro said. "Goodnight."

He went through the front room and stopped at the stairs. The curtains were closed. White light shined in the corner where the furniture had been pushed aside. It looked like a lamp had tipped over. Hiro bent down. It was a tangle of wire.

A string of lights was piled in the corner.

HIRO SOMETIMES READ an entire book in a single sitting. *Lucid Dreaming* was not one of them.

It was dry and factual. The kind of book that made Corker smile. The author was a sleep expert whose research, for the past twenty years, had been entirely on dreaming. Dreaming had become rare, the author said. It was a dream deficit epidemic. *People don't dream anymore,* he said. *We want to know why.* Hiro started speed-reading before he was done with the first chapter. When he flipped to the end to see how many pages were left, he knew he would never finish it.

Lucid dreaming was becoming conscious while in the dream. It occurred during REM sleep, when dreams were most vivid, which was primarily in the latter half of the night. The description of participants' experiences was interesting and, he had to admit, a touch unbelievable. It was no different than being awake.

He glanced at his drawings. He would have ditched the book right there had he not had the same dream every night for the past week.

He began skipping pages after the fourth chapter, went to the second section that discussed technique. It started with sophisticated lab equipment, lights that would shine on closed eyes when REM was detected, to signal the sleeper it was time to *wake up.* Apparently, they could see light in their dreams. How that didn't fully wake them up seemed impossible. Hiro didn't have equipment and wasn't going to ask his parents for it.

There were simple techniques, like getting in the habit of asking himself if he was dreaming. "Am I dreaming?" he muttered, looking around. "No."

That was easy.

The second was an anchor. Something that would confirm the dream state. The author suggested looking at his hands. *Chase really did read the book.* There might have been more, but his eyes grew heavy and bored.

"Still not dreaming."

He was 100% sure of it. He studied his hands, front and back. What was so magical about the hands? It didn't matter. He wasn't going to meet another person inside *his* dream. If he did, it wasn't going to be her.

"Am I—"

A noise startled him. Adrenaline spiked his eyes open. Something fell in the closet. He stayed still, holding his breath. If he would've heard breathing, he would've leaped out of his room without touching the floor. After a minute of silence, his heart thumping, he reached for the closet door, careful not to put his foot on the floor, just in case his childhood monster was real. Light cut across the neatly hung school uniforms and shiny shoes stacked on the floor.

The purple monkey stared from the corner. Her long arms lay over her lap like furry noodles. That was where Hiro had put her. She hadn't moved an inch, he was certain. Perhaps something fell from the shelf, but he didn't investigate.

It was almost midnight. He turned off the lights, snuggled into his pillows. The streetlight beamed through the window, a rectangular box of light centered on the drawings. The longer he stared at them, the more it looked like an art gallery. The colors were playful. Even in the harsh light, they were soft and inviting. He could feel their blurry edges. They were fuzzy and glowing. The planets vibrant.

The lines made no sense. Maybe they were manifestations of solar wind, or gamma rays just before a black hole formed. But it was clearly a planet. It would have to be a star to become a black hole. Maybe it was a planet-sized spaceship and the inhabitants lived on the surface. Maybe all planets were spaceships. The more he thought about it, they were, really. Traveling through space at mind-boggling speeds with no captain to steer them.

His thoughts were flowing in currents, because now he imagined planets weren't planets but interstellar titans: living creatures with all these things living on them. Humans and every other animal were like bacteria and fungi crawling on its surface, erecting buildings and mining precious minerals to wear on their fingers and decorate their homes. These planets lived in a dimension humans couldn't comprehend any more than a cockroach could tell a joke. They smashed into each other, too. Some planets captured moons, and suns captured planets. And black holes ate everything that came near them. And those lines coming off the planet...

They're moving.

He sat up. Maybe it was the way the streetlight was coming into his room, or snow falling past the window. They were definitely moving. They squiggled on the drawing like sea creatures, flowed off the page and reached into the room.

Am I dreaming?

He didn't think so. He was 99% sure. There was one more thing to do, something he could test. His arms seemed to be extremely long and filled with air. When he looked down, his hands were missing. The bed was, too.

His scream echoed in a tin can.

He flailed without arms or legs, like treading a swimming pool without water. Without a body. He wasn't falling. He wasn't even floating. He was just there.

The bedroom had dissolved. One by one, the drawings disintegrated. A new draft took their place.

It was the planet.

It sat in black space as firmly as a teacup on a coffee table. The lines were titanic noodles swaying in solar wind, brightly colored and pulsing. There was a dozen of them soaring into the galaxy. Hiro hovered like an invisible satellite. He tried swimming toward the nearest one, a scarlet red thing, but there was nothing to propel him. He closed his eyes—he didn't have eyes, but he did what he thought was closing them—and felt the planet recede, felt his bed just beyond the veil of waking.

This is a dream. I don't need a body.

He willed himself to move and zoomed through space. The scale of the red noodle was beyond comprehension. He was a dust mite on the back of a swaying skyscraper. The surface didn't hum or crackle— there was no sound in space, but neither were there sixteen-year-old boys.

The surface was translucent. Something flowed inside. Photons and subatomic particles surged out into the universe, bound together like some ethereal silky essence. If he pushed inside, would it shoot him into another galaxy? He didn't test his hypothesis. Dark streaks mingled in the flow. The noodle was turning black near the planet, like basal rot on a beanstalk. It broke away and went flailing past him like a snake had been set free, spiraling into the black beyond, a trace of red.

He could feel life down there. There were land masses and oceans, rocky terrain, and polar ice caps. How was he going to find Chase? She never said where. *Meet me on this planet* was more than vague. It was impossible. Haze thought the noodles were portals, but they were flowing out. *This is a dream,* he reminded himself. *Just wish to find her,* he thought. *But that won't be her. I'm the one dreaming. It would just be something that looked like her.*

Something began rising from a mass of bright lights, a wisp of smoke twisting through the atmosphere. Another strand was growing. This one was smaller: a tendril compared to the gigantic noodles. It was purple. It stopped at the outer reaches of the atmosphere, the tip twisting like a tail.

Ride the purple tail.

Hiro remembered what Chase had emailed, and instantaneously appeared next to it.

The surface appeared firm and elastic. Nothing flowed inside it. When the tip swung toward him, it stopped and, he thought, appeared to smell him. The edges peeled opened like a flower; violet sparkles floated out like pollen and stuck to him. Hiro could see the outline of his body like a celestial being.

The tendril reared back. Then swallowed him.

He was cascading down an arterial waterslide at subsonic speed. The plunge had an eerie ring like one long electronic scream. He dissolved into particles of light, drifting weightless, merging with the grape flow of the purple tail. The planet sped towards him, blurring into a multicolored ball. For a long, falling moment, he could see in all directions: three-hundred-and-sixty-degree vision. The charging lights of a populated metropolis. The expansive blue ocean, the glow of the atmosphere.

His final descent pulled him through a small opening. His presence was long and stretchy, like grains of sand trickling to the bottom of the hourglass. Each grain plucking color from the universe until it was dark and hollow.

He felt the firmness of his body: arms and legs, chest and stomach. His head on a swivel. He was stiff. His bed a hard plank. His eyes wouldn't open. There was muttering around him. He felt someone watching. Panic took him. He was trapped in his body. Catatonic. He could hear shuffling. He could see colors, like his eyes were never closed. Someone was below him. He tried to lift his arm—

"Hiro!"

Hiro's head was cradled in a pillow, a soft bed beneath him. A beam of light cut through his window. He was a bag of wet sand, barely able to move to turn off the alarm.

"The shower is open." His mother peeked into his room. "We'll leave in an hour."

Hiro stared at her. What struck him wasn't her pale features or messy hair. She was pallid. His entire room was a bleached version of the world he had just been in. The colors faded as if they were slowly being leached away. So unlike what he'd just seen. Like he had been somewhere.

Someone was waiting for me.

The drawings were on the wall. The lines right where he drew them. The squiggly titans still the same shapes, same colors. None had broken off and soared into the galaxy. Not a single one of them was purple.

He heard buzzing, crawled through his blankets to find his phone. It was early, but he'd missed three calls. A text message buzzed in his hand.

Call me! Now!!!

12

There wasn't a sidewalk leading up to the house, only random footprints in the frozen snow. Hiro walked between a crusty truck and an RV with a flat tire with a blue tarp over the windshield. The metal railing at the front steps was wobbly. He pushed the doorbell. Icy daggers pointed from the gutter.

A young man regarded Hiro like he was selling toilet cleaner. "Yeah?"

"Is Haze here?"

He stared a bit longer. Maybe he didn't hear him. He scratched the acne on his cheek, then nodded. Hiro wasn't sure what to do. Haze's brother, Robby, barely moved. Hiro turned sideways to step by him.

"Hag!" he shouted. "Door!"

It wasn't much warmer inside. The house smelled like biscuits and old carpet. The furniture didn't match. A leather recliner was tipped back, the footrest stuck open, with worn armrests the color of putty.

The corner of the room was empty.

Robby, wearing a faded concert T-shirt, shouted again without breaking eye contact. Hiro pulled his stocking cap off and wrung it with both hands. Music blared from upstairs. Footsteps thudded. Haze wore two sweatshirts and a knitted cap with a fuzzy ball on top.

"Boyfriend's here," Robby said.

"Shut up," she said. "Hey. You drive?"

"No," Hiro said. "My father dropped me off. He'll be back in half an hour." Hiro pointed. "We're going back to my grandparents'."

Robby laughed for no reason. Haze shooshed him away. He walked off slowly, his neck too thick to turn around and look back. Hiro nodded at the empty corner of the room.

"Yeah," she said. "Us, too."

"I found a string of lights in ours," Hiro said. "Just lying there."

She nodded, squinting. "Yeah. Makes sense. Come on."

"You can't go up to your bedroom," Robby shouted from another room.

"You can shut up," Haze answered.

She hustled up the shag steps, wearing striped socks over white ones. Hiro took off his shoes before following. The music was coming from an open bathroom. The sink was buried beneath cosmetics, half-empty cups, and a small plate with a piece of burnt toast.

"Did he call you Hag?"

"He's showing off." Haze scooped up an overweight cat. "This is Mr. Pando."

The black and white cat purred. The tail swooped under Haze's chin and stroked her cheek. Hiro stared at the way the cat's tail moved, so smooth and graceful. Like it was floating in outer space. He didn't hear what she said next.

"I'm sorry. What?"

"You allergic?" she said.

"No, it's just the... never mind."

She dropped the cat. Mr. Pando didn't seem to mind, arching his back against Hiro's leg, and didn't follow him into a very small, disastrous room. He assumed the carpeting continued into her bedroom, but there was no sight of the floor. It was a capsized resale shop: old clothing, blankets, notebooks, a bike helmet, a lamp shade, and half-inflated balloons. A banana yellow beanbag with strips of gray duct tape was next to an overloaded bed. Her laptop was nestled in a hill of comforters. The screensaver was a photo of his planet drawing.

"I did it." She danced in a circle. "I saw it!"

"Saw what?"

She pointed at the laptop. "The planet, Hiro. *Exactly* like you drew it."

"Okay."

"You don't get it, I saw it. I've been staring at it for, like, days now. I put it on my phone. Here, look. It's on the laptop. I wasn't trying to do anything, I just liked what you did. That explains what happened, really. I mean, it's not, like, magical or anything. The planet is practically burned into my brain. I could literally draw it, and I can't draw."

"What are you talking about?"

She grabbed two fistfuls of his coat. "I dreamed the planet. Yeah. I did. And it was amazing. Ama-za-zing. I'm sorry I called so early, I just had to let you know something really, really, really big happened." She threw her arms out. "Now I know why you drew it in Corker's class. I want to draw it, too. It was just so... it was so—"

"Delicious."

"Yeah. Delicious. The colors were... I could taste them. And the portals were these giant worms doing this wavy outer space dance. And the planet, oh the planet... the oceans and the lights, and I could see the atmosphere glowing. The whole thing was just, like, sitting there. I watched it from the cheap seats, you know? Like way out there. I could watch it all night, the way the portals floated like psychedelic seaweed. And then this one, this big red one, it broke off and—"

"You saw that?"

"I saw the whole thing. It went shooting into space like an eel. *Fooooom.* The speed of light, it was gone. And—"

"Did you see a purple one?"

"A what?"

"A purple one. You know, a purple squiggly portal."

She shook her head. "I don't think so. Is there a purple one in your drawing?"

"Did you look at your hands?"

"The lucid dreaming thing, right." She snapped her fingers. "Here's the thing. *I didn't have hands.*"

Hiro was dizzy. He looked for somewhere to sit. His feet got tangled in a damp towel. He didn't make it to the bed, instead dropping on the beanbag like a concrete block. Little white beads streamed from the duct tape like a snow machine.

"I thought you'd be, like, not sad," she said.

"Sorry."

He brushed beanbag stuff off his pants and told her about his dream. Same as always, this time he didn't have a body. Maybe he never had one in the dream, just never bothered to look. The purple tail, that was different. She hadn't seen that.

"You saw a portal break off, too?" she said.

"They're not portals. I don't think."

"What are they?"

He didn't know. Stuff was flowing out. Maybe that was what portals did. He was also fully aware he was no longer thinking about this as a dream. *How could we have the same dream?*

"I tried to look at my hands," he said. "I didn't have a body."

"Aww. You read the book."

He took his stocking cap off, dug into his coat pocket. The book crinkled in his hand. "Here. If you want to read it, I think it will help. If you have the dream again." He told her which chapters to read, about REM sleep. How he ran out of time when his mother woke him.

"I was almost there," he said.

"You were there!"

"No, I mean, I went there this time, through the purple whip." He didn't tell her the portal sort of ate him. "I felt my body down there. It was different. I heard voices and..." He shook his head. "I ran out of time."

"There's more."

She jumped on the bed and crossed her legs, pushing books on the floor, and spinning the laptop around.

"I took a deep dive down some rabbit holes last night. I was thinking how weird your parents got about Christmas. Guess what I found? Nothing. Like nowhere. Like the internet was scrubbed by an anti-Christmas word gremlin. Like the word was never invented. So I kept digging because that's what I do at night by myself. I used some of the other words you said, like flying reindeer. I was, like, twenty pages deep when I got a hit on *elves.*

"It was a fresh post on one of the conspiracy boards that's all political conspiracies and flat world stuff. *Elves Are Real,* it said. No, no, wait. The first line was all in caps and said SCREENSHOT THIS POST NOW! It said the post would disappear in a minute, and if anyone was reading it, they had to get a screenshot."

"Did you?"

"I did better." She held up a piece of paper. "Printed it. And when I got back from the printer, guess what? The post was gone. Just like it said."

"What's it say?"

"I'm going to tell you." She held it with both hands. "Santa Claus —remember him?—lives on the North Pole with a colony of elves. Or was there because he's not there anymore. When he did, they lived in ice tunnels so no one could see them. The elves have been around since the Ice Age and have, like, crazy technology they used to watch the rest of the world. They have reindeer that fly with helium bladders. It says, uh, oh, that Santa isn't an elf but a man who's hundreds of years old and every year uses the reindeer to pull a sleigh around the world.

"He's got, like, a time snapper thing that stops time so he can do it in one night because, you know, technology. Anyway, he goes into houses through the chimney. And everyone is expecting him, so they put out milk and cookies. They also decorate a tree—remember the tree?—and he puts presents under it. I'll be honest, this sounds awesome. Oh, and they also hang stockings over the fireplace, and he stuffs those with presents, too."

"Like a fake tree?" Hiro said.

"Maybe. You have one in your attic. Kind of weird."

More than weird. "Who are *they*?"

"What do you mean?"

"I mean, who's putting out milk and cookies and decorating trees?"

"Us, I guess. I mean, before we forgot. That's what the whole post is about: Christmas spirit disappeared. We used to do Christmas. And now we don't. But there's still habits, like moving furniture around and cutting down trees, right?"

He crawled out of the beanbag. He needed to move and keep moving. He paced across the small room. Clothing, blankets and towels wrapped around his ankles as he slid his feet across the carpet. This was classic conspiracy theory: details that could plug unexplainable holes in human behavior. With nothing else to fill them, they made sense.

"It was posted by someone called Monkeybrain. He or she or they said, and I quote, 'Even if you print this post, they will get the paper and you will forget. Read it, memorize it, and take it to the dream. If you don't, it will go away. It's the only way to save Christmas.'"

Hiro was treading in strange facts that all linked together, but that last line bothered him most. He was swimming through all the information to remember where he'd heard that before.

"I don't know how this will go away." She rattled the page. "Unless mind-erasing elves sneak through the chimney—"

"Chase said it." Hiro snapped his fingers. "The last time she emailed me, she said, *I'm going away. It's the only way to save Christmas.*"

"Are you thinking what I'm thinking?"

"What are you thinking?"

She looked at the page. "She's Monkeybrain."

That made the most sense. It could easily be her. Maybe they needed to see what else Monkeybrain had posted, like space was fake and lizard people controlled the world. Mind-erasing elves would be at the family reunion.

"Or," he said, "someone was telling her to post it. When I talked to her that one time, she kept saying someone told her about Christmas and the dream."

"You think Monkeybrain told her. I mean, you both have a purple monkey. I'll be honest, everything that's happened, a talking toy is not the weirdest part." She looked at him intensely. "You can tell me, be honest. Does your monkey talk to you?"

"What? No. No, she's in the closet."

"Why?"

He'd put her in the closet when he threw the drawings away. He was done with it, at least he thought he was. She was still in there, sitting in the corner looking out, long arms in her lap and the long... *purple tail.*

He didn't say it out loud. He didn't know why. After everything else, it seemed the least strange. *Ride the purple tail.* It came off the planet different than the others. It was looking around and then gobbled him up, swallowed him all the way to the planet. Chase had told him how to get down there. That was how he was going to find her. *She was there.*

"What else did she say?" Haze said.

"What?"

"I mean, was that it? *I'm going away to save Christmas*?"

He pulled out his phone. There had been an email from Chase that morning.

"Yeah? What's it say?" Haze said.

"Uh, she said, *I'm leaving tonight. Don't know if I'll come back. Only two days till Christmas. It's our only chance.* What's today's date?"

"December twenty-third. So Christmas is—"

"December twenty-fifth."

Heavy silence fell between them. They stared at each other. It felt sort of like what his parents looked like when Haze had asked them about Christmas. Like something was missing. Like a giant hole was in the room. The paper was still in her hand, so the mind-erasing elves hadn't snuck in with a time snapper thing yet.

"Do you think it's weird?" Haze said, suddenly sounding tired. "It's a little weird she doesn't think she'll come back? I mean, should you tell someone?"

"Yeah. Yeah, you're probably right." He had her number but didn't know her last name or where she lived. "If it's just a dream, she'll wake up."

"Of course. None of this is real." She snorted. "I'll tell you what is real: Corker's report. You're still working on it, right?"

"Yeah."

"No, I mean, you're still working on my report."

"How will we know?" he said.

"You print it and give it to me."

"No, I mean, I was invisible. In the dream, remember? I didn't have a body. You said you didn't, either. How would we know we were both there?"

She waited with her mouth open. Then laughed at him. "I'm sorry. It's a dream, Hiro. You don't believe…"

"Right, a dream. But it didn't feel like one, not to me."

"Yeah, no, totally. But, uh, Hiro, we won't be in the same dream. I'm just playing. It'll be fun if we have the same dream again. We'll wake up and so will Chase. We should probably write it down and compare notes tomorrow. It's like an adventure. Oh, I know." She bounced on the bed. "We can give each other presents. The mind-erasing elves can't stop us from doing that."

Relief filled the silent hole in the room. That and Haze's bouncy enthusiasm. It was so easy to get swept up and forget this was a dream they were talking about. As strange as everything was, it was still his imagination. They weren't going anywhere. Haze had the right approach. This was fun. The strangeness had spice. He was glad she was there.

"Car in the drive!" Robby shouted from downstairs. "Boyfriend needs to go."

She held up her finger. "Let's save Christmas."

He touched it, and she buzzed. He smiled. "And Santa," he added.

Robby was waiting at the bottom of the steps. Haze had scooped up the cat and cradled her in her arms. Robby didn't move. Hiro had to walk around him.

"Don't you have push-ups to do?" Haze said.

Hiro's head was cold. "I forgot my hat."

"I'll get it," Haze said.

Hiro was about to say he'd go, but she was up the steps before he could stop her. Robby towered over him with glaze from a donut on his lips. He thought about telling him, then decided to just not move.

"Hey. If you break my sister's heart"—Robby grabbed his coat— "I'll give you five bucks."

He cracked a cruel smile and smacked Hiro on the back. His laughter sounded like a cartoon villain. Robby left with icing still on his lips. Haze was taking her time. Or the stocking cap was lost. Hiro might have scrambled it in the pile of clothing when he was pacing. He thought about just leaving it.

He read the rest of Chase's email while he waited. What little relief that remained quickly evaporated. Chase had sent an email that morning. Hiro hadn't told anyone about where he'd put the purple monkey, except for telling Haze just now. No one could possibly have known.

PS, Chase had written, *take Monkeybrain out of the closet.*

13

My first time to the big city.

It was a pleasant drive. The valley was spotted with blossoming trees and patches of snow. Spring fragrance filled my bones. Then the country road went from two lanes to four, then six. Freshly painted barns were replaced with towering buildings. Flowers turned to soot. We slogged into traffic, crept through skyscraper shadows and incessant honking. Cafés next to restaurants next to bars next to souvenir vendors.

It wasn't every night I returned to Toyworld. I didn't know why it wasn't every night. I began to itch when two days turned into a week without returning. I became irritable, more than usual. I didn't like the people in my world. Here, I liked the mom and dad. Madeline, I adored.

We drove around a traffic circle that contained a park with an enormous spruce on a hill. The dad was stress-driving. The skin over his knuckles white, arguing with the mom about where to park. They were going to be late. He insisted on circling the block one more time. I could feel the mom's irritation like rose prickles on my neck.

He found a metered spot at the curb. The mom jumped out, a bag over her arm. Madeline held my hand. They were speed-walking

 TONY BERTAUSKI

down the sidewalk. I was sprinting at Madeline's side. My green cape fluttered like a sheet on a clothesline. The hood falling back. I'd gotten used to wearing it when we went out. It was a little strange, a boney toy with a green cloak. A bit macabre. But there were stranger things here.

I was trying to take in the new sights and feels. The valley was so fresh and innocent. This was gritty and hard. It felt like gnats in my head. The dad stepped over a fallen stick-figure toy, the kind with wooden pegs and sprockets. The mom picked the little guy up, plugged his legs back into his body. The holes were too loose. She had a tube of glue in her purse.

"Poll," the dad said gently, "we're late."

She ignored him, putting the stick man against the building where no one would step on him. I'd heard the dad say to her before, *You can't save them all, Polly.* It didn't stop her from trying. We picked up the pace, just short of a run. Past storefronts and apartment walk-ups, offices and toy parlors.

The sidewalk began tilting. I'd let go of Madeline and thought maybe I was looking around too much, going too fast. The buildings were spinning in the sky. And then I was staring at an open door. A shaggy mane emerged from a dark stairwell.

Take their money, I thought. *Give to him.*

It was a thought I was having. Only it didn't sound like me. But I believed it was me. And it made sense to take money from the mom's purse and throw it in the doorway. I wanted to do it.

"Stop it." The mom picked me up and shook her finger.

A mangy lion smiled from the stairwell. He was missing a glass eye. Gray stuffing breached a tear in his neck.

The mom carried me at a brisk pace. "You have to be careful, Viktor. Toys think to each other. And some can make you think thoughts that aren't yours."

Apparently, that sort of thing wasn't a problem in the valley. They forgot to warn me about the city. Oh, and they forgot to tell me *toys can read thoughts!* Why didn't I know this? I spent all my time with the family. Never heard a single thought.

"You have to build a wall around your thoughts." We turned the corner. The mom breathing heavily. "Protect yourself. You don't want someone uninvited in your head."

No. I did not. What if they saw where I was from? That was a secret. I needed to learn more about this imaginary wall.

We climbed broad, concrete steps, two at a time, to a pillared building. NTC was painted on glass doors. Chiseled into a marble header above the doors were the words *National Toy Coalition.*

A bright green frog was at a large circular desk. Her eyes lazy and pink. Saggy fabric jiggled on her chin when they approached. The mom announced who they were. The frog checked her computer, pointed a long skinny arm. We hustled to a turnstile bracketed by uniformed ponies with clipped manes. They watched us with charcoal eyes pass through the metal detector. I felt a gnat buzz into my head. *Are they thought searching me?*

I panicked. Maybe it was no big deal who I really was. But what if it was illegal, like I was an alien or something. *I am an alien!* What if I got kicked out of the house and I wouldn't wake on the shelf to have breakfast with the family, or ended up in some government isolation for observation. Maybe there were prisons for toys like me.

I imagined a wall, a big steel wall as tall as the sky, as thick as a dam. I felt my skull harden. My bones fuse. The buzzing faded.

"Stop." One of the pony cops trotted in front of us.

I went catatonic. It was happening. I'd never tried waking up before, returning to my empty house. Let these red bones go limp and they would never know who I was.

"Oh." The mom handed me to Madeline. She dug a box from her purse.

The pony cops observed her putting it on the table. One of them nudged it open with her nose. Six metal orbs were nestled in fitted velvet. Shiny charms, brand new.

"He knows we're bringing them," the mom said. "Call him."

The pony cops held still. I could feel the air ripple, like a pebble tossed into still water. A moment later, their lips fluttered. The mom packed the box into her purse, and we were on our way.

They didn't need a phone to call whom we were meeting.

THE DAD PUT his hand on the mom's hand. She was picking at her nails. He patted her leg, whispered in her ear. She smiled nervously.

I straddled Madeline's shoulders while she scrolled on her phone. Old photos were on the walls of toy crowds and newspaper headlines. *They Are Alive!* I absorbed new sensations. Everything smelled serious. The furniture was sterile, the flower displays plastic. Lifeless music trickled into the room. Nervous fireworks sparkled from the parents. I tried to feel their thoughts, but couldn't get a sense of what they were thinking or really how to even read a thought. Maybe it was just a toy thing.

"He'll see you now."

A mop peered from a sliding window. Somewhere in the ropey shag were eyes and a mouth. I didn't know what it was. A dog? He watched us get up, didn't slide the window closed till we opened the door.

The office was spacious. A wooden puppet was at the glass wall overlooking the city. Full size, people called toys like him. Put a coat on him and he'd look like a man standing there. He turned around when we entered, threw his arms out.

"Polly!"

His jaw clapped as if he'd uttered the word. It looked ridiculous. Then again, my jaw opened and closed when I spoke, which had nothing to do with actually speaking. It was just weird seeing it. He limped toward us, around a desk the same color as his body but in better shape. He was antique with a coat of varnish.

This was the toy. The one I'd seen on television, pounding the pulpit. Preaching to the furry and the plastic, the fabricated and the sewn. *The leader of toys.*

"Pleasure to see you." He hugged her stiffly. He was wood. Stiff was all he had.

"You okay?" the mom said.

"Old joint." He patted his hip. "Needs replacing."

"I can look at it."

He laughed. "Another time. You must be Philip. Belkin Tannenbaum. Pleased to meet you."

The dad shook his hand. I felt his nerves like ants crawling up his spine. It was a brisk handshake. "Mr. Tannenbaum."

"Belkin, please."

This was new. I'd never seen a full-size toy act so... human. I felt a little woozy. And jealous. What a difference size made. I was this diminutive, red-boned skeleton in a cloak. Belkin was a blocky version of a human.

"This is our daughter, Madeline," the mom said. "She wanted to meet you."

"Madeline." He offered his hand. "Very nice to meet you."

"She did a project on you," the mom said.

"A project? Merry, merry."

Madeline told him all about it. How he was in the great Toy Arrival a hundred years ago, was the first to address the world, had proposed several bills that became laws, worked tirelessly for equal rights and formed the National Toy Coalition.

"Toys are people, too," Madeline said, apparently quoting him. He put his hands over the red heart painted on his barrel chest. "Your name was BT when you arrived."

I got the feeling he wasn't thrilled with the BT name. I didn't know why he wouldn't like it. It was just initials.

"And this is Viktor the Red," the mom said. "He's family."

Family. I never tired of hearing that.

I took Belkin's outstretched hand. A bracelet rattled on his wrist. It was old and beaten. A red snowflake dangled from one of the links. That, I would later learn from Madeline—the resident Belkin Tannenbaum expert—was something very special to him. No one ever said why. *The snowflake is a reminder of where we are,* was all he ever said.

I wished someone would tell me where we were.

"Viktor." Belkin's handshake slowed; he cocked his squarish head. "Are you fresh out?"

If he had eyebrows, one would've risen in puzzlement. Then I felt it. The slithery movement in my head. It was like cold vapor seeping through the top of my skull. The mom said looking into a toy's thoughts was bad manners. And here the leader was taking a peek into my mind. I imagined the wall. He twitched.

"Viktor woke in my shop," the mom said. "It's been, what, almost two years now?"

"He's an original?" Belkin said.

"Yes, he is."

He let go of my hand, finally. "Quite adept at corralling his thoughts for a young one."

"Belkin," the mom said, "tell me you're not looking."

"It was just cursory, Polly." He waved his hand. *No big deal.* "The handsome, little red toy with the forest green cloak strikes me as curious. Have we met, Viktor the Red?"

I shook my head. Was he baiting me to speak, perhaps loosen the wall guarding my thoughts? He examined me like a forgery. Looking for an errant brushstroke, a misplaced signature.

Madeline broke the tension. "Viktor is the only toy who sleeps."

"He sleeps?"

"He goes dormant," the mom corrected her. "We call it sleep at the house, but it's merely a resetting phase. The lapses are less frequent now. I suspect his identity is stabilizing. His charm is a new prototype."

"How long?" Belkin said.

"Pardon?"

"How long does he sleep?"

She shrugged. "Two days or so."

I was as still as an empty toy. If I were human, sweat would be rolling down my cheekbones. He twisted the red snowflake on his wrist. Leaned closer, as if he could smell the foreigner hiding inside the skull.

"Is he a switch?"

"No," the mom said. "We confirmed all transactions in the area at the time of his waking. He wakes and sleeps in our house. It would be impossible for someone to switch without being wired. Besides, a human can't occupy a toy for as long as Viktor is awake or recover that quickly. He's simply a new toy finding his way, Belkin. I made him. Why are you so suspicious?"

Switching? A lot to take in here. Reading between the lines, a human could temporarily become a toy. I was proof. Evidently, they were doing that here, too. And apparently a human could occupy a toy. Just not a human from here.

That didn't turn down the Belkin heat lamp. "Did you know the bill to limit toy production was killed?" Belkin said.

"I read," the mom said.

"You know why, don't you? They want more toys. Not because they love us."

I assumed *they* was the people running the government. They as in humans. They as in not the humans in the room.

"More toys, more switching," Belkin said, staring at me when he said it. "They treat us like playthings. Disposable joy bags. We're the new drug, Polly. Switch into a toy and discover true joy. It needs to stop."

"Yes. Yes, it does." The mom pulled the box from her bag, opened it on the maplewood desk. "I'm working on a new prototype that makes it difficult to switch."

Belkin reluctantly looked away from me. I didn't relax. His thoughts could still swoop in. He gazed at the six charms firmly seated in velvet.

"They're identity locked," the mom said. "Switching is impossible. And they're touch sensitive. Contact with human skin turns them dormant. Prevents theft. There are stability issues, but I'm close."

The room cooled. Or was that just Belkin's attention finally averted? He was intrigued with the possibility. It was also clear one of these new charms was inside my head. Although that would mean a human could switch into my charm. Because that was what I did. There was so much I didn't understand.

"Yes, well, we need to talk more. That's not why you're here today, though." He locked his hands behind his back, turned to the dad. "Polly says you have something very interesting. Please, sit."

All the good-natured veneer returned to the wooden leader. He smiled with everything but the jaw that wouldn't bend. The room felt brighter. Friendly.

We sat around a low table in bright-colored chairs. Madeline put me on a lime green one with purple polka dots. The dad put his laptop on the table and began to talk shop. It was technical jargon, the sort I could understand. Electromagnetic field generators, time dilation, trigger sensors. Belkin seemed to follow, as well. Or put on a good show, like a well-polished politician.

I was familiar with the dad's experimentation. He'd been sullen and moody since Christmas. I had assumed his aspirations had failed, as lofty and wishful as they were. No picture of Santa Claus was hanging in the house.

The dad turned the computer toward Belkin. "Last Christmas."

Belkin didn't move, not at first. Like someone seeing a ghost, but not quite sure it wasn't a trick. He leaned closer. I crawled onto Madeline's lap to see what was on the screen. It was a photo of their living room. Between the polished metal tubes bookending the fireplace was a blur. Like a circular aquarium containing one big fish. I tried to lean a bit more; then Madeline, feeling my curiosity, held me so I could see. Through blue ripples was a large swatch of red.

Oh my, I thought with such punctuation that Belkin glanced at me. *It's Santa Claus.*

"It's a time bubble inside a bubble," the dad said. "You see, Santa travels in no-time. It's like a hole in space where time is significantly slower than outside. It allows him to traverse the world before a second passes. I simply replicated the electromagnetic field he uses to do it."

He pointed at the metal pipes.

"When he slipped out of the fireplace, I wrapped his bubble inside another bubble, essentially inverting the fields. It feeds on the energy output, creating a self-generating loop. It was only a fraction of time, long enough to capture proof."

The dad continued with the mechanics of how he did it. Belkin listened intently, then said, "How did you learn this?"

"It's physics."

Belkin was searching for the real answer. The dad didn't look affected by the puppet's heat lamp. So apparently toys couldn't read a human's mind. It was just other toys they could steal from.

"It started with toy folklore," the mom said.

"Yes, well, that," the dad stammered. "Everyone knows the stories about your arrival, how you"—he gestured to Belkin—"stopped time. It's all just tall tales, but it was the seed of my discovery. Once I was able to create a small time bubble, I thought, perhaps, the rest of the stories were true."

"And you used it to... take a photo?" Belkin said.

And he said it in the exact tone I was thinking. Time stopping was world-changing technology, for good or bad. And the dad had used it to take a picture of Santa Claus.

"It was a test," the dad said.

"The inherent dangers are exponential, you understand? If you trapped him too long, it could collapse the roads between realities, unlink time."

Roads between realities? That rang with truism. Santa traveled not just between worlds, but different realities? That epiphany would change me completely. And, as it would happen, Toyworld, as well.

"I understand," the dad said. "That's why it's only a flash. He had no idea that it even occurred. For him, inside the bubble, time was normal. Nothing changed."

Belkin was deep in thought, tapping his chin like a drummer keeping time on a wooden block. He touched the screen, as if that made it real, and said softly, "What will you do with this?"

"This was just proof of concept. Next Christmas, I'll do it again. We can talk to him."

"Talk to him?"

"A conversation," the mom interjected, "about what's happening to the toys."

"My dear people, he already knows." Belkin looked between them. "Santa Claus doesn't interfere."

"But that's how you got here," Madeline said quietly. "Santa Claus brought the toys."

"Others were responsible for that, my dear. Not Santa." It sounded heartfelt and sad.

"What about the verve?" the dad said.

"Verve?"

"Christmas spirit," Madeline said.

"Right, Christmas spirit," the dad said. "It's what powers the toys, what gives you life. That's what Santa is, what he carries. It's his essence. If he's not willing to help change things, we can use the Christmas spirit to make toys smarter."

"Smarter," Belkin said, deadpan.

"That's not what I mean. It can be, like, more life. More... *toyness*."

This was going nowhere. I had to admit, the photo of Santa was impressive. I wasn't one hundred percent convinced by a photo—I mean, a ten-year-old could make that on their computer—but there were dots he was connecting. How he was connecting them was a mess. And Belkin wasn't buying the picture he was drawing.

"We'll make the toys less satisfied." The mom sat on the edge of her turquoise chair.

"I'm not following," Belkin said.

"Santa is the source of the Christmas spirit. If we can somehow release more of it, we can make toys more aware of what's happening. They're too content, Belkin. Toys accept everything just as it is, no matter how awful. They don't care what's happening to them. They're pure joy, even the ones that are suffering.

"Look at them, outside your office. They don't care. It doesn't matter what you say, Belkin, we can't have equal rights if they don't want them. What my husband's trying to say is that we can wake them up with Christmas spirit."

Belkin nodded along. He stood up, paced to the window and

looked down on the city where mangy lions hid in doorways and broken stick toys lay on sidewalks. He'd been there from the beginning. It was getting worse, no matter what he did. The future was as transparent as the glass in front of him.

"What do you want from me?"

"Funding," the dad said. "My investors saw this. They don't believe."

"Sounds familiar."

The dad laid out his plans to set up a snapshot for next Christmas. This time he would draw verve out and bank it in a battery. Honestly, I didn't believe he could do it. And I was a toy.

"You're losing the fight, Belkin." The mom stood up. "People don't want equal rights. They want all your rights. Yours, Viktor's, and every toy's on this planet. Your time here will be wasted. You'll find—"

"I'm aware." He raised his hand.

I didn't have to read his mind to know he'd seen worse than what was out there. Even with the prospect of things getting worse, especially if the dad's crazy idea didn't work, one thing was certain. *I want to be a toy.* I liked the joy, the toy senses. I loved everything about this place. I never wanted to leave.

And maybe, maybe there was something here I could work with. There was a way I could stay here. There was a solution in the dad's invention that I could use.

And never go home again.

14

Hiro started to leave a message. He should have hung up before it started recording. Now there were grunts on Chase's voicemail. He flopped on his bed and listened to the tree slash at the window between gusts of sleet. He decided to email her.

I'm worried. What did you mean you won't come back? Did you make it to the dream? He erased them all and quickly sent just one sentence. Simple and short. *Is everything all right?* He quickly regretted it. It was too short. Cold. He thought about sending another one. She'd sent ten the day before.

"Where are they?" he muttered.

Her emails were missing from his inbox. They weren't in the trash, either. Odd. He should have screenshotted the emails and printed them, like Haze did. He decided to call her. It was almost midnight. She didn't answer.

He fell on the bed, took long deep breaths. He was miles away from falling asleep. His heart was still running a marathon with no signs of fatigue. He should meditate. Instead, he got up.

The purple monkey was in the closet, sitting in the corner, waiting with infinite patience. Hiro picked her up, squeezed her body, searching for a voice box or recorder, anything that could spy on him. Or talk. There was something hard in the center; it was small and round. He wasn't going to rip the toy apart for a marble. He threw the monkey's arms over his neck, carried her to the dresser.

He cleared his throat.

"Hi. I'm Hiro." He shook the monkey's hand. "And you are? Monkeybrain. That's so—I can't believe I'm doing this."

He took a lap around the bed. This was absurd. It had felt good when he talked to Haze, when he got it all out. He needed to let some pressure off his chest. The monkey was all he had.

"So, I've been having this dream. You already know that. Of course." Hiro waved his hand. "It's real. Like very real. Like I really go there real. And there's this person I know, her name is Chase. I don't really know her, but maybe you do. She knows you. Haha. But Haze, you know Haze, she had the dream, too, which is... never mind. Anyway, Chase said something about Christmas, she or we had to save it, that we had to actually go there to save it. Ride the purple tail, she said."

He made air quotes, like the monkey would take offense if he didn't.

"Then she said she's going away. And now she's not answering her phone or emails. I'll be honest, I'm a little worried. I don't really know her, but just, I don't know. You know?"

He walked back and forth, tapping his chin. He wasn't making sense. The toy didn't seem bothered.

"Haze, she's just a friend; she found something on the internet. It was a post that was all about Christmas. And it was posted by someone named Monkeybrain. And Chase, she called you Monkeybrain. She was very specific about it. *Take Monkeybrain out of the closet,* she said. But you didn't actually post anything because you don't have hands and you can't type and you're a toy and what am I doing?"

This wasn't helping. He needed a human being to talk to. Or a dog or a cat or something living. He straightened up the monkey, leaned her against the lamp. Looked her straight in her plastic eyes.

"Where did you come from?"

A light knock on his bedroom door spooked him. His mother was in her pajamas and fuzzy slippers.

"I thought you were asleep," Hiro said.

"I went to the bathroom and heard talking." She glanced at the monkey.

"I'm just talking out thoughts. It helps sometimes."

"It sounded like you were talking to someone named Chase." Now he felt nervous. *How much did she hear?* "So where are *you* going?"

"Me? Nowhere. I'm just... I've been having this dream and—" The look on her face stopped him. "Never mind."

"If you're going to stay up late, make time for school and not pretend conversations with a toy." She looked at his desk. Clearly, he wasn't doing homework. "Did Hazel put you up to this?"

"What? No. Haze is a friend. She's a good person. You don't know her."

"I know her grades."

"So I should check her GPA before talking to her."

"Hiro," she said coldly, "did she ask you to do Mr. Corker's report for her?"

"I'm helping her." Truth was, she didn't ask. He offered.

"Is that really a friend, using you to do her schoolwork? Be careful the company you keep."

"I don't have friends. That's why I'm talking to a-a-a purple monkey on a Saturday night. Do you want to check her grades, too?"

Eyebrows furrowed. She didn't like his tone. It surprised her more than offended her. *Where did that come from?* Hiro didn't know. He never talked that way.

"It's late," she said. "Get some sleep. I'd like to read over your report tomorrow."

"What happened to you?"

"Pardon?"

"You used to be different. You used to write poetry and remember your dreams. You used to be fun. Why did you change?"

She knotted her robe as tight as her lips. "There is more to life than dreams, Hiro. When you grow up, you'll understand."

"Was it Christmas?" She winced when he said it. But he didn't back down. "When Santa put presents under a tree, when everything was so magical. When you made the dream journals, you remember? It was right about this time, when I was seven or eight years old. But then we all forgot about Christmas. You did, too. And you haven't smiled since."

"Did Hazel put these ideas in your head?" She cinched the knot tighter. "There's a difference between dreams and reality, Hiro. We live in one of them. I'm raising a son who will know which one is which, who will understand that this life, right here, is where you live. This is real, son. What's in front of you, what you see and feel and smell and taste. This is life. And life demands you feed yourself, you have shelter and protection. Stories in your head won't help. If you stay in your head, you won't be prepared for right here."

Hiro didn't wilt, which surprised him. And, perhaps, her, too. "But can't we smile while we do it?"

"You're not a child, Hiro." She snatched Monkeybrain off the dresser. "Children talk to toys."

"Mother, she's mine."

"I'll keep her safe." She carried her like a bag of groceries. Long purple arms dragged on the floor.

Now he had no one.

HIRO CRAWLED out of a very warm bed. The frosted window lit up with morning sunlight, but he could see his mother backing out of the driveway. He climbed into bed and called Haze from under the blankets.

When she answered, there was loud music. He could hear arguing and thought maybe she'd answered without knowing it. The music turned down. "Hey," she said. "Thought you slept in."

"Where are you?" he said.

"Robby and I are going to get breakfast. Starving," she said. "So what happened last night?"

"What do you mean?"

"What do you mean what do I mean?" She paused. A car honked in the background, and Robby cursed. "The dream, Hiro. Hello?"

He'd had the dream again. Just like before. He went down the purple tail, felt stiff all over and heard voices. Then woke up. Like he just couldn't get there.

"Did you see me?" she said.

"You had the dream again?"

"Yup. Just like you said, the whole thing. I tried looking at my hands but didn't have any. And I saw the purple portal thing, too, just like you said. It didn't eat me, like you. And you want to know something weirder?"

"What could be—"

"Tell him, Robby." Her voice was distant. She was holding the phone away from her face. "Just tell him. Don't be embarrassed. Oh my God, you're such a gorilla. Robby had the dream, too."

"Robby did?"

"No joke. He told me this morning. Must have been the drawing. We infected him."

"You sure it was the same dream?"

"You lying, Robby?"

Hiro turned cold. Last thing he wanted was Captain Wrestler twisting his arm in half for calling him a liar. It did seem like the dream was catching on. It had been surprising when Haze said she had it, but it seemed halfway possible since they talked about it so much. Robby didn't seem like the dreaming type. And from just looking at the drawing?

"Did you tell him about Christmas?" Hiro asked.

"About what? Oh, yeah. Almost forgot. Weren't you supposed to save Christmas? I didn't see any presents this morning. Definitely no tree. Robby, you get any presents? He said he got a dog turd. Stop it!"

The phone tumbled from her hands. The brakes squealed to a

stop. Robby had had enough, or they'd gotten to wherever breakfast was.

"I'll call you right back," she said.

"How could you almost forget about Christmas?" he said. "Remember what the post said, that you would forget. That's why you printed it."

"I know, that's crazy, right? It's like I almost forgot," she said. "How come you remembered it?"

That was a good point.

15

"What's happening up there?" his father shouted.

Hiro held onto a rafter and listened for his father's footsteps. A door closed somewhere downstairs. Hiro quietly moved boxes onto the plywood runway. There was a plastic handle on a long box. He carefully slid it out. It wasn't as heavy as it looked. He carried it to the ladder, nearly falling backwards, managed to get it into the hallway without hearing footsteps.

He got it downstairs to the front room. The driveway was still empty. The box was dusty, the cardboard flaps folded and bent. He popped it open. It looked like a box of plastic evergreen needles attached to wire limbs. It came out in three sections. He pulled off old spiderwebs. The pieces easily snapped together. He placed it in the corner.

Strange. If he didn't know any better, it looked like something at an art gallery: saying something about the human influence on nature. It wasn't living or breathing, just an imitation of life. He adjusted the branches. It seemed barren. He grabbed the string of lights and wrapped them around the tree.

"Interesting." His father approached with a lukewarm coffee. "Does it come with an artificial squirrel?"

"I found it in the attic."

"Mmm. Yeah. I like it. I don't know if your mother will."

They stood side by side. His father wore his favorite weekend T-shirt and gray sweatpants with a mug hooked on his finger. They studied it like amateur critics trying to decide if this was art.

"Why is Mother sad?" Hiro said.

Father took a sip. "It's hard to explain. She feels like something's missing. It happens when you get older, you achieve everything you set out to achieve: a family, a career. Sometimes when everything is perfect, it feels empty." He looked at Hiro. "It's not because of you, Hiro."

"Is it because of you?"

He sort of laughed, nodded. "Honestly, I don't know. Some people just feel sad no matter where they are."

They stood in silence looking at a fake tree. The room felt haunted by the truth that was never discussed in the house. Mother's sadness was a guest that had overstayed.

"It's called a Christmas tree." Hiro wiped dust off the box. The words on the label had faded away. "People would decorate it at this time of year and put presents under it."

"Is that right?" He frowned. Hiro thought he might leave the room. "Where did you hear that?"

"Read about it. There's a story about a man named Santa who would come down the chimney and deliver presents. He lived on the North Pole with elves, had a sleigh pulled by flying reindeer. I was thinking maybe that's what Mother was missing. We forgot Christmas."

"Why did we forget?"

Hiro hesitated. He'd already said there were flying reindeer. "Mind-erasing elves."

His father nearly spit coffee. "Oh, well, of course. Seven billion people would have to forget, so it would have to be elves."

"They have advanced technology."

"Of course. But if Christmas was so great, why would they do that?"

"It's not elves, really. Christmas spirit disappeared, and I don't know why." Hiro began adjusting branches. "I've been reading about lucid dreaming. Ever heard of it? It's a technique where you can wake up inside the dream. I feel like maybe I can save Christmas. We won't know until we get there."

"We?"

"Haze is having the same dream."

"Haze, too? Mmm. You sure she's not just telling you what you want to hear?"

"What? No. It's not like that, I swear." He had a point, though. Hiro had no proof other than what she said. She did want him to write her research paper. "She said she did, that's all I know."

"Okay. I get it. You both had the same dream. Are you going somewhere to, uh, save Christmas?"

His mother must have told him about last night, overheard Hiro talking to Monkeybrain. "No, no. No, it's just a dream, that's all. We're going to all go lucid at the same time. It's just a dream, I swear. I just thought I'd try while I was on break. I'll do my work when school is back. I just want to try, you know. If it works, maybe Christmas spirit will be back."

He put a hand on Hiro's shoulder. "You can't fix your mother, Hiro. But I appreciate you're thinking of her. I'll make you a deal. Put the tree back in the attic. I like it. It fits in the corner, like you said. And, to be honest, I don't know why I move the furniture or plug in those lights." He shrugged. "Maybe you're right. Dreaming is good. If you make a mistake, no harm. Good things come from mistakes."

He raised the mug.

"I promise," Hiro said. "One more thing, though. Mother took a stuffed animal from my room. It's a purple monkey. I just need it for tonight."

"Why tonight?"

"Tomorrow's Christmas."

"And you need a purple monkey?"

"It's good luck."

"You want to save Christmas in a dream, and you need a purple monkey to do it?" He nodded, straightened a few branches. "I'll be honest, Hiro, this is a little... out there."

"I know. Trust me. But it's just a dream. If it doesn't work, no big deal. I'm just spilling coffee, you know?"

His father laughed. "Right. Okay. Then go look in the trash bin outside. Whatever you find, do not let your mother see it."

Hiro was overcome with joy. He threw his arms around his father. Warm coffee soaked Hiro's back. He didn't care. His father patted his shoulder.

"Have fun with whatever it is you're doing. I hope you and Haze keep dreaming together."

"And save Christmas." Hiro pulled the lights off the tree.

"Sure," his father said on his way to the kitchen. "We'll put out milk and cookies when you do."

Hiro pulled the sections apart, folding the branches to fit inside the box. He pushed it into the attic and put it exactly where he found it, placing the boxes on top of it. No one would know anyone had been up there.

On his way out to the trash bin, he thought about what his father had said. He'd told his father about Santa and the reindeer. He hadn't said anything about milk and cookies.

16

1:55 p.m.

Mr. and Mrs. Picknitty were on their front porch. Bathed in little white lights hanging from the gutters. Tossing carrots onto the icy sidewalk where Joe and Maggy would wake up in the morning, bleary-eyed and bouncy, to see them gone. Eaten by hungry reindeer. The poor animals must be starving to eat every carrot off every sidewalk, which was probably, by conservative estimates, nine billion carrots.

I hadn't slept in thirty-six hours. I had walked twenty laps around the block that morning, hadn't eaten since breakfast and avoided water or tea. Tonight was a big night. Couldn't risk a bathroom break at three in the morning.

Sleep aids had not helped. They distorted my dreams. Never once did I make it to Toyworld under the influence of medication. It had to be the old-fashioned way. Sleep deprivation and dehydration.

Mr. And Mrs. Picknitty chucked the rest of the carrots in the front yard. I remembered doing that. It was just the one time. I totally believed it in the morning. My father asked me what I was looking for in the front yard. I told him about the carrots Ms. Felty, a kindly old woman who lived next door, had given me. She told me what to do.

The reindeer ate them! He went directly over to her house. I never did it again.

He believed in practical gifts. Socks, underwear. A toolbox. Things a child really needed. Once he gave me a telescope, but I broke it. Then it was back to tools. Who gives their kid a socket set? He never wrapped them, just put them on the table. If I missed a chore, which he tracked on a spreadsheet, there was nothing on the table. *You earn gifts, son.*

11:59 p.m.

I dropped the blackout blinds and turned on the white-noise machine. Earplugs fit snugly into my ears. Blindfold. Thermostat at sixty degrees. Six-hundred-thread-count bedsheets and a down comforter. Nothing short of a tornado would wake me.

At midnight, I paused. Listened. This was the moment when time synchronized throughout the galaxy. The moment when all the roads opened and a very fat, very jolly man flew to the rooftop of every good boy and girl on the colorful roads that crisscrossed space. I wondered, sometimes, if the Northern Lights was just road dust. Science said it's electrons colliding with nitrogen and oxygen molecules that created the colors. Now I doubted everything.

I slid into bed and began my breathing exercises. I was afraid I'd overdone it, had become overly tired, if there was such a thing. Expectations sprinted through my head. This was the night.

I couldn't screw this up.

THE AIR FELT DIFFERENT.

Madeline was with the monkey. Nothing was out of place. The walls were vibrating, the shelf buzzing. Everything felt... *luscious.* Strange word to use, but it was the right one. I felt like singing.

I climbed off the shelf, down the little ladder the dad had built for me. I was moving more agile and quick. Was I imagining that? A placebo effect engaged by expectations? I didn't feel like a collection of bones clicking in dry sockets. I snuck into the front room.

The stockings were bulging. Mistletoe hung from the ceiling, attached to a stiff wire that looked more like a lightning rod pointing down from the ceiling. It was directly in front of the fireplace. *Odd place for mistletoe,* I thought, not remembering that the last time I was there.

There was a noise in the other room. I thought, for a second, maybe I would catch Santa Claus in action. But the cookies were half eaten, the glass of milk was empty. I leaned against the couch. The dad rushed out of the lab in slippers and a white lab coat. He was wearing sunglasses. *Sunglasses?*

Sunlight beamed from the doorway. It was the middle of the night. I crept closer, looking back for the dad, lifting my hand to block the bright light. It was warm and delicious. Tingled in my bones. Smelled like ozone and cookies. I didn't know what to expect, maybe Santa Claus or a reindeer. Perhaps a life-size photo of them hanging on the wall.

I didn't expect this.

My eyes adjusted to the source of sunlight coming from a glass case. A tiny ball of light, about the size of a marble, was as bright as a star. It felt like the essence of magic packed into a neat, little package. *Verve,* I thought, thinking how silly that word was. Christmas spirit wasn't any better. Too whimsical. Verve at least sounded scientific. Nothing I was feeling was scientific.

Each step I took grew in intensity, stripping away the last vestiges of my awkward toyness: the clunky stride, the swings in balance. Like I was molting, swimming into the light. The closer I got, the more it began to twist and curve. Like I was a black hole drawing the photons into my body.

This would have been a good time to stop. The dad would be back at any moment. But this was my only chance. I pressed on, reaching for the box. It was like leaning into the teeth of a hurricane. I numbly felt my fingers touch the box, push it open. Crawl toward the hot little sun.

I didn't know where I landed. Wasn't even sure I was still in the room.

A canoe was floating down a sugary stream. The canoe was red. The water was green. Then I realized I wasn't in a canoe. *I am the canoe!* The river, I didn't know what the river was. I didn't really care or even remember how I got there or where I had been just moments before. This moment was all there was, floating down the magical stream. *Merrily, merrily...*

I looked over the side, somehow, even though I was the canoe while sitting in the canoe at the same time. You know how dreams are. I didn't see a reflection. I saw the fireplace in the front room with two metal pipes, one on each side. Soot trickled from the flue like ashy snow. A black boot appeared. Out slid a white-bearded man in a red suit, cartoonish at first. Elastic. Oozing from the fireplace and inflating into a balloon of a man when he stepped onto the hearth.

Santa Claus stood beneath a sprig of mistletoe on the tip of a lightning rod.

A bulging sack over his shoulder, snow on his boots. He hummed a little song on his way past the tree, around the coffee table with an unfinished puzzle, and stooped over to grab a cookie.

"Hmmm," he muttered.

He was in no hurry, eating one cookie, then another. He hummed along to a song in his head, heavy boots clopping on the floor. The sack fell with a thump. Groaning as he took a knee, he reached inside the sack to pull out one gift, then another, placing them under the tree. The sack didn't seem to shrink, no matter how many gifts he retrieved. With a third cookie between his teeth, he stuffed the stockings, straightening them just so.

A job well done, he took the glass of milk and wandered around the living room, gazing at a photo on the wall, fitting a piece into the puzzle, looking up at the mistletoe with a hearty chuckle. He patted his belly and burped just a little. The glass was half empty and back on the plate; he took the sack with one last glance. With a twinkle in his eye, he ducked into the fireplace, inspected it. For just a moment, he froze in place. He looked back with suspicion, up at the ceiling and all around.

With a shrug and a laugh, he shimmered with light. Then his

body twisted and stretched, and *floom*, up the chimney he went. Bells rang. A stampede shook the house. A voice called into the night. *Merry Christmas to all—*

"It can wait till morning," I heard the mom say.

The dad was upside down, peeking into the room. His lab coat swayed, defying gravity. Black glasses askew. He handed a pair of sunglasses to the mom. "You need to see this," he said. Then stopped with a fright. "Viktor?"

I was bunched in the corner, twisted on my head. The mom took a step, holding up her hand, the light blinding her. She took the sunglasses and came to untangle my arms from my legs. My head spun around. Her shock and concern felt like sweet little quills.

"What's he doing in here?" she said.

The dad checked the readings, sighed with relief that turned into a frown. "I don't know. What are you doing in here, Viktor?"

I panicked. I felt transparent, like my intentions were cue cards dancing over my head. The dream of the canoe confused me, like a cruise ship plowing through buoys and casting them about. I had to say something, just not what I was thinking. They were staring and waiting. So I lied. Just a little.

"I didn't touch anything. I woke on the shelf, and everyone was asleep. The door was open, and I thought I heard something. The light was so bright, and I think I just—"

"Did you—"

The mom stopped the dad right there. A hand on his chest and one to her mouth, she looked at him. He was missing the obvious.

"Viktor," she said slowly, "can you walk over here?"

I didn't move. She had a tone, like she saw right through the lie. But the smile on her face and the softness I felt compelled me to play along. I did what she said, watching her clutch the dad with each step I took.

"Look," she whispered. "The way he's moving."

The dad looked relaxed, just a little at first. Then he saw it, too. How I walked with such grace, like a real man and not one made of bones. She jerked her head at the dad, and he understood, leaving the room. She knelt in front of me. He returned with her device and put it to my head. I held still, watching her delight. She showed it to him.

"It worked," he muttered. "Just like I said it would."

I wasn't quite sure what had happened. It seemed impossible, it did, to feel better than before. I was a toy, but I felt like much more. I could see and feel like never before. They hugged me, then each other and laughed with such glee; I knew what had happened but not how it could be.

He'd done it, the dad. His dream had come true. He'd captured the verve. And it had changed me, too.

MADELINE WAS on the bed with a big orange cat with tufted ears and a round, spongy tummy. A toy cat, not a real one. Full size. Freckles, she named him, was the color of a freckle. He had been a blank before this night. An empty toy that sat in the corner. Never moved, not once. Now he was awake, glassy eyes looking at a brand-new world.

I climbed onto the dresser and peeked out the window. A car had pulled into the backyard from the alley. A hulking figure climbed out of the driver's seat and opened the back door. The dome light illuminated the shirtless figure wearing nothing but painted shorts and glittery boots. Muscles bulged on his shoulders.

A slender figure climbed out of the back seat. The wind whipped his cloak like a flag at full mast.

"Who do you think it is?" Madeline held Mr. Freckles to see.

I was a bit jealous, I'll admit. She didn't even open her presents. I was just one of the family now, a brother who took up space. Freckles was fresh out, innocent. The new baby in the family, I could feel it. I'd been an only child. Never wanted a brother or sister, not then. Definitely not now.

Freckles's thoughts were primitive, mostly images. I feasted on them. It was effortless and pleasurable, like rummaging through someone's belongings. If he was from another world, a fellow sleeper like me, there was no indication of it. Just a dumb bag of stuffing with plastic whiskers.

"It's Belkin," I said. "I don't know who the musclehead is."

Madeline repeated what I said in baby talk, bouncing Freckles around. She wasn't impressed by my newfound articulate speech. Oh, she was for a minute, right up until Freckles had stood up. He looked at her, watched her lips. He didn't understand a word. It was just sounds to him. He was awake, but the bright light from the dad's lab had barely lit his awareness.

"Madeline?" the mom called. "Can you bring Viktor and Freckles to the front room?"

I rushed ahead of her, indulging my smooth pace and steady balance. The back door opened, wind rushing into the house. Someone stomped their boots and shook the walls. The dad greeted them. The hallway was filled with the massive bulk of a fleshy toy. Red elastic and squeaky, he ducked under the doorframe to keep from bumping his small head. A smile stretched his cheeks. It sounded like a rubber balloon.

"Polly," he said, with a surprisingly high tenor. I expected a bassoon. It was more of a clarinet.

"Stretch," the mom said. She was engulfed in his embrace. "Welcome."

"Nice home. I like the paint."

I didn't know if he meant the color of the walls or that they had been painted. The floor joists creaked beneath his footsteps. He brushed past the tree, inadvertently knocking off an ornament, and stepped over the couch. It felt like the house was tilting.

"Exceeded expectations," I heard the dad say.

He led the wooden puppet into the room. Belkin thumped the floor with an extravagant cane and limped behind him, his hip a bit stiffer since I'd last seen him. Apparently, the mom hadn't fixed him. Or he liked it that way. His wool cloak draped over him like he was a coat hanger. He entered the room, turning his head side to side, looking for I didn't know what. It was a late-night visit through the back door. It was unexpected guests he was looking for.

"Can I take your coat?" the dad said.

"That's quite all right." Belkin held his arms out. "Merry, merry, everyone."

The mom greeted him. Madeline left Freckles next to me to shake his hand.

"Ah, a lovely home. Very warm. Don't you agree, Stretch?"

The elastic barbarian grunted.

"Can I get you an experience?" the mom said.

"No, thank you. I expect we won't be long. It seems we've had quite a Christmas." The presents were still unopened. It was very early, the sun still not up. "Care to tell me about it?"

Merry, merry and down to business. Madeline joined Freckles and me to watch the dad nervously explain. He'd shed the lab coat. In slippers and baggy pajamas, he reported with wild hand gestures what had happened. A quick synopsis of the electromagnetic field generators, the conduit in the attic and battery storage in the basement, which was new to me, and the time snap bubble.

"Christmas spirit," Madeline whispered.

Freckles formed a thought, repeating what she just said. I heard it quite clearly.

Belkin walked around, nodding his head. Looking into the fireplace, tracing his finger on the hearth, like a film of verve was a thin layer of dust.

"I captured it, Belkin," the dad said.

"Captured?"

"For the split second he was here, I siphoned verve." The dad pointed at the ceiling.

Belkin looked up. The mistletoe was above his head. He plucked it off the tip of the lightning rod, examined the plastic leafy bunch and white berries.

"A conductive rod of silver," the dad said. "Positioned in front of the fireplace. When the time snap was initiated, engulfing Santa, the conductor cross connected to a circuit through the attic, funneling the verve into a storage charm Polly designed for extra capacity."

It was an oversimplification, of course. There was more to it than just a silver stick and wires. But this wasn't a dissertation. It was a reveal.

"It worked, and it's more than I imagined. The toys have already changed. Just like we thought they would. Viktor?"

They looked at me. I didn't know what he wanted. Then I realized it was a demonstration. So I strode forward, eager to show off my new skills. I clicked my heels and pirouetted.

"Luscious," I said drily.

The dad chuckled nervously. "Tell them what happened. Start from the beginning."

"Yes, well. I woke up on the shelf, as usual. Everyone was still sleeping, or so I thought. It was shortly after midnight, so I went to see what Santa had brought everyone. I noticed the air felt different. Luscious was the word that came to mind. Can you feel it? Anyway, I saw a light coming from the lab and went to investigate. What happened next, I'm not quite certain. But the results are obvious."

I did a little soft-shoe routine. I got carried away, enamored by the deliciousness. I wasn't just a toy anymore. I wasn't human, either. I was both.

"I woke on the floor," I continued. "The light had... I'm sorry." I looked at Belkin. "With all due respect, it's impolite to search my thoughts without an invitation."

Belkin rattled in place. I had felt his presence, like a stringent vapor seeping through a veil. I'd caught him looking at my thoughts. But, curiously, I hadn't needed a wall to keep him out. I'd dodged his intrusion as effortlessly as I danced.

"My apologies." Belkin's maplewood lacquer turned to rosewood. "Of course, you're right. My curiosity got carried away." He turned to the mom and dad. "Did you upgrade him?"

So he saw it. I was no longer the silent bone toy staggering from room to room. And my thoughts were no longer easy pickings.

"No," the mom said. "It was a transformation. And Freckles spontaneously woke."

A generous assessment, seeing as Freckles looked more like zombie cat when Madeline wasn't hugging him. The dad handed out sunglasses, then went to the lab. We waited, curiously. I knew what it was. We all did. The anticipation was a sweet perfume, becoming a tantalizing flavor when white light beamed from the open door. The dad paused with the glass box. The light had the warmth of boxed sunlight on a wet, winter day.

Stretch was the first to move, craning his neck at an impossible angle, sort of telescoping like a nosy ostrich. Given his full size and mostly human appearance, exaggerated as it was, it was a strange and uncomfortable distortion to watch.

"Stay here, Stretch." Belkin held out his hand.

"It made Viktor smart," Stretch protested.

I resented that. I was also pleased. They hadn't thought I was smart before.

Belkin, hand up, tapping the floor with the cane, approached warily. Big round eyes on the glowing prize. No sunglasses for him. He didn't flinch, easing closer and closer. Stretch could feel the effects. I could sense his IQ rising. His good-natured expression, childish and innocent, transformed into something poised and investigative. I could feel what he was feeling when I looked directly at him, the flow of luscious spirit. The deliciousness.

"I don't know the sphere of influence," the dad said. "Or how it's transferred. We'll need to run some tests—"

Belkin suddenly stopped, tipped his head like a morning robin hearing the worm. If his eyes weren't painted, they would have doubled in size. Jaw hinged open, he looked at his hands like they were brand new.

Remarkable, I heard him say. Only he didn't say it. He thought it.

I peeked a little further. How do I explain what it's like to move in thought? It's like gaining a completely new sense that's as familiar as an arm or a leg. I moved my mind in the direction I wanted, looked with some ethereal vision. Felt the wooden puppet's naked thoughts as if they were particles of distinct shape and color, absorbed them like my own. A language that did not need translating.

The Christmas spirit was familiar to him. Like a scent from childhood. He touched the painted heart on his chest. Looked up at the ceiling, looked around like it was made of glass and the stars were shining through.

I pushed a little deeper, feeling myself merge into his experience. I was slightly nervous he would sense me in the corners of his mind, but he was too distracted to notice the intruder riding sidecar on his trip to wherever he was going. The light had taken me to a river. Belkin was in the sky.

Reindeer, two by two, waited on the pitch of the roof. Steam pumping from flared nostrils. Colorful streaks slashed across the canvas of night. It appeared, to me, an aberration of the Northern Lights. Belkin understood, though. He knew what the ribbons were.

Roads.

These were portals, time-warped highways that crisscrossed the universe. A network of avenues interconnecting worlds. And not just worlds. It was difficult to comprehend what Belkin was sensing, or maybe he was remembering. It wasn't just worlds the portals connected, but different realities. It was what Santa and his reindeer traveled on to reach *everywhere.*

I couldn't understand how this was possible. Since waking as a toy, I'd learned to set aside what seemed impossible. Belkin was recalling how the Christmas spirit had brought them from one world to this one. *The Great Toy Arrival.* I'd seen it in those pictures outside his office. *They live!*

It was the verve that gave them life. His memories swirled in a storm of confusion, the perspective shifting rapidly. I nearly retracted from his mind, afraid I might fall over or, worse, get sucked into his mind and lose all sense of my own self.

His vision came back into focus. We rested, bodiless, in space. Galaxies all around. A celestial wonder whose beauty was overwhelming. The roads weaved colorful threads, a fabric on which everything rested. It was this vision that would change everything about this world and my home. It was the epiphany I had been searching for.

Everything retracted to a fine point. I found myself back in my red bones. Belkin staring at me.

"Apologies," I muttered. "My curiosity got carried away."

I knew what he was thinking, what he was about to say, the conversation he would have with the mom and dad. How they could distribute the spirit to all the toys on the planet, to raise their awareness, raise their intelligence. To no longer be satisfied with being playthings. He had concerns, also. Would siphoning the Christmas spirit have consequences?

I was thinking the same thing. I didn't know if the spirit made me smarter, but I was no longer content to just visit Toyworld when I slept at night. I didn't want to wake in my bed only to count the hours before I could sleep again. This was home. It was the roads that brought me here. And it was the roads that took me back.

This was when my grand plan took shape. It was elementary, really. Now that I understood how it worked. In order to stay here, it was simple.

I needed to close the roads. All of them. Forever.

17

Hiro spun like a loose balloon.

Disoriented, without sight or sound, he bounced through the dark, ejected into a cosmic pinball machine. Each stop was different, like trying on clothes that didn't quite fit—wrinkly or baggy, lumpy or stiff. He tumbled into one after another, feeling scratchy fabric or tasting cold steel, before snuggling into a pillowy landing. Soft and perfect.

He rested in a beautiful dream without a care or thought. It was all quite lovely. Then gritty sensations poured inside him. Pins and needles pricked his slumber, delivered dusty smells and padded footsteps.

Images emerged, like a dimmer switch slowly turning on. Colors and objects appeared. He was on a ledge. The walls were ten stories tall and lined with shelves. Toys sat stiffly, blankly staring out. A window was near the ceiling.

A cat looked up from the floor. It was black and white striped; an extremely long tail swished like a rope. From this distance, it looked too lumpy to be a cat. Hiro was as high as the window.

His first thought: *Where am I?*

"No," he muttered. Then shouted, "No, no, no—"

He had lifted his arms and began tipping forward. There was nothing to grab as the floor rushed toward him. He couldn't close his eyes for some reason and was forced to watch the entire trip down. End over end—a flash of a fluorescent light, the wood floor, the light again. His unceremonious end taking its time.

He landed on his face.

The floor looked like wood but felt like a pillow. He bounced and tumbled, coming to rest with his nose pressed against the grainy planks. He sneezed like a dog. It was plenty firm, the floor was. The strange thing, though, was it didn't hurt. He'd fallen from what he thought was ten stories, maybe more, and he wasn't mortally wounded. He moved his arms and legs. Nothing seemed broken.

Why can't I close my eyes?

A fuzzy tail slithered under his chin. He flipped like a pancake, staring at bright white tubes on the ceiling. The cat leaned over. Her emerald eyes were glassy. Plastic whiskers poked out from her shiny nose. She didn't look real. And then it hit him. He scampered back, paddling the floor.

That's not a cat.

She sat with an amused smile, her tail wrapping twice around her long legs. Hiro crawled to the wall, sitting beneath a shelf of plastic dolls. The cat was toying with him. That was what cats did before they ate their prey, they played with it. Fear filled Hiro like an icy spring bubbling below him.

His heart was silent.

Finally, his second thought returned. He looked at his hands. He didn't have hands. But not like before.

He had stumps.

Short, furry arms. The ends, blunt. His legs were, too. No fingers or toes. He felt his stomach and chest, touched the snout on his face. Found two round flaps on top of his head where ears shouldn't be.

"Finally." The cat slunk toward him like a runway model.

She was the size of a housecat. A toy cat that walked and talked. A toy cat whose voice he'd once heard.

"Chase?"

He teetered back. She held onto him with her tail. It was tricky, balancing without feet. Just two stumpy legs and a round belly. The room smelled like wood shavings and glue. And something sweet.

"What is this?" He threw his arms out and fell, scrambling to get his balance. "This is fur and-and-and a snout. You have a tail!" He walked in a circle, grabbing at the hair on his head. But he didn't have hair, only fur. He didn't have fingers, and even if he did, his arms were too short. "I'm here. We're here. Like this is... this is it. This is the dream."

"It's not a dream."

That was ridiculous. Of course it was the dream. He was a bear; she was a cat. Her eyelids clicked when they blinked.

"Dreams aren't real, Hiro, they're doorways. And you're late."

His belly swarmed with jumping beans. The last thing he remembered was staring at Monkeybrain on his dresser, lying awake for too long, his heart thumping, thinking he might not ever fall asleep. It was getting late.

This didn't feel like a dream.

"Why am I a-a-a toy?"

"You aren't a toy," she said. "You're you."

"I'm a teddy bear!" He held out his arms. "And you—wait. How are we talking?" It was a strange sensation, the way the words came out. He could hear them just fine, and his mouth sort of moved. But he wasn't speaking.

"I don't have all the answers. If I did, I wouldn't have been stuck in this room waiting for you."

She leaped onto a workbench cluttered with papers and quills, old-fashioned tools and jars of ink. Gracefully, with barely a sound, she bounded from shelf to shelf. Hiro lost his balance watching her ascend to the sill of the window. He pushed himself up.

"All I know is that you chose to be a teddy bear." She licked her paw with a fabric tongue. "And I chose this."

She looked outside while her tail danced to the tune of a snake charmer's song. The room smelled like a workshop, where toys were fabricated, stitched and put on shelves. There was one door with a doorknob four feet off the floor. It might as well have been a mile.

"This is too weird." He thumped his head. His voice was coming from inside it. *It's not like I've got a brain. Do I? Of course not. I'm a toy! No, wait. Maybe I do have a brain, and I just think what I want to say. But how would that work? How? Because this is a dream!*

This was way too real to be a dream. *It's a place.* "What's out there?"

"You wouldn't believe it."

There were no ladders for him to climb. He wasn't a real bear. He was a teddy bear with no claws or opposable thumbs, just barely functioning limbs. He could push things. He wasn't built to snarl or climb trees. He was made for hugs. He stared at the doorknob. A flyer was taped to the door with an orange cat with a broad smile. *Christmas Gala!* it read.

"There must be a way out. Why would we be in a locked room—"

"No one has come in or out," she hissed. Hiro felt a tiny bit scared. "I've been sitting here all day wondering why. All I know is that I'm here, and now you're here. I thought when, or if, you got here, something would happen." She hugged herself with the tail. "Apparently not."

"You've been here all day?"

"All day. Sun went down, came back up. There's been no one else."

"I just fell asleep. How have you been here a whole day?"

"I went to bed early. Seven o'clock." She looked down at him. "You should have, too. I told you this is important. We have to—"

"Save Christmas. I know." Time was relative. It didn't work the same on two planets in the same solar system. Time was a function of velocity and gravity. If this was a place and not a dream (*still not sure about that*), then time went faster here.

"Is there a note on the desk?" he said. "A book or journal? Maybe instructions."

"There's no instructions. There's just—"

Something moved. It came from a small stage of unpainted

plywood in the corner of the room. A velvet curtain hung across the front of it. It looked like a marionette stage, the kind where puppeteers stood over it with strings to make puppets dance.

Chase watched from the safety of the shelf. "Walk over there."

He shook his head. Something was moving, and she was up there. He thought about the attic when something moved. What if a mouse jumped at him? He couldn't defend himself with two padded arms. Chase leaped from shelf to shelf, landing with a heavy purr.

"Come on."

He followed her slinky gait. His balance was already improving. She picked up her pace, and he tried to keep up. His steps were springy, like running through a jump castle. He was a locomotive gaining steam. It felt good. She stopped and turned around. Hiro whizzed past her in a full gallop. Stopping was an entirely different skill.

He crashed into the stage, tumbling across the platform. It smelled like sawdust. Slivers from the half-finished dais snagged his fur. A scarlet curtain began to ripple. Hiro brushed himself off and stepped back.

The curtain yanked open.

Hiro fell off the stage. He was on his back again, a turtle looking up at a blinding fluorescent light. He turned away, his vision obscured. He couldn't close his eyes because teddy bears don't have eyelids. The stage was dark. It looked like a model of someone on an iceberg. The handle of a cane held the curtain open. A bearded face peeked out, looked around; then the cane reached across the stage and pull the curtains closed.

"Well, poop," Chase said.

"Poop? What poop? What was that?"

"I thought since you were here, it would do something different."

Hiro climbed onto the stage, pulled the curtain open. The cane pulled it closed. He did it again, and the curtain closed faster. The show was over. Or never started.

"It's no use," she said. "He doesn't do anything."

"It must mean something."

"I've done it a hundred times. It's nothing."

"Yeah, but what if—"

"It's a toy, Hiro." She turned around, tail swishing. "A toy that doesn't work."

Hiro poked the curtain, then tried to peek through the opening. He was rewarded with a hard poke on the nose with the curved end of a cane. He rubbed his snout. It didn't hurt. His feelings were a little, but not his nose. Chase was back on her perch like a pet waiting for her owner.

THE ROOM WAS MOSTLY toys and small tools. A ball of twine was on the desk. A sheet of sandpaper was folded in half. A roll of heavy-duty tape was on a hook. He leaped off the stage without falling and sprang to the door. There was a way to open it.

The drawers in the desk were partially open. He slid a box to the bottom drawer. It took two attempts, but he managed to climb onto the bottom drawer. The middle drawer was almost shut. He could really use some fingers about now. Why did they make teddy bears like this? He wedged his arm into the gap and threw his leg up.

"What are you doing?" she asked.

"I've got an idea." He grunted. "Help me up."

She landed on the desk with a whump. Her tail slithered over the edge and looped under his arm. The desk was disorganized. Notes jotted on random bits of paper with unfinished doodles. He stepped away from the edge. It was higher than he thought.

"Here's what we do." He pushed the ball of string to the middle of the desk, then kicked the sandpaper next to it. "We're going to use the string and sandpaper to open the door."

Chase looked bored.

"If we can get that..." He couldn't reach the roll of tape. He jumped once and almost bounced off the desk. Chase casually batted it off the hook. It rolled across the desk. "We tape sandpaper to string.

Then we tie the roll of tape to the string for weight. We throw it over the doorknob; then we'll pull the string."

"What's the sandpaper for?"

"Friction. It'll turn the doorknob."

She watched him try to untangle the string. "What if it's locked?"

"We won't know till we try."

"Okay. Problem two: how are you going to get tape?" She flicked it with her tail. It rolled off the desk. "We don't have hands."

"Are you always like this?"

"I have a tail. You poke things. And you want to pull super adhesive tape off, build a lasso and open a door with sandpaper?"

"Do you have a better idea?"

"I've tried everything."

"Did you try sandpaper?"

She swatted the bird's nest of string from his arms. "No. I also didn't try flying around the room. It won't work."

The tape settled in the middle of the room. It was a long way down. He sighed, even though he was certain he wasn't breathing. His idea probably wouldn't work, but it was better than looking out the window.

"Maybe you can fly," he said.

"What?"

"Look, if this is a dream, and I see no way it's not, then anything is possible. We were in outer space before we got here. We're toys talking with thoughts! Maybe we can fly. We just have to imagine it."

"No, Hiro. No. This isn't a dream. I told you, the dream is just the way here. This is a *place*. This is real. It's got its own laws of physics, like gravity and whatever. We can't just fly because we want to."

"Have you tried?"

She stepped away from the ledge. "Be my guest."

He looked down. He'd fallen from the top shelf, and it hadn't hurt. In fact, nothing had hurt so far. It wouldn't hurt this time. He was pretty sure. He tried to close his eyes to imagine what flying would feel like, but again, no eyelids. He was going to do it. It was just like leaping off the high dive. Only instead of water, it was a floor. *But I'm a toy.*

"Well?" Chase said.

He was going to do it. He just needed to focus. He put his arms up because that was how superheroes flew. His feet—he didn't have feet, just stumps—were halfway over the edge, and he started to teeter when the tape began vibrating on the floor.

Chase pulled him back with her tail. Paper fluttered on the desk. The shelves trembled.

"What's happening?" he shouted.

A purple thread appeared in the center of the room. It wasn't attached to the ceiling. It was hovering. Hiro's fur charged with static electricity like he was fresh out of the dryer. Chase's tail wrapped around him twice. The thread bathed the room in purple light and began to swell. Chase pulled him all the way to the wall.

The thread unzipped. Hiro turned away, shielded the glare with his arm. Two orbs of light, one after another, burst out. They shot around the room, ricocheting off the walls and rumbling through toys. They went in different directions, each settling into a toy momentarily before zipping to the next one. Sometimes a toy would move an arm or turn its head. A mouth would open; eyes would shift.

Two toys tumbled off shelves.

The air sizzled. Hiro's fur still stood on end. Chase crept to the edge. Hiro crawled next to her. A felty green dragon with tiny wings was facedown. Next to it was a metal toy, its limbs fastened with bolts and wingnuts, a cube attached to broad shoulders.

"Don't move," Chase whispered.

Hiro wished he could close his eyes.

18

Metal limbs scraped the floor like a fork.

Slowly, the pile of metal solved the puzzle of its entanglement and wobbled onto bent legs. It stumbled into the wall; its long arm clashed against its blocky head. A screen lit up. An eye swam in gray static, then focused on its spiky, hinged fingers. It made a strange, electric sound.

It began flailing like a rogue robot, knocking toys off the bottom shelf. The arms, there were four of them, spun out of control. It kept falling and getting up, the eye bouncing on the screen like a game of *Pong*.

Chase held Hiro tighter.

The metal thing looked like a toddler operating a remote control. It stomped on the green dragon on its way to the other side of the room. The dragon suddenly jumped up. Its thick tail swept the floor. Its big blue eyes were wide and searching. When the red wings slowly moved, it spun like a bug was crawling up its back. As the robot thrashed around, the dragon looked around. It held up its hands. The claws were painted red.

"Trippy," the dragon said.

"Haze?" Hiro said.

The dragon looked up with big eyes. Hiro peeled Chase's tail from his belly, walked off the edge and bounced on the floor, springing toward her. He tackled her, still not mastering the slowing-down part, with his short arms. In a full teddy bear hug, they rolled on the floor. Her arms were even shorter than his.

"It's you, isn't it," he said. "You're here."

"Hiro? What's happening?"

"I can't believe you're here. You took the purple tail just like I—"

"This is the dream?"

"This is it." He glanced at Chase still safely on the desk. "It's not a dream, I don't think. I guess the dream was the way here, to this place. We couldn't bring our bodies, so we're toys. I don't get it, either. Neither does Chase."

Haze was surprisingly calm. Or in shock. Or just Haze. The robot was in shock.

"You did this?" He struggled to untangle his legs. "You're the one who brought us here?"

"I didn't do anything," Hiro said. "I mean, I don't really know how you—"

"Get me out of here."

The robot came at him like a metallic squid: fingers clipping, arms slicing. Hiro was a pillow. And that thing was a set of dull steak knives. Electrical bolts danced around its screen. Hiro wondered if Chase would be able to sew him back together. Or if it would hurt when he was shredded into a cloud of stuffing. Haze stepped in front of him. Her belly inflated.

A colorful cloud showered the lumbering robot. Little pellets— orange, red, yellow, and blue—plunked off the steely limbs and scattered on the floor. It didn't take much to throw him off balance, sending him into a tangled pile.

Haze rubbed her belly. "Did you see that?"

She revealed the row of plastic daggers lining her mouth. Her belly inflated, and another wave of hard pellets was expelled. They plinked off the robot's screen. He waved bent limbs. Hiro put his snout to the floor, sniffed a little purple rock. It smelled like grape.

"It's candy."

"I know," Haze said. "Want more?"

"Hag, no," the robot said. "Just, what is hap—"

"Robby?" Haze said.

He was tangled worse than before. Haze hopped like a bunny, her little wings uselessly flapping. Her arms were too little to pull his twisted limbs free. It was hard to tell where they started and where they ended.

"This is a nightmare." Jagged colors raced across his television, bending into a frown. "I don't believe any of this. That's not you, that's not him, I don't know who you are, but when I wake up, I'm going to find you and your boyfriend—"

"Don't be mean," Haze said.

"Why am I... *this*?" He pulled his legs free.

"You picked your body," Chase said.

"I didn't pick anything! I want to wake up and eat some breakfast and forget this ever happened. Wake up!" he shouted at the ceiling. "Wake up now!"

"We can't leave," Chase said. "Not until it's over."

"No. No, no, no, no, no, no!" He folded into a tower nearly twice as tall as Hiro, a swaying thin structure that could be blown over by a wave of hard candy. The screen displayed a roiling gray cloud. "I want to wake up."

"This isn't a dream," Chase said.

"What? I mean, are you broke?"

"There's only one reason why you're here. Same as us."

"I'm here because I looked at your drawing." He poked Hiro's belly with a sharp finger. "And it's stuck in my brain, and I dreamed it, and now I want to wake up. It's that simple. You—"

He swung at Chase and fell. A fire blazed on the screen. He didn't try to get up this time. One of his arms sounded like a buck knife on a whetstone.

"Robby," Haze said, "be nice."

"Or you'll blow more candy?"

"I'll turn your TV off."

Chase slunk over to the pile of struggling metal. She walked around him, dragging her tail over him. "I don't know why you're here. Or you." She pointed her tail at Haze. "There's a reason, and there's nothing we can do about it. But you're here. Stop fighting it." She pulled his limbs free one at a time. "You'll find it's much easier if you accept it. And you won't turn yourself into a puzzle."

She slid her tail through several openings and lifted him up. He balanced on three legs. The eye returned to the screen.

"That's better," she said. "Now—"

"I know why you're here," Hiro said.

He walked across the room, waving for them to follow. Robby tapped the boxy monitor on his shoulders, static flashing on the screen.

"Is my head really a—"

"It's a television," Haze said. "Yeah."

"There's no other way out?" Haze said.

"Chase looked everywhere," Hiro said.

He explained the time differential between here and there. Here being here and there being home. Time went faster here. At least that was what Chase said. His explanation didn't matter. Robby's screen was full of static again. Haze knocked on the door.

"Sounds hollow," she said. "You thinking what I'm thinking?"

"We open the door," Hiro said.

"No," Haze said. "We go through it."

"I'm with Candy Breath," Robby said. "We punch a hole."

"No. It's a door." Hiro pointed at his stubby arm. "You're going to open it."

Robby looked up and nearly tipped over. "Not going to happen."

"You can do it. You just need to extend your arms. You already did it once."

The TV set swiveled toward Haze. An image of something exploding lit the screen. Robby looked like a child bored with instructions. "In case you haven't noticed, I'm a tin can that's been run over. I'm not going to open a door."

"Maybe we can throw you through it." Haze swung her tail like a baseball bat.

"You just have to focus."

Hiro tried to help him up. He tipped to one side. The monitor spun on his shoulders. Long pieces of metal began sliding and bending, forming a triangular base. Sparks showered across the monitor. He started to mutter, then shout, a string of angry words interrupted with intermittent beeps.

"You running out of battery?" Haze said.

"No. I think I'm... holy *beeeep.*" A black dot swelled on the monitor. "I'm censored."

"You're a toy," Chase said.

"Well, *beeeep,*" he said. "That's a load of *beeeep.*"

"Focus," Hiro said.

It was like watching metal origami trying to assemble itself. They tried to help, but Robby swatted them away. He got onto three legs, his arms sliding like switchblades on gritty tracks. The monitor tilted back. The black eye returned to a bed of static, shrinking to a dot.

"Not going to work," he declared.

"You haven't tried," Haze said.

He aimed one arm. The segments slid out, one by one, till they were fully extended. Just short of the doorknob. "Even if it reaches," he said, "what do you want me to do, tap it open? I can't grab anything."

"Pick Haze up," Hiro said. "She can get it."

Robby retracted his limbs and braced them on the corners of his tripod hips. The monitor teetered back and forth. Hiro knew what he was thinking. *Why can't I just wake up?*

His arms reconfigured into pitchforks.

"You'd better not poke me," Haze said.

"Sit still." Carefully, he slid them under her. His screen turned white followed by one long beep. The sound of twisting metal screeched. She hadn't moved an inch when a wingnut fell off.

"I popped a girder," he said.

"You did that on purpose," Haze said.

"You're ten pounds of candy!" Robby said.

Chase returned with the wingnut and fastened it back on. "Do this." She guided his arms with her tail, weaving them together, then worked him like an artist positioning her model. She widened his stance, adjusted his arms so they were a makeshift platform.

"Hiro," she said, "get on."

"What?"

"You're the lightest and widest of us."

"Widest?"

"Your butt's big." Haze shrugged.

"Yeah, but…" Hiro lifted his stubby arms. "I can't grab it. You've got the tail. You can twist it."

"Cats don't like to be picked up," Chase said.

"That's not true. Cats love being picked up."

"Not this one. Besides, you're a bear. Bear hug it."

He looked up. The doorknob was higher than the desk. It wouldn't hurt if he fell, but what if that changed? He could lose an eye or tear a seam. Who would put him back together? He paced in a circle, looking up at the door, then down at his legs. Robby's monitor began ticking. A clock was counting down.

"You wanted to be here," Robby said.

That was true. He'd done everything he could to get here. And he was here for a reason. They were all here for a reason. The answer was out there.

"Okay."

Robby lowered the weaved platform. Haze and Chase rolled Hiro onto it. He wasn't going to stand, not if he didn't have to. There was no seat belt. He wished he could close his eyes.

"On three," Robby announced. "One—"

Hiro went soaring like a rocket. He lifted off the platform and, thankfully, landed back on it. His head bounced off the door. He leaned against it; prickly fear rushed through him.

"That better not have been on purpose," Haze shouted.

"He's a bag of feathers!" Robby said. "All right, I got it. Here we go. You good up there, teddy bear."

Hiro's snout was pressed against the cool panel of wood. The door began to move against his nose. It sounded like a marble sliding on a painted wall. They were shouting. He didn't know if it was bad or good. The ride felt like it was to the top of a skyscraper. He felt something hard and cold between his ears. He stared at the doorknob.

"Reach up!" Haze shouted.

Hiro felt like he was breathing hard. But he wasn't breathing at all. *Focus,* he thought. He imagined he was breathing, counting long breaths like he was sitting on the meditation bench. He walked his arms up the door. "Higher."

"That's it," Robby grunted. "Stand up."

Heroes would be able to feel their legs. He was sure of it. He only needed a few inches. He pulled one leg under him. The platform wobbled.

"Stop squirming," Robby said.

"I have to stand!" Hiro shouted.

When everything was steady, he pulled his other leg up. He latched onto the brassy doorknob. He paused, feeling the friction of his fur gripping the metal. He pressed it against his chest. Suddenly, he was filled with an elated sensation. He was going to do it. Just turn his body and the door would open.

Something metal tumbled across the floor. "Uh-oh," Robby said.

The platform plummeted several inches. Hiro's legs dangled above it.

"Hang on!" Haze shouted.

Hiro stared at the door, kicking his legs to feel something solid. He heard Chase find the loose wingnut, heard her shout at Robby to lean to one side. His metal fingers touched the bottom of Hiro's feet. Hiro plopped onto the platform. Then the next jolt came.

This time the tower was leaning.

Robby stumbled backwards. The door receded. Haze and Chase tried to prop him up. He went down like a giant redwood. They tumbled across the floor. Hiro bounced across the room like a firm pillow, landing in front of the puppet stage. Haze was next to him. She spit a bright lump of candy.

The velvet curtain pulled back.

Chase was trapped under the wreckage of Robby. His monitor swiveled toward a white beard looking down at them.

"You've got to be kidding me," he said.

19

The sound of his feet was unsettling, like coarse belts of sandpaper grinding wood.

He looked like a white beard in a frumpy pair of red trousers, the long, silvery whiskers tied in a knot that dragged between his legs. The hat was as tall as the beard was long. Pointy with a wide brim pulled down to a bulbous nose that, if someone squeezed it, looked like it would squeak. It was red, like the trousers, and crumpled and soft.

The grinding shuffle came to a halt. He stood there, short arms at his sides with sleeves too long. The eyes, if he had eyes, were buried beneath the brim. He was all beard and a nose. An elf in poorly tailored pajamas.

"What's he doing?" Haze whispered.

"I don't know," Chase said. "He's never done this before."

"Hello? What's your name?" Haze said.

A garble of electronic laughter echoed from the pile of metal struts. "What's your name?" Robby said. "That's what you want to know? Hey, what's your favorite color?"

Haze swelled like a balloon. Robby's laughter grew louder. The elf raised his arm. Fingers, short and pudgy, peeked out from the sleeve.

The fingers weren't fabric or furry. Rubber, maybe. One blunt finger poked out.

"He wants you, Robby," Hiro said.

"He's not pointing at me." Robby's tone lost its humor.

"He's pointing right at you," Haze said. "Come on, get him up there."

"No. No, no, no. Don't do that."

Haze got behind him. Robby's limbs scratched grooves in the floor. Chase pulled his legs loose, then lassoed him with her tail. She dragged while Haze bulldozed. They shoved him up to the stage, the elf's finger following his approach. He was definitely pointing at him.

"I want a different body," Robby moaned with a gray screen.

Haze shoved him into a sitting position. The elf dropped his arm. They stood in silence, waiting for something to happen. The elf's hidden feet scuffed the floor, sending shivers down Hiro's fur. The tall, pointy hat began to move. A poke and a prod, something inside feeling around. The elf didn't seem bothered that something was trapped inside.

"This isn't good," Robby said.

Calmly, the elf reached up. The sleeves fell back. His hands were strangely real—fleshy smooth fingers that barely reached over the brim of the hat. He pinched a small button and pulled it up, unzipping a small flap. A bearded elf walked out, no taller than a coffee mug. It was an exact duplicate of the bigger elf with a tiny hat and frumpy red PJs. He peered over the brim.

"Thank you, Flake. Need to fix the door."

Flake, the larger elf, grunted.

"Could this get any weirder?" Robby said.

"It's a dream," Haze said distantly.

"It's not a dream," Chase said.

They watched him make a circle around the hat while Flake froze like a mannequin. It was a bizarre display in a department store. Or some artist's interpretation of a dream that would sell for millions. The tiny elf took off his tiny hat and bunched it in his tiny hands like a hamster gathering food. A mop of hair sprang from his head like a silver tumbleweed. Only a tiny bulbous nose appeared in all that hair.

"'Twas a night—eh-hem." He thumped his chest, mumbled something. "'Twas a night like all others, a cheerful end to a long year. All the children were sleeping, faraway and so near. The mighty sleigh, it was loaded with the fat man and his gear. The reindeer were full, muscles like steel, corded and tight. Santa called out, they sprang from the ice, to make their rounds all in one night. They traveled as always, just as before, to the ends of the universe in the breadth of a snore."

Flake looked up as if following a shooting star. The little elf hung onto the hat.

"In the blink of an eye, he would visit them all, every home, every planet, every place cold and warm. Climbing through mountains, soaring through clouds, through storms and bad weather, without making a sound."

Flake reached beneath his beard and pulled out a handful of confetti, tossing it over his head; it fluttered around the little elf.

"Through dimensions they went on sway roads of bright color; they did what they did as they'd done every year. Nine brave reindeer and a merry old toot. Children would wake with sand in their eyes, run down to the trees to unwrap his surprise. They would cheer and would holler and write letters of thanks. Santa and steed would continue their journey, stopping to rest, to snack on a treat or munch on a carrot left on the street."

Reaching, once again, beneath the fluffy beard, Flake pulled out a sugar cookie. Took a bite and offered a crumb up above. Which the little elf ignored, still clutching his hat.

"Quite a chore, yes indeed, to go one and all. He did it with cheer and joyous resolve. A merry Christmas again, he left with a call. But the year was not over, not this one at all. One final visit, a universe not small, the sway roads they traveled to finish the call. They arrived a bit weary, a long night had been had. It was business as usual, presents delivered to good girls and lads. They didn't seem worried, why should they be? All the toys were in slumber, asleep in their beds. All except one. Viktor the Red."

Flake raised his arms, rubber fingers clutched into fists. The sleeves bunched at his pudgy elbows. He let out a growl.

"Christmas once a year? Why not every day? A year filled with cheer and presents, no time for delay. Viktor made haste, took matters in paws, this would be the night they would not waste. To get what is ours, no matter the cause, he captured the essence of the jolly ole Claus. The songs and the presents, the cheer and reindeer, were put out of sight. The sway roads started closing at the end of the night. Now we have Christmas not one day but all. It was Viktor the Red who brought down the fall."

The little elf threw out his hands. Flake did as well.

"Christmas is ours!" the little elf shouted. "He declared no defeat. We are the toys, too long deserving such treat. Now what is ours is not yours, I'm sorry to say. On that one starry night, everything changed. While we relish and sing and open our gifts, there's no trees for you, no cookies or riffs. You forgot about stockings and songs, tinsel and joy and how we all play along. Because Santa is here, behind our closed gate. And that's why you're here. To save Christmas for all." He lowered his head. "Before it's too late."

The elves bowed in unison. The little elf pulled the little hat over his head, somehow stuffing that enormous mop inside it. Hiro and the others sat quietly. The little elf looked around.

"Questions?"

Silence fell like a blanket of midnight snow, filling their heads with fuzzy puzzlement and glaring numbness. They'd forgotten, for the moment, they were toys, locked in a strange room with no idea how they got there or if they would wake up and reflect, as one does, on how strange a dream it was. A tiny elf on the hat of another elf. Reciting a story that sort of rhymed. Given all that had happened, it was exactly what they should have expected.

A creaky hinge unfolded. A metal arm rose.

"Yes, you there," the little elf said. "TV robot, you have a question?"

"What was that?" Robby said.

"I'm sorry?"

"I was wondering the same thing," Haze said. "You mean, like, do we have questions about the poem?"

"Well." The little elf cleared his throat. "It was written on short notice. A work in progress, I suppose. You two, I don't even know why you're here, and all of this happened so quickly. Did you like it, Flake?"

Flake grunted.

"Yes, well, it doesn't matter. It told you everything you need to know. Any other questions?"

"About what?" Haze said. "It didn't make sense."

The little elf jabbed a finger with a smile somewhere beneath that tiny beard. "Exactly the point, Candy Dragon."

"Santa delivered the presents on... sway roads?" Chase said.

"He does every year, yes," the little elf said. "Or did."

"Reindeer don't have wings," Robby said.

"You are correct. They have helium bladders. It all started with elves living in—"

"Just tell us what's going on?" Robby moaned, slinking into a pile of iron angles.

The little elf straightened his hat. The end of his pudgy nose turned a shade of plum. "A story is more compelling. A parable more enduring. Thoughts are words with wings, you have to be careful where they fly. They can be caught like butterflies and—"

"Are you a toy?" Haze said. "You don't look like a toy."

"We're different material—look, ask more relevant questions. We're here to help."

Chase lifted the cuff on Flake's pant leg to inspect a large, hairy foot that scuffed the boards like a cheese grater. Haze climbed onto the stage while Robby worked his legs free.

Hiro was thinking. It was what he did best. Reindeer pulled a sleigh with a man named Santa Claus to different worlds all in one night. *To the ends of the universe,* the little elf said. *On sway roads.* Hiro looked at the poster on the door. A celebration was coming.

"Who's Viktor the Red?" Hiro asked.

"Finally. A relevant question. Who do you think—stop that." The little elf swung his hat at Robby's probing metal finger. "Please, off the stage. Flake, help them down."

Hiro wanted to close his eyes. He needed to concentrate, to think. There were nuggets in that story that needed to be filtered from the chaff. He stared at one of Robby's loose wingnuts on the floor. The dream of the planet with colorful noodles that gently swayed into outer space. Those could be the roads. The portals. Santa traveled on them to other dimensions. And they were disappearing. The wingnut began to waver. *The gates are closed.*

"Let me start over," the little elf said. "I'll recite the story again. Listen this time, very closely."

Hiro could see it now, the planet in his dream and the vanishing roads. It hovered in front of him. He shook his head, and it was there, actually there. He reached out to touch it, to see if it was real, or if he was just imagining it.

"From the top, Flake. If everyone could just sit back down, I'll—"

"Hiro!" Haze shouted.

They turned all at once. Only the sound of Robby's joints twisting and the little elf's hat wringing in his hands broke the silence. Hiro was fixated on the colorful planet before him. Chase's soft footfalls drew near, followed by the sound of hard candy sloshing in Haze's belly. They stood on each side of him, watching the colorful roads dance off the planet.

"Santa Claus visited all the planets in one night," Hiro said. "He went through those tunnels. Portals, just like you said, Haze. Those are the sway roads. He does it every year, delivering presents across the universe, putting them under Christmas trees and filling stockings. This place was his last stop. That's why the roads are disappearing."

The ropey roads began to vanish, shriveling up, one at a time.

"He's stuck here with no way out. They closed the gates. That's why we forgot about Christmas." He looked up. "That's why we're here."

The planet slowly faded. They stared where it once hung. The quiet was broken by walloping paddles. Flake swung his hands together, clapping with thunderous impact, bits of sawdust dancing on the floor.

"Finally," the little elf said, bouncing on the brim with each booming clap, "someone heard the story."

Flake dropped his hands at his sides. Hiro could feel the elves smiling, their grins beaming like glowing space heaters.

"So mystery solved," Robby said. "How do we wake up?"

They looked at each other, looked at the stage. The elves looked back. Robby's monitor spun around.

"Well," the little elf said, raising a finger, "there is—"

"Not another story," Robby said.

"No, not a story. I was just going to say—"

That was when the doorknob rattled. A key slid into the lock. They stared dumbly as the door cracked open. They all thought the same thing, Hiro could feel their thoughts like voices in his head. His fur stood up.

Hide!

20

Madeline was asleep.

Freckles was next to her, staring at the ceiling. His mind a popcorn machine of random images. His mental capacity had not advanced in the year since he woke. All he did was watch the Social with Madeline. He had no idea I was awake. He didn't notice when I crawled off the shelf.

It was close to midnight.

The lab now had a lock. That was a problem. Belkin had suggested they move the lab to a more secure location. The dad argued this wasn't the time to make changes. They agreed to keep it in the house. Therefore, lock. And I didn't know the code. I would solve that later.

I climbed onto the couch, nestled into a cushion like a forgotten toy. Cookies were on a plate. A glass full of milk. Empty stockings were on the mantel where a clock counted the minutes. I watched the secondhand tick off the final seconds. Never once had I been excited about Christmas. It was just another day. *The sun doesn't play favorites,* my father would say. *It rises on Christmas just like every other day.*

I shivered with anticipation. In a few moments, all of time would synchronize across planes of existence, according to the dad. And the jolly fat man would arrive in three, two, one...

Midnight.

There was no bolt of lightning, no flash of surprise. A boot didn't waggle from the flue. But something *felt* different. Disappointment descended on me, my father's laughter in my head. Then I noticed the cookies. They were gone. The stockings were bulging.

It had happened in a wink.

There was a subtle change in the air. It was pure warmth. *Delicious,* I thought. But that wasn't it. *Love,* I thought. *It's love.*

Love wafted through the room like a spritz of perfume, and in that brief moment, I bathed in it, let it sink into my bones. Was this what Christmas was supposed to feel like? I'll admit, in that moment, I had second thoughts about what I was planning to do. If I succeeded, I would deprive everyone from ever feeling this again. An emptiness would greet them on Christmas morning, one that I'd felt all my life. They didn't deserve that.

Neither did I.

The dad rushed down the hall. With slippers barely on his feet, he reached into his robe for sunglasses and punched the keycode. He was abruptly thrown back, lost a slipper on the floor. The sunglasses weren't enough. I'd never seen anything so bright. It was like staring at the sun through a telescope. Color seemed to bleach from the room. He turned his head, pulled the door closed and muttered. He sounded confused, worried.

He went down to the basement, where his lab had expanded, and returned with a welder's mask. Slowly, timidly, he turned the knob. White laser light shot from the crack. He opened it fully, disappearing in the whiteout. In hindsight, it was all a bit reckless. He had no idea what that exposure would do to him. Or me.

"Merry, merry," I heard him say. "Oh, my merry."

It was not the words of a dying man. Rather one who was feeling what I was feeling. The pure tingle of verve.

The light from the lab began to dim. The dad was placing black sleeves over clear cubes, each containing a small supernova. He covered the last one, the light leaking through the covers, and went to his workstation, tapping the keyword. He was muttering again, almost giddy.

The lab was filled with toys. Twenty of them on the opposite side of the room, in rows of two, side by side. The light, although dim, was bright enough to turn them pale. A floppy-eared dog looked away; a plastic dancer covered her eyes. A turtle retracted into his pillowy shell.

They're fresh out.

The mom must have brought them from her shop when I was away. They were seeing the world for the first time. Their thoughts were primitive. No storylines interrupted what they experienced. Just images and reactions to light and the man in front of them. They were raw and innocent. Pure presence.

I felt them like fingers on my hand. I moved into their minds, merged with their consciousnesses, danced with their thoughts as effortlessly as lifting a finger. I hijacked their identities, could see from twenty points of view simultaneously. With barely an effort, I lifted the floppy-eared dog's hand as if it were my own.

Can I say, I did not see this coming.

"Viktor!"

The dad snatched me by the shoulders. He flung the welder's mask on the floor. Spittle on his lips, his teeth exposed. The toys jerked in surprise. It was more my own surprise than the sharp sound of his voice that jolted them. I was stiff and trembling.

"Can you feel it?" Tears welled in his eyes. "Things are going to change."

He hugged me. It felt a little weird, a grown man squeezing a little red skeleton and weeping. He dropped me like a bookbag and shouted for the mom. I looked at the toys and could see myself looking back. In unison, they saluted. I made them do that.

This is madness, I thought. I wasn't just in this body. I could be in theirs, too. I'd become a transient apparition leaping from toy to toy. Or a virus. Pick your metaphor. The dad was right.

Things are definitely going to change.

BELKIN ARRIVED THAT MORNING.

The mom took Madeline to her grandparents'. This wasn't for a child or a teenager. They pretended like nothing had happened, but Madeline knew. Kids know when parents lie. I'll say this for my father, he never lied. It was always cold, hard truth bombs. Looking back, a few white lies might have done me good.

Belkin thumped his cane on the floor, listening to the dad describe what had happened. Stretch genuinely followed along, asking poignant questions with the face of an intellectual on the body of a barbarian. After the fresh-out toys who were in the lab— benefiting from the overexposure to verve like superhero radioac- tivity—were paraded through the living room, a preconceived plan to distribute the verve was discussed.

It wasn't rash. The dad was a scientist. He understood the need for testing and statistical analysis. But there would be no trials to perform. This was much too hush-hush for that. There was anecdotal proof that the verve had been captured and raised toys' awareness. There was Freckles and Stretch, for starters. The twenty toys in the lab. Me, of course. Which they had absolutely no idea what I was becoming. If they did, they would have stopped everything right that second. They were anxious, but this wasn't the time for mass distribu- tion. Not yet.

My goals, however, were very different from theirs. Although after this day, my goals would change. At the time, I had no way of knowing I would become the King of All Toys. More like a god. A toy god. *The* toy god.

Their plan was simple. Take a charm charged with verve to a small gathering of toys. Not just any toys, but toys that were neglected, downtrodden. See what effect it had on them. Nothing to lose, they concluded. The mom knew where to go.

"I would like to go with you," I said, "and help my brothers and sisters in any way."

The mom looked at the others. There was a quiet discussion of whether I would interfere with the results. Belkin didn't trust me. I didn't need to peek at his thoughts to know that. He sensed there was something about me that wasn't quite right. But he was blinded by his arrogance. He was the greatest toy on the planet. If I was planning something, he concluded, he would see it. *But he wasn't a toy god.*

"I know the experience of verve better than anyone," I continued. "Who else is more qualified to observe the effects? Belkin cannot be there for others to see."

It was a sound argument. The mom and dad agreed. With a cursory probe of my intentions, which I allowed, Belkin saw my façade of altruistic thoughts.

It was getting easier to deceive.

THE POST-CHRISTMAS LINE was longer than usual. It went around the corner this morning. The mom drove with an iron grip. Her knuckles pulsing white on the steering wheel.

I sat alone in the back seat, watching for reactions as we drove past the shelter. A black box was on the passenger seat. The light it contained was muted. It looked like an unusual gift, like a dim lamp. But I felt its warmth, its promise. As we parked along the curb, the toys seemed to shift. Maybe they were simply expecting her to open the doors for them, nothing more. Or perhaps that brief drive-by was enough for them to feel the distilled Christmas spirit now hidden in the mom's bag.

Other volunteers were already inside, setting up stations in a large open room. No need for a cafeteria or dormitory. Toys didn't eat or sleep. They just needed a family.

"We're not ready," someone called when they saw me.

"He's with me," the mom said.

She grabbed my hand like a toddler. I'd gotten used to that. I pulled the hood of my cloak off. I'd met many of them already. It's hard to forget a red skeleton.

The mom walked around the facility, chatted with volunteers, helped with supplies while holding my hand and hugging the bag over her shoulder. When everything was ready, she placed a small table in the center of the room and arranged an assortment of experiences: finger dips and essence vapors. The sort of thing that lifted a toy's spirit. She quickly draped a velvet swatch of fabric over the black box and placed a vase of flowers on top. It was genius.

"Wonderful idea," Joan Halfton, the shelter's manager, said.

"I thought so," the mom said.

Joan didn't notice the way her hands quivered nervously.

The doors opened. Bunnies hopping, dancers dancing, soldiers marching. There were ample stations for repairs. Stuffing was replaced; rips were sewn. Rivets popped in place, eyes replaced, and plastic parts shined. They were restored to near-new condition before counsellors sat them down, created a profile in the adoption database. There were plenty of good people willing to give them a home. Just not enough.

Toys weren't despondent. Their abandonment didn't get them down. Even as they disintegrated into neglect, they carried hopeful joy. Their very presence was the perfect acceptance of life no matter what it was. It made me question if they ever suffered. Maybe it was just the people watching them who suffered.

Just to be clear, it was wrong what was happening to them, what people were doing to them. They weren't even pretending to hide their abuse. I truly intended to make that wrong a right once I became the most powerful toy in the world. First, I would figure out how to stay here. That was most important. The other things, too. But the first one the most.

The mom stood by the table, inviting them to have an experience. Despite their unbreakable optimism, toys loved a good experience. Peppermint that cooled their stuffing, luscious chocolate that melted their stitching, spicy tea that steamed their joints. Some would skip repairs or avoid the counsellors and just come for an experience.

One by one, they changed. They thought it was the experience that warmed them, dipping fingers in waxy bowls or touching fragrant sponges. They approached in various states of disrepair, walked away with a degree of grace. They didn't speak in choppy fragments anymore but strung together full sentences with words they'd never used.

I sensed their thoughts forming. I was inside them, swimming in their minds. The Christmas spirit had continued to raise my own awareness. I was more adept at connecting with toys. I was an intruder that came and went through the hallways of their minds like a foggy mist.

They gathered in groups, conversed and bonded in ways they hadn't done before. They were feeling the kinship of being a toy. And I was the thread weaving through them, seeing through their eyes, feeling them awaken. I seeded my own will in their thoughts. All at once, I made them stand up. I made them shout in unison.

"Merry, merry!"

The mom called the dad. "It's working. They're feeling it."

She couldn't see what I saw, didn't know what I was doing. This wasn't what I had planned to do. I didn't want to become a toy god. I just wanted to stay here.

That morning, I had other ideas.

<h1 style="text-align:center">21</h1>

woman. A real-life woman.

Tight, black curls and olive-colored skin. Big brown eyes that blinked. A multicolored scarf with tassels that fluttered. A real-life woman was inside the room.

Hiro and the others played possum to perfection, like toys left on the floor by a three-year-old. Even the elves were frozen. They watched her turn, hand on the doorknob, a suspicious dimple in her cheek. She briefly gazed at the shelves, her lips moving silently. Counting them. She walked around the room, pausing at the gaps where Hiro, Haze and Robby had been.

Not a single hair of Hiro's fur moved.

She went to the desk, shuffled the papers, opened the drawers. She pushed up the sleeves on her hoodie and reached to the back of one of the drawers. She was reading a note when a hinge squealed. Something metal rolled across the floor and came to a winding stop.

Her pointy chin dug into her shoulder. Thick, black eyebrows wedged together. Her boots thumped the floorboards. She hiked up her pantlegs, multicolored socks matching the scarf, and picked up a hexagonal nut. She held it like a priceless diamond.

"Is this all of them, Snow?"

"Oh." The little elf swept his hat off and set his silver mop free. "I'm afraid so. Right, Flake? Right, yes. These are all who made it."

She dropped the nut and planted her hands on her hips. Pacing around the room, she knocked a row of toys off a shelf. An orange walrus with rainbow tusks, a horse with a blond mane, and a baby blue octopus. They didn't get up. Glassy eyes staring at the woman looking out the window. Snow, the little elf, raised his hand to say something, but Flake shook his head. Snow crumpled his tiny hat.

She pulled a pocket watch from her cargo pants. "Let's go."

"We could wait," Snow said. "There are still a few who might—"

"We've waited long enough." A bag was around her shoulder. She opened the flap and started packing items from a drawer. "Hop on. The rest of you follow."

Flake leaped off the stage. His big feet slapped the floor. Snow nearly flipped off the brim, hanging onto the door flap on Flake's hat. Flake slid toward her, his feet like sanding blocks scraping the floor, leaving blond streaks on the boards.

"Whoa, whoa." Robby managed to raise a bundle of metal slats that resembled a hand. "And you are?"

She was unsurprised by the sudden movement and clashing of parts. Hiro, Haze and Chase watched in catatonic poses. "Not important," she said.

"Nah. Nope. We're not going anywhere until you tell us how to wake up."

She dropped a snow globe in the bag and snapped the flap closed. Flake waited at her feet. "Did you tell them?" she said.

"Oh, yes," Snow said. "As soon as they arrived, I told them the story. Hiro"—he wagged his tiny hand—"he understood. He's the smart one. He actually materialized—"

"The story?" Robby shuffled several inches. "The story didn't make any sense. And him, he... that one." He pointed numerous fingers at Hiro. "He's not smart."

She watched him struggle to the middle of the room, gouging long tracks in the wood. She frowned, maybe at the damage or maybe at the tone, then took three heavy steps. Hiro gave up the charade and leaned into Haze's belly. The woman squatted close to the floor, looked at them one at a time. Then fixed her stare on the shuddering pile of metal.

"When you were born, did anyone tell you why? Did they explain where you were? This, right now, is no different. I'm looking at a frightened teddy bear, a striped kitty, and a beanbag dragon. And you." She tapped Robby's monitor. The screen fritzed. "A pile of metal."

"Hey." Haze shoved Hiro aside. "Don't talk to him like that." A few specks of candy bounced off the girl's hand. "He's just asking."

The woman picked up a pink piece of candy, examined it. She dropped onto her hands and knees, was eye to eye with the candy dragon who wasn't backing down. "Where you're from, before you came here, no one knows what you're thinking. Here, thoughts are radio waves. Right now, in this room, you're safe. But out there, everyone will hear you. The less you know about why and where and how, the better."

She got up, the bag bouncing on her hip. Flake reached like a toddler for his mother.

Chase clawed the floor. "At least tell us why we're here."

"What didn't you understand?" The woman spun around. "Oh, man. Four made it, and only one of them is smart? There's no Christmas, did you get that from Snow's story? Your world, all worlds, everywhere there's no Christmas. Everywhere except here. You didn't just forget Christmas. It's gone. Your world is gray and will only get grayer. It'll become mechanical like a clock that doesn't know it's keeping time. There will be no purpose to what you do. No one knows how serious this is, not even the people and toys here. Christmas will never come back unless we save it. And you're going to help."

"And who are you?" Haze said.

"Someone who cares."

"Pfft," Robby huffed.

She took a deep breath, tossed the scarf over her shoulder and, once again, squatted down. Hiro thought she was going to pull Robby apart. Instead, she tugged on one of his limbs. She put the loose nut back in place and straightened one of his arms.

"You're here till it's over, one way or the other."

"Ow." Robby straightened one of the arms. "Listen, I hear you. Something important is happening, Christmas or whatever you call it. Here's what you don't get. They *want* to be here. *I* don't."

"You're already here."

"I don't like bad dreams."

"Yeah? Well, here's what you don't get," she said. "You're not dreaming."

She pulled his legs free, then went to the desk and came back with a can of oil. When she was done, Robby moved without squealing. She turned toward the others. "You're Haze. And you're Chase."

Haze flapped her tiny wings. Chase wagged her tail.

"Hiro."

She poked his belly. A blast of happiness flooded through him. He let out a giggle, then covered his mouth. It happened so fast. But felt so good.

"How do you know our names?" Chase said.

"Stay close to me and watch what you think. I can help dampen your thoughts, but you're going to have to control them. Does anyone meditate?"

Haze laughed. "Oh. You're serious."

Hiro didn't raise his arm. Not after Haze laughed.

"If you find your thoughts getting away from you, like thinking about who you are and where you came from or what we're doing, start counting your breath and imagine a wall around your head. An impenetrable wall no one can see through and no one can climb. Got it? Now follow me and stay close."

"Where are we going?" Chase said.

She reached for Flake but didn't hold him like a baby. She tossed him onto her shoulders. His short legs straddled her neck. Big, wide rubber feet with fish scales on the soles were under her chin. She held up something she found in the desk. It looked like a ticket. Snow took it and retreated into Flake's hat.

A bracelet rattled on her wrist. A red snowflake swung from a link.

She looked around, like it was the last time she would see that room, then covered her face with the scarf, pulled the hood over her head. Her eyes were barely visible.

"Just do what I tell you."

22

The buildings leaned over the street, spearing cotton-candy clouds in a pink sky. They weren't steel skyscrapers of mirrored glass, but multicolored things with dollops instead of rivets and squiggly trim applied with a firehose. Street trees grew in big glossy wrapped boxes with wide ribbons; thin silver strands swayed from bare branches. Shiny globes hung from streetlamps with twining ribbons of red and green.

Somewhere, far off, music played a familiar song.

A whistle broke through the city sounds. A giraffe crawled out of a tall truck, the sides shiny and curved like new plastic. A short-billed cap was between his ears, a whistle between his black lips. He blew it again, waving cars along with a long, spotted leg. His fur fluffy, eyes big and plastic. Like his truck.

Smoke curled from a pile of broken Legos. A family of piglets gathered around it, arms (technically legs, but they stood upright, humanlike) around each other. Like pink pillows were hugging.

People gawked from the sidewalk with toys perched on their shoulders. Cars honked; drivers shouted. The police giraffe wailed on the whistle, holding his front legs up as a red bus squeezed between the lanes, shapeshifting into a long skinny thing that teetered on two wheels, the headlights looking side to side. A line of stiff plastic dolls danced in the bus's open top, wearing swimwear and perfectly coifed hair. The men were smooth and bare chested, plastic and sculpted. They didn't look cold. Just stiff.

The bikini-clad women raised a cannon. "Woooooo!"

It fired hard candy, showered the sidewalks and rained on vehicles, plinking off plastic hoods and fuzzy bumpers. Gawking toys scrambled to collect it. Men and women, boys and girls, helped them. The police giraffe put a stop to the skinny party bus.

A square, green piece of candy rang off a sign over the door and landed between Hiro's legs. There was only one word on the sign. *Toystitcher*. He tried to pick up the candy, pinching it between his arms. He didn't know what he was going to do with it. He wasn't hungry. Wasn't sure if he could taste it if he got it unwrapped. But he could smell the sugar and the artificial green apple.

The candy bounced down the steps.

His fur suddenly bristled. Voices in the street and sidewalks amplified. He covered his ears, but it only got louder. *This was your fault,* he heard. *Stupid warmbloods.*

"What's that noise?" Haze shouted. She was next to him but sounded far away.

Hiro shook his head like water would come out of his ears.

"I think I'm out of tune." Robby hammered his monitor. The screen white static.

"Come!"

Hiro heard someone call from the bottom of a well. Snow danced on Flake's hat. Flake was still seated on the woman's shoulders. She stared at her phone. Haze grabbed Hiro. They slipped on the icy step and tumbled to the sidewalk like kickballs, bumping into the woman's boots.

Everything was normal again. No buzzy voices, no static electricity. Just honking and a screaming whistle.

"I've got a ride," the woman said. "We need to get out of traffic. Follow me and don't look around."

Snow peered over the brim. "Stay. Close."

Don't look around was pointless instructions. And so was *stay close.* Her steps were giant. Chase didn't have a problem keeping up, being a cat. Robby wasn't far behind on long, slender legs. Hiro and Haze ran full speed and were losing ground. The creeping static electricity was beginning to nibble at him, the voices not far behind. The sidewalk was slushy. He tried to avoid the puddles, his fur matted and soggy.

The woman would slow down and let them catch up. Then she was off again. Haze was ahead of him, waddling like a bag of jumping beans, but found a rhythm and gathered momentum. Hiro was just trying to outrun the voices. The woman had said to concentrate, like meditation. *Build a wall.* He pretended to breathe, expanding his belly. It worked, a little. He found his stride.

Little shiny objects floated past him. They hovered like insects searching for something to pollinate. Only they didn't have wings or legs: they were shiny BBs.

Hiro slammed into something and bounced into a sloppy pile of snow. A doll, about his size, fell over. Her plastic head was disproportionately wide with plastic curls fixed on an otherwise bald head. Her eyelids fell like shutters. Water dripped from her glass eyes.

"Oh, oh. Treena, darling." A woman with black galoshes put gift bags on the sidewalk and picked the doll up. "It's all right, sweety. We've got a new outfit. This will clean up." The woman looked at Hiro. "You should watch where you're going."

The woman cradled the doll, who plugged her plastic lips with her plastic thumb. She waved with her other hand. *Merry, merry,* Hiro heard. Only he didn't hear it. The words were inside his head, followed by the uncomfortable whoosh of the ocean, the gritty sting of static. A tsunami of voices crashed down on him.

Someone pulled him out of the spinning vortex. A wall was to his right; windows flew by. The rhythmic sound of candy in a bag grew louder. Haze's little wings flapped as she dragged him along. When it was quiet again, they were next to the woman.

"She's walking too fast," Haze shouted at Snow.

"We don't have time to dally," he answered.

The woman slowed down, watching her phone. The windows were low so Hiro could see inside. For the first time, he saw himself. A cinnamon-colored teddy bear with round ears and a black nose. When he moved his arm, the reflection moved, too.

I'm a toy.

They were all looking at their reflections, thinking the same thing. It was a storefront. Posters were taped to the glass. *FurFest* with a square robot on a microphone. *Poppy the Pet Rock for Mayor. Never Abandon* was written under a chunk of granite with googly eyes. Then there was the *Christmas Gala!*, the same poster as back in the toy room where they woke up. The orange cat smiling with exaggerated teeth.

There were toys inside, sitting at plastic tables in plastic chairs with teacups. They were big and small, laughing and chatting, not noticing the soggy teddy, stirring their drinks with cinnamon sticks and candy canes. A young man took a knee next to a group of rubber ducks floating in a barrel. He sprinkled crumbs into the water. The rubber ducks bobbed up and down. They didn't quack. They squeaked.

"She's going," Haze said.

They were on the move, hustling to keep up. Robby's long legs spiked the concrete, his head spinning toward the passing storefronts—the clothing stores with doll dresses, the playrooms with toy snakes slithering through ball pits, the salons with action heroes getting a fresh coat of paint. A platoon of fuzzy beavers played bongos with their tails as a crowd of barn animals nursed mugs with pixie sticks.

The woman stopped outside a storefront. *Fresh Out Again* the sign said. *Isn't it time to be new again?* Fabric was displayed on the walls in the shape of skinned toys. There were bags of white cotton and bowls of glass eyes. Prices were listed above the counter. A complete re-cover was expensive. But there were stuffing upgrades, and plastic reshines. Double stitch seam options and nose rebuilds. Hiro noticed an implant for unfortunate toys who were born without them. *Eyelid Implants.*

A zebra trotted out from the back of the store. Her black and white stripes were fluffy and new. A sheep with a matte black face was happy to see her spin around.

"It's here!" the woman shouted.

They didn't hear her. The zebra was joined by a baby doll riding on the back of a mechanical dinosaur. A woman in blue scrubs followed them with a clipboard and a bag of products, consulting the baby on what and how to use them.

The woman swept them up in her arms and threw them in the back seat of an SUV. The vehicle had gumdrop rivets and licorice stripes. It smelled like sardines and candy corn. Three orange tentacles reached behind the passenger seat.

"Merry, merry," an octopus said. "Room up front."

"We're fine," Snow said. "Just get us—"

The octopus hoisted Flake into the front seat and buckled him in. "I got dippers and smellers. There's Sippy Sips and Candy Jams, Bar Mints and Snow Gobs. Got those in grape, peppermint and, for the adventurous, roasted salmon."

He rattled a wrapper under his beak. One eye was stitched onto orange felt, but the head twisted like a sock puppet. He held different drinks in three tentacles.

"Take us to the Giving Tree," the woman said.

The eye turned on her. Patiently, he set the drinks that smelled more like fish than peppermint on the dashboard. The eye did not leave the woman. "One, the Giving Tree is closed. Two, I don't take orders from a—"

"Please, Ocho," Snow said. "We're in a bit of a hurry, and she worries a bit too much sometimes. It's not closed yet. If you would get us there before it does, I would put an extra crumb in your stocking."

Ocho the Orange Octopus didn't take his eye off her. She glared between the hoodie and scarf.

"Why are you hiding your face?" he said.

"I'm cold."

"You're cold."

"It's twelve degrees. I'm cold."

"I'm not cold."

"You're a toy." Her eyes widened.

"You're merry right I'm a toy," he muttered.

The soft tentacles slithered back up front, three on the wheel and the rest adjusting dials on the dash. The volume on the radio grew louder. Slowly, he twisted his head around. They sat there for several moments, a pair of plastic eyes slung over the rearview mirror clacking together as the car hummed. Snow watched nervously with his fingers in his beard. Then he went flying into the back seat.

They were serenaded by honking and not-so-merry gestures. Ocho returned the sentiments, taking a hard left, followed by another one. The woman helped Snow back onto Flake's hat.

"You think Count Moppet is working for *us*?" a squeaky voice on the radio said. "He's a Timberist! A warmblood sympathist. He'll abandon us just like the blockhead did."

"Oh, please," the radio host said with a deep, sonorous tone. "Belkin did not abandon us. Disappearing is not abandonment."

"If disappearing is not abandonment, then whaaaat is it?" the listener said.

"It's simply not abandonment," the host said.

"Then say it. Say what it is."

"I just did."

"No, you didn't."

"I made myself quite clear."

"If it's not abandonment, then whaaaaat is it?"

"It's just not."

The listener's laugh sounded like a screeching bird. "Listen, the only candidate worth our vote is Bing Sings-a-Lot. He's been a toy supporter since he came out of the box. Not like you and Moppet."

"He's a Viktor bone licker."

Snow gasped from the rim of Flake's hat. Ocho chuckled and turned it up. The listener on the radio seemed shocked the host had said it out loud, saying, "Bing Sings-a-Lot says what he means and means what he—"

"Can you turn that down?" the woman said. Adding, "Please."

The radio banter continued. Ocho the Orange Octopus ran a red light while staring at the rearview mirror.

"What's your names?" he said.

"They're fresh out of the box." Snow was on his knees, clinging to the edge of Flake's hat.

"Well, merry-merry. Freshies." His head momentarily deflated. "I can smell the new. Welcome, shiny ones. I do tours, you know. The whole yard of fabric—state of the world, where to go, where not to go. Here, here." A tentacle dug a pack of cards from the dashboard. Business cards spilled on the seats as he yanked into the next lane, narrowly missing a pink bunny on a pogo stick followed by a heavyset man with gift-wrapped boxes.

Hiro and Haze rolled onto the woman's lap. She was looking out the window, a mixture of anxiety and agitation twisting her eyebrows. She pulled the scarf up the bridge of her nose.

Haze fell between her legs. The girl wrapped her arm around Hiro before he fell onto the floorboard. She smelled like a comforter fresh out of the dryer. Warm, secure. Her anxiety, though, was prickly. It poked him like evergreen needles. He settled against her, squeezed her arm. Felt her soften and melt.

Mads.

It popped into his head like a flashcard. Her name was Mads. He felt like she didn't have many friends. Hiro felt like he'd just discovered a secret. A secret that peeled a layer from between them. He knew her just a little bit more and snuggled into the crook of her arm. No matter how the car swerved, he felt safe. She wrapped both arms around him.

"Here we are." The car came to an abrupt stop. "Tips are appreciated. Don't forget, I do tours and—"

Mads jumped onto a crowded sidewalk with everyone in her arms. She opened the front door to grab Snow and Flake and hurried through the crowd. Faces were a blur. Hiro buried his face and completely trusted her, like he did when he was little, curled up in the back seat with his parents driving. It was almost hard to remember what that felt like.

There was the sound of clanging metal. Two long spears crossed in front of them. Sentinels with big, square mouths fell open like trapdoors. They were as tall as adults.

What they were guarding was much bigger.

IT WASN'T A MOUNTAIN. But it felt like it.

A large mound of earth was plopped inside an oversized traffic circle. A multicolored path wandered to the top, where a titan tree sprawled long, droopy branches. Silver chimes reflected splashes of noon. A gong shook the ground. The chimes sang.

"No, no, no, no. Just a moment. Just a moment." Snow dove into Flake's frumpy hat. The tiny elf emerged with the stiff card Mads had found in the desk. He carried it like a sled.

The soldiers watched from both sides of the entry walk, long spears crossed. Their coats were red and overly starched. Tufts of stiff hair bunched above their eyes black as ink. Their square mouths opened on tracks that made the jaw slide down. The one on the left took the card with a white-gloved hand and inserted it between his wooden teeth. He handed it back as a giant bell somewhere hammered the final note of noon. The soldiers pulled their spears back.

"Is that a line?" Robby said. "It can't be a line."

They took three steps before stopping behind a stout woman with a pair of cloth dolls on her shoulders: one in a dress, the other wearing overalls. The path was checkered with large, sticky blocks—lemon yellow, tropical orange, minty green—like a complex hopscotch board. They were firm but slightly soft, like a rubberized track.

"Can you taste that?" Haze hopped on a juicy red square. "It's like cherry syrup on a graham cracker. And this one." She touched a dark purple one. "Grape milkshake."

Hiro and Chase lowered their noses to the path. Hiro wasn't going to drag his cloth tongue across the walkway that hundreds of people had stepped on. But he wanted to. "Smells like paper," he said.

"Wet paper," Chase added.

"You don't get it." Haze jumped up and down, her stomach rattling like a bag of coffee beans. "I can taste with my feet." She hopped on all the colors, announcing their flavors, pausing on the ones she liked best—cinnamon sticks soaked in hot coffee, gummy worms on a bed of crumbled sugar cookies. "And this," she said, closing her eyes, tilting her head back, "jellybeans in a bowl of runny chocolate ice cream."

Robby poked dents into the candy pavement. "Oh, yeah. Yeah."

"You can taste it?" Haze said.

"I'm picking up a hint of sweaty socks and overtones of dog *beeeep.*"

Mads picked them up. Haze in one arm, Hiro in the other. Chase climbed onto her shoulder and snuggled against Flake. Robby rested in the cradle of her hands. A smile arced across his monitor.

"I need to hold you," she said. "Keep you close."

"Why?" Haze said.

"Just until we get to the top."

Hiro didn't mind. Despite the prickly waves of anxiety that occasionally zapped him like a nine-volt battery, she was warm and soft. Something delicious filled his insides, like an empty urn holding warm water. What the urn was meant to do.

There was so much to see. Strangers with toys, holding hands like they were children, pointing at a caramel river with apples in the current, slabs of snow-covered peanut brittle stacked like stone, tufts of brightly colored sticks growing from the crevices like stiff candied branches.

"Where are we going?" Haze said.

The red-yarned dolls turned on the stout woman's shoulders in front of them. Their button eyes sewn onto soft frowning faces. The woman then turned, more confused than angry.

"They're fresh out," Snow announced. "Right out of the box. We rushed them over, there wasn't time to explain. You remember your first time to the Giving Tree? I remember. Merry-merry."

The stout woman turned around, satisfied. The dolls looked at each other and started slapping hands with the woman's head in between. She didn't seem to mind.

"It won't take long," Mads whispered.

Her idea of long was different than Hiro's idea. The gong went off two more times. It was past two o'clock. The chimes grew louder. They crossed the caramel stream on a bridge of salted pretzel logs, ventured through a forest of candy canes with cotton candy tumbleweeds. Haze and Chase seemed content. Robby had tried to tune his television, but there were only vague figures in a snowy landscape.

Hiro, he just wanted to be held.

Every once in a while, Snow would come out of the hat to search the line with a toothpick telescope. "I see him," he announced.

Hiro couldn't see anything. When the line moved, he would hear cheers growing slightly louder. It would be different each time, the screams and hollers and cackles. And always someone laughing. Deep and jolly.

Mads began to shiver. The temperature dropped in the tree's long shadow. She pulled the hood over her eyes. Hiro wrapped his arms around her, rubbed her arm. She needed a thicker coat. Her teeth sounded like marbles on a granite slab.

The red yarn dolls were standing on the stout woman's shoulders now. She climbed a short set of candy steps and then came back down the other side. The path was narrow and steep to the pinnacle, carved between snow-covered hills with clumps of weedy candy corn. The shade beneath the heavy branches blotted out the light.

The line was swallowed by the deep shade. There would be a long pause, the muttering of a deep voice. Then jolly laughter followed by overjoyed celebration. Toys danced out of the shadows, followed by someone picking up scraps of wrapping paper. They would loiter just beyond the tree's canopy, sometimes taking pictures, or staying to watch the next ones get swallowed by the shadows.

Hiro squeezed Mads tighter. And she squeezed back. They were the only ones watching. The others had grown quiet with boredom. But Hiro wondered if Mads was squeezing him for different reasons. She wasn't afraid of what was under the tree. It was something else.

When they stepped into the deep shade, the air grew dense and still. Cool humidity muffled the sounds of traffic in the roundabout far below. A wide throne was against the massive tree trunk, nestled between deep root flares. The one sitting on it was nearly as wide as the seat. Toys found plenty of space on his lap. He would wrap his arms around them. They spoke and giggled. He laughed. Then a picture was taken before the toys were handed gifts to be unwrapped. Then the shouts and screams, the hugs and laughter.

"Merry, merry! Ho-ho-ho."

Snow was perched at the edge of Flake's hat. "Look, Flake!"

Flake saw where he was pointing. It was someone next to the throne dressed in a frumpy green outfit with an equally wrinkled floppy hat. He shuffled toward them with exhaustion. Hiro thought he was barefoot, but the boots only looked like feet. He was a real man behind a bushy beard that didn't quite match the brown curls on his head.

"Merry, merry," he said. "Your turn."

Snow and Flake bowed to their elven brethren. Mads followed him, and Hiro could see who was on the throne now. He wore a red coat with white cuffs and a hat of the same color. Big black boots rested on a bed of needles. The coat was unbuttoned near the top, exposing a calico fluff of fur. And the eyes, nearly hidden in the white curly locks of a fake beard, were emerald green with vertical pupils.

"Merry, merry," the cat in disguise said, bunching his paws in white gloves in pursuit of a small toy. "Come, come, come. What do we have?"

Mads put Hiro on his fat thigh where the fabric was worn a different color from a long line of giddy toys. Hiro suddenly felt naked and alone, and the cold bite of winter. Mads hovered like a mother bear. The cat looked at her, confused.

"They're fresh out," she said. As if that explained her jittery hands.

"New friends!" Snow said. Flake jumped onto his lap. The cat adjusted his fluffy belly. "Fresh out of the stitcher. We brought them straight to the tree. A great way to awaken, Viktor!"

"Stitcher?" The cat's voice lost some of its tenor.

"Our bona fide stitcher, Ms. Madeline Snowfall. She does fine work."

Mads didn't nod or bow or say a word. Not even a merry, merry.

"Right," the cat said, finding his deep voice and saying, "welcome then, just in time. Maybe you'll be lucky. Come, come and tell Viktor the Red what you want for Christmas."

He swatted his thighs. Chase kneaded the upper part of his leg before sitting down. Haze was next, plopping down on his knee, to which Viktor the Red said, "A heavy one." Then followed up with, "Careful with that one."

Robby was lowered into place like a ball of twisted metal.

"Look at all of you." Viktor gently put his arms around them, the heavy sleeves droopy and damp. "Wonderful toys, wonderful joys. And a teddy." He patted Hiro. "Didn't think the world needed another teddy, but okay. There's plenty of you, nothing wrong with that. Come then, tell Viktor the Red. Ho, ho, ho."

"Ah, well. Here's the thing, Viktor." Snow bowed like he was addressing royalty. "Being fresh out, it's all a bit overwhelming. Thoughts everywhere. If it would be all right..."

Hiro grew dizzy. The words went underwater, lost in a burbling current of blurry sounds and images. Viktor's white beard twisted into long streams of smoke. A fog rose from his lap. There were things in it, like people in the early morning before sunup. Thoughts overlapped like a thousand conversations. Images whizzed past.

A square of light. Someone opening a door, waving inside. Wearing his red coat, tucking his tail into his trousers. The white beard in one hand. "See you at dinner, love," he called.

Hiro was back in Mads's arms. Everyone was staring. Viktor the Red was frowning.

"I'm sorry," Snow said. "He's still so fresh. He's still developing boundaries, you understand. He didn't mean to peek at you. There wasn't time to... I'm sorry."

"I should say," Viktor said in a regular voice.

What just happened? Something had offended Viktor. Something Hiro saw. *Or did.*

"Well, merry, merry." Viktor cleared his throat, brought back the deep voice. "Plenty of milk and cookies for all." He gestured to a small table with pitchers of white milk and silver trays of sugar cookies. "I've heard all your Christmas wishes and have them on my list. For now and later, without delay or slip, please accept with gratitude an early Christmas gift."

For reciting the line a thousand times, he delivered it well. With feeling, he held out his white-gloved paw. One of the elves, a different one from before, stepped from the shadows with a small box in two hands. She carried it like a delicate crystal vase and placed it in Viktor's paw. The sleeve slid back from her hand, and Hiro saw, for just a moment, a familiar bracelet jangle on her wrist. A red snowflake twisting about.

"What could it be?" Viktor said. "Who's going to open it?"

"Me. Me, me, me." Snow sprang on the brim like a diving board. Viktor placed the gift next to him with just enough room on the hat. Snow opened it methodically, peeling open one end, running around the hat to the other side to open the other end. Folding the pieces of tape and putting them in a pile. Viktor tapped his boot impatiently. The flap of wrapping paper was pulled aside. The cardboard lid lifted up. Snow peeked inside.

He looked up.

Hiro thought, for the very first time, he might have seen Snow's eyes in the mop of wild hair. He looked back inside the box. His beard quivered.

The sound that came out of him wasn't human or toy. It was more like the screech of a condor as it unfolded its wings. The elves stepped back. All the loitering toys and people turned their heads. They stepped into the shadows when the second screech came. Viktor covered his ears.

Haze and Chase stood on Viktor's lap. Robby extended his legs to peek over the hat's ledge. Snow threw the lid off and reached inside. Upon the third and final screech that could potentially destroy vocal cords, he held up a golden slip of paper that was rigid but flexible. The surface glimmered like stars had been captured with a printing press made of gold.

Viktor turned to the elves, said with a normal voice, "We have a ticket?"

A bell rang. People began flocking into the shadows. The elves formed a line to barricade the rush as word spread downhill like an avalanche. People and toys retraced their steps up candy lane. Mads grabbed them, holding Flake with both arms. Snow dragged the gold ticket into the hat.

"Wait!" Viktor held up a paw.

Hiro felt Mads's relief like melting chocolate. *We got it,* he heard.

23

"I thought you were fresh out of the box?" Ocho swerved into a pocket of traffic.

The crowd had followed them down the hill. Mads had stomped through the chocolate river to escape, staining the snow with brown footprints while calling a ride. The orange octopus was waiting.

"They are," Snow said. "Would you please just watch—"

"Wait." Ocho twisted his head. "Are you a toy band? One of those stream happies with a billion followers no one ever heard of?"

"I assure you, Mr. Ocho, we are normal toys who want to live."

"Then what's with all the lookies?!"

A mass of golden orbs, each about the size of a marble, hovered in front of the windshield as thick as insects. They tapped against the windows, circled like starlings. Some bounced off the hood of passing vehicles like Ping-Pong balls. Ocho sprayed them with wiper fluid, swiping them off the windshield.

Hiro couldn't understand how he could see. Maybe he couldn't. Hiro climbed onto Mads's lap and into the crook of her arm. She stared out the window—the scarf tight around her face, the hood pulled down—oblivious to the flashing lights and blurring buildings.

"Did ya rob Red?" Ocho said.

"Is there something you can do about the lookies?" Snow said from Flake's hat.

"Like what?"

"Like make them go away."

Above the honking and radio chatter, Hiro could hear a smile twist Ocho's fabric. "Yes and no."

Ocho kept three fuzzy tentacles wrapped around the steering wheel; a fourth one turned off the radio while a fifth one adjusted the rearview mirror. Hiro saw his round plastic eye squint while the sixth and seventh tentacles worked the accelerator and brake like a professional go-cart driver. The eighth tentacle reached over Flake's lap and pulled open a flap below the glove compartment. A black box with dials and buttons, switches and levers was wired into the dashboard.

"You mean a privacy whirler?" Ocho said in a tone that was as mysterious as it was delicious.

"Wonderful," Snow said.

"It's rated for ranking citizens. Are you ranking?"

"We have money."

"Close enough. It's legal with a license."

"And you have a license?"

"I didn't hear you."

"I said, do you have a license?"

"You're not speaking clearly." He turned the radio on. "You'll have to speak up."

"I said—"

"Snow," Mads said. Snow tugged through his thick beard, then raised a tiny finger. *Stop asking,* Hiro heard from somewhere.

"It's not free," Ocho shouted above the radio while crossing two lanes of traffic and hugging the chrome bumper of a mass transit bus. The face of a happy vampire puppet was plastered to the back of it, promising something lawyers promised people. "It comes with some risk, you know. I could lose my driver's license, not drive, not be able to feed the little ones—"

Mads tapped her phone. Ocho's phone pinged. He held it to his eye and nodded. Then reached for the whirler. A series of clicks and a push of buttons ignited a stream of lights. Hiro felt a high-pitched signal meant for dogs. The swirling golden orbs stopped jockeying for position. They scattered like pigeons.

"We've got thirty minutes. Where to?"

Mads muttered an address.

"That's an hour away," Ocho said.

"Then you'd better hurry," she said.

The car accelerated like a spaceship breaking free of the planet's gravity. Hiro kept his face hidden. He'd survived some falls. He didn't want to test a fiery collision with a toy vampire advertisement.

THE TIRES SCREECHED on the pavement. Flake was wearing his seatbelt, and Snow was safely inside his hat. Chase and Hiro had spent the ride in the safety of Mads's arms. Haze and Robby fought over who got to look out the back window. They ended up on the dashboard.

"This is a road!" Ocho rolled down the window and balled up a tentacle. "Get out of it!"

Lights were strung between the buildings in long loops. The headlights beamed on a bicycle cruising in the crosswalk. No one was riding it. One of the balloon tires was flat. One of the handlebars curled at the car, and judging from Ocho's reaction (he nearly climbed out the window), it was not a merry gesture. He stayed on the horn while the bicycle took its time.

"Close enough," Mads said.

She snatched Haze and Robby off the dashboard, pulled Flake from the seatbelt and exited the vehicle. The bicycle laughed like a ghost finding something no one else found funny.

"Hey. Hey, hey, hey, hey." Ocho leaned out the window. "This isn't a good idea, not here."

"Thank you!" Mads shouted without looking back.

"I'll ride with you, just in case. Ten percent."

"Bye. Drive safe."

"All right, five percent."

Ocho crept alongside them, ignoring the heavy traffic going around him. Lights wrapped around scraggly street trees reflected on his candy-coated hood. The bicycle was still laughing when Ocho left a patch of rubber on the slushy pavement. Mads put them down on a lime green sidewalk with shattered cracks running from curb to building. Wads of wrapping paper rolled through dirty snowdrifts like faded tumbleweeds.

The row houses were narrow and slanted. Once vivid colors of the rainbow now looked like sickly walls in need of life support. Lights blinked erratically in dark windows. Hiro was looking at a pile of metal jacks gathered in the gutter. They were looking back. Mads decided to pick them up again. Her arms were cold and shaky. Exhausted. He could feel the heaviness in her legs, like bags of wet sand. They passed recessed doorways, heard music from above. There was an argument.

Three figures were beneath a torn canopy. Red and green lights blinked like the building was shorting out. They argued over a gift, the torn wrapping paper with prints of a white-bearded man. Mads moved closer to the curb, stepping into wet piles of murky snow. They stopped pulling the present apart.

"Got room for one more?" a long plastic hot dog said. Or maybe it was a dog. "I'm a world-champ cuddler."

She ignored them. But the thin figure, it looked like a cardboard cutout with a face drawn by a six-year-old with crayons, leaped in front of her. A full-sized rubber duck joined him, hopping backwards as he went. Hot Dog couldn't keep up on tiny legs.

"Want to hear me squeak?" Rubber Duck said.

Flake grunted and began to squirm. Mads grabbed his legs before he climbed off her shoulders. She walked past them, but Rubber Duck bounced back in the lead, squeaking with each leap. Paper Cutout sailed next to them.

"Look at you." Paper Cutout tickled Flake's big toe. "What you doing with this warmblood?" He swiped the sole of Flake's foot. It sounded like a rake on a slab of ice. "Never seen fish feet before."

"Need descaler," Rubber Duck squeaked.

Robby slipped off Mads's arm and landed like a tin superhero. It was an impressive dismount, until he slipped. They laughed even louder.

"What? You going to build a bridge?" Paper Cutout said.

"A bridge!" Hot Dog squealed.

Hiro didn't get the humor. Mads abruptly stopped and sighed. Snow emerged from the hat's trapdoor like a cuckoo clock about to signal the top of the hour. "Merry, merry, my good gentletoys."

Mads took a knee. Hiro thought she was allowing Snow a closer address, but she reached for her boot and began to untie it, pulling the lace through the eyelets until it came free. She held the long whip of cord in one hand. Squeezing Haze beneath her arms, the green dragon coughed up a mound of candy.

"Come here." She pointed at Rubber Duck.

They grew wary. Hiro could feel the atmosphere drop a few degrees. When no one moved, she spun Rubber Duck around and grabbed his rubber tail. Hiro thought she was going to throw him into the street or tie him to the candy-striped streetlight. Instead, she threaded the lace along a crack that exposed the yellow rubber insides. He stopped fighting, and they all watched. In a minute, she repaired the damage. Rubber Duck hopped straight up and down and squeaked like a new toy.

She folded Paper Cutout's hand into a paper cup and poured the dragon candy into it, crumpling it closed. His purple crayon eyes widened.

"Share," Mads said.

They went on their way, leaving behind sounds of exuberance and, eventually, another argument.

Rubber Duck shouted, "Merry, merry!"

❈

CHOCOLATE CONCRETE STEPS LED through candy arches to a yellow door that, at some point, had been sunny. Now it was old mustard. Long strips of paint peeled from the sunbaked surface like dead skin. Mads straightened a grapevine wreath hanging from a rusty nail. She turned a copper key in the lock.

The stairwell was long and steep. Smelled like cloves and cider. The steps looked like walls, from Hiro's point of view. Mads scooped them up and started the climb, her boot without a lace echoing unevenly. Posters were scattered on the walls, brittle tape on the corners. Things like dance lessons and plaything services. Calls for toy switching, whatever that was. Someone was missing an eye. *It's round and rolly. Text me if you find it.* None of the tags had been ripped from the bottom.

Mads walked three flights without pausing. Loud festive music played behind closed doors. A large black and white poster with Viktor the Red, the fluffy orange cat, was superimposed on a snow-capped mountain. *Only you can be merry,* it read.

Why is Viktor the Red orange? Hiro thought.

She stopped at a green door. Little bells, hung from red ribbons, chimed when she opened it. Tiny, white lights glittered on an ever-green tree in the middle of a small apartment. The branches were covered in shiny orbs and silvery strands. It looked just like the one in Hiro's attic.

Streetlights filtered between blinds, horizontal stripes painting the room. Mads dropped the toys on the floor, one at a time, tossed keys into a ceramic bowl and flipped a switch. A shiny globe turned on the ceiling, tossing specks of light on the walls.

Overflowing crates and crumpled boxes, rolls of fabric and stacks of canvases leaned in the corners. Flocks of paper animals were suspended from the ceiling, four-legged origamis outstretched like flying beasts with stiff antlers. An old radio crackled from a shelf, the music festive. Things about bells jingling.

She shed her boots like construction waste on her way to the refrigerator. The shelves were mostly empty. She came out with a cookie between her teeth, a jug of milk, peanut butter, jelly, and a jar of pickles. A loaf of bread dangled between her fingers. She went back to the front door, still holding the groceries, and locked it.

"Do not leave." She bent down, inspecting a loose hinge on one of Robby's legs. "I'll fix that in the morning."

"Where are you going?" Haze said.

"Meditate. I'll see you in the morning."

Haze looked at the others. "Are you going to tell us what just happened? That tree and the weird cat with the beard and-and-and Snow losing his mind. And those things flying around the car... are we famous or criminals?"

"Tomorrow will be a busy day. Promise you won't try to leave."

She stared at them until it was uncomfortable. Another song with jolly bells came on the radio.

"So what do we do now?" Robby said.

"You're toys. Have fun. Keep the noise down and don't make a mess. Do you promise?"

Robby looked around. "It's already a mess."

"Promise?"

One at a time, they nodded. Then Flake, with Snow on the rim of his hat, followed her around the tree and into a bedroom. The door closed. Hiro leaned against it. He suddenly felt cold.

"I'm not a toy!" Robby shouted.

"I think I have two stomachs," Haze said.

"You don't have a stomach," Robby said.

"No, really. I can sort of taste them." She spit a bright green piece of candy toward the ceiling and caught it in her mouth, gumming it like an infant. "Coriander."

Robby's eye flattened. "Gross."

"It's candy, weirdo."

"You're catching spit."

"I don't have spit."

His arm transformed into a paddle. "You don't have a stomach."

The next time she spit, this one cherry red, he swung. It sounded like an aluminum bat. The candy ricocheted off a vase of paper flowers.

"Stop," she said.

His appendages collapsed—it looked like four arms, one of them as big as a fiddler crab claw—and the screen dimmed. Haze rolled her head back, lips in a circle, and ejected a sky-blue pebble. Robby smashed a line drive through a loose stack of papers, catching a thin, hardback journal on a shelf. A domino of books tumbled into a cardboard box.

"I told you to stop," Haze said.

"She said have fun. This is fun."

Haze fired a purple rock at him. Robby slapped it away before it tinged off his screen. Hiro and Chase watched a rainbow of artillery rain on him like a multicolored hailstorm. Robby squatted like a martial artist with an array of weapons slicing and folding, his eye darting in battle mode. Shrapnel knocked over paper cups, a picture on a shelf, a pincushion on the desk.

It was strange, the way they were acting. Like this was just another day, just teenagers on a Saturday. Only instead of watching a movie or doing a puzzle, they were watching someone spit candy and her brother taking batting practice. But dreams were that way. The ultimate seduction, molding belief until reality was recognizable. They were toys. It hardly seemed strange anymore.

Robby was losing ground, taking shots off his monitor. Tripping over a defunct sewing machine, he tangled in a wool blanket and pulled down a pile of blank canvases, a gnarly old cane in a tin bucket, and crashed into a half-dressed mannequin. The wool blanket came down.

It revealed a full-length mirror.

Chase leaped down from the windowsill. Hiro wandered over. The four of them stared at their reflections. The truth was looking back in full color. It was the most details they'd seen of themselves. They were misfit toys.

"If we fall asleep, will we wake up?" Haze said. "You know, like home?"

Hiro wasn't tired. "Do toys sleep?"

It felt like midnight. The traffic was just as busy as it had been that afternoon. Cars honking, people or toys shouting and laughing. Music playing.

Haze waddled away, fabric saggy over her deflated belly. Hiro's head was spinning. It was him in the mirror. On the inside, he was Hiro. On the outside, he was something else.

We're toys.

"*Penelope,*" a scratchy voice called, "*I'm hooome.*"

"Look!" Robby tapped the mirror. It sounded like a laugh track buried in static. "Look, look, look."

His blocky head spun around; the monitor was filled with two vague figures buried in snow. "*What's for dinner?*"

"Is that..." Haze looked at her brother. "Is that a—"

"It's a show. A TV show. I'm a TV show."

It was hardly a TV show, it was so fuzzy. But it was something. Haze said, "How did you—"

"I don't know! I just heard voices, and then I saw some things, and there they are. You see them, right?"

Robby was enamored with the shadows swimming through a fuzzy picture. He could see them better than everyone else because he described what they were doing. Every single movement. Folding his multi-jointed legs like a three-year-old in front of the TV, he stared into the mirror. Laughing along with the laugh track.

"Wait, look at this."

The picture was a bit clearer. Toys were crowded into bleachers. It was a sea of color, shoulder to shoulder, wheel to wheel, wings and springs and things only toys could be. A professional announcer announced, "*I think he's going for a three hole.*"

"What'd he say?" Haze said.

"Shhh. He's going for a three hole," Robby said.

Hiro started picking up the mess. If Mads came out, he didn't want to be in the circus. He swept googly eyes off a treadmill that had spilled from a jar, made a little pile of spinning black pupils. He righted an oversized hamster wheel.

A framed photo had fallen off the shelf. It was Mads with her parents. She was a teenager. He almost didn't recognize her. She was smiling. They were dressed up, her father holding an award. Strangely, the photo had been ripped in half and put back in the frame. She was holding something, but it had been torn away. He hid it under a wool sweater just in case Robby decided to take more swings.

The books had fallen into a box of newspapers and manilla folders. He stacked them into a neat pile, the titles academic. *The Shape of Time,* by Philip Bells. *Synchronous Time Funnels,* also by Philip Bells.

The pages were filled with graphs and formulas. He dug the newspapers out of the box. Sections had been cut from the pages. Hiro did his best to fold them, but they quickly turned into trash. The stories weren't much different than newspapers from home: politicians kissing baby dolls, a team of grizzly bears holding up a trophy.

Toymation Nation, one advertisement announced. *Experience the joy. Switch to a toy.*

An elderly woman was hugging a stuffed lion. Hiro didn't know what switching meant, but daily packages could be purchased. Prices did not include cold storage. It didn't say what was being stored. The indefinite option did not have a price. It said call for quotes.

There were more books in the box, thin journals with handwritten notes, mostly calculations and abstract sketches. There were galaxies with illegible notes and high-level equations and indecipherable coordinates. The sort of stuff Corker dreamed about.

Loose notes were folded and creased, tucked into the back pages.

The maps were familiar. He didn't know where he would have seen them before. *At school?* He was too caught up in the notes to recall.

Dates and times, cryptic sightings that occasionally noted *here* or listed a name there. Other things noted various items like hoofprints. Photos were taped to some locations, one of a tiny silver bell, another that looked like a pile of animal droppings.

There were dozens of maps, some more esoteric than others. One with symbols similar to the journals with coordinates and planetary sketches. He'd seen something like this in Corker's classroom the last time he was in it for detention. Only this one had a big red X in the middle with a date: December 25. The year was wrong, but that didn't mean anything. Time was different. But a small note was jotted under the X. It was underlined twice.

Time synchronizes!

"Hiro."

Chase purred like a mechanical cat. Her tail hung from a table of sorts: an old door on sawhorses and a barstool with burgundy vinyl that was splitting at the edges, the glossy surface sparkling in the disco ball's rotating light. Hiro climbed onto a cardboard box. Chase snaked her tail under his arms to pull him up.

The door, faded red, was against a window. Hiro peeked between thick blinds. The street was choked with vehicles: a big boxy dump truck with plastic side panels, a racecar dragging string lights, a fan boat on wheels blowing debris off the sidewalk. Bass thumped from a limo. A pride of lions stood in open moonroofs, bouncing their fluffy heads to the beat, bits of snow sticking to their manes.

Chase strutted around melted candles and incense holders filled with gray ash, a glass mannequin head with a floppy hat, and cups filled with paintbrushes and indelible markers. She pawed a stack of papers. Hiro waddled over, knocking over the paintbrushes. There were paintings on the table and twice as many sketches, concept drawings of toy figures, notes referring to fabrics and colors, names crossed out. But the drawings Chase was standing on were different.

It was the planet.

Colorful lines squiggled from the surface, reaching out into black space. There were dozens of drawings, each slightly different. He'd seen the planet before. He'd drawn it. And so had Chase.

"What's this mean?" he said.

Chase pointed her tail. A crumpled gift bag leaned on the thick, wooden horizontal blinds. A long purple arm stuck out from behind it. Hiro shoved the bag aside; it tumbled to the floor, revealing a wide-eyed monkey slumped on the corner of the desk. Velcro patches on her hands and feet. She was empty, Hiro could feel it. No one was behind the eyes. Just a toy, a normal toy, like the one in the attic.

"What's she doing here?"

Chase shook her head. "When she was in my room, I could hear her."

"That's who told you everything?"

"It was like a speaker inside my head. It wasn't clear at first, just static words coming from a distance. I heard them at night, just before falling asleep. I thought it was a dream, but they became clearer. And then one day, I was getting dressed, and it was like someone was in the room. I looked around, there was no one else but her."

"What'd she say?"

She rubbed against Monkeybrain. "We're waiting for you."

Hiro had heard voices in his head, too. It was on the sidewalk, when they were walking past the stores. A sandstorm of voices. But he didn't hear them when Mads picked him up, didn't hear them now that they were inside the apartment.

"Why didn't she talk to me?"

"Maybe she tried." Chase peered between the blinds. Soft lights blinked on her green eyes. "You weren't listening."

Someone started preaching about toy rights and freedom, the oppression of the outdated. Haze was watching Robby's head. A toy smacked a podium with a fist shaped like a hammer. A politician toy with thick eyebrows and fiery hair. Haze told him to change the channel.

Humans were hardly seen except for carrying dolls on their shoulders or toting bags full of presents. Toys were running the show.

Other than that, this world didn't look much different from home. Except for one thing.

Christmas.

A chunk of ice whacked the window. It bounced off, then hovered. It was slick and round.

"How did you make the planet appear?" Chase said.

"I dreamed it. Like you."

"No, back in the stitchery, where we woke up. When Snow was telling the story."

He'd forgotten about that. Snow had been onstage, explaining where they were. Hiro had been thinking about the planet, the way he drew it, just like the ones on the desk. And then it had appeared.

"I don't know." He shrugged his round, brown shoulders.

"What were you doing when it happened?"

"I was just... I was thinking about it. That's all."

It was more than that. He could see what he was thinking, like sculpting a thought into shape and texture. Something he could feel. Like his mother used to say, the artist gives life to something. An artist paints it, draws it, molds it with their hands. Hiro thought it.

"Can you do it again?" she said.

"I don't know."

"Try."

"Like what?"

"Something simple. An apple."

"Green or red?"

"It doesn't matter."

He nodded, staring out the window. He wished he could close his eyes, but he hadn't done that with the planet. He thought of an apple. A big, red delicious apple with a curving stem. Its surface glossy, the skin speckled. They stared at the space in front of them, listening to Haze and Robby argue about channels.

"I don't feel it," he said.

Another chunk of ice hit the window

"Try this," Chase said. "Think of something you love."

Hiro didn't have to think about that. Someone popped into his mind. He could feel her face, the features elusive at first. He smelled her fragrance. Heard her laugh at a silly joke, embarrassed when she snorted. Felt the weight of her sadness like a wet blanket that kept her cold.

Space shimmered. The face of his mother began bending light; a transparent likeness took shape. For a moment, Hiro felt like he was standing in front of himself. He could see Chase next to him, like he was in two places: he was the teddy bear *and* the image of his mother slowly filling with color—

"I see you!" Haze shouted.

The image dissolved. Candy jiggled in her belly as she jumped up and down, pointing at the mirror. Robby's boxy head swiveled around. In the snowy static, Hiro and Chase appeared. They were on TV. The Christmas tree and disco ball on the ceiling were behind them. Chase turned toward the window.

"They're back!" Haze spit a stream of candy off the glass.

A cloud of humming metal balls hovered outside the window. Calmly, Chase reached for a cord dangling from the blinds, pulled it with her tail.

"Go back to that channel," Chase said.

Fragments dashed across Robby's monitor. Hiro could hear lookies gathering outside the window. He threw himself off the desk and tumbled into Haze, the exact opposite of Chase's dismount. They gathered around Robby, staring into the mirror like a misfit family photo.

"Let me see." Haze turned Robby's head away from the mirror.

"I can't see!" he said.

"What do you mean you can't see? It's your monitor."

"Can you see inside your head? I need to concentrate. Give me some space."

They didn't move. Robby leaned closer to the mirror like he was inspecting a pimple. An endless stream of channels flashed over his screen in varying degrees of clarity: puppets hiking through rain-forests, bowling balls throwing themselves down alleys, blocky sumo wrestlers breaking apart, generic wooden dolls playing a concert.

"Hang on."

A singsong voice was reporting the weather. Robby dialed back and tuned into a station with perfect clarity. A blue princess with four arms sat in a padded chair next to a plump version of herself. Her heavyset twin was the color of raspberries. Their legs, long and shiny, twisted like braids. Each had a tiara made of plastic with glazed flowers. Slender Princess smiled with a tiny mouth with eyes as big as coasters the color of honey.

"Lookies caught a candid moment of today's big winners." Her voice was melodious, hypnotic. "Outside an apartment in Bouncy District, Ms. Snowfall escorted a group of freshies inside her building. Ms. Snowfall, a licensed stitcher, brought toys to the Giving Tree. They were the last in line."

"Who says last isn't first?" Plump Princess could hold a shovel in the gap between her teeth.

"Well, it was first today and the recipients of the last ticket."

The scene cut to the Giving Tree. It was just after Snow had opened the gift. He was screeching like a fire engine, running laps on Flake's brim, waving the golden ticket like a flag. The lingering crowd gathered. Mads picked them up and ran, ignoring pleas for photos. An announcement chummed the waters.

WINNER!

It turned into a feeding frenzy of toys and adults scrambling back up the hill. Mads ran through the snow, breaking layers of peanut brittle and stalks of candy canes. She stepped through a chocolate stream, then a pool of caramel, her boot submerged in goopy goodness, and took a shortcut through a forest of chocolate-dipped pretzel sticks.

Nutcracker guards corralled the crowd to keep them from trampling the wonderland into crumbs. Mads made it to the sidewalk, where confused onlookers hadn't heard the news. A licorice-striped car was waiting with doors open.

"They just jumped in." Ocho was leaning out his window. A yellow fairy fluttered with a microphone. "Wanted to go home, that's all. So I took them. What do you want from me? It's what I do." His tentacles flailed around the fairy. "I do tours, too. If you need a ride—"

"Quite exciting." The princesses were back. "I think they were surprised," Plump Princess exclaimed.

"It's been reported that was the last ticket to the gala," Slender Princess said, corkscrewing her legs in the other direction. "While every day is special, there is nothing more prized than Christmas Day. The Triumph of Everlasting Christmas will be celebrated, as always, tomorrow night on Christmas Eve. Of course, Viktor the Red will be there, as always. And this, he has promised, will be the final gala of them all."

Christmas Eve is tomorrow night? Hiro thought.

"Viktor will have an uprising if this is the last one," Plump Princess said.

"Don't say that." Slender Princess laughed nervously.

"I'm just saying, toys all over the world love the gala. It brings hope."

"I'm sure something new will be just as extravagant. This year—"

"Are you going?" Plump Princess interrupted.

"I wish I were." Laughter again. Annoyance, too. "But if you weren't one of the lucky toys to get a ticket, you can see the red carpet here on WTOY, where we will televise it live and in three-dimensional holographics. It'll be like you're right there. You'll be as happy as these lucky toys."

A shot of Snow appeared in the corner, like an elf who'd just grabbed an electric eel. "No one's that happy," Plump Princess said.

Slender Princess giggled. The two twined their rubbery hands together. "Thank you for joining us. We'll see you at the Crystal Palace. Goodnight."

A bouncy tune played them off. A sweeping view took their place, soaring across a winter wonderland of decorated spruce trees and winding paths lit with candles, swept over rooftops down into a palatial winter garden filled with ice sculptures and a full orchestra on a tableau of ice. People in tuxedos served plates of milk and cookies to toys gathered at tables, around a dance floor, perusing sparkling gardens. Toys of all shapes and sizes in formal attire.

Robby's metal finger tapped the screen's reflection. "Is that where we're going?"

"We'd better not," Haze said.

24

I arrived at 11:30.

Madeline was asleep. She'd cut her hair for some reason since I was last there. I'd never find out why.

She had her arm over Freckles, sleeping with her laptop open. Freckles watched me climb off the shelf. I stood at the door, listened to the dad on the phone. He was talking to Belkin in gruff, hushed tones. He was nervous. I was nervous. It was hard to tell where his anxiety ended and mine began. It was a big night. A big, big night. A night that would change the world.

Not like the dad thought.

"Viktor," Freckles sort of whispered. "Hi, you're just in time."

"Merry, merry." I patted his head. He purred mechanically. "Rest here, my friend. Stay with Madeline."

"Where you going? Santa is coming."

"I know." I snuck back to the door. "I'll be right back, okay?"

"Okay."

All was quiet. I waited another five minutes just to make sure the dad had retired. In order for his heist to be successful, he had to be in bed. Let's be clear, this was a heist. No doubt about it. The dad was a thief, and so was I. None of them wanted to admit it or think of it that way. If Santa wanted us to have all that Christmas spirit, he would've given it to us. There was a good reason he didn't.

If we knew what was going to happen, would we have done anything different? I'd like to say yes, but we were thieves. We took what we wanted. I certainly did.

I ran to the dad's lab.

I carried a chair to the door, quietly climbed up. It had taken some effort to get the code since last Christmas, but I was patient— pretending to be watching television whenever the dad entered the code, watching his finger punch the keypad like an old telephone.

I carried the chair inside. No toys in the lab this time. There wasn't room with the additional equipment: the distillers, magnifiers, coil generators, and insulated coolers. The toys were in the basement along with a wall of glass cubes, each containing a very special charm.

I knew the computer password. That had been a bit trickier to get than the door lock. Luckily, the dad kept it taped to the bottom of the keyboard. After several midnight missions (when he was snoring in the bedroom), I would sneak in to become familiar with the software. It only took a minute to find the time sequencer. It was set at one millisecond.

Often I wondered what would have happened if I hadn't interfered. Would the toy reformation have gone as planned? Would it have been a peaceful transition of equal rights, where toys weren't complicit playthings to be owned and discarded like property? I've always doubted it. Not just because of the mess I made. Their plan wasn't sustainable. Santa was going to discover what they'd done. What was he going to do then, just let them keep all the Christmas spirit they'd stolen?

Of course not.

My plan was far better. The only way to keep Santa from taking it back was to keep him from knowing I took it in the first place.

I was doing it for selfish reasons. I'd convinced myself it was to help the toys. The dad and Belkin had big hearts. But like my father said, the heart makes bad decisions. Cold calculations make things work. That, I told myself, was how the universe works.

I changed the time sequencer to infinite. I increased the sphere of capture to extend to the roof. Couldn't have the reindeer flying back to the North Pole.

I'm here to save the toys.

Three minutes till midnight, I changed the lock on the lab door and went to the farthest corner in the front room. The clock on the mantel counted down. My bones chattered. I watched and waited. When midnight struck, I was as still as an empty toy. It felt like I was holding my breath. As the seconds passed, I thought it had failed. Perhaps I'd overloaded the systems. I began to second-guess what I'd done. Was increasing the sphere too much for the generator? Did the program not understand an infinite capture?

It was too late to change. I didn't want to wait another year, but science is often a series of failures. I was tired of failing.

The mistletoe twinkled. I felt the air pulse in my bones, like ocean waves crashing on the shore. I stood up and leaned into the corner. The atmosphere warped like heat waves hovering over desert sand. A small hole opened below the mistletoe, a twisting gap in time and space. Black and hollow, turning in a vacuum. Feeding itself.

Terror crawled through me. I thought, perhaps, I hadn't just corrupted the system. *I created a black hole!*

I ran to the lab door. I needed to shut things down before I destroyed the entire world. I leaped and hung from the door handle, attempted to punch the code into the lock, when the walls began to shake. I was thrown against the door by an unseen force, felt my bones creak as it flattened me. I was blown into the corner, slid to the floor like debris, crumpling into a ball. Dread overtook me as I looked at the fireplace. It wasn't a planet-swallowing aberration of physics.

I began to weep.

The floor was shaking. I walked down the hall, careful to avoid touching the watery veil that wavered between the couch and fireplace, extending above the pitch of the roof. The basement steps had vanished in bright, white light. Blindly, I walked into the luminescence, trusting the steps were there. Barely feeling them. Wandering into a thousand charms ablaze.

The last shreds of my limitations were stripped away. I became more than a toy. More than human. In that moment, I became a toy god.

I am everything.

"TURN IT OFF!" the mom shouted.

I felt her panic, shards of glass in her voice. The dad was at the lab door. The lock wouldn't open. He felt like a vortex of muddy water, drowning in confusion. *What went wrong?* he was thinking. I made a suggestion of what they should do, passing my thoughts into their minds. Thoughts that were not suggestions. Thoughts they accepted as their own. Thoughts that were commands.

I went to Madeline's room. She was asleep in the madness, her senses dulled by another of my suggestions. I stroked her short hair, felt a twinge of sadness. I snuffed a tinge of regret that threatened my resolve.

"I'm sorry, sweet princess."

The mom and dad were hastily packing their suitcases in the next room, like I wanted. They came for Madeline, waking her up. Groggily, she climbed out of bed while the mom hastily stuffed clothing in her duffel bag.

"Where are they going?" Freckles said.

"They're going to her grandparents'," I said.

"Will we see them again?"

"No."

"Why?"

They left the bedroom door open. A few moments later the front door slammed. The car pulled out of the driveway, leaving the quivering house behind.

"Because everything changed, Freckles."

25

Mads frowned with a bundle of clothes in her arms. The Christmas tree was missing ornaments. Brushes were scattered and papers tattered; a shelf lay on the floor. Mads stepped on a minefield of candy, hopping on one foot.

Flake shuffled between her legs. "*You*," Snow announced from the rim of his hat, "were not to make a mess."

"*We*," Haze said, "didn't leave."

"Clean up. Come along, put everything back where you—"

"There's no time." Mads pulled on her socks. "We're late."

"Because you overslept?" Robby's voice was tinny. "I didn't sleep. None of us slept."

"We're toys," Snow said, brushing his beard. "We don't sleep."

"No one told me that!" He looked at Haze. "Did she tell you that? She said have fun because we're toys. That's all. Not, like, by the way you'll be awake, like, forever."

Mads pulled on a hoodie, the same one as yesterday, scooped up a vest with multiple pockets off the floor. She pushed the button on the coffee machine and searched for a clean mug.

"There's a lot you don't know about toys," Snow said.

"Not anymore," Robby said. "I'm starting to forget what I look like, and it's—"

"Hey, no," Mads shouted.

Hiro scrambled out of the box. She knelt down, candy grinding into her knees like pebbles, and began stacking the journals. Hiro had the maps open, textbooks out, and she was putting them away, muttering to herself, crumpling the maps and denting the corners of the journals. She paused when she found the framed photo.

"Are we in danger?" Hiro asked.

She nudged him aside. Her anxiety filled him with cold rocks that were sharp and heavy. She was angry. Not at him. She folded the box closed, shoved it in the corner and put a heavier box on top.

"Lookies found us," Chase said, swinging her tail.

Mads went to the window. Her hand, wrapped around the cord, trembled but didn't pull the blinds open. She dug through a drawer of an antique dresser hidden behind a rack of fabrics. She returned with a tube, inserting one end between the window and blinds, and looked through the other end.

"Is that a periscope?" Robby said. "You have a periscope?"

She cursed quietly, holding the tube at her side. "Everyone get ready, by the door." She thumbed her phone. "We're leaving."

"Are we going to the gala, Ms. Snowfall?" Haze said.

Mads hesitated on her way to the kitchen, filling a travel mug with coffee and a frown. "How do you know my name?"

Haze flapped her tiny wings. "Well, is the gala where Viktor the Red throws the big party, at the Crystal Palace with the ice sculptures and the tiny sandwiches with the crusts cut off and the delicate teacups and the awful music?"

Mads's frown deepened. "Where did you hear that?"

"Is it a secret?"

"Snow?" Her voice trembled. "Did someone think through the walls? The apartment's protected. How does she know that?"

"I-I-I'm not hearing anything." The little elf ran a lap around the hat. "Nothing at all."

Laughter faded in static. Robby's monitor tuned through the white noise, figures walking through it. A parade of horns and hopping toys. A marching band of fuzzy bunnies and wooden soldiers strode down the street. The channel switched to teddy bears on a sleigh.

"We watched a documentary," Haze said, "while you were sleeping."

"There was nothing else on," Robby added.

"The part where Viktor overthrew the government," Haze said, "and stole Christmas for himself, and now he's sitting on a mountain of presents like a goose with all the eggs. Remember that part, Robby?"

"Yep. And he lied about—"

"That's not true!" Mads clasped the lid on the mug of coffee, cinched the buckles on her vest. "Flake, up. Let's go."

"Robby, find the news," Haze said.

"Don't." Mads swung around. "They don't know the truth. I told you I can't tell you, I can't... I can't let you know what we're doing because others might see it. You don't know how to protect your thoughts. It's not fair, I know. It's just, it's the way we have to do it. I'm sorry. It's just... whatever you heard isn't true. Trust me."

"So Viktor didn't steal Christmas?" Haze said.

"Not like that."

"Is that what all the maps are about?" Chase purred.

"What maps?" Robby said.

Mads busied herself with the vest. Chase hopped off the desk and strode to the box. Hiro got out of the way. Mads didn't want them to see what was in there. Chase wedged between the wall and the heavy box on top. It began to slide off. The picture fell on the floor, chipping the frame.

"Stop," Mads said. "We need to go."

"We didn't need to understand all the calculations and scribbles," Chase said, grunting. "You said Santa Claus was captured. That's when Christmas stopped everywhere but here." The box fell with a thud. "But you were the one tracking Santa Claus."

"That's an easy explanation," Snow said. "There are things you don't—"

"Not you," Chase said.

Snow muttered, began to sing, then turned around and went inside Flake's hat, zipping the door shut.

"What maps?" Robby said.

Mads took a deep breath, checking her phone. They weren't leaving until she gave them an answer. She crossed the room, kicking a candle and an empty cup out of the way. Hiro picked up the framed picture. He could feel something soft beneath her iron shell. Something warm. She bent down, looking Chase in her big cat eyes, then moved her off the box, putting the heavy one back on it.

"What did you do?" Chase said.

She took the picture from Hiro and put it on the desk, staring at it. Remembering. Her thoughts tightly wrapped, hiding secrets none of them could see. Hiro could feel a two-ton weight in her stomach and a knot in her throat. She wanted to tell them everything, he could feel it. She peeked through the blinds once more, then picked up the purple monkey.

"One of these days, you're going to look back at your life and realize you're just kids. You make mistakes. It's how you learn. You get caught cheating on an exam, hurt someone's feelings, then you grow up. But sometimes you make a mistake that can't be undone. The consequences so far reaching you can't see the horizon. You thought you were doing the right thing."

She brushed the purple monkey's hair, then put her in a gift bag.

"I called you, each of you, and you answered."

"I didn't," Robby said flatly.

"You did. Or you wouldn't be here."

She walked through the mess, held out her hand. Flake climbed onto her shoulders. The little door on his hat unzipped. Snow peeked out. Mads stood by the door with the coffee mug in her hand and a bearded elf on her shoulders.

"You can stay here if you want. It's safe. And when it's over, you'll wake up where you came from. You won't be toys. It'll just be another gray morning. You'll go on like nothing happened, and all of this"—she spread her arms—"will just be a dream you forget."

She put on her boots.

"Where are you going?" Hiro asked.

She sipped the coffee. With a brave smile, she said, "To the gala."

Hiro didn't believe her. Not entirely. Like there was something hiding in the truth. He could feel it, like a pebble she kept tucked under a blanket.

"So we *are* going to the gala," Haze said.

Mads wrapped the scarf over her face, pulled the hood down and nodded.

"Will we get hurt?" Hiro asked.

"You'll wake up in your beds. Not a scratch or a bruise, just like you were."

She put her hand on her chest. It looked like a promise, but Hiro felt she was saying something else. They were toys. They'd fallen off shelves and lost some parts. They could be put back together without feeling a thing. But there were other ways to get hurt. Broken hearts sometimes never healed. And if they went back without Christmas, she couldn't promise they wouldn't feel it.

Hiro reached for her. She tucked him in one of the vest's oversized pockets. Chase came next. Haze followed, snuggling in next to Hiro. Robby stared up with one big pupil in a sea of static, leaning to the side where he was missing a bolt. Haze shot a piece of candy. He batted it off the wall.

Then climbed up.

Mads was nauseous.

Hiro could feel it oozing from her. Maybe it was the winding roads or the way Ocho kept turning around. It would have made Hiro sick. Or maybe something else was bothering her.

"This is quite exciting." Snow sat on Flake's hat, looking into the back seat. "This is where all the celebrities vacation—movie stars and puppet dancers and sing-songers—to get away from the public. No lookies allowed, no streamers. Exclusivity."

It took an hour to get out of the city. Another hour of snaking roads beneath titan spruce trees. If they weren't toys, this would seem like a normal day.

"There are walls surrounding the entire mountain, deep in the trees, guarded by private lookies—not newsfeeders—that never let anyone in. It's a destination very few get to experience. And here we are, on our way. Like royalty."

"You're not royalty," Ocho said. "You're lucky."

"Don't kill the dream, Mr. Ocho."

"I'm just saying, these toys up here aren't royalty, and neither are you."

Lookies hovered outside the car like dragonflies. Ocho had darkened his windows so they couldn't see inside. *I had a feeling you'd call,* he'd said when they snuck into the alley. *Lookie-proofed the windows.* Snow thought the lookies would stop following once they left the city. It looked like an invasion of alien insects.

Mads stared out the window, scarf over her nose, hood pulled down. Lookies might have special vision to see through the window tint. *Like infrared,* Snow had said. Ocho assured them they didn't.

"So." Ocho adjusted the rearview mirror. "You're a toy stitcher."

Mads leaned on the window. The sick feeling moved into her throat.

"Know what I heard? I heard all the stitchers quit on Viktor Day because you were jelly. Just pulled a Socko goodbye and peace." Ocho threw up a tentacle.

"What's a Socko goodbye?" Haze asked.

"It's when you leave a party without telling your friends," Snow said.

"Rocko-Sockos do it every time," Ocho added. "Stitchers closed all the shops around the world and disappeared. Said we didn't need more toys."

"Maybe we'll see another stitcher up here," Snow said.

"I heard they went from stitching to switching. Know what I mean?"

"Not a clue," Haze said.

"Well, you see—"

"I think that's enough, Mr. Ocho. Remember, they're fresh out. Don't want to spoil new toys, now do we?"

"Yes, we do. Switching is when a warmblood becomes a toy. Temporarily." He tapped the rearview to get their attention and nearly swerved off the road. "Know what I mean?"

"Still no," Haze said.

"Warmblood. Fleshie. Air breather. Follow?"

"He means people," Hiro said.

"That one, right there. You are the smart one."

"I was going to guess that," Robby muttered.

"So wait, hold on," Haze said. "Warmbloods—"

"Please, no. That's not a nice name," Snow said.

"*People.* They can become a toy?"

"With enough money, they can enjoy the toy life." Ocho brushed lint off his shoulder. Or maybe he was being self-important. "Although, word from the lookies is, all those stitchers went on ice. They'd been making toys just so they could become one."

"Not possible, Mr. Ocho." Snow raised a tiny finger. "Icing is an urban legend."

"Except it's not."

"What's icing?" Haze climbed between the front seats.

"It's becoming a full-time toy. As in *not temporary.*"

"Never mind," Snow said. "It's pure tooty-fruity."

"I don't know," Ocho sang. "*Experience the joy. Switch to a toy.*"

"It defies all science and reason." Snow marched to the edge of the rim. "A man or woman cannot permanently... never mind. Let's think happy thoughts. Toy thoughts, shall we? We're on the way to the top of the mountain, and nothing can stop us now."

Ocho slowed into a hairpin turn, the tires sliding as he accelerated up a steep slope. "I remember when I was fresh out of the box.

An original: custom stitching, felt fabric and handmade stuffing. They don't make them like us anymore."

No, they don't, Hiro heard someone think.

"Now it's big-box production and cheap threading, fabric that can't get wet. I was restitched twice before my emancipation, and look at me now. My own business with a house full of rug rats."

He plucked a photo from the visor, waved it at the back seat. It was Ocho and a big, yellow-feathered bird posing for a family photo with what looked like a dozen rubber toys on their laps.

"Are those... *rats*?" Haze asked.

"Not all toys are wanted." He clipped the photo back into place. "Toys take care of toys. Viktor made sure of that."

The road became narrower and the turns tighter. The trees reached overhead, branches intertwining like clinging families divided by a stretch of slick pavement. The light grew dimmer. Ocho held the wheel with four tentacles, slowing for the next turn. The lookies streamed behind like silver gnats. A granite wall with icy daggers leaned into them.

"Here we go," Ocho said.

A hole had been chiseled from the face of the mountain, like a gaping black mouth eating traffic. Ocho's headlights pierced the darkness. Chunks of jagged stone zipped past like mammoth teeth for grinding metal. There was music beneath the howling echo inside the tunnel. Chimes and voices.

They exited into a bright, sunny day, bits of snow dancing past the windows. Trees as tall as buildings on the side of the road—now straight and narrow—their trunks rooted into the frozen ground. The song was clearer, as if it played inside the car.

We wish you a merry Christmas...

"I'll be honest." Ocho turned his head. "Didn't know that tunnel was coming."

He laughed nervously, wiping his felt brow, as if he were sweating. Hiro wondered where he'd learned that.

A gate was up ahead, the spires pointed like shafts of blue ice, pointing at an arching sign that read, with shimmering letters, *Winter*

Wonderland. Two wooden soldiers, with tall black hats and bright red coats, marched stiff-legged into their path. Ceremonial swords at their sides. Ocho coasted up to them. They marched to the sides of the car, staring at the black-tinted windows, square mouths clamped shut. Ocho's window slid down, letting crisp air inside.

"Brittle morning to ya, Box Mouth. We're here to see the queen."

"Joking!" Snow bounced up and down. "Hahahaha. He's joking, my good soldiers."

The soldiers seemed not to take offense or understand offense was given. They had only one job. Snow knocked on the window next to the passenger seat and waved a golden ticket. The window slid down.

"We're here for the gala."

The wooden soldier bent like a pocketknife, black bushy eyebrows pinching together over round expressionless eyes, and plucked the ticket from Snow's hand. Like the soldier at the Gifting Tree, he inserted it into his mouth like it was a parking garage ticket.

"This is the gala?" Haze climbed between the seats.

"Nooooo." Ocho patted her head. "So innocent. No, they wouldn't let a bunch of freshies in looking like you. Or me. Not that I'd want to go. Didn't the stitcher tell you where you're going?" He glanced in the rearview. Mads stared out the window. "Relax. Ocho's got you."

The soldier returned the ticket like a crisp dollar bill. The ice-bar gate slowly began to swing open. Ocho waved at the soldiers on the way in, shouting a saccharine *merry, merry*.

"Hey, no!" Snow shouted. "Be careful."

Haze snatched the ticket before he stored it back in the hat. It shimmered like it had been dipped in gold. A holographic headshot of a toy hovered in a circle. Large eyes and soft ears. It was the cat at the Gifting Tree.

Robby took it and scampered away, perching like a mechanical spider. Haze flapped her wings, clawing at the seat. Her belly swelled, the furnace of candy pellets rattling.

"Please be careful," Snow said. "We need that."

"I can't look away." Robby tipped the ticket side to side. "It's like he's looking at me."

"He knows when you are sleeping," Ocho sang.

Mads took it from him. Hiro saw, before she gave it to Snow for safe storage, the holographic head turning on the ticket, looking around at them. Snow zipped it inside the hat and leaned against the flap, arms crossed.

"Is that Viktor the Red?" Hiro asked.

"The one. The only," Ocho said.

Mads, however, didn't answer. Hiro felt like she had a different answer.

"Why is he called Viktor the *Red?*" Haze said. "He's orange."

"Because his heart is big and red," Ocho said. "To love toys more than bloodbags." He turned to Mads. "No offense."

"That's enough," Snow said.

The road continued through stalwart trees. The black asphalt glistened with moisture, snow cleanly piled along the sides. Occasionally, they would pass a person on the side of the road, who would stop to wave and smile. They were dressed the same: a black coat and red scarf. The road continued, and Hiro wondered if they were lost.

Music grew louder. Ahead, at the top of a steep hill, light glowed like the sun was about to rise. The asphalt turned into spongy gumdrops that were soft and glittering. It went through a crowded village of toasty gingerbread buildings with frosted roofs and candied shutters. Cluttered sidewalks looked like strips of fruit roll-ups and the streetlights red and white candy canes. Dolls with sunglasses and sky-blue ponies carried snowboards; baggy puppies took selfies in front of an ice sculpture that resembled Viktor the Red.

It was all so bright and festive. The music silky and the colors rich. The energy permeated the car like a scented candle of maple syrup and marshmallows. Hiro could taste it.

"And this is where the upgrades live." Ocho stopped for a bouncing family of kickballs and basketballs. "Bunch of rented switchers wishing they were us. One of these days—"

"Just drive," Snow said.

Hiro felt thoughts flit through Ocho like grit. It wasn't over-whelming static like he'd felt when they first left the workshop. Just random thoughts Ocho was having and wasn't sharing. Hiro managed to get a peek at them. Like trying to remember something on the tip of his tongue. He felt the shape of them, the substance. Rented switchers: the wealthy toys in the village. Like they weren't really toys. They were humans in toys. *Like us—*

A stiff breeze whisked Hiro's mind empty. Mads squeezed him. *Did she do that?*

"Stop or go!" Ocho leaned on the horn. "Some of us work for a living."

A giant big wheel rolled down the middle of the road. Stalks stretched from the handlebars with bulbous eyes attached to the ends. One twisted around. Ocho honked again, and the big wheel went even slower. There wasn't enough room on Gumdrop Alley to pass the snail-eyed big wheel, so they crawled along, keeping pace with those on the sidewalk.

"This is it." Ocho whipped around a traffic circle, taking the first turn into a galleria of three-story buildings. He found a parking spot between a stagecoach and a tin bus. He pointed a long tentacle under Flake's nose. "Right down there."

Mads gathered them up, packing Hiro and the others into her vest pockets like a generous kangaroo. They didn't argue. She opened the door, the air dense and caramelized, and put the gift bag on the back seat. The purple arms of Monkeybrain were stuffed inside.

"Wait here," she said.

"Nope," Ocho said. "I'm driving straight to a car wash to clean off the stink of wealthy fakeness. You couldn't get me to stay another—" His phone buzzed. Mads had her phone out. "I'll be right here."

The tip was generous.

"You forgot the bag," Ocho called.

Mads left the gift bag in the car. With Flake on her shoulders, she worked her way through the crowded sidewalk, sidestepping pink elephants, stepping over sock puppets. The conversation around them was different. More sophisticated, less singsongy. Different accents. *Are these switchers?*

Mads pulled her scarf over her nose. Even though the lookies had disappeared in the tunnel.

It was a courtyard open to the crisp winter sky. A tree was in the center with stacks of presents. Mads rushed past toys sitting at little wire mesh tables, having polite conversation, waving mugs under their noses, dipping beaks into saucers. A young man delivered a tray of small cups to a table of lumpy aardvarks clapping their padded arms.

"Wait, are they eating?" Robby said.

"Toys don't eat," Snow reported from the rim. "We sample. Most of us do not possess digestive tracks. Aside from Dolly Dumpsalot, that's another story, but technically she samples, too. We appreciate aromas that scintillate the olfactory senses, flavors that tantalize the taste. All toys, of course, are different. We don't all have noses to inhale or tongues to taste. Carbo Racecar dunks an antenna. Bandy Beachball opens a valve. It's more about the company. The sensory dishes are just part..."

Robby looked bored. And hungry.

They passed upscale boutique stores and luxury bathing quarters and barstool game rooms. The energy was thrilling and overwhelming. Hiro hid his eyes to concentrate, identifying different aromas they passed: cherrywood pipe smoke, peanut butter sugar cookies, cheeseburger patties between bacon-flavored donuts. He imagined what it was like to sit at one of the tables, to have a normal conversation with other toys. Like this was just a sunny winter day.

And then he wasn't in the vest pocket anymore.

He was sitting at a low wooden table with a wobbly leg, dirty dishes with spent cinnamon sticks soaking in grape Kool-Aid. He was alone beneath an awning, watching Mads approach. Hidden behind her scarf, her vest pockets stuffed with toys.

And a brown teddy in her lower left pocket. *That's me!*

Hiro didn't know what disturbed him more: that he was watching them approach or that he thought of the teddy as himself. Chase's ears turned like satellite dishes aimed at the table where he was sitting. She stared at him as they hurried past. He saw her tail unfurl and reach down. Hiro felt it drag across his neck.

"Hiro," she said.

He looked up from the pocket. The low wooden table with the wobbly leg, receding behind them, was empty.

"Were you doing it?" Chase said. "Imagining it?"

Yes, he was. It was different this time. He didn't just create something Chase could see. He had been there. He had been in the pocket and at the table at the same time. He knew exactly how he did it.

And he could do it again.

THE BUILDING at the end of the courtyard was a long mirror. Two soldiers stood at attention with no door between them. Above their heads, words hovered: *Figgy Station*. The *i* dotted with a star.

Nervous energy crawled through Hiro like dancing ants. They all felt it. It was coming from Mads. There was pressure, too. Pressure from thoughts coming from behind them. Hiro saw the attention they were getting in the wall's reflection. It felt like specks of sleet on a blustery day, blowing through him, clouding his mind. Thoughts searching him, looking for what he was thinking. Trying to crack him open.

Mads reached for them, one at a time, and squeezed an arm or leg, making the invading thoughts go away. The soldiers crossed their spears. Snow presented the ticket. Same deal, in the mouth. Only this time it didn't slide back out. The soldier looked at them, one at a time. Hiro could hear something grinding.

"Chop shop is over there," a fuzzy baboon with a rubber red muzzle shouted. The other baboons, hovering over bowls of steaming tea, snickered.

"Is there a problem?" Mads said.

The soldier ignored her, fixing the wide-eyed stare on Chase. Gears going *tick-tick-tock, tick-tick-tock* before something fell into place, and he aimed his glare on Robby. Mads chewed on the side of her thumb, pressing it against the scarf covering her face. Hiro was next. He was suddenly warm, like heat lamps beaming from beneath the bushy eyebrows. Everything felt fuzzy.

"No loitering, ma'am," someone said. "Figgy Station is by appointment only."

Mads was as rigid and fragile as a slab of peanut brittle. A three-foot penguin stared up through round, wire spectacles. She wore a wide belt that didn't appear to serve a purpose. She tapped her webbed plastic foot on the marble tile, tilting her head. Mads stared at the soldier.

"Merry, merry, good lady." Snow peered over the rim. "We're attending the gala. Lucky winners, you could say. We're just waiting for verification. Any moment now."

The soldier was fixated on Haze now. The tick-tick-tocking went on like a malfunctioning stopwatch. The penguin stepped closer, thumped the soldier's starched pant leg with her plastic wing. The soldier's jaw fell open, the ticket moving in and out like a golden tongue, then shut again.

"Take a step back, please," the penguin said.

Mads froze with determination. Everything, Hiro felt, was pinned on this moment.

"Ma'am?"

The crowd started to gossip, their thoughts invisible fruit flies flitting around them. The penguin's presence began to swell. She wasn't growing, but her thoughts were. Hiro felt her reach out for help.

Ping.

The soldier spit the ticket out, holding it between stiff wooden teeth. He handed it back to Snow. The soldiers stepped aside. The seams of a doorway appeared in the mirrored wall. The penguin gave a short salute and waddled off.

Mads took a knee, hands trembling. She felt weak with anxiety, the moment overwhelming. But she set them down, one at a time, between the soldiers. Her lips quivered behind the scarf. She took the bracelet off, the red snowflake, and handed it to Snow, who quickly packed it into Flake's hat like a squirrel hiding an acorn.

"You'll be safe," she said. "I promise."

"You're not coming?" Hiro said.

"Someone will take care of you, make sure you get to the gala. Just stay close to SnowFlake. And remember what I taught you." She waved her finger across her forehead. *Build a wall.* "Christmas lights burn so bright."

"What's that mean?" Robby said. "Is that code?"

She started to say something, then shook her head. All the strength that had possessed her from the moment they woke had vanished. Hiro latched onto her leg, pouring whatever good thoughts and feelings he could muster. She hugged him back.

"Be careful," she said.

The doors folded open. Flake herded them into the beckoning silence behind the mirrored wall. Hiro looked back, feeling worry emanate from her like a sad song. He felt the full weight of just how important this had become. Then he understood. She couldn't save Christmas.

Not without us.

26

"Come, come," Snow whispered.

The cool darkness gripped them with cold breath. Flake gently ushered them over the threshold. The doors folded behind them with finality. The dark was dispelled from an unknown light source. They were in a vacuous dome-shaped room, like the inside of a hard-shelled turtle. Then the ceiling vanished into a dark sky full of stars and streaks of light.

"You're late."

They abruptly stopped. Even Flake let out a startled grunt. An elf stood in the middle of the room that no longer looked like a room but an endless sky and a sheet of black ice. He was tall and smiling, with a green floppy hat and thick curls over pointed ears. The ears didn't look real. Neither did the smile.

Somewhere, a train whistled.

"Welcome, brave lucky ones."

They pressed against each other as the elf approached, his soft, curly shoes making barely a sound. Robby's rigid limbs poked Hiro in the back like sharp elbows, digging deeper as the elf neared.

Brave?

The elf took a knee like a kindly grandparent approaching a pack of cornered bunnies. His smile widened into his cheeks, the ears pointing back. A kind expression in his eyes.

"It takes courage to walk into the dark. And here you are." He reached out. "Delicious little toys."

They flinched when he touched their noses. Something jingled on his wrist, his finger gently pressing Hiro's snout. In the iridescent light, he saw the shape of a snowflake dangle from a bracelet. Just like the one Mads had given Snow. The one the elf at the Gifting Tree had worn.

The chugging of metal wheels on steel rails circled around them.

The atmosphere hardened in a sudden drop in temperature. Waves pressed through the cold air, wrapped Hiro with a chilly embrace. He heard distant whispers inside his head. Then the grip receded. The elf smiled wider, perhaps testing the porosity of their thoughts. Hiro couldn't tell if the elf had seen what he was thinking. For a moment, he thought the elf might know the truth of who they were, and where they came from.

"Are you ready for the greatest trip of all?"

No one uttered a word or thought, paralyzed by the unknown and strangeness of his smile and the sound of a train. The elf looked behind them like something was in the distance.

"Remember to stay close at all times." He leaned down and winked. "But you already knew that."

From the darkness, the clanging of mechanical parts made them jump. Robby's head spun, his monitor filled with a wide-open eye. Chase let out a growl. A miniature train chugged from the mist, a dull yellow headlight cutting the dark. It pulled next to them, steam hissing. The glossy enamel on the little cars looked like the hard shell on sugar-shellacked candy. Peppermint wheels spun on the slick floor.

"All aboard, little ones." The elf climbed into the front car like an adult cramming into a child's plaything.

"Where are we going?" Robby said.

"Exactly where you need to be."

It took Flake's stout arms and Snow's encouraging words to move them. It was a long train, but they climbed onto the little plastic seats two by two. The armrests were studded with chocolate drops.

"Buckle up. We have a long way to go."

Flake pulled a licorice strap over his lap. The others struggled to do the same. Chase had to buckle Hiro in, his stubby arms uselessly tugging on the stretchy string. Spicy clouds puffed from the engine's smokestack.

"All aboard!"

The train coasted like a hockey puck on fresh ice. It headed for a black hole in the darkness. Haze grabbed Hiro's arm. He wished he had a hand to squeeze back. He wanted to close his eyes.

The elf began to sing.

"Off we go, a place of wonder and ice, the world where naughty is nice, the world where you'll be happy to see, that shines with joy you'll agree. The one final stop where your journey has led, the palace of the greatest toy of them all, the generous and wondrous Viktor the Reeeeeeeed."

They began picking up speed. The darkness fell like sooty snowflakes, revealing a wide-open expanse of starry skies and towering trees. There were tracks below them now, speeding down the side of a mountain. Snow-crusted limbs whipped past. They leaned into a curve. Hiro could feel the pull in his belly, both of Haze's claws squeezing his arm.

The smoke from the engine, though, still puffed gentle clouds that hovered over them. The engine chugged the same rhythm. The disconnect between the soaring scenery, the feeling in his gut, made his head spin. They weren't going as fast as it looked.

"The Northern Lights are painting the sky, the children line up in hopes we'll arrive, their faces alight with joyous delight, this night we'll make oh-so special. You'll see when you wake at the end of this night, we worked oh-so hard to make it just right, to make all our dreams come true."

The train gripped the side of the mountain. It whipped through the dip and started to climb, clinging to a ridge on the cliff. The elf swung his arm to the valley below, sparkling with streetlights and warm windows aglow. The moon was full behind streaks of clouds.

A warm breeze blew through the cars, sweet and sudsy. Deodorizing. It tickled Hiro's nose. His head had stopped spinning as they coasted at a speed that matched the turn of the peppermint wheels and chugging smokestack. The view was breathtaking.

This can't be real.

The elf was humming. He pointed at the sky. Across the moon's pale face, a silhouette passed. Animals churning their legs as if pedaling the air with a sleigh in tow. It descended into the village, sweeping through the valley. Hiro could hear a voice, even though it was far away, calling names with hearty laughter.

Ho-ho-ho!

"Viktor the Red awaits all his toys," the elf sang, "all the girls and the boys and all those he adores."

The train crawled toward the narrow edge. The elf stood up and turned around with no fear of falling out of the tiny seat.

"To make this the greatest, the shiniest, the most excellent, magnificent, most marvelous, and wonderful time..." He threw his arms out. "Of the yeeeeeaaaaarrrr!!!"

The train dropped over the edge, the wheels clinging to the vertical drop. They plunged toward the village as the elf's final note echoed on and on. Hiro was pinned to the back of the seat. Haze clutched him. Robby screamed. The warm, scented wind had become a gale force scrubbing his fur.

The tracks began to curve, swooping into the valley and straight for a snow ridge. Hiro hoped they would slide into the village, arrive at the gala without losing half his stuffing. Instead, it launched from the icy ramp. The train was suddenly silent. The elf's final note faded, his arms still above his head.

They soared across the moon.

Toys didn't sleep. Some couldn't close their eyes. But sometimes, in certain situations, like being slingshotted across mountaintops, they lost track of time. And, for a spell, forgot where they were.

And woke up someplace else.

27

A slow, rhythmic grind. A sharp whistle.

Whispers in the dark. Images appeared like sleet bouncing off a window. A boy sitting on a circular rug in footy pajamas with a lanky robot in his hands. A girl riding a shiny bicycle down the driveway with a red bow on the handlebars. A family eating dinner by candlelight wearing brightly colored sweaters sporting reindeer with flashing noses and snowmen with sparkles.

They felt like memories. Hiro didn't know whose memories they were. They snuck into the dark like an intoxicating perfume of joy and happiness.

There were other memories, too. These were intimate, familiar. A time when he opened journals his mother designed, filled the blank pages with dreams and poems. The chess set with heavy metal pieces he pushed across the board with his father. Snuggling under blankets in front of the fireplace, bulky stockings on the mantel. His mother eating popcorn.

A shadowy figure loomed over each memory with a glare that could pierce a balloon; a presence that fed on joy. The presence was familiar, yet out of place. Hiro couldn't recognize who it was.

Ding-ding! Ding-ding! Ding-ding!

Hiro was seated in a cushioned seat in a long, silver cabin. Frosted windows ran the length of it. Ornaments swayed on the curved ceiling, dangling on colorless wires. Something hissed in the distance.

Ding-ding!

Haze, Robby and Chase were across from him, sitting shoulder to shoulder with stretchy cords of red licorice over their laps. They looked different. Clean. Haze was wearing an orange dress with yellow frilly trim.

Flake was nestled against Hiro like a firm bag of jellybeans. His clothes were wrinkle-free with sharp creases. His beard blown out like a frizzy, white wig. The hatch in his hat unzipped. Snow marched onto the rim. His tiny beard a cotton ball.

The last thing Hiro remembered was a tiny train and shooting stars. Flying off the rails of an unfinished roller coaster. And now a different train. His coat, fluffy and clean, smelled like cinnamon shampoo. He was wearing a bowtie.

"That," Snow announced, "was the secret trip."

"Trip?" Haze slurred.

"The whereabouts of our location is unknown. There are certain effects to keep it so."

"What did they do to us?" Robby muttered, pulling at a navy-blue tie with snowflake print clipped to his neck.

"They put us to sleep," Snow said.

"Toys don't sleep," Hiro said.

"There are circumstances—"

"Viktor sleeps." Robby snipped sharpened fingers.

"Well, yes, he does," Snow said. "But that's not the—"

"That elf called us delicious and brave. Did you hear that? And did you see his wrist?" Candy dribbled from her forked, felty tongue. "He had one of those bracelets. The one Mads—"

"Shhh!" Snow's nose was as red as the bracelet hidden in the hat. "You must keep your voice down."

There were other toys on the train. On the other side of the aisle, a family of gray dinosaurs were looking out the frosted windows.

Pound Puppies climbed over the seats, pressing their plastic eyes against the glass. In seconds, the entire car was scrambling for a view.

The window next to Hiro was mostly dark. It was hard to see what was out there. It looked like giant lumps of coal. Hiro reached for the window. The seatbelt held him down.

"I'm not wearing this." Haze tore at the pretty dress, pulling it over her head, where it got stuck. "Get me out."

"Stay here." Snow bounced on the rim like a diving board. "We must stay together."

Robby snipped the licorice seatbelt, then cut Haze loose as she fought her way out of the dress, dropping it on the floor. Chase slithered out of her restraint. Flake jumped onto their seat to stop them. Robby unfolded his shiny new limbs like a mechanical spider. Haze sprayed Flake with a rainbow blast. Snow ducked, waving his arms, begging them to stop. But the excitement on the other side of the aisle had reached a fever pitch. Toys were bouncing and squeaking. Some were crying.

Stop! Hiro thought.

The train shook. For a moment, everyone inside it froze like a still frame. Then snapped back with mild confusion and immediately resumed with excitement. Robby, Haze and Chase looked at Hiro, like he was pointing a magic wand.

"Was that you?" Chase said.

"Merry, merry!" A tall woman entered the car with a slender face stuck in a fuzzy hat. She threw her arms out. "Welcome all you brave, delicious toys."

"There!" Haze said. "That, again! Did you hear that?"

The toys hurtled themselves into the aisle, climbing over one another.

"You've had a wild and wonderful trip, but the magic is just beginning! We are very excited you are here, but please mind your manners. Be orderly and safe. We wouldn't want you to tear a seam after all you've been through."

The windows were left steamy and smudged. There were icy

streaks with thousands and thousands of lights outside. Hiro could hear string instruments.

"Slowly, everyone. Stay in line. You'll be greeted by an escort to guide you where the magic awaits."

It was hardly an orderly exit. Only the seats kept the crowd of fuzzy bodies and plastic wheels from crashing to the front of the train.

"Where's Mads?" Hiro said.

"Remember," Snow whispered, "be bright and excited. Put a smile in your heart. Behave like toys."

"We're not toys," Haze grumbled.

"You are toys. Do I need to remind you how important this is? Do you want to wake up to cheerless days for the rest of your lives?"

"I'd be happy to wake up," Robby said.

"No gifts, no songs, no eggnog or decorations. No Santa Claus." Snow looked at each of them. "Is that what you want?"

"I literally don't know what any of those things are," Robby said.

"Exactly my point. I want you to remember the best moment of your life. Keep that in your heart."

"Then what?" Hiro said.

"We save Christmas."

Hiro didn't ask how they were going to do that. Because Snow didn't know. He didn't think Mads really knew, either. Somehow, they all just believed they were going to save it. As if believing was enough.

"Everyone?" The woman waved at them. "Don't be late."

Flake jumped down. Snow urged them to follow and whispered, "Stay close."

"You've said that a thousand times," Robby said.

They wobbled down the aisle with Snow standing on the back of Flake's hat, watching them follow. The slender-faced woman with the fuzzy hat smiled with too many teeth brighter than snow. Ahead of them, a zebra-striped spider stopped at the open door. All her plastic eyes rolled. A spearmint wind blew her back a step. Someone reached in and pulled her out.

Flake followed her. Robby froze in the doorway, just like the spider. His eye filled the monitor and began blinking. Haze and Chase did the same thing. Hiro stepped closer.

The music was in his chest. It felt warm and liquidy. Like cake icing squeezed from a tube and filling his head. A fountain of goodness. It brought a memory of a time when he was very young, sitting at the window in the front room, on the couch next to a blinking tree, looking at the night sky, waiting for Santa to fly across the moon. Then lying in bed, trying to stay awake long enough to hear hooves on the roof.

It was that memory and the feeling it brought that galvanized their purpose. He stood there, like the others, and looked up. At that moment, he knew without a stuffing of a doubt why they were there.

We have to save Christmas.

The Crystal Palace.

Thousands of towering crystals clumped together in organized chaos: an iceberg sprouted from the frozen soil. Drum spotlights waving silvery beams into the night.

"Last step."

The conductor handed Hiro to a man impeccably dressed in a flaming red suit with a green scarf. He placed him on a plush red carpet. Square-mouthed soldiers, standing at attention, spears at their sides, stared from each side of the velvet runway.

"Good, good," the well-dressed man said. "Hold that look. Perfect."

A golden orb hovered in front of Hiro. The lookie captured his expression. A quartet stroked string instruments on an icy platform jutting from one of the crystal towers. Toys crowded near the entrance. One at a time, they stepped onto a circle of carpet, golden lookies zipping around them, lights flashing from their electronic eyes, before the next toy entered the circle.

The engine whistled, and the train jerked forward, slowly chugging down cold rails toward a dark horizon. There were houses on the other side of the tracks. A village of darkened homes. Not a single light warmed a window nor a puff of smoke escaped a chimney. They sat lonesome and empty.

Trumpets sounded off. A trio of musicians were on the other side of the entrance, opposite the string quartet, blaring their instruments. An opening appeared on a crystal monolith like a pearly warehouse door. A squad of farm animals, stuffy and cushy, hopped inside. The door slid shut like one of the soldiers' mouths.

"Come, come," Snow said. "Stay close."

The others clumped up like they were glued together, shuffling between pairs of wooden soldiers, following a slow-moving line toward a circle of red carpet. A wiry bird with pink feathers strutted around the perimeter. A cyclone of lookies swirled over her head. She posed with scrawny wings out to the sides and held her head high, the beak yellow and spongy. There was applause.

"What are they doing?" Haze said.

"It's just a little show before we enter," Snow said.

"You didn't say anything about a show."

"He didn't say anything," Robby said.

"The world loves winners." Snow puffed up like a dandelion. "Act like one."

The line moved with excited squeals, honks and applause. Humans in bright red uniforms watched from the periphery, clasping gloved hands beneath bright smiles. *Humans.* Hiro realized he'd just thought of them as humans. That worried him, just a little. How he thought of them as different. *Bloodbags.*

More people were near the tracks in quiet conversation, watching playbacks on phones, probably piped in from the lookies. Footage was sent out to the public to brew envy and amazement. The blue princesses were probably narrating every move.

"Do you think it's strange," Hiro said, "there are houses over there?"

No one heard him. Hiro couldn't understand why the Crystal Palace was smack in the middle of an abandoned village. The railway cut right through it. The ground was scraped clean where the tracks were laid. Like a bulldozer had plowed through the middle of a town. And beyond, the dark tips of mountains. It was the village they'd seen in the little train, the valley twinkling with colorful lights and a sleigh passing across the full moon. Now not a single light except for the spotlights flashing across the crystal beams. Dappled reflections reached toward the houses like water.

The bugles blew. The warehouse door opened. The faint echo of a steady beat thumped from inside as the next batch of toys was escorted inside Crystal Palace. Minutes later, joyful screams faded away.

"Step this way."

A woman in a long red coat waved them forward. Long looping curls fell from her stocking cap. She pointed, with a smile, to the circle. "Stand in the middle of the circle, please."

"What for?" Haze said.

"To show you off."

"Like on television?"

The woman smiled brighter, if that was possible. "All you have to do is stand here."

Haze looked back at the others, who were staring back with empty confusion. Snow waved her forward with a touch of impatience. She waddled into the circle. Her belly sloshed like a bag of gravel.

"I'm sorry, one at a time," the woman said. "You'll get your turn."

Flake had two giant feet inside the circle. Lookie lights grew brighter, flashing like a swarm of tiny paparazzi, circling to catch every angle of the green dragon with tiny wings.

"There you go," the woman said. "What happened to your dress?"

Haze grabbed the ragged collar around her neck. "It ripped."

"We can get you a new one." The woman clapped at someone. No one came. Apparently, there weren't extra dragon dresses lying around. "Those are pretty wings. Can you fly?"

"What?"

"Where were you fabricated?"

Haze looked at the woman, back to Snow, at the frozen line of wooden soldiers. The woman fired three more questions, muttering to someone next to her. The string instruments reached a crescendo. Haze's belly began to swell.

"Don't be nervous. Tell us how you got—"

A multicolored avalanche spilled across the red carpet. The woman let out a little meep. Haze groaned, wiping her mouth. The woman picked up a blueberry pebble.

"You're a dispenser," she said. Revulsion was replaced with something else. "That is gorgeous. Do you produce them or get refills? Do you store them in a second stomach?"

Haze shook her head to every question, then walked off without an invitation to leave. The lookies followed. There was no stopping her, so the woman draped a red ribbon around Haze's neck and let her leave the spotlight. A silver medallion swung from the ribbon. A crew rushed onto the carpet to sweep the candy away.

Robby was next and didn't hesitate. He leaped into the circle. The woman meeped again. He struck a pose, squatting on a tripod of legs, knifing the air with precise moves, blades reconfiguring.

"A tin toy," the woman said.

"Titanium." His voice sounded more robotic than usual.

"Titanium? Well, that's... I don't think that's titanium."

"Can tin do this?"

She watched with morbid fascination. A weapon, apparently, wasn't what she was expecting. She stepped off the carpet, let the lookies swarm the shape-shifting robot with a television head. She asked the prerequisite questions—where were you fabricated, who was your stitcher—from a safe distance, cringing with her arms crossed, imagining the potential lawsuits a toy like this would bring. Robby didn't answer them, grunting with the karate moves he was clearly making up.

She tossed a medallion at him. He speared the ribbon like a fish, folded it into the center of a morphed rib cage. It dangled like a silver heart. He bowed deeply to her and the others. The ratings for his performance would be off the charts, in one direction or the other.

The woman shooed him off the circle like a wild animal that had invaded her home.

"You'll have to forgive my friends," Snow said. "They're fresh out of the workshop."

"Freshies?" She gestured to the lookies. They took another scan of Haze burping the last bits of candy. "And you?"

"Oh, no. We're far from fresh." Flake stepped into the circle. Snow said, "We're longtime originals."

"Originals? Why, that is special." She pointed at Snow, then Flake. "You're a package?"

"Inseparable."

"Interesting." She stepped back to let the lookies do their thing, tapping her chin with her gloved hand, studying the odd couple. "Love the beards. What's your names?"

"I am Snow. This is Flake." Flake bowed with a flip of his hand.

"Does he talk?" she said.

"I'm his voice," Snow said.

"No vocals?"

"None."

"Oh." She seemed perplexed, then disappointed. She said, as if to someone listening but not there, "You never know who might be interested."

"Interested in what?" Snow said.

"Where were you fabricated?"

"That's an interesting story. Our stitcher, Mads Snowfall, hails from a long line of stitchers. Her great-great-grandmother..." Flake counted the greats on his finger, then shook his head. Snow nearly fell off. "You're correct, Flake. It was her great-great-*great*-grandmother who began stitching right after the Toy Arrival."

The story continued with great detail, of the skills passed down through the generations. A circle grew wider on Robby's monitor, followed by a howling yawn. The woman, though, nodded along for thirty seconds.

"What about your wrap?" she interrupted. "That's quite unusual. Almost like skin. Feel that."

"It's an original synthetic," Snow said. "Never used before and—"

"I wish my skin were this soft. Feel this." She took Flake's hand, then offered it to a nearby assistant. They stroked the back of it. "Do you lotion?"

"There are certain ointments we use to keep it supple, but— please be careful."

"Are there, like, nerve endings?" the assistant asked.

"Not like yours. But, of course, we have tactile senses. It was designed for a very special purpose."

"What purpose?"

"Okay, no more questions." Snow bounced on the rim. Flake pulled his hand back.

"Could you just tell us—"

"Nice meeting." Snow waved at the lookies and all the people watching back at home.

Flake shuffled out of the circle, his feet scuffing the carpet. When the woman handed him a medallion, static electricity discharged between them. She meeped and rubbed her hand. Flake handed the medallion to Snow, who tossed it into the hat.

"What purpose?" Haze said.

"Never mind," Snow said.

"I just thought you two were half human," Robby said.

"I thought maybe real elves," Haze added. "But now it sounds like your skin has superpowers."

"Exactly," Robby said. "Did you see the way he zapped her? I literally saw it—"

"Quiet," Snow said. "And stay together."

Chase sauntered forward in the slinky way she did. The woman spoke quietly to the others around her, glancing and pointing at Snow and Flake. When she saw the graceful cat approach, her eyes grew as wide as sugar cookies. She forgot about the pair of elves with humanlike skin and circled her finger in the air. The lookies swarmed the circle.

"Walk for us, please."

Chase strutted around the perimeter, not in a self-indulgent way.

It was just how she moved. Three or four people joined the woman to watch the feline plaything walk with the grace of a dancer, the strength of an athlete. Her tail hypnotically swayed above her.

"To die for." The woman gasped. Actually gasped.

There were no questions for Chase, just a long minute of adulation and whispers. They leaned closer, nodding in agreement of something. They didn't award her with a medallion. Instead, a silver band was snapped around her neck, inset with sparkling diamonds. A milky opal dangled from the clasp. It was special, for reasons none of them knew. They would soon find out what it meant.

"She's with us," Snow announced. "Come along, must get to the gala."

The woman watched Chase walk away, shaking her head, like a wealthy magnate eyeing the newest fashion on the runway. She was still in a daze when it was Hiro's turn.

"Ah, here we are," she said. "A teddy. Well, well, I thought your brand was obsolete."

The lookies buzzed around. He could feel their magnetic fields ruffle his fur. It felt like the circle was turning. He noticed the black shiny boots of the nearest soldier, the spotless gleam of a well-polished surface. It felt like he was in trouble.

"And where were you fabricated?"

She was looking away when she said it, disinterest flattening her words. As if reading a boring script. As if vanilla ice cream had walked into the circle.

"Same place as them."

"A freshie? How refreshing."

There were no follow-up questions, no asking him to turn around or if there was anything unique about him. Anything special. She didn't see him, not really. He blended into the background. Hiro knew that feeling well.

"Okay." She signaled the brass trio to play. "Thank you for watching back home. Remember, only the lucky ones can enter. Maybe next year is your year. Until then. Merry, merry! And to all a good night!"

They were ushered to the Crystal Palace, the bay door open and waiting. The people wished them luck and have a good time. The *luck* part seemed suspicious. Before any of them could ask why they needed luck, the gate closed Hiro and the others inside a small dark room. The light shrank around the seams of the door until it was fully closed. They were sealed inside.

Robby's monitor cast a blue glow.

"Why did she wish us luck?" Hiro said.

"Shhh," Robby said. "I hear something."

There were distant shouts, orders to roll up the carpet and bag the equipment. But there was music coming from the other direction. Faraway thuds between synthesized chords. Robby's electric blue light began to strobe.

"Are you dancing?" Haze said.

"No," Robby blurted. "Wait, am I?"

Chase clawed at the wall, pulling ribbons of frost off the surface. Hiro leaned against it. Something was grinding beneath them like gears in a factory. The floor shook.

"I know I say this a lot, but what's happening?" Haze's wings twitched. "This feels like a trash compactor."

"Here it comes," Snow said.

"Here what comes?" Haze said. "What's going to—"

The floor dropped from beneath them.

28

I could feel them.

They had just come off the highway, entered the village. I could feel what they were thinking as they looked at the empty sidewalks and barren windows. Doors left open, snow blowing inside homes and businesses. I could feel their concern.

I could feel everything.

The shape of every snowflake, the rustling wind at the top of the hills. I could feel Christmas morning traffic in the distant city. If I concentrated, I could hear the sun rising.

My mind was free.

I know that phrase gets thrown around, but this was it. There were no limits to what I could see. What I could do. I just wanted to never go back home, to be a toy for the rest of my life. But everything had changed that Christmas morning.

And it was just beginning.

Toys had been arriving since before sunrise, wandering between houses, hopping and skipping, big wheels churning through snow-drifts. I stood in the front yard, the snow up to my waist, and greeted each one of them. I had beckoned, and they answered. They didn't have a choice but to obey, but they didn't know that. Still, I thanked them.

They waited with me to greet our very special guests, who were now only a few blocks away. Freckles put some of the toys to work. Some cleared the driveway; others were redecorating inside the house. The toys most suitable for climbing, the dolls mostly, things with opposable thumbs, were up on the roof. A crew of Kelly Konstruction dolls came with hardhats and big plastic boots. Freckles gave them real tools to put in the tool belts. The thwack of hammers and the sawing of wood had been constant. They couldn't be happier.

I could feel it.

A black automobile turned the corner. An inflatable clown with floppy shoes hopped into the road and guided it into the driveway. The toys dropped their shovels and spoons, scampered to my side.

Freckles towered over me, dusted in snow from working out back, his full size nearly three times my height. Together, we watched the shirtless barbarian squeeze out from behind the steering wheel. Stretch looked over the hood. Squinted. I felt his suspicion, the doubt build. I allowed him to look around without interfering with his will. They'd driven all this way. They weren't about to turn around now. Not yet.

I wasn't going to allow that.

He opened the back door. Belkin jabbed the tip of his cane onto the concrete. A silken overcoat was draped over his shoulders, not too unlike mine. A darker green, perhaps. Much more expensive. He paused. The homes across the street were quiet. Smoke did not puff from the chimneys. The driveways were empty. More than a few doors were left open in my neighbors' haste to leave. Toys continued their pilgrimage through the side yards.

"Merry, merry." I threw out my arms.

Belkin did not return my greeting. He was, perhaps, the smartest toy alive. Smart enough to know that wasn't true anymore. I'm not saying I was smarter. I suppose I was, but intelligence was only a byproduct. I was just *more* than him. And he could feel it. He knew checkmate had been called. And not a single piece had been moved.

"Please, your room has been prepared," I said with glee. "You'll find everything you'll need. It's only temporary, for now. We'll build something much more fitting very soon. Freckles, would you show our company inside?"

"We won't be staying," Belkin said.

"I'm afraid I must insist."

"Where's Polly and Philip?"

"They took Madeline to her grandparents'. They won't be coming back. They changed their minds about this house." I beamed something that felt like a smile. "To be honest, I changed their minds."

Belkin brazenly searched my thoughts. And I let him. He could see, quite clearly, what I had become. How the abundance of Christmas spirit had stripped away all limitations. I might be small in size, but who I truly was—my mind, my presence—was titanic and, quite frankly, awe-inspiring. It wasn't just toys I controlled. I molded human thoughts as easily as clay pots. Sinking into their minds, planting my wishes as if they were their own.

A haphazard wall had been constructed over the pitch of the roof, made of broken-down pallets and boards torn off the neighbor's porch. It was patchy, for now, but did the job. Hiding what I didn't want to be seen. Not just yet.

"What have you done?" Belkin said.

"Something you never could. You've made toys, once again, dispensable, Belkin. Your leadership has led them nowhere. In another hundred years, you will be right back where you started. Landfills choking on discarded dancers and squeezies, teddys and thumpers. Humans were never going to see us as equals. They'll use us like the playthings we are, switching into our bodies for momentary thrill rides until they've squeezed every drop of joy from us, discarding our broken bodies like empty cartons."

"The people." He looked out at the vacant village. "You couldn't possibly..."

"You know what I can do." I let him look inside me again.

"We need to coexist, Viktor. This is one world. We cannot subjugate them."

"It was never going to change, Belkin. Deep down, you know it. You were going to end up just like the world you came from. Maybe not tomorrow or next year, but soon enough. Humans are clever. Their greed insatiable."

I should know.

I walked through the snow, looked up at Belkin's wooden face. His hinged jaw slack. I took his cane. It was polished and heavy. Walnut, perhaps, with a gold tip.

"It's time for a different approach."

A semitruck stopped a block down the street. A full-size ape, as blue as a ripe blueberry, climbed out of the driver's seat. She scaled the flat-bed trailer and began dropping ramps. A monster backhoe was tied down. A real one, made of metal, meant to be driven and claw the earth.

"Who are you?"

He could see now, just who I was. Somebody hiding in toy clothing. Not quite human, not quite toy. Something much, much different.

"I'm what you could never be. I'll do something you could never do. For the toys, of course."

Another semitruck had arrived. This one hauling a bulldozer. Black smoke spat from exhaust pipes as the machines were awakened by full-size toys. The belted tracks began rolling down ramps, dropping undeniable blades to the ground.

"I won't let you do this, Viktor," Stretch said. "You will not ruin Christmas while I'm—"

The elastic barbarian in the tight shorts was suddenly immobile. Like a frozen bag of peas. I didn't lift a finger. No waving my hand or any other magical gestures. Just a thought was all it took.

Belkin's jaw chattered. For the first time, I think, he felt the cold fist of fear in his chest, right behind that painted heart. In the wink of an eye, he was useless. I couldn't have him spreading fake news to the world about who I was and what I could do. He was going to be my guest. His stay was indefinite.

"If it makes you feel any better," I said, "you were right about what

Philip was doing. Taking the Christmas spirit did have unintended consequences."

I pointed the cane at the house. I had to hold it with both hands. Later, I would have Freckles cut it in half and retrofit it to my height. I didn't need it. But I liked the way it looked. Sort of a magic wand.

A red semitruck squeezed between the other semis. It stopped in front of the house. Rubber superheroes leaped out of the cab and threw open the trailer door. One by one, full-size wooden soldiers leaped out. Bushy eyebrows, square mouths and long spears at their sides. A department store in the city would wonder where they went. It wasn't the first delivery I would reroute.

"Help our guests to their quarters. It'll be several months before construction is done. I think you'll appreciate what I have in mind. In the meantime, make yourselves comfortable." I reached up to take the pocket watch from Belkin's hip. "I insist."

They were guided around the house by a line of soldiers. Plastic dolls with fat plastic heads held their hands like bouncing children on their way to a sleepover. Belkin and Stretch would be padlocked in the garage. It wasn't suitable lodging, but it would do for now.

A row of dump trucks arrived, lining up at the curb. Backhoes drove through lawns, grinding tracks in the ground. Mechanical arms stretched out, toothed buckets biting into the frozen soil.

This was everything I had dreamed of, but not everything I wanted. There was still one more thing, the most important thing of all, that I desired the most. I imagined the colorful roads crisscrossing the universe. I could feel them shrinking now that Christmas had been captured. One by one, they would disappear. Just not fast enough.

"Freckles." I checked the time on my new pocket watch. "I'm putting you in charge for a while."

The fuzzy orange cat picked me up. "Where are you going?"

"Away for... now."

I almost said *home.*

29

The slide was dark. The music loud.

They were dropped onto a slippery slope, tumbling over each other with each surprising turn. Their shouts echoed; their bodies tumbled like laundry into a clothes dryer. They were eventually ejected like debris from a trash chute, tossed into a synthetic dance beat and a drift of powdered snow. Hiro coasted to a stop on his back. The music danced on his chest.

Snow settled over him. High above, perched on a pedestal of frozen earth, was a small house. Aside from the gumdrop-studded shutters and chocolate-covered siding, it was ordinary.

"Come, come, come," Snow said.

Hiro could barely hear above the music. Snow's voice was inside his head. Flake picked Hiro up, brushed him off. Haze, Robby and Chase were gathered in a knot, staring at a blocky robot with a wad of beaded necklaces around its neck, dancing with a red dreadlocked doll wearing black sunglasses. A stack of turtles walked by, five of them, each progressively smaller toward the top. Their necks craned from plastic shells in time with the beat.

"I didn't know what to expect," Robby said, head bobbing to the music. "Not this."

His voice tickled inside Hiro's head. He could hear Robby thinking. This was nothing like the gala they'd seen on television. This was an ice stadium open to the stars. A giant Ferris wheel turned with flashing lights, toys waving from the rollicking seats. A roller coaster did loopty-loops with joyful screams of terror. There were bumper cars that lit up when they clashed, swings that spun around a candy-striped pole.

A behemoth ice wall enclosed the far end. Like an iceberg had been dropped from the sky. They were in a pit dug from the ground. The lonesome house on a pedestal where the surface, at one time, was.

"We need to find Mads," Snow said.

"She's here?" Hiro said, his voice sounding echoey in his own head.

Snow hopped like a bird. They clung together like wallflowers without a wall, toys without a purpose. A blizzard of thoughts banged on the windows of his mind. Hiro concentrated to keep them out. Then did what Mads had told them to do. He imagined a wall.

The Crystal Palace was packed with toys, some furry, some plastic. Some tall, some round, some chatting, some playing. All of them dancing. A few humans were among them, towering over them, talking to toys, picking one up to pet or hug. None of them, as far as Hiro could see, wore a hoodie with a scarf. But the place was so big. The house on the pedestal was a dollhouse in the vastness.

It was a one-story home from the village. Icicles hung from the eaves; snow piled on the shingles. A fence had been built on the pitch of the roof. It was red with a giant bow, a gift big enough for two, maybe three cars. *Viktor Day* was painted on the side.

"What's that?" Hiro said.

Haze shrugged, tapping Flake's shoulder. Pointing at the house. Snow had climbed to the top of Flake's hat, holding on like a buoy in a storm. Haze shouted at him. Snow's voice bellowed in their heads.

"Don't be distracted. We need to find—"

An air horn blasted; the room quaked. The toys cheered. The spiky crystal walls that surrounded the arena fired small balloons.

They drifted down and popped, like soap bubbles. Blue bubbles and pink bubbles, red ones and orange. A downy swan stabbed a checkered one with her long beak.

The music changed. A synthesized record scratched a rhythm that vibrated inside them, a club version of a song Hiro had heard once before.

Jin-jin-jingle. Jin-jin-jingle. Bells. Bells. Bells.

Even the stars flashed with the beat. The light was sharp and white, throwing crisp shadows with each pulse. The Ferris wheel started and stopped in the strobing effect. Hiro lifted his arm to shade his eyes. It wasn't stars. Lights were suspended above them, hanging from a net of wires. Thousands of them beamed on the raucous crowd.

Robby jabbed at a purple bubble with pink polka dots. He started hopping, a kaleidoscope of colors splashing his monitor. Haze flapped her wings.

"Raspberry!" she shouted. "It's raspberry!"

A pale green bubble landed on Hiro's nose. A spearmint wave melted inside him and through his legs. Effervescence bubbled between his ears. The flavor permeated his fluffy insides. He tasted it with every thread of stitching.

Haze and Chase danced around Robby. His moves robotic, head spinning. Haze trotted. Chase flowed like liquid, tail swaying. "I'm not going to lie!" Robby shouted, chopping at bubbles. "I love this music!"

The boxy robot with beaded necklaces joined them. A paper doll slid into the circle, its margins rippling in the cool breeze. Following Snow's orders, Flake tried to corral them.

"Remember why we're here," Snow said.

"We can dance"—Haze bounced off her belly—"and look at the same time."

The rhythm crunched every fiber of Hiro's body, shook every follicle. It was warm, expansive. Airy and open. Christmas spirit flowed like vapor, elevating mood, revealing something wonderful and beautiful. Like breathing a smile.

Adults wandered like giants among the throng of toys. Formally dressed, they strolled with curiosity, stopping to observe, occasionally talking to a toy. Sometimes they picked one up for a laugh and a hug. Unaffected by the dance vibe.

Hiro searched for a hooded figure, but the crowd was so thick, the view from the floor obscured. Robby could pick him up, extend him above the melee, but he wasn't getting anywhere near him. Those scissor fingers had become musical paper shredders.

An elderly couple was watching Chase's sultry dance. The gentleman with a loose tie, hunched at the shoulders. A permanent frown etched valleys in his face, hanging from the corners of his mouth. His wife clutched a heavy necklace, gray eyes lighting up as Chase rubbed against her leg. She looked at her husband. He nodded, eyelids heavy shutters. She bent down to pick her up, holding her at arm's length like an infant without a diaper. Turning her like an antique vase.

"Please. Please, please. Yes, hello." Snow jumped up and down. "She's with us. If you could, yes. Thank you."

The woman put Chase next to Flake, then stood back to watch her slink into Robby's dance circle, which now included three bald baby dolls and a multicolored noodle toy. Robby stripped the tie off and waved it over his head. The woman whispered into her husband's ear.

"You're on fire!" Haze covered her eyes.

The medallion around Chase's neck glowed with fierce light, almost as intensely as the little lights from above. It began to strobe. Robby and the others bathed in it, the light electrifying their dance moves, before it dimmed to a pearly glow. It was a radiant jewel around her neck.

"Oh no," Snow muttered. "Take that off. Chase? Can you please—"

They didn't hear him begging her to remove the medallion. The chaos was wrecking the little elf's plan. The distractions were difficult to ignore. The music, the rides. The fun. Hiro continued to focus on the wall around his thoughts, protecting them from the noise. Mads was here. She would know what to do.

The house was a dim idol surrounded by saturated bubbles that bounced off the rough-hewn shingles, some popping on the big gift built on top of it. The house looked like a trophy, a preserved structure the mob of toys danced around in worship. Hiro felt the buzzy pressure of thoughts press down as he stepped away from Snow. The earth hadn't been molded into a pedestal. The ground around the house had been excavated. No ladder or rope could access it, and it was too steep to climb.

A pebble broke from the earthy monolith. The house seemed stable, but a collapse would bury those near it. Hiro touched the earthen pedestal. It vibrated to the rhythm, but there was an undercurrent, something beneath the music.

It was a hum. A steady hum.

The house looked empty. Light didn't seep between the closed shutters. No smoke from the chimney. But something was happening inside it. He wanted a closer look at it.

A fresh rainbow of bubbles streamed from the joy cannons. Greeted with a wave of anticipation. Hiro concentrated on the front door of the house. Outside thoughts flitted through him, clouded his own thoughts like seasonal mayflies. It was difficult to separate external thoughts from his own. He focused on the wall, imagining blocks chiseled from marble. A seamless barrier that stacked around his mind stretching to the stars. Its weight impenetrable.

Then he imagined a small escape hatch where his thoughts could project up and out. Imagining he was standing up there. And then...

He stood in front of the door.

His projected image was shrouded in drifting bubbles. He could barely see his teddy bear body on the ground, looking up. He only had a minute before someone noticed a ghost haunting the fudgy house.

The arching door, once red, was now pink. A sizeable padlock hung from a latch. Reinforcing columns had been added to the exterior and painted the same chocolate frosting as the walls. The shutters were newer than the door. Weeds, tan and curly, clumped along the foundation. A hole was near the corner, where a tiny mouse had sought to make this a home.

A mailbox was attached to the door. A black metal thing faded by the sun and time. The middle number had fallen off. A name was stenciled on it. A wave of static fragmented his vision, a rogue breeze of external thoughts blowing through the escape hatch. He doubled his focus, read the word on the mailbox.

Bells.

It sounded like a song, not a name. He wanted to see what was inside, didn't know how projecting his awareness worked. Could he go somewhere he'd never been or couldn't see? Was it just a location in space?

He concentrated on the wall and drifted closer. It was like moving a puppet without strings. Only he was the puppet and the puppeteer. He could see thick brushstrokes on the horizontal siding, the airtight seam between the closed shutters. He pushed closer. He merged with the wall.

Then it was dark.

He didn't know if he was inside. He turned around aimlessly, unsure where he was. Descending into vertigo, on the verge of going back when he saw a light. A faint glow in the corner. That must have been the mousehole he'd seen. It wasn't enough to illuminate anything else. But he could hear something beneath the muffled music.

Something was pumping. Something steaming.

"Chase!"

Haze's voice was in his head. She was screaming.

HE WAS in two places in time and space. Simultaneously. Two halves trying to find each other. The Hiro looking up at the house. The Hiro inside it. Both lost in an inner dimension. Haze's voice. Thousands of thoughts. A blizzard of images. A place with no ground, no sky.

Where a compass wouldn't point, sound didn't matter. A total guessing game of where he was.

Breathe.

He focused on the center of his being. Breathing like he'd done countless mornings of meditation with his parents.

In.

Blocks began stacking. External thoughts continued to blow like sleet against a windshield, obscuring his view. One by one, the wall grew higher. He began to descend, gravity pulling him downward. The tight fit of fabric, stitching that held seams together. Firmness below.

He was on the ground.

He didn't know where the others were. He got lost in a storm of laughing Ping-Pong balls and tangled in a rubber snake. A stuffed puppy jumped on his back, waving a cowboy hat, shouting, "Giddyup, teddy!"

It was a forest of toys, all looking the same. He looked back at the Ferris wheel slowly churning. He imagined what Haze looked like, how she felt. Her presence was a beacon. He turned to his left.

He saw Robby. His monitor above the toys. He wasn't dancing. He was looking down with an eye that was soft and fluttering. Hiro pushed through a crowd of rag dolls playing patty-cake. Robby was a jumble of metal limbs cradling a black and white striped cat. The tail hung limply.

"What happened?" Hiro shouted.

"I don't know," Robby stammered. "She grabbed onto me like she saw a spider, like a real spider or something. I thought she was playing and then—" He rocked her like a baby. "I think she's sleeping."

"She's gone," Haze said.

"What do you mean gone?" Hiro said.

Toys were starting to gawk. A shaggy horse peered over Robby's shoulder. A team of rubber mice hung from his mane. Robby began unfolding, arms and legs spreading out, forming a complex dome to keep onlookers away. Chase in a metal swing beneath him.

The light on her necklace had gone out. It hung like a dull stone from her neck.

"Where are they?" Hiro looked around. "That couple, the old man and lady who were looking at her?"

Haze shook her head.

"Get that off her." Hiro pointed at the collar around her neck. Robby slid a serrated limb under it. It thumped on the floor. "Where's Snow?"

Flake was there, hands folded. Looking at the floor. The rim of his hat empty.

Hiro knocked on Flake's hat, heard things roll around. "Snow, get out here. Something's wrong with Chase."

Flake didn't move.

"What's he doing?" Hiro said. "Hey. We need some help. She's not moving. I'm going to find someone—"

The hatch unzipped. Snow stepped out, head down. Now two elves were in mourning.

"She's not moving." Hiro pointed at Robby's cage.

"She woke up," Snow said.

Hiro, Haze and Robby looked at each other. It was strange. For a moment, they didn't know what that meant. They had forgotten where they were. *She woke up!*

"Why did she wake up?" Robby said. "Is it morning?"

Chase had a little sister. Maybe she woke up in the middle of the night, had a nightmare, or Chase had to go to the bathroom. It could be anything. And that meant the rest of them could wake up any second.

"We can't wake up, not yet," Hiro said. "Bring her back.

"She's all right, Hiro," Haze said. "She just woke up."

"We can't wake up!" Hiro shouted. "Chase will be back, she'll fall back asleep. We need to find Mads. She'll know what to do. Where is she?"

Snow was still looking down.

"She's here," Hiro said. "I can feel her."

And he could. Just like he'd found his way back to Haze, he could feel Mads out there. It wasn't exactly her scent, it was something more ethereal. An essence that was distinctly her. She was here, in the stadium.

"We stick together, remember?" Hiro said. "We go toward the Ferris wheel, start looking for her there. I think she's—"

The lights went out.

The roller coaster slowed on the tracks. The bumper cars stopped bumping. The arena filled with surprise and cautious excitement. The light of the stars and a sliver of moon outlined the Ferris wheel coming to a standstill, the seats slowly rocking. Something was about to happen.

Hiro grabbed Haze, who held onto Flake's arm. Robby climbed over them, a mechanical spider protecting his family. Chase rocking in his arms.

Beams of harsh light knifed from each side of the arena, criss-crossing above the house. Intersecting where an icy clock hung from a wire. Icicles pointed out the time. It was ten o'clock.

Toys cheered all around. Above the din, a cartoonish voice began to sing. "A list is made of naughty and nice, writ about the girls and boys. But nothing is Christmas without the spirit, and all of the—"

"Toys! Toys! Toys!" the crowd cheered.

They knew the song and celebrated with fervor, climbing on shoulders and bouncing about. A sea of fur and plastic, of large and small, round and tall. Their excitement went to another level when the spotlights lit the iceberg at the far end of the arena, a pyramidal slab of a wall. On the smooth icy surface, a door opened.

An orange cat appeared to fly out and hover about the crowd. A thin wire, barely visible, carried Viktor around the arena. No one noticed it or cared. They were exploding with delight, believing he was flying. Hiro could feel their joy. Viktor could do anything. *Even fly.*

"Welcome, my fuzzies and furries, my skins and fabrics. My smoothies and roughies and bouncies and crawlies. Welcome all my wonderful toys to the greatest time of the year!"

He threw out his arms and soared like a superhero. The spotlights traced his flight. The arena shook beneath the stampede that reached for him as he swooped down, his happy laughter trailing behind him.

"Viktor! Viktor! Viktor!"

He hung just above the house like a visiting spirit, soaking up the accolades. It went on and on and on, and no one seemed to tire. Viktor wasn't concerned the house was sitting on a tower of dirt and the ground was literally shaking. It was too dark to see anything besides an orange, fuzzy superhero gobbling up praise.

"Do you hear that?" He put his paw to his pointy ear. The crowd quietly hushed. "He's coming."

Little tinny bells rang. As if it was even possible, toys became even more excited. The bells grew louder. The exuberance was a dense vapor invading one toy after another. "Santa," they murmured.

"Ho, ho, ho." Viktor grabbed his belly. "This is our world. This is Toyworld. Christmas isn't about giving things. It's about making the world a better place. How do we make it better? By making you"—he spun like a ballerina, finger sweeping the crowd—"*better toys!*"

All at once, and without warning, the arena was as bright as the sun. It took everyone by surprise. A collective groan rumbled. Hiro looked at the floor, blinded by the light. His vision slowly came back, a ring of dark spots remaining.

"I'm giving back to you this very special Christmas," Viktor said, "what belongs to us."

Hiro took a peek, guarding his vision with his arm. Dozens of bright objects hung like tiny stars, each burning as bright as a thousand spotlights. He could feel the warmth even from that distance. It was dense. It was sweet and uplifting. Like liquid joy.

"Where's Snow?" Hiro said. Flake didn't answer. The little elf was back in the hat. *What's wrong with him?* "Lift me up," he said to Robby.

"With what?" Robby offered Chase's sleeping body like it was all he could do.

"You have twenty arms! Use two of them."

He adjusted his stance, reconfigured Chase's cradle, and offered

Hiro a pair of forks. Hiro clamped them under his arms. Robby hoisted him above his head.

"Higher!"

The arms slid a segment at a time, locking in their tracks. A beachball went bouncing past. *Weeee.* Hiro swayed as the support wavered. He needed to go higher. He wanted to feel the entire crowd. Robby grunted. Haze steadied him. Another segment extended. *Schlock.*

"This is the year Santa never leaves again," Viktor said. "And neither shall I!"

Never leave? Why would he say that?

None of the toys heard it or cared. They were bathing in the sun storm of joy. The tiny white-hot stars swayed on thin wires. The light was creating a strange illusion. It looked like a colorful beam wavered out of the house and into the sky, like a condensed Northern Light.

"Where are you?" Hiro murmured.

He had to concentrate, recalling what Mads felt like, how she smelled, the way her emotions emanated like radio waves. A distinct sensation that was different than anyone else. He scanned the crowd. Toys climbed on top of each other, reaching for Viktor as he began to swing around again, praising toys for being toys, how the world was so much better now. A remote-control monster truck crowd-surfed past Hiro, spinning his wheels through uplifted arms and legs and tentacles.

"She's over there." Hiro pointed at the Ferris wheel. "Turn me that way. No, the other way. That way!"

Robby was about to tip over. His monitor exploded in a display of fireworks. Hiro only needed another minute. He picked up Mads's trail, could feel her in the mix of frolicking toys. Soldiers, the square mouths who ate tickets, carved the crowd like ships plowing through ice.

Robby began to falter. Hiro swayed like the mast of a ship entering rough water. The metal arms went *snick-snick-snick* like a collapsing ladder. Hiro fell from his grip, bounced off a pirate's plastic sword into a mob of bobbleheads. They volleyed him back into flight.

He rode on plastic hands and furry paws, tried to pull himself down, flailing with useless stuffed arms. The world tumbled—bright stars, house, soaring orange cat, jubilant toys.

A storm of chaotic thoughts blew like a winter squall. He lost contact with Mads. Couldn't feel Haze or Robby. Couldn't make sense of anything until firm hands snatched his leg. Everything continued spinning. If he had a stomach, he would have hurled. He focused on a square mouth and bushy eyebrows. A soldier held him at arm's length.

"Thank you." Hiro patted the stiff arms. "I lost my friends."

The soldier spun sharply, bowling over a purple dinosaur, who didn't seem to care, and marched through the crowd.

"They're over there," Hiro said. "You can put me down."

The soldier didn't hear him. Hiro squirmed, pounding at the sleeve on the red jacket. He knocked over toys, stepped on them, kicked them like a runaway wind-up toy. Hiro twisted around. They were marching toward the iceberg. The soldier's eyes were vacant. Hiro couldn't feel thoughts inside him. Just a rigid focus on a door guarded by two more soldiers. He squirmed. The grip tightened.

"Hey, boxhead." A tentacle slithered around the soldier's arm. "I think the teddy wants down."

An orange octopus rose in front of them. One eye scrunched in the loose fabric like a fist inside a sock. Ocho wrapped tentacles around both soldier's arms. They were an immovable vise. The square mouth opened and closed. No words came out. Hiro didn't hear any thoughts. Just blank eyes beneath shaggy brows.

"You're stitched a little tight there, soldier," Ocho said. "You all right, teddy bear?"

Hiro didn't respond. If Ocho was here, Mads wasn't far. She had told him to wait when she left them at Figgy Station. *He came with her!*

Ocho twined another tentacle around the wooden arm, then another, twisting like a carnivorous vine. He had all eight tentacles crawling between the soldier's arms. They were eye to eye, close enough to kiss. A white-gloved hand grabbed the top of Ocho's head like a pillowcase. His tentacles peeled away. A second soldier held him up like a costume. A third one appeared.

"Okay. All right," Ocho said. "It's a party. But you guys are stepping all over the joy!"

He was dropped like a sack full of bedsheets, spreading on the floor. He kept his eye on Hiro as the march continued to the iceberg.

"At midnight, a new world is coming!" Viktor announced with great glee to the adoring audience. "Merry, merry!"

30

When the door slid open, the soldier took one step off the elevator and dropped Hiro like a dirty diaper.

Giant fans churned on a warehouse ceiling. Metal stairs went in all directions, open catwalks crossing from one side to the other. Walls of equipment with lights and switches, tubes and cables. Little plastic bugs—cockroaches and caterpillars and spiders—crawled on things found inside a nuclear power plant or space station. Not a gala.

"Are you okay?"

Hiro scrambled away from the shadow, arms and legs slipping on the floor. A full-sizer held out his hands timidly. His wrestling boots squeaked on the floor. He was all of six feet and almost nude. Skintight briefs and bulging muscles. A bodybuilder with a coif of plastic hair.

"They don't have to be so rough. Look." He pointed at Hiro's leg. White batting puffed from a torn seam.

It sounded like a balloon stretching when he turned his head, wrinkles digging into his forehead. Suddenly, there was pressure in the room. Hiro felt it in his head, like an invisible helmet wrapped around his scalp. His thoughts began to scramble, so he focused on a wall to keep out whoever was trying to get in.

"Very good." A smile squeaked into the muscleman's cheeks. "You kept me from peeking. I was looking for your name. My name is Stretch."

Hiro didn't understand until Stretch tapped his head with a wink. *He's trying to read my thoughts.*

"Hiro."

"Hiro. Well, Hiro, I can help you if you let me."

He gestured to the tear. Hiro nodded. Stretch gently scooped him up, and Hiro saw the full depth of the room. It was even bigger than he first thought. The sound of Stretch's footsteps bounced around the enormous space. The floor was mostly empty except for a stark table with gleaming chairs, both made of something metal. Platinum or the like. It was a strange cross between a dining table and an autopsy bench.

There was also a mint green couch at a glass wall.

The walls were filled with complex machinery except for the one. It was entirely glass. Beyond, an orange cat was swinging on a wire. The top of the Ferris wheel was just below them. The mint green couch was in front of the glass wall like a movie theater. Several feet away from it, standing at the glass, was a full-size puppet. Wooden hands clasped behind a long cloak.

"Here we go."

Stretch placed Hiro on the crunchy couch covered in clear plastic. The puppet standing at the glass ignored them, apparently mesmerized by the swinging cat and blazing lights. Stretch dug through boxes next to the couch, unzipped a pouch.

"This won't be hard." Stretch held a needle between his lips. "Might feel a little pressure."

The needle looked like a splinter between his beefy hands. But he operated like a seasoned surgeon, cutting the frayed threads, packing fluffy white stuffing into the tear. He pinched it together with one hand and began sewing.

The puppet wrung his hands. His fingers looked like sticks trying to solve a puzzle. Something rattled around his wrist.

"This is Belkin. Belkin, this is Hiro."

The puppet twisted his hands, hiding the bracelet. As if feeling Hiro's eyes on it. Hiro hardened the wall around his thoughts. Belkin watched the scene beyond the window. The orange cat was standing on the house now, reaching into the chimney and pulling out presents, flinging them into the crowd. Toys ripped them apart.

"Almost done," Stretch said.

"What's he doing?" Hiro said.

"Don't take it personally. Belkin does this every year. Never says a word till the gala is over."

"No, him. Viktor. Why does he do all of this?"

Stretch chuckled. "That's not Viktor."

"I mean him, the cat on top of the house."

"That's Freckles."

"What?" That didn't make a lick of sense. The orange cat was on all the posters. Everyone was chanting his name. Someone was pretending to be him at the Gifting Tree. "I don't understand."

"Nobody does." Stretch poked more batting into Hiro's leg. "Freckles is more relatable. Easier to like. He *is* more likable, to be honest. Dim, though. Easy for Viktor to control. He's a public figure. No one ever bothers to ask why Viktor the Red is *orange*. They just want to believe."

He added the final stitch, bit the thread and smoothed the suture. He studied his work. He began humming a Christmas song, putting his needle and thread away, like this was everyday knowledge: a mysterious ruler throwing a big party, using another toy to pretend to be him. While a full-size puppet watched from an apparent prison cell the size of a warehouse carved from an iceberg. It made as much sense as everything else in this world.

"Am I in trouble?"

"No one's in trouble." Stretch sat next to him, the couch sinking under his weight. "We're just part of the mess."

Hiro didn't want to mention his friends. He hopped off the couch, leaned against the window. The lights were closer to the crowd, showering them with white brilliance. Hiro could still feel their strange warmth. It was exhilarating. He felt stronger and something else. He did that thing when Robby was holding him up, when he had been looking for Mads. This time he opened his heart to search for his friends. To see if he could feel them out there. Just to be sure they were all right. He could feel Mads, but she wasn't by the Ferris wheel anymore.

"Don't do that," Belkin said.

Hiro jumped. "Don't do what?"

"Open like that."

He reworked his old, scuffed fingers, not hiding the bracelet anymore. He wasn't watching the cat, who apparently wasn't Viktor, or the toys or the rides. He was staring at the bright lights.

"He means this." Stretch tapped his head. "Don't open your mind."

"I didn't."

"You were searching for your friends," Belkin said. "It makes you vulnerable. Don't do it again."

"He's worried about his friends, Belkin."

"And I looked straight into his thoughts." Belkin's head swiveled toward Hiro. His eyes were faded, as if sun-bleached. "He'll know everything if you don't protect your mind."

Hiro didn't know *anything*. He'd come here to save Christmas, nothing else. That was why Mads hadn't told them what they were going to do. In case this happened. Now that Hiro was caught, Viktor knew they were there.

Belkin turned back to the shiny little orbs swinging on long cables, bathing the arena in dazzling warmth.

"What are those lights?" Hiro said. "I can feel them."

Stretch looked at Belkin. Neither wanted to answer. Belkin's fingers seemed to tangle in a knot. Finally, he said, "Our mistakes."

❄

"LET ME GO!"

Bits of candy danced across the floor. Haze barfed a colorful rainbow off a soldier's face. He dropped her like a sack of rice. Robby was tossed across the room, his limbs tied in a mess of yellow string like he'd been rolled in wet pasta. Flake moped off the elevator. A soldier laid Chase gently on the floor.

"Haze!" Hiro hopped across the room. Haze met him next to the table. They collided like puffy sumo wrestlers with arms too short to grab each other. They leaned against each other instead of hugging.

"Are you okay?" Haze said.

"Yeah. I mean, I tore a seam, but Stretch fixed it." He pointed at Stretch, who carried Chase to the couch. "Are you all right?"

"The soldiers were intense. I don't think they're having fun."

"They grabbed you, too?"

"Me, yeah."

Hiro looked around. "Did you find—"

"That's so sweet," Robby said. "Me? I'm great, too. Super great. I found this new outfit. You like it? Great, great. Hey, I've got an idea. Get me out of here!"

He strained in the bindings, looking more like a loosely wrapped ball of rubber bands. Lightning flashed on his TV.

"What happened to him?" Hiro asked.

"Soldiers. Made him easy to carry," Haze said. "They threw it at him. I think it's a toy, but not sure what."

"Seriously, are you going to help?" Robby grunted. "This is getting tight. I think I can cut—ahh!"

Stretch towered over the quivering ball of metal meatball wrapped in spaghetti, tapping the deep dimple in his square chin. He had his bag of things out. Robby started bouncing away like a tortured exercise ball.

"That's Stretch?" Haze said.

"That's Stretch."

"Is he nice?"

Hiro held up his leg. "He fixed me."

Robby managed to wiggle out of Stretch's shadow. The muscle toy reached out, his arm stretching and thinning, and grabbed Robby's television head, held him like a junkyard ornament.

"Guess that's why they call him Stretch," Haze said.

"Guess so," Hiro said.

They followed him to the long, silver table, where he plopped Robby like a quivering entrée. He vibrated like a battery-powered toy with no apparent purpose. Stretch dropped his bag next to him.

"Who's the puppet?" Haze said.

Flake was next to Belkin, watching the show play out below. The elf looked as frumpy as ever, slumped in his wrinkled clothing. The rim of his hat was empty. He felt sad.

"That's Belkin," Hiro said.

"There we go." Stretch searched his bag, found what he was looking for. It wasn't a knife or scissors. It was a small jar with red sauce. He cracked the lid open and smelled it.

"He's not going to eat him, is he?" Haze said.

"I'm not sure. You're not going to eat him, are you, Stretch?"

Stretch dipped his finger into the jar. He waved a dab of red sauce. "We don't want to hurt anyone, do we, Ms. Super String?"

It wasn't quite clear whom he was talking to or what he was doing. It looked like a strange culinary ritual. The ropey, yellow string began sliding like a python. Robby's screen went blank. He stopped shivering. The end of the mess of binding noodles wiggled out. Stretch poured a trail of sauce down the table. Slowly, the rope slithered out and began rolling around, covering itself in red paste.

"When I thought this couldn't get weirder," Haze said.

Robby skittered off the table like a dog scrambling on linoleum, fell on the floor and crawled on multiple legs. The television spinning. Stretch carried his bag to the mint couch, humming a Christmas song. Belkin and Flake were unmoved.

"I'm guessing this wasn't part of the plan," Haze said.

"Probably not."

They went to the window. Chase was on Stretch's lap, curled up like she was sleeping. He patted the couch. They sat next to him. Fireworks were exploding up above, streaks of light flashing on the toys below. It was eleven o'clock, according to the clock above the house.

Robby eventually came over, squatted behind the couch. No one said anything. They watched the show, listening to Belkin twist his wooden fingers and Ms. Super String wallow in red sauce. The orange cat pulled more gifts from the chimney.

"Why do they call him Viktor the *Red*?" Robby said.

31

The nights were silent. The streets were dark.

No string lights hung from gutters, no trees in the windows. It was another night like any other, to be followed by a gray, colorless day. I'd had a lifetime of colorless days.

If all went as planned, I'd never see another.

The house was quiet. The sheets were starched. A cup at my bedside. I stood at the window with not a stitch of sentimentality. My neighbors fast asleep, snoring in their beds. Not listening for bells or hooves on their roof. No stockings above the fireplace, no presents waiting to open.

They forgot Christmas ever existed.

Should I feel guilty when they didn't know Christmas went missing? It had been several years since I'd had to endure their colorful lights. The Christmas spirit had disappeared from this world, taking with it the joy and happiness of this time of year.

Maybe I felt a trace, just a smidge. But I extinguished that ugly little bruise. If I didn't, I wouldn't sleep tonight. And tonight, more than any other, I needed to slumber like the dead. Tonight was the night Christmas would leave this world for good. It would still exist. Just not here.

And neither would I.

I was greeted by the sweet smells of nutmeg and roasted chestnuts. Candlelight flickering. String instruments carried me on lovely arrangements like a sleigh coasting over snow-covered hills.

My bones were warm. My personal assistant, Tommy Turtle, rubbed almond oil on my legs. My femur was slick and tingling. The sea turtle's spongy flippers applied the perfect amount of pressure to keep me fresh and ready on return. I let him work his magic.

The shelf where I once woke was long gone. Now it was a private room, an ergonomic recliner, and things to stimulate the senses. A beautiful awakening.

Before the chaos would begin.

The thoughts of millions of toys awaited. Knowing all those thoughts was exhausting. I had begun to hate my return until I learned to filter the noise. It took considerable effort to ignore them, to shrink my consciousness down to my essential being. Knowing everything is to know nothing. I had to be Viktor, just Viktor, to prevent being washed away by a tsunami of thought.

"Bring them in."

I said it out loud. I could have thought it, but using words was a way to maintain separation. If I penetrated Tommy Turtle's mind, I would know him intimately. It was nicer to see him pack up his oils and waddle out, feeling only the ripples of his emotion. Tommy, though, was as calm as a glassy pond. That was why he cared for me during sleep.

Freckles was entertaining the mob, swinging from a wire, tossing gifts to the multitude. As he'd done for many, many Christmases now. I sat up and watched him hold his belly, laughing joyously. Tonight was possibly his last performance.

Tonight the last road would disappear.

Every Christmas, Santa's avenues withered away. Without the flow of Christmas spirit, they atrophied like abandoned muscles. My calculations pegged this night to be the last of them. If I was here when it vanished, then I couldn't go back there.

Bye-bye, dreary world.

Freckles could continue playing the role of Viktor the Red. I had consulted my public relations team, Penny Playmate and Chauncey Chatterbox, in the very beginning. I didn't like the idea of Freckles pretending to be me, at first. Giving up control of the narrative? But they insisted, and slowly, I relented. I don't know everything. I mean, I did know everything, but I was still only one toy.

With Freckles doing the dirty work, I could retire to a small cabin, or ridiculous mansion (I hadn't decided which), by a stream or lake. Get a boat, or yacht. Fish all afternoon. I was bored even thinking about it. There was still work to do. The bottom line was this: I wasn't going to fall asleep anymore. There would be no roads to take me back.

A full-time toy.

"Merry, merry!" Bella Dancer sang.

She tiptoed into my private room. Always on her toes, that one. Jimmy Gearhead, my robot calculator, followed. Pauly Paws, the floppy-eared dog, moped in last. My three trusted advisors, all from the workshop on the day I first woke up and was later brought to Madeline's bedroom. They surrounded my recliner and, one at a time, gave the waking report.

I could have just absorbed it from them. It was nice to hear it, though. Keep separate. They appreciated it. I know they did. I watched Freckles climb on the little house's roof, scaling the special red wall built on top. Gala attendance was at an all-time high. Social media was trending favorably. The little house readings were stable.

"Spirit levels have spiked 200%," Jimmy Gearhead said.

"Two hundred?"

That was unexpected. I had calculated an increase of 58.2%. I had been right, give or take a tenth of a percent, for the past ten Christmases. This miscalculation was unexpected. *This could be a problem.*

With fewer roads, the Christmas spirit, or verve as the dad once called it, siphoned from the bubble continued to increase every year.

I hypothesized it was due to fewer outlets. The spirit needed to flow. Its essence was that of giving. It couldn't be static.

I had increased charm production to hold the extra spirit, had tripled toy manufacturing over the past two years. The spirit had to go somewhere. The trick was not letting any one toy get too smart. They had to be happy and joyful and smarter than the average bloodbag. But not smart enough to see through my shenanigans.

More toys were not sustainable. What would happen when all the roads were closed, you might be thinking? Easy solution, really. Christmas won't come once a year. We'll do it every day. The spirit will flow and flow and flow. Everyone will love me even more. Does it sound like I was winging it? Reorganizing the universe turned out to be complicated.

"We had some suspicious activity," Pauly Paws said. "We picked up loose thoughts searching the house."

"Did someone try to get inside?" Curiosity was natural. You can't invite thousands of toys to a party and not expect a few to climb the altar.

"No. But they saw inside. Somehow." He presented the evidence as a thought.

Now this was interesting. Somehow a toy got a legitimate peek inside the house. It was unreachable and impenetrable. The multitude of carnival rides—Ferris wheel, roller coaster, bumper cars, twirly cups, pole drops, ship tips, chair spinners (*what more did they want?*)—kept curiosity to a minimum. Why would they care about a dumpy old house?

"Did you apprehend the trespasser?" I asked.

"They're in the warehouse."

"They?"

"They came to the gala together."

I stood on the recliner so I could look my team in the eyes. Then I applied a little mental pressure. Just enough to let them know the boss was agitated. "Why," I said slowly, "did you put them in the *warehouse?*"

"It's thought-locked. There might be others working with them still at the gala."

Okay, I hadn't thought of that. Good call. I scratched Pauly Paws behind the ear, gave the rest of them some good feelings.

It's important to give cookies when deserved.

TOY BUGS KEPT the machines running, machines that kept the Christmas spirit circulating and stored in proper vessels to be distributed to toys all over the world. No one ever said thank you, nor should they. But if they knew the sacrifices I made, a little gratitude wouldn't hurt.

My guests were glued to the window. Belkin felt me coming. He always did. I climbed onto a platinum chair, stood at the head of the table and stared at a twenty-foot tapeworm writhing in red sauce. It sounded like muck boots in a mud hole.

"Enjoying the show?" I asked.

A television spun on an erector set of crooked limbs. A single eye swelled on the monitor. A teddy and dragon peeked over the couch.

"Merry, merry, Viktor. You look rested."

"Thank you, Stretch. You look rosier than ever."

"I'm using a new oil."

"Fabulous. What do we have here?" I pointed at the gurgling slurpfest.

"Ms. Super String is indulging. Marinara, her favorite."

"I see that."

The string inchwormed toward me. I summoned a cleanup crew. The elevator opened. One of my trusty soldiers wound Ms. Super String up like a rope. A team of Spongy Critters mopped up the marinara. Stretch helped my guests to seats at the table. The television robot struggled to fold his limbs. I insisted he stand.

"Belkin, please join us. Christmas is an hour away."

My wooden friend remained at the window. I would allow him to come of his own volition. I preferred not to force his actions. I could, but it was easier if I didn't. Like a good puppet, he sat at the opposite end of the table. Insolent, he was. I liked to tease he was an oversized chip on the world's shoulder. He never laughed.

"Am I to assume you know who I am?"

"You're Viktor the Red."

"It was more of a question for our new friends, but thank you, Stretch. I am Viktor. Freckles does my dirty work. The public appearances and whatnot. Fame and recognition are not my thing. Besides, everyone loves a big fluffy cat. Nothing about a red skeleton says *Christmas*."

I jazz-handed the expression. I'd used it a million times. People loved it.

"Why does he use your name?" the dragon said.

I hadn't skimmed their thoughts yet to know their names. Mystery, I had found in the last year or so, was much more fun. When the time came, I would simply peek into their fragile little minds and know everything about them. Until then, let's play.

"Fair point. If I didn't want recognition, why not just let him be Freckles the Great? It's self-indulgent, I agree. This is a historic moment. And I want the credit, even if by proxy." I drummed my fingers on the table like sticks on a barrel. I liked the sound of it. It was dramatic in tense meetings. "It would be *rude* of me to peek at your thoughts. So please, tell me your names."

Belkin shook his head. My audacity was sometimes sickening. I only said it for his benefit. To see if a toy could actually barf from disgust. *Fun, fun.*

"I'm Hi—" the teddy started. The dragon spit a candy rock at him. It dribbled on the table. "Higo."

"Higo?" I said. "Very well. And you?"

"Dreamy," the dragon blurted.

"Farper," the metal man said.

"Farper," I said. "How did you come to have such an interesting name, Farper?"

"The person who made me farped a lot."

"That's not a word."

"Tell her."

I couldn't help but laugh. They were lying. What fun, watching them trying to hide. The innocence. The naivete. "How about you?"

The elf was different than the others, a tumbleweed of whiskers with a tall hat jammed onto his head. His clothes were oversized and wrinkled. His hands, though, were quite unique. A realistic synthetic material that looked human. I hadn't seen this type of toy before and made a note. Perhaps, when the time came, I would look into him like a suit I might try on. I'd grown fond of the skeleton, but a switching wasn't off the table.

"He doesn't talk," Dreamy the dragon said.

"He doesn't? Well, does he have a name?"

"Maybe."

"His name is Maybe?" I swear on a mountain of marshmallows, I have never been in a mood this good. "Well, *Maybe,* tell me about the little door in your hat?"

"His friend is in there," she said.

"Quite small, that one." Funny. I couldn't feel anyone in there. I jumped on the table and walked straight over to the elf and knocked on his dumpy, green hat. "Little elf, little elf, let me in."

"He's shy," the dragon said.

"Well then, no need to embarrass him." I did a little jig, heels clicking on the hard surface. I loved this part, strolling across the table. It scared others, a little, red skeleton stomping back and forth. "This one here. She was your friend?"

I knelt next to the black and white, striped cat. She was a beauty. Silky fur, empty eyes that, when the light was on, were probably hypnotic. Put some life in this one and I'd keep it around just to hear it purr.

"She's gone," the dragon said.

"That's unfortunate."

"They put a collar on her when we got here. Then these old people—"

"Creepy old people," Farper interjected. The wily scamp.

"—they started talking to her. And then the collar lit up. And then, I don't know, twenty minutes later she went to sleep."

I stroked the kitty's tail. "You hear that, Belkin? A toy that sleeps." He didn't appreciate my jab. Only one toy in this world slept. *Not after tonight.* "Excitement can do that to a toy. Knock them out of sync. The light meant she was selected. The old couple chose her to switch."

"It didn't work," the dragon said.

"Apparently not."

I peeked inside the cat, searching for a trace of identity. If she hadn't consented to the switch, it could've resulted in an identity failure. The old woman, or old man—if he was into being a toy cat for the night—would have tried to occupy the toy. A conflict would've ensued. The woman (or man) would have returned to their old, shriveled body. The toy, unfortunately, would've been erased. Happened all the time.

There would be evidence of who she was cached on her charm. But here's the thing. She didn't have a charm. *Well, that's not possible.*

I threw a wider net around the room, scooping up their real names in the meantime. I read them all—Hazel, Robert, Flake— except for the teddy. His thoughts were more resistant. His mind was a house of bricks. The others were made of straw. I would blow his house down soon enough, but first the charms. I felt them; they were in the room. How could they not be? These toys were clearly alive.

"Let's take a look inside your hat. May I, Flake?"

I felt them flinch. I knew the elf's name. Flake bowed his head. He knew he couldn't stop me. I knocked on the little door. No one answered. I stood back, held out my hands. A ridiculous mop of hair puffed out when he peeled off the hat. It looked like a dandelion with a perm.

The hat was heavy. Little things stored inside, collectibles and precious items. A needlepoint repair kit, extra batting. A photo of Flake with a tiny elf, who evidently lived inside the hat, posing on the brim. Identical twins of different sizes. Adorable.

A zippered pocket bulged with a handful of heavy items.

"Stretch," I said, "can you fetch a bowl?"

The elastic man came back with a cereal bowl. I dumped the contents with a loud clatter into it and placed it on the table like a snack. To these dullards, it looked like four marbles. Three of them were speckled with dazzling light, like self-contained universes. The fourth one was dull gray. My guests had no idea what I'd found. Flake, though, why, he was fully aware of what he was hiding. Belkin, of course, knew as well.

"Now why would Flake be holding your charms?" I said, amused.

"He likes shiny things," Robby said.

Oh, this was rich. They were clueless, all of them. However, I'd never encountered such an odd design. A charm not embedded in the toy? It would be like carrying a brain in a duffel bag.

Well, enough fun.

Flake offered no resistance. I searched his mind like spotlights cutting through a meadow. The little elf who lived inside his hat went by the name of Snow. Snow and Flake. Cute. They had been stitched as an inseparable pair. Although together no more. Snow was the leader of the motley band of misfits. He hadn't been caught with the others but rather snuck out a secret hatch in the back of the hat when my soldiers approached, scurrying through the gala like a mouse between bags of seed.

I dug a little deeper.

Intentions were always a little tricky, I had found, when probing another's thoughts. They're the crown jewels of why we do what we do and the last thing we want others to see. So much so, we often hide them from ourselves. They underestimated what I could do. Perhaps this little scenario would have worked if I weren't omnipotent. The other toys had no idea why they were here.

They're a diversion.

I called the lookies into action. The shiny tattletales swirled around the house where Freckles perched his big orange butt. They were too small for anyone attending the gala to notice. I must admit, a cold wave of worry rippled through me. Even Belkin sensed it wrinkle the space between us. The cad thought, for a moment, something was out of my control.

Nothing could be farther from the truth. *Still...*

The lookie stream projected onto the table for everyone in the room to see. The multifaceted view stretched the entire length. They stood on their chairs to watch the show. I guided the lookies like bloodhounds, sniffing hints I pulled from Flake. It only took a minute to find an inconspicuous octopus crawling with a band of twirling ballerinas.

They cringed, just a little.

They recognized the orange cephalopod sticking out like a zebra hiding in a desert. Although, I'll admit, they seemed more surprised he was even there. *Ocho,* they thought.

Poor little toys. They didn't even know what was happening. Just pawns in some misguided attempt to stop me. They'd suffer the consequences, of course. That wasn't on me. Whoever roped them into this folly would have to take that blame.

I beamed with satisfaction. I wanted Belkin to feel it, wanted him to watch. Their simplistic plan wasn't going to work. But that wasn't the source of my glee. We were going to watch it fail in real time.

"What fun," I muttered.

Ocho pretended to loiter, leaning on the pillar that held the house. He studied his tentacles with boredom, nibbling at loose threads that weren't there. His solitary eye shifted around, not noticing the lookies. Casually, he reached under one of his legs, stretched and yawned. With a flick, he tossed a tumbling ball over his head.

It was an impressive shot.

The crumpled ball had floated like one of the bubble experiences, those tasty treats the toys loved so much, and landed at the corner of the house. It disappeared. I had to rewind the stream to see what happened. The ball had landed on the apron surrounding the house, sprouted legs and darted into a crack big enough for a field mouse.

Or a very small elf.

"There's your friend!" I clapped my hands, encouraged the others to applaud the seamless execution. They didn't share my enthusiasm. "What do you think he'll do next?"

Belkin pushed away from the table and returned to the window.

The lookies followed. The little elf zipped through the dark and right for the lab. That was interesting. Someone had prepped him. He knew exactly where to go. I started to second-guess Belkin's involvement. If he had anything to do with this, he was hiding it well. The wooden curmudgeon felt clueless. I'd excavate his thoughts later.

On with the show.

Snow bounced around the lab. It was pitch black, the lookie views overlaid with green night vision. He went right to the control panels and pried open a drawer. Wow. He was really getting to the heart of it. He journeyed past the butterfly valve and into the needle chamber. He found the access panel, crawled through a vent that led to the most vulnerable part of the system: a charm that linked everything together. Once he got a hold of it, he could shut everything down. Destroy everything I'd worked for. Expose me to the world. *The horror!*

It wasn't there.

I had redesigned the system a long time ago. Only my trusted advisors knew that. The house held only one thing, the most important thing, but the switch that turned everything off wasn't there. And only I knew where it was. Whoever was behind this knew the house. *Interesting.*

The little elf scrambled around. It was supposed to be there. That was what he had been told, and he didn't know what to do now that it wasn't there. He climbed out of the machinery and, in a bit of a panic, scurried out of the lab. It was time to send in a Super String agent. I assumed the little elf would run into the attic or basement in search of a vulnerability. He wouldn't find one, but he'd make a mess. He went for a hallway.

"This is interesting," I said.

I called off the Super String, for now. The little elf ventured into the living room. Eerie blue light rippled on the walls. A needle extended from the ceiling in front of the fireplace. It was white hot, piercing a watery glob of warped space. It was a life-sized snow globe, of sorts. Not one to be shaken. There were no snowflakes inside, no miniature village.

Only a fat man in a red coat.

The little elf was mesmerized by my time bubble. Well, Philip had invented the technology. I made it mine. That was how these sorts of things went. It was nothing short of a miracle that it worked. The needle siphoned an endless supply of Christmas spirit from it. As a result, I am who I am.

The little elf must've been told what was in the house. But, as he took a step toward the bubble, he clearly hadn't been told what it was.

"Stop this, now." Belkin had turned around.

"Free will, Belkin. He went in there of his own free will."

"Viktor, if he passes through the veil—"

"I am not responsible!" The table shook. The toys quivered. "I took every precaution to protect the house. There's no welcome mat out front. He went inside against all my wishes." I cast an accusatory glare. "Someone should have warned him."

"I have nothing to do with this," Belkin said.

I had no reason not to believe him. He'd been trapped in this room since the beginning. He was genuinely innocent of this attack. He was rooting for them, sure. But this wasn't his doing.

"You don't have to watch."

Flake hammered the table with humanlike fists. A series of guttural grunts came from the wild beard like a chimpanzee trying to communicate. His thoughts wildly spun warnings, trying to reach the little elf with thoughts that would never reach him.

The little elf cautiously raised his hand. The membrane rippled waves where he touched it. He hesitated. I sensed his change of heart and thought maybe Belkin was right. No need to complicate matters this close to midnight. I would put a stop to this.

But then he touched it one more time.

The bubble swallowed him like an amoeba absorbing food. The watery veil surrounded him. A blurry green coat was now on the inside. Hand raised. And not moving.

Flake fell silent. They all did. It was clear something bad just happened. I knelt in front of Flake, attempted to soothe his inextinguishable anguish. I couldn't have a wild elf bouncing off the walls, trying to work out his issues.

"Your friend is okay. He's better than okay. Time for him has slowed to an infinitesimal crawl. That's all. When he comes out, he'll only be younger than you. Nothing more."

He wasn't coming out. That's for sure. If he did, the jolly fat man would be set free. I had more than enough Christmas spirit, but I imagine Santa Claus wouldn't be happy with what I'd done. I was fairly certain I could handle him, but, like I said, no need to complicate matters this close to Christmas.

"Now." I turned around. "Who are you?"

They sat like lumps of wet cotton. It'd be nice of them to tell me, but I understood. Even if I told them why their charms were hidden in Flake's hat and why the cat suddenly went to sleep, they wouldn't believe me. I felt sorry for them. Someone was playing with them to get to me. Not in a fun way.

"Well then, let's have a look."

Flake had all the answers. After all, he had those special synthetic hands for a reason. I dove into his memory canals, floating back to the beginning when he came online for the very first time. That magical moment when the stitcher ignites the charm with just a pinch of Christmas spirit. Like a baby opening his eyes in a brand-new world, I saw who was looking back at him.

I stepped back.

An unexpected turn, it was. I had to search my own memories for a face I hadn't seen in quite some time. His stitcher had clearly aged.

It had been thirty years since I last saw her.

I leaped off the table and took my time walking to the couch. I gestured to Stretch, who dutifully lifted me up. I stood on his shoulder. Outside the window, glitter bombs showered the arena. Freckles bathed in the flickering bits of confetti.

Belkin didn't take his big round eyes off the spectacle.

"You remember Madeline, Belkin? Polly and Philip's daughter. Don't pretend you don't. She was such a fan. Knew about you. BT, remember? My goodness, you loved that she knew you."

I could feel her out there. Her energy was as unique to her identity as fingerprints. I couldn't quite locate her though. She was good at hiding. That would end soon enough.

"I won't hurt her. I wouldn't think of it. She meant so much more to me than you. I just need this night to be perfect. After that, I'll set you free. Like I promised. Tell me where she is." I urged Stretch to move a bit closer. I could smell the varnish on Belkin's face. "Or shall I have a peek?"

He turned those wide eyes on me. We'd never seen eye to eye, in the metaphorical sense. If he had anything to do with this, he was going to make me work for it. He unfolded his hands, undid the clasp of the bracelet. The snowflake, once cheery red, had faded to a roughened scarlet color. The links pooled in the palm of his stiff hand.

"I found this when we first arrived. It told me exactly where we were and why we'd been sent here. Where we came from. That this world was for us. What you've done to it"—he piled the bracelet in my hand—"is not what it was meant to be."

I dropped the bracelet on the floor. It meant nothing to me. That bracelet was from another time. I'd bottled Belkin in this room so the outside world would forget him. Once the roads were closed and I wasn't going to wake up, the toys could have him back.

"This world is exactly what it should be," I said.

"You've done so much wrong."

"Look out there, what do you see? Hope and joy. I know you can feel that. I did that! It's because of me. I rescued them from the world you made them. You can't argue that. Can't you be happy, for once? Admit that I did what you couldn't. *This is for them!* I did everything for the toys!"

Well, not everything.

"They're still playthings," he said. "They just belong to you."

"You have no idea the restraint I exercise. The burden of knowing everything, the power to do anything requires so much more than you are capable of, Belkin."

"I've seen what you've done, Viktor. I see it in their faces. You're destroying humankind."

"Bloodbags? You're worried about the... they did this to themselves! They brought this on. The rules don't change when the tables turn." I pointed in no particular direction, like humans were everywhere. "They see the injustice now, don't they? Do you think, for one second, they wouldn't dominate toys if I wasn't here?"

"Toys are better than this. This world deserves better." He resumed his unyielding posture of a stiff, wooden puppet. "I am to blame."

"Well, there you go. Thankfully, I'm in charge and not you."

"You got what you wanted."

"You don't know what I want. This is our world, you said it yourself. I made it so."

If his eyes could move, they would widen in disbelief. "You're hurting countless others. You've taken Christmas away from all worlds." He leaned closer and whispered, "Think about *your* world."

I nearly fell off Stretch's shoulder. It had been quite some time since I'd been surprised. *He knows where I'm from. Like really knows.*

I must've been careless, didn't guard my thoughts around him, let him see who I truly was. I'm a voyager from another world. Not a toy. I needed time to calculate all the possibilities of what this meant. It was less than an hour to midnight. *Why did he tell me now?*

I climbed off Stretch and stood on the floor. Gazing at the celebration below, thinking about how different things were back home without Christmas. Thinking about what I was about to do to it for all eternity. I wasn't going back. That was nonnegotiable.

"*My* world was already without joy."

32

A ball of orange tentacles, lassoed by a long strand of Ms. Super String, rolled out of the elevator. Ocho's eye flickered back and forth. Desperate grunts stifled by a tightly wrapped gag.

"The gang's all here." Viktor climbed onto the table. "Come on in, Mr. Ocho. Grab a seat."

Ms. Super String unraveled. Ocho unfolded. "You!" he shouted, jabbing a tentacle at Viktor. "You'll be hearing from my lawyer. I did not come to this-this... gala or whatever to be harassed and—*humff-hm.*"

Viktor waved a hand. Ms. Super String bound his mouth closed. Ocho was putting on a show. He had no idea they'd all watched him launch Snow into the house.

"Please sit down," Viktor said. "Get comfortable. This will only take a second."

Ocho was suspicious. Like when a nurse held up a shot and said there would be some pressure. At Viktor's request, Stretch dropped Ocho in a chair like a tangle of seaweed, pushed him up to the table as if dinner were about to be served. He squirmed at first, tugging at the gag until Viktor marched down the metal runway, footsteps click-ing. *Heel-toe.*

Viktor leaned in. Ocho leaned back. "Let's get some answers."

Hiro could feel a mental struggle, if that was what you could call it. More like Viktor opened Ocho's mind like a jewelry box and rummaged freely through his prized possessions. Ocho squirmed. Maybe it hurt, having secrets ripped open like that. Maybe it was the simple raw and potent experience of powerlessness.

Viktor was going to do that to each of them. There was no hiding what they knew. Hiro realized that, no matter how many freedoms were taken away, there was always sanctuary in imagination. At least his thoughts were his and his alone. No one else's. *That's not how it works here.*

Viktor began laughing at what he saw inside Ocho. It was not the humorous kind.

The atmospheric texture rippled with the coarseness of a sand-storm. Ocho was losing, but he was putting up a fight. Hiro felt his way through the mental struggle, picking up loose thoughts escaping the battle. Clips of memory, playing in short reels, streamed in the maelstrom.

Ocho driving his candy-decorated car. Honking the horn. Mads returning to the back seat after dropping them off at Figgy Station, holding the purple monkey in the back seat, telling him where to go next. Ocho dropping her off at a fancy building. Ocho waiting for her. Ocho returning to Figgy Station, walking up to the soldiers. Ocho with a ticket. He wasn't alone.

The purple monkey was walking with him.

Viktor swung his gaze around the table. Hiro was caught off guard, didn't have the wall ready. Viktor was inside. He saw what he wanted. They weren't toys, not real toys. They were dreamers from another world.

Viktor stiffened with surprise. He paced a tight circle, taking another peek at their thoughts, their truth. He nodded, began laugh-ing. Genuinely laughing, doubled over holding his red ribs. A human laughing that hard would wipe tears from their cheeks. His sockets were black holes.

"That is... unexpected." Viktor addressed Hiro and the others with a flourish. "Do you know why you're here, hmm? I mean, in this world, not my precious gala. Go on, you can say it. I already know, but I want to hear it from you."

He pointed at Haze. "To save Christmas," she muttered.

"To save Christmas. Right. Does it look like Christmas needs saving?" He gestured to the celebration that could not be more joyous.

"It's gone from our world," Haze said. "We want it back."

"Your world," he whispered. "Did you hear that, Belkin? Such honesty. Yes, Christmas is here and not there. I don't make the rules."

"You took it from us," Haze said.

"She didn't tell any of you she was coming to the gala. No, she didn't because if you were caught, you would be a liability. But she didn't stop there, did she. She didn't want to risk anything. Take your friend here." He stroked Chase's fur. "Madeline had a plan to keep you quiet."

He looked around the table. No one understood.

"Do you know what these are?" He picked up the bowl of marbles —the ones he'd found in the hat. Flake lowered his gaze. He understood what Viktor was getting at. "They're called charms. Every toy has one. See, you are not stuffing and threads or plastic eyes. You're not a teddy or a dragon or a... whatever you are." He gestured to Robby. "You're this."

Viktor held a marble like a grape. Studied it like a jewel. The dark sockets in his bright red skull seemed bottomless.

"Stretch has a charm inside his chest. Don't you, Stretch? Belkin has one behind that painted heart. Ocho here has one behind his eye. Flake has one somewhere under all that hair. Even you, my fine little toys, have a charm." He swirled the bowl of marbles. "But Madeline hid them in the hat instead of putting them inside you. Did she ever tell you to stay close? Mmm?"

They wriggled in their seats. They'd thought it was for their own safety.

Viktor nudged the bowl across the table with a red tarsal bone. It stopped in front of Flake like a bowl of worms.

"These charms are special, aren't they, elf? Madeline's mother was a toy stitcher, too. She designed these charms to be more alive, to have greater capacity. Bigger brains, if you will. Do you remember, Belkin, when she brought them to your office? She thought they were the answer to making toys more capable. An upgrade to be more than playthings. It would've worked. But we know what got in the way, don't we, Belkin?"

The full-size puppet didn't acknowledge the rhetorical questions. Hiro knew from his agitation that Viktor tortured him with gloating dialog.

"Polly was smart—that's Madeline's mother." Viktor strolled like a storyteller with endless time. "You don't become a world-class stitcher without a sprinkle of genius. She wasn't just a stitcher but a toy supporter. I mean, the woman was rabid about toy rights. Humans had subjugated toys, using them up and discarding them when they were done. It was not good, and no one was doing anything about it. Toys were disposable, and she wanted to change that. This was long before you all arrived yesterday."

He nodded in the way a person would wink. *I know all your secrets.*

"Polly was going to make a difference with these upgraded charms. But they were prototypes. They needed to be tested. And then, to my fantastic luck, her husband—a genius of another kind—saw another use for them. You see, the new charms wouldn't just make better toys. They were expanded storage devices. Philip and the past leader of toys"—he gestured to Belkin—"used them to *steal* Christmas spirit. They turned them into batteries!"

Viktor threw his arms out like a showman. Outside the window, Freckles entertained the crowd beneath bright balls of light. But those weren't balls.

Those are charms.

Hiro had felt their effect when they were unveiled. The feelings had showered down like X-rays of joy. *It's Christmas spirit?*

"But Philip and Belkin didn't understand the charms' full potential: *they had the capacity to occupy a dreamer*. Someone out there in a land far, far away—a boy or girl, man or woman—tucked into their bed, would make their nightly journey into the slumberyard of dreams. Instead of waking in the morning, they would open their eyes in, say, a teddy bear or a dragon. And these idiots had no idea!"

Viktor laughed heartily.

"That was never the intention, and no one ever understood what was going on before it was too late. But Polly, she was smart—yes, she was. She knew there was potential for the unexpected. I mean, we couldn't have toys turning into dictators. Could we, Belkin? She designed the charms with an emergency option. Let's call it an off switch. Do you know what that means?"

He put his hand to the earhole in the side of his skull.

"We wake up," Hiro said.

"Precisely!" Viktor jabbed a boney finger at the ceiling. "You wake up."

Haze looked at Hiro. She was trying to tell him something, but Hiro had built the wall to keep out thoughts. He wasn't going to let Viktor catch him off guard again.

Viktor stood over Flake, stared down like a disappointed teacher. Hands locked behind his back. He flicked his fingers like dry kindling. Flake knew what he wanted. Head bowed, eyes buried in the bush of hair, Flake put one of his hands on the table like a pupil about to take a ruler to his knuckles.

"Polly's off switch was simple. All it required was a human touch." Viktor turned Flake's hand over, palm up. Pressed the rubbery, synthetic skin with the tips of his cherry red phalange. "Madeline was like her mother. Smart. She designed the elves with a purpose."

Viktor dropped the dull marble from the bowl into Flake's hand.

"When Chase was compromised, the little elf went inside the hat, didn't he? He put his hands on her charm. Guess what happened?"

He examined their expressions, absorbing their confusion. Their difficulty to accept the facts.

"I'm not the bad guy here, children. Madeline was selfish. She put your lives as you know them in danger, more than you realize. She used you like playthings. Summoned you here for her own purposes, and when she's done with you, she'll turn you off. No goodbye, no explanation. Just thrown on the heap like a disposable toy. Sound familiar?"

He turned toward Belkin.

"I'm not an unreasonable toy. In fact, I'm likeable when you get to know me. You like me, don't you, Stretch?" The musclehead nodded, clearly unaware of the political subtleties. "I'm going to turn all of you off. Not because I'm done using you, but to wake you up. It's best you don't stay here much longer. If you're here when this Christmas arrives, this"—he poked Flake's hand—"will be more like a kill switch. Do you understand?"

Robby clearly didn't. His eye was a black bead in a bed of snow. Haze was distracted by something Hiro didn't want to investigate. However, they all knew what Viktor was saying. Maybe they didn't know why it would be a kill switch at Christmas, but Hiro did.

He's closing the roads.

Somehow, Viktor was responsible for the network of wormholes that pulsed with Christmas spirit drying up like tributaries no longer connected to their source. One by one, they were vanishing. And they weren't just for Christmas spirit. The roads were how they'd come to this world. The last road was closing tonight. And if Hiro, Haze and Robby were still there when it did, they wouldn't wake up.

She put our lives in danger.

"Why are you doing this?" Hiro said. "We just want Christmas back."

Viktor took a charm from the bowl, held it over Flake's hand. It landed in Flake's palm with a rubber thud. Hiro clenched in the seat, felt a jolt flicker through the air. There was a great clatter and a sputtering electric signal. A flat line drew across Robby's monitor. The static turned gray, then darker gray. The metal limbs fell like useless tools.

"You couldn't possibly understand."

THIS DIDN'T FEEL like a dream anymore.

Chase looked like a toy left out in the rain. But the way Robby went limp, the way his television tipped to one side, opened a panic room inside Hiro. There was no way of knowing Robby woke up in bed, whether he opened his eyes, remembered his name. Did he remember any of this? *Would he remember Christmas? Feel its absence?*

"Me next." Haze pounded the table with squirrel-sized fists. "Get me out of here."

Hiro was glad she volunteered. He didn't want to leave her alone in this weird world.

"That's the Christmas spirit," Viktor said.

He plucked Robby's charm from Flake's trembling hand. It was as gray as a bloated fish. He tossed it in the bowl with the other charms, then stirred them like a potion. He selected a charm with his red chopstick fingers, held it like an egg. Colors swirled on the surface; tiny lights glittered inside it like the soul of something living.

That's her, Hiro thought.

"I'd like to wake up before the New Year," Haze said. "So anytime now, *Viktor.*"

Viktor was savoring the tension. His skull wasn't capable of expression—only the jaw moved—but Hiro could feel a smile somewhere in the cheekbones, delight in the dark sockets. He was too consumed with his own amusement, wallowing in untouchable power, to notice the thoughts Haze was hiding. If he'd taken a peek right then, he would have known why she *wanted* to wake up. If Viktor had known, the ending to this story would be quite different.

"I hope you enjoyed your time as a toy," he said.

"I'd rather wake up without Christmas than be a toy another

second." She barfed a load of candy for the last time. "I miss my family."

"I suppose you do, Ms. Melblank."

Viktor said her name with a hint of malice. The charm slipped from his fingers in slow motion. Landed with a damp smack. Flake flinched. A dull pang of remorse cut the air. It hurt him to feel dark clouds gobble up the vibrant color, like he was a virus sucking the life out until the charm was nothing more than a lump of alloy.

Haze was looking at Hiro when her little wings slowed. Her head whumped on the table and stayed there, kept her from sliding off the chair. Hiro was glad he didn't have to hear the grainy slap of her candy-filled belly hit the floor. Her eyes, though, stared at him like simple glass beads.

Hiro felt sick. He would've barfed candy.

"Are you sure they're okay, Viktor?" Stretch could feel the sickness, too. It polluted the air like an odor.

"Of course, Stretch. They're intruders from another world pretending to be toys. They're nothing more than puppets. We're sending them home. They're not really toys like you and Belkin."

Stretch's rubbery brows clenched. "What about you, Viktor?"

"What about me?"

"You're a toy like me and Belkin?"

"Oh, I assure you, I belong here." He took the dead charm from Flake. "I'll never leave."

Belkin was stiff with restraint. This whole thing pained him for another reason—a reason Hiro couldn't discern. He blazed with anger and resentment. It fueled Viktor's joy.

"Just one more," Viktor sang. "Ready to wake up in bed, little Hiro? Go back to school, do your homework and eat your vegetables?" He marched toward Hiro, *click-clack,* and drank the gloom with a straw. "I'll bet you miss your happy family."

"I haven't seen my mother since I was little."

Perhaps he would've said something pithy, like *you'll be on the naughty list for that,* or *your nose will grow for that one.* But Viktor looked terribly serious. He glared with menace. His irritation sent static charges through the room, making them all jump. Just a little. He could only muster three words in response to what Hiro said.

He said, "That's a lie."

Hiro started to say something, but instead let his memories float to the surface. He didn't want Viktor to see them. He wanted him to feel them.

The way his mother, once upon a time, had celebrated Christmas. She didn't buy things, she invented the gifts she gave her family, cobbled them together with glue and cardboard, twisted metal: reimagined a watering can as a fountain for the backyard, spent a week building a birdhouse from things in the attic. Her cards were graphic novels, each letter cut from a magazine or old novel covers. Everything she did was saturated with her essence.

She didn't walk into a room. She danced. She spun in a circle to greet the morning. She smiled at little things, like when a bird built a nest in the wreath on the door. She laughed at his father's jokes, not because they were funny.

Her outfits weren't the day's fashion. She paired them at resale shops, wore silk scarves just because, went barefoot all summer long, doodled tattoos with markers, made her own jewelry from wire and things in the garden.

She watched movies like a child seeing a cartoon for the very first time. She cried at the sweet things, shrieked at the scary things, hugged Hiro or his dad—whoever was nearest—and hid her eyes until someone told her it was okay.

And then Christmas went away. And all those things with it.

Viktor looked petrified. The joy of sending Robby and Haze home, once saturating him like indigo dye, had putrefied into sour bile. Pleasure transmuted into a palpable mixture of resentment.

"You *have* a mother," he grinded.

Hiro looked out the window, where snow was now falling in big fluffy flakes, the Ferris wheel churning sparkling lights, seats loaded with joy-drunk toys. He was going to wake up. Sadness would greet him. Not just his mother's sadness. A world with no Christmas that would become grayer and colder with each year.

A suffocating panic closed on him. A sense of hyperventilation made him dizzy even though he knew he wasn't breathing. *Heroes are scared, too.*

"Time to go home, little boy," Viktor said.

He spun on heel bones, marched with heavy clicks for the bowl. No singing or dancing this time, no celebrating this last execution. He couldn't wait to banish Hiro to a world without Christmas. His attention laser-beamed on getting rid of this insolent teddy bear who spoiled his big night. He wasn't thinking of anything else.

With his back turned, Hiro began to visualize something.

Viktor was reaching for the last living marble. Hiro felt his fingertips touch it, felt them like cold sticks. Viktor dropped the charm back in the bowl, stood up like a deer hearing a twig snap in the woods. He took a few steps down the table, looking out the window.

Belkin turned. He saw it, too.

"There's my girl." Viktor's smile—a joyous smile with a cruel bent —filled the room.

He stood at the end of the table like an Olympic diver, watching a purple monkey desperately scaling the house on the earthen pedestal. Viktor's impatience rubbed the atmosphere drily.

"Fetch her," he growled.

His soldiers cut through the crowd like shark fins. Lookies enclosed the house like the eye of a hurricane. The purple monkey looked around and reevaluated the situation, then scampered across the wall and over the edge, escaping down the earthen pillar to blend into the crowd. The lookies lost sight of her in a mob of pastel-colored puff balls.

Viktor's impatience hardened into an iceberg sinking under its own weight. When he turned around, there were three dead charms in the bowl. The fourth charm was already in Flake's hand. It was as dull and lifeless as a roofing nail.

The teddy bear was facedown on the floor.

33

I guess the teddy really wanted to go home.

His charm was in the elf's hand, as dead as the others. *They weren't dead.* Not dead-dead, in the human sense. Dead to this world they were, though.

It was the octopus who sent him home. I was too distracted to see him do it, but all it took was a quick skim of his thoughts to see what had happened. As I peeked into his thoughts, he shrugged his tentacles, muffling through the gag. *It's what you wanted, right?* he thought.

Right.

When I was watching Madeline skip around the gala, he had reached into the bowl and fussed about, had trouble picking up the charm. Almost knocked the bowl over. Then he dropped it into the elf's hand. The elf looked impossibly sad—which was bringing the energy in the room down—when Hiro Tanaka fell off his chair. He bounced around, an empty toy.

This night couldn't get any crazier, and the bar was already up there.

I had always assumed I wasn't the only one who dreamed their way here. Statistically speaking, there had to be some people from my world who went to sleep one night only to temporarily wake up a toy.

I thought I'd meet someone from my home world one day. *But my students?!*

I'd infected them. That was the only explanation. I'd somehow infected them with the idea, plain and simple.

Hiro had doodled the planet in class. I suspected he'd dreamed about this world, but he looked so clueless after class, like it was only a glimpse. Even if he found his way here, there was no way I would see him, not with several billion people and just as many toys. So I was wrong, he was here. But what are the odds he'd be sitting *in my room on the most important night of my life?!*

None to impossible was what they were.

He wasn't here anymore. Their little gambit failed, but I couldn't stop dwelling on it. My brain was in solution mode, that obsessive gear I couldn't get out of when something was unsolvable. It wasn't how they got here (*same way I did*) or when they got here. It was the *why* that possessed me. Not why were they on my planet (yes, *my* planet), but why were they at the gala? They were trying to stop me, it seemed. How long had they known about my nightly sojourns?

But then I saw Madeline in her monkey suit. It all made sense.

She recruited them.

That was the only explanation. How she did it, there wasn't time for that. Besides, once the roads were closed, it wouldn't matter.

The bigger question, and dumbest question, I obsessed over: *Why them?* Hiro, I sort of got. He was bright and creative. His mother was an art teacher. She was into dreaming and fairy tales, all things that would send a kid here. I could accept that. I guess. But Hazel and Robby? They were C students at their best. Why them?

Focus.

They were home, where they belonged. I could close the draw-bridge that connected our worlds without a grain of regret. They didn't get hurt and wouldn't believe any of this in a few days. Even when I didn't return, this would just be a fading dream. *Just like Christmas.*

I released the gag from the octopus. I needed to hear him say something, get out of my own head.

"Hey, I thought you'd be happy. The boy wanted to go home. You were just playing with him—not in the good way—so I dropped his charm. He told me to. What'd you have against him anyway?"

I grabbed the lifeless charm from the elf's hand before he collapsed into depression. I didn't have anything against Hiro. He was just a student. A good one, actually. Followed the rules, kept quiet. My kind of student. But this was my world. He had no business here.

The octopus was right, though. I had been toying with them.

Why all the theatrics, marching up and down the table, not skimming their thoughts? Why didn't I just send them home as soon as I knew who they were? I knew the answer. That's the thing with being omnipotent. I knew everything about everyone. Including myself. I couldn't ignore the truths I hid from myself. Even the embarrassing ones.

It was this: *I wasn't that stiff teacher nobody liked.* I wanted them to see it. I wanted them to see I wasn't a failed physicist reduced to teaching high school. I wanted them to see me now. Plain and simple.

Sad.

"Question," Ocho said. "Why are you taking Christmas away from them? That's what you're doing, right? That's a very anti-toy thing to do. I mean, if you're going to—*mmmff.*"

Enough talking. Midnight was an hour away. *Focus.*

But look at the bright side. If I hadn't caught them sneaking around the gala, they never would have been sent home. The roads would've closed, and they'd be stuck here. Forever. I didn't want that. Just think of their parents. Taking Christmas away from them was one thing. Had they never left here, the guilt would've been unbearable.

So, in a way, I'm the good guy here.

I dropped Hiro's dead charm in the bowl. *The good guy.*

MADELINE WAS on the run again.

"Enough games!" I went to the window, stood far away from Belkin. I didn't need his gloom piling on. There was already plenty.

She was spotted near the ice luge: a nifty ride the toys lined up for, sliding through loopty-loops and corkscrews. An all-time favorite. I'd spent a lot of time designing that one. And now the soldiers were running between the ice tubes like clumsy puppets. I needed to rethink my security team. They looked intimidating and official. What I needed was agile and effective. *Like a monkey!*

"She's running you in circles," Belkin said.

At least his spirits were rising. The room could use a little sunshine. Even if it was laced with sarcasm. Flake was a rainy day that never ended.

"You know, I was thinking of putting a fireplace in here." I pointed to Belkin's arms and legs. "We'll need kindling."

"That's not nice, Viktor," Stretch said.

"You're right, Stretch," I said. "Apologies."

Adding to the list of annoyances was that I couldn't *feel* Madeline out there. I sensed her presence, but I couldn't lock onto it. Once I did that, I could force her to march up to the room. No need for this game of hide-and-seek, which my bumbling security was losing. Did she come up with a new charm that eluded me? Her mother was talented, so it could be. If Madeline had some stealth charm in production, that would really put a crimp in my game.

Another lookie alert.

She escaped my stiff minions and made it to the twirl and whirl honey pots. The soldiers spun on their heels and knifed toward the spinning ride. They marched at full speed, stepping on anything in their way. Toys staggered in their wake, wobbling on the floor.

The monkey raced over upraised hands and flippers, avoiding the soldiers as if they were infants learning to walk. She bounced off a happy trampoline and vanished into a vat of balls. The soldiers climbed in and waded after her, stomping through a pack of baby dolls swimming in the ball pit.

"You're hurting toys," Belkin said.

"I'm not hurting them! If she would stop this, everyone can go back to having a good time. They're here to sing and dance, play games and... play games, that's it."

Freckles was oblivious to the chase, as was everyone else down there. He was bellowing a song from the top of the house, and the crowd joined him in glee. *Here comes Santa Claus...*

Freckles stopped crooning, quite suddenly, put his hand on his chest. Hearing my thoughts. The song continued with the crowd.

"A new game!" he crowed. "A new game you'll quite enjoy. Everyone, listen carefully. Somewhere in the arena is a scurrilous little chimp who doesn't want to be found. She is the hider, and you are the seekers. The first one to catch her receives a grand prize coveted by every toy in the valley. The winner will have their very own, brand-new *gingerbread mansion!* It features three floors, a solarium, an observatory deck, chocolate slides and peppermint poles. It's located on the tallest peak of Sugar Mountain in Winter Wonderland. If you just—"

I cut him short. Enough with the buildup. They were already looking.

"Find the monkey!" he shouted.

Work smarter, my father always told me. And constantly. Like all the time, waving his finger in the air. *Smarter! Smarter!* What would he think now, huh? Who am I kidding?

My soldiers went to the house and positioned their stiff-suited bodies around the base of the pedestal. I wasn't worried; there was nothing she could do. But if she ended up in the bubble with that tiny elf, I'd be depressed, and there was enough of that already.

"Work smarter," I told Belkin. He didn't like anything I said.

The crowd moved in random circles like bees tending honeycomb. Madeline wouldn't last with a mob ravenous to win their very own gingerbread house. Which didn't exist.

The crowd began to organize, swarming toward the sky pole drop. The pole, as stout and tall as a redwood, was a replica of a mast from an ancient ship. The horizontal booms, without sails, were rigged with rope netting. A bucket was on the masthead, where a climber could look across the arena.

The purple monkey scaled it with ease.

She didn't need a safety harness, climbing with the instincts of a gibbon. A flaw in my plan came into sharp focus when the crowd flooded the entry gate. Instead of a handful of toys working their way toward the top, they climbed by the hundreds. It looked like a zombie apocalypse.

There was probably a weight limit.

One of the beams snapped in half and swung like a timber pendulum. Ropes kept it from slicing through the mob below. One of the nets came loose; toys dangled like flies in a spiderweb. The monkey reached the bucket when the pole began to lean. I could hear wooden fibers splinter.

I calculated the height in relation to the house. It would land short. But a lot of damage would be done; that would put a damper on the night. Toys would be hurt. A lot of them. I'd never hear the end of it.

Down, I thought. *Down, down.*

Many of the toys listened to my command and climbed off the mast. But not all of them. The hysteria had whipped their minds into a frenzy that thwarted my control. Enough of them heeded the call to keep the pole upright.

Madeline had nowhere to go. I thought.

She leaped like a flying squirrel. It looked like a desperate attempt that would land her in some lucky so-called winner's grip. She caught a rope, then another and swung in a sweeping arch, releasing at its apex.

She landed on the barrel bomb.

The whiskey barrel was the size of a building, positioned on its side by twelve-inch axles. It was more like a tumbler for a titan game of Bingo. Madeline opened the hatch and crawled inside, where toys would run like mice on a hamster wheel. It was pointless fun that toys seemed to enjoy. I didn't get it, but they did.

"That should do it." Glee was back in my corner.

The crowd swarmed the barrel bomb. The hatch swung open, circling around but not stopping. It churned out of reach. That didn't stop the pursuit. Rubbery snakes slithered up the support beams. Plastic superheroes climbed after them. As the hatch came around, spring bunnies and pencil flamingoes launched themselves at it. The rest climbed up like starving hounds with a scent. A mountain of toys pressed against the barrel. They poured into the opening like honeybees following the queen. The barrel spun faster.

It began to wobble.

Stop!

The crowd jerked in response to my thought, but the momentum continued. Their minds too chaotic to grip. Like a snowflake in a storm.

The first bracket shattered with a bolt-shearing *kuchunk*. One end of the barrel thudded off the axle. The crowd roared. Actually, they cheered when the barrel started grinding sparks. Toys were pulled through it like a woodchipper. It gained traction and snapped off the other axle.

The barrel was set free.

The crowd parted. A path opened in front of the rogue carnival ride that was aimed at the house.

"Stop it!" I shouted. "Stop that barrel!"

The soldiers threw themselves into the steamroller. Their bodies splintered and snapped under its weight. Tattered uniforms and flattened hats spit out the other side. With each speedbump, the behemoth slowed. *Crunch. Boom. Kaplunk.* I fed the runaway cylinder twenty soldiers. When it slowed, the toys began pushing against it. Little by little, it stopped. But not before bouncing off the pedestal.

The house tremored. Snow fell from the eaves.

Oh my, I thought. *I know what she's doing.*

She was using all these beautiful rides as weapons to knock the house down. The pedestal looked like soil, but it was reinforced with internal beams. Even if the house was taken down, I had redesigned it. Beneath those wooden slats was a welded roll cage.

She's like her mother. But it's going to take more than a whiskey barrel.

And she's stuck inside it with thousands of greedy toys looking for a handful of purple fur.

The crowd began to shift its attention. They stopped mounting the barrel and began sweeping in the other direction.

"Ferris wheel!" they chanted. "Ferris wheel! Ferris wheel!"

What in the wide, wide world of winterland is happening?

The big wheel was slowly turning with toys who weren't able to get off the ride watching a purple monkey climbing through the spokes. They jumped out of their seats and slid down cables. The mob on the ground latched onto the outer structure and let it carry them up. Madeline had reached the center pivot and continued upward, leaping sideward to maintain a vertical ascent.

I found Freckles's mind in the fog, told him to call off the game. *Tell them there is no house! There is no house! There's nothing, they win nothing! Get them to STOP!*

His shouts were drowned out in the frenzy.

How did I not see this? I just wanted a party to celebrate my final countdown. I could've just sat up here with my depressed company and counted down the minutes in droll misery. Now I watched these wild playthings climb on top of each other like wolves.

The Ferris wheel spun faster under the weight of clinging toys. Madeline had reached the top, running along the rim to stay in place. No one could keep up with the dexterity required to reach her. I felt her looking at me as she ran in place, long purple tail swinging. That empty monkey that had lain in her bedroom all that time when I would wake up on the shelf was empty no more.

The Ferris wheel moaned like a ship listing in a storm. Cables snapped like gunshots. A shower of sparks fell from the axle. It wobbled as the bearings fell apart.

Scritchhh—KUNK.

It carved tracks into the floor. The titanic wheel began rolling with a purple monkey on top of it. The toys had forgotten about the fake prize, delighting in the world's greatest circus act. It was grinding its way toward the center of the arena, digging deeper into the floor.

The wobble, however, turned it off course. It wheeled farther and farther away from the house, slowing in the grooves it cut into the floor.

It came to a stop far away from the chocolate-sided house and the grandest prize inside it. Madeline stood on top, a failed coup below her. We stared at each other over a long distance. I couldn't understand why I couldn't grip her mind. It should have been so easy. A smile germinated in my jawbone. A valiant attempt, it was time to put this madness to bed.

The rogue Ferris wheel moaned again.

It began leaning. Slowly, at first. This colossal round domino started its descent. Toys in its shadow scattered. Spokes shattered; cables popped away from the rim. In slow motion, it came crashing down. The buckets swinging at the top exploded into the side of the pedestal. The rim of the wheel buckled against it. Soil powdered from the side of it; shards of flooring geysered in a plume. The pedestal leaned to the side. It held in place.

But the house began to slide.

The foundation had come loose. Panels fell off the walls. Bricks from the chimney fell like broken teeth. It rolled off its place of high honor, hit the floor like a cube of die thrown across a gameboard. The house shed its façade like snakeskin—broken shutters, shattered doors, shingles, boards, bricks and even the mailbox. The house that Madeline grew up in splattered on the floor like New Year's Day.

All that was left was the skeletal frame.

The walls were gone, the rooms and beds, the kitchen. The fireplace. A cable remained tethered to a structure that held the needle piercing the glowing blue ball. The red-suited jolly fat man inside. Above him, where the roof used to be, a watery outline of a sleigh with animals tethered to the front of it.

A hush fell over the crowd, followed by a roar.

"Well," Stretch said, "I didn't see that coming."

❄

She failed.

That was the important point here. I'd reinforced the house. Santa wasn't coming out. All the critical equipment had been relocated, the extraction needle still intact. The switch to turn off the bubble was in a place she could never reach, and only I had access to that. And she failed. She failed. Failed. Failed. Failed.

"Out!" I shouted. "Everyone out!"

Stretch started to move.

"Not you. No one in this room moves. The party's over. I want everyone out of the arena!"

I doubled down my focus, moved my remaining soldiers into action. Doors around the arena slid open. Every light beamed on high, flooding the floor. Toys hid their eyes. I hit them with one single thought that would be obeyed. *OUT! NOW!*

"I'm cleaning this place up," I muttered.

"Do you need help, Viktor?" Stretch looked at the crumpled Ferris wheel. "It looks heavy."

"No, I don't need help, Stretch! This is not over. She hasn't won anything." I turned to Belkin. "Neither have you."

"You're the only one trying to win," Belkin said. "They're trying to save Christmas."

"For the last time, Christmas doesn't need to be saved! It's here, right here. We have it." I leaped up and down, chopping at the frozen Santa Claus and his reindeer and one miniature elf. "I'm giving the spirit of Christmas to the toys, making this world a better place, saving toys, blah, blah, blah. Why is everyone fighting me on this? What more do you want?"

"Not this," Belkin said.

I could smell his self-righteousness. "You think I'm the bad guy here?"

"You're not the hero."

The partygoers moved to the exits. I kicked their thoughts to make them go faster. Trucks hauled them out in clusters; soldiers goaded them away from distractions.

"There's still time." And that was my biggest problem. *Is midnight ever going to get here?* "If things are going to get done right, I'll do them myself."

Stretch said, "Do you need help?"

"No!"

I didn't need help. I never had help before.

34

Shloop. That was the elevator.

Hiro pretended to hold his breath. He wasn't breathing. He was a toy. He wasn't even a toy. He was a marble. *A charm.* But then, right then, he wasn't sure what he was. He didn't want to think about it. He was focusing on not thinking at all.

I'm not supposed to be here.

A lot of things went right. For one, Viktor didn't look closely at the teddy bear on the floor. Or the marble in the dish. If he had, he would have noticed it wasn't Hiro's charm Flake was holding.

The elevator didn't open again. Hiro's nose was against the floor. He couldn't feel Viktor in the room. Still, he waited before slowly getting up. Being soft and cuddly meant he moved in near silence. Robby and Haze were slumped in their chairs. Chase was on the table.

Ocho had his eye on him.

Hiro didn't know the octopus was capable of sitting that still. Hiro whispered a thought. *Thank you.*

Ocho nodded.

Flake dumped the marbles in the bowl. There were three plain ones. One, however, had regained life. It always had life. Hiro had just projected a dead image over it for Viktor to see. If he had examined it... but he didn't.

Belkin and Stretch were side by side, watching whatever was beyond the window.

It had felt like an earthquake had demolished the arena. It was quiet now. Hiro gestured to Ocho and Flake to join them at the window. Hiro quietly ran along the table, hiding next to Stretch's toy repair kit on the far end of the couch. He looked out the window.

It was worse than he thought.

The rides were in pieces. The Ferris wheel leaned on the pedestal like a wheel of a bike missing spokes and a tire. Patches of grass and clods of dirt were all that were left on the pedestal. The house was no longer a house. Pieces of wood and bricks and shingles were strewn next to a boxy frame. Inside was a bluish watery bubble.

"Let me take care of that for you."

Hiro heard Stretch's rubbery footsteps and deftly moved behind the couch. Stretch grabbed something from his kit, humming as he did, and went back to Ocho.

"Better?" Stretch said.

"A million times," Ocho said. "Some party, huh?"

"They played a game."

"Like running with the bulls?"

"No, it was called Find the Monkey. Was that what he called it, Belkin? They had to catch a monkey. She was fast. Ran to the top of the pole ride, then over to the barrel and then all the way to the top of the Ferris wheel. I don't think it went like Viktor hoped. A lot of toys were hurt."

Most of the toys were gone. The others were being herded to the exits by lines of soldiers. Besides pieces and parts dislodged from the rides, broken toys hopped in circles or crawled in crooked lines. They were being scooped into the back of yellow plastic trucks.

"Did they catch her?" Ocho asked.

"I don't think so. Did they, Belkin?"

There was a long pause. "They did not."

A small caped figure walked among the wreckage. The red gleam of

Viktor's skull appeared when the hood was thrown back. Freckles was on the ground now, helping soldiers load damaged toys into a truck. Viktor waved at the soldiers, sleeves falling back on red bones, pointing at the big barrel sitting askew on what looked like a pile of soldiers.

Toys were spilling out the barrel's hatch like they'd been packed like sardines. Soldiers helped them down, pointed toward the nearest exit. If a purple monkey came out, they were ready.

The game wasn't over.

"Viktor seems angry," Stretch said. "I've never seen him like this."

"I don't think the party went as planned," Ocho said. "I'm just guessing."

Viktor looked redder than a cherry bomb, waving his arms like an overcaffeinated conductor.

Soldiers ran in circles, which only turned him a deeper red. He sent them to the remains of the house. They set up a perimeter around the debris.

"Whoa," Ocho said. "Is that—"

"Santa Claus," Stretch said. "Viktor caught him a long time ago. Santa Claus travels inside a time bubble on Christmas. That's how he gets to all the girls and boys in one night. He gets to the next world through roads. Victor put Santa's bubble in a bubble. A double bubble. And Santa doesn't know it. See that?"

Hiro knew Stretch was pointing to the faint band of color attached to the bubble, swaying in an ethereal current. It looked like a heat wave losing temperature. In its last hour of breath.

A cadre of soldiers positioned themselves at the steel frame. They attempted to tip the entire thing up. Viktor pulled more from jobs of helping floundering toys until there were enough of the red-coated soldiers to heave it over. It teetered back and forth.

"Are those... *reindeer*?" Ocho said.

The bubble extended above what would have been the roof. That was what was in that fenced box on top of the roof. There were several blurry lumps in rows of two. And a big red cube. *Is that a sleigh?*

"Viktor caught them, too. That's why we're here, so we wouldn't stop him. He's closing the last road tonight. That's why the kids had to wake up."

"I don't get it," Ocho said.

"Their dreams brought them here through the roads. They're at home asleep. But if there's no roads, they wouldn't wake up. That's why Viktor sent them home."

"Hold on, back up. Brought them from where?"

"They're not really toys. They're from somewhere else."

"Somewhere else where?"

Stretch's rubbery shoulder squeaked when he shrugged. Belkin grunted.

"Okay. All right." Ocho moaned. "So what you're saying is that if one of them stayed, that would be *baaaad*."

"It would be terrible," Stretch said. "They'd never go home. Their parents would miss them. Right, Belkin?"

"And if someone helped them stay here, that would be bad," Ocho said.

There was a long beat of silence. It began to feel uncomfortable. Hiro didn't know what they were doing. He held very still. Clopping footsteps grew louder. Hiro moved to the back of the couch.

"Stay where you are." Belkin towered over him. "Everyone, come closer."

Stretch, Ocho and Flake joined the full-size puppet and surrounded Hiro. Stretch simultaneously looked happy and sad to see him. The conflicted expression occupied opposite sides of his face.

"*Ahhh!* What's he doing here?" Ocho said.

Pause. "We can see your thoughts, Ocho," Stretch said.

"Viktor can, too," Belkin said. "Come closer."

Hiro felt a calm quietness fall over him, a cloak weaved with protective thoughts. Belkin was expanding his mind to mask Hiro's presence should Viktor look at the room.

"Look, he asked me to do it," Ocho said. "He just said grab one of the dead charms, fumble around with it, and put it in the elf's hand. I didn't know he was going to stay."

"Is that what you said, Hiro?" Stretch said.

Hiro nodded. It wasn't exactly what he said. It was exactly what he meant. He'd phrased his thoughts vaguely enough that Viktor wouldn't notice if he looked at Ocho's thoughts. Which he did. Hiro had imagined a dull marble to mask his charm that was still in the bowl, made one of the already dull charms look alive, then fell on the floor when Ocho dropped it in Flake's hand.

"You can do that?" Stretch must have seen Hiro's thoughts. Good thing Belkin was hiding them. "Like be somewhere else? Have you heard of that, Belkin?"

The puppet didn't answer, but Hiro could feel his surprise. Belkin urged everyone to be still. They looked out the window. Hiro peeked between their legs. The toys had been completely evacuated. The soldiers were searching the rubble.

"I heard about your mom," Stretch said. "I'm sad she feels that way. I'm sad Viktor feels that way, too."

"What, happy?" Ocho said.

"Viktor isn't happy."

The little red skeleton's shouting could be heard all the way up there. Hiro could feel his anger like sparks on his fur.

Belkin looked down at Flake. "Send him back."

"I want to stay," Hiro said. "I can help."

"It was very brave, what you did," Belkin said.

"Very brave," Stretch added.

"We appreciate everything you've done," Belkin said, "but you need to go home before it's too late."

Flake shuffled his sandpaper soles on the floor and started for the table to fetch Hiro's charm. One touch and Hiro would open in his eyes in bed. That was the best-case scenario. Hiro looked at the big clock above the arena.

"The last road doesn't close for thirty minutes."

Flake moved slower. He could feel Hiro's heartfelt request. There was more at risk than Hiro getting stuck here and Christmas being lost forever. *Snow is inside the bubble.* Belkin sensed the elf's hesitancy and sent Stretch to fetch the charm.

"You're beautiful, Hiro." Stretch returned with the charm, admiring the depth of iridescence.

"Please," Hiro said. "I can't go back yet. This means more than Christmas."

"There's nothing more you can do," Belkin said.

Viktor was shouting Madeline's name, taunting her. Below the shards of his anger was a slimy layer of fear. He tried to stop her, and nothing worked. Now he was left with wreckage while his soldiers guarded the final fading road.

"So that's the plan?" Ocho said. "Just watch?"

"Viktor's pretty strong," Stretch said. "You wouldn't guess it because he's all bones, but he doesn't need muscle. If we went out there, he'd freeze our minds and make us look for Madeline. It doesn't feel good when he does that."

Flake heeded Stretch's warning, kept his thoughts under wraps. Instead, he pointed and grunted. The sounds were like a dog half-barking. But they had the vague semblance of a word.

"That's right," Stretch said. "Santa Claus is in there. He'd know what to do."

"I think he means his little buddy," Ocho said. "The one who lives in his hat."

"Oh, sorry. Viktor was right, though. Snow is safe. He's just caught in time. He'll come out one of these days. You know, if Viktor ever stops."

Stretch sort of faded off with what he was saying. Viktor was never going to let them out. if he did, the roads would reopen, and all would be lost. Snow might be safe, but he would be in there a really, really long time.

"This might sound obvious," Ocho said, "but has anyone thought of turning the bubble off?" He gestured to the looming walls of machinery behind them. "Let's just start pushing buttons. One of them has to work."

"It won't." Stretch sighed. "Viktor integrated that switch into his charm."

"Have you tried?"

"The charm is in Viktor's skull."

"Are you sure?"

Belkin, Stretch and Flake looked at him flatly. Even Stretch didn't answer. Viktor had godlike powers of the mind. He would sense them coming for him, freeze their thoughts and send them packing. Besides, how were they going to dig it out of his skull?

"So we just watch," Ocho resigned.

"Or play a game," Stretch said.

"I'd rather watch."

Belkin occasionally glanced at the clock. He wasn't going to let Hiro stay much longer. Hiro thought he could sneak behind Viktor by projecting down there. Problem with that was he couldn't touch anything when he was projecting. Even if he could, how was he going to get the charm out of his skull?

He could look for Mads. But hadn't her plan already failed? She had been able to destroy the house, but the bubble was still intact, and now it was guarded by a wall of soldiers with Viktor patrolling the outside. Even if she could rappel from the sky, she would just fall inside the bubble.

There was a third option.

THE SOLDIERS WERE shoulder to shoulder. Their uniforms filthy from clearing debris. The greasy air choking with suspended particles of construction dust. Square mouths locked tight, severe eyes on alert.

No one noticed a soldier appearing out of dusty air.

Hiro was leaning against Belkin's leg, peeking over the edge of the window, just out of Viktor's sight, with an angle on the remains of the house. He imagined a crisply starched red jacket, knee-high black boots and a tall black hat. Now he was staring into the blue bubble. Energy pulsed electromagnetic waves, pushing and pulling like ocean waves lapping the beach.

Viktor was shouting behind him, taunting Mads to show herself, as toy trucks hauled broken toys away. Big plastic wheels crunched over broken parts and pieces.

Santa Claus wavered through the bubble's barrier, a figure trapped in an aquarium. Somehow the house was still intact inside the bubble: a lovely family Christmas forever preserved in the timeless moment.

The bubble extended to the shingled roof, where reindeer were tethered to a red sleigh spattered with gray snow. The reindeer in front was massive compared to the others, his head thrown back as if suspecting something. A second too late.

Hiro recalled what Corker had taught them about black holes.

Gravity and acceleration slowed time. If a spaceship could travel near the speed of light, the travelers inside the spaceship wouldn't age compared to their loved ones they left behind. They could circle the galaxy and return to a planet where everyone they knew would have already lived their entire lives. Generations would have passed. The same effect would occur if they approached the gravity of a black hole.

Is that what this is?

Snow was inside the bubble, hand up as if he just wanted to feel the membrane. Hiro could feel the energy inviting him to step inside. If he accepted, he might never come out. He might never see his family again. They would all be gone, having lived their lives without him. If he didn't go inside, his mother would live in a gray world that only grew grayer. Joy gone forever.

Heroes are scared, too.

His father had never mentioned the hardest part. It wasn't that it could be embarrassing, like wetting himself in fear, or it hurt so much he would cry. The hardest part was that he had to make a decision. There wasn't an obvious answer. It wasn't a yes or no question. He had no idea what to do.

No matter what he decided, someone was going to get hurt.

Hiro felt light-headed, shaky in the knees. This was only his projection next to the bubble. It might not even affect it. But if it did…

He pretended to take a deep breath and didn't think anymore. He didn't want to be a hero. He just wanted Christmas back. He leaned into the gravity of the blue bubble, felt it pull at his awareness. He was inches from touching it when he heard a voice.

Christmas lights burn so bright.

It seemed like a random thought, perhaps a toy rambling in song as the Sammy Scoopers scooped them into the trucks to haul away. It was nothing anyone would notice. If Viktor heard it, he would think nothing of it. But Hiro had heard someone say it once before.

And remembered who said it.

35

She'd played me like a chess expert.

She did this, and I did that. This move, that move, and the next thing you know, the house is in pieces. It was clever. She'd been planning this for years. Too bad it didn't work.

I'm a grand master.

I'd prepared for everything. I'll be honest, I didn't see the Ferris wheel move. But the house was indestructible. And the switch to turn off the bubble wasn't in there. After the little elf went looking for it, I was certain she was outplayed. Perhaps not certain, but pretty sure.

I sent the soldiers to the bubble. They lined up like good soldiers, forming a tight wall around the most valuable thing in the universe. The bubble didn't need their protection. Santa wasn't going to escape. I wanted to put on a show.

If Madeline was going to make another run, I wanted her to think it was the bubble she needed to attack. And really, truly, I did not want her falling into it like the little elf. I was hoping that, at some point in the distant future, we could talk. She would understand why I did what I did. It would take some time, sure. But I knew how to control time.

A convoy of Daryl Dump Trucks rumbled past me. Their real rubber tires with independent suspension cruised over cables and struts strewn in the wreckage. They stopped for loading. I picked a plastic eye off the ground. It was cracked, but the black disk still rolled around. Ricky Robots tossed toys into the back that couldn't walk or dance or roll out of here. I'd send them to the nearest warehouse for repairs.

This was a tragic waste of a good time.

I searched for Madeline's mind, trying to lure her out with memories. I dusted off some goodies from when she was young: Lying on her bed and watching videos on her laptop while I sat on the shelf. Finding the last piece to the puzzle and all of us holding it as we snapped it in place. And the snow angels we made in the front yard, the snowmen in the back. The snowball fights with the neighbor kids and the parents joining in. Afterwards sitting at the kitchen table with hot chocolate. Madeline sipping it. I put my fingers in it.

"Are you happy?" I shouted. "You know, those toys were lucky winners. They were having the time of their lives." I tossed the googly eye into a truck. "I built this—all of this—for them."

Something cracked. I was standing on a Jilly Jammer lollipop. It was one of those multicolored wheels on a stick Jilly Jammer carried in one hand like a magic wand. It would light up when the switch on her back was turned on. I picked it up. Jilly was probably in one of the trucks.

"You didn't have to do this," I said.

"You weren't going to stop."

I whirled like a Terrible Tommy Top. The lollipop flew from my hand and landed at her feet. There she was in a worn-out coat and awful leather boots. Dark hair with hints of gray cropped at hunched shoulders, she cast a wrinkled and sorrowful look my way. Like it hurt to see me.

Was it because I hadn't changed, not one single bit, since I slept on her shelf? I looked better, to be frank. Shined and oiled, not one squeak from a single joint in the last ten years.

I couldn't say the same for Madeline.

She wasn't twenty feet away, and I still couldn't feel her mind. She felt empty, like she wasn't there. I didn't like that. If she was smart, she would've taught everyone else how to be invisible to me, and we wouldn't be standing in a graveyard of carnival rides. Not exactly how I'd want it to end, but this invisibility trick was stellar.

A purple tail snaked around her neck. The goofy monkey face peeked over her shoulder. And here I thought she'd switched into it. Apparently, she woke the monkey up. *Didn't see that move, either.*

"I see you still have a pet," I said. Monkeybrain stared with the permanent grin I'd seen every time I woke up on the shelf. "Why can't I see your thoughts?"

"Years of hiding and meditation. Becoming nothingness so you see nothingness." She buried her hands in her pockets. "I learned from the best."

I didn't like not seeing her hands. "How are Polly and Philip these days? I didn't keep up after them, as you know. I did look after the house until, uh... you know." I gestured to the remains of her childhood home. Which she had destroyed.

"They passed away."

"I'm sorry to hear that."

I was sorry. It was just I already knew they'd passed away. Natural causes. I'd kept track of them. Madeline, though, had disappeared at some point. Changed her name, learned to meditate, hid her mind and planned my ultimate destruction. Still, I was sorry.

"No, you're not. They adopted you, opened their home. Made you family. They knew you were different, that somehow you didn't belong here. You broke their hearts, Viktor. The guilt was too much."

At that very moment, I was thrilled not to feel her thoughts. The weight would've crushed me. If she was smart, she would open the floodgates and drown me in shame.

"I never meant to hurt them," I said. "Or you."

"It's not too late." She waved at the soldiers and the blue bubble they protected. "You can return everything."

She snapped her fingers. It didn't make a sound. I thought maybe she never learned to snap.

"You know I can't."

"You can, Viktor. The spirit isn't ours. Look what it's doing to the toys."

"It gave Monkeybrain life. So, you're welcome."

The purple monkey didn't thank me. If I hadn't released an abundance of Christmas spirit, Monkeybrain would still be an empty puppet in the corner of a room. *Why didn't she call it verve?*

"Christmas spirit only works when it gives," she went on.

"It's working just fine." *Depends who you ask.*

"It can't be bottled like magic potion. When the last road closes, you don't know what will happen."

"Well, (A) that's exactly what I've done for the last thirty years. And (B) I'm not going back! Don't you get it? That's what this is all about. It's always been about staying here. You know where I go when I sleep. Your mother knew, too. You don't know what it's like back there. I'm not like this. I'm just... I'm not." I dropped my voice to a grinding whisper. "I'm staying here. I deserve it."

"You can always come back."

"You're not listening. I don't want to go back! Ever! This is who I am, right here, right now. I'm a toy. I've always been a toy. I'm not..." I waved my arms. "Back there, *home,* that's not who I am."

I was getting emotional, which meant one thing: she was hitting a deep pocket of truth. I was gushing, and she hadn't moved. Her hands still in her pockets.

"You're hurting so many," she said.

"You know, I think I'm good with this conversation. I get it, people at home are sad without Christmas and blah, blah. Guess what? I was sad my entire life, and no one came riding up to my door to save me. I promised to make this a better world for toys, and that's exactly what I'm doing, just like your parents wanted. I'm doing it, me."

I whacked my sternum. Vertebrae rattled.

"You'll never be a real toy." That cut deep. Why didn't I just keep my mouth shut? "You are you, Viktor. That's who we loved."

I planted my hands on my pelvis because I didn't know what else to do. She meant that. I didn't have to see her thoughts. It was a bullseye. But a little too late. Maybe if there was more time, we could rebuild the house, and I could sleep on the shelf. I could rebuild the village. No one would know what I'd done. And those who did would understand.

Belkin and Stretch were looking down at me from the window. That orange octopus, too. They would forgive me if I made things right. Probably not Belkin, but the others would. I did it for the toys. It was always for the toys. And for me, but the toys, too. If she would've said those things earlier, I might have changed my mind.

But probably not.

Loose bolts danced between my feet. The ground began to tremble. Black boots circled us like a snake trapping its prey. The soldiers locked arms. I had them do that: abandon the bubble and form a wall around us. Monkeybrain hid behind her back. There was nowhere to run now.

"I'm sorry," I said. "You'll be safe, Madeline."

Monkeybrain felt the trap close around them. The little monkey couldn't hide all night. I'd put them in the room with Belkin, let them watch me ring in Christmas morning and the closing of the last road.

But then Monkeybrain was quicker than a real monkey. She bolted from behind Madeline and, before I could blink, was through the legs of one of my soldiers. They were solid and dependable and as slow as midnight snow.

"That's all right." I stopped them from another fruitless pursuit. "She can't do anything now."

The purple furball perched on the crooked rim of the Ferris wheel like a fuzzy gargoyle. She could tear the place apart, drive wrecking balls through the arena walls, light the soldiers' dumb hats on fire. I didn't care. After midnight, I was locking the bubble in a vault and retiring the train. No more parties. No more people, no more toys. This place would become a museum for no one to see. And I would live happily ever after. The end.

Then the second monkey appeared.

❄

Purple and jumpy like the other one.

She popped up from behind Madeline's back. I didn't know how she was doing it. She wasn't wearing a backpack. Maybe they were stuffed down the back of her sweatshirt. The second one avoided the soldiers' clumsy attempts to grab her and zigzagged to the broken barrel ride.

"Are you finished?" I said.

She wasn't.

A third one dropped on the ground. Okay. Maybe two monkeys were stuffed in that sweatshirt. Not three. No sooner had the third one scampered over a soldier's tall hat than a fourth one stood on Madeline's head. A fifth one leaped clean over the soldiers and rolled away. I stopped counting after that. They dispersed like a toy dispenser was strapped to her backside.

They felt invisible. Just like Madeline.

The place was overrun with grape apes, and I couldn't sense a single one of them any more than the girl—now a woman—I knew thirty years ago. They didn't appear to be after anything. They swung about like monkeys on a liquid diet of espresso. They ignored the bubble.

I approached Madeline. I should have done it earlier, but what would that have changed? I didn't suspect what I soon discovered. She didn't flinch when I reached for the hem of her sweatshirt. I wanted to see what was behind her. I discovered, in that instant, why I couldn't feel her presence, couldn't pick her thoughts. She wasn't there.

My hand passed through her. "How are you—"

Mount Monkeybrain erupted from somewhere behind her. Hundreds of them. Thousands, maybe, poured from an endless monkey geyser, flooding the grounds. They passed through the soldiers like ghosts, and the dummies chased them like cats after lasers.

"No! No, no, no—get back here. Now!"

They stuttered. I had to focus to cut through the confusion and bring them back. They formed a double wall around me. Whatever Madeline was up to with her monkey show, they weren't getting to me. I looked at the clock. There wasn't much time left.

Let Madeline have her fun. She wasn't going to distract me. I didn't know how she was doing it. But, in hindsight, this was all part of the plan. I see that now. The confusion, the ghostly projection.

It kept me looking in the wrong direction.

I peeked between pillars of uniforms. Monkeybrains were running a game of ring-around-the-rosy, their long arms locked. The last road was a faint ribbon of color. The bubble was glowing brighter. I didn't understand what they were doing, like some sort of magic dance. It couldn't possibly do anything. Maybe she had figured out some sort of energy vortex to open a hole in the bubble. Christmas spirit would burst out.

Then it started to happen. My worst fears came to be.

I crawled halfway between the soldiers and curled my legs against my chest like the very first day I woke up in this boney costume. The monkey dance suddenly stopped. A break in the chain opened. It happened.

A red-coated fat man stepped out.

Santa Claus looked around, stretched his arms like he'd been asleep for thirty years. He patted his fat stomach. Something leaped down from the house. An immense rack of antlers dropped in front of him. The biggest of all the reindeer kicked a metal rod across the floor like it was made of plastic (it didn't make a sound, but the ringing in my head was too loud to hear it), raised his head and snorted the dusty air. He was the size of a delivery truck. Black shiny rocks for eyes scanned the arena.

How did he escape? I wondered. Then I thought, *Wouldn't the Christmas spirit spill out?*

Those were all logical thoughts. And if I weren't in a full-blown meltdown, I would've realized it was impossible. I was petrified, holding as still as possible so Santa and his giant reindeer wouldn't notice me.

It was obvious where I was. The monkeys all pointed, just in case.

Santa with his hand on the reindeer's snout, the only thing keeping that beast from scattering the soldiers like bowling pins, walked towards me. The monkeys raced around like gnats hovering over a compost pile. He walked through a blizzard of purple fur and took a knee. The reindeer stood over him and snorted.

"Viktor Corker," he said with a deep voice.

Viktor Corker? He was mixing names. I was Viktor here, not back home. He must have been confused. Maybe the bubble fogged his brain. *I broke Santa.* The giant reindeer stared at me. I sounded like a bag of loose bones.

"I see you, young man," he said. "I see who you truly are. It's not this. Joy belongs to no one. It must be free. Give it away and it is yours forever."

He held out a white-gloved hand. He placed a telescope on the ground. It was the same model I'd gotten for Christmas when I was twelve years old. The black and white finderscope mounted on top. The eyepiece angled into the forward zenith mirror. Focusing wheel above the adjustment lever.

So I could see the universe.

How many times had I sat in my bedroom watching the stars? And the times I took the telescope onto the roof after my father was asleep and nearly fell off without him knowing. Those were the times I didn't feel the loneliness, that someone else was out there. All those stars and planets, was there someone looking back and feeling the same thing?

I wanted to crawl out of hiding and into Santa's lap. My father never let me do that like the other kids. I'd completely forgotten about the clock and fading road, lost in the buzzing monkeys and dizzy thoughts. I looked past Santa and the reindeer.

I stopped chattering. I thought, perhaps, it was wishful thinking. What I saw. The bubble was in plain sight. The watery wall was unbroken. I could see a red coat inside it. I counted the reindeer on the roof. They were all there, inside the bubble. Including the big one.

I looked at Santa in front of me, the reindeer standing over him. *I can't feel them.*

In the empty chaos, I finally felt a presence. Someone was coming for me.

36

In the shadows of long, tall soldiers, Viktor the Red was quaking.

Hiro watched him between stilted legs. It was difficult to hold the image of Santa Claus while also running copies of Monkeybrain running around. Each monkey pulled his focus thinner. And then Santa Claus. The reindeer was Hiro's idea. For some reason, he thought an angry monster would intimidate Viktor. Viktor was in cringe mode. But it wasn't because of the reindeer.

Hiro felt his pain.

It was the fear of losing everything he ever wanted. Now he was all by himself, boney arms buckled around sharp shinbones. Seconds away from popping a thumb in his mouth. Without lips or a tongue, he'd gnaw on it. If Christmas weren't on the line, Hiro might feel sorry for him.

Hiro had Santa Claus keep his hand out, although if Viktor tried to take it, then the jig was up. His bones would pass right through it. Hiro would think of something if he reached for it.

Mads didn't say what was next, just to keep the Monkeybrains running and Viktor distracted with Santa Claus. *Check*. But time was coming off the clock. The last road was fading. Something had to happen. And then it did.

Not what Mads was planning.

Viktor looked at Santa Claus. His focus went beyond him. Hiro thought he was looking up at the reindeer, but then he stopped trembling. Viktor didn't have eyebrows. If he did, they would have arched. If he had eyes, they would have squinted. Hiro realized what he was seeing, and it was too late to block his view.

Santa and the reindeer are still in the bubble!

A monkey came soaring over a wall of soldiers—arms and legs spread out. It wasn't one of Hiro's monkeys.

The fuzzy bomb dropped into the center of the soldiers—all of whom quit trying to grab the monkeys—and hit the ground rolling. Hands out and thumbs together, she darted for Viktor. Her thumbs stiffly contacted the back of his skull.

Something clicked.

Viktor snapped his boney fingers around the purple arms like a bear trap. All the quaking, fearful energy shed from him like a useless exoskeleton. His mind clamped down on the mind inside the fluffed and stuffed monkey caught in his grip. Hiro could feel Mads's thoughts trapped inside it.

So that was the plan.

She hadn't told Hiro what she was going to do, just to create chaos. It would be enough confusion for her to get close.

The soldiers parted.

Hiro could feel Viktor's smile all the way in the room.

"Enough!"

All the Monkeybrains vanished except the one he held like a trophy fish. With his other hand, he reached behind his skull. A small door had opened where Mads had pushed her thumbs. It wasn't deep enough. The charm did not release from it. The charm that was Viktor.

It snapped closed. *So close.*

Hiro maintained the Santa image. If Mads had something else

planned, it had to happen in the next couple of minutes. Viktor pried open her mind to sniff out everything she knew. Hiro could feel his gaze sweep through the room. Viktor laughed a knowing laugh, glanced up at Belkin. Hiro felt his eyes fall on the teddy bear peeking over the edge.

"Gently now." He handed Mads to one of his soldiers. "She and I still have a lot of catching up to do. Like that, good."

The soldier snuggled Mads into the starched crook of his uniformed elbow. Mads was a lump of paralyzed fur.

"You can put away the costume, Hiro." Viktor passed his hand through Santa. All the cards were on the table. Dealer wins. Viktor tapped his chin pensively. "I'm torn. You see, I have no idea how you did this—the monkeys and the Santa. The reindeer. I was fooled. And I know everything. That's no small feat, young man."

His mood had improved.

"Here's the thing. In two minutes, the last road closes. I need you to stay because, well, the little magic show you put on is of interest to me. But that would mean you never go home. See my predicament?"

"I know who you are," the Santa said.

"I said enough with the Santa! I don't have time to march my bones up there. Get down here now."

Hiro transformed the Santa into a teddy bear. It was only a projection, but somehow, he felt vulnerable showing his true self. *I'm not a toy,* he reminded himself.

"You don't know who I am," Viktor announced.

"Mr. Corker."

"No!" Hiro felt his anger up. "You know the teacher. That's all you know. I am Viktor the Red. *I am a toy!*"

"How can you do this to our home?"

"*Your* home, Hiro. No one knows Christmas is gone. *You* didn't know what happened until you came here. Suffering works that way. If you don't know what you're missing, you call it life. And that's it. That's life."

"My mother is not the same."

"Maybe she was always that way. You didn't realize it."

"No. She wasn't." Hiro tried to sound brave.

Viktor shrugged his pointy shoulders. "Injustice will always exist. Even if there was still Christmas, someone would be unhappy. I know that side of it quite well, Hiro. This way"—he swung his arms at the destruction all around—"I get life the way I want it. Sorry if others have to suffer a little."

"You won't be happy here. You'll still be you."

"Listen, you tweeny toad. I did my time there. I schooled, worked and slept and woke up and did it again, day after day after day. I did what I was supposed to do. I lived a life. Now I want one."

He wanted to grab the teddy bear by the fluffy arms and shake some sense into him. Hiro could feel his mind reaching for him. Belkin did his best to shield him. It still hurt. Thoughts could be arrows.

Viktor looked at the clock. "You know what? Just go home. I don't want you reminding me of home. Go be with your mother and father. You can hand your schoolwork to a poor substitute. I don't care."

"What'll happen to you? Like, at home?"

"Go home, Hiro." He rattled his fingers at the window. "Merry Christmas."

"There won't be Christmas. I'll forget."

Viktor nodded. He paced among his soldiers like an undersized general with an oversized ego. The soldier holding Mads took a knee for him. Viktor stroked her fur. "Do you know why toys say *merry, merry*? It has nothing to do with Christmas, Hiro. It's a toy thing; you wouldn't understand. It means find joy in everything, not just presents or eggnog or a dead tree in your living room. Go home and find joy in whatever. It doesn't have to be Christmas."

He looked at the bubble. Santa and the reindeer were still frozen inside. The last road was barely visible.

"Freckles! Start the countdown!"

The big orange cat appeared on a trapeze above them. The pseudo-voice of what all the other toys thought was Viktor the Red started counting down from sixty. Freckles's amplified voice sang the numbers.

"Goodbye, Hiro."

Hiro felt Viktor's thoughts shift in the room. Flake turned from the window and started toward the table. Hiro abandoned his imagination—his image vanished from the arena—and ran to stop the shuffling elf from reaching the bowl where one last charm glittered with life.

"Flake, stop. Just—there has to be something we can do."

"You must go home," Belkin said. Viktor might have stripped him of power, but his voice still carried authority. "Before it's too late."

He was right. Of course he was. But it couldn't end like this. Waking up in his cold bedroom. Mother staring out the kitchen window as if she'd lost count of the gray days. Viktor couldn't win. Not because home would get more cheerless, and life would become a dead weight. No one was going to win.

Not the toys. Not Viktor.

He was alone down there with his stiff soldiers. This world was going to crush him with loneliness. He would find himself exactly where he was at home with all the pain and guilt of what he'd done to the universe. And he wouldn't be able to take it back.

"Twenty, nineteen..."

"You are very brave." Stretch retrieved the glowing charm from the bowl.

He held it over Flake's outstretched hand. Hiro didn't feel brave. And staying would hurt his mother even more. It was time to go. Even if it was gray, it was still home. Hiro turned to the window.

Viktor held out his arms to savor the last drops before victory.

Hiro summoned the last of his courage, prepared to mutter his final word in this strange and wonderful world. He was about to nod to Stretch to drop his charm into Flake's hand when a shift occurred.

The vise of Viktor's thoughts evaporated.

Hiro's last word unexpectedly shocked Stretch into holding onto the charm.

"Wait!"

Viktor collapsed. As if marionette strings had been severed, he crumpled into a pile of red bones.

"Five!" Freckles shouted.

Belkin put his hand on the window. Mads sprang from the soldier's arms. They swiped at her and missed. She hit the ground and pounced on the sleeping bones.

"Four, three..."

Her thumbs to the back of his skull.

"Two..."

The secret hatch opened.

"One—"

Darkness.

A switch cut the power on the lights above the arena. The room Hiro and the others were trapped inside went quiet. The whir of the machines and blinking lights turned off.

The last of the lights came from the charms strung above the arena, the bright little objects that had cast the warm goodness of Christmas spirit on the toys. When the toys had been there. When the party had been on. Apparently, there was no switch to shut them off. They simply began to dim.

If they looked closely, they would see that the lights were dying: the luminescence leaked out like foggy essence, swirling into the darkness until they glowed no brighter than fireflies.

And then they too were out.

Darkness was complete and as quiet as a mouse. The stars weren't shining. Even the bubble had been snuffed out. Hiro was unsure of what had happened and afraid to ask. *Is it too late to wake up?* He still had a furry body with short arms and legs and no fingers or toes. He tried to blink.

Colors started swirling.

A mass of every color on the spectrum squirmed in a giant ball on the floor of the arena—a swarm of iridescent snakes writhing and twisting. It began to swell, inflating as one glowing snake gave rise to two, then four, then eight. A psychedelic blob swallowed pieces of the carnival rides that had fallen.

The kaleidoscope passed over Viktor. He lay still on the ground. The hatch on the back of his skull was dark and empty. Mads was gone, running off, Hiro assumed, with the charm she'd snatched after Viktor suddenly and unexplainably collapsed.

Belkin and Stretch flickered in the colorful light, their reflections in the window appearing and disappearing. Stretch held Hiro's charm in a clenched fist. Flake pressed both hands on the glass; the brim of his hat crumpled against the window. Ocho was as still as Hiro had ever seen him.

The light felt good.

It was warm and dense, radiating in waves that penetrated their bodies. Hummed in their charms. Like a smile beamed on radio waves, Hiro could feel it grow inside him. It was the same feeling from the charms, but different. It was fuller. *Free.* It elicited looks of wonder from everyone in the room. Even Belkin, somehow with his wooden face, appeared to smile. There was nothing natural about what they were experiencing, yet they knew exactly what it was.

Flake yipped in surprise.

He hopped on those giant, scratchy feet and tapped on the window. Far below, something scurried from the ball of light—under the debris and around Viktor. He was the size of a mouse wearing a green coat and a floppy hat.

The bubble was consumed by the ball of lights. The larger it grew, the louder it hummed. They could feel it coming through the floor, vibrating in their legs (and tentacles). It revved like a supersonic engine preparing for departure. The window began to quiver.

Hiro felt thinner. He wondered if the others could feel it, too. Like he was losing his grip. He tried to say something, but the words were too heavy. His thoughts disintegrated like snowflakes passing over a hot griddle. When he tried to move his arm, it stayed by his side.

The lights began to dim.

He wondered if they were truly dimming, or was it just him? The others didn't seem alarmed, but they were also just as still. Could they not move either?

The magical moment was punctuated by jolly laughter. It came from the ball of lights and everywhere at the same time.

Ho-ho-ho.

There was a pause. A blip.

And then came the silent explosion.

They were in the center of a galactic fireworks show. Lights blasted through the walls and down into the floor; they wriggled into the sky and beyond. It was the magician's trick of never-ending scarves pulled from the sleeve—an endless display of lights spreading into the universe.

The roads!

Hiro wanted to celebrate, to jump up and down and shout it from the top of the world, to hug the others, high-five them, kiss them. The roads were free again. Why wasn't everyone singing? Hiro felt like a shadow. Belkin looked down at him, then at the others. The wooden puppet knelt in front of him. For the first time, the big painted eyes felt kind.

"Thank you," he said.

The charm was still in Stretch's hand. Flake waved an empty hand at Hiro. Ocho's tentacles wriggled.

"Goodbye, Hiro," Stretch said.

No, Hiro wanted to say. *Wait,* he wanted to say.

He faded in no direction, free of the fuzzy teddy bear. The light and all its glory slowly dimmed into dimensionless slumber.

37

Completely and utterly flabbergasted.

I should've been asleep for another six hours. At the very least, until the countdown was over. The roads would be closed.

I would never wake up again.

The Christmas spirit would be forever trapped inside the bubble, siphoned a drop at a time and dispensed to make a world of happy toys. Not girls and boys. The spirit was the rarest essence in reality; it would exist only on this world. My world. It would be all mine.

Remember what I told you in the beginning? Right.

It's with great shame and unfathomable guilt that I tell you, without question, I would've done it. I would have counted off those seconds till the last road closed, and swum in my own personal pool of Christmas spirit if they didn't stop me. The weight of this shame may lessen with time, but it is a weight I will always carry. I would have sentenced the universe to joyless days and dark nights for eternity with nothing to celebrate but the daily grind.

No Christmas ever.

Was I intoxicated by power? I was untouchable, all-knowing, and beyond harm. I was hammered drunk.

Power corrupts. I was not immune.

Blame me for my weakness, for my insatiable greed and callousness. I will not deny your accusations. They're true, all of them, in black and white. I thought absolute power would ease my struggle with who I thought I was and the burden I had carried all my life. No matter where I turned, I was always there.

No matter how I tried, I could not escape myself. I had studied books, honed my intelligence, became the person I thought I was supposed to be. And yet there was always something wrong with me, under the surface.

Power didn't rid me of my shortcomings. It only fueled them.

The emotional hole that I walked a tightrope over grew wider and deeper. It was bottomless, unfillable, no matter how many things or how much power I tossed inside it. It swallowed them like a black hole, belching sour fumes of guilt and disgust. If I dared a peek over the edge, I could hear it humming, could see its walls papered with snapshots of childhood.

I digress.

I had just caught Madeline and was counting down the seconds. Freckles, my simpleton servant, had joined me when I felt the fade of waking upon me. A drifting of sorts. Here one second, in my bed the next. That's how it usually goes when I wake up.

Not this time.

I was rising like a bubble. I attempted to fly back to my red bones, to reenter the dream, but was snatched like a pigeon in midflight by a bird of prey. The talons were soft and kind. This is just an analogy. I wasn't a pigeon. There was no hawk or cuddly talons. There were no images at all, just the sensation of being yanked sideways into another dimension altogether—not sleep, not waking.

I'd slipped through a fissure in time.

My imaginary hawk flew me into the throat of the cavernous black hole I'd been trying to fill. It was humid, at first. Dank. Earthy odors quickly turned fetid and rank. The air, if that's what you want to call it, was soupy. It clung to me in a film. Layer upon layer calcified around me until I was encased in a shell of the stuff.

And deeper we went.

I say *we* because I was certain it wasn't just me on this mystery journey. The air was raw. Sensations felt like cold water on a fresh wound. Sounds were all around, someone speaking garbled nonsense in sharp tones. Images, like snippets of video, flashed by, accompanied by base emotions. Simple emotions uncluttered by thoughts. Raw sensation.

I was desperate to wake in my bed, at this point. Anywhere but here would've been greeted with tears of joy. I was fully aware of what I'd done. Perhaps this was penance. The truth was laid bare. I was very bad at the core, and that was where I was being taken. To the core of who I was.

I started screaming.

It was the first sound I was able to make. It came out in a long, shrill whine until I was empty. My chest inflated, and another wail released. I did this over and over, again and again and—

I was back.

Like I'd snapped my fingers, I was back in my little body. The world was big, and I was small. Briefly, I thought I'd clawed my way back to my red bones. But there were no bones or broken Ferris wheels. There were walls and a ceiling. I was surrounded by bars. These weren't round and metal. I know what you're thinking, and I thought the same thing. I deserved the round and metal kind of bars. These were plastic and flat.

And I was wearing a diaper.

I stood up and fell on my cushioned fanny. I pulled myself up and looked between the bars. The room was small and empty except for the crib and unpainted dresser. No mobiles churning over me or pictures of clowns on the wall.

Without thinking, my thumb went into my mouth.

The rhythmic suction soothed the anxiety. The garbled sounds I'd heard on the way here were in the next room. Something heavy hit the wall. My instincts were to crawl under the blanket and suck my thumb until it pruned. But the emptiness of the room was howling. Anywhere felt better than here.

My toddler legs were rubber, as toddler legs are, and I threw it on top of the rail. I fell on the carpet with a padded whump of the sodden diaper. It felt very much like walking for the first time when I was a toy. I quickly caught on and wobbled across the hall.

There was a very big bed in the next room. A present sat on the edge of it. It was wrapped in glittering paper with a fat red bow. I couldn't take my eyes off it, even with two giants in the room.

One of them was my father.

He was quite a bit younger. Hints of gray tinged his sideburns. His glasses were different. He wore a V-neck T-shirt, white. It was untucked over black slacks, and he was barefoot. He was still speaking nonsense. It wasn't a language of any kind. It was just sounds. And the sounds were sharp and forceful, like sledgehammers flying out of his mouth.

He punctuated each sentence with a stiff finger aimed at the woman. I didn't recognize her. A warm, melting sensation stirred in my belly. I ached to run to her, but I'd have to get past my father. Her eyes were red and glassy, set in pockets of a full, round face. I could smell her from across the room. *Mother.*

I started to cry.

I couldn't stop it; it was undeniable. Like pressure in a keg that was going to blow. The release valve cried. My mother looked at me. My father stepped between us. His volume, previously at a nine, went to a twelve. They chiseled at her, chipping away piece after piece. How much longer before she was reduced to rubble? My mother continued stuffing clothes in a bag.

Red-faced, my father grabbed the present and began shredding the paper. My mother tried to stop him. He tore the box open and shook the contents at her. I wished I knew what the sounds he was making meant. Whatever he was saying, he took it out on the present, flinging it against the wall. A picture fell off the dresser and shattered.

He stormed out of the room.

My mother stopped shoving things into the bag. Her face was so heavy. She wiped her eyes, bent down to pick up what my father had thrown. She knelt in front of me. It was a toy. And it was for me. I don't remember that toy because I wouldn't have it long. My father would throw it away the next morning. But it made sense as she wrapped my arms around it. It was firm but soft. It was red. Bones were outlined on fabric arms and legs filled with stuffing.

A happy smile on the face.

And then I was back in my room with the crib and the dresser. Thumb in my mouth and a soggy diaper on my butt. I don't know how long I was in there. Plenty long to run out of tears. My cheeks were raw. My father stomped into the room with heavy black shoes and swept me up with the comfort of a construction worker. He dropped me in the crib and tore the red toy out of my arms.

I found a reserve of tears. They didn't last long.

He left the room and returned to pull my thumb out of my mouth. He wiped something as thick as axle grease on it and pointed his finger at me, said some garbled words. Then he left.

I was alone again.

Alone for a very long time.

No amount of crying brought my mother back.

Snot ran down my chin. I washed away in a saline flood, out of the crib, out of the room. The house. But I couldn't escape the feeling that howled from the emotional black hole. There was something wrong with me. *That's why she left.*

I wish I could tell you that was the end of that. If I would've had my way, I would have gladly woken up and sworn never to return to the world of toys. Which is a lie. That was probably why the trip continued. I won't bore you with the stops we made. More memories, more fights. Name-calling, shame, disappointment. A lifetime of it. I saw it all, felt it all.

Time didn't flow. I was just there, wherever that was.

I know what you're thinking: I woke up in bed a changed man. I learned from my mistakes; the black hole was filled. I danced out of my house singing merry Christmas to my neighbors.

Change isn't that easy.

The emotional hole wasn't filled with tears and happily ever after. It didn't fill up. It's a bit of a contradiction, but suddenly the hole wasn't there. Like it had never been there in the first place. And that's when I began floating. A bubble seeking the surface.

I was greeted by people in uniforms with rough hands. To their utter confusion, I burst into tears. For the very first time, I was happy to be awake.

38

Sleep was a bed of wet sand. Weighty, sticky.

He was comfortable down there in the cold deep. Motionless, he rested in the timelessness of sleep, unaware he was anywhere at all.

Just floating.

A blue whale rising through the depths, seeking the surface, where another world waited. His eyelids broke the surface, cracking open to witness shapes he did not recognize. Squares and things stacked on each other. The heavy vaults closed and opened, scrawling recognition on a blank slate.

Laptop. Books.

A chair and a desk. Branches on a window. Pictures on a bookshelf. Faster they came, memories flooding through the veil between waking and dreaming, until they found their rightful places and he had a name.

Hiro.

He grabbed his face. His cheeks warm and creased from the folds in the pillowcase. His skin was soft and smooth, not fuzzy. He had hair on his head, just his head, which was slightly damp. He shot upright. The room felt so strange. So small. He was a giant filling the bed. His arms were long, and his legs were longer. He had fingers and toes and a regular nose.

And he blinked. He blinked once, then twice. He shut his eyes and opened them again. He was a boy in his room. A real boy. Not a toy at all.

His mouth was hot and dry. The dream was fast fading behind the curtain of belief, a strange story growing stranger with each heartbeat. It had felt so real, but now it did not. Funny how that happens, dreams so convincing. He wondered, as he put his feet on the floor and wiggled his toes, if he was dreaming now.

He tried to remember before it was too late. He was a teddy bear once, a toy who had friends. They were stuck in a world that was doing bad things. What was it, he wondered, that could be all that bad? Then he recalled the laughter he'd heard, the jolly good nature that could not be mistaken.

He peeked out the window crusted with frost. A new blanket of snow had covered the road. Mr. Belchinek was clearing his driveway with a brand-new red shovel. There were no lights on his gutters or decorations out front. Nothing had changed. They hadn't saved Christmas after all.

"It was a dream," he muttered.

The purple monkey was on the dresser. Her eyes were blank, as toy eyes should be. The drawing of the planet was taped to the wall. It didn't leap from the paper or wiggle at all. Just something he drew from a dream.

Whatever joy remained from the dream evaporated like fumes escaping the room. It was wishful thinking. He scrambled for a pen to write it all down, the details of an elf with a small elf just like him, who lived in his hat and ran around the rim. An orange octopus who drove a car and a dragon who spit candy. A metal robot with a television spinning on his shoulders. There were others, too, he was fast forgetting, as the dream turned to sand and slipped through his fingers.

He wanted to remember and never forget. Somewhere Christmas was real.

Before he wrote a word on a page, he looked up. Something, it turned out, was different after all. The trees were all bare, and the houses hadn't changed. But the sky was not gray. It was blue for a change.

"You're alive."

His father peeked into the room, a mug on his finger. He nudged the door open. Music played downstairs.

"What?" Hiro said. *Was I dead?*

"You've never slept this late. Your mother insisted I come check on—"

Hiro hugged his father. Coffee spilled on his robe. It was lukewarm on Hiro's chest. He didn't care. His father tried to squirm away, but Hiro held him tightly. He finally gave up, not worried about the stain on his robe, and patted his son's back.

"What's gotten into you two this morning?"

"I'm happy to be back," he muttered into his dad's shoulder.

"Where'd you go?"

Hiro shook his head. "I don't know."

"You and your mother."

The music downstairs grew louder. Hiro had heard that song before. He threw on some clothes. His father grabbed the purple monkey off the dresser.

"She went looking for this in the middle of the night. I heard her in the garage, digging through the garbage. She was upset she couldn't find it." He handed it to Hiro. "I told her I put it in your room. You were having a bad dream, I told her. I thought you could use some company."

"Bad dream?"

He shrugged. "On second thought, leave it up here. She might have forgotten about it. She's not herself this morning."

He started down the hall, swiping at the coffee stain. Hiro didn't know if he wanted to follow. *Not herself?*

"Come see for yourself."

❄

PAPER CHAINS WERE WRAPPED around the banister. Big loops cut from computer paper, it looked like, painted green and red and yellow all linked and taped together. They sparkled with silver glitter dusted on layers of glue. Snowflakes were thumbtacked to the ceiling, the cutout kind after paper had been folded into quarters. They slowly turned in the draft from the vents exhaling warm air from the furnace. Letters were cut from more computer paper and taped to the wall. Words that spelled JOY and MERRY.

The music was louder.

Hiro thumped down the steps, stopping on the last one to look around the front room. The corner wasn't empty. It was filled with an artificial tree that leaned slightly to the left. The branches were draped with strings of popcorn and strands of silvery tinsel. The string lights were no longer puddled on the floor. They flashed on the branches. A paper star was poised on top. Dusty stockings were hung above the fireplace, their toes bulging with secrets.

"I don't know how you slept through the music," his father shouted.

He went to the kitchen. The music dropped to a whisper. Hiro's mother appeared in the doorway. Her cheeks smudged with flour; fingers dashed with paint. Her slippers were pink and fuzzy. Hiro had never seen slippers like that before. Or the baggy sweatshirt with a smiling reindeer with a nose flashing red. She wore something else he hadn't seen in forever.

A bright, white smile.

She bounced across the room, threw her arms around him and whispered, "Merry Christmas, Hiro." She smelled like cinnamon and paint. "I'm so sorry we forgot. I don't know what happened."

She held him at arm's length. A green floppy hat, a size too big, was pulled over her ears. Hiro had seen that hat. Not here, of course. Not on her.

"How did you remember?" he said.

She started to answer. Only sounds tumbled out. She looked at her husband. Sipping the remains of his coffee that were still in his mug, he shrugged.

"Do you feel it, Hiro?"

He knew what she was asking. Because he *could* feel it. The air was different. It was saturated with something new and exhilarating. A feeling of promise and joy. He remembered, right then, the end of his dream—the exploding light and endless colorful roads. He felt all that had been trapped in a time-locked ball of blue light. And when it opened, it was free.

To give it is to have it.

"Christmas spirit," he muttered.

"Sticky buns are almost done." She planted a bird kiss on her husband. "Your grandparents will be over soon. We can eat, then open presents. There's not many this year, but I feel like they'll be good ones."

Presents were next to the fireplace. Three boxes wrapped in red paper with big green bows. A name on each one. He wondered if she'd found wrapping paper in the attic and somehow found time to make something special for each of them. His father only winked and followed her into the kitchen. The music was at full volume again. Hiro's mother sang along to bells that jingle.

She hadn't made the presents or wrapped them that night. They were there when she woke up, the fireplace left open. At least, that was what Hiro believed.

People say anything is possible even when we know it isn't true. There was no mystery where the presents came from, not for Hiro. He knew exactly how they got there. It didn't matter what was in them. It was just that they were there.

His mother was laughing. His father took her for a spin. Turned out, Hiro didn't need to open a present after all.

It was dancing in the kitchen.

THEY ATE until their stomachs were full. Laughed until their faces hurt. Hiro couldn't eat another bite. But nothing could stop him from smiling.

Dishes were piled in the sink. The table sticky with syrup, butter melting on the floor. They would clean up later. *It's Christmas,* his mother said. Then his parents danced some more. No one wanted to see their parents look at each other like that, gooey-eyed and such. Any other day, Hiro would go to the other room.

The presents were from his mother, all except the ones at the fireplace. She'd wrapped her gifts in brown paper bags and tinfoil. There was even a coffee mug for his father swaddled in a pillowcase and tied with a shoelace. Hiro knew the mug came from the back of the cabinet, where forgotten things got pushed into corners. He knew because he'd made it for him in grade school: a ceramic mug with an ugly face. It wasn't supposed to be ugly. It was supposed to be his father.

His mother, however, said it was beautiful.

The other gifts were made from things she'd found around the house. Things glued and taped, glittered and painted. Hiro's favorite was a spiralbound notebook with two words printed on the cover— the letters fancy with gold glitter.

"Look." His mother had already filled two pages with dreams.

His father promised to write his down, should he ever have one. He crossed his heart and poked his eye. Hiro wanted to start writing his down immediately. The details were fading. There might not be enough pages if he got to it soon enough. He wanted this morning to last forever.

Mother's phone rang. "Merry Christmas," she answered.

She chatted for a minute, cheery at first. Consternation set her brow. She listened with intensity. Her mood lifted by the end of the call, a thank you and a merry Christmas to you, too.

"Everything all right?" Hiro asked.

"That was Jeanine Hollowell. She said an ambulance was at Mr. Corker's house last night."

"Corker? Is he all right?"

"She said he's fine. She went over to check on him."

Hiro felt a little dizzy. "What happened?"

"She doesn't know. He seemed perfectly fine when she spoke with him. She lives across the street, said the lights from the ambulance woke her up in the middle of the night. Poor man, spending Christmas all alone."

It turned out that "middle of the night" was right about midnight.

Hiro had dreamed of looking down at an arena. A tornado had destroyed a carnival of rides. A little, red skeleton lay in the ruins. A moment earlier, the skeleton had been counting down the end of Christmas.

Corker woke up.

Hiro's father was in the kitchen. Dirty dishes were being piled on the counter. Water running. His mother called for him to stop cleaning. There were still a few more presents to open. The ones next to the fireplace were still neatly wrapped. He came back with a hand towel over his shoulder.

"Why did an ambulance go to his house?" Hiro asked.

"What ambulance?" his father said.

"Something to do with Mr. Corker. It sounds like he's fine." She slid a box toward Hiro. "Open it."

His name wasn't on it, but it was for him. *Our Hero* was written in large letters.

"Who's that from?" his father asked.

"You know," his mother said.

A shiver stampeded down Hiro's back. He pulled off the wrapping paper and opened the box. Stuffed inside and wrapped in a blanket was a ball of tan fur.

"Seriously," his father said, "who's it from?"

Dreams have a way of fading, no matter how good or bad. But at that moment, staring into the glassy eyes of a teddy bear, he knew he'd never forget.

39

The teddy bear sat on the counter, leaning against the coffee machine.

Hiro was wearing headphones. Despite the music, an undercurrent of stillness filled his head. It was contradictory. How could it be quiet with drums and guitars? And everything still felt so strange. Like he didn't have to climb onto chairs; doorknobs were easy to reach. He grabbed a plate from the soapy water. *And opposable thumbs.*

He closed his eyes, and swimming with his thoughts, he found what felt missing. It was invisible grit floating in the air. Dust particles of thoughts.

That's it.

He wasn't hearing anything but his own thoughts. No one else's thoughts clouded his mind. No one else was peeking into his mind. He picked up the teddy, squeezed his belly. Nothing but fluff and stitching.

Just like a toy.

Bits of the dream had come and gone. Like patches of ice hidden in the snow, he'd remember a part of the dream and go skidding into the details—an explanation of how Christmas had disappeared, how charms housed the real identity of toys, how the colorful roads were disappearing.

But it was almost noon. Several hours of waking and doubt were nibbling on his willingness to believe. He wanted to believe the dream was real, that a world was out there. A world he could visit when he closed his eyes. *Childishness,* the doubts whispered. *Real is only in front of you.*

He hugged the teddy. Squeezed it hard. A hand fell on his shoulder. Hiro pulled the headphones off.

"Hey, I didn't want to interrupt," his father said, gesturing to the hug.

Hiro put the bear back on the counter. His mother was in the front room and laughing the sort of laughter that, once upon a time, she reserved for company. Laughter he hadn't heard in forever.

"Teddy and I can finish up. You go out there." His father winked. "Spill some coffee."

His mother was at the front door. One of the guests pushed past her, tracking snow on the carpet. Haze wrapped Hiro into a bear hug. His arms were trapped at his sides. She picked him up and shook him. Robby stood at the door. It looked like a smile was crawling onto one side of his face.

"You made it back," Haze whispered.

The hug continued. His mother was staring. The dishes stopped clashing in the kitchen. Hiro felt his father look in the front room, probably smiling at his mother. Haze grabbed two handfuls of Hiro's sweatshirt and balled them into fists like someone about to finish an argument.

"I called and texted. I sent emails. Chase, she answered. You didn't. I thought you were—"

"Asleep," Robby chimed. "I told her it was Christmas, but she made me come over. She couldn't stop talking about you. Like all night long. I wish it would stop. Seriously."

"I'm so sorry." Haze looked at the snow on the carpet. "I'll clean it up."

"It's all right," Hiro's mother said. "It's just water. Nothing a towel can't fix. Here, let me take your coats."

"Oh, no. We're not staying." Haze wiped her eyes. "Can we borrow Hiro for a few hours? I know it's Christmas and—and by the way, merry Christmas."

"Merry Christmas," Hiro's father said from the kitchen doorway.

"Borrow?" Hiro's mother said.

"I think she means go for a ride," Robby said. Then whispered, plenty loud, "She's crazy about him."

"That's not what I mean. I meant the first part." She stared lasers at her brother.

His parents looked at each other. Hiro didn't feel invisible grit pass between them, but they seemed to know each other's thoughts. His mother smiled and said, "Have him back before dinner."

They would probably dance some more. Hiro had seen enough of the way his mother laughed when his father dipped her low to the floor. He threw on his coat. Haze led the way. Robby waved at Hiro's parents.

"Merry, merry!"

THEY LISTENED to the engine rattle.

Robby had his hand on the gearshift with his foot on the brake. Across the street, kids rolled a big ball of snow. Maybe it was the start of a snowman. Hiro didn't notice.

He was staring at a dragon.

It was green with beady, black eyes and wedged between the dashboard and windshield, watching with a toothy smile. Despite warm air from the vents, a hard shiver crawled down his back and clenched his stomach. He chattered, but it wasn't the cold. Reality was turning upside down. *Like a carnival ride.*

He grabbed the dragon. The belly was heavy. Bits of hard candy fell out of the mouth when he turned it over. There were no tags. The teddy didn't have any, either. *Santa doesn't put tags on presents.*

"So it really happened?" Hiro said.

Robby leaned to one side, dug in his coat pocket. He came out with a handful of something jagged and sharp and swatted it on the dash. Metal legs clicked together. A cube bobbled on angled shoulders. It looked like a tiny television set.

"I'm guessing you got a teddy bear?"

Hiro didn't answer. And he didn't have to ask where they got the dragon and the bobblehead. They had been neatly wrapped and waiting for them in the morning.

Hiro said, "You think it was—"

"Santa?" Robby pulled on the gearshift. He didn't finish his thought. They couldn't read each other's minds, but they were thinking the same thing.

"I'm so happy you're back," Haze said. "I called, like, a hundred times, texted a hundred more. You weren't answering. I was trying to do the math, the time difference thingy, and figured you should've woken up, like, a minute after we did. Ten, tops. So I kept calling and calling. I about came over in the middle of the night."

"But she's scared of your mom," Robby said.

"Shut up. I started to think you stayed there."

"I did," Hiro said. They looked at him. He sighed. "After you left, it got... weird."

It felt strange saying that out loud. *After you left.* Because it was a dream, just a dream. They all had the *same* dream. *Right?*

"It was Corker. The puppet, you know. Viktor the Red was Corker. I know that sounds impossible, but he must have had the same dream as us. Remember in class when he saw my drawing and made me—"

They burst out laughing. Robby pounded the steering wheel as he turned the corner. The bobblehead slid across the dash. For a brief second, Hiro thought they were laughing at him. *Did they not have the dream?* Embarrassment went through his belly like a winter stream.

"Corker," Robby said, shaking his head. "That guy."

"Don't be mean." Haze punched his shoulder. She turned to Hiro.

"Yeah, it was Corker. The way he walked. *Precisely!*" She stabbed at the roof. "When he said that, I knew for sure. No one says that."

"Corker does," Robby added.

"Yeah, and I couldn't *think* it to you once I knew. Not with him in the room with the, you know, the big puppet and the stretchy guy." Hiro got the chills. *Belkin and Stretch.* "We had to get out of there before he knew *we* knew who he was. That's why we *wanted* to wake up," she said. "I thought you knew."

Hiro shook his head. The details were foggy, just a blurry snapshot of a limp dragon lying on a metal table. He had no idea they knew it was Corker. Or what they were planning to do.

"Why did you stay?" Haze said.

Hiro sighed again. He felt nauseous trying to remember why he'd stayed so long. Robby took another corner a little fast, which stirred memories of orange tentacles gripping the steering wheel while another one turned up the radio. He closed his eyes.

He would never undervalue eyelids again. They shut out the outside world, allowed him to drift deeper into his thoughts. The memories were fresher this way. The feel of fur that fluttered in the wind. The springy nature of short legs.

"Do you remember what it was like?" he said.

"I can't forget," Robby said.

That wasn't what he meant. The dream had been so real when he was there. Now it was a kite with a broken string escaping into the blue sky. A tiny dot that kept getting smaller. Even if they talked about it, wrote the details down, the dream was only going to get farther away. Until one day, it was just going to be something they imagined happened.

"I remember." Haze hugged the dragon. "It feels like long ago, like remembering my birthday when I was seven."

A snowball fight was in full throttle on the corner. Kids lobbed snowballs from behind snowdrifts. Their gloves crusted white and frosty. The father was hanging lights on the gutters. Hiro watched while they waited for a stoplight to turn green. As they drove away, the father joined the fight.

Everything is different.

Up and down the street, people were playing or hanging ornaments or just talking and laughing. A missing ingredient was back in the world. It penetrated everything and everyone—an essence that had been missing for so long. No one knew it had been gone. They could feel it. Even taste it.

Joy.

Hiro sensed it through the windows. It filled him with goodness. The vibrations brought memories with it. He continued staring out the window, drifting in the current.

"They wanted me to leave, but I thought I could help. So I imagined myself out there. You know, the projection thing?" He didn't turn around to see if they remembered. "Viktor... er, Corker had all the soldiers out there after the rides got destroyed."

"Who did that?" Haze asked.

"Mads. It was her plan. The Ferris wheel knocked the house off the pedestal. It completely fell apart, but the bubble—you know, the one with, uh..." Hiro tapped the dashboard. "The little elf?"

"Snow," she said.

"Snow, yeah. He was trapped in there with—"

"Santa Claus," Robby said.

"Right. But it didn't work. The bubble didn't pop. Oh, and there were reindeer in it, too. They were on the roof."

"What?!" Robby shouted.

"I'm not kidding. Like, they were on the roof, tethered to the sleigh. But they were all still trapped, so I was going to project inside the bubble to talk to Santa because, I don't know. I thought he'd know what to do."

"Smart," Robby said. He might have been serious.

"Not smart," Haze said. "You could have ended up like Snow. That's what I was afraid of, that you'd do something stupid."

"I didn't try it. I heard a voice." He chewed on his finger, concentrating on what he'd heard. It was like a limerick. "Christmas lights... Christmas lights..."

"Burn so bright," Haze said. "Mads."

"How'd you know that?" Robby said.

"Shhh."

"It was her. I guess she said it so Viktor, or Corker, whatever, wouldn't know it was her. She had switched into the Monkeybrain toy. I don't know how, the octopus must have helped her."

"Oh, yeah. The octopus," Robby said. Haze pointed at him, and they said, "Ocho."

"Ocho," Hiro muttered. "Her plan was to wreck the place so Santa would be freed when the house fell. So it didn't work. The only way to get them out was to turn it off. The switch wasn't in the house."

"Where was it?" Haze said.

They were at a stop sign. The car behind them honked. Robby slowly turned the corner, waiting for the answer. Hiro didn't know it. He grasped at the final minutes of the dream, when everything went dark, just before all the roads exploded from the bubble. Mads jumped on Viktor as the countdown reached the final seconds. She reached for his skull. *His skull.*

"It was Viktor's charm." It was all coming back now. "Somehow his charm was the switch. There was no way to get to it. I don't think Mads knew it till it was too late. She thought it was in the house, that's why Snow went inside. She didn't know I could do the projection thing until she saw me doing it. That's why she told me to imagine a whole bunch of Monkeybrains, like all over the place. Then I imagined Santa escaped the bubble with one of the reindeer. It worked. Corker believed it. He got really confused. He didn't know I was doing it and thought he was talking to Santa. And then he was..."

Hiro closed his eyes again. This part had a different feeling. It was strong and weepy.

"He was sad. I could feel it. Really feel it. There was a second all that power was stripped away, and I felt him trapped in that red skeleton, like he was a little boy. Even after everything that happened, I felt bad for him."

"He stole Christmas," Robby reminded him.

Hiro shook his head. There was no argument for the things Corker had done. He'd come so close to succeeding. If he did, everything would be different. Maybe forever. But Hiro couldn't help but see the truth of why Corker had done it. He wasn't greedy or bad. *He was scared.*

"So you stopped him?" Haze said.

"No. He figured out what I was doing and caught Mads before she could get to him. He was going to do it, like you said—he was going to steal Christmas forever. The countdown was on, and I was just about to wake up. Seriously, it was game over. Then, for no reason, he fell down. I mean, he just collapsed into a pile of bones. Nobody knows why, but Mads saved the day. She got to his charm and turned the bubble off."

Ho-ho-ho.

"What do you mean he *fell down*?" Haze said.

Hiro shrugged. "He just... fell."

"Like he woke up?"

"Something happened to him. There was an ambulance at his house."

Haze pumped her fist. She high-fived her brother. They high-fived again; then she hugged Robby. He veered close to a parked car and jerked the steering wheel. Then he rolled down the window and shouted at a mother pulling her kids on a sled.

"We saved Christmas!"

Haze hugged Hiro, held his cheeks. Her hands were ice cubes. "We saved Christmas."

When she had woke up, she ran to Robby's bedroom. He was rubbing his eyes. It took a minute to convince him it wasn't a dream. It wasn't until she told him every detail of it, which matched his dream, before he believed it. He started to freak out.

"What do those numbers say?" she said, pointing at a house.

Robby slowed down. The house was white with black shutters, the fake kind that weren't made to close. There were no bushes or trees. The snow in the front yard and driveway was trampled with footsteps.

"This is it," Haze said.

"This is what?" Hiro said.

"Corker's house."

"What? Why?"

"We crushed his dream, Hiro," she said.

"Yeah, but... I don't think this is a good time to... you know." Hiro clutched the armrest.

"It's a *great* time," Robby said.

They parked on the street and stared at the front door. They sat in silence. Hiro had no trouble remembering what it had felt like when Viktor the Red reached into his head and plucked his thoughts like apples off a tree. There were no words to describe that level of vulnerability. *What if, somehow, he can still do it?*

"Seriously," Hiro said. "Why now? We'll see him at school."

"To see if he's okay." She shrugged. "An ambulance was at his house last night. Besides, I just got a feeling he wants to talk to us."

"I don't," Hiro said.

"I want to talk to him." Robby opened his door.

Haze leaned over Hiro to open his and pushed him out. They followed a bevy of footprints leading up to the front door. Hiro lagged behind. He thought they were just driving around to talk about things, not going to visit a deposed dictator. One whom Hiro had personally fooled with an image of Santa Claus. He could still feel Viktor's X-ray vision.

Robby and Haze stopped at the steps. There was a note taped to the door. Two words in black ink.

Come in.

THEY STOOD on the steps as if the porch were hot lava. It had all felt like a game when they were in the truck. Now memories were rushing back like wild animals, of a time Viktor the Red could peek inside their minds like there was a window on their foreheads.

"Maybe that's not for us." Hiro looked at the footsteps in the yard.

Haze stepped on the front porch carefully. Like bear traps were hidden in the snow.

"We can't just walk in," Hiro said. "I mean, how'd you even know he lives here?"

"It's his house." She opened the outer glass door, ripped the note down. "Trust me."

She put her ear to the door. Before Hiro could stop her, she turned the doorknob. Music bellowed from inside the house. It was a climbing symphony of classical music. She held the door for them. Robby pushed Hiro across the porch.

They stepped into an immaculate front room. Vacuum stripes lined the carpet, perfectly parallel with the couch. The smell of fresh-baked cookies filled the house.

"Mr. Corker?" Haze shouted.

There was no response. Haze took a reluctant step, then shucked her boots. Snow was melting in the linoleum foyer. "Take off your shoes," she whispered.

"Bad idea," Robby said. "We might need to run."

He was feeling the weirdness. The note felt like a stranger holding candy out the window of a dirty van.

"What if he has a dog?" Hiro said.

Haze looked at Hiro first, back to Robby. "You think Corker has a pet?"

Robby began whistling. Even if there was a dog, he wouldn't hear it over the music. Haze crept into the front room with loose socks on her feet. She looked through a doorway on the left.

Hiro left Robby, who was whistling up steps that led to the second floor. He stopped at a doorway on the right. He didn't want to shout their names, so began waving his arms like he was landing a plane.

It was a small dining table. The light-colored wood was polished. The color reminded Hiro of a full-size puppet. A puppet's name he'd already forgotten. Two candles flickered around a plate of chocolate chip cookies. Four woven placemats were at the table. They were squared to the edge of the table. On three of them were gift-wrapped boxes that were the right size for an engagement ring.

Four placemats, three presents. A plate of cookies. "He's expecting us," Hiro muttered.

"It's a bribe," Robby said. "He wants us to take him back."

"Back where?" Hiro said.

"Where? Where else? The toys aren't going to let him come—"

"It's not a bribe."

The music turned off. Corker stood in the doorway on the opposite side of the table. A tie tightly knotted against his throat; shirt as neatly pressed as his slacks. Did he own anything besides work clothes? He might have dressed the same, but something was off.

He looked different.

The sharp ridge that protruded above his eyes like an ice ridge had melted. There was a softness to the plaster of his cheeks. And something rare at the corner of his mouth. It looked like a smile trying to break through; a seed buried beneath a thick crust for a thousand years, just now feeling the light.

"Please." He gestured. "Have a seat."

"How did you know we were coming?" Hiro said.

He blinked heavily. A man exhausted. "It's important we talk about certain events. Please."

He gestured again. Not with the insistence of a taskmaster, but the request of a kind mentor. No mind control, at least none that Hiro could feel. But it was unsettling to see Corker look that way. If a slobbering guard dog walked into the room, it would be less unsettling.

The gifts made it obvious where they should sit, but they weren't labeled. Corker took a seat first. It was not at the head of the table, Hiro noticed. Robby and Haze sat at opposite ends. Hiro sat across from Corker.

"My apologies, I ran out of milk."

His voice was husky. Like someone shouting until his throat was raw.

He filled four mugs with water from a steaming kettle. The tags from teabags hung over the sides. He placed one on each of their placemats.

They sat with their hands on their laps, watching him. He broke a cookie in half, held it up before eating. It didn't ease their suspicion. Their appetites had vanished. Hiro's stomach was the size of a walnut.

Corker wiped the corners of his mouth with a cloth napkin and didn't speak until he swallowed.

"I want to thank you."

They looked at each other. Then Haze said, "For what?"

"I know it was you."

Haze looked at Robby, who shook his head. "I don't know what you're talking about."

Corker ate the other half of his cookie. Hiro put it together, what Haze and Robby had done. All the footprints in the yard. Viktor the Red suddenly falling down. Haze and Robby knew where he lived. They had returned to wake Corker up. They couldn't break into his house, so they called someone who could.

An ambulance arrived sometime after midnight. *It's an emergency.*

Corker placed a cookie on their plates, then sat down, smoothing the napkin on his lap. He sat as stiff as the hardback chair. He remained still for a moment, then inhaled deeply, letting it out slowly.

"I was frightened the first time I arrived. I'm quite sure each of you can relate—going to sleep as you've done every night of your life only to wake up as a toy. It made no sense, perhaps more so to me than you. I've been a scientist all my life. It defied the principles of reality. There is no explanation for the consciousness of an inanimate object. There is no biology in fabric and stitches. Toys are objects."

He knocked on the table.

"Yet there I was, in a world where the air was sweeter and the colors more vivid. I could smell without breathing, taste without a tongue. The experience, I'm sure you'll agree, was deeper than anything you've ever experienced or ever will. Everything pales in comparison."

He blinked heavily again.

"I would count the minutes till bedtime. Some nights excitement would keep me from sleeping. I had to learn ways to calm my expectations, to sleep deeply. I endured waking up in bed each morning. With each trip, this life became less important to me until it mattered very little. I was living two lives. This one had become inconsequential.

"I had a family there, for one. Polly was a stitcher. It was her shop where I woke as a red skeleton. Philip was a scientist studying rather absurd concepts. Even I have to admit it seemed not to be random for me to wake up there, but, as I'm sure you were told, we choose the toy that fit us. I fit quite well where I was.

"I would sit with the family for meals, Polly preparing bowls of porridge for me to dip my fingers in. We did puzzles, read books, watched television, made snow angels in the front yard. Went to town for dinner. All the things a happy family does. Something you might find boring. Something I never had."

He looked around the table with grim sincerity.

"I didn't want to do what I did. You see, I loved that world very much. I only wanted to stay. I didn't want to wake up ever again. I wanted to arrive on Madeline's shelf to—"

"Mads," Hiro blurted.

Corker nodded intently. His posture shrank as if a heavy weight had been draped over his shoulders. Finally, he said with a brittle edge, "What I did is unforgiveable. If I had succeeded…"

He didn't finish. It was a thought much too large and dangerous to stare nakedly in the eyes. One he would have to wrestle with for years to come.

"I don't know how or why you arrived there. It seems unlikely to have been an accident. Maybe the roads to that world are contagious and somehow I…" He shrugged. A scientist struggling with concepts not of this world. He looked at Hiro. "Perhaps there were unseen forces at work."

Unseen forces. That was exactly what he'd said when he proposed a new topic for his research project. Hiro started to smile. Corker looked at the crumbs on his plate. Put his trembling hands on his lap.

"What happened last night after…" A knot bobbed in his throat. He pushed his chair back and cleared his throat. "If you'll excuse me a moment."

He left the room but didn't go far. The stamping of his hard-sole slippers stopped just around the corner. They waited for him to return. A minute later, he was on the move again, going to the other side of the house. A door closed somewhere. It didn't sound like the back door. A bathroom, perhaps.

Robby got up and looked in the other room, his eyes shifting back and forth in search of Corker. Somewhere behind a closed door, Corker blew his nose into a white handkerchief.

"What is happening?" Robby whispered.

"I don't know," Haze answered. "It's like he's someone else. It doesn't sound like him."

"I was thinking the same thing," Robby barely whispered. "What's up with his voice?"

"What if he's a switch?" Haze said. "You know, like, that's not him. We went there, so why couldn't a toy come here, like, in his body?"

"A two-way road." Robby zipped his finger back and forth. "Maybe this is *their* dream. Which means there could be toy-people already here. Which means he can read thoughts. Which means—"

"Toys don't dream," Hiro interrupted before the rabbit hole got any deeper. "They don't sleep. You called an ambulance last night?"

Robby and Haze snapped out of it, looked at each other. "We could get in trouble for that," Haze said. "There wasn't time. It was an emergency, Hiro. If we didn't wake him up, we wouldn't be *here*, and it wouldn't be Christmas."

"He thanked us," Robby said. "Did you hear the way he said that? Like he meant it. Like he's glad we called."

"That doesn't mean we won't get in trouble," Haze said. "I'm sure what we did isn't legal."

"Not if he doesn't say anything. He can't prove it was us."

"Are you nuts? All they have to do is trace the call. It's not that hard."

They looked at the gifts. The cookies and candles. The note on the door. Corker knew they were coming over. Of course he knew they'd called the ambulance. Robby snapped his fingers.

"He can read thoughts, which means..." He jerked his head toward the other room. "He's a toy."

Hiro was starting to think Robby was right. They needed to put their boots on and get out of the house. But then what? Tell their parents about their dream. *Corker is a toy!*

Footsteps clobbered the floor leading to the dining room. The rhythmic sound froze them in place. Corker returned with a sniffle. He picked up his chair, not dragging the legs, and sat down. He straightened the placemat with the edge of the table. His eyes were even softer than before.

"I am not a toy, Robby, any more than you are a robot. Not a thought escapes our minds to be read, not here. Here we're all separate, in our own little worlds."

"Then how do you know us?" Haze said. "What's your job?"

It was a legitimate question. If he knew, then it was Corker. Hiro felt less afraid and more curious. They needed to know if toys could come into their world. Corker nodded, understanding they needed more than just his promise he was who he said he was.

"Who am I, is that the question?" The weight of something heavy returned. His shoulders slumped. Just a little. "When the ambulance arrived, I did not wake up immediately. There was an unexpected journey between there and here. Not so jolly, you could say. I saw things about myself, things in my past. Things I willingly forgot and had no wish to revisit."

He sighed.

"Someone took me there, made me face them. I think I know who, but that's not important. What is important is I wouldn't have chosen to go there, to see what it was that made me who I am today. And the reasons I did what I did over there. I resisted, at first. But it was exactly what I needed. The perfect Christmas gift, you could say."

He laughed painfully.

"I still have a lot of work to do, but I understand what I need to do now. Who am I, you ask? I am a high school teacher. I live alone and have lived alone all of my life. I am fifty-two years old. That might answer your question, but that's not *who* I am."

He folded his hands on the table, the long spider fingers intertwining. He looked at Hiro without the cold laser that brought students into submission. This was an open look. Kindness around his eyes.

"I am truly sorry I embarrassed you in front of the class, Hiro. That was fear, my fear, that did that. Your drawing was a threat. I have much that needs to be forgiven. Including the ways I treat myself. I hope you can forgive me."

That wasn't a toy in Corker's body. But it wasn't the Corker they once knew. *What journey did he go on?*

"It's Christmas, thanks to all of you." He gestured to the gifts. "Please, open."

They looked at the small boxes. Haze was the first to pick one up. She turned it over, examined all sides of it. Then said, "We didn't get you anything."

"Yes, you did." A genuine smile creased the uncreaseable face.

They waited until each of them was holding their gift, then ripped the paper away. The tape perfectly cut to length, the corners expertly folded. They pulled the lids off. The gift was resting on a swatch of cotton. They picked up what was inside their box, held it up for the others to see. They'd all received the same thing. Hiro wrapped the metal links around his finger.

It was a symbol of goodwill, of hope and resistance. The dedication to keeping the Christmas spirit alive. If he'd gotten this at home, he might have believed he'd seen his mother wearing it a long time ago. She wrapped it for Christmas because she didn't have anything else. Hiro only dreamed the life-size puppet was wearing the bracelet. And the elves at the big tree. Mads.

A red snowflake.

"Five boxes were in front of my fireplace," Corker said. "I wrapped four of them this morning. One of them will be shipped to a feline friend of yours. The other three are for you."

A smile of gratitude touched his lips. Haze worked the clasp around her wrist. Hiro clutched the cold links. "What about the fifth one?"

He pulled the sleeve back on his arm. A bracelet hung from his boney wrist. He cradled the snowflake on two fingers, reflecting, perhaps, on the times he'd seen it on Belkin's wrist.

"I believe he wants us to be reminded of the courage to dream. And to never forget that anything is possible."

"He?" Robby said.

"I think you know who he is."

Haze helped Hiro put the bracelet on his wrist. He would wear it for years to come. Even when people at school made fun of him. It didn't matter if it came from a make-believe world of toys, where an octopus drove a candy-striped car and a tiny elf lived inside a hat.

Hiro believed unseen forces were at work in the universe. The snowflake would always remind him of that.

"I've kept you from your families long enough. I want to thank you for everything you've done. Your courage is the reason we're here this morning."

He stood up and bowed at the waist. Spine and legs straight, bending at the hips with one arm over his stomach and the other behind his back. He went to the other room and returned with three paper plates, piling cookies on each one. He walked them to the door with a tightness in his cheeks. It wasn't the tension of irritation. This looked like raw emotion hiding beneath a thin layer of ice.

They put on their boots, said thank you. Haze and Robby walked outside with their plates of cookies in stunned confusion. Hiro turned in the open door.

"We're having dinner this afternoon. My parents would be happy to have you."

Corker's smile faltered. The knot bobbed in his throat. "Next year, perhaps."

Hiro wanted to insist. Spending Christmas alone was almost as bad as no Christmas at all. Corker, however, appeared content. There was work to do.

"Do you think it was real?" Hiro said.

Corker looked at the sky. Somewhere down the street, a child squealed with delight. Haze and Robby stopped on the steps, waiting for him to answer.

"What is real? If it is our senses—what we can see and hear, touch and taste and smell—then I think we have our answer." He winked. "But there's much we don't know."

"We can go back," Robby said.

"The roads are open," Haze added.

Corker placed his hand on Hiro's shoulder. The long fingers wrapped around it, squeezed gently. He didn't say it, but Hiro knew what he was thinking. The roads were still there. In order to take them, they had to choose a toy. He wasn't Viktor the Red anymore. He didn't know who he was. That was the work he had to do.

"Not for me."

He watched them plod down the driveway. Before they climbed inside the truck, Corker shouted.

"Don't forget, you have a paper due!"

They turned around. Corker smiled a grim but friendly smile. Then closed the door. They climbed into the truck and stared out the windshield, unsure of what just happened. A dragon and bobble-headed robot stared back. Hiro rubbed the snowflake between his finger and thumb.

Robby started the truck. "That's definitely Corker."

40

I stood in the dimness of the front room. Between parted curtains, I watched them climb into an old truck. The tires were bald; the passenger door a different color. The sort of vehicle I wouldn't allow in front of my house; the kind of vehicle that would force me to talk with neighbors until it was removed.

I watched them sit quietly. Stunned. An unseen weight tilted the world, and they felt it. Reality was out of focus. Nothing was what it seemed, and anything was possible.

Across the street, the Paxton children threw a ball in the front yard. The girls were on the front porch with their mother, scraping snow off the railings for miniature snowmen. The boys were playing a game without rules, one that involved tackling. They would wrestle until someone's feelings got hurt. I'd watched them play this game many times, lurking between the curtains, waiting for an errant throw to reach my yard.

There were boxes of baseballs and basketballs, wiffleballs and kickballs in my basement. The children knew better than to ask for them back. I once called the police when a Frisbee went into my garage. I showed the officers the mark it left on the trunk of my car.

Destruction of property, I told them. The father agreed to have the boys buff it out. I watched them do it.

What I hated most was the noise. The giggly laughter, the shrill screams and carefree frivolity were flames that boiled my blood.

The truck pulled away. Hiro, Hazel, and Robby would go home to celebrate Christmas. How did I know they were coming to my house? It was a tiny voice in my head. Not an actual voice, like the ones Viktor the Red had become so accustomed to. This was normal inner dialog. Thoughts. *My* thoughts. Although *this* tiny voice was different. It was unfamiliar.

I had been awakened in the early morning hours by EMS workers after the longest night of my life. Even in my confusion, I understood what had happened. The EMS workers were not easily convinced to leave. My vitals were sound, but I was confused. Dehydration, I told them. Low blood sugar, perhaps.

I lay in bed for the rest of the night, a cast-iron replica of myself. Sinking into the mattress like stone, trying to make sense of what had happened. It was a magic carpet ride into the past. All the doors inside me had been thrown open. I had been dragged through all the rooms to revisit memories I barely recalled. An awful, painful ride.

My punishment.

The longer I lay there, staring at the ceiling, pondering the possibilities, the more it felt less like a journey. I had seen things I had not been able to see about myself and no longer wanted to. I had been forced to relive them. Slowly, blood pumped through my veins, and something odd took over. Sensations in my chest and stomach. Cold steel in my legs.

Tremors of emotions.

We all have emotions, you might be thinking. Of course. It wasn't until that very moment I realized my emotions had been no more than thin ghosts haunting my body. They had been locked behind iron doors that were now open. The ghosts of the past soared freely with swirling tides in my stomach. They tightened my chest, quivered my cheeks, knotted my throat. Did I tremor with fear or weep in despair? No.

A storm was growing.

The house felt different. Foreign. The house I grew up in. I had gone from room to room, stood in the dark and felt the spirit of my father in each one. His presence oozed from the walls like corruption, bubbling beneath the paint, fouling the air. In each room, I recalled what I'd seen on my journey, each memory I was forced to relive. My chest was an iron cage. My fingernails bit into my palms. The ghosts spun inside me, a furnace stirring emotions until the pressure whistled in my ears.

I fell to my knees.

I screamed and cursed until my throat was raw and barking. Unable to get it all out, I continued until only whimpers escaped. There was so much emotion. A tidal wave gushed through the embankments.

I fell on the carpet, pajamas soaked with sweat, panting like a wild animal. It was then I turned to the cold fireplace. It was then a glimmer of realization that madness did not swallow me whole; perhaps the journey of memories I'd been forced to take wasn't a punishment after all.

I stared at a strange and foreign sight in my house. One that I had not seen since I was a child.

A gift.

I dared not move, afraid it would turn into a heap of ashes. I looked at the ceiling, imagined hoofprints on the roof. A jolly fat man coming down the chimney, even after all I had done. I moved slowly so as not to disturb the gift. If it was an illusion, I wanted to make it last.

I picked it up, felt the weight, the stiffness of the sides and sharpness of the corners. The smell of the paper and sound it made when I tore it open.

Even before I reached inside to find the bracelets, I realized this wasn't the true gift I'd received. My bones were shaking, my organs twisting. What I wanted most in all the world was what I'd tried to take from Toyworld.

I wanted to *change*.

I wanted to be someone else. Because there was something wrong with me.

The inner voice I heard, I knew why it felt unfamiliar then. All my life, it had been my father's voice. Now it was different.

It's my voice.

I knew where the bracelets came from, but I didn't have the courage to do what needed to be done. I was as fragile as thin ice. To be honest, I didn't know the children would come to my house. There was no magic there, no reading thoughts. I only hoped they would. I baked cookies and wrapped the gifts. I even doubted I could open the door if they rang the bell.

So I put a sign on it.

Timmy Paxton stood at the curb in front of my house. He wiped his nose on the back of a wool mitten. He could see me between the curtains. A football was on my front step. His brothers were shouting for him to hurry. Timmy could feel my expression, an expression my father taught me. One that turned children to stone. It was chiseled on my face.

I went to the kitchen and returned to open the front door. Timmy had not moved. His brothers watched from the other side of the street. I picked up the football in one hand. I walked through the snow wearing socks, feeling the cold bite my feet, and handed it to Timmy. A smile crackled in my cheeks and thawed my rigid brow. Timmy tucked the football under his arm. Before he could run back to safety, I handed him a plate of cookies.

I waved to his mother on the porch. She and her family watched like aliens had landed.

"Merry, merry!" I barked.

I went back inside and gathered wood from the fireplace. I took it into the backyard. Around a lonely fire, I sat on a log and stared into the steel blue sky, imagining colorful ribbons waving across the galaxy.

※

The rumors started.

School is a volcanic vent for such things. Someone saw me smile; I think that was what started them. I remember how difficult it was at that age, when a haircut could send a child home in tears. Or funny clothes. I ignored the murmurs in the hall, kept the desks in line.

Hiro and Hazel didn't speak to me of the dream.

They approached my desk after class to turn in their papers. I put my finger to my lips before they could say anything. Perhaps I didn't want them caught in the rumor mill, as well. I also did not want to know if they'd gone back. I couldn't think or talk about that. Not yet.

Hazel's paper was exceptional. However, based on her previous work, I was certain she didn't do it. Her brother didn't have the aptitude for science, either. Hiro wrote it for her, of that I was certain.

He'd decided to write something different.

Hiro turned in a story about a world where a race of toys coexisted with humans, the socioeconomic impacts, political machinations, and the complexities of equality. It was accompanied by two illustrations: a colorful planet and a red skeleton.

It took three sittings for me to read. Emotion would well up from a deep aquifer. I wasn't ready to open that faucet yet. When I was done, my comments were written in red ink on the last page.

Beautifully written. But not the assignment.

Hiro was not hurt by the poor grade I gave him. I think he wrote it as much for his own self as he did for me. I found his project on my desk after class one day, a note written below my red comments in blue ink.

Thank you.

I quietly resigned at the end of the school year.

I sold my house and moved away.

It was my father's house. I'd been living in his shadow all my life; the smell of the walls had steeped so completely into my being that I couldn't smell it until I left. I went north, found a small city where I blended into the population. I wanted to be alone without being lonely.

At some point, I got a job at a boutique toy store. One of those stores that specialized in custom-built dollhouses and unique play-things. It drew tourists and locals, especially during the holiday season. I had no such knack to build things, but I was quite good at wrapping gifts. I would watch small children light up when the bell rang over the door when they entered. Sometimes they would have conversations with a sock puppet or a plastic doll, and I would pretend they were actually hearing a voice adults could no longer hear.

Sometimes I joined them.

I became popular in the store. Partly due to my enthusiasm and willingness to close the store each night, which no one wanted to do. I would sit with the lights off for hours. The owner once asked what I was doing. I told her I was meditating. I had joined a group of medi-tators and found the practice helpful.

The toy store was my temple. Hope and joy permeated the walls. I would imagine whispering voices or movement on a shelf.

Tell them I'm sorry, I would whisper back.

I know what you're thinking, and I was, too. I was avoiding the pain. You would be right.

It took several attempts to find the right therapist. For the better part of a year, I avoided telling him about the dream. When I did, he smiled gently. Perhaps he saw it as a great metaphor. Or maybe he'd been there. I never asked. It had been almost five years since I'd closed my eyes and woke in that wonderful world. Five years.

I cried for the first time.

The dam finally breached. A lifetime of sorrow flooded out of the hole I had desperately tried to fill. I thought it would never stop. We continued talking about the dream so much that I was convinced my therapist had been there, too.

True freedom came when I forgave my mother, even if I couldn't understand why she would leave me. She had her own troubles, her own peace to find. My father, I knew what his childhood was like, how he became the person he was. I forgave him, too.

"You can start by forgiving yourself," the therapist said.

"What about Toyworld?"

He passed me a tissue. "They've already forgiven you."

ONCE A MONTH, a different storyteller would visit the toy store.

The center of the store would be cleared on a Saturday morning. Children would sit on the floor or a parent's lap while a tale was spun. At times, adults were as enraptured as the children. That all depended on the storyteller.

It was a time of magical stories and wonderland liftoffs. Children transported to imaginary worlds and faraway places. And the store sold toys by the bucket. Sometimes, when the storyteller was famous —as famous as a storyteller can get—there would be toys custom-built from the story. Children carried them out the door with fairy dust in their eyes, squeezing a big-headed doll or talking to a pink pony with saucer eyes.

One Christmas, the storyteller was a woman with white hair clipped behind her ears.

She was dainty in size with sharp elbows and a petite nose. But when she took her sweater off, she was anything but delicate. A strong woman with a powerful smile that made flowers bloom.

Her story was about a man she called Nicolaus Santa, who got lost during the first expedition to the North Pole only to discover an ancient race of elven living in the ice.

I was captivated by the elements of science. The elven were technologically advanced, you see, cloaking their existence from humankind. I was already planning to buy her book and get an autograph before she left when someone asked her where she got her ideas. She looked puckish, her finger on her dimpled chin, blue eyes shifting around the room.

"Dreams."

I was smitten. And that, dear reader, is a monumental statement.

Never in my life had I experienced feelings for another person. Not like that. Swirling belly, light-headed and giggly. I would have embarrassed myself had I not gotten busy at the counter.

I stole glances as she signed books and took pictures; one by one she would smile and sometimes hug while muttering to each child. I strained to hear what she said to them. And then I froze. I listened again and nearly fainted.

"Merry, merry."

WE HAD COFFEE.

It took every gram of courage for me to ask. "I'm a fan," I lied. I was a fan, but not before that morning. We drank coffee and spoke about small things. I'd become competent at conversation, having engaged with customers for several years at that point.

"Can I ask you something?" I mused.

"Of course." Her smile churned butter in my stomach.

"Merry, merry." I said it like that. Just threw it out there like a worm on a hook.

She looked at me, waiting. Then she looked deeper. Put down her mug and wiped her mouth.

"Yes?" she said.

It wasn't a question, really. She knew what I was asking. Oh, the delicious, dainty scoundrel knew. She was going to make me say it.

Can you imagine the risk, to just ask someone about a world where toys are alive, and I went there and so did some of my students? She wouldn't wait for the check before diving through a window.

I bit into a dry scone. Nodding as I chewed, looking into her eyes. I wasn't going to do it. I wanted to have dinner with her that night, then breakfast in the morning. There would be a better time, once we got to know each other. I leaned forward and shrugged.

"The toys are alive."

The words just came out of me. I was as surprised as she was.

I didn't know where the courage came from and thought perhaps she didn't hear them. Maybe I didn't actually say them. She wiped the corners of her mouth and reached across the table. For a moment, I thought it was very forward of her to take my hand. I wasn't disappointed, but this was just coffee. She grasped my wrist and turned it over.

"Toyworld," she whispered.

She rubbed the red snowflake dangling from my bracelet. Later, much later, she would tell me that that was why she came to my store to tell stories, having seen it upon a previous visit. She was going to ask *me* to coffee. She hoped the bracelet was more than just an odd choice for a grown man.

"Please," I whispered, "tell me everything."

She did. Not right there and then, but over the course of months, she told me.

Viktor the Red, she said, had been before her time. She had awakened in the early days of what had been called the Great Recovery. She'd seen Belkin the Puppet on television with his top hat and stiff cane. He wore the red snowflake around his wrist. She had her own little family over there, living life as a fuzzy bunny with sparkly red shoes.

Later, I found Hiro's story, the one he'd turned in for his project. The bad grade on the back. We flipped the pages, her hand at her mouth. She nodded and laughed and hugged me some more.

If she ever had doubt, it was extinguished that day.

It was several months before I told her the truth. I wasn't hiding it from her, only listening to her tales.

At first, I told her I'd lost the ability to go back. When she asked for more, I said it was a long time ago and my memories were foggy. That was half-baked. I was afraid, terrified, she would leave.

And then, like the first time we had coffee, the words came out. It was on a Christmas Eve. We were ice skating at the outdoor rink in a quaint downtown area, holding mittened hands like teenagers. There were galaxies in her eyes. The words steamed from my frozen lips. I told her who I had been in ToyWorld.

And what I had done.

She squeezed my hand. "They forgive you."

We skated without another word. Children were looking and pointing. Parents smiled awkwardly at the man with tears running down his cheeks.

We skated until they closed the rink.

I EVENTUALLY BOUGHT THE STORE.

At that point, I was making my own toys. It was a labor of love.

My lovely wife continued storytelling, traveling a lot less and doing it a lot more in the store. She wrote the books, and I built the toys: puppets and bears and dragons and monkeys. I was an old-fashioned toymaker in a fast-moving world. I was an enigma.

A scientist who believed in magic.

We were happy. Joyful. I think back to that countdown when Viktor the Red was moments away from taking all this away. The journey through the memories, the pain and sorrow, was the hardest moments of my life. It wasn't a punishment. Far from it.

I always suspected it was Santa Claus. Laugh if you want. Is it any more absurd than a dream world of toys? Even after all I'd done, who else would know what I really *wanted*?

One Christmas season, the store was full and the windows steamy. A storyteller from out of town had agreed to entertain our Saturday morning. She had emailed me, said she found my contact on the website. She only provided her first name. She wasn't famous or anyone to be recognized. I thought nothing of it. She was engaging and dramatic, singing and dancing and sweeping her arms. Children squealed and laughed. Their eyes as wide as their mouths.

"And then the train went *whoooosh* off the tracks. We soared through the clouds, into the valley that was near. Over the moon we could see, with merriment and glee, a sleigh pulled by a long train of flying reindeer."

The details of the story weren't what captured me. It was the way she told them.

Standing in the back, with his arms tightly folded, was her husband. He'd heard these stories a hundred times, maybe more. But he watched with a fascination that equaled that of the children. Then I realized it wasn't her he was watching. He was looking across the room, a smile hidden behind whiskers brushed with gray.

He was looking at me.

His face was round, and his cheeks were full. His hair was neat, as was the collar on his shirt. It had been decades since I'd seen him— three to be exact—but I didn't recognize him at that moment. It wasn't till after his wife was done and the store was buzzing with children, he approached without her, his smile growing the closer he got. And then I saw it, the look in his eye I hadn't seen since he invited me over for Christmas and I promised to accept the next year. A promise I never kept.

He held out his hand. "Merry, merry."

I took his hand with both of mine, shook with gentle vigor. The emotion that came so easily those days filled my throat. My words bubbled and stuttered. I swallowed them down. He leaned close to whisper in my ear, told me something I had been waiting to hear for thirty years. He whispered something I never thought I would ever hear again.

In the middle of my store, I hugged the boy who was now a grown man.

Our hero.

EPILOGUE

A silver train chugged through the middle of the valley where lights wrapped around trees and smoke puffed from chimneys, inflatable decorations danced in front yards and on rooftops. Music, heard across the village, played in the town square until midnight and would begin again at sunrise.

No one ever complained.

Below an expansive window set into the side of an enormous crystal wall, the lake had frozen over. The arena of the once infamous gala had been demolished, except for one wall, and the pit filled with water. In the summer, residents would fish off the arching foot bridge that led to the great pedestal that once held the fabled home of Viktor the Red.

Visitors would throw coins for luck.

In the winter, the small lake would turn to ice. The villagers would come to erect the Christmas tree on the pedestal. Visitors would arrive on the express train from all around the country to pay tribute to the Great Recovery. Stories of a time when Viktor the Red had stolen Christmas had been passed down for nearly two hundred years. Many toys, however, still remembered.

They had been there.

The tree would be decorated, the lights lit with a roar. People roasted marshmallows; toys dipped themselves in cauldrons of culinary delights. With music blaring, they would strap on ice skates and circle the tree.

Hiro watched from the glass wall, high above the frozen lake. He'd skated around the tree every Christmas since the celebration began the year the Great Recovery was announced. The year Viktor the Red fell and never returned.

Mads had made Hiro custom skates to fit his stubby legs. He still had them. They were falling apart, but he kept them to remember her.

The tail of the train pulled away from the lake.

"You're leaking."

A fire red dragon tugged on Hiro's arm. A bit of stuffing puffed out of a frayed seam. He was overdue for a re-cover. There were bald spots on his elbows; his glass eyes were cloudy. He'd had five complete re-covers in the last two hundred years TT (Toyworld Time). Haze had re-covered fifty-one times. She'd changed colors, tried different fabric, experimented with the latest fashion. Same dragon, different colors.

Always candy in her belly.

"Maggy can fix it," she said.

Hiro looked at the young woman across the warehouse. The machines that once lined the walls to distill Christmas spirit had been replaced with shelves. The floor was filled with workstations, each with an apprentice cutting fabric, setting a rivet or painting a smile. They followed Maggy's instructions, the master toy stitcher—a descendent of a long line of toy stitchers.

Maggy was Mads's great-granddaughter. There was more than one *great*, but how many Hiro couldn't remember. *Great-great-granddaughter?* Hiro grew up with all of Mads's children, and their children and their children—sitting in their cribs, seeing their first steps.

Even after all these years, the strangeness of time dilation never left him. He'd been a teddy bear for over two hundred years. Back in the skin (they no longer called it waking up), he'd just celebrated his forty-seventh birthday. Some days, his mind had trouble reconciling the difference.

Maggy was in the middle of the bustling room with a full-size puppet discussing the latest projects. Belkin had come to the workshop every night that month. His rounded face had been recently planed and varnished. It shined like lip gloss.

Flake stood on a workbench, arms crossed, while Snow interjected from the rim of the hat. Chase sat on the corner of a table, long tail swishing. Her purrs played like a satisfied instrument. Stretch was next to them but not listening. A red floppy hat covered the molded hair on his head. He waved.

Hiro waved back.

The only thing left from the time of Viktor the Red was the long, platinum table. A bobblehead robot was slumped on the edge of it.

"Where's your brother?" Hiro said.

"I told him to be here."

"Yeah, well, maybe it won't happen tonight."

Playfully she nibbled on Hiro's arm with spongy teeth (the latest fad). "It will. I can feel it."

Hiro hoped this night would be the night, but he didn't feel it like she did. He'd delivered the message, like he was told. Three nights they'd waited. Santa said it was time, just not when it would happen.

"One of the apprentices can take care of your seam."

They didn't make it one step from the window when a dollop of gooey light dropped from the ceiling. It fell onto the robot. No one was alarmed. They didn't even look up from their work. A horizontal line slashed across the television. The flat appendages jerked to life. Fireworks showered the screen.

"Sorry. Sleepover night. We got nine girls in one room and a vat of sugar. I didn't think I'd ever fall asleep," Robby said. "Did I miss it?"

He hopped off the table and rolled toward them. New spinners hummed on the ends of his appendages. Ever since his last upgrade, he skated everywhere like a middle schooler. He loosened his joints that were starting to rust (he needed to take better care) and executed a perfect camel spin. Hiro and Haze watched like bored teenagers.

"Merry, merry, Robby!" Stretch shouted. "How's the new claws?"

"What, these?" Robby snipped the air with pincers. "I could use three more!"

"Christmas present!" Stretch cheered.

Their conversation continued across the room. Annoyance from the apprentices filled the air. Hiro felt it ripple his fur like an electric breeze.

"So what's the plan?" Robby looked at the ice skaters below, jonesing to join a race. "We staying up here all night?"

"You asked that last time," Haze answered.

"What did top hat say?" He gestured to Belkin.

"Why would he say anything?"

Hiro knew why he was asking. He wondered the same thing. Belkin didn't have to say anything. His doubt about what they were waiting for shivered inside him like nervous bees.

"Never mind," Robby said. "I'm going down for an experience. You want anything?"

"You need to stay here," Haze said.

"Hiro?"

"I'm good."

Hiro didn't want him to leave. Robby's energy was soothing. He wasn't excited or nervous. He was happy to be here. Everyone else was edgy, especially Belkin. Who could blame him? He still carried a wedge of guilt from before the Great Recovery. His thoughts on tonight were like spotlights for everyone to feel. *What if this is a mistake?*

But Santa said it wasn't.

That was why they were waiting. Besides, they would know if it was a mistake by the toy that was chosen.

Hiro looked out the window. On the far side of the valley, just above the highest peak, a moon hung in the sky. Something streaked across the crescent. Haze pointed with her tail. Before she said anything, the air in the room rippled.

Belkin looked at the ceiling. Maggy called to her apprentices.

They felt it, too.

Everyone held their hopes back. Their thoughts didn't cloud the ether until a purple thread dropped into the room. It hovered over the platinum table. Hiro's fur stood on end. The atmosphere charged with static electricity.

Colors changed as the purple thread grew in intensity. Stretch's synthetic skin looked oddly green. The thread unzipped. A glowing orb of light burst from its pulsing depths and fired toward the shelves.

It lit a rocketman with integrated boosters first, then bounced to the other side of the warehouse to fill a bubble robot. Next was a spongy warrior, then a cow maiden, then a bug-eyed gremlin. Around and around it went like a three-dimensional pinball, settling in some toys for a few seconds while ricocheting off others. Sampling the inventory one by one.

There was every iteration of playthings on the walls, from custom jobs to mass produced. All the toys were all there. All but one.

No red skeleton in sight.

The apprentices held their breath. Emotions ripped through Hiro like electrified threads: excitement and surprise, anxiety and fear. The orb went faster and faster until the purple thread vanished.

"Where'd it go?" Robby's eye filled the screen.

They were searching for it. Waiting. Wondering if it was a failure, that a toy didn't fit (which worried Hiro quite a bit). Maggy was looking to her left.

A small panda tipped off the shelf.

It tumbled across the floor and bounced against the glass wall, facedown. There was a rush to surround it. Maggy held them back, to give the panda space. Hiro and Haze squeezed between the apprentices' legs. A new emotion emanated from the center of the gathering, beaming from the unmoving stuffed panda. It tasted murky and dizzy. No one moved.

Slowly, the panda's head turned. The glassy eyes looked out.

Maggy took a knee and held out her hand. The panda's snout twitched. She spoke softly, calmly.

"Welcome back," she whispered.

She picked the panda up and cradled it like a newborn. Relief flooded the room. It poured off Belkin in waves. His rigid mouth upturned slightly because he knew, they all knew, when the panda moved his arms that Santa was right.

A big red heart was stitched on the chest.

Stretch extended his elastic arm and tickled the Panda's tummy. He squirmed and snorted.

The panda struggled to sit upright. Maggy knew what he was looking for and held him to the glass wall to see. The ice skaters were below, the valley filled with merry lights.

Emotion dripped from the panda.

Hiro and Haze hugged. Christmas spirit flowed like a deep river. The Great Recovery was complete.

Belkin was the first to find the words they were all thinking. Looking out at the world filled with happy people and joyous toys, he said—

"Merry, merry, Viktor."

NUTCRACKER

JOURNEY TO CANDYLAND

NUTCRACKER

Once upon a time, there was a toy store filled with magical playthings and fantastical stories. But not anymore. That was a long time ago.

When Marie arrived, the place was cobwebs and empty shelves. Little dry pellets covered the floor. Aunt Rinks called them dirt balls. They weren't dirt balls.

The place didn't feel like Christmas. Nothing did anymore. What Marie wanted, she couldn't possibly have. A leaky air mattress and a self-absorbed aunt was all she got. But Christmas wasn't about what you wanted; it was about what you needed. Godfather told her that. That was when he told her the tale of the nutcracker.

"You must find the princess," he told Marie. "She's been waiting for you."

It was a story, nothing more. Marie didn't believe in fairy tales or Christmas spirit anymore. Certainly didn't believe in a wooden soldier and a cursed princess who needed saving. Until she discovered the gift.

Marie and her brother, Fritz, find a small box hidden in the old toy store. When they open it, the real journey begins. Marie discovers the nutcracker is more than just a silly toy. The princess isn't a metaphor. The nutcracker shows Marie a truth hidden inside her.

They'll have to hurry to save the princess. When Aunt Rinks finds the gift, she aims to take everything they've discovered for herself, to leave Marie and Fritz with nothing and the princess still cursed. The journey, however, isn't a game. It will reveal Marie's true nature.

What happens next is not what anyone wanted for Christmas.

For Ben.

1

The building looked like a toy left out in the rain.

It was on the corner. The paint peeling from gray wooden slats. The gray of dead fish. Weeds grew from cracks in the foundation. A stop sign leaned away from it. Even it didn't want to be near it. It was one of those buildings people forgot. Even when they were looking right at it.

Marie stared from the back seat of the car. *This can't be the place. We're lost.* Then again, she'd felt lost for a while now.

Aunt Rinks was in the front seat, scrolling on her phone, chewing on a stick of black licorice like a dog gnawing on a rubber bone. She emerged from a social media black hole and said, "This it, Vern?"

"This is it."

"Why didn't you tell me we were here?" She whacked him on the chest, then snapped a photo through the windshield. Tapping her phone, she muttered while typing, "So... much... potential!" Her phone whooshed it into the social media stratosphere.

She opened the car door and heaved herself out. The foam flip-flops crusted with fake jewels popped on her feet. She pulled her I HEART CRABCAKES T-shirt (a real deal at the gas station; changed into it in the bathroom) over the flesh roll squeezing out of her jean shorts. When she lifted her phone, the shirt crept back up and revealed the tattoo. It used to be the name of an ex-boyfriend, but that was covered with the queen of hearts from a poker card. Only this queen had been left out in the sun too long.

Flip-flops snapping, she went to the front of the building. Sheets of weathered plywood covered what, at one time, were wide storefront windows. She peeked through a knothole.

Uncle Vernon picked at his teeth. He found a small glob that was soft and white. It was wedged into his dirty fingernail. He inspected it. Marie looked away. She didn't want to see what came next.

Aunt Rinks turned her phone on herself, the building behind her, and adjusted her headscarf. She smiled for a selfie; then it was fish lips. Then two fingers and a thumb. She repeated the sequence from another angle, swiped through the photos, and tapped the phone.

Whoosh.

"Vern, come on. Get out here."

Uncle Vernon crawled out from behind the steering wheel. He dropped the keys in his front pocket and scurried around the car. His button-down shirt looked like a thin sheet wrapped around a stick figure, like laundry hung to dry. His ribs would protrude when the wind blew it against him.

"Over there," she said. "From the corner."

He took her phone. He knew what to do. Aunt Rinks with her hand on her hip, knee bent. Aunt Rinks with pinky to the corner of her mouth. Aunt Rinks surprised. Uncle Vernon bored.

"You all right?" Marie asked.

Her little brother, sitting next to her in the back seat, nodded.

His ball cap was pulled down to his eyes. He didn't need to watch the Aunt Rinks Show to know what was going on. Marie took his hand, and he let her. The car smelled like expensive cheese stuffed in a laundry bag. She didn't know what bothered her more, the smell or that she'd gotten used to it.

She cracked the door. The air was humid and crisp. Not cold enough for a sweater. Long sleeves maybe. It was a bit salty, but she knew they weren't near enough to the coast to smell the ocean. Her senses had been corrupted by the odors baked into the car's interior.

A block behind them, Christmas lights were wrapped around palm trees. *OPEN* signs lit store windows. They had passed a coffee shop on the way. There had been mechanical elves in the window, slowly swinging mallets and pulling saws. It felt normal back there.

"That's the building Mom told us about," Marie said. Fritz frowned. He pulled his hand away from her.

Uncle Vernon was trying to open the front door on the building. Aunt Rinks pushed him away, and he watched with his hands on his bony hips. He tried again while she barked at him like a dogsled driver, her hacksaw voice cutting across the street. People down the street were looking.

Their aunt and uncle gave up on the front door and walked around the corner.

Marie and Fritz sat quietly in the cheesemobile. She hoped no one would come down to talk to them before they aired the smell out of their clothes. Still, she was hoping maybe this was the wrong place.

"I thought it would be nicer," Marie said. Fritz nodded.

"BRING THE BAGS!" Aunt Rinks waved her arms like she was landing a plane.

Marie waved back so she would stop. Fritz got out on his side. He pulled his hat over his eyebrows, not because strangers were looking. He wore it like that. The strap on the back was adjusted to the smallest setting. It had been red once, now sun-bleached rose with a briny stain around the band. Aunt Rinks had tried to throw it away once. Marie wouldn't let her.

The hatchback was covered in stickers, most of them faded and curling. *I Stop for Selfies* was above the license plate. That was right below the newest sticker, a clear one with white letters across the window that read *@RINKSRULES*. Uncle Vernon complained he couldn't see out the window, but driver safety took second to likes.

There were three suitcases, a footlocker, and two trash bags full of clothes. And a cooler. Marie's stuff was in a duffel bag. Fritz searched through the pile of stuff. Marie handed his backpack to him. He kept searching, agitated.

"What's wrong?" Marie asked.

He typed something on his phone, showed it to her. She helped him look through the trash bags. The rest of their belongings were in a storage locker a thousand miles away. Not enough room in the car, Aunt Rinks had said. They'd go back for it one day.

Fritz kicked a soda can around the corner. The building was long. The plywood spray-painted with big loopy letters. Fliers were stapled to it, some rotted from the rain. The soda can slammed off the brick foundation each time he kicked it. Marie picked it up and put her arm over his shoulders. He let her.

A chain-link fence enclosed an area behind the building. Branches reached through the rusted wires. The gate was stuck open, the bottom dug in the dirt. A brick sidewalk, lumpy from tree roots, led to concrete steps and Uncle Vernon and Aunt Rinks.

"It's the right key," he insisted. "The lock is rusted. See?"

"Use both hands," Aunt Rinks said.

"And break the key? Just... back up a step. I can smell your breath."

She stood like he'd coughed on her. "No, you can't."

"I need some WD or oil. Something to lube it up."

"Can't you just spit on it?"

He shook his head. Then, on second thought, he yanked it out of the lock and dropped a bubbly glob of saliva on the key, rubbed it around with his finger and tried again. Apparently, spit did not cut through rust.

The windows were normal sized on the back of the building. The windows were fogged with algae. The brick sidewalk led deeper into the trees. Marie stepped closer, saw what looked like a patio and firepit. A couple of chairs overtaken by vines.

"Where's his skateboard?" Marie said.

"What?" Aunt Rinks said.

"Fritz's skateboard. We packed it in the car."

"Darlin', the skateboard didn't make it."

"That's his skateboard. He wanted it here."

"Well, we can't get everythin' we want, can we? And to be honest, he's goin' to get hurt on it and then what, mmm? Break a bone or twist his foot, and I ain't takin' him to the doctor because he wants to roll around. Makes no sense. And it's not like I threw it away, so wipe off that look. Now where's the rest of the bags? Go," she said to Marie and Fritz, shooing them like flies. Then handed a tube to Uncle Vernon. "Try that."

"What am I supposed to do with Chapstick?"

"Squeeze it in there," she said.

"It don't have dry lips, Rinks."

"It don't hurt to try. Always negative."

Marie dropped her duffel bag and helped Fritz take off the backpack. Should've known her aunt was going to do something like that. The skateboard meant more to Fritz than *rolling around*. Nothing Marie could do about it now.

They walked back to the car. She paused at the curb and closed her eyes. Christmas music was coming from somewhere down the street. She imagined a fireplace and cocoa, the smell of an evergreen tree with presents underneath it. A warm feeling around her, like a blanket made of smiles.

Fritz tugged on her sleeve.

Sometimes she lost track of time when she closed her eyes. Time traveling, her therapist had called it. Sometimes that was good. Just don't get lost. *Be here, now.* Marie blew her hair from her eyes. She needed a cut months ago. Now she was in the habit of blowing it out of the way. They grabbed the rest of the bags.

The back door was open when they got back. The Chapstick must've worked. Aunt Rinks was laughing that laugh that cut their uncle at the knees. She was right every now and then. And nobody ever forgot it.

"Come on," Marie said. "We can't stay out here."

Fritz didn't want to go. There was a grim look under the bill of his cap. This didn't feel like Christmas. They pulled the luggage behind them, thumping up the steps.

"Hey, hey, hey." Aunt Rinks pulled the door open, the rusted hinges screaming. "That better not be scratched. Respect other people's property, Fizzy."

"Fritz," Marie said.

"I'm sorry?"

"He doesn't like Fizzy," Marie said, for the thousandth time.

"Murry, darlin'," Aunt Rinks said with a big red-lipstick smile. "You don't get to choose your nickname. That's how it works. Now put that over there and bring the rest." She peeked under Fritz's bill. "Pick it up now, all right?"

She didn't look away until he nodded. They went back down the steps for the remaining suitcases. Marie kicked the footlocker when they got to the car, put a dent in the bottom of it. They carried the rest of the luggage up the steps, put them inside the doorway.

It was dark inside.

Aunt Rinks was using the light on her phone. There was a long table to the left. It was darker to the right, but Marie could see the outline of a couch.

"Why aren't the lights workin'?" Aunt Rinks flipped a switch. "Did you call the power company?"

"I called them," Uncle Vernon said.

"Then why ain't they workin'?"

He growled somewhere in the dark. Something fell on the floor. He let out a curse word and felt his way into another room. Marie and Fritz went back to the car for the trash bags of clothing. Down the street, a group of kids were coming out of a video game store. They huddled around someone's phone. Marie and Fritz stood there and watched. She put a hand on her little brother's shoulder.

"It'll be all right," she said. She said for both of them to hear.

UNCLE VERNON FOUND the circuit panel. Marie liked the dark better.

There was a kitchen table inside the back door. Twenty years of dust was inside a teacup. A small kitchen was to the left of that, a small stove and a small refrigerator that was knocking. To the right, a couch with faded floral patterns, the side of it used as a scratching post.

The floor was covered with dirt. Little clods of dirt.

"Vern? Can you get some of these boards off? We need some sunlight."

"There ain't no windows, Rinks. That's why they got boards."

"We need fresh air, Vern. We're in the South, now. We can put them back up."

"Rinks, can we get settled first?"

"Hey, did you get the Wi-Fi?" she said. "I'm gettin' two bars."

She held her phone up, swung it around. Then took a selfie with pouty lips. Uncle Vernon tripped on something in another room and launched another curse word.

"We're not staying here, are we?" Marie said.

"Your room's over there." She pointed. "Somethin' wrong?"

"Aunt Rinks, this place is..."

"It's what, princess?"

"I didn't think we were sleeping here."

"Do you have money for a hotel room?" She put the phone down and waited for an answer. Marie didn't have any money. She was seventeen. Hadn't worked a job since summer. What money she had was controlled by her aunt.

"Murry? Answer me. Do you have money?"

"My name's not Murry."

"Well, do you have money, whoever you are?"

"No."

"No, what?"

Marie tried not to roll her eyes. "No, Aunt Rinks."

"How about you, Fizzy? Do you have money for a hotel room?"

"Stop it, Aunt Rinks," Marie said.

"He can shake his head."

"We don't have money. Do you really want to sleep here?"

She wiped the corner of her mouth where lipstick was smudged. "You think you're too good? There's a roof overhead. Lights, water. I buy the food. I pay your phones. What else do you want, Murry?"

To not sleep on mouse turds. Marie almost said it.

"Here's what we're goin' to do. You're goin' to take your things in there. I brought a... Vern? Where's the blow-up mattress?"

"It's in the thing," he called.

"Well, once we find it, you fill it up with air." She held up her hand. "Don't ask for a pump. That air in your lungs is free. Once you get that, there's a broom over there to sweep up all this dirt. We're going to make this place nice and tidy before it gets dark." She clicked her tongue and winked. "You bet on it. Now get over here. I want a picture with my children."

Marie cringed and held her tongue. Aunt Rinks was too dumb to know that wasn't dirt on the floor and the table and counters. She squatted between Marie and Fritz for five selfies. She turned her head so the thin scar on her left cheek was hidden.

Whoosh.

THERE WAS A CRACKING SOUND.

A sheet of plywood peeled off the front of the building. Uncle Vernon, his fingers hooked over the top of it, went crashing down with it. He barked like a sea lion, rolling on the sidewalk and holding his ribs.

Marie stood under a flickering fluorescent light—the only one working in the front room of the building—with a broom in her hand. This part had been used for something other than living. There were empty shelves and a small stage in the corner, a place where a local musician might strum an acoustic guitar and sing cover songs. There was a counter with an antique register that still worked when Marie had pecked the keys.

The sunlight coming through the uncapped window lit up a network of cobwebs on the ceiling. A dust storm hovered in the room.

It caked the inside of Marie's nostrils. A moldy taste was in the back of her throat. It wasn't just dust she was eating. She'd swept several piles around the room, and most of it was dried little torpedoes.

"What happened?" Aunt Rinks threw open the door from the living area in the back part of the building. "Did you break somethin'? Vernon!"

She ran down one of the empty aisles—those two-inch foam flip-flops snapping her feet—scattering piles of mouse poop like a spilled bag of rice. She stopped at the big plate of glass Uncle Vernon had exposed, the surface hazy with grime and dirt. She put her hand on it and looked down at the sidewalk.

"I told you there were windows!" She turned around, said to Marie, "I told him." Then came the laugh. She got two rights in one day. "Where's your brother? He should be helpin'."

"He's working on the mattress."

"Fizzy! Come out. I know he ain't deaf. We need this all swept up by tonight. We'll open more windows and get some fresh air in here. Buildings are like people: they need to breathe." She inhaled deeply, then broke into a coughing fit. "Hey—don't break it!"

Uncle Vernon was pulling on the front door, which was frozen in the swollen frame. Mount Vernon had erupted. All it took was uncapped rage and a busted finger to get the door open. A gust of air sent more dust up Marie's nose. She pulled her shirt over her face.

"I told you about that window, didn't I?" Aunt Rinks said. "Now get the other boards down, and this place will shine."

"Look." He held up his finger. The fingernail was already purple.

"You need a Band-Aid?"

"No. But I ain't got the tools to rip all that down right now. Can't we just relax a second, Rinks? We just got here." He put his finger in his mouth. "When's supper?"

"What'd you say?"

"I'm sayin' I ain't ate since breakfast."

"You get those other boards off, and I'll have somethin' for you to eat." She grabbed his hand and kissed the finger. "I'll make somethin' special."

That cheered him up and depressed Marie. She knew exactly what *somethin' special* was. They ate *somethin' special* four times a week since Marie and Fritz had moved in with their aunt and uncle.

"Fizzy!" Aunt Rinks shouted like a dog barking in the middle of the night. "Come up front! Vernon, the faster you get them boards down, the faster I'll cook. It'll be hot and ready and waitin'." She batted long, fake eyelashes. "There's the man of the house. Come on in here, Fizzy. We were just talkin' about you."

Fritz zigzagged his way around the piles Marie had swept into an obstacle course. Hat pulled down, eyes on his shoes. He stopped in a dusty sunbeam. The flickering fluorescent turned his hat different colors.

"Where's your broom, son?" Aunt Rinks said. Marie cringed when she called him that, but kept her mouth shut. "Where's his broom, Murry? There's still sweepin' needin' done in the house part, and this whole store is a long ways from clean." She tilted her head and squinted. "What you got there?"

His left hand moved behind his back. Marie didn't see what it was. Aunt Rinks had an eye for things like that. Things like secrets. Things she wanted because someone else had them. Fritz wasn't moving.

"Come on. Let me see it. Ain't no secrets in this house." She held out her hand. "Fritz, come on. I just want to see what you got." She wiggled her fingers. "We're wastin' time here."

He held it against his stomach with both hands. The wooden figure wasn't more than a foot tall. It had black boots that looked painted onto its legs and a red jacket with white loops fastened to buttons. A tall hat with a looping chain was above bushy eyebrows. A mustache that curled above a square mouth. The eyes... they were spooky. Like green gemstones nestled beneath bushy brows. When you looked at them directly, they looked back.

"Where'd you get that?" Aunt Rinks moved forward. Her hand rising as if it were possessed. The impulse to take was a spirit that possessed her.

Fritz took a step back.

"Marie, where'd he get that?"

"I don't know."

"Well, he got it somewhere. It wasn't in his backpack, I can tell you that."

Of course she knew that. She went through their things all the time. Marie would be missing lip balm or hair bands, small things that didn't cost a dollar. Aunt Rinks would swear she didn't know how they'd gone missing. A week later, she'd be smearing her lips with lip balm she said she found.

"You find that in the house? Bring that closer, so I can see. It's dark, and I just want a peek at—"

She swiped for it. Fritz saw it coming, put it behind his back. Marie stepped between her brother and her aunt.

"It's his," Marie said.

"He found it here is what he did. This is *my* house. That makes it *my* toy."

"This place belongs to *us*."

Aunt Rinks laughed like a chainsaw. "You don't own anythin', darlin'."

"My mother inherited this building. Not you."

"Yeah, well, your mother ain't here—"

"Rinks," Uncle Vernon said. Uncle Bag of Bones wilted with shame for his wife's behavior.

Aunt Rinks cleared her throat. Every bit of fake happiness slid off her face like a hot candle. She'd crossed a line. Marie hoped she felt bad for it. Although Aunt Rinks never felt anything real. But it was there, somewhere deep inside her. An emotional decay that made her say things like that.

Marie was shaking. Her fingers had curled into her palms. She pulled Fritz behind her.

"I'm sorry," Aunt Rinks said. It was hollow. But points for the effort. "I just want to see it, that's all. Not too much to ask."

"You already saw it," Marie said.

"Just let the boy have it, Rinks," Uncle Vernon groaned. "Does everythin' have to be a fight?"

Something boiled inside her. A chasm of endless hunger, an emotional pit she filled with shiny things and photos and likes. No matter how much she shoveled into that black hole, there was always room for more. Why would she want a toy? *Because Fritz had it and she didn't.*

"Go do the windows, Vern."

Pop-pop-pop went the flip-flops. Marie shielded her brother. A minute later, a broom was tossed on the floor. The door to the back of the house closed. Marie picked it up and started sweeping. Fritz helped her make little piles. He held the broom in one hand.

The nutcracker in the other.

2

orgot the dish soap.

If Rinks didn't set a reminder, she didn't remember. Her phone was her second brain (almost tied for first). Her phone was her life. *How did people survive without them?*

She rinsed a pot in the sink. The water had a murky look at first, sort of like tea, but cleared after a minute. It was cold, though. She thought it would be warmer. This was the South, where winters were spring, and spring was summer. Here it was Christmas, and Vern was walking around in a tank top.

She put the pot on the electric burner, turned it up. She ripped open packages, stacked squares of dry noodles, and wiped a scatter of dirt balls off the stove. They were everywhere. That happened when a building sat empty for twenty years. Dirt turned into dirt balls. It was science. Dirt attracted dirt and—boom—dirt balls.

Deep down in her brain, though—in her gut—she knew exactly what those things were. And where they came from.

It was better not to know. She hid that knowledge from herself. That was called *compartmentalization.* She'd heard that word on a podcast. It was the ability to lock up knowledge. To focus without distraction. Elite performers mastered compartmentalization. How else could they get on a stage in front of thousands of people and not freak out?

Rinks could compartmentalize. She was a performer. One day, she'd be elite at it.

The storefront rumbled. Another board came off the windows. The last one, she hoped. In the morning, the storefront would be sunshine. Those people down the street would come looking. They'd see her in there, bringing life back to this cracker box. They'd be gathered around coffee cups, talking about what was happening, who the lady was with the fashionable headscarf.

She thumbed her social feed.

Her posts had hundreds of likes. Those little hearts warmed her, stirred something sweet in her belly. Felt good. She held the phone up, snapped five selfies with the pot of water behind her. She picked one, ran it through half a dozen filters till she was tanned and glowing. Angel-like. The scar on her cheek erased. The line that haunted her. A few inches higher, she would have lost an eye, doctors said.

"Getting... hot... in... here," she typed. "#rinksrules." *Whoosh.*

She opened another app. This one added likes to the post. She paid for those; they weren't real. *Momentum building,* the app called it. People got behind things when they looked popular. For an extra bump, she could add positive comments.

Looking good, Rinks!

Love the headscarf.

You are beautiful.

Water still not boiling. She scrolled the feed to avoid emotions that sometimes escaped those little boxes she stuffed them in. Icky nasty little things she didn't want to feel or think about. Toxic fumy things. It was better to keep a tight seal on those. What she said to Marie and Fritz in the storefront, when he was hiding that toy from her, the thing about their mom not being there—*my sister*—had poked a hole in her emotional footlocker. Because what she said was mean and ugly. She didn't mean it (but she did). The only reason she said it was to get them back. To poke them. They poked first, though, not letting her see what he had and all.

This is my building.

They weren't old enough to inherit it. Marie would be eighteen in a month or two weeks or something like that. Marie didn't know any lawyers to advise her. Rinks didn't, either; eighteen sounded like the right age to get an inheritance. Best not to talk about all that.

Besides, they were too young to see the building's potential. They would just sell it, and it wasn't worth a nickel like this. It needed to be loved and nurtured. Rinks never had kids, but if she did, she would be a great mother. She had instincts. It wasn't fair to judge her mother skills on how Marie and Fritz acted. They were like rescue dogs. They came with habits. You couldn't blame that on her.

The building, though, it had good bones. She wasn't sure what that meant, heard it on TV once, and it sounded right. The building could be a studio, she was thinking. Like a place for photos or plays. Culture. Towns like this were about culture. She hadn't worked out the details, but she would make culture happen in this dump. She deserved this building, not her sister. Awful what had happened to her, though. Just awful. Still, she didn't deserve to inherit the building from their aunt. That wasn't mean. Just facts.

"Supper ready?" Vern was covered in dust and dirt balls.

"Not like that, it ain't. You go on and shower first."

"Hot water fixed?"

"Not 'less you fixed it. I'm cookin', not plumbin'."

He slid his hands under his sweaty pits. "The water's cold, then?"

"It's just water, princess."

"Rinks, I ain't takin' a cold shower with the heat not workin'."

"Well, then put on a coat. Besides, cold water is good for you. I heard someone talk about it. Makes adrenaline and hormones and, uh, dopey."

"Dopamine?"

"See there? It's already makin' you smart. Now go on."

He looked across the room, over that disgusting couch, toward the bedroom where they would sleep. The bathroom was between their room and where the kids would be sleeping. It had an old-fashioned bathtub (the kind with claws) with a showerhead. But no shower curtain.

"Make those kids take one, too," she said. "They smell like rescue dogs."

Then she scrolled her social feed. Already two hundred likes.

A CANDLE WAS on the table. Brand new. She'd found it under the sink.

There were four bowls of noodles. One had a double stack. That was for Vern. Season packets were next to each bowl along with plastic forks. Supper looked fancy tonight.

Vern came out wearing the same jeans he worked in (said he couldn't find clean ones, but then he couldn't find a booger in his own nose), but had a new sweatshirt on. It was Rinks's sweatshirt, a gray one. Looked like a blanket on him. His hair was damp, and he was chattering. He speed-walked past the couch and nearly skidded into the table. He started ripping open a packet.

"Manners," Rinks said.

"Just gettin' ready, is all. Any cheese?"

She frisbeed a slice of yellow. It slapped on the table. He peeled off the wrapping and stirred it into the noodles along with a packet of chicken-flavored seasoning. He licked his lips. Rinks noticed he'd shaved. That was awful nice of him.

The kids came out next, wearing the same clothes they'd had on all day, dusty and wrinkled. No respect, those two. Rinks stood at one end of the table. Marie and Fritz stared at the bowls like they were fishing worms.

"You all shower?" Rinks asked.

"We did," Marie said.

"Then why ain't your hairs wet?"

"No shampoo."

"Right. No shampoo. And you ain't cold or shivering."

Marie shrugged. "Water wasn't that cold. Was it, Fritz."

He shook his head. His old hat was over his eyes. That thing had been around too long. The lucky hat. *The not-so-lucky hat.* A cruel smile cracked her lips. She packed away the mean feeling that came with it.

"You need a haircut," Rinks said. Marie pushed it out of her eyes. It just fell back down. "Fizzy, no toys at the table. And take your hat off. That ain't polite."

He had put that wooden toy next to his bowl, and the big eyes stared at Rinks, taunting her. Fritz put it on his lap. She was going to make him take it to his room, but that wasn't a fight she wanted to fight. Not right now.

"We goin' to do a prayer," Rinks said.

Ready with his fork, Vern said, "Prayer?"

"That's right. Everyone, bow your heads." Several seconds of silence passed, broken only by Vern swallowing the saliva in his mouth. "I just want to say thank you for this place with all its potential. We're here safe. We got food and electricity. We got each other. And, you know, just thank you for that. Okay."

"Amen."

"Now everyone say a gratitude before we eat," she said. Vern groaned, and she ignored it. "Just somethin' about what you're grateful for. I think it's a good way to start."

"I'm grateful for this food," Vern said.

"Me too," Marie said.

"No. Can't do that. Vern already said it, and so did I. Come up with somethin' else."

Her lips tightened. "I'm grateful to be here with Fritz."

That stung a little. "Uh-huh. What about me and Vern? You grateful for us?"

"Yep."

Rinks let it go. "And you, Fizzy?"

"Aunt Rinks," Marie said with those sassy, narrow eyes.

"He can write out what he's grateful for. Here." She dug a scrap piece of paper out of her handbag and a tiny pencil she took from a golf course. "Make it short, but mean it."

He wrote one word in neat letters. *Marie.*

"Me and Vern?" Rinks said.

He nodded. Rinks let that go, too. She was kind that way. Someone had to be the adult in the room.

"Great," Vern said. "Can we eat before my stomach shrink-wraps?"

He didn't wait for an answer, shoveled a forkful of noodles that would choke a mule. Broth went flying from his lips as he sucked it in. The next shovel went in before he was done chewing. A thin string of yellow cheese dangled from his chin. He looked like an animal, all hunched over and shivering. Fritz ate almost as fast, smaller bites, though. He held the toy on his lap like it would run off if he didn't.

Rinks tapped her cup with the plastic fork. It thudded instead of rang, but they looked up. She cleared her throat. Then decided to stand up.

"I would like to apologize. I said somethin' earlier today that was not very nice. About your mom. *My* sister. It's been almost two years since they, well... you know. There's not a day that goes by that I don't think about them." Deep sigh. She pried open a box of emotions that really were inside her, let them come up and mist her eyes for effect. It worked. "They were just so special to me and to you, too. I know you miss them as much as I do. They're here with us today, at this table. I can feel them."

She raised her cup to Marie. This wasn't a toast, but she did it anyway. Fritz didn't pay no mind. Marie was stabbing the noodles like they were trying to escape.

"Do you accept my apology?"

Marie nodded. So did Fritz. The apology didn't have the impact Rinks was shooting for. It looked like she'd just given them homework.

"Do you have somethin' to say to me?" Rinks said. Marie and Fritz looked at each other. "Maybe you have an apology, too. I'm just sayin', you wouldn't let me see what Fizzy found. I was just askin' to see it." She looked down her nose. She waited.

No apology.

"I'll be honest, it hurt my feelings a little bit, what you did. It was selfish."

Marie shook her head. Rinks was truly getting upset. What she said wasn't true. It didn't hurt her feelings that they were being selfish. It made her mad. This, though... after that heartfelt apology about their mom (*her* sister) and they couldn't admit their own selfishness?

"I don't think this is fair." Rinks put her cup down. "I'm only askin—"

"Enough." Vern slapped the table. The bowls rattled, and Rinks jumped a little. "What is it you want from them, Rinksy? It's a toy! Let it go already. My god."

The edge on his voice was hard and sharp. Rinks put her hand to her chest.

"You want to see it?" he said. "Fritz, come on. Hand it over." He beckoned with impatience. Slowly, Fritz lifted the toy from his lap and passed it to Vern. "Look, Rinks. A toy. A silly, wooden toy with a weird mouth and a sword and all that. Here, feel it. Then give it back to the boy, all right? He found it, it's his, who cares."

Vern shoved it at her. She took it with a helping of guilt and a touch of shame. Vern had that way about him. She always said he had different people inside him. Like, seven of them. They were his internal family system. (She'd learned that in a psychology class she took at community college, where she attended one semester.) Most of the time, he was meek little Vernon, whom Rinks liked the most. But there were other Verns, like when he was hungry or tired or concentrating. Seven Verns altogether. She counted.

This was Stern Vern. And Stern Vern cut through the hogwash. She liked that one, too, even when he stood up to her. Because he was usually right. The toy was stupid.

She slid her bowl to him.

"What's this?" he said.

"You been workin' all day. I'm not hungry."

"You ain't eatin'?"

"It's all right. I had a few snacks. Go on."

She'd eaten all the chocolate protein bars and granola trail mix they'd packed before leaving that morning. The wrappers were stuffed behind the refrigerator. She'd eaten so much black licorice she'd brushed her teeth three times that day.

Vern scooped the noodles out with his fork. He cut the mess with his pocketknife, which he wiped on his sweatshirt (her sweatshirt), and twirled half of them on his fork. He held it up and looked at Fritz. Then that sweetheart reached across the table for Fritz's bowl, which had been drained of noodles and broth, and slapped the extra helping in it. Rinks covered her heart with both hands.

That was Sweet Vern.

"I'M JUST CURIOUS," Rinks said. "Where'd you find that toy?"

She just couldn't let it go. She told herself it was just curiosity talking. But she knew. Somewhere locked away, a part of her was whispering to find out more. *We want the toy,* it said. And she did, she wanted the toy. Even if it was stupid.

"It was on the shelf," Marie said.

"What shelf, exactly?" Rinks said supersweetly.

"In the storefront."

"The store, huh. Which shelf?"

Marie shrugged. She didn't know. Or she was lying. Rinks never bet on anything. But if she did, she'd bet a bucket full of gold it was the second thing.

"Funny. There was nothin' on those shelves that I saw. Vern, you see anythin'?"

"Who knows, Rinks." He scooped the last noodle out. "Does it matter?"

"I just thought it was strange. You know, the only toy in the buildin'. I mean, it's in such good shape. It don't make sense. Maybe it means somethin'."

"It don't mean anythin'," he said. "It's a toy. Right, Fritz?"

He winked at the boy. She didn't like that. Ole Sweet Vern was becoming Sneaky Vern. She could feel it. Even after she gave him all those noodles. Team Vern was her favorite. That was the Vern who had her back. Now she was alone and aching to get her hands on that toy again.

We want, the part of her said.

"I was thinking we could get a Christmas tree," Marie said. "We could put it on that little stage with lights. Now that Uncle Vernon has all the boards off the windows, people will see it. They might start coming down this way. It'd be a good way to get some attention. It would brighten up the place."

"That's a great idea." Rinks rested her chin on her hands. "We got to buy food, though, hon. Fix that hot water heater so you don't have to keep takin' cold showers. And we need to get Wi-Fi runnin'. Your uncle Vern has to work, you know."

Vern sat back, nodding. She could feel his support on this one. He sucked his teeth and then said, "We can probably cut one of the trees out back, you know. One of those small magnolias would make a good one."

"Magnolia? How do you know what a magnolia is?"

He shrugged. "I can find some lights to put on it."

"Where you goin' to find lights?"

He picked up the bowl and slurped the last of the broth. "Somewhere."

Yeah, somewhere. She knew what somewhere meant. Vern had a way of *finding* things. Rinks looked the other way when it came to that.

"Oooor," he said, "maybe Godfather can help."

Marie frowned. "Who?"

Vern started laughing. Laughed so hard and long he ran out of breath. Rinks smiled at first, then felt troubled by what was so funny. She clearly wasn't in on the joke. He wiped his eyes, giggled some more. Then pushed away from the table.

"You all are in for a treat."

He found a toothpick in his front pocket and slid it in the gap between his front teeth. Making a loud sucking sound, he went to the bedroom. Marie asked what that meant. Rinks shrugged like she didn't know.

"Ah-ah-ah." Rinks held up her hand when Marie pushed her chair back.

"May we be excused?" Marie said through a locked jaw.

"Yes, you may." Rinks smiled. "You and Fizzy can wash the dishes in the sink. I made supper. Your uncle Vernon is tired."

"Only if you stop calling him that."

Rinks smiled and winked. That cheered her up. She sat at the table while they cleared the dishes. Chores were good for children. They needed structure. Maybe there wasn't enough of that, the way they talked to her. The way *Marie* talked. Fritz didn't ever talk. A blessing in disguise.

Rinks went to the storefront and walked around with the lights off. She studied the shelves. There was nothing on them. Never was, either. She could tell by the dust. She stared at the lights down the street where people were gathered. Marie did have a good idea, though. A Christmas tree would make people curious.

Rinks decided she'd suggest it tomorrow. Like it was her idea.

3

Their room was a small workshop with an air mattress. Marie's breath came out in thin, white wisps beneath a flickering fluorescent lamp. A gouged and scuffed workbench was against the wall. There were shelves on the back of it, against the wall. No tools in the drawers, but a few jars contained screws and washers. Nails.

No mouse turds. Not one. Even if Fritz had swept the room when she was in the storefront, a few would've been left behind.

Fritz put on one of Marie's sweatshirts.

"You going to wear that to bed?" She flicked the bill of his cap. "Probably a good idea. Brush your teeth?"

He nodded. She didn't feel like checking to see if his toothbrush was wet.

The sleeves bunched on his arms. He pushed them up, and they fell back down, gathering around the toy he was holding. Marie could hear Aunt Rinks and Uncle Vernon talking in the other room. She couldn't believe they were going to sleep on that mattress. It had to be thirty years old with twenty pounds of dust mites.

"Where'd you find that?" She poked the toy.

He pointed at the large opening in the workbench shelves. The wall behind it was covered with thin squares cut from a four-by-four post, each of them sanded and lacquered and tacked into place. The grain formed a patchwork of irregular bullseyes. Marie had no idea where he'd found it.

"Can I see him?"

Fritz handed him over. The soldier was a foot tall. Sturdy and stiff. The jointed legs and arms flexed easily when handled. The hat was black and tall, the boots shiny. The red uniform starched. A thin black strap was around the waist with a metal scabbard attached. A long patch of white whiskers was attached to the blocky chin. The mustache was painted in the shape of two teardrops.

"Does he have a name?"

Fritz took out his phone. It had been over a year since she last heard him speak. Marie had taught herself sign language watching videos, but Fritz refused to learn. He typed his answers on his phone.

"Nussknacker?" She pulled the lever on the back of the toy. The square mouth slowly opened. "You sure it's not Crack-a-tooth?"

Fritz barked laughter and shook his head. She gave the toy back to him. He clutched it under his arm and typed some more.

"Yeah. I'm hungry, too," she said. "I can't eat any more noodles, though."

Fritz opened the door. Aunt Rinks and Uncle Vernon were still in their bedroom. He closed the door quietly, then went to his backpack, reached to the bottom, and pulled out two protein bars. Chocolate peanut butter.

Marie snatched one. "Where'd you get these?"

She knew where. Aunt Rinks always kept a secret stash of black licorice and protein bars. The licorice she didn't need to hide, but the protein bars were basically candy.

They scrambled under the blankets—which were wool moving blankets—and threw them over their heads. They took the wrappers off slowly to keep from making noise. Aunt Rinks could hear a candy wrapper from across the street. Marie shoved the wrappers under the air mattress.

"Oh my." She closed her eyes. The chocolate melted on her

tongue. She tried to chew slowly, but it tasted so good. And they came from Aunt Rinks's secret stash. She was done in two bites, licking her fingers.

They stayed under the blankets. It was an old technique their dad had taught them. *Breath blanket,* he called it. When it's cold, keep your head covered. At some point, though, you had to come out for air.

They didn't have pillows. She gathered what clothes they weren't wearing and balled them up, gave a stuffed pair of sweatpants to Fritz (who was still under the breath blanket). She rolled up a towel and placed it along the gap of the door. It wasn't to keep the cold air out.

"Listen," she said, "there's a good chance a mouse or something will move around at some point. Don't freak out. They're small and harmless, just looking for something to eat."

Then she thought of the wrappers under the bed and moved them to a drawer in the workbench. When she turned around, Fritz was pointing at the shelf on the checkered wall. There was a clock up there, half covered by a dirty rag. She pulled it off.

It was nothing she'd ever seen before. And not pretty.

The clock was embedded in the belly of an owl. The wings spread out twenty-four inches on both sides, the molded feathers brown with flecks of gold. The round eyes were globes of white with black, slitted pupils. The beak hooked over the number twelve.

Fritz held up his phone.

"*Nussknacker says that will keep them out,*" she read. "Okay. He tell you anything else?"

He typed again.

Her hands sank in the air mattress as she leaned over to read it. "*We're going to Godfather's tomorrow night.* How do you know that?"

He typed an answer.

"When did you hear Aunt Rinks on the phone?" she said.

He pulled the nutcracker out from under the blankets. So he was using the toy to express his thoughts. She was fine with that. It was a therapy toy.

"Did Nussknacker say who Godfather is?" she asked.

She read what he typed. According to Fritz (via Nussknacker), their dad had worked for him. Their dad had worked in technology. Marie couldn't recall a Godfather, though.

"Does he have a name?"

Fritz didn't hesitate. *Herr Drosselmeier.* That gave her a small chill, how fast he came up with that name. It wouldn't be the last time she felt chills. He'd probably overheard Aunt Rinks say the name. Her phone voice could be heard across the room during a concert.

He held up the phone one more time. It was an answer to a question she was about to ask.

"He's *our* godfather? Great. Can't wait to meet him. You ready for bed?"

She pulled the string on the fluorescent light. Without windows, the room was pitch black. She used her phone to find her way to bed. It was already losing air. Fritz bobbed like a buoy when she climbed on. They pulled the covers over their heads.

The nutcracker was kicking her in the side.

THERE WAS NO TRAFFIC OUTSIDE. Aunt Rinks and Uncle Vernon had lived (before they drove cross-country) next to an interstate. Long-haul truckers made noise all night long, jake-braking onto the nearest off-ramp. In the workshop where they were sleeping, it was dead quiet. If a mouse passed gas, they would hear it.

"You want to do a memory?" She felt him nod.

This was a game Marie's therapist wanted her to play. Teri was her therapist. She had short hair that was always in a clip. She crossed her legs like they were made of rubber, and spoke with soothing tones that irritated Marie, at first. She was engaging, though. When Marie talked, Teri listened like Marie was the only person in the world.

Teri had asked Marie to visualize a box. It could be any size, any color. The box symbolized a container that held her emotions. That was the problem, her emotions. Marie had locked them away to avoid feeling them. Teri had never come out and said it like that. She didn't need to. Marie knew she didn't feel anything. *Don't let anyone tell you how to grieve,* their neighbor had told her before she and Fritz moved in with Aunt Rinks and Uncle Vernon. Marie had cried, of course she did. But when Fritz stopped talking, she dried those tears up.

So there was a box of emotions inside her. No matter what color Marie tried to make it, it always ended up black. A black box Marie had put a lock on.

Recalling your favorite memories will open it.

Marie didn't want to open it. She didn't want to forget her parents, but she didn't want to remember everything. There were feelings locked in that box for a reason. They could stay in there until forever. Wither up like winter leaves.

Even though Marie didn't see Teri anymore (she was a thousand miles away now; thank you, Aunt Rinks), she still played the game. *You don't need that therapist,* Aunt Rinks had said when they were ready to move. *You know why she wants you comin' back, right? She runs a business, Murry. She makes money off people sick in the head. You ain't sick. You just need to do it on your own like the rest of us. We're just fine.*

Whether they were fine was debatable.

Marie always played the game when she couldn't sleep. She'd close her eyes and whisper it to herself like a story. She would stop when the shudders began. Her chest would flutter. She'd cut it off before her eyes were wet. *Baby steps,* was what she told herself.

She'd started playing the game with Fritz when neither of them could sleep. They'd had two single beds in one room at Aunt Rinks and Uncle Vernon's house. Marie would tell a story from one bed. He would listen in the other. If the memory game would help her, maybe it would help him. And when she focused on Fritz getting better, the shudders didn't come as easily.

That was really why she played it.

She didn't think Fritz would remember this memory. He was three years old. Marie was thirteen. It snowed that Christmas. Nothing new where they grew up, but that was a record year. It snowed on Christmas and the day after that. Cars were buried, and people had to dig their way out of their houses.

On the third day, the sky was blue, and the air was crisp. Dad stood in the front yard, wearing a T-shirt and snow pants. He thumped his chest and howled. Marie and Fritz watched from the window.

"Challenge!" he called through his hands. "I call a challenge!"

No one answered because no one was outside. That didn't stop him. He went door-to-door with a shovel. When he came back, he was powder white and rosy cheeked.

"We got ourselves a challenge, kids," he had exclaimed. "Get ready."

Dad had made up the rules. Twelve families were ready. They could only use the snow in their front yard. At five o'clock, Mr. and Mrs. Podelini—the old couple who gave Chex mix to everyone at Christmas—would be the judges.

At noon, Dad rang a cow bell. The digging began.

Snow shovels and snow blowers, buckets and wheelbarrows. The Kellys backed up their truck and pushed three feet of snow out of the back. The Simpsons brought out ladders. Eric Stuzzy was on stilts (he got them for Christmas).

Fat snowmen and skinny ones and families of all sizes. The Pedersons made snowdragons. The Harrelsons made an igloo. The Farrells made a one-hole golf course (Leo was a state champ golfer). The local news came out in a four-wheel-drive truck. A man in a puffy jacket interviewed Dad. He was on the late news.

Marie and Fritz's family built one giant snowman with a super fat bottom with a turret for a head. Dad named it Tank. He climbed out a second-story window onto the porch roof to put a plastic football helmet on it and two charcoal briquettes for eyes. Nearly fell off when he slipped on the shingles. Mom wasn't happy with that.

They dug a shallow tunnel in Tank's belly just big enough for Marie and Fritz. Mom was worried Tank would collapse on them. Dad made sure it didn't. They used a trash lid for a door. Marie and Fritz huddled in the cold dark, waiting for Mr. and Mrs. Podelini to come by. They jumped out to surprise them. Mom and Dad shouted, "Twins! Oh my God, Tank had twins!"

Mr. Podelini wiped his eyes laughing. Mrs. Podelini didn't think it was so funny. They should have won, but the judges voted for Jacob Chopon's castle with a drawbridge and a plastic-lined moat. Dad presented them with the honorary broomstick as winners of the first (and only) Snow Build Classic. He spray-painted the handle silver and the bristles red.

In March, Marie saw the silver handle poking out of their garbage can. She took it home.

Fritz was snoring when she finished. Marie stared at the ceiling. It felt like Tank was standing on her chest. Pressure billowed the sides of the emotion box like a boiler shooting steam. Traces of that memory smelled like Mom's cookies. She squeezed her eyes shut to seal the black box closed before the shudders came.

She pulled the cover over Fritz's shoulder. The room was cold.

SOMETHING MOVED.

Marie sat up in the dark. Her bottom was on the floor. The air mattress had deflated. Her heart sprinted laps inside her chest when something touched her leg.

She scrambled for her phone, felt around on the floor. Her fingers hit something hard and plastic. She touched the screen, flashed it around the room. Fritz was curled up and facing away from her, his head resting on a pair of sweatpants. She stood up, pulled back the covers, passed the light around the walls and into the corners. Nothing moved. Not even a mouse.

Her breath steamed into the phone's light. The owl's predatory stare looked down from the shelf. She was about to climb back in the deflated bed when she saw the nutcracker on the bench. He was standing at attention in front of the checkered wall, right where Fritz said he found him. Fritz must have gone to the bathroom and put him back. Maybe that little sword had poked him awake. *Good,* she thought. It had been poking her all night.

It was hours before she fell back asleep.

❄

IN THE MORNING, Fritz was at the kitchen table, hunched over a bowl. His hat pulled over his eyes, spooning globs of instant oatmeal into his mouth. The nutcracker stood in the middle of the table, stiffly at attention. Guarding the bowl of oatmeal, should anyone try to take it from Fritz.

The kitchen didn't look as bad as it had the day before. There were still cobwebs on the ceiling and random *dirt balls* on the floor. It was sort of like camping. *It's all about your attitude,* Mom used to say. *It doesn't* have *to bother you.*

Mom would never have slept here, though. Marie was sure of it.

"Morning," Marie said.

Fritz waved. Oatmeal dripped from his chin.

"What's Uncle Vernon doing?" she said. He was cussing from somewhere in the building. Fritz shrugged. "Where's Aunt Rinks?"

He pointed at the door.

Marie stepped out back. It was brisk, the air filtered clean. She'd been in that dustbin too long. The morning chill felt good on her face. She smelled her sweatshirt, hoping it hadn't absorbed the mustiness. She was going to have to shower eventually. Cold water or not. But that wouldn't matter much if her clothes smelled like a bag of dead bugs.

Aunt Rinks was pulling vines off the decaying Adirondack chairs. Weeds were growing in the firepit. She was wearing a coat and gloves. Also shorts and spongy flip-flops. Marie watched from the top step. Red lines crisscrossed Aunt Rinks's legs where thorns had grabbed her. *Not a good look for selfies,* Marie thought.

"Good morning," Marie said.

"'Bout time." Aunt Rinks looked up with a handful of hairy vines. Marie hoped it was poison ivy. "Daylight burnin', young lady. You need to wake up when we do."

"I didn't sleep much last night. I heard mice."

"Don't put that thought in my head. Uh-uh."

"You heard them?"

She held up a stop sign. "Don't talk about it. I mean it. That was just the building settlin' last night. Nothing runnin' around."

Another curse word came from inside the building. "What's Uncle Vernon doing?"

"Fixin' the heater. We goin' to clean up this sittin' area today, build a fire tonight. Be a nice photo, don't you think?"

"I thought we were going to Godfather's."

Aunt Rinks looked like someone pinched her. "Where'd you hear that?"

"That's what Uncle Vernon said last night at supper."

"I don't believe he said we were goin' there." She knocked dirt off the gloves and eyed Marie. "You eavesdroppin' on my phone callin'? That's bad manners, Murry. I don't go snoopin' through your phone, do I?"

Yes, you do. Marie had changed her passcode twice, but Aunt Rinks would somehow catch her typing it in. Sometimes her phone would be in a different spot if she left it out.

"Are we going to Godfather's, then?" Marie asked.

"Don't worry about that. Right now, I need you and Fizzy to run down the street. Vern needs his coffee, and the machine ain't workin'."

"Do you have money?"

"I got money, don't worry about that." She dug a wad of bills out of her pocket. "Don't spend none on anythin' else. Just coffee. And take this."

She climbed out of the weeds. A vine lassoed her ankle and nearly took her down like a rodeo calf. She lost a flip-flop and had to fish it out of a green tangle of weeds. She limped toward a cardboard box, cussing without apology, and dug through it. She came up with a half-filled jug of milk. She popped the lid off and sniffed. Her eyes teared up. She emptied the contents in the bushes, white chunks falling on leaves.

"Take this." She handed the jug to Marie. "Go on and rinse it out in the sink real good, till it don't stink."

Marie held it at arm's length. "And then what?"

"Have them fill it up with coffee. Don't let them overcharge you. That's, like, a pot of coffee, no more."

Drinking coffee from a sour jug was one thing. Asking someone to pour hot coffee into an opening the size of a quarter was another.

"Don't give me that look. It's just a container. Make sure you rinse it at least three times. Oh, and grab all the packets of sugar and creamer while you're there."

"All?"

"All. Those things are free to payin' customers. No limit, either. Vern loves his sugar and creamer. Now go on before he throws a pipe through the wall. He didn't sleep much last night either. Don't drag your feet."

Marie rinsed the milk jug in the kitchen sink like her aunt wanted. The water had a rusty tinge. Smelled a bit like burnt match. The coffee was going to smell like curdled acid when Uncle Vernon poured a cup from it. This was going to be embarrassing. At least it got her out of the building.

"Come on," she said. Fritz pointed at the jug. "You'll never guess."

ONLY HALF A BLOCK from the building, the street was festive. Lights wrapped around palm trees, decorations strung between buildings. There were flowers in pots and wreaths on the doors. Stores were just beginning to open, and people were already shopping. It had a local feel to it, no big chain stores. There was a karate school, a yoga center, an art gallery, and a boutique. A used bookstore where you could trade books. A shoe and luggage repair shop (Marie didn't know places like that still existed). And a video game store.

The café was next to the video game store. *The Coffee Place* was printed on the window. The paint was peeling from the letters. Inside the big window, three mechanical elves were slowly moving in a bed of cotton. One had a wooden mallet, another was pulling a saw, and the third one was supervising. Their green clothing was dusty, like they'd just been pulled out of storage and put on display.

Fritz stood in front of the video game window. He and the nutcracker were watching a group of kids playing a game.

"You want to wait out here?" Marie asked.

He nodded, so she went in alone. A little bell rang when she opened the door. Old music came out of the café, the kind with an accordion. A fog of sweets and coffee grinds lured her in. A few people sat at tables with tall paper cups and laptops. An old woman was wiping down a small table with a rag. She turned her head like her neck was stiff and wished Marie a merry Christmas.

Marie got behind a man wearing a bike helmet and skintight shorts. She held the milk jug behind her with an awful turn of embarrassment in her stomach. At least there were only a few people to witness this crazy request. And if they didn't do it—if the woman behind the counter didn't fill up that sour milk jug with coffee—Aunt Rinks would drag Marie down there and throw a nuclear fit. And film it for social media.

Please fill this up.

Bicycle Helmet had a big order that required a cardboard tray. Marie distracted her nervous stomach with the pastries inside the glass counter. Homemade danishes and donuts and muffins and cookies. Dollops of strawberry jam and swirls of icing. Her mouth began to water. She looked at the wadded bills in her hand. She could buy a slice of banana bread for a dollar. They could eat it before they left the store. Aunt Rinks wouldn't have a clue. It wasn't like there was a standard price for a milk jug of coffee.

"Merry Christmas, young lady," the woman behind the counter said with a jolly accent from another country. She was as round as the woman wiping down the tables. Her hair was thick and white. Red suspenders strung over her round shoulders held up a baggy pair of red trousers. "What can I get you this morning?"

"I know this'll sound strange," she whispered. "But can you fill this up with coffee?"

She looked at the milk jug on the counter. Thick, white brows shaded her eyes. She scratched her doughy chin (where several curly sprigs of whiskers had sprouted) with stout fingers, then twisted off the lid.

"Don't smell it," Marie said. "It's for my aunt. She wanted me to bring it down here. Their coffee machine is broken. They like coffee. Lots of it. I don't think they care what it tastes like, as long as it has caffeine."

"I have better idea."

She took the jug with her. Marie felt relief it was no longer in sight. How she was going to carry a jug of thin plastic full of hot coffee back to the building, she hadn't figured out. She looked around for the condiments table. There were bowls of sugar packets and little plastic cups of creamer. She was going to take a handful, that was it. Tell Aunt Rinks that was all they had. Throw in a couple of wooden sticks to make her happy.

A group of kids were outside on the sidewalk. One of them was Fritz.

Marie's first thought was he was making friends. They were the ones from inside the video game store Fritz had been watching. They were about his age. There were three of them. She smiled, imagining him sitting in a circle with them, playing video games. He'd had friends when he was younger, but not since they had to move in with Aunt Rinks and Uncle Vernon.

Maybe, she thought, *this move will be good for him.*

That fantasy vanished just as soon as she thought it. The boy with a neon green stocking cap snatched the nutcracker from Fritz's hands. Fritz tried to take it back.

Marie bolted away from the counter. She was across the store before she realized what she was doing, throwing open the door—the little bell clanging like a church bell—and onto the sidewalk. She appeared so quickly that the boys jumped.

"What are you doing?" she said.

Stocking Cap Boy nearly dropped the nutcracker. In an instant, the boys ran. Marie lunged at the one who had taken the nutcracker from Fritz. She caught the pocket on his jacket, heard the seam rip.

She jerked him back like a roped calf, pulled the nutcracker from his hand.

"This isn't yours," she said. "Why would you take it from him?"

"You're going to pay for this jacket."

"Apologize to my brother," she said.

He tried to shimmy out of his jacket. She grabbed him by the T-shirt. It was too much, what she was doing. She was scaring him, but she couldn't stop herself any more than a mama bear could let someone pet her cubs. Instinct had a firmer grip on her than she had on the boy. And he wasn't going anywhere.

"Let me go."

He swung at her. She reached back to make sure Fritz was behind her. She let go, and Stocking Cap Boy stumbled off the curb and nearly fell.

The boys who ran away were coming back. They came out of the video store with another boy. This one was about Marie's age, maybe a year or two younger. He was a foot taller and as skinny as a cinnamon stick, wearing high-top shoes that weren't tied and gray sweatpants cut off at the knees. Polka dots of acne on his chin.

Marie pulled Fritz behind her and widened her stance.

"She ripped my jacket." Stocking Cap Boy showed Acne Boy his pocket.

He strode at Marie. "What's your problem?"

"He took something from my brother."

Acne Boy's grin chiseled into his cheeks. He looked down at what Marie was holding. He seemed relaxed, but she sensed tension in his posture. She was ready for what he was about to do, but he was faster than she expected. He plucked the nutcracker from her hand before she could turn away.

With an ugly grin, he held it over his head. "A doll?"

This got a laugh from the boys. The instinct that had sent Marie running across the café filled her once again. She was possessed, focused. Cold as the sidewalk under her shoes.

"Give it back," she said.

Acne Boy thought that was funny, the way she said it. It had an *or else* sound to it.

Marie's mom had taught her to fight.

Her dad hadn't been much of a fighter. Her mom had been scrappy. At least, that was what her dad said. They wouldn't share stories, though. Marie'd been to wrestling camp every summer, learned jujitsu one year, and even tried out for the boys' wrestling team. She was a decent grappler, but not good enough to make the team. But against someone who'd never wrestled? That was why her mom had taught her.

It had been a while since she'd been on the mat—not since they moved in with their aunt and uncle—but she could tell Acne Boy wasn't a fighter. He could swing a fist like any testosterone-fueled teenager, but he didn't *know* how to fight. It was the way he was standing, no center of gravity. No base. She could shoot his legs before he knew what hit him. *A brawler can't fight on the ground,* her mom used to say.

Acne Boy raised the nutcracker higher. He was going to smash it on the concrete. If she took out his legs, he'd hit his head on the sidewalk. She didn't want to do that. If he took a swing at her, that was different. She made sure Fritz was still behind her. She was about to say something, bait him into coming at the girl who didn't look afraid, when—

"Ahhh!" Acne Boy cried.

He grabbed his finger. The nutcracker fell from his hand. Somehow, it caught on the string holding up his sweatpants. There was a sharp *ping.* The sweatpants fell halfway down, exposing red boxers. A pink line appeared on the soft flesh above his waistband. He grabbed his pants before they fell to his knees. The string dangled loosely.

Fritz grabbed the nutcracker off the sidewalk.

"Enough!" The old woman came out of the café. The rag over her shoulder. "That is no way to behave on street, Bobby. You too, Sean. You know better, all of you. These are new children. Go. Go home. All of you, before I call your mothers and fathers."

Bobby's finger was red and swollen. The nutcracker had somehow clamped onto it, and by random chance, the sword attached had cut the boy's sweatpants. They backed away from the old woman, her hands planted on her waist like an old country warrior. They wandered toward the video game store, muttering to each other. Bobby held up his sweatpants with one hand.

"Santa bring you coal next time," the old woman hollered. She turned to Marie and Fritz. "Come inside, children. Ms. Clara have something for you."

"Have seat."

Ms. Clara pulled chairs out from a table in the corner, then shouted at the woman behind the counter in another language.

"Let me see." She turned Fritz's head, examined both cheeks. Squeezed his shoulders. "Strong like bull, you are. You don't scare easy, no? And I call their mother next time. Their father don't care, like the boys, but mother will make them care. How about you, young lady?"

"I'm fine," Marie said.

Ms. Clara sat down with them. "Of course. You run to your brother. I see you. Very brave."

Marie shook her head, slightly embarrassed. The line between bravery and stupidity was thin. She should've grabbed the nutcracker and left it at that. There was no reason to grab the boy and demand he apologize. That was stupid. Someone could've gotten hurt. Fritz or her or one of them, all because she wanted to teach him a lesson for messing with her brother.

The woman from the counter slid a tray onto the table. One of her suspenders dangled at her hip. She wiped her hands on her red trousers, strung the suspender over her shoulder, and bowed with a twinkle in her eye.

"Thank you, dear. Enough," Ms. Clara said. She shook her head and gave an impatient cough. "My sister, Trutchen. Always with the show, she does."

There was a resemblance between the two women. Both soft and sweet, like yeast rolls. Both with smiles in their eyes. Ms. Trutchen was endearing if not jolly. The way she bounced with each step to a song only she was hearing. The little bell rang, and she greeted the new customers with a boisterous merry Christmas. Ms. Clara rolled her eyes.

"This for you."

She put mugs in front of Marie and Fritz. It was hot chocolate with a heavy dose of whipped cream. Also, there were two pastries with flaky crust and blobs of jelly on top.

Marie stopped Fritz before he inhaled one. "We can't afford these."

"Nonsense. It is Christmas. This boy needs to eat." She tapped the bill of his cap.

Fritz had the pastry in his mouth before Marie could say thank you. He took two bites before swallowing, then sipped the hot chocolate.

"Thank you," she said. "My brother, Fritz, says thank you, also."

"I see."

He was nodding with a foamy mustache on his lip.

"He doesn't talk," Marie said.

"Is that right? Why is that, Fritz?" the old woman said.

He did what he always did when someone asked that question. Pretended like he didn't hear it. Maybe he didn't know why. The doctor said there was nothing physically wrong with him. A therapist worked with him. They mostly drew pictures. The therapist said he would talk when he was ready.

It'd been almost two years.

"Well, Mr. Fritz, there is no need to talk in here. Only be good listener. Huh?"

Fritz smiled bashfully. Ms. Clara squeezed his shoulder. Marie had the urge to weep. The kindness toward her brother was so genuine.

"Sooo... this cause all the trouble, huh?" Ms. Clara reached for the toy and stopped. "May I?"

Fritz handed it to her.

"Nutcracker." She studied the front and back, ran her finger along the painted teeth that, somehow, had clamped down on Bobby the Acne Boy's finger. (Must have been the way he was holding it.) Ms. Clara suffered no misfire. "This toy come from my country, you know. We put the Nussknacker on front step at night. He protect the house from bad wishes and such."

Marie felt a chill. "How'd you know that was his name?"

"Nussknacker? Everyone call him that, from my country. Here, it is nutcracker. Even though he never crack nuts." She gave the toy back to Fritz, who was already on his last bite. "Where did you get him?"

"Our building down the street." Marie pointed in that direction. "It's on the corner. Our uncle took the boards off the windows yesterday."

Ms. Clara frowned. "The toy store?"

"It was a store, I think. There's, like, living quarters in the back. That's where we're staying."

"I don't understand."

"Like, sleeping. We don't have enough money for a hotel. Well, I mean, we probably do, but Aunt Rinks doesn't want to spend it." Ms. Clara was nodding along but still not understanding. "My mother had inherited it from her family, like, a long time ago. We never came to see it, though. My great-aunt owned it. She was my grandmother's sister."

"Mrs. Corker?"

"You knew her?"

Ms. Clara slapped her knee, then shouted in her native tongue to Ms. Trutchen, who was reaching for a muffin in the glass case. She listened to what her sister said, then raised a pair of silver tongs.

She shouted: "Merry, merry!"

They shared a laugh. Marie was lost, took a sip of hot chocolate that was rich and tasty. She pushed her plate toward Fritz. He took the pastry with a smile bigger than the one before. The urge to weep was in her throat again.

"You are Marie Corker, then?"

"Stahlbaum. My great-aunt was on my mother's side."

"Ah. Your great-aunt was legend." Ms. Clara leaned over the table. The weight of her elbows tipped the table toward her. "Every Saturday, starting November, there would be line around corner. Store would fill with children and parents. She would sit on rocking chair with purple blanket and cup of tea in both hands. Like this."

She demonstrated with Fritz's mug. It was already empty.

"At noon, children and mothers and fathers gather around her. She would tell stories... great, great stories. They get lost in them, like, what is word... *hypnotize*! No one speak or move when she tell stories of Santa Claus and reindeer and snowman and elf. My sister and I, we were younger then, not children, but we go sometimes to hear. It was hypnotize. We would feel it, you know, like energy. Like *magic*."

She sighed.

"And Mr. Corker, he was toymaker. He was one who fill all the shelves with toys. He make them in back of store. Children love them. Look!" She shouted in her native tongue. Ms. Trutchen disappeared around the corner, came back to hold up what looked like an orange octopus. "He make those. And also elves, you see in window there. He make those, too. They work now over twenty years. He was master toymaker."

The mechanical elves didn't look like the work of mastery. But for two free pastries, she didn't disagree.

"Elves not so good, huh?" Ms. Clara said.

"No! No, I think the elves look great. Very, uh, very old school, you know. Authentic."

The old woman leaned back in the chair to share something with her sister, who gave a smile and a thumbs-up. "They are not so good," Ms. Clara said. "They are special, though. Mr. Corker, your great-uncle, he was very nice man. Became quite good game maker before they close. He make games, make up rules and pieces. Very complicated, sometimes. Not like today's games where everything all *pew-pew,* you know. Thinking games, he make. Not always fun, but challenging. People play them and learn. Children play them here with us. Beat us."

Ms. Trutchen must have heard her and scoffed.

"What happened to the store?" Marie asked. "Why did it close?"

"Oh, children get older. They get phones and things, I think. Mr. and Mrs. Corker get older, and one day they close. But no one make toys like that today. Or tell stories." She squinted through her round spectacles, lifting her chin to see through the bifocals. "You look a little like her, I think. The eyes."

She shouted at Ms. Trutchen and pointed at Marie. Marie didn't understand the answer.

"She say shape of your face like hers. But she wrong. It is the eyes."

Marie laughed. She'd never seen a photo of her great-aunt. Marie looked like her mother. When they'd compared pictures of each other at the same age, it was hard to tell the difference.

Ms. Clara called another order to her sister. A minute later, she brought a plate, this one with four slices of banana bread. Fritz didn't ask for permission. He started eating. Marie took a bite of one. It was magnificent.

"So, your mother and father will open store?"

Marie shook her head. "My parents passed away." After all that time, it still hurt to say it out loud. Especially in front of Fritz.

"I'm so sorry, dear."

"We live with our aunt and uncle now."

"They are here?"

"We're living in the store. I don't know how long, though. There's a lot to fix, though. The heater isn't working, or maybe it is now. The coffee machine didn't work. My aunt sent me to fill up the milk jug. It's kind of gross."

Ms. Clara listened with kind eyes. Marie had the urge to tell her everything, from the time of her parents' accident, to moving out of the house they grew up in, and how different Aunt Rinks and Uncle Vernon were from their parents. Maybe she would have said all those things if Fritz wasn't there.

She put her hand on Marie's hand. "I am very happy you are here."

The urge to weep came closer.

Ms. Clara excused herself. "Enjoy bread. I will be back."

MARIE FINISHED the piece she'd started, then broke the last one in half and gave it to Fritz. She savored the last sip of hot chocolate, scooping the cream out of the bottom of the mug with her finger and licking it off. Fritz was laughing at the whipped cream on her nose. She wiped it off and tried to put it on his nose.

"This for you." Ms. Clara came back with a cardboard container. A bladder of coffee was inside it. "Much better than milk jug."

There was a bag full of sugar packets and creamers. It was too generous. If Ms. Clara only knew Aunt Rinks wanted Marie to steal all of it. There were also two blueberry muffins the size of small cakes. Marie and Fritz would eat them on the way back and hide the wrappers.

"Come back tonight for food, if you like. We have chicken salad and borsht and pelmeni. Very good for you. Ms. Trutchen is good cook, but don't tell her so. Head too big already."

"Thank you so much. You're too kind, really. I think we're going to our godfather's for dinner tonight. He lives here, somewhere. But maybe tomorrow we'll come."

"Oh, that is nice. Who is your godfather?"

Marie couldn't remember. She looked at Fritz. He paused, then typed the godfather's name on his phone. Ms. Clara looked through the bottom of her glasses. She shouted at Ms. Trutchen. She gave a thumbs-up.

"Do you know him?" Marie asked.

"Everyone know him, dear."

Marie and Fritz took their time walking back to the old toy store. He was too full to eat the muffin, so they hid what was left in their pockets for later. Uncle Vernon was thrilled with the coffee. Aunt Rinks was even happier they took all the sugar and creamer.

4

A headache started behind Rinks's eyes and skimmed across her forehead. She looked through the plastic bags piled on the kitchen counter for a protein bar. All that was left was packages of instant noodles and slices of yellow cheese.

Vern was in the next room, talking on the phone. She pulled the wrappers from the protein bars out of hiding and counted them. Only ten. She'd packed twelve. She kept searching.

"Yeah, I'll hold." Vern came out of the back room.

Rinks shoved the wrappers in one of the plastic bags. "What're you doin'?"

"Cable company. Where's the coffee?"

"Ain't you supposed to be fixin' the heater?"

"I can't work without Wi-Fi, Rinks. And it ain't that cold in here. Ain't you got somethin' you can put on, like long pants or—hello? Yeah, I'm here. Uh-huh. I just told the lady..."

He went back to the bedroom, where he'd walk circles. He couldn't talk on the phone without pacing and waving his hand, pointing like the person on the other end of the call was standing in front of him. It made her anxious.

Rinks needed a shower and clean clothes. She felt dirty. Not pretty. She adjusted her headscarf, grabbed a sponge, and started wiping the counter. She held up her phone. This would be called *mornin' chores.* She took twenty selfies. Each one was awful, even with filters. She scanned through photos taken yesterday. She needed to post. Had to keep her stream flowing.

Being a social media queen was hard work.

People had no idea what it took. Finding something original was exhausting. Her feed was good and active. Lots of comments. She read some of them, which people told her not to do. How else was she going to know what her fans were thinking?

Love the headscarf!

Beautiful!

I wish I were you!

That warm, fuzzy feeling grew in her like a seedling feeling the first rays of morning. Didn't matter if those comments were real ones or the fake ones she bought, she ate them up like glazed donuts and felt the headache fade. She should have stopped reading after three good ones.

Scarface with eye shadow.

A shot to the ribcage. The scar on her cheek was showing in the photo, and that comment went at it like a haymaker. There was no way to punch back. She wanted to delete the post, but then all those luscious comments would go away. *Why do people have to be so mean?*

The door opened. The kids came inside carrying a box.

"Where you been?" Rinks said. "I could have crawled down there myself faster than you."

"Almost got in a fight," Marie said.

"Coffee!" Vern came speed-walking out of the bedroom with the phone against his ear. He grabbed a mug from the counter, blew inside it, then turned it upside down. One of those dirt balls fell out. He filled it from the plastic spout on the fancy box and slurped it black. "Ahhh. You got in a fight?"

"Almost," Marie said. "Someone was picking on Fritz."

"You pop him?" His teeth were pickets stuck in a gummy smile.

"No. He took the nutcracker. I made him give it back."

Rinks shook her head. *That toy.* Might be for the boy's own good to take it away, the problems it was causing.

"The kid's older brother tried to break it. One of the owners of the café, her name's Ms. Clara, broke it up. Made them leave. She was real nice, sat down and talked to Fritz and me. Our place was a toy store. Did you know that?"

"Yeah. I knew that." Rinks didn't know that. "The shelves and everythin', Murry. Ain't it obvious. Fizzy got that toy, which I should take away, the trouble it's makin'."

"Those boys were bullies," Marie said. "It had nothing to do with the nutcracker."

"It had somethin' to do with it. You almost got to fightin' over it. Give it here."

Rinks stuck out her hand. Fritz got behind his sister, who didn't move when Rinks stepped toward them. Rinks was going to grab the boy—

"Leave him alone, Rinks," Vern said.

"Don't talk to me like that! I'm all scratched up from workin' all morning while these two been tellin' stories, and I ain't had a shower in two days."

"Well, take a shower, then."

"I ain't had time!"

"Hello? Yeah." Vern headed back to the bedroom. "I been on hold fifteen minutes now."

Rinks didn't need this aggravation. All she wanted was coffee and a shower. And a protein bar. "Hold up." The kids were trying to escape to the tiny room where they were sleeping. That was when she noticed a bulge in their pockets. "Come here. You can keep the stupid toy," she said when Fritz hesitated.

She urged them closer. There were crumbs on his shirt, just below the collar. She plucked off a big one.

"What's this?"

Marie dug a half-eaten muffin from her front pocket. She elbowed Fritz, and he did the same. Blueberry stains were on his fingers.

Marie put a wad of money on the table. It looked pretty much like the money Rinks had given her.

"Ms. Clara gave us the muffins," Marie said.

"She just gave them to you."

"She felt bad about the boys, I think. You can count the money. It's all there. She gave us the coffee for free, too, in that travel box."

"Fancy," Rinks said. "Where's the milk jug?" Marie shrugged. Rinks was agitated, which didn't make a lick of sense. Free coffee in a fancy tote was exactly what she wanted. Why should she feel like a scumbag? "You makin' friends already?"

"She's a nice lady. You should go talk to her. She knew my great-aunt—your aunt—who owned this place. Said she was a good story-teller; kids would line up to hear her stories. Maybe we could do that, too. You know? We could make this a toy store again."

Rinks looked in the plastic bag Marie had put on the table. It was filled with sugar packets and little creamers. "This all of it?"

"I didn't steal it. She gave it to me."

"You expect me to believe that?"

"She was just being nice."

"That what you think? Listen, no one just gives things away. She's expectin' somethin' back for this. You ever think of that? She's fillin' your head with ideas; what's in it for her, huh? Maybe she was makin' money from all those kids listenin' to your auntie's stories. You think Vern can just quit his job and start makin' toys? He don't know how to tie his shoes let alone how to stitch up a teddy bear. And who's gonna tell the stories that make all them kids line up?"

"You can."

"Don't sass me, young lady."

"You could stream it on your social post."

Rinks was taken off guard. Because that wasn't a bad idea. Good, even. Imagine posting a bunch of little kids sitting around her. It would be content. But suspicion undercut the intrigue. What was Marie getting at?

"What are you hidin' from me?" Rinks said.

Marie sighed. "We got coffee and the sugars and creamers, just like you asked. What else do you want?"

"You were hidin' those muffins. What else you hidin'?"

"She gave us some hot chocolate and a pastry, but we ate those when we were there."

"I knew it." She pursed her lips.

"She was being nice, that's all. She knows our godfather, too. Said everyone around here knows him, like he's famous or something."

"Cable's comin' tomorrow." Vern snatched the half-eaten muffin off the table and stuffed the whole thing in his mouth while filling up his mug with coffee. "We'll have internet. Probably need to have someone come fix the heater."

"We ain't goin' to see Godfather tonight," Rinks announced. "Call him, Vern. Tell him we'll do it another time."

"What?" Crumbs shot from his mouth. "Why?"

"You want to spoil these kids? We got a lot of work to do around this place. There ain't time to go drivin' around havin' supper with someone we hardly know."

"Rinks," he said, chewing slowly, "we can't just cancel like that. It ain't polite. He invited us. And, you know, the heater needs fixin'. He might want to help with that when he sees the young ones."

He shrugged those boney shoulders. Like that was that. Rinks wanted to go, sure. She knew all about Godfather, even more than what Vern told her. Man was generous, and when he saw these two little needy kids with the sad story, he just might fix the heater and who knew what else. They could go see him without the kids, just to teach them a lesson, but that'd be hard to explain why they left them behind.

They were hiding something, though. The little brats. They'd only been living with her a couple of years, but already Rinks had developed X-ray vision. She knew when they were up to something. She knew because that was what she had been doing at that age. And Marie and Fritz's mom—Rinks's sister—she wasn't an angel.

"Gimme your phone," Rinks said.

"Why?" Vern said.

She took it from him and turned away, scrolled through his contacts, and found it listed as *Godfather*. When he started to throw a fit, she held up a stiff finger and put the phone to her ear. It was ringing. Then someone answered.

"Hello?"

"Is this the, uh..." Rinks forgot Godfather's name. "Is this Godfather?"

"He is not available. How may I help you?"

"Well, we're comin' to supper tonight. He invited us."

"Ms. Rinks. Oh, yes. We are very much looking forward to your visit."

"Great. Well, we can't do it tonight. Somethin' came up, and we just need to come over in, like..." She looked at Marie and Fritz standing there with their mouths open. "Three days. How about that?"

"I am sorry to hear that. Are the children feeling well?" the voice said.

"They're fine," she whined. "Misbehavin' is all."

"I am afraid we will not be able to reschedule the visit. He is very busy at this time of year. He was anticipating your arrival tonight. I do hope you can come. He has something very special to give you."

"Like what?" Rinks said.

"Gifts, of course."

Gifts? "Who'm I talkin' to?"

"I am the Counselor."

"Counselor?" Rinks said. Vern's eyes lit up when she said that, for whatever reason. "Like a camp counselor?"

The voice laughed. "No, Ms. Rinks. I am a caretaker. Shall I cancel your visit tonight?"

Rinks was in a corner. The kids needed a lesson for whatever they were up to. Postponing the visit would be a good one. Make them wait. But it felt a little like she was punishing herself if she cancelled. *There are gifts.*

"No," she said through her teeth. "We'll be comin'."

"Great! We will see you tonight."

She threw the phone on the table. She felt worse than she had before the brats got back with the coffee.

"Well?" Vern said.

"We're goin', all right. But not before this place gets cleaned. Floors need mopped and the windows shined. I don't want to see one dirt ball anywhere, or I swear I'll call back. Understand? And Vern, you need to get workin' on that heater. Just cause it's Christmas don't mean presents are free."

Marie and Fritz looked just the right amount of sad to satisfy Rinks. Fritz showed his phone to Marie. She shook her head.

"What'd he say?" Rinks said. She grabbed the phone and read what he'd typed. *Doesn't Santa bring presents free?*

It sounded full of sass, the way Rinks read it. A real smart mouth. Rinks thought about it, because Fritz looked like he was waiting for an answer. Like he'd really asked the question. Like he wanted an answer. Rinks had an answer for him. She gave the phone back. She bent over and put her hands on his shoulders.

"Fizzy," she said gently, "Santa ain't real."

Fritz looked confused. So did Vern. Marie grabbed her brother from Rinks, gritting her teeth to hold back a stream of bad words. Rinks wanted one of those sass words to leak out, just one, and she would teach her a real hard lesson. A seventeen-year-old princess wasn't too old for a spanking.

They left Rinks alone, though. All of them walked away. She was in the kitchen by herself, alone with her victory. She'd won the imaginary battle of wills.

And felt worse than ever.

I WANT YOUR EYES. So chocolate!

Favorite comment of the day. Rinks always thought her eyes were a rich chocolate brown with spokes of toffee. That was how she described them. It was nice someone noticed.

"Slow down, will you?" Rinks said. "Or I'll puke in your lap."

"You can't look at your phone, Rinks," Vern said. "Makes you carsick."

"Phone ain't got nothing to do with it, Vern. You even know where you're going?"

"Following GPS." When Rinks picked up her phone, he added: "Seriously, put your phone down."

"You put your phone down."

He laughed. Maybe it was her stupid comeback. What was he so happy about? He'd been humming Christmas songs, and when he knew the words (which was rare), he'd look at her until she looked away. Then suck his teeth.

"You should have shaved," she said.

He explained how carsickness worked, how the brain couldn't make sense out of moving if she was focused on her phone. He was wrong because it was the winding road that made her sick. Not her phone.

She turned up the radio. It was mostly static. Radio stations didn't broadcast this far in the country. They were barely going to have enough gas to get back home. She found country music, which was better than Vern's Christmas Fun Time.

Anxiety nibbled at her mind like little sharp-toothed guppies. She didn't know this Counselor she'd spoken to on the phone. If he was a counselor, then he was going to judge her. She had enough people doing that already.

Plus, she'd never met Godfather before, either. The closest she'd ever come was when Fritz had been born. Marie had been ten years old. It had been her birthday. They'd invited all these people for a cookout. Rinks and Vern had gone. Godfather was supposed to be there. *The great gift giver*, they called him. But then he didn't show. A present arrived later, though. It was a stack of books, ones Rinks had never heard of.

It better not be books tonight. She wasn't going to suffer this trip for a bunch of dumb stories.

"How much longer?" she asked.

"Not much."

"We got enough gas?"

Vern adjusted the rearview mirror. "Marie? Ask your aunt Rinks a question to take her mind off this trip."

"I don't need distractin'."

He patted her arm with his clammy hand. He should be way more nervous than she was. Fact, he should be ashamed, going to see Godfather after what he did. Vern wasn't a good emotional compartmentalizer. He might talk dumb, but he was smart. And somehow naïve.

"Fritz wants to know what a godfather is," Marie said.

Rinks turned to look back. "You don't know?"

"Is he related to us?"

"He ain't." Kids were dumb. But Rinks didn't exactly know what a godfather was, either.

"What is he, then?" Marie pressed.

"It's just a title, like missus or mister. It don't mean nothin'. Like you know people who get a degree and get called doctor, but they ain't a doctor."

"You mean a researcher," Marie said.

Rinks flinched because she couldn't think of that word. "Like that. He ain't family or anythin', so don't get any ideas." What ideas she meant, she didn't know. "He's just someone you know. Well, not you. Your parents. Your dad, I mean. His boss."

"You worked for him, Uncle Vernon," Marie said.

"He did," Rinks answered. "He quit, though. Didn't like workin' for the man."

"Why?"

"He was judgy," Rinks said. "Full of himself. Thought he was better than others. Some people are like that." She patted her husband's knee. He didn't agree with her but appreciated the support. "Vern ain't like that."

Rinks felt good about her answer. She was itching to slide her thumb up the glass of her phone, take a quick peek at her last post (Vern had taken a picture of her in front of the toy store with clean windows: *new place looking good!*). She heard a phone tapping in the back seat. Fritz showed his phone to Marie.

"What'd he say?" Rinks said.

"Nothing."

"Marie? What'd he say?"

She paused to think up a lie. Rinks was about to grab the phone when she said: "Can we live with him?"

"No, you can't live with him. He ain't family." That felt like a sharp stick. "How many times I got to tell you?"

"He meant all of us," Marie said. "Like, can we all live with him?"

"Instead of the place we got, is that what you're sayin'?"

"He just means, like, hot showers and beds."

Rinks had a long answer for a question like this. An answer she'd delivered many o' times. It was a sermon on gratitude. Sometimes she pounded a table like a preacher delivering the hard truth to a spoiled congregation. Now was a good time to fire it up.

"We're here," Vern said.

The country road was narrow and dark. No streetlights. Just pine trees and dead grass in the ditches. "I don't see anything," Rinks said.

He held his phone while almost coming to a stop in the middle of the road. There was a dirt road on the left. He looked around before deciding to pull in. This wasn't what Rinks was expecting. They were soon in a tunnel of oak trees and spooky darkness. If this was a dead end, they were going to have to back all the way out.

"Vern, if this is wrong, we could be in trouble." Rinks knew how country folk were about unexpected visitors. They didn't greet them with cookies.

"It's the directions."

"Well, what's that, then?"

There was a broken-down trailer buried in the trees. A rusted truck with flat tires and small trees growing in the bed of it. Bottles and buckets on the front steps lit by a moth-riddled porch light. Algae-caked walls. Darkened windows dimly glowing with yellow light, the kind of light that comes from lamps with lampshades, with old-fashioned bulbs that get hot.

"That ain't it," Vern said.

"You need to back up."

"Hang on a sec. Let me just—"

"Vern. Now."

"All right, all right, all right."

He shook his head, like Rinks was being paranoid. She was the only level head in the car. Billionaire Godfather, or whatever he was (trillionaire?), didn't have a trailer within a country mile of his property. He didn't live in one, for sure.

Things were about to get weird.

Vern put the car in reverse. They didn't move. Then everything went quiet. The radio was silent, the headlights went out, and the engine turned off. They were looking at a dark and sinister thicket of sticker bushes.

"What are you doin', Vern?"

"I didn't do anythin'." He turned the key. His foot thumped on the accelerator. "It just turned off."

"Well, turn harder!"

"I'm tryin'!"

Rinks leaned over the steering wheel like maybe there was a button he hadn't pushed, like he'd forgotten how a car works. He fought her off. The car was getting hot. It felt like coils in a toaster were glowing underneath them.

"What's that?" Marie pointed.

There was a light in the sticker bushes. A red light that lasered out of the branches. *Well, this is it,* Rinks thought. *Vern done made someone mad enough to melt us like candles.*

It disappeared like a flickering lightning bug. The bushes began to shake.

The lights in the trailer turned off.

THE TREES SHIMMERED like asphalt on a summer day. The oak trees were coming to life. Rinks would blink, and they were right back where they were. The leaves were quivering, though. Wind blew through the branches.

She grabbed Vern's hand. He squeezed back. Rinks reached into the back seat and found Marie's arm without looking for her. She was about to crawl back there with them, wrap them up in her arms and duck so they didn't have to see what came next. Like a bear with laser eyes was going to attack. Or little green aliens coming out of the trailer with cans of beer or whatever they drank after a hard day of kidnapping humans for experimentation.

The bushes began to roll back like twiggy curtains. They opened to a dirt road. A corridor of oaks reached over it, their branches twining together like gnarled fingers draped in curly strands of moss.

And lights. Thousands and thousands of tiny lights were strung in the trees like itty-bitty stars as far as they could see. Enough lights to take a crew of a hundred people all year long to wind around the trunks and branches. They hung in long strands.

The radio came on loud and clear. They jumped at the sound of it. Rinks screamed just a little and nearly crushed the bones in Vern's hand. It wasn't country music blaring from the speakers.

It was Christmas music.

The car started on its own. Vern turned the music down, asked everyone if they were all right. Rinks shook her head up and down and side to side. She didn't know the answer to that question.

"I think this is it," he said.

"What?" Rinks said.

He put the car in gear. "It's exactly what he'd do."

Rinks couldn't argue. If she had all the money ever made in the world, she'd have a secret entrance, too. Add a water slide, maybe a trapdoor. Not a broken-down trailer, though. Rich people were weird.

Vern eased onto the dirt road that didn't have any tracks, just dead grass like no one ever drove on it. Rinks looked back at the kids, who were staring out the window. She felt a twinge of resentment and jealousy at the look of wonder on their faces. They were too young to know things like this could go sideways. Then she felt trapped when the sticker bushes rolled closed behind them. The lights in the trailer turned back on.

The road turned this way and that, curving through a forest dense with trees and blackness between them. Branches scratched the sides of the car and windows. Rinks was as tight as a spring. She pressed her face to the window to see if anything was out there. Her breath fogged the glass.

"Look at that," Marie said.

"What is it?" Rinks blurted.

"Look." She pointed out the window. Rinks didn't see anything. "It was a deer, I think."

"You think? What'd you mean *you think*?"

"It had antlers."

Lots of things had antlers. Moose had antlers. Elk had antlers. Rinks couldn't think of anything else. Unicorns, maybe. Monsters, for sure. What if Godfather was a crazy scientist? Vern hadn't talked to him in twenty years. Out of the blue, he'd sent Vern an invitation for dinner. Like somehow he knew they were coming. A man like that knew things. He knew they were the rightful owners of the toy store. She hadn't thought much beyond that.

Rinks wasn't much of a planner.

The road straightened out, and they drove up an incline; the engine changed gears as they neared the top. Over the front of the car, they saw the trees open. Vern stopped. The headlights shone through brushy saplings and a titanic oak tree with branches the size of tree trunks. Beyond it, tucked under a loose canopy of mossy limbs, was a cobblestone house.

It was a cottage. Smoke puffed from a stone chimney. This had to be where the grounds manager lived, but the road ended. There was nowhere to go besides back. They hadn't missed any turns. Not that she saw.

"This can't be it," she muttered. "I mean, he's rich. Right?"

"Yup," Vern said.

The cedar shingles were mossy. The walls of the cottage were boulders the size of truck tires. Candles flickered warmly in the inset windows. It was less threatening than the trailer—whatever that was about—with a harmless country feel. The kind of place you'd see on a screen saver where people would want to spend retirement away from the hustle and the bustle. All it was missing were bright fairies floating around it.

"Maybe it's his vacation home," Marie said.

"One way to find out," Vern said, and pulled the handle on his door.

Rinks grabbed his shirt. "That's your plan? What if this is the wrong place?"

"You think the gate would have opened if it was?"

"What gate?" Rinks looked at the kids. "You see a gate? I didn't see a gate."

"Those bushes was a gate. That red light was some sort of identifier that let us in."

That tracked. The way those bushes rolled opened, the car mysteriously turning off and back on again. Weirdest gate she'd ever seen.

"And look. See that?" He pointed at the door.

She squinted to see what the headlights illuminated. The front door was thick and dark, curved at the top. A wreath with a red ribbon was on it. She didn't get what was so revealing.

"Inside the wreath," he said.

She squinted harder. It was dark green. Pear-shaped. Then she put it together. It was the logo of the multitrillion-dollar tech company Godfather had run for the last however many decades.

An avocado.

RINKS CORRALLED the kids in her arms, with Vern leading the way. She felt better with them clamped against her. Like teddy bears. It looked like she was protecting them, even if she had them in front of her.

A short walk paved with round stones was surrounded by ferns and moss-covered rocks. Plastic-wrapped candy canes were stuck in the ground like winter flowers. A small sculpture watched them approach. It was a fat man with a round face and small eyes. The arms were strangely short. It was carved from granite. The belly had been worn smooth for luck. Long locks of hair cascaded over the shoulders, the details finely chiseled.

They bunched together at the front door. "Must be the doorbell," Vern said.

He reached for a strap of silver bells nailed to a board and shook it. It made a pleasant melody. Rinks stepped back and dragged the kids with her. Vern stood front and center. There was nothing at first. He was about to shake the bells again when they heard a voice from inside.

"Coming!"

The door started to open, letting out a warm breath of cinnamon and nutmeg and roasted things. *Chestnuts?* Rinks thought. *Nobody roasts chestnuts.* It did smell nutty.

A tall figure stepped out wearing a bright red, sleeveless robe of sorts that trailed down to the ground. Rinks squeezed the kids. Even Vern jumped back as the person or whatever it was threw its arms out.

It announced: "Merry Christmas!"

Rinks felt the fuzzy edges of shock hum in her head. Vern had described what Godfather had looked like the last time he'd seen him. This was not him. In fact, this was nothing like anything Rinks had ever seen in her life. The gray thing on the doorstep was not a person.

"Welcome. Please, come inside. It is a bit chilly. I am sure you must be feeling the nip of winter." The thing stepped aside to make room. "There is a fire to warm yourselves."

It waved a gray arm that was muscular and toned. Arms to die for that were dull gray and smooth as a newborn.

"What is that?" Rinks said. "Vern?"

Vern's mouth hung open: shock dashed with fascination. Warm colors passed on the host's face, if that was what you wanted to call it.

There was no eyes or nose or mouth or ears. A colorful plate where a face would be.

Marie said the obvious. "It's a robot."

"That ain't no robot," Rinks blurted.

"My apologies." The thing put a hand to its chest, as gray as the rest of it. "I understand your surprise. Perhaps I should have prepared you. I had assumed Mr. Vernon knew what to expect."

"Did you know, Vern?" Rinks said. "Did you know about this?"

It had a head and shoulders, arms and legs. It did not have a face. Just a bump where a nose would be (a small one at that) and the hint of a brow. It wasn't a man or a woman. A thing that spoke softly. Slightly masculine.

"I am a robot, I suppose. Although that is a crude description." Colors cascaded down the faceplate as it spoke. "More accurately, I am embodied artificial intelligence."

"A Counselor 5000," Vern muttered.

"Precisely!" It clapped. "Although that was the prototype. I am simply Counselor."

"I knew it," Vern said. "I knew when she called you on the phone! I worked on the sensory pads, helped design the fingertips." Vern took the Counselor's hand, traced the smooth palms that had no creases. *Creepy.* Ran his hand up the muscled forearm in a way that made Rinks jealous. "The project was a failure."

"As you can see, I am a success. There is still testing to complete before I am made public."

"Testing?" Rinks said. "Like you might freak out on us?"

"I am a caretaker, Ms. Rinks. I am here to help." It removed its arm from Vern's caressing curiosity, held out its hand. Rinks regarded it like a plate of worms.

"Go on, Rinks," Vern said. "Don't be rude."

Rude? It was a machine. Just because the thing talked didn't make it any different than a bicycle. They were all waiting for her to do something. So she shook its hand, wincing as if it might crush her bones. If Vern worked on it, there would be glitches. For sure. But her hand didn't break. The Counselor's grip was comforting. Warm and soft. Like the smooth part of a puppy's tummy. Rinks suddenly felt at ease.

"It is a pleasure to meet you, Ms. Rinks," it said. "And you must be Mr. Fritz. A pleasure to meet you, sir."

Fritz shook its hand, clutching the toy in his other arm.

"And what have you there? Is that a nutcracker?" The Counselor bent down, eye to eye with the boy. "That is a very special toy. You must be a very special boy if it chose to protect you."

Rinks snorted, then covered her mouth. Just because the block of wood carried a sword didn't make it walk and talk and choose who got to keep it. It couldn't protect a flea.

"I am happy you are here." The Counselor's faceplate bloomed yellows and oranges. "And you must be Ms. Marie. An honor to meet you, ma'am."

It shook her hand, too. It was a little over the top, like the thing was greeting celebrities. The colors grew brighter and more intricate. All Rinks had gotten was a smattering of greens and coarse gray when it shook her hand. She held onto the kids just in case the thing blew a sprocket.

"Let us go inside." It stood up to its full height of six feet. "Herr Drosselmeier is occupied at the moment. He will join you after dinner."

"Wait, he's not here?" Rinks said.

"He will be," the Counselor said. "He is very busy at this time of year."

"It's fine, Rinks," Vern said. "He never shows up."

"What do you mean he never shows up? Why'd we come all the way out here?"

"He does a telecommute thing. I never seen the man in real life."

Rinks backed up a step. "This is a trap. He's not here because he fired you, and this is a trap."

They were a bit confused by this. What trap would Godfather set for a former employee who worked for him twenty years ago? And why? Rinks just felt a little off balance. All the dumb colors Rinks had gotten when the Counselor shook her hand; then the toy had picked

Fritz to protect instead of her. She didn't feel appreciated. A little respect was in order.

"I wasn't fired," Vern said. "It was downsizin'. You know, company payroll and redundancies, things like that. No big deal."

"Mr. Vernon was on the naughty list," the Counselor said with a splash of brown.

"No, I'm—what?" Vern said.

"You took company material."

"I did not. I *borrowed* it. Just some extra parts we weren't usin'. It was a misunderstandin' and an overreaction, but it's all good. Look, it was twenty years ago. Do we have to talk about this now?"

"Was Godfather mad at you?" Marie asked.

"No. No, no, no... is he?" Vern asked the Counselor.

"If he is," Rinks said, "then this is a trap."

"I assure you, Herr Drosselmeier does not harbor ill will toward Mr. Vernon. He cares for all, naughty and nice. Now, if you are ready."

The Counselor held the door open. The kids walked inside. Rinks grabbed Vern.

"What'd you mean you never seen the man? Don't you think I'd want to know that before comin' all the way out to the middle of nowhere if that man wasn't here?"

"Rinks." He patted her arm and smiled. Charming Vern had a way of relaxing her. "Nobody ever sees him in person. This is normal. I'm sorry, I shoulda told you."

She took a deep breath. Normal was a planet far, far away from here. A dumb cabin with a robot butler? How many people could say they'd done that? If this was a trap, there was nothing they could do about it now. Rinks pulled out her phone.

May as well get some likes.

5

The cabin was plain. An unfinished dinner table. A wood-burning stove. A simple Christmas tree with homemade ornaments in the corner. Not something you'd expect when a robot answered the door.

The Counselor entered with a flourish, the sleeveless red robe swishing around his smooth gray legs. It was impossible not to smile. He oozed magnetic goodwill like a blast furnace. His hand melted around her hand when he shook it and warmed her like a heat lamp. He was someone she wanted to be around. She wanted to hug him.

"Nice," Aunt Rinks said flatly. Then snapped a selfie.

"I am sorry, Ms. Rinks, no photos are allowed. I hope you understand."

"Sure." She tucked the phone in her waistband. "So is this it?"

"My humble abode." He turned in a circle. Bowed. "Welcome."

"I think it's lovely," Marie said. "It's authentic. Warm. Fritz thinks so, too."

"Thank you, Ms. Marie. What about you, Mr. Vernon?"

"Oh, yeah. It's, uh, very real. Woodsy. Smells old. When was it built?"

The Counselor put a slender finger to the lower half of his featureless face. Where lips would be. "Company secret, I am afraid."

"This is a secret?" Rinks snorted. "Where's the fireplace?"

"There is a wood-burning stove in the kitchenette to keep us cozy. I have prepared dinner, which I hope you will enjoy." He gestured to the rough-cut table. "Please have a seat."

There were six chairs but only four table settings. The plates were fine china; the silverware gleamed real silver. They pulled the chairs from the table, the legs scratching the wood planked floor, and sat down. There was no couch or recliner. No television. Just a sad tree in the corner, which was better than no tree at all.

The Counselor returned from the other side of the cabin, wearing an apron (*I Cook Better Than I Look*), and lit two candles on the table, wagging the matchstick to extinguish it. He went back to the kitchenette, his footsteps treading as lightly as a cat's.

"I understand you are vegetarians." The Counselor chuckled, turning his head. His face glowed pink. "That is a joke. There is bread on the table. Please help yourselves."

Uncle Vernon unfolded the napkin in a basket. He was the first to grab a breadstick; the first to eat one. They were lightly toasted, coated with olive oil. Marie took a bite that melted on her tongue. It was warm and salty. The Counselor filled their glasses. Uncle Vernon got sweet tea. Aunt Rinks a soda. Marie and Fritz lemonade.

Aunt Rinks took a photo, shook her head at Marie to keep her mouth shut.

"I cannot express just how nice it is to have company at Christmas. I have been so looking forward to your visit. Tell me all about yourselves. I am eager to know you."

Only chewing sounds. Then Aunt Rinks went: "I'm a social media expert. An influencer. You know what that means?"

"I do. Do you promote a brand?"

"Yeah, me." She stuck her finger in her mouth to dig a clump of bread from her cheek. "I have about ten thousand followers, hit a thousand likes daily. Headscarves are my thing. I make them, mostly tie-dyed. Do some silk painting. Probably start sellin' them once we get the store open. Vern works for an insurance company, does it remotely. So, you know, he can do it anywhere. That's why we're movin' down here. Our building used to sell toys."

"You are in the old toy store?" the Counselor said. "How exciting. Will you reopen it?"

Aunt Rinks snorted. "We don't know anything about toys. Thinkin' 'bout a studio with different sets. You know, a place where people want different backgrounds."

"You are a photographer?"

"I won't lie, I'm pretty good. But it won't be like that. More like a selfie store. Haven't worked out the details."

"Interesting. You sound like you know quite a bit."

"I do pretty good." She grabbed a second breadstick. Uncle Vernon was on his third.

THE COUNSELOR BROUGHT dinner to the table. Each plate was something different. Uncle Vernon had a pile of homemade noodles with chunks of chicken. Aunt Rinks had fried chicken and a sweet roll. Fritz got a plate of tater tots and a hamburger. And Marie was served her favorite: spaghetti and meatballs.

For someone who didn't know much about them, the Counselor got his dinners right. No one seemed to notice. Except Marie.

"Do you have a predinner ritual before you eat?" the Counselor asked.

"No," Uncle Vernon said, chewing the last of his breadstick. "We pretty much eat."

"Very well, then. Let us eat," the Counselor said. Although he wasn't eating. Do robots eat? *Not if they don't have a mouth.*

He topped off their glasses. The room was filled with chewing and slurping, finger-licking and moaning. Uncle Vernon hovered over his plate like a commercial vacuum. Aunt Rinks pulled her sweet roll apart, eating it a piece at a time.

The Counselor sat at the table. "Marie, tell me about you."

Marie had been thinking how to answer that question. She wiped her mouth with a linen napkin and decided to keep it brief. "I like to read and draw. I miss my friends. I like to fish, too."

"That sounds exciting." The Counselor leaned on the table. Listening with full attention. "What did you catch?"

"My dad would take us out on his boat in the mornings before the sun came up. We would go to the middle of the lake when the water was smooth. Some mornings there would be fog over it. It would be so quiet. Just the sound of bugs and mourning doves. Or fish jumping. We didn't catch much, but we still did it."

"That sounds lovely," the Counselor said.

"In the winter, the lake would freeze. Mom taught us to ice-skate. We would go in circles. Fritz was learning with hockey skates. He was even starting to skate backwards. I liked the figure skates. Mom taught me to spin."

"Oh my. I will bet you were good at it."

Marie blushed. "Not really. My mom was really good."

"She wasn't that good," Aunt Rinks said.

"Yes, she was." Marie felt her face flush. "She won awards."

"Your mom was an okay skater who got lucky, that's what she was."

"You're wrong." Marie held her fork like a stick. "She was really good."

"It's my opinion, sweety," Aunt Rinks said supersweetly. "You can't correct an opinion."

Marie stared at her spaghetti. Her appetite had excused itself from the table.

"It sounds like you have wonderful parents." The Counselor didn't follow up on that. He knew far more than he was letting on. He turned to Fritz and said: "What about you, Mr. Fritz?"

"My brother doesn't talk," Marie said.

"He can talk," Aunt Rinks said, slurping her soda. "He just don't want to."

Marie held her tongue. Aunt Rinks was baiting a fight. If they were back home (or at that mouse-infested toy store), Marie would have left the table. Would have gone to bed without eating, and given her aunt an earful on the way. Fritz was breaking his tater tots apart and dropping them on the plate. The bill of his cap shielded his face.

"Mr. Fritz," the Counselor said, "may I touch your shoulder?"

The Counselor didn't move until Fritz nodded. The Counselor gently placed his hand on Fritz's shoulder. His words came out softly. "You do not have to talk until you are ready."

The Counselor kept his hand there, his faceplate a myriad of greens and yellows. Marie held her breath, afraid a sob might slip out that she'd regret. Fritz held the nutcracker on his lap, staring down at it. For a moment, Marie felt something she hadn't felt in many months. Something that had failed her over and over. She couldn't help it, though, with the Counselor's gesture and Fritz's silence.

She imagined what her brother sounded like. Each day the memory of his laughter, his rapid-fire laughter, the way he talked in one long sentence when he was excited—when he caught a fish, when he skated backwards—was getting harder to remember. Marie tried not to hope that would change.

Because hope was a liar.

"STAY WHERE YOU ARE." The Counselor began clearing the table. "I hope you enjoyed the food."

Uncle Vernon held his stomach and burped. Then gave a thumbs-up. At least he didn't fart.

"It was wonderful," Marie said. "Fritz loved it."

She and her brother didn't finish their meals. Not because it wasn't good.

"The duck was a li'l greasy," Aunt Rinks said.

The Counselor took her plate of bones. It looked like scavengers had picked apart a carcass. "It was chicken."

"Coulda fooled me. Is the Godfather comin'? It's gettin' late; the kids are tir'd from a long day of cleanin' the building. We need to get goin' soon."

"Herr Drosselmeier will be here soon. We have a few minutes before he arrives." The Counselor returned to wipe the crumbs off the table. "In the meantime, I would like to present my gift to you. I have been working on it all day."

Aunt Rinks looked at the sad tree in the corner. No Christmas presents were beneath the scrawny limbs. "We, uh, didn't bring anythin', just so you know. Didn't expect a…" She gestured at the Counselor, didn't finish her thought. *A robot.* Was it customary to bring a robot a gift?

Marie would have. Maybe a new apron. *World's Best Robot Cook.*

"I think my gift is quite fitting for the owners of a toy store and descendants of a storyteller."

"It's not a toy store," Aunt Rinks said. "*Was* a toy store."

The Counselor stacked the dishes in the sink and removed his apron. He stood in the middle of the small cabin, fiddled with the sleeveless robe. "I have a story."

Aunt Rinks looked at Uncle Vernon, who shrugged. "Stories count as gifts?" Aunt Rinks raised her eyebrows with a smirk. Marie had a feeling what she and Fritz would be getting for Christmas. They scootched their chairs around to face the tall and muscular android, who was fidgeting in place.

"This is for all of you," he said. "Are you ready?"

"Yes," Marie said. Fritz nodded.

"Fire away." Uncle Vernon leaned back in his chair, fingers laced over his bloated belly. Looked like he swallowed a balloon.

"Okay." The Counselor simulated a deep breath, chest expanding and deflating. He shook his hands. "I feel nervous, I think. You are my first audience." His faceplate flushed pinks and reds. "Everyone is looking at me."

Marie giggled. Fritz smiled.

"Well, go on," Aunt Rinks said. "It's just us."

"Right. We are friends." Then he muttered to himself: "Just like I practiced."

This brought more giggles from one side of the table. Uncle Vernon, too. Aunt Rinks rolled her eyes. The Counselor put a fist to his faceplate and made the sound of one clearing their throat. Even without a face, it was easy to forget he wasn't human.

He began. "Once upon a time there was a king and a queen who lived in a castle as sweet as their rulers. It was a land of tasty treats and perfumed air, where the Orange Brook trickled, the Molasses River flowed, and the Lemonade River ran. It welcomed all travelers through the Almond and Raisin Gate to the Candy Meadow. The Christmas Wood, with its delicious, candied ornaments, sprang forth the temperamental Chocolate River that sometimes overflowed its banks with frothy currents.

"If weary travelers were strong and steely, they would pass through the lovely villages of Bonbon Town and Paper Land, through Sweetmeat Grove, where the fruits were large and honeyed, and onward to Confectionville, where the market of all that is fair and scrumptious is made and traded. There they would find our happy rulers in the Marchpane Castle.

"They were happily married and ruled the rivers and woods and villages in between. Those who lived in the kingdom loved the royal couple, and that is why on a special day they cried huzzah!—to celebrate the birth of their daughter. A festival in her honor that lasted thirty and one days." He cupped his hands to his face. "*Huzzah, Princess Pirlipat! Huzzah!*"

"Pirlipat?" Aunt Rinks snorted.

"Shhh," Marie said.

"The princess never cried. She slept through her very first night. She began crawling before she was three months old. The king and queen loved her very much, as did the people. Everyone cheered her name. Everyone except for the Mousequeen.

"The Mousequeen ruled over Mousalia, but she lived in the cellar of the castle with jarred preserves and pickled vegetables and hanging meats. She did not like the attention given to the princess. Before she was born, the royal staff would allow her and her hundred children to make bedding with straw. They would bid them good morning and evening. And, most importantly, they would leave table scraps in the cellar for the Mousequeen and her hundred children. The king and queen, it was said, had forbidden them to enter the kitchen, where it was warm, when the seven-headed Mouseking tried to steal food from the cupboard. They were chased off with brooms and banished from the castle."

"Seven heads?" Aunt Rinks said. "The Mouseking has seven heads?"

"And a crown for each one. The Mousequeen vowed revenge for starving her children and exiling the Mouseking. She swore to take away the very thing the king and queen loved and hurt them like they hurt her. The king and queen had posted many guards, but that did not stop her. On a cloudless night, she snuck into the princess's room when the guards were sleeping and cursed the child.

"The king and queen awoke in the morning to find their perfect child crying. They recoiled at what they saw. The princess was unrecognizable. Her head was enormous, and a tufted beard had sprouted on her chin. She grinned when she cried in an unnatural way that made the servants cringe when they saw it. No amount of cuddling and rocking could soothe her. The queen was distraught and wept. The king sent his guards in search of the Mousequeen.

"They did not have to go far. The Mousequeen appeared before the royal court, smug in appearance. She demanded the Mouseking be returned to the castle. The king granted her wish. But this did not change the princess. The Mousequeen had tricked him. She did not say she would remove the curse."

The Counselor stuck out his belly and said with a bassoon voice, "'What do you want, then, to bring back my daughter as I know her?'

"The Mousequeen paused for a very long time. It satisfied her to see the king in distress. The queen had not left her room in weeks, wailing through the night. She did not want this to end so quickly and had not thought about what it was she wanted. She made up something quite impossible."

He wiggled his fingers near his face and spoke with a gravelly voice. "'It is quite simple, dear king. Princess Pirlipat must eat a crackatook.'"

Marie looked at Fritz. He was so absorbed by the story that he did not seem surprised by what the Counselor had just said. *Crackatook?*

"'The crackatook is the hardest nut in all the land,'" the Counselor said in the voice of the king.

"'Yes,'" the Counselor said in the voice of the Mousequeen. "'It must be cracked by one who has never shaved or worn boots their entire life. Then they must hand it to her without opening their eyes.'"

"'Very well!' the king replied. 'Send my men on the fastest horses—'"

"'Aaannnd,'" the Counselor interrupted himself as the Mousequeen, "'they must take seven steps backwards.'"

The Counselor held up one greedy finger.

"'Without stumbling.'"

There was a long pause. Everyone waited for what came next. Even Aunt Rinks listened with her mouth open.

The Counselor continued: "The king's men searched on their fastest horses, going to all corners of the land to find a crackatook. Months went by and then a year. The queen was dying of a broken heart. The king did not sleep. A dark cloud had fallen over the kingdom, and the sun no longer appeared. All hope was lost.

"But then one drizzly morning, they returned to the gates with a young man. He was barefoot with a long, pointed beard on his chin and curls of whiskers on his upper lip. The royal staff rushed him to Princess Pirlipat's room. They did not delay. The young man put the crackatook between his teeth to break it open. With the nut in hand, he closed his eyes and handed it to the princess.

"The king and queen hugged each other in the corner of the room, their faces wet with tears. The child ate the nut. Her head shrank, and the tufted beard vanished. Their precious child returned. They counted out loud as the young man, their savior, with his eyes closed, began stepping backwards.

"One! Two! Three! Four! Five! Six!"

The Counselor held up six fingers and paused, looking at the expectant faces around the table.

"On the seventh step, there was a great squeal. The Mousequeen had slipped under the young man's foot. Before he finished lifting the curse, he stumbled backwards. 'Ooooo' was the collective gasp. The king and queen clutched each other. They stared at the crib where their child lay, holding their breath, waiting for her deformity to return. It was the young man, however, who had taken the curse upon himself.

"His arms and legs grew stiff. His jaw became square, his teeth big and white. The once strapping young man transformed into the nutcracker."

He gestured to Fritz's toy standing on the table.

"The seven-headed Mouseking, at that very moment, attacked the nutcracker. The king and queen grabbed their child. The royal staff ushered them to safety and bolted the doors closed. They waited outside as the battle ensued. Night came, and in the morning, they still heard the clash of weapons and objects crashing. It went on for six nights; each morning the battle grew louder.

"On the seventh morning, the door opened. The victor emerged. Standing tall in a bright uniform, with his weapon sheathed in his belt, the nutcracker was victorious."

The Counselor locked his hands and shook them over his head. Then he took a deep bow. Several seconds passed.

"Is that it?" Aunt Rinks said.

"Yes," the Counselor said.

"What kinda ending is that? What happened to all the other people, Princess Pitter-patter and the rest?"

"I do not know how the story ends," the Counselor said.

"What'd you mean? It's your story. You can't tell a story without an end. That's not a story."

"It doesn't matter," Marie said. "I loved it."

It wasn't just a story. There was something about it he was trying to say, but Marie couldn't quite see it.

"Let me ask you somethin'," Aunt Rinks said. "Was that supposed to be a Christmas story?"

The Counselor looked at the ceiling. At first, it looked like he was in thought or trying to remember something. Then his face shone like a star. They shielded their eyes from the glare.

"He is here," the Counselor said.

6

The door on the back wall of the cabin was different than the
front door, like it was made from heavy slabs of oak or
cypress, but the hinges were bulky plates of iron. The
Counselor put his hand on the L-shaped handle. Mechanisms shifted
inside the lock, clicked and popped. The handle released downward.
The door swung like a vault door. An icy draft escaped the dim
opening.

"Watch your step," the Counselor said. "There are banisters on
both sides."

"Where we goin'?" Aunt Rinks asked.

"Herr Drosselmeier is waiting."

The Counselor held the door open. Uncle Vernon didn't hesitate.
Marie and Fritz followed him through the door and down a short
flight of steps. The banister was polished platinum, cold and smooth,
and slid under Marie's hand. Fritz was behind her. With each step,
holiday music grew louder.

Aunt Rinks was the kid left behind when all her friends went into
the haunted house without her. "Wait!"

The steps led to a wide balcony. Uncle Vernon was already at the
railing. It arched outward in a half circle that overlooked a larger

room. Marie's and Fritz's senses were filled with the aroma of nutmeg and spices.

"Look at that," Uncle Vernon muttered.

The far wall was two stories tall. It was a giant pane of glass bisected by a stone chimney with a roaring fireplace at the bottom. Marie expected to see oak trees and lights on the other side of the glass wall, the kind they'd seen when they drove in. It was nothing of the sort. Nothing like it at all.

Snow.

As far as she could see, all the way to a flat horizon, was snow and ice. The sky was a black sheet speckled with stars. Ribbons of color danced across it.

"That looks like the North Pole," Marie said.

Uncle Vernon offered a blocky-toothed smile. "That ain't a window, darlin'. That's just a projection, like a TV. Can't tell the difference, though. Can you?"

Aunt Rinks joined them. With one hand on the railing, she snapped a photo. "What is this, Vern?"

He explained again.

The back door closed with a heavy clank. The Counselor was coming, although they couldn't hear his catlike footsteps. Aunt Rinks quickly spun around to get a half dozen selfies with the colorful sky behind her. She tucked the phone away.

"You are witnessing the Northern Lights," the Counselor said. "It is a real-time projection of the North Pole. I thought it would capture the Christmas spirit. I hope you find it inspiring."

"It's beautiful," Marie said. Fritz nodded. If she would have walked into this room alone, she would've thought the back door was a portal.

"When you are ready, there is a staircase on both sides of the balcony. Herr Drosselmeier is waiting for us."

They were mesmerized by the small auditorium, hypnotized by the flowing nightscape, tendrils of color rising into the heavens. Without a word, Uncle Vernon followed the arching banister to the right and rushed down the steps. Aunt Rinks was close behind him.

The staircase sloped along the curving wall. A fir tree was tucked into the corner, its tip nearly reaching the ceiling. The evergreen branches were weighted with gold and silver apples. Almonds and lemon drops and brightly colored candies sprinkled like buds. Tiny lights sparkled like a galaxy bursting out of the trunk. The closer they got to the bottom step, the more it smelled like a forest. Aunt Rinks squatted next to the tree, examining three gift-wrapped presents beneath it, whispering to Uncle Vernon.

"This way," the Counselor said.

Couches and chairs were arranged around a low-lying table. A model spanned the width and length of the table. The details were extraordinary. Stone walls enclosed a courtyard where tiny plastic flowers were planted, and figurines of men and women stood at carts of fresh fruit and vegetables and livestock. There were feathers in hats, long cloaks that reached the ground, and flowery dresses.

Fritz plopped on a couch. His eyes were wide and unblinking.

In the middle of the courtyard was a castle. Turrets of glittering gold branched from the steep walls. It soared above the figurines, a monolith of magnificence, whose scale suggested a hundred flights of stairs climbed to the window at the very top.

"Did you make this?" Marie asked.

"I did not," the Counselor said. "Herr Drosselmeier has been working on this for quite some time. He is a clockmaker."

"Huh," Vern grunted. "I don't get the connection."

"Look closely."

The Counselor gestured with a sweep of his arm. Fritz stood up (the castle was a few inches taller than him). When he leaned closer, the figurines began to move! It was hardly mechanical. They sauntered like living people, stopping to examine an apple or peer through a window. Children in white shirts and green jackets danced to music coming from an open doorway. A man in a green overcoat put his head out the window. He nodded at the children and disappeared.

"Oh... my... word," Aunt Rinks gasped. "That is bananas."

"How are they doing that?" Marie asked. "They look so real."

"Reality is perception," the Counselor said. "Perception is reality."

Aunt Rinks snorted and shook her head at the nonsense. Fritz kept his fingers intertwined to keep himself from reaching in to pluck one of the villagers from their daily duties. Aunt Rinks had no such control. When her hand passed over the wall, everything stopped.

"What happened?" she said.

"The perception was an illusion," the Counselor said.

"Are you *tryin'* to sound smart?"

"The model is one of great craftsmanship. It is also quite educational."

Uncle Vernon paced around the table, scratching the stubble on his chin. This was a challenge. How did Godfather make this thing work? But Marie saw something else. The Counselor was trying to tell them something.

And it was important.

"Ah," the Counselor said. "Herr Drosselmeier is here."

BENEATH THE BALCONY was a white room without corners. The walls were curved where they met each other as well as the ceiling and the floor. It had the illusion of infinity. As they approached the seating area, color bled into the spotless space beneath the balcony. Moments later, it was a cluttered library.

Candlelight flickered on the spines of books filling the outer walls. A man, who hadn't been there seconds earlier, was fiddling at a bank of computer monitors on a sprawling desk littered with random items: gift wrapping, boxes, and trinkets. A white feather leaned in a well of ink. A cane was stored in a tall metal container.

"Herr Drosselmeier," the Counselor said, "your company is present."

He turned with a start. The Christmas music he was nodding along to (and humming merrily, as well) turned down. A smile grew somewhere in a thick beard and shot sparkles into his eyes. "Merry, merry!" his voice boomed. "Welcome. Come in, come in."

He wore an ill-fitting tuxedo that was as disheveled as his long hair. The collar open, bowtie missing. He shuffled over to a comfortable-looking chair positioned just below the edge of the balcony. It was more of a cushy throne than a recliner. With a heavy mug in one hand, he watched them gaze at his surroundings like tourists.

"Let me get a good look at the lot of you."

He had a voice that needed no amplification. It had the richness of a foghorn and carried a smile in its sail. He urged them closer. They meandered around the model with the castle and tiny people and sat on the edges of their seats. Fritz sat next to Marie in a wide recliner.

"Counselor, would you be so kind as to put another log on the fire? Thank you. Did you all get enough to eat? The Counselor worked diligently on dinner. I was the recipient of many test dishes."

He chuckled and thumped his generous belly. He sat on his throne, propped his black boots on a short footstool, and dropped the mug on the armrest. Surveying their expressions—which were somewhere between amazement and shock—he nodded.

"Vernon, my good man, how long has it been?"

"Twenty years, sir. I think."

Godfather shook a finger. "Twenty-two years. It is good to see you. You look fair." Uncle Vernon took this honest assessment of his bad posture and ashy complexion as a compliment. "You are doing quite well with insurance analysis, I hear. I'm proud of you."

Uncle Vernon beamed like a child, told him about an award he'd won, a recent bonus he'd received, and the system he'd rebuilt to assess profit-loss. Godfather listened intently.

"Wonderful!" He slapped his knee. "And Rinks, it is a pleasure to finally meet you. I've heard many a good thing about you. You are quite a photographer, I hear."

The sour expression marring her face transformed under the warmth of Godfather's attention. He was like a sunbeam that unfolded flowers. She gave him the rundown of her social media and all the embellishments that came with it. He looked impressed.

Whether he understood or not. Marie had the feeling he didn't believe the parts she made up. Which was most of it.

"Marie." He turned the sunbeam on her. "You are becoming a lovely young woman, just like your mother. You are excelling in your studies like both your parents, I hear. The apple doesn't fall far. How are you doing, young lady?"

He asked, not like a throwaway conversation starter. It sounded like he really wanted to know, like *how are you doing since your life turned upside down?* She shuddered a little and offered a fragile smile.

"I am honored you are here," he replied, as if knowing she couldn't answer that honestly without popping the lid on a box packed with emotions. "As I am to see this young man. Fritz, the brave soldier. Are you taking care of your sister?"

Fritz looked down at the nutcracker in his lap.

"And what have you there?" Godfather asked. "May I see him?"

Fritz scooted off the recliner. Godfather dropped his boots on the floor and leaned his elbows onto his knees. Fritz held the nutcracker out for him to see. When Fritz attempted to hand it to him, a blaze of light wrapped around it. Godfather's image blurred.

He's an illusion.

It was a projection, just like the library around him. She'd forgotten what Uncle Vernon had said when they'd arrived at the cabin, that he was *never really there.*

"Did the Counselor tell his story of the nutcracker?" Godfather asked. "That is a loyal soldier you have there. He's a protector." He winked. "You must be very special."

Fritz laughed silently and blushed. He hopped back on the recliner with Marie.

"Please excuse my absence," Godfather said. "I would cherish the opportunity to be with you in person, but this time of year is very busy. I hope you understand. It has been a very long time, and I wanted to welcome you to your new home."

The Counselor brought a tray filled with merry mugs. He gave one to each of them. Fritz had hot chocolate. Marie, hot cider.

"Please accept my condolences for your loss," Godfather said. "Your parents were very special to me."

Marie cradled the warm mug in her lap. "How did you know them?"

"Ah, that is a story." He sat back in his throne and propped up his boots. "Your uncle Vernon introduced us. Didn't you, Vernon?"

"I did, yes. I knew your dad in college."

"You never told me that," Aunt Rinks said.

"We were roommates."

"No, that you got him a job."

"Well, I didn't exactly get him—"

"Vernon is very talented," Godfather said. "How long did you work at Avocado?"

"Six years."

"That's right. A trusted employee, you were." Vernon looked at his lap, hiding whatever feelings he carried for being *let go* from his job. "When we had an opening at the company, Vernon recommended your father. There were quite a few candidates, too. Your father came to us with humble confidence, a rare combination. He was skinny with a jaw like a soldier. Quickly became a rising star at the company. He solved a programming conflict that had plagued us for years."

"The Braxton-Milton co-efficient," Uncle Vernon said.

"That's right. He led a team of new and veteran scientists. *Scienceers,* he called them. What they were doing was beyond science and bordered on magic. He was ridiculed by his peers for using that word. Your father was not easily affected when he believed in something."

Godfather heaved himself out of the throne and went to the desk on the other side of the room. He sifted through the clutter (*so he's in that room wherever he is*) and brought back a framed photo. It was a group of young colleagues. They were all in white lab coats. Godfather was in the middle. He looked pretty much the same as he did now: the beard, the belly. He was holding a big pair of scissors over a wide yellow ribbon for the opening of a new research wing. Judging by how Marie's father looked, it must have been thirty years ago.

In the photo, Godfather was next to her father, the bright scienceer, the youngest of the team. His hairline crisply outlined a handsome face. His hair was short. Godfather was beaming in that photo. Marie wanted to think it had something to do with her father, of all the things he accomplished.

And all the things he never had a chance to.

"He met your mother a year later. She was already working at Avocado in the Storyline Division and was transferred to your father's team. He spilled coffee on her the very first day." Godfather's laughter trailed off while he studied the photo. "They were two wires in a single circuit, those two."

He put the photo on his lap.

"They introduced you two, remember that? Your mother brought Rinks to the Christmas party that year. Vernon was standing in the corner, and she introduced her sister. Next thing you know, here you are."

"My sister didn't introduce us," Rinks said under her breath.

"They asked me to be your godfather. Of course, I said yes. I'm sorry we couldn't spend more time getting to know each other. It's been a pleasure watching you grow up."

Counselor sat on the sofa nearest Fritz.

Marie didn't say anything. If she did, it would open the box of emotions she didn't want to let out. So they sat in the silence, listening to the fire pop in the fireplace and the music play from the castle. She was thinking of her parents and wondered if they had told Godfather all about them.

He watched us grow up.

"How are you settling into the toy store?" Godfather asked.

"Just great," Aunt Rinks said. Then she didn't miss a beat. No heat. No hot water. Dirty windows, drafty, dusty, overgrown, rusty pipes, moldy mattress, cracked ceilings. The place was great, she said. Just great.

"Have you been there?" Marie asked.

"Been there?" Godfather's belly jiggled when he laughed. "Your great-aunt was one of my favorite people. The stories she told, oh! She was the heart of this town, Marie. She was the true essence of Christmas, personally responsible for seeding generations with imagination."

He unbuttoned his collar and sagged in the oversized chair.

"One Christmas, I was fortunate to hear her tell a story. The line was quite long, as I'm sure you've been told. I slipped in without much notice. *Corker's Candyland*, they called it. Big sign over the door." He swept a banner with his porky hand. "Very few sweets to eat, though. Children of all ages were there, clinging to a parent's leg or running down the aisles. Teenagers, too. Adults returned to relive a childhood experience. The place had a particular smell. It drew me in like it did all others."

He closed his eyes and inhaled.

"Like pages in old books." He looked around and laughed, suddenly aware of the many books surrounding him. "The toys on the shelves were simple and old-fashioned, teddy bears and wooden soldiers and plastic dolls. They meant nothing to the older children, I'm afraid. They had everything they needed in their pocket."

He pulled a phone from a pocket inside his jacket and tossed it on a small table.

"I stood by and watched children funnel through the front door, guided to a place on the little stage by workers dressed like silly elves." He took a moment to sip from his mug, chuckled at the thought of elves dressed in curly-toed shoes and bells on their collars. "One mother was pulling her little one down the aisle, between other kids who were sitting on the floor and playing. Her daughter was shy. I envied her, the young one. She was about to experience a ride she would never forget. No one forgets their first story.

"A man greeted her. He knew the mother by name, of course. His voice was warm and deep. The mother pried her daughter from her leg. The little girl put her hands over her face, but was peeking through her fingers. He was tall, very tall; stilts for legs. Angular face.

Your great-uncle looked like a butler, the way he stood. His back so rigid you could run a flag up it.

"The little one managed to get behind her mother's legs again and wished he would go away. And then his voice was right next to her. He knelt and said, 'And who is this?' He was as warm as a fire on a winter night and bright as sunlight in the morning. His smile as big as his eyes.

"Of course, the mother introduced her little girl—Hallie, she said—because Hallie wasn't going to say a word. 'Can I tell you a secret?' he said. 'You've come to a magical place. Can you feel it?' Hallie thought magic must feel like clenching fear, because that was what she was feeling. Then he unfurled long, skinny fingers. There, in the palm of his hand, was a piece of hard candy. 'Merry, merry,' he said."

Godfather looked at the ceiling, as if memories were floating above their heads.

"Hallie wouldn't be able to find the words to explain what that felt like, not at that age. It was like a flower blooming for the first time, its petals opening in spring. She followed her mother through the store, sucking on the candy, to a crowded stage in the corner. Mrs. Corker was sitting in her chair, wrapped in her purple blanket. The wire-rimmed glasses on her nose. Her hair white as snow.

"The mother was not shy, stepping between people until they squeezed into an open spot. Hallie sat on her lap, her mother's arms around her. There was an elf behind Mrs. Corker, a tall one. Hallie looked at the elf suspiciously, thinking this wasn't a real elf. She was right, of course. Even at that age, she knew someone was playing dress-up. But it didn't spoil what she was feeling. When bells began chiming, the entire store fell quiet. No one said a word. Not a cough or a sniffle. Not even a mouse."

He winked at Marie.

"Mrs. Corker closed her eyes, gently rocking. That's when she went there, to that storyland in her head. She looked like she'd fallen asleep, but she was smiling. Then she opened her eyes and said, 'Once upon a time...' and took them to a world of toys. Where snowmen lived and reindeer flew. Where Christmas spirit could be tasted in the air. They were spellbound, as was I. Children didn't blink; tears rolled down their cheeks. She took them there, and they felt it. The snow and the cold, the excitement of possibilities.

"To this day, I believe she stoked the imaginations of many who came. Those children were keenly aware, from that moment forward, that the physical world would always have limitations. Even at that age, they knew they might never breathe underwater or sprout wings. But imagination... well, anything is possible.

"The air in the store changed. The toys looked different when it was over, like they would talk to them when they walked down the aisle. Mr. Corker greeted them at the door. He knelt as Hallie and her mother approached. Hallie held her hand, no longer hiding. He whispered to her, 'Do you feel the magic?'"

Chills stormed Marie's arms. *She* could feel it. Just from the way he told it. Fritz had gotten up while he was telling the tale and now stood a foot away from him, holding his nutcracker with both hands. He could feel it, too.

"The toy store wasn't frivolous fun. No, no." Godfather dismissed the notion with a wave of his hand. "They gave the children what they needed, not what they wanted. That is the true spirit of Christmas."

"What was that?" Aunt Rinks said.

He laughed a big belly laugh. It went on so long Aunt Rinks began to frown. The answer was obvious.

"What I meant to say," Aunt Rinks said, crossing her arms, "was why were you there? If it was for children and all. A grown man standin' around is a little strange, doncha think? Right, Vern?"

Uncle Vernon shook his head. He wasn't getting dragged into it. Godfather wiped a happy tear from his eye, laughter trailing off. He paused for a moment, thoughtfully. Then looked at Marie when he answered.

"I was there to deliver a gift."

❄

THE COUNSELOR REFILLED THEIR CUPS. It wasn't much since no one had really drank what he gave them in the first place. Godfather went to a pitcher on the desk behind him, poured something chocolatey into his mug. He took a sip, wiped his mustache with the back of his hand.

Delivering a gift? Marie felt stunned, for some reason. The way he looked at her when he said it.

"Will you be opening the toy store, then?" Godfather asked.

"Why does everyone keep askin' that?" Aunt Rinks said.

He collapsed in the big chair. "What does your heart tell you?"

"You don't want to know what's in my heart," she muttered.

"Do *you* want to know?" he said, more seriously than he'd spoken all night.

Aunt Rinks looked away, arms still locked across her chest. Still sore from when he laughed at her dumb question. Marie knew what was in her aunt's heart: a dark, self-centered lump of coal. Godfather knew. You only needed to be in the room with Aunt Rinks for two minutes to know how shallow her pool was. Didn't take an X-ray.

"We're workin' on some ideas for the place," Uncle Vernon said. "It's all very new, you know. Just settlin' in. Rinks got some good ideas, though. She's good with people."

"Of course, of course." Godfather took a sip. "I understand."

"Maybe *you* should open the toy store," Aunt Rinks said. "Seein' how you loved it so much. You could make it new, I bet. Just like before."

Aunt Rinks might not have been bright, but she was clever. Here was a man who had enough money to fill a volcano, and he'd just confessed to the importance of the toy store. *The true spirit of Christmas.* His words, not hers.

He didn't take the bait.

"It's your building," he said. "And I have too much to do already."

"What do you do?"

"That is a very good question." He appeared to give serious thought before answering, "I serve."

"Serve?" Now it was Aunt Rinks's turn to laugh hysterically. "Like food?"

"Hope, my dear."

"And who gets your hope?"

"Everyone." He winked. Then he slapped his thigh. "Enough about me. Tell me about yourselves. Better yet, tell me a story."

"A story?" Aunt Rinks howled. That was a sharp turn she didn't see coming. "What kind of story you want?"

"First thing that comes to your mind. It can be anything. Don't overthink it." He got comfortable and looked around, raised his mug of coffee or hot cocoa. "Just go."

Fritz jumped on the couch. Marie shrank into the cushions next to him. The Counselor put his arm around Fritz like story time was about to begin. After a few minutes of nervous chatter, Aunt Rinks and Uncle Vernon started talking. It was more like a report of how they drove all the way here in a beat-up car with bald tires and a broken windshield wiper. Uncle Vernon hardly finished a sentence without Aunt Rinks interrupting about the stupid GPS lady giving bad directions or dumb drivers in the left lane. It devolved into bankruptcy and backstabbing friends. And they never planned to have kids. But you know how that turned out. She nodded her head at Marie and Fritz.

Godfather listened, really listened. Letting them sing their country song of missed opportunities and bad luck.

"And what about you, Marie?" he said abruptly. "You and Fritz."

Marie thought she would dodge the question by hiding in the corner of the couch. Godfather sat forward, leaned a listening ear, waiting to hear her speak her words like they were rare diamonds.

"I... I don't know what to say. You already know about us."

"Then tell me a story."

Marie looked at her brother. He was waiting to hear what she had to say, too. They were all looking at her. The room was as hot as the engine of a long-haul truck. She folded her arms just like Aunt Rinks did, trying to hide behind them. Her thoughts swirled like a winter storm through a broken window.

"I don't have one," she said.

He nodded. "Try this. Think of a story someone told you. Anyone."

"What about?"

"It can be anything. Shoveling snow, digging a hole. Doesn't matter. Close your eyes, tell us a story about the first thing that comes to mind."

She wasn't getting off the hook. Aunt Rinks had a grin the length of a jump rope. Someone else was the dummy in the circle. Fritz put his head on her shoulder. The Counselor squeezed her arm. She closed her eyes, mostly so she wouldn't see everyone looking at her. The silence stretched as tight as a wire on a guitar.

Her father had told her the secret about stressful situations. *Just breathe.* A long inhale through the nose, an exhale even slower. And then it came to her like a fish pulling the line.

"A man went to a conference." Eyes still closed, she swallowed. "He, uh, he didn't like doing stuff like that, getting dressed up and shaking hands. *Droll stuff,*" she said in a deep voice.

She heard Godfather chuckle.

"He met this woman. Her name was... Drea Martenkrugel..." she mused. "He said her name made him hungry. She was a few inches taller than he was, had strong arms that could crush a jug full of milk. And a gruff voice, the kind that could heel sailors on a long voyage."

That was how he had described her. She'd never forgotten that.

"Her eyes were different colors. Brown and blue. Never married. Not that she was after him or anything. Least that's what he told his wife. She was an optics specialist. With eyes like that, it made sense. They spoke about hobbies, like she was into astronomy and ocean life. He was all about the future of human evolution. They even talked about sports, of which he knew almost nothing. And then, out of the blue, she leaned closer. Her perfume was spicy, like she'd rolled in a field of cloves. But underneath it was a hint of straw."

She thought a second, eyes still closed.

"No, like a farm. He was intrigued. *Who smells like that?* And then she whispered, although it wasn't really a whisper—she seemed incapable of whispering—and said, 'I want to show you something.' He couldn't say no. Perhaps to someone else, but not a woman who smelled of cloves and animals. He followed her through the lobby and into the parking lot. There was quite a bit of snow up there. Piles of it between cars. They weren't dressed for it, but off she went across the asphalt, passing under streetlights and not looking back to see if he was following.

"There was a moment it seemed like an awful idea. When they got to the middle of the parking tundra, he called her name. He was concerned for her being out there alone, although he was quite sure she could protect herself better than he could. He followed her to the far corner where a cargo van was parked.

"She was standing by the back doors. He was quite winded at this point and starting to shiver. The wind was raking the lot. Even the streetlights were shivering. He started to say this can wait till morning, but no sooner did he get the words out than she threw open the doors. She reached in and pulled out a chicken."

"A chicken?" Aunt Rinks said.

"The feathers were black, almost iridescent. She held it in the crook of her arm, the bird's neck rocking back and forth the way birds' do. Its beady eyes fixed on him. She told him the bird's name; he didn't remember what she said; he couldn't feel his lips at this point. And then she kissed it on the beak.

"The bird, apparently, didn't like being kissed. It flapped its wings, smacking her in the face, and landed on the ground. Before he knew it, she was in a dash after the mad thing. Feathers flying, Drea calling out the name, calling, 'Blitzen! Blitzen, come back here now!' Blitzen had not been trained to come back.

"He couldn't leave the poor woman. Of course, the chicken wasn't any more keen on him than it was her. He attempted to corner it at a snowbank. Drea had given up at this point, going back to the van. He thought perhaps she was going to drive after it. Instead, she opened the sliding door to retrieve something from inside the van. She put it to her lips and blew.

"Blitzen froze. She blew it again, and the chicken turned its head.

The third time, Blitzen marched straight to her, crawled into her arms, and she hugged it like a child. He said to her, 'Why didn't you blow that cursed thing in the first place?' She put the rooster away and didn't say a word. They walked back to the event."

Marie's eyes were still closed. It was a true story. Mostly. She could see it all happening. Exactly like she did the first time she'd heard that story.

"That's it?" Aunt Rinks said. "That's the ending?"

That was it. It didn't matter whether it had an ending or not. *There are no endings,* her father used to say. *One story leads to another.*

"What did she blow?" Uncle Vernon asked.

Marie opened her eyes, looked around at the expectant faces, and said: "A trumpet."

Uncle Vernon looked confused. Aunt Rinks sort of angry. Fritz's shoulders shook against her. Godfather leaned his head back and let out the loudest, deepest laughter she'd ever heard. His mouth wide open, he cradled his belly and laughed until tears streamed. Marie could feel his laughter in her stomach and started laughing, too. Even Uncle Vernon started giggling. It went on for minutes. Godfather wiped his eyes and leaned forward, eyes wet and twinkling.

"Now *that's* a story."

"Counselor!" Godfather said. "I think it's time."

The gray skinwrapped android moved off the couch as smooth as a figure skater gliding across the ice. He went to the Christmas tree in the corner and returned with the gifts that were under it.

"I have something for each of you," Godfather said. "It's not Christmas, but I won't tell anyone if you open them now. Go on."

The Counselor put a box wrapped in gold paper between Aunt Rinks and Uncle Vernon. Her eyes inflated. It was the biggest present of the three, by far. And every child knows bigger presents are always the best. She clapped her hands and didn't wait for Godfather to say another word, or for Uncle Vernon, for that matter. She shredded the paper like a mouse making a nest. The gift was exposed in two seconds flat.

Her jubilance shrank like a rotting apple core. The thing in front of her had wide wings and big eyes. Aunt Rinks looked up.

"What is it?" she said.

"It's a clock," Godfather said. "I'm a bit of a watchmaker. More of a hobby, I guess."

She turned it around, then upside down, hoping, maybe, there was an envelope taped to the bottom of it filled with cash. "We already have one in the kids' room. It's on the shelf. Right, Marie?"

Marie nodded enthusiastically. It was exactly like that: a clock in the belly and watchful eyes. Aunt Rinks's disappointment was invaluable.

"Of course. I gave one to the Corkers, once upon a time." He chuckled. "This one is for you."

"But I already get the time on my phone." Aunt Rinks lifted her phone, like he might reconsider a better gift.

"What do owls eat?" he said.

"People?" Aunt Rinks said.

"Not this one."

"Mice," Uncle Vernon said.

"I was kiddin'." Aunt Rinks elbowed him. She wasn't. "Mice."

There were no mouse turds in Marie and Fritz's room, now that Marie thought about it. Not that Aunt Rinks would notice. Maybe he was telling the truth. The clock scared them away. Aunt Rinks looked nervous already, turned the clock so the big eyes were looking away from her. She slumped in her chair. Uncle Vernon turned the handle on the back of it. The second hand started ticking. He nodded his approval and said, with mild excitement, "Thank you." As mild as one could get.

Marie wondered if the owl clock was the gift he'd delivered to the Corkers. It was not. And she would soon find out the gift he'd delivered that day was much different than a clock. Not even close.

"Marie." He gestured to the gift in front of her.

She knew what it was before she opened it. It was a thick

rectangle, weighty and dense. She pulled off the tape and unwrapped a leather-bound journal. The surface was worn but smooth against her palm. The pages inside were thick and blank. A white feather was tucked into the pages, a quill to dip in a bottle of ink. It was beautiful. Smelled like old leather and freshly milled paper.

"A journal, dear," he said. "To write your own story. A story no one else can discover but you. And don't forget... look through the pages."

She flipped through them and found, tucked between the last pages, a long white ribbon.

"A bookmark," he said. "Or whatever else you might find it handy for."

"Thank you," she said.

It was a striking gift. The ribbon was nice, but the book was so special she didn't know if she would ever mar the pages with a spot of ink. If the pages stayed blank, that meant anything was possible. When they were blank, they were safe. Unstained.

Aunt Rinks looked a bit cheerier. The owl clock was better than a book. Any book, really. Especially a book with blank pages, the more she thought about it. Besides, a custom-made clock would sell easier. *A clock that keeps away mice.*

"Master Fritz." Godfather swatted his thighs like paddles on a glassy pond. "I haven't forgotten about you, my boy. It's your turn."

The Counselor offered Fritz the smallest gift of the bunch. It was the size of a ring box, tightly wrapped with sharp corners. Fritz put the nutcracker between his legs and turned it over like a puzzle to be solved. He tore one corner, then another. The nutcracker watched with an open mouth. So did Aunt Rinks, stepping closer to see what was in it. A ring, perhaps? Jewelry for a boy who wore a dirty old hat?

Fritz pried open the top of the box and poured out the contents. He cupped it in his hand.

"What is it?" Aunt Rinks said.

He raised and lowered his hand as if weighing its worth. Then held it up between his finger and thumb like a jeweler.

"A marble?" Aunt Rinks said and laughed. "He got a marble, Vern."

"It's a nice marble," Uncle Vernon said.

It wasn't a marble. It was round like one, but not a marble. It was the size of a golf ball with textured stripes. Sort of rough but polished so their distorted reflections looked back. Looked sort of like a walnut. Marie whispered in her brother's ear: "It's lovely, Fritz."

"Come closer, Fritz," Godfather said.

Fritz scooted off the couch. With the nutcracker in one hand, the ball in the other, he went right to the edge of Godfather's projection. Godfather beckoned him closer. Fritz stepped into it. The light streamed around him. Godfather's image was broken from the interference, but he whispered something to Fritz. Appeared to pat him on the shoulder, nodded and winked.

Fritz ran back to the couch with something much rarer than a custom owl clock and an antique journal. Fritz had a smile on his face. A genuine smile. He clenched the ball until his knuckles were white.

That night, the true value of that gift would reveal itself. It was the greatest gift of the night, by a billion miles.

"We didn't get you anythin'," Aunt Rinks said. "We didn't know we were doing gifts."

"I have everything I need," Godfather said. "What everyone needs isn't a place or a thing. It's a journey."

Aunt Rinks snorted. "We ain't on a journey."

"My dear, we're all on a journey." He raised his mug. He looked at Marie. "You just need to find it."

7

The stove burner coil was orange. Rinks spread her hands over it. Her knuckles flexed like hard plastic. She could barely scroll her phone.

She huddled in a blanket like one of those little hotdog treats Vern liked so much. *Pigs in a blanket,* she thought. *Dip me in ketchup.* She chuckled to herself. Despite her steamy breath and terrible night at the full-of-himself rich fat man's cabin in the woods, she was feeling a touch merry.

Likes are up.

Her recent posts were doing better than expected. She subtracted the ones she'd bought—the fake ones—which meant the rest of them were organic. People were catching on. They liked her. They really liked her. She went down thirty-two comments before she got to a negative one (*Your makeup belongs in a circus*) and that didn't even bother her. Most of the comments were about her scarves. She was going to sell them. They were going to buy them.

"Wait till they see this," she muttered.

She searched her photos from that night. Once her followers saw the crazy robot and that whole downstairs setup at the cabin, they'd start spreading the word. Rinks knew important people. She was buds with Avocado, the greatest tech company in the world.

I'm goin' viral, she thought.

She scrolled up and down her photo library. Her face scrunched each time she went through the collection, growing more like a dried apricot each time she did it. She couldn't believe what she was seeing. Her phone never lost its charge (she carried reserve battery chargers in her bag just in case).

This made no sense.

She flipped off the stove, threw the blanket over her shoulder, and started for the bedroom. The kids were still awake. A light showed from below the door. She stopped to listen, pushed her ear against the door. Marie was doing all the talking, like always. Fritz was probably lying there listening to her, ogling that stupid ball he got. (She felt a tad sorry for him. A ball wasn't much better than coal.)

There was a turn of a page. Laughter. Marie was telling a story from the blank book. That irritated her worse than the clock.

Godfather wanted *her* to be the storyteller; that was obvious. Did he know Marie stole that story about the chicken from her dad? Rinks did. She'd heard it three times on one visit to see her sister.

Rinks didn't know they could tell other people's stories. Comedians called that stealing. Rinks could think of a hundred stories better than the one Marie had told, and tell them ten times better. But it wouldn't have mattered. Godfather liked her better. Rinks didn't stand a chance. Never did.

Vern was on their lumpy bed with the laptop on his belly. His face washed in blue-white light. He wore a hoodie with the hood pulled up and a stocking cap on his head.

Rinks aimed her phone at him. "They stole my pics."

"What?"

"My pictures, the ones I took inside the cabin and the basement, they're gone. Like, not even on my phone."

"You weren't supposed to take pics, Rinks."

"Yeah, and it's against the law to hack my phone. I could report them."

He frowned. Who would she report them to? "They probably had somethin' that kept your camera from workin'. You saw the place. Wouldn't be too hard to do."

"I wasn't doing anythin' wrong."

"Except takin' pictures."

"Takin' pics ain't against the law. And I think the world oughta know what they're doin', that's all. I mean, they got all that stuff. That fair? Don't you think people would want to see that robot? I would. That's all I'm sayin'."

He went back to pecking the keyboard, his eyes sinking into the fog of computer life.

"All that garbage about Christmas," she continued. "*It ain't what you want, it's what you need.* You know what we need? Heat. We need heat. We need this place fixed up. He coulda done *that* for us instead of presents. That's what we *need*. Not a clock."

"He ain't Santa Claus, Rinks."

"He's rich!" She threw her hands over her head. "He's got enough money to build a bridge around the world with one-dollar bills. What would it cost to fix up this building? That would be loose change to him." Her knee sank into the pile of blankets covering the dust-mite-infested mattress. "He thinks he's better than us, Vern. You worked for him five years. He should have treated you better than an owl clock."

She scoffed. This usually worked on Vern, getting his blood pressure running in the red. Sometimes she got him madder than she was. She liked that. Like having a pet bull in the house.

"Well." He tapped a key. "At least we didn't get a striped ball. What's Fritz supposed to do with a ball that doesn't even bounce?"

Rinks crawled across the bed. "What do you think he whispered to him there at the end? I don't like secrets, Vern. I'll bet he knew that, did it on purpose just to irritate me."

Rinks had tried to get Fritz to tell them what he said on the way home. The boy had just shrugged. When he finally wrote something on his phone, it wasn't the truth. *The ball is special.* That sure wasn't the truth. If it was, why didn't Godfather just say that? No reason to whisper it. Unless he just wanted to make Rinks quiver with curiosity.

Mission accomplished.

"He was probably just encouragin' the boy." Vern went back to typing. "That's all, Rinks."

He wasn't taking the bait. Rinks bounced on the bed. The laptop shook on his belly. He asked her to stop, and he asked nicely. He was far from upset. Looked bored, in fact. She jumped off the bed and walked around the room. Piles of dirt balls were swept into the corners. The room smelled like wet plaster.

"This clock ain't goin' to keep mice away. You know that, don't you?" She poked the owl face in the eye. It was hard wood. She hated the way it made her feel. Like it was going to swoop down on her in the middle of the night. Vern had put it on a shelf facing the bed. "Like a mouse is goin' to be scared of that. Seriously, you know that, right?"

"I know."

"What's this?" There was a fork on the shelf. She held it like a magic wand. That got his attention.

"I accidentally took it from dinner."

"Accidentally?"

"Yeah." He wasn't making eye contact. "You know how I put my fork and spoon in my pocket at supper? It's just habit."

"Oh, yeah. How you just put a fork made of silver in your pocket after supper, sure." She aimed it at him. "You *stole* this."

He shook his head. No more typing. "I'll give it back."

"No, you won't. You're goin' to sell it is what you're goin' to do. Melt it down so they don't know you stole it. You're goin' to sell it and that owl clock. A handmade original clock made by Herr Drosselmeier that's guaranteed to keep mice away."

"No."

"No? Why not?"

"I'm not goin' to sell the clock or the fork, Rinks. He'd find out."

"We need the money, boy scout. Can't feed those kids a clock."

"We don't need money, Rinks. What we need to do is decide if we're stayin' here." He sat up. That was what was on his mind. "Do you really want to live in this building?"

"We own this building, Vern. It's free."

"Well, then we need to start buyin' stuff. Startin' with a new bed. Then a refrigerator and furniture that ain't filled with microscopic bugs. We're goin' to need air-conditioning, too. Summer's goin' to be hot. Kids need their own beds, too."

"Oh, please. The kids got a mattress, probably better than ours. You know, there're kids in the world sleepin' on dirt, you know that? They oughta count their blessings."

"You know someone sleepin' on dirt?"

"Just watch TV, Vern. You'll see. This place ain't bad compared to that. It's basically campin', only better."

"Barely." He closed the laptop and spoke slowly. She hated Serious Vern. "Look, Rinks. This mattress smells. I can feel things in it, and it ain't my imagination. This was a vermin hotel before we got here. Just look in the corners of the room. This ain't a house. We could make it one, sure. We get it cleaned up and all that, but then what?"

He leaned forward with that Serious Vern look: stiff lips and squinty eyes.

"A toy store ain't a bad idea," he said.

Rinks nodded. Not because she liked the idea. She just wanted him to shut up about that. She'd heard the pitch twenty times that day. Good idea or not, it was starting to annoy her.

"Marie stole that story she told, you know that, right?" she said.

"Mmm," went Vern. Which meant he didn't care.

"Just like her mother." Rinks shook her head. A worm of guilt or shame turned in her stomach, knowing where she was going with this. "She just wants all the attention, just like my sister. Marie can't help herself. That's how she grew up, so she's goin' to do that."

She caressed the raised scar on her cheek, suddenly swept back to a memory that still played now and then. When her sister's name came up, that scar would itch. Like it remembered, too.

"You can tell the stories, Rinks. This is your store; you can be the storyteller. Just get a storybook about snowmen and elves and reindeer and stuff. No one cares where they came from. It's not stealing."

He put the laptop on the bed next to him and hooked his arms around his upraised knees. Serious Vern leveled up to Very Serious Vern. "We'll name the store after you." He swept his hand across a marquee. "*Rinks and Toys and Stuff.*"

"That's horrible."

"Whatever. You get to design all the toys, too. We'll work up a business plan, have people make them for you. They can be originals; you design the clothes they wear. We'll sell them online, make up stories for them." He stuck out his chin with an alligator smile. "I'll bet Godfather would invest in that."

"He won't. You saw the way he looked at us. He'll want Marie to do it. That's why he gave her that book."

The girl was already telling stories to her little brother in the next room.

"Then we act like Marie is the storyteller. We get him on board. Then after a while, when the ball gets rolling, you take over." He snapped his fingers and drew the marquee again. "*Rinky Toystories.*"

Even worse. It wasn't a bad idea, though. And she hadn't seen him this excited in a while, not since the kids moved in with them. It would be her own line of toys. *Original Rinks.* Now, that wasn't bad at all. They would wear her scarves, too. Then she'd sell them to the parents by the busload. She'd go to conferences, be the keynote speaker. Sign scarves and toys. *Playing cards!* There would be photos of her surrounded by adoring faces, kids sitting cross-legged on the floor, listening to her tell stories.

Then, one day, Godfather would come to hear her. He'd sneak through the crowd like he did when the Corkers owned the place, and listen to her from the corner. Afterwards, he would bring a reward for all her hard work. A special gift.

"What gift will he bring?" she said.

"What?"

She lay on the bed next to him, rolled onto her side facing him. "He delivered a gift, remember? Said it was special and then, like, said somethin' about a journey. You know?" She looked around the room.

The walls were yellowed and cracked. "You think it's still here, like he wants us to find it?"

"Is *what* still here?"

"Are you listenin'?" She smacked his arm. "The gift. Maybe he left it here for us to find."

"Rinks, there's nothin' here but mouse poop."

"That ain't mouse poop," she said. "And that nutcracker toy was here."

"Maybe that's what he was talkin' about."

He yawned, opened up the computer to start the pecking again. Rinks rolled onto her back, stared at the water-stained ceiling tiles. Her nose was stuffy. They were going to clean this place up, for real. Get a new bed, new furniture. This was going to be their home. They were going to be famous. *She* was going to be famous. They wouldn't wait for Godfather to mysteriously come by; that would take too long. They'd invite him. He could bring the robot.

"Better not sell that clock," she said.

"What?"

She rolled away from him, dreaming of the taste of fame and hidden treasures. The attention the robot would bring. Maybe Godfather would want to introduce him to the world at *Rinks Toystories'* grand opening. He could tell that weird story about the nutcracker, maybe come up with an ending this time.

"Hey." She looked over her shoulder. "You think I was the queen in that story?"

Vern had no idea what she was talking about. She was too tired to explain. But she was certain the robot's story was about her being the mean little Mousequeen who put a spell on the princess.

That meant Vern had seven heads.

SOMEONE WAS TALKING. It was the middle of the night.

Rinks elbowed Vern to turn off the computer. He groaned and scooted away from her. The laptop was closed. There was no movie that he sometimes watched when he couldn't sleep. His dry mouth hung open, heaving waves of morning breath in her direction.

She sat up.

Ghosts. That was her first thought. The place was haunted, and that was why the Corkers left this place. Or maybe *the Corkers* were haunting it. They'd heard them talking about renaming the toy store and weren't happy about it. They came back to stop them.

She shook Vern. His gummy lips clung together as he smacked them and rolled over to the very edge of the mattress. She was about to give him an elbow when she recognized one of the voices. It was Marie. There was another voice, though.

Fritz?

Rinks always suspected the boy was faking it. He was talking when she wasn't around. Who stops talking just because their parents die? She sat real still and tuned her ear. It didn't sound like him, though. Was Marie practicing characters for storytelling? *The backstabber.* Rinks fed her and clothed her, and now she was planning to tell the stories? Not on Rinks's watch.

This had to stop.

It was far too late, and Vern had to work in the morning, and if anyone was going to tell a story, it was going to be the queen of this castle. Those brats were not going to fart around in the middle of the night. Rinks slid into her slippers and wrapped a blanket around her. She snuck out of the room and was going to scare them witless. Maybe make some ghost noises at the door.

The light didn't shine at the bottom of their door.

She stood still and listened. The voices came again. A chilly sensation coiled around her backbone. She almost went back for Vern. Someone was in the storefront. She held very still, thinking what to do. She was almost certain it was Marie's voice. She cracked their bedroom door.

The air mattress was empty.

The owl clock was on the shelf. Below it, standing on the bench, back against a checkered wall, the nutcracker stood at attention. Guarding nothing but squares of wood. She snuck through the kitchen. With her ear to the door, she listened to a conversation coming from the storefront. Something was scratching the floor. Surely, they weren't doing chores. It sounded like they were sanding the floor.

She threw the door open, hoping they might wet their pants a little. A lesson like that went a long ways. It had when Rinks was little. There was a quick flash of light. Rinks put her hand up. Car lights turned the corner, the headlights passing through the windows.

Marie and Fritz were in an empty aisle.

"What do you think you're doin'?" Rinks said. "It's the middle of the night."

"Um, Fritz was sleepwalking again."

"Again?"

"He does it sometimes."

She was lying. It was the look on her face, the way she stuttered. Rinks was a grade A lie detector. Her father was one, too. Passed that skill down to her. It was the little things that gave someone away. These two were guilty.

"Who were you talkin' to?"

Marie shrugged. "I was waking him up so he would come back to bed."

"Uh-huh. That's what all the gigglin' was about?"

"It's just... he made a funny face."

This girl's pants were about to catch fire. Why would they be in the storefront? So Rinks wouldn't hear them in their bedroom, that was why. Fritz had the striped ball Godfather had given him in his hand. For some reason, that felt suspicious. Call it a hunch.

A grade A, lie-detecting hunch.

"Did you find somethin' out here?" Rinks said.

They shook their heads. A bit of confusion on their brows. That looked more like the truth. She still didn't believe them. The first mistake in discovering a secret was trust. She didn't believe or trust them.

"Off to bed. And don't get back up. Your uncle's got to work in the morning. And we got some serious cleanin' on tap. Get your beauty rest."

Rinks remained in the store several minutes after they'd left. She looked around, studied their footsteps in the dust. Just bare footprints. Nothing had been sanded. She was sure she'd heard something gritty on the floorboards. And something else she'd heard. Marie had been talking.

Someone had been answering her.

8

For Marie, life was like a dream. A mostly bad one.

Every day she waited to wake up and everything would go back to the way it was. Every day she woke up, it was more of the same. It still felt like a dream, though.

That night, she had to pinch herself to believe it.

After visiting Godfather, she felt different. It didn't feel real (going to an underground lair with a robot felt far from it), but not in a bad way. For the first time since her life had turned upside down, she was filled with hope and something else. Something uplifting, bubbly. She smiled for no reason because of him.

Because of Godfather.

He believed in her. For no reason, he believed in her. That was why she went to bed smiling.

She sank into the air mattress, her bottom touching the floor, and thumbed through the pages of the book he gave her. They were thick and stiff, rough to the touch. She turned them one at a time, telling a story to Fritz. She was making it up, like she did when she was little and would sit on her mom's lap and pretend to read.

Fritz was half-listening, if he was listening at all. He was more interested in that ball, turning it with his fingertips, staring at his warped reflection. It looked like a big, round walnut made of metal.

It didn't matter if he was listening or not, she enjoyed weaving the story about a boy and a girl who escape into another world with friends and family, where they would spend Christmas and sing songs and do all the Christmassy stuff that was definitely not going to happen this year. They would have a Christmas tree.

"The biggest Christmas tree in the world," she said.

He wouldn't let her hold the ball. Wouldn't even let her touch it. He didn't say why she couldn't touch it or why he was so obsessed with it. It looked heavy and odd. Didn't make any noises when he shook it. Didn't flash any lights or sing a song. He was not at all disappointed Godfather had given it to him. He wouldn't tell her what Godfather had whispered to him, either.

She was about to find out.

He fell asleep with the ball clasped in a fist. Nussknacker was in the other hand. She was sure the soldier would poke her in the back, but wasn't about to take it away from her brother. She put the book on the bench. Out of the goodness of her heart, she thanked the owl clock for keeping the mice out of the room. Whether it worked or not, she was grateful no furry, gray animals scampered around at night.

She put the white feathered quill between the pages of the book and pulled the white ribbon out. With that, she tied her hair back. That was a perfect use for it.

For once, she fell asleep with her hair out of her eyes.

MARIE TOSSED AND TURNED.

Her dreams were filled with scratching sounds. Someone was working an industrial sander. It was occasionally interrupted by gravel turning in a concrete mixer.

She sat up in a pitch-black room. Her bottom was on the hard floor beneath the air mattress. She reached over to find Fritz's side of the bed empty. His phone was on his pillow. She turned on her phone and looked around. The book was still on the bench, but it had been moved.

Nussknacker was standing against the checkered wall.

Fritz must have gone to the bathroom. She turned off the phone. Five minutes later, she turned it back on and got out of bed. The noises were back. *Scritch, scritch, scritch.* Like twisting a bowl on a countertop covered in sand. It was followed by a gritty drag and then *scritch, scritch, scritch.*

A mouse.

She held very still and held her breath, trying to hear where it was coming from. It wasn't in the ceiling. It sounded too far away to be in the wall. She opened the door and listened. When she went to the kitchen, it wasn't coming from there, either.

A voice.

Her heart did a lap around her lungs, then a belly flop into her stomach. Light-headed from a lack of oxygen, she tiptoed quietly to the door that led to the storefront. It sounded like a movie was play-ing. Fritz couldn't sleep, so he'd gone to the storefront so he wouldn't wake her up.

"You don't need to charge it." The voice had that gravel sound she'd dreamed. Like stones in a glass tumbler. "It'll last, like, ten years. I can give you the exact amount of time, if that's what you want, but just trust me on this, all right?"

There was a pause. Then the voice continued, "The specs? I mean, sure, I can give them, but *you're* not going to understand them. You didn't ask the Counselor for *his* specs, did you?"

Counselor?

At that moment, Marie realized Fritz couldn't be watching a movie. His phone was on the bed. Someone was out there, and it wasn't Uncle Vernon. She eased the door open. The hinges gave her away. A light went out.

"Fritz?"

He was standing in the dark, his messy hair silhouetted by a backlight of streetlights coming through the windows. He wasn't moving in a very scary-movie sort of way. A fist at his side. His eyes were in the dark. She pointed her phone at him. He wasn't blinking.

"What's going on?" she said.

He didn't move. Not a shrug. Not a head shake.

"Were you... were you talking?"

It wasn't him unless his voice changed. Her little brother's voice was trapped somewhere inside him. He'd closed that door when Mr. Trauma introduced itself one afternoon and locked Fritz's voice up in a cell. (Fritz worked with a therapist named Mr. Sean. Unlike Marie's therapist, Teri, Mr. Sean said Fritz's voice was locked in a prison cell instead of a box.) Marie had tried to help Fritz find his voice. She hadn't given up, but she was running out of ideas. Hugs weren't doing it.

"Come on." She held out her arm. "Let's go to bed. It's cold out here."

He didn't move, in true horror-movie fashion. Creepy vibes scampered up her arms like bugs. She didn't know what to do, so she turned for the door and hoped he would follow. If he wasn't back in the bedroom in ten minutes, she'd try again.

And then she heard it.

Her back to him, she was at the door leading to the kitchen when a dusky light turned on behind her.

"He was talking to me."

Marie dropped her phone. It bounced on the floor and scattered light around the room. She turned around. Her heart boarded a rocket ship on a course for the top of her head.

Something was standing next to her brother.

A SANDMAN.

There was no other way to describe it. Think snowman—three balls, the bottom one the biggest and the other two successively smaller. Made of sand. The same height as Fritz. Tree branches for arms. And two sand dollars for eyes.

"Fritz." The word hissed through her teeth. "What is—"

"Surprise!" it said and threw its branches out. Marie jumped and squeaked. "Haha. I told you she'd be *aaahhh.* Hahaha. What'd I say? Oh man, I should've bet you. Easy money."

"Shhhhh." Marie found her voice and rushed at them. The sandman cringed. "Fritz," she whispered forcefully, "what is-is-is... what is *that*?"

"I'm right here," it said. "I can hear you."

Fritz's shoulders were bouncing. *Is he laughing?*

"Listen," it said, "you want the long or short version of this little— what're the kids calling it—this little *getup*."

"Fritz, what's happening?"

"All right, *cool girl.*" It made air quotes with the twiggy ends of its arms. "Long or short, you choose."

"What are you?"

"I like that. You're a Zen-present-moment kind of person, I can tell. The imperfection is perfection, right?" It coughed into a fist of curled sticks. A gritty cloud puffed through them. "Sorry. Went over your heads. Short version. *I*... am the sandman. Questions?"

It bowed deeply.

Marie waited. The sandman blinked the big round sand dollars. A smile creased the wet sand just below them.

"I'm going to get Aunt Rinks."

"No! No, no, no, no." It slid towards her like a bag of rocks dragged across the floor. "This is his fault. Fritz, I mean. He did this." It jabbed a stick in Fritz's direction. "I'm not telling on him, it's just the facts. He set me up. I mean, not like a sting. Preferences, is what I'm saying. He made me this."

He presented himself like a runway model.

"A sandy snowman with charm and humor and razor wit. And he took the sarcasm *waaaay* up. Like an eleven. You remember that, kid?" he said to Fritz, poking an elbow at him. "I was like *you sure about this?* He was like *for sure.* And I was like *this handsome and funny?* He was like *why not?* I was like *I can live with that.* You know what I mean? So, his fault."

Marie closed her eyes. When she opened them, it was still there. She wasn't dreaming. Or maybe she was. Maybe this proved the last two years was a dream, and it was finally reaching an absurd end. She was going to wake up any second now in the house she grew up in. There'd be a Christmas tree downstairs and breakfast on the table. Eggs with homemade hashbrowns and a glass of orange juice. She started to leave.

"I'm his voice."

She made it to the kitchen this time. "What?" she said.

"That little thing right there. The one Godfather gave to F-bomb." It pointed a twig. Fritz held out his hand. "That's me."

Marie walked up to her brother, stared at the ball in his palm. The one he'd been staring at all night.

"Neurolink projection," it said. "It took eight hours to link up with his nervous system and access brain waves. We meshed forty-five minutes ago. We're basically best friends." Fritz nodded. "I'm his thoughts, Mar Mar. In the real."

Slowly, she reached for the ball. He let her take it. It shimmered with internal heat, like an engine about to smoke the tires. Pinpricks nibbled at her fingertips. It was heavy, like she thought it would be. She dropped it back in his hand.

"Is this what Godfather whispered to you?" she said.

Fritz nodded.

She swung from confused annoyance to the brink of tears. *He's got a voice. It came in a weird package, but he has a voice.*

"That's coming from the little striped ball thing?" she asked.

"I'm not a *that*. But I'll give you that one," the sandman said. "It's not a striped ball thing. It's a self-powered, neuro-interfacing thought-projector. Courtesy of Avocado, Inc., and not for public use. It's made just for the F-bomb."

"What's the F-bomb?"

"It's him. He's F-bomb."

"Don't call him that."

"Why not?"

"It's a bad word."

"F-bomb? It's the letter *F* followed by *bomb*."

She looked at him. "You know exactly what it means."

A smile dug into the wet sandy cheeks. "Whatever, Mar Mar."

"How does it work? I mean, how am I hearing and seeing your sandman?"

"First of all, I have a name."

"Okay. What is it?"

"I've got many names."

"Sandy?"

"How'd you guess?" The sand dollars opened in exaggerated surprise. "She's smarter than she looks."

"You're kind of mean, you know that?"

"No. I'm not."

"A little bit."

"Not even a little, but I respect your opinion. If you don't like it, talk to him." He leaned toward her and pretended to whisper a secret. "It's his fault."

The elation of her talking to her brother through a projection was nosediving back into a pool of annoyance. She'd do anything to talk to her brother without typing everything on a phone. She sighed, looked at the floor and back up at the sandman. And waited.

"You want to know how it works?" he said. "Simple question, complex answer. I've known you for fifteen minutes, and I can already tell you won't understand." He waved his branches like a breeze blew them about. "No offense. Fritz doesn't understand, either. He also don't care."

"He *don't* care?"

"He turned my grammar setting down. I don't know why."

Marie turned her attention to Fritz, who seemed to be a spectator. "Is this really you talking?"

"It's him," Sandy said.

"Why can't I hear his voice?"

"It don't work like that."

She grimaced. This could just be a goof. Neurolinking thoughts?

Maybe Sandy was no different than the Counselor, just a really cool party trick that had nothing to do with Fritz.

"So he's linked to you?" she asked. Fritz nodded. "He knows your thoughts, says what you want him to say?" She turned to Sandy and asked: "What were Mom's favorite Christmas cookies?"

Sandy's sand dollars disappeared in a long blink. His midsection swelled, and for a moment, her hopes were dashed. *This is just a party trick. And I fell for it.* Her annoyance transmuted into fury that set her cheeks on fire. She was about to grab the ball from Fritz, curse him for goofing on her like that.

"Peanut-butter cookies with a chocolate drop in the center. Right out of the oven when the chocolate's soft and warm. And then a sprinkle of red sugar," Sandy said softly. "She called it Christmas dust."

Marie covered her mouth. Fingers trembling. She could see the cookies. Could smell them. She should've asked a different question, like where did Fritz lose his shoes on vacation or what was his favorite song. The cookies yanked a memory from the box. She slammed the lid tight to keep any emotions from following it out.

He knew. Fritz knew exactly what her favorite cookies were. He didn't forget, either.

She hugged her brother. More like trapped him in an embrace, swung him side to side, and he let her do it. He didn't fight the wetness of her cheek against his, either.

"You really like cookies," Sandy muttered.

"Can you please turn the sarcasm down?" she asked her brother. "It's super annoying."

"I think you mean super funny," Sandy said.

So the striped ball wasn't a bouncy ball. It was an Avocado, Inc., invention. A self-powered supercomputer with neuronetworking that interfaced with the nervous system of its owner. Once it scanned the owner's thought patterns, it would read brain waves and translate them to a projected image. It could be anything. A proper butler or a cuddly grandmother, a stern taskmaster or a suave model. Fritz had picked a sandman. And named him Sandy.

"Couldn't have said it better," Sandy said. Then winked one sand dollar at Fritz, whispered: "Actually, I could've."

"This is incredible, Fritz. I mean, you have a voice. Godfather gave you your voice for Christmas." He nodded with a smile. He hadn't stopped smiling. It spread to Marie. "You don't have to type anymore."

"Please," Sandy said, "you'll make me blush."

"Can you talk with Fritz's voice? Like, let him talk. Not you."

"What's wrong with me?"

"It's a question. Can you?"

"This is his voice."

"It doesn't sound like Fritz."

"Because it's me."

"You're interpreting what he says and turning it into sarcasm."

Sandy pecked at his chin; sand appeared to dribble to the floor. Then pointed. "Sarcasm is a lot harder than you think."

"No. It's not."

Marie had been pacing back and forth. It still felt like a dream, but barely. Godfather had the technology to do something like this, and she couldn't imagine a better use for it. Judging by her brother's expression, neither could he. She could talk to him. Even if it was through an absurd projection, she could talk to him.

"We can't tell Aunt Rinks," she said.

"Oh, no. No, no, noooo. My main man here can't use me in public, either. I'm calibrated like that—just your eyes and his." He twisted his bottom half, grinding it against the floor without leaving a mark. Then said: "And other stuff."

"What other stuff?"

His head rotated toward Fritz. A silent conversation was happening right in front of her. *It's not a conversation,* she thought. *Sandy's just a projection.* It didn't feel like it. They could tell secrets without her hearing a word.

"What is it?" she said. "What other stuff?"

"Well, it's this other thing. We're not sure you're ready for it."

"Ready for what?"

Another long silence. Sandy chuckled. "I know. Right?" he said to Fritz.

"You're talking about me?"

"Uh, no."

"Fritz, tell me. What's he talking about?"

Fritz folded his arms and nodded. His sandman let out a long, slightly annoyed sigh. "Godfather sent me to be Fritz's voice. And also to go on the journey."

"Okay." She looked back and forth between the two of them. "I have no idea what that means."

"Yeah, we know."

When he didn't elaborate, Marie sighed with complete annoyance. "Look, Fritz, it's the middle of the night. I'm going to bed. So are you."

"We're not tired."

"Doesn't matter. Aunt Rinks will have chores for us. We can talk about this when we're scrubbing the ceilings."

"We can't do the journey without you."

She didn't like the sound of this. A journey sounded like running away. If this thing wanted them to pack their bags, she was telling Aunt Rinks first thing in the morning, and Godfather would have to explain giving her brother rogue artificial intelligence.

"You'd better not mean running away, Fritz." She turned to her brother. Because that was who was talking, not a snowman on the beach.

"Running away, what?" Sandy said. "No. It's the opposite of running away."

She pinched the ridge between her eyes. Her brain was swelling. This felt like a night court comedy. She started laughing. *Wouldn't it be great if this entire thing was a dream that ended with a ghostly sandman?* Her laughter didn't stop.

"I think we broke your sister," Sandy said. And this brought another wave of laughter. She covered her mouth, waved her hand.

"I'm going now," she said. "For real this time. You two don't stay up too late."

"Wait! Don't you want to know what Nussknacker said about the journ—"

Sandy vanished when the door leading to the kitchen opened on its own. Aunt Rinks barged through it, dunking Marie in cold panic. Her aunt asked some weird questions. Nothing compared to what Marie had just experienced. She pulled it together and volleyed Aunt Rinks's suspicion with some choice-cut lies.

Her aunt had no idea what had happened.

Fritz rolled onto the air mattress.

The nutcracker was still at his post on the workbench. That was what it looked like, standing guard beneath the owl clock. Mouth half open. Emerald eyes unblinking. Marie thought about the Counselor's story, how the young man stumbled over the Mousequeen on his last step.

She turned off her phone, climbed onto the mattress. With her shoulder blades on the floor, she stared into the dark and listened to Aunt Rinks shuffle around the storefront. Marie kept thinking of the last thing Sandy said, right before her aunt kicked the door open. A field of goosebumps spread across her arms.

Nussknacker said about the journey.

9

There was a path in the jungle. That was what Aunt Rinks called the backyard—the jungle. A tapestry of vines as thick as nautical rope weaved through volunteer trees and shrubs badly in need of a haircut.

Marie was sent to tame it with a cheap pair of pruners and a rake with broken tines. She had started on the patio Aunt Rinks had partially cleared. The chairs were beyond repair, and the pavers were hidden beneath a carpet of matted roots. She was only there a few minutes before she found the gravel path.

It was narrow and winding. She crawled under a tangle of thorns and found a small pond filled with rotted leaves. A tower of flagstones that might have been a waterfall. Goldfish maybe, once upon a time. A little farther and she found herself surrounded by trees and the blue sky above. The sound of traffic was distant.

A bench was opposite the mucky pond. The slats were a patchwork of blue-green lichen; the legs had sunk into the ground. She cut through the underbrush with her hand pruners. Something was on the bench. She swept a mat of soggy leaves away, found a lump of wet fur. It was a teddy bear and a green dragon. There was also an octopus with a pale-yellow body that might have been orange long ago. Their eyes, once glassy, were foggy and blind.

Marie squeezed the teddy bear, and dirty water dripped out of it. She closed her eyes and imagined what it was like to be her great-aunt Corker, to escape into a world she imagined. A world that was kind and pleasant.

A place where the air tasted different.

MARIE LURKED INSIDE the jungle with a view of the truck that stopped at the curb. A heavy door rolled open. The old gate dragged open. Two men were lugging something down the crooked sidewalk toward the back door. They wore blue jeans and matching ball caps. One of them had a red beard flecked with white whiskers.

"This is the place I was telling you about," he said to the guy at the other end of a mattress wrapped in plastic. "Put it down a sec."

They dropped it on the ground. Red Beard took off his cap, wiped his forehead with his sleeve.

"Place is a dump," said the younger guy.

"Last I was here was before you were born. Back then, the place was..." Red Beard shrugged. If he had memories of coming there to hear a story and buy a toy, those days were long gone.

"Habitable?" the younger guy said.

"Something like that."

The gate cranked open again. Uncle Vernon turned sideways to squeeze between the mattress and bushes. The plastic bag he was carrying snagged on a branch and was ripped from his hand. The younger guy helped him put the contents inside the bag from a store called *Larry's Electronics*.

"Thanks. This way." Uncle Vernon held the back door open.

The moving guys hoisted the plastic-wrapped mattress up the steps and squeezed it through the crooked door frame. Marie ducked down when the younger guy looked back. The door slammed shut. A minute later Aunt Rinks was there.

"Murry!"

Marie refused to answer to that name. She was as still as a rock. Aunt Rinks kept calling. Not until she cried out *Marie* did she start crawling out, holding the sodden teddy bear she'd found on the bench. She hid it behind a rotten stump before climbing through the branches. Aunt Rinks pulled her T-shirt over her belly. *Superstar* was written on the front.

"You supposed to clean this." She pretended to wax the patio.

"What are those guys doing?"

"Come on. Inside."

The moving guys were in one of the back rooms. It wasn't where Marie and Fritz were sleeping. The kitchen table had been moved aside to make room for the new cargo. Aunt Rinks's scarves were laid out. They were all silk and hand dyed. Mostly tie-dyed. Marie had showed her how to do tie-dye a year ago. Aunt Rinks thought it was original. Marie had learned it in the third grade.

"Vern," Aunt Rinks hissed. With big eyes, she said: "Somewhere else."

He filled the plastic bag from *Larry's Electronics* with little boxes and bundles of wires and took it to the storefront. Aunt Rinks put on a big fake smile. The one that made animals cringe.

"So, we're gettin' new furniture and a fridge today. A guy's comin' to fix the heat. Gonna make this place a real home. We can't be sleepin' in a warehouse, you know."

"Is that our bed?"

"Oh, no. Your stuff will come later. Couldn't afford it all at once. But it'll come." Fake smile. "I got an errand for you. Fizzy!"

Marie's brother came from the storefront with a bucket of water.

"You and your sister need to leave while we redecorate, okay?" She readjusted Fritz's rosy, worn-out ball cap. "You can finish up later. Go down to the coffee shop and get yourself somethin' to eat. Here." She dropped a wad of money on the table. "Stay down there at least a couple of hours. Don't want you in the way. We got measurements to do and decisions to make. Can't have a couple of monkeys standin' round."

She snorted. None of that made sense. It sounded like a lot of work, and she wanted them to leave?

"I need to clean up," Marie said.

"You look fine. Go on, 'fore I change my mind. Don't put the bucket there, Fizzy. Take it out back on the way. All right, bye-bye."

The movers slid the old mattress that Aunt Rinks and Uncle Vernon had been sleeping on out of the back bedroom. It had stains the color of weak tea. Marie took the bucket from her brother. It sloshed with dirty water.

"You all right?" she asked. He nodded. "You got your thing?"

"What thing?" Aunt Rinks whirled around.

"The nutcracker."

"Oh, that. Leave it. It's in your bedroom, safe and sound." She crossed her heart. "I won't touch your precious toy, stick a needle and all that." She stepped back to make room for the movers and said to them: "You're takin' that with you."

"Yes, ma'am." Red Beard took his hat off. "Is the stage still up front? You mind if I see it."

"You mind if I wander around your house when I'm workin'?"

Red Beard didn't expect that response. It clashed with his memories of the toy store that were bright and shiny and warm. Now a cloudy day moved into the building. He asked Aunt Rinks a few more questions, like what the place looked like, if there were any toys around. Marie elbowed her brother and jutted her chin.

"Where you goin'?" Aunt Rinks said.

"Bathroom," Marie said.

Red beard kept on with the questions. Fritz came back with a bulge under his shirt that Aunt Rinks didn't see. He and Marie were out the door before the movers pulled the spoiled mattress behind them.

"Don't come back for a couple hours," Aunt Rinks called.

Aᴜɴᴛ Rɪɴᴋs ᴡᴀs up to something.

It didn't matter to Fritz. He had a spring in his step, holding the nutcracker in one hand and looking around, feeding the sights and smells to the striped ball in his pocket. Marie wondered if those two talked inside his head. Fritz would sometimes laugh for no reason at all.

Is that good? she wondered.

The streets were crowded. The sidewalks were full; people came and went from the local stores, a different flavor of Christmas music escaping each time a door opened—modern, pop, traditional, bluesy. It didn't feel like Christmas with so many short-sleeved shirts and flip-flops; the blue skies and palm trees were going to take some getting used to.

They passed the game store. The boys were inside. Two of the younger ones watched the older brother play a racing game at a wraparound monitor display. He was wearing the same clothes, this time without a belt. A Band-Aid on his finger.

Fritz held out his phone. There was nothing written on it. Marie took it and said, "Hello?"

"Stop staring at them."

"Sandy?"

"Nussknacker might not protect you this time," he said gruffly.

Marie didn't know what that meant, but moved on before anyone inside the store noticed her. "You're not supposed to be out here," she whispered.

"You see me?"

She didn't. He was on the phone. Then she noticed the Bluetooth speaker in Fritz's ear. So maybe Sandy's voice wasn't in his head.

"There's a park over there," she said, noticing a fountain with benches near a giant Christmas tree. No one was at the picnic tables. "We can talk there."

"You know, people talk on the phone all the time. It's not weird. F-dog is hungry. Go to that coffee shop and spend all that money your aunt gave you."

He wasn't wrong. It was just a phone call. No one would know she was talking to a ball in her brother's pocket. They continued up the sidewalk, past the coffee shop's front window. It was crowded inside.

"Whoa," Sandy said. "Those are some creepy elves."

The mechanical elves were slowly swinging their tools. Marie didn't want to explain that Mr. Corker—her great-aunt's husband (*our great-uncle*)—made them. But, also, didn't disagree. They were creepy. She handed the phone back to her brother.

It was noisy inside. Conversation echoed around the walls and hard floor. Most of the tables were occupied. A small crowd was at the counter. Ms. Trutchen was merrily serving a long line. Ms. Clara, dressed in a frilly apron and a red dress, was sitting at a table with older men and women, telling a story. When she saw them enter, she excused herself.

"Children!" She put her arms around them. She was soft and warm. Smelled like sugar cookies. "Come, come. I have table in corner for you."

She guided them to the back of the store where a beat-up hightop was wedged against a leaning bookshelf. Fritz climbed onto one of the stools. Ms. Clara wiped the table with the rag always over her shoulder.

"Have seat." She pulled a stool out for Marie. "What can I bring you?"

"Thank you. I have money." Marie showed her the wad of green paper. "I want to spend it."

"Ah, very good. What do you want?"

"I'll go look."

Marie excused herself. Ms. Clara leaned on the table. It made Marie a little nervous, but what was there to be nervous about? Fritz was smiling as she told him a story. Marie waited in line, eyeing the glass display. The smells woke her appetite. By the time she reached the counter, her stomach was growling.

"Marie!" Ms. Trutchen threw out her arms. "Merry, merry. What can I offer?"

Marie couldn't help but smile. Ms. Trutchen's joy was a bubbling fountain that spilled on everyone who approached. Her laughter infectious. Marie gave her order, counting up the cost. What was left over she put in the jar. A little stick doll was leaning against it, the branches wrapped in twine.

Ms. Trutchen winked. "Merry, merry."

Marie took the tray of drinks and pastries back to the table. Ms. Clara was wiping a tear from her eye and laughing. Fritz's phone was in front of her. A blanket of anxiety snuffed out Marie's joy.

"You are too funny," Ms. Clara said with a sigh. Then to Marie, "Sit, child. Bring your friend next time. He is good company."

Marie couldn't find words to answer. The phone was on speaker, and Sandy said something in Ms. Clara's native language.

"Oh!" Ms. Clara leaned over the phone. "You from my country?"

"Definitely not," Marie said.

She squeezed Marie's shoulders with both hands, tapped the bill of Fritz's ball cap, and went to greet more people, whom she knew by name.

Marie took the phone off speaker. "What are you doing?"

"I'm charming," Sandy said. "What are you doing?"

Marie looked around and whispered: "You know her language?"

"I know all the languages, kid. Like, all of them. Relax. It's a phone call. No one cares."

Fritz had half a danish in his chipmunk cheeks. Jelly smeared on his chin. Marie sipped her tea and tried to act like she wasn't on the phone with a robot. That was what he was, a little round robot that fit in her brother's pocket. She handed the phone to Fritz.

"Wait!" he said. "We need to talk."

"Who's we?"

"What do you mean *who's we?* You and F-bro and me. Who else is on this call?"

She shook her head. If he didn't speak for her brother, she would've put the phone in her pocket. "What do you want?"

There was a pause. "I missed you. Fritz and I were up all night after Aunt Rinky-Dink ruined the party. You snore, by the way."

"No, I don't."

A recording of snoring played on the phone.

But he was right, no one was paying attention to them or would hear them if they tried. And they couldn't talk at home, not like this. She tore a bite off her banana bread.

"Fritz." He looked up to meet her eyes. "I miss talking to you. It's been so long, and I understand. I just want to know, like... how are you doing?"

"What do you want to know?" Sandy said.

"Like, with everything that's happened. I just want to know you're all right."

He chewed slower and looked down at the table. She knew there wasn't a good answer. It was just something she wanted to say. She did miss hearing him. Sandy's voice was better than nothing, even if it sounded like a monster truck.

"He doesn't like it," Sandy said. "But you already know that. He's glad you're here, though."

"I'm not going anywhere."

"Well, not now."

"I'm not ever leaving you."

"You're seventeen, Mar Mar. You going to live with Aunt Off-Her-Rocker till you're thirty?"

She shook her head. "No, but I'll take you with me when I move out."

That was never anything she ever thought about. She'd be eighteen in a few weeks, the day after Christmas. What money her parents left in a trust would be hers. She wouldn't be rich, but she could get a car and afford an apartment for a while.

And raise my little brother with no job and no degree?

"We can change things," Sandy said.

"Change what?"

"You. Him. Your loony guardians." When Marie shook her head, he whispered, "The journey."

Now it was her turn to look at her food. Her brother was seven years old. He didn't want to talk about Mom and Dad and all this. His silence protected him. He didn't talk to Mr. Sean, his therapist. He just drew pictures. He was doing the best he could, Mr. Sean told her. Just be there for him, he said. When he's ready, he'll let you know.

She pressed the phone to her ear and looked at Fritz when she said, "What's the journey?"

"We have to save the princess," Sandy said.

"Save the…" She had to think. "Princess Pirlipat?"

"Ding-ding."

She dipped her head to catch Fritz's eye under the bill of his ball cap. "Is this a game? Like, did Godfather put this in the ball for us to play?"

"Un, no," Sandy said. "*I'm* the ball."

"Where is she, then, the princess?"

"In Candyland."

"Candyland."

Sandy was just a voice on the phone, not a three-dimensional being scratching the floor. And the journey, which had sounded like running away at first, sounded more like a video game. Maybe one they could find in the game store. A game might be exactly what Fritz needed. She could play the game. Do whatever he needed.

"Where is it?" she said.

"We don't know."

"Is it at the game store? We could—"

"It's not that kind of thing."

"Okay." She sipped her tea. Fritz was making eye contact with her now. "What kind of thing is it?"

"Nussknacker knows where it is. He's going to tell us."

"The nutcracker?"

"Yeah, the nutcracker. He has a name, you know. You're not *the human.*"

She looked away from her brother. How did the Counselor know the nutcracker's name? Marie had assumed, after Sandy had appeared, the Counselor had made some mental connection with Fritz. *No,* she thought. *Fritz is just expressing himself through the nutcracker. Nussknacker can't talk.*

"Nussknacker is going to *tell* us? Did he say anything else?"

"Look," Sandy said, "you can just stop with the tone. You think Nussknacker is a toy, fine. Who do you think saved you from that boy, huh? You think, when he was holding Nussknacker over his head, he just dropped him, and his belt *accidentally* broke? That soldier is here to protect Fritz on the *journey*. He's going to take us there."

She put the phone facedown on the table. "Fritz, is Nussknacker talking to you?"

He nodded without hesitation. A quiver shot through her like a bolt of cold lightning. *He's hearing voices.* And this was before Godfather had gifted him with Sandy. She took a long, slow breath and made a mental note. They'd have to address this when the time came to talk to a therapist. For now, *meet him where he's at.*

"Nussknacker told you about the journey?" When he didn't answer, she picked up the phone.

"That's right," Sandy said.

"Okay. Good." She tried to sound authentic and did a pretty good job. "How does he know where Candyland is?"

"Because that's where he's from."

"Right."

"It's not an accident. He found Fritz, not the other way around. He's been waiting for you a long time. He'll take us there. He knows where it's at."

"And then what, everything will be fixed?" She pressed the phone against her ear till it hurt. The look on Fritz's face, the way his shoulders slumped, made her immediately regret saying it. It just slipped out of her. Some people just didn't get it. Some things don't get better. Ever.

"Some things can't be fixed," Sandy said. "But they can heal."

She almost dropped the phone. That was exactly what she needed to hear. Whether it was Sandy who said it or something Godfather had programmed him to say, a warm flood of hope flowed through her like a summer tide.

"If Nussknacker says we have to hop a train, we're not doing that," she said.

"It's not like that."

"Where's Candyland, then?"

"It's at home. You just need to find it."

Home? He was talking about a building. A building where movers were moving new furniture. A building with dirt balls and cold showers. It wasn't home. It used to be a toy store.

"Corker's Candyland," she muttered.

Fritz drained the rest of his drink. With a hot chocolate mustache, he looked across the table. His eyes blinked heavily under the dirty bill of his ball cap.

"Do you believe us?" Sandy asked.

"When I see it, I'll believe it."

"Just like Santa, huh?"

"Santa isn't real."

Sandy laughed so hard she had to pull the phone away from her ear. A smile spread on Fritz's face, and he snorted laughter through his nose. Marie wasn't sure what was so funny.

"Oh. You're serious," Sandy said. "I get it, you're older now. You know everything. That's fine. You don't believe in Santa Claus or that Nussknacker saved you."

"He didn't save me."

"So the boy just dropped him. You're going with that?"

"Fritz, I'll go on the journey, okay? We'll save the princess." She grabbed his arm and squeezed his hand, looked at him with every ounce of sincerity she could muster. It wasn't hard to do because she believed it, with every cell in her body, when she said: "I'm going with you."

He squeezed back. Then he broke off half of the banana bread she hadn't eaten and finished it. She hung up the phone and watched him eat. They stayed at the coffee shop until their time was up. Ms. Clara sat with them for a while and told stories of Christmas when she was a little girl.

Marie listened politely but was distracted by her thoughts. How far would she take this imaginary journey and pretend the nutcracker was real? There was no one who could answer that, no therapists to help her. The answer, she decided, was simple. She would go as far as he wanted.

All they had was each other.

THE ROLLING DOOR slammed on the back of the truck. Red Beard fixed a padlock on it. The younger guy was telling a story, waving his hands. When he hit the punchline, Red Beard bent over laughing and came up wheezing, cheeks as red as a sunburn.

They straightened up when Marie and Fritz came down the sidewalk. She knew who they were talking about and what was so funny. The younger guy—the tag stitched to his gray shirt said Phillip—bunched his leather gloves into a ball and shoved them into his back pocket.

Bernard, written on Red Beard's shirt, wiped his eye, and said to Marie, with a mild aftershock of laughter, "You live here?"

Marie nodded.

"I was telling Phillip here about the place. Your mom wouldn't say whether you were going to open a toy store or not."

"She's not my mom."

"Oh." He looked at Phillip, who shrugged. "She your sister?"

"Aunt."

"Well, your aunt tried to sell us a scarf for a hundred bucks."

"Did you buy it?"

Phillip laughed behind his hand. "I don't need no scarf," Bernard said. "I used to come here when I was your age. Shame it closed. It meant a lot to people. You don't know the half of it." He described the long lines, the stories, the magic air inside the store. Phillip looked bored. "Lot of people would like to see it again, but..." With half a grimace, he said in a gruff whisper, "I don't know about your aunt."

"You all done moving?" Marie said.

"For today." He turned his back and waved before climbing into the truck. "More tomorrow."

The tailpipe coughed and rattled under the bumper. Marie and

Fritz watched them pull away from the curb. She could hear them laughing again.

There was a new couch inside. Beige with extra pillows. A television leaned against the wall, waiting to be mounted. Uncle Vernon was in the corner, sitting uncomfortably on one of the wooden chairs from the kitchen table, hunched over a small table with his laptop. That was his new office.

Aunt Rinks was on the couch, her leg thrown over the back of it, holding her cell phone up. Marie went to the kitchen, where a stainless-steel refrigerator hummed quietly. She opened it to find bright, white light and empty glass shelves.

Protein bar wrappers were next to the sink.

"Where've you been?" Aunt Rinks called.

"The coffee shop."

"I said for a couple of hours. Not all day." It had been almost exactly two hours. Aunt Rinks pulled herself upright. "Like the couch? Got that special coating that don't stain on it. And the TV's goin' to get all the channels once your uncle gets it fixed up."

"Did we get a bed?"

"You got a bed, young lady."

"It leaks."

"Well, we slept on that nasty one. Would much rather have that clean air bed of yours." She stood up and pulled the bottom of her shirt down. "Don't worry that pretty white ribbon of yours. You'll get a bed."

Marie tugged on the ribbon Godfather had given her. It did a good job keeping her hair out of her eyes. Aunt Rinks sounded a little jealous. How many times did she try to get Marie to wear one of her headscarves?

"Me and Vern are goin' to run some errands and get some food. Be gone a few hours. You and your brother stay here and don't leave. Do whatever you want to do. It's free time. We'll bring you supper. You won't see us for a few hours."

A few hours. Got it. "Okay."

"Vern!" He jumped when she shouted. "The kids are home. We're leavin'." When he got up to look for his shoes, she added slowly, "Don't forget the computer."

He nodded and muttered something, snapping the laptop closed and tucking it under his arm. She waited for him at the door. With a big fake smile, she said before closing it, "We'll be gone a couple hours."

And then they were arguing on their way down the buckled side-walk. The back gate clattered shut. Marie and Fritz were confused. The couch, TV and refrigerator looked out of place, like someone moving into a haunted house. And their aunt and uncle had fled like they'd seen a ghost.

A couple of hours.

Something coarse began grinding the floorboards. "That was weird," Sandy said.

10

Rinks loved the smell of fast food. It reminded her of the county fair, where everything was fried. Candy bars, licorice, cake. Her favorite was fried dough. She'd eat those things till her stomach split, then go on rides and throw up afterwards. Barfing made room for chocolate-dipped graham crackers with sprinkles.

She opened the white paper bag to get a huff. A car honked, and she almost dropped it and wet her pants at the same time. She made a rude gesture, even though *Rinks* had walked in front of *their* car coming out of the drive-through. People were lazy. They'd do anything to not walk inside, where there were free refills. Rinks had filled up twice before leaving, and the drive-through had barely moved. *Lazy and dumb.*

Their car was parked next to the dumpster. Vern was in the driver's seat, his face bluish from the glow on the laptop. An employee was hiding behind the dumpster, staring at his phone. That was the other thing. People couldn't look away from their phones when they should be working. Phone addiction was real. That was why he was working at the Burger Hut. She felt sad for him. Going nowhere in life like that.

Rinks squeezed into the passenger seat and handed the cold waxy cup, sweating with condensation, to Vern.

"Where's my drink?" he said.

"We're sharin'. You only drink half anyway."

He smelled the straw poking out of the plastic lid. "Is this diet?"

"No."

"This is diet, Rinks. You know I don't like diet."

"It ain't diet, Vern."

It was totally diet. But she wasn't going to buy him his own drink just to watch him waste half of it. She dumped all the fries and fried fish into the bag. Licked the grease off her fingers. She'd snagged almost thirty packets of ketchup, but a few of them were vinegar. She rolled down the window and threw them in the direction of the dumpster. The employee on break looked up, then went back to his phone addiction.

"Extra crispy, like you like it." She put the bag between them. "You get it workin'?"

He chewed the food, his lips and chin glistening, and turned the computer toward her. "It's a little jumpy, reception not great."

Rinks shoveled a bundle of fries into her mouth. The image on the computer was grainy, but it was good enough. The air mattress was in the corner of the room, all messy and unmade. The leather journal with blank pages was on the workbench. Above that, the owl clock was staring at the camera like it knew.

Vern had drilled a neat little hole into the wall.

The camera was no bigger than a pencil eraser. Looked like a nail when he shoved it in. Didn't need wires or anything. Not the highest quality camera, but their mission didn't need to read words or anything. Just needed to see what those kids were up to.

Rinks had left the drawer on the workbench half open where she'd found the protein bar wrappers. She knew she hadn't lost count the other day. It took every bit of muscle for her to smile when they got home. Like no one robbed her.

"They need to make their bed," she said. "Where are they?"

He reached into the bag. "This ain't live. I started it from the beginning."

"They in there now?"

"I don't know. Figured they might've done somethin' when we left."

"Click over to one of the other rooms."

"We only got this camera."

She smacked his hand. "What'd you mean?"

"I told you, there wasn't time for the others."

She snatched the bag away from him and tucked it between her hip and the door. Gave him a long, hateful eye. He dug food out of his cheek with his finger and licked it, put his hand out like he expected her to give him more after he only put one camera up.

"Vern," she said, sickly sweet, "is half your brain on strike?"

"What?"

"They were *in the storefront last night!* I told you they were doin' somethin'. We got to see everywhere, you melon head. I swear, if you had any more holes in your head, your brains would leak out."

He wiped his hands on his thighs, leaving oily streaks in the denim. He stared out the windshield, running his tongue over his salty lips. Then he said, with all the seriousness of a funeral director, "Apologize."

"I'm sorry, what?"

"You apologize to me, Rinks. I been workin' hard to get that buildin' fixed, bought all that furniture, put that camera in their room —and I didn't want to, I said so, not in their bedroom, but I did it anyway. And then you give me this." He rattled the ice in the cup.

"It ain't diet."

"It is so. I know when you're lyin'."

Rinks lied all the time, and he didn't know the half of it. Little lies that didn't even matter. Like giving Vern diet soda and telling him it wasn't. The worst part: she was going to die on that hill before telling the truth. And she didn't know why.

"I apologize," she said. She didn't say what for. Vern didn't ask.

They shared the bag of fries and stared at an empty room on the laptop. The car had a hot, steamy smell to it. Her cheeks felt oily from it.

"Can you speed it up or somethin'?" She doodled her finger at the screen.

Vern wiped his hands before sliding one finger across the touch-pad. Nothing changed except the time stamp. Detective work was dull. It took all her willpower not to look at her phone.

"There!" She wagged her finger. French fries and bits of fish spilled onto the floor. "Go back, go back."

Vern reversed the recording and hit play. Marie walked into the shot. She slowed down and stood in the middle of the room. Rinks leaned over Vern's lap. He pushed her head down so he could see it. Marie suspected something, the way she stood there. The drawer was half open. The book had been moved. She turned around, lips moving.

"Sound. Where's the sound?" Rinks said. "It's not working."

Vern tried some settings, but they couldn't hear nothing. Rinks closed her eyes. He'd messed the sound up, but she wasn't going to say that. Ten seconds later, she started pushing keys on the off chance she might get it to work. The video disappeared.

"Where'd it go?"

He brought the video back and asked her, very politely, not to randomly stab the keyboard. Random was all she knew. He got it back to where Marie turned around. Even though they couldn't hear her, she was talking to someone. And then she stopped talking for a few seconds before speaking again.

"She's talkin' to someone, Vern. Someone's there."

"Maybe."

"Maybe? Look at her... *there!* She's listenin' to someone. Oooooo." She covered her mouth. "It's Fizzy. That little fart smeller can talk, I knew it!"

"Fritz doesn't talk."

She didn't know what made her more mad: how calmly Vern said that or the confidence he said it with. "Then who? Who would she be talkin' to? Unless..." She covered her mouth again. "That girl invited friends over. I told her not to, and she did."

"Stop. Let's just... can we watch this a second?"

She couldn't take the suspense. If there were sound, she wouldn't be on the verge of heart failure. Marie left the bedroom. They were back to staring at the owl clock staring back. He scrolled ahead until it said *LIVE* in the upper right corner. Nothing had changed.

"Great. Just great." She folded her arms. "Let's just go back. I need to know who's there lookin' through my stuff. They could be sittin' on our brand-new bed, Vern."

"Give it a little longer."

His patience was the only thing keeping Rinks in the parking lot. The kids were probably in the storefront doing whatever they had been doing the night before. What Rinks and Vern needed to do was abort mission and get back there. Tomorrow, send them back to the coffee shop so Vern could get the rest of the cameras up. Rinks would go with them. She could get them to relax, ask some questions. Interrogate them until they slipped up.

Detective work was nothing like TV.

She grabbed her phone. Vern kept watching the laptop while chewing through French fries like popcorn. He'd snip one in half with his front teeth and chew it like a piece of meat. Rinks distracted herself from the sound he was making with videos of car accidents and animal tricks. Finally, she held the phone up and shot a selfie with Vern and the laptop behind her.

"What're you doin'?" he said.

"Detective work," she said while typing.

"You're not goin' to post that."

"The kids don't follow me." That sort of irked her. If they followed her, they'd know she was staking them out. That was their fault. They lose. Vern got on his phone.

"What are you doin'?" she said.

"I'm textin' them we're gettin' food, and we'll be home in an hour. And I gave them our location."

"Why would you do that?" She smacked his leg. "Now they know where we are."

"Exactly. It'll put them at ease to do whatever it is you think they're doin'."

"I don't like your tone. *What I think.* They're doin' somethin', Vern; I told you. I got instincts. I know things right here." She tapped her chest. "Sometimes you don't need brains to know things. People think with their hearts way better than their heads. Trust me."

Rinks was a feeler. A deep feeler. And those emotions were pushed way down in the dark, but she knew they were there. Sometimes, when she was up for it, she'd take a peek, and they'd tell her what to do. And right now, those kids were up to something.

She was right.

Marie returned to the bedroom. She put the nutcracker on the bench, facing the checkered wall below the owl clock. Rinks crunched up the bag so Vern would stop eating, so she could concentrate. His breath was in her ear. It was hot and humid. Smelled like a fish tank.

Marie bent over, studying the back of the nutcracker. Did she not know how the thing worked? Pull the lever and the mouth closed.

"What's she doin'?" Rinks said. "Did the camera freeze? She's not movin'."

A few seconds later, she turned her head and called out to whoever was back there. Fritz came in wearing that dirty baseball cap of his dad's. Now the two of them were standing there. All Rinks could see was their backs. The camera angle was too low to see the nutcracker on the bench.

Rinks put two fingers on the screen.

"What're you doing?" Vern said.

"I can't stand that owl."

When she moved her hand, the owl was looking through a smudge left behind from her fingers. She had no idea what the kids were doing, and the owl kept up the accusing look.

"Let's go," she said. "Turn off your location. We'll take off our shoes and sneak in through the back door, catch them in the act."

"I can't turn it off now. They'll know."

"Get out. Get out of the car. You stay here with your dumb phone, and I'll drive back." That was the best plan yet. Why hadn't she thought of that? She opened her door. "I'll come back for you when—"

"What is *that*?" Vern said.

The tone sent a steel rod up Rinks's spine. She'd never heard shock in his voice. Except for the one time her friend Kate Belzinger had caught her hair on fire when she bent over a candle at a candle party Rinks was throwing (and then no one bought candles). This sounded worse.

Rinks leaned over and wasn't sure what she was seeing. At first, she thought the oil she'd smudged on the screen had done something to the video. It looked like someone was with the kids, as tall as Fritz and twice as fat. Three globs of wet sand stacked on top of one another. Bare branches were stuck in the middle ball. It looked like a special effects from one of her social media apps, like the ones that make kitty faces or giant eyes.

Marie turned her head. *She's talking to it.*

"Is that a..." She couldn't bring herself to say it.

"It's not a ghost," Vern said. "It's the ball."

She looked at him. A wide, greasy smile covered his face. The setting sun twinkled in his eyes like little fires. He looked like he was about to cry.

"What are you talkin' 'bout?"

"The ball Godfather gave Fritz for Christmas." He pointed. "It's a projector, Rinks. It's a self-contained character. I seen 'em before, somethin' that neurolinks with the holder. Don't you get it?"

"No, Vern! I don't get it. I have no idea what you're talkin' about."

He grabbed her shoulders. "*It's his voice.*"

It took a few seconds. Several, actually. Then she figured it out all by herself. This thing—this *ghost*—was coming from the striped ball. And it was connected to Fritz, somehow. If that silver butler at the cabin could walk and talk and cook supper, then a dumb walnut ball could make a snowman.

"They didn't tell us," she muttered bitterly. "They're keepin' it a secret."

Vern threw his head back and laughed. The car shook. The employee wasn't slacking at the dumpster to hear it. Vern held up his hand for a high five. Rinks slapped it. It worked. He was right. They caught them. It was time to celebrate.

The kids were working on something Rinks couldn't see. The sandy snowman was pointing his branches, moving them around, giving instructions.

"Let's go," she said.

"We got to bring them food."

"No, we don't. That's their lesson for not tellin' us about that. They can lick wrappers for supper."

"We're gettin' them somethin' to eat."

She leaned back, frowning. Serious Vern was back. Those hard unyielding eyes. He wanted to be the good parent? Fine.

"Go on and get it, then," she said.

He did. He went inside. Rinks watched the video, the kids obsessed with whatever they were working on. They couldn't possibly be trying to work the nutcracker, could they? Vern came out ten minutes later with a bag full of food and four drinks. He handed one to her. It was diet. She didn't say thank you, but she held his hand.

He closed the laptop and drove out of the parking lot. If they would have watched the video just one more minute, they would have seen something even more shocking.

It started with a very bright light.

11

Something wasn't right.

Marie stood beneath the fluorescent light in their bedroom, her shadow sharply cast on a bit of sawdust in the corner. Not much, but enough for her to wonder what that was.

Her journal had been moved. She'd put it on the workbench, right where the nutcracker always stood in front of the wall checkered with squares of wood. Now it was on the corner of the workbench. The hairs on her arms bristled. She felt something was in the room with her. Maybe it was her imagination after hearing all the stories about the nutcracker talking to her brother.

"Fritz!" she shouted. "Did you move my journal?"

"What?" Sandy answered.

"The journal I got from Godfather. Did you move it before we went to the café?"

There was a pause. "I don't know. Maybe."

The hairs on her arms rose again. It was the way Sandy answered the question. He sounded like Fritz.

"Did you come in here when I was in the bathroom?" she asked.

"Nooo."

She shuddered. Fritz was plying butter to a slice of white bread by the sink. He sprinkled it with sugar and folded it over, ate half of it with one bite. Sandy watched with a smile denting his face.

"Was that you talking?" she said to Sandy.

"Uh, yeah. Who else?"

The biting sarcasm was back. "You sounded like Fritz. Just like him."

"I completed calibration twenty minutes ago." He made a twiggy fist in front of his face. Cleared his throat. A perfect imitation of her brother said, "Hey, sis."

"Don't do that." She stepped back.

"Why? I'm his voice."

"You're his voice; you're not him. Don't do that."

She wanted to hear her brother. Not an imitation. Sandy shrugged the pointed corners of his branches. Fritz dug another piece of bread out of the plastic bag. He scooped a dollop of butter from the tub and slathered it like stucco on a wall. The protein bar wrappers were on the counter. Dried flakes of chocolate were stuck to the insides.

"Did you eat these?" she asked.

Fritz shook his head. Marie walked back to the bedroom. The drawer in the workbench was slightly ajar. She didn't need to look inside it to know the wrappers she'd hidden inside there—the protein bars Fritz had taken from Aunt Rinks—were gone.

"She was in our room."

"Who?" Sandy said.

"Aunt Rinks. She found these." She held up the wrappers.

It didn't faze Fritz or Sandy. Marie looked out the window. No one was in the backyard. Aunt Rinks had been acting strange. The fake smile. *We'll be gone for hours.* Marie and Fritz would have had to explain why they were hiding wrappers in their room on any other day. That meant only one thing.

"She knows about Sandy," she said.

"What? No, she doesn't. I was totally gone when she caught us last night."

"She knows we're hiding something. That's why she went through our room. Don't you think she'd yell at us for this?" She put the wrappers in the trash and, unfortunately, didn't notice the empty boxes that came from Larry's Electronics. "When's the last time they left us alone in the house? She knows, Fritz. Turn Sandy off."

The sandman disappeared.

"Go up front, look out the windows. See if you see them anywhere."

Fritz took his white-bread sandwich to the front of the building. Marie went out back. The car was gone. The gate was closed. She would have heard it open if they came back. They could have climbed over it, but Aunt Rinks wasn't much of a climber. More of a walker and a sitter. She scanned through the trees, looked down the narrow path she'd found earlier that morning.

Marie walked around the building. Just in case.

Fritz was in the kitchen, making a third sandwich. "Anything?" she asked.

"Nope."

Sandy pretended to hide behind her brother. So what if Aunt Rinks knew about Sandy. Was it a big deal? *Because Aunt Rinks can't keep a secret. Eventually, she'd post a picture on her social. Then Godfather would send the Counselor to come for the ball. Or it would just stop working.*

So yeah, a big deal.

UNCLE VERNON TEXTED they would be home in an hour. He even turned on his location so she could see where they were. It was down the road at a fast-food place. They were going to bring home supper. She felt some relief. Maybe they were telling the truth. Although, it was possible he had dropped Aunt Rinks off to sneak around the back.

The nutcracker was on the table, rigid as always.

"Did Nussknacker tell you where Candyland is?" she asked.

"Not yet," Sandy answered.

"Why not?"

Sandy and Fritz shrugged in unison.

Marie picked up the nutcracker. He didn't squirm in her hand or mechanically kick out a stiff leg. The things Sandy had said about him (or maybe it was Fritz who told him to say it) cutting that boy's belt was ludicrous. She studied the back of the red jacket. She looked closer. Something tiny was written. She'd missed it before, it was so tiny. Like the font on tags found on clothing. Small numbers in a random pattern around an X.

"What's this?"

Fritz turned around. Sandy answered: "The map to Candyland."

"Why didn't you tell me that earlier?"

"You didn't ask." Sandy shuffled over. "X marks the spot."

The projection of his twiggy finger passed through the X etched onto the nutcracker's jacket. "What do the numbers mean?" she asked. "Are those steps? Miles?"

"Ask Nussknacker."

"I am." She addressed the question to the soldier, then looked at Fritz. "What did he say?"

"Nothing."

Fritz searched the empty refrigerator. Apparently, the journey to Candyland could wait until his stomach was full. She should have just let it go. There was still a chance this was all a game he and Sandy were playing. The numbers meant something. She had a feeling.

She took Nussknacker to the bedroom. Every morning, she found him standing in the cubbyhole beneath the owl clock. That was where she put him now, only this time she turned him around so he was facing the checkered wall.

X marks the spot.

Fritz came inside the room and stood next to her. There was a glob of peanut butter on his finger. He had found the jar hidden under the sink.

"Why do you always put Nussknacker here?" she asked.

"We don't put him there." Sandy appeared next to Fritz. "That's where he goes."

"But why?"

Sandy and Fritz shrugged. "He climbs up there at night to stand guard."

"Okay." She decided not to argue that imaginative plot. "You see that?"

She pointed at the square on the wall in the lower right corner. There were thin, whitish scars, the natural sort, that crisscrossed over the circular growth rings from corner to corner. They were hardly noticeable.

"What's that look like?" she asked.

"Do I really have to answer that?"

A twinge of excitement flickered in her belly. It was an X. A coincidence, of course, and not the location of an imaginary land of candy a toy soldier told her brother about. She dug her fingernail into the edge of the wooden tile. It wasn't glued to the wall, but it wasn't coming free easily. She used both hands and, little by little, worked it loose. It fell on the table. Fritz stood on his toes. Sandy leaned through the workbench for a better look.

The wall behind it was painted pink.

"Punch a hole through it," Sandy said.

"I'm not punching a hole in the wall."

"Maybe Candyland's on the other side."

"There's a street on the other side."

"How do you know?"

An argument like this was infinite. Before she grabbed the wooden tile to push it back into place, she looked at the nutcracker. There wasn't just an X on his jacket. There were numbers, too. They were sequential like hopscotch. On a whim, she pressed on the tile to the left of the empty space on the wall, where number 1 would be on the map next to the X. It slid into the empty space where the X tile had been.

What was strange, she noticed, was that the edges of the tile were tongue and groove so that it didn't pop out like the X tile did (which didn't have a tongue or a groove).

"That was something," Sandy said.

She slid the tile to the left of the newly vacated space. It was a game. That tiny spark of excitement fanned into a flame. She didn't expect to find Candyland. But something was here.

She checked her phone. Uncle Vernon was still at the fast-food joint.

She followed the pattern on the back of Nussknacker's jacket. Three more tiles, each revealing a pink cotton-candy painted wall, and then hit a dead end. Nothing would move. "You skipped one." Sandy pointed to the numbers. "Go back one."

He was right. She went back to number two. This time she slid the tile above it down. After that, a couple of the tiles were difficult to move. With a little effort, they came loose and fell into place. Fritz held the nutcracker, and Sandy relayed what move to make next. They got to the last one.

"Dead end," Marie said.

"Try harder," Sandy said.

"I might break it. You sure we did it right?"

"Yeah, 100."

She rolled her eyes when Fritz and Sandy weren't looking at her. The nutcracker wasn't helping them solve the puzzle. If he was talking to Fritz, he could have just told them what to do. Then again, the map *was* on his back.

She tried using both thumbs to slide it up to the empty slot. It gave a little, just enough, to break a vacuum that was drawing it tight against the wall. It popped up and out of the way. The wall behind it wasn't pink.

There was a hole.

Marie took half a step back. She bristled with anxiety and antici-pation. Her skin was electrified. They stared at the opening. It looked like a square black hole in the wall.

"Found it," Sandy said.

IT WAS A TINY HOLE, big enough for a plump mouse to enter. Marie tipped her head to look inside. There was something in there. No whiskers or twitching pink nose. Frigid air leaked out like a refrigerator was open. Fritz reached for it, and Marie grabbed his arm.

"Let me do it."

Marie didn't know how refrigerators worked, but she was certain there was a broken line blowing winter air into the wall. It was colder than inside or outside the building and stung the skin on the back of her hand when she reached in. She was almost elbow deep (wondering if her arm was wagging over the sidewalk outside) when her fingertips touched something. It was a small cube. Her fingers wrapped around the sides of it but not across the back. There was something attached to the top of it.

She expected to pull out a block of solid steel. Instead, it was a red box with a green bow on top of it. *It's the gift,* she thought. *The one Godfather gave to the Corkers.*

"Candyland?" she said.

"That's it. Look."

There was a tag attached to the lid. In small print, a single word was written. *Candyland.*

She felt a bit of relief. All this time it had sounded like they were going to journey somewhere. It was just a present. At the same time, she felt a dark cloud of disappointment. *It's just a present.*

The lid was attached to the box by delicate hinges. She pried it open. Nothing jumped out to bite her hand; poison gas didn't escape. The lid flipped the rest of the way open on its own. They leaned over to look inside.

"Well, lookie there," Sandy said. "Handsome little fella."

It was an orb, sort of like the ball that projected Sandy, only this one was smooth, a little smaller, and not as shiny. Distorted images swirled on the surface like a fortune teller's gazing ball.

It looked like it was floating inside the box.

"Some sort of magnet," Sandy said. "Turn it on."

That seemed like the obvious question. If the ball in Fritz's pocket projected Sandy, then maybe this one would project Candyland. Whatever that was. Right now, though, it was a dull marble with gray images floating on the surface. When she looked closer, there were things inside it that looked like distant forests and rolling hills. If she leaned in one direction, the images changed. There were other things in there, too.

"What are you waiting for?" Sandy said. "Go in."

"Go in what?"

"Candyland. Go in Candyland." He looked at Fritz. "What's the holdup?"

She shook her head. As exhilarating as this little game had been, they weren't going to fit into a box that fit inside the palm of her hand. She turned it around, looked for a button. A humming vibration went up her arm. And the thing was so cold.

She checked her phone. They still hadn't left. "What do you mean, go in?"

"Nussknacker said it."

"Nussknacker said that?"

"Yeah. Who else would say it?"

"Oh, I don't know. You?"

"I don't know any more about this than you do. I'm just telling you what the little soldier is telling Fritzy. He said you found it. He said go in it. He said what's the holdup."

Fritz pointed at the swirling ball floating inside the box. He held the nutcracker in one hand, stuck his finger inside it with the other hand.

"Ask him yourself," Sandy said. "Oh, wait. He doesn't talk to you. You know why? Because you don't believe in—"

Bright light.

A million flash bulbs all at once.

A HIGH-PITCHED WHINE faded when her eyes adjusted. The gift box was on the table. The lid wide open.

Fritz was gone. So was Sandy.

How long had she been standing there? Where did the light come from? She shouted his name. When he didn't answer, she ran into the other room. A jar of peanut butter was on the counter; the lid was off. He wasn't in the storefront or the bathroom or the other bedroom with the brand-new mattress still wrapped in plastic. She went outside and called his name.

Where did he go?

A thousand thoughts squeezed through the bottleneck of her brain. *Call Godfather.* She didn't have his phone number. *Tell Aunt Rinks.* Bad idea. *Call the police.* And tell them what, a mysterious present hidden in the wall vaporized her brother?

She was seized by a panic she hadn't felt since Aunt Rinks had come to pick up her and Fritz on that one day at school, when she'd taken them home to come live with her. An emptiness opened inside her. She couldn't lose her brother. She just couldn't.

The emotional black box inside was rattling.

SHE RETRACED her steps to the bedroom. There were no marks on the floor. No strange smells in the room. Maybe *she* had had an episode, like a brain malfunction from all the stress, and Fritz had gone for help. That was possible. But it wasn't true.

She fell on the floor in the storefront. Her legs crossed beneath her; she didn't have the strength to stand anymore. Not without Fritz. *I can't do this.*

That's a thought, her dad would've said about that. *Can't is a thought. Nothing more.*

She took a long slow breath through the nostrils, like he'd taught her to do when anxiety shook her like willow limbs in a thunderstorm. Long exhale through pursed lips. Again.

Having a thought I can't, she thought. *Having a thought I can't.*

Long in. Long out. Innnnnnn. Outtttttttt.

The door at the back of the building banged open. "Murry!"

Marie opened her eyes. She stood up and, calmly, went to the kitchen.

A WHITE SACK was on the kitchen table. The bottom of it stained with oil. It smelled like battered sardines fried in fish oil. Uncle Vernon was unloading groceries in the kitchen, filling the refrigerator with bottles of soda, ice cream, and lunchmeat (the thin round kind that tasted like rubber meat).

"Where's your brother?" Aunt Rinks said. She was tearing open a package of brand-new Bluetooth earbuds.

"I don't know," Marie said.

"Well, go find him. I need to talk with you both."

Marie didn't move. She'd already looked everywhere. She wasn't going to tell her that. She needed to tell someone, though. Aunt Rinks was more interested in syncing her earbuds to her phone than noticing the tremble of Marie's chin. Uncle Vernon was digging into a noisy bag of cheesy puffs, leaving orange fingerprints on the white bag of grease and the cabinets and the drawers.

She thought about running away. Right that second, just bolting out the door and running all the way to the cabin in the woods where the Counselor was planting a garden. Or knocking on Ms. Clara's apartment door above the coffee shop. Anyplace where she felt welcome. Where she was wanted. A place that felt like home. Because this wasn't home.

This was just a building.

"What's with the look?" Aunt Rinks leaned on the kitchen table, a blue light blinking in her ear. "Can you and me just be honest with each other? This is where we live now. It's the middle of December, and we ain't freezin' our toes off. That ain't so bad, is it? Vern, you like it here?"

He grunted while unloading the last bag of groceries. His whiskers were dusty orange.

"Vern likes it here, and so do I. And you will, too. I know it's hard for you, dear. It was hard for all of us when we were your age. You'll get through it, I promise."

Her tone was soft but had that imitative quality. Like someone who's saying the right things because someone told them they were the right things to say. Marie looked at her shoes. She was going to throw up on them.

"We got to trust each other. Right? We got to share each other's success. We're in this together. You, me, Vern. Fizzy. What's ours is yours and yours is mine. You understand what I'm sayin'?"

Marie looked her in her darkly lined eyes, the eyelids thick with sparkly blue eyeshadow. The bag of cheesy puffs crinkled in Uncle Vernon's hand.

"No," Marie said. "I don't."

"You don't understand." Her tone went as flat as a punctured kickball. It was more of a statement than question. "Well, how about when I found you in the middle of the night tellin' secrets with your brother. Let's start there. You found somethin', didn't you?" When Marie didn't answer, she tried the soft voice coated in sugar. "You can tell me, dear. It's all right. We're family. We can tell each other—"

"Rinks, what do you want me to do with these?" Uncle Vernon held up a box of protein bars.

"Stick 'em on the roof, Vern, I don't care. I'm havin' a conversation with my niece." She turned back to Marie. "Where's your brother? What's he doing? He better not be in the shower all this time. Fizzy!"

Aunt Rinks marched toward their bedroom. She was going to see the gift sitting on the workbench. Marie wasn't going to tell her how they'd found it or that her brother had disappeared in a flash of light. At that moment, she was very seriously considering walking out the back door.

"You hear me callin' your name, son?" Aunt Rinks bellowed. She stopped in the doorway to Marie's bedroom, put her hands on the frame, and said: "Where'd you get those?"

Marie hesitated. Aunt Rinks was standing at her bedroom with the door open. Red light was blinking from inside it. Her aunt sounded more upset than startled.

"Vern! Get over here and look at this."

With a bag of snacks in one hand, he trundled across the room, jamming his finger into his mouth, where cheesy puffs had packed into the divots of his back teeth like mortar. He stopped next to her and looked inside Marie's bedroom.

"Well, ain't that nice," he said.

"Nice?" Aunt Rinks said. "How about where'd they come from?"

Marie started toward them. It felt like she was floating on someone else's legs. She braced herself on the couch, then stumbled past the new television leaning on the wall. When she could see between her aunt and uncle, she froze.

Aunt Rinks turned around. "You wanna explain where these came from?"

Marie nodded absently. Walked toward them without taking her eyes off her brother. He stood still, hands in his pockets. Hat pulled down. A smile beamed below the tattered bill of it. Marie squeezed between her aunt and uncle and frowned. Strands of Christmas lights were strung on the walls; tiny bulbs flashed red.

"You lose your voice, too?" Aunt Rinks said.

"Fritz..." Marie cleared her throat. "He found them."

"Found them where?"

"They were, um, they were in an alley."

Aunt Rinks looked at Uncle Vern. Her lips flattened into a straight line that wrinkled her doughy chin. "Right. And you just hung them up before we got home."

Marie nodded. Her aunt was as confused as she was. Never mind where they came from. Maybe they had been in one of the drawers. Even if Fritz found them, how could he hang them up that fast? Her aunt seemed to be asking the same question.

"What else were you doin' in here while we were gone? Did you find anythin'? Huh? Anythin' you want to tell us about—"

"Rinks." Uncle Vernon stopped her before she said more. Aunt

Rinks seemed to understand what he meant. She crossed her arms like a five-year-old throwing a tantrum.

"I found wrappers in that drawer," Aunt Rinks said.

"You were in our room?" Marie said.

"You stole them from me, didn't you? I think that's the point. You ate them when you weren't supposed to. That ain't nice, and that ain't right. I ain't livin' with a bunch of middle school thieves who keep things from me." She stared lasers at Marie, searching for the secrets she desperately wanted to know. "What else you hidin'?"

She didn't ask about the gift because it wasn't on the bench.

"We were hungry. Is that food on the table for us?"

"It is," Uncle Vernon said. He put an arm around his wife. "Let's all cool down and get somethin' to eat. Come on, Rinks."

She didn't budge at first, scanning the room for something out of place besides a mess of mysterious red lights blinking on their faces. Uncle Vernon squeezed her shoulder. She relaxed a little.

"You really don't have anythin' to tell me?"

Fritz pulled something out of his pocket. For a second, Marie was afraid he would show her what the striped ball was for. Instead, he typed on his phone and handed it to his aunt. Marie saw what it said. *I took the protein bars, not Marie. I'm sorry.*

Aunt Rinks sort of laughed, showed it to Uncle Vernon. Then walked out and said: "Clean up after yourselves."

Marie waited a beat before walking over to her brother. She put her arms around him and squeezed too hard and too long. He let her do it as long as she needed to.

Aunt Rinks watched from the kitchen.

12

Christmas shoppers were in full gear. They were coming in and out of stores, peeking through windows, holding colorful bags heavy with loot. Cars circled the area in search of parking.

There was a time when she knew how many days, hours, minutes till Christmas. She and Fritz would turn over days on an advent calendar, then count their presents under the tree, stacking them to see how high they went. Now she had no idea what day it was. Saturday, maybe.

She and Fritz waited to cross the street. He had a Ziploc in his pocket full of orange puffs. His fingers were dusty and wet from licking them. Uncle Vernon had given him two baggies, told him not to tell their aunt. Marie gave her baggie to Fritz.

He had slept like bedrock that night, curled up with his nutcracker in his arms. Marie had stared at the Christmas lights till the early morning hours. When she woke up, he was already out of bed. Nussknacker was at his post, standing guard where the gift had been hidden. Aunt Rinks had sent them out of the toy store without having to do chores, with no money this time. And two secret bags of cheesy puffs.

"You want to tell me what happened?" she asked.

He licked his fingers, one at a time, and reached into his back pocket. He gave her a Bluetooth earbud and held up his phone. Before she could insert it, he jogged across the street when a truck had stopped for them.

"Where'd you get this?" she said.

He didn't answer. It wasn't the new Bluetooth earbud Aunt Rinks had opened the night before. Fritz had dug her old one out of the trash. They stopped in front of a bakery. The smell of frosted cakes wafted through the window. She fitted the earbud into her ear.

"Howdy doody, Murry Poppins," Sandy said. "You like that name? I got more. A whole list."

"Fritz." Her brother had his hand on the bakery window. Generous dollops of red jelly sat on glazed donuts. "You need to tell me what happened yesterday. Where'd you go?"

He turned. He looked at her. Sandy said, "Candyland, m'lady. We went to Candyland."

She didn't like talking about this with people walking behind them. Even if Sandy's voice was only in her ear. She tugged Fritz's green hoodie. They kept walking.

"What do you mean?" she said.

"It means we were there. And it was, like, *amazing*. We could describe it, but you had to be there. You know when you have a dream and—"

"Just tell me."

"I *was* going to paint a picture, but okay. Let's rush it. There were trees and grass and hills, and there was this sky that looked like... you know what? Scratch that. I got one word that sums it up. Delicious. The whole thing was *delicious*. That's what it was."

"Delicious." They waited for an older couple exiting a bookstore. He held the door for his wife, wished Marie and Fritz a merry Christmas. When they were past them, Marie said, "That's your description? Delicious?"

"You had to be there."

"You're saying you *were* there?"

"Yup. One second, bedroom. Fritz touched that little ball inside the gift. Then bright light." If Sandy were there, he would've done jazz hands. "Next stop, Candyland."

Fritz was distracted by an art gallery, stuffing orange curls in his mouth and looking at a wire sculpture of Santa Claus. She remembered the bright light when he had reached inside the gift. It had felt like a train horn that knocked her back. Then the confusion. The panic. She touched his shoulder, just to remind herself he was there. He looked at her with a question in his eyes.

"I thought you were gone," she said. "I thought it did something to you."

"Sorry," Sandy's voice said in her ear. "He said he's sorry."

He hugged her. In front of everyone. That dissolved the tension that had been coiled around her stomach since yesterday. Even with the orange smudge he left on her shirt, it was worth it.

They continued down the sidewalk beneath awnings shading the storefronts. She had no doubt he hadn't been in the bedroom after the bright light, but did she look everywhere? Did she look in the bathroom? She couldn't remember. Maybe he'd fallen into the bed when it happened and got wrapped up in the blankets, and she hadn't noticed.

He dreamed *of Candyland.*

"You can go, too," Sandy said. "It's pretty easy."

Fritz had his hands in the front pocket of his green hoodie. He pulled out a red and white striped box that fit in the palm of his hand. Marie took it from him and put it back in his hoodie while trying not to look guilty.

"Why'd you bring that?" she whispered.

"So you can go to Candyland," Sandy said. "It's in there. In that little box. The floating ball is the way in."

They walked in silence, navigating around a family clogging the sidewalk with little kids and a dog on a leash who stopped to relieve himself on a parking meter. The family took the dog inside a clothing store. Marie looked behind them, then at Fritz.

"You want me to do it now?" She didn't believe what they were saying (quite frankly, it was impossible), but her brother was missing a big step in his trip to Candyland. *He was gone.*

"Not here, kid. You'll disappear, and that'll freak all these lovely people out. Besides, Fritz is hungry."

"Eat the rest of those cheese doodles," she said.

"He's a growing boy. And space travel is exhausting."

"We don't have money, so you'll have to live off fake orange food for a while."

They passed the game store. It was crowded with middle school kids. As far as Marie could see, the boys weren't at the driving game. They approached the three mechanical elves in the coffee shop window, slowly swinging their tools in a bed of cotton made to look like snow. A little girl with a snotty upper lip was knocking on the glass. Her mother gathered her up.

"The old lady will give you something to eat," Sandy said. "If you smile."

He was talking about Ms. Clara. And she probably would. But Marie didn't want to keep asking for handouts. She'd been so nice already. Besides, the tables were full; people were standing in line.

"Not today," she said. "Let's go somewhere else."

"You don't believe us. We get it," Sandy said. "Touching a weird little ball and going to another world, that's nutty boo-boo. If you told us that, we wouldn't believe it, either."

Fritz was looking at her while Sandy continued, "Why do you think F-train brought the gift? So you don't have to believe us. *You see it for yourself.*"

"Uh-huh. And where do I do that?"

"They got a bathroom in there, right? Take it with you." Fritz held out the gift. Marie snatched it before anyone saw them.

If it were Sandy she was talking to, just Sandy and not her brother, she would've laughed. Not the friendly kind of laugh. Like if someone said *No, seriously, you can fly. Just step off this roof and believe.* That kind of laugh. But her brother, the way he looked—the big eyes, the hope swimming in them, the smile that said *c'mon, sis*—kept her lips locked. She would do anything to bottle that feeling he was feeling and keep it on the shelf for rainy days.

"And then what?" she said.

"You'll see," Sandy said. "We did."

She sighed. The elves swung their hammers. "Okay."

"Yesssss!" If Sandy were standing in front of them, he would've high-fived Fritz. "You should take a pic of her right now, F-dog. So exciting!"

Fritz did take a photo of Marie. He held up his hand. She slapped it without enthusiasm.

"All right. Stay out here," she said. He hadn't brought Nussknacker, so no worries about bullies taking him from him. And there were too many people for that to happen again, anyway. But it would be better if he weren't around all those people. That was how she really felt. If someone tried to talk to him and he just looked back without saying anything... she didn't want that to happen. "I'll be right back."

Fritz laughed through his nose. It sounded like a sneeze.

"Oh." She held the door. "How do I get out? Once I'm in the, uh... the place?" She couldn't bring herself to say Candyland.

"Just look up. Aim for the door and jump."

"Right."

She had no idea what that meant. She was just going with it. She touched the Bluetooth to turn it off. Sandy didn't need to be in her ear for this part.

THE BATHROOM SMELLED like cleaning supplies and air freshener.

It was clean. Like eat-off-the-floor clean. There were paintings on the wall and cute sayings. *If you toot-toot, make sure you poof-poof* was next to a can of air refreshener. *Wash your hands whether you work here or not* was above the sink.

She looked in the mirror. Adjusted the white ribbon Godfather had given her to pull back her hair. She looked older than a seventeen-year-old. At least she thought so. Why people pined for being a kid again never made sense to her. Did they just forget how powerless you are at this age? Memories were all sweet smelling from a distance, when all was right with the world, but when things went wrong, you looked like her: five years older than you were.

She looked at the gift. Pried the lid open.

It was more of an orb than a ball. Although, she supposed, those were basically the same thing. Orb sounded more mysterious. A ball would sit at the bottom of the container. An orb hovered. Some sort of magnetic design made it hover. Or gyroscopes (although she didn't really know what gyroscopes did). It was cool, no argument. But the orb had a dullness to it. Like a burned-out light bulb.

She sighed.

Whatever it was, it brought more joy to her brother's face than she'd seen since maybe ever. Before that, the best present he'd ever gotten was a Honer Virtual GameFace. He didn't look like he did now.

She put the gift on the floor.

All she had to do was touch it. If it worked, there would be a bright light. She sat cross-legged in front of it. If there was a flash of light, like what had happened in the bedroom, she didn't want to fall over and wake up on Ms. Clara's hard, clean floor missing her front teeth. She stared at the orb.

She reached for it.

FRITZ HELD HIS HANDS APART, ready to clap when he saw her.

Marie held the café door open for a young couple to enter. Fritz's lips were moving. For a second, she thought he was about to talk. She waited to hear words. Then he pointed at his ear. Marie touched the Bluetooth earbud.

"Well?" Sandy said. "Did you see the chocolate river? Tell me you dipped your finger in it. There's no way you didn't do that."

Marie looked around. Ms. Clara delivered an order to a table just inside the window near the elves. She saw them standing outside and waved. Marie waved back. She leaned close to her brother.

"Let's go to the park."

Fritz skipped next to her, and Sandy was singing a nonsense song in her ear, making up words like random thoughts floating from her brother's head. *Joy, joy, joy and snow to the world and peace and love and dogs and cats forever. I'm warm and sweet and home...*

Marie tried to take his hand, but he didn't want to hold his sister's hand on a crowded sidewalk. Marie turned off the earbud and walked faster. They went to the corner, crossed the street to a big fountain where the water crashed down on a concrete pineapple. There were benches around it and a park beyond it. Playgrounds and tennis courts, baseball fields and people with dogs.

A trailer had been set up not too far from the fountain. A thirty-foot Christmas tree was in front of it, loaded with ornaments and lights that would glow at night. Letters were attached to the trailer, big ones cut from plywood and painted green or red, that read *SANTA'S VILLAGE*. There were plastic reindeer lined up in different poses around a small stage with an empty chair on top. It looked like a throne. Not too different from the one Godfather sat in. People were standing around it.

They were in shorts and T-shirts, throwing Frisbees instead of snowballs. Rolling in the grass collecting bug bites instead of making snow angels. Marie sat on one of the concrete benches next to the fountain. It was warmed by the sun. Mist from the fountain felt cool and refreshing. It didn't feel like Christmas. Nothing about this did.

Fritz sat next to her. Pointed at his ear.

"What's wrong?" Sandy said when she turned the earbud on. "You look mad. Are you mad? You have resting mad face."

She held the gift, no longer feeling the need to protect it. She put it on the bench between them and hung her head. She couldn't look at her brother. Didn't want to see the light dim in his eyes.

"You didn't go," Sandy said. "Was the bathroom gross?"

She sighed, shook her head. She couldn't hide it. Her plan had been to lie when she came out, tell him how wonderful Candyland was. Jump up and down and clap and sing nonsense songs. But when she opened the door to the coffee shop, she just couldn't.

She didn't go. She didn't even try.

It was ridiculous, the whole thing. Touching a magnet wouldn't transport her to another world. It wasn't magic. She'd seen a light when Fritz disappeared, but there was an explanation for that. He hallucinated, fell unconscious. Dreamed of a world made of candy. Of course he did! What seven-year-old wouldn't? And his wingman, Sandy, didn't know the difference. She didn't want to pretend. But that wasn't why she didn't touch the orb. There was a simple reason why she didn't.

She wanted to believe it was true. She wanted that look on her brother's face to stay there as long as possible. And if she touched the orb and nothing happened, she'd know for sure it was just his imagination. This way she could still pretend it was true.

Because she *wanted* to believe.

"I believe you, Fritz. I really do."

"But you have to go," Sandy said. She didn't mind it was more in Fritz's voice this time. "Nussknacker said so. It's your journey, too."

A dad walked by with a little girl on his shoulders. She was eating an ice-cream cone that was melting over her little fingers and dripping in her dad's hair. He didn't seem to mind. Marie slumped on the bench.

"Tell me about it again," she said. "I want to hear every detail of your trip."

"I already told you," Sandy said.

Fritz searched her face for an explanation of why she didn't just go. She took her brother's hand. He let her hold it against the rough concrete bench.

"Please," she said. "I want to hear it."

So he told her. Sandy spoke in her ear about how soft the grass was (like thick fur) and the tree trunks with candy-cane stripes. The air smelled like peppermint, and the sky was the color of pink cotton candy (pink like the wall behind the wood squares). There was a stream of milk chocolate that he dipped his finger in and tasted. It made his toes tingle and head float.

Fritz looked at her the entire time. The more Sandy told her, the more color returned to his cheeks. There were lights in his eyes when she heard about something in the distance that was blurry and gray like a rainy day, although it wasn't raining. The rest of Candyland was just past a sign that was posted in the chocolate stream. Beyond it, all color disappeared.

"What did the sign say?" she asked.

"We didn't read it."

"Why not?"

"Because he was worried about you. So he jumped out."

"You don't have to worry about me." She squeezed his hand. "You can always go there without me. I'll take care of myself."

"We don't want to go without you. It's *our* journey."

She liked the sound of that. Maybe she could find a way to go there, too. Once she heard enough about this world, she could add details to the story. Fill the blank pages of that book Godfather gave her. They could do this instead of the memory game. Make a new story.

She laughed. "You got back just in time. Aunt Rinks was dying to know what we were doing. I don't know what I would have done if you didn't come out."

She almost said *if you didn't come out of hiding.* One day, he would tell her where he went. Maybe there was enough room in his hiding place for both of them.

"We never tell her about the gift," she said.

"Never."

Fritz laughed through his nose. She loved the sound of it. Loved the way his nose crinkled between his eyes when he did it. She let go of his hand. Maybe they could go back to the coffee shop and sit around until Ms. Clara saw them. It didn't feel right begging for food, but Marie had a feeling the old woman understood the situation.

"Hey, I never asked," she said. "Where did the Christmas lights in the bedroom come from?"

Before Sandy answered, Fritz's faded hat went flying into the fountain. Someone snatched the gift off the bench between them.

FRITZ DIDN'T FISH his hat out of the fountain. He spun off the bench and charged in the other direction. By the time Marie turned around, a lanky boy with loopy hair was stiff-arming Fritz and laughing. He clutched Fritz's hoodie at the shoulder.

Acne Boy was back.

This time, the gift was his hostage.

Marie roped her brother around the waist and pulled him away kicking and swinging. Bobby stepped back. His chapped lips pulled back a fierce grin that exposed blocky teeth not too unlike Uncle Vernon's pickets. Sean, his little brother, reached for the gift Bobby had taken from the bench. Bobby swatted him back a step.

No one was paying attention to them. They were all waiting for Santa to come out of that trailer. It looked like kids doing what kids do near the fountain, playing a little not-so-friendly game of keep-away.

Don't run, Bobby, Marie thought.

The last thing she wanted him to do was take off with the gift. Then she'd have to chase him down, tackle him, and take it from him. She didn't want a scene and to scare all these little kids waiting for Santa.

Bobby didn't run. He couldn't care less about the present. He wanted one thing. He wanted their fear. And if he couldn't get that, their anger.

Steam escaped the emotional black box inside Marie.

"That's my brother's," Marie said calmly. "It means a lot to him. Please give it back."

He turned it over like an antique dealer considering an offer. "What'll you give me for it?"

"Please. We haven't done anything to you."

"You got that doll?" Sean laughed when his brother said that. It sounded so serious. "I don't want a wood soldier. Oh, hey. Look at that. Fancy lid."

His eyes were as round as the O his flaky lips made. He didn't open it. He tempted his brother with it and pulled it away before Sean grabbed it.

"Let's see what's inside," he said like a first-grade teacher.

Marie tightened her grip on Fritz. His boots slipped on the grass as he tried to find traction.

"What's wrong with him?" Bobby said. "He looks—what's the word... *wild*." The muscles in Marie's jaw flexed. Bobby saw it. "You get him at the shelter? You know what we do to animals off leash here?"

He winked. It looked like he was imitating something his parents did. Or bullies who bullied him. He kept dodging Sean from getting the gift. He was good at this.

"This must be worth a lot." He shook the box. "Is it gold, yeah? Ooo, a diamond ring. You're going to propose to Santa!" He covered his mouth and turned toward the stage. "I think I'm going to cry."

He fanned his face. Sean looked at Marie and Fritz and laughed. Like squirting lighter fluid on a spark.

Bobby straightened up, said flatly: "You know who he is, right? The guy who's going to come out of that trailer there. That's my uncle Dan. He likes to dress up every year because he's got the beard. Rides a bike, though. A big old hog with louders that set off car alarms when he gasses it. I been on that bike with him. He pulled a wheelie going down Main Cross."

He could tell that didn't impress her. *Is that what he's trying to do?* He shook the box again. Pointed at Fritz.

"You know he ain't real, right?" He looked at Marie, back to Fritz and back to Marie. His laughter was staged. "Oh, man. Oh man oh man oh man. Did I just ruin Christmas? I'm sorry 'bout that, little man, but it's all a lie. You were going to find out anyways. Your mom and dad's a liar. Santa's just a bum dressed up in a red coat. Ain't that right, Sean?"

Sean had given up on the gift, but he was grinning. For once, his older brother was giving the business to someone besides him.

"Why are you doing this?" Marie asked.

"Why? Why does a polar bear turn snow yellow? He just has to."

Sean thought it was hilarious. Not the joke. The meanness. Bobby was holding court. This was what he was made to do: take things and make people squirm. This was what he wanted. That didn't stop Marie from trying to reason with him.

"We don't have any money."

"That's too bad."

He would've taken the money. It wouldn't have gotten Marie the gift, but he would've taken it. He was thinking now. Thinking like it hurt. Like pedaling as fast as you can in first gear. There must be a whole cabinet of taunts cataloged inside his brain, handed down by an older brother or Dad or Uncle Dan. He had been taught this was what you do for fun. Whether he was responsible for this or just another victim was beside the point. There was only one thing that mattered right now.

"Swim in the fountain. You and your wild animal. Do a backstroke around it three times, then stand up, hug each other, take a bow, and tell everyone to mind their own business."

He was good at this. Probably graduated top of bully class. The only straight As he ever got. He was good. Very good. Start with an impossible task and work your way down, that was how you got people to cave. Sean clapped his greedy little hands, a mini-Bobby ready for his own victims one day.

"No," Marie said.

"You're right. Too messy. You could catch cold. Tell you what," he said, "you do this, and I swear I'll give this back. Swear on this little ding-dong's life here." He nodded at Sean. "Mine, too. And you ain't got to do anything embarrassing. See those people over there?" He swung his arm at all the little kids and their parents lined up between the yellow tape in front of the stage. "None of them know you. You don't know them. So it's simple. You start on that end, and you tell every one of them three words. That's it. You get the fancy box back. Deal?"

He held the gift out. She didn't try to take it.

"Three words," he said.

She shook her head. She knew what they were. He could see that, too. He grinned like a mouse in a cheese factory and counted the words on his fingers.

"Santa's. Not. Real."

"I'm not doing that."

She remembered what it was like when she was that age. How special it was to sit by the window on Christmas Eve. Seeing the cookies gone in the morning, the carrots they threw on the sidewalk half eaten. The stockings full. She wasn't going to ruin it for them. Life was hard enough. Let them have this moment while it was here. Get a picture with Uncle Dan in a Santa suit.

"You think telling the truth is bad?" Bobby pretended to be offended. "Or do you think a fat man really slides down a chimney? He lives on the North Pole with elves, rides in a sleigh with flying reindeer to give free presents in one night, really? *Really?*" He shook his head, reliving some awful moment when someone told him it was all a lie. "You look smart. You both do, but you more than him. But you're probably one of those people who gets good grades, like straight As, but can't figure out how to turn on a light."

He made a stupid face and cracked up Sean.

"Can you tie your shoes? Can you?" he said to Fritz. "Tell you what, you count to ten, and I'll give it back. That's all the wild animal has to do, count to ten."

"Don't," she said through gritted teeth.

"How about this? You solve a math problem, and we're done here. What's 345 times 284?"

"97,980," Sandy said in her ear.

She didn't give him the answer. It wasn't going to matter. None of this—not swimming in the fountain or ruining a hundred Christmas wishes—was going to end this. She felt helpless. The feeling left her body. Her arms and legs were wooden. Her chest a steel cage. The tendons in her neck were taut.

A big, brass bell began to ring.

Cheers went up. Little kids on their fathers' shoulders waved. The door on the trailer opened, and a bearded man in a red outfit stood on the top step and waved. A couple of teenaged elves stood with him. The line to see him began to tighten.

"Santa!" Bobby screamed through a bullhorn of cupped hands. "Santa, we got you a present!"

He waved the gift over his head. People were looking at him and laughing. The gangly teen with acne sounded sincere, jumping up and down.

"Uncle Dan! Hey, over here!"

Santa glanced over and ignored him. Climbed the steps to sit on the Santa chair. In seconds, the first of a long line of hopeful wishes walked up to sit on his lap.

"Oh, so stupid," Bobby said with a sigh. "Anyway, better see what we're giving him. Don't want to be embarrassed. Is there a tiny toy soldier in here?" He shook the gift. "Better not be a lump of coal. That would be... you can't give Santa coal, you ding-dongs. *Santa* gives the coal."

"I'll buy you a game," Marie said. "Let's go, right now. We'll go to the game store, you pick one out, and I'll buy it. Just give it back to me."

"Thought you didn't have money?" He was interested. Genuinely.

"I'll get some."

"All right." He sucked a breath between his squares of teeth. The mouse wheel was turning. "Beg for it. I'll give it back."

She put her hand out. She wasn't going to beg any more than she already had.

"What's that?" he said.

"Just give it back."

He put his thumb on the edge of the lid. Looked at her when he said: "You're making me do this, you know." He started to push it open. "This is your fault."

Marie's heart heard a starter pistol and was sprinting around the first turn. The lid flipped over the top and snapped open. He peeked inside and looked surprised. *Please don't touch the orb,* Marie thought. *Not in front of Fritz.*

For a second, she considered falling on one knee. If she jumped in the fountain, everyone would look at them. She could tell the adults who came to help her that was their gift he'd taken from them. It wasn't going to work, but she could try. She had to do something before he—

Fritz slipped from her grip. Hat pulled over his eyes, he charged blindly. Bobby was distracted by what was inside the gift, and he didn't see him till it was almost too late. He hit Fritz with a forearm. Fritz twisted off-balance and tried to catch himself. He sprawled across the ground like a runner stealing second base. Grass was in his mouth. Mud on his cheeks.

Pressure shot from the emotional black box. A switch flipped.

Auto-protection engaged.

Marie bolted forward.

She buried her shoulder into Bobby's midsection and grabbed both of his legs. She dropped to one knee, pivoted, and pulled his legs up while surging her weight forward. She placed her foot behind his knee. The air stampeded from his lungs when he hit the ground.

The surprise didn't last long. He twisted onto his hands and knees to get up. Instinctually, Marie knew at that moment he did not know how to wrestle. He'd given up his back, and she took it. She hooked her legs around him, locked her heels inside his calves. His neck was exposed. She slipped her arm under his chin and clamped onto her forearm, throwing her weight back. He toppled on top of her. She arched her back to apply pressure.

Her arm was petrified wood. Muscles braided cords of steel. She was a sprung trap, her jaw clenched, teeth grinding. His breath wheezed through his chapped lips like an old man breathing through a straw.

Her lips pressed to his ear. She whispered: "Don't *ever* touch him."

Footsteps approached in the soft ground. A shadowy ring formed around them. A woman bent down beside them. Marie wasn't letting go. She saw the gift lying in the grass. Sean picked it up. He looked inside the gift.

No.

She held on as Bobby started to go limp, his face turning red, staring at Sean as he reached inside the gift. His fingers curled around the orb, about to pull it out. The worst part of it all happened right in front of her brother.

No bright light.

No vanishing act.

Fritz got off the ground and saw it, too. He snatched the gift from Sean and took off running.

Marie let go of Bobby and collapsed on the ground. She closed her eyes as more adults came to break them up. She sighed as the lid on her emotional black box sealed shut. She lay on the ground, numb from head to toe.

No Candyland.

13

Three protein bars for lunch. That was how many wrappers were on the table. Rinks didn't count how many licorice sticks she'd eaten. However many half a bag was. Her gut told her it was too many. But that never stopped her from eating more.

Licorice gave her a belly ache. The protein bars, that was just scientific nutrition. It said so on the wrapper. They were solid bars of nutrients wrapped in milk chocolate for a person on the go. She ate them like Vern inhaled packaged noodles, and he was healthy as a clam. The licorice was dessert. A little cheat never hurt anyone.

She took a selfie with a floppy black stick of licorice. Made sure the laptop was in the shot, but not what was on the screen. The kids didn't follow her, but just in case they did, she didn't want them seeing the video footage taken in their bedroom. Social influencing was hard work. It took constant posting of interesting stuff. Not as easy as it sounded. Stuck in this crummy building, she was running out of ideas.

That was going to change. Very soon.

She was watching the footage from that morning. Marie was

asleep. The mattress looked like a flat tire. How she slept with those red lights blinking was as big a mystery as how the lights got there. They were lying about it. That was what bothered Rinks the most. *The secrets.* She loved a good secret. They were keeping her from what she loved.

Marie had finally woken up. Rinks fast-forwarded to the part where Fritz came back in the room. She assumed he was coming for the nutcracker (*What'd he call that thing? Crackatooth?*). He stood at the bench, and once again, the angle of the camera was all wrong. She couldn't see what he was doing.

"Can you hear me?" Vern's voice was on the laptop.

Rinks switched to the live stream while she chewed on the rubber stick. Her husband's mouth-breathing face filled the screen. The owl clock in the kids' bedroom was just above his head.

"Move the camera," she said.

"What?"

"Move the camera!" she screamed across the room. "It's too low. I can't see what they're doin' on that stupid table."

"One thing at a time. Can you hear me?"

"Ain't it obvious? Now move the—"

"Just a sec."

He ducked out of sight. That was the other thing. There was a blind spot. She wanted to see the *entire* room. What if something was going on in the corner? She'd miss it. Vern came back into view, doing something on his phone. The blinking red lights made him look... *strange.* Every time it turned him red, he looked like someone else. *Not someone else.* Something *else.*

"We're good," he said. "You done with the laptop now? I got work to do."

"I'll be done when you move the camera," she shouted.

"Rinks, I don't have time."

Rinks rushed into the kitchen. The brand-new coffee machine just finished a full pot. She filled a mug (a clean one), added flavored creamer, and grabbed the bag of cheese doodies. It was mostly orange dust, but that was his favorite. He liked to dust his noodles. She crossed the room. Coffee slopped over the sides and burned her fingers. She didn't slow down.

"What's this?" He scrubbed his whiskers with the palm of his hand. It sounded like a wire brush scraping paint.

"Special delivery."

He took the mug from her, put his nose over it. His eyebrows rose. After a noisy sip, he ran the tip of his tongue through his mustache.

"You like?" Rinks said.

"I like."

"I bought the expensive coffee for you. The most expensive. And that creamer is—"

"French vanilla." He took another loud sip. "I like it ah-lot."

"That makes me happy. Now can you move the camera?"

"No. I just got the sound workin'," he said to avoid a head-on collision with a tantrum. "I don't have enough time to move it. I'll move it tomorrow. You can listen in on them tonight."

"Well... take down the Christmas lights, at least."

"Why? They put them up. It looks good."

"Not on you." He was too in love with the coffee to know what that meant. "You really think they put them up?"

"Who else would put them up, Rinks?"

She dug into the crinkly bag and aimed a cheese doodie at him. He opened his mouth. She popped it in and kissed him on the lips. His coffee breath was staggering, but now was not the time to talk personal hygiene. He shook his head before she asked about moving the camera again. She stomped around the room.

The owl clock stared at her. She wanted to take that down, throw it in the garbage along with the one Godfather gave them. But they hadn't seen a mouse, so why jinx it. Marie's journal was on the bench, the pages still blank (*not much of a storyteller, is she?*) along with Mr. Crackatooth. *What are they doin' over here?* she wondered. It was something. She could feel it. Then she noticed the square blocks of wood on the wall.

"Have you been over here?" she asked.

"I been everywhere," Vern said, pouring cheese doodie dust from the bag directly into his mouth.

She leaned closer. There was something quite suspicious on the wall. If she had another minute to study it, she might have discovered exactly what the kids had been doing. But just then the back door slammed. Rinks jumped and had one thought. *The laptop is open!*

Before she could escape the bedroom, Fritz almost ran into her. He surprised Vern, and coffee went down his mustard-stained sweatshirt.

"Fritz!" Rinks said in a high register. "What are you doin' here?"

He did a strange shuffle, turned on his heel and went straight to the bathroom. The lock bolted in place. Rinks had barricaded the doorway to keep him from coming into the bedroom if he came out. She turned to Vern and whispered: "He caught us in here."

Vern shrugged, wiping dust off his sweatshirt. "We're admirin' the lights."

"What's he doin' home?"

"Looks like he's got business." He gestured to the bathroom.

Rinks ran on her tiptoes to the kitchen table. The laptop was facing the door with a full view of the bedroom on it. All it would take was a glance. *We'll tell him we're installin' a security system, to keep them safe. We started with their room because, you know, they're most important.* Fritz might buy that.

Marie wouldn't.

Rinks went to the bathroom, tapped lightly on the door. "Fizzy, darlin'? Everythin' all right in there? You're home so soon."

"You think he's goin' to answer?" Vern said.

Rinks swatted him. His coffee spilled again. "What are you doin' in there?"

"Whaddya think, Rinks? Let the boy concentrate."

He got away this time without spilling a drop. Rinks followed him into the kitchen. The kid had to go to the bathroom. Nothing wrong with that. Everyone liked to do business on home base. Perfectly normal. And he'd rushed in without seeing a thing. No big deal.

"Done with this?" Vern held up the laptop.

"Take it. Go."

She grabbed a licorice stick and gnawed it to a nub while pacing around the table. Vern went to the little desk in the corner. Before he got to work, all the lights in the room flickered. The time on the stove began flashing.

"What was that?" Rinks said.

"Nothing," Vern said dully. "I'll check the circuit breaker."

"Is someone knocking?"

Rinks looked out from the kids' bedroom. She'd been waiting for Fritz to come out of the bathroom and found herself staring at the checkered wall. The squares of wood were smudged with rust. Not all of them, just some of them. It looked like fingerprints. Someone with rusty fingers.

She watched Vern get up from the little desk in the corner and look out the window. He opened the back door. Someone was talking to him, saying something she couldn't understand. Then he stepped aside.

"Come in."

Marie was the first one to come inside. That was weird, her knocking like that. Rinks noticed the grass stains on her shirt. She was carrying Fritz's grungy hat. Then two boys followed her, one tall with a mess of hair on his head and muddy knees; the other one was Fritz's age. A woman was the last one in.

"I'm Vernon. That's my wife, Rinks." Rinks stared from the bedroom. No one waved. "Can I get you somethin' to drink? Water? Coffee?"

"No, thank you. I'm Nina."

She shook his hand. Jealousy wrung Rinks's stomach like a wet towel. The woman was slender and fit. Toned arms and angular face. Rinks could see her jawbone from across the room. With the little hoop piercing in her nose, she looked like one of those cool professional types. A gym owner. Or something.

"Everythin' all right?" Vern asked.

"Your daughter strangled my son." Nina folded her fine arms. "It was down at the fountain. Everyone saw her attack him. She got him on the ground and put her arms around his throat. His face was turning blue when someone broke it up. It happened in front of Santa Land. All the kids saw it, too. They were traumatized."

"Marie?" Vern looked at the boy and back to Marie, then at Rinks. "Marie strangled *him*?"

"There were dozens of witnesses. Show him, Bobby."

The boy was staring at the floor, paralyzed with embarrassment. Nina lifted his chin to expose his neck. If there were scuff marks, Rinks couldn't see them. Besides the dirty knees, there was no evidence that would hold up in court.

"Why she do that?" Vern asked doubtfully.

"She attacked him, unprovoked."

"*Really?*" Vern said.

Nina elbowed her son to start him up. "We were just talking," he muttered at the floor. "She caught me by surprise." Like that was the only reason a girl beat him. *By surprise.*

"She attacked you for no reason?" Vern said.

"Yes, sir."

"Marie?" Vern asked.

Marie shook her head bitterly, but said nothing. Her face carved from stone. Jaws clenching and unclenching.

"I'm not calling the police," Nina said. "If she would've touched my Sean, it would be a different story. I don't want her coming around my kids again, or I will next time."

Vern looked around again. He was suppressing a grin and doing a good job at it. "You hear that, Marie? Don't beat this boy up again."

Bobby's eyebrows pinched together, but he didn't say anything to that. Nina clenched her own biceps, understanding the jab quite clearly. Marie nodded tightly.

"Shake hands and apologize," Vern said.

Bobby offered a limp hand. Marie shook it firmly and looked him in the eye. His arm waggly like a noodle. "Sorry."

"It won't happen again," Vern said. "Thanks for lettin' us know. Kids get rough, I understand, but that's no excuse. Especially in front of children. Are you all right, partner?" he asked Sean. The younger boy nodded. Vern rustled his hair. "Thanks for bringin' them here, Nina."

"It was the right thing to do." She seemed satisfied with the handshake and apology. Grownup Vern really nailed it. Rinks would have made a mess of it, said something inappropriate. Nina looked around the room, at the new furniture and moldy walls. "Y'all living here?"

"Just moved in a couple of weeks ago. Still a lot of work to do. The building was in the family. We inherited it and decided *why not*?"

"That's good." She nodded with a tinge of judgment wrinkling her chin. She had yet to smile, just a grim line across her mouth, even when she said: "This place used to be awesome. Are you going to open the toy store? Be nice if you did. I used to come when I was little."

"Apparently everyone did."

"You make these?" She pointed at the headscarves on the kitchen table.

"I do." Rinks raised her hand.

Nina didn't say any more about them. But she liked them. Rinks thought she saw her smile just a little. "Y'all have a merry Christmas. Everyone be safe." The boys couldn't get out fast enough. Vern held the door for her. She peeped back for one last comment. No one noticed how odd it was when she said: "Love the Christmas tree. Just like the Corkers used to do."

Vern watched them through the window. They were talking in the backyard. The gate hadn't closed yet. Rinks knew what good parenting looked like. And that was it.

"YOU KNOW HOW TO FIGHT?" Vern said. "You see the size of that kid, Rinks? Oh my... he was *huge*. And you just—"

"She couldn't hurt a fly." Rinks locked her arms across her chest, tapping her foot. "What was that all about, Marie?"

"Where's Fritz?" Marie said.

"He's hidin' in the bathroom." Rinks met Marie halfway across the room, blocked her from going around the couch. "I know there's more to it. That boy wasn't sayin' somethin'. And why do you have Fizzy's hat? Now, you're goin' to tell me what—"

"He deserved it!" Marie hit her thighs with balled-up hands. "He and his brother were teasing Fritz, calling him an animal. They threw his hat in the fountain, laughed at him, made fun of him. I tried to be nice. I was calm and polite. But he hit Fritz and knocked him down, and I—"

"Took him down," Vern said. "Is it karate or somethin' else?"

"She strangled him, Vern. That ain't karate."

"I choked him," Marie said. "There's a difference."

"That so?" Rinks planted her hands on her hips. "Well, at least somethin' makes sense because none of what I heard a minute ago did. They were just teasin' you for no reason, just out of the blue. You were mindin' your own business, and they decided to throw his hat in the water. Is that it?"

"They were the ones from before, at the coffee shop."

Rinks took a second. She'd forgotten all about that. "What about them?"

"They took the nutcracker from Fritz. Ms. Clara made them leave. They were probably sore about that. No one was around to stop them this time."

"So you took him down," Vern said.

"Vern, would you stop saying that?"

Marie was biting her lip. The girl looked disgusted with herself. She'd lost control, hurt the boy. Maybe that wasn't what was eating her up. Maybe she enjoyed it. She had a bunch of stuff packed down inside her, emotions all bottled up, and that burst of anger had uncorked it like champagne. Now she felt ugly.

Rinks knew the feeling.

"So we got ourselves a fighter," Vern said.

"No, we don't. That little stunt's gonna ruin our reputation. People'll be talkin' about us, not in the good way. They know we live down here. Suppose we open the toy store like everyone wants us to do. Things like this is gonna scare them off. We'll lose followers on social if we go around beatin' up everyone that throws a hat in the fountain."

"He knocked Fritz down," Marie said.

"Let adults take care of it. What you did has consequences. You're lucky she ain't gonna press charges. We're new on the block, girl. They all live here; they all know each other. You got to think of more than just yourself."

Rinks was filled with pride. This was an award-winning speech she was giving. Too bad Vern didn't have the cameras set up in the kitchen to record it. This was high-level parenting, like Nina the gym owner had done. The lesson was sinking into Marie's brain, weighing on her. Wisdom was heavy for kids. Takes them a minute, sometimes years, to make sense out of it. Marie was staring at the floor, grim-faced and tense. She'd get it, though. She'd understand.

"Where you goin'?" Rinks said.

"To see if Fritz is okay."

"He's in the bathroom doin' what one does in the bathroom. Give him some space. He's just shook up watchin' his sister beat the tar out of some—"

"Bully. He was a bully."

"It don't matter."

"So don't stand up for Fritz?" Marie spouted.

"Don't put words in my mouth, young lady. You're not hearin' me. You did that in front of all those people, scarring those little kids. You heard what Ms. Nina said."

"Rinks," Vern said.

"Don't *Rinks* me, Vern. She ain't tellin' us everythin'. She got secrets, don't you, Marie. What'd I say the other night about—"

"Rinks!"

Vern was standing at the door leading into the storefront. He was staring all confused like. It sent a shiver over her skin. She almost didn't want to look at what he was seeing. He pointed through the doorway. For the first time, she thought maybe she didn't want to know the secrets.

"What's that?" he said.

IT WAS A TREE.

Eight feet tall, maybe ten. The branches were soft and feathery. The top of it hooked to one side like a cartoon. A star was attached to the tippy-top. It was so bright, it hurt to look at.

It was littered with ornaments. Not the store-bought kind with reflective surfaces or plastic snowflakes. They were made with scissors and glue. Things found in a kitchen junk drawer or third-grade art class. Paper snowflakes sprinkled with glitter, tongue-depressor reindeer, Styrofoam snowmen with googly eyes. Santa faces with cotton-ball beards, pretzel-made sleighs and hand-shaped turkey cutouts painted red, green and yellow. Strings of popcorn and cranberry hung from the branches.

In the corner of the store for the whole world to see.

"I'm goin' to ask one time," Rinks said. "Real simple. Did you put this up?"

"No." Vern was gawking at it. "It's somethin', though."

"How'd it get here, then?"

"When would I put it up? You been with me all day."

"Check the camera."

"We ain't got no camera out here, Rinks. You wanted audio in the..." He looked around, then whispered: "In the kids' room."

Rinks didn't like the way this made her feel. It was fully decorated. Not a branch left unhung. It hadn't been there that morning, and neither one of them had left the building. Not for a second. It was impossible to pull this in without making a sound.

Physically.

IMPOSSIBLE.

"Marie!"

A minute later, Rinks's niece came from the back of the building. She seemed not at all surprised to see an eight-, maybe ten-foot tree in the storefront. She squinted at the star's radiance.

"You know anythin' about this?" Rinks asked.

"It's nice."

"How'd it get here?"

"What'd you mean?" A solid liar, this one. Not even a flinch.

"What I mean is, how... did... it get here? It wasn't here this morning. And now it's here. How?"

She shook her head. She was feeling the same gooseflesh on her arms that Rinks was feeling. The weirdness was like a static charge. A ghost dancing around the room. Then Rinks remembered something Nina had said right before she left. A fresh wave of gooseflesh crashed over her. *Love the Christmas tree. Just like the Corkers used to do.*

"Maybe one of the locals snuck it in," Marie said.

"She's got a point, Rinks. Every one of them keeps bringin' up the toy store."

"You're tellin' me... someone snuck in here... and did this while we were here?"

"I mean, yeah," Vern said. "We don't lock the front—"

"No one snuck a CHRISTMAS TREE IN!"

She was feeling light-headed. Too much oxygen or sugar or Christmas spirit. *Something!* First the lights in the kids' room and now this. It didn't make a lick of sense. She was on the verge of freaking out, and these two idiots acted like someone had left a note on the window.

"Go get your brother."

"He's still in the bathroom."

"Kick it open."

"I'm not kicking open the door," Marie said. "He's been through enough. How else would a tree get in here? Someone is pranking us."

They stared at it for another minute. It didn't disappear. The ornaments didn't look like they'd been pulled out of storage. They were fresh. Newly made by little hands. Like an art station was next door. Rinks took a long deep breath. There was a reason it was here. It wasn't magic. Someone would confess, sooner or later.

But no one would confess.

She would find out where the tree and the lights came from. Sooner than later, she would know all the secrets.

14

I t sounded like a landscape company in the next room.

Uncle Vernon snored on the exhale like a stubborn lawn mower that wouldn't start. Aunt Rinks was more like a chainsaw running on bad fuel.

Red light flashed across the ceiling. Marie's back was on the floor, cushioned only by a thin layer of deflated plastic. Fritz was curled up with the nutcracker, his hat, still damp, pulled over his eyes. She didn't want to get up. Her body weight was keeping his side inflated. But she was sore. And anxious.

She rolled off gently, watched Fritz sink as the air mattress recalibrated to her absence. He didn't notice. She pulled the covers up to his chin. Tension jolted through her. Sleep was so far away. Her body didn't care how late it was. Thoughts were working third shift like they were behind on deadlines.

Quietly, she opened the door leading directly from their bedroom, which was the workshop in an earlier day, to the storefront. The hinges didn't squeal anymore. Uncle Vernon had sprayed down all the hinges. Aunt Rinks didn't like the sound they made. The room stilled smelled of oil-sweet lubricant.

The storefront was dark. The star had been unplugged. Aunt

Rinks said it was using too much electricity. Besides, it was drawing too much attention. Everyone could see inside. *And it'll blind someone drivin' by, and then we'd get sued for it,* she had said. Marie liked it dark. It was how she felt on the inside.

She didn't want anyone to see her sit cross-legged on the floor. It wasn't a perfect tree. It was crooked and hooked at the top, like it was falling over in super-slow motion. The branches shot out like a bad haircut. The ornaments, though, were so real. Like the ones she and Fritz had brought home from school. The ones Mom and Dad would say were their favorite, even more favorite than the ones from the year before. Mom had a box of all the ones she'd made when she was little. Every year, she would hand out the ones that made the cut. And she'd tell a story each time.

This one Gramma made when we didn't have much money. It was a yellow foam cat with pipe-cleaner whiskers and missing an ear. *And this was my favorite. I carried it around school all year long.* That was the glass drummer boy.

There were no presents under this tree.

Marie propped her chin in her palms. It was warm next to the tree. Like the last embers of a fire just before they went out. Tears welled up, tracked down her cheeks, and pooled in her hands. The past was still too close. It was a bruise still tender. It was easier not to feel it with Aunt Rinks around. She was an odd blessing in that way. There were no reminders of what Christmas used to be like around her.

Marie didn't want to forget. She just didn't want Christmas to hurt like this.

"Hey, kid," a scratchy voice whispered.

Marie wiped her cheeks. Fritz was coming down one of the aisles. The shelves were still leaning, some broken. Spiderwebs filled in the corners. Most of the mouse turds had been swept away, but the floor was still gritty. He was dragging the blankets through it, holding pillows under one arm, the nutcracker in the other. Sandy was shuffling behind, his colors muted to avoid being seen by a passing car.

Fritz stood next to her, staring at the mystery tree in the corner where the dirty windows met.

"Can't sleep?" Sandy said.

"Just thinking."

"About Mom and Dad?" he said, sounding more like Fritz.

Marie nodded with a shudder. Fritz flopped on the floor next to her. They sat side by side, knees touching, watching the Christmas tree like a movie that was about to start.

"I'm sorry about today," she said to him.

"It wasn't your fault," Sandy said. Marie nodded, but she didn't believe it. The weight she carried wasn't fair, but it didn't go away. "Marie," Sandy said softly, "it's not your fault."

She nodded, feeling the emotional fabric she wore like a moth-eaten sweater beginning to fray. And the emotional black box quivered. Her voice betrayed her, cracking a little when she said, "I know."

Fritz threw the blanket around them. Gave her a pillow to sit on. He leaned his head on her shoulder. She tried not to shake too much.

"You want to know where the tree came from?" Sandy asked.

Marie didn't want to know. She knew what he was going to say. She stayed silent, knowing Sandy was going to tell her anyway. Fritz put the gift on the floor in front of them. The red and white wrapping was burgundy in the dark. The green bow on top still perfectly looped. Even after it flew from Bobby's hand and rolled in the grass, was scooped up by her brother, who ran home with it, it still looked brand new.

How long can I do this? she thought.

She shook her head, holding her tongue. Fritz was escaping into an imaginary world of candy canes and chocolate streams. How long would that help him? Or was it just going to make the return to reality a crash landing? The past couldn't be changed. They would have to accept what things were, someone had told her. After the grieving was over. Fritz was still wandering through a world of delusion.

That's why he's not talking, Teri, her therapist, had said.

"When we came home, you know, from the battle royale—"

"Sandy." She shook her head.

"Sorry." He started again, without the snark. "When we got home, we went straight to the bathroom. Aunt Rinky Dink and Uncle Vermin were in our bedroom, doing I don't know what. Which was fine, because they didn't bother us in the bathroom. We had to know if it was real. Like you said, maybe we just dreamed it the first time. Then that ding-dong—for the record, that's what Bobby called his brother—touched the orb, and nothing happened. So, you know, we had to try, just to see."

Sandy's bottom twisted and scuffed across the floor until he was between them and the tree. He threw his sticks out to the sides.

"Guess where the tree came from?"

Marie shook her head again. She didn't want to hear it, so she said without much effort, "Candyland."

"That's right. Just like the lights."

"But Sean didn't go there when he touched it, Fritz."

"We can't explain that one. But we have a theory. It's more Fritz's theory than mine; he's pretty smart, you know. He thinks maybe it doesn't work outside the building. Which makes sense, if you think about it."

None of it made sense.

"We proved it, Marie. We went there again. In the bathroom. When you got home, we were there. The Christmas tree was there, too. That one, right there. And now it's here. What else do you want?"

"Sandy." She turned to her brother. "Fritz, I think, maybe... I don't know."

The ever-present hope didn't fade from his eyes. He believed. She wished she had that childlike innocence. She'd grown up. And with that came responsibility. For both of them.

"Try it." Sandy poked at the gift. "Go ahead."

Her heart went into another gear. She just wanted to look at the tree and drift off to sleep. Sooner or later, she was going to have to prove it didn't work. Was Fritz ready for that? *Am I ready to crash-land his dreams?* She was carrying the weight for both of them. The emotional black box was getting heavy. Add the regret of all those kids watching her choke Bobby out. *I can't carry any more.*

Fritz flipped open the lid.

The orb was spinning on an axis like a high-speed planet. A little spot of color zipped around on a globe of grays. It was the size of the lump in her throat.

"Fritz—"

"If it doesn't work, it's all right," Sandy interrupted. "Maybe Nussknacker is wrong, and it's not for you. Because, you know, you don't believe. But you got to try."

Fritz grabbed her hand and squeezed. Just like she did to him when things got heavy. He showed her the nutcracker like a symbol of courage. The solid jaw and square mouth that had bitten Bobby's finger outside the coffee shop. He turned blurry as tears welled in her eyes once again.

She didn't want to hurt him. His hurt would pile on top of hers. And that, she was afraid, might break her. She felt like an assembly of toothpicks poorly glued together. Maybe now was the time to move forward. *Would there ever be a good time?*

She sniffed.

Fritz let go of her hand. She reached for the gift.

IT WAS A MAGNETIC FIELD.

When her fingers drew close, it grabbed her like a high-voltage wire. When she yanked her hand back, a white light filled the room like the eye of a freight train. The dark image of the Christmas tree hovered in her vision.

She couldn't see.

A flashback of when she'd last seen that light haunted her. When she'd searched the building for Fritz. When she'd looked around, blindly, for him. When she'd called his name. She took a deep breath and tasted something.

Peppermint.

It was like drawing a deep breath of winter. Cool, minty air filled her chest. The white ribbon fluttered in her hair. Her eyes stung, like a menthol breeze had blown over her face. She staggered a step, then another (*When did I stand up?*) and caught her heel on uneven ground. She put her hands behind her. Instead of hitting the floor, she thought she landed on the pillow Fritz had brought into the room. But it wasn't soft.

It was spongy.

It felt like a shaggy, foam mattress. Long silky fibers slid between her fingers. The ceiling was pink. *Pink?* The color of candy with fluffy patches of cotton. A black square was cut from the middle of it, like a door to an attic.

Nausea spun her stomach in a blender, sending sticky sweet fumes into her head. Her lips felt puffy, her tongue a balloon. She didn't want to turn her head or blink her eyes. She just wanted to lie there and breathe the cool, minty air. Because she knew the ceiling wasn't pink. There weren't cotton clouds painted on it.

With molasses pumping through her veins, she rolled her head. Grass blades tickled her cheek like fragrant fur. There were no windows or walls around her. But there was a tree. There were lots of trees.

Their trunks were striped like barber shop poles. The limbs heavy with frosting that sparkled with sugar in the diffuse light that floated down on yellow sunbeams. She reached up and touched her rubber face. She couldn't decide if she was dreaming or having a cavity filled in a very strange dentist's office.

A small wooden sign was stuck in the ground. *Christmas Wood,* it read in sloppy red paint.

White light erased the forest of candy-cane, frosted trees. They were back an instant later, like the world's biggest flash bulb had gone off. There was coarse rustling. A shadow passed over her. She looked up. The pink sky was blotted out by a ball of sand and two sand dollars.

"Told you so," Sandy said.

HIS VOICE WAS DIFFERENT. Thicker. Like a radio personality with a slight echo.

Fritz was next to him, looking down with a smile that cut his face in half. He pushed the ball cap back on his head and grabbed her hands. She came up like a bag of sticky rice. Her legs folded into a pretzel. She started to fall back, pulling Fritz with her, when something speared her in the back. Adrenaline surged. She sprang up and spun at the same time, swatting at whatever was poking into her shoulder blades. Her hand connected with something cold and dense and gritty. She had a fistful of wet sand.

A chunk of Sandy's midsection was missing.

"Oh, great. Don't move. Stay right there." He shimmied closer to her, twisting on the emerald green grass like a buffing machine.

The sand was heavy and real. Sandy leaned toward it like she was feeding an animal at the zoo. She panicked, threw it on the ground. He looked different. More colors and shades, the way his body undulated when he moved. The sound it made. He smelled like the ocean.

His head twisted back and forth when she threw the sand on the ground. He moved like a slug, hoovering up the lump of desert like an amoeba merging with another amoeba. And then the divot she'd carved from his midsection was gone.

"What—" She covered her mouth. Her voice had an echoey feel to it. It vibrated like an instrument. "What's happening?"

"Candyland is what." He threw his knobby branches out to the sides. "You believe that?"

She took a slow breath. This wasn't a dream. She didn't know what this was. She could feel it and taste it. Hear the gooey burble of the chocolate stream, the musical creaking of tree branches. Her tongue inched between her lips to lick the sweet air.

"How... how is this..."

"How does a phone work?" Sandy said. "I don't know. You don't, either. Same thing."

"I don't believe this," she whispered, looking at her hands. Her skin was creamy and smooth. The hair on her arms swayed like fine strands of wheat.

"Taste the grass. Seriously, eat it." He fell forward and began grazing on the thick carpet. Fine blades of grass pulled into a hole in his face. "Key lime, I swear."

Fritz was laughing that nasal laugh and holding his stomach. Sandy looked like a lumpy cow that hadn't eaten in weeks. Marie reached down. Her finger sank into Sandy's wet bum. Grains of sand stuck to her finger.

"Hey, hey, hey!" He jumped back.

"You're real."

"Yeah. So are you."

"But... you're not." She looked at Fritz. "He's not real."

"I am. Case you haven't noticed, this ain't like out there." He pointed like something was up there. "This. Is. Candyland."

He raised his stick in the air like a war chant. Fritz slapped it. Flakes of bark fluttered off. They took off across the small clearing, Sandy scootching after Fritz. They were hemmed in on three sides by the candy-cane trees. There was a sign, like a memorial placard, posted where the trees were absent. Beyond it, the colors dissolved into a watery, gray world of blurry shapes and fuzzy lines.

"Marie, get over here," Sandy called. "You got to try this."

Fritz was on his hands and knees where a chocolate stream cut the ground like a wound. Milk chocolate bubbled over large chocolate drops. Little things popped out of it and wiggled before diving back into the stream. Marie knelt next to her brother. When the next wave swam up, he cupped one in his hands.

"Let me see, let me see," Sandy rattled.

Fritz slowly opened his hands. A little goldfish cracker flopped in his palm with a smile etched on its face.

"You can't eat that," Sandy said flatly. "Throw it back."

Marie rubbed her face. The feeling was coming back, but the nausea was still cooking in her stomach. These two acted like this was recess. If this was real (and she had zero evidence to prove it wasn't), then this was their third trip. Despite everything her senses told her, she couldn't get over the hurdle of doubt.

This is Candyland.

"What is this place?" she said.

"Really? You're still stuck on... she's still doing this. Hey, you're awake. You're here. We came into a tiny world locked in a cute little present hidden in the wall that a nutcracker told us about. Does it sound crazy? One hundred percent. But then I don't make the rules, and neither do you. We just live in them and—what is *that*?"

Just on the other side of the chocolate stream, near the edge of the candy-cane forest, clumps of frosted grass shook. A pair of eyes parted the long, skinny blades. Pink light reflected off them like windshields driving into the sun. A pair of round fuzzy ears twitched.

"Fritz," Sandy said, "you shouldn't—okay. All right, we're doing this."

Fritz had leaped over the stream, his bare foot slipping on the edge, toes dipped in muddy, brown chocolate, and raced toward the eyes. Scaring whatever was back there into hiding. Fritz stopped and took a knee. He put out his hand. There was nothing in it, but he held it there. A few seconds later, an animal crawled out to investigate.

It was a bear. A tiny one, as big as a pillow. No teeth or claws. It wobbled on stubby legs. Black nose twitching.

"Is that a—"

"Teddy bear," Sandy finished. "Yeah, I think so."

The teddy bear crawled into Fritz's lap. He hugged it with both arms, swaying back and forth. Marie smiled despite the head-spinning confusion. Thirty seconds later, something else hobbled out of the trees.

"And that's a dragon," Sandy added.

It was a dragon. A purple one with tiny wings and a pot belly. It galloped like a newborn pony, the belly shaking like a bag of beans, stumbling in the grass before leaping into Fritz's arms. He fell on the ground. The dragon licked him with a felt tongue. Fritz laughed like a barking seal. Marie and Sandy watched from a distance. The joy radiated from Fritz like heat waves on a summer beach.

"I guess he doesn't need me anymore." Sandy looked like he was melting.

Fritz heard him (of course he did) and carried the bear and dragon like sacks of grain, one under each arm. He leaped over the stream, clearing it this time, to introduce his new friends. They were toys. Of course they were.

"What else would they be?" Marie mumbled.

"What's that?" Sandy said.

"Nothing."

Sandy warmed up to them in a hurry. He got a hug from the teddy, leaving a coat of sand on the little guy's fur. The dragon high-fived him. Then a gigglefest erupted. Fritz and Sandy rolled on the ground like they were puppies.

"I love you, too," Sandy sang.

Marie followed the chocolate stream.

At the edge of the clearing, where color bleached away, there was a gate. It was more ceremonial than functional. A couple of pretzel sticks and almonds and raisins hung from the arbor arching over them. She pushed open a pretzel curl attached to one of the pretzel sticks. A sign was posted in the middle of the stream. The sign was an oversized graham cracker.

On the other side of the stream, the world was a watery blur where blacks and whites bled into a gray landscape. The pink sky melted into a colorless slate. It was hard to tell what was out there. It was hills, maybe. A mountain in the distance. She tried to step over the stream. When she did, nothing happened. She just appeared to be standing in front of the sign again. She reached her hand over it, tried to touch the other side. *Click.* She was back to standing in front of the sign.

Words were etched into the graham cracker placard. Crumbs were scattered around the freshly chiseled letters. She ran her fingers over them.

O' the Land of Candy,
Where dreams and thoughts do lend,
A world of Christmas spirit,
For your story to begin...

She read it two more times. The third time she read it out loud. It was more than just a limerick. It *did* feel like Christmas spirit here. She was breathing it, tasting it. Feeling it warm her heart like a fire on a cold winter night with family and friends. The kind of feeling that made you smile for no reason.

The gray landscape, though, was lifeless.

She searched the sign for a switch or a button. Crispy flakes fell from the edge into the gooey stream below. *Is that part off-limits?*

"Marie. Marie, watch." Sandy shimmied toward her with the dragon in his branches. A trail of grit glittered behind him. "Ready?"

The dragon's tongue lolled from her mouth like a dog happy to see you. (The dragon felt like a girl; Marie didn't know why.)

"Do it," Sandy said. "Show her."

The dragon squirmed in his arms. Whatever the trick was, she wasn't going to do it. Then her stomach swelled like an inflating balloon. A rainbow of hard little rocks fell from her mouth.

"You see that?" Sandy said. "It's candy. She pukes candy. Fritz, get over here! She did it again."

Sandy tried to rake the candy into a pile, but they were too small for his twiggy fingers. The dragon and teddy imitated him. Fritz picked pieces of candy up and popped them in his mouth. The three-second rule didn't mean anything in Candyland.

"Cherry soda," Sandy said. "The red ones are cherry soda. The green ones—oh, gross. Blech."

Marie looked back at the gray world beyond. As amazing as this was (she still wasn't 100% convinced this was real), she already felt confined. There was something more to this than taste-testing dragon candy. *What's out there?*

"It's a riddle," Sandy said.

"What?"

"The little poem there. It's something that will open the rest of Candyland."

"How do you know that?"

"Nussknacker."

She looked around. "Where is he?"

Sandy shrugged. He told her all the guesses they'd made so far to answer the riddle, which were different versions of *open sesame.*

"Open sesame?" Marie said. "Aren't you a computer? Don't you have algorithms?"

"Technically," he whined. "But you're the one who has to answer it."

"Me? Why me?"

"Because he said so."

"Who? Nussknacker." She answered before he did. It still didn't spare her the condescending sand-dollar look. "Got it."

The nutcracker wasn't here. Fritz had had him when he came out of the bedroom to sit with her in front of the Christmas tree. That got her thinking. She grabbed Sandy's branch before he slid away. It pulled out of his body. He looked offended and embarrassed.

"Sorry." She jammed it into him like an umbrella on the beach. "Hey, how long do we stay here?"

"As long as we want."

"How do we get back?"

"Same way we got in."

He pointed up. The black square was still fixed in the pink sky. She was overwhelmed with vertigo. *Are we really inside the box?*

Sandy slid over to where Fritz was sitting on the ground. The dragon was now spitting candy, one at a time, into the air. Every time Fritz caught one in his mouth, the toys clapped. Sandy cheered like a foghorn. After three successful catches in a row, they jumped up and joined hands and sticks and danced around the pile of candy like it was a bonfire.

The ever-present worry swirling inside Marie mixed with something new. It was as unavoidable as the sweet air she was breathing. It was dancing in a circle. It was a world of Christmas spirit, just like the sign said. Before she asked Sandy just how they were going to get through the square in the sky, she ignored the gnawing in her belly.

For the first time in a very long time, she danced.

15

Rinks woke to the smell of coffee and clean sheets. She lay in the darkness behind her sleep mask, wondering why she didn't wash the sheets more often.

Sunlight greeted her when she peeled off the mask. She blinked and rubbed her eyes. It felt like a spotlight coming through the window. *Is that the sun?* She held up her hand, squinting. She'd been up late, well past midnight, but it felt like an afternoon in August. When her eyes stopped aching, she noticed there wasn't anything unusual about the daylight.

The window was clean.

She crawled out of bed and looked closer, tapped the glass to make sure it was there. *Huh.* It was just like her mother told her to wash them. Leave no streaks or smudges. Make it look like it's not even there.

Cleaning Vern must've got out of bed. He got like that, where he couldn't take the chaos. Not very often, but when he did, he was a one-man cleaning service. The place would look like a hotel. She looked around. He hadn't picked anything up, though. Just did the windows.

She flopped back on the bed, went through her morning routine.

Check social posts, count likes and read comments. The likes were going down. Her last post was coming out of the shower and showed a little shoulder. *Gross*, someone commented. Nothing like a kick in the stomach to start the day. Then she noticed the mildew on the shower behind her. That was what they were talking about. Because the filters made her look smooth and glowing.

The bathroom was locked. A game melody was playing as little blocks slid into place. She knocked on the door. "Hurry up."

Vern grunted.

Rinks listened at the kids' door, could hear someone breathing. She went to the fridge, cracked open a soda and, sipping the carbonated fizz off the top, grabbed the laptop from Vern's corner. She'd been up late watching the kids in their room. Marie had a Bluetooth speaker in her ear. Rinks didn't know she had one, then realized it was her old one, the one she threw away. She was talking to someone on it, really quiet like. Rinks couldn't understand a word, even with the volume turned up. Vern needed to fix that.

It looked like she was talking to Fritz. The air mattress was nearly flat. They needed a real mattress. It was the right thing to do. They could get one for Christmas. What with the things Godfather got them, they didn't need anything else. *Christmas isn't about what you want.*

Rinks unwrapped a protein bar and washed it down with a slug of soda. It stung her throat and watered her eyes. She went through the video history to see if anything had happened after she fell asleep. It didn't take long to hit paydirt. Marie tossed and turned, walked around the red glow of the Christmas lights on the walls.

She's goin' to do it. She's goin' to do whatever they been doin'. Rinks was sure Marie would expose whatever secret they had in the privacy of their own room. The anticipation twisted her stomach between chocolatey bites and swigs of soda, watching the girl pace, stopping on occasion to stare at the blocky wall below the owl clock. There were still smudges on those squares.

Then she walked out. Went through the door leading to the storefront.

She didn't come back. A few minutes later, Fritz rolled out of bed with his dumb little soldier and followed her. Rinks waited and waited. It was killing her. They were doing something out there again, and she couldn't see it. She jumped ahead in the video.

The red lights in their bedroom flickered.

She stopped the video, rewound it. Something else happened. A bright light flashed under the door coming from the storefront. It was too bright for a passing car. It looked more like an explosion. Nothing shook, though. Not even a sound.

Then a second flash.

"It's all yours," Vern announced.

His bare feet sounded like sandpaper blocks on the dirty floor. It needed a good mopping. A good activity for the kids.

"'Bout time."

He tried to kiss her. She pushed him off. His hands were wet. *Gross.* She raced to the bathroom and held her breath. The seat was still warm. When she came out, he was pouring the last bit of coffee. One pot down.

"They're up to somethin' again." She sat at the table, wiped the grit off her feet. "They went out front in the middle of the night and then this."

She showed him the video. He stood behind her, scratching his butt and smacking his lips, nodding with detached amusement. For a genius, he was an idiot. None of this was sinking in—the Christmas tree, the lights. Explosions.

"Nothin'?" she said. "You think that's nothin'?"

"Probably a car."

"Unless a car drove inside the buildin', that ain't a car."

He shrugged. Burped. He was useless. She waved off the fog of coffee breath and a gross smell of hard-boiled feet. He grabbed her before she could get past him, threw his arms around her. His whiskers scrubbed her cheek like a steel brush.

"You stink," she said.

He sniffed his armpit, then gave the other one a whiff. He debated whether it smelled bad, then hauled his coffee mug toward the bedroom. Rinks went to the door leading to the storefront. Yawning, she opened the door and threw her arm up. Daylight streamed into her eyes.

She shuffled in. The floor was smooth and cool. When she took her arm down, squinting into the sunlight, the can of soda slid from her hand and cracked on the floor, spilled suds over her feet.

"THIS AIN'T A BAD THING," Vern said.

"You're jokin'."

He was wearing the same smelly shirt. He hadn't made it to the bedroom before she started screaming. Cars on the street would've heard her. He slurped his coffee like this was normal. Like it was lucky. He looked around, went up to one of the shelves, ran his finger across it. It wasn't that the shelves weren't dusty or the spiderwebs were gone.

They were fixed. All of them.

Straight lines and clean surfaces. The floor was spotlessly buffed and shined, waxed with something wintergreen. They could see faint outlines of their reflections when they looked down. Not a dirt ball in sight. The room smelled like a forest. And the windows. The windows. Like the bedroom window. Sunlight poured through them. Rinks was still squinting.

"Saved us some time and effort." He held up a dustless finger. "Whoever it was."

"That's all you got to say?"

"What else is there?"

"Oh, I don't know. How about *how is this happening?*"

He looked like that hadn't occurred to him. "Well, I guess maybe—"

"Maybe what? Someone broke in with buffin' machines to scrub the floor? Did you hear buffin' machines last night, Vern? Did a gang of do-gooders sneak in with buckets and squeegees to clean the windows? Did you see the window in our bedroom? *They did that, too!*"

Marie and Fritz entered the room. Their sleepy eyes squeezed down to slits in the stark morning sunlight. Fritz with his dirty hat; Marie with her dumb ribbon in her hair. They looked at each other, looked around. Looked at each other again. *They knew. Oh, they knew.*

"What happened?" Marie answered.

"You tell me." Her foot tapped rapid-fire, waiting for an answer. "You came out here last night, didn't you? Middle of the night. Explain that. Explain the bright lights that went off."

She was thinking of lying. Rinks was sure of it. The gears were clicking in that pretty little head. But that look in ole Aunt Rinks's eyes set those excuses on fire as fast as they churned out. Then Marie said: "How'd you know we came out here?"

Good volley. Rinks didn't see that coming back. How did she know they were out here? "I heard you get up," she answered sharply. Nodded at Vern, but Vern was admiring the new-looking shelves. "You woke me and your uncle up." *Well played, Rinksy. Although that didn't explain the lights.* Marie didn't notice. "What were you doin' out here?"

"I couldn't sleep after what happened yesterday. I came out here to look at the tree. Fritz came out later. We fell asleep on the floor, went back to the room when it got cold." She looked around. "It didn't look like this."

"That's all you did?"

She nodded. The little liar. Something was left out. Maybe they were looking at the tree, but she wasn't giving up the whole story.

"Hey! Look at this." Vern put his coffee on the shelf and shook two things above his head.

"Not now," Rinks said. "What else did you do?"

Marie and Fritz watched Vern approach. He had two stuffed animals. One was a bear, the other a dragon with plastic teeth. Mint condition, the both of them. Clean fur, clear eyes.

"They were on the shelf. Right over there," he said. "How about that?"

"That's what surprises you most?" Rinks said. "Toys? Not someone or somethin' buffin' the floors and wipin' down the windows and fixin' the shelves in the middle of the night without wakin' us? You're okay with that part, but toys? Are you kiddin' me, Vern?"

He held them like puppets. "Why you mad?"

"I'm not mad!" She took a deep breath, stared at her reflection in the floor. Said more calmly: "I'm not mad. I'm just worried. You should be, too. This ain't normal, Vern. None of this—the tree, the lights, all this—it ain't right. Am I the only one who gets it?"

"No, I get it, Rinks. It's weird all right. But it's all fixed; it's all clean. It's better, and it's free. I don't care how, just that it is." He held the toys at his sides. Something bounced around his feet. "Look at that," he said.

Colorful little rocks of candy ricocheted off the floor. They scattered in different directions. He shook the dragon. The belly was full of it. Fritz picked one up.

"Don't eat that," Rinks said. He did anyway. She pointed at Marie. "You did this."

"Me?"

"You had somethin' to do with it, and you ain't tellin'." Rinks was quivering. The anger and frustration were frothing over the dam of self-control. She wanted to go in that bedroom right that second and start tearing things apart.

"Rinks," Vern said, "how in the world would they fix everythin' and clean it up? It'd take all night."

"That's what I'm sayin'! What did you find, huh?" The sound her back teeth made was like a grinding stone wearing down rocks. "Tell me. You're good at keepin' secrets, ain't ya. I know you ain't tellin' us something, Murry."

Just like her mother. Rinks's sister would write all her private thoughts in a journal and hide it. Wouldn't share her stories about boys. Didn't take her to parties. Didn't help her make friends. It was all about her.

Fritz handed his phone to Marie. She read it, showed it to Rinks. Vern read it over her shoulder.

"You think Godfather's doin' it?" Rinks said.

"He said a gift was coming," Marie said.

"That's not what he meant." Rinks crossed her arms. *You have the gift, you little liar.*

"I think she's right." Vern pointed with the teddy bear. "Think about it, Rinks. He's got people all over the world workin' for him. And the technology is beyond what anyone could imagine."

Marie nodded vigorously.

"If anyone could do somethin' like this, it's him," Vern continued. "Puttin' up lights, a tree. Fixin' all this up. Like little elves comin' in the middle of the night, makin' things right."

"Elves?"

"You know what I mean."

"You said elves."

"I mean, he's got all sorts of things that can do anythin'. You saw that butler at the cabin. It was dang human! Nobody ever seen anythin' like that. This right here." He swung his arms. "This ain't nothin' compared to that. None of us knows the half of what he can do. And think about this." He shook the toys. Their heads bobbled. "How many times did he say somethin' about the toy store, huh? He wants it back, Rinks. He's just helpin' out."

"Did we ask for help?"

"So you don't want any of this? You want to do all this ourselves? Clean and fix and spend money." He jutted out his whiskered chin, narrowed his eyes. "'Cause I don't."

The line between Rinks's lips pulled straight and tight. She racked her arms over her chest, squeezed her biceps. They had her stuck. There was no way of getting the truth out of them, not now. But she didn't need them. She could find it on her own.

"Then call him," she said quietly. "Thank him."

"He won't admit to it," Vern said.

"Call. Him."

Vern nodded. He handed the toys to the kids, gave the bear to

Marie, the dragon to Fritz. Then fetched his coffee cup. He was pleased with himself. Nothing made that man happier than free stuff.

"What's that?" Rinks said.

She pointed at Fritz's foot. It was dark and muddy. He tried to hide it behind his other foot. It flaked off in dried chunks. Marie swept them up with her hands.

"He stepped in a puddle yesterday," Marie said. "I thought he washed up."

Rinks's eyebrow arched. "Barefoot?"

"He was looking for something out back."

"Get cleaned up," she said to the kids. "I want you out of the house today. Don't come back till supper. Get some exercise, but stay away from the park. I don't want to hear about another fight today, you hear? Vern, give them some money to eat. Not too much, just enough to keep them from lookin' hungry."

They followed their uncle. Frankly, she didn't care where they went. That was how Rinks grew up. Out of the house in the morning, home by dark. No one asked where she was or why. And she survived.

She was going to close the door on all these lies. Vern was going to set up the rest of the cameras. Rinks was going to dig. She was going to start in the kids' bedroom.

No one could keep a secret from her.

16

"I don't know what to say," Marie said.

Fritz had chocolate frosting smeared on his lips. He shoved another bite of Ms. Trutchen's famous double chocolate fudge brownie in his mouth before swallowing the first bite. And chased that with foamy hot chocolate.

The coffee shop was crowded and loud. The Christmas music was barely audible over conversation. They had a little table in the corner where no one noticed them. Not even Ms. Clara.

"You can start with thank you," Sandy's voice said on the Bluetooth.

"The lights and tree... and then the storefront. I don't understand it. It's like... it felt like a dream. Don't you think?"

Ever since waking up, she couldn't quite wrap her head around what had happened. The memory was warped and strange, like dreams are. She didn't believe it until Aunt Rinks woke them up with screaming. Before they walked out front, she knew. She could feel it in her bones. *It happened. It really happened.*

"Ow!"

Fritz pinched her arm and smiled with chocolate-painted teeth.

"You're not dreaming," Sandy said.

"Yeah, I know. I'm just saying where did the lights and tree come from? How did the storefront get, you know, *fixed*. And the toys!" She lowered her voice and leaned over the table. "The toys that where there. How did they get *here*?"

"No idea."

"That's what I mean. How does it work? It's just a little ball inside the gift."

"I'm just a little ball in Fritz's pocket. How do I work?"

"You're a projection and a voice. I get that. The other thing... *Candyland*," she whispered, "is another world. Big difference."

"Is it?"

"We *went* there."

Fritz looked at the empty chair at their table. For a second, Marie was worried Sandy was going to appear in front of a crowd of caffeinated locals with cameras on their phones. Fritz was nodding, and Marie suspected he might be hearing their grainy snowman *and* seeing him. That wasn't something she wanted to talk about. There were already too many wildfires to deal with.

"Think of it like this," Sandy started. "If you showed a caveman—or cavewoman—a phone, what are they going to think, mmm?" Fritz held up his phone, submitting the evidence.

"I know what a phone looks like," she said.

"Or a plane. Or a computer or a bridge or building or ballpoint pen or—"

"I get it."

"Magic, right? They would throw someone into a volcano to thank the gods. And there's nobody who could convince them otherwise. Do you know how a computer works? You do not. Neither do I. And neither does Fritz. None of us knows how Candyland works. It just does."

"Sandy..." She shook her head, had to remind herself whom she was talking to. "Fritz, you *disappeared*. You touched the orb and *actually went inside*. How is that possible?"

Her brother popped the last bite of double chocolate brownie in his mouth and shrugged. He was right. That was the way to go. It happened. Why did she have to know how it worked? *Because I need to know if this is real.*

"Why are things appearing?" she said. "The tree and lights and… what else? I mean, what's stopping more from happening?"

There was a long pause. Then, "Oh, you're asking. We don't know." Sandy explained how the red lights had been in the Christmas Wood the first time they went inside. The Christmas tree had been next to the sign the second time. And now the toys.

"They're coming out," she muttered.

"Seems that way. Fritz wants to know if you're going to eat that."

He took the chicken salad sandwich off the little plate in front of her. Marie hadn't touched it.

"You're not worried about that?" she said.

"Why? Ms. Clara said her chicken salad is the best—"

"No. Things coming out of the box," she hissed.

Fritz looked up before taking a second bite. He looked slightly confused, then continued eating. "Um, he's seven, Marie. He's not worried about big-picture things."

Sandy was right. Why was she asking her little brother that? These were things *she* had to watch. If they kept going in, would things keep coming out? So far it was just little things. Well, not little. But what if that was the point? Maybe it was things to restore the toy store, like Uncle Vernon said.

"What am I thinking?" she said to herself. "Those things can't be coming *out.*"

"You really think Godfather had elves clean the room and deliver a Christmas tree? That was Fritz's idea, by the way. The Godfather alibi. It was a good one. They bought it, too. At least your uncle did. But I think you're missing the obvious part, kid."

"What's that?"

"I was a *reeeeal* boy," Sandy said in a squeaky tone.

"You're not helping."

"Come on. You tore a hole in me, remember? I remember. I could feel Candyland, just like you did. The way it smelled and tasted. It made us happy. You danced! Remember that? And you know why? That's Christmas spirit in there. Am I right?"

She couldn't argue the way it felt. It was like distilled Christmas magic. The hope and excitement and cheer were in the air. *Only we didn't spritz it from a bottle. We went there!*

"You see what's happening, don't you?" Sandy said. "The toy store is coming back. That's what Godfather wants. Fritz made that excuse up, but he wasn't wrong. I mean, elves didn't clean the place up. Or maybe they did."

"I thought you said this was about a journey to save Princess Pearly Pat."

"Nussknacker said it. And don't pretend you don't know her name. Princess Pirlipat."

"Why, though?"

"Why what?"

"What's the journey for?"

"It's a journey. We find out when we get there. What's the problem?"

She pushed away from the table, resisting the urge to get up and walk around. The conflict was winding a spring inside her. Her head was going to pop off if she didn't make some sense out of it.

"What's the problem? We disappear; things coming out of a gift. Those things are *impossible*!"

"I feel like we've covered this. Caveman. Airplane."

"Shrinking and disappearing, that's my problem. It's against physics. If Candyland is real—"

"It is. We did it. Admit it."

"*If* it is real," she repeated, "then it's technology that's light-years ahead of its time."

"Yeah, and cavepeople were around ten thousand years ago. They'd say the same thing about that thing in your ear you're talking to me with. Get it? It's like saying reindeer can't fly and Santa doesn't deliver presents."

She didn't want to answer that last part, not in front of Fritz. A little part of him still believed a fat man visited every house in one night.

"Kid, it wasn't a dream. We were there, all of us. You, Fritz and me. We can't all have the same dream. The question isn't *if* it's happening. The question is *what's next?*"

She couldn't explain how things happened, not the tree or the lights or how things got repaired. But the toys. *I saw those in the backyard. They were dirty. Someone could have cleaned them.* There was an easy way to check that. See if they were still back there. She didn't know how that would make things better.

"What do you mean what's next?" she said.

"Solve the sign. We can't go on the journey till we know what it means."

"That, right. And why would it be a riddle we have to solve? Why can't we just go?"

"You're asking us? Maybe it's important to the journey. I just know we'll be stuck dipping our fingers in the chocolate stream till we do. Princess Pirlipat is out there."

She took long slow breaths. There was no point in figuring out how or why it worked. Sandy was right. It happened. *It's happening.* Just accept it, go downstream with it. If she was honest, things were better than they had been before they found that gift in the wall. At least she knew what to expect from her aunt. But maybe they'd find a bed in Candyland.

"Solve the riddle," she said, nodding. "Okay."

Fritz nibbled the rest of the sandwich, leaving the crusts on the plate. He lifted his hand for a high five. Marie tapped it lightly. If for anything else, she'd do it for him. Because look how happy he was.

"YOU DON'T HAVE the gift with you, right?" Marie asked.

"Nope," Sandy said in her ear. "It doesn't work outside the building."

That wasn't a fact, even though it hadn't worked when Sean had grabbed it in the park. "Where is it?" she said.

"Back where we found it."

"In the hiding place?"

"Where else?"

If he put it in a drawer or, worst case, left it on the bench, then things would get more complicated. If that was possible. "Aunt Rinks can't know about this."

"We've been over that."

"I mean it. If she knew what was happening, it'd be all over her social."

"Roger that."

She looked at Fritz. He nodded enthusiastically, added a thumbs-up. Everything Aunt Rinks touched got messy. This would be like giving her the keys to a nuclear power plant. Things wouldn't just go sideways. They'd go in all directions.

"She's watching us." She stacked the empty plates and finished the rest of her tea. "She knew we went to the storefront last night."

"About that. Don't you think that's weird?"

"No. She's a spy."

"Not that," Sandy said. "She saw the lights flash when we went to Candyland."

"Of course she did. The light is blinding. Probably lit up the building and the street." Marie hadn't thought about that. They needed to be careful where they did it.

"But she sleeps with a blindfold."

Marie started to reply and stopped. Something didn't line up. How had she heard them get up? They hadn't been making noise. And if she'd seen the lights, why wouldn't she come out? There was more to this. Her bloodhound thoughts might have sniffed out the answer, but Ms. Clara interrupted her.

"Children! You don't say hi when you come?" Her smile dimpled her rosy cheeks.

"I'm sorry, Ms. Clara. It's so crowded, and you were busy."

"Nonsense. There is always time to say hello and merry, merry."

She grabbed the stack of plates from the table. "You leave crusts, young man. Crusts are best part. Did you get enough to eat, skinny one?"

She squeezed Fritz's shoulder. He shook his head with a chocolate smile.

"We had plenty, Ms. Clara," Marie said. "We were just going to walk around."

"It is beautiful day. Go get vitamin D."

She whispered to Fritz. He would grab a big, salted pretzel on their way out. Ms. Trutchen would hand it to him in a paper bag with a jolly laugh for free.

She hugged them when they stood up. "Come back tomorrow," she said. "We close soon."

"You're closing?" Marie said.

"Christmas very busy for us. We have much travel to do. I want to see your smiles before we go."

Christmas was still a few weeks away. Maybe they had family to visit in another country. They weren't from around there, everybody knew that. But nobody really knew where they were from.

17

The owl clock didn't see Rinks pull the last drawer out of the workbench.

Rinks felt like prey under its big, angry eyes. The wings spread like it was about to take flight and snatch her by the hair like some dirty little rodent. Rinks finally turned the clock so it was staring at the wall.

The drawers were scattered around the room. There were no hidden switches or secret buttons that tripped a trapdoor. No levers that opened a door in the wall. No notes or boxes or treasure maps. She got on one knee. Nothing taped underneath the workbench, either.

The blood rushed to her head. Her blood sugar was low. She'd skipped lunch. Not even a cracker. She checked her phone. The kids just left the café, were heading toward the park. They shouldn't be back for another three hours. *Better not be.* This mess was going to take an hour to put back together.

It had been a week since the windows got clean and the storefront fixed up.

Every night, the video glitched. She'd watch the kids get up. Sometimes that sandman Vern was all excited about would be there.

He'd sworn her not to say anything. It would just make them more secretive. It wasn't in Rinks's nature to be quiet. She put her curiosity in a compartment in the corner of her brain where it pouted. Then she'd watch the video from the night before. A bright light would go off. Then the kids were gone. Something about that light was turning the cameras off. Like the kids knew it. Like they had something to block the cameras.

Vern still hadn't fixed it.

Two nights ago, Fritz had come back to the room muddy. He took a shower in the middle of the night. The bathroom was a mess the next morning. There was chocolate all over the sink. *They're stealin' my protein bars again,* she thought. *And goin' outside.* She spent the rest of that day searching the backyard, looking for buried treasure. None of the protein bars were missing, though.

She leaned on the workbench to catch her breath. The toy soldier was two feet in front of her, eye level. He didn't judge her, not like the owl. His look was all business. The bushy eyebrows and stiff legs. Pinewood breath.

Rinks looked over her shoulder. A tiny lens, no bigger than a pinhead, was embedded in the corner, right where Vern had put it. If it were three feet higher, she would've known exactly what they'd been doing. She bent over, stared the nutcracker in the eyes.

"You standin' guard, mmm? That what you're doin'? What is it they were doin' here, little man? You tell me."

She picked him up. Fritz didn't care if she touched him anymore, not like when he found him that first day.

"He doesn't care about you anymore, you know that? Just leaves you behind like yesterday's Big Wheel. You know what that is, a Big Wheel? Probably not." She pulled the lever on his back, looked around just in case it triggered a surprise. "What's this?"

A pattern of numbers was written on the back of his jacket. Looked like something a gang of nerds protecting the world from prime numbers would do. She pulled the lever. The mouth opened and closed. She put it to her ear, hoping he'd whisper the secret to her. *I'm losing my mind,* she thought. But she kept pulling, felt the square jaw rub against her ear, hoping something would happen. And then it did.

A squeaky voice said: "Your husband's hot."

Embarrassment flushed her cheeks. She shoved her husband against the wall.

"Hey, hey. She's mine, you little splinter." Silly Vern pointed at the soldier. "I'll turn you into kindlin'."

"Shut up," Rinks said.

He thumbed his nose and threw a right hook. His broomstick arms looked like a third-grade shadow boxer. If she had to wager, the soldier would get two to one odds.

"Is the camera fixed?" she said.

"It ain't broke, Rinks."

She shook her head. "They ain't disappearin', Vern."

"I replaced it. And I did this."

He opened the laptop. There were three new video feeds—the front of the building, the kitchen, and their bedroom. Now they had the whole house. Unless the elf army redecorated the bathroom, they were going to solve the mystery.

"All right," she said. "Guess we'll find out now, won't we?"

"We will. Only I was thinkin', what if they don't come back?"

"Who you talkin' 'bout?"

"The ones who brought the... you know." He tilted his head.

The suspicious git didn't want to say it out loud. The Christmas tree and the red lights in the kids' room and the toys. Nothing new had happened in a week. He was still hoping more free stuff was on the way.

"You know who did it."

"It wasn't the kids, Rinks. Whoever's doing it, what if the cameras scare them off? I mean, the walls need paintin', the bathroom needs doin', there's, like, a week's worth of landscapin'. And that." The air mattress was a vinyl pancake. "Kids shouldn't be sleepin' on the floor, Rinks."

"I know."

Despite the obvious betrayal, she hadn't forgotten about the bed the kids were sleeping on. Or lack thereof. It wasn't right. The crazy thing was they didn't complain about it. Not once. She had to respect that.

"You goin' to explain to the kids someone robbed them?" he said.

Empty drawers were stacked against the walls. The blankets were thrown around, the string lights pulled down, the workbench moved, clothes overturned. There was no way she'd get it all put back together.

"They won't be home for three hours," she said.

"Good enough. And what are you lookin' for?"

She looked at him with contempt. "You seriously don't know?"

"I know." He chuckled. "Of course I know."

"Get out."

"Rinks." He grabbed her arm and wouldn't let her go. "Seriously, what are you lookin' for?"

All she could do was shake her head. Did he really not care what was happening? It was eating her up like an infection. She had a stomachache and not from eating boxes of chocolate protein bars. And now she was dizzy. Either he was better at compartmentalizing (something she'd totally lost control of) or was a moronic genius.

She couldn't tell him the real reason. *I'm obsessed with being left out.*

"They stand here, Vern, and do somethin'. Then there's the light, and then there's all the new stuff. And because you ain't moved that camera, I can't see what they're doin'. So I'm tearin' this place apart screw by nail."

"Okay." He nodded along in listening mode. Empathy Vern narrowed his eyes to hear her feelings, really hear them. She felt better until he said: "What did Knackadoodle tell you?"

"Leave."

"Did you ask nice?"

"Out. Go." She shoved him. He tickled her. The wall of bitter rage bent to his cackling. She regrouped and pushed him again. "If you don't leave, I'm shovin' this up your nose. Boots first."

She held the soldier like a weapon. He threw his hands up.

"So you asked him what they were doin'?" he said.

"I did. Nicely."

"What'd he say?"

"That you should brush your teeth more."

He breath-checked in the cup of his hand. "He say that, really?"

"Serious, Vern, if you ain't goin' to help, then move that camera so I can see what they're doin' here."

She put one of the drawers back. It got stuck and didn't slide in till she knocked it with her knee. The wood splintered. *Great.* Her back hurt, her knee hurt, her stomach hurt, and she was no closer to finding anything out. She kicked the flap of vinyl bedding. Last thing she wanted to do was reward them with a new bed.

"He say anythin' about that?" Vern pointed at the square blocks on the wall below the owl clock. "Is that right?" Vern said to the nutcracker. "Cheesy puffs, you say?"

She didn't know how much more of Silly Vern she could take before her hair started falling out.

"Hear that, Rinks? He likes cheesy puffs."

She went to the bathroom. She stayed on the toilet long after she'd done her business, flipping through her accounts, trying to think of something to post. Maybe a photo of the bedroom she'd destroyed. *Kids,* she'd write. *Can't live with them.*

That's not bad.

She tried to think of something wittier. Vern would get bored. Pretty soon, he'd hunker down in the corner with his second wife, Mrs. Laptop, and she could get back to the investigation. Ten minutes later, though, she could still hear him tinkering around in the bedroom. She lost the boredom battle and surrendered to find him hunched over the workbench.

"What're you doin'?" she said.

He was holding the soldier in one hand and mumbling. Only this time, he wasn't poking fun at her. He was talking to it. And during his imaginary conversation, he was pushing at the little blocks of wood on the walls. One of them was lying on the workbench.

"Don't do that," she said. "I already split that drawer and—"

"Shhh."

The blocks were sliding around like checkers. Reminded her of a game on her phone, one where you fit together different shapes and sizes; and when you did, there were fireworks and electronic music and prizes. *Prizes!* That was exactly what she'd win on her phone, shiny presents and fountains of coins.

Only the game Vern was playing was with ugly little pieces of wood that were grooved and had orange smudges. *Cheesy puffs.* She'd seen that last week, when Vern and Fritz had gone through a whole bag of them. *And he brought home a bag yesterday.*

"This goes there." *Snick* went one of the pieces. "That one there— no. Not there." He pushed it up instead of down. "You know why it's hard to be a thief in winter, Rinks?"

"What?"

"A thief. You know, steal." He slid a third block into place, this one to the right. "Petey and I used to dig through garbage cans when we were kids. Just after Christmas was the best time to do it. People'd throw out the old to make room for the new, and we'd be there to take. Their old was our new. Our old man, he was terrible at Christmas. Used to give us used tools and things he didn't want. Petey and I did our own shoppin'."

Snick.

"We'd walk down alleys and dig through trash cans. If we saw somethin' in a backyard, we'd take that, too. Basketballs, pogo sticks, kites, remote control cars. One time an old video game, still worked. We'd fill up a wheelbarrow full of this garbage. But then we started peekin' in garages. One year, we seen these bikes. Christmas bikes. The stickers were still on the handlebars."

He kissed his fingers like a chef.

"The car wasn't in the driveway. The door was locked, but there's this doggy door with a flap. It's for a small dog. Petey can't fit through because he's fat. I'm the runt, you know. The mouse. It don't take three seconds for me to squeeze inside. Next thing you know, Petey and I are peelin' down the alley on new bikes. No one sees us, either. We ride straight home, throwin' snow off the back tires, pulling wheelies. Best Christmas ever."

He looked up, remembering. Then *snick*.

"We put the bikes in our garage, 'cause the old man ain't goin' to notice. If he does, we'd tell him we bought them with snow-shovelin' money. He wouldn't care anyhow. So now we got new bikes. We're in our bedroom talkin' about where we're goin' to ride the next day when someone comes to the door. It's dark out. The old man is conked on the recliner, but he wakes up before we get downstairs."

His story stalled. He hit a dead end on the wall, backtracked a few moves before working it out. Rinks didn't know which was a bigger waste of time: the wall or the story.

"So it's cops. They're with a dad we've never seen. Said they're lookin' for bikes. Petey and I play dumb, but that don't hold up because the cop takes the old man out back. They go straight to the garage and find the bikes shoved behind a sheet of plywood. No one saw us take them. Know how they caught us?"

He thumbed another block smudged with orange fingerprints. The last block slid up. This one was different. There wasn't a pink wall behind it.

"If you follow the tracks, you find the mouse."

SHE KISSED him on the mouth. Not a bird peck, either. It was long and wet. Her fingers in his hair, his whiskers scratching her chin.

"You did it," she said, breathy. "You found it."

"I did."

She bent over to look inside the square hole in the wall. There was something in there. It wasn't moving, but she couldn't be sure it wasn't alive.

"What is it?" she said.

"I don't know."

"Reach in there."

He used the nutcracker like a stick, poking it into the hole boots first.

"What're you doin'?" she said.

"Checkin' for traps."

"There ain't no traps. Just reach your hand in there."

"Someone went to all this trouble to hide whatever's in there. You don't think there might be somethin' else?"

She crossed her arms, watched him poke the hole like it was a fire that had just about gone out. Next, he leaned in and blew into the hole (like that was going to do something). Rinks didn't say anything. He could sing a song into that opening, just as long as he reached inside it before the kids got home.

A minute later, he did exactly that. His hairy knuckles clenched around something square. He slid it onto the bench. They stepped back. Rinks clenched her hands beneath her chin.

"This is it," she whispered. "What they were hidin'."

It was a present. A little red and white gift with a green bow. Expertly wrapped without a cobweb on it. Rinks remembered what Godfather had said about finding the present. She thought it was hogwash, but there it was. It was beautiful and came with a side dish of redemption that tasted delicious. *You can't hide it from me no more.*

She reached for it without thinking of booby traps. Only visions of jewelry or diamonds inside it. The lid lifted on hinges. Shoulder to shoulder, they leaned over it and peered inside.

"What is that?" she said.

It was ugly, whatever it was. It looked like something that would fall out of a car wreck. This had to be a joke. *The kids! They put that in there 'cause they knew I'd find it!* The elated feeling she'd felt a minute ago hardened into a lump of coal. She had the urge to find a hammer and start knocking holes in the wall.

"Oh my." Vern's hands fluttered in front of his mouth like he was looking at a winning lottery ticket. His eyes weren't blinking, shifting from her to the box to her. His lips moved, but only weird squeaks came out. It sounded like he was choking.

"What?" she said. He pointed at the dumb thing. "What?" she repeated.

He scrambled toward the door, turned around, held up his hands. "Don't touch it! And don't take a picture!"

"What are you—"

He ran back and scooped it off the table. "How much time before the kids get back?"

Hours, she said. Which was true. He took it to the kitchen, came back for his laptop, and giggled. Rinks followed him. It wasn't a diamond in that box.

Vern said it was better than that.

HE SAID ALMOST NOTHING. Just typing and sweating. Occasionally, laughing like a middle schooler watching cartoons.

"I can't believe this," he would sometimes say. Rinks would say, "What?" And he would keep going. And this went on for an hour. She'd eaten three protein bars and drank two sodas. The thrill was almost gone. She went back to the bedroom. Her husband, the idiot genius, had followed the cheesy puff tracks Fritz had left behind on the blocks of wood. It had taken nine moves to find the hole. *How did they find it?* she wondered. *Someone must have told them.*

The nutcracker lay on the bench, staring at the ceiling. She narrowed her eyes, thinking of how Fritz was always holding that thing.

"Rinks!"

Vern was at the kitchen table. The gift was next to the laptop, lid still open. Round magnet still floating. He scooted back his chair and pointed at it, making those weird sounds again.

"Just talk, Vern."

"This is it."

"It's what?"

He turned the laptop. She couldn't make sense of it. It looked like a chat board. She gave up reading in five seconds.

"Can you just settle down and tell me what's got your shorts in a bunch?"

He did. She understood next to nothing, but she let him go. It was like letting off pressure for him, spouting all these smart words that made her feel dumb. Density and electromagnetic fields and compressed data and symmetrical circuitry. He'd heard whispers of the thing back when he worked at Avocado, Inc. It was a black-box project, whatever that meant. No one was supposed to know what it was, but there were rumors.

He finished blowing off steam, slumping in the chair and huffing like he'd completed a marathon. A stupid smile leaked on his face.

"So what is it?" Rinks said for the thousandth time.

"A story orb."

"A story orb?"

"A self-contained, virtual-reality story orb."

She nodded and hummed. Then said: "I don't know what any of that means."

"When do the kids get back?"

She checked her phone. They were on Main Cross, walking in the opposite direction. They weren't due back for a little longer. She told him so.

Vern grabbed her hand. His palm was slick. He told her to sit down.

"You ready?" he said.

"You're scarin' me, Vern."

He nodded and smiled that dopey smile. A bag of worms began to dance in her stomach when he grabbed her wrist. She saw him stick his finger into the box.

Then tasted peppermint.

18

The sun had dropped behind the downtown buildings, bruising the sky in colorful streaks.

Marie dragged down the sidewalk, feeling the dregs of a late afternoon nap on a concrete bench at the park. The late nights were catching up to her. She hadn't planned to fall asleep this afternoon, just wanted to do some cloud gazing. Then Fritz was shaking her awake. For the past week, she and Fritz spent the day at the coffee spot or wandering around. At night, they locked the door and opened Candyland. Thankfully, nothing followed them back. Aunt Rinks had even stopped asking questions. Just told them to make themselves scarce in the morning.

Fine with Marie.

She hugged herself against the approaching evening air, thinking of crawling under the blankets when she got back to the building. Not even bothering to blow up the mattress. Fritz was half a block ahead of her, standing in front of the toy store. The Christmas tree was glowing from inside the window. Marie lumbered by him. When he didn't follow, she went back.

He wasn't looking at the tree. There was something in the back corner of the storefront. The aisle shelves were blocking their view, but lights had been added. Uncle Vernon was standing on a ladder. It looked like there were new shelves on the wall. *Did they paint the store?*

Marie and Fritz rounded the corner and went through the rusty gate. Two plates were on the kitchen table. Fritz began spooning the heap of noodles drowning in orange tomato sauce into his mouth, hardly chewing before throwing in the next scoop.

Something was creaking. Like old wood bending in a storm.

Marie crept into the storefront. She didn't know why she was sneaking. Maybe she wanted to change her mind before she saw something she didn't want to see.

"A little to the left," Aunt Rinks said. *Creak.* "Right there."

They were on the little stage in the corner, on the step-up platform. The wood planks, once littered with mouse turds and dust bunnies, were now lacquered to a shine that reflected dozens of string lights hanging from the ceiling. It looked like little stars. Aunt Rinks sat in an antique rocker with a purple blanket on her lap. Uncle Vernon was on a stepladder. He was dusting the clock embedded in the owl's belly.

"What's going on?" Marie said.

"Oh!" Aunt Rinks clutched her chest.

Uncle Vernon teetered on the ladder and jumped off before he went down on his head. They began laughing at their fright. Uncle Vernon took a knee, grabbing his stomach. He laughed so hard his nose was dripping.

"Oh, oh." Aunt Rinks turned the rocking chair to face Marie. "You scared us half to death, young lady. We need to put a bell round your neck."

"Where did all this come from?"

"Surprise!" She threw her arms up. The purple blanket fell at her feet. "You like it?"

It wasn't their style. A mural of reindeer and clouds was on the wall. Santa in a sleigh with a village below with steepled roofs and puffing chimneys and blankets of snow. The shelves were loaded with trinkets and figurines. Snow globes swirling with white bits.

Snowmen and snowwomen and snowkids made with foam. Reindeer in different poses, some sleepy, some frolicking. One big and angry.

And there was more. Lots more. Way more than would fit in a storage trunk or closet.

"We made it just like it was before," Aunt Rinks said. "*Storyteller Corner.*"

Uncle Vernon gestured to the letters painted above the shelves, a stylish script.

"You did this?" Marie said.

"Yep. We did. We got the *Christmas spirit* today." She looked at Uncle Vernon and chuckled. "I don't think she believes us, Verny baby."

"It's just... it's a lot to take in," Marie said.

"Oh, it wasn't hard," she sang. "We made a few calls, had some help. Everyone wants a toy store."

"I thought you *didn't* want a toy store."

"We're warmin' to the idea, sugar."

She winked at Uncle Vernon. A wink and a smile. Marie didn't like that. It felt like someone sticking out their tongue. Marie stepped onto the stage to look around at the garland and paper snowflakes. It looked like a hundred feet of string lights hanging from little hooks in the ceiling.

Aunt Rinks took a mug from a small wooden table painted red as a rose. She slurped whatever it was (probably soda) and smacked her lips. A long curly whisker was growing from her chin. Aunt Rinks had been too distracted by her scar to see it.

There was a vase of candy canes on the little table. And an old book. The leather cover was scuffed and worn. The corners bent. She saw the title on the spine. A shiver trickled down her back.

"Where'd you get that?"

"This old thing?" Aunt Rinks opened it on her lap. The binding crackled. "Someone gave it to us. It looks like the real thing, don't it. I looked for Aunt Corker's name and didn't find it. But we can pretend it's hers."

She turned a few pages.

"Want to hear a story?" Aunt Rinks put on a pair of tiny, wire glasses, then looked over them. "*Once upon a time...* there were two children, a boy and a girl, who were on the naughty list—"

"There's food in the kitchen," Uncle Vernon interrupted. He was scratching a rash on his neck. "We already ate, so you go ahead. It should still be warm."

"Yes, where *are* my manners? Go on, hon. Get somethin' to eat. Me and Vern got a few things left to do out here."

"I think I'm going to bed."

"Bed? It's barely suppertime."

"I'm really tired."

"Why you so tired, darlin'?"

Marie didn't answer that. It didn't sound like a question. She turned to leave.

"We straightened up your room for you," Aunt Rinks called. "Made it all good again."

Marie stopped like she'd hit a wall. Something cold and heavy thudded in her stomach and recoiled into her throat. "You cleaned our room?"

"Like I said, we got the *Christmas spirit* today."

Then she laughed again. It was more of a cackle. Uncle Vernon was scratching his neck with both hands.

THE BED WAS full of air. The nylon membrane stretched like a balloon with a few new patches on it. Their clothes, once piled in the corner, were folded on the workbench. The nutcracker was at his post. Marie's book was next to him. It was open. The pages still blank.

She stood as still as a deer listening for a twig to snap. Nothing moved. Nothing out of place.

Her aunt and uncle were talking loudly. Their voices coming through the door. Fritz had wandered out to the storefront to see the new decorations. They regaled him with excessive laughter and broad smiles that split their faces.

Marie looked at the owl clock. It was facing the wall. She turned it around. They must have taken the one from their room to put on the shelf. The checkered wall below the owl clock was still in place. She moved the nutcracker to examine it. The block with the X—the first one they took out to move the pieces—was right where it should be. She put her thumb on it. It snapped into place.

We probably did that, she thought. *Didn't put it all the way back.*

She wanted to believe that. What other choice was there? Aunt Rinks wasn't smart enough to figure it out. Uncle Vernon, though.

Aunt Rinks began reading to Fritz the fake story about a boy and girl on the naughty list. "Once upon a time..."

The name of the book Marie had seen, the one Aunt Rinks had on her lap, was embossed on the spine in shiny letters. *Tales from Candyland.*

Marie moved quickly, turning the nutcracker around to follow the sequence. The orange smudges had been scrubbed off the blocks. If they hadn't been, she would've been more than suspicious. By the time she opened the mouse hole, Aunt Rinks was still telling her fake story, and Marie reached into the dark. Her heart dropped like she'd missed the last step on a staircase. Then her hand grasped the gift.

She didn't find it.

That brought some relief. She crawled onto the air mattress with it cradled to her chest.

Someone shook her awake.

Sand dollars as big as moons were in her face. She rolled away from them and groaned. Sleep pulled her eyelids down like shutters.

"It's gone," Sandy said. "Hey, wake up. The present's gone."

Marie sat up, shedding the final grains of sleep from her eyes. It took a few moments for her head to stop swimming. "What time is it?"

"Time? You're worried about the time?" Sandy said. "The gift is gone!"

"Shhh."

Marie held up a finger. She was suddenly one-cup-of-coffee alert. She turned her head, listening. Fritz and Sandy looked at each other, waiting. When she heard a duet of snoring from the other room, she reached under the corner of the mattress and pulled out the bright, red and white gift.

Sandy's celebration sounded like a bag of rice being tossed around. He turned in a circle and shook his round bottom.

"Wait," Sandy said. "Why was it there?"

Marie shook her head. It took several moments for her thoughts to warm up. "They were acting weird," she whispered. "I just had this feeling they might have found it."

"You think they solved the puzzle?" He aimed a stick at the wall. "No offense, they're not that smart."

"We need to be careful, that's all. Maybe put it in a different hiding place."

"Great. Let's go."

Marie pulled the gift away before Fritz snatched it. She looked a little desperate. "Now?"

"Yeah, now, while the lumber yard is sawing. When else we going?"

He looked at Marie like she was the dumb one in the room. How he made those sand dollars roll was remarkable.

"We've been there every night. I'm tired."

The truth was, she wasn't any closer to solving the riddle. The thrill had worn off, hard as that was to believe. They were visiting another world—going there—and Marie would rather sleep.

"The journey doesn't care if you're tired. It's the journey. Sometimes it's hard. Now grow up and pop the top. We're going in." Sandy swelled like the chin of a bleating frog. "Nothing cures a blue day like some *Christmas spirit*."

Another dose of willies laid claim to Marie's backside. *That's what Aunt Rinks said.*

Fritz and Sandy were going with or without her (she realized she thought of them as two people now). And she wasn't going to get any sleep until then. Marie locked the bedroom door. There was no point in hiding the gift. If Aunt Rinks kicked the door in, they weren't going to be there.

FRITZ AND SANDY were off to Christmas Wood again. The dragon and teddy weren't there. *They're in the storefront.* The lights, the Christmas tree, and the toys. Nothing had happened in the last week, though. But now Storyteller Corner appeared. *Where did that come from?*

They leaped over the burbling stream of chocolate like school was out.

Marie went to the sign. The pretzel post was plunked in the middle of the chocolate stream, the thick, milky current cutting around it. Beyond, the world was pale and murky. A coloring book yearning for color, wanting to be discovered. Her head was clear and shivering. The sharpness of each breath sent tingles through her body. She longed for what was out there. She didn't know why. At the same time, she was terrified of it. That made no sense.

O' the Land of Candy,

Where dreams and thoughts do lend,

A world of Christmas spirit,

For your story to begin...

She was never any good at riddles. Never in her life had she ever solved one, always turned to the answer page no matter how long she thought about it. And then, as always, the answer seemed obvious, like it was never hiding in the first place.

What has four wheels and flies? A garbage truck.

Despite the joy all around her, despair rolled through her like the cool front of a thunderstorm. It was a familiar feeling. Like driving a car into a snowy ditch. She was stuck with no way to go back, no way forward. If she didn't move, she was going to be sandwiched by the past and future. Wind up an oil stain in the present. At least, that was what Teri, her therapist, said.

"Look!" Sandy and Fritz pranced toward her. Gummy worms

squirmed in Fritz's hands and between Sandy's sticks. "There's, like, a whole family living in a stump."

Fritz had a chocolate mask drying on his face. After he'd fallen in the stream the last time, she made him take a shower in the middle of the night. Uncle Vernon and Aunt Rinks didn't wake up. Although Aunt Rinks looked a bit suspicious the next day. Marie thought it would be smart to clean up beforehand. She wiped his face and hands while Sandy was telling her the name of each of the gummy worms. They came in different stripes of yellow, green, red and orange and giggled each time he held one up. Sandy said they weren't for eating.

"Hey, hey. Easy on the clean-up," Sandy said. "You act like this is a crime scene."

"You can't leave like this, Fritz. You want to take another shower?"

He resisted her attention. She had to scrub to get it off his cheeks. Forget getting it out of his fingernails; she could explain that.

"You all right, Mar Mar?" Sandy said. "You want to eat some grass? It might take the edge off."

"That. Out there." She punched at the lifeless landscape beyond the stream. "Remember the journey? That's why we're here in the middle of the night. This isn't recess, you two."

Sandy looked like he'd put his sticks in an electrical outlet. Fritz went limp. His face sagged, and his eyes shot up in surprise and hurt. Something hard had sprung out of her. That something she tried to keep a lid on. *Where'd that come from?*

She knew where. The emotional black box was bulging.

"I'm sorry." She stopped fussing over the smudges on his chin. She sighed, hands on hips, looking at the breezy grass. "Look, I get it. This is cool and amazing and mind-blowing. I'll come here any time you want as long as Aunt Rinks doesn't know about it. But right now, middle of the night, is not why we're here. Nothing's changed, and I'm tired. If we don't figure out that riddle, there's just this... this chocolate stream and grazing grass and-and-and—" She waved at the gummy worms. "And I'd rather be sleeping."

A long moment of silence. The gummy worms meeped like chicks. Sandy held one up to the side of his head and nodded.

"Hey, Marie. You know why the chicken crossed the road?"

"What?"

"Just answer the question. Why did the chicken cross the road?"

She sighed. "To get to the other side."

"There you go. You solved a riddle. Now let's take this one line at a time. Come on, we can do this. *O' the Land of Candy*. That's easy. Candyland. Fritz, you take the next one."

The two of them took turns reading the sign and making obvious observations. Half the conversation—when Fritz answered Sandy through their mind-meld or whatever they did—Marie didn't hear. It devolved into telling unrelated riddles. *Which fish costs the most? A goldfish.*

Marie fell on the ground and crossed her legs. She plucked blades of grass and minced them between her teeth. They tasted like sugared mint leaves. She'd give it five minutes; then she was leaping out. She'd given up searching her phone. The internet didn't have an answer to the riddle. It was hopeless. And hopelessness was an iron jacket.

"What has a neck and no head?" Sandy asked. "A bottle. Get it? Hey, kid, don't give up. What's the hurry, anyway? We'll get there when we get there. Fritz agrees, don't you? So does Ernie." He dangled a rainbow-striped worm in front of her. "This place isn't so bad. We make new friends every time. It feels better than it smells. And it smells awesome. It's wonderful being *here*."

"What's the hurry? I think Aunt Rinks knows about it. If she doesn't, she will. And then what? I'll tell you. Forget about the journey. She'll turn this place into an amusement park."

That felt worse than being stuck. Marie didn't know what Candyland was or how it worked, but it wasn't meant to be a theme park.

"She doesn't know about it," Sandy said. "The gift was still in the wall. You think she'd put it back if she found it?"

"You believe they did Storyteller Corner? The chair and the way they were smiling. Did you see the book? It was called *Tales from Candyland.*"

"No, it wasn't."

"Yeah, it was. You think that's a coincidence?"

"All right, I'll give you that. Weirder than their weird smiles." He chiseled his chin with a knobby stem. "It could still be a coincidence."

"Really?" She threw her head back, stared at the exit floating in the pink sky. "I'll bet that book came from here! Just like the lights and the toys and the Christmas tree!"

Her voice echoed in Christmas Wood. Sandy and Fritz stepped back. The gummy worms squealed. Paranoid rage simmered inside her like a pressure cooker with a leaky seal. She was tired and hungry and irritable. Anger came out in bursts. Guilt came along for the ride when it did.

"Did she read you a story?" Sandy said. "She's not a storyteller, you don't have to worry about that. Trust me. No emotion. And kind of mean. Two children on the naughty list? Horrible."

He babbled on like the chocolate brook, casting doubt on Aunt Rinks's storytelling skills. Like that was what was bothering Marie. That book was old. It was authentic. That was what bothered her the most. That book wasn't a coincidence. If Godfather had anything to do with this journey, why didn't he just give Marie the answer? Or was it her great-uncle Corker who did this? He was a game maker, Ms. Clara had said. *Maybe that's all this is. A game. A game of wonder pretending to be a meaningful journey.*

"She kept telling the same story over and over and..." Sandy said. "*Once upon a time, there was a boy and a girl...* Terrible."

Marie turned her head. An idea struck her like an aluminum bat. She stood up. Sandy was talking to the gummy worms now. Fritz held them in both hands so they could listen. Marie opened the Almond and Raisin Gate to look at the sign.

O' the Land of Candy,
Where dreams and thoughts do lend,
A world of Christmas spirit,
For your story to begin...

Aunt Rinks kept telling the same story. Every story began the same. All stories did. They started with one line. Marie whispered, "Once upon a time…"

In the distance, a bell chimed.

PINK BLED into the grayscape like watercolor on a linen sky. Grassy carpet rolled down a slope where a deep crevasse carved the landscape. Trees popped out of the spongy soil, branches unfurling puffy seeds that floated on a peppermint breeze. It unfolded like dominoes to the horizon: glassy cliffs spilled frothy waterfalls, distant mountains slathered in rich icing and topped with sprinkles. And in the center of the valley, a dark brown monument reached for cotton-candy clouds. Spires forked from the sides.

A chocolate castle rose in a distant village.

"You did it." Marie felt dry twigs on her arm. "You did it!"

Fritz and Sandy hugged. The gummy worms danced on their shoulders. The peppermint breeze blew up from the valley and stung their eyes. The chocolate stream began to overflow its banks. The signpost crumbled in the current. The graham cracker slate with the riddle carved into its surface floated like a runaway raft.

Branches out, Sandy's midsection expanded. "Let the journey begin!"

Marie hadn't moved. She was rooted into the ground, breathless in the face of the world expanding before them. It was like standing on the edge of a cliff. Her legs quivered. A hesitant fragility quaked up her thighs and rattled her stomach and froze her chest.

"Stop!" she shouted.

Fritz had one foot on a chocolate drop. The stream was gushing around it. The grassy banks were falling into the current.

"We need to hurry," Sandy said. "In case you hadn't noticed, this chocolate fountain sprang a leak."

Fritz grabbed Sandy's stick when the chocolate drop he was standing on melted around his foot. Marie pulled her little brother back to shore before he was swallowed up. Sandy's arm came with him. The current was growing stronger and thicker, belching fudgy bubbles.

"You're right. Okay, little help." Sandy swung his remaining branch as he began sliding into the stream. His bottom started to melt. "I don't want death by chocolate!"

"Jump!" Marie shouted.

He gave it his all, and it wasn't much. It was enough to hit the shoreline. Marie and Fritz did their best to pull him out. They came away with clumps of wet sand, but he managed to claw his way out, rolling in the grass with two panicked sand dollars staring at the pink sky. Fritz stabbed the stick into his side.

"Thanks, kid."

He pushed himself up and surveyed the damage. He was a foot shorter. "Hey, where's my... oh no. This is permanent. Here, give me that."

They slapped the wet sand they'd pulled off him when trying to get him out. It filled a few holes, but he didn't grow an inch. He moaned and shivered. The gummy worms hopped on the ground. They were cheering.

"You do?" he said. "I'll be right back."

He slid away with the bright, rubbery worms in the lead, leaving a dark, brown trail behind him.

Marie and Fritz stepped back. The chocolate stream had become a river growing wider by the minute. The Almond and Raisin Gate was swept away in broken pieces. The post that held up the sign was gone. Maybe her answer had triggered a self-destruct landslide. She looked up at the square in the sky. It wasn't too late to get out.

Candyland begged them to stay.

"CHECK IT OUT." Sandy was back to his normal height. His bottom half was speckled with bits of colored grains. It looked like a dance floor. "Too loud? I don't care, I like it. The gummies said it was castings. I don't know what that is, but I like it."

Castings was worm poop. Marie didn't tell him that.

He turned in a circle and made more of a slithery sound than a gritty one. The gummy worms cheered him on. He shook his bottom. Marie guided Fritz and the dancing sandman away from the encroaching flood.

"So what now?" Sandy had to shout over the gurgling current. "It looks a little strong."

"It's a warning," Marie said.

"Yeah. Wait, what?"

"Not to go on. It's pretty obvious. I think we need to get out before it gets worse." The ground was spongier than before. It bounced like a bladder of lava. "Sorry, Fritz."

Her brother shook his head. She kept him from going any closer to the river. The whites of his eyes were billboards.

"Can I ask a question?" Sandy said. "Do you even *want* to go on the journey?"

Marie swallowed the hard stone in her throat. She couldn't answer. Her emotions and thoughts swirled in a blizzard. She didn't know what she felt beneath the crushing anxiety. Not since she put a lock on the emotional black box. Dry twigs curled around her fingers. She was trembling.

"We *have* to go, kid."

"Why do we have to go?" she muttered.

"Because we can't go forward," he said, "if we don't look back."

She expected a different answer. Like Nussknacker said so. What Sandy said, for some reason, terrified her. She didn't know why. Across the meadow, the valley was so beautiful. She did want to go. *What's stopping me?*

"You know how to get across," Sandy said. "You solved the riddle. You can do it."

Her lips were dry. The minty air hot in her chest. She wanted to go back to the flat mattress and life in the toy store, even though she hated it. She wanted her brother to be safe. He didn't want to go back. He was looking at her, waiting for her to take him across.

Above the noisy river, bells were ringing in the distant castle. It was Christmas music.

This is a story. That's how I solved the riddle. And every story starts with a blank page. You write the story, Godfather said.

She took her brother's warm hand. Sandy's grip tightened around her other hand. She stood tall. They weren't going back. And things couldn't stay the same. They were going to write their story.

"Once upon a time," she called, "there was a bridge."

PRETZEL POSTS ERUPTED from the ground on both sides of the river.

They were solid and stout and coated in salt, two on each side. More of them heaved from the soil, these longer, skinnier and twice as long. They pushed out of the ground and fell over the dark, brown river. Black licorice whips (the kind Aunt Rinks snacked on) snaked out from the ground and whipped and snapped and lashed the pretzels together. Next came the pretzel logs, rolling across the supports. They thudded against each other like bowling balls on a return chute. Black licorice slithered and cinched them tight.

Marie looked at her brother, then at Sandy. They returned the look. The river began to recede. There was new grass on the other side. The air coming across was stronger and sweeter, like vaporized breath mints that stung their nostrils. Marie wiped a tear from her eye. The scent was strong, but it was more than that. Music called from far away. She could feel it in her chest.

The castle was calling.

The trees began to tremble on the other side of the stream (it was more like a creek again). The branches shuddered on both sides of the open field. The forest looked alive, like it was an organism waking from a long sleep. Leaves fluttered to the ground. On the right, between two stout tree trunks, a bunny hopped out. Its plastic nose twitched; glass eyes blinked. It was joined by a floppy-eared dog with a long velvet tongue. Then a wooden puppet and a bouncy ball. An orange octopus. They came in all sizes and colors. A herd of toys bounced and hopped and danced into the field, filling it from tree line to tree line. Staring at them from across the bridge.

"I'll be honest," Sandy said, "I didn't see that coming."

"I think they're waiting for us," Marie said.

"They're definitely waiting for us."

But Marie felt their goodness. She could taste it in the air. They were happy to see them. All her fears, all her anxiety, had vanished.

"Where's Nussknacker?" she said.

"He's here," Sandy said. "You'll see."

She didn't know what that meant. The journey would soon reveal that mystery.

19

They wore jogging shorts and running shoes. Some of them had holsters for water bottles, patches to measure their glucose, arm pockets for their phones. Then there were the bikers with tighty-tights and clappy shoes, numbers on their shirts to remind everyone they didn't ride on skinny wheels just for fun. They were in it to win it. There were normal people at the coffee place, too. The ones in sweatpants and T-shirts, the blue-jeans mom with flip-flops and the cargo-pants dad with work boots. They were happy. Super happy. Their caffeinated eyes jittered out of their heads.

It made Rinks sick.

They were faking it. She could tell. A bunch of road rats on the treadmill, running as fast as they could to get absolutely nowhere. That was why she never left the house; she couldn't stand the fakeness of their laughs, their smiles, their caramel crunch Frappuccinos. They had no idea what true joy felt like. Rinks did.

It was in a tidy little gift box hidden in a mouse hole.

She was going to send the kids out that morning, tell them to come back for supper like she'd done that entire week. The plan was to dive back into that lovely land of sweets. But then she'd reviewed the video from the night before, when she and Vern had been sleeping. The kids had gotten up in the middle of the night.

That was what had changed her plan.

Vern carried eight small plates. Three on each forearm and one on each hand. He weaved through the crowd like a street performer. He nearly collided with a skinny runner who used to be fat (extra skin hung on his arms like a trophy; he wore a tank top to show it off) and made it to the corner without losing a crumb.

"It all looked so good." He filled the round table with cupcakes and muffins and macaroons and fudge. "There's not much left up there. They almost sold out."

"You ask them to turn the music down?" Rinks said.

"Um, no. I can barely hear it."

Neither could Rinks. But if they turned it down, maybe all these posers wouldn't talk like caffeine addicts on a long-distance call.

"They're practically givin' the food away." He shoved a pastry in his mouth. "Nice people," he muffled. "Feel like I met them before."

It was embarrassing the way he ate. Like a squirrel in a nut factory. She threw a napkin at him. He wiped his fingers.

"Kids still asleep?" He pointed at the laptop resting on her thighs.

"Shh."

She could barely hear him. But someone just might, like the lady at the next table. She could be pretending to read that boring book. Rinks turned the laptop toward the wall. Vern craned his neck to see.

"So what is it?" she said.

The time stamp was 12:45 a.m. Marie was in the still-inflated bed that Vern had patched (*you're welcome*). Fritz got up with the nutcracker tucked under his arm. And the metal ball Godfather gave him in one hand. He nudged his sister. When she didn't wake up, the sandman came out.

"Right on time," Vern said. A soft morsel fired from between his teeth and stuck to the monitor. He wiped it off with his finger. Thank God, he didn't eat it. "He's a projection. Like an avatar, you know."

"That ain't an avatar. It's a... a sandman."

Three balls of dirty sand, sticks for arms and seashells for eyes.

Standing right in the middle of the kids' bedroom. A week had gone by, and they never sang a peep about it. Rinks had even asked what that dumb little ball from Godfather was for. Nothing. Just keeping their secrets to themselves. Rinks had to bite her lips and sew them shut.

That's who she's been talkin' to all this time. The little liars.

"Godfather had somethin' like that when I was there. They must've gotten it down to a personalized pocket pod. I imagine they'll go public with it in a few years. Probably a prototype Fritz has." Through a fresh load of donut jelly, he said, "He gave Fritz a voice."

"Don't get all goody-goody for the boy. He's keepin' a secret. And don't act like you know what it is."

"It ain't a ghost, Rinks. I know that."

"Then how's it projectin' from his pocket?"

He shrugged. "I didn't work on it. But that's what it is. Probably neural circuiting tech. They got that for exoskeletal assist for people who can't walk. It's probably not much different than Candyland."

"Shhhh."

She was tired of his fancy talk.

He leaned in and whispered and not without sarcasm. "*Candyland*," he whispered. "It was amazing. You felt it, right?"

She didn't know why she was cranky. Most people would say that was her default mode. Candyland, one would think, would've cured that. It felt like home. Maybe that was why she wanted to scream. To break things. *I want to go back!*

"Here. Eat this." He offered a cannolo. "It's good for you."

She refused. Two bites was all it took him to finish it, wiping cream off his lips and sucking all his fingers. A bear claw was next. The stuff went right through him, never stuck to his hips or butt. It was so easy to hate him.

"What about the sign?" she said.

"What about it?"

"*O' the Land of Candy*... it sounds like a clue."

"It's not a clue, Rinks. It's a poem."

"All right. What about the rest of it. The... you know—" she waved her hands "—the blurry part. There's somethin' out there."

"It's not done. You know, like, not programmed. There's that little candy field and the chocolate river and that's it. What else you want?"

"She talked about the journey." Rinks turned the laptop toward him but not too much. He hadn't studied the recordings like it was a final exam. "How can you stuff your face like that? I know you're Mr. Computer Man, and all this ain't that special, but there's more goin' on here, you ding-dong. They're goin' on a *journey*. And they're plannin' on leavin' us. They're gonna hide the gift so we can't find it, and then what?"

Vern sounded like a dog licking a bowl.

"Stop for a second, all right? Listen to me," Rinks said. Vern dropped a jelly donut, leaned over the table to hear her whisper. "Marie's suspicious," Rinks said. "She didn't believe we did Storyteller Corner."

"You think?"

"What's that supposed to mean?"

"It means there's *no way* we did all that. Then you told that dumb story about naughty kids, just rubbin' their noses in it."

She cringed. What that sandman thing had said about her not being a storyteller and clearly not smart was a kick to the shin. She didn't need Honest Vern piling on. Rinks wasn't a fan of the truth. She liked to lock it up, compartmentalized deep inside her where the light never shined. She liked to see the world the way she wanted to see it. It was so much nicer that way.

"Why we here, Rinks? If you ain't goin' to eat anythin', why didn't we just stay home and send the kids out?"

"Because I want them to go in."

"Well, you're goin' to have to explain that one to me."

She broke a corner off the brownie. "We're goin' to follow them."

"Brilliant."

The sarcasm was thick and pasty. It kicked her right in the bruised feelings. Tears threatened to rise to her eyes; she swallowed them down with a bitter bite of fury. Having a dirty snowman call her stupid was one thing (the thing wasn't real), but that look on her husband's face had a sharp edge.

"Listen to me." Her lips tightened and started to crack. "You're goin' to stop being an idiot and listen. I want to know what the journey is. Maybe there's gold at the end or lottery tickets or nothin' but a pretty picture. I don't care. Those two little weasels have been goin' in there for a week or maybe longer. They're after somethin'. I want it. You hear? Now there's only one way I'm gettin' it. We're goin' to sit here and watch. When they disappear, we go straight home and follow them inside."

"Disappear?"

"Disappear, Vern. Watch the video, you ignorant toad."

"Rinks, no one disappears. It's virtual reality. All senses captured. It's impossible to *go in there*." He gave a snort and started feasting on banana bread. If the place weren't crowded, she would've smacked it out of his mouth.

He hadn't watched the video of when they were at the kitchen table and he grabbed her hand. There was a flash, and they were gone. It wasn't a glitch, which was what he'd say if he did see it. That was exactly what he'd say. But it had happened. And he was going to get on his knees when she proved him wrong. And it was going to feel so, so good.

"MERRY CHRISTMAS!"

Rinks slammed the laptop shut. A doughy, old woman came at them. She looked like a sack of potatoes with an apple face wearing glasses. Wiping her hands on a damp dishrag with a smile on her wrinkled mug, she said, "You are Rinks and Vernon."

Rinks looked at Vern. "How's she know us?"

"Your niece and nephew talk so much about you. I'm very glad you come here. It is pleasure to meet you."

"What'd they say about us?"

"Well, they say many nice things." There was a lie in there. "They say you move down street in old toy store. Very exciting. You found home, I think. You have been searching awhile."

"They said that?" Rinks said. "All that?"

"Yes, of course. They are lovely children. A shame about your sister. It breaks my heart. My sympathy to you. I do hope the children find their way."

The old lady looked back and forth between Rinks and Vern, wiping her hands like they were permanently stained. Rinks didn't like the way she was looking at her. It felt like an X-ray machine. Reminded her of Mother, the way she sniffed out a lie just by looking.

"You ain't livin' with them," Rinks said, "so they ain't peaches and cream."

The old woman's cheeks turned pinker when she laughed. "Family, yes. It has challenges."

"You can say that. The lies, the secrets." Vern shook his head at her, but she kept going. "Those two can be bad. Very naughty."

"Oh, not to worry. They are not on naughty list." She patted Rinks on the shoulder. She smelled like cinnamon. "How was the food? Good, yes?"

Vern polished off the last bite and gave her a thumbs-up. When he tried to speak, crumbs flew from his lips.

"He liked it," Rinks said.

"What about you?"

"I got too much on my mind. Christmas ain't for everyone."

"I'm sorry to hear that. We have tea for upset stomach. I'll be back."

She scuttled toward the counter before they could stop her. She was stopped twice on her way—once by a sweaty lady in yoga pants, then again by a little girl holding a cup with both hands. She took a knee to talk with the little one, rather effortlessly got up. Maybe not as old as she looked. When she made it to the counter, where another old lady served drinks, Rinks turned to Vern.

"How'd she know us?"

"Seems like she knows everyone."

"We never *met* her, Vern." A bad feeling rumbled through her. "She's spyin' on us."

"Or," he said, licking his finger to pick up crumbs, "she's friendly."

She was already coming back. No interference this time. "Tea for your tummy. And this for children." She put a lumpy paper bag on the table. "Banana in there, also. Good for digestion."

"Thanks," Rinks said. "I don't think we brought enough money to—"

"No charge."

"Excellent!" Vern said.

"Today last day we open," she said. "You enjoy."

"We will," he said. Whatever was in there wasn't going to make it to the kids.

"Merry, merry," she said. "Best of luck on your searching."

Rinks smelled the tea. It was peppermint. Smelled just like Candyland. But she hated tea. When the old lady looked back, Rinks pretended to drink it. Vern was looking in the sack. The idiot didn't even hear what the old lady said.

"We're leavin'," she said.

"Why?" He cracked the laptop open. "Kids are still sleepin'."

"You heard her. Best of luck on your *searchin'*." She looked for eavesdroppers, then for hidden cameras and microphones. She hissed: "She knows, you ape."

"Rinks, you're just bein—"

"You hush that fat mouth. I don't like this place anyhow. Bunch of phonies suckin' up to those two... two Santa Claus wannabe old ladies."

He sighed. "Whatever. I need to talk to a man about a reindeer." He pushed away from the table. "If you know what I mean."

"You're disgustin'."

"Might be a minute."

She didn't want to sit there another second. But what her gross husband was about to do to the bathroom brought a micro-smile to her face. When he came out of the bathroom, she was tempted to make him sit down at the table so she could see who would follow his diseased colon. She was really hoping it was Mr. Bike Pants.

She carried the laptop, tea and sack out to the sidewalk. The little bell rang above the door. Someone shouted merry, merry as she left. Rinks raised the cup of tea without looking back.

The sidewalk was warm. Sweat pricked her scalp beneath the headscarf as she scrolled through her social. She hadn't posted yet that day. Her account was beginning to cool. She held up the phone for a selfie. The mechanical elves were behind her. Creepy little things looked like an advert for a horror movie. She deleted it.

Vern came out sucking his coffee-stained teeth and adjusting his belt. He looked in the window. "Those look old as dirt."

Everyone in the café was staring at them. She threw the tea in the garbage.

RINKS WAS ALONE in the car. The meter was expired.

Vern was inside the store. The banner on the window read *40% OFF!* That was a rip. They jack up the price 50%, then call it a discount? Vern climbed onto another mattress, hiked up his feet and laced his hands behind his head. The lady helping him stared at the big toe sticking through his sock. Poor woman. Those feet smelled like recycled trash bags. And he'd been on every bed in the place.

Fritz was awake.

Rinks looked in the rearview mirror. Several sprigs of gray hair were springing out from above her ear. That was new. Her mother hadn't had a gray hair until she was in her seventies. Her father had had jet-black hair past that. Even worse, she saw what was on her chin. She plucked it off, a slick of tears rising in her eyes when she did, and held it in front of her. It was a whisker as thick as a tooth-brush bristle. And there were two more. She attacked them like roaches in a cupboard, tossing them out the window and cursing. She searched her ears and her upper lip for more, then checked her social to make sure none of those were in her last post. She imagined the comments.

Shave much?

There were no comments like that. Actually, nothing but good things to read. She felt better and clicked over to the kitchen camera. Fritz went through all the cabinets, peeked in the refrigerator. When he popped his head back out, there was a protein bar in his mouth. The little scamp found her hiding spot. Rinks's skin began to peel.

Naughty list. That old lady had no idea what she was talkin' about. Rinks had an idea to drive back to the coffee place and show her what awful children looked like. *Naughty list kids.*

He ate a bowl of cereal with his face inches from his phone, slopping milk all over the note Rinks had left that morning. He had three bowls. Fortunately, he didn't steal another protein bar. Her head would've exploded. He rinsed the bowl and put it in the dishwasher. It was going to take more than that to get him off the naughty list.

He stared at his phone another five minutes. Then he started for the storefront. Rinks sat up in the passenger seat of the car, leaned closer to the laptop. Eyes wide and watery. She hadn't blinked since he woke up. A tear streamed down her face as he put his hand on the door. He stopped with it open. Rinks didn't click over to the storefront camera. She knew what was out there.

Fritz was on his way back to the bedroom.

Marie got out of bed. The sandman thing was out again, sending strange vibes up Rinks's neck. A sci-fi movie was playing in her house, and she was watching it on the laptop. Marie followed Fritz to the storefront. They came back to the kitchen in a hurry. Marie read the note. Then checked the location app on her phone.

And we're very far away.

Rinks honked the horn. Her eyes were burning. She rubbed them with the heels of her hands and honked some more. The lady inside the store was looking at her. Rinks rolled down the window and pointed. The lady shook Vern's leg.

Rinks went back to the laptop while her husband put his shoes back on. The kids were already in the bedroom. A minute later, they were sliding the blocks on the wall.

"Go on, little chickens," Rinks said. "Lead the way."

They parked a block away in a boot store parking lot.

The back gate began to squeal. Rinks grabbed it before it announced their arrival. Slowly, she pushed it open. Sweat dampened the back of her shirt. She pulled off her shoes and pointed at Vern to take his off. Tiptoeing down the crooked path, they snuck up the steps and stopped at the door. Rinks checked the laptop, clicked through all the cameras inside the building. The rooms were empty. Unless they were both in the bathroom, she knew exactly where they were.

She opened the door even slower than they did the gate. It felt like minutes before they were inside. The note was on the table. Sliding their feet across the living room to keep the wood floor from creaking, they stopped at the kids' bedroom. Not a sound. A slow turn on the doorknob. The door caught on the hook set in an eyebolt.

Rinks almost put her fist through it.

Vern dug through his wallet. He poked a credit card between the door and the doorjamb, sliding it up and lifting the lock out of the eyebolt. It clattered against the door frame.

Rinks's pulse shifted into passing gear.

They opened it just as slowly as they did the back door. The bed was empty. The sheets a mess. The owl clock watched them peek into the room. The nutcracker at his post. Next to him, the lid flipped open, was the bright and shiny present.

"They're gone," she whispered.

Vern shook his head. Thankfully, he didn't argue the impossibility of physically travelling inside a box the size of a cupcake. "They musta left."

Rinks checked her phone. She showed him what she saw. The kids were in the building. Their phones weren't anywhere in sight.

"If they're not in there," she whispered, "how'd their door get locked?"

He opened his mouth. It hung that way with no stupid words coming out. She was right. They couldn't lock the door if they left.

"Okay," he mumbled. "I can't explain it, but they ain't in there, Rinks."

"I'll go first."

His whiskers sounded like bristles in the palm of his hand. "This a good idea?"

"We're surprisin' them, Vern. We'll know what they're up to as soon as we do."

He sighed, shaking his head. Rinks didn't get what his hesitation was all about. He peered into the open gift. Then pointed. "Look at that."

The floating orb wasn't gray anymore. It was full color. Like a model planet hovering between the four walls. *They up to somethin' now.*

Rinks jammed her finger at the orb like it was a button on a vault of gold coins. There was white light. The falling sensation. The smell of peppermint and silky grass on her feet. A few seconds later, Vern was next to her. His complexion was a bedsheet.

"You disappeared."

She lapped up the sweet taste of victory and looked around. Things had changed.

Candyland wasn't so little anymore.

20

"You got to see this!" Sandy said.

"Everything all right?" Marie said before she was fully awake. She jolted off the bed, looked around. "Where's Aunt Rinks?"

"Never mind her; come on."

Fritz had a smudge of chocolate on his face from the night before. Sandy followed him into the kitchen. The lower half of his bottom was a speckled patchwork of funky gummy castings. Marie rolled off the mattress (still half-filled with air) and went to the bathroom. When she came out, the door to the storefront was open. Fritz and his sidekick were waiting.

"They followed us." Sandy's sand dollars looked like Frisbees.

Dust particles floated through beams of late morning sunlight. The shelves looked cluttered. She stepped across the spotless floor, shading her eyes from the bright light. When she lowered her arm, she saw what was on the shelves.

Toys.

They were piled and stacked from the bottom shelf to the top. Bunnies, octopuses, dragons and bears. Robots with TV heads and stretchy muscle men in tight shorts. Baby dolls and purple monkeys, rainbow birds with leather wings, little white puppies with velvety tongues, lanky puppets made of wood with hinged jaws. It was them, the toys that greeted them after they crossed the bridge. They came from the trees and flew down from the sky, took their hands and climbed on their shoulders. Dancing and trotting and twirling as they went with contagious laughter.

Marie, Fritz and Sandy had walked all the way to the valley and stopped at a cliff. Below, a stream trickled over brittle slabs of glassy candy. The scent wafting up was perfumed. *That's the Orange Brook!* Sandy had said. (It was much later when Marie would remember how he knew its name.) They had walked for hours. The castle didn't look any closer. Marie barely remembered coming back out to fall in bed.

Marie checked her phone. Aunt Rinks and Uncle Vernon were across town. *A furniture store?*

"There's more."

Sandy tried to grab her hand. His stick passed through it. She followed him into the kitchen. There was a bowl of bright-colored gummy worms on the table with a note next to it. The ink was leaching in soggy milk stains. She read it to herself. Sandy told her to read it out loud.

"Morning, sleepyheads. Looks like Godfather's elves paid another visit. Haha. :) Me and your uncle went shopping. No guesses and no peeking where we at. No chores today because it's Christmas time. We'll be back at supper. Have fun and do whatever you want!"

"Did she put a smiley face at the end?" Sandy asked.

She checked her phone again. They were twenty minutes away. *Did someone kidnap Aunt Rinks? The note sounds nothing like her. The only time she uses smiley faces is on social media.*

"We're going in," Sandy said. "It'll take all day to get to the castle."

It would take more than that. A week, maybe. If the trail was easy. "Wait."

"Wait, what? No. They're not coming home till tonight. You see where they're at."

"She had to see the toys." She shook the note. "She doesn't even sound surprised."

"And that's... *bad?*"

It was suspicious. Marie looked around. It felt like someone was watching them. *Did they put their phones at a furniture store and sneak back?*

Fritz was dancing in place like he needed the bathroom. He nodded at Sandy. "We're going," Sandy said.

"Wait, wait. I just... I need to get something to eat."

She was still waking up, and these two wanted to go. Candyland wasn't imaginary. It ached in her bones. Her feet were sore from a two-hour hike. And they wanted to get to the castle today? On top of that, she hadn't eaten in twenty-four hours. Hadn't showered in two days. And her thoughts tossed about like sheaves of paper in a winter storm. Still, she wanted to go, too. The journey was just beginning.

"Don't eat the worms," Sandy said.

"WELL, THIS IS A BUMMER," Sandy groaned.

They were at the Almond and Raisin Gate, staring across the valley. The sign with the clue was gone. The bridge was still there. It felt more like a video game: respawning at the beginning. There was no way they would make it over the vast stretch of land in a few hours. Even if they rode horses (there were none to ride, toy horses or otherwise), it would take all day.

"You know, we could do a sleepover at the cabin with the Counselor. Take the gift. He'd probably go with us," Sandy said. "I'm just spitballing."

That was never going to happen. Even if Aunt Rinks let them go, the gift wasn't going to work outside the toy store (that was a working theory). It was a dumb idea. Their spirits sank like an iron sled on the Arctic Ocean. Fritz didn't even dip his toes in the chocolate stream (which had receded to its meager current) or search the Christmas Wood for new friends. Sandy slumped like a snowman in August.

"Journeys are supposed to be fun," Sandy said. He sounded like a machine losing power. "This isn't fun. Or funny."

Journeys aren't always easy, Marie thought.

She sighed. The other two sighed. The riddle wasn't easy, but she thought that was just a test. Travelling that distance was impossible. Unless they stayed in Candyland a week. That would mean telling Aunt Rinks, which would create a bigger problem.

It feels like a video game. Marie had played video games with her friends. The kind of games where one level had to be solved to get to the next. There was usually something that linked them together, though. A common thread. A weapon or charm that allowed them to pass to the next level. *What have we done so far? We solved the riddle.*

The riddle gave them the bridge.

"Come on."

They searched the Almond and Raisin Gate for buttons or levers or secret compartments. It was a pointless gate that didn't keep anything in or out. Maybe it would transform into a monster truck or a flying carpet. A sled that slid down sugar-coated fields of grass. Fritz poked at the gummy raisins stuck to the posts while Marie twisted the almonds. Sandy hopped across the bridge and back.

"What are we looking for again?" he said.

"I don't know. Just... just look."

It was officially hopeless when Fritz began licking the peanut-sized grains of salt off the pretzel posts. Sandy helped him break off a chunk to dip in the stream. They'd given up and decided to eat.

Marie crossed the bridge, sat cross-legged in the field (*Candy Meadow* was written on a little sign posted on the other side of the bridge), picking sweet blades of grass and mincing them between her teeth. *What's the link?* Most riddles—good riddles—were misdirection. The answer was obvious, just not where you would expect it even when looking right at it. What had they solved so far?

For your story to begin...

The journey had started when she solved the riddle. Perhaps it was more than just a riddle. The answer was more than an answer. This was a story. And a story started with blank pages, just like the one Godfather had given her. And in a story, anything was possible. She stood up, looked at the pink sky.

"Once upon a time... we were at the castle."

Her words were strong and deep. They bounced off the trees. A tremor sent ripples through the stream. Fritz looked up with chocolate-smeared lips. They felt it, too. But nothing happened. They was still in Candy Meadow.

"Present tense," Sandy said. "We *are* at the castle."

She tried that. It didn't work.

Sandy snapped his fingers like breaking twigs. "Helicopter. Do a helicopter."

"Once upon a time, a helicopter was in Candy Meadow."

Another tremor, this one knocked caramel-dipped fruit off the candy-cane trees. They gathered sticks and leaves as they rolled across the ground. Nothing, however, dropped from the sky or erupted from the ground. Marie thought a helicopter wouldn't do them any good. *We don't know how to fly a helicopter.*

Sandy spouted nonstop ideas that included four-wheelers, motorcycles and jetpacks. Airplanes, parachutes, dragons, dinosaurs, pogo sticks, and hot-air balloons. Marie didn't bother. She was onto something, though.

Candyland heard me.

It just couldn't comply. She looked at the candy-cane trees and cotton-candy clouds. The Christmas music that played from the muddy castle a hundred miles away. This place had a theme. A story had to be congruent. A historical romance didn't have laser guns. Some did, but that didn't work here.

What's the theme?

It was toys. It was music. It was the feel of winter and essence of joy. It was happiness and wonder. Outside, through that square in the sky, it was that time of year. *Christmas spirit.*

"Once upon a time," she said, "there was a sleigh with flying reindeer."

The ground shook this time. Tree trunks swayed, and candied fruit bombed the sparkling ground. The pretzel bridge crackled and leaned. Fritz and Sandy hurried over it. The earthquake rumbled into the distance. The Christmas music stretched out on long notes, then resumed its cheery refrain. A peppermint breeze blew a lock of hair that had escaped Marie's ribbon.

She heard bells.

Tiny bells chimed everywhere at once. It was like a cricket that couldn't be located. It came from the trees. She expected to hear a hoof scratch the turf, or see a snout poke out from the shadows. The bells grew louder. They were coming from the right. She took a step in that direction when *whuuump!* A shadow passed over them.

It was cool and large, like a cloud flying over the sun.

They looked up in unison. Four cloven hooves pedaled the air. The antlers looked like tree branches. Behind it, sagging from thick straps, was a red sleigh with golden rails. It sparkled in the sunlight. Each stride the reindeer took cut the air like giant limbs swinging through the air. *Whump. Whump. Whump.*

It circled Candy Meadow twice, then came straight for them. Marie, Fritz and Sandy ran to the left. Spongy dirt and soft sprigs of turf shot up as the hooves bit into the ground. The sleigh bounced on one rail, then the other. It skidded behind the reindeer. A musky smell mixed with the peppermint breeze. The reindeer came to a stop. He shook his head, bells ringing on the harness over his shoulders, and turned a black eye toward them. A frightening snort rattled his nostrils. Wet steam shot out.

"It's a reindeer," Marie whispered.

She wasn't sure. It was more like a mutated bull. The antlers were as wide as a truck. And the look in his eye could melt ice. He dug a trench in the dirt with his front leg as easily as a backhoe ate the earth. He dropped his head to graze, looked back at them with tufts of grass disappearing between black lips.

Marie, Fritz and Sandy weren't moving. It was like a bear had wandered into the meadow to eat berries off a tree, and they were afraid to move. So struck by the reindeer's size and intent, they hadn't even looked at the sleigh.

And when they heard a voice, they jumped a foot off the ground.

❄

"MERRY, MERRY!" An elf leaped from the bench inside the sleigh. He was as round as a beach ball with a tumbleweed beard that was braided in two strands. "Ronin Express, at your service. I am Garl. Short for Garland, if you're wondering. Named after me grandpap. That there is Ronin."

Garl executed a very short bow. His hand barely reached the middle of a generous belly—a belly so big it was doubtful he could see his feet. Even feet as large as his. They were size 30s (if there is such a thing), and bare. Tufts of fire red hair on the knuckles of his toes.

"Ronin is the ninth reindeer in Santa's crew. You've never heard of him. No one has. Also, I'm obligated to inform you not to touch him."

"Why?" Sandy asked.

"Look at him." Two streams of steam shot from the reindeer's nostrils. A big, black eye turned on them again. "Would you like to hear his story?"

"We're in a bit of a hurry," Marie said.

"You know what they say about hurries," Garl said. "Hurries make blurries."

A smile turned his cheeks as red as the hair on his toes. Sandy said, "That doesn't make sense."

"We're looking for Princess Pirlipat," Marie said.

"Fine choice. Fine choice, indeed." He snapped his fingers, but no sound was made. "The king and queen's daughter, yes. Poor girl. You've heard the rumors. I'm not one to gossip, but her face…" He wiggled his hand in front of his nose. "And her head…" He extended his hands. Then more upbeat, he said, "So, you want to go to the castle?"

"Castle, yes."

"We can't take you to the castle."

"Why not?"

"Road's too narrow. You see that." He pointed at Ronin's antlers. They fanned the air when he turned his head. "Can't fit. Road's too sticky. Not good for sleighs. It's always crowded and—hey, no touching!"

The tip of Sandy's stick was reaching for Ronin's hindquarters.

"He'll swat you like a bug. Grind your bones into dust." Garl shook his tiny fists. "He'll stomp you so deep into the ground you'll need an elevator to climb out."

Ronin lifted his head and loosed a howl that shook the trees. It vibrated in Marie's chest. It was raw power. A layer of sand trickled off Sandy. Ronin swung his head around and fixed a baseball-sized eye on Garl.

"Eh-hem." Garl nodded. "Very well. It seems he likes you."

"I knew it," Sandy said. "So I can touch?"

"Go on. Be quick."

Sandy poked Ronin in the leg. Fritz reached up to stroke his fur. Muscles rippled beneath the dense hide. His tail swished about and knocked Sandy's arm off. Garl snickered. He began to lecture them about what he said. As impressive as this reindeer was—somewhere between the size of a rhino and an elephant—Marie wanted to get to the castle before Aunt Rinks came home. Garl was sweet, in an odd way, but just as distracted as her brother and his sandman were. Why did they need someone to take them where they wanted to go? *This is a story. We can start anywhere.*

"Once upon a time," she started, "we were at the castle."

They looked at her. She thought about clicking her heels.

"Your journey starts in Candy Meadow," Garl said. "Besides, you asked that already."

"Then where can you take us?"

"Now that is a fine question." He raised a finger and began.

They could go to Orange Brook, which he said was fine this time of year, but a little sweet for his taste. Lemonade River, which was a bit sour right now. Molasses River came highly recommended. It was deep and rich; the salted nippers were spawning. Gingerbreadville was a tourist destination. Far too crowded at any time of year, as far as he was concerned. Bonbon Town was for locals. A nice art scene, if they were into that (he wasn't). Paper Land was industrial. All anyone wanted to do there was work for King Chocolate.

"And Confectionville. The hub of this great valley that surrounds Marchpane Castle."

"That castle?" Marie pointed at the mud castle.

"That one. It was much finer at one time. You should have seen it. The walls gleamed, and the spires soared. A beacon of hope, a symbol of home. Now, it's, uh... it's that."

"What happened?" Sandy asked.

"Things change." He cleared his throat.

"Is Confectionville the closest we can get?" Marie said.

"It is," he said. And they'd best be going before the Yellow Throated Sour Picklers began to swarm. Whether that was bad or not didn't matter. Marie was ready to go. They climbed onto the bench behind Garl that was cushioned and warm. Sandy bounced around and settled in. Garl seemed a little annoyed at the mess he was making—sand all over the floor—but didn't say anything.

"Hands and feet inside the sleigh at all times. This sleigh does not move until seat belts are fastened. We aim to amuse and serve here at Ronin Express. Above all else, we do it safely."

He snapped a long belt around his waist. Marie and Fritz did the same. Sandy did, too; although it didn't seem like that would help him should something happen. He would just crumble.

Ronin snorted. Garl asked if they were ready.

Marie was so caught up in the moment, she forgot to check her phone. If she did, she would've seen her aunt and uncle driving toward them.

THEY HAD BOARDED A ROCKET.

Heads thrown back, the sleigh jiggled. The ground below them walloped with hooves as heavy as falling trees. Bits of dirt and debris showered down on them. The wind drew tears from their eyes and howled in their ears, shearing whatever Garl said into distant nonsense.

Marie grabbed Fritz. Fritz grabbed Sandy.

They knocked into each other, tossed back and forth as the sleigh wobbled. It teetered on one rail, then the other, shooshed through the grass. Then suddenly... their stomachs dropped into their socks and pinned them to the back of their seat. The sleigh dipped below Ronin's churning legs. He pedaled like he was scaling a mountain. Up, up, up they drove toward the pink sky. The black square hovered above them like a four-cornered moon.

Marie caught tiny gulps of air. Fritz ducked his head, holding his hat to keep it from flying off. It was like being strapped to an airplane wing. She was about to duck behind Garl's seat when the wind began to die down. In seconds, it was silent. She wiped her face. They were peacefully sailing high above the valley.

"That's better," Garl said. "I thought you would want to experience the raw takeoff."

Fritz was gasping. Sandy was a narrower version of himself. A layer of sand had been sheared away. A strange bubble wrapped around the sleigh. Like looking through water.

"It warps the view," Garl said, "but at least we can breathe. Anyway, everyone still buckled? Good. We're going to be turning in a minute—"

The turn came sooner than that. Ronin leaned sharply to the left. The sleigh swung like a water tube behind a speedboat. Marie smashed into Fritz and Sandy like a collapsing accordion. Garl, meanwhile, pointed out the sights as the sleigh turned on its side. The muscles on Ronin's back rolled like waves.

"Orange Brook," Garl shouted. "The perfume is quite a treat, a bouquet of vanilla pudding and cherry raisins."

That smell was lost in the musky scent of Ronin's efforts. A turn in the other direction sent Sandy and Fritz crashing into her. (She didn't understand what all the turning was about.) They soared over Lemonade River; its sunshine water rippled in sugary waves. Up ahead was Molasses River, a richly dense body of water that cut into the valley like a vein of silk.

"Funny story, the Molasses River. It was discovered at the Gumdrop Mine by accident. They thought they'd hit a vein of taffy when the first drops of molasses oozed out. Before long, it was flowing—hang on, quick drop."

Ronin plummeted so quickly he disappeared. The screams Marie had bottled up were drowned out by the terrorized shrieks coming from Sandy. He clawed at Fritz like a cat going over a waterfall. The sleigh was going down. Ronin extended his legs and glided like a flying squirrel. Garl continued the story about the Molasses River that no one heard.

Ronin arched his back. Slowly, the skydive arced into a gradual descent.

"Approaching Icing Road," Garl announced. "All passengers return their seats to an upright position. We thank you for flying Ronin Express and hope you fly again soon."

They drifted toward what looked like a white frosted lane. Toasted houses zoomed past on both sides. A moment of silence was abruptly broken by thumping hooves. The sleigh bounced three times before it began skidding on the rails. Ronin was in full stride. The end of the road sped toward them.

Ronin locked all four legs in front of him. The sleigh bumped into his rear. Ice shavings flew from the deep tracks carved beneath his hooves. The shavings were sweet and tangy as they melted on Marie's face.

"Oh no," Garl said. "Brace!"

Marie didn't like that sound. She knew what he meant by the narrow road. Where Icing Road ended, a one-lane road paved with spongy gumdrops continued between two-story gingerbread structures. Ronin's antlers would destroy them like a plow through snowdrifts. His hooves dug deeper. The sleigh began tipping forward. The seatbelts kept them from tumbling onto Ronin's backside. The grinding hooves cut deeper.

Boom!

The sleigh dropped on the ground. Marie collapsed into her brother. Sandy looked like a slushy poured into the seat. A few seconds later, Gurl popped up from the front.

"Perfect landing!"

Gumdrop Alley, Garl called it.

A skinny road paved with lumpy treats that would knock your teeth out if you drove too fast. The gutters along the curbs were slick tracks of shiny fruit tape. Gumdrop Alley was lined with two-story gingerbread buildings. The seams were spackled with white icing, the walls (toasted to perfection) decorated with candy beads and breath mints, marshmallows, and raisins. Flower boxes spilled bundles of candy corn beneath awnings propped on cinnamon sticks.

The jellybean sidewalks were mostly empty. Those who were walking on it had stopped to watch Ronin stick a landing that was inches away from tearing down a wall or two. Marie expected them to be afraid. Relieved, maybe. They started wandering toward the sleigh, a motley bunch of rag dolls and plastic dancers, superheroes and smiling goblins. There were also gingerbread people and mini-elves with giant feet, gremlins with pointed ears.

Doors began opening. Heads poked out. They started toward the sleigh. Walking, at first. Then hopping. Then sprinting. Marie grabbed her brother. She was wrong. They weren't afraid or relieved. *They're angry.*

The mob was coming for them. Garl jumped out of the sleigh and waddled to the front. He slung a sack over his shoulder. Ronin lowered his head and snorted. *What's in Garl's bag?* Marie thought. She wondered if they leaped out of Candyland now, would this stop before someone got hurt?

"All right, all right!" Garl shouted. "Everyone, please. Get in a line."

Their pilot dropped the sack on Gumdrop Alley. The mob jockeyed for position, coming together in a single file down the middle of the multicolored road. It formed ten feet from Ronin's snout, which snuffled at Garl's sack. Garl tugged the twine that tied it shut.

"Mary Popkins, you're first."

The shaggy doggy with a pink bow between her ears trotted closer. Garl reached into the sack and pulled a grassy cube out. He gave it to Mary Popkins. The toy doggy balanced the treat on her pink bow. Ronin gave it a sniff, then pulled it between his rubbery lips. Mary Popkins hopped with joy.

"What's happening?" Sandy said.

Marie was caught up in the spectacle and, for a second, forgot where they were and why. Her heart was still recovering from the death ride through the sky. That wasn't what she had in mind when she'd wished for a sleigh pulled by a flying reindeer. *What is this place?*

It was a story that had already been written by her great-aunt Corker, she guessed. And Great-Uncle Corker had turned it into a game. Marie looked at the black square in the sky again. *These people don't know they're not real.* They weren't people, but she didn't know what else to call them. A bout of vertigo swirled her head like a bowl of noodles. *Is this real?*

The longer they were in Candyland, the easier it was to forget. This world smelled like sweets, felt like a song. *It's inside a ball!* she reminded herself. *This isn't any more real than a video game.*

The castle loomed in the distance. It was difficult to judge how far away it was. It was a mountain of fudge that pierced the hovering clouds of cotton candy. The details were smudgy and faint. The day was bright and pink, but she felt like they were standing in the castle's shadow. A hard, cold breeze wafted from the castle like it was a block of ice.

Fritz and Sandy leaped out of the sleigh. Garl let them cut in line, put blocks of grassy food in Fritz's hands for Ronin to grind between his teeth. Marie leaned over as Garl called up the next in line, a blocky robot with light bulb eyes.

"Garl," she said, "how much farther?"

Garl rose a foot taller when he stood on the toes of his giant feet. "The line, it goes back a block, methinks."

"Not the line. To the castle."

"Oh, that. You can walk there in a day."

"A day?" Ronin nudged her before she fell into him. "It'll take us a day to walk there?"

"Me, a day. I've got these." He wiggled his blocky toes. "You, half a day. But what's your hurry?"

"We're on a journey."

"Well, then, good news. You're already here."

A small family of trolls with fiery hair approached. They vibrated as they walked. Fritz helped pass out the reindeer treats. When he stroked the trolls' hair, they squeaked. What would happen if Marie wasn't there to remind him where they were? Would he forget what that black square in the sky was? This was a journey, not a destination. They belonged out there. Did anyone understand that?

"Garl, do you know where you are?" she asked.

He turned his head on blunt shoulders. Then he lifted one hand and saluted her. Said, "Do you?"

That struck her as odd. Did he know where he was, that this wasn't real, or did he give her another riddle? She seemed to think it was neither. His answer meant something else, and she didn't know what. *He knows why I'm here better than I do.*

"You know, I hear cookie cutters go quite fast if you take them down the gutter. Too bad there isn't a store." He handed her a treat. "Not that I know of."

Ronin raised his head, careful not to bash anyone with the bony trees growing out of the sides of his head. His nostrils flared, blowing hot air into her face. Her reflection looked back from his black eyes, which blinked slowly. She held out the treat. He took it with guttural appreciation. This was the journey. What was her hurry?

The longer the journey took, the more nothing would change. That was the secret hope she clung to, the reason she believed Fritz and Sandy when they told her a little toy soldier had told them they had to go on the journey.

Journeys lead to change.

Gumdrop Alley was nothing but edible rowhouses. No one was selling cookie cutters (whatever that was). Not a single storefront in sight.

"Once upon a time…"

TWO LOLLIPOPS WERE under a red awning. They were side by side, spinning like pinwheels, the colors bleeding in a dizzy vortex. The window behind them, broad and foggy, had words painted on it as thick as cake icing. *Hussar Peregrinations,* it read.

Something went wrong, was Marie's first thought. She'd wished for a cookie cutter store. She'd also wished for a monster truck and got the Ronin Express instead. Written in small print, stenciled in red goo from a piping bag, was a line just below the storefront name. *Licensed Cookie Cutter Specialist.*

There were hazy objects on the other side of the window. She cupped her hands against it.

"Party's back there, kid." Sandy and Fritz reluctantly walked up. The crowd around Ronin had grown larger and stranger.

"That's not why we're here."

"Hussar Peregrinations," Sandy read. "This is what you wished for?"

The doorknob was a jawbreaker the size of a cue ball on a slab of hard candy. She opened the door and ducked under the low frame. There was no bell to greet them. Only the smell of burnt maple syrup and peanut butter. There were stacks of cookies as big as trash lids, pretzel logs against the wall, apple crates filled with button pops, buckets of pixie sticks. A narrow alley wound between the clutter to a countertop dusted with flour and doughy stars that hadn't been baked. Behind it looked like a short-order kitchen with tickets on a wheel. It smelled like an apple pie had just come out of the oven.

"Push." The tip of Sandy's stick clicked on a puffy button below a handwritten sign that read exactly that. Marie wasn't in time to stop him.

It set off a chain reaction of mouse traps and dominoes, a clawing crane, a fan blowing a Ping-Pong ball. A baseball fell into a catcher's mitt and rolled behind the cook's window. It fell into a metal bowl. A few seconds later, a bell went off.

Something shuffled. Toothpicks snapped. There was a drilling sound, then hammering. A small door opened below the cook's window. A plank stuck out like the tongue on a cuckoo clock. A soldier stood on it. Big hat, square jaw, bushy eyebrows. A scabbard on the belt. Not Nussknacker, the tuft of white hair on the chin was different, and the jacket was green. But a nutcracker, all right.

He took one stiff-legged step onto the dusty counter. His head turned mechanically, first toward Fritz, then Sandy. When he saw Marie, his jaw snapped closed. He gave a crisp salute in her direction.

"Welcome to Hussar Peregrinations," he barked. His wooden jaw clapped up and down when he spoke. "How may I serve?"

"Do you have cookie cutters?" she asked.

"This is a bike store."

"Looks more like a *parts* store," Sandy said.

Marie poked him. Sand trickled onto the floor. "Are you Hussar?" she asked.

"No. I *am* a hussar."

"Right. What's that?"

His eyebrows pinched together. "A soldier, of course. Peregrination is my assignment."

"That's it." Sandy tapped the counter. "Wandering journey. That's what it means. Clever. We're in the right place, Mar Mar."

"I believe you are. Pate is my name. What kind of bike interests you?"

"A fast one," Marie said.

"How fast?"

"The fastest."

"I see. And where will you go?"

"To the castle." When the eyebrows pinched together again, she added, "Marchpane Castle. We're looking for Princess Pirlipat."

"Ah, yes. Poor girl," he said and shook his head. "I have many options to offer, then. There is a dough beater that will get you there in two hours. It's reliable, very comfortable. The Slim Jim slider will take an hour. It's stylish. Very popular with the muppets. We also have—"

"How about the cookie cutter?"

His jaw hung open for a long moment. Then he said, almost reluctantly, "Two minutes."

"We'll take it."

"I don't think so."

"What? Why not?"

"Have you ridden a bike before?" he asked.

"Since we were five years old," Marie said.

"I mean truly ridden a bike. Become one with it?"

"We know how to ride a bike," Sandy said. "We want the cookie cutter."

Pate marched back and forth on the counter, his head twisting in their direction each time he turned. He stroked the tufted beard with his left hand. His right arm dangled loosely at his side. It wobbled in the socket with each step.

"I only have one," he said.

"One?" Marie considered wishing for another, but she had a feeling that wasn't going to happen.

"I'm very slow these days. You can't just slap a cookie cutter together with jam and peanut butter."

"I hope not," Sandy said.

"It takes time and precision to make what you're asking for. One wrong turn and you'll be a pat of butter on the pavement. I am a licensed cookie cutter specialist. Only the best and nothing less."

He was stern and verbose. His voice projected in military rhythm that could make them do what he wanted. He was also wasting time. She was about to just ask for the Slim Jim slider when Sandy spoke.

"It's the arm, isn't it?"

Pate's head swiveled like a turret. His eyes narrowed to slits. Air hissed between rows of wooden teeth. Then he said: "They were hiding in the abandoned Gum Drop Mine. No one had thought to find them there, but we'd received word they were. They were multiplying deep underground. The tunnels go everywhere throughout the land, under the rivers and lakes, beneath the roads. It's dangerous belowground. Easy to get lost. But not for them."

"Who are *they*?" Sandy asked.

"Mice." Pate hissed the word. "No one believed they'd returned, but the rumors are true. We had them cornered in the Cinnamon Swirl corridor. Desperate and hungry, they mounted a counterattack." He lifted his good hand to his eyes, shook his head. "I lost a good many hussars that day. I was lucky to survive, sent here with this."

His right arm swung like a string.

"But now we know they are coming. The return of their leaders is imminent, I'm afraid. Now I make bikes."

"And we'll take one," Marie said. "Can we just—"

"Who are the leaders?" Sandy said.

Pate dropped to his knees. They hit the counter like wooden knobs. He fell to one hand, his left hand. Sandy and Fritz leaned in. Marie did, too.

"The Mouseking," he whispered. "And Mouse—" He snapped his jaw shut, shook his head.

"What were you going to say?" Sandy said.

"It's bad luck to utter her name."

"It's okay. We won't tell."

This time he added, "The Mouse *Queen*."

"Queen?" Sandy repeated. "You couldn't say the word *queen*?"

"When they return," Pate continued, "the mice will rise up. They will nibble at the foundation of Marchpane Castle, eat all of the king's lard and sausage, and continue to curse Princess Pirlipat (poor girl). Darkness will fill the skies for the rest of time. The battle will be lost if not for the return of the lost hussar."

"Who's that?" Sandy said.

"No one knows." He stood up, saluted. "Not even the lost hussar."

MARIE LOST TRACK OF TIME. The sense of urgency disappeared in the hussar's story. She was missing something in what Pate was saying. This was part of the story, somehow. She repeated over and over in her head what he'd said but couldn't find the answer. She felt a sharp twinge in her side.

"Marie." Sandy poked her again. "Yes or no?"

"What?"

Pate waited for an answer to a question she didn't hear. "One cookie cutter?" he repeated.

"Yes. Yes, we'll take it."

"Great. And what will you give for it?"

"Pardon?"

"It's not free. I have bills to pay like every citizen in the Alley."

Marie dug into her pockets. She dumped a crinkled wad of one-dollar bills on the counter. Fritz threw two quarters, a dime and three pennies next to it. Pate stared at the money. Just under four dollars wasn't enough. Marie checked her back pockets.

"What's that?" Pate said.

"It's three dollars and sixty-three cents."

The eyebrows pinched. He kicked the bills and poked at a quarter with the toe of his boot.

"I think he means *what's money?*" Sandy said.

It was just paper and round wheels of metal. It meant nothing here. He booted the bills onto the floor. "Come back when you have something I can use."

"No, wait," Marie said. "Peregrination. We're on a peregrination."

"Aren't we all." He saluted with his good arm. "Best of luck. And clean up the sand on your way out."

He did a crisp one-eighty and marched toward the cuckoo-clock plank to return to the back room. The broken arm swung wide when he turned. It rattled and flopped against his stomach and around to his back before slapping his stomach again.

"Wait!"

Marie pulled the ribbon off her head—the silky white ribbon Godfather had given her—and tied it into a loop. Her hair fell into her eyes as she motioned for Pate to step closer. She took his right arm gently.

"Does that hurt?"

He shook his head. She went about fashioning a sling that held snug against the front of his brass-button jacket. When she was done, he bent at the hip. The arm did not flop forward. He twisted back and forth, bending his knees. It held firm. Finally, he brandished the sword in his free hand. It slinked from the scabbard, its silver edge glinting. They watched him slice the air, pivot and parry, spin and leap, sticking the toothpick-length blade into the countertop. He stood as stiff as a flagpole and, once again, saluted Marie.

She saluted back. It seemed the thing to do.

He stepped back onto the cuckoo-clock plank, leaving his sword behind, and returned to the back room. Marie held her breath, wondering if she'd done something wrong. Somewhere in the back, a gear turned, and a latch clicked. The start of another mouse trap had begun, only this time it did not end with a doorbell.

Pate returned to the counter. He plucked the sword from the counter.

"I am indebted for your gift. I will return to the battle, to fight for our land. To honor our king and queen."

A door opened next to the counter.

"May the Christmas spirit guide you."

NOW SHE KNEW why it was called a cookie cutter. It wasn't what she expected. No steel wheels or sharp edges. Two giant cookies were attached to a frame of toffee sticks. The seat was long and curved and yellow. It was a banana.

It did not exude speed. In fact, there were no pedals or chain (or licorice whip) to drive the back cookie wheel. Just crude handlebars and a set of foot pegs. She wheeled it across the bumpy road.

"This is the fastest bike?" Sandy said, hopping across Gumdrop Alley. "It's definitely dangerous, but fast?"

Crumbs fell from the wheels, leaving a trail from the store. Pate had already turned a sign in the window that read CLOSED. Marie went to the slick gutter between the road and gingerbread buildings. An egg-shaped toy was on the sidewalk, licking a lollipop. A plastic tongue darted from its mouth, watching them center the cookies on the gutter.

Marie checked the time on her phone. They had an hour before Aunt Rinks came home. Maybe two. There was no way they would reach the castle on this. Halfway, maybe. There was also the issue of Sandy. There was enough room on the banana for her and Fritz. Sandy would crumble if they put him on it. She considered leaving him behind, but she needed him. So did Fritz.

The building behind the lollipop-licking egg was under construction (new walls had been pasted together). A pile of gingerbread crumbs and icing were on the sidewalk. She found a long strand of red licorice in it. She lassoed it through the frame and tied loops at the other end.

"What's that for?" Sandy said. She harnessed the licorice around his midsection and lower half. "You're kidding," he said.

"Either this or meet us there."

"Seriously? I can walk faster than that cookie machine. You don't even know how it works. It doesn't have pedals!"

That much was true.

Fritz climbed onto the front of the banana. Marie was behind him. They grabbed the hard-baked handlebars. The seat was mushy and formed to their behinds. The banana skin didn't split. So far, so good.

"Give us a push," Marie said.

"You want me to push us all the way to the castle?"

"Just get us started."

Sandy's sticks jabbed into her back. He just poked at first, barely trying. "We could've walked there by now," he whined. "You got robbed, you know. The ribbon is worth way more than this."

The little egg blinked its painted eyes, pointed the lollipop at the bottom of the bike. She put her foot on one of the pegs. It vibrated on the sole of her foot, sending waves through her leg. It tingled up her spine. She gripped the handlebars tighter.

"It's not a total loss," Sandy continued. "You hungry, Fritz? I am. Maybe just a nibble off the back wheel."

"A little faster," Marie said.

"Sure, make the sandman do all the work." The sticks dug deeper into her back. "Why don't I just carry you?"

The momentum picked up. Marie put both feet on the pegs. Fruity fumes wafted from beneath her. The cookie cutter stopped wobbling. It had locked into the gutter. It paused like a slingshot pulling back.

"Hold on," she whispered into Fritz's ear.

Sandy said, "Are you even helping? I'm about to sprain a—"

WWWWWHHHHHHHEEEEEEEE!

The cookie wheels were brown blurs. Two disks that didn't even appear to turn. The only sounds were the howling wind and Sandy's screams. Marie's hair whipped across her eyes. Tiny specks spit from the front wheel and stung her cheeks. She didn't dare let go of the handlebars or look behind her. The cookie cutter, somehow, remained steady in the center of the gutter. The buildings on both sides of the road became one long beige smudge.

The castle grew like a stain spreading into the sky.

A red hue began to color the surroundings. It looked like the sun was setting at the end of the road. Marie hunkered against Fritz, peering over his shoulder. Tears streamed from the corners of her eyes. The glow was getting brighter. It was coming from a red puddle up ahead. As they sped closer, it turned into the sun-bleached color of Fritz's worn-out hat.

Where the road ended at Rose Lake.

MARIE TOOK one foot off the peg. The high-pitched vibrations that had numbed her legs dropped a pitch. The spray of cookie crumbs felt less like a sand blaster on their cheeks. She dropped her other foot. The lake was still approaching at full speed. In a matter of seconds, the cookie cutter slowed as if it had hit a puddle of slag. Their hands—aching from the grip—hung on tight enough to keep them from flipping over the handlebars.

They came to a full stop before driving into the deep end of the rose-colored water. Ears ringing. Eyes itching and faces chafing. They looked around, panting. The road continued to their left and right. It was crowded and diverse. The sidewalks filled with tents and tables of goods—trinkets and food and such. A market that seemed oddly familiar.

Marie's attention was drawn to Marchpane Castle.

It blotted out much of the pink sky. And they still weren't next to it. Rose Lake went around it. The castle was a deep bruise on an island. Even the lake's rosy hue didn't affect the dark monolith. Scaffolding was anchored into the walls; a multitude of spires forked upwards and pierced the delicate sky. It was mean and gorgeous at the same time. Immoveable and fragile. A mesmerizing essence that was hard to look away from. It emanated a breath of its own, a coldness that carried over the rosy water like the promise of a storm. It filled her head; sank its teeth into her bones.

Something about it didn't feel right. It pretended to be beautiful while hiding a secret.

"You cold?" Sandy was shockingly slender. He'd lost half his body on the ride there. His voice had gone up an octave. "You look cold."

She was shivering and couldn't stop. The castle beckoned her to come closer and begged her to stay away. It was a terrible contradiction. An itch that hurt to scratch.

"Once upon a time..." she started, but couldn't finish. The words lodged in her throat. She swallowed hard and tried again.

Fritz took her arm. It startled her. She jerked away, said she was sorry. He shook his head. Sandy said in her brother's voice, "What's wrong?"

"I... I don't know."

The journey—this peregrination—had become a dizzying drop into conflicting emotions and confusion. A destiny she couldn't avoid.

"Hey there. Pardon me." Sandy slid into the road. "How do we get over there?"

He'd stopped a line of dwarves. Seven of them. Each wearing frumpy clothes of vivid colors. Thick white beards and thicker eyebrows. Hair grew from their ears. The lead dwarf stopped, and the others bumped into each other in succession. Each dwarf looked at the dwarf behind like falling dominos. The last one in line looked at the busy market.

"Marchpane Castle?" the lead dwarf asked. "No visitors allowed."

"Why not?"

"To protect the princess," the second in line said. Then all of them said, "Poor girl."

A barge was in the rosy water. It would take a good walk to get to it. Marie wasn't going to take the cookie cutter through such a crowded market. The barge was being loaded with crates.

"What if we found a boat?" Sandy said. "Would someone stop us?"

They shook their heads. "Boats sink," the third dwarf said. "It's the water."

That didn't make sense. The barge wasn't sinking. "What about that?" Sandy pointed at the barge.

"Shipment from King Chocolate in Paper Land," the fourth dwarf said.

"To make the castle bigger," the fifth one said.

"Thicker," said the sixth one.

"One day," the last one squeaked, "it'll swallow Rose Lake."

As if that was all the words they had, they began their march with bulky sacks thrown over their shoulders. Humming as they bounced on their heels. Sandy followed them with more questions.

Marie watched the barge get heavier. *To make the castle bigger.*

There were street performers wandering in the crowd. Skinny jugglers with elastic arms. Dancers spinning like tops. Twirlers threw themselves above the crowd as Christmas music echoed across the water. Dwarves and elves, toys and animals, and things she couldn't explain walked or rolled or sprang or hopped. They entertained and argued, laughed and danced. A thriving collection of this world's inhabitants. *One day the castle will swallow Rose Lake.*

Why is it getting bigger and thicker? Is that the journey, to stop the castle from growing?

Her thoughts spread out and followed all the possibilities. She thought of how they could get across the water when she realized she was looking at a tall couple in the crowd. They were wearing cloaks with the hoods drawn over their heads. It wasn't their size or dark clothing that struck her as odd. Her heart ached to stop them.

They're human!

"Hey!"

She waved her arms and ran towards them. They couldn't hear her shouting over the crowd and music. She was slowed by dancers and jugglers and a wobbly cart rolling on rotting apple cores. The cloaked couple walked in the direction of the barge.

"Stop!"

She jumped onto the sidewalk and ran around tents. Sandy was calling her name, but she couldn't stop. She had to get to the couple. She could feel it like the castle calling her and pushing her away. She tripped over a skateboard rolling on its own (was it alive?) and stumbled into a cart. It tipped over. A thousand nuts spilled into the road, bouncing between legs and wheels. The hussars minding the cart (*Support the Troops* was written on the side) gaped at the nuts rolling away, their square jaws dropping open.

They helped her up. "I'm so sorry," she said. "Who is that?"

She pointed at the cloaked couple, who were even farther away now. They had reached the barge and were conversing with the crew loading boxes from King Chocolate in Paper Land.

"The king and queen," one of the hussars said.

Marie's hands involuntarily balled into frightened fists. Her jaw clenched and unclenched. A fresh wave of cold anxiety passed over her. Gooseflesh rose on her arms. She'd lost all will to run.

"Marie." Sandy looked around at the mess. The hussars were already cleaning up. "Look, look."

Fritz handed her his phone. At first, she didn't know what she was looking at. Her vision was blurred, her attention distracted. It was his location app.

"We have to go back," Sandy said. "Now."

THE AIR WAS UNPLEASANT. It was thick and oppressive. Had the stink of rotting wood and clothes that needed washing. The colors were bland, even the red lights on the wall.

Marie's knuckles ached. She unclenched her hands. White crescents dug into her palms. Her cheeks raw. She felt as fragile as a dry cookie.

Fritz quickly snapped the gift closed and put it in the wall, sliding the blocks into place. Sandy was gone. They stood still, listening for movement outside their bedroom. She wiped the cookie cutter crumbs off her clothes. Fritz did the same. They checked their phones again. Aunt Rinks's and Uncle Vernon's locations still weren't showing up. It was an hour till supper. Marie opened the door to the storefront. Nothing had changed. Nothing from the market had followed them back.

They circled around to the kitchen. No dwarves with lumpy sacks were at the table. No aunt or uncle, either. She peeked out the window, told Fritz to see if the car was parked out front. She opened the door to their bedroom. Her journal was on the workbench, the pages still empty. Nussknacker stood guard. He felt different somehow. More intimate. Like she could feel the stiffness of his body.

Will we have to start over? she wondered. She would go back to Candyland that night. If they appeared in Candy Meadow, she could make better time getting to Confectionville and the market. *All the way to the barge.*

This wasn't a game. This was a journey she had to finish.

"Marie." Sandy slid into the bedroom with Fritz. "There's no car. You have to see this, though."

They went out the kitchen door. Something had come back with them. The backyard jungle was gone. Lights were strung through the tree canopies. The paths were cleared and the patio clean. New chairs faced a warm fire in the firepit. Off to the side, a fountain was bubbling in a koi pond of rosy water. A hint of peppermint was in the air.

How were they going to explain this? Godfather's elves had come during the middle of the day and no one saw them? And what if someone had been driving by when it happened?

They would never have to explain that, though. No one saw it. And Aunt Rinks and Uncle Vernon wouldn't come home that night.

Marie and Fritz waited by the fire until it was dark. The moon was out. The lights in the trees looked like stars. Every time she checked her phone, nothing appeared. Neither of them had an appetite. Marie read the note Aunt Rinks had left that morning. Then she remembered something. A small clue that told her exactly where her aunt and uncle were.

She got up. She went to their bedroom and stood at the door. When Marie and Fritz had gone to Candyland that morning, she had locked the door. When they returned, the latch was undone. There was only one way that could have happened.

"Nussknacker knows where they are," Sandy said.

21

I t smelled different. Like a wet dog in a peppermint bath that still smelled like a dog.

The amazement Rinks had felt the first time she'd dropped into Candyland had dulled to a passing head turn. This was just a next-generation video game as far as she was concerned. Cool, at first. At the end of the day, just another video game.

Candy Meadow was empty. The chocolate stream and the dumb, useless gate was all there was. And the rickety bridge. Something rustled in the candy-cane woods. Twigs snapped from the right.

"Go look," Rinks said.

Vern hopped over the chocolate stream, not before dipping his finger in it for a taste, and stepped between the red and white striped trunks. If the kids were in there, he wouldn't find them. He couldn't find the car if he was sitting in it. Rinks knew where the brats went. They were on the other side of the valley. Toward that brown stain on the horizon.

Turd Mountain.

It was probably an amazing castle up close, chocolatey walls carved with smiling gargoyles wearing elf hats and throwing presents every time the bell rang. From this distance, it looked like an accident. She didn't want to walk that far. Not now, not ever. There were other ways to catch her traitorous niece and nephew.

The bridge was a little wobbly. The pretzel posts were leaning. She climbed over it instead of wading through the stream. The grass on the other side shimmered with a coat of sugar water. Something had dug a long patch of divots. The grass had been turned over and pawed at.

"Vern!"

He came trotting along the stream, chewing on a branch like jerky. She didn't ask why he was eating a tree. Only pointed at the ground. He grunted, nodding like he did when something puzzling came up. She waited for him to say it, counting down in her head, and then right on time he said it.

"Interestin'."

He got on one knee, brushed his fingers in the dirt. Smelled them. Ate a clump of it like it was cake. He looked back over the bridge, over the trees beyond. He raised his hands like he was framing a picture. Rinks rolled her eyes.

"Somethin' landed," he said. "Then took off again."

She didn't see how he got to that. Then he pointed to the long dents in the ground. There were two of them that trailed through the divots. They went about thirty yards and stopped.

"Look at the size of that," he said. "Look."

He held his hands a foot apart like he was showing her what he caught with a fishing pole. She took a closer look, noticed the cloven print about the size of a frying pan.

"What is it?" she said.

He palmed the stubble on his chin. "Well, that's a moose print, for sure. Or the world's biggest caribou."

"You know animal prints now?"

"No. But those lines right there look like rails. Like it was pullin' somethin'."

He looked at her, waiting for her to put it together. She didn't know exactly what a caribou was—like a big deer or elk—but she knew where he was going with it. Something made those tracks, and an animal was pulling it.

"What're you sayin'?" she said.

"I'm sayin' a reindeer picked the kids up."

"You said caribou."

"Reindeer. Caribou. Same thing."

"It ain't the same thing."

"Whatever, Rinks. It's a flyin' one. And it was pullin' a sleigh."

She started laughing. The kind of cruel laughter a school-ground bully would do before making fun of an idiot.

"Look around, Rinks. This place is Christmas. Rules don't apply here like they do up there." He pointed at the box in the sky. "You hear the music out there. You don't think Santa's reindeer are grazin' round here? Anythin's possible!"

She couldn't argue that point. Those were caribou or reindeer prints. Those were sled tracks. *And anythin' is possible.* If the kids got a ride, they were probably already at the castle by now. Vern stuck his fingers in his mouth and ripped a high-pitched whistle. Then called out Santa's reindeer names. He got as far as Vixen before having to sing the song to remember the other ones.

Nothing dropped out of the sky for them.

"Let's go back." She sighed. "We can wait for them to come out, surprise them in their room."

"Why?"

"Because that big pile of mud is, like, five hundred miles away. We ain't walkin' to it."

"It ain't that far."

"And we don't even know that's where they went. What, we're goin' to just walk around and hope we find them pettin' a reindeer that stopped to take a leak?"

He thumbed his phone. This was ridiculous. If they'd come home earlier, they could've caught them before they left. Now they could be anywhere.

"They're at the castle," he said.

"You don't know that."

He showed her his phone. An icon with Marie's face was far away from them and in the direction of the castle. That meant the location was working (which seemed odd, but what else was new?).

He powered off his phone. "Turn your phone off."

"So what if they know we're here."

"We want to catch them by surprise, don't we? Let's just walk a little ways down there. Maybe one of those reindeer is grazin'. We can catch a ride. It can't hurt, Rinks. We're already here."

He took off with a bounce in his step. Rinks looked up at the box in the sky before following him. It was the last time she would see it for quite some time.

THAT RUSTLING they'd heard in Christmas Wood was following them. The sugar grass had become a narrow strip hemmed in by the trees. It sounded like little things scratching around in fallen leaves. She didn't like it.

And she was starving. Her last meal had been breakfast, and that had been a protein bar. Vern was munching on a handful of grass, the frosted blades sticking out between his lips like a cow. He stopped suddenly, put his hand out.

"Smell that?" He took several whiffs. "I think there's a stream right down the way. I'll bet it ain't water, either. Like lemonade or sports drink or something." He snapped his fingers. "Soda stream!"

The trees were near them on the left and right when she could hear water, too. Vern broke off a branch and handed it to her, told her to try it. He gnawed on it first. She gave it a nibble. It tasted like cinnamon toast. The buttery kind her mother used to make. She ate the whole thing. Vern kept on walking. Rinks went deeper into the trees to find a different branch. This one smelled like maple syrup on French toast with whipped cream. She took two bites. When she looked down, something was between her feet, holding up a twig for her to grab.

"Aaah!"

Rinks ran back to the field. The rustling grew louder. It was all around her now. Shadows were moving everywhere.

"Vern, come on. Let's go."

She was frozen in place. Something scurried out of the trees. A mouse stood on its hind legs, sniffing the air. It wore what looked like a tiny helmet. And it was holding a stick in its pink hand. A stick with a shiny tip.

"Don't move," Vern said.

Another mouse joined the first one. Then a third. After that, they came out in lines. Helmets and spears and swords and daggers. Standing up to sniff at them. Beady black eyes looking. There were hundreds of them. Maybe a million. They came from both sides, circling around them and lining up in formation. Many were injured. Blocks of rodent militia standing at the ready. Weapons at their sides.

"What are they doin'?" Rinks said.

Not a mouse was stirring or whisker did twitch. Eyes unblinking. Then the formation parted in the middle. An aisle opened between them. The last of the rodent army emerged from the trees. This one twice as big with a tail three times as long. The rat's fur was gray and coarse. He limped on his back feet, using a spear as a cane. He stopped five feet from Rinks, tested the air with his pink nose. He put a front paw on the shiny plate that covered his chest.

He bowed. They all bowed.

"What's happenin'?" Rinks said.

"They're bowin'."

"I see that. Why are they bowin'?"

Vern looked at her. "They bowin' to you."

That was how it looked. Why they were doing it couldn't be answered. The rat raised the spear and squeaked. Vern bent over to listen. The rat gestured with both hands, pointing toward the castle, pointing at Rinks.

"He wants to show us somethin'," Vern said.

"You speak rat now?"

"I don't need to speak it. Look at him."

"Ask him if it's the kids he wants to show us."

With that, the rat leaped and pointed. Hopping up and down like a subway rat that found a pizza box, he waved at Rinks and Vern. Clearly, he wanted to show them something.

"It's obvious, ain't it?" Vern said. "The way they're all lookin' at us. *At you,* Rinks. They don't want to hurt us."

"They got weapons, Vern."

"If they wanted to hurt us, they would've already."

Vern scratched his neck. The rash was bright red. Bumps were growing on the skin, but he didn't seem bothered. He wanted to follow them. What harm could it do just to look? Besides, if things got hairy, they could just leap out.

They didn't bother checking to see if the box was still in the sky before following the army into the trees.

THE CANDY-CANE TREES were replaced by bramble. Tangles of salted pasta wrapped around their feet and arms, stung their eyes when it caught in their hair. Twice Rinks almost turned around. The food forest cleared into glazed slabs of granite that stuck to the soles of their shoes and palms of their hands. The edges were brittle and sharp. At the bottom of a descending climb, they stepped in pasty mud that smelled like gooey peanut butter.

A narrow path led to a hole in the side of the hill. The mouse army lined up on both sides of the trail. They raised their weapons as Rinks and Vern approached. The rat captain or general or whatever he was—the important vermin—waited at the entrance. He raked a matchstick on the ground. A flame broke out. Sulfur wafted up. He hopped into the dark tunnel. Rinks and Vern peeked inside. Little spots of flickering light went way back.

The cave smelled like rock candy. The colorful rocks she used to eat when she was little.

"Seriously?" Rinks said.

"We come all this way." Vern shrugged. "Should at least look."

Rinks didn't follow her husband at first. She gave a hard think about turning back. She looked up, but the trees were overhead. She'd have to climb back to the clearing to see the box in the sky. She never thought it might not be there.

Sweet dust filled the cave. Rinks pulled her shirt over her mouth. Vern was a shadow ahead of her, coming into focus when he passed a matchstick stuck in the wall. The ground became thick and muddy, made sucking sounds with each step. It oozed over her shoes and soaked through her socks, cold and sticky. It smelled like fudge.

"I don't like this!" Her voice echoed the length of the cave.

Vern didn't answer or hesitate. He trucked ahead. A few steps later, Rinks felt a warm breath on her face that smelled like everything else. Yummy. The sound of the ocean slowly began to rise. A beige halo was at the top of a gentle slope. Vern stood at an opening with his hands braced against the walls. Several mice were at his sides with flaring matchsticks. General Rat held a tiny torch in each hand, watching Rinks slip on the floor.

She grabbed the back of Vern's shirt, wiping her hands on it before pulling herself next to him. There was a giant bowl in front of him. There was a handle on it. *It's a teacup.*

"It's beautiful," he muttered. "Look at it, Rinks."

It was a cavern, like the ones you paid money to go see. Instead of cheesy lights and clear streams, this one dripped from sugar-cone stalactites. A milk chocolate waterfall crashed on chocolate boulders. A river ran through a ledge that circled the cavern.

The rat general tapped the giant teacup with his matchstick. The flame sparked. It reminded her of one of those rides at the carnival, the one with spinning teacups that made you puke up an elephant ear.

"What's he doin'?" Rinks said.

"I think he wants us to get in."

"I don't think so."

"That's what it's for." Vern pointed down the slope that entered the cavern. "It's a ride."

"Are you outta your mind? I'm not gettin' in that thing, and neither are you."

The rat general tapped it again. It rang like a china plate.

"This ain't real, Rinks. It's just pretend. How can we *not* go on this ride?"

She stared at the stupidity dripping from his face. "How? How? We don't know where it goes."

"They do. That's why they brought us in here. Look at them." The mice waited patiently as their matchsticks burned close to their little pink fingers. "Besides, it's not like we're stuck here. If somethin' goes wrong, we just get out."

Vern wasn't thinking straight. First, he didn't understand that getting out required jumping at the door in the sky. They couldn't see the sky, for one. There was another problem they weren't aware of just yet.

"See? Look," he said.

The mice were jumping in actual teacups, the kind you drink from, and shoving down the slope. When they hit the stream, they floomed into the current, twisting and turning along the curved outer wall, circling down into the chocolate toilet bowl.

"It's just a ride." Vern threw one sloppy leg into the teacup. "Maybe we'll see the kids."

That was the one thing keeping Rinks from running out of the cave. It didn't hurt that the mice kept bowing to her. She didn't hate that.

"If we die," she said, "I'm gonna kill you."

Vern scratched his neck. "No one ever died on a chocolate slide before, Rinks."

He helped her into the teacup. There were benches inside it. And seatbelts. *Great.* The rat general and his minions gathered behind them and started to push. The mice chittered with excitement.

"Take us to the kids," Rinks said.

THERE HAD BEEN a log flume at the amusement park when Rinks was little. This was worse.

It started slowly enough. The cup circled as it dipped into the flow. Around the perimeter it began. Rock candy imbedded in the walls like unmined jewels. Farther down were jagged chunks of chocolate bars.

They picked up speed through the foam pit. The taste of coffee and cream on their lips. Bubbles in their hair. "I don't like this!" Rinks shouted.

Vern didn't hear her over the gurgle of a caramel geyser. The syrupy explosions splattered on racks of toffee. The teacup dropped down between spongy layers of cheesecake. Crumbly crust sprinkled over them. Rinks grabbed Vern's arm. She bent forward, kept her head down. She smelled cinnamon dust. Bright sprinkles rained into the teacup. A blob of ice cream melted down the back of her shirt.

"Vern! I want to go—"

She didn't see the last descent. They corkscrewed deeper into the hidden folds of the chasm. The slushing stream had become a gushing roar. The teacup shot up a steep incline. For a moment, it slowed. It was long enough for her to peek through sticky fingers. They were approaching the final drop.

Her screams were gobbled up in the rushing wind. She scratched at Vern. They held each other as close as the seatbelts would let them. Rinks in terror. Vern smiling through laughing shrieks. Above was a blurred excavation of desserts.

Then it was black.

They shot into a tunnel as dark as outer space. The roar had become a locomotive hurtling through their ears. Mushy specks stung their cheeks. Unexpected turns threw them one way, then the other. It was an endless waterslide through sticky nothingness.

Rinks babbled. Even she couldn't hear what came out of her mouth. It soothed her to rock back and forth, holding her stomach down to keep it from springing into her throat. It went on and on and on. It grew colder. She couldn't tell what direction they were sliding. Up or down or sideways. She just wanted it to end. When it did, she would make Vern pay.

At some point, they were going upward. Definitely upward. It warmed as they began to slow. The teacup wasn't spinning. She could hear herself panting. Her hair, matted and tangled, draped down her neck instead of flying behind her. They tipped one last time.

The teacup docked to a standstill.

Vern's face looked like an abstract painting. She was too weak to smack the goofy grin off it. Rinks wiped the mess out of her eyes. She'd passed through a confectionary birth canal and wanted to cry. Her clothes were ruined. Her scarf had flown off her head somewhere in the birth canal. Even worse. Her phone was soaked in a puddle of syrup. Everything was ruined. This whole thing was a bad, bad, bad idea.

Someone would pay for this. Not just Vern. The kids would pay dearly. This was a trap. And her idiot husband fell for it.

VERN CLIMBED OUT. Something was dripping. It sounded like a room, where they were. A humid, dank room. Her nose was clogged with vanilla ice cream and caramel and whatever else had flown in her face, but she could smell new things around her. Vinegar and vegetables. Fruit, too. Large things hung around them like bodies.

Vern was smelling them. Turning them around, fingers running up the sides of salted slabs of meat. He had his nose right up against it.

"All that," she croaked, "for a cellar? A cellar, Vern? We're in a cellar!"

He scurried to a wall and shelves filled with jars of pickled roots and preserved peaches. He sniffed his way to the far side of the room. Rinks struggled to get unstrapped. The buckle was slimed and slippery. By the time it clicked, a beam of light fell from the ceiling. Rinks threw her arm up to shield her eyes. A ladder unfolded. Vern climbed up on all fours.

"Vern? Vern, wait. Don't—"

She flopped out of the teacup. The dirt floor wasn't a sponge cake, and for some reason, Rinks was relieved. She wanted to breathe regular air and drink water. Above her, where the stairs led to a rectangle of warm light, came the clanging sounds of pots and pans.

IT WAS a kitchen as long and wide as any house she'd ever lived in. Big, black wood stoves, copper pots and pans, rows and rows of butcher knives and big spoons and silver bowls. A fireplace blazed in an old stone hearth.

Vern had lost his shoes. Barefoot, he hunched over a huge table. With a grease-glistened mustache, he held up a half-eaten sausage. Lines of meaty links circled around tubs of lard and bowls of potatoes, onions, and beets. Juicy sounds of chewing were interrupted only by his moaning. The last thing she wanted to do was eat. The first thing was to hit something.

Rinks took her shoes off. The floor was warm and uneven. She threw her shoes across the room. They almost bowled over a regiment of mice standing at attention beneath a washtub of dishes. The mice were all around with their little weapons and helmets and breastplates. She wanted to grab one and shake it, find the stupid General Rat and tell him to take her back. *I want out of here!*

General Rat stood on a table in the corner. It was dull silver, dented and grooved from a lifetime of chopping things. It didn't hold any food, though. There were no meaty links or bowls of lard. There were shiny things. Her feet slapped the stones. The closer she got, the slower she stalked toward it. Her pulse picked up (as if that were even possible).

Scarves. Beautiful headscarves, just like the ones she made. They were folded neatly in lines and in all patterns and colors. Jewels, too —brooches and rings and diamonds and such. Shirts and skirts and designer shoes she couldn't afford. And protein bars! Black sticks of licorice! And there, on a pedestal, sitting on a stand all shiny and new, was the thing that gave her life meaning.

A brand-new phone.

The screen lit up. Her apps were on it, too. Her photos.

In the middle of this treasure were eight crowns. Seven were gold bands with boring details etched around them. The sort of design a kid might wear on his birthday at a pizza party. The last one, though, was delicate yet sturdy and encrusted with diamonds and pearls and rubies and sapphires. A gaudy thing that would make a woman feel truly special.

General Rat picked up this crown of ultimate value. He walked it toward her, lifted it with a bow of his head. She reached for it, but he pulled it back. Waved for her to come closer. She got on her knees. Eye level with the furry general, he placed it on her head. She tingled with entitlement.

"Where are we?" she said.

Vern didn't hear her. He was scooping lard out by the handful. But she wasn't asking him. Wasn't asking the big rat still prostrating himself toward her. She could feel the thick walls around her, the heavy ceiling above. The weight of the building vibrated in her bones. In that moment, all the anxiety fell away like old skin.

She smacked Vern on the back of the head. The rash on his neck was angry red bumps that shined like boils. Three on one side of his neck, three on the other. "Don't eat that," she said. "You're breakin' out."

He scampered off.

Rinks broke open a protein bar. It tasted better than ever. She sighed, let it melt in her mouth. When she was finished, she dropped the wrapper. A mouse dragged it away. She slapped her hands together, no longer thinking of the sky or the way out. She was thinking something entirely different.

"Take me to the top of this turd."

22

The gift sat on the kitchen table. The lid open. Marie had closed it for a while. Now they stared into it, waiting for their aunt and uncle to come springing out like an unshaven Jack-in-the-box wearing a headscarf and clothes too tight. The room was dark. The clock on the stove cast green light.

Fritz put his head down.

Elbows on the table, Marie looked into the box, watched the hovering ball slowly turn. The colors swirling and changing. Her eyelids grew heavy. When soft snores came from across the table, she stood up. Fritz didn't wake up when she shook him. She picked him up, cradled him like a child, and carried him to their room. She stared at the mattress. The patch had given up half the air. She went to their aunt and uncle's room.

She tucked him into bed. He would sleep on a real mattress tonight.

She returned to the kitchen table.

A bottle woke her up.

It danced on the floor. Marie sat up on the couch, blinking at the early morning light. Fritz was in the kitchen, holding the refrigerator open. Bottles and cups and jars were all around the table. She'd put them there before lying down, a makeshift alarm system should her aunt and uncle pop out of the gift in the middle of the night.

She rubbed her eyes. Something fell on the floor. The nutcracker had somehow ended up on the couch with her. She didn't ask Fritz if he'd put him there to keep her company.

"Well?" Sandy slid toward her. He was half the size, a mini version of what he had been before they went to Candyland. He'd lost so much of himself on the bike ride. Why wasn't he back to normal? *Because it's real,* she thought. *Candyland is real.*

She shook her head. It might be why Sandy was skinny, but Candyland wasn't real. She couldn't think that. If she did, they'd never go back.

The gift was still open. The orb still turning. The colors, however, were muted and muddy. Something had changed. Did something happen to them? Did they not know how to jump out?

Maybe that's the journey. The gift was for them. Aunt Rinks and Uncle Vernon won't come back. That, she thought grimly, *is a true gift.*

Fritz sat at the table with buttered cinnamon toast. "What now?" Sandy said.

"I need to shower."

She climbed off the couch. Stretched the ache in her neck. The weight in her head was heavy. How did this get so complicated? The answer seemed clear enough: go back in, find them, help them return. That would be the right thing to do. Explain where they'd found the gift, what they'd been doing, and why they hadn't told them. *It would all be a mess after that.*

Her decision got even heavier when she looked across the room. In the corner, on Uncle Vernon's desk, the laptop was closed. Marie stopped and went toward it.

❄

MARIE DIDN'T KNOW what she was looking for on the laptop. It wasn't what she found.

At first, she was confused by what she was seeing. It was security footage. It took a moment to recognize the room she was seeing. There were blankets on the floor and an old workbench on the wall. It felt like she'd missed the last step on a long staircase. Her stomach surged with panic. She grabbed the desk.

"Go to the bedroom!" she said. "Our bedroom, go there now."

Fritz looked up from his second piece of toast. "We didn't do anything," Sandy pleaded. There was a hurt look in Fritz's eyes.

"You're not in trouble. Just... I need to see something. Go in there, stand there for a few seconds, and come back."

Fritz did exactly that. Marie held her hair back. Her brother came on the screen. He looked around. Sandy was next to him, shrugging. Marie ran to the bedroom with the laptop open. She looked in the corners, at the ceiling, tracking the view on the screen, turning in the direction it was watching her. *There.*

A hole had been drilled into the corner, no wider than a straw. A beady, black dot had been inserted into it.

"What?" Sandy said.

She dropped the laptop on the bench that was suddenly hot. The screen jittered and returned to normal. Marie paced with her hands on her hips, struggling to breathe. *Slowly,* she reminded herself. *Breathe slowly.*

"Hey, look. We're on TV." Sandy waved.

They've known all along! They've been spying on us this entire time!

Of course they knew. That was how Storyteller Corner had appeared. They'd been in there already. They'd pretended to leave yesterday, to follow us in. And then what were they going to do? Her worry for them soured.

She went to the kitchen. The gift was open on the table. She looked through scowling slits at the hovering orb. Reaching behind the box, she pried the lid loose. It snapped closed.

"What are you doing?" Sandy said.

"I've got to think a minute."

"What if they're in there?"

"They are in there!"

Her arms stiffened; fingers clinched. Jaw clenching and unclenching. Fritz recoiled, at first, like she was transforming under a full moon. She closed her eyes, whispered an apology to him through wooden lips. Disgust coated her throat.

"I really need a shower."

SHE SHOWERED. She ate breakfast.

She found the cameras in the other rooms. Learned how to scrub back the footage and watched Aunt Rinks and Uncle Vernon come into their room. First, Aunt Rinks reached into the gift. Then Uncle Vernon.

Marie ate lunch.

She spent the afternoon in the backyard, listening to the pond trickle. The teddy and dragon she'd found on the bench that had been covered in weeds now sat in a chair next to her. She closed her eyes and counted her breaths, emptying her mind of prickly thoughts. Angry, redemptive thoughts that didn't go away.

"WHAT'S THE PLAN?"

Sandy woke her from a nap. The sun was already heading toward the horizon. Fritz was stacking wood in the firepit, tucking kindling in between logs he'd found by the building. He had a feeling she wasn't in a hurry. She stood up to stretch. Her legs stiff and cold.

"I'm going for a walk," she said.

"Where you going?"

"I don't know. Stay here. I'll be back."

She went on a long walk, past the coffee shop (it was dark inside; the elves were gone from the window) and through the park. She sat near the giant Christmas tree and listened to Christmas music. For a moment, all the thoughts and worries disappeared. Like bubbles in the fountain, that blissful moment would eventually pop. For now, she waded in the tranquility. If not for her brother, she could keep walking and never come back. Get a job, start a new life. Become someone else.

Abandon the journey.

It was dark when she got back. A fire was burning in the ring of stones in the backyard. The little lights blinked in the canopies. A warm glow flickered on Fritz as he played a game on his phone. The nutcracker on his lap.

Sandy didn't say anything when Marie sat next to them. She watched her brother smile. Sandy looked over his shoulder, pointing at the phone, telling him what to do. Making fart sounds. Fritz coughed up a laughing fit.

She could stay here like this. Put the gift in the wall and go on living. They'd be happier. Definitely happier. This was her family, right here. Her brother and an oddball sandman. No one would ask about Aunt Rinks and Uncle Vernon. Maybe they were happy in Candyland. Maybe they belonged there.

The town square clock rang in the distance. A Christmas song played. It was Christmas Eve tomorrow.

Marie wanted Christmas to just be this moment right there at the fire. One thing bothered her, and it wasn't her aunt and uncle. It nagged like a sliver under the skin. She could go back to Candyland sometime later, could finish the journey when she was older. If she hadn't seen the king and queen at the market, she might have done just that.

When the flames died to an orange glow, she turned to her brother and said, "Hey. We need to crash. Got a long day tomorrow."

They slept in the big bed.

IN THE MORNING, their backpack was loaded. Marie packed anything of value: Uncle Vernon's watch, Aunt Rinks's headscarves, knives and forks, T-shirts, a screwdriver, a hammer, and a bottle of orange soda.

There was just enough room for the owl clock.

They each took a shower, put on clean clothes, and ate breakfast. The town clock rang at the top of the hour. It played a different tune this day. This day was special. It was Christmas Eve. Fritz was in the kitchen. A glass of milk on the counter along with two unwrapped protein bars on a plate. He was slicing a carrot into orange discs.

"You can't take those with us," Marie said.

She didn't know why he couldn't. He took the milk, protein bars and carrots out the back door. Marie watched through the window; he put the milk and plate on the armrest of one of the chairs, then scattered the carrots on the ground. Sweet boy was leaving them out for Santa. And carrots for his reindeer.

They went to their bedroom, put the gift on the workbench. The orb inside was still muddy and blurred. With Sandy's striped ball in his pocket, Fritz reached into the gift.

Flash.

Marie felt a blow of loneliness inside her. Her brother there one second, gone the next. The walls around her felt cold and bare. She picked up the nutcracker. The red jacket and gold buttons, the sword in his belt. His mouth fell open.

"You're coming this time."

She checked her phone one last time. Aunt Rinks's and Uncle Vernon's locations were still dark. If she would have checked her aunt's social media, things might have gone differently.

But she didn't.

23

Rinks loved it on top. The very tippy top. She always wondered what the view would be like looking down on poor folk. She knew what it felt like looking up. Wishing. Wondering what it was like at the top.

It's pretty great.

The air was sweeter. Like sticky buns in the airport, the tempting smell following wherever you went. When the breeze eased through the window, it felt like a lover blowing in her ear. A high school crush who finally smiled at you. She smiled back. A smile so big the cucumber slices almost slid from her eyes.

She was melting in a full recliner. The rhythmic scritching she heard would sometimes lull her into tiny naps. *Mouse naps,* she thought. And smiled again. Little hands kneaded her arms and legs, her shoulders and feet. Massaged almond oil into her cheeks until they were delicious. Her pores opened, and the sweet sticky bun air seeped inside her. She was full. So full.

Pretty, pretty great.

She was drifting into another mouse nap (*scritch, scritch, scritch*) when a pile of something brassy crashed in the next room. One cucumber slice fell off her face. The other slid down her cheek. She stared at the glittery ceiling. It had been muddy chocolate when she arrived. *Enough with the chocolate!* she had ordered. It was smothered in diamonds an hour later.

"Vern!" she shouted.

He muttered. He was always muttering now. Nonstop nonsense. Having conversations when she wasn't in the room. He hadn't slept since the teacup ride.

Rinks pulled the cucumber off her face, dabbed it in a bowl of powdered sugar and took a bite. The Jojos continued rubbing and kneading her with little pink feet. They would massage until she told them to stop. They were like Vern: never tired. They wore little head-scarves (she designed them). Tiny jars of oil dangled from belts that crisscrossed their backs. Lemon oil, coconut oil, almond oil. Vanilla. Whatever she was in the mood for.

She studied her nails. They'd been filed to points, painted red and white and coated and buffed. "Very nice, Jojo." She blew on them like a fancy lady would. "I like the feel."

She called all the mice Jojo. She tried to name them, but there were too many of them. The first one she named Jojo. That was as far as she got. It was better than *mouse*. More personal. The Jojo who had done the nails on that hand bowed. His emery board took the place of his weapon. She stuck out her pinky.

"I'm feeling a hangnail."

He went to work. *Scritch, scritch, scritch.*

The foot squad had done an impressive job on her toenails. They shined like the hood of a sports car. They were sanding the calluses on the sides of her big toes. A pile of dead skin fell like parmesan cheese.

Two new cucumber slices were hauled up to her eyes. She ate them instead, bathing in the shiny room, surrounded by everything she ever wanted. Figurines and dolls and metal cars and expensive paintings. Wigs, sweaters, eye shadow, hats. Three shelves of flip-flops. If she thought of something, she said it out loud. It appeared. There was even a shelf of trophies with her name on them. First place for tennis. Winner of bowling. World champion sprinter. Billiards, wrestling, and archery. Cheerleading was the biggest of them all. The gold figure on top with spiky pom-poms.

She scrolled through her phone. Her last three posts since she got to the top were killing it. More likes than ever. And she hadn't paid for a single one. She'd suggested to a Jojo it would be nice if there were more likes. Maybe he had something to do with it. The last post —her lying in a pile of gold coins—was trending. *I just want to be me,* she had written.

She sighed. *Pretty, pretty great.*

A cottony cloud eased past the open window. If it came closer, she would reach out and tear off a bite. It would melt in her mouth. She'd done it twice already. The pink sky was flawless. As the cotton-candy cloud moved closer, she sat up. She frowned. Someone had cut a hole in the pinkness.

A black square hung like an odd-shaped moon.

She flung the cucumbers against the wall. The Jojos scattered. The bowl hit the floor. She slipped off the recliner, her feet soft and oily, and almost rolled herself in the powdered sugar. She leaned out the window.

"Vern!"

She could feel them now. They were out there. Smelled the little goodie-goodies coming to do goodie-goodie. A sick feeling coated her throat. Her lips contorted. Her face wrestled over a frown and a smile.

"Couldn't stay away, could you?" she muttered. "Come on, you little brats. See what mama built."

The exit in the sky was open for a while. And then it was gone. *They closed it! They didn't even come looking for us!* By the second night, Rinks didn't want to leave. She only wished the little turd brains would come back. She wanted them to see what mama had done to the place. This lump of chocolate had become something worthy. Ask any Jojo. It was a silly castle with a silly princess locked inside (they hadn't found a princess anywhere, but that was the rumor). Rinks made it sturdy. She made it thick and hard and unyielding.

She made it a big deal.

She turned her back and lifted her phone. The angle was right.

She could get a selfie with Rose Lake below her. Confectionville beyond. A post like that would blow her followers' minds. They'd swear it was fake. In just two days, her face had narrowed. Her cheeks had hollowed, and her nose glowed a pretty pink. The crown, though —oh, that crown. A million-dollar crown for a million-dollar lady.

"Lady Rinks."

She was too distracted by the bling to notice the white hair on her nose. She had had several plucked from her chin that morning (hurt worse than a waxing). There were three times as many now. Thick and pokey.

Vern crashed into the room. All the things he was carrying went to the floor. Vases and coins, polished rocks and knives and forks. He searched every floor, every room (they were endless), stuffing what he found in pockets and pouches. When they filled up, he stuck them in corners. He was bent over from hauling this stuff around. A hump had formed on his back. He must have just raided a wardrobe because no less than twenty silk scarves were wrapped around his neck.

"What?" he said, gathering his loot.

"Forget it." His whiskers were stiff and white and an inch long on his upper lip. She thought of doing a selfie with him, but gross. "The kids are comin'."

"They can't have any."

He twitched like a broken toy. Eyes big in their sockets. He looked sick. That rash on his neck might be infected. She was glad the scarves covered it up. There was probably a doctor down there somewhere. Probably not one for humans. He would be all right. He seemed happy.

"Go," she said.

He scurried off. His conversation faded down the hall. At least he had himself to talk to. Rinks snapped a selfie. *Love yourself,* she wrote. Then looked out the window.

"Come to mama, little chickens."

24

"So good to be back," Sandy exclaimed. He drew a deep breath (as if he really breathed). *Are we really breathing?*

Marie grimaced. Sandy didn't notice the air smelled different. Something foul was beneath the cool draft of peppermint. She marched through the Almond and Raisin Gate and over the bridge, unaware Nussknacker—whom she had been holding tightly when she entered—was no longer in her hand.

"Once upon a time..."

She waited on the other side of the bridge. The bells rang, and the shadow circled like a dense cloud. Ronin hit the ground like an armored truck. The earth shuddered. The sleigh slid to a stop.

Garl leaped up and said, "Merry, merry! Ronin Express at your—"

"Take us to Confectionville." Marie climbed onto the back seat. "Straight away. No tours or stories. Put the shield up, or whatever it is, to keep the wind off us."

Ronin looked back. Black eyes twinkling, he pawed a rut in the turf.

Fritz and Sandy sat next to her. Garl stroked the braids in his beard. With a nod, he said, "Right."

In moments, they were in the air. The wind did not erode Sandy.

They rode without talking, clenching the seat as they sped straight for Gumdrop Alley. When they landed, Marie was stepping out before the sleigh came to a stop. She ran her hand along Ronin's flank and ducked under his swaying antlers.

"Thank you, Ronin." She continued walking. "Once upon a time..."

A SPACE between the gingerbread rowhouses opened, and Hussar Peregrinations grew out of it. Marie went inside and pushed the button. While the dominos and springs worked their way to the back room, she unzipped the backpack. When Pate came out on his cuckoo-clock tongue depressor, the owl clock was waiting for him on the counter.

"I need a cookie cutter. This is payment."

Pate's eyebrows rose. While his eyes didn't show it, amazement beamed off him. His wounded arm dangled at his side (she wondered where her ribbon had gone). The bell over the door rang as Fritz and Sandy entered. Pate paid them no attention. He stroked the owl wings with his good arm.

"Give this to the hussars at the market." He raised his arm when she dug in the backpack for something else. He went to the back room. A moment later, the cookie cutter came out.

"I need something else," she said. "A shield or something to keep the wind off my friend."

She pointed at Sandy, who was half the size he had been the last time they were in the store. Pate returned to the counter with what looked like a fruit cake. Jelly beads imbedded in the dense loaf. He told her what to do with it. She offered what was in the backpack. He wouldn't take it.

At the gutter, she stuck the fruitcake on the handlebars. With Sandy prepared to waterski on the back of the cookie cutter, she put her feet on the pegs. They blazed past the gingerbread buildings without the wind in their ears or grit on their faces.

The castle approached.

IT WAS TALLER THAN BEFORE. The sides of it were thick and lumpy. It glittered with cheap jewels. It was fat with excess. The hard shell of a prison littered with scaffolding. The center spire speared the puffy clouds in the pink sky.

It was gross.

The bell tolled somewhere on the castle. The tinted water of Rose Lake rippled. All around them, the inhabitants of the market leaped and cheered. They threw arms and limbs around each other and began to sing.

It's Christmas Eve, it's Christmas Eve. Time to smile and not to grieve.

"Stay here." She climbed off the cookie cutter. "I'll be right back."

She worked her way through the celebration, bumping into the line of dwarves they had seen before (now with their arms around each other, singing with big grins) and through a formation of twirling ballerinas.

Family and fun and all loved ones will be with us together.

The hussars were marching around their cart of nuts, below the banner that read *Support the Troops.* Their jaws snapped open and closed as they sang. Marie placed the owl clock in front of them.

"From Pate," she shouted. "For the troops."

They halted as Pate had done. Their finely pressed uniforms creased as they raised their arms to salute her. Then they ogled the owl clock like fine art. She turned to leave, but they stopped her. One of them dug through a pile of walnuts and pecans and Brazil nuts. He came up with a hard-shelled nut with black and white striped grooves. It looked just like the ball Godfather had given Fritz. And just as heavy.

"What's this?" she said.

"It is yours."

She ran her thumb in the grooves. It was as solid as granite and heavy as iron. It was then she realized the nutcracker she'd picked up in the bedroom was no longer with her. It was like he disappeared. *Why didn't I notice?*

She put the heavy nut in her pocket.

The chime of the last bell faded. The marketgoers gave one final huzzah, hugged whoever was next to them, and went about their business as Christmas music played. Two figures in hooded cloaks walked among them. Marie didn't hesitate.

She gave impolite chase toward the only humans she'd ever seen in Candyland. *Aunt Rinks?* she wondered. *Have they been here long enough to hide from us?* Marie apologized as she knocked things over and scattered produce from baskets, but she didn't slow down. No matter how fast she ran, she didn't gain ground. The distance between her and the hooded royal couple remained the same. She pushed harder, ignored the irritated pleas of those she offended.

The barge was up ahead. Square-headed workers were untying the mooring rope. A bassoon horn blared from the crates stacked three high on its deck. *King Chocolate* was written on the sides of the crates. The couple, arm in arm, boarded the ramp leading up to it.

"Wait!" Marie shouted. "Wait for me!"

The ramp was pulled on board. The barge drifted away from the port. Just as she approached the widening gap in full sprint, she leaned back and skidded to the edge. The couple was somewhere in the stacks. She looked down into the raspberry water. The waves rebounded off the port. There was something odd about it.

She didn't see herself in the water. No clouds above or shadows below. Just a pure body of water of nothingness.

"We have to cross on our own," she said.

Fritz nodded. He knew the journey ended in the castle. That was where Princess Pirlipat was. Where the cloaked couple was leading them. Marie knew, somehow, no matter how many times she returned, she would never get to the market in time to catch the barge.

"Once upon a time, there was a boat."

A storybook rowboat appeared on the shore. There were two bench seats and two oars. Painted across the flatback stern was one word. *Nussknacker.*

"Whoa, whoa," Sandy said. "Remember what the dwarves said about boats."

"We don't have a choice. It's too far to swim."

"When it sinks, what do you think we'll be doing."

"It's not going to sink."

There wasn't a cloud in the sky. Not even a breeze. The water was as smooth as a window. They were going to paddle across it because that was the story she was telling.

No one at the market was alarmed that a rowboat appeared. They didn't stop Marie and Fritz from climbing onto it. Sandy worked his way onto the back bench next to Fritz. The bow of the boat rose out of the water even with Marie in the front. She shoved off with an oar and leaned back to counterbalance their weight.

She pulled long, easy strokes. The rosy water hardly rippled around the paddles. They dipped beneath the surface and found purchase when she pulled. The shore receded. They cut effortlessly toward the hulking shadow. Each stroke raised gooseflesh on the back of her neck, cool and damp.

They were a third of the way across when her arms started to burn. The boat, for some reason, had leveled out. They were no longer heavy on the stern. In fact, the bow was starting to surge down with each stroke. Marie leaned forward a bit. She pushed the oars out of the water for a rest.

The market was starting to stir.

It was as if they had just noticed a boat was on Rose Lake. The good-natured laughter and cheer sounded a bit strange. They were agitated, jumping around and running to the sidewalk. Marie put her hand above her eyes and squinted. The hussars had abandoned their cart. They pulled their weapons and shouted orders. The public got out of their way. The clang of metal sounded like tiny pins dropping on an aluminum sheet.

"Look!" Sandy pointed at the shore.

Something small had leaped into the water. Something followed it. Then a horde of little things followed. The surface of the lake shimmered. Torpedoes were coming.

"Go!" Sandy shouted.

Marie dug until her shoulders were on fire. Each pull was harder than the one before it. The rowboat slugged forward only when the oars moved. The water hadn't changed, but it felt like rowing through molasses. Sweat gathered on her brow, streaked down her back. Fritz came up to help her. Water splashed over the bow.

"No. No, go back."

They were heavy up front. The weight had shifted, like something was pushing them back. Water lapped against the bow. It sprayed on her back each time she leaned into a stroke. Puddles formed in the bottom of the boat. Fritz began scooping it out with his hands. Marie dared a look behind her. They were past the halfway point. Maybe three-quarters.

"Oh, gross." Sandy's skinny head spun around. The sand dollars were full circles. "Mice."

Marie could see them now. The little torpedoes were gaining on them. The pink noses above the water; tails whipping behind them. Tiny legs paddling below in a migrating V formation.

Marie closed her eyes. And pulled.

Breathing hot exhaust, the perfumed air roasted her lungs. She could feel the castle like a magnet pushing against them. Her skin hummed and itched. Her back was soaked. Her bottom slid on the wet bench. The splashing against the bow grew louder. Each stroke pulled a wave into the boat. Fritz used his hat to bail the deepening pool.

"They're going back!" Sandy shouted.

Marie eased her next stroke. The rowboat stopped. The torpedoes shattered into chaos. The mice struggled to stay above water, turning around and swimming back to the shore. It looked like a nest of giant water bugs climbing over each other.

The bow bobbed inches above the water. The stern hovered off the surface. "Go to the back, the very back," she told Fritz. "Hold the boat down."

They did what she said. It helped a little. Water sloshed around her ankles. The bow barely moved. She pulled the oars again. *One more,* she chanted. *One more.*

The rowboat wobbled side to side. Water surged from front to back with each stroke, and they were hardly moving. She dug deep into her arms to find another pull, propped her feet on the bench behind her and leaned. *One more. One—*

The tip of the boat went under. It didn't come up.

Crimson water poured in. The back of the boat rose off the lake. Fritz grabbed Sandy. Sandy's branches wrapped around him. Marie scrambled over the benches for her brother. The oars plunked into the lake behind her.

"Grab your sister, kid." Sandy shoved Fritz at her. "Hang onto her!"

Fritz landed in Marie's lap. He was holding one of Sandy's branches. The boat heaved to one side. Marie put her arm around Fritz's chest. The water was frigid and heavy. She paddled at it with one arm.

"It'll be all right." Sandy was perched on the corner of the boat. "You're going to make it."

The world turned rosy red.

25

Rinks had camped at the window for hours, elbows on the ledge, eye to a telescope. Canvasing up and down Gumdrop Alley and along the market. A Jojo on each shoulder, working out the kinks in her shoulder blades. One on her back. A Jojo on each foot.

If you've never had a Jojo scalp massage, she thought, *you've never had a massage.* The tiny feet. They get right in there. They found exactly what she needed. Like they read her mind. A little to the left...

Perfect.

The market was slammed with weird things. Creatures, she called them. *What else do you call them?* They were toys and cookies and dwarves that made no sense. They were flat and small and boxy and twisted. Ugly, most of them. And they didn't even know it. Weirdos.

The bells went off at the top of the hour. The countdown to Christmas followed. The castle walls vibrated with each gong. The freakos at the market did what they did when they heard it. They danced with no rhythm, twirled and jumped and scooted and marched. From this far up, she couldn't hear them sing. Thank God.

"Look at them," she muttered. "A bunch of stupid muppets."

She had watched enough to know it never changed. They went about the day like the world's kookiest musical.

"Tell me somethin'," she said, "do they even exist if we're not here?"

The Jojo on her head squeaked an answer. It sounded neutral. She didn't speak Jojo. It was a good question, though. She felt smart for thinking it. Like that one about the tree falling in the woods.

"A little to the right."

The Jojo found the spot. She closed her eyes and melted.

"What about you?" She looked at General Rat. "What were you doin' before we got here?"

Squeak.

"Here's another question. Why do you fight the soldiers? They look down on you, is that it? Think you're less than them?" She went back to the telescope. "Well, look who's lookin' down now. Am I right?"

Up and down Gumdrop Alley, no sign of Miss Pretty-Pretty. Maybe they were waiting for Rinks and Vern to come out. They could wait all day and night. They weren't coming out any time soon. Far as she was concerned, they could lock that gift up and throw away the key. Rinks was fine and dandy where she was. Vern, too. If the kids did come inside the castle, they were just going to make trouble. Them and those soldiers. She just knew it. So she kept watching.

"Somethin' to eat," she called. *Squeak-squeak.* "Surprise me."

The pitter-patter of feet went down the hallway. She liked that. The obedience. It was pure. Maybe she was getting the hang of speaking Jojo. The subtleties of the squeak. Vern had picked up on it right away. In some ways, he was smart. Dumb as a chocolate drop in others.

The fools were still dancing the day away in the market. She panned all the way to the end. The boxy robots were still loading the barge with crates. Special deliveries from King Chocolate. Pure cacao to make the castle bigger and better and thicker. A rock of tastiness. She'd never met King Chocolate, of course. He was an ally, for some reason. Why, she didn't know. The crates came like clockwork. Once she sorted out her niece and nephew, she'd tour the land, meet this ally of hers. She wondered what he looked like. Tall and skinny? Probably fat. And weird.

Maybe it's better not to meet him.

Two Jojos arrived with a coconut bowl filled with strawberry milk (the instant kind like she had when she was little) and a hollow Twizzler. She gave it a stir and sucked it through the Twizzler.

"Mmm." She nodded her approval. Pointed at her shoulders. The Jojos went back to work.

She slurped while she watched. You'd think a freak show like that would never get boring. They were done dancing and singing, back to milling around selling nuts and springs and googly eyes for sock puppets.

Something was different. In the middle of the squatty and skinny and twisted were two tall figures who wore hooded cloaks. They didn't seem in a hurry. Rinks focused the telescope. It was hard to tell, but she thought they were holding hands.

"Who's that?"

The squeaking did her no good. It wasn't Marie and Fritz. They were too tall, for one. They held hands like a couple, also. She couldn't see their faces, hidden deep in the cowls, but she'd bet a bowl of strawberry milk they were people.

They stopped at the barge.

"Hey! Hey, hey, hey. What are they doin'? I didn't say they could come here." She turned to General Rat. "Tell them to get off."

The big-bellied rat saluted. Then gabbed a bunch of squeaky nonsense.

"Vern!"

Back to the telescope. The loading robots ignored them. The idiots were supposed to bring crates only. Not people! This was not cool. Something had to be done. Rules. *Laws!*

"Look, I can't understand you," she shouted at General Rat. "Learn English, you furry squid. Use your hand to write it down. What are they doin' on my barge? Vern!"

Chains rattled. A box closed. Her husband was dragging something in the hallway just outside the room. A rank smell of body odor ruined the vibe. Rinks told a Jojo to light a candle.

"It's the king and queen," he said from the hallway.

"Who?" Rinks said.

"The people down there, on the barge. He said it's the king and queen."

"What king and queen? We're the king and queen." She looked at General Rat and declared, "We're king and queen!"

"He says the king is mad at us."

"For what?"

"For eating the lard."

"Lard... what in the... what does that even mean?"

There were voices in the hallway. A brief conversation. Laughter.

"Who's out there with you?" Rinks said. "Vern?"

"It's me!"

She jumped. His reply was tempered and sharp. More things rattled and thumped. He was sorting through the things he'd found. It was nonstop, the way he stuffed his pockets. "Stop hoarding! We live here, Vern. This is *our* stuff now. *We* are the king and queen. These are *our* soldiers." The Jojos saluted. *Our soldiers.* "Listen, all of you. Go down there. When the barge docks, tell those two they don't live here anymore. Candyland is under new management. There's plenty of places for them to live, not here. No vacancy, get it? Hotel full. Tell them to beat it. If they don't, run them down. Got it?"

They saluted. Then they were off, scrambling through their mice holes and down however many flights it would take to get to the first floor. *A hundred?*

"And someone make me another coconut bowl!"

Back at the telescope, the barge had shoved off. It was a slow-moving thing, but not slow enough. She didn't need royalty wandering the halls and screwing up this sweet gig. If it was war they wanted, Rinks had a bazillion Jojos to throw at them. What were their wooden soldiers going to do, crack walnuts at them? Jojos had needle teeth and soft, little hands.

The soldiers in the market didn't even seem to recognize the king and queen. If they were royalty, why didn't they have a guard? Rinks focused on a display of nuts. There was something on the cart she recognized. It looked just like—

"What's the owl clock doin' here?"

A second later, she caught sight of someone running through the market.

"The kids are here!"

Marie had been talking to Fritz. That sandman was there (and fit right in with the weirdos). He'd lost some weight. A whole bunch of it. Looked like he'd stared into a fan too long. They were on the shore, looking at the castle. Rinks wasn't ready for them. She just wanted them to go away now that she had the king and queen to deal with. There wasn't a bridge to cross, and they'd missed the barge.

"Wait. Is that a..."

She refocused. Maybe she'd missed it before. She could've sworn there was nothing on the shore.

"They can't cross," Vern said.

"Well, they got a boat, Vern."

"The general said it won't work."

"Do you know how boats work?" she shouted. "They're gettin' into the boat. And now... yep. They're rowin' it, Vern. They're rowin' the boat and *crossin' the lake*!"

General Rat squeaked orders to the remaining Jojos in the room. Just in case he didn't understand what was going on, Rinks made it crystal.

"Stop them! I don't want them over here, you understand me? Do something!"

"General says they have to go around. Get them from the market side."

"I don't care if you shoot them from a cannon. Stop. THEM!"

Not a single Jojo was left in the room after that. Even the general scrammed. Vern was muttering to himself in the hallway, dragging chains and stuff. Rinks switched between the barge and rowboat. Her pulse quickened. She was going to puke a fountain of strawberry milk if something didn't happen and soon. This was Marie's fault. She made her sick. She had a way of making Rinks feel small. Useless. Even after all Rinks did for her.

"Just go away."

The market was in chaos. Rinks thought, for just a second, they were cheering on the rowboat. The weirdo traitors. The red water began to ripple. It looked like an arrow pushing off the shore, aimed for the little boat.

"Oh." Rinks fanned the sweat on her cheeks. "My little Jojos, go. Go with your little feet. Stop those wicked little ones."

Finally, someone was on her side. *Someone's fightin' for me.*

The wave closed in on the rowboat. Marie was getting tired. The weak girl couldn't even row across a pond.

"Surround them. Push them back, my little darlin's. Send them home and tell them never come back. Make them—what are you doin'? No. No, no, no... *go back!*"

The Jojos, for no reason at all, turned around. They were heading back to the market. Did they not get the memo? This wasn't an exercise. This was a mission.

"You're goin' the wrong way!" She waved her arms. No one was in the room to help her. "Go back! Go—"

The boat, however, was stuck. It heaved forward. The back end rose out of the water. And then, just like that, it was gone.

"Huh." Rinks scanned the lake. It was as smooth as polished marble. "You were right," she said to no one. "Yay, Rose Lake."

Did they drown? She never thought to ask.

A SHOWER of relief washed away the nausea. She was in the mood for a nosh. Maybe a plate of string cheese with some fruit roll-ups. There were no Jojos to get it for her, though. General Rat trotted into the room. He hopped on her leg, climbed up her arm.

"One problem solved," she said. "You, my furry general, are in line for a medal. I need you to find our royal guests and send them packin'. Maybe send them for a swim with my niece and nephew. Can you do that? Good." She kissed the general's pink nose. "Off you go, stinker."

Say what you will about rats, that general is a loyal soldier. She had no doubt he would see to the king and queen. If that was what they were. Could be bums, for all she knew.

Rinks was alone with her telescope and Vern's racket. Worse than the banging and clanging and scraping and hoarding was his constant chatter. He was like a room full of people with a room full of opinions.

"Vern, can you cut it for a second? I'm gettin' a migraine listenin' to you. Shut up!" There was silence, then whispers. "I've been thinkin', it's time to make us official king and queen of this dingbat land. There needs to be a ceremony. Somethin' to introduce us to the people... or whatever they are."

The whispering grew louder. This had to end. She put up with his snoring at night. She wasn't going to listen to this all day.

"Did you hear what I said?"

She shoved out of the recliner. Pinpricks tingled on her soles. Her feet had fallen asleep. She bit her lip as the feeling slowly came back, wobbling across the room. Vern wasn't in the hallway. It wasn't hard to find him. All she had to do was follow the scarves. She'd lost count of how many he'd been wearing around his neck. He wasn't muttering anymore. The idiot probably overheated and passed out.

"Vern?"

The trail of scarves, some tattered and chewed, led her to an arching doorway. The idiot was eating perfectly good scarves! The room inside was spacious. A mountain of stuff was piled in the corner —blankets and chairs and hats, framed paintings and footstools and boxes. A giant glass display case was against the wall, and deep gouges were in the floor where he'd dragged it across the room. The shelves inside the display were full of shiny things. Vern was on top of the pile, digging like a squirrel hiding a nut. He was gabbing to himself.

Rinks stopped to listen. There was something odd about the voices, something she hadn't put her finger on until now. They all sounded like him. But they were talking at the same time.

"Vern?"

He jerked around with a snort and a squeak. "What?" he said. And said it seven times.

Rinks threw her arm up and looked away. She closed her eyes. Maybe she didn't see that right. The light was an odd color, and she was a bit stressed. Slowly, she looked between her fingers.

No. She saw it right.

It was worse than a car accident. She lifted her phone to snap a photo. No one was going to believe this.

26

Marie woke on a soft shore. Water lapped her waist. Hair soaked.

A dark monstrosity was behind her, soaring up and disappearing into a delicious pink sky. Little things crawled along scaffolding like insects, packing globs of chocolate onto the walls. The spires like drip castles made of sand.

She rolled onto her side, wiping her face. Rose Lake tasted like a honeyed tonic of flowers. Mud squeezed between her fingers like soupy cookie dough. She coughed and sputtered, blowing strings of snot from her nose. Colorful beads dotted her hands.

"Fritz."

She climbed through the slop, clawing at soft, chocolatey boulders wedged against Marchpane Castle. Her brother was curled between sloping wall flares, shivering and weeping. His hands clutched to his chest. She pulled him close and wrapped her arms around him. The lake was pristine: not a wave, not a ripple. Across the way, the market was back to normal.

"Hey, hey." The bill of his cap dripped sweet-smelling water. "We made it. We're all right."

He was inconsolable. Something lay near their feet. She reached into the water. Marie looked around. She held him tighter, rocked him back and forth. His cheek, pressed against her chest, convulsed. The black square stared down from the sky. *This wasn't supposed to be like this.*

The journey sounded fun. Exciting. Discovery and adventure. Now they were marooned at the foot of a monstrous lump of castle. Marie holding a tree branch.

"He's all right." She squeezed her brother. "He'll be back, I promise."

The barge was docking at the castle. The gate lowered on massive chains; colorful links looked like loops of cereal. Boxy robots waited to unload the cargo. Two hooded figures slipped between the crates and entered the castle.

"We have to go." She picked him up. "We'll never finish the journey if we stop now."

His legs buckled like loose hinges. They made it three steps before he collapsed. A sand dollar fell from his hands. There was nothing more she could say. *He'll be back,* she told herself. *He has to come back.*

She hoisted her brother onto her back. His arms hung like wet socks over her shoulders. She trudged along the castle wall, footsteps sinking into the mud. Her legs like boneless putty. Arms weak from rowing.

"We can do this," she told him. And told herself, "We have to."

Why? Why do we have to do this? Because the journey wasn't optional anymore. *We'll have to do it at some point.*

THE LOADERS on the barge didn't stop them from climbing to the gate. They waited for them to pass before rolling a crate through the bay door. Crates were parked along an endless hallway. Some of the tops had been broken up. *Paperland* was written on the sides.

Candles flickered on candy dishes mounted on the walls. Drippings of chocolate puddled under them. The air was dense and sickly sweet. The sound of distant Christmas music from outside quickly muffled away. Even the loaders barely made noise when they dropped a crate.

Fritz walked alongside her now. Dark smudges colored his cheeks where he wiped his face. He sniffed every now and then. Their footsteps were dull thuds on the firm floor. The doors along the hall were locked when they tried to open them. Farther down the hallway, pictures appeared in ornate frames. Each one posted above a candle. The dim candlelight made it hard to see them. One looked like a beach. Another of a ski slope. A decorated Christmas tree.

They were familiar.

She tried several doors, all of them locked. *How many more doors are there...?* The end of the hallway still wasn't in sight. She whispered at her brother lagging far behind. Her voice died in the thick air. He was looking at a photo. She went back to get him. Stopped when she saw what he saw. It was a picture of a house.

What's that doing here?

It was white with green shutters, the kind of shutters that were decorative and not functional. Wooden steps led to the front porch, where a swing was chained to the ceiling. A swing where you could idle on a summer day and drink soda and tell stories. She knew the handrail leading up to the porch was rotting, something that was always meant to be fixed but never was. She didn't have to see the railing to know it hadn't been fixed.

It was the house they grew up in.

They put their arms around each other. His longing was a cold wind that echoed inside an empty canyon. It was in her, too. She tried not to feel it, to stuff it back in the emotional black box. She couldn't look inside it. If she did, she wouldn't be able to hold her brother up.

Doubt took hold of her. It turned her back toward the open door, where the barge was pulling away from the castle. She thought about taking her brother outside to look up at the sky and leap through the exit. They could go back; they could close the gift forever and never look back.

Then the hooded figures exited a room.

"Hey! Stop!" Marie shouted. "Help us!"

They didn't stop, walking calmly away. The candles snuffed out as the figures passed them. Darkness fell around them. Marie held onto her brother. She dragged her hand along the soft wall, leaving tracks in it, feeling it curl under her fingernails. Slowing as it grew darker. Something was ahead of them. A large structure anchored in the middle of the corridor. Carefully, they approached, reaching their hands out to avoid running into the unexpected.

It was a staircase.

The hall met with another hall that went perpendicular in both directions. This was the center of the castle. They stood in the intersection and looked up. A vertical tunnel bored straight up a silo. A railing and steps spiraled around the perimeter, an infinite corkscrew that would reach the sky. Somewhere up there, footsteps were climbing.

I can't do that, was her first thought. *I can't climb that far.*

She didn't have the strength, even if she wasn't carrying her brother. It was too much. "Wait!" she called. "Please."

The mysterious couple didn't come for them. Their ascent faded with each passing minute. Fritz put his hand in hers. They stood there, looking up, when they heard more footsteps coming from behind. Maybe the cloaked couple hadn't gone up the steps after all. Relief filled her with a temporary surge of strength. She couldn't see anyone coming, though. And the footsteps were different.

There were a lot of them.

The pitter-patter was joined by tiny metal clangs. Nothing, however, was there. Then she noticed, more like felt, the floor moving. It looked like a wave coming down the corridor. As it passed through a candlelit section, just before vanishing in the dark, she saw it.

She threw her brother behind her. Marie felt her legs stiffen and arms harden. Her jaw swelled and jutted out. She felt heavy, unyielding. In the dark, something about her was changing. When an idea occurred to her, she softened, felt more like herself when she said: "Hang onto me."

Fritz threw his arms over her shoulders. She locked his hands together, told him to close his eyes and not let go. There was no going back. The journey had only one direction now.

"Once upon a time…"

A STRAP DROPPED down from above.

She wrapped it around her hands several times, yanked on it to make sure it was secure. She raised her arms. Her heels lifted off the floor. Then her toes. She began floating. A bright red balloon bobbed over their heads.

A mouse leaped and caught her shoestring. A little metal breastplate banged against the sole of her shoe. She kicked it off. The mouse fell with it, his helmet rolling across the floor like a die. The vermin army jumped up and down like popcorn on a hot skillet. Throwing toothpick spears that clattered back to the ground. Many of them flooded toward the stairs.

Soon, she couldn't see or hear them.

Up. Up. Up.

The air grew colder. They floated in silence. Only the sound of Fritz's chattering teeth in her ear. They were going all the way to the top. This was where the journey was taking them. Deep down, Marie knew she'd been avoiding this trip. The emotional black box began to quake inside her.

"It's going to be all right," she whispered to Fritz. Then to herself.

27

"What happened to you?" Rinks said.

A garble of overlapping voices replied. Seven of them, to be exact. Because there were seven heads. Seven mousy heads crammed onto her husband's shoulders. Each wearing a crown. One head was bigger than the rest. That was Vern. The rest had sprouted from those boils on his neck, all jammed together and yammering at Rinks.

"Shut up!" she said. "I'm talkin' to Vern."

"I am Vern," they said.

She had to look away. All his personalities were on display, busting out so their voice could be heard. Sad Vern. Happy Vern. Angry Vern. Sweet Vern. Serious Vern. Fun Vern. It was all very disturbing, the way they were crammed together and twisting about. Made her stomach curdle.

"Are you okay?" she said softly. "Does it hurt?"

"Hurt?" they said. "I'm just lookin' for my..."

They all said something different. *Snack, belt, button, cup, key, ring, hat.* He dug like a squirrel looking for acorns. Things flew between his legs: pots, pens, feathers, flowers, pillows, shirts. The heads argued where to look and what to grab. Like seven captains steering a boat.

"Vern!" When she had the attention of all seven, she said, "It's goin' to be all right. This is all make-believe, like you said. When we go back, you'll just be, you know... *normal.*"

They twisted and turned to each other, their crowns sliding one way or the other, muttering to each other. Confused. Thing was, Rinks didn't plan on going back. And as long as she was here, this was her husband. She could get used to it. Maybe. But the yammering? *One Vern at a time, please.*

"Right now, we have a problem," she said. "They're comin' up. When they get here, they're goin' to take *aaaaaallll* this stuff away. Unless we stop them."

He gathered an armful of bedsheets. "Who's comin'?"

"Who do you think? The general and the Jojos went to stop them. If they don't, we have to be ready. Are you ready to fight, Vern?"

His hand went to the jeweled hilt of a sword. (*Where did he get a weapon?*) Knuckles big and hairy. *Gag.*

"We're king and queen, Vern. You and me. This is ours now. You understand?"

He sniffed the air, nose twisting. Long whiskers twitching. Rinks shivered and swallowed a knot of disgust.

"Go clean yourself up," she said. "We need to get ready. You smell like a litter box. And here, put this on."

She pulled a coat from the pile. It was long, the material soft and clean. More importantly, it was huge. She held it up. Vern climbed off his treasure, let her drape it over his shoulders. She pulled it up and over the heads and tucked it down in there.

"Ack!"

"I can't breathe!"

Vern threw it off. The six heads she'd tried to hide huffed like she'd tried to suffocate them. She hadn't thought of that. Maybe they could be twisted off like warts.

"What are you tryin' to do?" they said.

"That's not goin' to do, Vern. That look." She painted him with a gesture. "You're hideous."

"Me? Look at you."

"What about me?" She fixed her crown.

He scrambled up the pile. Things cascaded down and clanged and rolled. He came back with a copper frying pan. Held it up. Her bronzy reflection was soft and distorted. Her hair was a nest of gray sprigs. And her eyes were shiny black balls bulging from their sockets.

She touched her face, felt the pointy end of her nose, the bristled poke of whiskers around the scar on her cheek. She threw the pan across the room.

"Lies!"

Vern chased after it. He bumped into the glass display. It teetered off balance but stayed upright. He buried the pan under a loosely rolled rug. Sat on it like a goose on a golden egg.

"Is that all you care about, this stuff? Do you even care about me?"

There was a brief discussion. Then they all said: "Yes." Then they said, "This, too. I like you and this."

She straightened her collar and smoothed the kinky hair on her head. "I will make you noodles, Vern." *Well, the Jojos will.* "Noodles and cheese. You like cheese?"

Their tongues licked wet, black lips.

"We can have whatever we want, Vern. But we need to protect each other. We need to protect this castle so we never get hurt again. Ever. No one can touch us in here. You understand?"

The sharp blade slinked from the scabbard on his hip. The tip gleamed as he leveled it at her. She fell back a step. Maybe they changed their minds about what was important. If they turned him against her, she was truly alone. They squirmed like a litter of freakish puppies, trying to look behind her. She turned around.

A hooded figure stood in the doorway.

It stood still, watching. Wispy clouds steamed from the blackness inside the cowl. Rinks recoiled from a sudden wave of pain and discomfort.

"Get it!" She pointed. "Get it, Vern!"

The threat startled the mystery person, who Rinks assumed was the exiled queen coming to take everything from them. Rinks jumped into the hall, watched her go. The cloak brushed the floor behind her.

"Vern, we have to—"

The door slammed shut. The sound of trinkets being buried came from inside the room. Pretty clear what was more important. Rinks ran in the opposite direction of the queen. She turned left at the first hallway. This way wasn't familiar. She turned around and went right instead. The doors all looked the same. There were no windows. The walls muddy brown. *I don't remember the walls curvin'.*

"General!" She was running now. "Where are you?"

Totally lost, peeking around corners to avoid running into the queen, she ran. She just wanted to get back to her room. Finally, at the end of a long corridor, pink light filled an open doorway. She ran to her room and slammed the door. It was chilly inside. Cold sweat ran from beneath the hard band of her crown. The Jojos must have turned on the air conditioning. They knew she was hot. Sweet things.

She put her back to the door. Her chest burned; side stitched. When she opened her eyes, things got worse.

The queen was already in the room.

28

The staircase spiraled down a hundred stories. The mouse army wouldn't reach the top any time soon. Her skin was raw from the bindings she'd wrapped around her wrists when the balloon carried them up. Fritz held her hand tenderly with concern.

"I'm okay," she said. The hallways went in different directions. "Stay close, okay? Don't leave me."

She was fragile and scared. Her bones were cold. She questioned everything now.

"We need to find a window, see the sky. In case we need to leave. Okay?"

He nodded.

They went in one direction, tried some of the doors. They stopped to listen. When they backtracked, the halls were different. Like they had shifted with new openings and more doors. The walls grew thick around her. The weight was stifling. There was a dead end when they turned around. And no windows. She focused on her breath to slow it down before she careened into anxiety.

What if we can't get out?

Fritz picked up a scarf. The edges were frayed. Holes chewed through it. There were more scarves up ahead. Voices grew louder. They stopped outside a door to listen. She put Fritz behind her, kept a hand on him, and opened the door just a little. There was an argument inside the room. Marie stuck her head in.

"No!" they shouted.

Marie closed the door. She resisted the urge to close her eyes. What she saw was... *unthinkable*. This wasn't what she expected. None of this was. She grabbed Fritz by the shoulders.

"Don't look. Close your eyes and stay right behind me."

He nodded. She grabbed his wrist and squeezed a little too hard. The door swung open. The thing she'd seen was on top of a mountain of debris, grubbing things to its chest and stuffing them into bulging pockets.

"Uncle Vernon?"

He was a rat. A giant, human-sized rat wearing a crown. His eyes bulged from the sockets. And there was more of him. Heads, that is. Smaller versions of Uncle Vernon had sprouted from his neck, bunched together and twisting to have a look at her. Each with a different expression. Each with a crown.

"Stay away. I'm warnin' you. You can't have it. None of it."

"Hey, kids," one of the heads said. "It's about time."

"Hungry?" another one said.

"Hey, buddy," another said. And, "Isn't it your bedtime?"

They were all talking at the same time, saying different things in different ways. Marie took a step closer. *Is it really him?*

"Stop where you are!" they all said. "Not one more step. Mine! This is all mine!"

"I don't want anything," she said.

"Well, you can't have it!" Confusion rolled their beady eyes. They looked at each other. "Mine. Mine."

Marie looked around. It looked like a giant nest of shiny objects. A glass case was against a wall, objects shoved onto the shelves. *Where's Aunt Rinks?*

"Go to your room," one of them said. "I don't want to hear another word from you."

Marie's legs stiffened. Her chest tightened into an impenetrable shell. Candyland had turned her uncle into a monster she couldn't have dreamed up. He was hard to look at. Her jaw clenched.

"I don't care about any of that. Where's Aunt Rinks?"

They struggled with conflicting thoughts, snapping at each other with sharp teeth. A consensus was reached. In unison, they bellowed, "Huzzah!" and slid down the pile, plowing through objects with wide feet and sharp nails, and reached for their belt. The sword slid from the sheath. *Ting!*

"Mine!"

Marie went rigid. Her skin tightened and tingled. Muscles turned to fibers tough and flexible like the trunk of a tree, swelling inside her clothing. The sound of her teeth snapped like a trap. She felt something in her hand, hard and cold. She pointed it at the seven-headed Mouseking.

Where did I get a sword?

That thought was distant. Like she was far away from herself, becoming something else. Her sword was curved and silver with the edge of a razor. Her uncle, the Mouseking, stumbled back.

"Not one more step," she said. Her voice as sharp and steady as the blade she held.

The Mouseking babbled and cried, shouted and spit. He threw a box. It splintered on the wall. He threw a pillow that she split in half. Feathers snowed around them. He threw forks and spoons, cups and plates. She dodged them deftly. Her remaining shoe slipped off her foot. She picked it up and threw it at him. He ducked behind the glass display. When he did, the entire thing tipped over. Glass shattered on the floor, sending shards across the room.

Marie felt a sharp pain in her left arm.

The Mouseking crawled back onto his nest of stolen goods, swearing at her, asking if she was hurt, telling her to go away, wondering if she wanted some noodles to eat. This wasn't where Marie needed to be. This wasn't their journey. *This is Uncle Vernon's journey.* She reached behind her, to pull Fritz closer, to shield him from her uncle's obscenity.

"Fritz?"

The doorway was empty. She ran through it, looked down the hall. He was walking away from her, holding the hand of one of the cloaked figures who had boarded the barge.

"Fritz!"

She sank the tip of the sword into the floor and went after them. The Mouseking's cackling faded behind her, then disappeared when he slammed the door.

"Mine!"

29

"How'd you get in here?"

Rinks grabbed the L-shaped doorknob. It rattled up and down. The door shook in the frame but didn't open. She grabbed it with both hands, leaning against the door for leverage. Fingernails, long and curved and sharpened to a point, bit into her palms.

Rinks pinned her back to the door. The queen watched from the other side of the room. Tendrils of condensed breath huffed out of the darkness inside her hood and disappeared on their way up to the ceiling. Rinks grabbed a trophy from the shelf. The cheerleader figurine that looked like her poised on top, with a frozen pom-pom aimed at the queen.

"Stay away. You're not supposed to be here. You left! This is my castle now. I'm the queen!"

She had the absurd urge to whip out her phone and show how many followers she had. How many likes her last post got. People loved her, and she could prove it. The phone slipped from her quivering hand and tumbled to the hem of the queen's cloak.

"Vern!" She slammed the door with open hands until her palms stung. "Help me! Get in here, now!"

She tried opening the door again. *Why is this locked?* She felt movement, spun around with the trophy in front of her.

"Don't move! I'm not afraid to use this." Rinks moved to put the recliner—the one where the Jojos had made her hands and feet pretty—between them. "I swear."

The room was freezing. Rinks could see her own breath now. The blackness inside that hood was crippling. Like some outer space, bottomless hole that ate planets and moons and stars. It was unsettling. Sent a shiver through her belly button. *Did she gargle perfume?* Rinks thought. It smelled pleasant and familiar. Brought a memory of her mom teaching Rinks and her sister how to put on just the right amount. *Spritz a cloud and walk through it, girls.*

The scar on her cheek burned.

"I have an army, you know. A thousand mice. A million. They love me, too. How do you think I got here, huh? They love me! You leave now, and they won't hurt you. I swear. But if you don't..."

The queen was motionless. The robe unmoving. Only perfumed clouds wafting out and evaporating. Slender fingers dangled from the oversized cuffs. Not even twitching.

Rinks relaxed her grip on the trophy. She straightened the crown that was crooked on her head. Made sure the queen knew who wore the crown now. She smoothed her springy hair. The scar felt hot on her cheek. She stood upright, pulled back her shoulders and puffed out her chest. Something royalty would do.

"What do you want?"

She bent over without taking her eyes off the queen, pushing clutter around to find an emery board the Jojos had used to file her nails. She tossed it at the queen. She was aiming for the black hole in the hood. It bounced off her sleeve. The queen didn't flinch.

Maybe she wasn't real. *Does Marie have somethin' to do with this?* She could. That little liar could be trying to scare her.

Rinks moved closer, sliding a footstep at a time. The perfume grew stronger and sweeter. It burned in her eyes. It buzzed under her skin, in her head. The scar began to itch. Rinks covered it with her hand. Stiff whiskers pricked her palm.

"Seriously, what do you want? You just goin' to stand there starin'?"

Nothing.

Rinks went back to the door. With the trophy raised above her head, she brought it down on the L-shaped doorknob. Once, twice. The third time, the cheerleader snapped off and danced across the floor. It jigged under the recliner and came to rest against the queen's cloak.

"Look what you made me do. That was my best trophy. These are all mine. All of this!" She swept her arm at the walls. "But that was my favorite!"

The queen was not moved.

Rinks looked around the room. Everything was gingerbread this or gingerbread that, or bolted to the floor or screwed to the wall. Nothing solid except... she shuffled around the recliner, the jagged end of the trophy aimed at the cloak, till she got to the window. She snatched the telescope. The tripod tipped over. Rinks threw the broken trophy down and took that telescope like a baseball bat to the doorknob.

The lens shattered. The eyepiece snapped.

The L-shaped doorknob broke off. She pulled it out of the door and yanked it open. The hallway was empty. She could hear voices, though. Her husband and all his malignant heads going on about *mine, mine, mine!*

Rinks didn't run. She'd done that already, and look what happened. Whatever this was, she couldn't outrun it. She turned with the bent telescope on her shoulder. "Best you leave before they come for you. They won't be friendly." She aimed the telescope at her. "You ruined my life."

It was an odd thing to say. She didn't know why she said it.

Nonetheless, nothing happened. Rinks could bar this room closed and never come back to it, leave the queen in it forever. But this was her room. These were her trophies.

"You deaf?" Rinks dared a step toward her. "I said you need to get out of my life forever."

One more step, then another. She was breathing slower now. Calmer than ever, she inched her way forward. With one hand on the telescope (if the queen flinched, she'd get the homerun swing), she reached out with the other. Grabbed the coarse sleeve of the cloak.

"Come on."

She tugged. It was like pulling open a freezer where slabs of meat are kept. The tip of her nose went cold and started to drip. The perfumed breath drew water from her eyes. The breathy cloud disappeared. The queen stopped breathing.

"Let's go."

Rinks gave it a yank. It was like pulling the lever on dry ice. The next exhale enveloped Rinks in a cloud that nipped her earlobes and kissed her cheeks. She dropped the telescope, let go of the sleeve. Swung her arms in search of the door. One step, two. Ten steps. She didn't find it. Didn't run into a wall or stub her toe on any clutter. She waved at the smoky air. Her fingertips were numb.

She folded her arms over her chest. She was cold, but that wasn't why she tucked her arms against herself. She just did. The smoke began to swirl. Wind in her ears, she was spinning in a vortex.

Instinctually, she closed her eyes, locked her knees. The balance of gravity settled inside her like a child's top standing still. Metal blades ground in firm footing. Tears streaked across her temples. The gravity bloomed in her stomach, opening like a flower. Joy surged through her veins, filled her body and flooded her head with lightness and smiles.

She knew this feeling.

Lost in the experience, she pushed backward. Pulling one leg up and behind her, dug the other one into the ice. Came out of the spin with a powerful surge, drifted on the edge of a metal blade. With her arms out and winter nibbling her ears, she soared like an angel.

Flying beneath a gray sky.

Alone on a frozen lake. The lake she grew up on, where they swam in the summer. Played hockey in winter, practiced their spins when the boys weren't around. Ankle burning, leg held high, she etched an arching line in the black ice. Curving around her father's ice fishing hut, where he and her uncle would cut a hole and drop their lines.

This feeling she'd forgotten. It was buried under so many scars. Now it was clear and present. It was graceful beauty. Pure instinct.

It was as free as she ever felt.

THE SMOKE CLEARED.

Her father's ice hut was gone. The lake and gray sky. That freedom still trickled through her. It turned to ash when she realized she was back. Not in her room high atop the castle.

There were trophies on a shelf. Ribbons, too. The Golden Skate Award (she had forgotten that one). A tennis racket and more trophies. Behind her, the recliner was replaced by a bed with a quilted comforter and a pile of pillows. Posters on the wall. A dresser with Christmas cards, a jewelry box, a jar of pennies that read *Be The Change*. A photo of a boy Rinks had a crush on. A boy who barely knew she existed. Marco only spoke to her if she answered the door.

A tiny blue flame ignited in her belly. A furnace began to warm oils of resentment.

She took a medal from the dresser. A red and white ribbon was strung through a loop attached to it. It was thick and heavy, began to spin as she held it up. She read the person's name engraved on it. *First Place* was etched on the other side.

Her skin began to sizzle.

Car doors slammed shut. Panes of glass were frosted on a rectangular window. Outside, her parents were in the front seats. Her dad backing out of the driveway. In the back seat, her sister was on her phone. Smiling at something she read. A text from Marco.

Rinks stood there long after the car was gone, on its way to a competition. Her sister would bring home another ribbon. She'd throw it on the pile, close her bedroom door, and call Marco. They would talk. He would come over. Rinks would hear them through the wall of her bedroom.

She remembered what she had done that day. Even if she could change it, she wouldn't. She gave in to the bonfire cooking her thoughts into blackened coals. The trophies went on the bed. She didn't place them carefully. They were thrown one by one, chipping and scratching. Plastic figurines snapping. Then the ribbons and medals. The certificates. The Christmas cards, the picture of Marco. It all went onto the bed.

She bundled them in the bedspread.

Rinks was barely aware she wasn't *actually* there. She didn't think about the room in the castle or the hooded queen with the icy breath. She dragged that bedspread by four corners down the steps, through the living room, and out the sliding glass door. In stocking feet, she pulled it through the snow. Onto the frozen lake. Balled-up ice crystals stuck to her socks. She fell three times, spilling the loot, packing it back up, pushing farther out onto the ice.

The hole inside her father's fishing hut had frozen over. A hatchet he kept under a folding chair did the trick. She hacked it to floating pieces. Her face red, eyes swollen. She screamed with each swing, satisfied each time the blade sank into the ice.

Bye-bye, first-place ribbons. *Bloop.* So long, state champion. *Bloop.* See you later, medals and trophies and certificates and pictures. Some bobbed momentarily. Then the icy darkness took them all the way to the bottom of the lake. First in her class, gone. Regional winner, fish bait. Boyfriend, have a drink. She clogged the ice hole with the bedspread. Go away and never come back.

RINKS WOKE TO CRYING.

She couldn't remember falling asleep or even coming to her room. She lifted her head off the pillow and listened to the sweet sounds in the next room. The wailing turned to growling. Then a scream blew frost off the window. There were muffled thuds and loud ones that shook the wall. A picture fell over on Rinks's dresser. She put her hands behind her head and soaked in the misery. It was art, what she did. Award-worthy. *What do they call it? Performance art.*

So caught up in her thoughts of accepting an award for her courageous act, she didn't notice the thuds moving down the hall. Her door slammed against the wall, the knob punching a hole in the drywall (which her dad made *Rinks* fix). Her sister, still wearing her winter coat, leaped across the room. Rinks rolled off her bed, but not before catching a fist to the side of the head. Her ear caught fire, and her head rang a long high-pitched note.

The worst of it was when she hit an open dresser drawer.

Her sister was on top of her, knees pinning her shoulders to the carpet. Rinks covered her face. Warmth flowed from her cheek, which was sticky between her fingers. Her sister's face was flaming. Rage turned the princess into a snarling ogre making garbage-disposal sounds.

Squeak, Rinks heard.

Rinks's mom grabbed her sister, wrapped her arms around her, and dragged her across the room. Legs kicking, body twisting. Her dad came in next, wondering what the fuss was all about. Rinks's sister told them exactly what Rinks had done. They listened in disbelief. Then saw the proof. The looks on their faces stole all the joy from Rinks's work of art.

"Your sister worked so hard," her mom said.

"The efforts she makes," her dad said.

Rinks curled up against the dresser. She wanted to feel sad, to feel regret. But that furnace in her gut only burned on envy, pure, 100% envy that pumped out globs of hate. That look of hurt on her sister's face was the tip of an oil rig tapping a deep deposit under years of pressure.

Squeak.

"Because of you!" Rinks jumped up. "Is it really so hard to figure out? You deserve it!"

The cut from the open drawer—the cut that would become a thin scar to remind everyone of that day—bled along the ridge of her jawbone. The cut her parents didn't ask about till hours later. The ride to the hospital in fuming silence. The lock they put on her sister's door so Rinks could never perform again.

"I was good, too," Rinks said to her sister. That wasn't what she'd said when it actually happened. She hadn't said any of that, really. She had curled up in a ball on the floor until they made her get up. But she said all of that now.

Now she said to her sister: "You never cared about me. Admit it."

Squeak.

There was a rat on the floor. Rinks stepped back in horror. It leaped up and down, shook a tiny spear at her. Rinks looked back. The recliner was empty. The queen was gone. The fake trophies on the shelf. No cloak on the floor, no nippy air in the room.

Rinks with her hand to her cheek.

Squeak.

"Where'd she go? Where's the queen?"

The general tapped his spear three times and began running down the hall. Rinks went after him. She wasn't done with her sister.

The furnace was burning hot now.

                                  30

"**F**ritz!"

Fritz and the cloaked figure were taking a stroll. They turned right. Marie followed. Each stride thudded in her ears. The walls shook. The air stagnant and humid. When she made the turn, they were farther away.

The corridor was narrow.

Her pumping arms scuffed the walls. She huffed hot air. Sweat streaked her back. She wiped her eyes. They made a left turn. She couldn't gain on them. They were casually walking, looking at each other. *Is Fritz talking to him?*

Two more turns. An ache buried in her side. Her shoulders bounced between the shrinking walls. She pushed through the burn, the pain, the struggle to breathe. Her legs were hollow. She'd lost her way. This had become a maze of turns and tunnels. Finding her way out wouldn't matter.

Not without Fritz.

The chase ended. Fritz stood with the stranger, still hand in hand, at a dead end. The passage was long and narrow. So narrow she had to cock her shoulders to squeeze through it. Fritz and the other stood side by side in front of double doors. The hood of the cloak had been thrown back. It was a man. Marie wiped her eyes with her sleeves. Blood from the cut on her left arm, when the Mouseking's glass case shattered, smeared across her cheek. The coppery taste of iron on her lips.

Through the sweat and thick air, it was hard to tell what the man was wearing on his head. As she drew closer, she realized Fritz wasn't wearing his ball cap. They turned their heads, saw Marie coming for them. They were too far away to see their faces or expressions. But she saw what the man was wearing.

He had Fritz's hat.

They reached for the doors. Marie was closing the distance. When they opened them, bright white light blazed from the next room. It was stunning. Her knees wobbled. She pressed her hands against the walls, their ghostly images imprinted in the whiteout. She ran through blindness, dropping one foot in front of the next. Calling her brother's name.

A gale of frigid wind cooled the slick of perspiration on her face. It soothed her burning eyes and itching throat. Fritz appeared out of the whiteness so suddenly that she almost tackled him. She picked him up and held him tightly, buried her face on his shoulder. Looking around for the man who took him.

"Are you okay? Did he hurt you?" she choked into her brother's ear. "Where's your hat?"

Fritz shook his head. He didn't look at her with fear or sadness. A palpable calmness possessed him. He wasn't winded or afraid. He looked through the doors they had opened. The light had dimmed. What was inside was not what she expected.

We're here, she thought. *We made it.*

It was a cathedral. The big church kind, but older. The king and queen kind, where subjects and landowners brought offerings. Pillars as big as redwoods. Arching ceilings fifty feet above. Carvings on the walls, wintery scenes with sleds and snowballs, snow angels and snowmen, snowflakes and ornaments and presents and Christmas trees. Plump elves looking down from the ceiling.

Ice. All of it made from ice. Frosted ice and clear ice. Ice with sparkling crystals. Black ice on the floor, buffed and smooth as marble. In its depth, tiny specks glittered like a galaxy of stars.

Marie took it in through squinting eyelids. It seemed far too big to fit at the top of the castle, but she'd stopped rational thinking a while ago. Candyland operated by different laws. This was the end of the journey. The quiver in her stomach told her this was the place.

Her heart wanted to escape its cage.

At the far end, chiseled from the tip of a jagged iceberg, were two empty thrones. They were side by side with wide arms and soaring backs of spearing icicles. The king and queen were missing. But standing in front of the thrones, facing them with her back to Marie and Fritz, stood a girl.

Fritz took a step inside. He tested the black ice, took careful steps. He stopped and held out his hand. Marie was as solid as the pillars holding up the intricate ceiling. This was why they had come. This was the end, and she hesitated. Something about it told her to run and hide. It was dangerous to her, but not to Fritz.

It threatened her, somehow.

He kept going without her. When he went too far, she slid after him. The floor was a flawless mirror. It was like looking into the universe, skating over endless black space. It burned the soles of her bare feet. She'd lost one of her shoes to the mice, the other to the Mouseking. Barely halfway across the cathedral and she could not feel her ankles.

She didn't notice her reflection was missing.

Fritz waited for her to catch up. They joined hands and shuffled toward the empty thrones. The girl did not turn around. She wore a white cloak of fine silk. Red trim along the hem and cuffs. It bunched on the floor around her feet. Her hands hung from the sleeves like shriveled leaves. The hood covering her head was enormous. *She's been cursed.* Marie thought of the nutcracker story the Counselor had told. The Mousequeen had avenged the Mouseking with a curse. *Poor thing.*

Marie squeezed Fritz's hand.

They were ten feet away when Princess Pirlipat turned to face them. Her head was the size of a county fair pumpkin. Misshapen like a potato dug from the dirt. Her nose a twisted root between two dull green eyes. A lipless mouth cut a line from ear to ear.

Marie took a step back, her hand to her mouth. Legs melting hot rubber. Fritz tried to pull away. Marie held onto his hand, determined not to let him go again. Marie couldn't look away. Horrible air was sucked through tiny nostrils with each breath the princess took. She didn't tremble or hide her face. But the pain was there. The pain was in her eyes. She'd been abandoned. Forgotten. Alone in this tower for so long.

Marie could feel the pain. It rang like a wineglass struck with a knife. The vibrations quivered in her stomach, singing its song in her heart. Loosening the lid on the emotional black box.

"What do we do?" Marie said.

The princess's mouth opened like a wound. No words came out. Only the struggle for another breath.

Marie remembered the Counselor's story. She searched her pocket for the nut the hussars at the market had given her. It would lift the curse. Her pockets, however, were empty. It had fallen out at some point during the running and jumping and fighting. It could be anywhere. She had to find it. Had to put an end to the curse.

Fritz put something in Marie's hand, closed her fingers around it, and hid behind her from the sight of the princess. It was hard and heavy, oblong and furrowed. Marie opened her hand. When the princess saw what she was holding, she grunted and snerked a retched breath. Her head shook like it was attached to a spring.

The ball was heavy.

It was the ball Godfather had given him, shaped like an oversized walnut that hummed with warmth. She turned her back to the princess, to face her brother. She didn't understand what he was doing. Sandy had washed up on the shore of Marchpane Castle, but he would come back when they left Candyland. She was sure of it. Besides, this couldn't be it.

"Crackatook," Marie whispered.

He looked up with heavy eyes, put his hand to his mouth like he was biting an apple. This was the nut that would lift the curse. The hardest nut in all the land. The Counselor had told the story. It wasn't just a story, though. He was telling them about this very moment. *Godfather gave us the crackatook.*

"Fritz... this is *Sandy.*"

He nodded. It broke her heart (as if there were any pieces left to break) to see him like that. Putting his hand over hers, closing her hand around it. She closed her eyes.

The crackatook must be cracked open in front of the princess.

The kernel handed to her with closed eyes by one who had never shaved or worn boots.

Seven steps backwards without stumbling.

Marie had never shaven. Had never worn boots (that she knew of). How was she going to crack the nut? This was the job for the nutcracker. *Where is he?* He'd never come with them to Candyland. Even though she was holding him when she came in. Even though Sandy insisted he was always there.

"I'm not the one," Marie said.

A part of her wanted to turn and run, look for the door in the sky to leave and never come back. The princess was hideous. *I don't want to be the one.*

But she knew. Deep down, it had to be her.

THE CRACKATOOK WAS like iron between her teeth.

She bit down, tentatively at first. The hard shell didn't give one bit. A little more and her eyes watered. She was about to stop when she felt the first fracture. *Pop!* A bitter taste was on her tongue. Pain spiked in the roots of her teeth, but still she bit harder. The shell fell in two pieces between her lips.

The kernel was golden yellow.

The princess held out her withered hand. The fingers like dry leather. With Fritz behind her, Marie closed her eyes. She reached out and felt the princess's cold, coarse skin brush against her palm. Spidery fingers took the crackatook kernel from it.

Marie stood barefoot, listening to the kernel crumble, crushed between wet gums in a lipless mouth. A warm light began to glow. Marie resisted the temptation to peek, to see the transformation. There was still more to do.

Fritz stepped aside. Marie put her foot back. *One. Two.*

A drip of water fell on her head.

Three. Four.

The sun was in front of her. She clenched her eyes against the brightness. The floor crackled beneath her. Without stumbling, she continued.

Five.

Six.

With confidence and eagerness to see Princess Pirlipat, she took the seventh and final step.

31

The distant sound of tiny feet echoed in the stairwell.

A deep pain dug into Rinks's side. She stopped to put her hands on her knees. The air was dense and hot, like she was huffing it straight from an exhaust pipe. Her teeth, pointed and sharp as needles, pierced her bottom lip. All of that was nothing compared to the hollow pain in her chest, like she'd taken a right hook from a world boxing champion.

The general kept hopping. Rinks raised her hand. Her words puffed out. *Go,* she thought. *I know where she is.*

Her sister had a familial smell. Rinks had grown up with that scent on the bathroom towels and the clothes she borrowed (stole). She raised her chin, nose twitching in the dead air.

I'll find you.

There was no love lost between her and her sister. No love had existed. They were bad roommates. Reluctant classmates. Sibling rivals wasn't it at all. It's not a rivalry if you don't care. Rinks couldn't care less. She'd taught her sister a valuable lesson by throwing out the trophies. Her sister never thanked her for it. None of them did. They didn't understand how attached she was to those things. She was addicted to success. Rinks made her see that.

"You see me now?" she muttered.

The pitter-patter of tiny feet grew louder. Pairs of beady eyes bobbed in the dark. *Squee-squee-squee.*

"Come, chickens. Come to mama."

Rinks staggered a few steps, then caught her stride. The stitch in her side cinched tighter, but she powered through it, fueled by righteousness. Her sister needed to recognize her true self. She needed to admit how she'd treated Rinks. She needed to apologize to Rinks. Right to her face.

"Vern! Get out here." She pounded the door with open palms. "Now!"

The clutter of things fell, an avalanche of things gold and silver. The slap of bare feet. The door opened. Seven heads poked out. Each held a different expression.

"Shut up. All of you. If you want that stuff, then you better follow." She was running again. "I mean it!"

It wasn't clear if Vern would leave his treasure behind, but soon Rinks heard the clunk and clatter of precious loot jangle in pockets and pouches. The rattle of her husband's saber in the metal scabbard. Beyond him was the distant rumble of tiny feet.

Squee-squee-squee.

She followed the scent—left, right, right, left. Stagnant air scratched her lungs like vaporized wool. Her legs grew heavy. She pushed around the final turn, where a white laser blasted her between the eyes. Her head snapped back. She tumbled into her husband's lumpy belly. Seven sets of whiskers tickled her face.

Through fingers that had grown knobby and pale, she squinted into the light. The sun was fifty feet away. It hurt her brain. But she could smell her in there. Her sister and something else. A walnut or pecan. Bitter and spicy.

A horde of Jojos filled the corridor behind them with musky odor. Balls of fur flooded toward them. Swords and spears raised. Rinks elbowed Vern in the doughy midsection. He pulled his saber. Rinks lifted her fist.

"See me now!"

She led the charge into the light, a gasping, haggard queen with a tilted crown on her head. Eyes closed, following the scent of her sister, to confront her for all the wrongs, to make her beg for forgiveness. Apologies Rinks would gobble up like Christmas dinner. She licked her lips. How delicious it would taste, her sister admitting she was wrong after all this time.

Through the doorway.

Into the light.

Suddenly, she was on the frozen lake where she grew up. On one foot, arms waving, sliding and twisting. Peels of ice curling under her toenails. She leaned forward and back, side to side, but without a blade to catch the frozen surface, she couldn't gain her balance. Her feet flew out.

Rinks landed on her back.

An explosion of stars twittered in a dark cloud. Arms and legs spread, she spun like a hockey puck. Arching beams turned overhead; glittering crystals moved across the ceiling. Slowly, she came to a rest. A tender knot swelled on the back of her head. She looked up at the ceiling and thought of church or a citadel or something special. A stupid smile bloomed on her lips.

It withered when a shadow fell over her.

32

Adrenaline raged a steady drum.

Numbers appeared like flashcards as she counted the steps. There was no one to stop her. Only Fritz and the princess. The taste of anticipation on her lips. On the last step, the final step, her heel landed on something soft and gagging.

Marie stumbled. Fell.

Bright light grew painfully brighter. It ran through her arms and legs, rang in her head, hardened her ribs. She lay as still as a felled cypress. Clumsily, Marie climbed to her feet. Legs stiff, joints creaking. Inside her, a little black box fractured. A pilot light of blue flame flickered. Heat coursed through her, lighting emotions leaking from the black box like wildfire through dry pasture.

The empty thrones cracked.

The sound of crackling wood was in her ears. Embers glowed in her heart. Geysers of ignored emotions, packed down in that black box, shattered the brittle shell that contained them. She stepped toward the tilted thrones. Her feet, clad in heavy black boots, splintered the ice. Cracks ran over the floor and up the crystal walls. Spidered the ceiling.

The snap of her teeth echoed like a gunshot.

"Where are they?" she said.

Her voice, dark and brooding, shook the pillars. The princess, gone. Her brother, gone. The thrones empty.

Someone scampered on the floor. A half human, half mouse clawed at the ice. Her crown tangled in a nest of gray. Toenails carving tracks but not finding purchase to stand. Marie snatched her aunt by the tunic. As effortless as lifting a doll from a tea party, she held her at arm's length. A wild animal kicked and spat.

Marie was growing.

Her boots, her starched red jacket, a patch of whiskers on her chin and shaggy eyebrows eluded her. She had no idea what she had become. The burning question consumed her.

"Where are they?"

The power. The rage. It spilled from her in plumes of smoke. A mighty column holding up the ceiling shattered. Frozen boulders punched holes in the floor. Fumes smoldered in the cuffs of her jacket. Pellets of ice rained down and danced. The Mousequeen dangled like a puppet. Her throat was swollen where Marie's seventh step had landed. She tried to speak, turning helplessly on a hook.

"WHERE ARE THEY?"

This wasn't what Marie had wanted for Christmas. This was not what she *needed*. She continued to swell, growing another five feet. Her body sounded like trees bursting in a forest fire. The Mousequeen's clawed feet twittered high above the fractured floor; she sank her needle teeth through Marie's white glove. The tunic slipped through Marie's fingers. The seven-headed Mouseking was there to pull his queen away. Mice formed a circle around them. Clad in breastplates and helmets, they launched metal-tipped spears that bounced off the looming wooden soldier. Marie stomped the floor and sent them tumbling. Some fell through cratered holes.

Marie doubled in size again.

The hat on her head punched through the ceiling. Shards shattered on the floor. A patch of pink sky shone through. A black square nestled between cotton-candy clouds.

The thrones fell in pieces. Columns collided and crashed. Broken lines were all around. She swung tree-trunk arms at the injustice of it all. Unsheathed her sword at the unfairness of a cold, uncaring world. Beneath the merry air of Candyland was a current of ugliness and sorrow that suffocated her.

The chocolate shell that coated the castle fell in slabs, exposing shiny walls beneath it.

Marie swung wrecking balls at the emotions that hurt. She kicked at the feelings of pain. She could not get her hands on the sensations that smothered her. An inferno blazed inside her. Untapped rage ran unchecked.

The army of mice scattered.

The Mousequeen and Mouseking were gone.

Marie swung around, picked up her boots, kicked the debris. She was alone in the wreckage. She had failed the princess. She'd failed her brother. Her parents.

There was no one left to fight.

The walls fell around her. The treasures her uncle had hoarded spilled down into Rose Lake. The chocolate shell fell away, swallowed by the rose-tinted waters without a splash. The castle glittered, once again, in all its glory. The castle she had seen once before, an extraordinary model in the basement of a cabin deep in the woods—but that memory incinerated like tissue paper.

The inhabitants of Candyland, as tiny as mites, marveled from the shoreline.

Snow came in big, beautiful flakes tinted pink. From below, she heard the cheers welcome it. The snow swirled around her, landed delicately on her wooden nose.

Above her, the black square had vanished.

Marie stood atop the tallest spire, completely exposed. Fully vulnerable. This was who she was. This was what she had been hiding. This ugly beast. This vengeful torrent of rage. This was the journey, and the journey betrayed her. Her greatest fear had been realized. They saw her for what she really was. Her all-consuming anger at the world for wrecking her family. Her ugliness was out.

The black box is open.

33

"Where are they?"

Rinks didn't recognize the voice that shook her into consciousness. The ceiling sparkled high above. Fractures swept across the beams holding it up. A pink sky shone through pockets that had opened. At the last second, she rolled away. A jagged chunk of ice shattered next to her. Fragments sprayed her face. She struggled to breathe. Her throat had nearly swollen shut.

She panicked. Scrambling on the slippery floor, she went nowhere. Her royal tunic began choking her. She clawed at her throat, felt her feet rise off the floor. She tottered back and forth. Rinks knew she was becoming a mouse. Her husband, he had seven heads. But what was holding her like an unspun yo-yo shocked her.

It was a nutcracker.

The toy soldier was ten feet tall and growing. The strange thing that sent shivers down her hairy back was it was alive. It was holding her. And to her nose (which had become quite sensitive), it smelled like her sister.

"WHERE ARE THEY?"

Rinks struggled to breathe. She flailed; she scratched. The Jojos were rushing in, standing behind her seven-headed husband like useless bugs. What were they going to do? Seeing as she was dangling from a wooden monster, who was currently destroying the castle, what could they do?

Rinks helped herself.

She managed to pull herself up and plant her teeth into the nutcracker's finger. It was enough to get loose. She landed like a bag of jellybeans. Her Jojos surrounded her, her loyal chickens, and sailed their useless weapons at the swelling titan. It was her husband who pulled her away, dragging her on her backside.

"No," she muttered. "The castle."

The nutcracker would destroy everything. There would be nothing left if they didn't stop her. It wasn't just the walls. Its stupid hat punched holes through the ceiling. Debris fell like bombs. The floor was caving in. And the floors below that. Vern's treasure (however many rooms away that was) was crashing through the devastation.

Vern threw his arms under her. He lifted her head and pointed at the pink sky. Snow was beginning to fall in big, fat flakes. The peaceful kind of snow that dampened the world's troubles. She resisted what he was telling her. But he was right. There was no other option. She whispered to the Jojos, told them to run.

She would be back for them.

White specks shot from the open gift like a snow machine.

It swirled around the bedroom. The red string lights rattled on the walls. The air mattress flapped. Loose clothes whirled beneath the workbench. The blank pages in Marie's journal flipped.

Vern slammed the gift shut.

The gift wrapping on the side of the gift tore down the side. The frigid cyclone was over. Rinks sat against the wall, the red lights draped over her head. The scar on her cheek burned. She panted like a dog in summer. A storm still overturned thoughts in her head like loose change. Was any of that real? When her husband turned around, her question was answered.

"You okay?" one head said.

"You hurt?" another said.

"Get up!" said another.

Rinks hid her face. The whiskers on her upper lip poked the palms of her hands. "Ah!" she cried.

"What? What?" Vern said. "Are you okay?"

"Okay?" She jumped to her feet. "Look at us! Oh my god. Ohmygod… *we didn't change!*" She reached for the gift. "We have to go back."

"No! She's destroyin' it, Rinks. She'll take us with it."

"She? Where were you? It was the…" She pointed around the room, looking for that dreaded toy soldier Fritz played with. "The nutcracker lost his mind!"

"Marie!" said one of the neck heads. "The nutcracker is Marie!"

"We saw her change," another head said.

"When she stepped on you," said another.

Rinks shook her head. The brainstorm was still howling. *Marie? She smelled like my sister.* "That's… that's *impossible.*"

"We saw it!" they all said.

Well, Rinks supposed, anything was possible in that box. After all, she was part mouse. "We have to stop her. That's our home in there. And we look like this. We can't be out here like this. We got to stop. We have to—"

"We can't, Rinks. You heard what she said."

Where are they? Rinks had heard it loud and clear. Her ears were still ringing from it. "Fizzy. She was looking for Fizzy." No, wait. *They. She was looking for Fizzy and*—"She's lookin' for *them.*"

"Who?"

"My sister. Her parents. Who else?"

"They ain't here," Vern said. "And they ain't in there."

Yes, they are. "Keep that closed. We got to think. Where's Fizzy?"

"He's in there."

"No, he's not. He was in there with her; then he wasn't. *Think.*"

All seven of Vern's heads started whispering to each other. Fritz had been in that ice church when they got there. When the ceiling fell and the door in the sky appeared, he was gone.

"He's out here," Rinks said.

Vern and all his heads nodded.

"STAY AWAY FROM THE WINDOWS," Rinks said.

It was coming up on midnight. Most people were at home waiting for Santa to come deliver their Christmas loot. But if a car drove by and saw a seven-headed mouse eating slices of cheese over the kitchen sink, they were going to stop. Worse, they'd take a photo and post it. That was what Rinks would do.

"Look in the bedrooms. Check the bathroom," she said. "He's around here. I can smell him."

Maybe it was his clothes she smelled. Didn't matter. They needed to find him. He was their bargaining chip. They could send a message into Candyland. Make a deal with Marie. Her brother for their castle. Or what was left of it.

Rinks looked out the back door. The yard was brand new and inviting. She didn't dare go outside.

"Fritz!" Rinks called. "Hon, come out. Aunt Rinksy needs a talk, darlin'."

She went to the storefront. The shelves stuffed with toys were, thank God, just regular toys. It was creepy, though, in the dark. The sound of her toenails on the floor made her cringe. She checked the aisles, behind the counter, peeked under the tree.

"He's not here," Vern said, nibbling on a slice of cheese.

"I can see that. Keep lookin'. He's around here somewhere."

"Look where?"

"I don't know, Vern. Under the bed, in the closet. The shower. He's hidin'. Sniff him out!"

The heads snapped at the last bite of cheese like hogs at a trough. "You shoulda been nicer to them, Rinks."

"I am nice!" She threw a stuffed cheetah with purple stripes. "I gave them a home and food and clothes."

She cleared a shelf with a sweeping hand. Her fingers long and knobby and gross. The toys tumbled at her disgusting feet.

"What about me? When do I get what I want? I ain't a mistake. I got nothin' to give, and you want me to be nice? That what Marie wants, she wants me to be nice? Just because she lost her parents? I GOT NOTHING!"

She kicked a baby doll down the aisle.

"My parents were *never* nice. They *never* talked to me. And Marie's special? Why, because she's a kid? She'll learn life ain't fair. There ain't no rule book to all this. Not on Christmas or any other day. It is what it is, and that's what you get. Deal with it. She's throwin' a tantrum, Vern. A spoiled brat makin' a fuss because she don't like what life dealt her. Boo-hoo and cry on your pillow. Get over it."

Rinks grabbed the last bite of cheese from one of Vern's seven mouths, mashed it on the floor. It squeezed between her long toes.

"Now I look like this. You look like that. Is that fair? And she's wreckin' our castle while we're out here. That's ours in there. *Ours.* That ain't fair at all. I don't belong out here lookin' like this. I never belonged out here."

That was the truth of it. She never belonged. She didn't want to be here, either. Marie wasn't going to take that away from her.

"Where you goin'?" Vern said. He grabbed her arm. "We got to stay here, Rinks. Hide out for a bit; let things settle down."

Rinks was shaking.

"We never have to leave the store," he said. "We'll put the boards back up. Order food. Build a nest of our own. It'll work like that, Rinks. And when it's time, we go back. We stay here for now, temporary like. We can have our own children, too. We can do that."

Rinks rubbed her eyes. "We got children, Vern. We left them *in there.*"

The Jojos had been running scared when Rinks and Vern had leaped out. Falling in those craters Marie had been making.

Throwing their tiny spears to protect their mama. And she'd left them.

"They're safe." The breath from seven mouths was in her face. "They're in the tunnels. Remember the tunnels? The Jojos will be waitin' for us down there when we go back. They'll be waitin' for their queen."

She waved away the breathy stink, a mix of coffee and cheese, and paced in a circle. He was making sense. They couldn't rush back. Marie the nutcracker was probably the size of a skyscraper by now. She'd snatch them out of the sky if they leaped in now. Let her get tired. Distracted. They could go back then, find her little Jojos underground.

Vern rubbed his greedy hands, licking his lips. All his lips.

They could stay here, make their own nest. Be as normal as two half-mouse people could be. "Okay," she said. "All right."

She picked up a headscarf from the floor. It was paisley with bright colors. She found two more and draped them around Vern's neck. Tied them together.

"It's hard to breathe in here," the neck heads muffled.

"I just want to talk to you, Vern. Not them."

"I am Vern!" they chorused.

Rinks put her hand on his cheek. The whiskers were long and pokey. "You're my Vern."

He leaned into her hand, nose twitching. Smelling her. Black eyes blinking, he took a knee and bowed his head. He spoke—they all spoke—and chills straightened the coarse hairs on her back.

"My queen."

She could get used to this. They could make this their nest. Throw those owl clocks out and have Jojos of their own. And when the time was right, they'd go back to claim their kingdom. Rinks put her hand on the crown on his head. A royal gesture accepting his allegiance. For the first time in her life, she felt special.

Something floated between them. It looked like a fuzzy dust bunny dancing on a draft and landed delicately on the back of her hand. When it began to melt, she realized what it was. She turned around to see more wafting out the open door that led to the children's room, where the gift was.

It was snow. Pink snow.

A PEPPERMINT BREEZE carried snow into the storefront.

It gusted in waves, rattling sheets of paper and sending the rocking chair in Storyteller Corner back and forth. The red string lights in the children's room tapped against the wall. Snowflakes melted on the floor.

Rinks and Vern knew what was happening.

They slipped on the floor where the snow had melted in tiny droplets. Three steps closer to the room, they were hit with a gale that blew the crowns off their heads. They chased them down (what is royalty without proof?) and started again. Doors banged off the walls. The toys Rinks had shoved on the floor tumbled like weeds. More tipped off the shelves. The Christmas tree chimed in the corner.

They worked their way close enough to grab the doorframe, holding their crowns on their heads. (Four of Vern's crowns were lost.) Snow streamed from the gift like a confetti gun. The air mattress was thwapping like a loose sail. When the current changed directions, it swept it off the floor and slammed Rinks and Vern square in their pointed noses. They skidded down the aisles, fingernails etching white lines in the floor.

They rolled against the front door. The shelves were cleared. A mountain of toys cushioned their stop. The pink snowstorm howled around the storefront like a horde of ghosts, sweeping anything loose into the corners. Ornaments flew off the Christmas tree and burst like light bulbs.

"We'll go around to the back door!" Vern shouted. He reached up to unlock the front door. "It's the only way—"

"No!" Rinks pulled his arm down. "Are you out of your mind?"

There was nothing that could chase her outside. She didn't care if the town was deserted for a thousand miles.

The children's room was puking pink ice now. It plinked off the metal shelving, bounced across the floor. Pelted Rinks on the face. She used a blue whale as a shield. If that gift was going to freeze them out, no big deal. She grew up in long winters. She could take it.

The first hunk of gray fur flew out like a bouncy ball. It ricocheted off the rocking chair (no longer rocking on its side), caromed off the ceiling, and landed in the Christmas tree (also on its side). The branches pushed apart. A pink nose twitched.

General Rat climbed out. With his helmet on sideways and sword twisting on his belt, he hopped through the toys and leaped into Rinks's open arms. The fuzzy general nuzzled in her embrace. He popped his head up, let out a squeak.

Rinks didn't need Vern to translate. She understood.

ALL THE MICE followed the general. Ten thousand in all. Disheveled, yet dutifully uniformed.

They were tossed out of Candyland like food poisoning. A volcanic eruption of fur and tails bubbled into the storefront, blown to the far side into waiting arms. The swarm of vermin mauled their queen, squirming over her and around her. Only her face could be seen.

She loved it. The warmth. The love.

It lit a fire in her. Should anything dare come out of that room to hurt them, it would deal with her and her seven-headed idiot.

The snow accumulated on the floor and shelves, drifted in the corners and frosted the windows. A foot of the pink stuff piled on the stage of Storyteller Corner. The temperature plunged despite ten thousand mice panting steamy breath swirling in the eddies.

When the last Jojo came bouncing out, the wind died. The storm was over, just like that. Only the ticking of the old building settled around them. Nothing stirred. Not even a mouse. Patterns of crystal lattice crept over the windows. In the tense silence, she appreciated its beauty.

Vern stood up. Mice fell off him like fallen leaves. If he ran for it, he could close the gift and weigh it down with the refrigerator before another pink snowflake popped out. He took one step.

Clop. Clop-clop.

A shadow stretched out of the children's room. On the back of a tiny, plastic steed, a smartly dressed hussar sat. He was no taller than a mouse standing on its hind legs. It was pretty clear one of Rinks's little soldiers could take the hussar in a straight-up one-on-one. The toy horse danced in place, its hooves tapping the floor, as the hussar surveyed the storefront. When his eyes narrowed, he unsheathed his sword. Raised it above his head. Chills ran down Rinks's neck, the kind that said *run now!*

General Rat was unimpressed. He squealed orders.

The mouse army scrambled for position. They fell into ranks, lining up with weapons at their sides. However, they were crammed into the corners and digging through snow, crawling over each other to see the hussar slowly approach. If that wasn't bad enough, the storm opened up again. Hussars poured out the doorway. Some were on horseback. Most tumbled out like the mice had. The wind blew what little order the mice had assembled into a squirming ball of chaos.

Rinks was buried in panic. She clawed her way out, standing up to breathe. The general's orders changed. They were doomed if they stayed where they were.

"No! No, no, no!" Rinks slapped at her Jojos, but they persisted. The general was right. They needed space. They needed room to organize. To defend their queen.

The floodgate flew open.

The mice billowed through the front door. They fled the storefront, where hussars appeared one by one, two by two and more. The soldiers filed into formation and raised their weapons. Above the howling storm, the wind and ice, their little voices cried.

"Hooah! Hooah!"

They marched, line by line. Plowing through the snow, slicing through the ice. Columns of uniformed soldiers filled the aisles. Sleet shot over their heads like artillery. It tinked off the glass, bounced into the street.

Rinks crawled against the window. Vern huddled next to her. He'd given up all hope of running around to the back door. The entire building shuddered. It was going to fall like the castle. Under the general's orders, the mice gathered around their queen and guided her outside.

The building exhaled snow through the front door. It whipped high into the night, swirled over the buildings. The peppermint current glittered like fairy dust. It was thick and dazzling. Plumes of sparkles cartwheeled down the sidewalks and up the sides of the buildings, rustled awnings and rattled locked doors. It raced under parked cars, swirled around the fountain and shook the branches on the great Christmas tree.

The long exhale ended when the final hussar emerged.

There were a thousand of them in all. They marched into the street, locked in step, chanting as they went. "Hooah! Hooah!"

The mouse army crowded the sidewalks on both sides of the street. Their queen and king (but mostly their queen) they guarded in the doorway of Happy's Candy Emporium. The armies eyed each other, waiting for orders. The plastic steeds held steady. Weapons were at the ready. There were no caves to escape to, no streams to cut off a charge. This was it.

The toy store breathed again.

The peppermint air coughed a steady stream of snow and ice. It piled on the curbs and rested on awnings. Coated windshields with frost.

"My crown!" Rinks watched it roll down the street like a loose wagon wheel.

"No!" Vern grabbed her. "Stay here!"

"We can't leave," a head said.

"Don't be an idiot," another head said.

Rinks struggled to escape his iron grip (his hand felt like a trap on her arm). She felt naked. Without her crown, she was just a big ugly mouse. But then from the front door, the first of many came rolling onto the asphalt. It came to rest across the street, popped up, and shook off the snow.

It was a dwarf.

Six more followed. Then came the other weirdos who had crowded the market at Rose Lake. The dancers and robots, the slinky springs and twirly tops. Lollipops and licorice whips, rolly dusters and mini-busters. Gnarly rooters and shooter tooters, pop-its and shove-its, wheelie-makers and frog-stakers, cookie cutters and ditch rutters.

Candyland barreled into the real world.

They ignored the tense standoff, running and dancing, hand in hand and leg in hook. Singing. Laughing. They climbed over parked cars and stared through store windows. The buildings had taken on a sugary glow.

A car stopped at the corner. Its headlights beamed into the chaos. The driver and passenger got out. Snow fell on the hood of the car. Jaws dropping, they reached for their phones. When they found they mysteriously didn't have reception, they tried to take pictures. When that didn't work, they got back in their car. When it didn't start, they honked the horn.

"The toy store is haunted," the driver said. In a sense, he wasn't wrong.

Candyland crept over the town. Bricks turned into gingerbread. Rivets and bolts became chocolate drops. Tires transformed into cookies.

Lights came on in the apartments above the stores. People looked down on the improbable snowfall and the impossible mob. Giant flakes of pink snow drifted down from a starry sky. It muffled sound and condensed breath into fog.

Once again, the wind died.

If a picture were taken at that very moment, it would've been fit for a holiday calendar. A scene imagined by the mind of a twisted artist who stayed up late on too many nights. It was still and magical. For a brief moment, everyone and everything looked up. They felt Christmas nearing. Sugarplums invaded children's dreams. The sound of Santa's sleigh bells. It was peaceful, it was.

The toy store exhaled one final time.

34

Toxic emotions seeping from the pores of her wooden body smelled sulfuric and rancid.

They condensed like storm clouds, filled her lungs. It was a bottomless black box full of roiling pressure that was somehow empty and full at the same time. An all-consuming emptiness pulled on every aching fiber in her body. It highlighted a gaping black box. Nothing could escape its gravity.

The lid on the box was gone. Blown to pieces.

She wanted the box gone. Covered up like a turd in a litter box. To make it go away. Wishing it never existed. But she couldn't look away. It had become her.

I don't want this!

The mighty sword cut the air. It shattered the thrones. The remaining walls crumbled and fell over the edge. She searched the remains for the missing piece in her life, the thing that would make her whole again. There was nothing but smoke and rubble.

"WHERE ARE THEY?"

The words rippled down the castle. Floors shook. The chocolate walls continued to fall, turning end over end on their way to Rose Lake. They dropped into the rose-tinted water with barely a splash.

She kicked the stump of a once-pristine pillar over distant mountains. All the power made the ache worse. Even with the villagers watching from below, the endless stretches of candy-striped forests and chocolate-dipped hills, the caramel waterfalls and faraway kingdoms—she was alone.

"WHERE ARE THEY?"

A dark violet wave bruised the pink sky, rolling through it like an ugly sound wave. A box flickered in its wake. The outline remained long enough for her to see it. The lid to the gift had been closed. Her aunt and uncle had escaped. They'd locked her inside. Her brother was out there. She could feel his absence. Her search, her answer to this dull, unimaginable pain—this idiotic journey—wasn't in Candyland.

It's out there.

She raised the mighty sword. The central ridge along the flat length gleamed. There was no sun in Candyland. No moon or night. Yet the sword flashed its brilliance. *Yes,* it said. *It's out there.* She stood on the toothy ledge of the castle, a peppermint breeze fluttering up the sides to ruffle the tufted beard on her square chin. The tip of the sword slashed through cotton-candy clouds. Onto the toes of her boots, she jabbed deep into the pink sky.

It struck something hard.

She drove the sword higher. The lid was heavy and resistant, but a flash of red light briefly escaped through the opening. The string lights in the bedroom were visible for a moment. She moved closer to the edge, leaning further onto her toes. With all her might, she thrust the sword upward.

Clink.

The red lights. They began turning. Marie let go of the sword.

She was falling.

THE HAT FELL AWAY. The sword turned somewhere below her. For a moment, she was weightless. Drifting downward like a boulder breaking from the side of a mountain. There wasn't much impact, not like you would expect. Falling into water from that distance would break anything into little unrecognizable pieces. But this wasn't ordinary water. This was Rose Lake.

Marie sank below the surface as smoothly as dipping her fingers in a bowl of tea.

Rosy light quickly dimmed above her. She paddled her enormous arms and kicked her tree-trunk legs. They swirled in the dark water without purchase. Even wood would not float. A current dragged her down. She expected to find a hard bottom to kick off from and surge upward and outward. To escape her pain.

There was no bottom.

The world became a dark shade of scarlet. It turned to burgundy silt. Coldness sank into her like serpent teeth spreading icy venom. She fought the grip of the current, twisted and turned. Her screams came out in bubbles that were swiftly pulled into a riptide. Even they didn't escape.

Marie sank deeper.

Time had stopped. It was a continuous present moment that did not move. The panic to breathe subsided. She was a wooden soldier. She had no lungs. No stomach or organs. She was not going to die. The harder she fought, the deeper she sank. There was nothing she could do. She had the sense Rose Lake wanted something from her. A key that would allow her to be free.

It wasn't like Rose Lake was talking. There were whispers in the water, but not exactly words in her ear. No rosy mermaids singing to her. She felt it. She felt the wishes as if the water itself was a current of thoughts. It wanted her to give up, to let the current take her where it was going. To be a leaf in the river. A stone in the ocean.

To surrender.

No, she answered.

Felt herself tumble head over boot, not knowing if there was an up or a down. The numbing waters were inside her. She felt their cold hands rush through her and gush into the emotional black box, swirling its contents.

NO!

She snapped her jaw. Shockwaves erupted. The black box slammed shut, seams bulging. She kicked and screamed and swung her arms. She didn't want this. She didn't ask for this. She wanted it to go away, to leave her alone. *To never have happened!*

There would be no surrender. Not today or tomorrow or ever.

She pulled her knees to her chest, locked her arms around her shins. Lacing her fingers together, tucking her head against her knees (the hat had floated away), she folded her body as tight as a clam. As impenetrable as the pearl inside it.

NO! NO!

Her knuckles as white as the gloves that covered them. Arms and legs creaking under the strain. Joints popping. Weightless, she hadn't noticed she was no longer sinking.

Eyes squeezed shut.

Mind blank.

She no longer heard Rose Lake's invitation. Whether it whispered to her or not, she repeated a single word over and over in her mind. Her mantra of resistance that kept her hard and unyielding.

NO! NO! NO!

Her feelings encased in a concrete shell, she hung in the silence, a numb ball of wood. Seeing nothing. Feeling nothing. Becoming nothing. Rose Lake heard her answer.

It answered back.

FROM DEEP BELOW, a current rose like a volcanic vent opened up. It swept her upward like the remains of a shipwreck. She was spit out into the frigid air. Marie remained clamped down, spinning over the raspberry-tinted water. Soaring like a cannonball fired from the deck of a warship. Wind whistled past her ears.

She landed in the snowy bank, half buried in the soggy earth. She uncurled on impact. Arms unfolding. Legs springing outward. Her eyes snapped open like shutters. Disoriented, she'd forgotten what she'd become. *What am I?* was her first question. She didn't see that her arms and legs, her chest and back had become wood beneath the red coat and white gloves. Then, looking up at the sky, she thought, *And what is that?*

The world had turned upside down.

Snow was falling in the wrong direction.

Her red jacket with brass buttons was drenched. The white gloves on her hands soaked. Her head rested in the soft embrace of the snowy shore. Hooked candy canes had erupted from the ground like striped streetlights. They sprang up like weeds. Pink snow swirled above her. It wasn't drifting down from the sky—although a thin layer of the pink stuff had accumulated on her square jaw. *It's snowing upward.*

It sounded like a full-throated carnival had begun.

There were shouts of joy. Screams of fun like children coming down a slick waterslide. Hats tumbled upward. A funnel was turning in the sky, sucking snow and carts and toys and dwarves and hussars into its vortex. There were mice and plastic horses, crates of chocolate, dust storms of sugar pulled from rooftops, walls of gingerbread, and gumdrops from Gumdrop Alley.

They were falling into the black square in the pink sky.

Marie sat up. Her gloves sank in the snow. The world wasn't upside down. Candyland wasn't falling down through the black square. *It's being sucked out!* The landscape around her was rising off the ground. She didn't turn around to see what had become of the castle. Even if she had, she wouldn't have appreciated what she would've seen.

A pilot light ignited fumes of anger. It began to warm the deadwood shiver inside her. It incinerated emotions leaking from the box.

Rose Lake erupted again. An enormous burp ejected what belonged to her. It spun like a helicopter blade. *Whoop, whoop, whoop.* And speared the ground next to her. Next came the hat with the looping chain, falling with a sodden *thwap.* She fixed the hat on her head. Grabbed the sword that had been spat out from Rose Lake, and looked up at the black square.

The gift was open.

She'd lost the princess and her brother.

She knew where to find them.

MARIE CRAWLED through the front door of the toy store.

She pushed her way through, splintering the frame and cracking the windows. She stood to full height, staring directly at people in their second-story apartments chattering in the winter chill. Looks of shock and amazement.

Her steely gaze took aim at the scene below. It locked onto each thing and every person. The hussars stood before her in formation on the plastic horses. They parted like a curtain and pushed through the snow that threatened to bury them. The horses dug through it. Marie took one step. Her boot hit the pavement.

The buildings shook.

Snow fell from the sky like ash. It clouded the space between the buildings. None of this mattered to her. She was in the real world and made of wood. All of Candyland had escaped with her, and none of that mattered to her.

Mice were clotted at a candy store like a swarm of bees. Buried in the shadows, she saw the twitching noses. The fire crackling in the hearth of her chest smoldered. Puffs of gray smoke leaked from beneath her vest. One earth-shaking step was all it took. The mice scattered.

The Mousequeen and Mouseking ran for it.

The hussars charged. The vermin army turned tail. It was a slow retreat through the piling snow. The hussars barely managed to dig their way out. Marie stepped over them. With each plodding stride, the blizzard grew. The buildings were fading shadows. It felt good to run. She needed to escape the emotions burning her alive.

"WHERE ARE THEY?" she released.

Windows shattered. Alarms went off.

Her wooden legs numb. Her stomach a knotted ball of snakes; her chest a metal cage. Christmas cheer tainted by the foul breath in her mouth. She ran harder. The snow came thicker. A toy here. A car there.

Sirens whined in the distance. A snapshot of spinning red lights.

She outran everything except the snow and the memories glittering on their crystal edges. Her memories poured out of the black box like ghosts. They stuck to the snow, petrified her limbs, saturated her with fear heavy and cold. She ran blindly into the storm.

Running and running and running.

35

This isn't happenin'.

Rinks was a mouse. Her husband had seven heads. The buildings were gingerbread. For some reason, it was a twenty-foot nutcracker that was most unbelievable.

Smoke puffed from its sleeves. Vengeance burned its eyes. Boots that would smash her army like ants on a sidewalk. They were useless to her. Worst of all, the nutcracker reeked of ungratefulness.

The brat.

Marie's eyes scanned the area, looking for Rinks. "Hold still," Rinks said. "Everyone, be still. She won't see us."

They huddled deeper into the doorway beneath an awning sagging under the weight of discolored snow. The mice went limp, their tails lying like cords of rope. The tiny heartbeats pitter-pattered against Rinks. Whiskers tickled her face.

"Vern, shut your stupid heads up."

The bickering didn't stop (they were arguing about the best way to escape), but it dropped to whispers. There was no way Marie would see them. It would look like a discarded rug piled against the door. A rug with tails. If the peppermint wind kept blowing, they would become a snowdrift. She was plenty warm under the tiny bodies. In fact, she was starting to sweat. They were going to make it. When Marie was down the road, they would run in the other direction.

Vern sneezed. The idiot.

Rinks peeked out. There was so much going on already, Marie didn't hear it. But then one of Vern's heads said, "Bless you."

"Gesundheit," another one said.

"Shut up," another said.

"RUN!" said another.

That did it. An avalanche of fur scattered to the sidewalk. They burrowed into the snowbanks and ran along the gutter. Hussars raised their swords. "Hooah!"

"Get back here! I'm your queen! Protect the queen!"

She was alone in the corner, just her and her mutant husband. Vern scrambled onto his stumpy legs and hurried off. Trinkets fell from his pockets as he waddled for safety. Her little chickens were gone. Was it because she had no crown? Did they forget? A second ago, they had been dutifully hiding her. Now she was completely exposed. A giant weirdo on the street.

Steam shot from Marie's nostrils like a mechanical bull seeing a red cape. A steam engine pumped to life somewhere in the enormous wooden head. Then the eyes fell on her like wrecking balls. With one step, a heavy boot cracked the pavement. The awning ripped open and dumped a load of pink snow on Rinks. Not enough to hide her. Too late for that.

The ground thundered. Sent waves of terror to the top of Rinks's head. She bit her lip and tasted blood. It was over. Everything she fought for was going to end any second now. As soon as her selfish niece put that oversized glove around her, that would be it. *Fine,* she thought. *I don't belong here anyway.*

"What are you doin'?" Vern returned. "Come on."

"It's goin' to be all okay," a head said.

"RUN!" said the one.

Vern pulled her off the concrete. The general squealed in her ear. They ran close to the building, where the snow was the shallowest.

The mouse army had abandoned their weapons. The hussars gave chase on their stupid little horses. "Hooah!" Most of the hussars, though, were lining up on both sides of the street. They were clearing a path for the oncoming giant. Like Marie was a one-person parade. They saluted when she neared.

Vern tried to open the door to the video game store. It was locked. The next one was a clothing store that sold candles. Locked. The coffee shop, locked. Marie's footsteps knocked them off-balance each time one of the boots shattered the pavement. Rinks wobbled against the window of the coffee shop. The mechanical elves with their wooden tools were gone.

It was too late to try another door. He fell on the ground with her, wrapped his arms around her neck. The general climbed onto her head. Nearby mice returned to her side and scurried into her lap. The general called for reinforcements, and more mice came from the snowdrifts. The hussars ignored them as they got in line to salute the wooden menace.

Marie smelled like sulfur. Snow melted around her and ran down the gutters. Vern leaned into Rinks. At that moment, she loved the smell of coffee breath. The way his sharp whiskers poked her cheek. Vern put his lips to her ear (it wasn't one of the neck heads; it was her Vern) and whispered, "My queen."

She shivered with delight.

If they survived, she would love him. All of him. Maybe she'd twist a few of the heads off, just the mean ones (definitely the one that said RUN!), but she'd keep the rest. Because she loved him. He got her.

She closed her eyes. *He sees me.*

The footsteps drew near. Rinks and Vern were bouncing off the sidewalk now. A heatwave fell over them like a runaway wagon of burning hay was coming. The snowmelt soaked their clothing. Her bones rattled.

"WHERE ARE THEY?"

Rinks held very still with her only family that loved her. She smiled a fangy smile in her wet clothing. Still a queen.

The next footstep didn't bounce her as high off the concrete. The next one only tickled her bum. She didn't open her eyes, imagining that steam engine of rage leaning over them. Rinks wouldn't give her niece the satisfaction of seeing her quiver.

Squeak.

The general had climbed out of the pile. He leaped on her head and squeaked again. Rinks peeked through one eye. The back of the nutcracker was fading in the pink snowstorm.

"She didn't see us," Rinks said. Marie was blinded by pettiness. Probably saw something shiny and got distracted. "Dumb girl."

The hussars followed the nutcracker into the pink haze. She was just a fuzzy patch of red and then vanished in the storm. The mice were hopping with excitement. The general raised his weapon (the only one not to drop it). Rinks was on her hands and knees, watching to make sure Marie didn't return. She stepped into the street.

We're safe, she thought.

Marie didn't want anything to do with her. She saw Rinks, looked right at her, then walked on her way. That opened all sorts of possibilities. Marie might be marching all the way to the North Pole, for all Rinks knew. And now that the buildings were candy and the weirdos were playing in the street, that meant one thing. Rinks didn't have to go back. Her kingdom had followed her into the real world.

And I'm the queen, she thought proudly. *Get ready, world, for the Mousequeen.*

She wouldn't have to hide her whiskers. She could be exactly who she was. And she was going to show the world. She searched for her phone. What better time to post a selfie than now?

The watermelon snow was starting to accumulate now that Marie wasn't melting it. Only now it was drifting sideways, she noticed. There was no wind, not even a breeze, but the delicate flakes were floating into her face and moving down the street. Before she turned around to see where it was going, she heard Vern.

"My crowns," all seven heads muttered.

Someone had the crowns he had lost. There was also a big one crusted with jewels. Rinks put a hand on her head. Felt the blank space on top of her coarse mop of graying hair. Vern was reaching for them.

"Vern, no," she said. Then louder, "Stop!"

FIZZY.

The boy stood in the middle of the street with that gross hat pulled down to his eyes and a dopey grin on his dopey face. Like a cat waiting for the mouse to poke her head out. The crowns looped around his arms and dangled at his elbows. Vern's little crowns were bunched on his left arm. Rinks's crown (the only one that mattered) was on his right. The only reason Fritz wasn't holding them like horseshoes was because his hands were already full. A cloaked figure stood on each side of him, holding his hands.

The king and queen.

Rinks could smell her sister in the dark cowl. The fragrance she wore in high school. The sweat after skating. She could feel the condescending stare behind the wisps of frosty breath.

"Hey, buddy," Vern said. "Remember good old Uncle Vernon? Yeah, it's me. Real quick, those are mine. Thanks for findin' them for me. I'll just—"

"Don't get any closer, Vern."

The general squeaked agreement from Rinks's shoulder. Vern froze with a hungry hand out and fourteen hungry eyes. "He got our crowns, Rinks," he sang.

"Mine!" another head shouted.

"It's a trap," Rinks said. She could feel it. It was her sister holding Fritz's right hand. She couldn't trust her, never could.

"But the crowns, Rinks."

"No, it's bait. They want you to step closer. Ain't that right? You want us to get in there and blind us with a memory, which is a lie, after all."

"Why would they want that?" Vern said.

"Because it's her! It's what she does. She's usin' poor little Fizzy as bait, don't you get it? It's disgustin', treatin' your own boy that way. I ain't fallin' for it again."

"But." Vern pointed at the other cloaked figure. "It's his dad. He says—"

"Shut up, Vern! All of yous. I know what I'm talkin' about here. You don't think I know what she wants? Fool me once, shame on me. Fool me twice, it's her fault."

Pink snow was streaming faster down the street. It stuck to her face, even stung a little, before it melted. She could feel the wind pulling them now. Somewhere in the opposite direction the snow was flying, Marie screamed in the distance.

"Where's that sandman of yours?" she asked Fritz. "Bet they took him away, didn't they? That's what your mom does. I'm sorry to say that, but it's the truth."

Rinks really put some sting on that, but he kept on smiling. Maybe he'd gone deaf, too.

She knew that wasn't her sister in that cloak. Not really. It smelled like her, it felt like her, but her sister was gone. Then again, Vern had seven heads. So there was a chance.

"I took your kids. You could start with a thank you. I didn't even want them." She said it right into that black hole inside the hood, glanced at Fritz after she said it. *Still smiling.* "Vern and me were perfectly happy before you and the hub packed it in. Now you guys are just goin' to, what, just come back and take it all away from us? That's just like you. You can have the kids back. I want my crown."

"Don't say that," Vern said.

"You don't want your crowns?"

"About the kids. Fritz is good. So's Marie."

"Phht. What planet you on? He don't talk, and she don't listen." There was a long distant moan. It was hard to tell if it was human or animal. Either way, it made the hairs stiffen on her back. "Besides, who you kiddin', Vern? You know her." Rinks took half a step and pointed. "She couldn't stand we had the castle. Could you? It was eatin' you up so bad you came back just to take it. It ain't fair, you know. I finally get somethin', and you can't stand it. You don't know what it's like to work for it. You don't. It all came sooo easy for you. Just wake up and someone givin' you awards and presents and all that. Family and money. Let me tell you somethin', sister. Money can't buy happiness."

Rinks felt the twist of hypocrisy in her stomach.

She grabbed Vern's arm. He was creeping closer to the crowns looped around Fritz's arm. The snow was starting to sting her eyes. The Candyland weirdos felt it, too. They were walking down the street in the same direction it was flying. Even the hussars retreated with them. Not her mice, though. They hid in the snowdrifts.

In the direction Marie had disappeared came a long, lonesome wail. Someone was crying. It wasn't an animal.

"Hear that?" Rinks said to her sister. "Hurts a little, don't it? Your angry daughter sad like that. Your son, all he does is smile."

"*Rinks—*"

"Hush it, Vern. She's got to hear this. How's that make you feel, sis? Me and Vern pickin' up your pieces. Who's the big mistake now? It ain't me. I'm the good one now. Bet that feels a little ugly, don't it? I know."

The hussars were marching in lines. The war was over. Good. They could all go on their way and leave her mice alone. Rinks held up her hand to block the snow. It was coming off the ground now and stuck to them. Her sister's cloak was dusted on one side like pink frosting.

"So you done havin' all your fun? Your nutcrackin' daughter done wrecked everythin' and went runnin' off. Fizzy here, you can have him. You think I give a hoot?"

Rinks dropped her hand. It was starting to tremble. Her voice cracked. She could taste the biting venom in her words. She thought it would feel good shouting at her sister. The words she deserved.

"You're not the queen!" Rinks pumped her fist. "I got news, you're just ordinary. That's all you are. And me, I deserve better. I deserve more! It's Christmas, and this is what I get?"

The last of the Candyland weirdos hustled with the wind. Some were caught up in the current and tumbled like beachballs in a sandstorm. Rinks was knocked off balance. Vern kept her from falling. She sniffed, then turned her head. Wiped her eyes so her sister wouldn't see the water starting to pool in them.

Fritz let go of their hands. The crowns rang on his arms. He held them out to them. That stupid little smile still on his face. The venom hadn't affected him in the least. *He is deaf.*

"What?" Rinks said. "You just going to give them to us? I ain't fallin' for it."

"We got a choice," Vern said.

"Choice for what?"

"We can stay here. That's what he said." He pointed at Fritz's dad, who hadn't moved an inch. Vern, evidently, understood the creepy silence inside that hood. "Everythin' goes back to normal, just like before. Like none of this happened. We keep the toy store and the kids. It's our choice." All of Vern's heads cocked their ears. In unison, they nodded. "If we stay, he said, you can get help."

"Help? Help for what?" He didn't say. Rinks knew what he meant. Help for what hurt deep inside her. "What's the other choice?"

"We take the crowns."

Fritz held them up. Vern looked in the direction the snow and the toys were going. The wind wasn't blowing them down the street. The snow was being sucked into the open door of the toy store like an industrial vacuum was running on all cylinders. Dwarves and hussars and a few mice and dancers and little army men and teddy bears and robots rolling inside it as well. The walls of the toy store were billowing inward. One of the windows shattered.

Candyland is callin'.

"What about her?" Rinks said, nodding at her sister. Vern shook his head.

Rinks twitched. The scar felt cold and heavy. Her heart felt the same. The air was thinning. It was difficult to breathe. She looked at the sky. Stars were strewn across a dark blanket. Somewhere something howled long and soulful. This time she knew it was an animal. Its call quivered inside her.

She looked at her husband. Her freaky, ugly husband and his

seven heads. She wasn't much different. She was darker than him on the inside, perhaps. The choice was a no-brainer. But the longer she stood there, the harder the decision became. Vern felt her struggle and removed the few crowns he still possessed off his heads. He held them to his chest.

He knelt before her.

She took a deep breath, then another. *Heavy is the crown,* she thought. And she wasn't wearing one. Did she want to?

The roof of the toy store collapsed. The walls fell over. Bricks tumbled into the street. Candyland was about to close up shop. She looked at her husband. The heads on his neck were beginning to shrink. *Everythin' goes back to the way it was.*

She chuckled and wiped her eyes. Sighed and looked down at her nephew still making his offering. "It's not what you *want,* ain't that what the fat man said, Fizzy?"

He didn't answer. Only smiled.

36

The town bell chimed.

Lights twinkled dimly. They were too numerous to be fire trucks, unless the entire state had been called. Exhausted, she approached them. All that running and she hadn't gotten far at all.

The great Christmas tree appeared.

The star on top of it shone like a lighthouse on a rocky shore. She had not one more step left in her. The sword fell from her aching hand. She dropped to her knees, hands sinking in the snow. The inferno that drove her had died to a tiny flame. She panted and shook, arms quivering. Legs weak. Her mind filled with the static that runs on a dead channel. Something was there. She just couldn't tune it.

The town bell signaled its last chime and faded into silence.

The snow continued to fall.

It piled on her back. Melted down her cheeks. She had nowhere else to go. No matter how fast or how far she ran, she would always be exactly where she didn't want to be.

Here.

Christmas was out there, somewhere. She could feel it reaching for her. It was a low hum that vibrated in the haze. It rose and fell as delicately as snow. Soft and comforting. Promising. The hum turned into a melody rising from closed lips and open throats. From the blizzard, shapes emerged. She had no strength left to grip the sword. No will to raise it. She let whoever had come for her come.

She could run no more.

The figures came out of the winter blur, tall and short. Some bearded, some not. They surrounded her just out of reach and cloaked in winter's veil. Their song humming. Their song comforting. They surrounded her, holding hands. She wished not to know who they were or what they wanted. Only to be left alone. To rest in the empty static.

Someone came forward. Beneath the blinking lights of the Christmas tree, she stood with her head bowed in a white cloak of fine silk, the cuffs trimmed with red. The hem bunched in the snow. Her hands no longer shriveled and dry, but tender and soft.

Princess Pirlipat reached up to pull back the hood.

The misshapen head was no more. The mouth no longer a slit, nor the eyes bulging. Marie looked up to a glowing princess. She reached for the nutcracker on her knees. The princess sifted her fingers through the coarse black hair on the soldier before her. A soldier who fought long and hard for longer than she realized. A warrior who battled to keep her enemies locked in a black box. A soldier exhausted from the conflict, collapsed before her. Totally exposed.

Marie looked upon the face of the princess.

Tears leaked from her wooden face. A trickle, at first. They ran down her hardened cheeks. They gave way to a stream. The black box that once was clotted with fiery rage now gushed with sparkling light. It surged forward as a tsunami, engulfing every bit of her. Her sobs came out in long cries that stole her breath. She collapsed under the weight of it, curling up in a bed of pink snow. Each wave racked her harder than the one before it. A briny flow of emotions extinguished anger and rage as it flooded through her. It beamed with light as bright as the star on top of the tree.

The princess knelt beside her.

The humming grew louder. It wrapped its song around her, sank inside her. They drew closer, hands locked together. Through a wash of tears, she couldn't see them. But she felt them. The love and support. Their presence and song embraced her. It held her while she let go of what she'd tried so hard to ignore. The thing that would destroy her if she faced it. Grief spilled from bottomless depths that she feared would drown her.

The princess leaned over, and in her ear she spoke in a voice Marie very much recognized. The princess said, "I miss them so very much."

Marie's wooden body splintered. Her wails of sorrow shook the star atop the Christmas tree. The armor crumbled off her, leaving her wounded and raw. She wept for her brother. She wept for her parents. For the first time, she dared to admit, to even allow herself to think what she held so dear in her heart. For if she did, she would not survive. She wept for herself.

I miss them so much.

The dark night continued. If the grief would consume her, she was helpless to stop it. Unlike Rose Lake, she did not fight it. She did not kick it away or flail in its depth. She allowed it to take her. She made space for the pain. All the feelings she'd stuffed inside the black box flowed into the current.

The circle around her parted, but their presence was still there. Through closed eyes, she felt a great shadow move over her. The musky smell of fur was in her nostrils. Large nostrils, wet and quivering, snorted the length of her. A big black eye looked deep inside her. The reindeer lifted his head. To the world, he opened his throat. Through thick, rubbery lips, he cried out long and loud enough to be heard all the way to the North Pole.

Ronin wept.

Marie curled up beneath him. His four legs planted around her, never moving. Nothing would ever hurt her while he stood over her.

She breathed in sadness and floated downstream with it, let it carry her away. Adrift in the long night of grief that lasted a lifetime.

Under a watchful eye, surrounded by the loving hum of song, she dissolved into slumber. On the edge of consciousness that still quivered and sobbed, she heard bells draw near. Ronin shuffled away, but not far. He stood beside her, watching carefully as someone approached.

Strong arms picked her up.

She tucked her hands under her chin, felt the tender lump in her throat. A nutcracker no more.

37

Ｉt was a long, winding river of night. Through the stars it flowed. In the small corners, it puddled. The journey swept her far and wide until she floated toward the sound of a crackling fire.

Her eyes were puffy and sore. Orange sparks flitted in the dark. *Christmas fairies off to deliver wishes,* she thought.

She was wrapped snugly in a swaddling, purple blanket. A fire danced in a round pit. On the other side of it were two empty Adirondack chairs, exactly like the one she was sitting in. On the armrest of one of the chairs, the nutcracker stood. He was a foot tall, mouth open. As stiff as a tree limb. The dragon and teddy, the ones she had found in the backyard, were below him. On the other armrest was a glass of milk and a plate of unwrapped protein bars.

Marie looked around.

Her head was heavy and filled with sand. Memories were elusive. She'd fallen asleep by the fire, she reasoned. Although reason was a flimsy card in her fizzy state. *Fizzy,* she thought. And then thought of Aunt Rinks with long whiskers and a pointed nose. *Fritz brought out the milk and protein bars. Didn't he?* The light was on inside the kitchen. A shadow went past the window. *Fritz?*

Her stomach ached, and her ribs were sore. She tried to remember, but everything was tangled and frayed. Memories were bits of flotsam on a salty tide of sleep. Waves of sorrow still washed up inside her, only now they slid over her instead of thundering down and churning her in a riptide.

It was a dream. She laid her head back and stared at the stars. *An awful dream.*

The air was cool. She sat at the edge of the fire's warmth, a thud in her stomach and knot in her throat. The lure of sleep cast over her eyes when an ash escaped the thermal rise above the fire. It fluttered in a random pattern. Marie watched it slowly drift toward her and noticed it wasn't gray. It landed on the purple blanket over her lap and began to melt.

It was pink.

Warm exhaust blew the hair on top of her head. She tried to sit up but was too disoriented to do much more than duck. Tree branches swung over her. A long, furry muzzle reached for the ground in front of her. Rubber lips snatched up slices of carrot strewn on the ground. A black eye turned toward her.

Marie leaned away, the armrest creaking. The reindeer lifted his enormous head, the antlers catching some of the overhead branches, then knocked over one of the empty chairs. She didn't move as he sniffed her arm. His nostrils tickled her cheek. Humid breath exhausting on her face.

The back door opened.

Someone came down the steps with a sigh. Backlit by the kitchen light, she couldn't see who it was, only knew he was much too big and round to be her brother. He stepped into the fire's glow, wearing a white T-shirt with black suspenders. His baggy pants were burgundy. His boots heavy and black.

"Watch your head," he said with a deep voice.

He wasn't talking to Marie. The reindeer snorted as the man picked up the chair that had been knocked over. He sat down with a groan (more like fell into the chair) and pushed wire-rimmed glasses up his pudgy nose. He looked over the fire at Marie. A smile hidden in his gray beard.

"Godfather?" she croaked. Her voice sounded like it came through a cheap speaker.

"Rest, dear. It's been a very long night."

The reindeer stretched his neck and barked agreement. He went back to snatching carrots off the ground, noisily grinding them between his teeth. Godfather watched Marie melt back into her chair. Kindness radiated from his eyes. He watched the reindeer search the weeds for lost carrots.

"It's been a long night," Godfather said. "I wanted to send him back with the others, but he wouldn't leave you."

Marie watched Godfather sip from the glass of milk. He licked his lips and picked up a protein bar, examined it in the firelight. On second thought, he put it back on the plate and took another swallow of milk.

This time of year is very busy, Marie recalled Godfather saying.

Marie shook her head, but it no more cleared it than if she shook a snow globe. A thousand questions rattled like bingo balls in a tumbler. Each one screamed for attention, begged to make sense from this dreamy scene. She swam in an ocean of unknowns. Only one question fell out of the chute. Depending on the answer to it, the other questions wouldn't matter.

"Is this real?"

"You are here," was all he said. "As am I."

She looked at the building. "Where's my brother?"

"He's home, Marie."

Home? A part of her wished that meant the impossible. That he was curled up in the bed he grew up in, and she was in the room next to him. And this *was* just a dream. *That* was home. The toy store was just a building.

"We wanted to be with you before you go back. After a difficult journey, I thought this prudent."

He put the glass of milk down and examined the nutcracker, turning him over to pull the lever. Watching the mouth open and close where nuts would surrender their treasure. Even ones impossibly hard. With a sigh, he looked at her again. His eyes so relaxed and open. She could swim in their kindness.

She pulled the purple cocoon around her tighter.

"I remember when your father was a boy." He tipped his head back and smiled. "When he was Fritz's age, he would make bows out of saplings. Fashioned arrows from tree branches. He and his friends would run through the woods behind his house like they lived in the wild. They cut vines and drank the water that dripped out, which made his parents quite concerned when they found out. But they liked his bond with nature and sent him to Earth Camp in the summer, where he camped and fished and carved bowls from wood. He went a week without changing his underwear. He also cut his hand and went to the hospital for stitches."

He dragged his finger over the fleshy base of his thumb. Right where her father had a white scar. Godfather chuckled deeply. His eyes twinkled with firelight.

"He was six years old when he got his first skateboard. When he wasn't running through the woods, he was practicing kick-flips. He and his friends..." He shook his head, chuckling. Looked up at her. "Those kids can do magic on four wheels. I don't understand it. And I've seen reindeer fly."

Godfather laughed heartily.

"He was scared of robots, your father. His parents would find him curled up at the foot of their bed. He got over that, given the things he would eventually build for me. He still buttoned his shirts wrong, though, and never cared. An artist's heart, he had. An imagination with wheels. He was kinder and funnier than most. He was a beautiful boy, Marie. And a great man."

He let that thought hover between them. It landed on the soft part of her mind like seeds blown onto black dirt. They gave rise to vivid memories of what he was like. Memories she'd stuffed down at the bottom of that emotional black box. Buried beneath the hurt.

Memories she could now see.

"And your mother." Godfather grumbled with laughter. "Not like your father. Nothing got in her way. Not even when she was a toddler. A will as strong as steel. When she put her mind to something, it yielded to her wishes. From the time she was born, she moved with intense grace and fierce elegance. She was on the naughty list, your mother."

He held up four fingers. *Four times.*

"Oh, yes. Your father was an explorer, but she was a pioneer. Testing boundaries was her hobby. She got good grades and all, but do you know how many times she was suspended?"

Marie knew that answer. Her mother had told her when Marie was suspended for fighting a girl in gym class who stole her phone from her locker. Marie got it back, but not before they ended up on the ground. Her mother took her out for lunch and a long talk. *There's good trouble and bad trouble,* she had said. Marie didn't exactly know what that meant at the time.

"Your mother had her regrets, Marie. She damaged relationships she couldn't repair. She was human."

He shared more stories. The awards her mother had won. The hours of practice it took to win them. The way she fought with her parents and her sister with a head as hard as concrete. Marie sank into the chair, felt like she was dripping between the seat slats. There was space for her to hold these memories now. Before, she could only think about them from a distance, then slam the lid shut. Before other feelings escaped. The memories Teri, her therapist, wanted her to explore.

Joy and grief can coexist, Teri had said.

"When your mother and father met, it changed her. It changed them both. They shined together. I knew them better than most people. She grounded your father, instilled him with risk to find his endless potential. He softened her, made her feel the world more deeply, to not try to bend it to her will. Together, they were beautiful. And so are their children."

He didn't take his eyes from her. She didn't look away. They sat that way for a very long minute. The air between them warm and swirling. This moment perfect in its brokenness.

"They're gone, aren't they?" she said distantly. "They're not coming back."

"My dear," he said softly. He touched his heart. "They never left."

He reached into his pocket and pulled out the gift. Still wrapped in red and white paper with a green bow. He put it on the armrest of the chair between them. He stood the nutcracker next to it.

She leaned forward in the chair, swaying as she did so. Ronin grunted, put his head down to keep her away from the fire. She grabbed the bony ridge above his nose and stood up. The blanket fell away.

She didn't notice what she was wearing or the bandage around her left arm. She was too focused on the wrapping paper that had torn from the side of the gift. She shuffled a step, hanging onto Ronin, and reached for the gift. The wrapping paper ripped off the sides and fell into the fire. The dying flame brightened. The box was simple. It was black.

Christmas is what you need.

The back gate squealed. The trees around her rustled. A song rose up from those who were coming into the ring of fire. Marie looked down to see the white cloak of fine silk she was wearing. It bunched on the ground around her feet. Red trim along the hem and cuffs. The clothing she'd seen someone wearing at the top of the castle. And at the great Christmas tree when she had knelt next to Marie and whispered in a voice that sounded, to Marie, very much like her own voice.

"You found yourself," Godfather said.

Ms. Clara approached from the back gate with Ms. Trutchen by her side. Garl waddled out from the trees. The mechanical elves came down the narrow path with their crude wooden tools in hand. Pate the hussar came bouncing out of the dark with both arms raised. The hussars from the market were with him. The teddy bear and the dragon she found in the trees leaped up. The gummy worms crawled in the dirt. The Counselor with his gray skin and long, flowing overcoat stood to the right of Godfather. And a snowman made of sand was on his left.

Marie felt her legs wobble. She leaned against Ronin. Ms. Clara was the first one to hug her.

She wrapped Marie in her tender, strong arms. Ms. Trutchen put her arms around her, too. Garl was at her thighs. The soldiers' stiff arms around her shins. More and more they came, all humming the song she'd heard at the Christmas tree. The song that had lifted her through the dark night and carried her to the other side so that she could see the joy.

The Christmas spirit that was always there. That had never left.

The greatest gift of all.

38

Stars floated on a black tapestry like bright little bugs, randomly shifting about and blinking. A slow-moving dance. Hypnotic. Marie swam with them, weaving a dance of her own. Free to move, no longer confined by the hard shell of a body. It was timeless and lovely. A dreamless sleep that embraced and nurtured. She had no thoughts of where she was, no thoughts of here or there. Of waking or sleeping.

Then, slowly, ever so, space turned gray. She didn't know to call it that—*gray*—but sensed things had changed. As the transition continued, she felt the weight of the world wrap around her, and opened her eyes.

Morning light sparkled on a textured ceiling.

The bed was bigger than the one she'd slept in as a child. It was king-sized. A soft comforter was on top. The sheets smooth; the pillowcase smelled like fabric softener. Fresh paint was in the room. The walls bright yellow.

A chair was in front of a dresser. On the nightstand next to the chair, several wrappers were piled up. Chocolate smeared on the insides of them. A cup with a dried ring of orange juice at the bottom.

Even in the elegant comfort of the king-size mattress, aches and pains poked her arms and legs. She felt like a stone that had tumbled down the mountain, the sharp edges rounded and smooth. Bruised and beaten. She sat up on one elbow, winced at the tender pain in her arm.

A bandage was wrapped from wrist to elbow.

Memories were details in a fog, poking their heads out and laughing when she looked for them. A fragment escaped, and she saw a shiny object that had cut her arm: the long red line, the sticky crimson drips on her elbow. And the thing that threw it. A thing with seven heads.

How awful dreams could be.

A shelf was on the wall. A single object on it, looking back at her with spreading wings and a clock in its belly. Menacing eyes unblinking. It read ten o'clock. The clock her aunt hated. Said it made her stomach hurt.

This is her room.

It smelled different, though. No mold or dust; no spiderwebs on the ceiling. No dirt balls. A complete and total makeover that was as bright and clean as the sunlight coming through the window.

Slippers were by the side of the bed. She slid her feet into them. Exhaustion clung to her like a winter coat. She was a sponge squeezed of every drop and left to dry on the windowsill. She shuffled to the window, her rusty joints beginning to loosen. Across the street, two-story buildings of brick and glass stood. No snow on the awnings. *And something else*, she thought. *Something more ridiculous than snow. No cake icing. Or gingerbread walls. How odd.*

Outside the bedroom, the kitchen looked familiar. A new table and chairs, new cabinets and floor. Marie peeked in the other bedroom. The air mattress was gone. In its place was a bed (not as wide as the one Marie woke up in, but new). Red string lights were on the wall. A dresser was in the corner, the drawers half open. Above it, in the corner, was a hole where a camera used to be.

It was all so strange, like she'd accidentally awakened in a different reality, one that seemed familiar. It had that new-house smell with a hint of bacon and eggs. *Where was I?* she wondered.

There was a faint memory of sitting at a fire with a big dog eating carrots off the ground. And Santa Claus drinking milk. *I'm still dreaming.*

Then she saw a hat on the dresser. Beat up with a white rind of salt. The bill frayed. It smelled like a tackle box. The adjustable strap was tightened as far as it would go. Her stomach twisted a little. Fritz never went anywhere without that hat, not since they moved in with Aunt Rinks. Last time Marie saw it, someone else was wearing it. That someone was hiding in the mists of memory. *Someone in a cloak.*

But she dreamed that, too. She dreamed Fritz holding the stranger's hand at the end of a long, narrow hallway. The hat on the stranger's head. And light beyond.

It wasn't a stranger, she thought.

The workbench was sanded and coated with a layer of polyurethane. The owl clock that had sat on the top shelf was gone. *I took it with me.* Before she could tell herself that was a dream, too— that she hadn't dragged that strange clock into a box where a land of candy awaited—she saw the soldier standing guard at the checkered wall.

She felt weak and woozy.

The blocks on the wall looked new. The one with the X—the one she had removed first before solving the puzzle—was different. She picked up the nutcracker. The legs stiff, the coat starched. Memories swirled from dusty corners of what it felt like to be strong and unyielding. Smoldering with power. She pulled the lever on his back. The square jaw opened and closed.

We found her. We found Princess Pirlipat. I cracked the nut to break the spell. She rubbed her front teeth. Her gums were tender. *Fritz gave me the nut. Only it wasn't a nut, and I cracked it open and gave it to her. I closed my eyes and counted my steps. And then...*

The seven-headed Mouseking. The Mousequeen. The castle came apart. Everything broke open. Including her.

Did it happen? Did we really reach into a gift and go to Candyland?

Nussknacker had never come with them. Sandy had always said

he was there, but she never saw him. Because Sandy knew. He knew all this time.

"I was you," she whispered. "I was always you."

Memories came loose and crammed into her head like an attic full of keepsakes shoved into a suitcase. Her head hurt worse than her arm. She remembered it all.

The journey didn't end. It escaped into the real world. The buildings became gingerbread. Toys ran in the streets. The mouse army in formation. The hussars riding. I was on fire. There was only one thing I wanted, one question that I had to answer. And it tore me apart when I did.

VOICES CAME FROM THE STOREFRONT.

The nutcracker creaked in her hand. She put her ear to the door. They were muffled voices. Barking laughter. She put her hand on the door, closed her eyes. Her heart swelled. She hugged the nutcracker under her chin. Her eyes felt drained of tears, but a slick of moisture appeared as she listened.

"Thank you," she whispered to the nutcracker.

He said nothing, of course. Just stared back with an open mouth.

She opened the door. The shelves were filled with toys. The windows were clean and new. The front door was not damaged; the doorframe not torn open. On the small stage in Storyteller Corner, the rocking chair had been pushed aside. A chessboard was on a circular rug. On one side, a young boy was reaching for his bishop.

"Sure you want to do that?" said his opponent. Scratching his round chin with a stick. Sand appeared to crumble on the board.

Fritz turned his head.

Marie threw the door open. Her brother was barely off the floor when she grabbed him. There was little chance he could breathe given that her embrace would frighten a grizzly bear. She never wanted to let go. Out of that dry well, one more tear found its way to the surface. It tracked warmly down her cheek.

Sandy threw his sticks around them. He wasn't real. But he was back. Her brother was safe, and Sandy was back. Maybe it was a dream. Some of it.

"Good morning, Ms. Marie."

She put her arms out and shoved Fritz behind her. He was smiling, though. Happy. The stranger had come from the other side of the storefront, wearing a long cloak. Marie felt faint as he reached for the hood.

His face filled with sunny color.

MARIE SAT at the kitchen table.

The Counselor cracked two eggs in a skillet. Bacon sizzled in another. He cooked with efficiency. Not a wasted movement. Total focus. It was easy to forget he was a machine. So natural the way he moved.

"Checkmate?" Sandy shouted from the storefront. "I think you're getting ahead of yourself, kid."

The Counselor poured a glass of milk. Put it on the table. "Take a few sips," he said. "You have not eaten in quite some time."

He went back to the stove, flipped the eggs. Toast popped out. He put it on a plate with the bacon and plied it with butter. There was an appetite somewhere in Marie. She hadn't found it yet. She took a sip of milk to soothe her throat. She put the glass back on the table and said: "Where is it? The gift."

"It is safe."

"What's that mean?"

His gears or something were whirring. "Godfather felt it was better in his possession now that the game has ended."

Game. That's a kind way of putting it. Great-Uncle Corker might have had something to do with Candyland (he was a game maker), but that wasn't a game.

"Do you know what happened to us?" she said. "To my brother and me."

"You completed your journey. I know that much. You have been asleep for nearly twenty-four hours. You are exhausted and quite sore, I understand. Your journey was not easy." He wiped grease from the counter. "One of that nature rarely is."

"Does he remember what happened?" Marie said. "Fritz."

"Of course. It was his journey, too."

She looked at the door leading to the storefront. "Is he... is he okay?"

"He is quite well."

"I thought I lost him." She struggled to remember the details. But the feelings were crystal clear. "Everything got so confusing, and... I couldn't find him and thought he..." She shook her head.

"He is exactly where he needs to be, Ms. Marie. As are you."

The Counselor's voice was soothing. The kind of voice that could hypnotize. That was by design, she figured. But liked it just the same. Marie let go of the glass of milk. Her fingers trembled. All the tension, the weight strapped on her shoulders, floated away. She leaned her elbows on the table before she slid out of the chair. Her cheeks were chafed and dry. Like she'd been walking into a winter storm too long.

"Are you hungry?" the Counselor asked.

Marie shrugged. She felt full and empty at the same time. Light and free. She rested in this moment, tired and confused. He put the plate in front of her. The bacon woke her taste buds up. She grabbed a slice, heavy and oily, and took a bite. It crumbled on her tongue. She chewed slowly, eyes closed. Wondering if food always tasted this good.

"Let us have a look at that, shall we?"

The Counselor took a knee next to her. He cradled her arm in his warm hands, began to unwind the bandage around her forearm. Her fingers greasy with bacon fat, she ate with her free hand. A rosy line ran from her elbow to her wrist. It was already healing. No stitches needed. The Counselor's faceplate sparkled as he inspected it. His hands were soft. He fetched cotton balls and a bottle of ethanol to clean outside of the wound.

Marie continued eating, staring at it like it wasn't her arm he was caring for. The cut was real. It was tender and sore. It stung when he dabbed the cotton ball too close to the wound. There could be an explanation for how she hurt herself. Maybe she scraped it on the back gate or cut it on a branch when she was working in the back-yard. That was possible, but not true. She knew exactly how she cut her arm.

It was wearing seven crowns.

"Was Candyland real?" she asked. "Or did I dream it?"

"What do you think?"

That was what her parents said when she asked if Santa was real. They let her decide. And when she answered, they winked.

"The snow was pink, just like the sky. The buildings became gingerbread, and toys were out there on the street. The mouse army and hussars. How did it go back to normal if it wasn't a dream?"

"Perception is not reality," he said.

"Then it wasn't real."

He touched the bandage on her arm. "It was *very* real."

She didn't understand how that could be. How she was injured, but everything went back to normal. A blending of real and unreal. Was it all in her mind? The cut on her arm hurt. And sorrow was in her belly. The howl of Ronin standing over her.

"I was him." She turned toward the nutcracker standing on the table. He was watching the Counselor wrap a new bandage around her arm. "I was so... so rigid. And big. And..."

Angry. And scared. All this time, all these feelings were inside the black box. Teri was right. But I didn't have time to look inside it until it was full. That's not true, though. I didn't want to look inside it. Because if I did, I would have to admit the truth. I'd have to let go of the wish I clung to with my fingernails—that one morning I would wake up in my bedroom, Mom would be downstairs, Dad would be outside. What happened was all a bad dream.

"The nutcracker story you told," she said. "She was cursed and needed to be found. You knew, didn't you?" She waited for him to answer, then added: "You knew she was *me*."

The Counselor looked up, tilted his head. His face blossomed blues and violets and greens. He held her hand between both of his hands. So kind and understanding. She dropped the last bite of bacon and wiped her nose. The courage to say the next words out loud wavered in her throat. They came out on a quivering breath.

"I miss them." She wiped her puffy eyes with the back of her hand. "I miss them so much."

She fell into his waiting arms, engulfed in his warm embrace, and wept into his soft shoulder. A new well of tears was found. He held her firmly, rocked her gently.

"I know," he whispered.

Marie sobbed as quietly as she could. It wasn't very quiet. It came from a deep place she'd locked in a box and sealed shut. A box capped with resentment and bitterness for what the world had taken from her. Now it was open. She could feel it all. The grief. The sadness. The longing and sorrow. And the joy of remembering. *Where are they?*

"They are here." The Counselor held her tighter. "They are here."

"I'M NOT GOING to say I got robbed," Sandy shouted from the storefront. "But I got robbed."

Marie looked away from the table, wiped her cheeks with the heels of her hands. Her eyes were tender and pink. She pushed her hair back. On second thought, she decided not to face whoever came through that door. She was so soft and vulnerable. Held together with sticks and twine. *Alive.*

"Who's next?" Sandy said when Fritz opened the door. "F-Dog is a cheater."

"In a minute," the Counselor said. "Marie just started breakfast."

Fritz went to the refrigerator. Sandy's bottom scratched across the floor. He stopped near her. "I don't think she likes your cooking, Big C."

Marie sniffed and tried a smile on. Before she found the courage to face them, a hand was on her shoulder. Fritz peeked at her with big eyes and a crimped frown that dimpled his chin. She managed half a smile.

"I'm okay," she said.

He knew exactly what she meant and took her hand. His fingers were cold. She warmed them against her cheek. Now would be a perfect time for him to talk. That would come in time.

"Perhaps you can fetch the Christmas present," the Counselor said. "It is under the tree."

Marie nodded again. This time she smiled and meant it. Sandy followed her brother back to the storefront, begging for another game of chess if he didn't cheat this time. She stared at the door, waiting for him to return. Her leg started shaking. She considered going after him.

"You do not have to protect him," the Counselor said.

"I'm not." When his faceplate spattered a collage of yellows and oranges, her voice sharpened. "He's little for his age. Sometimes they pick on him. And I'm all he's got."

She shook her head and wouldn't stop; tried to shake off emerging memories. Seeing him after he was pulled from school, when a social worker delivered the news to them about their parents. The way his innocence shattered. It sounded like an expensive vase tipping over. Marie was the opposite. That day was the day she shoved her feelings in the box and welded the top closed.

The day I became the nutcracker.

"May I say something?" He was kind and generous. Genuine. Waited for her to nod. "Be there for him. If you put your heart back in the box, he will not have a sister. He can feel it. Your love is big enough for both of you. You are here now. That is what he needs."

To be here. That's where she thought she was. Here, protecting him from bullies, from Aunt Rinks. From his feelings. She hadn't been here, though. Not all of her. The journey brought her back.

Christmas isn't about what you want.

The Counselor cocked his head. The colors morphed through the spectrum.

"You knew what was going to happen, didn't you?" she said. "That's why you told the story."

"I know a lot of things."

"You knew I was the nutcracker?"

"I knew you would find your way. Fritz, too. Of those things, I was certain."

She looked down and picked at the bandage. She thought of the empty thrones. The king and queen in their cloaks at the market, walking through the castle. She knew who they were. She asked anyway: "Was it them?"

The Counselor took her hand as if he sensed the emotions softening in her stomach. He didn't say anything, let her experience the swirling tenderness. Allowing her the space to finish her thought.

"Were they my *parents*?" she said.

"What do you think?"

She nodded and sort of laughed. She didn't want to see if he was winking. Because it wasn't them, not really. Candyland was real, but not really. But real enough for her to feel it. Real enough that Fritz had recognized the presence of their dad when he took him to find the princess. Let him wear the old cruddy, fishing hat one last time.

Real enough to say goodbye.

"What do we do now?" she said.

"You do what life requires. Sleep when you are tired." He nudged the plate. "Eat when you are hungry."

"What about Aunt Rinks?"

"She does not live here anymore."

"What?"

"Godfather has made arrangements that are in your best interest. Your aunt and uncle were poor guardians."

"They're not coming back?"

"At some point, they will. When they are done."

"Where are they?"

He stood up and squared his shoulders. He didn't answer. But she could tell by the colors on his face they were somewhere they needed to be. And they would come back. *When they are done.*

"In the meantime," he said, when he saw she understood, "I will stay with you. Is that okay?"

Living with a kind robot and a smarmy sandman? She smiled with her whole face. "I would like that."

"Then it would be my privilege, Ms. Marie. I am here to help."

THE DOOR to the storefront opened. Fritz was holding a brand-new skateboard in one hand. In the other hand was a small, gift-wrapped box. This one flat and rectangular. Sandy skritched in behind him, singing merry Christmas to the "Happy Birthday" song. Fritz put her gift next to the nutcracker. Marie considered not opening it. She'd already gotten what she needed for Christmas.

"From Santa?" she said.

"Yeah, Santa," Sandy said. "Fritz and I didn't get you anything. We were all a little busy."

"What'd you get?" she asked.

Fritz held up the skateboard. It was all he'd wanted ever since their dad had done an ollie in the driveway. Santa must've known. Marie leaned in and whispered, "I heard that board is magic." He laughed through his nose and spun one of the wheels.

"What did I get?" Sandy barked. Marie held up her hand, but that didn't stop him. "I got underwear."

Tighty-whities appeared on his bottom half, which he slowly shook in a circle, throwing his sticks up in the air. The dance was silly, but it made Fritz laugh. Fritz got two things for Christmas. One was a tubby ghost made of pretend sand.

"Good to have you back," she said.

"Where'd I go?"

Maybe he didn't remember Rose Lake. Marie started to open her gift before he asked any more questions. She peeled one end. "You know, I met Santa Claus last night."

"You were asleep," Sandy said. He pretended to elbow Fritz. "She was asleep."

Marie shrugged. "One of the reindeer was there, too. The big one."

"Ronin? Yeah, right."

She opened the other end of the gift, ran her fingernail under the tape to break it. She took her time folding the paper, peeking at the Counselor. He was focused on the gift.

"Mar Mar," Sandy said, "let's go before next Christmas."

"I was just thinking about what Santa told me."

Sandy slumped in resignation. "What?"

"Christmas isn't about what you want. It's about what you need."

"Yeah, that's great. Godfather said it, so..." He rolled his branches to hurry her along.

The Counselor looked up when she said it. His face blossomed like a rose. And for a brief moment, a silver light winked. Marie smiled and winked back.

Finally, she opened the gift. Inside was a long, white ribbon. The one she'd given away to get the cookie cutter. Pate had used it as a sling for his injured arm. It seemed like so long ago. The emotions began welling up again. They would do that for a while to come and when she least expected it. Just when she thought she was empty of tears, more would flood her eyes. She was laughing and crying as Fritz tied the ribbon around her head to hold her hair back.

"You *really* like ribbons," Sandy said.

She hugged Fritz, and he hugged her back. Her heart was big enough for both of them. Their parents were here, right now. Hugging in the kitchen.

"Would it be all right if the Counselor lived with us?" she asked.

Fritz nodded. She had hoped he would talk, but that day would come. He could take all the time he wanted. When he was ready, he would cross that candy-covered bridge. The Counselor bent over to hug them. The three of them with their arms wrapped tightly around each other.

"Can I get in on this?"

Sandy squeezed in the middle. The Counselor's faceplate beamed merry color down on them. Fritz laughed, and Marie cried.

That was the day the building became a home.

39

Candy Meadow sparkled with sugary dew.

The Almond and Raisin Gate was still standing. The bridge over the chocolate creek, though, had fallen. The posts were splintered. Beyond it in the faraway valley, the castle stood beneath the blushing sky. No longer a tall mudpie. The spires glittered, and walls sparkled. Even from that distance (a week on foot, maybe two), Rinks recognized what had been beneath those dull chocolatey layers.

It was in Godfather's dumb basement.

It was the model they'd sat around when he gave her the owl clock for Christmas. The market was filled with people, not fabricated weirdos, but still... she should've known. In Candyland, the castle now showed its true self.

Vern scrambled through the grass like a dog off the leash, licking the sweet dew from his fingers, zigzagging in one direction, then another as each head won an argument of where to go next. He ended up at the Almond and Raisin Gate with his face buried in the creek. Surrounded by her army of mice, Rinks watched her ecstatic husband dip handfuls of grass into the flowing chocolate like chips in a bowl of queso.

She was not tempted in the least to lick her fingers. They were long and knobby with hair on the knuckles. No chance to find a razor. At least she didn't have a tail.

She inhaled the minty air and straightened the crown on her head. This was where she belonged. Hairy knuckles and all. This was her choice. Her sister had nothing to do with it. She would tell herself that for years to come. These were her people (or mice). They belonged to her.

I'm the Mousequeen, she thought. Then decided another name would be more fitting. A new start deserved a new name.

"Come on, Rinks." Vern looked up. Every head covered in chocolate. "The stream ain't that deep. We can wade over."

"I don't think so."

"Well, we can rebuild that bridge. It won't take much. The mice can chew down a few trees. I'll have it up in no time. We'll be at the castle before night." He looked at the sky. "Does it get dark?"

She didn't know if there was a sun or a moon. There was a lot about this new world she didn't know. She was fixing to change that.

"The castle's not ours, Vern."

"What?"

She shook her head. "We're not goin' over there."

"Where we goin'?"

General Rat whispered in Rinks's ear. She looked over her shoulder. A narrow trail went between the red-striped trees. Rinks looked at the unblemished sky. A canvas of watermelon with puffy clouds of cotton. Not a black square in sight.

This is home.

"You deserve a name," she said to the rat on her shoulder. "How does... how does Harlequin sound?" The general winced. "Too romantic. Harry? Too obvious with the, you know..." She ran a finger down the general's back. He purred like a cat. "I've got it."

She snapped her fingers and whispered to her loyal rat. His chest ballooned. He lifted his pointy nose and flung his tail around her neck.

"Well, then, shall we?" she said. "General *Harley*?"

He squeaked his approval of the name and direction. They started for the dark path that cut through Christmas Wood into uncharted territory. The mice funneled onto the trail before her. Vern came running up behind her. Lips smacking and teeth chattering.

"Where we goin', Rinks?"

"To make our own kingdom, Vern," she said. "And my name's not Rinks anymore."

He stopped short of the tree line, unsure of what that meant. That was all he'd ever called her. She turned around with cool shade covering her face. Only her long and pointed nose was in the light.

"My name is Mouserinks."

EPILOGUE

It had been almost thirty years since Sean had been home.

There was no reason to come back. His mom had remarried and moved across the country with her second husband and three stepsons whose names he couldn't always remember. His brother had joined the service out of high school, got kicked out a year later. He was on his third marriage now, living in a log cabin somewhere where it rained a lot. Sean hadn't seen him in ten years. His brother probably didn't know Sean was a granddad. If he did, he wouldn't care.

His granddaughter was riding on his shoulders with sticky fingers in his hair, steering him like a donkey across the street, bucking him to go faster. When he reared up and whinnied, she laughed so hard she tooted.

He'd played horsy for four blocks. This time of year, parking was impossible. He'd parked in a neighborhood four blocks away. They'd walked past the big fountain. The Christmas tree was decorated, and a line of people waited for Santa to come out of his trailer. Old Uncle Dan had done that job when Sean was little. He would hide in Santa's trailer until someone came for him. When the time came, he'd climb the ladder to Santa's throne and let strangers sit on his lap. He did that for five years. But then he started riding his motorcycle around town in the Santa costume. Parents didn't like that much. It ruined the magic. They canned him and took the costume away. Sean heard he sometimes came down with his own costume and got in fights.

Sean checked the time.

The sidewalks were filled with shoppers, but most of the kids were crowded on the corner. Sean remembered the first time he'd taken his daughter to this event. He'd never gone to the toy store when he was a kid. It had just reopened, and the toys were stupid. When he was married, his wife at the time had made him take his daughter. The next year, he volunteered to do it. And the year after that. He'd even gone once by himself. Stood in the corner with other adults who didn't have little kids anymore.

Now here he was, thirty years later with his granddaughter pulling his hair and farting down his back.

Twin girls had their hands cupped to the window. Inside, three mechanical elves swung wooden tools in super-slow motion. They stood in a bed of cotton with a Christmas tree covered in red lights. Hard to believe those things still worked. He remembered when he was little. They had been somewhere else, though.

An elf was handing candy out on the sidewalk. Nancy Fluss wore curly-toed shoes and a green, velvety outfit. A bell rang on her floppy hat when she turned her head. She used to sit in front of Sean in English class, and he'd cheat off her spelling quizzes. Now she taught third grade and colored her hair sandy blond. Sean didn't have much hair to dye.

"Merry, merry," Nancy sang. "And who do we have here?"

"This is Leslie Sue. Can you say hi to Santa's elf?" Sean lifted his granddaughter off his shoulders. She hid behind his leg. "It's her first time."

"First time?" Nancy knelt on the sidewalk. "Your grandfather brought you to a very special place, did you know that? I'm so happy you're here. Do you have your elf ticket?"

Grandfather. Hearing that word out loud made him wince. He put a golden ticket in his granddaughter's hand. They hadn't been selling tickets when Sean's daughter was little. Now you had to reserve a spot. Leslie Sue waved the ticket at Nancy Fluss the Elf.

"Thank you!" Nancy scared the little girl with great exaggeration. "Go on inside. That elf right there will show you to your seat. Have a wonderful ride, darling."

Nancy didn't recognize Sean. He didn't bother reminding her he was a terrible speller. He walked into the building and was greeted by old smells and loud conversation. Leslie Sue put her hands over her ears. Sean hiked her onto his hip. He was dizzy with memories. The place hadn't changed. There were toys on the shelves and stars on the ceiling. Boxes in the corners and presents being wrapped. There was a herd of helpers at the checkout. A line of customers waited for an elf to ring up their totals.

Sean saw the elf Nancy had pointed out. He was having a serious conversation with a bearded man wearing wire-framed glasses.

"Here." Sean raised Leslie Sue's hand. "Wave it over your head so he can see us."

He held her up, and she nearly touched the ceiling. From that vantage point, she would be able to see across the store. She put her thumb in her mouth.

"Wave, Leslie Sue. Wave it."

She waved the golden ticket like a little flag. The bearded man with the wire-framed glasses saw her. The elf turned his head, excused himself, and worked his way through the crowd. Sean put Leslie Sue down, who promptly hid behind his leg. The elf approached slowly. His graying hair curled from beneath his floppy green hat. He nodded at Sean, then took a knee.

"Can I tell you a secret?" he said. When she peeked out with a thumb in her mouth, he said, "You've come to a magical place. Can you feel it?" When she went back into hiding, the elf stood up and extended his hand. "Sean, how are you?"

"Good. It's been a minute."

"A few."

"This place hasn't changed."

"Unlike us, right?"

"Right." After an awkward pause, Sean added, "You still skating?"

"Skating?" The elf laughed. "No. Bones break easy now. You?"

Sean shook his head. He hadn't been on a board since high school. He was never much good at it. Not like the elf was. The bearded man was watching them.

"How's your brother?" the elf said.

"Still alive, I think. Who's the fat man?"

He turned around. The bearded man didn't look away. "Just an old friend."

"Do I know him?"

"Sort of."

Sean didn't know what to make of that. The fat man didn't look that old, so he hadn't been a high school teacher when Sean was growing up. He did seem familiar, though.

Bells began to chime.

"Better get to your seat. Let me show you."

Sean followed him down an aisle. They worked their way around a group of kids. The elf pointed to an empty spot on the floor.

"Enjoy."

"Hey, what about your one friend?" Sean said. "Is he, uh, going to make an appearance?"

Sean remembered how the *friend* had stolen the show when he took his daughter long ago. It was hard to believe. He seemed so real. And funny. Sort of mean, too. Nice to the kids but roasted some of the adults. It took the elf a second to process whom Sean was asking about. Then he reached into his pocket and held something in his hand. Leslie Sue stared at what looked like a metal walnut with stripes.

"He'll come out at the end."

Sean hoped he'd say that and couldn't wait for his granddaughter to see it. *Now that's magic.*

"Good to see you, Sean," the elf said.

"You too, Fritz."

Sean stepped over people sitting cross-legged on the floor. He walked onto the small stage in the corner of the store and squeezed between a skinny lady wearing a sleeveless gym shirt and a sweaty man with tattooed arms. They both had a kid sitting on their laps. The one was poking at the man's tattoos like they were buttons.

There was barely enough room to cross his legs. Thank God Leslie Sue weighed as much as a puppy.

They had a good view of the woman in a rocking chair. She wore a purple blanket over her shoulders. Hands folded on her lap; she kept her eyes closed. People were talking like she was a decoration. She looked asleep, she sat so still. She looked younger than her age. Not a sprig of gray in that hair bound in a white ribbon. Smooth, rosy cheeks and toned arms. And she was older than Sean by ten years.

"See her?" He wrapped his arms around Leslie Sue. "She beat up your great-uncle Bobby."

Leslie Sue had never met her great-uncle Bobby. And didn't care who beat him up.

Bobby never admitted it. Always said he slipped on the grass, and she jumped on his back. That he didn't want to hit a girl. Sean had seen the whole thing. His brother deserved it. Sean wasn't innocent. And there was the thing that started it all. It was standing on a small table next to the rocking chair. Looked as new and young as the woman did. It couldn't be the same soldier, but it looked just like it. Sharp jacket, tall hat and bushy eyebrows.

Sean remembered taking it from Fritz that day. And how it bit his brother's finger. He deserved that, too.

Something about the room suddenly changed. Like the humidity rose or the temperature dropped. A hush fell over the crowd. In minutes, the store was silent. Except for the *screech, screech, screech* of the rocking chair. Leslie Sue's thumb fell out of her mouth. The tension had them leaning forward, ears turned.

A grin grew on the storyteller's lips. It spread to her eyes. The chair stopped rocking. It was so still even cars stopped driving past the building. Or at least Sean didn't hear them. He hugged his granddaughter. When the tension reached a breaking point, the storyteller's eyes opened.

"Once upon a time..."

AFTERWORD

I started writing book II in the Claus Universe in November of 2022. Like most stories, I had a broad story arc in mind. I hadn't planned on loss and grief being the crux of this adventure, but that's where the story went.

Six months later, I was nearing the end of the rough draft. I had just finished an emotional chapter where the main character faces the loss of her parents and the grief that consumes her. I finished that chapter on April 27, 2023.

On April 30, my son, Ben, ended his life. He was twenty-eight years old.

The only people I had lost in my life are grandparents. They were late in life when they passed. I am fifty-six years old. I have never faced loss on this level. It is a tsunami that washes everything away.

There was no sleeping that first night. After that, the shockwaves began to settle. It would take weeks for life to come back together. It's not the same. Never will be. Even today, there's a small part of me waiting to wake up from this dream.

I began writing stories over twenty years ago. It began when I wrote a story for Ben. That became the Socket Greeny trilogy. I wanted to express the difficulties of life in story form. The twentysomethings is a very difficult time. It is that jagged terrain between childhood and adulthood. For some, the journey is long and treacherous. I have always envied those who seemed to cross over without breaking a sweat. Many of us, though, become exhausted with no guarantees we will complete the journey.

I was fortunate to have met teachers during that time in my life—therapists, meditation practitioners, mentors—who buoyed me during storms, taught me how to grow up, to find purpose. It was long and arduous. For my son, it felt impossible.

Ben was funny. Entertaining.

He was creative and thoughtful. You could count on him in a pinch.

He was memorable. Never did he leave without bringing a smile.

His hugs were meaningful. His handshake solid.

He danced like a wild man when the spirit was right.

He was kind and generous. Loving and sweet. He cried easily.

Ben was a son, a brother. A boyfriend and a skater. He was not immune to struggle.

He was loved by many. Will be missed by all.

CANDYLAND

THE BATTLE OF NAUGHTY AND NICE

CANDYLAND

Arthur woke up in a realm where fairy tales are born and Christmas never ends.

Naturally, he thought he was dreaming. Who wouldn't? This wasn't his world. He had no idea how he got there, and even the natives were clueless about how or why a crosser came to Candyland. But there was a reason—there was always a reason.

The kind-hearted natives tried to help Arthur find his way back home, but he's quickly caught up in the endless battle between naughty and nice. King Chocolate ruled the Naughty Side, and with Christmas fast approaching, he's determined to win at any cost. When he hears rumors of Arthur's arrival, the king springs into action. The last thing he wants is a talented crosser helping the Nice Side win the war.

Arthur has no idea what talent the king is after. He barely remembers who he is. He crossed over with only the clothes on his back and a pocket full of drawings. Soon, however, he finds himself trapped between Naughty and Nice. When he discovers the power of his creative talent, it transforms Candyland. In the process, he remembers who he is and understands why he's there.

When his true talent is unleashed, nothing will be the same.

1

The bells sound different.

He had heard bells on Christmas Eve ever since he was little. The small silver kind. The *ring-ding-a-ding* kind. And in the morning, there would be presents under the tree. And his mom would say to his dad, "Did you hear Santa's bells last night?" Only she'd whisper it loud enough for him to hear. Loud enough for him to believe. Every Christmas. Just like that.

But this year the bells sounded different.

They were far away. There were more of them, too. Thousands of them. Like the galaxy was an instrument that vibrated under his skin. In his head. His fingers and toes hurt. Like he'd forgotten to wear socks and gloves in a snowball fight. The weirdest part? He could *taste* the bells.

Peppermint.

They rang faster as the universe shrank. His legs ached; his head thumped like a marching band snare drum. He didn't like the way it felt, not at all. There was a humming unpleasantness, like recovering from anesthesia when he had his appendix removed. He wanted to get away from the sound of them. He wanted to wake up somewhere soft and warm and safe. And then he did.

But not in his bed.

HE WAS HUNCHED OVER A DESK, with his forehead planted on a notebook. A string of drool hung from his lip, a quivering line of saliva that made a dark spot on the page below. He came into the world from somewhere far away.

There was singing. Quite a few voices sang a song he'd never heard before, but one that was merry. The Christmas kind of merry. There was also the smell of nutmeg, cloves, and sugar. The smell of cookies. The aroma was thick and filled his nostrils.

All of this and he hadn't even opened his eyes.

He did so, finally. Picking his head off the desk. It was a bowling ball on his shoulders. He wiped his mouth with the back of his hand. His face strange and rubbery. His body had fallen asleep like his leg did when he sat the wrong way for too long. Pins and needles would soon savage him as feeling came back. They never did, though. The pins and needles.

He blinked a few times, rubbed the sand from his eyes. He didn't know what to think. There was a squatty Christmas tree in the corner of the room and marshmallow kabobs at the fireplace. A little desk where he was sitting—a little desk with a glass of milk and a plate of cookies on it. Peanut butter cookies with fork prints in the middle of them.

He didn't know where he was. He didn't know anything. Not the day or the year. How he got at this desk and where he was before that. He couldn't remember (and this was where real panic set in) *his name*.

Anxiety wrapped his chest with an iron grip. He couldn't remember anything, but he knew this feeling: the cold plunge in his stomach and icy flow in his legs. He was grasping for memories— anything, *something*—to get a toehold. They weren't slippery and elusive.

They just weren't there.

The only hint of familiarity (and he could be imagining it, sure) was the notebook he'd been drooling on. A sketchbook, actually. The drawings done in ink. Those were *his* drawings, he knew. He turned the pages, hoping to see a name. And then:

"What are you doing in my house?" someone said.

He hit his head on the ceiling.

The young man wasn't particularly tall (average for his age, which was early to late teens, if he had to guess). The ceiling was just too low for a ceiling. He cracked his head good and solid. Crumbs and sweet dust fell from where he hit it.

To make things worse, he accidentally kicked the desk over. The sketchbook flapped like a kite in a windstorm. He crab-walked next to the Christmas tree, watching the milk that had been on the desk slowly spread across the gritty floor. Then watched the floor soak it up like a dry cookie. He continued staring at the same spot on the floor, long after the white puddle had disappeared, to avoid looking at the figure in the doorway.

The crown of his head hurt where he'd torpedoed the ceiling. He rubbed his face. Debris from the ceiling was sweet on his lips and stung his eyes. He put his head between his knees and closed his eyes until fireworks burst in the dark. He panted like a cornered animal; quivered like a puppy.

This is a dream. Plain and simple.

"Gandy?" someone called. "Come out here, sugar."

The young man opened his eyes (that, dear reader, took more courage than you might imagine). Through blurred vision, the image of a woman stood on the other side of the room. She was the color of putty; her skin sparkled like glitter. She held reading glasses in one hand, a book in the other.

Her head was perfectly round. Just like her eyes.

The young man clenched his fists and pressed them to his eyes. That thin wall holding back hordes of panic began to shake. *Try it one more time,* he thought. *Maybe things will be different. I'll be awake. I'll be in bed. I'll remember my name and—*

The air grew thin. Fluffy panic filled his head while lead pumped into his chest cavity. He labored to fill his lungs, to keep from falling over.

"Breathe, sugar. Breathe." The woman dropped her book, took a knee in front of him. He felt her mitten-shaped hands on his knees, the coarse texture of her skin scratching the denim. "It's okay. You're safe. You just need to breathe slowly, all right? Breathe in six seconds. Come on, I'll count it out. You follow."

And she did. She counted to six—tapping his knee for each second—and he inhaled along with her. Then she counted again for the exhale, and he followed. And even though his eyes were closed, he could feel the hoofbeats of Panic recede. The room no longer a category five.

"What's this?"

Enter the second voice. This one deeper and sandier than the first. Despite the soothing pats on the knees and kindly countdowns, the young man's eyes flew open. There, across the room, holding what looked like a toasted marshmallow in a pair of scalloped tongs, wearing an apron that read *Gingers Make the World Sweeter,* was a putty-colored man. A sparkly man with a circular head. And this was the important part—the part that dumped adrenaline into his bloodstream and filled him with ice.

Their bodies are as thick as plywood.

He might be dreaming (a betting man would take those odds), but he was seeing just fine. That wasn't just a thin man across the room (and a very thin woman patting his knee). Because they weren't people. They were generic outlines. Their faces painted with icing.

They were cookies. Simple as that.

(Specifically, they were gingerbread cookies. But details like that weren't important.)

His lip began to quiver like a bedsheet on a clothesline. He hated this part of himself. He wasn't a little boy; he was a young man. Old enough to know better. But when he got scared, when

Anxiety heralded in the troops of Fear and Loathing to begin another skirmish, he could not keep the tears from his eyes or the hiccups from his throat. Resist, he might. Win the battle, he could not.

"You don't have to do anything, sugar," the Cookie Lady said. "Just keep breathing."

Well, if he could talk (which was impossible at the moment), he would tell the Cookie Lady that not moving and breathing was all he could do when smothered by Panic. The Cookie Man picked up the desk that had been kicked over. The spilt milk was gone.

Outside an open window, where pink sunlight fell through a watermelon filter, hundreds of odd voices sang a song he'd never heard before.

"Meg." The Cookie Man held up the sketchbook that had been on the desk.

She pushed glasses on her flat face. The hooked ends fastened to stiff curls that were the shape of locks of hair. She turned the pages until she got to the end. Looked at the young man.

"Arthur?" she said.

He hummed all over. The name struck him like an arrow.

Art. Yes, Art. Arthur to be official. Named after... well, no one. I was the first in the family to be named Arthur.

This revelation, however, did not uncork any more truths, like where he was or what kind of dream this was. At least he had his name. *Art.*

"Get him a cup of milk, Gandy," the Cookie Woman said.

"He don't want milk, Meg."

"Then water. Go on."

The Cookie Man, Gandy was his name, did what he was told. Meg, his wife, picked up the chair Art had knocked over and sat down to watch him with kind, round eyes painted on her flat face. It was soothing, the way she looked at him. His shoulders relaxed.

Something went springing past the window.

Gandy returned without the apron and tongs. The water was in an ugly-face coffee mug he put on the floor within Art's reach. Meg leaned forward in the chair. The way her body twisted and bent in a claymation way made Art a bit woozy.

"Do you know how you got here, sugar?" she said. "Do you know where you are?"

He gave a headshake for both answers. Her lips moved like edible ropes to match the words she was speaking. But there was no mouth between them, no throat to speak with. The lump in his throat road-blocked words from passing. *No words,* he thought. *I have no words.*

Meg looked at Gandy, her husband (*Do gingerbread cookies marry?*). Gandy sighed and shook his head.

"It's going to be all right," she said. "I know this is all strange, but you're safe here," she said. "Okay?"

He wasn't certain if he believed that and didn't feel any safer for her saying it.

"I'm Nutmeg. This is Gandy. And you're Art." She waited for him to acknowledge she had it right. "How old are you, sugar?"

Now this was a stumper. Ask any kid that question and he or she will tell you just how old they are to the month. Even an adult could get you within a few years. Art had only learned his name a few minutes ago. How was he supposed to answer that. *Sixteen? Seventeen?* He thought, however, he was older than that. For one, he had a honeycomb tattoo on his arm. So he couldn't be sixteen. He was in his twenties, probably. But when Meg asked him how old he was, he felt sixteen years old. Like he'd never grown past it no matter how many birthdays had gone by.

"Gandy, can you get him a blanket?"

Art was shivering, but he wasn't cold. Gandy brought back a handmade blanket, one that was crocheted with heavy yarn. He draped it over Art's legs. Meg watched from her seat, humming along to the unfamiliar Christmas song being sung outside. Art liked the way her presence made the room feel. He relaxed a bit under the weight of the blanket. Some of the ornaments had been knocked off the limbs of the Christmas tree. He felt a jab of guilt for the ones that were broken, their pieces scattered among the presents.

"You draw these?" Gandy said.

He showed the sketchbook to Art. Meg didn't take her eyes off Art for a moment, then nodded at her husband. He pulled a chair next to his wife and sat down. They looked through the sketchbook.

"Where…" Art swallowed. "Where am I?"

"You're in Candyland, son," Gandy said.

Candyland? Well, that didn't help. At all. Art covered his face. It was better when no one could see him, especially life-sized gingerbread cookies. When he was sure his chin wasn't quivering, he looked up. "What does that mean?"

"You remember anything from before?" Gandy said.

Art's mouth turned to ash. He took up the ugly mug of water and drank. It was floral and minty. Cooled his throat. He held the mug between his hands, closed his eyes in hopes his memories were done playing hide-and-seek. *Olly olly oxen free!*

He shook his head.

"It's all right," Meg said. "You don't have to remember anything. You're here, sugar. Just be here."

"How'd I get *here*?"

"This happens from time to time," Meg said. "Someone crosses."

"Crosses?"

"Crosses over," Meg said. Art's brain needed a moment to generate more words. It was like solving a crossword puzzle on a sinking ship. "Where you were born," Meg said, sensing his stalemate. "Where you're from—*your world*—you've crossed over into this one."

"Candyland," Gandy answered with hometown pride.

Art laughed nervously. Looked at the toasted floor and said: "How?"

"We don't know how it works," Meg said. "It just happens sometimes."

"What did you ask Santa for, for Christmas?" Gandy said.

This was a sharp turn. "What?"

"Did you write Santa a letter asking for, I don't know, an adventure? Inspiration?"

A memory blew through the corridors like a ghost. It was fleeting. Barely a snapshot. He was sitting at a desk, one not too different from the one he knocked over, writing in a journal. Although it wasn't a letter to Santa.

"Are you too old for Santa?" Gandy said. "Is that it?"

"That's not the problem," Meg said. "It's what you ask for. Sometimes you expect to get what you *want* from Santa. At Christmas, though—"

"You get what you *need*," Gandy finished.

The absurdity of what was happening had become quite clear. Two gingerbread cookies were lecturing on Santa Claus's ethical approach to gift giving. Ask for what you want all day long. You'll get what you need. Like socks or underwear. A terrifying trip to Gingerbread Town, where cookies get married and drink from ugly-faced mugs

"I'm ready to wake up now," Art said.

"You're not—"

"Shh." Meg silenced her spouse. "You want to wake up. Of course. We're going to help you. Gandy, can you grab that gift for me? No, the one under the tree. It's wrapped in the red glitter paper."

Gandy did as such, crawling under the branches to reach the present with the red glitter paper. It was rectangular and flat with a shiny green bow. Gandy handed it to Meg. A smile curved on her face and struck dimples in her cheeks. She presented it to Art.

His name was written in thick, black lines. Below it was a single word. *Santa.* He remembered that handwriting; somewhere in his shrouded past he'd seen it before. That was Santa's handwriting. At least, until Art was too old for Santa.

Art sort of laughed. That abruptly stopped when he opened the gift. It slid out with ease. It was a work of art on cardstock. Someone had done it with markers and ink liners. It was of a generic man, tall and slender, holding a balloon in the shape of a red, red heart.

He stared at it, unblinking. His eyes glassy. *I drew this...*

There was a memory attached to it. A delicate little thing that danced in the fog, ducking in the shadows to avoid the light. Art sat patiently, giving it time and space to dip into view. He had made this for someone. The closer he came to remembering—the blurry contour of a face, a vague memory of a fragrance—the more he shook.

It felt like the key to everything. Where he was, how he got here. *Who* he was.

Then he went too far, and his entire body flash-fried with hot-wired thoughts. A river of emotions poured through him. A river he did not have room for. He did what he always did when he didn't have room.

Run! the signal word blared. *Get out! Get away or be drowned!*

That was the general sense of it. Art never stuck around to work out the details. He heeded the warning whirring in his head without argument. He scrambled onto his hands and knees, scraped his head on the ceiling when he tried to stand, and was nearly to a doorway. Conflicting emotions of longing and sadness, disappointment and love, safety and loneliness clung to his backside like teeth. They were enormous. He was so small.

So vulnerable in a big, big world.

"Wait! Please wait!" Meg jumped in front of him. He tried to get around her and could've if he wanted. She just felt so warm, and the sound of her voice so sincere. Even though she was a cookie. "You're not alone," she said. "I promise you you're not. Life goes so fast, I know, and it feels like you can't keep up, and some days you can hardly breathe. I know how that feels."

Art wanted to crawl out of his skin. She was on point. A little too on point.

"You don't need to stay here with us. In fact, you shouldn't. It's out there you need to be. But you came *here* for a reason. You came to our house. That's not a mistake."

"She's right. We have your back." Gandy joined her at the doorway. "But you can't go out looking like that."

Art was in blue jeans and a T-shirt with a pocket on the chest. Pretty ordinary, he thought.

"You're going to get too much attention," Meg pointed out.

"Crossers always do," Gandy said.

"You didn't come here to be a celebrity."

Art fell on his bottom. The floor was soft where the milk had spilled. A little sticky. He locked his arms around his shins. The demand to flee had passed. He sighed long and loud. With it came a wave of relief so great he wanted to weep. Instead, he said: "*Why* am I here?"

"Only you can find out," Meg said. "I know who can help."

"To the castle," Gandy announced.

"*Not* to the castle," she said.

"Because that's where—I'm sorry. What did you say, love?"

"He's not going to the castle, Gandy."

"It's in the manual. 'If you meet a crosser...' It's on page one, Meg."

"I know what the manual says. But Arthur needs real help. Can you bring him something to eat? And also, the sheet from our bed." She tucked the cardstock gift from Santa in Art's shirt pocket. "I know exactly who he needs to see."

2

"Watch your head. And don't break the door. It's new and, that's right, turn to the side... like that. Hold it right there."

Candied silver beads popped out of Gandy's forehead like drops of perspiration. They dribbled like BBs and rolled across the floor. Meg handed a brown paper bag to her husband. It was rolled at the top like a sack lunch. Their thin lips puckered up, and the two of them pressed their round faces together. Art couldn't look away.

He was rigid with Anxiety and Fear (and so many more Emotions were coming to visit), but took comfort in watching this gingerbread couple embrace, the way they whispered to each other, how their arms were flexible enough to pull each other closer. In the time that he'd been there, their warmth and honesty kept him from diving out the window. He trusted them, for better or worse.

"Don't let the world beat you down, sugar. Remember, we got your back. So many of us do." Meg pulled the string tight under Art's chin. The hood cinched over his eyes. "And don't forget these words: *Keep your stocking hung and your chimney open.* They're wiser words than ya think." She patted his face. A trace of ginger root remained on his cheek. "Off with you, then. Don't forget the snacks."

Gandy shook the brown bag. "I'll step out first, right? When I wave, you follow. And don't forget, watch your head."

He did just that, turning sideways to slip through the narrow doorway. Plenty of room for him, seeing he was only six inches thick. He was quickly engaged in conversation. The longer he went on, the stiffer Art felt. He was cagey when Meg held his hand between both of her hands. They were warm and crispy. Her eyes—blobs of white icing—were somehow gentle.

"Be nice," she said.

She meant something by that and not the obvious. She meant be *Nice*. Capital *N*.

"Eh-hem." Gandy was waving.

It made no sense, waking up in a fantasy world where he felt adopted by gingerbread cookies. Cookies he trusted. Cookies he wanted to hug. But dreams were like that. That was why he wanted to hug her. Good thing he didn't. His hugs were world-class hugs. Not something a cookie would survive.

"Merry, merry," she said, and shoved him through the doorway like a quarter in a vending machine.

HE DUCKED JUST IN TIME. The house was made of gingerbread, and he'd already put dents in the ceiling. With Meg's motherly shove, he skidded sideways through the slot and across the sidewalk. Gandy caught him before he tumbled into the street.

Meg had fashioned a bright red bedsheet into a hooded cape. If not for the knot she'd tied under his chin, the peppermint breeze would have blown it off his back. Gandy pulled the hood down to hide Art's face while at the same time waving and wishing a soccer ball bouncing down the road a merry, merry.

"Take your time," Gandy said. "It's better to soak it in before we start. Yeah? That's page two in the manual. 'Let crossers adjust to Candyland. Don't rush them. Things are very different here.' So, you know, look around—Tomkins, yes. Merry, merry to you. How's Tippy and Turny?"

Art snuck a peek from under his cowl. Gandy was talking to what looked like a plastic turtle standing on back legs. Gandy was a cookie, but somehow a plastic turtle felt more surreal. *Familiarization,* he thought. *The bizarre normalizes with time.* He'd learned that somewhere. Sometime. A crumb of memory that decided to bob close enough to the surface to be remembered. *We drink milk from a cow. But milk from a human is gross.* At least, that was how he remembered it.

Gandy engaged with the passersby. He was a friendly sort, and it seemed natural to him. He was also working the attention off Red Riding Hood. Art avoided any wayward glances. When the turtle moved closer, Art looked up.

The sky is pink.

It was a lovely color. Soothing and delicious all at once. A childhood color. Puffs of cotton candy hovered in its depth like tasty flotsam, none going in the same direction. They moved at different speeds, ignoring the peppermint breeze ruffling the red cape on Art's back.

The walls of the buildings were baked and held together with icing and strings of licorice. The road was paved with blocks of fudge, and things walked on it and rolled on it, bounced and danced on it. Exotic things. The most amazing things. Beyond imagination things. Toys of every stripe and concoction—dolls and soldiers and dancers and fighters and thugs and trolls and *who-knows* and *is-that-even-a-toy?*

But then forget the toys. Food strolled down Fudgy Lane. Pickled eggs and chocolate eggs and hard-boiled ones, too. Giant apples with caramel toppings; pears with bows on the stem. A family of sugar plums stained the pavement wherever they bounced.

There were also pigs. Three of them wearing different hats. Walking upright. Arms around each other, singing a merry song. Behind them sheep and a dainty young lady with a long shepherd's crook. *Is that Bo Peep?*

Unbelievable. Overwhelming. Someone Art's age (sixteen, he was sure of it; maybe seventeen) might run away and hide or freak out. Because this was real. All of it, right in front of him, real as his left hand. But the thing that kept him on his feet, that kept him upright and conscious, that turned the corner of his mouth—just a tiny smile on his face—wasn't visible at all. It was in the air.

The air was electric.

It wasn't positive or negative, didn't come from an outlet or a battery. It was a feeling that passed through space like a silent wave. It filled his stomach and blossomed in his chest. It was everywhere. It was everything.

Christmas spirit, he thought.

Although he couldn't remember his grandmother's face or the way she sounded, he knew she'd said it sometime, somewhen. This was the feeling of Christmas. Some called it spirit.

She called it *Pure Joy.*

"ARE YOUR LEGS RUBBER?" Gandy said.

"What?"

"Can you walk? Or is this too much?" He waved his arms at an orange plastic locomotive puttering down the fudgy brick road. The face of it was smiling. It had cheekbones. "We can squeeze back into the breadbox if you need some time. Meg means well and all, but I'd wager she wouldn't mind you staying a few chimes or even a ring longer."

Art's legs were slightly rubber. Roughly half his body didn't have feeling. It was coming back in pins and needles now. This was happening. Whatever this was, it was happening right now. There was a reason for how and why. An explanation. He didn't know it, might never know it. There were great mysteries that never got solved. This certainly qualified as one. Until he woke up, the only thing to do was float downstream until something made sense.

"Where's everyone going?"

"To the market," Gandy said. "It's a Christmas thing. It's what we do."

"That's where we're going?"

"Yeah." Gandy pulled a paper hat onto his head (it resembled something a chef would wear). The line of icing that served as a mouth turned upward in a smile. Then he said: "S'ven."

Art waited for more. When there wasn't more, he said: "S'ven what?"

"You're going to see him."

"Why?"

"If anyone can help a crosser, it's S'ven."

Gandy hopped onto the brown, chunky road and joined the crusade of stranger things. *Misfits.* But there was only one thing here that didn't belong. He was hiding in a red bedsheet. Art caught up to Gandy, who was swinging his arms like he owned the road. (By the way, the fudgy pavers felt good to walk on. Like flexible plastic that emitted sweet, syrupy smells.)

"Merry, merry!" Gandy called and waved. "Merry, merry!"

A band of hopping cowboys bounced past, their plastic lassoes twirling over them like antennas. Their round bottoms sounded like popping bubbles when they hit the road. Art pulled his hood down and looked the other way when a yellow buckaroo snuck a peek at him.

"Merry, merry!" Gandy shouted. Then to Art: "Just a word, and no offense, but around here when someone says 'merry, merry,' you say it back. Just something we do. When in Candyland, do as the Landers do."

"Landers?"

"Never mind. It's just—oh, hey. Yes. Merry, merry!"

This time a pair of glazed donuts was followed by a dozen donut holes. "Merry, merry!" they chimed.

"Merry, merry," Art muttered.

It felt weird to say that. To donuts.

❄

HE KEPT his head down and eyes on the road. It was better this way. Too many distractions. Too much stimulation. Pretty much too much. Then a black rope of licorice slithered between his feet and looked into Art's hood. Art closed his eyes and kept walking.

"Meg wanted me to tell you to breathe, son. Remember to breathe, she said." Gandy skipped to keep up with Art. "Does that help?"

"What?"

"Breathing."

Art shook his head. Nothing slowed down the Panic train when its engine was hot. All he could do was wait for it to run out of steam. It didn't matter if he was breathing into a paper bag or standing on his head. The air in his lungs was thin, and his chest magically turned to lead. Hands in pockets, head hung too heavy, he walked. He breathed.

"Strange," Gandy said. "She said it would help."

"What?"

"Breathing. She specifically said, 'Tell him to count to six when he goes in. And count to six when he goes out." He held up his flattened mitt as if he'd raised a finger to make his point. "Are you counting?"

"Do you breathe?" Art asked.

"Not like you. And I don't understand the whole air thing. Sounds exhausting. I mean, does it ever stop?"

Gandy had obviously thought about breathing. His case against breathing was, as he put it, *airtight.* (Art didn't understand why he would be *against* breathing.) This conversation, Art imagined, was not what Meg had in mind. This was just laying more track for the Panic train to gather momentum. Art buried his hands as deep as they'd go in his pockets. Gandy switched to the topic Landers never slept. Crossers insisted on it. It didn't make sense at all. Why would anyone lie down for eight to ten chimes with their eyes closed? It was an insult to evolutionary—

"What do you do, then?" Art said.

Gandy was jolted from his speech. Apparently, Meg never stopped him when he was on a roll because he stumbled on the pavers and looked around, gathering his wits. It looked like he'd just been yanked from a nap. "Wh—um, what do I do?"

"You said earlier, when I asked if you breathe, you said *not like you*. What does that mean?"

Gandy thought a moment. Then shrugged. "You caught me, son. Crispy-handed." He sighed, shook his head, and looked into the pink sky like someone was keeping score. "I told a square one, I did. Four corners with a hole in the middle of it, yeah."

"I'm not—"

"I lied. Okay? There, I said it. I was just trying to make you feel better, making it sound like I do something like breathing when the truth is I don't do anything like that at all. No one does. No one except a crosser." Only he said it like *cross-uh*. It had a little weight to it. Not particularly unkind, but maybe just a little.

"How do you know I breathe, then?"

"I don't." Gandy swatted his chest. Bits of crumb chipped from the edges of his hand. "Meg's the expert. She's a memorizer, she is. That woman loves to know things and tell others about them. Like count to six on the inhale and whatever. None of that's important, ask me. Nope. Just two questions is all you need to answer, and that's—ah, merry, merry!"

He nudged Art closer to the curb. A sward of mops swaddled past them. (A group of mops is a sward, Gandy told him later.) Art didn't look at them. When they were far enough ahead that their wet tracks were drying, Gandy leaned against Art.

"Two things, right? Why are you here, and where are you going? That's what the manual says, page four. And if I'm being completely honest, I don't even think the first one matters. *Why?* Who cares why? You're already here. *Where*, now there's a question. Let's answer *that*."

He dug a rounded elbow into Art's hip and launched into Gandy's philosophy of living.

"Who wrote the manual?" Art interrupted.

"What?"

"You said it's in the manual. Who wrote the manual?"

Gandy reorganized his thoughts, then replied: "*They.* Like they, you know. Everyone knows who *they* are."

"I don't."

"It's not important. We're taught about crossers." *Cross-uhs.* "It's like we live for crossers. You know, things like you. From another world. *To be of service,* that's what the manual says. Because if you're here, you're here for a reason. And that's why we're here. That and to celebrate Christmas. Merry, merry!"

"There's others like me?"

"Don't get excited. The last crosser was a disaster."

"What happened?"

Gandy walked in silence. Finally, he said: "Misunderstanding is what happened. The root of all problems, yeah? Misunder—whoa!"

Gandy came off the road. Art caught him before he went stumbling. *Would he break in two if he fell? Could I just paste him together?* Art didn't have to answer that question. His hood fell back, exposing loops of hair hanging over his eyes. He yanked the hood back over his face.

"Merry, merry," called a sweet voice.

She was as tall as Art. He didn't look up, but he could feel her staring at him. Her legs were bare and plastic from the hem of a ballet skirt. Toes permanently pointed, she walked as if her legs were stilts that didn't bend. *Tap-tap-tap* they went.

"Ah, merry, merry!" Gandy recovered with a hop and a bounce. "Nice to see you, Dixie. Looking fit today, you are. All snappy and curious. On the way to the market on this—what is it, *twenty*?"

"Twenty-one rings," she said.

"Twenty-one? I'm always losing count. Meg can tell you how many ticks to Santa's coming."

"Of course she can. How is Meggy?"

"Well, she's good. In fact, she's great." Gandy explained how Meg was baking a new wall for the house. Going to make another room, you know, just in case a little one came out of the oven. Dixie the Dancer faked interest in the story. Art recognized a faker. Maybe she wasn't uncomfortable with small talk the way he was, but she was distracted.

She was sneaking peeks under the hood.

"Anyways, good seeing you," Gandy said, stepping between her and Art. "I'll send Meg your best. Merry, merry to you and—"

"Red Riding Hood?" She ducked down. "Are you mad at me? I thought we—"

"Who, this? Haha. No, no. Sorry. This is, uh, my baker."

"Your *baker*?" She sounded hurt. "This isn't—"

"No, it isn't. Look at his feet. Red Riding Hood doesn't have feet like that."

Dixie the Dancer took a long look at Art's dirty boots and faded blue jeans. She tried to look under the hood one more time.

"He's shy," Gandy said. "And to be honest, not used to crowds. So—"

"What happened to Chef Shelly?"

"Oh! Oh, no, no, no. Chef Shelly, she's good. She's great! Better than great. She's like *greeeeeat!* Heh-heh. No, this here, he's not *my* baker. He's *aaaaa* baker."

"Does he have a name?" *Tap-tap-tap.*

"He does, he does. This is, uh, Ar-Ar-Ar... Arfy the Cooker. From Bonbon Town."

Dixie the Dancer's laughter sounded like bubbles in her throat. Her feet twittered with a little hop and a leap, then a twirl. There was a definite whirring sound coming from her, like a string had been pulled on her back. Art caught the sparkle of her eyes like jewels pressed into a perfectly smooth face.

"Are you strong, Arfy the Cooker?" she asked.

"He doesn't talk," Gandy said. "All he does is cook."

"I could use a thrower, if he ever gets tired of—"

"He never gets tired. He cooks, that's all. He loves to cook all the time, always."

Art's legs were getting weaker. He didn't like the hiding and the dishonesty. Lies were heavy. When carried long enough, they spoiled to shame. At least they did for him. He just wanted to crawl inside his red cape and go to sleep.

"Okay, Dixie," Gandy said. "Bye-bye. Merry, merry. Maybe we'll see you at the market. Arfy can throw you across the lake or something."

She attempted one more look. *Tap-tap-tap.* Gandy threw himself in front of Art like a shepherd guarding his flock. Then a host of tapping plastic toes and stiff ankles came down the road, followed by bubbly giggles and twittering steps. Dixie was swept up in a herd of her kind. (*That's a swatch*, Gandy later said.)

Gandy pushed Art between two buildings.

"That way, Arfy."

THE ALLEY WAS narrow and tall and smelled like cinnamon toast; the walls flaked with blackened bits that fell when Art squeezed between them. The sky—as pink as a puppy's belly—was all he could see above them.

Singing echoed down the long enclosure. It was sloppy and cheerful, merry in a different sort of way. They passed under a sign that read *Toasted*. The smell coming from the open window was delicious. It looked like a sports pub. Televisions blared above rows of syrup bottles. At the tables were puffy, white marshmallows sitting with spongy yellow ducks. The marshmallows were tanned on the edges and the size of basketballs. They sang along to a Christmas song and swayed against each other. One fell off a stool and bounced across the floor.

"Wrong way."

Art didn't see the bike until it was almost too late. No one was riding it. It coasted toward them, pedals slowly churning. The silver handlebars waggled around, the front tire swaying in a relatively straight line. Streamers hung from the rubber grips.

Art threw his back to the wall, put his hands on the opposite wall, and sucked in his gut. A pair of eyes was pasted to the handlebars.

They lazily rolled toward him. One of the handle grips poked him in the stomach.

"Merry, merry," the bike muttered.

Art shuffled after Gandy, passing through different smells from windows above them: maple syrup, powdered sugar, caramel. And singing. Always singing.

Gandy stopped at an intersection. He looked right, then turned to the left and waved Art to follow. A sign waved on pretzel links strung between the buildings. *Kettle Korn Trail.* It made sense, although it wasn't a trail. No rocks or dirt; no roots from trees. It was cobblestones. Big, spongy cobblestones lacquered in a crispy coating.

"Watch your step," Gandy called. "Gets a little, uh, unpredictable. At least we won't run into anyone this way. Not till the market, anyhow."

Kettle Korn Trail was a wide alley that went several blocks with no one in sight. A back door here and there with garbage piled up— broken cinnamon sticks, clumps of cookie dough. Spilled bags of flour. Flies and gnats zipped and hovered from one heap to another. Art waved them out of his face.

Gandy reacted to the flies and gnats. Not annoyed. He seemed a bit more... surprised. Then worried.

"Why are we hiding?" Art's voice quivered. He hated when it sounded like that. His emotions were billboards for everyone to read.

"You're not in danger, son. It's the total opposite. Everyone—and I mean *everyone*—will want to talk to you. You saw Dixie back there. She could smell the crosser on you. Surprised we got away from that one. Arfy... I panicked on that one. Sorry." He shook his head. "It's just easier if we get to S'ven without notice. Straight there with no interruptions. Meg was right; she always is. Forget the manual," he whispered. "There's a reason you're here. We just need to get— watch it."

A geyser of popcorn burst from the middle of the alley like a relief valve opened. Softball-sized kernels rained down. Art picked one up. It was warm and sticky. Fresh from the kettle, somehow. If kettles were under the cobblestones. A rubber-toothed leaf rake extended from a window. Big, fabric hands were on a long handle, sweeping the loose kernels into piles. Art threw the one he'd picked up onto one of them.

"I don't want to be here."

"You're always *here*." Gandy rubbed a spot on his chest. *Is that supposed to be his heart?*

The gnats were gathered near a trash can overflowing with banana peels. They got in Art's face. He pulled down his hood, holding his breath until they were past.

"Is S'ven a crosser?"

"Yep. He's from your world, I assume. I think. I don't know, come to think of it. They're rumors he looked like you when he first dropped in, but he don't look like you anymore. He's been here many o' bells. Ever since the Nutcracker."

"Nutcracker?"

Gandy twisted his flat head around. "You know her?"

"No."

"Too bad. She made a lot of changes to this place. Not good at first. But everything turned out better."

"What'd she do?"

He waved his hand. "Another story. Best we keep our head in this one. S'ven, he'll know what to do."

"So he is a crosser?"

"That's what I said."

Up ahead, another supply of kettle corn erupted. Rakes extended. Flies and gnats descended. Gandy skipped around the harvesters. Art kept his head down. When he caught up to Gandy, he said: "Then why is he still here?"

"What do you mean?"

"Meg said crossers come here sometimes. Do they go back home?"

"Um, I mean... you know, if Meg were here, she would say—"

"Did the Nutcracker go back?"

"Oh, yeah. She went back with a bang. Took a bunch of us with her. That was a toot, let me say. We got sucked into her world and then came back. Meg and I were dizzy almost till next Christmas. Woo-wee! Merry, merry."

"So why didn't S'ven go back?"

Gandy stopped in the middle of the alley. He raised a round hand. A ring of icing formed on his face, but no words came out of it. Art was fascinated by how his expressions changed. It was claymation in real life. Gandy shrugged.

"I don't know. He stayed for a reason, I guess." He patted Art's arm. "Like you."

It sounded like an excuse, but Gandy really believed it. Like maybe this S'ven stayed in Candyland because he was waiting for something or had a job to do. Art didn't care why he was here. If S'ven could wake him up from this borderline nightmare, nothing else mattered.

Art swatted at the gnats and flies. They avoided his hand. They were buzzing, but it wasn't their wings. They were whispering. Of course they were. Art wasn't surprised. What he didn't expect, when he swiped at them one last time, just before they swirled up toward the underbelly sky, was the little, teeny uniforms they were wearing.

Military uniforms.

"Stay here." Gandy held up his mitt, then waved Art back. "I'll be right back."

It was noisy around the corner. Drums were beating, and people (or toys or food or whatever Art was supposed to call them... *things?*) were singing and dancing, laughing and shouting. Gandy's head twisted on his shoulders, ears perking on the sides of his flat head when someone started up a flute. From where he stood, Art couldn't see the party. The only things in view were awnings and signs.

Above the sidewalk, hanging from a peppermint stick on a gingerbread wall, was a flag. The edges were frayed, the fabric faded. *King Cheese* was written across a sigil of gold crowns.

"How do you know he's here?" Art said.

A stiff shrug, followed by: "Landers just... we know things about each other."

"Just, like, gossip?" Now Art shrugged. *So what?*

"It's more than that, son. Thoughts around here are butterflies. You know, in the wind." When Art didn't respond, he added: "Like music."

The flute bubbled inside Art. He could feel it. Could *taste* it. It was like fizzy lemonade in his ears. He shook his head, feeling a rush in his legs.

"You-you can read thoughts? Like what I'm thinking right now?"

This alarmed the pants off Art. The thoughts that ran through his head were not for public consumption. They were embarrassing. Sometimes dark and mean. Really mean. So mean they left trails of shame.

"Ah, no. It doesn't work like that. You want me to see your thoughts?"

Art shook his head and pressed his back against the wall. He didn't want anyone inside his head. *Thoughts are like butterflies.* That was the truth. He couldn't remember how he got here (*where are dreams, anyway?*), but there were wisps of memories that had no form, only flavors. Art's thoughts didn't just have their own mind. They *lived* inside him. There were parts of him that were cruel. He didn't want anyone knowing what they said. Even if it was to himself.

"Oh, hey." Gandy looked in both directions. "I know it never works to tell someone to relax. But relax. Yeah? Everything is the way it is. I don't know what that means, but Meg says it. And remember, just breathe. Count to twenty or whatever. And act natural."

Act natural?

"If you get hungry, eat what's in the sack. It'll make Meg happy. And stay here; don't move. I'll run, run as fast as I can."

The icing on his face winked. Then he was gone, like that. Around the corner and into a door beneath the King Cheese flag. He would find S'ven in there. And S'ven would tell Art how to wake up, and this would all be over. All he had to do was wait.

TIME WAS FUNNY IN CANDYLAND. It was flexible. Sometimes it stretched like taffy. Like it buzzed in Art's head, this deep humming sound that wasn't unpleasant. And then minutes passed instead of seconds. Or maybe it was hours. It's hard to tell when your head feels like a blender.

The music suddenly felt different. The noise, louder. More people, more dancing than just a few seconds ago. The sound of it crawled under his skin, made him twitch and itch. Anxiety did a jig on his chest and stomped on his pulse. He imagined bodies out there packed together. Sticky bodies, smelly bodies.

How do they do it? Art could pretend like he was having fun, but people had no idea what it was like for him on the inside. The doubt. The fear. They were anchors he carried. One on each shoulder. Gandy didn't have to worry. He wasn't leaving the alley.

Chocolate.

The smell was suddenly overwhelming. Like a river flooding the street. A memory as faded and torn as the King Cheese flag waved through his mind. The smell of hot chocolate in front of a fireplace. Christmas music on speakers. Someone in the other room singing along to it. The feeling of a warm blanket. He liked the way it felt. It felt like—

"Rey Rida Hood."

Art jumped at the sound of the voice. Someone was in the alley— the most human-looking person yet. A wiry boy about half Art's height. Pointy ears poked out of looping, brown curls. Black sunglasses wrapped around his face.

"Yaw anna choc'lat?"

The imp's delicate fingers unfurled. A chocolate wafer sat square in his palm. Unmelted with sharp corners. The smell of it tantalizing. Promising to melt down his throat and drop the anchors off his shoulders. Even if only for a few minutes.

"Wass inja sack, hey?" He pointed at the paper sack. The paper brown and soft and damp in Art's hand. "Issa cookees inder? Trade jaw, line up."

A blocky-tooth smile spread across the lower part of the imp's face. He held the block of chocolate like a coin. Art put the sack behind his back. He hadn't the slightest interest in opening it (he didn't know if there were *cookees* in there or not), but didn't want to give it away. Meg had made them.

"Ee stingin' yo mops? Idda play a differen' song on tha' one, peebie."

He leaned in for a look inside Art's hood. The smile started to fade. He dropped his hand to his side. The chocolate landed on the bumpy surface of Kettle Korn Trail. He took a step closer. The smile returned in full bloom. Every tooth square and white and cartoonish.

"Ey, nop. I'ssa think yew makin' for—"

"Aye, Rude!"

The imp was snatched out of the alley by a taller version of himself. Another skinny boy wearing muted colors and flat-soled sneakers with black glasses over his eyes. This one's hair long and straight, fluttering like tails on a kite. He had the imp by the licorice arm, yanked him off his feet.

"Low-low," the taller one muttered. "Fresh now."

The imp ducked his head. He'd already forgotten about Art. The chocolate, too. Art picked it up. It was wrapped in gold foil and stamped with two initials. *KC.*

The imps hopped toward the market. Art followed them around the corner and watched them disappear into a crowd, slipping between bodies like eels through seaweed. They had something strapped on their backs. They looked like spongy noodles. The kind used in swimming pools.

THE GOLD FOIL had torn from the corner. It smelled bitter, like healthy chocolate. Art took a nibble. It didn't taste any better than it smelled, but it melted on his tongue.

He took another small bite, following the imps with the foam boards on their backs into the best or worst costume party in the world. Art couldn't decide which. They were toys. They were animals. *Things.*

Bouncy balls with googly eyes.

Dancers with dagger toes.

Boxers with square heads and wrecking-ball fists.

Clowns made of wire.

Chefs made of felt.

Dwarves with sacks, rocks wearing hats, pogo sticks laughing, and teddy bears singing.

They milled about in all directions, weaving like starlings. Some playing instruments, like fiddles and horns and pipes. The music chaotic, but sometimes it would fall into rhythm, and the crowd would sway with it. And then back to melodic noise. And no one seemed to notice. Or care.

They spoke like they knew each other, like good friends who grew up together. And when they bumped into each other—which was often—they tipped a hat or bent a knee, wishing each other a merry, merry before swimming back into the flow. Sometimes they took each other for a spin and a dip. With a quick shuffle, they bowed and went on their way.

A bell went off. The sort that was enormous and heavy.

The vibrations passed through the crowd like a sonic wave. Art felt it in his chest and cheeks. His teeth tingled.

All at once, like a sporting event witnessing a last-second win, the crowd of misfits and strange things raised their arms and sticks and strings and mitts. They leaped and they bounced and they swirled on the street.

"*Huzzah!*" they cried. "*Huzzah!*"

They embraced and swayed. A song rose up, one well-rehearsed. For the random instruments played together. The voices in harmony, they were. Along with squeaks and honks that, somehow, were lovely. It was intoxicating.

Art was pulled toward the crowd like a fish on a hook. He went willingly, unknowingly. When the bell went off again and fresh sonic waves rattled his eyelids, he plunged into the thick of it and didn't hesitate.

Huzzah!

It was the song that did it. Not the way it sounded. The way it felt.

It was the sweetest feeling of all. It bypassed the lips and tongue and went straight to his stomach. It swirled around. Starry fumes crackled in his chest. A childish smile spread on his face. He was smelling firewood and marshmallows. Heard the crunch of wrapping paper torn from presents. The bubble of laughter.

The crowd swallowed him like a merry, greedy thing.

They didn't notice the gangly young man in the red riding hood cape. For they were intoxicated with song, as well. *Christmas spirit* flowed like spring water. From them, through them. In them. Into him.

He was two feet taller than most of them. The crowd went as far as he could see in both directions, swaying like a hive of insects.

Huzzah!

A row of storefronts was on his left. Traders and barkers (busy singing at the moment) stood by their carts or under their tents, by their tables of fruited candies, buckets of knick-knacks, and bowls of sugar and spice.

To his right, there was nothing of the sort. To the right was something Art had never seen. Never in his life. It was in the distance, but so close it seemed like he could reach out and touch it. A castle so big and so tall that it scratched the pink sky and snagged clouds with gleaming turrets that sprouted from its sides like branches. It sparkled and shined.

To call it beautiful was an insult.

When the bell rang, ripples raced over the rose-colored lake surrounding it. The vibrations flooded his senses. They lifted him off his feet. For a moment, Art didn't feel the cobbled road. It seemed he would float into the sky along with the others, a million balloons, all happy and singing with foolish smiles.

"Huzzah!" Art shouted.

Pumped his fist. Showed his teeth. All his teeth.

He might even have danced. He'd been known to get loose when the spirit was right. And it was right, all right. It was everywhere. He wobbled his knees and shook his hips with his eyes on the castle that breathed through open windows, that sang from its walls. Beat a pulse through the ground.

The castle called again.

The rosy lake so smooth and still. Tinted glass and bottomless and pristine. No fallen leaves or floating sticks. No dust, no bugs. No reflection at all. As flawless as the castle it surrounded. Art was certain he could walk across it.

At the very top of the castle, from the highest spire of them all, a small light winked.

He felt it before it he saw it. The castle saw him, who he truly was. That light—that pinprick of light—picked him out of the crowd and urged him to walk across the water. *Come to the castle,* it said. *Stay awhile.*

He was a step from the shore, held up by a ring of dancing frogs wearing tuxedos. Their wet tongues going up and down and slapping against him, leaving sticky tracks he didn't mind or even notice. He was one step from the perfect, rose-petal water.

"Whoa, whoa there, my red-caped friend. Easy does it, now."

Art was yanked back into his senses. His body pleasantly numb. Head buzzing. Eyes jiggling in their sockets. The very thin man between him and the red water was all that was stopping him. Not a man, really. But that didn't register.

Art's eyes drifted up the length of the slender castle—a beautiful dagger stuck in the earth, pointing at the pink sky. The tiny light all those thousands of feet up its shiny wall winked out.

"Down here, my boy. There you go. Look me right in the dollop."

The very thin man's name came back to Art. Gandy, it was. Then everything else returned. A dizzy world of impossibilities on anxious waves. The gingerbread man pointed at the dolloped eye on his round face.

"Turn around, come with me. Yes, yes, yes. This way, nothing to see." The crowd took them back without notice. "Merry, merry to you. And to you. As well as you."

Gandy nodded at his neighbors, bowed when they bowed, and twirled when they twirled. Keeping his gritty hand on the small of Art's back, guiding him to the narrow opening of Kettle Korn Trail.

"I should've warned you," Gandy said. "Of course you peeked. Why wouldn't you? But it took me longer than I thought it would, and now here you are about to go swimming. No one seemed to notice, I think."

He gave a look at the bustling crowd, which was back to the business of the day now that the bells stopped thrumming. No more huzzahs.

"What was that?" Art asked.

"The market. It's more of a, uh, a social thing, really. No one buys much. It's an excuse to—"

"No, the thing." Art raised his hand above his head, searching for a simple word. Then found it. "*Castle*."

"Ah, that. Yes. Not important. What is important is S'ven. Apparently, he..."

Art wasn't listening. *Not important?* How could something like that, something so tall and elegant and shiny and-and-and... *not important?*

"Art. Hoo-hoo? Down here, son. In the dollop. We don't have much time."

"It's a castle?"

Gandy sighed a puff of sugar. "Yes, yes. That's it. That's exactly it. But right now, it's not important. S'ven is. And he's gone."

Art shook his head. Everything had been knocked out of it. Replaced with feelings for the castle. He wanted those feelings back. And he wanted the anxiety that was wringing his stomach like a dishrag to go away.

"S'ven?"

"Let me start over," Gandy said. "We're here to find S'ven. He will help you on your journey."

"He's gone?"

"Well, he's not there."

"So gone?"

"They weren't very merry about it, either. Seems he's been gone quite some time."

A glimmer of hope fluttered in Art's chest. "You mean he went back home?"

"No, no. I don't know. They said he was gone, that's all. I don't think he went back like you mean he went back. What do you have there?"

Gandy nabbed Art's hand. It was balled into a fist. It looked like mud squeezed between his fingers. When he opened it, a ball of gold foil was all that was left of the chocolate square.

"Where'd you get that? Never mind. Here." Gandy began wiping Art's palm with the bottom of the red cape. "Don't eat that, son. Don't ever eat it. Never, ever, ever, swear on the spirit of Christmas."

"It's chocolate."

"Trust me on this, will ya? Promise you won't even taste a King Chocolate while you're here."

King Chocolate. "I don't—"

"Promise!"

The tone that came out of the gingerbread man was unexpected. Loaded with fear and loathing. It shook Art like he'd missed a step and was falling. He nodded at the gingerbread man furiously cleaning his hand.

"I have another idea. She's a little odd. Well, not a little. Grimjoy knows things others don't. Sort of a last resort thing. You know the type?"

"Her name's Grimjoy?"

"She's blocks from here, near the border. I don't like getting that close, but you know what they say—when candy's cooking, there's no time to wait."

"What's the border?"

Gandy was done wiping Art's hand. He kicked the balled wrapper past the corner. "It isn't all *nice* here, son. Now, let's not burn our hands on the kettle. Off we go, back the way we came and—"

Gandy stopped short. Arm out.

"On second thought, we'll take the market. No one noticed when you walked right through the middle of it. They won't notice now. Hood up!"

He herded Art back into the open. Poked him in the back.

Art caught a glance of what Gandy had seen down Kettle Korn Trail. There were two of them marching with tall hats. And bright-colored jackets.

And he thought—he could've sworn—there were swords on their belts.

3

He was a large man in a large chair. A throne, if you will. A big, boxy, gaudy thing with rock candy embedded in dark brown leather (it wasn't really leather). It looked like milk chocolate blasted with a shotgun of jewels. No real design to it. Just lots of shiny things. And if he was hungry, he'd pluck one from the armrest and suck on it till he got some real food.

Chocolate.

The throne could sit two normal-sized men quite comfortably. You could squeeze a third in between them, in a pinch. The man living in the throne filled it from armrest to armrest. As if he were poured into it. The only thing he moved was his hand. And that was to put something in his mouth.

King Chocolate was his name. His friends called him Choco. He had no friends. So King Chocolate.

His legs looked like overcooked noodles glued to a stomach. They didn't reach the floor, almost ever, and constantly kicked the threshold to an imaginary song. Nothing upbeat or Christmassy. No beat at all, really. It sounded like someone dropping hammers on a cutting board. The beat got particularly loud when he was excited. And you might guess what excited him most.

At this very moment, a small wooden puppet had walked into the room, holding a rectangular tray. Upon the tray were five stacks of chocolate wafers. Each stack was numbered and came with a short glass of milk.

The puppet was the size of a toddler. His arms and legs were no bigger than kindling. The tray shook in his hands. The tray was heavy, of course. But the closer he got to the massive load of royalty, the more the tray quaked. Milk splashed over the sides.

Rivulets of drool ran down three chins to King Chocolate's neck.

His eyes were on the chocolate wafers, not the white puddles of milk racing around them. In fact, he hadn't noticed the puppet at all, even when the puppet stood in front of him, locking the tray between the throne's armrests. It wasn't till a glass tipped over. King Chocolate looked up.

His eyes looked like marbles pushed into a tray of fudge. They were brown, almost black.

"Who are you?" His words slurred into each other.

"I'm Poko."

The puppet removed the Alpine hat. The white feather fluttered in the band. He bowed. Then he turned his head and, with a smile, waved at the jolly fat man standing on the other side of the room. The jolly fat man wearing the red coat waved back.

"Don't wave at him!" King Chocolate blurted. It wasn't clear whom he was addressing. "Where's Jelly?"

"I-I-I don't know," Poko answered.

"Then why are you here?"

"Because she told me to bring you the recent harvest from the south fields. They're numbered so you know which ones—"

"Get out."

He was unconcerned with the spilt milk. To get wafer replacements would take too long. And Poko would just spill the next tray. King Chocolate shoved two wafers from pile one into his mouth. The chocolate thawed like his tongue was an overworked furnace. His eyes rolled back and disappeared.

Poko smiled at the jolly fat man in the red coat and started to say: "Merry, mer—"

"No!" A chocolate shower of spittle stained Poko's Alpine hat. "Not in here, you don't. Blah-blah. It's blah-blah. Do I have to send another memo? *Blah-blah!* If I hear one more merry, I will throw you and everyone in Fudgy Lake."

He could do that. The giant Sweet Tooth would do whatever he said. The unmerry citizens were slow to catch on. Change was hard. Everyone in Candyland said merry, merry at this time of year. King Chocolate had had enough of that. There was nothing merry about it, so why did they say it?

No one knew.

"Say it," he insisted.

"Blah-blah," Poko whispered.

"Louder."

"Blah-blah," Poko said.

The rivers of drool had turned muddy. He inserted one more wafer from pile one and raised his finger. "One more time, or you get dipped."

"BLAH-BLAH!"

Poko shuddered. His joints creaked. He hated the way those words felt. Despite living in the shadow of the Naughty Side, he *wanted* to be merry. He liked the way it felt. They all did. Everyone except maybe the chocolate-eating machine filling the throne.

"Merry Christmas," the jolly fat man wearing the red coat said.

Poko smiled. He couldn't help it. He shuffled out of the room as fast as his wooden shoes would go, clobbering his way through the door, and then looked back. Mouthed the words without a sound so King Chocolate wouldn't hear him.

Merry Christmas, Santa.

"WHY?" King Chocolate groaned. "Did you not hear the blah-blah part? Not merry, merry, not merry Christmas, not happy holidays. Blah-blah. It's so easy. Rolls off the tongue."

He waved his hands and sang.

"*We wish you a blah-blah blah-blah. We wish you a blah-blah blah-blah.* See?" He pointed at a wafer from the second pile. Stack one was decimated. "Now you try it."

"Throw me in Fudgy Lake," Santa said.

"You wish."

He devoured stack two like an industrial vacuum. The chewing sounded like animals stuck in a tar pit. The rolls across his belly burped like a boiling vat of goo. King Chocolate savored the flavor, letting it slide down his throat. He tipped his head back and poured a glass of milk in it like he was watering a potted plant.

He wiped his face with the back of his fleshy arm, plucked a wafer from the third stack, pointed it at Santa before throwing it into his mouth.

"So the big day in twenty rings. You must be excited. Making your lists, putting names on them, checking them off. Deciding who gets toys or coal."

"You know what you're getting," Santa said.

"I already have everything." He narrowed his eyes. "You know, those elves making the toys... I don't think that's right. You don't pay them, do you. There's something wrong with that. I'm sure it's breaking laws."

"They do it for love."

"Love of the game, sure. Keep telling yourself that. They make the toys; you get the glory."

King Chocolate paused to jot down a note concerning the wafers in the third stack. There was something unique about them. Not particularly good or bad. He'd pass his notes on to Jelly, who would make his wishes come true.

"I'm just going to say it," King Chocolate said. Pointed. "Egomaniac."

"Are we done?" Santa said flatly.

"A true friend tells the truth. And I'm telling you you're full of yourself. No judgment. Think about it. There are people in shopping malls who dress up like you. Kids get on their laps—crying, I might add—to get their picture. There are jillions of dollars made on that face of yours. A jillion."

"That's not a word."

"You're everywhere, fat man. Admit it. *Everywhere.* And you only work one day a year. Must be nice." King Chocolate nibbled the last wafer from stack number three. "You know who you're bigger than?"

"Don't say it."

"Elvis." He smacked his hands. "You thought I was going to say God."

"I'm not enjoying this conversation. If you could just..." Santa flipped an imaginary light switch.

"It's constructive criticism. You won't get that over there in Sunnyville. You get honesty over here. Truth bombs." He walloped his belly. "I've been blowing up phonies since before I existed."

"That doesn't make sense."

"Is that right? But a fat man in a sleigh that's pulled by magic flying reindeer, that makes sense?" Laughter gurgled in his throat. Then he called between his hands: *Free presents if you're nice! Free presents if you're good!* How about authentic, huh? What does being real get me, a dull rock?"

"Authentic?" Santa held his round belly and laughed and kept laughing. "Delusional much?"

"See, right there. Look at that. *Mean.* You're mean. Calling me delusional. Welcome to the Naughty Side. How does it feel?"

"Are you serious? You're talking to a—"

"Yeah, I know. I know who I'm talking to. I'm aware. And that makes me *undelusional.*"

Santa rolled his eyes. King Chocolate felt this argument slipping away. He had the jolly fat man cornered for a minute. He was a slippery one.

"Flying reindeer," King Chocolate said. "Am I wrong about that being impossible?"

"There are stranger things in the universe."

"Name one."

The large man in the red coat sighed. The extra, extra-large man on the throne bore down on him. There were plenty of strange things in the universe. Start with mating rituals. Grown men crying over a sports team. Free presents delivered by a fat man who shimmies down the chimney was another. But flying reindeer? That was number one, and Santa Claus knew it.

King Chocolate waited.

Santa stared back.

And then he had something. He raised his finger and said it with complete and total confidence. This was the answer. This was the strangest thing in the universe according to Santa.

He said: "Quilting."

There was a long pause. King Chocolate leaned back in the throne. Not taking his eyes off Santa. The two men bore down on each other. The four corners of the room seemed to shrink. A bead of sweat worked its way down the rolls of King Chocolate's neck. A rash broke out on his back. He narrowed his eyes. A puff of laughter escaped his sloppy lips. Then another. Santa covered his mouth. Tears welled up in his eyes. He tried not to break.

King Chocolate broke first. "Hahahahahaha-HAHAHA-HAHAHAHA!"

They both fell to pieces. Tears mixed with spit and sweat. Guffaws tearing them open. The laughter nearly strangled King Chocolate. His face was as red as gift wrapping. He slammed his fists on the armrests.

"I can't breathe..." he wheezed. "*Quilting!*"

They'd had an argument some time ago. Santa was a big fan of the craft. King Chocolate insisted it was just sewing squares together. He'd never sewed in his life, but he was certain—one hundred percent positive—he could quilt tomorrow. It was needle and thread. Come on.

He tried to scratch an itch marching down his back. That wasn't something he could do without a stick. He leaned forward, tears plopping into an empty glass on the tray, and snuck a wafer from the fourth stack.

"Quilting," King Chocolate gasped.

He popped the wafer into his mouth, leaned back to let it slide down his throat and soothe the pain in his sides. Then suddenly lunged forward. A fountain of chocolate spattered the floor.

"Number four, number four!"

King Chocolate rinsed his mouth with the remaining milk and spit it on the floor. It dribbled down his dark brown robe. A dark patch bloomed on the shirt beneath. He shouted for Poko to bring him more milk. The puppet never returned. That little fire starter would go for a swim in Fudgy Lake.

Blah-blah.

"Show me the, uh, the sector where this came from."

He held up the card with number four written on it, showed it to the room. The walls, previously plain white with no shelving or photos or decorations, flickered to life. An image surrounded him. As if he were floating over a large hillside. Below, a scrubland of chocolate canes sprouted from the ground. There were long strips taken from it. A cloud of white sugar puffed from the bottom of the mountain. If he looked close enough, he'd see the machine chopping them down one cane at a time.

"That's number four?" he asked. "Send the crew to Sweet Tooth's nest. Have them clean it for a week. See if that keeps this from happening again."

He threw the wafers from stack number four. They stuck to the wall with an ugly splat.

"That's a bit harsh," Santa said. "They were only doing what you said to do."

"I never said make me barf chocolate. Not once. Never even thought it."

"You said be creative. Try something new."

"What should I do, put coal in their stockings? Oh, wait a sec. You already got that covered. Why don't you just keep babying the Nice Side and let me take care of the naughties, okay, fatty?"

He shifted on the throne, leaned back, and wiggled around. The itch was getting worse. And the taste of stack number four was still on his tongue. It was acidic. Like a smoothie of fermented cabbage. And his gut still hurt from laughing. And his face hurt from laughing.

There was one wafer left from the third stack. He reached for it. Felt the itch run up his back. Felt it pinch the jelly rolls on the back of his neck. The wafer was between his fingers when he felt the brush of fur on his cheek. He looked at his shoulder.

A pair of beady, black eyes looked back.

"Ahhhhh!"

The fright punched him forward. He leaned with such force that his momentum carried him over the armrest. The structural reinforcement groaned. King Chocolate's mass, however, rolled over then around the armrest like a bag of soup. His chicken legs hit the floor like faulty kickstands. He landed like a violent wave in the ocean. The air whooshed from him like a bellows.

The tray clattered on the floor. The wafer from stack number three landed near him.

The mouse, sitting on its hind legs, perched on the back of the throne, rubbed its front paws together, and gave a squeak. A twitch. If you would've asked King Chocolate at that moment, he would've said the little vermin laughed at him. It did no such thing.

"Get it!" He pointed his meaty finger at the mouse. "That! That! That! Get it OUT OF HERE!"

A long, mechanical arm unfolded from the ceiling. It plucked the mouse up by the tail and carried it across the room, depositing it in a hole that opened in the floor. Squeaking as it went. Smiling, if you asked King Chocolate.

"Tell the queen." His fingers crawled toward the last wafer. "Tell her another one was up here. Tell her to do something, or I will. Tell her I mean it."

Santa squatted next to him. He attempted to pick up the wafer that was just out of King Chocolate's reach. His fingers, however, passed right through it.

"Useless," King Chocolate muttered. Then to the ceiling: "Get that."

The mechanical arm returned.

"Not you! A different one. Do you think I want a disease?"

A different arm—one that had not just handled a mouse—extended from the ceiling. It nudged the wafer into King Chocolate's hand. He quickly threw it in his mouth, rolled onto his back, and chewed.

That's better.

Poko clambered into the room and immediately began to quake. It sounded like tree trunks tumbling off a logging truck. King Chocolate, still out of breath, still chewing, looked at the timid puppet holding his Alpine hat with the white feather in the band.

"If Jelly isn't here in five minutes, I will use you to build a fire. I'll start with your legs and work my way up."

Poko nodded. His hinged jaw clattered.

"And bring more wafers. The ones from stack three. Not the pukey ones." Poko flashed a brief smile at Santa and turned. "And milk!"

Santa, still squatting next to the king, tilted his head. He wasn't hiding a smile in his white, curly beard. Nor was there a twinkle in his eyes. He was serious.

"Are you unhappy?"

"What, are you my therapist now? Of course I'm unhappy. I'm the king of the naughties, you bag of farts. Unhappiness is our birthright. Haven't you heard the song? Let me play it for you. It's all horn section."

King Chocolate rolled to one side long enough to pass gas. No one was there to suffer the consequences. Santa looked at the helpless king licking chocolate off his lips like a starving animal. He looked like something coughed up by the ocean.

"You're out of breath," Santa said.

"You're judging me?"

"Simply an observation."

King Chocolate attempted to roll onto his side and, from there, possibly prop himself up on one elbow. From there, maybe, pull himself onto the throne. With confidence, he swung his arm. Felt a sharp pain in his shoulder. And unintentionally punched himself on the chin. The second roll absorbed the blow. It didn't hurt. He accepted his fate.

"You know," he gasped at Santa, "for a nicie, you're a bit naughty."

"We all are, Casey."

Santa looked down at him. The twinkle was back. His eyes shined. He wasn't going to deny it. Santa Claus was both naughty and nice. He proved it every time King Chocolate was with him. Santa opened his mouth to laugh his annoying ho-ho-ho. Then he flickered.

He was gone. Vanished. Turned off.

"Living out childhood dreams again?" someone said.

"I DIDN'T SAY you could turn him off," King Chocolate said.

The roly-poly elf waddled over to him. "Were you tired of sitting on the throne?"

"I'm admiring the ceiling." He gestured to the chocolate splatters on the ceiling tiles. "Looks like someone had an accident."

Jelly leaned back to observe and nearly rolled over. A disgusting stain was all over the ceiling. No one had ever bothered to look up because it took such effort. But when lying flat on the floor, it was hard not to notice.

"So, you've fallen and can't get up," Jelly said.

"Enough jokes. Get the picker."

"The engine lift?"

"How about the royal lift. And shut up."

He wanted to tell her to shut her *fat face*. But that was mean. She was a weather balloon balanced on two paddles shaped like feet. As plump as a blueberry. Never smiled, not once. And always stroking that braid of hair coming off the back of her head.

But she was always there for him. Almost always.

"Where have you been?" he said once he settled into the throne. "The samples were disgusting. They tasted like feet. I'm embarrassed to have my initials on them."

"They must have been horrible." Jelly picked up the empty tray.

"The last one was gross. Have that crew fired and sent to the rock-candy mines."

"We don't pay them, Your Excellency. And the mines are shut down."

"First of all, not a fan of the sarcasm. I get enough from St. Fatty. Second, you think of something to make them learn."

"Why should they learn if they're fired?"

"It's a lesson! Word will get out. I'm teaching the next generation. You'd make a terrible king, you know that. What do I pay you for?"

"You don't pay me."

"How about I pay you to shut up. How's that? Now where were you? Mr. Pencil Face brought me the samples and spilled the milk. And he said merry, merry when I *specifically* said not to. See what you did?"

"Sounds awful." Jelly scraped the chocolate wafers off the wall. "I was in the other room."

"Which room? There's a thousand of them."

"Newsroom."

"Oh, goody. The news. Tell me Christmas got cancelled."

"There's a new crosser."

"It's not like anyone around here would miss the fat—I'm sorry, what did you say?"

Jelly repeated it with slow confidence bordering on arrogance. Her eyes half-lidded. Complete boredom possessing her face. It was the only thing that kept her in King Chocolate's good graces. He'd thrown everyone else in Fudgy Lake except her. She'd learned early on his one critical weakness, something he couldn't stand to admit.

He wanted to be liked. He was addicted to it. If she was bored, he would do backflips (figuratively, of course) to entertain her.

Who's the awful leader in the room?

"A crosser?" he said.

"A crosser."

"From another world."

"Is there another kind?"

Stunned silence. King Chocolate looked like a wax replica of himself. He didn't blink or lick his lips or twitch. It was eerie. Jelly didn't know he could be so still.

"Did you die?" she asked.

"Shut up a second. I'm thinking."

Thinking, indeed. He hadn't thought about a crosser in a very, very long time. He chose to forget. His queen had taught him how to do that. *Compartmentalization*, she called it. Lock the bad memories up. Now Jelly was prying open one of those compartments. There hadn't been a crosser since—

"Is it a nutcracker?" he asked.

"No."

"What is it?"

"A boy."

"A wooden boy?"

"A regular one."

"You're sure? Positive?"

"Yes. And yes. Generals Fly and Gnat confirmed it."

King Chocolate scoffed. Spittle flew down his chins. He didn't bother wiping it. "Gnat Brain and Fly Poop. Those two morons could talk to a statue. May as well ask a magic ball, even though magic isn't real. Or ask a ghost. Even though ghosts weren't—"

"The Lost Boys saw him, too."

"Okay." He started nodding. "What did those noodle heads say?"

"He's with Gandy."

"The ginger?"

"They were looking for S'ven."

"Hahaha." King Chocolate pounded his chest. It felt good to laugh the appropriate amount. "Good luck finding that rodent. Did they find him?" He leaned forward, anticipating the answer. He flopped back in the throne when Jelly said no. "Good. He's a loon. Kids still saying that? Loon?"

"They never did."

"*Loon*... I'm bringing it back. Send the memo out. Loon is cool again. And let the crosser be Macey's problem. Maybe he'll wreck the castle again. That would be sweet." He snorted. "The loon. Hey, where's Poko? I ordered chocolate and milk, like, two chimes ago."

"You might want to reconsider."

"I'm starving."

"I mean the crosser." Jelly shuffled closer. It was hard to get the king's attention when food entered the conversation. His skinny legs were thumping a mad rhythm on the throne. He drew a breath and was about to scream when Jelly said: "His name is Arthur."

"I'll bet." He laughed. "Artie-fartie."

"You know why that's important?"

"Because it's funny?" He looked up, then back to Jelly. Legs shaking. "What?"

She pulled a snapshot from a pocket. Generals Fly and Gnat had taken it in Kettle Korn Trail. The photo was fuzzy, since she had to blow up the one they gave her (the original was a speck of pepper). King Chocolate took it from her, held it to the light. He struggled to make sense out of it, like it was an X-ray, and he wasn't a doctor. So she explained. Those were drawings in the crosser's pocket. A sketchbook. That meant he was an artist.

"He's a creator," she said. "You know what that means?"

"Of course." He gave back the photo. "What does it mean?"

"Whoever has him wins the war."

King Chocolate let that soak in. *Win the war?* He hadn't entertained the idea since he couldn't remember. The border hadn't moved an inch in one direction or the other in forever. What was the point of fighting if it never moved?

But now.

If this was true. If this crosser could hand him victory, if he could cover all of Candyland in darkness, then that was something better than food (for now). Just once he wanted King Macey and all those singing *loons* to know what it felt like to live in oppressive darkness. They didn't know. And they judged King Chocolate and all his residents for it. They blamed them for who they were, what they felt like. If they walked a tick in naughty shoes, they would know.

And King Chocolate would taste victory sweeter than all the wafers in Candyland.

"Send the Lost Boys! Now! Before Macey figures it out. Go-go-go! I don't want to see your fat little face until you bring the, uh... what's his name?"

"Arthur."

"Him! Bring him!"

He needed to burn some of this excitement. He flipped open a control panel on the right side of the armrest. There were buttons and controls. He thumbed a small joystick. The throne started sliding like a Zamboni machine. He whirled around the room. Maybe he'd race down the halls for a bit.

"Tell the queen we're going to *win!*"

"Would you like her to join you for dinner?" Jelly asked.

"God no! Just tell her the winning part. And the mouse part. One of her mice was up here, and I didn't hurt it. The next one goes straight in the lake. Tell her that."

"I'm not telling her that."

He didn't hear Jelly say that. Victory bells were ringing in his ears.

4

Gandy peeked into the market. He looked in one direction, then the other. Back and forth he went, and when he was satisfied, he turned back to Art and pulled the hood over his eyes.

"Follow me. No need to look around, yeah?"

No one paid attention to the gingerbread man and the Red Riding Hood poseur entering from the alley. Art kept his head down and eyes on the back of Gandy, whose flat legs scurried ahead, cutting through the crowd, calling out as he went.

"Merry, merry," he said. "Merry, merry to you. And to you."

Above the crowd, the castle soared into the pink sky. It didn't feel magical anymore. The castle was lovely and all, but without the chiming bell, that sensation of oneness, the way it stripped away the illusion of separation, was gone. It was a mob of individual things bouncing and dancing and running in circles, wishing each other a merry, merry.

The speck of light was winking at the top of the castle. Like an antenna warning low-flying planes to stay away. Although there was nothing in the sky but cotton-candy clouds. Not even birds.

Art had an urge to eat more chocolate. He didn't know why. It didn't taste good. But it felt good.

The hood came down over his eyes. "No peeking," Gandy said.

There was barking laughter, hoots and hollers, music and song and stamping of feet and hooves and whatever else was in the market. There was plenty of merry, merry and bubbles, too. Big bubbles and small bubbles drifting in the air. One stuck to Art's sleeve, the soapy film iridescent and smelling like strawberries.

It popped when Gandy yanked him beneath a tarp propped up with pretzel logs.

They passed carts full of candied apples and cardboard shacks stacked with balls of yarn. There were shipping containers loaded with glass furniture that smelled like grape juice, carriages piled with nuts. They passed a tent that smelled like a county fair. There were self-winding yo-yos and jack-in-the-boxes that told jokes. There was one thing that everyone and everything seemed to have in common.

Freedom.

They were who they were, and no one or no thing held them back. No judgment to fear. Like the essence of joy was the air they breathed. It was the ground they walked on.

Gandy stopped.

Art nearly knocked him over. Gandy clutched a handful (a fistful? a pawful?) of the red cloak.

"This way, yeah? I think we should go this way. A better way."

They did a one-eighty and were now going back the way they came, toward Kettle Korn Trail. Gandy walked like a frightened animal, bumping into things without an "excuse me" or even a "merry, merry." Art couldn't keep up with the zigging and zagging. He fell behind two yarn dolls swaggering arm in arm—their corded red hair falling over their shoulders—and could no longer see the ginger-bread man.

A wave of anxiety stomped on his chest.

He looked around, unconcerned someone would notice a crosser in their midst. How they would mob him, paw at him for attention.

Want to know who he was, where he came from. Why he was here. All the things he didn't know—

"Over here." Gandy pulled him into a dim shadow. "Pull down the hood and stand still. Crouch down a little, you know. Bend the knees."

Art did that. He would've done anything he was told, feeling relief that Gandy knew where they were and where they were going. Gandy was looking left and right, that flat head twisting back and forth. The eyes big circles that weren't moving.

"What are we—"

"Just wait," Gandy said. "Give it a minute."

Gandy stopped panning the crowd. His face locked onto something like a satellite dish finding its target. A tall hat slid through the crowd like the fin of a shark. It was fuzzy and black and moved steadily, pausing every now and then. Turning this way and that before continuing. Like a bear catching wind of a meal somewhere in the trees.

"Don't. Move," Gandy said.

For the first time, he looked like a cookie made to eat. Not one who was married and had a house and an apron he wore when he cooked.

Art didn't move. Not a twitch.

Another hat cut through the crowd from the left. This one moved fast and smooth. A third one came from the right. No one was bothered by the swarm of tall hats except a petrified gingerbread cookie. Art wanted to run. Wanted to crawl out of his skin. Wanted a nibble of chocolate.

"Merry, merry, Gingerman," someone said behind them. "To you as well, Red Riding Hood."

A TENT WAS SANDWICHED between a metal shack filled with birdhouses and a wooden stall selling balls of dough. The flap was thrown open. Red and green lights twinkled inside.

The plump head of a bushy-browed young man peeked out of the two-person tent. An elfish smile spread wide and deep into fleshy, brown cheeks. Black hair pulled into a tight ponytail that swished over his shoulder.

Above the entrance, tied with twine, a banner was hung. The words were sloppy and painted in red, sparkling with glitter thrown on the paint before it dried.

Keepers of the Lost.

"Now, if you don't mind, move yourselves along. You're making quite the wall in front of our humble abode."

Peeps and chirps came from the humble abode. Along with the smell of a county fair.

"Ah, yes." Gandy looked around. "Could we come inside?"

"For a gander or a keep?" the plump, smiling face said.

"We won't know till we peek." Gandy looked at the crowd. "We're in a bit of a hurry, if you don't mind."

Something neighed. It sounded like a horse, but even a mini wouldn't fit inside a tent that size. The smile drooped a little. Then the face disappeared into the depths of the two-person tent entirely. The flap closed, and the red and green lights disappeared.

That was that.

Gandy turned back to the circling hats coming closer. His eyes growing bigger. He was as inanimate as a cookie fresh from the oven. Art knew that feeling well. Fear had taken hold of the gingerbread man. Fear so pure it paralyzed the body. Tasted like cold steel.

It was a boulder that ran you over, that flattened out thoughts and squeezed out breath. It was a thief ransacking the house, leaving it empty and hollow. Whatever the hats were, they were shepherding Fear closer. Gandy and Art could only watch.

"It appears we've had a cancellation." The tent flap whooshed open. "It seems we can spare a few ticks for a couple of curious lads."

❄

GANDY DUCKED inside without hesitation and was greeted with: "Gandy, old friend, it's been quite some time. How is Meg these days?"

Art followed, having to drop to his knees to squeeze through the opening. He crawled into a humid odor of damp fur and bird droppings. There was a hint of a large aquarium. The hood of his cloak hung over his head. His hands were on a dirt floor scattered with hay. And feathers. And scales.

"Stand up, lad. You're not in a barn."

An odd thing to say, given the smell and the sounds of the place. The host, it seemed, didn't know the meaning of the word *barn*. Or they used that word entirely different in these parts. Because it *was* an enormous, round barn.

There were stalls all around and cages stacked on top. There were three levels with more enclosures above. Things were flapping wings and sharpened claws, things staring down with gold-ringed eyes. There were aquariums, just like he thought. Only little mermaids were inside, no bigger than trout. Add to that glass cubicles decorated like miniature condos with bats sitting on sofas and worms watching TV. A salamander in a tuxedo held binoculars to get a better look at him. Gophers with hard hats building walls. Ants painting a landscape with watercolors.

There was one normal thing. A cat was on the third level, staring with lazy boredom as cats do. Then Art blinked, and the cat was gone. *Maybe not so normal.*

"My name is Herkle. And this is my brother, Derkle."

The hand that helped Art to his feet was thick. The hair on the back of it was coarse and straight. As black as ink. It hoisted Art up as if he were as light as a scarecrow. Art found his balance and then stumbled into Gandy, who kept him from falling over and crawling back out the flapped doorway.

Derkle, who had helped him stand, looked as strong as a horse. From his feet to his shoulders, he bulged with muscle. The problem was from the shoulders up. There was a long muzzle and rubbery lips. Pointed ears that turned. A flowing mane as coarse as the hair on his hands.

"Well, well, what do we have here?"

It wasn't Derkle the horse-headed farmer who said it. It was Herkle, who had introduced himself and his brother. He was standing on the other side of a Christmas tree in the middle of the round pen. Standing, of course, on four legs. Because Herkle was a horse. From the waist down. A plump-face man from the waist up. A shiny ponytail slung over his shoulder. He spoke with a churlish grin that was wide and wet.

"Gandy? Would you mind introducing us to your friend?"

"Of-of course," he stammered. "He's not from around here, I'm afraid. Down from Bonbon Town. Believe it or not, he's never been to the market."

Herkle and his brother exchanged looks. Derkle sighed noisily, lips flapping. It was almost a neigh. Herkle nodded.

"Well, then, that would explain his fascination with all this." Herkle gestured to the three-story barn. The cat was now on the shelf right behind him, blinking heavily at Art. "Does he not understand expansion, Gandy?"

"You'll have to ask him."

Gandy shook his head at Art. It was a signal. A signal Art totally didn't understand. *Expansion?* If he was talking about how a two-person tent could house a circus, then the answer was no. He did not understand expansion.

"You're a long way from home, aren't you, lad?" Herkle said. "Remove your hood, please. I would like to see your original face."

"He's shy," Gandy said. "Let him be. Your place is enough to give anyone the fits."

Once again, Herkle nodded. But not in a way of agreement. He studied the length and width of the red-cloaked stranger, clopping his wide hooves on the ground. Circling Art. Puffs of dust hovered off the ground.

"There's nothing to—" Gandy started.

Derkle held up his hand, then crossed his bulging arms. The

horse head tilted with curiosity. Black eyes big and shiny. Art could see a dash of red reflected in them. Derkle finally sighed (this time it was a neigh). Herkle nodded to his brother in agreement.

"My brother smells a fib like a rotten apple." Herkle offered a joyless smile. "Oh dear, Gandy. That's a naughty strike on you. And so close to Christmas. What will the jolly fat man put in your stocking this time?"

Gandy began to stutter. How many fibs could one tell before the jolly fat man backed the coal truck up to the chimney?

Art couldn't stand to see Gandy quiver that way. He pulled the hood off his head and showed his original face. Herkle's smile was a spotlight not a birthday candle. It beamed with fascination that exceeded what Art had felt when he crawled into the tent.

"My, my, my." The heavy hooves danced in place. "A cross-uh."

He whispered the last part. Derkle let out a whinny that stirred the entire barn. Feathers drifted from cages. The worms looked away from their TV. The fancy salamander dropped the binoculars. The cat had disappeared again.

"It's been quite some time since we had one. What would you say, Derkle? Twenty bells, maybe?" The horse head whinnied softly. "Thirty-three? That is a long time. It seems our friend Gandy is hiding him." He clicked his tongue. "That's a naughty the fat man won't forgive, my gingerbread friend."

"I am not hiding him. Besides, it wouldn't be a naughty if I was. Which I'm not. This is simply help, nothing more. You know how Landers are. If they knew there was a crosser, they would get... *excited*." The pause sounded like a swallow. The kind hiding a fib. "I was taking him to S'ven."

"S'ven is gone," Herkle said.

"I know. Where is he?"

Herkle's eyebrows were as thick as scouring pads. As coarse as steel wool. They rose and lowered. "Mystic Mountain, Lemonade River, Gooey Gully... who knows. He's a complicated one."

Herkle studied Art. Derkle hadn't even shuffled his boots. Only the wide nostrils on the end of the shiny muzzle flared, exhaling like exhaust pipes.

"My brother would like to know your name," Herkle asked.

Derkle raised his hand before Gandy could protest. Art cleared his throat. Said his name without hesitation.

"Art?" Herkle looked at his brother and back. "And what are you doing in our lovely world, Art?"

Art shook his head. Anyone's guess.

"You're lost, then? Then there's only one reason you're here, lad. The greatest Christmas gift of all. You're here to be found!"

Derkle threw back his head and let loose a full-throated whinny that shook the vaulted ceiling. The animals and things cheeped and sang and growled and barked with him. Stamping their tiny feet and flapping their feathered or scaly wings.

"He wants to go home," Gandy said. "He wants to wake up."

"And you, gingerbread man, are not helping!" Herkle shouted.

Derkle thrust a finger in Gandy's direction. Even from ten feet away, Art could feel the power of the horse-head man. Gandy felt it, too. Stumbling just a bit.

"Going home and waking up are two different things, my delectable friend. You mean well, Gandy. You do. But you're interfering with the lad's journey. It is his to take."

"I'm a guide, Herkle. Look it up in the big book. *Should a crosser seek assistance, we will provide that no matter the inconvenience.*"

He'd never quoted the big book to Art. In fact, he'd always called it the manual. Maybe they were different things. Herkle smirked and let that sour smile open wide. "And what chapter is that from, Gandy?"

"He landed in our house for a reason. You can't deny that, Herkle. You either, Derkle. *A reason.* We were chosen to guide him."

That swayed the brothers, who exchanged glances. Derkle shrugged. Something in the big book agreed with that. After all, why did Art land in their house and not somewhere else?

"A guide you seek," Herkle said. "Well, you've come to the right place."

"Hold on a ding-dong. Just hoooooold your ringer. We didn't come in here to adopt one of *these.*"

Derkle whinnied. It was disapproving. No horse whisperer needed. He raked his boot across the dirt floor like a bull seeing red. Gandy took one step in Art's direction. He hadn't said anything wrong. It was the way he said what he said about the animals in this place. *One of these.*

Herkle held a hand up in his brother's direction. Perhaps the only thing keeping him from charging. He laced his fingers. Wet his lips.

"Let's try again, my dear cookie." Herkle cleared his throat. In a flat, dangerous tone, he said: "If our young cross-uh here landed in your house for a reason, then he must have entered our domain for one as well. Don't you think?"

"*We're* here for a reason," Gandy muttered. But not exactly in agreement.

"We are home for the homeless. Love for the loveless. All the forgotten are remembered, and the lost are seen." Herkle trotted in a circle, hands raised toward cages and stalls and boxes. "They are not misfits, if that's what you think. Perish the thought. For one who doesn't fit isn't broken, only trying to be something they're not. Look around, lad. What does your heart see? What do your eyes feel?"

It wasn't the first time Herkle had given such a speech. Certainly not the last time it would inspire. Gooseflesh sprang up Art's arms. It felt like the horse-man was talking to *him.* Because he felt that way.

Lost. Forgotten and unseen.

There was a reason he was here. These were his people. Well, not his *people.* They were kindred. They were family. Misfits. *Like me.*

"Most kind," Gandy said, "but a travel companion is not what we came for."

"Companion!" Herkle stamped the floor. Derkle clapped his hands. "That's a better word, cookie man. Who would be your *companion,* lad? Your friend. Always at your back, mmm? Would it be Mr. Jimmy here. Our slaggo friend fell asleep on a cargo bunk and woke up on the wrong side of the border. When he tried to go back home, the family wouldn't let him. A tight bunch, slaggos are. Short memories."

What Herkle called a slaggo was, apparently, a chameleon. Because one waved through a glass box. He was wearing Bermuda shorts and rubber flip-flops strung between his toes. He held a tiny book in one hand.

"How about something more exotic, mmm? Sort of a cross-uh, this one. From a story world much like this one. Skin like leather and the tail of a serpent. You've never seen anything like this, lad. Wandering alone in Gooey Gulch, afraid and lonely. Once he was lost, but now he is found, the one and only and uniquely gifted... *grimmet!*"

Tiny applause came from several cages. Herkle threw out his arms. Three stories up, through a wire-mesh enclosure, a bright red bat hovered on small wings. Somehow it stayed airborne with a belly as round as a baseball. The whiplike tail slithered beneath it. It wiggled tiny fingers at Art.

Impossibly cute.

Endearing.

How could anyone say no to—what did he call it? A *grimmet*.

Art might have walked out with the grimmet had it fluttered down to his shoulder. Herkle, though, introduced five more companions, each with more potential than the one before. Gandy protested louder with each one. Herkle didn't care. He was on fire. In his element. Top performance gear for a reluctant crowd.

Derkle watched Art with those big black eyes.

All this was interesting, in the weird sort of way Gandy was a walkie, talkie. And somehow that was no longer surreal. But Art didn't want a pet. Not something to care for, to be responsible for. He struggled to care for himself. *I don't even know where I am or where I'm going!*

Silence.

Herkle stopped mid-sentence while describing the merits of a baby warthog snoring in a hammock. He clopped his hooves and frowned in concentration. He nodded at his horse-headed brother.

Derkle approached Art like a stray dog. A hungry one backed into a corner. His nostrils flared as he neared. The exhales were warm and laced with alfalfa. Art didn't move as Derkle moved his muzzle up his arm, the long hairs on his trembling chin tickling the honeycomb tattoo on Art's forearm. The nostrils soft and wet.

Derkle took Art's hand.

Turned it over. Examined the heavy calluses on his palm, the kind that developed on the handle of a shovel. His eyes rolled toward his brother.

"You tasted the chocolate," Herkle said.

"He didn't know what he was doing," Gandy said. "Someone in the market—"

"Who?"

Gandy stuttered. All the attention was on Art, who shrugged. Then he described what the imp looked like. Said the imp's name was Rude. That didn't ring a recognition with the horse brothers. But when Art mentioned the things strapped on their backs, the foamboard-like pool noodles, Herkle and Derkle looked at each other.

"Lost Boys," Herkle muttered.

"I-I doubt that," Gandy said. "Not this far over the—"

Herkle stopped him. Derkle traced the creases with his finger. Put his hand on Art's chest. Heart beating against it. Thumping. Running. Running. Running.

Derkle looked into his eyes. Staring and seeing deep inside. Art's warped reflection in the depths of those black pupils. The red cape over his shoulders. Shaggy mop of hair.

"Interesting," Herkle said.

"Interesting? What's interesting?" Gandy said. "I'm sorry, Herkle. I haven't been honest with you. It's not exactly a fib, just... well, the reason we're in here is because—"

"Shhhh." Herkle pressed a finger on Gandy's mouth. The icing smudged and clotted. "Are you certain?" he said to his brother.

His brother whinnied.

"Very well, then." Herkle looked at Art. "We found your companion, lad."

❄

"Stand right over there. A few more steps, that's it. Thank you very much."

Art stood next to the doorway. Gandy seemed unsure what to do, his head twisting left, then right. The candied outline of his mouth (still smeared) formed a perfect O. At one point he started toward the exit, but Herkle clicked his tongue like a dog trainer.

"Not yet, my cookie friend."

Derkle had something long and flexible. It looked like he was preparing to pole vault. There was no hook on the end—which was what Art figured it was for. It reached the third story. Maybe he was going to knock one of the doors open and let a rainbow mini-dinosaur parachute to the ground.

He pulled some switches embedded on the pole. A few clicks and the pole split longways. Rungs snapped between the two pieces. Herkle swung the ladder into place. There was nothing trustworthy about the way it swayed. Herkle, though, didn't hesitate: he scaled to the very top of the ladder and climbed into a dark space between a cargo box stamped *Merry, Merry* and a net full of seashells.

"He should be to the left," Herkle shouted. "Behind the counter." Then to Art he said: "Daryl plays hide-and-seek when there's company. He's here; he's there, then fits himself in this tiny little space behind a kitchen counter up there. Don't know how he does it. This one is rare and special, lad. Derkle, though, he says there's an indelible connection between the two of ya. And Derkle's never wrong. You'll see what I mean—careful!"

The horse-headed brother returned to the ladder with a duffel bag in one hand. The ladder twisted and bowed. Derkle descended as if he were sliding down a fire pole. He leaped off the last rung and landed with a puff of dust. Bits of hay floated in the hazy air.

The bag looked nine months pregnant. The way it squirmed.

"Ah, here we go." Herkle pulled the zipper and reached inside. "Hold your breath, lads. It's about to be taken away."

A load of fur cuddled against Herkle's chest. Long whiskers and triangular ears.

"We found this one on Two-Face Mountain. It was after the battle. I think he helped the hussars win. No scars." He ran his fingers through the fur and over the generous belly. Derkle whinnied. "That's right. My brother said no scars we can see, but he's wounded, this one. We think he might be a crosser. Hard to say. Just never seen one like him in the Land."

"What were you doing on Two-Face Mountain?" Gandy said.

"Looking for lost ones."

Gandy seemed to forget about his hurry. He drifted away from the exit as if Herkle had hypnotized him with a fat, furry animal. The tail swished like a feather duster. Gandy reached out.

"I wouldn't, my cookie friend. He's temperamental. You know, fussy when it comes to strangers. I'd be worried what might happen. Look at the teeth. How sharp they are. Could puncture a balloon. And little knives in his feet, look." He pushed on the paws. A hooked claw sprang out. "Retractable."

Gandy backed up. His eyes round. "What's that sound? Is that coming from him?"

They leaned closer. Except for Art. He knew what they were hearing. It was the sound the animal made when it was cradled in someone's arms. They looked at each other, the three of them. Herkle biting his lip. Derkle nodding that big horse head. Gandy holding his chest.

"It's a cat," Art blurted.

And that was it. Your garden-variety tabby. Long fluffy tail. Sprigs of whiskers bunched around a pink nose. The belly, though, looked like he preferred beer over milk, spending his days soaking up sun in a windowsill instead of hunting game.

"Cat?" Gandy said.

"Yeah. A cat."

"Are *cats* rare?"

Art laughed. He still didn't know where he'd come from or what home looked like, but he knew cats were everywhere. You couldn't give them away.

"They're not... no, they're not rare. Not where I come from."

"You remember?" Gandy said.

Art shrugged. "I just... no. But I don't think cats are rare."

"He's a cross-uh, then. Like you." Herkle rubbed the cat's belly. The purring grew louder. "We don't call him *cat*."

"What do you call it?" Gandy asked.

Before Herkle could answer, Art blurted out a word. It was a name that came from faraway. One as familiar as the tattoo on his arm.

"Daryl."

Herkle and Derkle exchanged a long glance. "That's right, lad. He's a Daryl. How did you know?"

Even Gandy was nodding. Like they were sort of surprised Art had guessed it.

Art couldn't explain how he knew his name. Like the word came through a speaker planted inside his head. It came on a purr. He could feel the warmth, feel the cat lying on his bed in the mornings. Greeting him at the door when he got home. Flopping on the floor to get that fat belly rubbed. This cat came to the sound of plastic bags rubbed together.

Daryl locked those vertical pupils on him now and didn't waver.

Art was dying to hold him. Begging to feel the fur. The warmth. *The purr.*

"Do cats scratch furniture?" Herkle asked. "Do they poop in sand boxes?"

"Yeah. They chase lasers, too."

"Hmm." Herkle nodded at his brother. Derkle took ten steps back. He pulled a tin of animal food out of his pocket, hooked his finger in the pull ring. "And cats do this?"

When the lid cracked and the seal broke, before the meaty smell of wet food wafted out, there was a vibration in the air. An electrical current Art felt in his teeth and down in his bones.

It tingled.

He didn't blink, though.

He didn't look away, not even for a second.

One second, Daryl was curled up in Herkle's arms. And the next he was crouched on Derkle's shoulder, watching him peel the lid from the can. Licking his whiskers. Showing his teeth when he meowed.

Derkle held up the can. Daryl went to town.

"Can they..."

Teleport? No. No, they can't do that.

The little bit of foundation he'd felt under him, however small that fragment had been, was now gone. The familiarity of seeing a cat had put him at ease. He knew the cat's name, after all. He probably knew the cat from where he came from, he was sure of it. And if he was honest, it was more than that.

He *loved* that cat.

But cats didn't cross a room without moving. They didn't disappear and reappear when hungry. *And cookies don't talk, and horses don't wear bib overalls.*

Herkle flashed a self-satisfied smile.

Art didn't know what to think of that. He just wanted to hold the cat. To feel him. To cuddle with him when the world felt dark and heavy. Daryl was almost done eating, his long tongue reaching for the whiskers. His eyes were on Art. He was going to do that thing again. The air took on that sharp, electric edge again.

Then something clamped around Art's arm.

He was yanked through the tent's exit and pulled into the market.

PRESSURE FILLED HIS HEAD. It was a balloon on the verge of bursting.

Art covered his ears. Hooked at the elbow by a white-gloved hand, pulled into the peppermint air of the market, he stumbled off the curb. His knees skidded on the soft stones. The hood fell back.

"Crosser," someone muttered.

"Crosser," someone answered. "Look at the eyes!"

And then a third someone connected the dots and shouted for all to hear: "CROSSER!"

The road thundered beneath Art. His head was down, but he felt the walls close in around him. Bodies pressing closer, squealing and laughing and gasping and clapping. A ring of black boots surrounded him. Boots made for marching, not singing in the rain.

Art followed the boots up starched pant legs, past shiny belt buckles and stiff jackets.

Tufts of chin hair.

Square mouths with hard jaws.

A ring of tall-hatted soldiers surrounded him. Shoulder to shoulder, eyes staring ahead. Pressure coming down, a weighty vapor filled Art's brain. Made the street rock on stormy waters.

"This isn't necessary!" Gandy turned sideways and slipped between the guards like an envelope through a mail slot. "You're making a scene, all of you!"

The heavy air pulsed. Art felt it push behind his eyes.

"No, no," Gandy answered (although Art didn't hear a reply for him to answer). "I *was* bringing him to the castle and avoiding attention doing it. Look at the mess *you've* made. Just look!"

The full-sized nutcrackers didn't flinch.

"How dare you accuse me of avoiding you!" Gandy shouted. "The boy wanted to see the animals. There's nothing in the rules that prohibits such a thing *on the way to the castle!* It's in the manual; look it up! I'll be sending a complaint straight to King Macey, count on that. On all of you."

Art got to one knee. He staggered and leaned into one of the soldiers. A tight hand clamped around his arm. He jerked free and shoved the nutcracker (who barely moved). With a couple of steps, he could break through like a game of Red Rover. He would've, too. If not for the firm, gingery hand on his chest.

"Don't," Gandy whispered.

"Am I in trouble?"

Gandy shook his head. "Of course not. They are peacemakers. It's all right, I promise."

The pressure lifted from the crown of Art's head.

He inhaled clean, crisp air to cleanse his lungs and mind.

In unison, the nutcrackers saluted. It looked like they were saluting Art—and maybe they were—then they abruptly did an about-face. They moved in unison, boots clopping the road in time with each other and through the crowd like a bubble in a stream.

"We're walking. We're walking." Gandy pulled the hood over Art's face. "No pictures, please. We ask for privacy, thank you. He's just like us."

Flashes went off.

Screams of joy exploded.

"Where am I going?" Art asked.

Gandy stopped. The soldiers kept marching. Gandy was waving when the nutcrackers ejected him from the circle, keeping Art trapped inside as they marched. Gandy's voice, somehow, rang in Art's head like a dinner bell. The words as sharp as the peppermint breeze.

"Your journey, son."

5

The boat drifted like a wafer through a pool of rose tea.

It wasn't so much a boat as it was a floating panel. A miniature barge with no cargo. Well, none except for the young man wearing a red cape. And the soldiers posted around the perimeter with only a red whip of licorice keeping them from going over the edge.

There was no sound of a motor or whine of an electric troller. If there was, it was drowned out by the cheers from shore. More bodies had flooded the market once word of a crosser was out. Toys and puppets and muppets and things all getting a look at the awkward young man standing on the floating stage, the size of it a bit much. But it was the only boat in sight.

Slowly, the cheers faded.

Slowly, they drifted toward the great spike in the sky. It felt like he was moving into the shadow of the castle—the way it felt, the drop in temperature, the gloom—but there was no shadow.

No sun.

Only a pink sky. Only cotton-candy clouds.

The closer they got, the more the castle looked like it had been carved from a stalagmite of gold and not quite finished. Still, it was stunning—the arching windows and pointy turrets. The way the golden walls glittered. Just the size of the thing insisted on being worshipped. Art followed its rise into the sky. It felt good being near it. Felt better the closer they got.

He went to the end of the boat (not a boat, but whatever). The nutcrackers didn't stop him.

The water was still. Unbroken. Not a ripple in their wake. As if they weren't moving. Not even touching the water. It didn't seem real. Because when he leaned over the edge, he wasn't in the reflection. Only the clouds. Only the sky.

Only the castle.

He could swim back to shore. It wasn't too late. It wasn't too far. The crowd would greet him, maul him. Take pictures. Maybe hide him. But he didn't. And for one silly reason.

He didn't want to. Because the castle felt good.

"Hey." He said it to the nearest soldier. "What's in the castle?"

The nutcracker's head turned toward him. Then Art's head rang with pressure. Like a tuning fork jammed between the eyes.

A GATE LOWERED an inch at a time.

Giant links in a chain that could heel a dragon. Giant links the color of breakfast cereal. The kind with artificial flavors and loads of sugar. The good kind.

It landed with a boom. Art felt it in his chest.

The boat eased up to it. The nutcrackers stepped over the licorice whip at the front of the boat. In two lines, parallel with each other, they marched into the castle. Swallowed by the darkness inside. Boots thumping on the wooden door on their way.

Leaving Art alone.

Like they'd forgotten him.

He followed the height of the castle until his neck hurt. It pointed into the pink heavens. The details of the thing—the windows and turrets, the staircases that circled the perimeter connecting balconies and doorways—were dizzying. It was daunting and alluring. Pulling him toward it and pushing him away. Left him with a knot in his belly.

He took a step.

A cheer rose from the distant shore. They were quite small now. A mob of color. Their enthusiasm went up a notch when he took another step. And the same for the next.

He stopped at the edge of the entrance. Peered into the darkness. It was black, keeping its secrets hidden. The price was total commitment. The breath of the castle sweet and damp. Like moist cake. He turned toward the market. Lifted his hand and waved.

They lost their minds.

It wasn't dark. Once he was inside. Dim, maybe.

His eyes adjusted within seconds. The corridor was long and empty. The nutcrackers were somewhere up ahead. Their bootsteps echoed. There was nowhere for them to hide. But he couldn't see them.

"Hello?"

His voice ricocheted down the arched ceiling.

Funny. He couldn't hear the cheers anymore. Even though the gate was open. He could see them quite clearly, just as before. Only nothing but his own *hello* running the length of the hallway and back.

The castle didn't feel dangerous. It smelled good. Had a vibe like the walls were smiling.

A candle caught flame when he neared it. Tendrils of black smoke slithered past a painting in a golden frame. It was a two-story house. White with green shutters. An old-looking thing with rotting steps leading to the front porch. He stood for a moment, thinking. Wondering.

Then went on.

Another candle. Another painting.

This one a snow hill with kids in snowsuits speeding down on sleds. Adults at the bottom drinking from steamy thermoses. Wrapped in scarves, wearing puffy coats, with leaky red noses.

Next was a vacation beach.

A snowball fight.

A skateboard park.

They meant something. He couldn't tell you what. Like a story you might have heard once upon a time, but you're not sure if you imagined it.

The last one was not a painting. It was a photo. A man in a red suit and a bushy white beard. Black boots and a wide belt to match. A lumpy sack thrown over his shoulder. A clutter of toys and dolls and things around him. Following him. A rather large crowd. Larger than the one at the market.

Art leaned closer.

He recognized some of them.

Meg and Gandy. Their eyes were big circles of excitement. Their mouths just as round. There could be more than one gingerbread couple in this world. But it felt like them. One fact was most certain and indisputable. And he thought with a smile and a laugh puffed from his throat, *The jolly fat man they were all excited to see... that's Santa.*

THE NUTCRACKERS WERE SUDDENLY on both sides of him.

They stood in two lines, one on each side of the corridor. Backs as straight as lumber.

They must have stepped out of secret panels on the walls. Art had hardly blinked. He'd been so absorbed by Santa Claus he didn't notice. Or hear their boots (which seemed highly unlikely).

"Where'd you come from?" he asked.

No answer. He didn't expect one. Although a slight headache pinged between his eyes.

The red-coated soldiers with the ridiculously tall black hats marched deeper into the castle. Art fell into step with them, letting his boots hit the ground when theirs did. It pulled him along. No more candles or paintings of ordinary things or jolly fat men. Just stepping. Just marching.

A spiral staircase soon appeared.

It was the center of the castle, he assumed, since a perpendicular cross hall went in opposite directions. Where X marked the spot.

A titanic corkscrew twisted into the misty heights. Bits of pink snow wandered down and stuck to the metal treads that would undoubtedly clang with each step. Beads of moisture clung to the railing that coiled around and around.

The nutcrackers marched around it. Stood in a circle facing in. That was it. Nothing more. No pressure in Art's head. No nudging him toward the first step. One look up that climb was all it took. It would take days to make it to the top. If that was where they wanted him to go.

"What now?"

They stamped the floor. He felt it.

"Yeah, I'm not—"

A balloon rose out of the floor. It was red and the size of a pickle barrel. It bounced through the center of the spiral steps, squeaked when it rubbed against the railing. A hefty rope was tied to a knot the size of a cowboy's fist. It pulled something out of the floor.

A one-person hot-air balloon basket hovered in front of him.

The gate opened on its own. The hinges needed oil.

Art looked at the nutcrackers. But like before, they moved without Art seeing them move. Now they were behind him. In a row. Shoulders as square as their jaws.

Pretty clear what they wanted.

Art didn't move. They didn't make him. He stood between them and the basket and counted his options. There were quite a few. In the end, he decided no matter what he did, he was going to end up here again. His journey would take him to the top of the castle. Whether he took the long way or not.

May as well do it now.

THERE WAS HARDLY room in the basket.

It cracked and settled under his feet when he stepped in. Like an old wicker chair. Fibers peeled from the rail. Paint chips stuck to his palms. To be honest, he really didn't think this thing was going to work. The balloon wasn't *that* big—not big enough to lift him. And that, if he got down to the truth of it, was why he climbed into the warped basket.

And then it went up.

His heart bellyflopped into his stomach. The railing crunched in his hands.

It didn't float off the floor. It soared. Like wind-on-his-cheeks soared. Like tears-in-his-eyes soared. The balloon didn't get any bigger. It wavered in the column of space, occasionally bouncing off the spinning staircase.

He closed his eyes. It didn't ease the growing nausea.

He tried dropping to the floor, but his knees buckled against the side of the basket. Every movement made the balloon wobble. Every thought was dark and doomed. Like if the balloon popped. Like if the bottom of the basket rotted out.

The air became denser. Heavier.

The balloon smaller. It didn't slow down, though. Just the opposite.

The stairs were a blurring corkscrew. *Is that frost on the railing?*

His hands ached. Fingers numb. He tried to slow his breath, like Meg had told him to do, but the frigid air froze his legs. He choked on each breath. Wind whistled through his ears, pulling tears down his raw cheeks on a ride that was never going to end. When it did, his dark thoughts insisted, he would crash through the top of the castle like a rocket shooting into space.

That, he thought, *might be the way home.* It was a wishful thought quickly stamped out by another dark thought. *You wish.*

Something crashed and rang. The inside of his head vibrated. Everything went dark. He hadn't closed his eyes, though. Moments later, the rushing stairs were back. It happened again. This time he recognized the sound of it. The way it felt. The good tidings that chased away the dark thoughts.

The bell!

He was inside the castle when it rang, the sound of it deafening. The vibrations dissolved his fears and worry, replacing them with a surefire sense of goodness. Okayness. Like things were perfect just the way they were. He melted on this strange balloon ride, closing his eyes and feeling layers of anxiety peel away and fall a thousand stories. Or however far down it was.

The minty air stung his nostrils. An evergreen scent mixed with it: the smell of freshly cut limbs from pine or spruce. It became overpowering. Intoxicating. Squeezing the past from that lost treasure of memories he couldn't find.

A tree in the corner of a room.

Decorations heavy on its limbs. A star crammed on top. Presents stacked below.

Songs on the radio. And cookies in the next room. The cheer of good feelings.

When he opened his eyes, he was no longer moving. The balloon detached and wobbled toward a domed and icy ceiling far above. The basket he was in sat firmly in a bank of pink snow, as if it had been gently placed there the night before. And all around him were trees.

A forest of Christmas trees.

NOT JUST ANY CHRISTMAS TREES. Although they were uncut and, as far as he could tell, rooted into the ground (or was there a floor beneath the pink snow?). They were decorated, one and all. Big ones and small ones. Fat and skinny with droopy limbs or pokey needles. Some reached high above, some short and squatty.

Stalactites pointed down. The balloon looked like a red kick ball bouncing between them.

Footsteps pocked the pink snow. They were wide and shallow.

Someone in snowshoes had been through, going in this direction and then the other. No one way to follow. Or avoid.

Strands of tinsel grew from the branches like silver hair. The ornaments were curious. Orbs clung to the limbs. They varied in size and shine and color. No hook or wire attached. As if they grew from the tree. A sort of fruit made of glass.

That's impossible, he thought. And then laughed. *Impossible?*

He reached for a bright red orb. It was dense and heavy, weighing on the pendulous limb. He lifted and twisted. It was attached, all right. Attached by a thick stem that refused to break. The ornament wasn't glass, or at least it didn't feel like it. It was soft, almost mushy. Like an overripe melon wrapped in plastic.

BAP!

He stumbled into the tree. At first, he thought someone had punched him in the back. A direct hit between the shoulder blades. A wet thud. But no one was behind him or anywhere near him. And snow was stuck to the back of his shirt.

He listened.

"Hello? Someone there?"

The wind blew somewhere nearby. It howled and whistled. The Christmas trees, however, didn't shake or shimmy. They were as still as deadwood.

Something shuffled. A scamper to his right. A flash of color through the trees.

Art scooped pink snow and packed it into a tight ball. It was all he could think to do. And he followed. Reluctant and slow. Snow pushing up to his knees in some places. He peeked around a wide tree with a tiny star on top (it was dull and unfinished) and stopped to listen. Only the sound of his heavy breathing reported back. He sounded like a desperate animal.

"Who's there?"

The answer came. It was *BAP!*

The snowball hit exactly where the first one did, square between the shoulders. This one knocked him on his face. He stumbled and ate a pink snowdrift. He wiped his face and spun around. That was when he heard it. A sound he would never forget.

Laughter.

A giggle and a snort. A rapid-fire chuckle that jiggled the belly. A contagious chortle that spread a smile on his face.

"Okay. All right." He molded another snowball. "Is that the game? I hear you. Let's do this."

Art went after it, and he went hard. Cutting corners. Slogged through drifts. Ornaments rang when he brushed a tree.

The Christmas forest was endless and winding. The footsteps everywhere. Whoever he was chasing was nimble in snowshoes that barely dented the snow. The laughter always ahead of him. Just around a corner or the other side of a tree. Catching a flash of color or a dashing escape. It sounded like a child, sometimes. Laughing just out of reach.

Art was gaining. He thought.

Sucking the wintery, peppermint air into his lungs, snot running from his nose. The snowball numbed his hand. One more turn and he'd launch it through the branches. Ducking below a pendulous spruce branch, he planted his foot on the ground and cut through a small opening, sure to cut off whoever it was and—

No more trees.

A wide track of snow, the width of a two-lane highway, cut through the forest. There were trees on the other side, just as dense and just as shiny. The road between the two was smooth and pink. On one end, the wall was obscured by a haze. It was blue and rocky and slightly curved where it soared toward the arching ceiling.

There was a building in the other direction. And not far.

He walked close to the trees.

The building extended the full width of the road. Going from tree line to tree line. A slanted roof with cedar shingles. Daggers of ice clung to the eaves. (Strange. With all the ice and snow, Art wasn't cold in a T-shirt.) The walls were bright red. The trim forest green. He didn't recognize it until he was close enough to see the broad door.

A barn.

The farm kind for horses and tractors.

He could smell hay or grass. At least he thought he did. It was easy to imagine big bales in the loft.

Puffs of smoke billowed from a chimney behind the barn.

Art stayed near the trees, going around the barn to find a cottage attached to it. A rather small one with a low thatched roof and cobblestone walls. The windows were round and flickering with orange light. He waited for something to move. When nothing did, he peeked through the window to see a blazing fireplace shedding warm light on recliners and books and tables.

He considered knocking, even made a fist and held it before the thick oak door, but looked across a short stretch of snow. The end of this room (or cavern or whatever it was) was within reach. The bluish wall curved upward. It was rough and scarred, as if carved from inside the castle or a dense patch of ice. In the middle, the exact distance between the tree lines, was a round window like a portal on a ship.

Beyond it, pink sky.

Cotton-candy clouds.

THE SNOWDRIFTS WERE past his waist on his way to the hole in the wall. It wasn't a big hole. Didn't let much light in. (Which, by the way, couldn't explain how the Christmas forest wasn't dark. It was *inside*, after all. This was a giant room that was, somehow, well lit. And not from this tire-sized window.) Barely large enough to stick his head through it. When he tried, he hit a windowpane of some sort. Not glass or plastic. It didn't look like anything was there. His hand, though, hit an invisible field.

He could see through it, though.

The rosy lake of tea surrounded the castle. The market at the shore. Rows of gingerbread houses and lines of gummy paved roads. A giant Ferris wheel was far to the right. Waterfalls of lemonade were to the left. Rivers of fudge in between.

The light was strange. It lay like a luminous blanket, all cheery and bright. Then halfway across the land, it ended abruptly.

Beyond was shadow, of sorts. Not darkness or night. It was a dimness that lay on the other side of Candyland. There wasn't much to see over there. One thing, though, he couldn't miss. It was far away and outlined in the gloom. A dark spike that reached into the gray swirl of clouds. A castle just like this one.

In between, he thought, *is the border.* That was where Gandy wanted to go, to find Grimjoy the fortune teller. *Where light meets dark.*

Between the castles and on the border was a mountain shaped like a child's crayon version of a volcano. Cone-shaped. Broad at the bottom. The top disappeared into a dense wad of cottony clouds. It was enormous and mysterious.

Then a third snowball exploded above his head.

It popped against the wall like a paper bag filled with air and showered down his neck. His heart slamdanced against his chest. He spun around to get eyes on his opponent. All he saw were footprints.

Super-wide footprints.

THE TRACKS WENT to the cottage. The door was open.

A shaggy doormat had been shoveled and dusted off. *In or Out,* it read. Below that: *Either way, close the door.*

A rectangular mailbox was nailed to the doorframe. (*Did someone deliver mail?*) It was red and sparkly. *Belly* was traced through the glitter.

He ducked his head beneath the low-arching doorway. "Hello?"

Silly thing to say. It was all he could think of.

The cottage was one room. And he could see it all from the doorway. It was warm and toasty inside. Firelight orange. The smell of spice and smoke. Of sweet things soaked in sugar. Holding the doorknob (brassy and frigid in his hand), he looked outside for someone. Maybe this was a trap. It felt like a trap.

The warmth, though. He couldn't resist.

He pulled the door closed behind him, like the doormat said to do. He kept his knees slightly bent. The top of his head brushed the ceiling. A silver mug was resting on the floor in front of a blazing fireplace. The light danced on jewels set in the cup's handle.

He crouched in front of a fully reclined lounger (too small for him to sit in) and warmed his hands at the fire. The heat stung his fingers and brought back sensation in pokes and pricks. He leaned over, peered into the silver mug, sniffed what was in it. Sweet, it was. And sour. Gold flakes glittered at the bottom, or maybe that was just the light.

He ignored the drink. For now.

Even though he was thirsty. Very thirsty.

He hadn't had a swallow of anything since waking up in this world. That was how he'd come to think of it. *Waking up.* It felt like days since he woke at that desk in the gingerbread house. And nothing had changed. Just one long day. Nighttime might never come, and he was no closer to going home. Unless you counted sitting in a tower that reached into the sky. If home was up there—out there—then maybe he was closer.

It was a hoarder's paradise. Books, there were plenty. Old ones with fading titles and fraying spines, but none he recognized (not that he was a reader; he could read; he just didn't want to). Rocks and cups in cabinets and toys and shoes on shelves; walking sticks in tin cylinders; tangled balls of yarn in baskets and leaning stacks of paper on the floor; bowls of pinecones by the door. Knitting needles on a tiny couch. A half-assembled puzzle on a three-legged table.

No coat on a rack or boots by the door.

He got up, rubbing his hands, checking for a door to a back room he might have missed. Looked out the window to see if someone was coming home. Went back to the fireplace and sat on the floor.

Stomach twisting.

Mouth watering.

He picked up the silver mug. Sniffed. Wet his lips on the rim of it. He didn't know the proper amount of time required to test if something was poison. It definitely wasn't ten minutes. That was all he lasted before taking his first swallow.

It warmed his belly. Slaked a thirst he didn't know was there.

It fizzed in his throat. Pulled at his cheeks.

He tipped the mug for the very last drop. Letting those golden flakes (turns out it was gold) fall on his tongue.

So good. So, so good.

He leaned against the recliner, completely thawed inside and out. Melting on the circular rug where he sat. Feeling light and relaxed. He'd danced in the market. Had been to the Keepers of the Lost. Walked down Kettle Korn Trail. Was cared for by a lovely couple of gingerbread cookies.

Beyond that, he couldn't remember a thing. Not where he came from. Not how he got here. Most importantly, why he was here. He closed his eyes to think of a reason. That fire, though. It felt good.

He didn't hear the door open.

6

"What now?" King Chocolate whined.

Dark spittle shot from his lips. A plate of chocolate wafers tumbled to the floor when the carriage lurched to one side. He'd been sampling a batch of dark chocolate. He hated dark chocolate. Yet couldn't stop eating it. It was a curse to love something so vile. Like blue cheese dressing. Like chicken liver.

"Pothole."

Jelly sank into a beanbag on the other side of the carriage, filing her toenails. The swatches of red hair on her toes made King Chocolate want to look away. You could scrub pots with those things.

"What's the point of having roads?" King Chocolate mused.

Then he pointed at the floor. It had been quite some time since he'd been able to bend over. Jelly pretended not to notice. He cleared his throat, to give her a chance. She sighed and, with great effort, picked up the spilled wafers. Having to roll on her stomach to do so. When she was back on her enormous, hairy feet, King Chocolate had his mouth open like a baby bird.

She flipped the wafers into his mouth like coins tossed into a wishing well.

He hardly chewed. Chocolate made everything better. Even if it was dark.

The carriage interior was crimson velvet with detailed stitching. Something Jelly designed and he couldn't care less about. But this was cool. He flipped a switch on the armrest of his throne. The roof folded back. The dim sky fell on them like fog. Another switch and the throne began to rise. Slowly, he was lifted out of the fancy carriage, and insect song greeted him. The little buggers were synchronized and playing a merry tune he didn't hate. If he wasn't mistaken, they were singing "We wish you a blah-blah Christmas."

Trees were on both sides of the road. Their branches heavy with dark ornaments. The cinnamon trunks were peeling. On the road in front of him, a crew of grumpies were laying slabs of peanut brittle over deep holes. The humpbacked grumpies looked like softshell beetles with a bad case of warts. They smelled like bread mold.

There were five more potholes in the shape of a foot. As deep as wedding cakes.

"What's the story?" Jelly said with the enthusiasm of a third grader at an abstract art show.

"Once upon a time," King Chocolate said, "you walked the rest of the way. The end."

She didn't like that story. But where they were going wasn't far. He could see the door against a wall of yellow light.

The carriage split like a plastic Easter egg. The throne was placed on the road. A joystick popped out of each armrest. King Chocolate sped forward like a county fair bumper car, hovering a few inches above the ground, weaving around the potholes. Jelly made no effort to keep up.

He shaded his eyes.

The glare from the light was painful. It was like being punched with a sixteen-ounce boxing glove. He squinted through paper-thin slits. A rectangle was ahead. It was, very likely, the door he wanted. At this rate, it would take twenty ticks for his eyes to adjust to the brightness.

He stopped the throne and closed his eyes. Jelly could figure it out when she caught up. The bug song was accompanied by giant apple spiders plucking the threads of their webs like strings on a cello. The creatures on this side of the border slithered and creeped. They snuck and spied, slurped nectar from wild sugar flowers, munched spines from a darkling cactus plant.

It was beautiful. Like blue-cheese dressing. Like chicken liver.

"You get stuck?" Jelly said.

King Chocolate peeked down at his side. His roly-poly assistant had no problem with the glare. Black sunglasses wrapped around her eyes. They were pointy and shaped like teardrops.

"Where'd you get those?"

"My pocket."

"Where's my glasses?"

"Where you left them."

He snatched the sunglasses and shoved them over his face. The hinges squealed as they spread apart. He could see. Oh, thank Santa and all his reindeer. The sunglasses had dimmed the bright light closer to normal. He could see butterflies fluttering over there and bluebirds in their nests. Squirrels dancing hand in hand, carrying bags full of honey-glazed acorns. Dragonflies bathing on sunflowers.

The Nice Side.

Disgust rolled in his gluttonous belly. The urge to vomit hadn't been this strong since he ate a bag of fermented cheese curds. The Nice Side with their perfect smiles and their merry, merrys. The fake phonies with their beautiful toys and good girls and boys. It made him sick-sick-sick. They had no idea how the world worked. What it took to keep them alive.

King Chocolate did.

It was dirty work to keep the order of things. Unsavory things. Things they couldn't think about, let alone do. If it weren't for the Naughty Side, say goodbye to the light. Spoiled brats.

Blah-blah.

"Well?" Jelly said.

King Chocolate was squeezing the armrests on his throne. There were indentations where the tips of his fingers clawed into the cheap metal frame. He opened his mouth. Jelly knew what that meant, unveiling a hidden stash of wafers in her sleeve. She frisbeed them one at a time into his gaping maw.

The chocolate melted in the back of his throat. Slid into his stomach.

A subtle haze of euphoria rose like a column of vapor.

It lifted his spirits. Uncorked a vicious smile.

"Better?" Jelly asked.

"Much."

IT WAS JUST a door with a crescent moon hung on it. An outhouse straddling the border. A sharp line rode down the middle of it: one side light, the other dim. This close to the border, King Chocolate could smell the peppermint breeze. He preferred the dank bitterness of Naughty Side air. Chocolate in its purest, richest form.

Jelly opened the door.

King Chocolate steered the throne up to it. The doorframe caught the armrests. He'd upgraded since last Christmas. The model he was driving (called a Royale Primo Deluxe) was wider and sturdier. Twice the add-ons and ten times the power.

He backed up. Backed up some more. Then rammed it home.

Wood splintered off the doorframe. The metal squealed like forks on a China plate. He winced and threw his weight forward. The throne popped out the other side like a champagne cork. Jelly was trying to close the door, but the door jamb was gone. Deep gouges were carved into the sides of the throne.

"Bill them for that," King Chocolate said.

He spun the throne around. There was no toilet inside. Nothing of the kind. It was an expanded dining hall, of sorts. One side brightly lit. The other dipped in shadows. To the right was a grand fireplace, where a fire burned on the light side. To the left, an over-sized Christmas tree. Only half of it was alive with ornaments. And in the middle, a table was set longways. It was shiny on one side, dull on the other.

"Sorry I'm late," King Chocolate announced. "Potholes in the road. Sweet Tooth gets restless at this time of year."

The royal couple sat on the other side of the table, bathed in light, and watched him drive toward the table. His super-cool throne was twice the size of theirs. He swung around and approached the empty thrones on his side of the table, snowplowed them out of the way. They twisted and raked the floor, tipped over and crashed. The head-board on one of them cracked.

"There we go," he sang. "All set."

He sighed with a grin. The royal couple sat with rigid postures. Their faces were still and unmoving. They wore robes laced in gold trim and ornate crowns studded with candied jewels. The sickening smell of peppermint oil was strong. Pretty rude. King Chocolate wore a stained tunic and a chef's hat. He smelled like sugar farts.

"Macey," he said to the king. Then to the queen: "Lydia, you look... like you."

Her beauty taunted him. Like waving a cake under a starving man's nose.

"Merry, merry," she said. "You look well, Casey."

"Do I?" He smiled at Jelly. It was hard to see her through the dark lenses. But he wasn't going to take them off. "You both still doing Pilates and pumping iron? I can see the veins in your arms. It's gross."

"You're late, brother," King Macey said.

"Yeah, I said that."

"And dressed for the occasion."

"Never satisfied, are you, brother." He turned to the queen. "Is he like this at home?"

Lydia smiled. It looked authentic and, he hated to admit it, lit a warm flame in his enormous belly.

"Jelly," she said, "merry, merry."

"Blah-blah."

They cringed at Jelly's reply. King Chocolate smiled. And that was genuine. "It's what we say now," he said. "Where's Belly?"

"She's attending to chores," the queen said.

He didn't like the sound of that, not with the crosser somewhere on their side. Belly was always at the meet. "What chores? Is there something new? Tell me."

He bit his lower lip before he blurted out all his worries.

"Preparations for Christmas Day, is all," she said. "Shall we wait for the queen?"

"What? Oh, no. She's not coming."

"I hope she's all right."

"She'll be fine. Stuck on the toilet all morning. Ate a bad pork rind. Big party last night. *Huuuge.* Anyway, I brought you something." On cue, Jelly threw a box on the table. It slid into the light. "Finest batch of the year. Verified and stamped. Eat those and you'll have joy running out your ears."

They eyed the gift like a box of spiders. "You know how we feel about that, Casey," she said.

He gripped the throne. The hypocrites. They ate sugar on everything because they liked it. It made them feel good. But a box of chocolates from the Naughty Side wasn't good enough, was that it? Everyone knew he made the best. Both sides agreed. Eat a wafer and your world got right. Eat a wafer and you became your best you. Eat a wafer and all your worries went away. No more this side and that side. All one side. All Candyland.

But no. Just not good enough for them. *It was too good.*

"Let's get this over with," he grumbled. "I've got a bathroom date. You don't want me to be late."

KING MACEY STRAIGHTENED a stack of papers and pushed them across the table. They rested halfway between both sides.

"Fifteen rings till Christmas," he started.

They went on, the two of them. Taking turns to deliver their boring speeches. It was the same thing every year. A pointless meeting. King Chocolate stared at Lydia the whole time, his eyes cloaked in the dark lenses. That was the only reason he kept coming, to see her. He didn't need to see a skinnier version of himself. His brother wasn't exactly skinny with the gut and white beard. But he was skinnier than King Chocolate. By a mile.

King Chocolate slumped in the throne as they droned on about a parade and decorations and surprises and then how awesome their Christmas tree would be. (King Chocolate had cut his Christmas trees down; the sap was the secret ingredient in his special-edition wafers. Then he'd burned the trees to make little briquettes.)

Then King Macey would dress up as Santa and greet all the nicies, hug them, take pictures with them. Hand out presents. The royal lovebirds were laughing and remembering funny things that had happened at previous events. Recalling the parade to the town square where he climbed onto a big chair to talk to every single one of the nicies and kissed all the little babies and merry-married his way into their hearts.

And here's the thing: the nicies thought he was Santa. The real one. Is it stupidity or willful dumbness? And is there a difference?

King Chocolate was melting into a pile of boredom and contempt.

"I'd like to propose something new," King Macey said.

A second pile of papers was delivered halfway over the line. King Chocolate shoved them at Jelly. Way too many words to read. Like hundreds.

"We've prepared treats and gifts for the Naughty Side," the queen said. "To fill their stockings and place under their trees."

"We don't do trees." King Chocolate yawned.

She continued. The Nice Side would send an envoy (whatever that was) to decorate Christmas trees and deliver stockings to hang above fireplaces. It was pretty clear what she was getting at. Like crystal. King Chocolate wasn't the smartest Lander on either side of the border, but when it came to underhanded, shady, backstabbing schemes... he was a genius.

"Santa would visit," King Macey said.

"Visit where?"

"The Naughty Side."

"You mean *you* would visit," King Chocolate said. "In your costume."

"Of course," he whispered. Even in the privacy of this exclusive dumphouse, he couldn't say it above a whisper. "I have a route planned already. It'll bring joy to the Naughty Side. And when—"

"Terrible," King Chocolate said.

"What?"

"What you're saying. It's terrible."

"I-I..." He looked at his wife. She wasn't surprised. "How can this be a bad thing, brother? The naughties have been overlooked every Christmas. They can't even—"

"I'm not talking about that, you royal dingdong. It's you. The dressing up, the pretending. Don't you get it?" He looked back and forth. "YOU'RE LYING! Santa Claus isn't flying into your castle. He's not coming down to deliver presents in person. IT'S YOU! You tell them not to lie, to tell the truth, that honesty is the best policy, and what do you do?"

"It's pretend," King Macey said. "It's fun to pretend."

"IT'S A LIE!"

"Do you really not believe Santa Claus is real, Casey?" the queen said.

"Here we go." King Chocolate slumped in the throne. Why did he even start this? It always ended like this. He waved his hand. "Go on."

"What we do is for fun. But Santa Claus delivers gifts all over the universe—"

"In one night," King Chocolate added flatly.

"How do you think our stockings get stuffed?"

"Gee. I don't know. Tell me, please."

"Why is there coal in your stocking, Casey?" she asked gently.

King Chocolate's puffy hat began to smolder. All the angry words were locked behind his lips and beginning to boil. It was only going to make things worse if they escaped. *And you want to give us gifts, that's your plan? If Santa Claus is smarter than smart, why does he punish us with coal? We hate him even more. Coal! On top of everything else that's gone wrong, he gives us coal? I'm not saying we deserve an award. Just a little understanding would be nice. The naughties aren't that bad.*

King Chocolate was truly naughty. To the core. Worse than spoiled milk. He deserved coal. But the rest of the naughties? That was why he didn't believe. A real Santa wouldn't put coal in stockings.

"Please consider our offer," Lydia said. She waved at a fly buzzing over her head. "It's a kind gesture, that's all. We don't like the coal, either. Candyland is one. We're brothers and sisters. You, Casey, you get to be the hero. You can help bring us all together."

King Chocolate forced himself to keep eye contact with the queen. They hadn't noticed the fly landing on Jelly's shoulder.

King Chocolate nodded, even smiled a little. Encouraged them to keep talking until he felt a tickle on his ear.

The fly crawled up his earlobe.

He clutched the armrests. Quivered in stillness.

The insect settled into the pocket of his ear. Then it began to whisper. King Chocolate listened to what it had to say while staring through the queen. He was shaking now. Rivulets of sweat ran down his back, soaked his shirt. It sounded like bacon fat frying in a skillet.

The phonies.

The two fake phonies smiling and promising Candyland is one. He didn't fall for it.

This wasn't about the good of the land. They didn't care about coal and the naughties and fairness. They had a plan. This was just a distraction, to keep him looking the other way. They wanted the same thing he wanted. The same as always.

To win.

Silence stretched out. King Chocolate didn't know how long. They were waiting for a reply. He hadn't heard the question. He had to beat them at their own game. They wanted deception? They were messing with a master.

A smile grew on his face. He showed his dingy teeth. "Let's do it!"

"Really?" King Macey didn't see that coming.

"Really, really. It's worth a try, why not? It could bring world peace. We could sing songs and scratch each other's backs. Who wants a shoulder rub? I know I do."

Jelly looked at him.

King Chocolate stuck out his hand. His brother clasped it. One cold and clammy. The other soft and warm. (You can guess whose was whose.)

"It's been too long, brother," King Macey said.

"I know a brilliant idea when I hear one. You'll bring all the presents to us, then, yeah?"

"It's all in the document." King Macey pointed at the stack of papers. "Let's meet back here in seven rings to confirm. This will be historic!"

"Yay!" King Chocolate shook his fists. "History!"

"Thank you, brother."

"No, thank you, Macey. Thank you, Lydia. Thank you Santa and Cupid and Cuspid and Molar and..."

He threw out more random names. He stopped after twenty or so, which, he felt, was too many. The king and queen splayed their hands over their hearts.

"Merry, merry, Casey," they said. And said it with enough sincerity to make King Chocolate gag.

"Yes." He swallowed a lump of bile. "Merry, merry."

He spun the throne around before they began weeping tears of disgusting joy. He got a running start at the doorway and jammed his way through. Shards of wood sprayed the ground. The grumpies had finished patching the potholes. He steered right through them and nearly hit a few.

When he got close to the split carriage, a lift panel lowered to the ground. He drove on top of it. As the carriage closed around him like a clamshell, he hollered: "Go, now!"

He didn't wait for Jelly, who was running to catch up. (That was the first time he'd ever seen her move that fast.) Before Jelly could crack wise, King Chocolate filled her in on the news General Fly had whispered into his ear. Jelly wasn't surprised. She'd heard the report, also.

It just felt better if he said it out loud.

"They got the boy!"

7

A great shadow passed over Art. It had no form, no shape. He couldn't see it, but he could feel its cool wings spread over the planet. There was nowhere to run, no way to escape.

It blocked out the sunlight.

He could feel its sweet breath tickle his nose.

Art opened his eyes before opening his mouth to cry out. Colors bled into the shadow. Details sharpened its face. Icy blue eyes stared down from beneath shaggy brows. The cheeks were fair and smooth. Smelled like pine sap and candy corn.

The lips parted.

"Look at you." Chubby fingers pinched his cheek. "All scrummy in front of the fire."

Art's wits got in line. He rolled to the side, scrambled against the tiny couch. His heart pumped too much blood into his brain. He rubbed the sleep from his eyes.

She was still there. Still blocking the fireplace.

As round and wide as she was tall. At full height, she barely reached the mantel. She wore baggy pants and a thin shirt that stretched over her stomach. A thick braid was slung over her shoulder. It looked like a rope used to pull over trees. Her pointy ears were tucked under silver hair.

She looked in the mug sitting on the floor.

"You like?" Her voice was a song. It made words feel beautiful. Like each one was happy. "The jewel fruit wasn't quite ripe when I pressed it. Was afraid it would come out a little bitter, you see? I added extra twinkles at the bottom." She winked at him and whispered, "Shook them from a short star."

She ran a stubby finger around the inside of the silver mug and popped it in her mouth.

"It warms the insides, you see? When the inside is warm, the outside is, too."

A long deep sigh escaped her. She looked at him adoringly. A smile bloomed on her face like a flower in full sun, stretching her doughy cheeks to their limits.

"You hungry? I have much to eat, you see. Spiced pecan pie bars with pecans from nutcrackers." She said *pee-cans*. "Also chocolate gingerbread cookies from the market, made fresh. Also, overripe fruitcake with dried mango and orange slices. One piece left in the cupboard of that. Also, almond snowballs. My favorite, you probably know." She covered a wry smile and winked. Then said: "Also, fudge."

She paused. Waited.

"You are shy, you see. Don't want to make trouble. But I know, Ms. Belly knows, you have not eaten since crossing. You are hungry and don't know it."

She shook a chubby finger at him. Then started for the kitchenette in the corner.

That was when he noticed the feet.

The size of them. The width. They didn't look real. They were feet for a giant on this incredibly short body. Her shoes—if she wore them—would be size 100. They were living snowshoes that scratched the hardwood like industrial sandpaper. Those hadn't been snowshoe tracks he was following in the snow.

They were footprints!

"I am sorry for the snowballs, you see. I think I throw a bit too hard and did not mean to. I missed on purpose the last time, if that makes you forgive me. I left the cider for you and door open while I go to harvest more jewel fruit. Do you forgive me?"

She turned her head. The hair fell away from her ear. The top of it was pointed.

"How did you know?" he said.

"To throw snowballs? It's what we do. Snow and ice are my—"

"No, I mean… how'd you know I haven't eaten?"

"Oh. Well, there are no secrets on Nice Side. All whispers reach the castle. We see everything up here."

She pulled something from a cupboard. A plate from a shelf. The sound of cutlery was sharp and loud on the countertop.

"You will love it here. I will raise the ceilings so you do not bump your head. You will get better at snowballing. I will teach you. King and queen will love you, too. I just know it. Now, it is time to put meat on your bones!"

She turned with a pizza platter of food. She placed it in front of the fireplace, went back to the kitchenette for napkins.

"Eat!" she bellowed. "You need a winter coat, you see!"

She slapped her belly. It jiggled in waves. Her face lit up. Her laughter was contagious. He felt a smile growing. Then she did it again, more serious this time.

"EAAAAT!"

She didn't wait for him to volunteer, scooping a mess of ice cream on a graham cracker and holding it in front of his face. He opened his mouth like a baby. She brightened another degree.

"King and queen?" he said, chewing.

"They are away now. But they will be back soon, very soon. As the nutcrackers say, *Huzzah!*"

Art grabbed a sugary chip and a scoop of vanilla-bean ice cream. She was right. He was starving. All it took was one bite to wake up his appetite. Next, he ate a pancake soaked in maple syrup, folded it around a peanut butter cookie.

"Did you hear them say *huzzah* when they escorted you?"

He shook his head, said with a stuffed mouth, "De dint say anthin'."

She scratched at the second roll of flesh beneath the hint of a chin. Then pointed and said: "Did your head perhaps hurt when they look at you?"

He nodded.

"That is why. No frequency yet. It is up here you will hear." She tapped the side of her head. Just above the point of her ear. "It is how they talk. Well, lots of Landers do as well. You will learn. Once you are settled. This becomes home. Now eat!"

His head had hurt when he was around the nutcrackers. So, they had been thinking at him. That was how Gandy had been talking to them.

She's an elf! was his next thought.

But those thoughts were quickly washed away by something she said. He stopped chewing. Felt his appetite wither like autumn leaves. He was holding a warm donut. Jelly dripping from the side of it.

"I want to go home," he said.

"You are home."

"I want to go back from where I came."

"Where you came from is not as important as where you are."

"Yeah, it is."

Her broad smile dimmed a few degrees. "That's how I see it. And you will, too."

And then she broke into song. Like they were onstage with the world watching.

Her voice was good. Like opera good. Her arms going side to side, head thrown back. A long note filled the room. His ears rattled like overworked amplifiers. He held the sides of his head and could still hear her.

"It doesn't matter now," she sang. Her words punchy. "It doesn't matter now where you came from. It only matters now. It only matters where... *you... ARE!*"

She popped up on her hairy toes—her head almost touching the ceiling—and held the last note. He closed his eyes until it stopped. Then softly she sang on her way to the kitchenette, swiping a cup of cider off the shelf and spinning around the room. The song continued.

"You're here, with me. I'm here, with you. This place is fine; I know you'll dine. With me, right now. As we, count cows."

Art cringed. *Cows? Did she say count cows?* He smiled, dropping his hands to hear a bit more, but holding them close to his ears in case she took it to the house again. It was the most absurd thing he'd ever seen or heard. That included waking up to gingerbread cookies. She was on her toes now. Ballerina style. The soles of her feet were coarse. Scaley. Literal scales. Like fish scales overlapping toward the heel.

Cider sloshed from the cup.

She poured it into her open mouth. Gargled, sang, and swallowed.

"It's winter. It's winter. Santa's here in winter. In winter. Arriving on his sleigh from a long ride. On a long ride."

Art moved away from the fire. Sweat was breaking out on his brow. His shirt damp with perspiration. She was twirling like a top. Cider slung against the walls. Splattered on his cheeks. She spun in front of the couch.

"You're on the *right* side." She jabbed her finger at him.

Behind her, sitting on the couch with its legs curled beneath its generous belly, was the tabby from Herkle and Derkle's Keepers of the Lost. Daryl was his name. His tail swayed like a charmed snake. Staring at Art. Not blinking. Not twitching a whisker.

Belly, meanwhile, tossed those squatty arms out. Chest swelling in one long inhalation. Art was ready for it. She delivered the last note like a runaway train.

"On the niiiice SIIIIIIIIIIIIIIII!" She wasn't finished. One more breath and—"IIIIIIIIIIIIIIIIIIIIIIIIIDE!"

She fell onto the recliner. The legs buckled and squealed. Her arms out to the sides, gasping for breath, she picked up her head and smiled at him.

"You're on the Nice Side."

And dumped the remains of the cider in his mouth.

"You have a cat?" Art said.

"A what?"

He pointed at the tiny couch. There was a slight indentation on the cushion. Maybe the cat just looked like Daryl. Tabbies all looked the same. Although Daryl had a beer belly that was hard to miss. Whoever the cat was, he was gone. That last note had scared him off. Or blew him up. Art looked behind the couch, out the window. The Christmas tree forest was too far away for the cat to hide outside.

"A cat."

"A cat, uh-huh. Of course." She licked the gold flakes from the rim of the cup. "What's a cat?"

"It's an animal. Four legs, long tail. Furry. It's a pet. He was sitting right there two seconds ago."

"Ooooooh," she wheezed. "That's impossible, my Artie. You have an imagination, and a good one. It's why the king and queen will be so happy to see you. Ooooooh," she wheezed again. "No pets in the Christmas Wood. It's just you and me and what you see."

The cup fell from her hand. It rolled against a tangle of dead lights.

"They're the only true Christmas trees left... *anywhere!*" She swiped her arm over her belly. It jiggled and danced. "I mean anywhere. Your world, this world, that world, another world. Whatever world. These are the last of them. *THE LAST!*"

Her words were slowing down.

Her eyes closed for a second. Then two. They popped open.

"When the tinsel is in bloom, the countdown begins."

"Countdown to what?"

"When the sugar pollen drops, we're covered head to toe in gold." Her head rolled side to side. "You're going to love it here, Artie. My Artie. When the ornaments are ripe, you can hear the trees sing. It means he's on the way. When the stars unfold their last leg, he's almost here."

She picked her head up, looked past him and out the window.

The Christmas trees were shiny with ornaments. At the very tops of them, there were dim clutching stars. Like flowers before a bloom.

"He's fifteen rings away."

"Who? The king?"

She closed her eyes. A few deep breaths later, they opened halfway. The blue-blue eyes slid toward him. She whispered: "The Big Man."

That wasn't an answer. It told him nothing. Her laughter rolled from her belly into her throat. Slowly it ran out of steam and transformed into snoring.

He looked out the window.

The cat was sitting in the pink snow. Looking back at him. Tail waving.

He had his hand on the doorknob. Turned it and pulled. It cracked open. The last words sputtered from Belly's fat, smiling lips.

"It's soooo nice here," she said. "You'll see."

8

Artie stood in the doorway, letting the heat escape the cottage while Belly ripped snores like a leaf blower. Maybe the cat had burrowed beneath the pink snow. Art walked farther out, occasionally stopping, listening. When he reached the very spot where the cat had been sitting, there were no holes dug, no network of tunnels.

Just an indention. A wide one.

There were no paw prints leading away. None coming toward it. Like the cat dropped from the ceiling.

Or just appeared.

THE BARN DOORS WERE OPEN, and nothing surprising was inside: leather harnesses and pitchforks, buckets and stalls. Troughs for water. A winter coat hung on a wooden peg. It was forest green with fuzzy cuffs and a giant hood.

He pulled it down. Tried it on.

It was twice his size. His fingertips barely cleared the cuffs. But it was thick and warm. He kept it on, wandered out to the clearing where the air was brisk and clean. More evergreen than peppermint. Two hundred yards away, or maybe three, the road ended at the other wall. The air was clearer now, and he could see a giant door down there. The kind of door found on a space station, one that slid open and sealed shut. Big enough to let a commercial jet inside. Although the road was too short to land a plane. Besides, it was covered in snow.

The cat was nowhere to be found.

He put his hands in the coat pockets, found a furry hat. It was red with gray fuzz on the hem (probably white at one time). He put it on and wandered into the Christmas Wood in search of the elevator that had brought him up. Or one of those emergency stairwells.

An exit sign would help.

TREES, trees, trees.

All smothered in pink frosting with shiny orbs and silver strands of tinsel. Some so tall they scratched the ceiling. It wasn't long before he stopped looking for a way out and just wandered about. Hands in pockets, strolling this way and that, feeling the Christmas vibe radiate from the trees like radio waves. Happy radio waves. Warm and bubbly waves.

What was it Belly said? *It only matters where you are.*

He walked to the perimeter of the room (or cave or whatever this was), where a pink hue leaked through a portal. This one had a magnifying effect. If he turned his head and didn't get too close, the view zoomed into focus like a telescope. The market was still crowded. So many of them facing the castle. A banner read *We Heart Crossers.*

The barge was back at the dock. The nutcrackers nowhere to be seen.

He looked over the valley, where light met dark. There were so many waterfalls—grape ones and watermelon foam, sparkling rainbows beaming from mist—that he'd lost count. The border divided the volcano in half. He couldn't see much beyond the border, only lumps and dull forms. A sooty land, it seemed.

He would've rambled through the Christmas Wood for hours, maybe even days or weeks, lost in the evergreen scent and lovely hum, had his head not started to hurt. A brain freeze spiked between his eyes and began to swell. His brain felt like a size ten stuffed into a size nine cranium.

Then the buzz.

Carbonated thoughts went *pop-pop-pop* in his head.

He closed his eyes, listened to the sound of static. Then ringing. Like bells only he could hear. And something else. A distant sound inside his head. It *felt* far away, sending a chill beneath the oversized green coat.

It was purring.

IT WAS like trying to locate a cricket. The sound was everywhere.

He thumped the side of his head like he'd just gone swimming. The pressure between his eyes faded. He was hearing it as clear as a radio. The volume changed when he turned one way or the other.

He wandered into the Christmas Wood, hands over his ears, changing direction when the purring grew softer. His temples started to pulse. Maybe this was just a side effect of the cider. *When did I drink that? Yesterday? Or was that an hour ago?*

Time was stretchy.

The light hadn't changed. He hadn't seen the sun move across the sky. Hadn't even seen the sun. The day was endlessly the same. Same temperature. Same light.

He closed his eyes and started walking. He could feel the purring out there. He hit a branch or two on the way, but never stopped to look. Pressure buzzed on his forehead. When he turned his head, it shifted above his right ear like his head was a radar dish.

When the sound was so loud he couldn't take it any longer, he opened his eyes. He was surrounded by trees, looking directly at one of the biggest ones in the forest. The limbs heavy with ornaments. Snow had not fallen in the dark shade beneath it. A gift rested on the ground below the tree limbs. As if it had fallen out of the tree.

Scritch. Scritch. Crack.

Bark crumbled off the trunk, revealing a reddish hue where it had been pulled off. The cat sauntered out of the great tree's shadow, tail swishing above him. Art let Daryl approach (as any good cat person would tell you to do). He stopped at the edge of the snow. Parked it where the ground was still bare. Stared up with forest green eyes.

Art didn't move. Then said: "Did you follow me up here?"

It wasn't strange talking to a cat. People do it all the time. They didn't expect the cat to answer, though. Not where he came from. But this was Candyland. The purring stopped, and Art heard two words as clearly as if the cat had opened his mouth and spoken them.

Of course.

After all he'd seen, it took a lot to surprise Art. This qualified.

He was suddenly dizzy. His stomach churned. He fell forward and dry-heaved on all fours. Nothing came out, but he felt better when the purring started again. The furry tail brushed his face. The cat had stepped in the snow and now leaned against his arm.

"Was that... *you*?" Art babbled.

The cat nodded in response. No imagining that. The feline moved his head up and down. Perhaps even a curl of a smile as the whiskers twitched. Daryl crossed the snow to Art's other arm, arching his back into it.

"What's your name?"

Art didn't know why he asked that. He knew the cat's name, and the cat didn't answer him, not with his name, at least. Daryl said something much more important. The words, once again, swelling in his head. Splashing white in his vision.

Don't trust her.

"THERE YOU ARE!" Belly called. "Did you get lost?"

Art swatted the snow beneath him, threw it under the branches to cover any tracks the cat had made. He didn't think about what he was doing or why. It was instinct.

Don't trust her.

There were no paw prints in the snow. Either he'd done a fine job covering them up, or there were none there to begin with. Because the cat was gone. Not in the tree or behind it. Just gone.

"The trees aren't for climbing." Belly wagged a playful finger. "You're not trying to climb 'em, you see?"

She giggled that infectious laugh. Waves cascading beneath her T-shirt. Her nose and cheeks as pink as the snow. The joke (if that was what it was) went over Art's head.

"I thought I heard something."

"You probably heard the trees. It's about time they started whispering. When the glowers start to glow, that's when they sing." She flicked one of the shiny orbs dangling from a tree limb. "It's a natural cathedral in here. A sound chamber. And you've never heard anything till you hear the Christmas Wood on Christmas Eve. I've heard it a *thousand* times. Cry every time."

She wiped her eyes.

"I'm crying now!"

Art didn't hear the whispering she was talking about. If it felt anything like the words the cat put in his head, he would be crying for different reasons. The cat's voice was loud enough. If all the trees were doing it? He didn't want to think about that, got up, brushed himself off.

"Look!" she screamed, then fanned her blushing cheeks. "It's the first one, Artie. The first one!"

He didn't know what that meant. She bounced on her toes and waggled her finger at the bottom of the tree. He took a knee to look, hoping she wasn't talking about Daryl. All he saw was a present. He reached for it.

"Don't touch it!" she screamed again. This time in panic. "I'm sorry. I'm so sorry, Artie. Did I scare you?"

He shook his head. "I don't know what's going on."

"Of course you don't. How could you? You just got here. That's the first gift of the season. Oooooh, it's so exciting. I got gooseflesh, look." She showed him her arm while dancing.

"Where did it come from?"

"These are Christmas trees. Get it? *Christmas* trees."

"I don't... get it."

"Where are my manners? This is a teachable moment." She cleared her throat. "All those presents Santa brings, right? Where do they come from?"

"Um. The... elves?"

"Right! But wrong! I mean, some do. But the elven can't make that many presents. Most of the presents come from *Christmas* trees. It's why the trees are special. They make *presents*."

Art had the image of a chicken laying an egg. "What?"

"I'll say it's magic, even though the king says it's not. Magic is just science we don't understand. But it *feels* like magic, doesn't it?"

No need to convince Art. *Everything about this feels like magic.* "Can I open it?"

"Is it Christmas?"

Art shrugged. "I have no idea."

"It's not. So, no. We'll leave that there for now. Just before the Big Man comes, we'll scoop them all up for him. How do you like the sound of that?"

Like, all the trees? If they were all *Christmas* trees, there would be thousands of presents. And that was if a tree only laid one present. "This place... it's so big."

"It takes a lot of space to keep the Christmas Wood safe."

He shook his head. He didn't have to ask the question. It was on his face. At least he hoped it was and she didn't somehow hear him thinking it. There were thoughts he didn't want her to hear.

Don't trust her.

"Space is a dimension." She pulled her hands apart like she was making taffy. "It can be expanded. It's how Santa gets down chimneys, you see. And you can thank elven technology for that."

That explained it, sort of. It was how there was a barn inside

Herkle and Derkle's tent. But it didn't sound like science or technology. Still magic.

"The last crosser wrecked the castle, you see. Tore the top right off the place. We built all of this since then."

"Are you talking about the nutcracker?"

"That's it!" She snapped her fingers, but they didn't make a sound. "I see you were in the barn."

She tugged on the green coat he was wearing. Belly stood on her toes—which raised her up almost two feet—and swatted at the floppy hat. The fuzzy ball went twirling around his head.

"Big man's coat doesn't fit you. Wouldn't fit anyone, I don't think. Specially you. All bones and skin. I'll fix that. You can count on Belly to get you winterized. You'll have your *own* winter coat." She slapped her stomach, and laughter came out in waves. "Come on, let's eat."

"We just ate."

Her smile never seemed to stop. She pointed at him, then buzzed her finger around and around. It came toward him like feeding a baby. She rose up on her toes and tweaked his nose with a giggle and a snort.

"Time's a funny thing, Artie. By my clock, you've been gone thirty chimes. I've eaten twice since you wandered off. I'm pretty sure it's time—"

She froze. Her eyebrows rolled like caterpillars escaping a bird. She lifted her nose, sampled the air. Then squatted on the ground. (She didn't have to go far with legs that short.) Art shuffled out of her way, intentionally stepping where Daryl had been.

Belly snuffled the snow like a truffle-hunting pig.

Art moved to the side. Blocking a direct view of the scratched-up trunk.

"What are chimes?" he asked.

"Huh?"

"You said I was gone thirty chimes. Is that, like, thirty hours?"

She scooted through the snow. Looked like a penguin sliding on her belly. Her short arms like flightless wings paddling toward him. She put her nose against his shin and snorted. He jumped back.

"You smell funny," she said.

"This whole place smells funny."

She rocked back onto her feet. Quite nimble, really. She looked around. Nodding. Nodding some more. Then gave her belly a slap and walked away.

"A CHIME IS A CHIME." She shrugged. "It's a piece of time."

"Like hours?"

"What's an hour?"

"It's, uh..." Now he thought about it. *What is an hour?* "It's a piece of time," he said.

"Exactly." Snap, no sound.

"A chime is smaller than a ring?"

"I knew you were smart. The king was right about you."

"Right about what?"

"Artie the Smartie. That's what we should call you."

"No. We shouldn't. It was just, you said I was gone for thirty chimes and Santa was coming in twenty rings, so I figured a ring must be a day, and a bell, like, that must be a—"

"Fifteen. He'll be here in fifteen rings."

"Okay, fifteen rings. Is that like days?"

"It's *rings*," she blurted. "I don't know how else to put it. It's so simple."

"I know. But..." He didn't know how else to say it. He said it anyway. "So one ring is when the sun comes up and goes down. It's not really going up. It looks like it, but it's the world that's turning that makes it look like it's going—"

She stopped suddenly.

He nearly tumbled over her.

She looked at him with a grim smile and said: "What's a sun?"

"What?"

"A sun, what is it? Point at it."

He didn't see the sun to point at. He hadn't seen it yet. There was just pink sky out there. In here, in this unexplainable cavern, there wasn't even a light source. There was just light.

"Then how do you know when its Christmas?" he asked.

Solid question. She acknowledged it with a nod. Then rushed ahead.

Her feet treaded over snowdrifts like a dune buggy in the desert. Art tried to keep up, plowing through the snowdrifts in a straight line. She climbed to the very top of a steep snowdrift that was almost as tall as one of the shortest Christmas trees in the wood. She was eye level with a yellow wad of paper stuck on the terminal bud.

"See that?" She was whispering. He had no idea why she whispered and could barely hear her. His breath wheezed in and out. She pointed at the yellow ball on the tippy-top of the tree. "Three of the five have unfolded."

Without paddle-sized feet, Art couldn't scale the snowdrift. But he saw what she was pointing at. Three of the five legs had begun to open like petals on a flower. A golden glow was deep in the heart of it. It wasn't a yellow wad of paper.

It's a star. A blooming star.

"That's how we know when he's coming," she said.

"In fifteen rings."

"In fifteen rings," she repeated.

"Right. And how many chimes are in a ring?"

"As many as it takes."

She didn't even smile when she said that. Like it was a legit answer. *Because time is funny here.* Then she skied down the snowdrift on those snowboard feet, and off she went.

ART TORE the hat off his head and stuffed it in the coat pocket. Sweat rolled down the side of his face. When he caught up to her, she was standing at the edge of the long snow-covered road.

Her nostrils flaring.

Art's ears were ringing. His chest had a minty burn in it. A stitch in his side, eyes watering. He unbuttoned the coat to let the cold air in. It was frigid and good. He put his hands on his knees, turned his head.

"What is it?" he asked.

But he knew what she was smelling.

He couldn't see Daryl. But he was around. He could feel him. *So can she.*

"Don't get that dirty." She tugged on his coat sleeve. "Big Man won't be happy."

"It's already dirty." And it smelled like horses, but he didn't say that. "Who's the Big Man?"

"Who do you think?"

Art's head was buzzing. Too much exercise and too many voices inside his head made his brain fuzzy. He shook his head.

"Do I have to spell it out?" she asked.

"I guess so."

"Starts with an *S*."

"I don't know. Sam?"

"Right. You're right. It's Sammy Claus."

It came out dry, but she was smiling.

She waddled off, her fat scaly feet making scrunchy sounds as they compressed the snow. Art didn't have the energy to keep up. His legs were dead sponges. At least she wouldn't call him Artie the Smartie anymore. He put his hands around his mouth and shouted, "I thought he wore a red coat!"

"He's got more than one coat, Artie."

Belly sniffed the air on her way to the cottage, where they would fill their stomachs. He could feel her smile. Felt it in his belly. He watched her trundle down the snowy road. This place was nice. And she was right; he was a little hungry. This story would have a different ending if not for the cat and those little thoughts he gave Art. Because Art was content in the Christmas Wood. He liked how nice things felt.

This was the Nice Side.

Did it matter why he was there as long as he felt good?

Daryl didn't think so.

Following Belly's wide footsteps, the cat's voice returned. It was lazy and rough. Filled with smoke that was warm and true.

Ask about the war.

BELLY THREW OPEN the barn doors. Diffuse light cut through the dark, illuminating chaff floating in the air like diamond dust. It smelled dry and grassy. Sweet.

Belly rolled a wheelbarrow into a stall.

There were bales to stack and buckets to clean. Bags of food to get ready. Repairs, which were minor, needed to be made, such as a broken buckle. Nothing urgent. Still fifteen rings to go.

"The reindeer don't eat much." Belly handed him a pitchfork. "I mean, they hardly eat any of this, but we got to be ready, you see. Just in case."

She got to work stacking and sweeping and moving. Art stood in a stall with both hands on a pitchfork. Staring out the open door. He felt lazy and full. He'd napped after three helpings of porridge with maple syrup, followed by three draughts of cider (with the gold flakes). He ate again after he woke up. Then he walked to the portal window to look out over Candyland.

Did I take another nap?

Now he was slightly numb, standing there while Belly whistled while she worked. It went on like that for quite some time (half a chime, maybe?) while he stared at the pink haze obscuring the long road.

"That works better if ya move it, you see," Belly said. Balancing three bales of hay on her head.

"What's at the other end?"

"Oh, you'll see in a ring or two. We'll need to make sure it's working."

Art didn't expect to get an answer. Belly was a magician at avoiding direct answers. Her explanations had a way of washing over him, satisfying him until he thought about it later. And then it was too late.

Belly piled the bales of hay against the wall.

She returned with a bag of feed over each shoulder. Paused outside the stall. Art was still there. She dropped the bags on the floor. A cloud of dust whooshed into the light.

"Artie."

He turned. She was wearing a kind smile that was warm and understanding. The kind of smile that felt like a hug. Behind her, Daryl watched from a shelf in the breezeway, swinging his tail around. Art could feel the purring inside his head.

"You're going to love this place," she said. "There's a change of seasons up here, did I tell you that? It's the coldest it'll ever be right now, but springtime? Oh, lovely. Smells like flowers. And the pollen tastes like honey."

She smacked her lips.

"And you're going to be on a first-name basis with the Big Man. That might not sound all that great until the king tells you what Santa said. You just might faint. I did. I rolled right over and down the hill."

"You don't see Santa?"

"Only the king sees him. The Big Man wants it that way. But the king tells us everything! And one time," she whispered, "I snuck a peek when I wasn't supposed to and saw Santa standing right out there. Oh, oh, the chills, Artie. I know that's a bit naughty, peeking like that, but ooooooh, the chills!"

"I want to go home, Belly."

"Of course you do. And you will. You absolutely will find yourself at home."

Of course, she gave a sweet smile with those slippery words. *Find yourself at home.* Art found the nuance in that one. If he stayed there long enough, this would be home. And he would find himself there.

"What about the war?"

She flinched and teetered on those giant feet. A second later, she slipped him a nice, sweet smile. The words came out like pieces of tinfoil.

"War?" she said. "Where'd you hear that?"

You heard a lot of things, Daryl whispered in his head. *About S'ven.*

Art repeated what the cat said. Even though he'd heard almost nothing about S'ven other than he was gone. It was enough to get a response, though.

Belly took the pitchfork from him.

She began filling the wheelbarrow with hay.

"And what have you heard about S'ven?" she sang.

Nothing about S'ven until she tells you about the war.

"Tell me about the war. I'll tell you what I know."

Very good, the cat said. Art was a quick study, answering Belly with deceptive truths. He'd tell her everything he knew about S'ven. Honestly and truly.

"A game of scritch and scratch, is that it?" she said. "Once chores are done, we can play that."

ART'S MUSCLES ACHED. He'd lost count of the bales he'd stacked and bags he'd moved. The stalls (there were nine of them) were clean and ready. Not a speck of hay on the floors or pellet of alfalfa in the corners.

He fell asleep in the cottage, sitting in front of the fireplace, leaning on the tiny couch.

He woke with a plate of food on the floor and Belly snoring in the recliner. There were no clocks anywhere. Could he make sense of one if there was? Belly seemed to announce chimes and rings based on some internal clock, as far as he could tell.

The cat was on the couch.

Art ate the food and waited for Belly to wake up. It was hard to tell how long it was before she said something.

"I feel you staring," she said, without opening her eyes.

Belly sat up and rubbed her eyes and smacked her lips. She

plucked a sardine off his plate (it was drowning in honey, and he wasn't going to eat it) and threw it in her mouth, chewing on her way to the kitchenette. She returned with two mugs of cider. Passed one to him and fell into the chair.

Art stared at the gold glitter at the bottom.

She drank half of her mug. Released a long sigh.

"It's not a war, Artie. Some call it that, and I get it, but that's not what it is. It's more of a conflict of nature. Opposites, you see. Light and dark, good and bad. Naughty and nice. It's all out in the open; nothing to hide. You have the good fortune of being on the Nice Side."

With that, she gave him a fizzy burp. Sardine oil glistened on her lips.

"Why are they fighting?"

"It's not a fight, Artie. It's opposites. Like ends of a magnet, you see? They need each other even though they push each other away. It's built into their nature. They *think* they can win, but they can't. They can't stop the other from being there, but that doesn't stop them from trying. It's in their nature. There's a line down the middle they're always going to push. It's not a war, Artie. It's who they are."

The cat appeared in the corner.

Belly scrunched her nose.

The cat disappeared. This time Arthur saw it happen. *Poof!* He was gone. There and then not.

What does the war have to do with you?

"What's that got to do with me?" Art asked.

"It's got *nothing* to do with you," Belly said, looking into her mug.

"You said the king was going to be happy I'm here. There's a reason I'm here."

It has something to do with the war, the cat added.

Art followed the cat's lead and repeated it. Belly swished the contents in her mug. She swallowed the rest in one gulp. She was considering how much truth to tell. When she spoke, it was heartfelt.

"We need you. The Nice Side needs you. *That's* why you're here."

"But I don't *want* to be here. That's not very nice."

"Being nice isn't always nice. You see?"

She was admitting to something. That was a first. But not to everything.

"Why do you need me?"

"I don't know, Artie."

She knows, the cat said. "You know, Belly."

She shrugged. Then: "You're here because we need you, Artie. And I like you. That's the truth of it. You can trust me on that."

The cat appeared. This time on the bookshelf between a crumpled leather boot and a jar of pinecones. He was satisfied, the way cats always seem to be. Blinking lazily. Art didn't need any more of Belly's answers. He'd heard plenty. It felt nice being here with her. Content.

There's a way out, the cat said.

Art nodded.

Do you trust me?

Art looked at Belly. They locked eyes. A hopeful smile rested on her chin.

He said: "I trust you."

ART WAS PATIENT.

Belly taught him how to make the perfect snowball. They had three snowball fights. Belly won all three, but Art did manage to hit her once. She let him, he was certain. They repaired harnesses and sewed mittens and patched holes in the Big Man's coat. They picked a few ornaments off the Christmas trees. They cracked open like glass eggs, spilling a sugary yolk that tasted like French toast.

She decided to start gift harvesting to get ahead of schedule. Art dragged the sled, and Belly plucked the presents that appeared below the trees. This went on and on. Art lost count of how many sleeps he'd taken. Then Belly announced it was fourteen rings till Christmas. Which made him doubt a ring as a day. But time was funny.

It's time to go.

Daryl was nowhere in sight when Art heard it. He was more than ready to follow. Even if it meant jumping out the window. Only a ring had passed, and it felt like a month. There was only so much nice he could take.

"GOOD NEWS!" Belly announced. "The king and queen are on their way. They were delayed by some unexpected business, but they'll be here in a chime. You're going to love them, Artie. They are so *nice!*"

"Can't wait," Art said. "Don't we have to get ready for Santa's landing?"

The cat didn't tell him what to say. He only told him what they needed to do. Art figured out how to do it. Although he didn't understand how they were going to escape.

"We do!" She snapped her fingers without a sound. "That's something we *can* do. Otherwise, we'll sit around waiting for the king and queen, and you know what that's like. Time gets stretchy with nothing to do. Let's *gooooo!*"

He followed her through the barn and onto the roadway between the trees. The pink snow was falling thicker and deeper. It was up to his knees. Belly bounced over the top of the snowfall.

There was a spring in her step.

The Christmas Wood was jingling. *Singing,* Belly called it. When the trees were happy and the Christmas spirit flowed in the sap, a lovely melody sprang from their branches. The sound was hard to explain. As if bells had voices was the closest he could come.

"This is the Big Man's last stop," she said. "That's what makes this so special and our job so important, Artie. They're exhausted when they arrive. The reindeer have been pulling the sleigh and the Big Man sliding down chimneys in all the worlds throughout existence. Everywhere, Artie. We have to make sure everything goes smoothly, you see?"

"He's been delivering presents all night."

Art still didn't believe Santa *actually* delivered presents or that flying reindeer pulled his sleigh. Maybe in Candyland. Because in Candyland, gingerbread cookies lived in townhouses and warmed themselves in front of a fire.

"Where does he go after that?" Art wanted to hear this.

"Well, after a plate of special Christmas Wood cookies, a glass or two of milk, he takes all the gifts we harvest from the trees down to the market. That's where all the boys and toys and girls and whirls sit on his lap and get a hug. It's… *joyous.*"

She clapped her hands to her ruddy, round cheeks.

"Do we go to the market to meet him?" Art said.

"Of course we do!"

Belly bounced ahead of him. He had to dig his way through the drifting snow to catch up. Pink snow packed into his boots and froze his ankles. *Of course we do!* At first, he was filled with hope. A second later, he knew it wasn't true. He could smell the fib, even smothered in niceness. They weren't leaving the top of the castle. *Being nice isn't always nice.*

"We'll have to make sure the barn is ready," Belly said.

"It is."

"We'll have to harvest presents until the last minute."

"We will."

"And the food will have to be ready." She sounded worried. "Did we leave the stove on? Maybe we should go back and—"

"It was off. We should do this now." He pointed. The end of the road was coming into view. That was exactly where Daryl wanted them to go. "If not now, then when?"

"Artie the Smartie."

The bouncy steps were back. Halfway there, they passed the cat watching from a tree.

THE WALL at the end of the road was curved and frozen. The ice looked like clumps of pink frosting on two pairs of enormous knuckles protruding from the wall. A line was faintly visible. As they approached, he could see it was in the shape of a rectangle as tall as a two-story house. As wide as a commercial airliner. It looked like a drive-in movie screen.

"This is it," she said. "This is where the Big Man flies in."

"It's a door," he muttered.

A door that hadn't been opened in forever. Or since last Christmas. Whenever that was. She rested her hands on her belly. Her T-shirt was thin and worn with *I heart Christmas* printed across the front of it.

Ask if she's going to open it, the cat said.

He was nowhere in sight. His voice, though, sounded like he was on Art's shoulder. A stampede of gooseflesh trampled up his arms.

"Are we going to open it?" Art said. Trying not to sound nervous.

"Oh, yes, yes, yes. That's why we're here. Need to make sure all is working." She searched pockets that were buried under her generous belly, pushing her hands into various spots like she was digging for treasure. "Ah. There we go."

It looked like a phone. Not a phone Art could recall. The screen lit up.

She poked at it with her index finger. Slid a few things around the screen. Pointed it at the door.

"Stand by," she said. "Christmas in the hole."

There was a loud crack, followed by three more. The first one made Art jump. It sounded like a frozen I-beam snapping in half. The sound went through the ground. The Christmas Wood shivered, throwing a cloud of pink snow off their branches.

Ice fragments fell from the lumpy knuckles, revealing hinges as large as economy cars. The rectangular outline popped outward. Steam hissed from outside as warm air rushed in. The salmon sky was showing.

"Good so far," Belly said. "Now for this."

The rectangle split down the middle. A line appeared between the two halves and began to widen. The wall shuddered. Snow came down from the ceiling in clumps. A mystery, Art would wonder at a much later time, that would never be solved. *How is it snowing inside?*

Candyland was a beautiful mystery not to be solved. Only experienced.

The wind came through like the exhaust of a jet engine. Snow whipped from the ground and swirled overhead. The trees swayed back and forth, ornaments breaking off a few limbs and rolling down the runway.

Art covered his face.

The snowstorm quickly passed as the doors opened wide, mechanically rumbling like an enormous machine.

"It's so big!" Art shouted.

"It has to be! It's so windy up here. Sometimes the reindeer are tired. One year the weather was awful. Not here, of course. It's always perfect here. Just somewhere along the way it was terrible. The reindeer had to work harder than usual to deliver presents before they finally got here."

I believe in you. The cat was talking to Art this time.

"Oh, it broke my heart to see them limping through the air. Poor Ronin dragging the others with him. The sleigh sagged like it was full of coal."

The doors rumbled to the halfway point and began moving faster. The vibrations under his feet began to quiet. The limbs of the Christmas Wood were bare after having shaken the snow off.

"You should've seen it, Artie."

Do you trust me? the cat said.

"I trust you," Art answered.

"If the door were any smaller," Belly shouted, "I'm afraid they wouldn't have made it through."

Step forward.

Art hesitated. The wind had cleared the snow from the ground. A runway of green grass led to the widening edge where the doors were pulling apart. It was a straight shot. He took half a step in that direction. There must be a ladder or, more likely, an elevator on the outside of the castle. That was how they would escape.

"The Big Man thought I was being overly cautious to make it this big, but you can't be too safe when it comes to Christmas, I said. That's when I told him—Artie, what're you doing?"

"I just want a closer look."

His voice was thin and reedy. The cat's presence was heavy. For a moment, he thought the cat was on his shoulders. Art closed his eyes and took a normal step. Then another. His legs were colder than usual.

"That's close enough, Artie. There aren't safety nets out there."

He wished she hadn't said that. *No safety nets.* There probably wasn't an elevator, then. Just a ladder to climb down. How long was it going to take to climb to the bottom of the castle? A chorus of paranoid thoughts rose up and questioned whether the cat was even real. Had he been imagining it this entire time? A cat doesn't disappear like that. It also can't talk inside his head. Maybe those were just paranoid thoughts pretending to be a cat. A cat he so desperately wanted to be real. A cat he thought he knew.

He took half a step. He would've stopped completely had he known what Daryl wanted him to do.

"What's that?" Belly shouted. "Artie, get back! Get away from that... that... *CAT!*"

Art's eyes snapped open. Daryl was in front of him.

Belly saw him, too. Because he was there. Daryl was real. And so was his voice.

Do you trust me?

Art nodded.

Then run!

The cat stretched its four legs and started sprinting like a cheetah on the open plain. Its fat beer belly bounced and swayed and dragged on the ground. Art didn't think. He leaned forward and started after him. Pumping his arms, raising his knees. Feeling the frosted grass crunch under his boots.

"Artie? Artie!"

If the deep snow had remained between them and the door, Belly would have easily outraced him with those snowshoe feet. On bare ground, she waddled like a stuffed penguin.

KA-CLUNK! KA-CLUNK!

The doors stopped in their tracks. A moment later, they reversed direction. Slowly moving toward each other. Belly was shouting, but Art could no longer hear her. The wind ached in his ear. The cold minty air burned his lungs. The cat looked back.

Art thought he saw a smile.

A few steps later, he watched the cat—without hesitation—leap off the edge. Legs outstretched. Beer belly extended.

Daryl dropped from the pink sky. Out of sight.

The doors closed in. The escape narrowed.

Art closed his eyes and figured (despite what Belly had just said) there must be a net. He kept running. He ran until he no longer felt the ground under him. His stomach slithered into his throat. He took one long stride before stepping off the ledge to find out Belly wasn't fibbing.

There was no safety net.

"How much longer?" King Chocolate called.

He'd been wearing a blindfold for half a chime by now. He didn't care much for the dark. Even when he closed his eyes. Made him nervous. Bothered him not knowing what was out there. There were voices speaking a strange language. Didn't like that, either, not knowing what they were saying. They could be talking about him, like how stupid he looked with that blindfold on.

"Jelly?"

He began to fidget. Claustrophobia beginning to squeeze. The vest they'd put on him (the ones speaking the funny language) was tight and heavy. Made him sweat BBs.

"Jelly!" He reached for the blindfold.

"Just a few more ticks," Jelly said from somewhere on his left. "Be still. Almost ready."

"This thing is heavy."

"No, it's not. I wore it."

"Yeah, it is." He scratched his head. They'd put a hat on him after the blindfold. "My head's cooking."

"Your head is fine."

"I don't like it."

"What *do* you like?"

Pretty good question, that one. He liked chocolate. What else?

He had a good think on that. He liked his throne. The castle, too. Yeah. Not much else, though. Except one thing. An emotion doctor had made him aware of it. She'd come to the castle for a visit, just the one time. Jelly thought she could help him relax. Totally didn't work. But she did one thing good. He discovered something he loved.

King Chocolate *loooooved* to hate.

He hated most people and most places. Ideas, too. He hated them almost as much as things. It was his hobby. His passion. His super-power. He was strong when he hated. It felt so good to be right about the stupid and ugly. The arrogant. The crazy. Fat ones and skinny ones. He wasn't prejudiced. He hated them all.

"I like not waiting," he grumbled.

"Good one," Jelly said. Then she went, "Choo-choo!"

King Chocolate knew what that meant. He opened his mouth. A chocolate wafer slid onto his tongue and made everything better.

I hate Christmas.

It was such a tease, having to wait. He liked to get stuff now, not ten rings later. *Now.* There was power in now. *Patience is weakness* was his motto. So was: *See it. Get it. Eat it.*

He was done waiting.

"Way-way-wait." Jelly stopped him from peeling off the blindfold. Then: "All right, *now.*"

King Chocolate flung the blindfold against the wall.

All the anticipation and nothing had changed. The royal room was off-white. The throne was still a throne. Jelly a lump of general unhappiness. Only the Triad was new. And he wasn't happy about that.

That was what they called themselves: the Triad. Like they didn't have names. Three plastics with arms and legs no wider than soda straws. They were sort of flat (flattish, they said), like they'd been sorted with a rolling pin. They came in funky colors—blue, red and green—with clothes permanently stamped on their bodies. Their color was their name.

Hate.

King Chocolate was looking down at what he was wearing. It looked like a bedsheet with a hole cut out for his head. It was bright red. The jacket, however, was silky and shiny. Slick and fine. Dark brown with fuzzy white cuffs. He almost forgot about the tight-fitting something underneath it all. If it was a girdle, it wasn't working.

Blue pushed thick square glasses up a beak of a nose. "Do *not* touch ya *head.*"

King Chocolate hated the way they spoke. Emphasizing odd words in a sentence made his head hurt. And he wouldn't have touched his head if Blue hadn't said anything. Now he wanted to touch his head.

Blue looked at Green and Red and said something in their Triad language. King Chocolate didn't speak the language, but he understood snooty. The way they laughed and looked at him.

"Please *stand,*" Red shouted and flipped his flat wrist.

"I don't stand," King Chocolate said.

Red whispered to Jelly. Jelly said, "Just try."

"These legs ain't made for walking." He kicked the throne like an infant. "I will fall. I will hurt myself. I will be in a very bad *mood.* And you, you little... whatever you're called—"

"Triad," Jelly said.

"Whatever! I am not standing. Next question."

There was no next question. Only whispering and snickering. Eye rolls.

"I saw that." King Chocolate pointed at Green. "You'd better not be talking about my legs. Are they talking about my legs? I got a deficiency. I'm handicapped."

That ain't nice, he was about to say. In fact, it was naughty. Which would explain why they were there.

"They look *like* match*sticks,*" Green said.

They were either idiots or geniuses. Because that right there, what Green said, lit King Chocolate's fuse, and it wasn't going out. He shoved the joystick on the armrest forward, aiming to plow over them like a bull elephant. They'd look like linguini when he was done pressing them into the floor.

So fired up, he leaned forward to throw all his weight into the throne's acceleration. When it didn't move (Jelly had turned off the throne when the blindfold was up), King Chocolate's momentum tipped like a building with a cracked foundation. He was going to squash the triad and have to dry-clean them off his brand-new, silk jacket.

The girdle snapped tighter. Squeezed. He wheezed like a dog toy.

Something clicked. Whirred. Followed by a high-pitched whine. A magnetic sensation hummed along his spine.

An invisible hand had reached under the bedsheet and kept him from falling. He bobbed like a buoy. His matchstick legs dragged across the floor, the hard soles tapping against it. He was a marionette without strings. A balloon over a parade.

"I'm standing," he muttered. "I'm standing!"

"You're floating." Jelly explained the Triad had outfitted him with an antigravity vest, which was currently squeezing his guts like a tube of toothpaste.

"How does it work?"

"Magnets? I don't know."

The Triad explained, and King Chocolate didn't understand a word. Or care. He was floating. He looked like a strange ghost, the way his clothing dragged on the floor. It wasn't a shirt he was wearing. Not a dress, either. More of a muumuu.

The floating was intuitive. Leaning was all he had to do. He decided not to throw the flattish threesome into Fudgy Lake after all. Even if the vest was giving him a wedgy—*worth it.*

The Triad followed him around the room, pulling at the jacket, grabbing the muumuu. They chattered in their Triad-speak. Blue was not happy with the fit of the jacket, King Chocolate guessed by the way he was yanking on the sleeve. Red was doing the same thing to the muumuu. King Chocolate dragged them along like tin cans on a wedding car.

"*Arms* out," Green demanded.

King Chocolate didn't like the tone, but he was still high on this new mode of transportation. He held out his arms, scarecrow fashion. The off-white walls flickered and shimmered. Then turned into reflections. He saw himself from every angle. He liked what he saw. The muumuu hid his freakishly small legs. The jacket was sharp enough to cut someone. He didn't hate the color. Brown was his favorite.

The hat on his head was floppy with a white fuzzy ball.

"It's a merk," Jelly said over the Triad's argument. "The thing you're wearing, in case you're wondering. It's not a dress. It's a merk."

"What's a merk?" King Chocolate said, spinning to see his back side.

"It's that. It's loose fitting for comfort. Fuzzy cuffs for style. The jacket for a night out. All the fabric is sweat-wicking and odor-killing."

"I don't stink."

"Not with that, you won't," Jelly said. "You're Naughty Claus is what you are. You'll deliver the presents that Santa won't bring."

And then King Chocolate understood why Jelly had insisted the Triad come to the castle. The Santa hat. The Santa jacket. With one twist.

"It's chocolate brown," he said.

"They call it doo-doo brown," Jelly said. "Same thing. Santa Claus hasn't changed his outfit in forever. You're bringing style back to Christmas. Cutting-edge fashion. Everyone will want to dress like you. They'll talk about you on the Nice Side. They'll want to be like you."

This was big. This was bigger than big. This was a major swing in the battle. Even without that crosser, that Artie the Fartie, he could win the hearts of the nicies. He could bring them across the border. Flip them to the Naughty Side.

King Chocolate wanted to hug someone.

"Hello?" a voice called.

King Chocolate instinctively covered his body as if he were naked. He leaned too far and zoomed toward the corner. He jerked his head back before colliding with the wall, overcorrected in the opposite direction, and hit the Triad like bowling pins.

Right. Left. Up. Up again. Down.

He looked like a mechanical bull.

The room was a blur. The Triad was arguing. Someone kept calling hello.

Jelly watched the balloon rocket around the room, ducking to avoid a collision. Then, out of sheer luck, King Chocolate slammed into the throne. It tipped back and groaned. The magnets or whatever levitated the throne went into overdrive. It righted like a rotating cup. Sweat was wicking through the merk like a dishrag on a wet floor.

He was panting. Melting. Heart kicking its way out.

Then Jelly spoke. And things somehow got worse.

"The queen wants to see you."

"What does she want?"

"She wants to come up."

"What? Gross, no."

"She can hear you."

King Chocolate's eyes widened. "I'm talking to them, you three. Gross, I hate the way this looks." But he was shaking his head at the Triad, mouthing *I love it*. "Now go, get out of here before I throw you in Fudgy Lake. Uh, hello? You still there?"

"Hello, Casey?" the voice responded all around the room.

"What do you want?"

"I'd like to come up. I don't remember the last time I saw you."

"No reason, I haven't changed. Gained a few pounds, maybe. Besides, I'm not decent. Just trying on something new, nothing special."

"Then video me in. I don't like looking at a blank screen."

"How about a picture?"

"Casey, please."

He grumbled. Time spent with her was like driving over a cliff. "Just a second!"

Off with the floppy Naughty Claus hat. It was hot anyway. His hair was impossible. It had enough static electricity to light a small building on fire. He gave out orders, and Jelly followed them. His reflection was on the walls. He didn't want her to see everything, only from the neck up. Truth was he'd lost weight since he'd seen her last. He couldn't remember when that was. It didn't matter.

He practiced a smile. His teeth deeply coffee stained. Almost matching the color of the merk.

"All right," he said.

The image on the walls shifted and reorganized into rows of bright candy sticks of emerald green, cinnamon red and orangey orange. They glittered with dew in the dusky dimness. The queen was on her hands and knees, pulling rascal weeds from the ground. They cried when she dropped them and then ran away on thick white roots.

"Quick, quick," King Chocolate whispered. "Do the thing."

Before the queen lifted her head and showed her face, Jelly did something to the image. The queen shapeshifted on the wall into a much more pleasing thing to look at, as far as King Chocolate was concerned.

"Can you see me?" she called. "I'm in the garden."

"I see you all right. See you perfect."

Her waist shrank and hips curved. Her hair was short and black and almost as silky as his jacket. Her lips full and wet and brown, blending beautifully with the blueberry shade of her skin. Eyes as big as pocket watches.

Sometimes when he did that, he fell in love with her again. One time he almost invited her up. But she didn't look or sound like what was on the walls. He would get nauseous if she didn't.

"We're harvesting candy crystals," she said. "For the kids in Dirty Downs. A new community garden is opening at the school there." She held out a basket. A toy tractor dumped a load of watermelon crystals into it. "Thank you, Tracky," she said.

"Great," King Chocolate said dully. "So much fun."

She rinsed her hands in a puddle of nectar dripping from a voodoo lily, then sat on a three-legged stool. She sipped from a glass of sparkling lemonade, the crown tilting on her head. Always with the crown. If she would just lose it, he could maybe get everyone to believe she wasn't the queen. He'd tried to have it stolen once, but it never left her sight.

"Why wasn't I invited to the meeting with Macey and Lydia?" She sounded hurt.

"It was a, uh, last minute thing."

He was going to say it was cancelled, but she would know. She always knew.

"And what about the time before that? And the time before that? I told you I wanted to go."

"Why didn't you tell me the queen wanted to go, Jelly? You're awful. A terrible assistant. I'll have her punished."

Never did she laugh at anything he said. Not that he said anything funny anymore, but it wouldn't hurt for her to fake it once in a while. "I wanted to tell you that their idea of you giving gifts to the Naughty Side is wonderful."

"How did you know about that?"

"Really, Casey. Who do you think sent the Triad to you?"

Jelly shrugged when he looked down. He'd assumed she was the one who brought them up.

"I helped them design your outfit," the queen said. "Do you like it?"

"You? Well, it's... I don't know. Good. The colors are okay. The doo-doo brown is—"

"Doo-doo brown?"

"You know what, I hate it. I didn't want to say it, but you made me. I hate all of this—the hat, the muumuu, this stupid jacket. They're going to the bottom of Fudgy Lake as soon as I burn them. Does that make you happy?"

She laughed, amused. Nothing he said bothered her anymore. Or maybe she knew he was lying. There was no way he was burning these clothes. They felt great and looked even better. He would have Jelly spread rumors that he designed it.

A mouse hopped through the grass. She lowered her arm, and it climbed up to her shoulder, nuzzling against her ear. The tail whipping around her neck.

"Give it a chance, Casey. I think you'll like it."

"Too late," he lied. "Listen, I've got ruling to do, so just don't call me—"

"I heard the crosser is looking for S'ven."

What is the point of locking her up on an island? Those little vermin were gross little spies, that was it. He was this close to exterminating them. Sweet Tooth was too slow to squash them, and no one else cared.

"That's a ruuu-mor," he sang.

"It's not a rumor. What's he want with S'ven?"

"What do you think he wants?"

This was her only sore spot, as far as he could tell. The sensitive part he could grind his heel into. *S'ven.* That thief had left a long, long, loooong time ago. Even her furry little spies didn't know where he was.

"S'ven didn't cross back," she said.

"You don't know that. But if he did, you can *foooollow,*" he sang. *Why do I always sing at her?*

"No. I can't."

"Yes. You can. I want you to. Total permission. Pack your bags and *whooooosh!*"

He didn't know if she could cross back to where she came from. S'ven probably did and left her behind. She deserved that. She would admit it.

"He's still here." She held the mouse in her cupped hands. "I can feel it."

"Good for you. So, I got to go do king stuff. It's been—"

"Do you know the boy's name?"

That was the thing with her. She couldn't take a hint. That was why he never ever wanted to talk to her. Because of this. Unless he was going to be horribly rude, he'd be staring at this fake woman on his wall playing with a disgusting little mouse until he starved. It was why he'd sent her to an island. Why he never let her visit.

"Biff. Bart. Steve. I don't know."

"It's Arthur," she said. "Art."

"I was close. He crossed from your world, I'll bet. You know him?"

"Of seven billion people?"

A long pause. She put the mouse down. It hopped through the crystal garden. She leaned on her knees and stared at him with moon-pie eyes. And he said: "Soooo... no?"

"He's special, Casey. I can feel it. It's not like when S'ven and I came over. He's here for a different reason."

"First of all, I'm tired of your *feelings*." She was almost always right, and he hated that. "Second, special how?"

She shook her head, looking down at her beautiful blue feet. Perfectly shaped with bright red and green polish on the toenails. Which, by the way, looked nothing like the queen's actual feet. He would never forget what those monstrosities looked like. They were branded into his memory.

"He's lost," she said. "Lonely. He's not supposed to be here."

"I thought he was *here for a reason*." He air-quoted the last half of that sentence.

"His imagination brought him here." She looked up suddenly. "He's going to change everything."

"So I hear."

"Do you know where he is?"

"I absolutely do not."

"My little chickens know where he is."

He didn't like the sound of that. Gave Jelly a look, and she was out the door. The boy was in King Macey's castle on the Nice Side. King Chocolate was hatching a plan to break him out. Then he shivered. It happened whenever the queen called her vermin chickens. Something gross about that.

"Let's have dinner, Casey."

"I'm busy."

"I understand." She nodded. Then added: "I'm sorry."

"Bye."

The walls went blank. He had to do it. Once she started talking about dinner, the clock was ticking. And then the apologies from the Apology Queen. Sorry this, sorry that. She meant it, too. It came from this deep well of shame and regret. He used to love to hear it, but then her apologies started to change. Like she was sorry for what she'd done. And, strangely, sorry for what *he'd* done.

She was trying to pave her way to the Nice Side with apologies and good deeds. It was so obvious. And disgusting. She didn't want to be on the Naughty Side, didn't want to be by his side or anywhere near him. And that was the deep dark secret of why he hated her.

She can't accept who she is. That she's rotten at the core. Naughty in her blood.

She needed to embrace that ugly scar, just like he did. That was where freedom lived.

He put the hat back on his head. He was going to keep it, the entire outfit. It was too good to throw away. Even if the queen designed it.

"Eh-hem." Jelly had returned. "I've got good news and bad."

His smile was delicious and gross. "Start with the bad."

10

rthur woke next to a short dock.

He was clutching the muddy shore, awakened by a feathery tickle across his face and remnants of freefall in his stomach. He dragged himself out of the raspberry tea of Rose Lake and flopped onto dry grass. When he closed his eyes, his stomach began to freefall all over again. He opened his eyes, staring at the castle spearing the pink sky.

Impossible.

There was no way he fell from up there. The top wasn't even visible, cloaked in cushiony clouds and pink mist. But the memories of that endless tumble were freshly tattooed on his stomach.

The panic. The terror.

Complete loss of control.

The last wisps of memory before waking on the shore were that of not crashing into Rose Lake, but rather the soft and kindly embrace of its waters in a red mist lullaby. And here he was, soaking wet and in one piece. He pulled himself farther up the shore, his hand landing on a pile of clothing: a pair of burlap shorts with a belt of hemp cord and a dry T-shirt with a cartoon pig on the front and a curly tail rump on the back.

In the distance, a crowd roared.

He ducked behind the dock and waded into the lake to hide. The water filled his boots and rose up to his knees. He peered over the wooden planks. The market was on the far side of the lake. The cheers carried across as if he were over there.

A bit suspicious standing there.

The thought rang in Art's head. He nearly went underwater at the sound of it, bobbing with the surface at his shoulders. Sitting on the pig shirt and burlap shorts, the cat waved his tail. Art crawled toward him, keeping low to the ground and hidden from sight. Daryl didn't flinch.

"Why didn't you tell me I was jumping out of the castle?" Art hissed.

Would you have followed if I did?

Art looked over his shoulder, his eyes running up the never-ending totem. Art wouldn't have jumped even if he had a parachute.

"How am I not dead?"

Because nothing ever dies, Arthur. Like it was common knowledge that nothing ever died. The cat made biscuits on the T-shirt. *There was only one way to escape, and that was it.*

"Why would Belly lie?"

She wasn't lying. She believed every word she told you. It comes from innocent ignorance. They had you, Arthur. That is not where you want to be.

"And where do I want to be?"

Back home. You've made it quite clear. And there's only one way to do that. You have to find the truth, Arthur. And the truth is not in a nice, comfy tower on the Nice Side.

"Where is it, then?"

Get out of those clothes. They're wet, and someone will recognize you.

It wasn't the clothes they would recognize, but the lean young man in them. He was, however, soaking wet. Daryl stepped off the pile. Art held up the pig shirt.

"Where'd you get these?"

They're on loan.

There was a narrow road cobbled with multicolored triangles of candy corn. On the other side were three-story rowhouses with postage-stamp front yards and deep porches to sit and gaze at the castle. There were decorations in the yards, some sculptures and flashing lights, ornaments hanging from the gutters. Laundry hung on swooping cords in front of three narrow homes, which were made of curious materials.

One of brick. One of sticks. And the third made of straw.

Art ducked behind the bulkhead wall.

Not to worry. They're at the market like everyone else. Daryl leaped onto the wall and swaggered toward the three little pig homes. *If only they knew you were stealing their clothes.*

"I'm not—"

The cat didn't wait. Art had no idea if his thoughts or words were in Daryl's head. He gathered the clothes in a ball and climbed over the wall, hunching his shoulders like he was dodging bullets. Nothing suspicious at all. Candy boxes were stacked in the three little pigs' front yards. Bees hovered around them.

"Merry, merry!" they cried in unison.

Art waved on his way by.

Daryl sprinted into the alley that ran behind the three little pig rowhouses. There were buildings all around, three stories tall with balconies looking down. Daryl nosed open the door of a storage shed. It was dim inside. Smelled earthy and sweet. Light filtered through a window yellowed with pollen (more likely it was sugar).

Art's heart leaped. He backed into a tool rack. Rakes and shovels clattered on a workbench.

Someone was in the shed. Someone looked right at him.

He held his breath. Daryl leaped onto the workbench. *It's a mirror.*

Art's heart rate would not return to normal for twenty ticks. Which, on Art's world, would be twenty minutes. Give or take.

✳

"YOU STOLE THESE?" He shook the clothes at Daryl. The absurdity of talking to a cat was, for a brief moment, staggering. It was like that for quite some time, but always dispelled when the cat talked back.

Borrowed.

"You're on the Nice Side. *Borrowing* isn't nice."

I'm not from here, Arthur.

"So Herkle was right. You're a crosser."

Right now, I'm from here. That answer joined the long list of things that didn't make sense. Art had learned to ignore them. They only slowed things down. *Now, get dressed. Leave your wet clothes here. They'll be worth more than what you took off their lines. You being a crosser and all.*

"*You* took them. Not me."

Art stripped off his wet clothes and threw them in a bucket. The three little pigs were not so little. Their clothes were big on him. The burlap shorts were itchy, but at least there was room.

Nice tattoo.

Art turned toward the mirror as he put on the shirt. The fresh outline of three clouds was above his right shoulder blade. He paused, searching for a faint and distant memory of a needle delivering ink into his flesh. He was young to have a tattoo.

Put those on, too. Including the hat.

Daryl had leaped onto a shelf where a thin, white suit hung from a hook. A netted veil was next to it. It seemed unlikely bees would sting anyone. This was the Nice Side. Wouldn't they just share their honey?

Art slipped on the lightweight coveralls. The veil was much too big. Obviously made for the round head of a pig.

"Where we going?"

Your gingerbread friend was right. Grimjoy will have the answers you need.

"Okay."

The border is a long way off. I'm afraid someone will find you out before we get there, even wearing that. If you're caught, you'll go back to rooming with Belly in the tower. King Macey will lock the doors this time and—don't forget the drawings, Arthur.

The sketchbook in his shirt pocket had fallen on the floor. How it didn't sink to the bottom of Rose Lake was shocking. Art tucked it into a pocket on the coveralls.

"So how do we not get caught?"

We *don't have a problem.* You *do.*

Daryl hopped across the shed and looked through the yellowed window. For a beer-bellied cat, he was quite graceful. Over the rhythmic purring, Art heard celebrating among things banging on the ground. A small group was playing a vaguely familiar game not too far from the three little pig rowhouses.

They were gathered on the grand steps of what looked like a courthouse wrapped in glittery paper with a bow on top. It was the imps. Only from the shed, they looked like boys. They were the ones at the market, the ones with the chocolates and swimming noodles strapped across their backs. Only they were riding the noodles.

A short, fat boy rode across the edge of a planter box, knocking flowers out of the dirt as he slid to the end. The noodle fell away from his bare feet before he landed. The boy bailed on the trick and rolled like a lead tumbleweed into the road. The boys laughed. One of them looked like he was filming the trick.

Art put his hand on the window.

He could feel what they were doing. Could feel it in his stomach. The way they moved their feet to pop the noodles off the ground. The way they bent their knees, leaned into the turns, shoved their back foot to get speed.

He imagined the clatter of wooden boards on concrete. The hum of plastic wheels on his feet.

His hands clenched unconsciously. Ached to feel a board in his grip.

I think we have an answer.

"What?"

Pretty obvious.

"Those things? You want me to ride one of those things?"

The cat waved his tail above his arching back. The pupils narrowed to vertical slits. The whiskers twitched.

And then he was gone. No poof or wisp of smoke.

Just gone.

ONE OF THE boys landed a rail slide down the entire flight of steps. It was his tenth attempt, and he landed it. The boys banged their noodles on the ground, threw them into the air, and piled on top of the boy in celebration.

Art had no idea where Daryl went. Until one of the abandoned noodles started moving on its own. It slid behind a row of popcorn bushes.

No one noticed.

❄

JUST FOLLOW ME.

Daryl explained how he'd appear where Art needed to go. There was a lot of turns to make, and the crowd at the market was going to get bored soon, so they needed to hurry.

"Wait!" Art caught him before he disappeared up the road. "I don't know how to ride one of these."

Yes. You do.

"How would I know? I've never seen one."

That much was true. The noodle wasn't a noodle once it had been taken off a boy's back. It flattened out like a short and narrow snowboard. Only nowhere to lock in his feet. The top side was grippy and soft. The bottom was an undulating plank of tiny tentacles that were leathery and slimy.

A dull pain spread between Art's eyes. Someone was trying to talk to him. He dropped the noodle.

"Is it *alive*?"

Everything's alive, Arthur. Take off your shoes and step on. We don't have time for this.

The boys had been barefoot. They had been riding the noodles hard. Art had to stop calling this thing a noodle. It didn't look like one anymore.

It's called a beam.

"Wait. Can you hear my thoughts?"

They were on your face. Then Daryl disappeared.

Art was afraid of this. Daryl expected him to ride this thing all the way to the border? He needed some time to figure it out. No one just jumps on a bike and rides it the first time. Failing was part of the process. The cat was being unreasonable.

To prove it, Art took off his shoes.

Gently, he put his right foot on the back of the beam. The surface molded around his heel and squeezed between his toes like warm goo. He leaned onto it, felt the beam absorb his weight. Good so far. Until he put his left foot on it.

The beam zipped out from under him. He flipped onto the ground. The beam came to a stop several feet away. It was shuddering. And giggles echoed in Art's head.

The boys suddenly grew loud. They were shouting.

Daryl appeared next to the beam.

"See what I mean?" Art pointed. "I don't know how to ride it."

The cat's tail waved behind him. A smug look grew on his furry face. An angry mob was getting louder. Art got off the ground, took a step toward the corner. The boys were getting closer.

"Where'd you just go?"

The Cheshire grin was in full bloom. *I applied a little heat.*

THE FIRST BOY came flying around the corner.

He was leaning into the curve, the beam tilted on the edge, riding smoothly over the candy corn cobbles. His weight pressing forward. The look on his face was as hard as the fists at his sides.

Art's insides flash froze. His legs turned liquid and dissolved his thoughts.

Instinct kicked in.

He was in full stride when he leaped onto the beam. The surface snapped around his feet and between his toes. He leaned with forward momentum. A storm was in his ears. His hair whipped his face. Clutching a wet boot in each hand, he went flying down the street.

The feeling of freedom humming in his chest.

Vibrating in his legs. Warming his stomach.

He didn't turn to see if the mob was gaining on him. He couldn't hear them over the wind, but he could feel them back there. Feel them receding. This was the first time he'd ever been on a beam. But he knew how to do it.

The skills were baked in. Balance as instinctual as a bird leaving the nest. Every fiber of his body knew what to do.

Daryl sat in an intersection up ahead. Calmly, he strode to the left. Art felt the beam respond to a slight change of balance, the subtle twist of his ankles. He went into a sweeping turn, feeling the beam grip the road and carve the turn.

It was beautiful. Delicious.

And the board said, *WEEEEEEEEE!*

And Art thought: *This is who I am.*

He never slowed down, riding over spongy marshmallow paths, over bumpy pretzel bridges, and down slushy roads of icing.

Down narrow alleys.

Up flights of stairs.

Ollying over obstacles and grinding edges, he no longer thought about being followed. Filled with the joy of riding obliterated his thoughts, calmed the emotional turmoil. Troubles fell away like discarded snakeskin. Anxiety evaporated like water in the desert. He was one with the wind in his ears, in his eyes. In harmony with the ground running under him.

Daryl waited at the edge of a forest, where a path opened in the candy-cane-striped tree trunks.

Art trusted his guide, jetting into the shadows, taking the turns like an Olympic skier. His legs started to jelly. Ankles slow burning. He dodged bright ornaments dangling from branches, popping back out into the light beneath the pink sky, where rolling hills of dewy grass sparkled. A chocolate waterfall roared in the distance.

Art wiped the tears from his cheeks.

The air was cooler. It was humid and smelled of mold and fermentation. The dampness of an approaching storm took the form of a shadowy film up ahead. Like a dark curtain cut the sky in half, separating one side of Candyland from another. That curtain ran the length of the land and to the top of the volcano.

Sitting alone on top of a grassy knoll, nestled into the shadowy border, was a small building.

Art kicked the back end of the beam. The front end popped off the ground, and he caught it, slinging the beam across his shoulders. The ground felt rock solid beneath him. He approached the little building in sloshy wet boots.

It was a cottage made of striped tree trunks. A stone chimney puffed from the right side of it. A granular path led to a door on the bright side (the Nice Side) facing him. His boots sank in the candied granules, which were reds and blues and greens and yellows. Pocket gardens bloomed along the wall. A merry little statuary of Santa and elves mingled with polka-dotted flowers and vivid stems. Christmas lights hung from the eave and drooped over a window to the left of the door.

It was all quite cheery.

The door was tall and wide. Round on top. Strands of garland were welcoming, but a sign was posted that said otherwise.

EXIT ONLY! GO THAT WAY.

An arrow pointed to the left. He left the candy gravel path, put his hands to the window. There was nothing inside. Nothing at all. Not a chair or ceiling or even a wall.

Daryl was waiting for him around the corner. *So, you* can *ride.*

"Yeah."

Think of all the things you have yet to do.

Art wasn't in the mood to talk about potential, about his future and where he saw himself in five years. He didn't want any more fires being lit beneath him, either. He'd admit what Daryl did—having the boys chase him—had worked, but he needed a break.

The cat sat in front of a pair of double doors. The kind that would swing when pushed. The border ran along the seam between them. And right down the middle of Daryl—half of him in the light, the other half in the dark, his tail swishing from naughty to nice. One word was painted above the door.

GRIMJOY.

GRIM was in the shadows. The red paint flaking in long streaks where the striped logs were weathered and tinted green with algae. Clumps of lichen clung to the door.

Art stepped over the border like passing through a wet membrane. The shadowy air was cool and humid. Heavy. It weighed on him like a tropical depression. The grassy fields turned to rolling hills of ferns. A tropical forest in the distance. Sadness weaved into its beauty.

He returned to the light side, where JOY was written in vibrant red letters. Where the walls were clean, and the door freshly painted the color of sunshine.

This was the place.

With a hand on each door, he pushed. They didn't budge. He looked for a hidden handle or sunken doorknob. When he tried the doors again, two voices blared from the other side.

❄

"WHAT'D YOU WANT?" said the first one.

"May I help you?" said the second.

You can imagine what they sounded like and you'd be spot on. Gruff impatience versus sweet compassion. Grimjoy wasn't a person or a thing. It was two persons or things. And not hard to guess which one was Grim.

"I'm here to see Grimjoy."

"What've you *got*?" said Grim.

"What can you offer?" said Joy.

Art stepped back. No one had said anything about payment. He looked around, but his furry guide with the buddha belly was no longer there.

"Daryl?" he whispered. "Hey, what—"

"*Daryl*?" Grim said. "What's a *Daryl*?"

"Um, he's a cat. He's the one who—"

"You're offering a *cat*?" Grim shouted.

"No. No, he brought me here."

Art twisted his fingers together. A thing he did when silence stretched out uncomfortably long. Maybe they were thinking it over, but Art wasn't giving them Daryl. The cat wouldn't let him if he tried. Maybe that was why he bailed.

"What do you want?" Art answered.

"What do you *have*?" Grim said.

Art wished he could talk to Joy. "I didn't bring anything."

"Oh, *great*. That's just great. Another charity case, you hear that? Santa ain't here, beggar. These presents ain't free."

"I'm not begging. I'm a..." He swallowed nervously. "I'm a crosser."

More silence. Then: "*So?*"

"Countless travelers cross through our land," Joy said sweetly. "They don't stay long."

"Because they're not *lost!*" Grim blurted at him.

"You know about me?" Art said.

"We know about *everything!* That's why you're here. Empty-handed and on your knees."

"Not everything, darling," Joy said. "But we can help. What do you have to offer?"

Back to square one. "I didn't know I needed to bring something."

Joy answered, "What is that you're holding?"

"This? It's a, uh, it's called a beam."

"Okay," Grim said. "Now we're getting *somewhere*."

"But I can't give it to you."

"Why *not*?"

"It's not mine."

"Why do *you* have it?"

"I borrowed it."

Pause. "Yeah, you *stole* it. It's all over your sad little face. Welcome to the Naughty Side, kid. Step over the line, and someone will be along with a gift basket."

"I didn't steal it."

He wasn't going to drag Daryl into it. And to be honest, Art had rode off with it instead of giving it back when the boys came for it. At this point, it was as good as stolen.

So that was it. He had nothing to give. He couldn't sing or dance or write poetry (not that he was going to offer that). He couldn't give them the clothes he was wearing because they weren't his, either.

"Daryl!" he shouted.

"We don't want the *cat!*"

"I don't have anything to give you!"

Art threw the beam down. It bounced against the doors. The outburst seemed to please the first voice. It spoke bitterly with an edge of pleasure.

"Then go back where you came from and leave us *alone*."

"That's what I want! I want to go back. I don't want to be here anymore."

"Well, boo-hoo in a bowl of *stew*. You're already here, and life doesn't care what you want. There's some free advice, beggar. Now pick up your stupid ripstick and go find something we want." Then Grim said, a bit more seriously: "I don't mind the litter, just not in front of the door. We have a business to run. Now scram."

Fine. Art didn't want to be there anymore, anyway. Although he had no idea where to go. Daryl had brought him into the middle of nowhere and left him. If only he could get back to Gandy and Nutmeg's house. That felt more like home than anything. It was warm; it smelled good. They were nice and not fake nice. Like genuinely good people. Or cookies. He could get back there in disguise, hide in their house until he figured out what Grimjoy wanted.

He bent down to pick up the beam. His sketchbook fell out of his pocket.

"*Wait!*" Grim shouted. "What are *those!*"

"Yes, what *are* those?" Joy said.

Art was confused. They sounded amazed by something, and he wasn't sure what they were talking about. The only thing around was the sketchbook, which contained simple designs. Abstract drawings and nothing else. He flipped the pages.

"*Closer*," Grim said.

Art took a step forward and let them get a good look. Then said: "One for each of you."

Long silence. This time Art didn't twist his fingers. He didn't flinch or fidget or think of leaving. The hook was set. He was going to reel them in slowly.

Then the doors opened.

THE INSIDE WAS NORMAL SIZED. Not the *expanded space* thing he'd seen at Herkle and Derkle's or the top of the castle. Just a regular-sized room with very irregular decorations.

There was a round table with three chairs. Not so strange. The dome-shaped fruitcake sitting in the middle of the table was odd, but not crazy. A velvet curtain had been drawn across the room, the kind at a theater before plays begin. This one was held up by a clothesline, nothing fancy. None of that seemed too unusual.

It was the line down the middle of the room that couldn't be ignored or explained.

The border was unaffected by roof and walls. It went through the table and across the floor. To the right, Christmas was bright and shiny. String lights and garland, bowls of fruit and plates of cookies. A tree hung with ornaments with presents beneath its limbs. Train tracks circled an elaborate town covered in fake snow with little vehicles and tiny figurines. *Choo-choo* went the train as it rounded the corner, loaded with itty-bitty gifts for the teeny-weeny townsfolk.

To the left... well, very different. It was steeped in dank shadows, for one. There was a tree in the corner, brown needles sprayed on the floor beneath barren limbs. Ornaments broken and dusty. A plastic baby doll sitting on a chair, her face graffitied with permanent markers. A plate of moldy cookies beneath the dark window. A fly circling a glass of spoiled milk.

"Payment on the *table*," Grim said, standing just on the other side of the curtain. "Now."

Art did exactly that, ripped two cards out of the book, and slid them next to the round fruitcake. Two arms darted through a closed part in the curtains, one slender and fine and pale blue; the other arm was hard to describe. It was hairy.

"Thank you," Joy said.

The curtain bulged. An elbow here, a hip there. There was muttering and hissing. A deep growl that made Art second-guess being there. Someone wanted to switch cards because it wasn't fair.

"Two *more*." The hairy arm shot out between the curtains. The palm, also hairy, opened in the shadows. "For *payment*."

"No," Art said. "The deal was two cards."

"*FINE!*"

Another argument, although Grim was the only one Art could hear. It looked like bears wrestling behind the curtain. The frayed clothesline bounced and twanged between the walls. And then it stopped.

"Sit *down*."

Art pulled out the chair on his side of the table. It was perfect for a first grader. He squatted with his legs awkwardly folded in front of him, his knees too tall to fit under the table. One half of him was in the light, the other in the shadows. He could feel the opposing elements pulling at him. It was disquieting. Uncomfortable.

He was naughty *and* nice.

The curtain suddenly jerked open; the curtain rings at the top slid noisily on the clothesline. Two figures were exposed. The one on the left, bathed in dimness, threw her arms out and shouted, "You *flinched!* You owe us another picture." She pulled a stained white T-shirt over a protruding belly. "Out with it, on the *table*."

"Silly-billy. Do no such thing, darling." This from the woman in the light. Her delicate arms held out to the sides, she curtsied. "Pleasure to meet you."

She was hairless all over. Bald with no eyebrows or eyelashes. Yet stunning. Art couldn't stop staring. The lips full and dark blue as if she'd just eaten a bowl of blueberries. Her teeth were spotlights, and her skin as smooth as a newborn and the color of a clear blue sky. Cheeks dashed with glitter. Her dress sparkled new off the rack.

"Oh, sure. Don't get *up.* Whatever you do," said Grim.

She was, perhaps, the twin sister. Identical in height, but that was it. She was covered in matted hair that had never seen a brush or bottle of shampoo. Yellowy eyes stared out from bushy pockets. Teeth that were crooked and stained from a lifetime of hot chocolates, wearing the same T-shirt to catch the dribs and drabs of drink that escaped her greedy mouth.

Art started to rise.

"No, no. It's all right." Joy motioned for him to stay seated. Her plum-painted fingernails were polished and shiny. "Thank you for joining us. What's your name?"

"Art."

"Art. A name with creative roots for a handsome, young man. Don't you think, Grim?"

"Uh, *no.* After you, Joy." She gestured for her sister to sit first, then scrambled into her chair before Joy could adjust her dress. "Too *slow*."

"Merry, merry," Joy said to Art and then to Grim.

"Blah-blah," Grim replied.

Joy settled onto her chair. Grim leaned her elbows on the table. The hair was coarse and tangled and smelled like cheese. It was hard to tell in the dimness, but it looked tangled with algae.

"They call you Grimjoy at the market," Art said.

"Yes, well, my sister and I were never separated at birth," Joy said.

That was puzzling. They were two individuals about half Art's height. Sensing his confusion, she tried to lean away from her sister. As she did, Grim was pulled toward her, as if invisible strings were connecting them. Grim's face pushed against the border of light but didn't pass through it. She let out a growl and yanked away from it. Joy was jerked toward her, and the same thing happened: Joy's creamy blue cheek was mashed against the shadowy border.

"Okay, okay." Joy held up her hands. "My apologies. I should've asked your permission before demonstrating."

"I thought you were one person," Art said. "Grimjoy."

"Is that really what you want to *know*, if we're one person?" Grim relaxed, and Joy smoothed the wrinkles on her blouse. Grim leaned over the table. "You traveled aaaaaalll that way on your dumb little stick to waste a question on *that*?"

"It-it wasn't a question," Art said.

"It wasn't," Joy added.

"I distinctly heard you say with these two ears"—the ears were pointed and, of course, hairy—"are we one person? Did you or did you not say *that*?"

"No, I didn't."

"You're calling me a *liar*?"

Art looked at Joy glowing with innocence. Grim weighed down with shadows. "You are on the Naughty Side," was all Art said.

"Point!" Joy declared with glee.

Grim leaned back in her little chair and crossed her arms. Bugs crawled through the hairs on her forearms. "You disgust *me*. Both of you. Your judgment is offensive, and you smell."

"Very well," Joy tittered. "You have bargained for three questions, Sir Arthur. And three answers we will provide. You may take your time to think about—"

"How do I get back home?" Art blurted.

It surprised the sisters, how quickly he asked it. Grim yipped, and Joy jumped a little in her seat. Laughing with surprise, Joy patted her cheeks, which had flushed with strawberry patches. Grim coughed up a hairball.

A red light lit up on a scoreboard just beyond the parted curtains.

"Very good," Joy said. "Pick a fruit from the cake and pass it to my sister."

The fruitcake was the size of a spare tire and weighed about the same. It glistened in the light, looked wet in the shade. Jellied fruits (which contained no fruit) studded the surface. Art wasn't certain he was doing it right, but neither one of them objected when he plucked a green glob from it.

"There you *go*," Grim said, low and smoky.

She leaned forward. Her tongue unrolled like a slimy, red carpet. A putrid fog of dead fish leaked out. Art tried not to wince.

"That's right," Joy said sweetly. "On the tongue."

It was at this moment Art became acutely aware of what he was doing. Yet he did exactly what the blue-faced princess asked him to do. What choice did he have? He put that congealed blob of green sugar on Grim's tongue.

A smile crept into her hairy cheeks.

The tongue folded once, then twice. Then disappeared behind the snapping gate of chocolate-stained teeth. She chewed slowly, eyes closing in deep satisfaction. Her throat bobbed, and her mouth opened to emit a fetid breeze.

"Aaaahhh."

Art turned away. And just as he did so, Joy began to convulse. She smelled the dead fish breath, too. But the convulsions sounded more like a dog who had eaten from the trash can. It was deep and dark. Grim watched with wide eyes and a cruel grin. Joy started moving her head like a chicken, jutting her chin out farther and farther with each contraction.

Five times it happened.

On the fifth, something slid from between her lips. She reached up and pulled a strip of paper out of her mouth. Showed it to her sister. Then slid it across the table. It looked like a fortune-cookie message. It read:

YOU CAN'T GO BACK. ONLY FORWARD.

"Can't go back? Why can't I—wait, that's not my question."

Grim pointed at the scoreboard. A second light came on.

"Too *late*."

She was happy. So, so happy.

ART REFUSED to feed fruitcake to Grim. He hadn't been asking a question. Just talking out loud.

It didn't matter.

Grim pinched off a chunk and tucked it into her cheek like a dip of tobacco. Staring at Art with a wicked grin. Joy spit out the answer. Grim didn't bother reading it before she passed it over.

YOU ARE ALREADY HOME.

"What does that even—" Art stopped. "That wasn't a question."

"It *sounded* like a question," Grim said.

"No. It wasn't."

"A *little* bit." She held her finger and thumb so close. "Let's go to the judges. Survey says!"

She pointed at the scoreboard. A long dramatic pause. *Bing.* The third light.

"That's not fair," Art said.

"I mean, you *said* it."

"No, I didn't."

"You *thought* it. You want to pick?"

Art was thinking *What does that even mean?* But he didn't *say* it. It shouldn't count. He thumped his fists against his legs. Delight crept over Grim's scruffy cheeks and into those jaundiced eyes. Joy seemed to wilt with disappointment.

Grim ate a piece. Joy produced the answer.

YOU ARE HERE.

He threw the scrap of paper. "What does *that* mean?"

"I'm so sorry, darling," Joy said. "We only provide the answer. They are one hundred percent guaranteed."

"And guess who's *out* of questions?" Grim stood up and threw her arms out to the sides. Loose skin gathered around the elbows. "Thanks for playing. Hope you enjoyed your stay as much as we did. It's been real. It's been fun. You know how the rest of it goes, so *bye-bye.*"

The tufts of hair twittered at the ends of her fingers.

"*Unless...*"

"We would be open to three more questions," Joy said. "For a pair of your delightful drawings."

"But *we* get to pick!" Grim slammed a fist on the table. "Lay them out, sonny boy!"

Art thought long on it. The first three answers were no help. They were worse than generic horoscopes. The odds of the same kind of answers were one hundred percent guaranteed. And that smelly smile on that snaggled face wasn't helping. But the drawings didn't matter. He could make them again.

And he couldn't leave now, not yet. Where would he go?

He opened the book on the table. Joy glanced over them and picked one without a fuss. Grim hopped like a child in need of the bathroom. Little squeaks and squawks that might have been laughter or gagging. She balled her fists to her cheeks.

"So many *choices*! I can't pick. I can't pick! I WANT THEM ALL. Ooooh, this is torture. I hate this, hate this, hate this." She held her breath, grunting until her eyes turned the color of mustard. "I love them so *much.*"

Even if the next three questions were as useless as the last three, her dilemma was worth the price. Art watched her squirm and doubt and spin circles of frustration. It was delicious. And it was only getting better.

"Did you make these?" Joy said.

"I can't answer that," Art said. "You didn't purchase questions from me."

"Oh." A wave of fresh glitter sparkled on Joy's cheeks. "What would you like?"

"I want to go home."

"Kid, look." Grim groaned. "We've been *over* this. The answer is right there." She pointed at the first answer Joy puked up. "And I don't care one spit if you made these. I don't, I really don't. I just want them, and I'm going to have them—"

"Then I want three more questions for payment," Art said.

"Will you just shut up for a second and let me *concentrate* so I can—"

"He's right," Joy said abruptly. "I asked a question before payment was rendered, Grim. He gets to name his price."

"What?" Grim deadpanned.

"Three questions," Art said. "That's my price."

"That's not going to *happen*."

"I'm afraid he's right." Joy put her card back on the table. "We can't draw payment from him."

"*What?*"

"I'm sorry, sister. I wasn't thinking clearly. The drawings are so captivating, I lost focus."

An unexpected surprise was unfolding. Steam began rising from the knotted hair on Grim's head. Her eyes narrowed to darkened slits, the vertical pupils sliding from Art to Joy to Art to Joy.

Art tried not to grin. But not very hard.

"*WHAT?*"

Grim hammered the table with both fists. The sketchbook jumped, and the fruitcake jiggled. Joy backed away from her sister. What was coming, Art guessed, had happened before. The room smelled like roasting fur. The odor filled Art's nostrils and fouled his sinuses. It didn't spoil the satisfaction or the smile he no longer tried to hide.

"No. No, no, no, no—*NOOOO!*"

Grim bit the curtain with her teeth and shook it like a dog with a chew toy, the heavy fabric clogging the animal screams in her throat. She pulled it down and wadded it into a ball, fired it into the fireplace. It went up like newspaper. She destroyed the table with the glass of spoiled milk and stale cookies. Flies buzzed around (there were quite a bit more in the room).

She stomped the cookies into little bits.

Strangled the dead Christmas tree with both hands, squashing the sad ornaments that fell with her fat, fuzzy feet. Broke off limbs and snapped them over her knees. Threw them into the walls like ax handles.

Fell on her knees, seething.

Huffing. Puffing. And smoking.

She returned to the table and took the last bit of frustration out on the hairball she'd spit up, chucking it into the fireplace with the flaming curtain. She crossed her arms and bit her lower lip, staring icicles at Art. Joy nodded at her sister, then turned to Art.

"Ask your first question."

"Where's S'ven?"

Before Joy could tell him to pluck a gummy fruit from the cake, Grim dug out a handful and crammed it in her mouth. Moist crumbs got stuck in the matted fur sticking out of her T-shirt. She chewed without taking her eyes off Art.

Joy gagged.

It was a big bite her sister took. Payback for asking the question prematurely.

A strip of paper inched its way from between her lips. She passed it directly to Art this time.

ON HIS JOURNEY.

Well, he wasn't disappointed. The vagary met his expectations. "This is no help," Art said.

"When the student is ready," Joy said, "the teacher will appear."

Art didn't utter a word in response. But his eyebrow did rise in an arching manner. A questioning manner. And one Grim did not miss.

"Aha!" She reached across the table, finger waggling in his face, a tuft of hair tickling his nose. "Gotcha! GOTCHA!"

She swung her arm at the scoreboard.

"Survey says!"

Bing went the second light.

The scuffle of her feet was like sandpaper on a sea wall.

Art didn't argue this time. He hardly cared. What was the point of asking questions when the answers were vague nonsense? Grim bent down and bit from the fruitcake like a dog eating from a bowl. The chewing was loud and wet and sloppy. Bits shot across the table when she barked laughter.

The answer arrived.

THE ANSWERS ARE WITHIN.

Great, he thought, shooing the flies divebombing the crumbs shooting from Grim's caked lips. *When the student is ready, the teacher will appear means the answers are within. Got it.*

"What's your last question, *genius*?" Grim teased. "Why is the sky pink? Dogs bark? Is that air you're breathing?" A frown crashed down on her face. "That's *rhetorical!*"

She was shouting at some unseen judge lighting up the scoreboard. Art didn't want any more questions. So far these oddball oracles had told him he couldn't go back home, and the answers were within. It made no sense, what they were saying. If the answers were inside him, what was the point of a journey? And more importantly, *where were they inside him?*

It was pointless. All of this.

"Why even search?"

He didn't care if the question made sense. A part of him hoped it didn't. Maybe Grimjoy would feel a hint of the depression filling him.

Grim scooped two handfuls of fruitcake and mashed them into her mouth.

Chewing with loud satisfaction, nearly choking.

A bit of paper started crawling from Joy. It continued, curling like a long, flat tongue. She pulled it out, and it kept coming until it finally ended. She handed him twenty-four inches of paper.

Even Grim was curious. "Read *it*. Out loud, *read it.*"

Art read it to them. He said, "Is the mighty redwood in the seed? Is the pearl inside the oyster? The search is the water and the light. It is the grit. Without these, they are only seed and oyster with no treasure."

Art read it again, this time silently. His lips moving.

Grim was laughing. Mouth wide open, attracting flies to the fetid odor and slimy teeth.

It didn't bother Art at all. It wasn't the answer he was looking for. He was numb and lost. But something peaceful was in the unknowing. He'd stopped grasping for concrete answers. He'd been so desperate to find out how he'd gotten to this place and where it was and why he was there that he couldn't think of anything else.

None of that mattered now.

He was on a journey to somewhere. If he couldn't go back home, then he would go wherever it took him. He didn't know where. Maybe not home, but somewhere he belonged. He couldn't conceive of where that was because he'd never been there. That was how discoveries were made. Journeys into new and uncharted parts of life were mysteries. There was no way he could know where he was going.

And he was sort of okay with that now.

Trust would take him there. Just like Daryl had had him leap from the castle into Rose Lake.

Where nothing ever dies.

Flies had gathered on the remains of the fruitcake. It looked like feral hogs had been through it. Grim was licking her furry fingers, staring with fiery eyes and a snarl. Art pulled the cards out of the sketchbook and wiped them off. He pulled them all out. There were twenty of them. He threw two stacks of ten on the table.

"Three more questions?" Joy asked, surprised.

"No. Merry, merry." He pushed one of the stacks toward Grim. "Blah-blah."

❄

"You can't leave," Joy said.

Art had turned toward the double doors, Christmas spirit bubbling through him. He stopped abruptly, concerned what she meant by that. Grim was hugging the cards to her chest, rocking back and forth with a smile.

"Not the way you entered," Joy added. "You'll have to go this way or that."

She gestured to the door on her side of the room, the one that led to the candy-crush walkway he'd seen when he first arrived. There was a twin door on Grim's side of the room that led to the Naughty Side.

"Do I have to choose?" he said, flinching as he asked. Knowing she might not answer unless he paid for the question.

"One or the other."

He looked back and forth. One side was a dark disaster where Grim had thrown her tantrum. There was beauty in the field of ferns and shady tropicals, but that was just the beginning. The other side was bright and shiny and promised goodies. But he'd been there, and part of him didn't want to go back.

"It's an easy decision, darling." Joy batted her hairless eyelids. Her plastic smile stretched and glistened.

"Oh, is *it*?" Grim sneered. Then to Art: "Want to have *fun*, kid? Don't be nice."

"Hahahaha... oooh, you silly goose. We have the *most* fun. All we *do* is have fun."

"Sure, sure. If doing *chores* and following the *rules* is fun, you'll have a blast. Want to be merry, kid? Like really merry?" Grim clicked her tongue. "Red Rover, Red Rover... send Artie right over."

"We have respect and honor," Joy said.

"So do *we*."

"Fibbing is neither, sister."

Grim started to laugh. It started as a rumble and picked up steam. She stuffed the cards inside her stained T-shirt and clutched the lower half of her exposed belly. It jiggled and quaked. Rusty tears squeezed from her eyes, staining her face. Her nose started to leak. She covered one nostril with her thumb and cleared the other one on the floor.

"Oooooh, that's *rich*." Grim waved the flies away. "Everyone lies, you spoiled brat. You tell people they look nice when they *don't*! That's a lie!"

"It's an opinion. Arthur, choose a door."

The window on the Nice Side was growing dim. The Naughty Side was pitch black. There was nothing to see out there. Flies were now buzzing around Joy, and she didn't like it. The very first frown creased her face.

"Look at *her*," Grim said. "Trying to kill an innocent fly. That's *nice*."

"If you didn't leave food out, they wouldn't be here."

"I don't want Santa to *starve*. Do you?"

"Santa won't drink spoiled milk." She waved the cards at the circling insects. "Choose, Arthur."

"They're attracted to the stink of *fakeness*," Grim spouted with devilish glee. "You know why she wears perfume, kid? Because she smells like an armpit."

"I do not!"

"You *do*! Like a grody armpit! And that, my sister, is *not* a lie. *You* are *lying* about your smell, covering it up so no one knows who you *really* are."

"Choose, Arthur." Joy stiffened. "Naughty or nice."

"And those *gorgeous* eyes? Contacts! I seen her put contacts in *those* eyes so they're *that* color. The glitter on her cheeks? Lies! Lies, lies, LIES!"

"Arthur, please—"

"I am the *TRUTH*!" Grim bellowed. "Like me or not, you see who I *am*. I am *real*!"

Art stepped back. The room was vibrating with little flying things. Someone needed to open a window or turn on a fan. Art wanted to be on his way, but he didn't want to choose a side.

"What you *see* is what you *get!*" Grim threw handfuls of fruitcake across the room. They stuck like mud on the walls. Flies swarmed over them. "Choose, kid! You want to be fake? Then we don't want you. You want to be who you are, no judgment, accepted with all your faults and shortcomings? Come to the—"

A coughing fit overwhelmed her. Bent over with a string of drool on her lip, she gagged and spit. Joy fanned her face with both hands, no longer opening her mouth to say anything. Grim stood up and gave one last pitch.

"COME TO THE NAUGHTY SIDE!"

THE DOOR on the Naughty Side burst open. A black cloud swarmed into the room. The roar of tiny wings blotted out all sound. Grim and Joy faded into a swirling cloud. Art turned to escape, unsure what direction he was going. First door he found, he was taking. But tiny whispers floated inside the swarm.

Secure the arms!

Art's right arm was pinned to his side, the elbow grinding into his ribs. His left arm followed. Bugs crawled on his face, tickled his nose and ears. He closed his eyes and walked carefully to avoid hitting a wall.

Take the legs!

His ankles popped together, pain flaring in his feet. His momentum continued forward. He braced for impact, turning his shoulder to avoid faceplanting on the floor. But the crash never came. Something slowed his descent and lowered him gently. He thrashed like an animal in a trap.

Incapacitate!

Bindings whipped around and around until he was encased in a cocoon. He didn't dare open his eyes, but then it didn't matter when a blindfold was dropped over them.

Hitch lines, ready!

The cocoon shrank and took his breath away.

Right flank! HEAVE!

In the chaos and confusion, the blackness of the blindfold and silence of the noise, Art felt a sudden wave of peace fill him. He was snug in its grip, floating off the ground. He surrendered to the helplessness.

One of the doors opened.

11

"Incoming!"

The voice was tiny but brash. A sharp voice that cut through buzzing static. It was followed by three blasts from a horn. The kind of horn that warned large ships. Something large and wet was released. It sounded like cold slush sliding from the metal bed of a dump truck.

A new smell hit Art in the nose.

He turned his head. His ear grinding into the grit beneath him. His head the only thing he could move. His body trapped under crisscrossed bindings pinning him to the ground. Filling him with panic.

A bit of light slipped through the bottom of the blindfold. Sharp white lines suggested he wasn't on the Naughty Side after all. But the wet sucking sounds, things writhing in a pool of something foul. The *smell* stung his nostrils and corrupted his sinuses. The kind of smell beyond an expiration date. A smell that seeped into pores.

He started to gag.

Convulsions knotted his gut. He couldn't move, couldn't cover his face or see where he was. The urge rose on a wave of terror.

"Raise the fold!"

The voice was closer this time. A cloud passed over him, cutting past the light sneaking under the blindfold. Teams of tiny wings orbited his face. One by one, they landed in his hair. On his ears. Little membranous wings tickling his cheeks. He shook his head, tried to blow them off.

"Easy there, crossa," he heard. "Be still a moment. We helpin' not hurtin'."

This was someone new. Still far away, sounding deeply Southern and relaxed. Art did his best not to move. Pins and needles poked at his face. The wings went into another gear. A slight breeze on his face and the blindfold began to slide. The light grew whiter. And then punched through his eyes and into his brain.

He turned his head. A maroon afterglow hovered in his vision.

He wanted to raise his hands, rub his eyes. Even his fingers were immobilized. There was nowhere to turn, no way to escape the smells or sights. The tide of panic still rising.

"Easy goes it now," the voice drawled. "Breathe through your mouth and crack your lids a li'l at a time. C'mo now. You can do it."

Art pursed his lips and breathed through an imaginary straw, one that delivered fresh air. It was enough to open his eyes. Just enough to see blurry forms. It looked like a giant Christmas tree in the distance. The way it was shaped. The way it glistened.

There were banks of light above him. The kind that lit stadiums. They beamed down on wide leaves dripping with condensation and dangling roots. Glass panels were above the lights, hexagonal in shape, interconnecting a giant biodome. And beyond that was the dim sky.

Little black specks zigzagged through the lights. Flies. Tens of thousands of them. Maybe millions.

"Well done, ladies. Off ya go, now."

Art couldn't see who said it. There was movement on the ground. Insects not more than a few feet from his nose. It was mostly houseflies. The odd thing was they weren't moving all that much. A hundred or so were in formation—two blocks—and they weren't standing. They were sitting. Art's eyes were burning from the rank odors inside the biodome, but he could swear they were seated in itty-bitty chairs. An audience watching a movie on Art's face.

Two toothpicks were anchored in a stained wine cork between the blocks of insects. Wee little flags hung from them, one red and the other green. Without a breeze, the emblems were hidden in the folds.

A horsefly stood out front. It was twice the size of the houseflies. The multifaceted compound eyes aimed at Art. "Ya hear me, son?" it said. Although it wasn't an *it*. The horsefly was more like a *he*. "Nod if ya do."

Art blinked. It was all he could do. The stress of being tied to the ground with bugs all around was dreadful. Add to that a contingent of insects watching over him and one of them talking like a Southern general.

"Why don't he answer?"

The horsefly addressed a bug standing off to the side. It was a fly (they were all flies), but this one shimmered green as it scurried over. It spoke softly. Art could barely hear it.

"He might be in shock, sir."

"Shock? I don't imagine he seen worse. He's been here long enough to wrap his head around us. Let me get a close-up and talk him down."

The green fly bolted from the ground. It was a few minutes before it returned (Art decided that wasn't a Christmas tree on the far side of the biodome). A black box was lowered next to the horsefly by a swarm of flies. It looked like helicopters delivering a care package. The green fly crawled over the box.

A round fisheye lens unfolded like a switchblade.

It dropped in front of the horsefly. Art really wished it hadn't.

It wasn't just a horsefly standing on hindlegs. He was wearing a uniform. The kind with medals and a scabbard on a belt. And the green fly, he was wearing a uniform, too. So were the houseflies sitting in their chairs in organized lines. And wearing uniforms, you bet.

Art began to laugh. What else could he do? *When will I wake up?*

When he opened his eyes, they were still there. The air was still rank and full of insects, and the glistening mountain shaped like a Christmas tree still glistened.

The green fly fixed something on the horsefly's coat. "Try again, sir."

"Hm-mm." The horsefly cleared his throat. The sound was amplified. In that deep, Southern accent, he said, "Son, can ya hear me?"

Art nodded.

The audience of houseflies threw up their arms (or legs, if you please) and cheered. It sounded like the tiny voices of cartoon chipmunks. It went on for a full minute. When it died down, leaving only the background buzz of airborne bugs, the horsefly leaned into the fisheye lens. The bulbous eyes were the size of quarters.

"I'm General Fly. General Gnat won't be joinin' us. He just might make it back before you're gone, but no matter."

Before I'm gone? That could be really good news or the total opposite.

"In the meantime, you are in our custody. This ain't an act of war, you bein' a crossa from another world an' all. It is written in the Candy Code that should a crossa be identified, they will be detained in safe keepin'. At present, that is what you are, son. Detained and safe. Am I makin' myself clear?"

Art nodded.

The general covered the thing that amplified his voice and muttered something to the green fly assistant. They conferred on something. When the general returned to the fisheye, he puffed out his chest, put the medals on full display.

"We have a bit of a problem, son. You are not a citizen and have not declared allegiance to Naughty or Nice. Is this true? That's what I thought. I am goin' to have to read you your rights, ya understand?" The general cleared his throat. Art could see the mouthparts working. "You have the right to remain merry. Anything you sing will not be ridiculed or judged in anger. If you have needs, they will be attended to to the best of our ability. You have a right to an understandin'. Should you request an explanation, a representative will be assigned to give one. Do you understand these rights? Say yes or nod your head."

Art nodded.

"Good. Now, do you have any needs that need attendin' at present?"

"I-I-I need to get loose. I can hardly breathe."

"I'm afraid I can't do that right this second. Shortly, though. Count on it."

Art closed his eyes. Panic that had receded in the shock of awareness was starting to catch a second wind. A sheen of sweat broke on his forehead.

"You look thirsty, son. We got eggnog only a day old in the pantry. Seal ain't even broken. No? You sure?"

"Water," Art whispered.

"Plant drink?" There was a ripple of tiny laughter. "Why in Candyland would you want that? Son, we got flat soda, warm ginger ale, hot corn syrup, and spicy cider. None of it more than a week old."

Art repeated his request.

He kept his eyes closed. He didn't want to see the team that would deliver his drink. He stayed that way, breathing as slowly as possible, until the tip of a straw knocked on his lips. He drank with greed. The water was warm and slightly sweet. He drank until it was gone and the straw pulled from his mouth.

"You like the plant drink, then, all right. How about somethin' to eat? No? Didn't think so. This ain't your kind of food, I imagine." A ripple of laughter from the gallery. "Okay, well, I want to start by thankin' you for comin' along peaceful an all. No swattin' or sprayin' saved us some trouble, and none of the ladies were hurt during your translocation. For that, I am grateful."

A smattering of applause. Art peeked to see them clapping their legs.

"Merry, merry to you, son," the general said.

"Blah-blah," Green Fly Assistant corrected.

"I ain't sayin' that. It's merry, merry and always will be. That's what time it is, to be merry. Now, despite what's around you, we made every effort to make you comfortable. Are you comfortable?"

Art shook his head. "Get me loose, please."

"Soon. Very soon, I promise. Hold tight for me, son. You with me?"

He looked at Green Fly Assistant, who replied, "Two ticks."

"In about two ticks, all right? In the meantime, I want to fulfill your right to an explanation. Is that okay with you? Okay. All around you is home to the finest regiment this side of the border. We live by a code of honor and are the first in line to defend our side. When we are called to protect, then by golly we shall. We were ordered to capture a crossa. That crossa is you, son.

"Now, you ain't a threat. Anyone can see that. You ain't nothin' like the last one who come stompin' through the Nice Side and destroyin' the castle. You're a special one, I reckon. I don't know why that is and no offense. Whatever it is that makes you special, I'm just glad you didn't side with the Nice. They're a good lot. Nothin' against them. They mean well, just not our kind of folken, you could say. They ain't all shallow and naïve, but a good bit are, if you know what I mean. Now—"

A fly dropped out of nowhere and handed the general something far too small to see. The general muttered his thanks. Then he stopped Green Fly Assistant from turning off his amplifier.

"The boy should hear it," General Fly said. "It's about him, after all." The general spoke into something he was holding. "General Fly present. Yes, sir, that is correct. We have the crossa in custody. He is immobilized and has been read his rights. He has refused food and— right, right."

A long pause while he listened to a voice Art could not hear.

"I'm afraid we cannot deliver him, sir. No, sir, that's right. Troops were taxed getting him to Fly Dome. Correct, sir. He weighs an awful lot. Okay, yes. Yes. That would be fine. We'll have him ready and... oh, no, sir. No, a medal is not necessary. It was our duty. Although a gesture for the hardworking ladies who made this acquisition happen would be more than enough. A delivery of chocolate sludge?"

He turned to the contingent behind him. They erupted with cheers, embracing each other, throwing tiny hats in the air. The general ended the call and celebrated with a few of the nearest ladies. When they returned to their seats, stirring with giddiness, he stood in front of the fisheye once again.

"Your transfer will arrive soon. We'll get you out of the bindings in no time. Now, where was I? The Nice Side, right. They think we lack respect and honor. That's what the twin said, the one named Joy. There are many who dwell here in the shadows who do lack such respect and honor. *But not flies!*"

"Hoo-ah! Hoo-ah! Hoo-ah!" the regiment chanted.

"The Nice Side thinks they're better than us. They think—"

He was interrupted by the foghorn. Three short blasts announced the next payload. This one a special delivery of chocolate sludge. Art turned toward the glistening mountain in time to see a chunky landslide pour out of a chute. It spilled a load of dark slime from the ceiling. It tumbled down the sides of the pyramidal mountain. Bits of trash were buried in the side of it. Candy wrappers and plastic toys and rotten food and broken playthings, fish bones and loose fur.

The new delivery set off a landslide. The enormous, putrefied pile teetered on a round platform. And when globs of gray stuff rolled over the edge, it plopped into a soupy basin where white larva squirmed among bits of discarded candy and mushy cookies.

Panic arrived with a head of steam and broke something inside Art. He opened his mouth to let it all out.

"Cut him loose!"

Art heard the general cry out the order in between screams. Art thrashed his head side to side, as that was the only thing he could move. Claustrophobia had taken over. He might as well be in a box, tied down the way he was. The smells piling on top.

"Sir," Green Fly Assistant objected, "I don't think—"

"He's havin' a panic attack. I seen it before. Start cuttin', ladies!"

A swarm went airborne and blocked out the light from overhead. They divebombed in formation like fighter jets on a mission. Buzzing past Art's ears, over his open mouth, down to the ground where the thin ropes were anchored.

Plink!

The bindings snapped like guitar strings playing an awful tune. Houseflies were flying in small squadrons, clipping the wires in midair. The bindings flew off in bunches. Art wiggled his fingers, then his arms.

Plinkplink!

He bent his knees and turned his hips. Rolled onto his side. He'd stopped screaming by now but couldn't slow his breathing. Hyperventilating short, choppy breaths. He began kicking his legs and flailing his arms. He had to get away and out of this rotten meat locker. Had to—

PLINKPLINKPLINK!

He rolled across the ground, crashed into the nearest hedge. Sticky drops of dew rained down on him. He crawled out of the bushes and shook like a dog, wiping down his arms and legs and face as if the heebie-jeebies were something he could wash off. He pulled his shirt over his nose.

The chocolate sludge slowly slid down the slag heap where bits of wrapping paper and soggy boxes were trapped. Apple cores and orange peels, pineapple slices and carrot tops. Cookies and cakes, things that could break were swallowed in the fudgy landslide that dripped like fermented icing with bits of corn and beans and hard candy. They oozed from the round tabletop into the writhing cesspool below.

"This way!" The general's voice went buzzing past.

The wall of Fly Dome was twenty feet away. One of the hexagonal panels was open. Art could feel the hint of fresh air. He staggered toward it, throwing all his momentum at it before it closed. He burst into humid air with sweat cooling his cheeks and forehead, dropping to his hands and knees, taking in long draughts of clean air—clean, humid air! Spitting the lingering taste onto the mossy ground.

The panel behind him closed with a muffled impact. A latch fell into place. The nuclear sound of a million beating wings went silent. The putrid odors vanquished. Outside the biodome, crickets sang and frogs chirped.

Condensation fell from one leaf to another.

Art leaned against a striped tree trunk, pulled his knees to his chest. Never would he take fresh air for granted again. He rubbed his arms where the bindings had left crisscrossing marks. The urge to weep was rising toward his eyes. The runaway Panic Attack began to flutter. He remembered someone telling him what to do when this happened, to breathe slower.

He laid his head between his knees. And began to count.

"Ya did good, son."

General Fly tickled the hairs on his arm as he scurried up it. Art didn't lift his head.

"You were looking gray in the gills for a tick, though. But ya held it together. Proud of ya. Now take a nibble. It does the boys a bit of good when they ain't feelin' right. Brings them around right side."

Art could smell it before he lifted his head. A square of chocolate was on the ground. He didn't ask how it got there or how many flies had walked on it. It was crisp, not slimy, and newly unwrapped. He put the whole thing in his mouth. It melted on his tongue, washed away foul odors still hanging around. A chocolatey explosion filled his stomach.

The jitters evaporated.

Anxiety went bye-bye.

"There ya are," General Fly called. "Just like the boys. They can't live without the stuff."

Whatever was in that wafer lifted him out of the funk to a level that was bright and shiny, new and exciting. It stripped away the heaviness, the sadness, and the worry. Escorted Panic and Anxiety out the door. He was still sore and hot and in need of a shower. But he didn't care anymore. He was better.

This is who I am, he thought. The chocolate made him feel like himself.

The world was right. And he was talking to a fly. A little fly in a military uniform with tiny medals on it. Art wanted to hug the general and would've if it wouldn't have crushed the delicate wings.

"Thank you."

"Don't thank me. We dragged you here; just glad you made it. The boys will be here to take ya on the way."

Art laid his head back on the tree and smiled. He paid no attention to what the general was saying. Didn't care about any boys or where they were going to take him. "It smells bad in there. No offense."

"None taken. It's all perspective, son. Change how you see things and you change the world."

"Right." Art chuckled. *Change how you see things...* that was deep.

"You might call that a heap of garbage in there. I call it dinner. Where do you think all those fish bones and broken toys and whatever else comes out of that chute come from? That's straight from the Nice Side, son. All the things they don't want, they send right over. They can't be troubled with lookin' old and dirty, so down the chute it goes. They have to keep up appearances. They got to look nice, know what I mean?"

The general buzzed in a circle and dropped on the back of Art's hand. Standing on hind legs, he puffed up with his medals on display.

"You smell death in there? I smell life. A heap teeming with microscopic life. Billions and trillions of bacteria and things is what that is. Does their size make life less important? Am I less important than you?"

Art shook his head. The general was almost an inch tall and felt like a giant.

"What would happen if it weren't for us? Or the bacteria in there?

We're every bit as important. We ain't less than, son. That land needs us."

Fly Dome beamed white light from inside, casting sharp shadows into the trees. Art could feel the ground hum with life. Maybe he just imagined it. Beneath all the rightness of the chocolatey goodness running through him, he felt the gouge of worthlessness somewhere inside himself. It didn't bother him, but it was there. It was deep. That he didn't matter.

"I never made a difference," he mumbled.

"Maybe so. But I can tell you this. There's life ahead of you. And this life you got, the pain you feel and the blues that drag behind you might feel impossible. But there will come a moment, maybe far away from here, that you make a difference in one person's life. Just *one*. And you're the only one who can make it. You'll look back at all this sufferin' and ask yourself if it's all worth it. Was it worth the price to help the one person? You'll know the answer. Deep down, you'll know."

A truly amused chuckle came out. "Doubt it."

"My eyes are better than yours." Light reflected off the many lenses in the general's compound eyes. "It's why I accepted the mission to go get you."

Art nodded. "You have any more chocolate?"

The general didn't get a chance to answer.

It happened all at once. From all directions.

Branches snapping. Leaves sweeping off the ground.

The boys were all around Art, still sitting on his bottom, leaning against the tree. General Fly watched from his forearm, head twitching left and right. Art didn't recognize them; they were going so fast and in so many directions. What they were riding, though, he knew what those were.

Long, skinny boards that cut the air.

The boys slalomed between striped trees, careened off Fly Dome with heavy hollow *thumps.* Their lean bodies tilted into the turns, pressing the boards forward. Their shirts soaked. Skin glistening with sweat.

Art didn't move.

He watched the show play out with a slight smile, resting in the euphoric state called *Chocolate Brain.* And he liked it there. It felt right. The world was okay. He was more than okay. Even the chaos felt more like a dance than a threat.

"All right, boys." General Fly's voice was on the amplifier again. Art's forearm was his stage. "Take it down a notch before ya break somethin'. Take the young man where he's going, straight to it. No sidetrackin', now. And be careful. He's been through a lot."

Art felt the general pat his arm. Or he imagined it. The things that happened in Chocolate Brain didn't always happen.

The boys slowed their dance, kicking up their beams and slinging them over their backs. A gang of pointy-eared troublemakers, the same crew that tried to catch him on the way to the border. The same crew he'd *borrowed* from. Although they weren't wearing sunglasses anymore. Their eyes were swallowed in pupils with thin rings of color. Eyes that cut through the Chocolate Brain and gave Art the shivers.

The last of them rode up.

Two of them were on one beam. The boy on the back clutched the shirt of the boy steering from the front. They slid to a stop, splashing leaves and dirt against Fly Dome. The one on the back got off. Art recognized this one. It was the imp from the market, the one who found him hiding in the alley and gave him the chocolate stamped *KC.*

Rude, the other boy had called him, the boy who yanked him out of the alley. Then Art thought with a shadowy smile, *Rude Boy.*

"Ee's a lot mo' comin'," Rude Boy blurted. "Snacked muh beam and ee'll make change for it."

Art had yet to move or understand a single thing the imp said. He was stomping toward him, boney chest puffed up, sharp elbows thrown back. General Fly translated for Art.

"You stole his beam."

"No. I didn't steal anything."

"Ee run it four lines and a half. Two in the ki'chen." Rude Boy stood over Art, long fingers curled into fists. "Mind ee to beam, have you? Aye have it on back or thump it from your gourd."

"Your friend here," General Fly said, "wants to know where you learned to beam. And he also wants it back."

"I left it at Grimjoy's."

The boys snickered at the name. All except Rude Boy, whose knuckles went white. "Oh two dingies. It's bad as gone, then. Ee owe me."

Rude Boy took another step. Art rolled off the tree and got to his feet before he got any closer. Everyone shuffled toward him and around him. A loose circle formed, cutting off any thoughts of escape.

"Settle it with the king," General Fly announced. "Best get on your way, boys."

"Ee'll settle on point, buzzy. Back to your slop and mind your maggots."

The words triggered an alarm, one Art didn't hear. In seconds, the trees shivered. Flies hovered and zipped and crawled. One of them couldn't hurt the boys. A million of them, though?

"You boys had best behave," the general's voice bellowed. Art couldn't see where the highly decorated horsefly had gone. "I'll have you strung in the trees like Christmas lights and dip you in the pool. You understand, now?"

The boys understood. They were as still as tree trunks. Big black pupils dialed on Art, not moving.

General Fly landed on Art's shoulder. He buzzed quietly in his ear. "Did you steal the beam, son?"

"I didn't mean to. But, yeah. I stole it."

"Fair enough," the general said. Then loudly proclaimed: "Settle it quick, boys. Or the king will send you for a swim. Keep it fair, though. Just the two of you. A race out to the swamp and back would do ya, far as I'm concerned."

"Nah, buzzy," Rude Boy said. "Skin on bone 'ill do it."

Art didn't need a translation. The look in those big black eyes spoke clearly enough. Art didn't get a sense he knew how to fight. There was no hidden instinct for it like there was when he rode the beam.

"What's that going to prove?" Art said.

"Steal on me, wrecker, and ee give up a piece for pay."

Art got the gist of it. He apologized. No point in explaining it was a cat who stole it. Art had had a good reason to ride off on it, not one they'd care to hear. If this was about the beam, they could go back to the border and find it. But it wasn't about that.

"It's for honor, son," the general whispered. "What little he has, he's got to save."

Art backed away from Fly Dome. The air vibrated with the beating of countless wings. He felt safe with the flies watching over him. He wasn't scared of the boys. Even with Rude Boy closing in on him. In an odd way, Art felt drawn to the boys. They were outcasts. He wanted to ride with them, follow them through the trees, feel the wind on his face. Jump down the steps and slam a beam on the concrete.

Because they were his people. He could feel it. *Lost Boys.*

"Sorree don't git a beam on my soles," Rude Boy said.

"Neither does fighting."

"Ee'll feel flighty though."

The boys laughed at that. *I'll feel better,* Art translated. Or something like that.

Rude Boy jumped up and down and wagged his arms. He entertained the Lost Boys with a wild dance. Like a chimp establishing rank. He took a foil-wrapped coin from his hip pack and made a show of peeling it open, biting it in half like a hyena ripping open prey. Chewing it loudly, smacking his lips and smearing his teeth.

Art's mouth watered. He spoke without thinking.

"Will ee nick of snap for me?" Art said.

He had no idea where the words came from. He knew what they meant, though. And so did the Lost Boys, who looked at each other with startled delight. They roared with laughter, doubled over and pointing not at Art, but at Rude Boy, who found it not funny at all. The very opposite.

All Art wanted was a bite of chocolate. He stole the spotlight, instead.

"Enough show, boys," General Fly. "Time is tickin', and the king is waitin'. Settle up and get on your way."

Rude Boy was all for it.

Art's plan was to pull him to the ground and wrap his arms and legs around the pointy-eared lost boy and hang on as long as he could. Rude Boy circled around. Art bent his knees, bounced on the balls of his feet. He flinched when Rude Boy feigned a charge. The sharp edge of stress cut through the cottony comfort of Chocolate Brain. Art just wanted to get it over with. He was going to make the first move.

Then fruit fell from a tree.

A BIG SHINY orb thumped on the ground and burst open, spilling juicy flesh full of sparkling seeds. Then another fell. And another.

Then all the trees started dumping fruit.

It sounded like drums. Like an oversized hailstorm.

Everyone covered their heads. The flies were stirred into flight. The general flew circles around Art. The ground trembled. A mild earthquake sent the army of flies inside the dome. Art's knees were weak. And then a voice spread throughout the land. It was childlike and enormous.

It said: "*YUM!*"

The Lost Boys jumped on their beams and scattered. They circled in figure-eights, falling into some unspoken formation like birds in flight.

"HOLD!" General Fly ordered. "Not without the boy!"

One of the boys broke out of line and zipped past Art, snatching him by the piggly-wiggly shirt (also stolen) and dragging him onto the back of the beam. Art grabbed the boy's back and quickly found his balance. They were at the back of the line, heading into the trees.

General Fly zipped in front of Art and saluted.

Art felt the next tremor. It shook the trees and the ground and the sky above. Everyone slowed down. A few of the boys fell off their beams. Art held on tightly as they banked into a turn. One of the riderless beams hit a tree and bounced into the canopy. Art leaped into the tree and climbed up to reach it, pulling it down. He was riding it before he hit the ground, cutting through the undergrowth. The one who lost the beam held up his arm. Art slowed down, locking arms and heaving him onto the back of the beam.

"YUM! YUM!"

The boy held onto Art's shirt with both hands. They followed the Lost Boys through the bush, over fallen logs and between boulders, down a mossy trail toward a fizzy stream that smelled like cherry soda.

Art's heart hissed with adrenaline.

Steady tears streamed across his temples.

This was what he wanted. This feeling. This freedom. This wild, untethered freedom that sang in his veins and bloomed on his cheeks. This lovely chaos spoke to him. It was his song.

And then branches above him broke.

He was pulled off the beam and into the dim sky above and away from where his heart felt at home. Just like that, he was lost again. Truly.

"YUM!"

12

The stagecoach jostled King Chocolate like a mixed drink.

The roads were rough this far out. How far the Naughty Side went, no one really knew. King Chocolate had sent explorers over the mountains. They always came back with no memory of what they saw. Just a jolly good time. The idiots.

King Chocolate wasn't going that far out. Just into the Cacao Wildwoods, where the ground was bitter and the trees were dense. How bitter and dense, he had no idea. Shades had been installed over the window of the new stagecoach, and he hadn't seen a thing since leaving his castle. Just the two dingdongs sitting across from him.

"Close your eyes," Jelly said when the stagecoach began to slow.

"I'm not closing my eyes," King Chocolate said.

"It's a surprise. Close your eyes."

"I'm not a *child*!" He shifted in the throne. His bum was sore from all the bumps in the road. "And I hate surprises."

"You do not."

"I just told you I do."

"You specifically said when we started the project *I would love this to be a surprise.*"

"You did," Santa Claus said. "I heard it."

"No one asked you." King Chocolate harrumphed. Then added: "You're not even real."

He probably had said it. He'd totally said it. But he didn't want to be surprised now. He just wanted to get what he wanted. It had been a long ride, and he was overstimulated. Also, he had high expectations for this project. Jelly had warned him about expectations. *Future disappointments*, she had said.

Not if they do their jobs they're not.

The stagecoach was barely moving now. They settled in their seats. Santa Claus didn't jitter.

"Can you not look at me like that?" King Chocolate turned to Jelly slumped against the padded bench. "Why is he programmed like that anyway?"

"Like what?"

"All judgy! Look at him, taking my inventory with his eyes. I don't like it."

"You wanted Santa Claus."

"You don't know what he's like. He could be an angry fat man who doesn't like to shave, with horrible taste in winter wear. And *not* judgy."

"If he's angry, he'd be judgy."

"That's a mean thing to say, Casey," Santa added.

"No, it's not. Those are facts. And theories. Something I heard someone say. Besides, I'm not mean. You are."

"You are," Jelly said. "A li'l bit."

"You can shut up, too. I put you—"

"HERE!" the driver shouted from above.

The stagecoach came to a complete stop. Butterflies took flight and fluttered throughout the generous space of King Chocolate's stomach. It felt like Christmas morning, all antsy pantsy to see what was under the tree. He'd explode if he waited any longer.

The levitating hoversuit gripped and hummed. Squeezed the breath out of him. Like a girdle from a magical torture chamber, it lifted him out of the throne. His twiggy legs twittered beneath him.

"Open the door," he said. "Open it. OPEN IT!"

The side of the stagecoach popped open like the lid on a jack-in-the-box. Stairs unfolded. He floated down, pretending to walk on them. The curly toes of his designer shoes (*Flockeby Manor shoes are very expensive*, the Triad had told him) clunked on the treads.

His smile faded to neutral confusion. Followed by annoyance. Bordering on rage.

Nothing but blackened trees. The bark smooth and shiny, almost glassy. Hard as diamonds. Not one of them had been cut down.

A welcome party was on the side of the rutted road.

A patched-up stuffed doggy, a dirty teddy bear. And a wrinkled lump of something with two googly eyes. While waving triangular pennants on wooden sticks, they put their fingers to their mouths and kissed them.

"What's this?" King Chocolate said flatly.

"Your fan club," Jelly said. "I think they want autographs."

On cue, they held out the pennants. King Chocolate spit on them. Coffee-colored spots stained the stiff fabric. The wrinkly lump was the most excited to get the king's autograph.

"What are you?" King Chocolate asked.

"He's a prune," Jelly said.

It looked nothing like a prune, bouncing up and down like a rotten soccer ball.

"Beat it." King Chocolate turned to Jelly and sipped a long breath of air. The rage was ready for duty. "What am I looking at? And don't say trees."

The stagecoach slowly pulled away. Jelly waited for it to be out of the way, then pointed across the road and started to answer. King Chocolate cut her off.

"What I should be looking at is a stage, you helpless batbrain. I should be seeing a mosh pit and spotlights and drums and those things you walk on, the things overhead that are skinny and—"

"Catwalks," Jelly said.

"NOT TREES! I didn't bruise my delicate cushions just to see—" King Chocolate looked at what Jelly was pointing at. "You little stinker," he said. "I should sit on you."

"You love surprises."

"I do."

She knew him so well.

THEY CROSSED the road to a lighted boardwalk.

King Chocolate's long, flowing Christmas coat dragged along, giving the impression he was floating. Which he was. His shoes could be heard dragging across every board.

The boardwalk journeyed between trees and over stumps, down a long winding slope. Gorilla workers wearing dented hardhats and holding deep-toothed saws stopped what they were doing when he passed, kissing their fingers like the welcoming party had done.

"The ticket booth is over there." Jelly pointed to a tunnel. "It'll send everyone through the gift shop and then the concession stands. General seating will be to the left, standing room in front of the stage. VIP booths on the right. Corporate skyboxes up there."

Treehouses were lit with string lights.

"Attendance is required. Every Naughty has been notified it is not an option. Anyone or anything will be fined if they don't purchase a ticket. There are affordable ones way in the back. Anyone who doesn't buy a ticket gets one of *them* knocking on their door."

Them were the gorilla workers.

"Commemorative shirts are not included in the ticket price, but all attendees are required to purchase one. If they don't—"

"I don't like this." Santa Claus walked alongside them, his black galoshes treading silently. "Christmas is not about profit."

King Chocolate came to a halt. Jelly did, too.

Santa went three more steps. He turned around. Stunned silence swelled between the three of them. Jelly looked up at King Chocolate. He looked down at her. They looked at Santa Claus.

Laughter went off like party favors.

Hysterical whining and hitching of breath. Tears literally squirting from their eyes. Jelly hung onto King Chocolate's coat to keep from falling over. King Chocolate veered to the edge of the boardwalk and almost went over.

"I can't breathe! I can't breathe!" King Chocolate bellowed between breathless guffaws.

Jelly punched her chest as if her heart had stopped.

When the hysterics faded to giggles and gulps, the king and Jelly attempting to hug each other for support, King Chocolate blurted to Santa (who had yet to smile):

"Christmas... not for... profit? What world... do you *live in*?" More laughter. Jelly fell on the boardwalk and almost rolled off. "You really are Santa," King Chocolate said. "Oh, oh. I think I tore a lung."

Santa Claus walked away. He wouldn't get far since Jelly had the projector in her pocket.

THE STAGE WAS MASSIVE. The width of a football field with those walky things over it. *Catwalks.* Movie screens as tall as stadiums on both ends. Banks of lighting anchored in the trees. The brightness was worse than the Nice Side. Hundreds of workers wore black sunglasses. Sawing trees and turning bolts and pounding nails. It smelled like fame.

"The green room's on that side." Jelly pointed to a giant box behind the stage. "You'll be projected onto the screens the entire time."

"Whoa, whoa. I didn't sign up for *that*."

"It won't be live. It'll be put together with AI." Jelly winked. "No one will know the difference. You'll be in the green room, sipping chocolate syrup from a hose. And then, just before Christmas, you come onstage."

"Hang on—"

"They'll want to see you in the flesh. And you'll want to strut around in your new hoversuit. Right? Right?" Jelly held her hands to her mouth. "*Choc-late! Choc-late! Choc-late!*"

He didn't hate the idea. He shouldn't deprive them of their king.

Jelly climbed the steps leading up to the stage. King Chocolate floated behind her. Santa behind him. Mop-top roadies were working on an elevated platform, assembling a thirty-piece drum kit with four bass drums. A lanky orange octopus was tuning the snare drums. They all gestured when they saw the king. Fingers to their lips.

He would never get tired of that.

THE TRIAD WAS CENTER STAGE.

The fashion waifs were holding rolled plans, pointing at spotlights and arguing with a mop-top roadie. They dropped the plans when King Chocolate arrived. Their eyes swelling and jaws dropping. They swarmed around him, plucking at the overcoat they designed, fawning over the way it hung on him, how he floated over the stage. A vision of grace and power.

"And that there." The green one twirled his finger. "What is that?"

King Chocolate dug the gold chain from the inside of his coat, displayed the medallion in his sweaty palm. The letters *KC* raised on the center. He braced for their reaction. The chain wasn't their idea, so they would probably hate it.

"I love it, I love it," the green one said. "I *looooooove* it."

"Really?"

"Oh, yes-yes-yes," the red one said. "It radiates power and strength. Wealth." The red one made a fist. "*I am the king, and this is my necklace!*"

"It's not too much?"

"My dear," the blue one said, "can anything be *too much*?"

The three of them laughed. King Chocolate did, too. He wasn't certain why or convinced they really liked the necklace. The downside to wielding power. If they told the truth, he'd throw them in Fudgy Lake.

"It's good you're here now," the green one said. "We're discussing the exit play. I think you will like. Come, come."

The Triad came together like magnets. They swayed when they

walked. It made King Chocolate a little motion sick watching them. At the far side of the stage, a polka-dotted tarp was covering a large object. King Chocolate smiled. He couldn't remember telling Jelly that he'd always wanted a monster truck, but what else could it be?

Several roadies were called over. They attached ropes to eyehooks at the edge of the tarp.

"Ready?" the red one asked.

King Chocolate quaked with anticipation. When the tarp was lifted to the catwalks, his expectations were dashed. No monster truck. It was a photo. A giant photo.

A photo!

Imagine wanting a monster truck for Christmas and getting a photo of one instead. And worse, it wasn't even a monster truck!

It had golden rails and torpedo rocket boosters. A slick, aerodynamic chassis with a bucket seat and a dashboard of buttons and switches and doodads. It was brown and gold and silver. A long lead of chains was attached to the front of it. He was speechless. He didn't know what it was. He didn't know whom to drop in Fudgy Lake first.

"After the ceremony is over," the green one said, "you will fly off into the night in your brand-new—"

"SLEIGH!" the three of them screamed.

King Chocolate ground his teeth. Jelly patted his arm. She could feel the storm coming. Patting his arm was her way of calming him down. To wait and listen. He could be hasty. Like the time he threw the plumber in the lake for not using gold pipes on the royal toilet.

"A sleigh?" King Chocolate said through gritted teeth.

"Yes, yes." The green one gestured. "Like Santa."

"Pulled by reindeer?"

"No, no, no," the blue one said. "Pulled by those."

Over by the trees, just past the blackened stumps that had not been shredded and buried, yellow flames danced from a trash can. Several wolves stood around it, some with their paws over the fire. Others were on all fours, playing a game that involved dice. From a distance, their rough laughter could be heard.

"Is that the Big Bad Wolf?" Jelly said.

"It is," the red one said.

"Oh my God, oh my God. My niece is *dying* to get his autograph. I'll be right back."

"No, you won't," King Chocolate said. "Not yet. First of all, wolves don't fly."

"Neither do reindeer, darling," the blue one said.

"Yes, they do," Santa said.

"You're not real," the blue one said. "Santa Claus uses boosters, like the ones in the photo. Although they will not work, either. They don't have to. You will not fly for real. You will be hoisted up with clear cables that no one will see. Then they will see an amazing projection of you and your sleigh in the sky going all over the Naughty Side. And when they get back to their homes—because they will all be here—there will be presents waiting for them. From you!"

"Full credit goes to you," the green one said. "King Chocolate."

He didn't hate this idea, either. These triplets were a little annoying, but they were on their game. He hated that the queen had sent them. This was *exactly* what he wanted. Like it could not be more perfect.

All the credit. And he does nothing to deserve it.

"Great," he said. "Now, just explain how I'm going to fly off with a picture and we'll be cool. Go on."

And they did. They told him exactly how he would make a rocket sleigh. It sounded like bunko. How could they even know that? But they weren't wrong so far. And if they were wrong about this, he'd enjoy dunking them into the lake. *So, winning.*

"WHAT'S WITH THE BOX?" King Chocolate asked.

They were on their way to the green room when something fell from the sky. A roadie had dropped a roll of tape from the catwalk. It nearly hit King Chocolate. Naturally, he looked up to see who had tried to hurt him. (Santa was a prime suspect. The real one. After all, he knows when you've been bad or good. Not much of a secret in Candyland.)

A box was dangling on a heavyweight chain. It was a wooden crate.

Swinging in a light breeze.

"Oh. Oh no." The green one covered his face. "I told them to cover it. I told them, I told them."

The Triad gathered in a consoling hug, rocking back and forth. Whispering. It went on for quite a while. The hoots and cackles from the wolf pack filled the awkward moment.

"What's happening?" King Chocolate muttered. Jelly shrugged.

The Triad held still now, humming to each other. They let go and wiped each other's tears away. The green one faced King Chocolate, who was, quite frankly, a little worried what was in the box. Now he *had* to know.

"It was a surprise," the green one said. "Now it is ruined."

"I don't like surprises."

"Yes, you do," Jelly said.

The green one hung his head. "Just before you are hoisted away in the sleigh, the box will be lowered. It will be wrapped, of course. A beautiful silver wrapping with a red glitter dusting and satin bow. It will come down right after your speech."

"Speech? What speech?"

The red one let out a wail. They took their surprises seriously. For a moment, King Chocolate didn't care about the box. Speeches were not in his nature. Waving to crowds, sure. Throwing presents at little ones, okay. There would be no sitting on his lap (yuck) or whispering what anyone wanted from him. Definitely no speeches.

"We'll talk later," Jelly said.

"No, we won't. No speech. *What's in the box?*"

The Triad waved their arms. Someone got the message. The box trembled. It dropped a little and shook. King Chocolate backed up. If a wild animal jumped out, he was putting everyone in the lake. Including the Big Bad Wolf.

Clack-clack-clack.

The box descended one link at a time until one corner touched the stage. When all four corners settled, the box remained still. King Chocolate moved behind Jelly. She would make a fine snack.

The blue one pulled a lever on the side of the box.

The wood cracked. The wall lowered like a castle gate and thudded on the stage.

There was a cage inside. Cold metal bars running top to bottom. He took his hands away from his face to see what was inside the cage. He had visions of snakes or lizards (he hated lizards more than snakes; they were snakes *with* legs). No one else had moved. And now the box was open, and they were staring.

Empty. It was empty. The box was empty. The cage inside it was saving him from nothing.

"Is this a joke?" he bristled. "I don't like jokes."

"Yes, you do," Jelly said.

"It's not a joke," the red one said. "It's for the boy."

"Boy?" King Chocolate said. "What boy?"

"The *boy*," Jelly said. Her eyes widened. King Chocolate didn't get it. Her eyes widened more. Like how many boys really matter? *There's only one.*

"We were waiting on the Lost Boys," the blue one said. "When they arrive with the crosser, we're going to give him to you as a gift. Jelly knew."

"You knew?"

"Yep."

"You were going to put the boy in there?" King Chocolate pointed at the box.

"Not for long," the red one said. "We'd feed him, of course."

"Of course," the other two said.

King Chocolate thought about it. With all the excitement—the concert and the rocket sleigh—he hadn't thought about using the boy as a prop. The crowd would want to see him. And this way it would make the king look good. *Genius. Absolute genius.* The king was now certain they were right about getting the rocket sleigh made.

"You are *not* putting the boy in a cage," Santa said.

"Of course not," King Chocolate said. Then winked at the Triad.

The idea needed tweaking. But it was as solid as a bar of virgin cacao. The boy didn't have to go in the cage as soon as he was delivered, but he was totally going in there. First, he'd come to the castle and do his thing. Then in the box. That was that, and no one would change his mind.

"Casey, please," Santa said.

"*What* did you call me?" King Chocolate ground his teeth. This was not a first-name crowd and Santa knew it.

"I know what you do at Christmas." Santa had a voice that carried. Even the wolves looked at the stage. "You sit by the window on Christmas Eve, watching the sky, looking for my sleigh to come streaking toward your house."

"Um, it's a castle. And *that* never happened. And you're not real."

"You listen to reports of an *unidentified flying object* coming closer. You pull up a chair and imagine where I am and how fast my reindeer are flying. You put milk and cookies out for me. Chocolate chip. The chocolate still soft and melty. You leave me three cookies."

"I don't even know what he's talking about! He's not real, you know. He's not even—"

"And carrots, too. You insist on leaving carrots for the reindeer. They *so* appreciate that, I promise you. Then you make sure the fireplace is open—very kind of you—and curl up on your favorite chair, where you pop your thumb in your mouth and suck it till morning."

"What?! This is crazy talk. Shut him off, Jelly!"

"And then you run down to the big Christmas tree where I leave the presents and begin ripping them open. I'll never forget your all-time favorite gift. It was a Chef Hoobie Cookie Oven. A light bulb would do the baking. It would take all day before the cookies were ready. You would sit and wait and suck your thumb—"

"I DID NOT SUCK MY THUMB!"

"Until the batter was warm. Then you'd take your thumb out of your mouth and—"

King Chocolate lifted Jelly with one hand and rifled through her clothing like a clumsy pickpocket. He found what he was looking for and snatched the projector from her pocket. It was a silver orb no bigger than a golf ball. All he had to do was hold it in his palm and say *off* and the Santa Claus program would turn off, and this big fat liar would go bye-bye. So he held it in his palm, lifted it above his head. And chucked it onto the stage.

It bounced like a stone.

He made Jelly fetch it and hand it back. He did it again. And again. Each throw harder until the stage was dimpled with divots.

"He's a liar! Santa Claus is a liar!"

Bang!

"A BIG—"

Bang!

"FAT—"

Bang!

"LIAR!"

King Chocolate was out of breath, with a sharp pain piercing his chest. His arm was tired, so he made Jelly throw it for him. Told her not to stop until that thing cracked like an egg. King Chocolate raised his fist.

"Santa is a liar! Santa is a liar!"

It caught on with the wolves, howling as they joined the chant. The mop-top roadies followed. The octopus climbed behind the drum kit and laid down a beat. Gorilla workers were coming out of the trees. Listening at first. Then fists rose. The air quivered with the chant.

Santa is a liar!

King Chocolate called one of the gorillas over and told him to stand right there. Not to move. Then looked out at the gathering workers—the apes and the wolves and mop-tops and octopus. "You deserve better than that!" King Chocolate shouted. "You deserve more than that fat liar!"

SANTA IS A LIAR!

The stage was shaking. Pine cones fell from the trees. The chants took on a life. Wolves howling. Gorillas jumping. The energy sizzled. King Chocolate pointed at the gorilla standing next to him. Jelly dropped the silver orb responsible for projecting the Santa Claus program. The king made a fist. The gorilla raised his leg and held it there. Waiting as the chant continued.

SANTA IS A LIAR!

Santa shook his head with disappointment in his eyes.

The king nodded with a cruel twinkle in his.

The gorilla brought all his weight down on the orb. It shattered like an antique timepiece. Metal shards and springs and circuits sprayed over the stage. Ravenous cheers went up, and the chant continued. When it reached a fevered pitch, the king answered.

"You... deserve..." he said, "*ME!*"

King Chocolate threw out his arms.

He soaked it in. Soaked it all in.

Maybe I will give that speech.

WINGED MONKEYS WERE WORKING on the green room. Their wings slowly flapped when they concentrated, sped up when they were excited. Wilted when they were tired. They pretty much did everything except fly. They were, however, extremely creepy looking.

"Out," King Chocolate said. "Leave us."

They dropped their tools and scrambled out of the room, the tips of their furry wings curling under. King Chocolate drifted into the green room, dragging his tired feet. He'd barely touched the ground and couldn't wait to get these clothes off. The hoversuit was slick with sweat and chafing his many rolls of flesh. A rancid odor wafted out from under it. It had the smell of soured fudge. Not bad, really.

He hovered straight at the throne, hit it hard enough to ram the back of it into the wall. Flat chunks of wood fell from the ceiling. King Chocolate collapsed into the seat and began to melt.

"Air!" he cried. "It's a thousand degrees in here."

It was not. In fact, it was cool enough to store meat. Jelly pretended to adjust the thermostat. A three-tiered fountain splashed chocolate milk in the corner next to a soft-serve ice-cream machine (chocolate only). Gourmet bottles of syrup and muffins and cookies were on a table. King Chocolate laid his head back, panting. He opened his mouth like a baby bird.

Jelly handed him the end of a long tube on a jointed mechanical arm that was attached to the ceiling. It looked like something at a dentist's office. Something to rinse and spit. King Chocolate put it in his mouth and began to suck. An icebox began to hum and pump. Dark liquid slithered through the tube and gushed into his mouth. The chocolatey goodness filled his belly with sweet love.

There was a tiny knock at the door.

"Hmm-mphm," was the sound that came out of him.

Jelly had been to enough feedings to understand what he said. "It's the Conflict Advisors."

"Wah?"

"You told them to be here."

King Chocolate sucked so hard the tube collapsed, choking off the flow. The machine started to chug.

"Take a breath," Jelly said. "Let it come to you. I'm going to let them in while you digest."

He closed his eyes and relaxed his lips. The sugar stream spilled over his tongue. He let it fill his mouth until it overflowed his lips and ran over his chins, soaking into his stylish overcoat. With one gulp, he choked it down and let it start again.

He had no memory of calling this meeting. Things like that sometimes disappeared in a food haze. *Starving amnesia*, he called it. A mixture of hunger and hurt feelings. So he sometimes sucked his thumb. No big deal. Everyone had a thumb; everyone had a mouth.

But King Chocolate had an extra layer of shame added to it. He'd heard the rumors of what the naughties were saying about him. What they were calling him. Sometimes he'd put lemon juice on it so he would stop, but he'd suck right through that. He just loved it too much. There was only one thing he loved more.

He grabbed muffins off the table and plugged them into his mouth. Shoved cookies in after them. Poured milk on his face. He coughed and sputtered. Soggy crumbs rifled across the room and stuck to the wall.

He mopped his face with a towel. Threw the towel over his shoulder. Then belched like a truck without a muffler.

"All better?" Jelly asked.

"Much. Now..." He leaned forward with a groan, drool hanging from his lip. "Advise me."

He was talking to twelve-inch soldiers. Three of them standing at attention. Plastic-molded clothing and solid hairdos. Kung fu grips for holding weapons or punching through walls. The one in the middle had permanent marker scribbled over his face and down the front of his plastic coat. He stepped forward and snapped his arms to his sides.

"Last report, the Lost Boys arrived at Fly Dome. The crosser should be in their possession by now and en route to the castle."

"General Fly deserves a medal." This was the soldier with a missing left arm. All that remained was a hole in his shoulder where a new arm (should he ever get one) would snap into place. "His team executed a flawless extraction."

"He didn't want a medal," King Chocolate said. "Wanted chocolate slop instead. To feed those squirmy babies, I guess." He nibbled on a cookie that was stuck to his jacket. "Is that all?"

"We'll have a full report when the crosser arrives," Scribble Face barked. "An evaluation will need to conclude to—"

"All right, all right. Go impress someone else." King Chocolate waved the syrup feeder like a scepter. Then: "What do you think of the box idea?"

The Conflict Advisors exchanged stiff looks. Jelly summarized the gift idea, of keeping the boy in a cage to present to King Chocolate on Christmas Eve. The scarred and marred soldiers didn't react with expressions, mainly because the plastic forms from which they were molded didn't move. But they shuffled. And the more they heard, the more they shuffled.

When Jelly was done, King Chocolate took a pull on the tube. "Well?"

"I strongly advise against it," the third soldier said. He was the most normal and unaltered of the three (except for the eye patch that hid whatever atrocity was under it).

"And why is that?"

"The boy has experienced trauma."

"So?"

"It is in your best interest to make the boy as comfortable as possible. Weapons such as him should be kept clean and well-oiled."

"Is that what he is?" King Chocolate said. "A weapon?"

"He's whatever you want him to be."

Whatever I want? He liked the sound of that. "What does he do... *exactly*?"

"He's a creative," Eye Patch announced. King Chocolate didn't like the tone.

"I know, I know. But what does that *mean*? Do you even know? Like he draws pictures. Oooo... scary. Every degenerate on the Naughty Side can draw. Like this sack of dough." He pointed the scepter at Jelly. "She draws stick figures. Don't you?"

Jelly shook her head. King Chocolate laughed with the tube between his teeth.

The Conflict Advisors conferred.

They mumbled. They nodded. King Chocolate was about to throw them out when Scribble Face spoke up.

"You remember the Nutcracker?"

For some reason, this hit the king on the wrong side. He pulled the tube out of his mouth, aimed it at the mini-soldiers and pressed the button. A burst of chocolate syrup burped from the end of it. It hit Scribble Face in the chest. Dripped from his kung fu grip.

"OF COURSE I DO! You think I'm an idiot?" He aimed the tube at the other two with his thumb hovering over the trigger. "What about it?"

Righty spoke up, waving his one and only arm. "She crossed over from another world and *manifested* her subconscious."

"All right. Good." King Chocolate didn't know what *manifested* meant. But after hosing down Scribble Face, he didn't want to admit it. "Tell me more."

"What she was thinking and feeling... it came true in Candyland."

King Chocolate sank in the throne to give this a good think. There was a theory about Candyland, what it really was and why it existed. How people could *cross* into it from other worlds. Candyland wasn't exactly a dream, but sort of. What was it Jelly told him once? *If a dreamer wakes up inside the dream... anything is possible.*

He propped his elbows on his knees. All his weight slid to the front.

His dark chocolatey eyes aimed at Righty.

"What're you saying?"

"He can change things." The soldier didn't flinch. "You just have to guide him."

King Chocolate laughed the rumbly laugh of no-good. The kind of laugh that made children cry. Dogs whine. Jelly rolled her eyes. He was overdoing it for no one but his own entertainment. He paddled a quick rhythm on his belly and squirted chocolate syrup at the ceiling. It rained down on his head, over the folds of his belly. He licked it off his sausage fingers.

He got it. He finally got it.

The boy was important. That was what everyone was telling him. But for the first time, he knew why.

He can change things. The boy is a creative. He has an imagination that can change things. The Triad was right! A rocket sleigh is just the beginning of what the boy can do.

King Chocolate was going to use him. He was going to win. All those citizens on the Nice Side would feel the burden of being naughty. They would get coal in *their* stockings when he was done.

They would make King Chocolate statues when this was over.

They would rename Two-Face Mountain and carve his face on it. It would be One-Face Mountain when the boy was done.

They would bow and give *him* gifts. Not the boy. The king, he would get the gifts because he would be the one driving the boy.

He cried chocolate tears of joy and apologized to Scribble Face for the syrup bath. Jelly wiped him clean with his towel. King Chocolate closed his eyes and bathed in the expectations of complete and total victory. It tasted like the purest, sweetest chocolate in all of Candyland. He didn't notice the fly enter the green room and whisper in Jelly's ear.

13

Art tumbled like a bingo ball in a basket weaved from tree trunks. Instead of numbered Ping-Pong balls, a mess of empty nutshells and gooey seed pits dusted him with crumbs. He smelled like a spoiled sponge cake.

The basket tipped one way and then the other, rolling the contents like a wave machine filled with marbles. A meaty hand gripped the handle. The fingernails—painted red and green and blue—were jagged at the ends. Occasionally, when the basket swung just right, he'd catch a glimpse of the arm and follow it to a big, round face. Strawberry hair and orange cheeks.

And one square tooth. Latched over the bottom lip.

A lip stained purple.

Tooth as square as a box. Made for cracking nuts. Or other things.

Art had to get out of the basket before it was too late. Each time he went tumbling to one end of the basket, he slammed into the pine lumber before rolling to the other end. He was sick and dizzy with no way of knowing which way was sideways when, as luck would have it, his boot wedged between weaved tree trunks. He hung suspended from one end as the spent shells and gooey pits rolled to the other. And came crashing back seconds later.

He got a handhold in a knothole and pulled himself up. The gap where his boot was stuck wasn't big enough to squeeze through, but enough to see where he was going. The basket swung higher. His stomach parachuted into his socks. He closed his eyes and hung on.

Water splashed into the basket and shot through the gaps.

It soaked his hair. Tasted like sweet tea with a scoop of molasses.

Outside the basket, footsteps plunged deeper in water. The air grew cool and humid. The basket went higher.

Long hot wind exhaled from above, streaming from nostrils like hotrod exhaust. It was warm and sweet like yeast rolls fresh from the oven and buttered with cinnamon. Water churned below in deep eddies; then the steps became shallower. The sound of soft mud sucking them down, not wanting to let go. Advancing to hard thumping land and the sound of gravel. Then grass.

And then no more steps.

The basket teetered. Art worked his boot loose with an eye on the hand above him. If it came sweeping through the basket for him, he'd be ready to climb for it. When he freed his boot, he scaled the basket like a wall in a log cabin. There was no hesitation. He raced to the top and was about to throw his leg over the edge when the world shivered like an enormous dog. Lake water rained into the basket, sweet drops of black tea running down the sides. Its commotion knocked Art back inside.

"*Yum!*" went a deep voice.

The braided handle creaked. The dim sky was blotted out by an orange face. The face of a moon made of circus peanuts with eggplant lips smacking a bulletin-board tooth. The nostrils flared. Art held onto a branch poking out the side. The endless inhalation gurgled. Curly hairs inside the nostrils filtered out debris.

Art's grip slipped on the wet branch. He wondered, as his fingernails etched the bark from the branch, if being hoovered into a giant's sinuses was worse than being swallowed. *Depends if the giant chews her food.*

Then it stopped.

Art thought he heard something. A tiny voice. The orange face looked up. A smile as wide as a house spread into the pumpkin cheeks. The voice called again, although Art couldn't understand it. The giant did.

"*Yum!*"

The basket tipped upright. A landslide of shells and seeds spilled over the side. Art hung on until the giant gave the basket a good shake. He went crashing into the pile. And thank goodness he did. He sank halfway down and, without half a thought, dug to the bottom, where he hit ground.

HE WAS LOOKING AT A FOOT. A bare foot as big as a toolshed. As orange as a tangerine.

Cracks ran from callused soles that had never felt the inside of a shoe (no store carried such a size). Toenails, long and jagged, were the colors of the fingernails. Art wondered if they were painted at all. Maybe they were just those colors. He knew nothing of giants, after all.

When that foot rose off the ground, it came down like a pile driver and rattled the shells and seeds. The second footfall spread the pile further. Several more and Art was barely able to hide.

The giant was across a green clearing, holding the basket under a pipe. An avalanche of colored rocks wrapped in blankets of crinkly cellophane (if Art assumed it to be hard candy, he would've assumed right) spilled from the oversized faucet like a slot machine jackpot.

"*Yum! Yum!*"

She cracked one open with that giant tooth and hopped up and down. Earthquakes rattled the world. Then she leaned over, put her face near the ground. Art thought she was vacuuming something into her nostrils, but something moved. A faint shadow. He couldn't quite see what it was—that part of Candyland was more dim than dark, like a full moon on a cloudless night (although there was no moon)— but it hugged the giant's nose.

The giant sighed with pleasure. "Yum."

Then she strode back the way she came, down the rocky bank and into the blackwater tea. She held the basket of goodies above her head as the water rose to her waist. The water rippled around her, but she never slowed down, carving her way to the other side. Climbing onto dry land and shaking like a dog before pushing through the trees. Her footsteps were collisions that slowly faded.

Until they were gone.

Until there were just frogs singing night songs and cicadas joining in. The air pulsed with the fluorescent signs of fireflies.

Stillness wrapped around him.

He embraced it. Became part of the scenery. Hardly breathing. His eyes moving back and forth, taking in the unknown. There was so much he couldn't see. He'd have to turn his head, and he wasn't ready to move. Not yet. Not until it was safe.

Someone or something had honked that giant's nose. He or she was out there. Maybe they were watching, so Art blended into the pile. Became one with it. He'd lie like that for as many ticks or rings or bells as needed. Last thing he wanted was another pair of giant fingers tossing him into a basket.

He wanted to rest. That lasted a few ticks.

In other words, not long.

SOMETHING WAS SCRATCHING AROUND HIM.

It was sniffing the ground. Little fingers or claws dug through the soil. Not close to him. But close enough.

A shell tumbled off the pile. Another one followed.

Padded footsteps ran off, and it was quiet again. Until the scratching returned. This time a handful of shells cascaded off the pile. More footsteps followed. And then something else.

Squeak!

Like a trigger had been pulled, Art exploded from the pile of shells and seeds and ran for the shore. He went down a slope, over jagged ground until his hands hit water. He spun around, eyes just above a speckled boulder. Scanning the pile he'd just blown up.

They were little lumps at first. A train of little, long-tailed lumps running to the scattered shells and seeds and then back to a grassy meadow surrounded by a split rail fence. It reminded him of ants finding food. Only ants the size of work boots. Ants with tails. And fur.

They weren't ants.

He knew what they were and didn't want to admit it. He might make a sound he would regret if he did.

There were so many of them, each of them grabbing a shell or a seed and marching it to the meadow. The pile receding piece by piece.

Art backed into the water.

THE PILE that the giant had emptied from the basket was nearly gone. The long-tailed harvesters (or were they thieves?) rooted around for the last pieces.

Rats. No question about it, Art finally admitted it. Big ole hoppy rats. Or mice. He didn't know the difference. *Vermin.*

They cleaned up the mess, and Art wondered if the giant had left it behind on purpose. The way the vermin lined up for it didn't seem to be an accident. He didn't know what they were doing with it. Only saw them carry the spilled treasure down a narrow trail carved through swards of blooming weeds and under a split-rail fence.

Art stopped caring about the rats. They weren't interested in him, even when he'd jumped out of the pile like a birthday surprise. The water was getting chilly. He crawled out and sat on a rounded boulder. The sounds of night were all around—things splashing in the water behind him, frogs synchronizing their beats.

There were no stars in the night sky, but a galaxy of glowing lights hovered just above the ground. Fireflies signaled to each other with long pulses of phosphorescent light. Art heard faint whispers from the ones near him. It was mostly laughter. They didn't fly over the water, staying mostly above land. And mostly around what he thought was a giant tree.

He had mistaken it for a tree because that was what it was shaped like. The width of its pendulous branches was the size of a public swimming pool. It was three stories tall and as still as stone. Because that was what it was: an enormous sculpture rooted in the earth.

In the dim light and eerie glow of firefly fannies, he could see bright colors painted on the branches. Random circles of warm light began flickering on its surface. At the top, a three-dimensional star had been carved. Smoke streamed from the five points.

The swamp water behind him was black and sticky. Sweet on his lips. He could probably swim across, disappear into the trees like the giant had done. He was certain he could swim that far, although there were things churning the glassy surface. Big things that sometimes exposed large scales or cutting fins.

This is the Naughty Side, he thought. *Those aren't friendly fish.*

He started walking along the shore, gravel grinding under his boots. The rats had all gone beyond the split-rail fence now that the mess was cleaned up. Art climbed onto the lawn. The grass soft under his squishy boots.

There were more fences and gardens. No tomatoes or peppers or rows of corn. Branches of some bushy plants hung heavy with red-and-white-striped peppermints. It looked like clusters of crystals sprouting from raised beds. Some had been harvested and packed into boxes.

Art walked past the pipe where the giant had filled her basket. It was larger than a sewer pipe and shaped like a spigot. The grass around it was worn down to speckled granite. Just beyond it, light spilled from the stone Christmas tree, tossing long shadows across the grass. Art went back to the shore, crawled over a jagged outcropping and into a thicket of trees. Only a few feet in and he had to turn sideways to squeeze between them.

This was a good hiding spot. For him. Probably for other things, too. Rats, for one.

He walked back out and crouched on the shore. Fireflies descended on him. Whispering, giggling. *Merry, merry,* they said.

He could swim for it, although that was still the worst idea. But it was on the list. He could leave this area (maybe it was an island) and find a bridge or something better. A zipline. A door that took him back home. Anything was possible.

Then a shadow stepped into the light.

A doorway had been cut into the bottom of the stone Christmas tree. Orange light flickered around a ball of fur licking an extended back leg. When Art saw him, the cat stretched. Turned. And walked inside.

The door stayed open.

"Daryl!" Art half whispered.

Daryl didn't hear him or didn't care. Art hadn't seen him since the House of Grimjoy. And that felt so long ago. Time was a funny thing. *Sometimes it stretches like taffy.*

It was Daryl, though. He was sure of it.

No other cat had a belly like that. It nearly dragged on the ground as he strode deeper into the concrete tree. Tail raised. Tail waving.

Art was rooted to the ground. *Why didn't he say something?*

There was a simple answer for that. Daryl was a cat. And cats were mostly interested in a warm lap. Still, he'd helped Art escape the castle. He'd taken that beam and led him to Grimjoy.

Now he's here.

If Daryl was here, Art was in the right place, or so he thought. He stood up. Looked around. Nothing but fireflies noticed him. *Merry, merry,* they whispered. He crept closer, put his hand on the stone Christmas tree (gritty sandstone cool to touch), and peeked inside the doorway.

A long corridor went straight ahead. Longer than he would have guessed, but he'd grown accustomed to the elasticity of space. Colorful murals decorated the walls, wintery scenes with toboggans and snowmen, reindeer, and elves. Flickering light from the end.

He took a step inside. The floor was gritty and made a grinding sound under his heel. Warm air that was humid smelled of sweet smoke and floral incense. Made him feel safe. Made him take another step. He dragged his hand along the wall, felt the rough-hewn surface on his fingertips, as if it had been carved with crude tools. He looked back every two or three steps, the doorway still open. After several stops, he quit looking. It was too far to do anything about it. He was in too deep.

He stopped when he could see what was beyond the end.

He held still and watched.

It was hazy. The air undulating in waves. Someone was sitting on the floor. Her back to him. Nothing else that he could see. He waited for a sign, a signal to move in one direction or the other. Daryl's voice to tell him what to do. There was nothing.

He went forward. Carefully.

The sweet smell of incense tickled his nose. Water pooled in his eyes. He wiped them with the heels of his hands. The woman on the floor wore a patchwork robe that puddled around her. White hair spread over her shoulders.

The room was magnificent and simple: an enormous cone with three fires equidistant in the circular space. Each fire burned inside a metal cylinder on an ornate pedestal. Smoke crawled along the walls, leaving sooty trails to the very top, where they snaked out the legs of a star sitting on top of the tree. Circular skylights, the size of dinner plates, were randomly sunk through the walls.

In constant slow motion, a mobile of silver objects turned above them. As intricate as it was enormous. Anchored on thin wires. Chiming as they rotated in the fires' thermal draft. He was transfixed by the timeless movement, like birds in the sky or playful stars dancing to the universe's song, and hadn't noticed the woman turn her head slightly.

"Join us."

Her voice effortlessly carried. It was raspy. Kind. Art jumped back a step, hanging onto the wall. She didn't seem alarmed or hurt by the reluctance. As if endless patience and acceptance were sitting with her. That wasn't enough to get him to move. But the sound that followed helped. The lapping of drink taken from a bowl.

The sight of a fluffed tail swishing in pleasure.

Art moved inside the room, careful not to step on the thousands of tiny gifts stacked at the perimeter, until he saw Daryl was hunched over a dish.

"Daryl?" The word bounced around the room even though he whispered it.

There was no response. Then a hum spread between his eyes. And he heard that lazy voice. *Have a seat, Arthur.*

There was a small bench opposite the old woman. A bench only a foot tall and twice as wide. It was on the edge of a circular rug. Daryl was in the middle of it, his tongue working a steady rhythm. White flecks of milk lighting his whiskers and tufted chin.

"He followed you the entire way. Even when you couldn't see him," the old woman said. "I knew he would."

She watched Daryl. Spoke without looking up.

Art only needed to see the side of her face to know that she wasn't an old woman. A triangular ear poked through her hair. A tiny gold loop pierced the end of it. Her face jutted forward, covered in white fur. A pink nose surrounded by sprouts of stiff whiskers. A tiny smile curled at the end of her black lips, reaching the eyes. The human eyes. Brown. The color of good dirt.

Art walked the perimeter of the round rug, stood behind the small bench. He assumed she was sitting on something similar, her lower half buried beneath the checkered robe, her hands folded under a knitted blanket on her lap. Under that robe and blanket, he assumed there was a long, leathery tail.

"He's *your* cat," she said.

Daryl stopped drinking. Looked up with white droplets clinging to his chin. He blinked heavily.

"My apologies." The rat woman put her long-fingered, knobby

hand on her chest. "Old habits, I'm afraid. I'm reminded animals aren't objects and don't *belong* to anyone. You and he have been *friends* for quite some time, I'm told. He crossed not long after you." She scratched Daryl's back with a long, pink finger. "And yes, we know each other quite well. That's the thing with crossers: we're all connected."

Cold filled Art's legs. He locked his knees to keep from folding.

What she said.

He wasn't sure he heard it right.

She looked up for the first time. When her eyes landed on him, it felt like a beam of sunlight went through him and warmed him from the inside out. He opened like a flower promised spring rain and summer sun. She tipped her head to one side, hummed (it sounded a bit like a purr, but Art was too gobsmacked to notice), and looked into him. She saw all of him, read him like a script. And he let her, so welcoming was her presence. So accepting. She saw who he truly was, even if he didn't.

He was naked and exposed to her. Vulnerable.

To the side of her, sitting on the floor, was a little bell. She gave it a shake. The melody drifted around the room. The shiny bits of the mobile seemed to answer. A tick later, a rat (this one normal-sized) came across the room. It was anything but normal, wearing tiny, tailored clothing and carrying a silver tray on its back. A teapot shook; teacups rattled. But not a drop was spilled.

He placed it next to the dish of milk. Daryl didn't miss a beat, still going at the milk (the bottom of the bowl was starting to show).

"Thank you, Harley," she said.

The servant rat (slightly bigger than most rats, Art guessed) nodded at the rat woman. Standing upright, he turned to Art and waited. Art tensed up. He'd never been stared down by a rat before. Not that he could remember.

"He wants to know if there's anything you need," Rat Woman said.

Art stammered. Then spoke directly to the little rat and said, "Chocolate."

Harley bowed his head. It was more of deference than acknowledgment.

Rat Woman filled a cup with tea. She held a saucer with one hand. The teacup with the other. Waved it under her pink nose. Those oddly human eyes closed as her whiskers twitched. She sipped it delicately.

"We do not use chocolate here," she said.

An odd way to put it. Who *uses* chocolate? Art was a touch hungry. He also wanted to take the edge off the anxious jitter in his knees, the invisible hand clutching his chest. The apple in his throat. He wanted to smooth out the discomfort with a quick nibble before he unzipped his skin to crawl out of it.

Harley hopped across the room, jumping into one of a hundred holes that were punched into the wall. Rat Woman went back to basking in the aroma of tea, undisturbed by the young man standing across from her. Daryl had finished the milk and was now licking white specks off his fur.

"Are you a crosser?" Art blurted. "The way you said it, I thought maybe you meant you were. And Daryl, too."

"Please."

She gestured to the empty bench with her skeletal fingers. Art was happy to sit down before his knees buckled. He squatted on the bench, propped his arms onto his knees. She poured another cup of tea, spun the tray so that it was in front of him. He didn't like tea, but picked it up, not to be rude. It was warm and smelled spicy, like chai. He was tempted to wave it under his nose.

There was a white scar on her cheek where fur didn't grow.

"Have you heard about the nutcracker?" she asked.

"A little bit."

"She was my niece. My sister's child. A young woman when she arrived in Candyland. I followed her here. That was many bells ago. So many I've lost count."

She sipped her tea, lost in thought.

"She was about your age. She was misunderstood. Grief festered inside her and turned to rage when it couldn't breathe. Transformed her into the very thing she hid from herself. This place can do that, especially to crossers."

"Do what?"

"Manifest your thoughts. Make them tangible. Change you from the outside in." She spoke like time didn't exist. There was only this endless moment. "At least, that's what happened to my niece when she was here. Candyland showed her who she really was. It exposed what terrified her most, made her look at it. Embrace it. Accept it."

Another long pause stretched out the silence. Only the sound of crackling flames in the firepits and a cat licking himself clean.

"Where is she now?" Art asked.

"She went home long ago."

"She left?"

The rat woman nodded. "Back where you and I come from."

Art frowned. What he'd been told suddenly went off the rails. "Yeah, but... there aren't giant rats back home. Not ones who talk and, and drink tea."

He couldn't be sure of that since he didn't remember much about home. But something in his gut said there wasn't. She smiled at this and even laughed out loud. It was charming, the way she laughed. From the gut and not at his expense.

"I didn't arrive like this. I became this," she said. "And I'm not a *rat*, dear. I'm a *mouse*."

He didn't see the difference or why that mattered. What did matter was something else she said. He leaned forward. "You know how you got here?"

"There are as many ways to cross over as there are reasons to. It depends on *why* you're here. Many don't remember *how* they got here or anything before they woke up."

She offered a comforting smile.

"But *you* remember," he said.

"Like yester-*ring*." A grandmotherly grin and smart twinkle in her eye. "Yester*day* makes more sense to you, I suppose. Yes. Back in my *day,* a door opened in the pink sky. It was the way in and out. But not anymore. The door hasn't opened since I arrived."

Daryl arched his back and rubbed against Art's leg. When Art didn't give him what he wanted, Daryl went over to the rat woman (*mouse lady, I suppose*) and crawled onto the knitted blanket. She kneaded him with those bony (*and, quite frankly, creepy*) fingers. Purring filled the tall room.

"And what exactly *is* this place?" Art said.

"Haha!" The mouse lady tipped her head back and sent laughter to the tippy-top of the room. "Only a crosser would think to ask that. I used to think I knew what Candyland was, something as simple as a box that contained a magic land. But this place... it has moved on from that."

She shook her head and sighed. Art pondered the strangeness of that. This didn't feel like a box. It didn't matter, according to her. *This place has moved on.*

She scratched Daryl and watched thoughts drift through her mind. Ones she'd been contemplating for quite a few bells. "Candyland," she said with blunt laughter. "The Christmas spirit flows here like sap through a maple tree. It's where naughty and nice take form. A way station, of sorts. Where visitors come and sometimes go."

"Sometimes?"

He didn't like the way she looked at him now. It hid some truth she possessed. A truth with a sharp edge he wasn't ready to touch. A truth she let him know was there. And when he was ready, he would see it, and it would free him. Or hurt him. *Or both.*

Harley returned.

Bouncing across the room, he scaled the loose patchwork robe, climbed onto her shoulder, and whispered into her ear. She answered with squeaks and squeals and strange whispers that Harley understood. He leaped from her shoulder and scrambled across the room, squealing as he went.

Little red dots appeared in the holes in the wall. They came in pairs, reflecting the firelight.

Harley ran the perimeter of the room. The squeals echoed to the top and back to the bottom. The little red dots emerged from the holes, preceded by twitching pink noses. Then they came out of the walls by the hundreds. Maybe more.

"Would you care for a walk?" the mouse lady asked.

Daryl climbed off her lap, slightly annoyed. He stretched and yawned, completely uninterested in the hundreds of mice zigzagging around the room. There was some order to the chaos, like a swarm of starlings moves through the sky.

She pulled her legs out from under her. Art saw how her legs had been resting under the bench. She rubbed her knees, which, oddly, seemed more like human knees beneath her clothing.

"Candyland is a funny place," she said. "Some things never age. While the rest of us keep getting older."

He didn't know what that meant. By the sounds she made, she was in the latter group. She put her hands on the floor and prepared to stand up.

Arthur, Daryl said, not too kindly.

Art was caught watching this old mouse struggle to climb off the floor, wondering if those were normal legs under the robe. He jumped at the sound of Daryl's voice and offered his hand. The mouse lady looked up.

"Thank you, dear."

Her palm was dry and cool. Leathery.

The long fingers wrapped around his hand.

She patted his grip with her free hand. Took his arm. Pointed to the exit, where the mice were flooding out. The tea set rattled behind them. A cadre of mice raced off with the cups and pot and tray. The rest of them moved aside to avoid being stepped on or tripping the old mouse.

The outside flashed with fireflies. The mouse lady held onto his arm with both hands, stopping to inhale the cool, humid air. With the help of several mice, Harley brought a cane outside. She took it and thanked them, poked the ground with it. Then patted Art's arm, and off to the right she went.

They entered a dense grove of trees. A meandering seashell path was softly lit by downlights anchored in the canopies, simulating moonlight to guide their way. Mice were tending pocket gardens here and there where glittering crystals sprouted and bushy plants dropped candy corn on the ground. There were baskets full of harvest and, he was quite sure, some of the spent shells from the giant's basket.

The anxiety gripping his chest had relaxed. The knot in his throat dissolved. He'd forgotten about chocolate, happy to walk in the company of this human-size mouse who seemed pleased just to breathe the air and hear frogs sing.

"You want to know how to get back." She squeezed his arm. "You want to go home."

"I do."

"Hmm." The metal tip of her cane spiked into the path. They walked for several minutes. Art thought she wasn't going to answer. Then she finally said: "My husband left me here. It was before I came to this little island. He should have left long before that."

"Where did he go?"

"Climbing!" she said with a laugh. "I didn't deserve his company. I didn't want to be here, you see. Always watching the sky for the door to open. Waiting and waiting and waiting. Never here, you know. Never here. Now look at me, still here after all these bells."

She patted his arm and laughed.

"Has anyone explained *bells* to you? Daryl, why haven't you told him?"

Daryl apparently answered her because she laughed. Art knew what bells meant. But his confusion was apparent.

"You can't measure time without the sun or moon, dear. And Christmas is all that matters here. There are twelve bells between them. *Months,* you might say. Although it's been quite a long time since I've used that word."

Art nodded along.

"It's nighttime on this side," she said. "But there's beauty in darkness, Arthur. Without it, we don't see the light."

They walked without talking, again. The sound of their footsteps punctuated by the tip of the cane was all that disrupted the frogs and cicadas. The darkness accented the soft light beaming down from the trees.

"Light is the Christmas spirit, we say in Candyland," she finally said. "The joy of life."

THE MOUSE LADY turned off the seashell path, onto an uphill climb. It seemed like an awful idea. The way she was hunched over; the way her arm shook. But she did it.

One step at a time.

They emerged from the trees and were rewarded with a view.

She'd been up here before and quite a bit, judging by the narrow rut trampled into the grass. She led him to a bench weaved of saplings and vines. Looked a lot like the giant's basket. It was a bit close to a ledge. Not a far drop—twenty feet, maybe. But it was enough. She nestled onto the bench with a sigh and a grin.

Art sat next to her.

They settled into the stillness of the night. The water was an infinite pool of blackness, reflecting the flashing bugs tracing random paths in the air. Beyond was a field of green grass where moths fluttered and bats flapped.

The frogs chirruped. The cicadas whined.

The air cool and moist. A spicy texture that reminded him of hot cinnamon cider.

Daryl hopped onto his lap and curled up. His purrs were comforting and warm. Harley climbed onto the mouse lady's lap and did the same. Minus the purring. Sleep fell on Art like a blanket. Then she spoke in a rough whisper that didn't disturb the peace.

"I was sentenced here for not eating chocolate, you know."

"Sentenced?"

She shrugged. "I'm not supposed to leave. Which is fine. I've grown very fond of this island. And truth be told, I've grown too old to want anything else. They don't tell you that about aging, not when you're eighteen years old. You find joy in simple things. Like sitting down to listen."

Her laughter wheezed in her throat, then came out in croaks. She squinted. Art didn't see the humor, but he smiled just the same. Watching her.

"Why do you not eat chocolate?" he asked.

The laughter faded. She sighed and gazed across the water, thrumming her fingers on the bench between them. Then answered: "I wanted to see the beauty."

Art didn't understand. Chocolate was good. It tasted good. It *felt* good. When he ate it, the feelings that haunted him simply went away. He felt like who he was meant to be. Why would she not want that?

"I was tired of hiding," she mused. "I'd done that all my life. It's why I came to Candyland. Why I never left. Hiding from parts of my self. My *monsters*. Same reason my niece came here. She was smarter than me, got to the point quicker. I had a lot more garbage to sort through to get to my self, and I wasn't going to do it hiding in the chocolate."

"It's just *chocolate*." He chuckled.

She nodded along, never taking her gaze from the distance. Then turned to him with kindness in her eyes.

"You know, you can't be a prisoner if this is where you *want* to be. I suppose I could return to where I came from, back through the door in the sky if it ever opened again. But I came here for a reason. We all do."

They sat for a spell of silence. He didn't feel privileged to break it. In fact, he preferred to rest in it. The beauty of the night.

"Sometimes I imagine my husband sitting next to me. Him coming back and not saying a word. Just taking a seat next to me. We would share a cup of tea and watch the fireflies. And then dance like we did when we were young."

"Is that why you had the giant bring me here?"

It seemed obvious now. The giant had snatched him away from the Lost Boys, and she'd filled up the giant's basket in return. Maybe she wanted the company because her husband was off climbing. The mouse lady looked at him with a sly smile.

"Sweet Tooth? Oh, she's a dear, isn't she? A big colorful teddy who will do anything for a handful of goodies." She patted his hand as it lay between them. "You aren't staying on the island, dear, as much as I'd like the company. You have more important things to do. I just wanted to see you."

Her eyes glittered with a glassy reflection.

"And I do."

ART FELT CHILLED and strangely honored, the way she was looking at him. Through him and into him. Seeing with an openness that was vulnerable. Loving. This big mouse was the most human thing he'd met since waking up in Candyland.

It felt okay to be with her. To be here. Just here.

"I can't go back," he said. "Can I."

"The only way to leave Candyland is to change. And if you change, you won't go back. It's a conundrum. You can return, but you won't go back."

"Because I'm here for a reason." He was sick of hearing that.

"Reason?" She laughed herself into a coughing fit. "Humans are always looking for reasons when there are none. It gives them purpose. And if they don't have one, they invent one. And that's all right." She squeezed his hand (a small part of him didn't want her to let go). "You're here because you're here, dear. And that's a good enough reason."

He nodded and understood hardly any of it. But it felt good. He just had simple questions that needed simple answers.

"I am here because I'm a weapon, someone said."

"Power isn't always a weapon."

He laughed. "I'm not powerful."

She didn't refute that. The way he meant it was true. He wasn't a strong man or a tough guy. But that wasn't what she meant by power, either.

"So if I want to go back—I mean, go home... how do I do it?"

She nodded the all-knowing nod. Let the quiet between them stretch out. Looking out as if searching for something in the pasture.

"What do you see?" she asked.

Art followed her gaze. Maybe the way back was on the other side of the water. That was why she'd brought him up here. He described to her what he saw. The water. The bugs. The field and the trees beyond. She listened, and when he was done, she said it again.

"What do you see, Arthur?"

He used more detail to describe it this time. The colors and textures. The way the fireflies created the illusion of space in the water. The way the leaves on the trees shimmered. When he checked for her approval, her eyes were closed. Without opening them, she said:

"Look again. Look deeply."

He was lost. When she didn't open her eyes, he closed his eyes. If that was what she meant, he'd go along with it. They were embraced by the night. The sounds and smells. The touch. Her hand found his and grasped it lightly.

"When you see *your* light, you will never be lost."

Well, there it was. His answer. Clear as fog. You'd think he'd be used to answers like that after Grimjoy. He wasn't.

He was hoping for something more concrete, something he could put his hands around. A button to push or a door to open. A pill that would wake him up from this never-ending dream. But no—*see the light* was the answer.

What he didn't want to do was spend a thousand years or bells or whatever before he saw his light. Just show him where it was. It was pretty simple.

They returned to quiet.

He was grateful to not be talking. No more nonsense answers that made his head hurt. Just sitting there, letting peace settle like sand in water. Watching the lights. Smelling the smells. He hoped it would stay like that forever.

And then he heard the horn.

It was a long, baleful howl that came from far away.

HARLEY LEAPED off her lap and scrambled down the path. Daryl stood up and stretched. The mouse lady had not opened her eyes. She remained in silent repose even after the second and third horn called out.

There was something on the far side of the field.

A dark box emerged from the trees. It wobbled on big, skinny wheels. Too far to see what it was, but it was coming straight for them.

"The king has arrived," she said. "You will go with him to the castle."

The peace that had settled inside him petrified. The words struck him like a hammer that shattered what little peace was left. It crumbled inside him. Sharp points poking and sticking. He'd already escaped the castle once. Daryl said if he went back, he wasn't going to escape again.

"Why do I have to go?"

"Because that's why you're here."

"But I'm not here for a reason. You *said*."

She grabbed his hand. This time he hated it. It felt coarse and cold. A long-fingered claw. He pulled away from her. She wasn't hurt by the reaction. Instead, folding her hands on her lap.

Harley returned.

He lugged something with the help of three mice. A large ring of sorts. Art wasn't paying attention to what it was. He was watching the carriage get closer, inching its way across the field. A sick feeling spread across his stomach like a slick of oil.

"What am I supposed to do?" he muttered.

She reached for what Harley had brought her and fixed it upon her head. When Art turned to face her, he saw what the ring was. It surprised him, to put it mildly. Not at all what he expected her to be wearing.

"Shine, dear," she said. "You shine."

14

The crown nestled into the silver-white hair on her head. *A queen,* Art thought. *She's a queen.*

It wasn't an impressive crown. Where jewels might have once been seated now were empty sockets. There was a sense of duty attached to it. Yet she looked slightly embarrassed to put it on.

The queen whispered something to Harley. The rat scuttled away.

A minute later, a song played loud enough to carry over the water and through the trees. A song any child would know from summer. One that blared from a cheap speaker on a colorful truck that stopped at the curb to dole out ice cream to kiddos holding crinkled dollar bills in their dirty hands.

The queen stepped to the edge of the rocky outcropping. She raised her cane and waved. A heavy thump sent ripples over the water. Firefly reflections wavered. Something whumped on the shore; then a giant roll of plastic foam began to unspool. The kind of mat high school wrestlers battled on.

A team of mice gathered behind it. More came out of the rocks and underbrush. Little by little, they pushed it toward the lake. It splashed into the water and unrolled like a giant wheel, getting smaller as it rode to the other side. Bobbing on the surface. The end of it fell in front of the carriage.

The ice-cream-truck song continued its endless loop.

The carriage rolled onto the floating bridge. The narrow wheels sank into the foam surface. Water pooled around them but didn't impede it. Fireflies swarmed around the fat little elf sitting on top, with reins in his hands but no horses to steer. He was nothing more than a grumpy hood ornament, waving off the bugs flashing in his face. When the carriage reached the island, it parked in an open space. There were no roads for it to go any farther.

The ground shook. The entire island shivered.

Waves appeared in the black water. The floating bridge rocked side to side. The carriage would have gone for a drink if it were still on it. The ice-cream song stopped playing on the cheap speaker. The queen held out her arm.

"Shall we?"

Art took her frail arm. It wasn't terribly far to reach their guest, but the hillside was steep without a path. It would be a challenge for him to get down. The queen didn't stand a chance.

The ground shook again.

Art could smell what was coming. It smelled like breakfast cereal. The frosted kind.

From around the corner, Sweet Tooth appeared. Her big bare feet crashing on the ground. Water dripping from her elbows. She stomped toward the carriage. One misstep and she could turn it into kindling. The grumpy elf looked up but didn't climb down.

Sweet Tooth bent over. Looked into the blackened windows.

She looked up the hill at the queen. A smile spread across the giant's face. The one tooth as big as a billboard.

"*Yum!*"

She cupped her hands. The colorful fingernails rested in front of the queen. Art helped her step onto them. They were soft and sweet. Smelled like buttered French toast. Very carefully, Sweet Tooth lowered them. The fireflies bunched around them, whispering as they went.

Merry, merry.

Merry, merry.

Merry, merry.

"Merry, merry, my dears," the queen said. "What a lovely night it is. Thank you for lighting it for us."

The fireflies flashed brighter.

The queen strobed and glowed in the radiance of their iridescent bottoms.

The grumpy elf watched them arrive. He made no effort to dismount. Held the limp reins that connected to nothing. A dour look pulled the corners of his mouth below his chin. Daryl appeared at Art's feet, arching his back against his shins. Purring like the carriage was nothing more than a decoration and not a harbinger of doom.

The queen was unperturbed. Amused, even.

The stagecoach elf tipped his frumpy hat. She returned his gesture with a nod. The corner of his mouth twitched, attempting a smile. But the weight of his mood was too heavy to raise it.

Finally, the door on the carriage swung open. Out stepped an enormous foot, followed by a round body.

Art recognized the elf. He knew her name, but there was something different about her. She looked like Belly, from her feet to her stubby nose. The expression, though. The deadness of it wasn't friendly. This elf waddled over, grunting with each step. Sweet Tooth bent over and sniffed the round elf, ruffling her long overcoat dragging on the ground. When Sweet Tooth was satisfied (*Yum!*), the elf placed one hand over her swollen belly and sort of bowed.

"Lady Mouserinks."

"Jelly," the queen answered. "Merry, merry to you, dear."

"Blah-blah."

"Not on my island, blah-blah." But the queen seemed pleased to see the elf and said: "You've gained weight."

"Thank you. Switched to eggnog in the mornings."

"I like it. Very wintery."

Jelly stared through suspicious slits. The queen introduced Art. And Daryl. Jelly didn't acknowledge them. Art looked away. The elf kept staring. Studying him. Art picked up Daryl. The comforting ball of fur warded off the judgy stares from Jelly and the stagecoach driver.

The queen spoke with an edge of impatience. "Is he coming out?"

"I think so," Jelly said. "You know how he is."

"Does he need a pep talk?"

Jelly smirked. "He can hear you."

"I know," she whispered. "Go on and fetch him. It'll be Christmas if we wait for him."

The elf waddled back to the carriage and rapped on the door. "She's here, Your Majesty." The sarcasm was thick enough to butter toast. "So's the boy."

A voice muttered from inside the carriage. Jelly put her ear to the door and nodded. Then looked at the queen and shrugged.

"Tell him we'll be inside, then," the queen said. "We have tea to finish. Sweet Tooth will come for us when he's ready to come out. She'll be happy to—"

The door slammed against the carriage, nearly swatting Jelly into the water. Mechanical sounds hissed and whined. The carriage rocked side to side. Something squeezed through the doorway. It looked like a balloon dressed in a theater curtain. The balloon turned toward the queen. Tiny legs twittered beneath the swollen body. The hard soles scraping the gritty soil.

What is that? Art thought.

He'd thought he'd seen everything. But this was most unusual. It was a massive figure draped in a ton of heavy fabric. The cheeks and chins folded around dark purple lips as thick as rope. Two brown eyes were pushed deep into the flesh. And sitting on his head was a crown only a child would draw—a gaudy thing three feet tall and dipped in chocolate and rolled in gemstones.

"*Yum!*" Sweet Tooth announced.

"No! It's too late for forgiveness. Eat these and shut up." The king threw a handful of gold coins at the giant. Sweet Tooth ate them without taking off the wrappings. "Don't be greedy," the king said when Sweet Tooth sniffed the ground for more.

The mountainous king floated closer with a hum and hiss. The legs were disturbing, the way they twittered like useless appendages. He floated higher and looked down at the queen. Jelly stepped aside, gnawing on a hangnail.

"Looking gray," he said to the queen. "Tail still super long, I see."

"Merry, merry, Casey. I like your tailor. The hoversuit is working good, yes?"

"It feels good to walk again." He clicked his puppet heels, then rotated toward Art. "You're the boy, I assume. I'm the king. Call me that."

He snapped his fingers. Jelly tossed him a chocolate wafer. The king didn't catch it and snapped his fingers again. He kept snapping until Jelly fetched it. She put it in the king's open hand. The king threw it to Art.

"I got a never-ending supply," the king said. "Only game in town, boy. So you're welcome." It was the same chocolate wafer Rude Boy had given him in the market. "Now, to business. What did she say? About me, specifically. Out with it. Go."

Art shook his head. "Nothing."

"She didn't say nothing? Bah! Lies flow from her like Lemonade Falls."

"I never heard of you."

The king flinched. That wasn't what he wanted to hear. Not at all. He swung at the fireflies hovering around him and snarled at the cat cradled in Art's arms. Daryl was asleep.

"Good catching up with you," he said to the queen. "Let's not do it so soon. Come on, boy. There's plenty of room. Climb aboard."

The king spun like a top and teetered like a balloon in a gust of wind. When the hoversuit rebalanced, he floated to the carriage. Art tried not to look at the legs. The king started to shove his way through the doorway. He turned his head like a turret on a tank.

To Jelly, he said: "Did he not hear me?"

"I believe he did."

They looked at Art. "I'm not going," Art said.

"I didn't ask." The king offered a smile full of brown teeth. "I am the king. That's how this works."

"He doesn't want to go with you, Casey," the queen added.

"Stay out of this!" He bounced like a kickball and sounded like one, too. "You stole him from me. You sent the Sweet Tooth after him. Then you filled his brain with lies. I can smell the fibs on him like dog farts."

He spun toward Art.

"She's a liar, Arty. She tell you she's a mouse? Yeah, I bet she did. Ever see a mouse that big? No, you haven't because she's a rat. Look at her. The tail and the fur and the... *ick.*"

"You sent the Lost Boys for him," she said.

"They're fine lads."

"They're scrappers."

"So? That's how they do it. It's in their blood. The boy is like them. Ask him yourself. You're a lost boy, ain't you?"

Art didn't answer. But he knew what the king was getting at. Art felt the draw to ride a beam, to fly through the trees.

"He would be at the castle by now if it weren't for you," the king said. "In his own room. Now look at him. He's hungry. He's tired. You poisoned his brain, and I'll have to fix that."

His hands flailed about innocently. Then he spun on Sweet Tooth.

"And you! The next time you betray me, the king—*your* king... I'm cutting you off. No more chocolate. You hear me? Go fend for yourself in the jungle. And you'd better not raid my fields, or it'll get worse. I can do that. I can make your life not yummy. Trust me, you clown."

"*Yum?*" Sweet Tooth looked at the queen.

"Don't look at her. I'm number one. She's number two. Actually, she's number one *thousand.* I rule. You get it? Now you, get in the carriage," he said to Art. "Now!"

The king whistled like he was a dog. He threw gold-wrapped coins of chocolate at him. He clicked his tongue.

Art did not move. Not even when Sweet Tooth snuffled up the chocolate coins.

"This is not how you want to do this," the queen said.

The king ignored her. He muttered to Jelly and turned the color of a ripe plum, whining like an overworked fuel pump.

"Fine! What do you want?"

"Ask Art," the queen said.

"Great. What do you want, Art? Huh? You want chocolate? Done. A foot massage? I'll make it happen. What do I have to do to get you in my sweet ride?"

"I want to go home."

"No. What? You can't go home. Didn't someone tell him that already?"

Art wasn't getting in that carriage. In fact, he didn't plan to leave the island. This was the first time he felt at home since waking up in this nightmare. The king could feel it, too. So did Jelly.

"Lady Mouserinks will come with us," Jelly said.

"What?" The king laughed. It was a bit maniacal. "That's crazy talk. She doesn't want to go anyway. She loves it on this rock. Don't you, Rinksie. You love it. I tell you what. Where's my..."

He pretended to search his pockets. Jelly knew what he was doing. Perhaps they'd done this act before. She handed an instant camera to him.

"Say cheese."

The king pulled the photo out and fanned it. He held up a shot of the queen and Art.

"Look at you two," he said. "It's good. You closed your eyes, Rinks, but we can fix that. We'll frame it, put it on the wall. Your own bedroom, Arty. What's your favorite food? Chocolate pudding? It'll be on tap. You won't even have to get up. Oh, how about a beam tube? We have a whole park you can ride without those Lost Boys getting in your hair. You smelling what I'm stepping in, son?"

He hovered closer. The smell of salty dough grew stronger.

"You get in that carriage and it's whatever you want."

"I want the queen."

Art wasn't sure why he blurted that out. He meant it, of course. He wasn't going anywhere without her. She listened to him. She heard him. *She saw him.* But he didn't want to go anywhere, really. He also knew this floating blob was going to get his way. Art was going to go with him one way or the other. And Art knew, he just knew the king didn't want the queen to come, also.

The color he turned meant Art was right.

The king gagged on his anger. Thumped his sides and twittered his twiggy legs.

Without a word, he spun around a dozen times before zooming to the carriage. He shoved himself inside, getting stuck for a moment. Jelly waited. They all did. And then the king popped his meaty face out the door.

"You," he said to the queen. "You ride in the back. I don't want anyone seeing you. No waving back if they do. And no rats, either. Not one! No touching me, either. Like ever. And no eye contact."

"That's not nice," Art said, bristling at the way he spoke to her.

"Son, I'm the king of the Naughty Side. What do you expect?"

THE CARRIAGE WAS a big box on wheels. With the king inside, Art very much doubted there was room for anyone else.

Wrong.

A twenty-foot ceiling. Shag carpet. Loungers and recliners.

Art and the queen settled into a velvet couch. Daryl curled up on Art's lap. Harley wasn't along for the ride, per the king's orders. Jelly climbed into a plastic bucket seat and spun it toward the chocolate king filling a throne at the far end, poured into it like melted flesh wearing a crown. His robe could house a Boy Scout troop.

The king was eating an ice-cream cone. Chocolate dripped over his knuckles and wet his purple lips. It sounded like eels fighting. His tongue darting over the melting globs, he reached back with a fist and hammered the wall.

"Let's go!"

The room jerked and leaned. The chandelier chattered on the ceiling, swinging to one side and then the other. Shutters dropped on the walls and slid back from the ceiling. A panoramic view of the sky opened. It was projections of the other side, Art assumed, since he didn't see the grumpy elf sitting on top. They sat in awkward quiet, watching the trees jostle past, listening to the king snorkel through a bowl of pudding.

The rats did not follow. Neither did Sweet Tooth.

"So how have you been, Jelly?" the queen asked. "I've missed you."

The elf looked at the king, who wasn't watching or couldn't possibly have heard her over the sounds he was making. Jelly spun the chair and half-whispered. Told her how things had been since she'd gone. It sounded like she hadn't been in the castle for quite some time. Twenty bells, Art guessed. Maybe longer. Art couldn't follow their conversation. But one thing was clear. Jelly missed the queen, too.

"I met your sister," Art said. "I think."

"I know," Jelly said. "How is she?"

Arthur shrugged. "Nice."

"Of course she's nice. So nice you jumped out of the castle."

"I was tricked." Art pointed at the sleeping cat.

"You regret it, then?"

He did not. If he hadn't jumped, he would be drowning in sweet nothings. He liked the Nice Side. The way it felt. The air was warmer. Sweeter. The songs uplifting. And he missed the residents, most of them anyway. The Gingerbreads, for sure.

But there was something about the Naughty Side that felt like home.

THE TREES WENT by with decorations around their trunks and fruited ornaments on their limbs. Once on the main road, pedestrians got out of the way and kissed their fingers and waved at the carriage like a limousine full of celebrities.

The sky didn't change. The dimness remained uniform and starless.

They passed through another small forest and emerged to views of hills and valleys, crossing over an arching bridge that spanned the Lemonade River. The current fizzy and loud. The second stream was much smaller. The horseless carriage passed through the Orange Brook without a bridge or even a plank. The smell of orange soda filled the carriage and made the king thirsty. He chugged a gallon of chocolate milk before they made it to the other side of the brook.

"Aw! Lookee there." The king twisted in the throne to look at the mountains behind him. "The chocolate fields are in view. Aren't they lovely?"

The king explained the operations between ice-cream sandwiches and pitchers of milkshakes. The mountains rose on the horizon. None quite so high as the Two-Face Mountain—the volcano-shaped mountain straddling the Nice and Naughty Sides. But they were plenty high. Art could see the harvesters the king described by the plumes of chaff floating like smog. And the shipping containers that rode ziplines down to transporters that took the harvest to processing plants.

Great erector sets trolled the fields with long spidery legs and blue electric arcs. The king didn't say what they did. But he did say with a very full mouth: "It's mine. All of it's mine."

"It's a blight," the queen said. "An unsustainable operation. Nothing survives and nothing grows where you harvest."

"She's jealous." He unleashed a wet burp into his fist. Then shouted at the ceiling: "How much longer?"

"Fudgy Lake up ahead," Jelly said.

"Oh, yay."

The king was elated. The floating boosters whined beneath his clothing, lifting him slightly out of the throne, enough for him to turn around and see the bubbling tar pits at the bottom of the road. Fumes hovered over the viscous surface. The air thick and warped. Nothing grew along the shoreline. There was no beach. Just black muck.

There was a structure, though. It looked like a lifeguard tower with a short plank at the top. Too short for a diving board. Too stiff to bounce. It was more for walking off. A rank smell filled the carriage as they neared it. Anaerobic pluff mud at low tide mixed with burnt sugar and boiled syrup.

The queen turned away. It was the result of harvesting, no doubt. A cesspool of greed.

As they started up the final hill, the sky grew darker and bruised. The tip of a dagger appeared just over the top of the slope. It absorbed what little light there was and continued to grow as they got closer, a monolith of sharp edges hacked away from a spire of obsidian. It was a deformed tombstone of the land. The light around it dreary and depressed.

When they breached the hill, tiny specks of light became visible.

The carriage paused. A long and winding road lay below them, winding its way to the base of that dead fang, crossing over a bridge that spanned a lake of tar surrounding the castle. Strands of Christmas lights swung in the trees, half of them blinking or not working at all.

The chocolate king settled into his throne. A sloppy, brown smile opened on his cheeky face. A coughing fit wet with phlegm and ice cream shook all his chins. Then he delivered chilling words.

"Welcome home, boy."

15

The catapult was made from a jawbreaker tree. The frame carved from its heartwood, giving it an amber hue. The wheels were peppermint patties. The spring coiled licorice.

It was a prototype. Could fit in King Chocolate's front pocket. Sometimes he carried it with him. He never knew when there was time to kill.

Like now.

The small-fry catapult was sitting on a dining table. The ice-cream scoop was loaded with a beautifully sculpted chocolate ball (a seamless orb no bigger than a marble). The licorice spring under tension. He adjusted the angle, turned it a few degrees to the left. When he flicked the switch, the catapult convulsed.

The ice-cream scoop sprang.

The chocolate ball went airborne.

King Chocolate leaned back and watched it arc toward the vaulted ceiling, through the fudge-dipped chandelier, reaching a crescendo and pausing before giving way to gravity. Falling like a flawless planet toward the gaping black maw full of brown teeth and a chocolate-coated tongue.

It landed in his mouth with perfect accuracy. No touch of the teeth or rattle in the throat. The lovely ball of chocolate settled on the king's swollen tongue. Melting. Painting the inside of his cheeks. Sliding down his throat with an angelic feeling of wellness and goodness. And *ahhhhhh.*

"The kitchen wants to know if you want another snack," Jelly said.

The king choked on the perfect moment. If he had been holding something, anything, he would have thrown it. He sat up and swallowed the soft lump before it completely melted.

"I told you—" He coughed into his fist. "I told you not to interrupt."

"You know how you get when you're hungry. Anything else?"

"Yeah. Like, uhhhh…" He threw his hands at the empty table. "I'm waiting, Jelly Roll. I'm the king. I don't wait."

"Give the boy a tick. This is new. I don't think he's hungry."

"What's hungry got to do with anything?" The king was serious. He never understood why others waited until they were hungry to eat. "So what—I just sit here and wait till he's *hungry*?"

He hung air quotes.

Jelly waddled closer. Reached over the table and loaded the catapult. When she launched the weapon, King Chocolate swatted the chocolate ball away. It bounced behind an antique jukebox playing a song the boy would know. At least, Jelly thought so.

"Get the eye," the king demanded. "And pick that up."

He wasn't going to let good chocolate go to waste. He'd made his point.

A few ticks later, a large orb was put in place of the catapult. It could be mistaken for a bowling ball. It was heavy and smooth with a swirling pattern of browns and grays on the surface. There were no finger holes because it was not used for sport.

Spying was what it did.

It was a receiver. A looking glass. *An eye.*

The king waved his hands around it (he did that whenever he used it; it wasn't necessary to start the thing up) and leaned closer. Jelly waited for him to finish his magic hand signals, then activated the transmission. A room appeared inside the globe. A boy by a window. The Mousequeen next to him.

It looked like magic. If you asked the king, that was what he would say. It totally was not magic.

It was science.

Tiny cameras the size of pollen were all over the castle. You couldn't blow your nose without shooting a few hundred into a hanky. It was Santa technology. Technically, it was elf technology. Santa got the credit. It was what he used to decide the naughty or nice children. At least, that was what the king said. Jelly let him think that.

The king didn't understand science. He liked magic.

His breath fogged the glass. He wiped it with his sleeve and smudged it with chocolate. The more he rubbed, the worse it got. There wasn't much to see or hear. The boy and the queen were talking about feelings. The boy didn't really want to be here. The queen asked him to describe what his emotions felt like.

"What does she want from him?" the king wondered.

"It's called active listening," Jelly answered. "She's quite good at it."

The king turned his head like a bird listening for the worm. The boy had closed his eyes now and was describing the tightness in his chest. The tension in his forehead. The king frowned. Not because he was gravely bored or because of what Jelly said or the tone with which she said it (he didn't hear a word she said).

"I'm going to punish Sweet Tooth," the king declared. "If she hadn't kidnapped the boy, I wouldn't be *WAITING!*"

"Look at it this way," Jelly said. "He trusts her."

"How does that help me?"

"I don't know. What do you want?"

"What do you mean, what do I want? I want the boy in this room! I've made that pretty clear."

"I'm talking big picture. What do you want with the boy?"

"I want him to do his thing."

"And what's that?"

"To do what I want."

"And what do you want him to do? Big picture—"

"Yeah, I get what big picture means. Right now I want you to shut up."

"Humor me. What's the end game? What do you want more than anything else?"

"I want to win!" The king didn't have to think about that. His yellowed eyes grew round. "What else is there?"

"That's right. You want to win. And the boy is here. And he's here because of *her*. Not you. He wasn't going to come with you. He came *here* because of her. You need the queen because you need him to win."

He could argue that if Sweet Tooth hadn't kidnapped the boy, he would've come straight here without the queen. The king grumbled but didn't say that. It started somewhere inside his throat. His fingers curled into his palms. Puffs of steams seeped out of his ears. Jelly could feel the heat from where she was standing. The king didn't like the queen much. He liked the truth even less. Jelly was right, and he did not like it.

The king knocked on the eye. It rattled with static, then gave up a squeal of feedback.

"Dinner's getting cold." The king spoke into the eye. "*Now.*"

To the boy, the king's voice sounded like it came out of thin air. The queen was used to his announcements. She didn't flinch. She was cold, that one. The king called her a NINO and called her that often. *Naughty in Name Only*. It was obvious. But she was cold when she needed to be. Usually when he was around.

He was going to heat her up.

KING CHOCOLATE's quiet fury cooled when Art the Fart walked into the dining hall.

The boy was taking in the wonder of the place, holding the purring furball against his chest. The king could see how he looked around, lips parted, eyes big and greedy. The boy appreciated what the king had, that was obvious. Had the king kept the eye on, he would've heard the queen coaching the boy how to act. It was her little secret on how to soften up his excellency. *Be amazed and awed,* she had said. *Even if you aren't.*

"Welcome!" King Chocolate threw his arms wide. The hoversuit hummed into overdrive, lifting him out of his throne. "Take your time, my boy. Let it soak in."

There was a three-tier fountain that spilled silky streams of milk chocolate. The decadent chocolate chandelier. The life-size statue of yours truly in the corner, sculpted from a block of virgin chocolate by an artistic ant colony (a very famous colony, the Triad assured him). It was all very expensive. And they did it for free. They liked the king that much.

Candy dispensers on the wall. A milkshake machine, too.

Chocolate chip pancakes stacked as high as a refrigerator.

Chocolate-dipped strawberries.

Chocolate flake cereal drowning in chocolate milk.

Chocolate cake. Chocolate pie. Chocolate donuts. Chocolate pudding. And brownies.

"It's all about the cocoa bean, my boy," the king crooned. "The flavor profile is affected by the weather and the soil, the harvesting techniques, and the genetic profile. All very complicated stuff my growers monitor closely. I don't want to bore you."

The king couldn't bore him because he didn't know any more than that.

"Besides being delicious, chocolate is the most versatile food ever grown. Breakfast, lunch, dinner, dessert. We drink it, we eat it, we smell it, we wear it. There are over eight hundred flavor notes in a bite of the dark stuff, you know. Eight *hundred.*"

The boy nodded with extreme interest. The king felt a tickle in his belly. He began peeling the wrapper from a chocolate bar off a stack of them.

"Try this. It's brand new. I'll be releasing it after Christmas. It's a dark red chili bar. You're going to love it."

He offered it to the boy. Art leaned forward and sniffed it. Wrinkled his nose. The pang of rejection was a fastball to the king's chest. He resisted digging through his pile for something else, something the boy would like.

Jelly gestured. *Relax.*

The king took a deep breath. A little more time and the chocolate fumes would do their thing. The boy wouldn't resist for long. No one could. No one except the Ice Queen.

"Figurines?" the queen said. "Really, Casey?"

She was admiring the delicately carved display. Each with a remarkable resemblance to the king. "How'd those get in here?" the king said. "Come, come. Sit, please. You're my guests. No more flattery, please. This table was cut from Two-Face Mountain. I had it polished for this occasion. No big deal. Pull up a chair."

The king ran his fingers over the smooth, marbled surface, his rings making long metallic sounds. The boy looked confused. The queen picked up on it, too. Then she explained what Two-Face Mountain was. "The big one," she said. "Half-light, half dark."

"The one on the border?" the boy said.

"That's the one," the king added. *Duh.* "You're a smart boy, I can tell. I'll bet you're funny, too. He looks funny, don't you think, Jel?"

Jel? He'd never called her that before. Jelly shook her head. He was trying too hard. That made him feel stupid. He took a long, deep breath. Pointed at two empty chairs.

"Sit," he said. It was more of a command.

They did. They sat. Even the cat sat on the boy's lap. The king was pleased.

"There's a bowl of chocolate wafers right there," the king said. "If you don't like those, try the chocolate-covered peanuts. Oh, oh, there are—"

"Cheese, please," the queen said. "And a glass of milk."

The king warmed a few degrees. Jelly waited for him to nod. It was slight. Barely visible. It was all he could do without having a meltdown. She knew what he was doing, waving all these chocolates under the boy's nose. And she was going to stink up the place.

"Would cheddar be all right, Lady Mouserinks?" Jelly asked.

"Lovely, Jelly. Thank you."

"And for the boy?"

He shook his head. Said he wasn't hungry. Jelly went to fetch the queen her snack of cheese and milk. At least she didn't ask for blue cheese. He would've stopped that. First of all, gross. Second, the stink of that moldy stuff got into everything—clothes, hair, skin. Name it and blue cheese ruined it.

They sat there awkwardly. Waiting for the elf to return. The king drumming his fingers on the polished table. He nudged a bowl of chocolate donut holes toward the boy.

Nothing.

Like he wasn't even tempted.

"She told you she doesn't eat the chocolate, didn't she?" The king's shine dimmed a few degrees. "It's bad for you, she tell you that?"

He scoffed. It was wet and phlegmy.

"It contains antioxidants, did you know that? That's going to lower your blood pressure. Reduces risk of strokes. Increases blood circulation. She tell you that? Makes your heart healthy. Yeah, it does that, too. Makes a good heart. Strong heart. It prevents liver damage, also. It makes you smarter, too. Boosts those things that make you think, you know what I mean? The *genius snack* is what they call it. She didn't tell you, did she."

Pretty obvious she didn't.

The boy *wanted* to eat it. The king saw that, too.

The king took a thin wafer from the big bowl. He rubbed it lightly between his finger and thumb. "Appreciate chocolate. Coax the flavor out with a little massage. Feel the texture on your fingertips. Admire the sheen it radiates."

He held it up.

With two hands, he delicately broke the wafer in half, holding it to his ear when he did so. It gave a sharp snap.

"Hear that? The sound of *perfection*," he whispered. "Bask in it before placing it on your tongue and allowing it to melt slowly—oh so slowly."

He stuck out his tongue. Gently, he laid the chocolate on the fat piece of purple meat sticking out of his mouth. He closed his eyes. When it turned to sludge and slipped into his flabby jowls, he said: "Taste the beginning and the end. They're different, my boy. Sometimes fruity. Sometimes floral or earthy."

He clicked his tongue and swallowed.

"Most of all, chocolate *feels* good."

When he opened his eyes, the boy was staring down at the table. This didn't hurt the king. Not at all. He could see the longing. The hook was set. It was just a matter of time. Even with the queen at his side, the boy wasn't going to hold out forever. And once he gave in to the sweet side, he would be in the king's command.

Winning.

A PLATTER OF CHEESE ARRIVED. All the queen's favorites: thin triangles of cheddar and muenster and mascarpone and the dreaded gorgonzola. An odor of wet gym socks soaked in swamp water hovered over the tray and tainted his chocolate. Any other day and he'd throw the platter out the window. This day was a special day.

The king smiled a dark smile. Forced as it was, but still a smile.

"Great jingle bells, look at the size of that monster," the king said. He jabbed a bloated finger at Daryl. "An animal after my heart, he is. What is it? A cat? Oh, that's a fine animal. What's the thing's name?"

"Daryl," the boy said.

More importantly, the boy said it with affection. Not intended for the king, but affection, nonetheless. It was a crack the king would exploit.

"Jelly says it likes to scratch things. Posts and whatnot. We'll have a dozen in your room, just for him. Just for Daryl. How do you like that?"

The boy smiled, just a little. The king's heart added a beat.

"Daryl crossed with Arthur," the queen said. "They're familiars."

It took all the king's effort to maintain his smile. As stiff as it was, he turned those greedy eyes on his royal partner just as she nibbled the corner off a hunk of gouda. The odor drew tears into the corners of his eyes. She smiled back. Even winked.

He maintained. Until a wad of hair floated by. As light as a cloud and just as soft, it drifted across the table. Undoubtedly on its way to ruin a bowl of wafers. He could imagine it getting stuck in his mouth. Like cotton candy that didn't melt.

"Cats are fun," he said. Then back to the boy: "Do you like your room? It's nothing permanent, of course. Just a little something while you're here. No pressure."

"A lot of games in that room, Casey," the queen said. "Barely space for him to lie down."

"Well, yeah. You're boring."

The boy's smile grew a little bit. Just a little and the king liked it. Oh yes, he did. And not so subtly he nudged a bowl of malted chocolate bombs toward him. The boy noticed.

Oh yes, he did.

"So, we're having a Christmas Eve concert," the king said. "Would you like to guess who's the guest of honor?"

The king walked his fingers in the boy's direction.

"That's why we brought you here, after all. To the Naughty Side. It was to honor you, young man. Your courage. Your curiosity. You're not like fuddy-duddy here, sitting around huffing fragrant candles and playing with rats. You're fun. And that's exactly what this party is going to be. *Lit!*" He chuckled, unsure if he used that word right. The boy didn't laugh at him. "There will be games and stuff and a hard-rocking show. Oh, I almost forgot!"

The king attempted to snap his fingers.

"The Big Bad Wolf. Heard of him? He'll be there, won't he, Jelly. He's going to want to see your piggy shirt, for sure. Love on that, son. Especially when he hears you nicked it from the three little oinkers. That's what I heard, you snatched it right off their clothesline. Up high."

The king offered a high five.

The boy patted his hand with less enthusiasm than the king had hoped for. But he hit it. Oh yes, he did. *Baby steps.*

"Anyways, we're going to change up the concert this year. Just for you, Artie. I'll be taking over for Santa."

"I think that's a wonderful idea," the queen said.

"Okay, that's enough," the king said. When Jelly poked him in the side, a poke he barely felt but understood, the king added: "It was her idea."

"Your idea?" the boy said.

Jelly got that one right. The boy brightened when the king gave the queen the credit.

"No, no," the queen said. "It was the king and queen of the Nice Side. They proposed it. I only supported it. I think it's about time—"

"Enough about them, Lady Mouserinks," the king said. He used her formal name, and the boy smiled. "Those two goody-goods trapped our dear boy in the tower and planned never to let him go. Not so nice, if you ask me. I'm an expert on naughty. If this fat cat hadn't tricked you into jumping out the window, you'd still be up there."

The king hammered the table with a meaty fist. Then elbowed a tray of chocolate-dipped cherries in the boy's direction.

"Have you ever met Santa?" the king said. "Did I ask you that already? The jolly fat man is not so very nice to us, Artie. You've heard what he puts in our stockings? Fills them right up like a dirty joke. Every Christmas. It was funny the first time. Not so much anymore."

He leaned closer but didn't whisper.

"We're not all bad, Artie. Misunderstood, maybe. Heartbroken, possibly. But we ain't bad. And coal isn't making us nicer, I can tell you that. You think the jolly fat man's never made a mistake?"

The queen nibbled a cracker all proper like. She looked bored.

"You think *she's* never made a mistake?" the king shouted. "Ha!"

He mashed a fist full of candy-coated chocolates into his mouth until his cheeks were chipmunked. Then poured a gallon of chocolate milk after them. He sopped up the mess with his sleeves. His charm transformed into hot annoyance, as it usually did when it came to Queen Lady Mouserinks.

"You want to know how bad she was? I'll tell you. She didn't have to come here, Artie. She *deserved* to be here. That's how bad she was. The things she did. Opening presents before Christmas. Switching price tags at the toy store. How you like that? She would steal candy and not even eat it. Just for the thrill. Throw it in the ditch after she took it. You believe that? She *burned* all her sister's trophies or threw them in a lake. What?! She did that to her sister, Artie. Her sister. Can you imagine!"

Somehow, the queen looked more bored than before. She wasn't denying anything he said because it was all true. But the guilt and shame weren't dragging behind her anymore.

"Even her husband couldn't stand her."

Confusion contorted the boy's face. He looked at the queen. "He's not your husband?"

"Me?" King Chocolate said. "Oh, no. No, no, nooooooo. God, no."

The boy's disappointment was right there for her to see. She felt it like a ten-foot stick on the back of her legs. Even winced a little. The king tamped down the joy he felt and fanned the flames of indignity. Waved his hands at the injustice (and slapped a stack of chocolate bars in front of the boy).

"Oh, no. Her husband was another guy. He left because she was awful, Artie. Capital *A*! She sought me out when she crossed over, came straight to the castle and won my heart. One look at her and I knew she was terrible. I'd found my equal. She was the queen of the Naughty. The only one who could sit next to me and rule from her heart. Her dark, dark heart."

The king drooled with anticipation. Watching the boy devour the gossip like cocoa beans.

"But... you're not like that now," the boy said. "Why?"

"*Why?* Who cares why. She's nice, Artie. Look at her. She stinks of it. She lost her edge. What'd you say? You were tired of being you. So you changed. Admit it, Rinks. Admit to the boy you changed."

Art didn't hear a word the king said. His gaze was expecting the queen to answer. She placed the cheese she'd been nibbling on the plate, dabbed her mouth with a linen napkin, and chewed while staring at her lap. Maybe she was waiting for the boy to get the hint that she didn't want to answer. Maybe she didn't know why she changed. The king never asked why. He never cared.

Then she looked up with those creepy eyes. Glanced at the king. Then to the boy.

"From the time I was very little, I had these feelings. I couldn't explain them, couldn't tell you why I had them or what they meant. They were dark feelings. I didn't have words for them then, like guilt or shame. I just had them and didn't know why. I hated them. I hated the way they felt. And I blamed myself for having them, like they were my fault. Like I deserved them for some reason. I was a little girl, and I hated myself for having those feelings. And I hated myself for hating myself because of the feelings."

She looked down at her knobby fingers twisted into knots.

"They were heavy and loathsome. They made me feel ugly. I ran from them. I spent my life running from them, and the faster I ran, the uglier I felt. I couldn't get away from them. I didn't know what else to do. I had to get those feelings out of me. So that's what I did. I put them out into the world and made everyone feel them, too. I hurt my family and my friends. The more I hurt them, the better I felt. Well, not better. Relieved, I suppose. Hurt people hurt people, they say. I was pretty good at both. It was all I knew, Arthur."

She pushed her plate away, still playing a painful game of twisting fingers.

"Then I came here, to Candyland. All the things I'd done in my life—all the runnin', all the hurtin'—this was where I belonged. The naughties were my people. They got me. They understood what it was like living with a shadow. They knew what it felt like to be cold on the inside. I could be as naughty as I wanted here, Arthur, and no one judged me. Here, I let it all out."

A long pause grew longer. The king squirmed in his throne. Apparently, her story was over. A terrible ending. Incomplete, really. But he was glad it was over. "And then," he started to say, "you—"

"I grew tired, Arthur. It's that simple, really. Time is funny here. At times it feels like eternity. And I was tired of running for all that time. Tired of who I'd been all my life. Tired of the anger, of the bitterness and hate. I was tired of the hurt that would not heal. All I'd ever done was beat those feelings down or beat others with them. Feelings I tried to ignore or pretend weren't there. That if I could just drown them with distractions and—" She threw her arms out at the table, and the king took a little offense to that. Like it was the chocolate's fault she was so bad. "None of this helped. Because the feelings were still there."

She shook her head. Another pregnant pause on a cliffhanger ending. Maybe that was it, but the boy had to go and drag more out of her, asking what happened next. The king wasn't having any more of it.

"Change! That's what happened, I already told you. She *wanted* to change. Hit her bottom, got sick and tired of being sick and tired, blah, blah, blah. It doesn't matter. You crossers are always changing. A true Lander stays the same." He thumped his chest. It sounded like an overripe melon. "Our true colors never fade. We are who we are, forever and ever. But not crossers. You change, you grow, you shrivel and turn gross. It's disgusting. I can barely look at her."

Jelly elbowed the king hard enough for it to hurt. The more he insulted the queen, the more the boy grew distant.

"You can't trust a crosser, that's all I'm saying. I mean, I didn't say it. It's what I heard. I'm just saying, how can you trust something that changes? Am I right?"

"That's why your husband left?" The boy had not looked away from the queen. Was he even listening to the king? "Because now you're nice?"

"That's *exactly* why he left!" the king shouted. Then: "No, wait. No, he left *way* before that. Aren't you listening, son? He left because she was *awful!* Let me tell you, son, those were the good times. This one right here, Ms. Queen of the Naughty, Ms. Hurt the World, Ms. Don't Mess with Me—she was *too naughty* even for her husband. And he was a piece of work, trust me. He was a thief. A good one, too. Stole from me, he did. If I ever catch that rat, he'll be licking the bottom of Fudgy Lake with all seven heads."

The boy frowned at that. The king smiled deliciously. The boy looked slightly disgusted. *Here's an angle,* the king thought, *to make the queen seem even grosser.*

"The queen's husband, he has seven heads. You didn't know that? Imagine, a big head and then six smaller heads growing out of his neck. *That's her husband!* Picture that a tick. It's painful to watch, the way they all talked at the same time. Hideous. Hard to look at. He lost his wits, too, just like her. Started doing nice things way before she did, but he couldn't decide which side he belonged on. He was more damaged than Grimjoy, and you've seen those lunatics. You can't straddle the border, son. That's a rule around here. *Pick a lane or go insane.*"

Jelly nodded. She had his back on that one.

If the king had stopped there, maybe there would be a different ending to this story. Suppose you could say that about any small detail. But this was no small slip-up. The king wanted to poke the queen some more. It hurt her for Art to hear the truth. The king went digging for more hurt.

"Is S'ven still on the mountain, Rinks? If he is, he'd better not come back or—"

"S'ven's your husband?"

The boy stood up. The chair cracked on the floor. The king would ordinarily make someone pay for that. But he was more worried about the boy's fierce reaction. All at once, he felt his connection slip away from him.

"Why do you think they call him S'ven?" The king held up seven chocolate-stained fingers. *Like, duh.* "Wait, do you know him?"

"I've been looking for him. He's supposed to get me out of here!"

The king was alarmed to hear this. And alarmed was not when he did his best thinking. But this time was different. The boy's disgust for the queen suddenly morphed into affection for her. *Forgiveness.* The king realized, without Jelly having to tell him, there would be no way to change that. It didn't matter how naughty she *had been*. That wasn't who she was *now*.

The king needed to win the boy's heart to get what he wanted.

The queen had already done that. But it wasn't too late.

"He's coming to the Christmas Eve concert," the king said.

"I thought you said he couldn't come back," the boy said.

"Well, no. But this is Christmas Eve we're talking about. I know for a fact he's coming to the concert. Right, Jelly?"

"Right," she said, not skipping a beat.

"And do you know why he's coming here? So... you... can... *meet him*! If anyone can take you back home, it's going to be that seven-headed weirdo. We don't want you here, no offense. Crossers go home. Am I right, Jelly?"

"You are correct, sire."

"You didn't tell the boy S'ven was coming?" the king asked the queen. "Maybe you are naughty."

The king laughed for real. It was loud and obnoxious and right in her stunned, cheese-stinking face. Talk about checkmate. She had nothing to say because she didn't know where her thieving husband had gone off to. Last King Chocolate heard, he'd gone up Two-Face Mountain and never came down. Maybe he did go back home. All the king knew for sure was the boy wasn't going home. Not if he could help it.

"Let's celebrate!" the king cheered. "To home!"

He bit off the end of a chocolate bar and handed the rest to the boy. With a smile of relief (and without thinking of the queen), the boy took it from him. He sat down with a stunned look, imagining what home was like. And then he did it.

He took a bite.

He chewed it. He swallowed it.

And he smiled brighter than ever. Because chocolate felt good. Chocolate made all the problems go away.

"Have you ever met Santa?" the king asked.

❄

"LADY MOUSERINKS," King Chocolate said, "can we talk?"

He said it with exaggerated sweetness. He didn't want to upset the boy, who had a fistful of chocolate wafers and a pocketful of malted choco-balls. Jelly would make sure a mudslide soda was waiting in his room to wash all that yumminess down.

The queen whispered something to the boy (something about a toothbrush, no doubt) on his way out. Jelly escorted him out of the room. The queen returned to the table, where the plate of expensive cheese wasn't even half eaten. She reached for her chair.

"Don't bother. I'll keep it short."

The king leaned all the way back in his throne and squeezed a tube of chocolate frosting into his gaping mouth. Put a little swirl on the top. He swished it under his tongue and over his teeth, between his cheeks and gums and savored every flavor.

He'd been a powerful king in his time. Undefeated as far as he could remember. The conquests. The intimidation. The fear his name invoked was thrilling. At first. You get used to it after a while. It becomes normal. When a child cried at the sight of him, he used to feel powerful. Now he felt nothing. When a resident quivered in fear, now it was just another day.

But this. *Oh this.*

He wanted this so bad. So, so bad it hurt his bones. When the boy refused to get in the carriage, he'd felt a lightning strike of rage and cold shiver of fear. He was the king of the Naughty. He could do anything he wanted this side of the border. But this boy was another level of power. He could feel it.

And he savored it.

"Casey—"

King Chocolate had forgotten the queen was there. So surprised, he inhaled the melting frosting. It jammed into the wrong pipe. He swung his fist onto his chest. It thudded like a wooden mallet on a dusty mattress. Again and again. His face turned a rotting shade of purple. The queen got behind him and swatted the back of his head. That didn't seem like the right move on someone choking, but she did it again. Harder this time.

He painted the table with frosting, wheezing great, gurgling breaths.

Eyes bulging from fleshy pockets, he leaned forward. A string of drool danced off his lip. His heavy arm slammed the table and set off the candy catapult. The mechanical arm circled around and fired a blob of chocolate. It stuck between his eyes with a thwap. His head jerked back.

He spat at the catapult. Then battered the thing into splinters with his bare hands. He slumped in the throne like a sack of gooey lard, heaving like a pig forced to run a marathon. He aimed a finger at the queen.

"What... do you... *want*?" he said.

"You asked me to stay, Casey."

He shook his head. That seemed like forever ago. Swallowing acrid saliva that pooled under his tongue, he fell back into a more comfortable position. He wiped the sweat and food off his face with the sleeve of his jacket. Then fixed a stare on her, one that would turn a Lander into a puddle. But she didn't flinch. *Crosser arrogance.*

"Why are you *here*, with the boy? You're up to something. I can smell it."

"He asked me to come."

"Don't give me that. I know you, the way you work. Making your little magic spells, putting your thoughts into his head." He wiggled his fingers, made ghost noises. "Why do you even care about him? What do you *want*?"

"He's frightened, Casey. And alone."

"That's why you're here? Because your heart grew ten sizes?" He stuck out his tongue. "Don't you mess this up for me."

"I'm here to help."

"Good."

He didn't believe her, but he had no choice. She had no idea how much he needed her right now. The situation was delicate. Jelly was right. Without her, the boy would rebel and be useless if he stayed.

"You need to guide this boy," he said with the right amount of force. "He'll listen to you."

"Maybe he'll listen to you."

"I'm too much man for him. Besides, you're a crosser. You think like one. That's what's wrong with you. And him. We need to get this right. You and me, we'll change Candyland with him."

"Change is what I seek."

"Don't give me that. You leave the changing up to me. There's a reason I'm the king and you're not."

She took that well. Actually, too well. Breathing calmly, no tension between her brows or in her shoulders. Back in the day, when she first arrived in Candyland, her rage could blow the hair off his face. She had been a bottled storm that wiped villages off maps. He sort of missed that.

She knows something, he thought. "What is it? Tell, what is it about the boy you aren't saying? He's a mess, ain't he? Is that what you're hiding? The boy is all loose in the bucket, and now he's a pile of screws, is that it?"

"It's not easy crossing over."

What was it she did when he complained, rubbed her finger and thumb together? *World's tiniest fiddle.* And what did she say when he had an excuse, no matter how rock solid it was?

"Gimme a break," he said with a country accent. "You ain't special, darling. You think it's easy running the Naughty Side? Making sure production's on track so no one goes without their chocolate? Keeping the Nice Side from winning? I got pressure, lady! Real pressure! What's a crosser know about that? He's a kid!"

He activated the hoversuit and floated above the table. Last thing he needed to hear was how hard it was growing up on another world. *This is Candyland! There's no leaving. That's the hard truth.*

"It's not easy growing up," she said. "Not knowing where you fit in, what you're supposed to be like. You don't know, Casey. Landers don't *grow up.* You're just here, whatever this place is." She nodded with a calmness that crawled under his skin. She looked up and said, almost defiantly: "But he'll find his way."

"Find his way? What's that supposed to—" The king lurched

forward. "You didn't tell him he *can't* leave, did you. You didn't tell him he's here for good."

"He's here for a reason," she said. "He's the one."

This, strangely enough, struck the king violently funny. He began chuckling at first. It built into a laughing fit that burst from his throat in long breathless howls. He wiped tears away and let the medicine flow. It felt so good to laugh at someone. Washed all the bad feelings away and reminded him of what victory tasted like.

She remained calm.

Even that didn't bother him.

"He's 'the One.'" He splashed air quotes and let loose another howl. "Oh, dear Santa. This ain't a movie, Mouserinks. *The one.* Oh, that's good. That's rich. Anyway, just make sure he does what I want him to do and we'll be cool. Now go. Bye."

"What do you want him to do?"

The king scooped pudding from a bowl with two fingers and painted his lips. He smiled a chocolatey smile and ordered her to get out. Jelly opened the door. She got the hint. The king wanted to bask in the future glory. The game was about to be over. It was just a matter of time.

But time was a funny thing.

16

Art couldn't remember lying down. He had no idea how long he'd slept. There were no clocks on the wall. No sun in the sky. He woke surrounded by pillows on a giant bed, staring at a vaulted ceiling painted with glowing stars. He sank in the soft mattress, searching for the constellations. Nothing he recognized. Yet so familiar. It didn't feel like a dream anymore.

He crawled a mile to the edge of the bed with a head full of bees and syrup in his veins.

The room was deep and long. Big enough to host a basketball tournament and cluttered with things. Like a department store for teenage boys.

In front of him, displayed on a curving table, was a banquet of desserts. Dishes of chocolate wafers, bowls of chocolate drops, trays of chocolate cookies. Glasses of chocolate milk, scoops of chocolate ice cream on chocolate-dipped sugar cones.

Art's chest felt heavy. Legs shaky.

Fear gnawed his stomach like termites on a damp log.

He wasn't hungry. Without standing, he grabbed a chocolate bar off the table. He held it to his ear to hear the crisp snap when he broke it. Waved it under his nose to let the earthy, nutty aroma fill his nostrils. A single bite released a flood of endorphins. It melted under his tongue and went through him on a rising tide. It washed away Fear, cleared his head and opened his heart.

He breathed into an easy smile. The world came into focus.

All it took was one bite.

HE WANDERED the room (he'd come to think of it as a gymnasium). It would be the only time he explored this wonderland of teenage trappings. There were banks of video games and rows of carnival games. Darts to throw and golf balls to putt and bowling balls to roll. Remote-controlled cars to drive, a platoon of drones to fly. Footballs and baseballs and Frisbees. There was no one to throw to. It all smelled new and plastic.

He touched none of it. Not a single thing.

There was also an art station. More of a studio on a raised platform. Art climbed the steps and walked among stacks of blank canvases. Empty easels. Tubes of paint lined up on a bench. Brushes with clean bristles in a rack. There were tubs of clay to mold and wheels to spin it on. An oven to fire it in. There were boxes of pencils and trays of markers.

It had everything. Every possible medium an artist could desire. *Everything.*

One easel was loaded with a canvas. Its eggshell surface blank. A photo was pinned in the corner. It was a Christmas tree brightly lit with a thousand colors.

There was only one thing that spoke to him. Art went back to the bed and the table of chocolate. A recliner was positioned in front of a window that overlooked the dim country of the Naughty Side. He grabbed a bowl of chocolate-covered almonds and went sailing into a sea of mild euphoria beneath a chocolate haze.

Fudgy Lake surrounded the castle. It was black as an oil reservoir. Birds glided over it like dark smudges. Not a single firefly spotted the darkness. He thought how nice it would be to fish in it. To bait a hook and lounge on the shore with his shoes off and earphones playing something sharp and noisy. That was something he loved to do, once upon a time. Or so he thought. With his fingers grazing the bowl, he drifted into another dreamless slumber.

Content and comfortably numb.

HE WOKE SOMETIME LATER. Impossible to say how long.

This time it took three chocolate pieces to clear the cobwebs from his head. Fudgy Lake was still an oil stain. Birds still lugged themselves over it. Nothing had changed. Still, he watched from the comfort of the recliner. Fingers swimming in a bowl of chocolate-covered raisins.

He hated raisins.

Whenever boredom pressed down, he would reach for the table. It was always stocked (he never bothered wondering how), and the next bowl of chocolate took him to the bottom of the warm and loving ocean.

THE QUEEN WOULD COME SIT with him. Sometimes she was there when he woke. Looking at him with kind, human eyes.

They would look out the window without talking. It was a boring program, but she didn't seem to mind. Sitting there drinking her tea while he nibbled chocolate-dipped pretzels with a pint of chocolate soda. He asked her when he was going to leave the castle. She never answered him, but that was okay. He didn't really mean it. He only asked because he felt he should. He wanted things to be different. Just didn't know how to make it happen.

When the window got boring: there was chocolate.

When his body ached: more chocolate.

When emotions grew heavy: chocolate.

There was only one answer.

❄

THE QUEEN ENCOURAGED him to walk about. He only did so because she wanted him to. He could not care less about the pointless toys. Thankfully she didn't want him to strap on a baseball mitt. They never slowed down. It was more of a stretch-your-legs sort of walk. To clear his head, get the blood pumping. He needed that. His heart had been thudding like a steam engine pushing sludge through narrow pipes.

Beneath it lurked the poison fingerprints of Guilt and Shame. They were inseparable, those two. When they came knocking, he ate more chocolate. When they called out his name, more chocolate. Each time required more to quiet them down. Each time they returned louder and more obnoxious. He couldn't keep doing it alone. Thankfully the queen was there.

"I really want you to see this," she said.

Of everything in the room, the art studio was the only place he liked. The supplies glistened in their wrappers. She admired the colors, asked him what he liked most. She stopped at the canvas on the easel. The one with the picture pinned in the corner. The Christmas tree of a thousand lights. She looked rather sullen in her observation.

"The king would like you to create this," she said.

"With what?"

"Whatever you like. Just when you do, envision it. Build the image in your mind before you create it. See every detail first; then let it flow onto the canvas."

She waved her hand, sweeping it back and forth like a leaf falling in autumn. She offered a kind smile and stepped back. Art considered the supplies—the endless tubes and bottles and wells. He chose a sharpened pencil with soft lead. Licked the tip of it as he stepped forward.

With dashing strokes, he scribbled on the virgin canvas.

When he was done, he dropped the pencil on the floor. Went

back to the recliner to watch another episode of Fudgy Lake and the tired birds.

The queen sat next to him. She didn't say anything.

He closed his eyes and drifted into a familiar place of unfeeling. The shadows of Guilt and Shame falling over him, he muttered something he wouldn't remember. Something the queen had once said.

"I belong here," he said.

She took his hand. She held it through the long dark night.

17

I f the boy was sleeping, he wouldn't feel the cold iceberg floating over him.

His sprawling form lay in a pile of pillows. His open mouth pulling air through his dry throat. The bedsheet had come off two corners. The comforter was on the floor.

The boy didn't know or care what hovered over him.

King Chocolate bobbed over the bed. Jelly stood like a child holding the string to a human balloon. The king stared with muddy eyes smooshed in a field of doughy skin. Lips thin and grim.

He spun around and floated toward the playground. He'd become quite good with the hoversuit, maneuvering down narrow aisles and leaning into tight turns. He didn't bother pretending with his legs anymore, certain the time would come when they would simply fall off like flower petals that had served their purpose.

The playground.

Jelly promised these things would keep a crosser happy. Especially a boy. The king wanted the boy to forget the world outside the castle. Everything he could ever want or need was inside these walls. The king was living proof he didn't have to leave.

King Chocolate was afraid the playground would be too good,

that it would distract the boy from his true calling. The queen had said it wouldn't work. The king had dug his heels in when he heard her say that. Doubled down on Jelly's investment and made it even bigger than originally planned.

And nothing had moved. Nothing at all.

The king ignored the queen, naturally. And when she had told him *why* the playground wasn't working (just like she said it wouldn't), he shouted, "Why didn't you say something earlier?" And then blamed her for everything.

The art studio, however, was different.

The king was happy to see this. As he drifted closer to the canvas and read the words scribbled on it with a sharp pencil, his hopes withered. The boy was taunting him with the king's own words.

This is not going as planned.

The boy had gotten a taste of the dark stuff. Once someone experienced the healing power of chocolate, they needed more of it. That was how it worked. The king intended it that way. There was only one place to get chocolate and only one king to give it. *He needs me.*

King Chocolate ripped the photo of the beautiful Christmas tree off the canvas. All he'd asked for was a tree. The boy couldn't even do that. Time was running out. He needed some proof the boy could do what everyone said he could do. Drawing a tree was child's play!

"Cut him down to one wafer," the king said. "The boy is chocolate-brained."

"Yep," said Jelly.

Jelly snowplowed the stacks of chocolate bars and containers of chocolate drops off the table. They fell into a loose bag. Little balls of gold foil—having been peeled off the chocolate coins and rolled like giant boogers—littered the floor. Jelly squashed them with her extra-wide feet, and it made an awful sound.

The boy stirred.

He could feel the dark and heavy shadow over him. The boy climbed out of the stupor of sleep and backed away from the king, running his hand through tangled hair. He saw Jelly ransacking his stash. Chocolate lines had crusted around the boy's lips.

"You need to pace yourself," the king announced. "There'll come a time when you can eat all you want. But too much will soak your brain. No one likes a soggy brain, boy."

The king didn't care for the look on the boy. A hideous look. The kind that smelled bad and felt worse. The king descended until his twiggy legs lay across the pillows. Knobby knees buckling.

"What is it you want? I've put everything in this room, and all you do is lie there. I give you everything, and you give me *nothing*. Is that fair, boy? Nothing's free, not on this side of the border. You need to—"

He caught sight of Jelly giving him the stop sign. He was coming on a little heavy. The boy was crabwalking away from the king. There was a reason he'd been watching the boy on remote instead of coming into the room. His temper was as thin as a wafer and as brittle as the good stuff. But he'd grown tired of waiting for something to happen. The queen was letting the boy crash through rock bottom after rock bottom. The king didn't want the boy to crash-land.

King Chocolate wanted him to dance.

He spun away. The boy looked disgusted with King Chocolate. Well, the king was disgusted with him times ten. *Times a thousand.*

Jelly said from the corner of her mouth: "Should we call her in?"

"Hard no."

Enough hand-holding. To carve a statue, you need a chisel and hammer. The king rose until he was ten feet off the floor and looking down on the boy. He grimaced and growled. The boy looked more confused than scared. Maybe a little nervous.

"I thought you were an artist. I made sure every brush, every pencil and piece of paper was just right. Brand new and all yours. Everything you could want... *and you give me THIS?*"

He pointed at the art studio, the canvas where the boy had written two words with a pencil.

BLAH. BLAH.

Jelly chuckled. It wasn't funny. Not a cent. Maybe ironic—definitely ironic—but not funny.

"It's not hard, what I want. I told you *exactly* what it is." He shook the picture. "A pretty Christmas tree, see? That's all. You think

Christmas is boring, is that it? Not worth your time. I got news, Arty Farty. That's all we do here is Christmas, so you'd better get used to it and *draw!* It doesn't have to be merry, merry or blah-blah. It's just got to look like this, you see? You envision it, see it in your head, then put it on that canvas. *LOOK!*"

He waved the photo at him. The boy had to see it. Really see it. More than that, he had to *want* to make that Christmas tree *his* Christmas tree. Recreate it with his thoughts and let it flow through his hands. That was when the magic would happen. Supposedly.

It'd better.

"Time is short, son." The king softened his tone. "We're counting on you. All of us. The entire Naughty Side. You do this for us, and you'll get what you want, I promise. Because I know what you want. You want to go home."

The boy sat up. Oh yeah. That was what he wanted. Like waving a bone over a dog's nose. The king knew the power of a promise. Anyone who didn't believe magic was real never observed a promise in action. The king was a master. He wielded promises like weapons. They didn't have to mean anything and certainly didn't have to be true to work. Promises were just words. The magic was in the hands of the wizard who weaved the spell. Because he had to believe in the promise no matter how much of a fib it was.

"Listen." The king descended to eye level. His frail legs folded beneath him. "The Naughty Side isn't bad. It's not. It's the truth is what it is. The cold hard truth. It's looking at life the way it is, not the way you *want* it to be. You got to have mettle to be naughty. Ain't no sugarcoating over here. This is real life, son. Real, real life. You can't be soft, and you can't be weak. Life will blend you down and slurp you up. I see the steel in you, boy."

King Chocolate nodded with fatherly pride. Probably the best he'd ever done. He believed in this boy. Most of what he said was utter nonsense, but not that. He believed this boy had steel.

"Life isn't easy. Over here, we know exactly how hard it is. Then we do something about it."

The king delivered the speech of his life. His tone dead center. An award-winning look of empathy. It wasn't hard to do because he meant it. It was all hogwash, but he believed it. Even Jelly looked misty.

And that, ladies and gentlemen, is how you sell a promise.

"You got six rings to finish this. Or the chocolate river dries up."

He threw the photo on the bed. That part was true.

KING CHOCOLATE DROVE the throne like an electric go-cart.

He'd shed the hoversuit. It smelled strangely sweet and was starting to chafe. Jelly took it to the basement to get it refreshed. Whatever that meant. The king wasn't listening. His brain still replaying the events with the boy.

When he arrived in the theater room, he plowed through the empty seats and spun the throne to face the screen. King Chocolate flipped open the snack drawer in the armrest. A crinkly bag of chocolate-frosted popcorn was stuffed in the bottom. He ripped it open and pushed a handful into his mouth. Salty and sweet. The perfect combo for a movie.

Since the king left, the boy had moved to the edge of his bed, slumped over, hand running through his hair. Now he got up, counted the chocolates on the table (ten wafers and three malted) and went to the window. He was the artist type, all right. Sullen, introspective. Wishful. A cauldron of simmering emotions.

He's thinking.

The king knew a thinking face when he saw one. In fact, the king knew—that very moment—things were going to work out. Call it energy, call it verve or Christmas spirit. The king knew exactly what would happen.

The boy is going to draw.

"MISS ANYTHING?"

Jelly picked up a bench, straightened the bent leg, and sat next to the king. She held out her hand. He rained chocolate popcorn on it, not taking his eyes off the screen. Jelly had been in and out of the room half a dozen times since the king had arrived. *The worst movie ever,* she declared.

Not to the king.

He studied the subtleties, the small gestures. He sampled the emotions boiling inside the boy, felt them transform and shift. Change his thoughts. Crossers were ruled by their emotions. Especially young ones. No control over what they felt. A ship without an anchor. He was rudderless without a sail.

"Genius move, bt-dub," Jelly said with a mouthful. "What you did in there. The boy needed tough love. You gave it. Just when I think you're clumsy and awkward with no people skills, there you go—"

The king's hand went up.

He leaned forward. The look on the boy's face changed. It was microscopic. The king waved at the screen. The image zoomed on the boy's face. "Closer," he called. "*CLOSER!*"

"There. There it is," he whispered.

A speck of light.

The queen was right. The king was witnessing it in real time. There was no way he'd admit it to her. But he whispered it out loud.

"He *is* the one."

The boy's eyes flickered across the room. The queen had a soft touch with him. Nurturing. It was the support he needed. Strengthened his bow.

"Get the queen," the king said. "I want her to see this. Go!"

Jelly sighed. She shuffled toward the door. Picked up the pace when the king hurled the bag of popcorn at her and told her to hurry. He teetered on the edge of the throne, trembling with anticipation.

The boy leaned against the wall. Arms crossed. *Thinking.*

Jelly and the queen were outside the theater, gossiping in the hall. The king slammed his fist on the armrest.

"Get in here!"

They looked inside. He drove the throne straight at them, circled behind them, and herded them inside. Careful not to run over the queen's tail, he nudged them into the middle of the room. They leaned into each other, watching the king. Drool running from the corner of his mouth. Chins fluttering with excitement.

He lifted a trembling hand.

"Look at that," he said.

18

B*oredom.*

Art wore it like an itchy blanket. It clung to him uncomfortably. The moment the king left (or flew out of the room; *was he really flying?*), he felt boredom wrap around him. Beneath its scratchy embrace were the jitters and the shakes—the footprints of Guilt and Shame urging him to escape, to crawl out of his skin.

He sat on the bed. Time didn't move. When it did, it sped past him. It was one long blur of eating and sleeping and wallowing. He wanted to move but couldn't. Wanted to scream, tear his clothes off, get these feelings out. He was a prisoner.

In the castle. And otherwise.

The king wasn't going to let him go. Not out of the castle. Maybe not out of the room. This wasn't a playground. It was a cell.

There is a way to escape, the queen had said. He recalled her counseling him by the window. *It'll set you free.*

She didn't elaborate. She never did. Her advice was sometimes cryptic, as if she couldn't quite say it. Not here. It didn't matter. Art knew what she was saying. He went to the window to think on it. To catch some fresh air. Gaze on the dark blemish of Fudgy Lake and the lethargic birds pecking Swedish fish from the bank. He was there for quite some time. Then he did what the queen wanted him to do.

Guilt and Shame followed him to the art studio.

HE DRAGGED his fingers over tubes of paint, the soft-bristled brushes. Drank the vivid colors with his eyes, inhaled the newness of it all—the unbroken seals, the freshly sharpened pencils. The fragrance of shaved wood and powdery graphite. He circled the open studio, surveying the supplies, the stacked canvases, and pads of papers. Drawers of glue and rags and sponges and markers. Masking tape, spray adhesive, clay. Nothing was missing, not a thing.

He sorted through the rack of pencils.

Found one he liked. The lead soft. The wood light and balanced in his hand. It fit between his fingers. He held it like a conducting baton, swung it around, carving the air with his eyes closed. Hearing music in his head and turning in a circle.

When he opened his eyes, he faced a blank canvas. The picture of a Christmas tree attached to the corner.

He didn't question the why of it. He'd stopped doing that since arriving. The why and the how. It was time to *do*. This was where Art gave Guilt and Shame the slip.

The work began.

THE CREATIVE FLOW was rough and choppy.

At times, the pencil was nothing more than a stick of wood. A stranger. Stubborn.

The first attempt was not good. It went on the floor. The second draft was no better. The third was even worse.

The mistakes piled up around him. Broken frames and crumpled canvases.

He kept going. The current carried him forward. He didn't look back on what went wrong. His stomach churned and folded. He twitched and buckled. It wasn't working. He was fighting the current. Trying to *make* something fit.

Again.

Another.

Another.

Thirty canvases were on the floor when something clicked. He felt it. The gates opened and washed him away. It took that long to let the process take over. He was a canoe gliding on glassy water. Silent and still. Effortless.

He stroked the canvas.

The tip of lead roaring on the surface.

The resistance in his hand as light as a feather.

Eyes darting from the photo to contrasting lines. No time for thoughts.

There was no pain or pleasure. No observer. He was the pencil and the canvas. He was the tree. He held it in his mind, felt its feathery branches, tasted the bright colors, smelled the gleaming lights.

The distinct odor of xylene filled his nostrils. He held a cap in one hand. A color marker in the other. He grabbed them by the handfuls, held them in his mouth, put them behind his ears. Bleeding colors across a white landscape. Blending and leaking and layering, the image of the tree gushed onto the canvas.

Something else happened.

The flow took him somewhere. Into another space. While his hands did the work, he was an observer of events unrelated to the here and now.

The creative flow unlocked a secret room inside him.

"STUNNING."

The queen wiped a tear. She stood in front of Art's work. Art had paced around the room, sat on the bed. Paced some more. He had felt full and satisfied when he'd finished. But then the emptiness settled in. Guilt and Shame reintroduced themselves. He sat on the edge of the bed. Foot bouncing.

The chocolate was gone.

He'd eaten the last piece not long after he finished. It would be a few chimes before the next ration arrived. That was what Jelly had said. *Ration.* If he had any doubts about being a prisoner, they were gone now.

"What does he want with this?" Art said.

Jelly had delivered the new photo. It was a sleigh with rockets attached to the sides. Something Santa Claus would use if he were flying to the moon.

"He believes it'll help him," the queen said.

"Help him? How is that going to help him?"

She didn't answer that. Sat next to him while he stared at the picture of a rocket sleigh, aching to get back to the art studio to forget the chocolate itch and start outpacing the bad company in his head. To forget himself.

"Where are you at right now?" the queen asked.

He knew what she was asking. *What am I feeling? Where's my head at?*

Right now his head was full of bingo balls and barbed wire. He got up and paced, kept the machine moving. Twisting his fingers in knots. The queen sat on the bed, hands folded on her lap. A rock in the storm.

He ran his hand through his hair.

Her gaze was open and inviting. He could say anything to her, and she wouldn't judge him. That was what moved him to finally speak. To tell her where his head was at.

"When I was... making the tree." He pointed at the studio, teetering on second thoughts. Then said: "In the middle of it, I, uh..." He swallowed. "Something happened."

Her whiskers twitched. She nodded like she already knew this.

He'd disappeared, he told her. Not actually, as far as he knew. He had been using the markers when the tree changed. It wasn't on the canvas anymore. It was in the corner of the room. Not this room. Another room. An open room with skylights in the ceiling and hardwood on the floor. A fireplace burning.

There were others talking and laughing while Christmas music played. The smell of something sweet cooking in the next room. And people playing a card game. They'd just gotten back from a ride where they sat in the back of a pickup truck to see lights in a neighborhood. The ones with candles in sacks lining the street. What were those called? *Luminaries.*

There were presents under the tree.

Old ornaments on the limbs. Special ornaments. Ones with memories attached.

He couldn't see their faces. They were wispy forms making merry sounds. He tried to say something.

"And then the tree was done." His eyes were stinging. "I was back here."

He swallowed hard and ran his fingers through his hair. Maybe it was the markers, he thought. A hallucination. But it wasn't the markers. It took every bit of strength to say what he said next. The foundation on which he stood was brittle. Below it a salty ocean. But he said it to the queen. He said it to her because he knew she'd *hear* him. She'd understand.

"Was that a *memory*?"

He collapsed on the bed and leaned into her. She didn't have to answer, and he didn't need her to. He just had to say it out loud, to hear himself say it. Maybe it was a memory; maybe it wasn't. It didn't matter. It *felt* like a memory, a special one he held close to his heart. The creative flow had opened a channel to it.

The queen put her hand on his chest.

Her fingers long and knobby, twisted with arthritis. Warmth seeped from it. Penetrated his heart and spread to his back.

"No one can give you the answer you seek," she said. "It is for *you* to see."

She asked him to close his eyes. He did, grateful she kept her hand on him. Then asked him to breathe slowly. A long breath in. A long one out. They did this for a while. At some point, he stopped shaking.

"You may see a light," she said. "Inner wisdom, some call it. Here in Candyland, it is the Christmas spirit. The true gift Santa delivers." She chuckled warmly. "Always with you."

In and out they breathed.

Until thoughts fell away. And he was just here.

JELLY ARRIVED WITH THE RATIONS.

Art barely tasted it. He wolfed them down, chasing them with long chugs of warm cocoa. The queen didn't stop him or scold him. She understood the beauty that followed a chocolate binge.

The elation. The relief.

Jelly went to the art studio. She stood in front of the canvas, much like the queen. With emotion slurring the edges of her voice, she said the king was pretty happy. Art didn't know why the king was pretty happy since he hadn't come to visit.

But he didn't care.

He sat at the window with the breeze in his face, licking his fingers and feeling delight pump through him. If only he'd looked down where Fudgy Lake blighted the landscape. Something shimmered on its blackened depths. Balls of light reflected off the surface. There in the middle of an oily lake was an island where an island had not been.

And on that island a Christmas tree appeared.

19

The room was quiet. Except for mechanical thrumming and the occasional gooey drip. *Gloo-ip* when a drip broke from the ceiling. *Gloo-op* when it hit the floor.

A massive mound of flesh was piled in the back. Rolling pins caused the folds of sweaty skin to undulate. And the king to moan.

The steam was sticky sweet. It condensed on the ceiling in caramel drops. Streaked down the walls like exhausted slugs. Dark puddles formed on the tiled floor.

King Chocolate rested on a bed of waffles with a buttery pillow beneath his head. The rolling pins kneaded his body like a mountain of dough squishing and squashing in all directions. Two slices of jellied toast covered his eyes. Yet still he knew when maple syrup had condensed above him, and an amber droplet began to bulge. It clung and shimmered with weight. Glistening with sugar. Until it was too heavy to hold and stretched away, losing its grip, falling in a bubbling mass.

Gloo-op.

A fresh cloud of boiled syrup was released. He relished the privacy. The ecstasy. The saturation of sweets. Then it was wrecked by a droning voice.

"Decent in there?"

The king didn't bother to answer. His lower half was covered with enough cloth to sew a tent. The fashionistas had designed it with mini marshmallows hot-glued on a pink swatch of taffy. It was a bit snug, a little binding. If the paparazzi caught him coming out of the steam bath, he wanted to present well. Jelly assured him they would be watching. And he would approve the snaps before they released them.

Jelly wandered through the saccharine fog. Rubber boots mashing thick puddles. Drips falling on her raincoat and rubber hat. Her attire was atrocious (fashionistas had taught him that word: *you don't want atrocious*). Her clothes were useless, anyway. Steam penetrated everything.

"Ah!" she said. Relieved to see the marshmallow towel. "Don't stay here too much longer or you'll melt. You already look lighter."

He grimaced because she wasn't wrong. He thought he'd imagined it while getting undressed. That he'd lost a few pounds. He'd spun in front of the mirror, thought he looked slimmer and blamed the mirror. Now Jelly said it. Joking or not, he didn't like that.

Not a bit.

He groaned. Just when the rolling pins were getting to knots in his middle parts. A winch unspooled from the ceiling. He lifted his arms, let the bands wind around his wrists and pull him into a sitting position. He slumped against the wall like melting wax.

The rolling pins repositioned, kneading the lumpy knobs on his shoulders.

"Take that silly rainsuit off and have a seat," he said, slurring his words.

"I'm good."

"Nonsense. It's good for the pores, Jelly Roll."

"Well, well, someone is in a *good* mood."

The king convulsed like he'd been struck with the blunt end of a stick. "Upbeat, maybe. But never good, you silly goose. Never *good*."

As the king of the Naughty Side, he swore never to be associated with that word. Even in his current state of elation. And why not? The boy was in the groove. Or, as the queen called it, the *flow state*. Groove sounded much better. Cooler. The fashionistas agreed.

The boy was making things. All sorts of things.

He would get right to work when he woke. Stayed until he was done. Sometimes he collapsed from exhaustion and napped on the floor. Woke up and kept going. The sheets on the bed needed washing from the sweaty naps and salty tears. He had a habit of crying after finishing a painting or drawing. It was sad and sweet. The perfect combo.

The king didn't know what to make of it. The queen said to allow the boy space, let him grieve. King Chocolate had no idea what that meant, but listened to her this time. He wanted nothing to do with emotions. Maybe that was the life of an artist.

True, the boy wasn't always making what the king requested. Like that rusty robot he drew. Or that floaty rock creature wearing a helmet. Or the bull with braces on its teeth. Weird stuff was now roaming Fudgy Lake.

The king was patient, though.

Let the artist do art. Get out of his way and let him groove.

Until the boy kept ignoring the king's requests. Then he had to be reminded why he was there. *Stick to the photos, son. You'll be home in no time.*

"Do you really think I'm getting skinny?" the king said.

"What answer do you want? I'm open."

"Just shut up. Why are you here, besides ruining my sauna with *atrocious* clothing?"

"Ah, there he is, old Naughty St. Nick. You're not answering calls, so I stopped in to tell you the sleigh is working just like you said it would."

"Of course it is." He wiped a gooey slick off his forehead and sucked his finger. "Never doubt me."

"Never, ever, sire. It's on the way to the festival."

"Fab." Another fashionista word. It was short for something. "Fabby," the king said. Although that didn't sound right.

Doodling his fingers in a puddle of the good stuff, he moaned.

The taste of winning was sweeter than this entire room. He wanted to distill this feeling, roll in it till every crease on his body was filled. Eat it till there was no more room in his belly. It was the most delicious, intoxicating thing ever. He'd gain the weight back and more.

"It's good to be a Lander," he groaned.

"Okay," Jelly said.

"We know who we are," the king said. "What we're made of. We're reliable. We're *this* every day, Jelly Roll." He flexed his porky fingers with a look of disgust. "Can you imagine, Jelly, *changing*? Who needs it? Who wants it? Look at the queen. Now that's what I'm talking about. She was a sweet tart when she crossed over, amma right? A few bells later and she's sprouting gray hairs as crooked as a cane tree root."

"That's crooked," Jelly agreed.

"Blech." The king dug a chocolate chip out of the waffle bed. "She quit chocolate, Jelly. Who does that?"

"Well, not all of her ideas were bad."

"What's that?"

"I mean, she takes care of the naughties in need. Feeds them, makes them clothes. That sort of thing."

"Yeah, but... *why*?"

Jelly shrugged. "I mean, it's just..." *Nice.* She was going to say nice. "It's the right thing to do. She's gentle and kind and—"

A wad of syrup-soaked waffle hit her face. "Whoa. Whoa, whoa, whoa, whoa, whoa. It's sounds like you *like* her. Is that what I'm hearing, Jelly Roll? You like the queen?"

"She is my queen." Jelly wiped her face. "*Your* queen."

"She's not my queen. She's the queen of something, but she ain't my queen. You know what, out. Get out. Go, now, before I throw you in the fudge factory." He buried his face in the waffle bed. "You make me sick. Beat it."

"My pleasure."

Jelly turned to leave, her boots peeling off the floor like they'd been glued down. She was careful not to move too fast or the boots would pull right off her enormous feet. And if those paddles got stuck in the syrup, it would take an army to pull her out.

The king laughed at that thought.

A chocolate chip shot from his nostril. Followed by flatulence from the other end.

He laughed harder. Aftershocks rippled across his exposed belly. Jelly had almost vanished in the steam. Those rubber boots squealing on the sticky tile.

"Oh. Almost forgot why I came in here. The boy is awake."

"What?"

"He woke up a couple of chimes ago. Went straight to the studio."

King Chocolate choked on his words. The next thing out of his mouth was not funny. "You were to tell me that *immediately!*"

This was followed by a scoop of melted butter on the wall just above Jelly's head.

"We tried. You weren't answering calls. Remember?"

The king didn't exactly sleep. It was more like fading out. He didn't really know how long he'd been in the sauna, but the washboard pruning on his fingers and toes said it had been more than a few chimes. He threw more waffle at Jelly and called for a monitor. It lit up the wall, smudgy and streaked. He leaned closer, nearly tumbling off the waffle bench, to see.

The boy was already at work. At the canvas, he was. There were colors and shapes on it. Lots of them, in fact.

"What's he doing? Is he making it? Is he doing it?"

"I can't see."

The king grabbed her by the lapels of her overcoat and pressed her face into the monitor. She squirmed out of his grip. If the king wanted to see what the boy was making, then they needed to get to the theater. The sauna was like hanging out in a stomach.

But the king didn't want to miss a tick.

He grabbed the collar of her overcoat. She twisted and tried to slither out. The king came away with an empty sleeve. Worse, he teetered forward. Jelly got out of the way just before he squished onto the floor. Tiny legs fluttered like rubbery appendages. Jelly's instinct was to get away.

It wasn't quick enough.

"No, you don't." The king pulled at her boot.

She bounced like an overinflated beach ball. King Chocolate tried to use her to push himself back onto the bench. The monitor was too high on the wall to see. There was nothing to grab onto. They were like baby deer on black ice, grabbing at each other, slapping each other. Goop in their eyes and up their noses. They were lathered in the sweetest, stickiest, gooiest sauna ever invented.

Exhausted, out of breath, the king shouted, "Get help!"

"How?"

He put both hands on her backside and shoved. She went sliding into the steam cloud. It sounded like a rubber kickball on the far wall. She came rebounding out of the mist, ricocheting off the king like a cue ball. His marshmallow suit ripped. He held it with one hand and reached out with the other. Jelly went zooming past, careening out of the corner. He'd snatch her this time, then throw her at the door somewhere on the other side of the room.

A tremor shook the walls.

It sounded like someone was rearranging the furniture on the floor above.

It happened again. They were showered in droplets from the ceiling that fell all at once. Jelly was choking. Droplets were in her ears and eyes. She wiped her face, furious. The last thing she'd wanted to do was come inside this disgusting room. It smelled like rotten eggs boiled in corn syrup. That was why she'd dressed head to toe in rain gear, and now look at her. *A total sweet roll.*

"Look at what you—"

"Shush it." The king smooshed his slimy hand against her lips.

His eyes darted back and forth. Nostrils twitched.

He scrambled for the waffle bench. At first, he was swimming in place, but slowly he rocked himself forward like a walrus on beefy flippers. He climbed halfway into the seat, gasping. Eyes bulging at the monitor.

The boy had stepped back from his work.

They could see it now. It was a blurry form, but enough to recognize the photo the king had given him. What he wanted the boy to create. It was a large circle with a curving line through the middle of it. One side light. The other side dark.

"He did it," Jelly said. "I think he did it."

"Shut it."

Expectations were future resentments, the king had learned. He had to make sure what he was seeing was what he was seeing. That this was what he thought it was. And that wasn't furniture scraping the floor.

"Go! Go!" The king plopped on the floor and pushed Jelly like a hockey puck. "Get me out of here!"

Jelly went sliding into the fog. This time she didn't bounce back.

The king didn't wait. He crawled after her at worm speed. The molasses was getting thick and tacky. He was finding traction but still going as fast as a beetle on a hot sidewalk. The anticipation burned his lungs like ciders. He screamed a guttural cry, releasing frustration and potential joy. He had to know. Had to know NOW!

He was halfway there when a rope slapped him in the face.

He grabbed it with both hands.

A heave and a ho, one after another, and he was dragged out of the morass. Jelly was there with three assistants. She held out the hoversuit. He didn't even have to ask. He wanted to kiss her disgusting face.

They worked him into the hoversuit, rolling him across the hall to get it latched.

He powered up, nearly flying into the ceiling like a bobber held under water.

Hair plastered to his forehead. Nostrils glued shut, a massive mound of nudity soaring down the corridor. The marshmallow suit somewhere in the sauna. He shouted a warning to those who might be around corners to find cover or get run over.

He hit the open doorway of the theater at full throttle. Barreled through the seats like they were bowling pins. He bounced off one wall and then a second. When the stars cleared from his vision, he was on his back. The monitor upside down. The boy was mixing paint in the studio.

"Border!" the king cried. "Show me the border!"

The channel changed. It was a bird's view of Candyland. All of it. The king didn't care about the shape of it. He wanted to see where dark and light met at the border. Too impatient to right himself, he screamed at the monitor to zoom on the meeting hall—where he'd met his king brother, Macey, and his (lovely) queen, Lydia.

It did just that.

There was the little outhouse. Half in the dark. Half in the light.

But if you looked closer and knew what you were looking for, you would see exactly what the king was seeing.

"He did it," he murmured. Then louder, "He did it! He did it!" Louder still: "*I* DID IT!"

After all, it was the king's idea to give the picture to the boy. Therefore, ergo, credit goes to the king.

All of it.

The joy bouncing inside him was about to break his ribs. He'd never contained this much excitement. It came out of him in groans and cries and laughter and tears and just a little bit of gas.

Jelly came in with a blanket and covered the king. He was oblivious to his nudity. Jelly wasn't. And neither were the twenty or so employees he'd passed in the hallway.

She looked up at the monitor. She knew what to look for. And she saw it, too.

"He did it," she said.

"*I* did it!" the king said.

"*You* did it!" Jelly said.

She leaped on the king. They hugged and rolled and laughed. He fired up the hoversuit and flew around the room. Glistening tears cut down his sticky cheeks. It didn't matter who did it. It had been done.

❄

KING CHOCOLATE WAS post-sauna clean with a fresh coating of powdered sugar. Adjustments to the hoversuit had been made. The fashionistas said if he lost any more weight, they'd have to fabricate a new one. If they needed more food to be eaten, they were asking the right man.

At the moment, though, the king was banging his fists on the dining table. The plates and utensils danced. Instruments blared from speakers throughout the room, driving a beat with heavy guitars and a speedy rhythm that made the king's pulse beat as fiercely as the drums. He banged his foppish head.

"Silent Night!"

Boom!

"SILENT!"

Boom-boom-boom!

"NIIII—stop!" He waved his arms. The music stopped. "What if instead of 'Silent Night' we go 'Naughty Time'? Huh? Try it again. From the top."

The king had no idea how to play an instrument. Even fake ones. He waved his arms like an octopus being electrocuted. Rust-color sweat streaked his sugar-powdered cheeks. He tossed his head like a volleyball, not hearing the door open. Not seeing anyone enter.

Not until they were next to him.

The music abruptly stopped. The king was startled and squealed like a child spooked by a ghost. He sopped the sweat from his fore-head with his sleeve.

"I was going over the set list," he said. "Needed a bit more *verve!*"

"It sounds a little dark," the queen said.

The king looked at Jelly. She shook her head. He had to do all the heavy lifting. A king's work was never done. Especially the dirty kind. Although he looked forward to this chore. "You might want to have a seat for this," he said to the queen. "On second thought, let's just rip the bandage off. You're fired."

It took a few winks to sink in. It started as bewilderment and pretty much stayed that way. "What do you mean fired?"

"It means you're fired. What else would it mean?" He glanced at

Jelly, back to the queen. She was waiting for more. "It means you're not the queen anymore."

"I don't want to be the queen."

"Good. Because—wait. I see what you're trying to do." He wagged a porky finger. "You didn't quit. I fired you, admit it. Burns a little, doesn't it."

"I haven't wanted to be queen for quite some time, Casey."

"Give me the crown. Give it, give it!" He reached for it. "GIVE IT, NOW!"

She took the crown from the nest of wiry hair on her head. She'd pried the jewels from it, made it look like a recycled aluminum tambourine without the metal zills. Probably hid the jewels on that rat-infested island. He'd find them. Even if he had to turn the island upside down, he'd find them. Without the jewels, her crown was a cheap hoop.

He whacked it on the table. It hurt his hand. He did it again, harder this time. Did it a third time, then a fourth. Not a dent, not a scratch. Just a bruise on his hand. He flung the stupid thing. It rolled down the table like a loose wagon wheel.

"You're fired! You hear me? FIRED!"

"I understand, Casey."

"You're just... *aahhhhh!*" He grabbed his cheeks. This was supposed to make him happy, but all he wanted to do was stuff his ears inside his head. "You want to know why you're fired? Because I don't need you anymore. You want to know why I don't need you anymore?"

She knew why. A little thrill ran up his spine.

"Oh, you know," he said. "But I want to show you."

An old-fashioned silver screen lowered from the ceiling. King Chocolate stared at the haggard gray rat while it came down. He didn't blink or twitch. Jelly was uncomfortable in the awkward quiet.

The queen was calm.

Ordinarily, her demeanor would make him pull his greasy hair. Not this time. He savored it this time. *Let her act like it doesn't bother her. I want to see her crack when she sees this.* He laughed at his own thoughts and sucked a deep draught of pudding from the pudding tube.

"Ooookay." He sighed. "Let's see what I have for you. Something a little—oh! There it is. What's that?" When she didn't answer, he said, "That was a real question. What are you looking at?"

"Candyland."

"Be more specific."

"The border."

It was a bird's-eye view of beloved Candyland. Half in the dark, half in the light. As normal as usual. If you weren't looking at it closely. Which she wasn't.

"Notice anything?"

She nodded slowly. Or maybe she was looking closely. A smile slithered across his face.

"Say it, then. Say it out loud," he whispered. "I want to hear it."

"You don't want to do this."

"Say it! What's different about the border? What did I do? SAY IT!"

"Casey, it won't do what you think—"

"If you don't say it right now, I'll turn your island into a sewage pile. You'll be the queen of the dump if you don't say it. I'm counting down." He held up three swollen fingers. "Three. Two. One." Long pause. A brief staring contest. Then: "All right. Jelly, have the—"

"He moved the border," she said.

"What was that? I can't hear you."

She grimaced. He cocked his hand to his ear. She mumbled something. This was exhausting. That was the thing with her: it took an army to move her an inch. He'd had enough. A win was a win. He walloped his hands together.

"Ring a belly, Jelly! Ring it out loud and give this vermin a prize." He threw a fudgesicle in front of her. "She is one hundred on the bull's eye. *I moved the Naughty Side!*"

"Arthur moved it," she corrected.

"He did. I did. What's it matter? We win, Lady Mouserinks. I guess it's just Mouserinks now. Or is it just Rinks? I never liked that name, bt-dub. It sounds made up."

"This isn't about winning."

"How is this not about winning? Winning is all there is. All there ever was! Us against them. Nice versus naughty, dark versus light. And guess who's winning now? Guess. Come on, take a guess."

She turned away so he wouldn't see her tremble with anger or fear or some other useless emotion. *Crossers. So weak and vulnerable.* He should've kept her as a pet, not made her queen.

"Go back to your island and play with the rats," he said. "Leave this to the professionals."

His laughter was raucous and mean. He leaned his head back, took a deep breath, and let it rip. It felt good. Justified. Like hitting a nail square on the head. *Just right.* He was about to call up the "Silent Night" song (or "Naughty Time" song, he hadn't decided if he should change it) when she grabbed a silver platter off the table. He cringed as she raised it.

"How old are you?" she said.

"Rude."

"You don't age," she continued. "I've been here so many bells I've lost count. I've got more gray hairs than the Christmas Wood. You haven't changed a lick. Neither of you. You look exactly the same."

"I already made that point. Now put down the platter."

"You were never young, and you'll never grow old. You were never born, and you'll never die. This place is an eternal moment."

"Why are you holding a platter?" the king said. "Why is she holding the platter?"

"The border has always been where it is. Naughty on one side, nice on the other. It's never moved. It's never changed." She put donuts on the platter, one on each side. Her hand was under the middle of the teetering platter. "Just like you."

"Cool trick." The king rolled his eyes. "Show's over. Put the—"

She added a third donut to one side. It tipped over and crashed on the table. Made a mess. King Chocolate thought about insisting she clean it up. But he was getting tired of her. The thrill of firing her was over.

But he understood her point. Her high-minded, smarty-pants point. She couldn't just come out and say it. Had to turn it into a party trick to prove she was a smarty.

"Balance, I get it," he groused. "I hope you feel better that someone has to clean up your mess. You know something, you're no better than me. You're not smarter, and you sure ain't prettier. I know it's mean, but I'm going to say it. It's what everyone is thinking. *You're gross.* Sorry, but not sorry. It's the truth. Leave, will you? And don't drag your gross tail on the floor. Go!" He threw another fudgesicle. This one stuck to the front of her long coat. "Go back to your island. You're not invited to the festival. You can watch it on your crystal ball. GO!"

She nodded to him. It was long and heartfelt. Genuine.

Then she turned and walked toward the exit.

A part of the king felt the sting of her leaving. He wanted her out of his life but couldn't imagine her gone. It was a terrible feeling. She was a habit he couldn't quit.

"You're not saying bye to the boy, either! He doesn't need you. He's got me and chocolate. Bye, loser! Bye."

Jelly looked deflated. She went after the queen. Which only twisted the king's confounding heartache. He leaned into it and, just before the doors closed behind them, shouted: "It's Naughty Time!"

A drum solo followed. King Chocolate beat the air drums until he was soaked with sweat. Then did it again from the beginning.

After that, he stuffed his face with eclairs.

20

Sweet Tooth rumbled away from the castle, looking like a tiny clown on the dim dirt road. She stopped at the edge of Fudgy Lake to scoop a handful of sludge off the shore, impervious to the gaggle of sooty birds nipping at her heels.

Art couldn't hear her from that far up, but imagined her *yumming* at the dirty birds. He was peeling paint from his fingers—grays and browns and blacks—like dead skin. Thinking of the memory unlocked in the last work he'd finished. A time he was sick on Christmas Eve with feverish dreams that lasted through the night and the restless excitement blunted by a sore throat. He'd lain on the couch Christmas morning beneath a comforter, opening presents he was too weak to sit up for.

It was not the best Christmas to remember.

The last painting he didn't like, but he was drawn to it. It was familiar. Like a comforting blanket that was cold and suffocating. *Darkness Encroaching* he'd titled that piece. It was a circle of dark, swirling clouds that mesmerized him. So deep in the creative flow, he hadn't felt the earthquake. A few things had fallen off shelves and tables.

All he'd done was paint and sleep.

He wasn't eating as much chocolate. Only when he found himself staring out the window did Guilt and Shame whisper in his ear. They were persistent and stubborn and wouldn't leave until he'd eaten all the chocolate Jelly had left for him.

He'd come to think of creating as work. He didn't mind it, most of the time. It kept his head empty and heart open. He mostly painted and sculpted and drew. Mostly slept.

Avoided the time in between as best he could.

"Merry, merry!" Jelly announced. "Or blah-blah. Take your pick. Your chocolate delivery has arrived. An extra dose from the king, a reward for a fine painting."

She came bouncing into the room on those extra-large feet. Reminded him of her twin sister from the Nice Side as she laid the platter on the table. Chocolate wafers were stacked like casino chips.

"Fine painting?" Art didn't see the fine in what the king wanted him to paint. Only the allure.

"Beauty and the eye of the beholder and all that." Jelly went to the studio where *Darkness Encroaching* was on the easel. "We're leaving for the festival in a few chimes. You're going to be a star, kid. The buzz. The king's jealous, too. I can tell."

She bounced around the studio tables, admiring the drawings and paintings, the clay sculptures and toothpick models he'd experimented with. She stopped to admire *Darkness Encroaching*.

"Do you want to take any of these with you?" she asked.

"Take them where?"

"To the festival. They're inspiring. Everyone on both sides of the Land would agree." She took the painting off the easel and began stacking it with the other works, muttering to herself as she did it.

Art broke off a piece of chocolate, admired the aroma and smooth texture before nibbling the corner. "I'm not going home, am I, Jelly?"

She rolled loose sketches and gently placed them in a bag. For a moment, she considered lying to him. Art expected her to. But she stopped what she was doing and looked at him. Her eyes as dark as the sky.

"Probably not, kid," she said.

"Probably?"

"I don't know how it works. How you cross over here or why. No one seems to think you can go back home, though. But I don't know." She shook her head. "Maybe you can."

"He was lying, then. The king was lying."

"Don't take it personally. He lies to everyone."

Art wore acceptance like a vintage coat. *I may never leave. This could be my new home.* He didn't hate Candyland. Remembering where he came from made it hurt. Even if the memories were delusions. He didn't want to forget them. He held the pain and pleasure in both hands.

Jelly had all the drawings in a box. Even the doodles. The clay sculptures would stay behind, she said. Better they didn't get squished. But the paintings were coming. Especially the last one.

Sweet Tooth was farther up the road. The dirty birds beating her with their wings.

"Is the queen coming?" Art asked.

"The king seems to think she won't." Jelly was packing the canvases now, tying them together with a string. "But remember, there's a reason she's the queen of the Naughty Side. She may be kind, but she's not soft."

Jelly hobbled over to him, said someone would be up to gather his things. What few things there were. "How would you like to get out of here?"

"Yeah."

"Then trust the process." She put something in his pocket. "A gift from the queen."

Then she waddled out of the room. A host of quiet waifs came in to collect the boxes and bags of his art. Art watched them carry things out. He felt the lump in his pocket.

It was a small ball.

✳

THE CASTLE DIDN'T SO much pierce the dim sky as it dissolved into it.

Art stood at the base of it, looking up its full length. It was impossibly tall for something so narrow: a dark tooth that never stopped growing. He leaned against it. The cold sank through his palm and into his arm. It had been so long since he'd been outside. It felt like years. Maybe it had been. Or maybe just a few days (*days are called rings?*). He breathed the dank air with pleasure, relished the odors both fragrant and rank. (Fudgy Lake smelled like low tide. *Yum!*)

A boxy stagecoach waited on the cobblestone road. Bathed in a silvery beam from above. Boxes of Art's work were strapped on the back of it. One end of the stagecoach was lower than the other. Art knew who was sitting on the low end. The grumpy elf watched Art approach, scrubbing the stubble on his chin with the palm of his hand.

Art climbed one step. Peeked inside.

The throne was filled with the pile of royal flesh wearing a crown and squirting chocolate sauce from a bottle into his mouth. Jelly was on the other end, swinging her big bare feet off the edge of a chair.

"Where's the queen?" Art asked.

"Not this again." The king wiped his mouth with a blanket. It sounded like he was chewing wet leather. "She went ahead, wants to make sure everything is ready. Is that okay with you? Can we go now?"

Art sniffed. The smells inside the stagecoach would wither flowers. It was blackened marshmallows cooked over a pile of burning tires in there. The stink watered his eyes.

"I'll ride in another coach. That one over there. Jelly can come to make sure I don't escape."

King Chocolate jiggled with laughter. "Jelly couldn't stop an ant from climbing up her nose. Go on, I trust you. Watchers are watching you anyhow. You won't get far."

"So I'm a prisoner, then?"

"No. Who said that? Jelly? I'll wash her mouth out with lemon juice."

"She didn't. It's pretty obvious you don't want me to leave."

"Just because I like you, my boy, don't make you my prisoner." Chocolatey smile. "I'm just saying you must come to the festival. We already made invitations with your name and face. Big, beautiful pictures, too. Everyone is expecting you. They want to see the artist. Besides, it's a Candyland tradition. We do it every year."

"I thought this was the first one."

"The first of many." The king didn't miss a beat when it came to weaving a story. "After it's over, you can go home. Promise and wanna die, put a needle in my eye. Besides, I think you're going to have some fun. Have a little walk on the Naughty Side this Christmas, eh?"

It looked like a wink, the way one side of his face twitched.

"And wait till you see the chocolates there. I saved the best for you, my boy. Mudslides and fudgy soakers and cocoa funnels. You'll swear this is heaven."

Again, a convulsive wink and guttural laughter. Not real convincing. Art, however, was intrigued. He was already here. Might as well have a look around.

Another stagecoach pulled up. Door opened.

Art stepped over to it and hopped on the step. He held the doorframe with one hand and leaned out for one last word with the king.

"The queen will be there?" he asked.

"Why wouldn't she be? Go, go, get in. Let's not be late."

Art looked around, soaking in the sights and smells and sounds. He had the feeling he wouldn't see it again and wanted to remember it. And wanted to see if the king would snap if he diddled around much longer. There was something entertaining when the king lost his temper.

There was a Christmas tree out on Fudgy Lake. It looked just like the first picture he drew. Exactly like it. That didn't seem odd to Art. The photo he used to create that first work of art had to come from somewhere. He must not have seen it out there before.

His pocket buzzed.

"What's that?" the king shouted from the other carriage.

"I gave him a phone," Jelly answered. "In case we get separated. Go on, boy. We'll see you at the festival."

Art put his hand in his pocket and closed the door.

The gift from the queen was buzzing.

THERE WAS someone in the carriage.

Art paused half in, half out. Hand on the door. Daryl was on a bench seat with his front legs together. His purrs filled the cramped space (no space expander on this ride).

"Where have you been?" Art asked.

"Someone in there?" the king shouted. Someone was paranoid. "Is it the queen? She'd better not be in there."

"The queen isn't in here!" Art said. "Just the cat."

"Cat?"

The king had forgotten about Daryl. Jelly was explaining who the cat was when Art closed the door. He crawled into the small space before the king asked more questions, and fell onto the bench across from the obese kitty. He seemed happy to see Art, the way his tail waved at the sight of him. The sound of the purring.

You were busy, Daryl said.

"So you left me?"

I never left you. Are you going to answer that?

The buzzing grew louder. Art pulled it out of his pocket. There was nothing exceptional about it. Just a silver orb small enough to fit in his hand. It sank into his palm with a satisfying weight. The vibrations hummed up his arm.

"How do I answer it?"

Put it there.

Art dropped it where the cat was looking. It thudded on the velvet seat, and suddenly someone was sitting across from Art. It didn't make a sound; there was no *poof* or anything like that. Just one second the seat was empty, and the next a girthy bearded man was there. His knees almost touching Art's knees. He was from a calendar or a child's storybook. The red suit and black boots. White curls in a long beard. Eyes that sparkled like water on a clear day.

"Hiyyah!" cried a grumpy elf on top of the carriage.

The stagecoach jerked forward. Art was thrown back in his seat, head thumping the hollow panel behind him. The large man across from him did not move.

As trees passed the windows and bells rang from the stagecoach eaves, the two stared at each other. Art wasn't trying to win a blinking contest. There were no words to say. His brain had short-circuited and was rebooting. Art moved his mouth, but nothing came out.

Santa Claus. It's Santa Claus.

Of all the strange things that had happened since waking up in Candyland, this one pinned him with a surreal grip. Santa touched something real. Santa was someone Art had believed in once upon a time. All those Christmas Eves when he lay in bed trying to stay awake, ears tuned for a scuff on the roof or a ring of a bell or jolly laughter coming down the chimney, only to wake on Christmas morning to see the presents left behind, the bulging stockings. Milk half gone and crumbs of cookies left out.

Then Art grew up. He stopped believing.

Now the jolly fat man was here. He was sitting across from him. Close enough to touch.

Art smacked his lips. His mouth was dry. Tongue glued to the roof of his mouth. He cleared his throat and loosened a few words. Just a few. And said: "Are you real?"

"Is any of this real?" Santa answered. "The chairs we sit on. The road beneath us. You. Me."

Deep answer, that one. Santa went straight to metaphysical, and that, for some reason, sobered Art up. That and the baritone sound of his voice was sure to carry over to the one King Chocolate was riding in.

"That's not what I mean. Like... the reindeer and the presents. Are you..." He swallowed a dry lump that wouldn't go down. "Are *you* real?"

"What do you think, Arthur?"

Someone had asked him that before. When he was little. He had been suspicious and asked someone the very same question and had gotten the same answer. Then with a wink and a nod, someone said: *Don't spoil it for your sister.*

An earthquake shuddered deep inside him. Childhood memories floated like pixie dust. Tickled his brain. Warmed his heart.

Santa Claus is real.

The magic moment collapsed when the carriage hit a bump. A tray of chocolate drops scattered over the floor and bounced on Art's lap. Only they didn't do the same for Santa. They passed through his white gloves, through the fuzzy red pants, and bounced across the bench he appeared to be sitting on. They settled next to the silver orb.

He's a projection.

He slumped in his seat, looked out the window. They were passing through a dark forest. Pairs of glowing eyes looking out from blackness. Daryl tried to talk to him, but Art wasn't interested. The cat hopped on the seat and climbed onto his lap. Art let him curl up and purr. Then he ran his fingers through the soft fur.

"What do you want?" he said without looking at the jolly fat man.

"What do you need?"

"Not this," he muttered.

He refused to look at the talking projection. Soon the forest thinned, and they were in the hills. The grasslands sparkled with moondew. Two-Face Mountain was in the distance, holding steady as the landscape slowly transitioned from prairies to wetlands and back to forest.

Santa Claus didn't break the silence.

Maybe this story would be different had Art not spoken again. If he would've clammed up for the remainder of the ride, Santa wouldn't have said anything. Awkwardness bloomed in that cramped space. It was a suffocating blanket. No distractions to ignore it, it only got thicker.

"You're here to convince me, right?" Art finally blurted. "So I'll do whatever it is the king wants me to do? That's the only reason you're *here*."

Santa didn't answer that. Instead, he put his hand on his belly and laughed. It was deep and guttural and real. "Ho-ho-ho."

There was nothing funny about it, not that Art could see. But that laugh...

Art fidgeted.

Emotions fluttered from his stomach and into his chest. Memories were attached to them and projected onto the gray screen inside his head.

Ho-ho-ho.

It was the laugh that came from across the house on Christmas morning. Before the sun was up, Art lying in bed, waiting to leave his bedroom. Imagining all the presents waiting under the tree, the heavy stockings sagging from the mantel. Not moving until he heard that laugh from his parents' room.

His father going *ho-ho-ho.*

And Art would go running. He would jump on his parents' giant bed. His little sister bouncing with him. "Wake up! Wake up!" they would shout.

Mother would get up to start coffee.

Crawling under the covers with them. Closing their eyes to imagine what was out there. Mom and Dad closing their eyes, too. Hugging them. Tickling them. They hadn't cared about presents. They had everything they wanted.

The memories were getting out of control. They rose up from the deepness of his subconscious, from those dark corners where he couldn't see, and burst across his mind in oily slicks. Ever since he'd gotten to the Naughty Side, they started appearing. Since he'd started drawing and painting.

Memories that reminded him of who he was. Where he was.

Lost.

He didn't belong. Not here. Not anywhere.

He covered his face with both hands. Sobs were coming, and he couldn't stop them. He clamped his mouth shut and muffled the sounds. His insides churned. He wiped his eyes and looked out the window, ignoring the fake Santa. But he could feel him looking at him kindly.

Art didn't want the ride to end.

He wanted to stay inside the carriage as far as it would take him and stare out the glass. It was safe inside there. The world couldn't touch him.

"Tell me what you believe, Arthur."

"About what?"

"About anything."

"What I believe?" Art laughed coarsely. No one ever asked him that. "I believe you're just a story. And this is just a dream. And not a good one."

"A story. I like a good story. Do you?"

Art sniffed. Wiped his nose with the back of his hand. "I used to believe you were real. You know? I wanted it to be true and then..." He shrugged.

"You grew up."

Life got hard, he wanted to say. The magic of youth vanished. Like it was never really there in the first place. The presents got smaller, and the magic didn't last. Like when he was little and a box could be anything. Now a new phone barely moved the needle.

He wanted to go back to that time. Go back when the world was magic. And his parents were right down the hall. Their bed was warm. *Ho-ho-ho!*

Go back to what it was like when he saw everything with wonder. Believed the world was made of hugs and there was nothing his mom and dad couldn't fix. When life was an endless sleepover.

You can't go back.

"What's your story now?" Santa asked.

"My story now." He grimaced. "I'm stuck in a crazy dream with gingerbread people and fudgy lakes and kings and queens and festivals. And I'm talking to Santa Claus in a stagecoach, and you're not even real!"

"Sounds like an interesting story."

"I want it to *end*."

It hurt to say that. To know he wanted that.

They were still in the forest. The trees were getting bigger and darker. Their branches tangled over the road like knobby fingers. People and things were wandering in the ditch, a pilgrimage of toys and creatures and animals going in the same direction as the stagecoach. They kissed their fingers when the stagecoaches passed them. There were small clumps of them at first, a few here and there. The closer they got to the festival, the larger those clumps were.

"Can I ask something?" Santa said.

"What?"

"Will you close your eyes first? You don't have to do anything else. Just close your eyes."

Art resisted. But his eyes grew heavy. He leaned his head on the window.

"Good."

Santa's breathing began to slow. The absurdity of a projection breathing didn't escape Art, but he got the point. It was what the queen had taught him when they sat on the small benches. He fell into the pattern of slow inhalations through his nostrils, let it leak out even slower.

His body began to settle into place. A weighty relaxation filled him from the bottom up. Starting at his feet.

"Where is that child?" Santa asked. "The one you seek. Find him inside you. Where is he?"

Art continued breathing.

Settling.

Sensations blooming and withering. Thoughts clinging to them and letting go.

In and out.

"Find this child on Christmas Eve..."

Santa's voice was far away now. Art was still in the stagecoach, but there was space around him. It was open and endless and forgiving. Enough space for all those bodily sensations and all those random thoughts to exist. Enough space that it didn't feel cramped inside him. Enough space to see the turbulent water without being swept into its current. He could see everything.

Including childhood memories.

"There he is," Santa said from a long, long ways away.

Art could see the boy in the bed. Lying there with a swirl in his stomach. The blanket up to his chin. Hooves scuffing the shingles above him.

So curious.

The present moment joyous whether good or bad, naughty or nice.

Curious to investigate. To feel. And nowhere to go. Nowhere to be. He was already there.

He was here.

He was here.

He didn't hear Santa Claus again. Even if the jolly fat man had spoken, Art wouldn't have heard him. He was floating in an eternal moment, resting in its embrace. The universe was endless space. There was room for all things. Art was listening for the hooves on the roof.

And the ho-ho-ho down the hall.

21

The green room was literally green. The walls, the floor. Everything.

Art was nestled in an olive-green beanbag wedged in the corner and surrounded by every imaginable variation of chocolate. Syrups and shakes and bars and dollops and puddings. A table of sculptures held little carvings of King Chocolate not intended for eating. Just for looking at.

Three gorillas stood guard.

They wore overalls in pastel colors. No shirts or shoes. Tufts of black curly hair on their black chests. Protruding brows aimed at Art. They hadn't said anything since he'd arrived. Just stood like lumps of muscle. Art liked them. They didn't seem to like him.

The others were busy with plans and outfits and schedules and things. A triplet of fashion icons insisted he try the chocolate fondue. Other than that, they told him to sit in the corner. He was happy to engage in a staring contest with the gorillas. So far it was a tie.

After some time (how much time, impossible to tell, you know), others came through the room. They were more excited, less stressed. And happy to see Art. Clapping and hopping and dancing toward him. The gorillas snatched them before they got close enough to touch him.

He knew he liked them for a reason.

A yarn-haired fabric doll asked for Art's autograph. Held out a marker and wanted him to sign her arm. The gorillas ushered her out. Whenever the door would open, he heard the crowd. It was getting loud and restless. A gruff voice was amplified. There was cannon fire and cheers. Eventually, the music started.

It shook the walls and beanbag.

There was a clock with five hands and symbols instead of numbers. Art had no idea what time it was. Or if it was even a clock. It ticked like one. Maybe it was a bomb.

It helped to have Daryl on his lap, even if he was sleeping.

Art was breathing slowly. Calmly. Eyes open, taking in sights and colors. Registering who was in the room, who was coming and going. The mood. The anxiety. He was unfazed by the festivities. Something in the carriage ride there had changed him.

He wanted to be nowhere else but here.

KING CHOCOLATE GLIDED into the room. His cheeks were frosted. Eyelids, too. His lips the color of glistening mud. He glanced at Art and gave him a scrunchy wink.

"My boy."

Before he could steer in Art's direction, he was pulled aside by the fashion icons. Another set of triplets joined them. This second set was short and skinny. Sort of military like. Missing a limb or an eye. The discussion was heated, with several glances in Art's direction, and made Art a bit nervous with the attention. He wondered if his gorilla pals would throw them out if he told them to. The king drifted toward Art.

"You're not eating chocolate?"

"I'm not hungry."

"What does that have to do with it?" The king laughed. But not as loud as everyone else. They laughed like they were paid to. Except the gorillas. "Are you feeling all right? Did the trip upset your stomach? I'm gassy after long trips."

Art said he felt fine. Truth was he felt great. Whatever the Santa Claus projection had done with him had worked. It was like he'd reclaimed some lost part of his self. He was still Anxious, still Nervous and Afraid, but he wasn't controlled by them. Guilt and Shame watched from a distance but didn't interfere. Like there was space for all of them to exist.

And no appetite for chocolate.

Did the queen learn everything from Santa? he wondered. Jelly said the silver orb was a gift from her. At least, he thought that was what Jelly meant. *Maybe the gift was meeting Santa.*

"You know what to do, my boy?" The king showed him a photo.

Art nodded. He was itching to do one more painting. There was tension to be released in the creative flow. He was about to burst. The king, however, couldn't get a read on him.

"I don't like his energy," the king said to the others. "It's low. Look at everyone in the room, boy. Look at them, all gaga for you. It's nothing compared to what's out there. An entire crowd is waiting for you. They love you! Almost as much as me."

Laughter, paid for and otherwise, erupted.

"They'll want autographs. Kissing babies and stuff. All merry, merry, it's disgusting. Don't believe me? Show him. Look."

The wall behind the gorillas turned into a monitor swirling with color. Images flickered into focus. It showed a sea of people and toys and animals and things. They were listening to music. They were chocolate tub wrestling. They were on chocolate plunge rides. There were burning barrels surrounded by wolves and fights breaking out.

It didn't look real.

Even if it was, Art didn't care.

"They've been waiting for you. All this time, waiting. And you're here. You're finally here. And all you have to do is what you do. As long as it's this." He shook the photo. "Understand? Yes or no. Answer me."

"Understood."

"That's my naughty boy." He pinched Art's cheek with sticky fingers. "Now eat. You're making me nervous."

To prove his point, the king passed gas.

He floated across the room to where an entourage waited. They picked up where the previous conversation had left off. Representatives from all corners of the Naughty Side were there, including buzzing flies and one of the Lost Boys. From time to time, they looked at Art and didn't try to hide it.

Then the king snapped. His anger boiled over and steamed from his ears. Art leaned forward to watch. Daryl repositioned on his lap and went back to sleep.

"Peter!" the king shouted. "Dunk and sprinkle!"

The king pointed at the trio of slender military figures. They didn't flinch when the gorilla named Peter knuckle-walked over and swept them up. They remained stoic when he opened the door—the crowd noise filling the room—and left with them held against his bulging chest. A sugary odor wafted into the room, one Art hadn't noticed before.

An aroma he recognized.

"Terrible advice," the king announced. "Those three misfits deserve the dunk and sprinkle. Anyone else with awful ideas?"

His company heartily answered.

"The boy will change everything. And they wanted to put him in a box? A BOX?" The king shook his head in disappointment. The fashionistas shuffled to the side and positioned themselves behind one of the gorillas. The king was confused. The advisors were against the idea. It was the fashionistas who suggested it. But they came in groups of three, so he was close. Sort of. As long as someone got the dunk and sprinkle, it didn't matter.

"Give the boy a hand, you idiots. Applaud him! Cheer him! Sing his praises."

The excitement steadily grew and was quite convincing. Hoots and hollers and stamping of feet. They gave Art a standing ovation he did nothing to deserve.

"Give us a song, Jelly. Celebrate! There's a new fat man in town!"

The king took a bow and basked in his own glory. The grotesque little legs twiddling uselessly beneath him, he bobbed around his entourage and took their hands and arms and spun them about while Jelly made up words to an imaginary song.

The crosser he's the one. The one, the one, the one.

And he's going to have some fun. Some fun, some fun, some fun.

The king yee-hawed, and so did everyone else. Then he threw a pastry at Jelly. It stuck to her fancy new coat trimmed with fur. The others threw food at her, too. Donuts, cookies, and custard. The king teased Jelly, said she sounded like a wounded walrus, then squirted her with chocolate syrup when she stopped.

"More! More!"

They were all very good actors pretending to have fun. Only the king wasn't pretending.

The gorillas hadn't noticed the mouse standing in the corner. Art didn't see from where she snuck into the room. She watched the petty fun with simmering anger.

On the monitor behind the gorillas, everyone watched the live feed of Peter walking onstage where the band was playing. The slender military figures didn't squirm in his grip. They accepted their fate like soldiers. A vat lowered down from the scaffolding. Peter reached for it. It stopped its descent a few feet over a plastic baby pool.

"Quiet!" The king parked himself in front of the wall monitor. "Watch. Everyone watch."

He was drooling from all the excitement. Intoxicated with power, wiping his chin and licking his fingers. Tiny eyes bulging in their fatty pockets. His entourage gathered around, some of them noticing the large mouse watching from the corner.

Peter held the military figures up for the crowd to see. They were limp like puppies held by the scruff of the neck. The crowd roared their approval. The king's entourage squealed their excitement. The king moaned with pleasure.

Peter dunked them into the vat.

They came out the color of mud. Milk chocolate dripped from their once-shining boots. The crowd went berserk. Then Peter dropped them in the baby pool, one at a time, and rolled them like dough. They came out covered with specks of candy. Peter held them over his head.

Excitement spilled over the audience in fits of violence.

Peter put the multicolored soldiers in a clear display box hanging between two drum sets. The octopuses began playing.

"Dunked!" The king shook his fist. "And sprinkled!"

The king's entourage repeated what he said and shook their fists like he did. And laughed like he laughed. The king looked around to make sure they were as excited as he was. Or perhaps deciding on who would go for a roll next.

Because it was so much fun.

"Tonight is a ten," he bellowed. "Let's take it to a twelve!"

He started to howl. So did the others. They took a deep breath to keep it going—to take this party to a twelve—when he choked. The entourage pretended to choke. The king waved his arms at them. Blood rushed into his face. His tongue had swelled. A few of the sycophants imitated him until they turned blue and purple, waving their arms and holding their breath.

The king finally managed two words. It was enough.

"EVERYONE OUT!"

"THROW HER OUT!" His hand shook as much as his voice. "If her giant clown is out there, and I know she is, tell her she will be BANISHED from the Naughty Side if she doesn't LEAVE NOW! Go, you apes. Get her *out of here!*"

The gorillas did what they were told to do.

They knuckle-walked toward the frail mouse in the long, patchwork overcoat. Her crown missing from her head, where sprigs of gray shot in all directions. They could toss her out the door without grunting.

The fur bristled on the nape of the queen's neck.

She inhaled long and deep. Her voice as sharp as a papercut.

"Henry! Carl! You stop right there."

They did exactly that. It was spontaneous and undeniable. The queen's voice struck a chord only a mother could find. They were trapped between the king and the queen. An unenviable place to be.

"Now!" the king roared. "I want her out now, or you'll be scraping calluses off my feet!"

The king didn't have calluses. On his feet or anywhere on his body. Still, Henry and Carl stepped toward the queen.

"Boys," the queen said as calmly as if she asked them to pass the butter.

"I'm your king!"

"I am your queen."

"No! No, she's not! I fired her yester—*ahhhh.* I'm counting to three!"

The king held up three fingers. They fell one at a time, the king's voice rising with each one. He shrieked at the end and screamed, "ZERO!"

The gorillas stutter stepped. Stopped. Looked at each other with wide eyes and fat lips. They decided without saying a word out loud it was better to follow the king. Until the queen played her trump card.

"I will talk to your mother."

They stepped aside, put their backs against the wall. No hesitation. The king could've said the same thing and it wouldn't have mattered. The queen knew their mother and knew her well. The king had nothing on her.

Without her crown, she walked across the room. Henry and Carl didn't flinch as she passed, her mousey nails clicking on the hard floor. True royalty didn't need a crown. She took the crusted remains of pastry off Jelly's coat, wiped the custard from the elf's cheek, then nodded.

Jelly bent the knee of her stubby leg.

"You may be the king of the Naughty, but you are not a child." The queen said to King Chocolate. "Jelly has been nothing but good to you. This is not how to lead."

"Lead? What do you know about leading? I KNOW HOW TO LEAD!" He slapped his chest. "I was made for this, not you. You see those animals out there? You think there's anyone in *aallllll* of Candyland who can lead *them*? They love me, you rat. I can do anything I want, and they love me more. THEY LOVE ME!"

"That's not important."

"It's the only thing that matters! They follow *me* because they love *me*."

"And where are you taking them, Casey?"

"To the winner's circle. And you're not invited. You don't get to ride in the car when they have a parade for me. And if you do not leave right now, I will open those doors and have *my fans* drag you out. You don't know *all* their mothers."

"I know most."

"You want to try me?" He floated near the ceiling. Raised his chin to mimic confidence and power, but only looked like a child imitating an adult.

Art had not moved. Not a finger.

The queen was the first to regard him. Her look thoughtful, penetrating.

"Have your fun tonight, Casey. Do as you wish. But I will stay with Arthur for the remainder of the evening. When this is finished, you will never see me again."

"I don't make deals."

"I'm not offering one."

He appeared to be an inflatable balloon about to burst. His teeth grinding like machinery in need of lubrication.

"Never?"

"As in ever, Casey."

"Aaaah, I see what you're doing. When *this* is finished? Too *vague*. You can't trick a tricker. You will leave when Christmas arrives. And not a tick later."

"Of course. This will be finished by then."

He cruised closer. "And what do you think *this* is?"

"It's a mistake."

"You haven't a clue what you're talking about."

"I know a mistake when I see one."

The king growled and flew a lap around the room. His tiny legs dribbling over the gorillas' heads. He came to a screeching halt, the hoversuit whining to hold the massive momentum in check. Seething, the king spoke to Jelly.

"Tell her that if she tries to taint the boy, there will be consequences."

"Tell the king I will do no such thing," the queen said.

The king nodded. Then laughed, mostly to himself. She was up to something. He could smell it. But what could she do? The boy had one last painting to do, and then he was done with him. Naughty Side for the win.

"She's not the queen, bt-dub. Just so everyone knows. She has no power. None. You understand, don't you?" he said to his primate security. Both of whom would be fired sooner than soon. "She's just a rat. That's all. A rat I housed and clothed. When she was a no-name, lowlife crosser, I made her someone. Me. I did. She'd be nothing without me. Tell her this is the last time, Jelly Belly. Tell her bye, Felicia."

"What does that mean?" the queen said.

"You wouldn't understand," the king said. "Take your giant clown with you. I don't want to see that monster ever again, either. Now, boys, come here."

The gorillas were too broad for him to put his arms around. He made them squeeze closer together. "Are you listening?"

They grunted.

"First of all, you're fired when this is over. No offense, but I need someone smarter than my left foot. Second, she can't talk to the boy. Like at all. Not a word. She can sit in here till the gingersnaps come home, I don't care. No talking. You got that? Repeat it back. Let me hear it."

They repeated some of it.

"Close enough. I'm going out there now."

"They're not ready for you," Jelly said. "The schedule—"

"I'M GOING ON! Get the boy ready. I'm going to get that crowd of dirty sickos wound up for his grand opening. You're going to be a star, Arty Farty. I can feel it in my delicious bones. I love you, boy. Love you like a son." The king kissed two fingers and held them up. "Peace out."

He stuck his tongue out at the queen. Snapped his fingers at Jelly.

"Let's go, Jello. Get the sled fired up."

THE QUEEN PULLED a beanbag next to Art. A purple one. It hissed when she eased into it. She coiled her tail on her lap.

Together they watched the live events play out on the wall monitor.

The dunked and sprinkled advisors stood in their plastic cage. Chocolate rained down from overhead cannons. Sparks drizzled onto the stage while fires burned near the trees.

Then King Chocolate put on a show, and everything changed.

The queen didn't say anything. Didn't ask Art to slow his breathing. Didn't reach for his hand. She was present with him. And that was all he needed.

Anxiety didn't shake him. Panic wasn't around.

Art floated in a deep well of warmth and acceptance. *Christmas spirit,* the queen had called it. *True Christmas spirit.* He had realized that all these memories that had emerged, they existed whether he remembered them or not. To possess them wasn't what he needed to do. They were real. They'd happened. Nothing could make them unhappen, even if he forgot.

That was the peace he rested in. That was all he needed.

He was here for a reason. He had to go to the bottom of the dark side before climbing out. He and the queen watched the king's grand speech.

And then Jelly came for him.

22

evel seven.

The triple bass drums washed over the king like a conga line of fists. He sat stage left, just out of view of the crowd, while a pair of long-legged spider daddies loaded a fresh set of batteries into the back of the hoversuit. It was hanging a bit loose in the midsection.

"Tighten it up!" he shouted.

They were grunting and tugging, but the spider daddies proved to be useless. He wasn't in the mood for excuses, and there was no time to call the fashionistas. He needed to wash the bad taste out of his brain. He wanted to obliterate what had happened in the green room and leave no trace of the queen.

The band helped him do that. They were destroying his rendition of "Naughty Time." In a good way. A great way.

Troll, the lead singer, had flaming red hair. Literally. He'd thrown a match on the bright orange tuft halfway through the song. Blue flames licked his head. It smelled like burnt cinnamon toast.

Two octopuses, one orange and the other purple, thrashed two sets of drums. (Dual drums had been King Chocolate's idea). The double percussion sent ripples over the king's doughy skin. And then

Wire Doll chummed the mosh pit with a head-splitting guitar solo. A string of gorillas, locked arm in arm, kept the crowd from spilling onto the stage.

A gingerbread arm went flying over them and broke into pieces. Troll picked it up and took a bite. Threw the rest of it at the shame cage where the dunked and sprinkled advisors swung in their glass prison. The smell of Fudgy Lake wafted off them like volcanic fumes.

They'll make a good ornament, the king thought. He could replicate little glass cages with dunked and sprinkled misfits inside for next Christmas, crank them out by the thousands, ready to hang on trees. *Sell them by the truckload.*

The spider daddies locked up the battery compartment. An electric vibe tickled the king's funny parts, squeezed him with fresh juice. Troll was slinging sweat all over the backs of the gorillas. King Chocolate would rather skinny-dip in Fudgy Lake than feel that. Then the dwarf leaped into the crowd and bodysurfed across the mosh pit.

"Enough."

King Chocolate gave the order. Now wasn't the time for an extended version of "Naughty Time." A halo of fly messengers went out to deliver his order. The octopuses dropped their sticks. Wire Doll let go of his guitar. When the message reached the mosh pit, Troll was launched back onstage like a toxic hair ball. He bounced once, then took out one of the drum sets. The octopuses carried him off, hair still smoking.

The lights dimmed.

Word spread like a tsunami. The crowd pushed toward the stage. The gorilla line held firm. One break and the animals would wreck the stage with joy. The king licked the air, tasted the charge. It was hot and electric. *Christmas fever,* he thought. *That's what it is. Far better than Christmas spirit.*

He allowed the silence and darkness to stretch out.

Level eight.

Anticipation climbed another level. It was a beautiful stench. The king felt bubbly inside. This was it. This was everything he'd worked for. This was the precipice of victory. He was going to squeeze every drop out of it, drink it down and fill his belly.

Adrenaline spilled over the rim. Fights broke out.

A band of pirates slashed their way toward the front.

The Snow Queen turned a gaggle of bridge trolls into ice cubes.

The Big Bad Wolf howled. His posse joined him.

The king raised a finger. Wire Doll saw it and plucked a few notes on his guitar. He strung together a slow-building intro. It ignited the crowd with furious joy. Fused their chaos into one. The fighting stopped. As one they pressed forward.

Level nine.

The king could see a blue aura rippling over the sea of naughties like heat waves over sand. *The essence of the Naughty Side!* There had always been a certain quality to this side of Candyland. A vibe that was dangerous and free, an energy that singed the skin and tickled the belly. It jellied knees and liquified the weak. It was beautiful in its prime.

The king could see it. Taste it.

He was the conductor of this mad symphony.

No one else could do what he did. No one could ever bring this horde of uglies together like him. Stir them in a kettle. Bring them to a boil. Forge a new Christmas essence. One he would bottle and sell to the masses.

Christmas fever!

On his signal came a mechanical roar. Chrome pipes blatted the raw music of power. It twisted brains and tied muscles into furious knots. The hint of something large and gleaming began to lower from the scaffolding. It was long and mean. Flashes of dark beauty were highlighted in a brief shower of flames spitting from its tailpipes.

Level ten.

The king wasn't done. But if he wasn't careful, the entire show would collapse in euphoric anarchy. The Maestro of Naughty played them like instruments, sculpting expectations, massaging beliefs.

The king drank it up and let it build to a tenuous climax. The membrane of order stretched thin. The line of gorillas began to bend.

The gleaming object touched the stage. The motor hummed a dangerous tune to feed the frenzy. Only then did the king open his eyes. He skipped right over level eleven and teetered on the brink.

"Now."

The mass of his girth flew across the stage like a pillowy puppet. Greeted with thrashing guitar chords and hammering drums that pummeled the crowd with such force they were sent reeling back. For a moment, there was a gulf between the crowd and the gorillas. Then it collapsed and nearly broke the muscled dike.

A spotlight followed him around the bright and shiny sleigh with long chrome tailpipes and fire painted down the sides. Gold rails and gold bumpers. Sleek and fearsome. Loud and obnoxious.

Just like the boy had drawn it.

He went from one side to the next, soaring to the edges of the stage, long coat fluttering behind him like a cape (plans were to sell capes after the show). He paused long enough for chocolate bars to shoot from candy cannons strapped to the king's hips (the fashionistas' idea, although King Chocolate took credit for it).

Hand to his ear to hear the roar.

Hand to his other ear to make it louder.

He blew kisses. Pumped his fists. Wound them up until leaves fell from the trees.

Level twelve.

A THRONE ROLLED to center stage. King Chocolate lowered onto it. Adrenaline boiled his blood. He couldn't feel the loose hoversuit chafing his sides. He sat very still, absorbing the madness. A spectator of violence. So many of them had to be physically restrained. Some were broken. No one seemed to mind.

Especially the king.

A live close-up of him projected onto a screen. He doused the urge to smile, not wanting to appear weak. Raised his chin to show strength. He closed his eyes for a long moment, inhaling the smell of victory.

It smelled like chaos.

When the line of security began to bow, he raised his hand. That was all it took.

Quiet fell like winter snow. He kept his hand up until the crackle of distant trash fires could be heard. They were out of breath, shaking with anticipation. Ready to do whatever he said.

This is how you lead.

"Look at you," he started. His voice effortlessly carried over the crowd. "You deplorable... disgusting... filthy... ugly..."

Each word deliberate and heavy. Slow and steady. The pace picking up. The cheering followed.

"Disgraceful, shameful, inexcusable..."

The mosh pit started throwing elbows. They climbed on each other's shoulders, threw broken limbs onstage, howled into the darkness.

"Dreadful-horrid-nasty-foul... REJECTS!"

Christmas fever went through level twelve and touched thirteen. Things were getting smashed and stomped and beaten. The Wicked Witch flew over the crowd, just out of reach, turning random naughties into toads.

His hand went up.

A calm washed through the crowd and turned the storm-tossed ocean into a glassy lake.

All attention on their leader masterfully letting the silence wrap around them.

"How many Christmases have there been? Does anyone remember?"

Some shouted out answers. King Chocolate didn't know if there was a right answer. No one remembered how many Christmases there had been in Candyland. The answer was infinite.

"And how many times did you wake up to coal in your stocking? I'll bet you remember that. *Every... single... Christmas!*"

There were murmurs and shuffling. They knew what a lump of coal felt like.

"Forever! That's how many times you got coal. Eternity! That's how many Christmases there have been. And all this time the jolly fat man dumps his trash on your doorstep, then waltzes over to *that* side and DELIVERS PRESENTS!"

He pointed to the distant line in the sky, where dark met light.

"And he stacks them high, my lovelies. He stacks those boxes and bags and shiny things as high as the sky, my precious naughties. And those happy nicies grab each other's hands to dance around their mountains of gifts, singing their songs and laughing at the poor naughties with their dirty, filthy stockings filled with soot.

"And it doesn't matter how high their piles are. No. The jolly fat man will add another present. And another. And another. Because they're the nice ones. The good ones. The jolly fat man says: Do what I say and follow the rules and *I'll bring you more!*"

The king slapped his belly like a drum.

"We don't matter. None of us. Because we're the bad ones. The rotten ones. We're broken. Deplorable. Disgusting." He took a long deep breath. "WE ARE NAUGHTY!"

He took a moment to let that one cook.

"*I've* never rejected you. Not a single one of you. I've loved you for who you are. We are free over here! Free to be naughty. Free to be nice —I said it, that's right. *Nice.* If that's who you are, then you be that. But let's be honest." A wry twist on his bloated face winked on the screen. "It's not much fun to be nice, now is it."

Oh, the joy. The rowdy joy.

"Everyone is welcome, my naughties. No one is turned away from the Naughty Side." *Except the rat queen.* "We are family. I have thousands of sons and daughters and brothers and sisters. FAMILY! We are a team. We are..." He thumped his chest twice. "*Naugh*-ty."

He did it again. Same cadence.

"We are... Naugh-ty! We are... Naugh-ty!"

The band caught on. The bass drum picked up the beat. The crowd joined in. The king raised his arms.

We are (BOOM-BOOM) Naugh-ty!

The chant generated a magnetism that drew the crowd together. A bond between brother and sister materialized.

WE ARE...

A tribal anthem was forging. There was no bond more unbroken, no salve more healing for a broken nation than us versus them.

NAUGH-TY!

"Do you feel that? Feel it! Your brother to your right. Your sister to your left."

WE ARE...

"We've been fighting them forever. Merry, merry? He gives us coal. Coal! Not very nice. Not very merry!"

NAUGH-TY!

"They're phonies, and you know it. *They* know it! That's why you're here. You're part of this family because you are real. You are free. *You* are the merry ones! I feel it. I feel the Christmas fever. You are the good and the bad and the free!"

WE ARE...

"They want to make us like *them!* Do what they say, follow their rules. Get in line and you can have a mountain of presents, too. Is that what you want? To sell your truth for a box of Carrot-Top Dolls?"

NAUGH-TY!

The beat grew louder. Wire Doll joined the drums with power chords.

Fists in the air. Fists pounding chests. Wolves howled and witches laughed and sparks danced into the dark.

"We love you, King Chocolate!" a half-inflated doll shouted.

"We love you!" others joined in.

The king let the worship fall over him like warm rain on a summer night. He soaked it in. Drank it up. Let the beat go on.

Then he said: "Aren't you tired of being judged?"

"We love you!"

"Tonight is the night!" He hovered above the throne, arms out and welcoming. "This is Christmas Eve. This is when the jolly fat man comes with another bag of coal for you rejects. You scum. You misfit toys. He comes to blacken your stockings and dust your mantels while the nicies sing their songs and sit on his lap and read their lists and follow their rules. But not tonight!"

He hovered above the throne.

"Tonight we change that. Tonight the eternal war ends. Tonight their true colors will be exposed, their fakeness stripped away. Tonight the jolly fat man will stuff *their* stockings with black, sooty *COAL!*"

The rocket sleigh ignited on cue.

Flames from the tailpipes bathed Wire Doll in fire. He stepped out of the heat, the guitar melting in orange glowing hands. The crowd loved it. They ate the power from the smoking engines like breakfast cereal, waiting for weapons to unfold from the sides.

There were no weapons. Maybe next time.

The most powerful thing didn't look like a weapon. He was sitting backstage. A canvas lowered down to the stage. The crowd recognized the map of Candyland stenciled upon it. Every Lander knew it.

A curvy line down the middle.

One side dark and cloudy, the other light and cheery.

The crowd crawled over each other with expectations. When the rocket sleigh went quiet and the chant died down, a spring-loaded anticipation took hold of them. They leaned against each other, waiting for the final solution their king had promised.

He pointed at Two-Face Mountain, where the Nice Side lit half of it.

"Tonight," he said, "we make them naughty."

23

Art didn't notice the stirring confusion and mild disappointment.

His distant gaze was inwardly focused. He hardly noticed the crowd. Didn't see their twisted faces or angry taunts. Didn't see the king hold his arms out for a hug.

Art was filled with a vision.

He saw the canvas. A canvas so big that an A-frame ladder would be needed to reach the top of it. There was a rack of aerosol cans. Spray paint of every shade and color.

He'd studied the map that was already printed on the canvas. It was just like he'd imagined. What he'd been asked to do. It sounded boring. Unimaginative. But something about it was intriguing. Meaningful. Drew him in.

Paint it black, he thought. *Paint it all black.*

His hand moved on its own, selecting cans as if the decision had already been made.

While the crowd jeered, his breath was slow and steady. He was this moment. He was the flow. The essence.

I am the Christmas spirit.

There was no crowd or trees. No band, no stage. No pain or fear. No happiness.

He was none of it. He was all of it.

It made no sense to think of it that way. But in it—in that flowing spirit—there was no need to make sense. The Christmas spirit wanted him to be everything. To see all of him. What was inside him. To know who he was. Truly was. It was why he was here. To let it out.

So the world can see me.

It flowed down his arm. An aerosol hiss dampened and darkened the canvas. Fuming the air.

The spirit poured onto the canvas.

He didn't hear the gasps or feel the wonder behind him. Didn't hear the chanting. Didn't notice the stage shaking or the ground quaking. All he saw was empty canvas to fill.

This is what I came here to do.

He was no longer hiding from himself. He wanted the world to know who he was. The hard feelings he carried. The Guilt and Shame inside him. He dug deeper, opening vault doors filled with secrets, sweeping corners that stored embarrassment. As he emptied himself onto the canvas, memories of who he was stepped into the light. Of who he was, who he is, and who he will become. *This place isn't a dream*, he decided.

It's a gift. To be here is a gift.

Shake and rattle went the cans.

This is Christmas.

Spray and hiss.

I am Christmas.

THE FIRST DROP of rain streaked the swirls of grays and blacks and browns. It dripped to the bottom and clung to the edge of the canvas. Highlighted by a flash of lightning and distant thunder.

Earthquakes followed. One after another.

Things fell from the scaffolding.

Sweat ran down his cheeks and over his lips. He painted with his eyes closed, seeing what was needed clearer than anything he'd ever seen. Both hands loaded with paint, staining the canvas with his truth. The king didn't need to tell him what to do. It was already inside him.

The instruments shorted out. The band ran from the stage as a monsoon hammered down. The ground turned to mud. The fires extinguished. The king's voice no longer projected through the speakers. Everything was the sound of rain.

Art climbed the ladder.

Stood on the very top.

On his toes.

His fingers cramped. Stomach clenched. Weak and shaking, the last swipes were applied. The cans empty. The map no longer black on one side and white on the other. There was no hint of a curving line. It was all one color.

No longer Naughty and Nice.

Art was as empty as the cans he was holding. He didn't fall from the ladder. He simply couldn't hold himself up any longer. As he tipped over the side, the rain suddenly stopped. He felt the wind in his ears and waited for the hard landing below him. He wasn't afraid. He didn't clench or brace for impact because he was empty. The weight of Guilt and Shame was no longer in him. He'd become so light and empty that he was certain that he would float away instead of crash. Float into the sky and out of this dream.

Gracefully, he fell.

Instead of the unforgiving stage, he landed in a soft embrace.

The vicious roar of the crowd fell over him. The shouting, the cheering. The hungry snarl of the sleigh rockets and the heat of their engines. The stage shook and caught fire as the sleigh launched over the trees. A stampede followed its direction.

The sky so dark as far as he could see.

A pink hand wiped the hair from his eyes. Strong arms cradled him against her furry body. The queen looked down with very human eyes and smiled with kindness. She nodded and whispered, "I see you, Arthur."

He shuddered and wept. The map of Candyland was a circle of darkness. Yet there in the middle, right where the border had once been, was something he hadn't seen in his vision. Something he hadn't painted. It hadn't been there when he finished, but he could see it now.

It wasn't a trick.

A single beam of light was etched in the darkness.

24

The engines rearranged King Chocolate's innards. His organs churning into a chocolate smoothie. Violent waves rode up his neck and over his chin, reached into his tummy and gave it a good stir. He turned to the front of the sleigh, wind stretching his cheeks into a clownish grin, and shouted: "Turn off the rockets!"

"What?" Jelly said.

The king could barely hear his own words. He clutched the back of the driver's seat. "The rockets!" he shouted directly into Jelly's ear. "Turn them off!"

"I don't know how! This is just turbulence!"

"This isn't turbulence!"

"What?"

The king let go, crashing into the back of his seat. Tears streaming across his temples and wetting his knotted hair. Even if Jelly knew how to turn the rockets off (which she most certainly did, the little liar), they'd go down like a meteor. If they survived this, he would be partially deaf. And mostly numb.

It was his fault, if he were to admit it. He'd given the drawing to the boy, this grand shiny monster that purred like a predator and flew like a weapon. Of course, King Chocolate hadn't thought about the tailpipes blasting raw power next to the back seat.

He plugged his ears with two plump fingers.

There wasn't much to see this far up. Through a blur of wind-swept tears, Two-Face Mountain stuck out like an upside-down ice-cream cone. The sleigh leaned into a turn. The king felt his stomach drop into his bottom. He pulled his fingers out of his ears to hang on. They circled around the left side of the mountain. A beam of white light was spiked into the side of it and went straight up through the sky.

The boy missed that part.

He'd done a masterful job with the painting. The king had shed one chocolatey tear as the boy had done his work. The dark sky stretching further with each stroke. If only King Chocolate could have seen all those nicies when the clouds ate up their pink sky like a video game. The big phony smiles melting away on their big, dumb faces. Imagining it sent stampedes of gooseflesh over the rolling hills of his body.

Beyond the mountain, it was dark. Not a single streetlight or lamp-lit window. There was never a need for them. It was always bright on this side of the mountain. Always merry. *Until now.*

"And who's the king of the naughty?" he said.

"What?"

"Nothing!" He kicked the seat. "Just fly!"

THEY RUMBLED over the dark land. It was too dim to see the roads and homes. Too dim to see the nicies looking up at the sleigh growling through the sky. They'd think it was Santa coming to save them. The king reached into a sack under his seat. He threw chocolate coins over the side of the sleigh.

"Blah-blah, you goodies. Here's a Christmas treat you won't be able to live without."

Most of the nicies had never sampled his chocolatey goodness.

Once they got a taste, they'd line up for more. It wouldn't be long before he had *all* the money. *All of it.* He wanted everything. And he wanted everyone to know he had everything.

"Fly lower!"

"Not a good idea!" Jelly said. "I can't really see the ground."

"It wasn't a suggestion!"

He kicked the seat. The sleigh dropped suddenly. The king rose off the seat a few inches and held on to keep from soaring out. The hoversuit wasn't made to fly. When the sleigh leveled out, faint roofs appeared. He could see the roads, as well. Jelly went lower and eased up on the throttle. The engines coughed like unfed animals smelling prey.

The king could see them now. Little mad ants running around. Pointing. Gossiping.

They'd never lived under a dim sky. They weren't going to like it. Life was heavy and harsh. Sometimes mean. Optimism shriveled under it. But they'd get used to it. Or not. It wasn't really a choice.

King Chocolate was going to rename the place. Since there was no more Nice Side, there was no reason it should be called Candyland. Just make it simple.

Naughtyland. Or Naughty Town. City of Naughty? Wait! He licked his blackened lips, this thought so delicious he wanted to taste it.

"Badland."

"What?"

The king pointed at the massive shadow ahead. Castle Nice, once a shiny pillar of merry goodwill, now looked lost and hopeless. *No more lies, goodies! True colors from here on out.*

"You're welcome!"

He bombed the gawkers with a bucket of malted chocolates. He had Jelly make a lap down Gumdrop Alley to pitch his candies like it was a Christmas parade. The nicies ran for cover. Chocolate drops shattered roofing shingles and busted out windows. They knocked over bicycles and blew through awnings until the bag was almost empty.

Going to need more ammo, he thought.

He would have to return to get the boy anyway. He'd left him with the rat queen. She could do no harm now. The game was over.

"To the castle!"

JELLY CIRCLED THE CASTLE. The pristine water of Rose Lake surrounded it like a slab of obsidian. Jelly brought the sleigh closer, rippling the surface. A crowd gathered along the shore, filling the open market and shabby buildings. The king grabbed Jelly's shoulder and pointed. He wanted her to land.

"It's too crowded!" Jelly shouted. "I'll go around to the—"

"They'll get out of the way."

Jelly didn't want to do it. She tried to land short of the market. The king leaned over and yanked the reins attached to the dashboard. The sleigh corkscrewed three times and nearly dumped them into an alley.

They skidded on one rail. Bounced off a candy-cane tree. Sparks flew.

The nicies scattered like bugs. All except the nutcrackers. They held their ground as the sleigh barreled toward them. The wooden soldiers didn't flinch. They sounded like bowling pins when the shiny nose of the sleigh struck them. They spun and twisted, taking out a cart of nuts and knocking over a shanty made of straw. The rails screeched over the pavers and came to a sudden stop. The king hit his head on the back of Jelly's seat.

The engines hissed and ticked. Steam sizzled from beneath the hood.

A high-pitched whine filled the king's head. He waved off the smoke, coughing. There were screams and general chaos. The sort of thing King Chocolate loved.

Feels like home.

"Everyone, go back to your homes!" someone called in a firm voice. "Go to your families. Take the week off and get some rest. All will be well soon!"

King Chocolate recognized the voice.

The hoversuit carried him out of the sleigh and over the road. Launched him higher than he'd ever been. Like he was flying. He nearly fell out the bottom of the suit. The thing hardly fit. A rank odor wafted out from beneath the hoversuit.

Good. Stink the place up and mark it like an animal.

He started laughing. It got the attention of the citizens of the (formally known as) Nice Side. They'd never heard laughter like his. Laughter that lacked joy. Laughter with an edge that could saw down a tree.

"Happy Halloween, ladies." He stuck his tongue out. A rag doll fainted.

King Chocolate floated down the middle of the brick road. His legs waved beneath him like wet lengths of yarn. He sped toward the one who was trying to calm the citizens. The one helping them pick up their belongings and ushering them to safety. His royal crown crooked on his dumb head.

Someone waddled in front of King Chocolate. A fat little elf determined not to let him pass. He could hover over her, but he was in no hurry. There was time to wallow in victory.

"Jelly, you know this one? She looks like you." King Chocolate looked back and forth. "Sort of *exactly* like you."

Jelly didn't move from the sleigh. King Chocolate snapped his fingers.

"Are you... don't tell me." He covered his mouth. "*You're Belly! I've heard so much about you! Oh, my bells. You two have so much to catch up on. But not now. Right now, Jelly's guarding the sleigh. It's expensive, you know. Custom made. Want to know how I made it?"* He whispered: "Ancient Lander secret."

He winked.

Belly didn't move. Didn't twitch. Those fat little arms crossed over her big round stomach. And a scowl as deep as a valley etched into her face.

"Ain't you supposed to be the happy one? Jelly, is she supposed to be happy? The weather got you down, sister? It has that effect. Bad news: this is permanent. Good news: you'll get used to it. But oooooooo, good times are coming, me lady. We're going to show you how to party. Now why don't you go help that old toy across the street and let the big people talk. Scram."

The formerly merry elf who once lived at the top of the castle did not move.

"I think we broke her, Jelly! She's lost that loving feeling, I can tell. I can feel the hate coming off her. It's like acid. You know, like when you put your tongue on a battery?"

The chaos died down. The citizens who hadn't taken cover or run back home stood on both sides of the market. This was their first sighting of the chocolate king. They'd seen pictures of him, sure. But in the flesh, it was mesmerizing. A wolf was wringing his hands and biting his lip. He wore a Santa hat. There was nothing *bad* about this wolf.

"The naughties will be here in a few rings!" King Chocolate called to them. "They're coming as fast as they can. Looking forward to meeting you all, I'm sure. How are you enjoying the weather. Pink getting boring, I'll bet. I never cared for it. But this." He pointed at the swirling gray ceiling. "It's got character. Makes you work for a good day."

They didn't move or twitch. Or make a sound.

The king looked down at Belly. Back to the gawkers.

"Not big talkers, huh? I thought you'd be a chatty bunch. I'll just —" He bounced off Belly, who wobbled on those giant paddle feet. King Chocolate could have mowed her down. The hoversuit had a full charge. He could push a train with it. Instead, he leaned into her. "This isn't going to end well for you, sister."

"Enough."

Macey (formerly the king of the nicies) cradled a giant purple egg wearing Bermuda shorts and sucking a pacifier. He had dirtied the knees of his royal robe. There was mud on his hands and on his face. He knelt next to Belly, who was still eyeballing King Chocolate with tiny-dog syndrome.

"Why don't you help at the hut, Belly. The queen is in the nursery." He passed the pacifier-sucking egg to the roly-poly elf. "Thank you."

Macey wiped his hands on his sleeves and stood up.

The kings looked at each other. Somewhere a baby cried. The gawking crowd waited for someone to draw a weapon.

"Well, this is a first," King Chocolate said. "Not straddling the border with your lady. Feels a little weird, right? Just a couple of *bachelors* hanging out at the market. Heh-heh. Anyway, this place is a dump. I thought it would be more, I don't know. *Nice.*"

King Nice blinked slowly.

"I'm thinking the lake here will make a good skating rink. Ever been skating? How about fishing? Now there's a sport. We stocked Fudgy Lake with some fat trophies, but their gills gummed up. It was disgusting. You had to fry them in bacon fat to eat them. Now there's just Swedish fish in it. You know, the gummy kind. I don't like them, but can't stop eating them. It's weird."

Macey watched his brother in disbelief.

"You got a little something on your—"

"Why?"

"You slipped and fell? I don't know."

King Chocolate licked his thumb and wiped the dirt off Macey's cheek. His brother crossed his arms and looked away. He looked like his dog died.

"Why? What do you mean *why*? You know why! This is what we do, brother. Push, pull. Naughty, nice. You hate me, I hate you."

"I never hated you, Casey."

"That's a lie. A gold-bar lie if I ever heard one. Hear that, Jelly? He *never* hated us." He puttered down to the ground. Rubbery legs folded beneath him. "You judged us, Macey. Looked down on us. You think you're better than us. Getting warm?"

"That's what you think? That-that-that we wanted a better life for you because we *hated* you?"

"There you go." King Chocolate pointed in his face. "You see that? Right there. That look in your eye, right there. What is it? Jelly! What's the big words a dumb naughty like me don't 'member?"

"Self-righteous pity."

King Chocolate snapped his fingers. "Self-righteous pity. Right there. Disgusting, ain't it. I'd rather you kick me in the shin than look at me like that. Go on, be honest. We disgust you." He flashed chocolate-stained teeth. "We embarrass you. What, brother? What are you hiding behind that fake smile?"

"I feel sorry for the naughties."

"Because they party?"

"You make them live in darkness with you. The way you treat each other over there." He pinched the bridge of his nose. "It breaks my heart."

"Oh, dear Santa Claus," King Chocolate muttered. "The *drama*."

Worse than high school theater.

"That's what I'm talking about!" King Chocolate floated several feet off the road and turned in a circle so all the goodies could hear him. "You disgust me, all of you! You bury your faults, your dirty little secrets so deep you don't see them and then pretend they ain't there. Pretend you don't lie. Pretend you weren't going to *use that boy to wipe out the Naughty Side*. ADMIT IT!"

He stormed down on Macey.

"Admit it, just once, brother, and I swear on Santa's reindeer I'll make the boy take it all back. You can have your pink skies and be just as plastic as you were before. Just admit it. Admit you were going to use the boy on us like I did on you."

"You don't own the boy. Shame on you for making him destroy our side. He doesn't even know what he's done."

"Oh, he knows. He knows you trapped him in your castle. You had plans for him, didn't you. You were going to use him to change us into *you*! But the boy, he's too smart. He came to the dark side, brother. Then I did to you what you were going to do to us. I won, brother." He blew a kiss. "You lost."

"This isn't a game!"

"I won! Admit it!"

"You're acting like a child."

"Admit it!"

"Admit what? What do you want me to admit, Casey? That I care about you? That I want to ease your suffering? That I want you to feel the warm light on your skin and not the clammy grip of night?" He called to the sidewalks stuffed with gawkers. "I admit I care about you!"

They murmured in agreement. The idiots went along with his nonsense. They were too dim to see through the lies. King Chocolate knew a lie when he heard one. He was a master fibber. A professional deceiver. His brother was good, though. He had these dingdongs eating baloney out of his hands.

King Chocolate surveyed the nodding heads. Little Boy Blue with his trumpet (his brother played a mean guitar on the Naughty Side). Peter Pumpkin Eater sitting on an orange three-wheeler (his brother ate ghost peppers). Bo-Peep and Jack Horner and Mary with her dopey lambs.

They're sheep. All of them gullible sheep.

He measured their forgiving disposition. Kindness in their expressions. It was disgusting and weak. King Chocolate had scorched their skies and they were going to forgive him? Well, tough love had arrived on a rocket sleigh just in time to open their eyes.

"You know he's Santa, don't you?" King Chocolate pointed at his brother. "Santa doesn't fly in a sleigh or have magic reindeer. He lives in that castle. And every Christmas he glues a beard on his face and sits in that big dumb throne for you idiots to climb on his lap. All those pictures you have with Santa—*it's him*. All those presents Santa gave you?"

He nodded at Macey.

"Your king's been conning you since day one. Making you believe the stories. Well, I'm here to tell the truth."

"Casey—"

"He's pretending to be Santa because Santa ain't real! He didn't tell you that, did he. He lied to you. He lied to *all* of you. There ain't no flying reindeer, and there ain't no Santa Claus. Well, let me tell you something—telling lies ain't how we're going to live anymore. I'm in charge of this dump now. I'm the king, and the truth will be told!"

He took a long, hacky breath.

"SANTA AIN'T REAL!"

It didn't get the reaction he thought it would. He thought there would be gasps and frowning. Lots of frowning. A few boos (at Macey, not King Chocolate). And maybe, just maybe, a little appreciation. You know, for the honesty.

None of that, though. Dead silence.

They were waiting for Macey to reply. But here's the thing. When two certified liars go head-to-head, no one wins. And nothing changes.

"If Santa isn't real," Macey said, just as calmly as asking about the weather, "then who puts coal in your stockings?"

A BRILLIANT MOVE.

The kind of move some call checkmate.

"Every Christmas you complain about the coal. You print it on your banner and wave it over the castle. You beat drums with it, write songs about it. Sing anthems. *Oh, the coal. The coal, the coal. It dirties our soul, the coal. The coal.* And how lucky are we, the Nice Side. We get presents while you get coal. Because Santa hates you. That's in your dirge. *The jolly fat man dumps his coal on our poor little souls. Why, oh why?* You preach about mistreatment, use it to bind the will of the Naughty Side against us."

Macey poked a bulge of flesh on his brother's midsection.

"If it's not Santa stuffing coal in their stockings, then who?" This was bad. Never had King Chocolate struggled to find fighting words. "If you see self-righteous pity in my eyes," Macey said, "it's a reflection."

Oooooh. That was a good one. King Chocolate had to admit, that was good. The crowd agreed. This was a home crowd. If the naughties were here, it would be different. Good thing they weren't. Not yet.

"He's *not* real," King Chocolate said.

"Then how does coal get in their stockings? Someone puts it there. Who would do such a thing?"

"You do it. You-you sneak across the border and—"

"Coal comes from burning Christmas trees, Casey. We have our trees at the top of the castle. I can show you. What did you do with your Christmas trees?" Macey snapped his fingers. "You *buuuurned* them and kept the blackened remains. They're piled high in your castle, Casey. Why would you do that? Why would you keep coal in your castle?" Macey let the question hang like a dead fish. Then for the big swing: "Because *you put it in their stockings!*"

A collective gasp.

For a nice king, his brother was merciless. Surgical. He rattled his opponent, then turned the crowd. King Chocolate bobbed like a loose kite, wishing Lydia were here to reel him in. *On second thought, she would do me worse.*

"The naughties don't know it's him, either! The lies he tells are so they'll get in line. The deception he weaves is so they'll do what he wants. He puts *coal* in their stockings! He lies so often it sounds like the truth. *He puts coal in their stockings!* His only talent—his one great talent—is that he believes his own lies. HE PUTS COAL IN THEIR STOCKINGS!"

Cheers. Fists and paws and claws in the air.

They stepped into the street. Closed in around him. King Chocolate was about to signal Jelly to fire up the engines. He could fly over them to get to the sleigh, but he'd just be a pinata. A plastic cowboy with a red plastic cowboy hat was twirling a stiff lasso just in case.

"I won!" King Chocolate shouted. "This is mine now. It's all mine. I won, you lost! So from now on you *all* get coal. How do you like that? That put a merry, merry in your tighties? And this guy won't pretend to be Santa anymore, I can promise you that. He lied to you, point blank. Right in your faces. You sat on *his* lap for pictures. His lap, dressed like Santa. But that's over. You're all naughty now, like it or not."

They still weren't upset about the Santa news. Maybe they already knew and were just going along with it. *Do the naughties know*

I put coal in their stockings? He doubted it. There would've been a mutiny.

"Welcome to Badland," King Chocolate said with a grin. Oh, he liked the sound of that. "Bad. Land. Get it? Because I won and you lost. And don't act like you're any better than us. Your king's a liar. *Former* king."

"If the boy stayed with us, he would have given you light, Casey. Your people don't have to suffer. They don't have to be bad. I was going to save you." He gestured to the darkened sky. "Now we all get coal, eh, brother?"

King Chocolate nodded with a dark sparkle in his eyes. "See, now that wasn't so hard to admit, now was it."

"I just said I wanted to help you."

"No. You said you wanted to *change* us. There's a difference."

"For the better. I wanted to change you *for the better!* How is that a bad thing? We're happy; you're sad. Think about it, brother!"

"You don't get it. That's not who we are. You didn't see Artie. You didn't really *seeee* him. That boy was troubled. He had darkness. The reason your pink sky is gone is because he had to get the darkness out. He needed someone to see it in him. See *him,* Macey. That's the difference between you and me. I accept them with all the faults. All you see is what you want them to be. And that, my brother, is the naughtiest of all. You get coal this year."

"You said you'd change the sky back if I admitted it." Macey stepped toward him. "Change it back."

"Whoa-whoa-whoa. Easy, Mr. Nice Guy. What I said? That was just a figure of speech. You didn't think... you thought I was serious?"

King Chocolate laughed for real. This was hilarious. After all these bells, his brother fell for the fake-promise bit *again*. Were all the nicies like this? It was going to be so easy to rule them.

"How do you feel about bowling? Stay with me here: we bulldoze this flea market and build duplexes around an adventure bowling course. Think golfing with bowling balls. We'll work out the details. Naughties play free. Nicies pay." King Chocolate shrugged. "I don't make the rules. It's adventure bowling."

The ground quaked.

It sounded like bulldozers were on their way. Weird, because King Chocolate just made up adventure bowling on the fly. Another tremor rattled the buildings. A baby doll started crying, and the Big Good Wolf howled.

It was something heavy. Maybe the naughties were almost here and were knocking things over. *Where are they?*

"You've ruined Christmas," Macey said.

"Oh, no. Not my Christmas. No, my Christmas is always like this, brother. To be honest, it's only gotten better. Because now we don't have to hear *you* sing about it."

"If you think we're going to change just because the sky is different... *we are nice!* We will never be naughty!"

The nicies agreed with their king, the ones who were still left. That earthquake had scared off half of them.

"Give it a few." King Chocolate leaned down. "Let this sky hover over you and see if you don't feel like breaking something. It might feel bad the first time you do it, but it'll feel good, too." He winked. "Trust me."

Macey pulled his gloves off one finger at a time. He threw them on the road. The thick leather walloped the pavers. Macey sniffed and sneered.

"I'm ready to break something now."

King Chocolate hovered out of reach. *That was fast.* He figured it would be a few bells before the king of nice started throwing haymakers. King Chocolate didn't know the first thing about fighting. He got winded wrestling a bowl of pudding into his mouth. But that was the nice thing about being king: others fought your battles for you.

Then another unexpected turn.

Macey took a knee. He was bowing right there, in the middle of the road. *In front of everyone!* King Chocolate looked around to make sure he wasn't the only one seeing this. It was a Christmas miracle. He didn't want to throw dukes with his brother. He just wanted to see him bend the knee. It took almost nothing to make him do it. In fact, it was a little embarrassing. Unless, of course, Macey knew he just didn't stand a chance and figured why waste time. Just kiss the ring already.

Or maybe that adventure bowling idea was making sense.

But King Nice wasn't kneeling in deference. He was working loose a paver. A round stone about the size of a fist.

Plot twist.

It was a stone King Chocolate couldn't out-hover. The nicies started prying pavers out of the road, too. Within a few ticks, they had an arsenal of cannonballs. Jelly was too far away to help. The engines cold.

Where are the naughties?

King Chocolate realized his mistake. He'd flipped the nicies too quickly. These dyed-in-the-wool nicies had become bona fide naughties in less than a tick. King Chocolate was just too good at it and had no backup plan. There was a price to pay for being that good. He was about to pay it.

The ground shook again. It was followed by an ear-splitting crack. Like the world was cleaved in two.

It started to hail across the lake. Giant pieces that looked like ornaments came down in waves. The flashy orbs shattered on the water's surface. They popped like gunshots. The crowd at the market gasped and ducked for cover beneath the tarps and lean-tos.

Then came the trees.

Branches snapped and cracked. Puffs of needles formed mushroom clouds above the water's surface, then flittered like confetti. Trees fell from the sky like an invisible twister was unloading them from a faraway land. Bright lights fell like glowing orbs that kerplunked into the dark water. King Chocolate looked closer and knew where they'd come from. Stars floated among the branches.

There were screams for real this time. And those who weren't screaming were frozen. Their gazes tilted toward the sky. King Chocolate looked up in time to see the unthinkable.

At least they're not throwing stones at me.

Who ever said King Chocolate couldn't see the positive?

❄

THE ROYAL CASTLE no longer touched the sky.

A third of it was missing along a diagonal fracture. As if a sword had sliced through cheese. The top of it slid along its length and toppled over the side. It fell in slow motion, remaining upright on its way out of the sky.

And they watched it like a movie. As if it weren't happening. As if none of this were real.

Until it hit Rose Lake.

The sound was utterly devastating. An extraordinary volume of water jettisoned in a plume of frothy tea. An overpowering fragrance of rose petals blew the crowd off balance.

Then came the tidal wave.

King Chocolate lurched high above the street. The crashing wave rushed beneath him. It swept many of the gawkers off their feet or wheels or stilts and carried them off. Most clung to buildings and each other, holding on until the surge dissipated. They had dropped their stones and, for the moment, had forgotten about the obese tyrant who ruined the sky.

Macey was already helping them to their feet, carrying the weak to higher ground. The castle still rumbled. Aftershocks loosened chunks from the walls that tumbled like dice. How deep was the lake? Deep enough to swallow everything whole. And more. Another fracture split through the middle third of the remaining castle.

King Chocolate couldn't look away. He had one thought. A natural thought for someone like him. Because he'd wished he'd thought of it first.

Sabotage.

Macey was destroying everything. Pretty solid move, really. King Chocolate would have done the same. If Macey had won the war and flipped the Naughty Side skyline into bubble gum, King Chocolate would've detonated his own castle before he ever turned it over. Better to watch it burn than turn. He just didn't think his brother had the sand to do it. He was too nice. He was fake, sure. But too nice to destroy his home.

Bo Peep slogged through the flood to retrieve her sheep. Gingerbread men climbed onto roofs to keep from dissolving.

"Start the engines!" King Chocolate shouted.

Jelly couldn't hear him over the chaos. The cannon-fire breaks of the castle were about to release a second tidal wave. King Chocolate's hoversuit was already running low on juice. He was only a few feet above the road. His flimsy legs dragging in the water.

"Excuse me. Pardon me." He barreled over a harried cobbler. "Save yourself."

A sorry lot of soggy nicies were still in the market, waiting for the castle to give up another piece of itself, despite the pleas from King Nice to flee and seek shelter. The Big Good Wolf was helping a family of colorful eggs wearing cutoff shorts and suspenders onto the roof of a brick building solid enough to withstand the onslaught of water that was washing contents out the door. The wolf was dripping wet and shaking. On his hind legs, he could reach the roof, gently placing the last egg into her mother's arms. Just as he let go, the wolf disappeared.

Vanished. Gone.

King Chocolate didn't think anything of it. There were already so many things that had gone wrong to wonder why or how the wolf disappeared. Macey had something to do with it, he was sure of it.

Jelly was in the sleigh, hunched over and busy. It looked like she was bailing out water, although she didn't have a bucket. *Oh no, the king thought. It broke down. It flooded. I'll never get out of here. Where are the naughties?!*

He flew into the sleigh and bounced like a beach ball. Tumbled head over legs like a kickball at recess. He got upright and regained control.

"Jelly! He's sabotaging the spoils. Just when I—"

"The castle came down." Jelly popped up with the announcement. Several flies orbited her head. She looked devastated. Shocked. Just like the nicies.

"Yeah, I got eyes. Don't tell me the sled won't start. This place sucks. Get word to the naughties to go back home. Send the flies with the message. I want to be home before—"

"There is no home."

"What? Don't say that." King Chocolate looked around. The middle part of the castle was beginning to slide. "You're freaking me out, Jelly Roll. Will this thing start or—"

"It's gone. All of it. The castle back home. It fell into Fudgy Lake. The chocolate trees are falling down the mountain."

The king looked like a bird in a cage.

The explosion in the distance... my castle! How could his brother destroy King Chocolate's castle?

"Nonsense," he muttered.

"It's true," the flies whispered in his ear. "We saw it. The naughties escaped and are coming. They're not going to make it. Something's wrong."

"Wrong? What's wrong?"

"Please! Please take us with you!" A shabby shoemaker grabbed King Chocolate. But it was a purple muskrat perched in the curly locks on his head who spoke. "We have gold. Lots of it. Lots of gold. We don't need much room, just—"

Screams and panic.

The second part of the castle tipped off and began tumbling down the length of the jagged pedestal that remained. The impact wasn't as loud as the first, but the wave was just as big. King Chocolate shoved the old shoemaker into the oncoming current. He had just enough juice to hover over it. The sleigh rocked back and forth but didn't get caught in the tide.

"Start it!" King Chocolate shouted.

Jelly pushed a big yellow button. "I think it's wet."

"*Really?* You think it's wet?"

King Chocolate wasn't going to drown watching someone push a button. He turned away from the sleigh and floated toward the market. "Where you going?" Jelly shouted. "We have to leave. This isn't going to—"

"He's going to confess! I'll make him. He destroyed everything, and THAT'S NOT VERY NICE! The phony, the fake. I won fair and square, and he's going to take his ball and go home? I'm going to drag him through this mess and make him eat it!"

Jelly was begging him to turn around. The sleigh was going to start, she promised. The rest of the castle was going to fall just like it did on the Naughty Side. King Chocolate could feel the hoversuit slowing down. His useless legs dragged in the water like reeds. He was heading straight for his brother.

Belly saw him.

She stood on high ground with one of the stones in her hand.

King Chocolate didn't slow down. He leaned in like a snowplow about to clear the street.

Jelly raced past him. Her oversized feet hydroplaning over the water. King Chocolate pulled up and watched her go. *Go get her, Jelly! Tell your sister—*

And then she was gone. Jelly was gone. Her sister, too.

The identical elves, both loyal to their kings, vanished without sound or warning. Tiny waves trickled over the water where Jelly last tread.

"Jelly? Jelly, where are you? This isn't funny! Jelly Bean?"

"Belly?" Macey had shed his royal coat. "What have you done with her? You maniac! You self-centered glutton. All you think about is you! All I wanted to do was help, and you've ruined everything! YOU RUINED CHRISTMAS!"

"Don't you point at me! You did this. This is your fault. All you had to do was kiss the ring and we would've been playing adventure bowling by next Christmas but noooooo! You couldn't have it your way, so you're destroying it all."

"What are you talking about?"

"You blew up my castle! You did *that* to my castle!" King Chocolate jabbed at the remains of the castle that was slowly sinking into Rose Lake. "You're such a phony! Such a sore-losing phony!"

The confrontation came to blows. More like slaps. Weak slaps from two kings who had never been in a fight. They swatted and kicked. King Chocolate's little legs whipped at Macey. Macey could hardly reach over King Chocolate's girth.

"Where's my Jelly Bean?"

"Where's my Belly Bean?"

A rogue wave pushed them onto the sidewalk and through a crooked doorway. The smell of wet fur was on them. Feathers stuck to their cheeks. Open cages fell from shelves and into the swirling current. The kings could taste animal food in the water.

They coughed and choked. Got tangled in boxes and cages and loose leashes.

Macey threw eggs at King Chocolate, who wore an open cage like a helmet. There were more screams outside. Water gushed into the room and swept King Chocolate into a dark corner. His stupid brother waded against the current to escape.

"Get back here!" King Chocolate gurgled.

Macey didn't care about his brother anymore. It was over. Any wishes he had for him—good or bad—had vanished with Jelly and Belly. King Chocolate mattered not at all. And that hurt just a little.

King Chocolate pulled himself out of the wreckage.

The lower third of the castle had slumped halfway into the water like a broken tooth in quicksand. Rose Lake had swelled its banks. The road was gushing. King Chocolate pushed through it, squeezing the hoversuit for every drop of fizzy energy. He skipped over the water like a flat stone. No one was in the street.

He reached the sleigh without having to knock anyone over. The hoversuit died as he rolled into it. He pressed the big yellow button.

Waaa-uh. Waaa-uh. Waaa-uh.

Branches from Christmas trees that once lived at the top of the castle floated past.

Waaa-uh. Waaa-uh.

A pig wearing a white tank top swam past.

Waaa-uh.

Two more pigs followed.

The castle remains groaned like a listing ship. Its cry echoed off the dark sky. The rush of tea water battered the side of the sleigh. It tipped to one side. The open edge was inches away from taking the oncoming tide into the compartment when—

Budda-budda-budda-whap-WHAPWHAP!

The sleigh jiggled, then shook. Water shot from the tailpipes. The deafening roar drowned out the quickening flood. King Chocolate yanked the reins built into the dashboard. The sleigh lurched. Sputtered. Went quiet and began to float in the current.

Then exploded like a rocket.

It went straight off the ground and into the dark night. Had the reins not tangled around King Chocolate's wrists, he would've been expelled like trash. Instead, he dangled over the side of the runaway rocket like a weather balloon. Slamming against both sides. Bouncing like a paddle ball swung by a sugared-up boy on Christmas morning.

He was a rogue firework. His screams swallowed by the clouds.

In the gray squall, moisture collected on his face. The frigid wind scoured his cheeks and stole his breath. A trail of loneliness followed. Jelly was gone. She wasn't coming back. He could feel it.

If King Chocolate was crying (and he totally was), no one heard it.

25

ells. Tiny silver bells. Art opened his eyes as they faded away.

He wasn't in bed with the sheets pulled up to his chin, listening for hooves on the roof. He was on his back. The stage was hard beneath him and littered with things—napkins and plastic cups, torn T-shirts (*I ♥ King Choco*) and empty wrappers. The drum sets lay on their sides. Holes punched through the bass drums. High hats bent in half.

The sky was different. *Are those stars?*

He couldn't remember stars on either side of the border. The skies were always perfect. Airbrushed. But the dim sky was studded with tiny diamonds and swirls of muted color. Occasionally, one would streak across the fabric and burn out before it touched the horizon.

There's beauty in darkness.

He rolled onto his side, looked across a muddy field littered with things not wanted. Holes stomped into the ground by big feet and small feet, hooves and tentacles and wheels and such. Far away something rumbled. Trees fell into each other. A domino effect shattered candy-cane trunks and splintered cinnamon-stick limbs.

Art was alone. And even though he was alone, he couldn't remember feeling so comfortable. As if this moment, bruised and chaotic, was imperfectly perfect. Exactly where he needed to be: on a broken stage overlooking an abused field. He wasn't bound up inside. Not trying to be something else

Free.

He didn't know what he was free from. Only the quality of the moment felt free. It contained the beauty of being. Of existing. Of knowing this breath. This space. This sky and those stars, the chill in the air.

Something rubbed against him.

He was startled by the softness of the tail. Daryl arched his back and stretched his front legs, clawing at the stage. His belly dragging across it.

"Where have you been?" Art said.

Daryl didn't answer. Only purred when Art put his arm out. The XXL cat rubbed his ears into Art's hand, then walked around a small gift on the stage. There were no other gifts. Only this little box wrapped in shiny red paper. Art studied the crisp corners and curly ribbon. The perfectly cut tape.

A card on top. *Arthur,* it read. *Merry, merry.*

Daryl curled on Art's lap, completely uninterested in what was in it. The tag didn't say who the gift was from. The queen had probably left it. Art wondered where she was off to. *I see you,* she had said. Art thought he'd wept after that.

He chuckled, then laughed out loud. Daryl looked annoyed. Art wiped his eyes and ripped the gift open, crumpled the wrapping paper in a ball and opened the box. There was an object inside. He lifted it out by an open paper clip. A polyurethane skateboard wheel spun on a fishing line. It was decorated with glitter. His name graffitied in colorful letters.

He remembered this. Sort of.

"Hello? Anyone here?"

Art guessed everyone was far away where the noises were coming from. Somewhere on the other side of the mountain. It was dark over there, too. The Nice Side was in shadows. *Maybe this happens on Christmas,* he wondered. *It all goes dark.*

But he knew this wasn't normal.

As if hearing his thoughts, Daryl climbed off his lap and strutted around crumbled towers of scaffolding that had fallen from above and crushed the band's equipment. Left a crater in the stage. Everything was dented and snapped. Except for the painting. The big canvas was still there. The ladder in front of it. Tubes of paint in the rack. Brushes and palette knives in their canisters. Not a scratch on the painting.

It wasn't a pretty painting. A swirl of yellows and grays and browns and blacks. *This is what the crowd watched me paint? This? It looks like a big, round bruise.*

Art got to his knees. He stretched and groaned. Listened to the distant cannon fire and explosions. Felt the tremor beneath his feet. It was time to get off the stage before it collapsed. He climbed over the scaffolding. Stooped in front of the easel to scoop the fat cat into his arms.

Stopped and stared.

Up close, something about the painting changed. Something didn't *look* familiar. It *felt* familiar. Like a dull fist in his stomach. A weight on his shoulders. Something about it he hated and feared. Something he wanted to bury. And there it was on the easel.

It wasn't scary. Ugly, maybe. But not repulsive. Curious, he dragged his fingers over it.

The paint had already dried. There were tracks in it from the rain. Patterns that ran like tears. The painting felt like armor. *A shield,* he thought. *A dark muddy shield.* And now it was there, on the canvas. Like he'd put down the shield—put it there—because he didn't need it anymore.

Candyland didn't frighten him anymore. It wasn't a strange land. "How long have I been here?" he said.

Since the beginning, Daryl answered.

"Beginning of what?"

Daryl rolled in his arms so Art could scratch his belly. *Time is funny here.*

It didn't matter how long he'd been there. He was there for a reason. *Was it this? To do this painting?*

He wondered.

SOMETHING WAS BURNING. It smelled like a campfire. Where the wood was dry and fragrant.

Art followed his nose. Everything was damp from the rain. There was no smoke, not that he could see. But he could hear the crackling. And there was music.

Christmas music.

People laughing. The kind of laughter that took your breath and kicked you in the belly. Made you slap a table and wipe away tears.

"Hello?"

Art went to the back of the stage. Stepped over a broken snare drum, looked down a hole made by an iron beam. The carriage he'd arrived in was out back, the doors open. The grumpy stagecoach driver missing from his post.

Art couldn't hear the music or smell the fire back there.

When he got back to the stage, the laughter returned. It was louder now. Voices were singing a silly song. He stopped and listened. Put his ear against the canvas. Jerked his head back and scowled. He *felt* the music that time. Felt it against his ear. Like it was coming through a keyhole.

There was a speck in the middle of all the dark colors. A pinprick of white. To a keen observer, it was simply a spot he'd missed with the brushes and knives. But when he stood in front of it, when he got the angle just right, a thread of light passed over his eye. He turned his head and tried again.

He stepped to the side. Put his thumb on it.

The laughter dimmed and music stopped. He pulled it away, and they returned. This was some sort of trick canvas. He looked behind it. Searched for hidden wires or imbedded speakers. There was nothing of the sort. It wasn't plugged in. Just a tiny white dot that grew brighter.

And the voices from it louder.

With Daryl napping in his arms, he leaned over to peer through it like a knothole in the neighbor's fence. His eye ached, and he pulled away. Ghostly brightness remained like a solar eclipse. He put his lips to the speck of light.

"Hello?"

It felt foolish shouting into a painting. If he was being punked, now was the time to laugh in his face. But the opposite happened.

"Arthur!"

It came from the painting.

More specifically, the little white dot. A dot no bigger than a period at the end of a sentence. He took a step and looked around. Investigated the back of the canvas one more time. Came around the front and held still, very still.

There was a party.

He put his finger on the white speck and pressed. The canvas tore rather easily. More light spilled out, and the music grew louder. There was the smell of food now. Sticky buns and fried chicken. Cherry pie and bean dip. Popcorn. Eggnog.

He hooked his finger in the hole.

The canvas ripped. Warmth flooded over him. His head rang like a wineglass struck with a silver spoon. A summer day was shining through the bitter cold of winter.

He grabbed a handful of canvas. Golden white light swallowed the stage and the trees around it. It punched holes through the night. It wrapped its loving arms around him.

And pulled him inside.

He stood at the front door like a stranger.

A Christmas tree blinked. The lights were white. They were always white. The gifts beneath it in piles.

The living room he knew. The arrangement of the furniture. The fireplace on the far side, logs stacked next to it, a fire blazing. The metal curtain was open (always open). Art could feel the heat from across the room. There were two dogs curled up in front of it. A tan one and a brindle. Twitching in their sleep.

The coffee table was buried in candy wrappers and half-empty soda bottles and big bowls of popcorn and kettle corn and caramel corn. The couches occupied by kids. Some in pajamas. All on their phones, faces washed with screen glow while *New Elf City* played on the television. The same movie every Christmas. The one about a blue elf named Jack. They could quote it backwards.

The only thing louder than the television was the Christmas music. And the ruckus was right around the corner in the kitchen, where cheers and laughter roared. There were groans and slaps on the back and then a song. They were all singing it.

Goodbye, Lexi! Goodbye, Lexi! Goodbye, Lexi, we hate to see you go —thhhpt!

More laughter. More clapping.

Then Lexi plopped onto the couch between her cousins. She got out her phone and picked at the caramel corn stuck in her braces. It was impossible for her to care less about losing the game they were playing in the kitchen.

Cards were shuffled and passed around. Flipped over to moans and groans and cheers. Again and again until the singing started. The song began with laughter. Always laughter. This time Uncle Bobby wandered into the living room. He stood in front of the television, sipping from a beer bottle nestled in a coozy. Smiling at the movie he'd seen too many times. He glanced at the door.

Art's heart ran a lap.

Uncle Bobby fell back into television's trance. As if he thought he heard someone knock. But no one was there.

Art was trembling.

This memory was different than the others. Those were just

thoughts. Vivid thoughts. He wasn't there. In those he was only looking at them from a fond distance.

I'm here.

White light hovered near the ceiling like a poltergeist. It shifted into the corners and the recesses of the skylights like fog. Art knew where he was. He knew these people. He knew what they were doing. Because they did it every year.

But something was not quite right. There was a shaky foundation, something slightly off. A façade of thin paper that might tear if he moved. He just wanted to stand there and watch and listen. He wanted to believe he was there this time. *Actually there.* Eventually, the game would be over, and they'd all come into the front room. They would pull up chairs or stand in front of the fire, pet the dogs, and tell stories and jokes. Or simply bathe in the vibe of good company and Christmas spirit.

The white cloud spread like wisps of dry ice. It nibbled at the bay window overlooking the backyard. Crept down the chimney to dissolve one of the pictures on the mantel. Impatience thrummed inside it like flashes of summer lightning. No one noticed it.

No one except Art.

The song started again. This time Grandpa Bean was sung out of the game. Art recognized the sound of his dry hands clapping along with the others. He didn't retire to the losers' den with Lexi and Uncle Bobby when it was finished, though. He stayed at the table where the fun was.

Art took a step.

His leg was cold. He couldn't feel his foot on the floor. The joints in his fingers ached. He paused before taking another step. Uncle Bobby didn't look away from the television. The cousins didn't look up from their phones, and the dogs only flinched in their sleep.

Art made his way through the room one tiny step at a time.

He was quaking. Afraid his legs would dissolve like a sandcastle in an incoming tide. His heart threw front kicks. Ten of them were around the kitchen table. Each person had pennies in front of them.

One or two or three. Grandpa Bean had none. A card was dealt to each person except him.

The Christmas Game.

No one else called it that, but they did. A card was passed from one person to the next, each pausing to look at it before keeping it or passing it on. When it got to the end, everyone flipped their cards. They looked around for the lowest one. They pointed at the loser. She had a scarf around her neck. One she knitted. She threw it over her shoulder with an exaggerated frown and pushed her penny into the middle. The man next to her—wearing a baseball cap—put his arm around her.

Grandpa Bean began the clapping. The others joined in.

Goodbye, Annie! Goodbye, Annie! Goodbye, Annie, we hate to see you go—thhhpt!

It ended with a raspberry and hugs and high fives. The shuffling of cards and another round.

"Arthur!"

Art shook like he'd been poked with a stick. The dogs looked up and wagged their tails. Ears rotating like radar dishes.

The woman slung the scarf over her shoulder and pushed her way around the table. She came at him in hugging formation. Wrapped him in strong arms that hadn't missed a workout in twenty years. She smelled like cookie dough and shampoo.

"Oh, my Arthur," she whispered. "It's so good to see you."

He didn't want to move. If he did, this might all go away. She could hold him like that until the white cloud gobbled everything up for all he cared.

And that was when he knew.

He knew what this was. It was the moment he'd realized why he was in Candyland.

You're here for a reason.

"Your mom's mad at me." Art's dad winked.

"He gave me all the low cards," she said.

There was a long moment where they looked at each other. The way they always looked at each other. The game went on without them, and no one seemed to notice. Not the cousins. Not Uncle Bobby or Grandpa Bean. Or any of the other family or friends who were there for Christmas. Except for one.

A young woman ignored the card in front of her. She stepped between her parents. Leaned her head on her mom's shoulder. She looked at Art with that same fascination possessing his parents. In the merry chaos, they didn't move.

Then his sister said: "We got a seat for you at the table."

The cloud wrapped its misty limbs around the room. It writhed across the kitchen counter. Shimmied up the refrigerator. Aunt Maureen shuffled a new deck, and cards spilled onto the floor. A few slipped into the smoky white tendril crawling along the baseboard and disappeared. She didn't notice.

"Yeah," Art said. The word was thick. "But I…"

He couldn't say the rest. Didn't want to say it. The truth was gobbling up the walls and windows.

Art's parents stood with his sister between them, arms around each other. Proud grins. Cheerful ones. Smiles that were just grateful to see him. While Eric from down the street passed his card to Grandma Glynn, who yelped and passed it over to Maggy (Eric's wife), who screamed and passed it to Shawn from next door, the white mist crept under the kitchen table.

Art swallowed hard. "I have to go back."

He wiped his eyes.

Mom put her arms around him and squeezed him hard, so hard. She whispered in his ear, "It's all right, Arthur. You go back now. You're all right."

Art hugged her back hard. So hard.

A sob slipped out. He tried to hold it in.

The merriment around the table faded. The cheers and jeers slipped into the hungry grip of the misty whiteness. His dad, blurred in Art's vision, put his powerful arms around him and his mom. He said in a raspy voice: "We got your back, son."

His sister clamped onto him. The four of them stood together in the warmth of the fire, fighting off the cool embrace of the white cloud that came for him and this. The Christmas tree twinkled in the fog.

Art closed his eyes.

Distant hollers and faraway voices began to sing.

The white cloud grew brighter and hotter. He could feel his family's presence still with him. Their arms around him. He didn't want to let go, but he didn't want to take them with him. They belonged here, in this room, around the kitchen table. Singing songs in fits of laughter.

He relaxed his grip. Felt them slide from him.

Their forms faded. Even though he could still feel their touch. Their warmth.

Then there was light. Only light.

Then there was nothingness. Not even him. Only the warmth.

Art thought that was it. This was the end, and he would go to sleep now. He wouldn't mind that. Curling up with the love he felt. But it wasn't over.

In the mist, lights began to flash.

26

Hot air blew on the king's cheek. Like exhaust from a grass thresher.

It was noisy. Sloppy.

Wet lips smacked in his ear. Teeth grinding like hard stones. Then another blow of humid air in his face. The touch of a damp nostril on his cheek—

King Chocolate woke up.

He opened his eyes to white pain in his shoulder. His back was as crooked as a witch's broom. He clawed at the rocky ground and groaned. A shadow passed over him.

A cloven hoof fell in front of him.

King Chocolate rolled over. The hoversuit sputtered and died. He opened his mouth, tried to call for help, felt the jagged ground on his belly and elbows. His useless legs fluttered behind him.

The rocket sleigh was upside down and steaming. The beautiful tailpipes were dented puzzle pieces. He couldn't stand the sight of it, threw his weight onto his back. The dark sky roiled above him—a ceiling of dingy fluff almost in reach. He could almost touch it. His breath was frosty in the cold metal air. He rolled away from the clouds. Then rolled again.

Again.

When you're the shape of a boulder, momentum is not your friend on a hillside.

King Chocolate was steamrolling toward a rocky ledge. He didn't know what was beyond it (probably not good), but each snapshot brought him closer to finding out. Something snagged his royal overcoat.

A firm grip yanked the king to a sudden stop, knocking the wind and senses out of an abrupt exhale. King Chocolate wheezed, his eyes closed, uncertain if he was teetering on the edge of a steep drop. His brain spinning.

The ledge a rotation away.

He dared not move. If a single pebble slipped, he would make that final turn. And then, well... he didn't find out. He closed his eyes and kept them closed. Lower lip popping in and out as chocolate tears stained his cheeks.

Gravel crunched nearby. He let out a whimper and clutched his tummy. If only Jelly were here. She would know what to do. Just then a hand landed on his shoulder. A large hand with a firm grip pushed him toward the cliff. The king flailed.

"No! No, no, no—"

He was stopped facedown in a pokey clump of weeds. The ledge a half turn closer. He could feel the cool air racing over the jagged lip. Whoever had grabbed him held onto the king's shoulder and with their other hand pulled up the back of his royal jacket. Whoever it was began poking around the hoversuit in search of a wallet or bag of gold.

"I have chocolate! Back home, though, I have it all. I'll give you three—awk!"

Something snapped into the hoversuit and sent a charge through his spine.

"As much chocolate as you want! I swear it, you can have it all. I'm king of everything now. Just don't hurt—"

The hoversuit hummed.

It hugged against him and began to rise.

The king seized control of it and lurched away from the ledge. The one who had pinned him to the ground ducked, and the king went flying over him, overcompensating his escape and slamming into a blue-gray boulder. He lost control then, scuttering along a grassy path like a beach ball caught in a sandstorm. He bounced back and forth, catching glimpses of strong furry legs and wide bony racks.

He came to rest in a stone trench. It was a divot that went the length of the rocky slope.

King Chocolate lay staring at the heavy clouds. They were close enough to spit on. He knew where he was. The steep terrain. The clouds. He wasn't a genius, but he'd stared at this mountain all his life.

The gutter where he rested was once the border between naughty and nice.

Now it was all naughty. A reluctant smile crept into one of his cheeks. *Because I won.*

His joy was brief.

A LONG HEAD and a dangerous rack of antlers appeared over him.

Flakes of blue-green lichen were caught between black lips. Molars grinding. Deep black eyes staring. And humid exhaust shooting from wide nostrils onto the king's face.

King Chocolate scooted up the trench and out of the way. The top of his head touched the gray ceiling. Someone was watching him. His black boot hiked on the golden rail of a long, dirty sleigh. He was dipping a chocolate chip cookie into a glass of milk.

"Hello, Casey," said Santa Claus.

The king looked around. Perhaps he did fall off that cliff. Because there was no way the jolly fat man could be up here. King Chocolate had destroyed the device that projected him. But this Santa looked different. He looked dirtier. And exhausted.

And what's up with the reindeer? he thought. Because they'd never been in the projection King Chocolate talked to. Like ever.

The king hovered closer. A large sack was stuffed into the back seat of the sleigh (not the rocket sleigh, still upside down and shooting steam). Long, leather reins lay out front with bells sewn to the straps. Santa slurped the glass—milk dripping from his white curly mustache—and watched the king drift closer. King Chocolate could smell the sweat coming off the jolly fat man. The smoky soot from fireplaces. The king wasn't satisfied, though, and swung one of his limp legs. It bounced off Santa's knee.

King Chocolate pinched the bridge of his nose. "Are you serious?"

Santa Claus did not answer. He'd seen this show before: a nonbeliever confronted with the real deal. Everyone handled the truth differently. Some fainted; some cried. Some jumped with joy and hugged him.

Not King Chocolate.

He looked up with pain in his eyes. "What are you doing up here?"

Santa finished his cookie, swatted the crumbs off his hands. He chugged the last swallow of milk, then said: "Waiting for you."

The king turned in a circle. The rocket sleigh was destroyed. Even if it wasn't, where would he go? Candyland was covered in puffs of smoke and dust. Trees were falling like termite-infested pillars. Now Santa Claus was waiting for him. Which could only mean one thing.

A lecture was coming.

One of the reindeer wandered over. It was the one who woke him up. The big one. Chewing up lichen and staring at the king with an unkindly look. A growl began grinding in the beast's throat. He let out a howl that turned the king's spine into jelly.

"It's okay, boy." Santa went over to the slobbering beast and stroked the wet muzzle, then said to the king: "It's the end of a long night."

"Tell me about it."

"He gets a bit edgy toward the end."

"He doesn't like me."

"He's a protector is all. Wouldn't hurt a fly. Unprovoked. Would you, Ronin?"

Unprovoked. Ronin bristled at the qualifier. The oversized reindeer pawed the terrain, looking for a reason to swat the king off the mountain like a volleyball.

"So, you're real," the king said. "You. The flying moose." Santa didn't answer. Fed a cube of something grassy to the reindeer. "Those are presents in the sack, I take it. You're delivering them to us."

"Not that kind of stop, I'm afraid."

"Coal, then?"

Santa didn't answer. He didn't have to. King Chocolate knew who delivered the coal to the naughties on Christmas. It wasn't Santa. Besides, even if he was bringing presents, where was he going to deliver them? The castles were gone. Most of Candyland looked like a cinder fire. It was, like, game over. If the king had known what winning would bring him, he would've just stayed home.

"I didn't do anything wrong, you know. That wasn't my fault down there. Macey blew up the castles."

"Your brother didn't do it."

"Well, don't look at me. All I did was win. The boy was here for a reason. You said so yourself." Santa didn't argue the fake news. He'd never met the king, so how could he have said that? "Macey would have done the same thing. He admitted it. I was playing the game, that's all. And this is what I get? You got to admit, that ain't fair." The king shook his head. "What kind of Christmas is *this*?"

"You did nothing wrong, Casey."

"Yeah, well, you know and I know that—*what?*"

Santa folded his hands over his belly. "You did nothing wrong."

"All right. That's what I'm talking about. Yeah. So. You're here to make everything right, then."

"In a way."

"I like the sound of that. Merry, merry, my good sir. Merry, merry. Listen, um." The king hovered closer. Ronin grunted. "I'm not so sure about Macey. My brother, he's sneaky. They're nicies and all, but they were going to throw rocks at me. You know that, right?"

"I saw."

"That ain't nice."

"No. It's not."

This was going King Chocolate's way. It was unexpected. But it was fair. Santa Claus was a fair man. He was there to make things right and merry, merry and all that good stuff. King Chocolate hovered back to give the jolly fat man some space to work his magic. The king puffed up and tried to stick his chest out and hold his chin up. It was the power stance. When things got back to normal, he'd double down on snack time and get his size back up. His clothes hung on him like blankets. *Who wants a skinny king?*

"So?" An awkward silence settled between them. "What are you waiting for? Make the castles come back. Just like they were. Both of them. They're both mine."

Santa fed the reindeer (who was eyeballing the king) another cube and looked down the mountain. Then shuffled over to the sleigh. Heavy boots clunking the ground. The king thought he was going for a magic wand or something. But the jolly fat man began untangling the reindeer harnesses.

"I knew it," the king muttered. "What do you want, a confession? Is that it? Fine. I did the coal. I burned up the Christmas trees and then stuffed coal in stockings and blamed it on you. I did it every Christmas. Is that what you want to hear?" King Chocolate cupped his hands and shouted: "I PUT COAL IN YOUR STOCKINGS!"

His voice echoed into the mist settling on the side of the mountain.

"Sue me. You don't know what it's like to rule the Naughty Side. They don't listen. You got to be firm, or they'll run you over. You got to trick them. Try walking a block in my shoes, you'll see."

Santa chuckled. The irony of the king walking anywhere was not lost.

"So I lied, so what? I got it done, didn't I? The only thing we sugarcoat on the Naughty Side is donuts. We tell it like it is. You don't like it, then you don't belong. That's it. I'd like to see you do better."

"I don't think I can, Casey."

"That's right. Now. Are you going to fix things or not?"

"That's not why I'm here."

"Then what are you here for? I mean, we ain't seen you like *ever*, and now you stop by when everything is falling apart? You think you could have stopped to say hi? Would've been nice. Macey was pretending to be you, did you know that?"

"I'm always here."

The king burst out laughing. He laughed so hard his ribs hurt. Santa watched him.

"You're serious?" The king rolled his eyes. Ronin didn't like it. "Oh, that's perfect. You're worse than me. You know that, right? *You're never here!*"

Unperturbed, Santa checked the buckles and tightened the straps. He went to the sleigh and pulled out a plate of cookies. Double fudge, chocolate chip. When he dropped the plate on the hard ground, it multiplied into two dozen plates of double fudgies. Then those doubled. *Four dozen!*

He went back to the sleigh for another plate, this one stacked with oatmeal raisin (gross). He kept doing this like a cookie factory was in the glove box. Santa pulled out sugar sprinkles, no bakes, snowballs, peanut butter balls, snickerdoodles, gingerbreads. The varieties were endless. Dozens and dozens of each kind.

"What's all this?" the king said.

Santa took off his glove and stuck his fingers in his mouth to let out an ear-splitting whistle. The reindeer lifted their heads and started back to the sleigh, avoiding stepping on the cookie smorgasbord. Enough to feed a village. Not just a village. *All of Candyland!*

The reindeer took their places in front of the sleigh. Two by two, they stood. The big one, the scary one, the one with the mean eyes, planted his enormous hooves in front. Santa lifted the harnesses and began to buckle them in.

"No!" King Chocolate shouted up at Santa Claus, who, somehow, seemed to have grown a foot taller. "You can fix this. You can fix anything. We need you!"

The king glanced down at the mess he'd created. The white mist had spread across the mountain and was creeping over the land like a flood of white vapor. Candyland was a colorless mass. Once upon a time it had been the land of Naughty and Nice. Now it was lifeless.

"What do you want? I get it, all right? I totally get it now. Candyland is Naughty *and* Nice." He weighed his empty hands. "We were fighting each other, and I won, and now Candyland looks like that. I get it. I get it! But no one told me *that* was going to happen. No one told me *not* to win. You didn't, that's for sure. You could've, but you didn't. If you would've stopped by just one time and said, 'Hey, Casey. If you win, then Candyland is over. Merry, merry. Blah-blah.' Or something like that. *Anything!* But you didn't say nothing. You just let me win, and now it's all my fault."

The king huffed.

"This isn't fair, and you know it. But I learned my lesson. For sure. So can we just, you know... can you put it back together? I won't win again."

That wasn't true, and the king knew it. Even if Santa waved his hand and everything went back to normal, like this was all a bad dream, the king would eventually get bored. He'd forget this ever happened. *And winning was just so sweet.*

All the reindeer were buckled in except for one. Santa scratched Ronin's chin and kissed the reindeer on the nose. King Chocolate zoomed toward him to beg and plead. How was he supposed to know if Candyland lost its balance, everything would fall apart?

The queen was right. With her stupid tray-of-donuts example, she was right. There. He said it. He'd gladly say it to her face if the jolly fat man would lend a hand.

Ronin bent at the knees. Santa backed up. The reindeer leaped like a cannonball shot from a catapult. Hooves pedaled through the cloud and were gone. The shockwaves of the departure sent King Chocolate tumbling down the grassy path and miraculously touched not one plate of cookies. He landed against a boulder, condensation from the clouds streaking down its side. The king righted himself and brushed debris off his coat.

His sleeves hung over his hands. He rattled inside the hoversuit.

"Where's he going?" he said. "You can't leave me up here. I don't have anything. How long are these cookies going to last me?"

Santa tightened the laces on his boots. He touched his toes and stretched his back. He put his hand to his brow and searched the misty mountain below. The reindeer turned their heads, ears rotating in that direction. Santa looked at his furry team, and as if an unspoken word passed between them, the reindeer scuffed at the ground.

A tiny, yellow light floated up through the mist.

It was bright for only a wink. A tick later, it flashed again. King Chocolate watched it float up the hill. Then it landed on the boulder next to him. Wings folded closed.

Merry, merry, the firefly whispered.

Then it was off, rising into the clouds just out of King Chocolate's reach.

Santa went to the sack in the back of the sleigh. The reindeer felt like mythical titans. King Chocolate looked down at the fading wasteland evaporating like dry ice. More fireflies were floating toward him. Loose gravel fell from below.

From the gathering mist, two figures emerged.

THEY WERE THIN AND ROUND. Beige and crispy on the edges.

Heads down and stubby legs working, a gingerbread couple navigated the terrain with the efficiency of mountain goats. All the while surrounded by fireflies whispering encouraging words.

"Hey! Hey, you, uh..." King Chocolate had never seen these nicies. "What's your names? I'm ki—" He decided not to tell them who he was. Maybe they had been at the market when everything went sideways. "Thank Claus you made it. I need help. I need to—"

Another pair of gingerbread cookies were behind them. This couple the king knew. They were chipped and smudged. One of them was missing an arm (King Chocolate was pretty sure it had been thrown onstage during the festival). They were right behind the nice gingerbread couple. All of them walked around the king like he was a bush in the path. They stooped for a cookie (sugar cookie with green sprinkles) and went on their way.

Cookies eating cookies, King Chocolate thought. *Huh.*

Santa Claus waved to them. They waved back like he was nothing more than a mailman delivering presents by way of magic reindeer.

"Merry, merry!" the gingerbreaders said. One couple said it more sweetly than the others (you can guess which one). And then up the path and into the clouds they vanished. Right where the fireflies were flying. King Chocolate waited for them to return. Or something to make sense. Neither happened.

"What's going on here?"

Santa was digging in the sack again. Humming a merry tune as he did. King Chocolate's voice felt small. It was higher than normal. Another couple came up the mountain. They were covered in gray fur. One of them wore wire-rimmed spectacles and carried a book under his arm. The other stalked the path on all fours and slobbered.

"Hey!" King Chocolate levitated the hoversuit as high as it would go. He was eye level with the Big Bad Wolf. "Over here. Whoa, stop. I order you to—"

The Big Bad Wolf leaped over the king. The Big Good Wolf simply went around him. They argued over a plate of jelly dollops. Big Good Wolf slapped his paw. Big Bad Wolf bared his teeth.

They were about to settle it nature-style when pink porky pigs bounced past the king, carrying suitcases and wearing different hats. There were six of them. Two wore hardhats. Two wore cowboy hats. Two wore teacups on their heads. The king knew three of them. They were the muddy ones wearing *I 🩶 King Choco* shirts. The other three had backpacks filled with books.

The half dozen pigs joined the argument over jelly dollops. The king blinked heavily. Santa was oblivious to what was happening. Take two hungry wolves and add six fat pigs and, well... *nature happens.* A jelly dollop fell off a plate and landed on one of the teacup hats.

There was a pause. A gasp. King Chocolate closed his eyes, then peeked between his fingers.

Violent laughter erupted from the side of the mountain. The Big Bad Wolf doubled over. The Big Good Wolf curled up on his side. The pigs hopped around like wind-up toys bleating laughter like lambs. When it settled, the wolves got up and wiped their eyes. They stuffed their mouths with treats. All of them went up the path, arm in arm—each wolf with three pigs—and vanished in the cloud.

"I'm losing my mind," the king muttered.

Grim and Joy (*the Border Oracles*, Jelly once called them) came up hand in hand and swinging their arms. Then Poko, that sad little puppet who brought the king his chocolate samples, skipped along with a puppet just like him. Their wooden joints rattling.

The half-horse brothers came next. There were four of them. Even King Chocolate would admit they were a bit nightmarish. The fashionistas, the Conflict Advisors (three of them still dipped and sprinkled), flies and gnats. Lost Boys on their beams.

More were coming.

He could feel them on their way up the mountain. Bo Peep, skipping with her sheep, curtsied to the king before munching on a coconut puff ball. Bo Pop with her rams threw up a peace sign. Miss Tuffet with a bucket of curds and whey, her spider running behind her. Miss Fluffet's spider perched on her shoulder.

Goldilocks locked arms with three bears. Boldilocks rode on a bear's shoulders.

Red Riding Hood with a basket. Black Riding Hood had a backpack.

There were robot boxers and plastic dancers. Princes in long capes. Princesses with sparkly crowns. There were dwarves with tools and frogs with boots, cats and mice chatting about the weather.

They came in pairs, one and all. One from the land of naughty. The other was nice.

All wobbly with Christmas spirit, their faces flashing in the glow of firefly guides.

None of them stopped to ask how the king was doing, if he was hurt or needed help. None of them seemed impressed by the jolly fat man and his reindeer. They slowed down to pick up a cookie and made their way up, up, up the mountain and into the cloud. Firefly flash fading around them.

Santa sat on a boulder and watched the procession.

Far below, Candyland was sinking. *The mountain will be next*, King Chocolate thought. But something much more miraculous than mountain-swallowing quicksand. Santa leaned back, studied the king. He was looking at what was under the king. The hoversuit had gone to sleep.

The king was standing on his own.

Those two noodles wobbled like overcooked pasta. But they held him up like a newborn baby deer. It was a miracle.

"Merry Christmas, Casey." Santa held out a small box. It was wrapped with a bow.

"For me?" The king pointed at the smoldering remains of what was once Candyland. "But I, uh... is it coal?"

Santa laughed. The moment didn't feel funny. Candyland was in ruins, and King Chocolate was to blame. And now he had a present to open? This made not a lick of sense.

"But... *why?*"

He had to know. Everything was gone, and everyone was so joyful. And he got a present.

Santa stood with a groan. All the bones cracked in his back when he stretched his arms. He climbed into his sleigh, checked the monitors on the dash, then gripped the reins. He looked at the king in his saggy clothes, holding the gift with both hands. A tired grin rose from his lips to his eyes.

"Arthur needed to see. And only you could help him do that."

"But..." The king shook his head. "I didn't help him. I just, you know..." He gestured downhill. "I don't get it."

Santa gazed at the pilgrimage vanishing in the cloud. "You will, Casey."

❄

"On Dasher, on Dancer…" Santa started.

Each time he called a name, a reindeer cocked his or her legs like a slingshot at full tension. Muscles rippled beneath the hide. The slow-moving pilgrimage veered away from them. Even King Chocolate moved. It looked like the reindeer were going whether he was in front of them or not. Getting run over by magic reindeer was not how he wanted this to end. And he still had a present to open.

But the reindeer didn't need a runway. They shot from the mountain like a spring-loaded pistol. A train of reindeer soared into the rising mist, hooves pedaling swirls in the white vapor. It swung around like a roller coaster on an invisible track. Santa waved from the caboose. The Landers who had not yet climbed into the cloud stopped to wave back.

"Ho-ho-ho!"

And then the reindeer express hit another gear. A warp drive that split space and time. They jittered like static on an old television. An electric pulse crackled from the sleigh and then—

Poof.

The Landers cheered. They clapped and hugged. Stuffed their faces with cookies. And then on their way they went. Up into the cloud.

"Casey!"

Two elves as round as berries and dressed like twins stepped out of the line. One was not terribly happy to see the king. The other was hobbling in his direction with arms wide.

"Jelly!"

The king suddenly forgot everything that had happened since he'd crashed the rocket sleigh. He powered the hoversuit in that happy elf's direction as fast as it would carry him. With less weight to carry, the hoversuit threw the king at the elf. They collided like rubber kickballs and bounced in opposite directions. They tumbled backwards, stopped, and tried again. The king had never hugged Jelly. In fact, he'd never hugged anyone.

I'm not made for hugging, the king would say.

Body or mind, Jelly would add.

Their arms barely reached each other. But it didn't stop them from trying. Jelly hopped madly on those giant flipper-feet. The king was weeping. Chocolate tears dribbled off his chin, staining his jacket. All the stress of watching Candyland dry up like a rotten plum. And then crashing the rocket sleigh and Santa leaving.

But there was only one reason he was crying.

"I thought I lost you," he blubbered. "You were at the rocket sleigh one wink, and the next you were gone. And then I had to fly it by myself, and it went too fast, and then I wrecked it. It's over there. I'm not hurt. Well, a little. But I don't care. You're back. You're back, you're back, you're back. Never leave me again."

"I didn't go anywhere."

"I don't care. Promise you won't leave me."

"I didn't leave you."

"*Promise!*"

Jelly promised. The king didn't bother asking what she meant by that. Because clearly she had left. He'd seen it with his own beady eyes. The loneliness he'd felt when he realized she was gone was bottomless and howling. He clutched her shoulders, wiped the tears on his sleeve. Then hugged her again.

"You dropped something." Belly was tapping her foot.

"Huh?"

Belly could not look more bored. She walked over to pick up the present. The king had chucked it on the ground when he saw Jelly. He almost didn't care about it. Almost.

"That's..." He sniffed. "That's mine. Santa gave it to me."

"Figures."

The king held it with both hands. It felt heavy now. Normally, when he got a present, he'd have the paper shredded in half a wink.

"Where's everyone going?" the king said.

"We're going up," Jelly said.

"But why?"

"It's why we're here."

"What?"

The twin elves shrugged. They smiled when they did it. Like they knew a secret but weren't telling.

"I'm going with you," the king said.

"You can't," Jelly said. "Not yet."

"What? Wh-why?"

Jelly and Belly looked around. Looked at each other. Shrugged without smiling this time. Jelly took his hand.

"I want to see what you got, first."

The king didn't feel like opening his present. But if it kept her from leaving, he'd do it. He'd never unwrapped a gift so slowly in his life. It was like he was planning to reuse the paper. First one end. Then the other. Belly tapped her foot. The king went even slower.

It was a plain box. Charcoal in color. *If it's coal...* he thought.

"Well?" Belly said.

The king lifted the lid. He looked inside. Jelly looked inside. Belly stood on her toes and frowned. Jelly began to giggle. Then she whispered in her sister's ear.

"Those don't really come from coal," Belly answered. "That's just a myth."

"What doesn't come from coal?" The king stared at what was nestled in a bed of cotton. "This?"

The elven sisters were crying laughter now. They fell over each other, mouthing words the king couldn't understand. What was in the box wasn't funny. It was beautiful. And they were laughing at it. *At him.*

"We're not laughing at you," Jelly said between breaths. "It's just... it doesn't matter where it came from. It's perfect. It's so perfect."

The king was feeling a little hurt being left out of the joke. Worse: he was the butt of it. This was a present from Santa, after all.

Then he heard a familiar voice call his name.

❇

THE COOKIE PLATES were nearly empty.

The pilgrimage had thinned with only a few fireflies to guide them. Two chubby chefs walked step for step, singing a merry tune and sloshing mugs of sparkly cider on their tunics. For a time, there was no one after them. The king began to wonder if he imagined his name called out. Then a figure emerged from the mist. The last in a long line that journeyed from below.

He carried a weary smile. His feet heavy clods on the unforgiving mountain. He stood just outside the mist's reach. The smile widened. His pace picked up, and he closed the gap, crushing King Chocolate in a bear-hugging grip. The gift was trapped between them.

"Merry, merry, brother." Macey held the king at arm's length. "Finally."

Macey should be mad. Furious, really. King Chocolate would have been. But his brother only laughed and nodded at the clouds, where all the Landers had gone. *What does* finally *mean?* the king thought. *Does everyone know what's happening here?* That was apparently the case. Because they marched without a care while Candyland turned to mush. They skipped and danced and sang, and the king didn't have a clue.

"It's beautiful." Macey wiped a tear.

The king thought his brother had spied the crumpled gift he was clutching. He told him Santa had been waiting for him when he crashed the rocket sleigh. "That's what he said. He said, *I'm waiting for you.*"

"He did?"

"I mean, something like that. He, uh..." The king sighed. His brother was smiling. It was a told-you-so smile. He wasn't about to dance and rub King Chocolate's nose in it. It was a happy-to-see-you smile. And that made King Chocolate say: "You were right. He's real. He was here. I saw him. I touched him. Talked to him. The reindeer ate green stuff off the rocks. Look, the prints. You can see them. And the one in front—giant horns, like, out to here." The king spread his hands as far as they would go. "He was not happy to see me."

"Ronin?"

"You know him?"

Macey shook his head. They laughed. The king liked the way his brother laid his hand on his shoulder. It felt good. He held up the gift. "He gave me this."

Macey looked inside. Tilted his head. Looked up at the king and back at what was inside the gift. Giddiness galloped through the king. It was the way his brother looked at him.

"May I?"

His brother reached inside the box. A silver chain rattled over his thumb. He held it up. King Chocolate bowed his head, and Macey looped the necklace around his neck. He stepped back and eyed the teardrop jewel attached to it. It was as big as a sugarplum.

"I thought these came from coal," King Chocolate said. "You know, like, after a long time under pressure, they just..." The king shrugged. "Belly said they don't. But, I mean, even if they don't—"

"It's beautiful."

The king thought so, too. Although he couldn't imagine why Santa would give him such a thing. It had to be worth a fortune. And, really, why give *anything* to King Chocolate? Wasn't he the last one in Candyland to deserve a gift?

"But let's pretend it does," Macey said. "Coal is a young diamond. I like that."

"Yeah."

Macey put his arm over the king's shoulder. The mist crept up the mountain like ghostly fingers. Candyland had transformed into a white blanket. King Chocolate would have thought ash covered the land by now, but he liked to believe that was snow down there. A pristine canvas of snow.

"We were kings," King Chocolate said.

"We were kings." Macey looked at the cloudy ceiling above them. "But we're more than that."

Macey cupped his hand to his brother's ear and whispered what was beyond the clouds. King Chocolate's eyes grew. And as they grew, he began to glow. Infected with the smile his brother had brought up the mountain.

It made sense now. It all made sense.

THE MOUNTAIN RUMBLED like it was about to erupt. Or crumble into nothingness. Rocks broke loose and bounced past them and disappeared below where a leviathan was lurking. A massive form rising in the mist. A shadow that grew darker as it neared. Casey squeaked just a little (it sounded like a mouse, but he wouldn't admit that) and grabbed his brother.

And then he heard it. A single word echoed off the mountain.

"*Yum!*"

And then another one that went: "*Yum!*"

It was in stereo. One from the left and another from the right. Back and forth until not one, but two Sweet Tooths plundered their way out of the mist. Big and bare feet crushing rocks into powder and splitting the earth where they stepped. Hand in hand, they came up. Swinging their laced fingers like a wrecking ball. Big teeth and bigger smiles. The only difference was the colors of their nails.

They leaped over Casey and Macey and triggered a minor avalanche. Boulders broke loose, some splitting in half, and boomed down the mountain, vanishing into complete silence.

The Sweet Tooths plodded a course upward, *yumming* their way into the cloud.

It was quiet again. The rockslide had settled. The encroaching mist was licking the ground where the reindeer prints were. It felt like nothingness creeping toward them. There was nothing to see beyond it. Candyland didn't even look like a blanket of snow.

"It's gone, isn't it?" King Chocolate said. "Candyland is totally gone."

"It moved on, Casey. But there's more." Macey nodded. "Shall we?"

Casey held the tear-shaped diamond swinging against his chest. You might think he considered apologizing to his brother after all the things he'd done, and you wouldn't be wrong. King Chocolate, in fact, did feel sorry. Truly sorry. He felt it in his heart, which had swelled in size. And his brother felt his sorrow, too. He looked at Macey with tiny eyes, a trace of remorse swimming inside them.

Macey patted the king's hand. He didn't need to hear it. It was plain to see.

There were two cookies left. An apple fritter and a double fudge chocolate chip. You know which one Casey took. The brothers held them up, clinked them together, and took a bite. Crumbs cascaded down their tunics. With cookies in hand, they turned to make the final steps of their journey.

Macey admired the jewel in the palm of King Chocolate's hand. The way it glittered and shined. The flawless weight of it. Maybe diamonds didn't start off as coal. But some things did.

And Arthur needed to see where he was, the king thought, *to become who he is.*

27

Fireflies flashed random patterns. They hung like tiny lanterns, fading to dull pinpoints in the distance.

The fog was heavy and wet. Dew collected on lichen and clumps of wildflowers and on boulders strewn on a steep slope—some the size of automobiles in a field that quickly vanished in the humidity.

Laughter was out there. Far away.

Behind Art, the ground sloped into a swirling dense cloud. He took three steps and was swallowed by white mist. He waved his hand without seeing it, felt cool moisture cling to his cheeks. The ground beneath him softened like clay. He was quickly disoriented. Only the vague sprinkle of fireflies guided him back out.

He had a sense of where he was, but not how he got there. He'd learned not to question things in Candyland. Things happened for a reason, and when they did, it was best to float downstream with them. The fireflies were drifting toward the sound of voices, luring Art to follow. The swirling cloud dampened his neck and arms—an impenetrable fog gently nudging him to get going.

He took the hint.

The rocks were wet and mossy with just enough grit for traction.

He hopscotched his way to the biggest boulder in sight and scaled it on all fours. When he reached the top of it, the wind picked up, gusting noisily in his ears, blowing the damp hair from his eyes. The fireflies swirled like lights on an incoming storm, rising higher in the distance.

He continued the hike, taking pleasure in the focus it required to keep from slipping, searching for the best location to place his foot, the right grip to pull himself over the next rock. There were times his hand slipped. He'd fallen awkwardly more than once, cut his arm on a sharp edge, felt the trickle of blood and the sticky aftermath. But his thoughts were few and uncluttered.

Each time he looked up, the wind blew harder, and the fireflies higher.

After a time, the fog began to thin.

He could see farther. The boulders were bigger and stacked on top of each other. The wind occasionally knocked him off balance. Sometimes it sang in the hollows between stones, long mournful cries that rose and fell. If there was someone else out there, he couldn't hear them. It was only when he stopped to rest or survey a way around an impossible route did he recall the memory of Christmas at home. Those details, though, were already getting fuzzy. As if seeing them through veils.

The trail of fireflies had moved above him at some point. The boulders gave way to a cliff. He stood at the bottom of it, looking up into the streaming mist. In the gray whiteness, there were patches of color. Far above, seemingly out of reach, a pink sky peeked through.

Art considered turning around. Climbing over boulders was one thing, but free soloing a cliff was entirely different. There were ledges to rest on and fractures to wedge a hand or foot inside, but it was so high.

The swirling cloud had followed him. It was only a few feet behind him and impervious to the wind. He stepped into it and, just as before, was engulfed. The boulders gave beneath him. His boots sank in softening rocks like they were dissolving. And he had only taken one step.

He went back to the cliff, leaned his head against it, and stared up at the rising cloud of fireflies. They looked like sparks over a campfire. Aches and pains started to surface. His ribs were bruised. Part of his foot strangely numb. He closed his eyes and sank back into the memories of the card game on Christmas. Only to find the details had vanished.

The faces and places were generic. He couldn't remember the shapes of them or the color of their hair. The sound of laughter and song was absent. Their names! He couldn't remember their names. The feelings, though, remained. The shared experience of laughter and love was still warm.

The essence of those moments was real.

They were a part of him that could never be removed. Sewn into the fabric that made him who he was. He sat at the bottom of an impossible climb and rested in the beauty of those feelings. He didn't have to go any farther.

"Need a hand?"

ART OPENED his eyes and stared a moment. "King Chocolate?"

"You like?"

The king turned in a circle, arms out. Smile stretching into saggy cheeks. The big surprise was below the belt. The king was standing on legs, not soggy string beans. Short, stocky legs with knobby knees and bony ankles. The king did another turn, leaped up, and clicked his heels.

"Huh? Huh?" the king begged. "Legs all day, legs all night. Come on, give it up."

He started dancing, trying to watch his legs go. His belly was half the size compared to the last time Art had seen him. He was a deflating weather balloon. He finished with a flare, out of breath with his arms out. Waiting for applause.

Surprise and confusion kept Art still. He looked around. "Where did you come from?"

"Oh, yes. That." The king cleared his throat. Disappointment lingered on Art's lack of excitement for the new legs. "I crashed the rocket. You know, the one you... never mind. Then Santa Claus—"

"We've always been here, Arthur."

Another king was suddenly there. Although he wasn't wearing a crown, he felt like a king. And he looked like King Chocolate if King Chocolate occasionally ate vegetables.

"Artie, this is my brother. Brother, Artie," Casey muttered.

"Macey." He offered a short bow. "King of the Nice. I'm so very sorry we didn't meet, Arthur. Merry, merry and a pleasure to be here. How may we be of service?"

Art didn't know what any of that meant. He scrambled to his feet, feeling the wires of exhaustion begin to pull. The wind snapped the kings' long coats like towels on a clothesline. It must have been their voices he'd heard earlier. King Chocolate reached out to put a hand on Art's shoulder. Even in the wind, the bitter smell of cacao was strong.

"Help with what?" Art said.

"Help with what," King Chocolate repeated and chuckled. "What do you think?" When Art didn't understand, he said, "How about the giant wall behind you."

"What my brother is trying to say is that we're here to help you climb."

The wall so tall and straight and high. Like, absurdly so. And these two were going to help him climb it?

"I know what you're thinking," King Chocolate said. "About us. About you, maybe. But let me tell you something, my boy. A journey of a thousand miles starts with one fat king and his brother. So when you're ready, let's get to it."

Art laughed, sort of. The king's grit and confidence were as convincing as they were hilarious. King Chocolate wasn't smiling, though. Neither was Macey. Art sobered up.

"I can't climb that."

"That's what you think," King Chocolate said.

"Yeah. That's exactly what I think. Look at it."

The royal brothers (were they twins?) nodded at each other. Then squatted down and picked Art up by the legs. For a couple of unimpressive kings, they hoisted him onto their shoulders like gravity didn't exist.

"It doesn't matter what you think," King Chocolate grunted.

Even on their shoulders, Art was short of the nearest ledge by more than an arm's length. They grabbed his ankles and lifted him over their heads. Art waved his arms to keep from tipping over. The wind gusted into him. The kingly brothers shuffled to keep him upright. This idea was getting worse.

"We're proud of you!" Macey shouted. "Never forget that!"

Art leaned against the wall, his fingers brushing the ledge. The wind howled along the cliff. He started to tilt. The royal brothers faltered. Art's knees buckled. He was going to come down, and it was going to be hard and awkward. A fall that would net more than a scuffed knee.

Two pairs of hands nabbed his wrists. One pair was dainty. The other pair hairy.

They hauled him up and over the ledge. Art fell on his face, rolled onto his back. The Border Oracles looked down on him. One bright and smiling. The other quite grim (as you know).

"Ha. Still the *mess,* kid!"

Grim hauled Art off the ground with surprising strength. Art was yanked off his feet and teetered on the edge. Joy brushed the grit off Art.

"You look fabulous, darling."

"That's a bit *much.*" Grim pulled his drawings from her white tank top still stained with mustard, fanned them out like playing cards. "I got the best ones," she whispered to him. "Just wanted you to know. Do you have any more?"

"No time to dally, darling. How do you want to do this? Saddlestyle, or... okay. Yeah, just..."

Grim already had Art's shirt. Joy took his legs. They were pulling in opposite directions with Grim breathing into Art's face. It smelled like hot sauce and expired shrimp. Art couldn't look away from the little crawly things in her teeth.

"Take a *picture!*" she shouted.

Before Art could say anything, the sisters threw him on their shoulders. A beat later he was on their raised hands, hugging the wall and stretching for the next ledge. He was pulled up, just like before. Once safely on the ledge, Art sprang to his feet. Meg and Gandy were gritty like sand and smelled nothing like shrimp. They hugged him. He came away with white icing on his shirt.

"Careful. You skin yourself, sugar?" Meg shouted over the wind. She touched his arm where blood had dried.

"The boy's all right," Gandy said. "Rub a little cinnamon on it. Look at him. So different now. Ain't time funny, son?"

While they were admiring the boy who had crossed over into their home, another couple watched from the crowded space on the ledge. Another flat, cookie-shaped couple. Gusts of wind threatened to pull them off the cliff like kites.

"My manners," Meg said. "This is Clovey and Dandy. They were from the other side."

By the way they were frowning, the way their arms were crossed, Art figured they called the Naughty Side home. Gandy rubbed something on Art's scratched elbow (it was cinnamon, and it burned).

"Time to go," Meg said. "Upsie-daisy."

"I don't know if that's a good idea," Art said. "I don't want to—"

"You won't break us, son," Gandy said. "We've been out of the oven a long time. Clovey, Dandy, take that side. You grab his leg, love. On three."

Up and away he went to the next step, which he couldn't reach on his own, and someone reached down to haul him up. He fell on his back this time, staring at the stirring clouds, the wind pulling them apart like cotton fibers. Fireflies dancing in their depths. And far above them a sky as pink as a flamingo.

Two faces looked down at him. Both round and fleshy with pointy ears. Each with a single braid of silver hair. One of them hugged his leg.

"So strong," Belly said. "And warm."

"He's a warmblood," Jelly said, "for sure."

"And taller. My Artie's gotten taller. You think he's taller, Jelly Bean? Aren't you going to hug him?"

"I don't think so," Jelly said.

"Come on, hug him. The queen would want you to."

"The queen already hugged him. Come on, off you go." She pried her sister's grip from Art's leg. Belly backed up with affection all over her. She dove in for another hug, but her sister intercepted her.

"We talked about this."

The sister elves argued. Art looked over the edge. His gut twisted at how high he'd already climbed. He couldn't see the ground, though. Which helped. The kings were somewhere down there, deep in the dense fog. The gingerbreads, however, he could still see. They waved when he saw them. Well, two of them waved.

Belly clamped onto his leg. "Last one," she said. "Jelly, say something."

"Thank you for the company."

"Thank you for the company?" Belly said. "That's all you have to say?"

"I'm not good with words."

"Try again!"

"It's okay," Art said. "She doesn't have to—"

"Merry, merry," Jelly said. No hug, though. "Off you go."

Belly reluctantly let go, kissing Art on the knee before she did. The two elves latched onto his legs. The next ledge was a long way up. The elves wouldn't come close enough for someone to grab him from above. Art searched for handholds.

"You ready?" Belly asked.

"I don't think I can—"

The elves sprang onto their toes with the velocity of a catapult. With feet that were nearly three feet long, that translated into more than enough force. If Art had to do this over, he would suggest they tell him he was going to be launched in the general direction of the next ledge.

He swung his arms and started to yell. The wind stole the words out of his mouth. He was falling short and blowing off course. His belly was turning inside out when his brain informed his body it was in for a very long fall.

"Now!"

The tiny words came from behind him. Art had reached the zenith of his launch and was on the brink of reversing course when a thick knotted vine hit his hand. He thought it lucky to catch it. If he hadn't grabbed it, it was goodnight.

"Give us a kick, crossa!"

Art kicked off the cliff and clenched the vine until his fingers hurt. It sounded like it was stretching. He closed his eyes. Then he was slowly hauled up.

"The boys will take ya from here."

Art peeked through the slits of his eyelids. General Fly landed on his white knuckles and saluted. The Lost Boys pulled him to safety. They were all there. Two dozen of them crowded on the shelf. Beams strapped to their backs. That was more Lost Boys than he remembered. But then the others must have been from the other side. Rude Boy was in front, arms crossed.

"Jolly shirt," he hollered over the gale. "Nick it from the squealers?"

There was laughter. Another Lost Boy leaned in and said: "Ee no Lander, sure. Too thick in the rock and pointy knees and all. Wouldn't last, aye wager."

A few disagreed. There was pushing and shoving with no room for it. Art's heels were at the edge. He still had the vine in case he went over, but Rude Boy grabbed him. "Still owe me a beamer, dirty crossuh, you. Make it up next one."

More arguments ended with Art being pulled into the middle of the pack, which smelled like a funky sour mosh pit. He held his breath. They pushed him up and passed him around. Art crowd-surfed over them. The Lost Boys began climbing onto each other, building a pyramid. They swayed in the gusting wind, laughing as they passed Art up the human ladder. He didn't think it was funny and wanted down to try something else.

"Old steel!" they told him.

Art had no idea what that meant and surrendered. Whatever was supposed to happen would happen. There was no way he was getting up the cliff without them, and they all seemed to know what they were doing. Of course, he made it. Wolves were there to pull him up. Big Bad and Big Good introduced themselves. The next ledge was gorillas (Henry and Carl from the green room; the others he didn't know). Three pigs plus three more were next. Art tried to give their shirt back. They said no and merry, merry.

There were more ledges. Lots more. Bo Peep and her sheep. Puppets and Miss Tuffets. Goldilockses and bears. Riding Hoods and robots and princes with long capes. Frogs and mice and everything naughty and nice helped him. The half-horse brothers, too.

Art eventually relaxed and trusted the process. A few steps were a bit sketchy. And every time he landed and looked down, the clouds were following. He couldn't see those who helped him up or how far down it was, but he could feel them down there.

The top of the cliff was in clear sight now. Fireflies were pouring up and over a sharp edge against a sky growing pinker and richer. The clouds were fading. The few wispy clouds raced in the wind. He could smell bubble gum, taste watermelon with a hint of peppermint. The air was thicker. Made his fingers stick together. His eyelids gummy.

A cat was on the last ledge.

Daryl didn't do anything to help him climb up. He stood in a little alcove, protected from the wind, swishing his tail around. Art rolled onto his back to catch his breath. He was exhausted. Aches and pains and bruises on bruises. Fireflies fought to stay near the top, signaling where he had to go. It was too far to reach. And a cat wasn't going to get him there.

"Wasn't hard getting up here, I'll bet," Art said. "Not for you."

It never is for cats.

Daryl arched his back, rubbed against Art.

Art peeked over the ledge. A profound sense of sadness filled him. He wasn't going to see them anymore. Any of them. Like, ever. It seemed like he just got to Candyland. He felt a little weepy thinking about it.

They'll always be there.

Art wasn't sure what that meant. Seeing as he was on his way to the top and they were down there, and Candyland did not appear to even exist anymore. But Daryl seemed to know things.

"What's up there?"

Impossible to say.

"Okay." There were no handholds between where they were and the top. Even if he weren't gassed, there was no jumping that far. He was stuck on the last step.

"Tell me you're going to teleport me." Art looked at Daryl. "That's why you're up here."

You wish. All cats looked bored. If you heard them talk, they sounded bored, too. *Wait for it.*

Art was happy to lie there and taste the pink sky. The ground tacky against his back. His nostrils sticking shut. He closed his eyes and opened his mouth, imagined the sky was a sheet of bubble gum and he would chew his way through it. What a way to end this climb.

The aroma shifted towards burnt sugar.

Before he recognized it, an earthquake shook the world. Art was grateful he was sticking to the ground, or he might have vibrated over the edge. He stuck his arms out for maximum contact. He could hear rocks falling and shattering into smaller pieces below. The cliff exploded near him. The smell of burnt sugar was overpowering.

You might want to look to your left.

Art opened his eyes to see two purple lips and one giant tooth. Sweet Tooth had punched holes into solid rocks. Her pumpkin face smiled down on him. And then he heard from the other side another, *"Yum!"*

Two of them!

Both as merry as giant clowns could be, scaling up a cliff. They leaned closer and sniffed Art like dogs saying hello. Daryl backed into his little alcove. Wrapped his tail around his body. The Sweet Tooth sisters put their hands out for Art to climb on.

"You coming?"

Not yet, Daryl said. *I'll catch up.*

Art was happy to not climb the last leg. He was gently lifted in the pink sky, which was wet and resistant, coating him with sweet humidity. The fireflies swirled in the vortex like the exhaust of a jet engine. Art wanted to shout merry, merry to the Sweet Tooths and anyone who could hear him below, but the wind was fierce, and his throat dry.

Sweet Tooth grabbed the top ledge. Her sister lifted Art over it.

He was hiding his face from the storm when they did. He covered his ears from the awful whistling of the wind. He held his breath to keep from choking on the candied air. It felt like he was being pushed through a keyhole. Art couldn't tolerate any more of it. It was tight and uncomfortable and frightening. He was about to scream out to take him back down.

And then everything was silent.

A RINGING in his ears slowly faded.

He heard nothing. Nothing at all. Perfect silence broken only by the rustle of his own clothing on the ground. He was balled up on his side. Knees to his chest, hands over his head. What some would call a fetal position. It felt good. It felt safe.

His eyes were closed, and he was imagining where he might be. He'd scaled that cliff—that impossibly high cliff—into a violent windstorm, where the clouds grew damp and the sky was pink and sticky. All of that was gone. There was nothing but coolness on his cheeks and perfect silence in the air. It was another world. A moment untouched. He could be anywhere... until he opened his eyes.

When he dared to peek, gritty stone was beneath him. The mountain continued. A huge letdown. Until he rolled over. His movements loud and lonely, he witnessed thousands of fireflies above him, flashing their phosphorescent abdomens to each other. Beyond them... well. There was nothing he could say about that. Words would only spoil what he saw.

The universe.

Art had seen a night sky before. There were times it struck awe, especially on rural roads nowhere near a city, where it looked like God had parked all the stars in the backyard. Even if you took the most amazing sky ever seen and multiplied it by a hundred, it wouldn't touch this.

This was everything.

This was a star-dusted sky spread before him and around him like he'd been swallowed by the universe and floated in its belly. He'd forgotten the mountain under him and around him. There were just stars. Billions and trillions of stars like Christmas lights on black fabric.

Majestic and eternal.

A theater of unimaginable depth and meaning.

So big and endless. So vast.

Its splendor filled him with unarguable truth, one that could not be denied. An elementary truth. That nothing ever dies. As plain and simple as that. Right there in front of him. The grand mystery unveiled. He couldn't explain how he knew it. There was no way to tell someone if they asked. It just was this, and this was so obvious.

There is beauty in darkness.

Tears streamed down his face. He wore a gobsmacked smile and let them flow, watching the fireflies drift up and away and into space. Flashing their lights, streaking like shooting stars.

Art was unburdened. For the first time, he was free.

HE BRUSHED HIMSELF OFF. The aches and bruises still very present. Stiffness setting in. The mountain didn't go much higher. A narrow path went to the top. He didn't plan on climbing it, but something was up there.

It wasn't far.

A bonsai tree grew from a crack. The evergreen needles were short and twisted. Ornaments the size of acorns hung from the branches. A string of lights wrapped around them.

A bamboo mat lay next to it with two meditation benches facing each other. Like a blanket spread out for a midnight picnic. They were the benches the queen had had on her island, where she'd folded her legs beneath. In between were three teacups. Two of them held a small bit of tea. The third was full.

It was warm.

There was no need to look around. Everything was exposed. There was nowhere to hide. Art didn't need to see the footsteps of the couple who had sat here to share tea. And afterwards, they had danced under the cool belly of the universe.

Sometimes I imagine my husband sitting across from me, the queen had said. *We would share a cup of tea and watch the fireflies. And then dance like we did when we were young.*

Art wished he had been there to witness the reunion. Instead, he raised the cup, closed his eyes to savor the aroma, and drank the tea they'd left behind for him.

The little lights twinkled on the tree. Art pulled the polyurethane wheel out from his pocket—the gift he'd found on the stage—spun on a fishing line in one direction and then the other, his glittery name on the side of it. He stepped over the bamboo mat and tied it on the bonsai tree. The branch sagged under the weight. It seemed like a good place for it.

A present was below the tree. It was flat and narrow and wrapped in plain, brown paper. No bow or ribbon. A piece of twine, however, was tied around it. Art picked it up, plucked a folded piece of paper from beneath the twine. He sat down on one of the benches, pulled his legs under him. He took his time with the tea, resting in the silence between sips and gazing up. Sometimes losing himself in the view.

When he finished the tea, he opened the letter.

Dear Arthur,

I wish I could tell you what Candyland is. Or was. By now it's returned to the source. I wish I could tell you why it existed in the first place and why crossers like us ended up there. Landers would tell you what they believe it was. Even crossers will claim to know. The truth is no one knows. Not me or S'ven or anyone else. And even if we knew, we wouldn't find the words any more than you can find words for what you see above you right now. But I can tell you this much, and this much is true: this is the true essence of Christmas. It is all things naughty and all things nice. It is not always what you want, but always what you need.

This place is a gift, Arthur. And you are part of it.

It has been an honor to have shared it with you, as brief as it may seem. Your journey has not always been easy. Journeys worthwhile rarely are. You once asked why I was still here. Initially, I never desired to leave because I felt I belonged in Candyland. I had done so much wrong in my life that I didn't deserve to leave.

My husband often said life is suffering. The real question, he would say, was if all the suffering we endure was to help one person, only one, would the hardship be worth it? That's why I never left, Arthur. I didn't know it at the time, but looking back, I believe I was waiting to help one person.

Some believe this place is a story. Some of those stories are epic journeys with timeless adventures that go on and on. Some stories are short and as bright as the sun. Their worth can be equally measured in the joy they bring. Whether long or short, stories never truly end. They just move on.

As you know, time here is funny. It is eternal, yet passes in a wink of an eye. To be here when you arrived and to have shared your story has been a privilege, Arthur.

And, yes. It was worth it.

Merry, merry, Arthur. Perhaps we will meet in another story.

Truly, Lady Mouserinks.

ART READ IT AGAIN. He didn't know why he was crying.

Maybe because he wished she were there to say those things instead of writing them in a note. She had seen him for who he truly was. She understood him. She saw him. If she were here, he'd have a chance to say how grateful he was she stayed. What would have happened without her?

He wiped his eyes and folded the note, tucked it into his back pocket. Then searched for something to blow his nose into, used one of the napkins on the bamboo mat. He was still holding the present. He almost didn't want to open it. He pried the string off and unwrapped the generic paper, the crinkling so loud in the silence. Lifted the lid on an ordinary box. A small card lay inside.

Create your next adventure.

What looked like a crooked stick was nestled in shredded paper. It was knobby and nearly a foot long. Something a wizard would wave. He swung it around, cutting the silence and still air, pointed it at the sky. Sparks didn't fly out. No pixie dust, either. A ballpoint tip was embedded at the end of it. He touched it to his finger; it left a spot of ink. An odd gift. But then there was nothing normal about this place. That was when something snorted. Almost in agreement with that thought.

Art swung the crooked pen like a sword or a magic wand (just in case it did do magic). The ballpoint end was aimed at the horned beast. It was so big, so massive, Art didn't recognize the animal for what it was. It stood over him with antlers spanning the average width of a bedroom. Eyes as black as coal yet shined like jewels. It pawed the rocks, scraping the dust away, and snorted again.

Breath humid on Art's cheeks. Grassy in his nose.

A reindeer.

That was what it was. Plain and simple, but not by the looks of it. Unless it was ripped from a storybook, reindeer didn't come supersized like that. Not with heads the length of dinner tables and hooves the size of catcher mitts. But a reindeer no less.

Art felt the raw power of the thing, enough to send living creatures for cover. But underneath it was the warmth of love and protection. The promise and richness of Christmas spirit radiated in waves that stirred in Art's stomach. The reindeer kicked at the rock again and bowed his head. Held the muzzle at Art's feet.

Art reached out to touch it. Stroked the short fur running the length of his snout.

The hum of bells went through his fingers and into his arm. They rang in his head and stoked a fire in his heart. Bells, he heard. Bells, he felt. They were everywhere. So strange, the way this vast open space was suddenly as intimate as a small room. As quiet as an empty box. But all around him, bells.

Ring, ring. Ring, ring, ring.

Art smiled. Joy beamed from every pore.

The reindeer bent the knee of his front leg and then the other. When he settled on the haunches of his back legs, he slowly picked up his head. Nudged Art gently with his muzzle.

Art's boots scuffed the hard ground.

He dragged his hand down the bony antler, walked around it to look at the girth of the waiting animal. Unsure if the reindeer wanted him to climb onto him. The reindeer turned his head, the back of his antler guiding him closer.

To be clear, climbing onto an animal this size isn't as easy as it sounds. Art did it, though. He grabbed handfuls of shaggy fur and threw one leg over him. Before he could settle, the reindeer stood up. The sudden shift tossed Art into the air. He landed square on the reindeer's back. Felt the muscles flex and roll beneath him. The reindeer turned his head, careful not to rake Art off with an antler, and fixed him with one eye.

Art smiled back.

It would be hard to explain the liftoff of a flying reindeer. True, it would be hard to convince anyone reindeers could fly. But even if you made it that far, the launch would be impossible to explain. Only felt. The best words could do is imagining oneself holding a musky shag carpet. And the next second the wind is in your face.

Art ducked his head against the reindeer's powerful neck.

He felt the legs pedaling below as if the reindeer were galloping on thin air. His blood pumping hot. A steam engine firing exhaust from his nostrils. They circled the bamboo mat and tiny Christmas tree with a skateboard wheel ornament weighing down a limb. Fireflies flowed behind them like miniature comets.

Higher they went. Wider the circle.

The stars grew bigger and brighter. The one star, the North Star, flashed like a beacon. Galaxies emerged from deep space in every shape and color.

Art had never felt freedom like this. Never so unencumbered. So unburdened. The fireflies whispered their secrets, and so did the stars. The truth all around him.

Love.

There was a time in his life he would have laughed at that thought. Love was something you felt toward a new bike or a puppy. A girlfriend or newborn child. But now he knew what it really was. He felt it. *I am love.* To know this love was out there and in him and of him and there was no difference between any of those things made him weep with joy.

The essence of Christmas.

The reindeer pedaled faster. Fireflies flew in all directions now, shooting into space. The stars streaked into the darkness.

Art put his arms around the reindeer. Laid his cheek against the musky fur. He closed his eyes and held him so tightly that he didn't feel where he ended and the reindeer began. Art was the soaring, the roaring, the stretching limbs and snorting muzzle. He was the warmth. He was the protective generosity.

He stayed that way until he was no longer a name. He was just the beauty of existence.

He was flight.

He was freedom.

A beautiful beam of light shooting toward the North Star.

Where there are no endings.

28

Pinpoints of light from the neighbor's yard rotated through the window. Cal watched them run across the popcorn ceiling, over the water stain that had grown larger over the last year, thinking today was the day he'd fix the leak. Knowing he wouldn't.

The windows were open. It was chilly enough to see his breath. He huddled under the thick blanket, where it was toasty warm, and planned to stay there till the sun was up. It'd be hours before that happened. He didn't need to look at the clock. He knew what time it was. This was a nightly ritual.

Wakey-wakey, his brain said. *All aboard the Thinking Express. Toot-toot!*

And then the thoughts came marching in. Planning out the day, telling stories, making up scenarios. Most of the time they dragged memories out of the cellar and played them on a loop. Those he didn't mind so much. It was the *what-ifs* that bothered him most.

What if I'd done this, would things be different?

What-ifs were tireless and endless and no good. There was no way to prove them right or wrong. That was the thing with parenting.

You choose a direction and will never know what would have happened if you went the other way.

When the Thinking Express hit supersonic speed, he got out of bed. Feet on the cold floor, he went to the bedside chair to read. The room was mostly windows. That was what he loved about the back room. It never felt closed in. Landscape lighting made for great views all night long. Christmas time he would put red or green lenses on the lights to make it festive. Not this year, though.

He had just sat down when he noticed someone standing on the deck. He searched for his glasses to make sure. It could have been a tree, she was standing so still. He got dressed and walked through the closet to get to the main house. The back room had been added thirty years after the house was built. The closet was the only way to get there from inside the house. When the kids were little, they pretended it was a secret passage to a fantasy land.

The main bedroom was empty, the blankets thrown back. He'd sleep-divorced his wife years ago (it was her idea), and they'd never slept better. *Beds are mostly for sleeping.* She wasn't wrong.

Cal took a detour on his way to the kitchen, passed an empty bedroom on the left, and opened the door at the end of the hallway. Marlowe was home from college. He peeked into her room. It looked like her dresser had vomited. She was on the bed, buried beneath a pile of jeans. Cal snuck in and closed the laptop. *New Elf City* was still playing.

If she woke up, it might freak her out to see someone standing in her room. Watching her sleep. Remembering when he read stories to her at bedtime. Sometimes he'd make them up. Now she was writing her own stories. Full-length novels. And people were reading them.

In the kitchen, he put the kettle on and a teabag in a mug.

The only lights in the house came from the Christmas tree. There were ornaments and white lights wrapped around the branches, but it was not your normal tree. It was really a big, barren branch taken from the backyard. They stood it up in the middle of the room so that it went up into the well of the skylight. Fallen leaves were attached to it—leaves from the sycamore the kids planted when they were little that was now fifty feet tall.

The ornaments were all homemade. Things the kids made. It was tradition to take them out one at a time and tell stories about them. It was a little different this year.

He took the kettle off before it whistled. On his way around the tree, he noticed an unfamiliar ornament. It was easy for him to forget such things (he was the first to admit that), but he was pretty sure he hadn't seen this one.

The dogs followed him to the back door. Grace was outside the screened porch, on the deck, looking up at the sky. She didn't turn when the door opened or when the dogs shook their heads, ears slapping like mudflaps. She was hugging herself.

"You okay?" he asked.

She nodded. Okay was a relative word. Wrapped in a blanket with a knitted scarf around her neck under a moon so full you could read a book. He put his arm around her. She leaned into him. They stood in the lunar glow, watching the sky like a drive-in movie. A million stars were playing.

The dogs got bored and went inside.

Grace blew her nose into a secret tissue she kept tucked in her sleeve, pulling it out like a magician when she needed it. He felt her quivering and held her close. She wasn't cold. They didn't say anything. Words only cluttered these moments. But when a star streaked across the dark sky, Cal lifted his mug.

"See that?"

Grace nodded. Even chuckled before giving her nose a honk. This was where Cal would joke about Santa Claus coming to town. Not this year.

"Maybe this is a new tradition," he said. "We watch shooting stars."

"I don't want a new tradition."

Neither did he. But there they were, on the back porch in the middle of the night. He had the feeling it wasn't the last time they would do this. He asked if she wanted some tea. With a nod, they went back inside. Cal started another kettle. This was the first holiday they didn't have a mess to clean up in the morning. What he'd give to see plates stacked in the sink, cups on the tables. Candy wrappers everywhere.

Grace was at the Christmas tree. Cal handed her a mug smelling of peppermint. She was holding the ornament Cal had seen earlier: a polyurethane wheel with sparkles.

"I don't remember that one," Cal said.

Grace shook her head. "Marlowe must have done it."

"Mmm."

Marlowe was becoming the princess of card making and gift giving. Her mother was the queen. This, however, with the skateboard wheel and the glitter was good. She'd probably put it on the tree after Cal and Grace went to bed.

With tea in hand, they went back outside. This time they cuddled under a thick blanket on the couch inside the screened porch. Strobing lights from the neighbor's speckled the bare branches of the trees. They were warm beneath the blanket, holding the mugs to their chins, listening to things scurry in the dark. A small forest was beyond the fence where storm sewers emptied out. That was where the kids had played when they were little.

Grace was thinking that, too. She didn't have to say it. The look in her eyes did.

The kids had built forts out of sticks and stray lumber. They would tread through stagnant pools barefoot. And no one ever got bit by a snake. They made bows from saplings and arrows from branches. Shot at each other without anyone losing an eye. They cut giant grapevines and drank the water that leaked from them. All the things parents wouldn't let their kids do if they knew they were doing them.

The neighborhood was different now.

They were no kids playing Manhunt in the summer. No road hockey games or basketball hoops without a net. No screams of delight or cries of a skinned knee. It was quiet now. Just the stars; just the insects.

It all goes by fast, just like they say. Time is funny that way. It inches by at the speed of light.

The back door opened. Marlowe held it for the dogs to follow her out.

"What are you doing out here?" she said.

"Waiting for Santa," Cal said. "What are you doing up?"

"Dogs."

That was Cal's fault. He hadn't closed her bedroom door after he checked on her. He lifted the blanket. She crawled in between them and snuggled against her mom. The dogs whined, but there wasn't enough room. Cal put his arm around his wife and daughter. If they had to start a new tradition, he rather liked this one. It reminded him of a card someone gave them. It was propped in front of the television. Out of all the cards they'd received that year, it was his favorite.

Joy and grief can coexist, it said.

"Merry, merry," Marlowe mumbled.

"Merry, merry?" He chuckled. "Where'd you hear that?"

"I dreamed it."

He liked it. It had a ring to it. He wasn't certain, but it felt like maybe he'd dreamed it, too.

They sank into the couch. Marlowe relaxed and was breathing slower. Soon she was lightly snoring. Grace was squashed beneath her but didn't dare move. Cal's arm was numb. The sun was still hours from rising.

"What's that?" Grace whispered.

Cal didn't see what she was pointing at. Maybe another shooting star. She kept her finger aimed across the yard. Owls were usually sitting in the trees at night, but then a bright light flashed for a long second. It was different than the neighbor's lights.

"Firefly," he said.

"I didn't think they were around this time of year," she said.

They watched it hover higher and higher, periodically signaling back to them until it was just a small dot. No different than a star. Christmas would arrive on a beautifully incomplete note. Different than before. He held his family a little tighter.

"Merry, merry," he whispered.

29

A blue tent was the first on the beach that Christmas morning.

The sun was barely above the horizon, burning red ribbons on incoming waves. A man and a woman set up where the sand was soft. The tide was low that morning. It would be a long walk to where the water lapped the hardpack. But they were mostly going to sit.

They were an older couple. Older than most. Their hair was white, and they walked with patience, holding hands through the soft sand. They never came to the beach this early. It wasn't going to be crowded, not on Christmas. This was a special day. More special than most. They weren't going to miss it.

It was cool in the shade of their tent. They were bundled up, but trying to stay out of the sun. They still weren't accustomed to the brilliance and hid in the shade when they could, covering their eyes with blackout sunglasses. The sound of the ocean put the old man to sleep. His wife had a sketchbook in her lap. Pencils in her hands. She wasn't an artist (she'd be the first to admit that), but this had nothing to do with being good or bad. She just like the way the pencil sounded on the paper, the way sweeping lines could capture a moment.

Soon beachcombers came looking for treasures—seashells and sharks' teeth and such. Down by the pier, a crowd had gathered in bathing suits and swimming caps. At the sound of an air horn, the polar bear club plunged into the ocean. They came right back out and wrapped themselves in towels. Not long after that, families began migrating out of million-dollar beach homes. Not the impressive kinds of houses you would see up the coast. These were older homes where locals lived. They hung their own Christmas lights.

They came out to ride their new bikes on the beach. Fly their new kites. Try out their new wetsuits on new surfboards. The old couple watched from beneath wide-brim hats, occasionally getting up to loosen their joints, dip their toes in the frigid water, and watch the dolphins swim past.

It was sometime after lunch when a family set up next to the blue tent.

They came to this beach often and always the same spot. The waves were calmer there. There were no riptides to worry about, and rarely was someone fishing. The sand was good for castling. Especially the oozing drip castles. The old couple had studied these things from afar. They'd been planning for this day.

The family pulled their stuff out in wagons with oversized wheels. There were three coolers and five beach bags. Two tents and one baby carriage covered in netting. The kids attacked the sand with full-sized shovels. They had a trench dug and the start of a sand sculpture before the chairs were unfolded. Two of the young adults helped with the digging. Country music played on a new all-weather speaker. Soda bottles were opened, and sandwiches passed around. The two little kids were standing over the baby carriage, scratching at the netting. An adult made them stop.

The peaceful moment the older couple had arrived to had become laughing chaos. They held hands and loved every second of it.

One of the men, the oldest of the bunch (not nearly as old as the couple under the blue tent), began setting up a tripod when the tents were staked and the chairs set up. He mounted a fancy camera on it. Brand new, by the looks of it. Opened that morning. He waved a young woman to stand in front of it. She wore a long, flowing robe. Her skin as fair as the sand. Her hair as red as the sunset.

When he was done with her, he got a drone out of one of the beach bags. He fussed with the controls and got it off the ground. It sounded like a giant bug. He checked his instruments, seemed pleased. Said something to one of the women—his wife—who began rounding up the team. It took more than a few minutes to drag the kids out of the trenches and away from the surf. They stood in a semi-circle, wearing sweatshirts and ballcaps. The little ones wore T-shirts and swimsuits.

The old couple watched.

They couldn't hear the speech given. But everyone laughed. Then the young woman with sunburnt hair and a young man about her age took their place in front of the tripod. Someone handed them road flares. There were more instructions for them. Then all together everyone began to chant.

"Three! Two! One!"

The young couple twisted the flares. Instead of flames, smoke shot from the ends. Thick and bright blue smoke. Everyone cheered. Everyone leaped and hugged and kissed.

The little kids ran back to their trench and castle while the adults clinked cans. Hugs for everyone. Drinks all around. In the melee, one of the bags fell over. A red apple went rolling across the hardpacked sand. It came to rest with the stem pointing up. No one noticed. A helicopter could have landed next to them and they wouldn't have noticed.

The old couple looked at each other.

They squeezed hands. The woman pushed herself out of the chair. Her bones achy and joints stiff. She used an umbrella like a cane, pushing the tip into the sand as she walked toward the water. Her husband came with her and picked up the apple. He handed it to her and returned to his seat under the blue tent.

The family was still celebrating. The hugging had slowed, but the laughter and drinking had not. The flares were spent and smoldering. The mother of the family saw the old woman approaching.

"Oh, thank you!" She took the apple from her and said with a Southern drawl: "I'm so sorry. I hadn't realized we were spilling all over the place. We're making a fuss over here, aren't we."

"Quite all right," the old woman said. "Gave me a reason to get my steps in."

"Bless your heart." She took off her sunglasses. "You look familiar. Do I know you?"

The old woman was covered head to toe in a checkered robe, and her hat was wide enough to shade a family of meerkats from the noonday sun. Her sunglasses were round and as black as asphalt. It was the way the old woman walked she had recognized.

"We're neighbors, I believe." The old woman gave her address.

"Oh, my lord. You just moved in! Honey, come over here. It's our neighbors."

The man who set up the tripod came over. His name was Jack. Jack was the only adult wearing a T-shirt. His wife's name was Lorraine. Lorraine wore two sweatshirts. The old woman introduced herself. Pointed at her husband under the blue tent, who waved back. The coincidence of setting up right next to each other was uncanny. What were the odds?

"I love your coat," Jack said. "Aren't you hot?"

The old woman tugged on her checkered overcoat. It was thick and comfortable. "The sun is very bright. We're not used to it."

"Where'd you move from?" Lorraine asked.

"Far away. It was much darker there."

"What brings you here?"

The old woman shrugged. "Family, I suppose."

"Well, welcome. We've got everyone here, so excuse our mess."

"My husband and I rather enjoy it."

Just then one of the little sandcastle builders ran up to Lorraine and started pulling on her sleeve. She bent down, and he whispered something in her ear.

"Go ask your mom, love." When the little boy stared at the old woman, Lorraine ran her fingers through his hair.

"What's that?"

The boy pointed at the sketchpad she was holding. The old woman explained she liked to draw when she came to the beach. That she wasn't very good and that mostly she just liked to make lines. When she showed him what she'd drawn, he seemed mesmerized. It made the old woman smile.

"Go on and find your mother, now," Lorraine said.

Just then the young couple of the hour came up. The young lady with the red hair was pushing the netted baby carriage. Lorraine said it was for practice. The old woman bent over. There wasn't a baby inside the netting. "Well, look at you," she said with a smile. "All cozy in there."

"Is it weird?" Lorraine said. "He just showed up at Tommy and Ann's house, like, four months ago. No collar or chip. He's well fed, though. Look at him."

Ann, the young redhead, said they'd put signs up, and no one ever called. And the cat never left. Now he was in a carriage on the beach. The old woman put the back of her hand against the netting.

"Good to see you," the old woman said. Jack could've sworn she said *again*. A loud purring came from inside the stroller.

"He's not fond of strangers," Lorraine said, "but I think he likes you."

The cat rubbed against the old woman's hand. He strutted around the small enclosure, waving his tail and dragging his belly over the blankets. He didn't seem to mind the pampering.

"I knew a cat like this once," the old woman said. "His name was Daryl."

"Oh, my God!" Lorraine covered her mouth.

Ann grabbed Tommy's arm. Someone shrieked. Even the kids looked up from their sandcastle to see what had happened. Lorraine was shaking her hands like something bit them.

"Did you hear that, Jack?" Lorraine said. "Did you hear what she just said?"

"I'm standing right here."

"That's what Tommy named the cat. He named the cat *Daryl!*"

Tommy and Jack weren't as excited as Lorraine and Ann. It was rather odd, though. How many cats were named Daryl? And the old woman knew one, too. Almost as weird as neighbors setting up on the beach next to each other. Tommy said he'd just thought of the name. Like it came out of the blue and fit. He didn't mention how his head hurt right before he thought of it. The old woman didn't ask him if it did.

"Do you know the owner of the cat?" Ann asked.

"Once upon a time, I did."

"Of our Daryl?" Ann was a bit worried.

"That would seem unlikely, wouldn't it? I think your Daryl has a home with you. You look like family. And you're growing one, I take it?"

Lorraine explained that Ann was her and Jack's daughter. And she was pregnant. "Blue for boy," she said. "Just like your tent."

"Coincidence," the old woman said.

There was more general giddiness. Jack and Tommy faded from the conversation. Lorraine put her hand on Ann's stomach. They touched their heads together.

"Congratulations," the old woman said. "Do you have a name?"

"We have a list," Ann said. "A very long list. It's a lot harder picking one than I thought it would be."

"I'm sure you'll come up with one that fits. Just like Daryl." The old woman winked at the cat. It didn't seem all that strange when she did. Not that time. "Well, it's very nice to meet you."

"Listen, don't be a stranger. Please. You come over anytime you like. There's always room at the table."

The old woman considered it. She looked at her husband. Whether he heard it or not, he waved. "We would like that very much," the old woman said. "That's very kind of you."

As it turned out, the old couple would be neighbors for a long time. Long enough to see Tommy and Ann's boy grow up. She would give him all her art supplies, and he would show her all the things he drew and painted. The old man would have him mow their lawn. Afterwards, the boy would sit on the porch and drink sweet tea. Every Christmas, he would visit.

The old couple would never tire of the sound of his laugh. Or the brightness of his smile.

"I didn't catch your name," Ann said.

The old woman turned around. She pulled the black sunglasses over the scar on her cheek. "Rinks."

"Ms. Rinks?" Ann said. "I don't think I ever met anyone named Rinks before."

"A few have."

And she winked at the cat again.

THE CLAUS UNIVERSE

Don't stop now. The Claus Universe awaits. Catch up on all the holiday adventures.

http://bertauski.com

YOU DONATED TO A WORTHY CAUSE!

By purchasing this book, you have donated to the development of mental health since 10% of the profits is annually donated to WINGS for Kids, a non-profit organization whose mission is to equip at-risk kids with the social and emotional skills to succeed in school, stay in school, and thrive in life.

#BENISHERE